DICTIONARY OF MUSIC

Da Capo Press Music Reprint Series

GENERAL EDITOR
FREDERICK FREEDMAN
VASSAR COLLEGE

DICTIONARY
OF MUSIC

By Hugo Riemann

Translated by J. S. Shedlock

Volume I
A-LIP

𝄋 DA CAPO PRESS • NEW YORK • 1970

A Da Capo Press Reprint Edition

This Da Capo Press edition of Riemann's *Dictionary of Music* is an unabridged republication in two volumes of the one-volume fourth edition, revised and enlarged, published in London in 1908.

Library of Congress Catalog Card Number 75-125060
SBN 306-70025-5

Published by Da Capo Press
A Division of Plenum Publishing Corporation
227 West 17th Street, New York, N.Y. 10011

DICTIONARY OF MUSIC.

AUGENER'S EDITION, No. 9200.

DICTIONARY OF MUSIC

BY

DR. HUGO RIEMANN.

FOURTH EDITION, REVISED AND ENLARGED.

TRANSLATION BY

J. S. SHEDLOCK, B.A.

LONDON:

AUGENER LTD.

DICTIONARY OF MUSIC.

A.

A, the name of the first note of the musical alphabet (A B C D E F G). The Italians, French, Spanish, call the same *la*, or (especially in old theoretical works) with the complete solmisation name *A lamire*, or even *A mila*. (*See* SOLMISATION and MUTATION.)

The **A**'s of the various octaves are distinguished from one another when written as letters by means of additions—first by the difference between capital and small letters, then by strokes over or to the right of the small letters, and under or to the left of the capital letters; or instead of the stroke—as now usual—the 8VA and 8^{VA bassa}, or even by 15MA and 15^{MA bassa}), yet the ordinary limits of notation are those of our present concert-grand pianofortes, with a compass from Double Contra *A* to five-times accented *c*. Compare the following synopsis, in which at the same time the usual letter notation of the notes is given. (The French call the great octave the 1st, the small the 2nd, etc.; and the Contra octave the minus 1st [− 1], and the Double Contra octave the minus 2nd; so they call our a¹, la³, and so on.)

The once-accented *c* (*c*¹) is the one situated in the middle of the keyboard—our orchestras

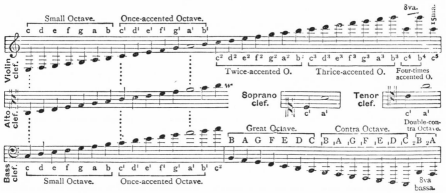

SYNOPSIS OF NOTES AND CLEFS.

corresponding figure; so that c̄, or *c*ᵃ, or c², bears the same meaning. The total compass of serviceable musical sounds extends from Double Contra *C* to six-times accented *c*, *i.e.* through nine octaves; but the very lowest and very highest tones of this giant scale occur only in the organ. They are not written down, but appear only as reinforcements of sound (in the 32-feet stops on the one hand, and in the smallest mutation stops, Quint ⅔ or ⅓, and Tierce ⅘ on the other hand. [*See* FOOT-TONE.]) The notation can indeed show these sounds (by generally tune from the once-accented *a* (*a*¹), indicated above in all clefs by a ○-note, which is given out by the oboe. The normal pitch of the same, which formerly was very uncertain, was fixed by the French *Académie* in 1858 at 870 single, or 435 double, vibrations per second (called Paris chamber-pitch, also "low pitch," to distinguish it from the considerably higher one in general use [different in different countries and cities]); the Paris pitch (*Diapason normal*) is gradually being everywhere introduced. At the International Conference held

In Vienna, Nov. 16–19, 1885, to establish unity of pitch, it was resolved to recommend this pitch to be officially adopted by the Governments of all the countries represented. In Germany and France the tuning-forks from which pianofortes are tuned give a^1 (or a^2), while in England they give c^2.—On the titles of old vocal part-books, **A** means *Altus* (alto part). In recent scores and parts, letters (A—Z, Aa—Za) are written as signs; so that, at rehearsal, a conductor may easily point back to any particular bar. In recent theoretical works (those of Gottfried Weber, M. Hauptmann, E. F. Richter, and others), letters are used with chord-meaning : **A** then indicates the *A-major* chord ; **a,** the *A-minor* chord, etc. In old antiphonaries, etc., of Gregorian song, especially those with Neumæ, an *a* written at the commencement indicates that the song is in the first ecclesiastical tone.— In Italian marks of expression and indications of time, *a* must be translated by "with," "in," "to," "at," "for," "by"; for ex., *a due,* for two (two-part). (*See* DUE.)

A♯ (Ger. *Aïs*), an *a* raised a half-tone

 ; and then in connection with

thorough-bass figuring $\left(\text{really } \begin{smallmatrix}\sharp\\a\end{smallmatrix}\right)$ it stands for

the triad of *a* with raised third, *i.e.* the **A**-major chord, and finally the **A**-major key. On the other hand, *a♮* or *a♭* denotes the *A-minor* chord, or the *A-minor* key. But this mode of indication is not general, and, on account of its ambiguity, little worthy of recommendation. (*Cf.* **A,** and KLANGSCHLÜSSEL.)

Aaron, (1) Abbot of the monasteries of St. Martin and St. Pantaleon at Cologne, d. Dec. 14, 1052; author of the treatise (in the library of St. Martini) "De Utilitate Cantus vocalis et de Modo Cantandi atque Psallendi," also (according to Trithemius) of another, "De Regulis Tonorum et Symphoniarum."—(2) P i e t r o, also written A r o n, a distinguished theorist, b. about 1490, Florence, d. between 1545 and 1562; a canon of Rimini, afterwards (1536) monk of the order of Cross-bearers, first at Bergamo, then at Padua, finally at Venice; published "I Tre libri dell' Istituzione armonica" (1516, also in Latin by G. A. Flaminio) ; "Il Toscanello in Musica" (1523, 1525, 1529, 1539, and 1562) ; "Trattato della Natura et Cognitione di tutti gli Tuoni di Canto figurato" (1525) ; "Lucidario in Musica di alcune Opinione antiche e moderne" (1545); and "Compendiolo di molti dubbi Segreti et Sentenze intorno al Canto termo e figurato" (without year of publication).

Abaco, E v a r i s t a F. d a l l', b. July 12, 1675, Verona; d. July 12, 1742, Munich, Electoral Bavarian Capellmeister ; he published sonatas for 1 and for 2 violins with *continuo,* and concertos for stringed instruments.

A ballata (Ital.), in the ballad style.

Abb., an abbreviation of *abbassamento* (*di mano*), indicating which hand is to go under in a crossing of hands in pianoforte or organ music. (*Cf.* ALZ.)

Abbandonatamente, or **con abbandono** (Ital.), with self-abandonment, unrestrainedly.

Abbandono (Ital.), with self-abandonment.

Abbassamento (Ital.), the act of lowering, or the state of being lowered.—*Abbassamento di mano,* lowering of the hand in beating time ; *abbassamento di voce,* lowering of the voice.

Abbatini, A n t o n i o M a r i a, composer of the Roman school, b. 1595 or 1605, Tiferno, or (according to Baini) Castello, d. 1677, Castello. He became (1626) maestro at the Lateran, from which post he passed to similar ones at other churches in Rome (del Gesu, S. Lorenzo in Damaso, Sa. Maria Maggiore, and N. D. di Loreto). **A.** wrote a large number of church compositions, of which some were for a great number of voices; four books of psalms, three books of masses, Antiphons for 24 voices (1630–38, 1677), and five books of Motets (1635) were published; he produced an opera at Rome in 1654, entitled *Del Male in Bene,* and another at Vienna, 1666, entitled *Ione.* He also assisted Ath. Kircher with his "Musurgia."

Abbellimento (Ital.). Same as ornament (q.v.).

Abbellitura (Ital.), embellishment, ornament.

Abbey, J o h n, celebrated Paris organ-builder, b. Dec. 22, 1785, Whilton (Northampton), d. Feb. 19, 1859, Versailles. **A.** built, among others, the organ for the National Exhibition of 1827, also the *orgue expressif* unfortunately destroyed at the Tuileries in 1830 (both designed by S. Erard) ; and in 1831 the one for the Paris Opera House, which was burnt in 1873.

Abbreviations are used in great number in notation itself, as well as in the marks of expression and indications of time. The most usual **A.** in notation are : (1) The employment of repetition signs (*see* REPRISE) instead of writing out twice a number of bars or a whole section ; also, instead of this, especially in the repetition of a few bars, the indication *bis,* or *due volte* (twice) is employed.—(2) In repetitions of a short figure, the sign ⚊ or ⚊, also ⚊.

(3) In repetitions of the same sound in notes of short value, the employment of notes of larger value with indication of the species of note into which they are to be resolved :

Played :

(4) In a pause of many bars with indication of the exact number over slanting lines:

(5) In an Arpeggio to indicate a method of breaking chords, previously used and written out:

(6) The octave mark is used to avoid many ledger lines for very high or very low notes:

after which the return to the ordinary position is indicated by *loco*.—(7) The mark c 8VA ... (over or under single notes, also merely 8), *i.e. con (coll') ottava* or *con ottava bassa*, is used instead of writing out octaves:

(8) In scores, when several instruments have to play the same notes, the indication *col basso* (" with Double-bass," *i.e.* same notes as D. B.), *col violino*, etc. :

instead of writing the same notes out again. Similarly, in piano music, when both hands had to play the same passage, but at different octaves, it was formerly the custom only to write out the part for one hand, and to indicate

that of the other—after a few notes to show the distance of the hands from each other—by " *all' unisono*," or simply " *unisono* " :

(9) The mode of performance (*legato, staccato*, etc.), if it remains the same through a series of similar figures, is frequently not written out, but indicated by *simile* or *segue*, *i.e.* corresponding to what has preceded.

Also signs for shakes, the turn, mordent, etc., are ∴. of the notation. (*Cf.* ORNAMENTS and SIGNS.) Abbreviations of marks of expression, indications of time, and names of instruments will be found under their respective headings. For ex., *B.C.* (*Basso continuo*) under **B**; *m.s.* (*mano sinistra*) under **M**; etc.

A B C, musical. (*See* LETTER-NOTATION.)

A-B-C-dieren (Ger.) is a term employed to express the singing of notes by their letter-names, a custom prevalent in Germany in elementary school instruction in singing instead of solmisation (q.v.).

Abd el Kadir (Abdolkadir), B e n I s a, Arabian writer on music of the 14th century, the author of three treatises, which have been preserved : " The Collector of Melodies," " The Aim of Melodies in the Composition of Tones and Measures," and " The Treasure of Melodies in the Science of Musical Cycles." (*Cf.* Kiesewetter's " Music of the Arabians " [1842], p. 33.)

Abd el Mumin (Abdolmumin). (*See* SSAFFID-DIN.)

Abeille, J. Ch. L u d w i g, b. Feb. 20, 1761, Baireuth, d. March 2, 1852, as musical director and court organist at Stuttgart ; was an excellent pianoforte and organ player and a prolific composer (operas, *Amor und Psyche* and *Peter und Aennchen* produced at Stuttgart [1801 and 1809], chamber music, etc.). Some of his songs are still sung in schools.

Abel, (1) C l a m o r H e i n r i c h, chamber musician at the court of Hanover, published from 1674 to 1677 three sets of instrumental pieces, " Erstlinge musikalischer Blumen" Allemandes, Courantes, Sarabandes, etc.), republished together in 1687 as " 3 Opera musica."— (2) C h r i s t i a n F e r d i n a n d, about 1720-37 viol-da-gambist at Cöthen, father of the two following.—(3) L e o p. A u g u s t, b. 1717, Cöthen, excellent violinist, pupil of Benda ; was engaged in the court bands at Brunswick, Sondershausen (1758), Schwedt and Schwerin (1770); he

published six violin concertos.—(4) K a r l F r i e d-
r i c h, brother of the former, b. 1725, Cöthen,
d. Jan. 22, 1787, London, the last performer on
the gamba, and a composer highly esteemed in
his time. He was a pupil of J. S. Bach's, at St.
Thomas's School, Leipzig. From 1748 to 1758
he was member of the Dresden court band;
after that he went on concert tours, and lived
in London 1759–1787, with the exception of two
years (1783–5) spent in Germany. In 1765 he
was appointed chamber-musician to Queen
Charlotte. His numerous sonatas, concertos
for pf. and strings, quartets, overtures, and
symphonies deserve mention.—(5) L u d w i g, b.
Jan. 14, 1834, Eckartsberge (Thuringia), received his artistic training at Weimar and
Leipzig (Ferd. David), became leader of the
orchestra at Munich in 1867, and one of the
principal teachers at the Royal School of Music
(violin, playing from score, etc.). A. published
violin compositicns and also a violin Method.
Died Dec. 8, 1895, Munich.

Abela, (1) K a r l G o t t l o b, vocal composer,
b. April 29, 1803, Borna (Saxony), d. April 22,
1841, as cantor of the "Francke" Institution at
Halle; he published a book of songs for schools,
as well as numerous choruses for male voices.
—(2) D o m P l a c i d o, prior of the abbey of
Monte Cassino, d. July 6, 1876, was an excellent organist and composer of church music.—
(3) P e d r o d e, teacher of singing of repute, b.
March, 1877, Barcelona. Tamberlik was one
of his pupils.

Abell, J o h n, famous English *evirato* and lute
player, b. about 1660, London, where already
in 1679 he was member of the Chapel Royal, d.
1724. The Revolution of 1688 cost him his
position; yet, after long journeys on the Continent, he returned to London in 1700, and
gained fresh triumphs. A. published two collections of songs.

A bene placito (Ital.), at pleasure.

Abenheim, J o s e p h, b. 1804, Worms, d.
Jan. 18, 1891, Stuttgart, a worthy member of
the court band at Stuttgart (violinist), appointed musical director in 1854; he wrote
many entr'actes, overtures, etc., but only some
interesting small pf. pieces and songs have
appeared in print.

Abert, J o h a n n J o s e p h, b. Sept. 21, 1832,
Kochowitz (Bohemia), received his first musical
education as chorister at Gastdorf and the
Leipa monastery, but fled from the latter place,
and, thanks to the aid of a relative, became a
pupil at the Prague Conservatorium under Kittl
and Tomaczek. In 1852 he was engaged as
double-bassist in the Stuttgart court band, and
in 1867 obtained, on the departure of Eckert,
the post of capellmeister there; in the autumn
of 1888 he retired from active life. Abert's
c minor symphony (first performed in 1852), his
Symphonic Poem "Columbus" (1864), also his
operas, *Anna von Landskron* (1858), *König Enzio*,

Astorga, Ekkehard, Die Almohaden (1830), besides
overtures, quartets, songs, etc., have won for
him a good name.

Abesser, E d m u n d, b. Jan. 13, 1837, Marjolitz
(Saxony), d. July 15, 1889, Vienna, a prolific
salon composer, opera *Die liebliche Fee.*

Abgesang (Ger., "aftersong"). (*See* STROPHE.)

Ab initio (Lat.), from the beginning. (*See*
DA CAPO.)

Abos, G i r o l a m o (also Avos, Avossa), composer of the Neapolitan school, born at the beginning of the 18th century at Malta, d. about
1786, Naples; pupil of Leo and Durante. He
wrote operas (1742–63) for Naples, Venice,
Rome, and London, which were highly esteemed
by his contemporaries. In later years, after he
had been appointed teacher at the *Conservatorio
della pieta di Turchini*, Naples (1758), he wrote
also many sacred works (7 masses, litanies,
etc.). Aprile was his most famous pupil.

Abraham, (1) *see* BRAHAM.—(2) D r. M a x, *see*
PETERS.

Absolute Music (i.e. *music per se*, without relation to other arts, or to any presentation
whatever outside of it) is a limiting term, which,
in recent times, forms the watchword to a
great party among musicians and friends of
music. A. M. is opposed to music-painting, to
presentative or programme-music, *i.e.* to music
supposed to express something definite. According to the opinion of a hyper-modern mi-
nority, all music which does not express some
definite poetical thought is mere trifling with
sounds. On the other hand, ultra-conservative
musicians utterly deny to music the power of
representing anything. As a matter of fact,
when music becomes symbolic, *i.e.* attempts by
means of certain formulæ or artificial imitation
of sounds intentionally to awaken certain definite associations of ideas, it goes beyond its own
domain and enters that of poetry or of the
representative arts (*cf.* Riemann, "Wie hören
wir Musik," 1888, "Catechism of Musical
Esthetics"), for the essence of poetry consists
in awakening and linking together by means of
conventional forms (words) certain conceptions,
that of the representative arts by the direct
imitation of objective phenomena; both, therefore, reach the aim of all art, that of moving
the soul, by indirect means, of which music need
not make use. The great power of music lies
in the direct emotions which it awakens, in the
fact that it is a free outpouring of feeling, and
calls forth feeling from player and listener without the intervention of intellect. (*See* Es-
THETICS.)

Abt, F r a n z, b. December 22, 1819, Eilen-
burg, d. March 31, 1885, Wiesbaden, attended
the St. Thomas School, Leipzig, and was to
have studied theology, but soon turned his attention to music, conducted a students' "philharmonic" society, and made successful at-

tempts at composition. In 1841 he became musical director at the Court Theatre, Bernburg, but went in the same year, and in a similar capacity, to the "Aktien" Theatre at Zurich, and from thence entered on his appointment of Court Capellmeister to the Duke of Brunswick (1852–82). In 1872, at the invitation of various large choral unions, he visited North America, and gained exceptional triumphs. The songs and quartets for male voices of Abt are not of great artistic value, yet frequently show his power of inventing flowing melodies. Some of them have become real folk-songs ("Wenn die Schwalben heimwärts ziehn," "Gute Nacht, du mein herziges Kind," etc.). Among his partsongs are some of poetic beauty ("Die Stille Wasserrose"). A number of his cantatas for female voices have also become very popular ("Cinderella," "Little Snowwhite," "Red Riding Hood"). In 1882 A. withdrew from active life, and retired to Wiesbaden.

A cappella (Ital.), in church style, *i.e.* for voices alone, without any instrumental accompaniment. (*See* CAPPELLA.)

Academy (Fr. *académie*, Ital. *accademia*), an exercise ground in ancient Athens where Plato was accustomed to assemble with his pupils, and discourse to them; the name then passed on from Plato's school, and in 1470 was seized hold of afresh by one of the learned societies at the court of Cosimo de Medici, which called itself the "Platonic A." Since then numerous other societies of learning and art have arisen, which have taken the name A. The greater number of the German academies are State institutions: the academies of Berlin and Paris consist of an almost fixed number of members in ordinary. The French *académies* consist of the *Académie française* (A. for French language and literature), the *Académie des inscriptions et belles-lettres* (for history, archæology, and classical literature), the *A. des sciences* (for natural philosophy), the *A. des beaux-arts* (A. of arts), and the *A. des sciences morales et politiques* (law, political economy, etc.). The *A. des beaux-arts* is richly endowed, and offers every year a number of important prizes: the science of music owes much of its progress to the competitions of this A. The Berlin A. of arts is a State institution (but entirely distinct from the A. of sciences), of which the School of Composition, the *Hochschule für Musik*, and the Institute for Church Music are branches. (*See* CONSERVATORIUM.) The Royal Academy at Brussels has also a branch for the fine arts; and since 1780 Boston possesses an A. of arts and sciences.—In a wider sense institutions of all kinds for education, especially the universities, and high schools for special subjects are included under the term A. Also musical academies claim a right to the name, although it is actually only borne by a few (Royal Academy of Music in London, Kullak's *Neue A. der Tonkunst* in Berlin, the

Academical Institute for church music at Breslau, etc.). (*Cf.* LYCEUM.)—Also concert societies and operatic enterprises have often taken the name of A.; as, for example, the Academy of Ancient Music (1710–92), a concert society established in London for the encouragement of ancient music; the "Royal Academy of Music," a company for the performance of Italian opera, established in London (1720–28), for which Handel wrote 14 operas; the *Académie (nationale, impériale, royale,* according to the Government in power) *de musique* at Paris is nothing more than the Grand Opéra existing since 1669, in connection with which may be named the *École royale de Chant* (1784), the germ of the present Conservatoire de Paris; and the Academy of Music at New York, a house devoted to opera, but especially to concerts. In Italy *accademia* is quite a common term for a concert, a musical entertainment.

Acathistus (Lat., from Gk.), a hymn of praise sung in the Greek Church in honour of the Blessed Virgin.

Accademia degli Arcadi, a society of artists (poets and musicians) founded at Rome in 1690. The members bore old Grecian pastoral names.

Accarezzevole (Ital.), in a caressing manner; equivalent to *lusingando*.

Accelerando (Ital.), accelerating the time; getting gradually faster.

Accent (1) is the prominence given to certain notes or chords by emphasis. The stress put upon the important notes of phrases, motives and sub-motives, which notes always occur at the beginning, or in the middle of a bar, or on the moment of any beat, has, according to the traditional teaching of metre and rhythm, been reckoned amongst accents (as a so-called grammatical or metrical, regular, positive accent); but as this stress is not an extra emphasis, but merely the constant rising and falling (*crescendo* and *diminuendo*) which is actually the basis of musical expression, it is confusing to mix it up with accent. Real accents are rather those extra reinforcements of sound which disturb the natural course of dynamic development (*cf* DYNAMICS, THE ART OF, and METRE, THE ART OF) occasionally turning it topsy-turvy, and which the composer generally indicates by special marks (*sf.*, >, ∧): A frequent and important A. is that *of the commencement*, the bringing into prominence the first note of a phrase or motive; this makes the thematic structure specially clear, but if continually employed when not demanded by the composer would become repulsive and obtrusive. Certain rhythmical formations, especially *anticipations by syncopation* of notes whose full harmonic effect is only realised on the following accented part of the bar, require accentuation (*rhythmical* A.); and in a similar manner complicated harmonies, chance *dissonances, notes suggesting modulation* must be made prominent (*harmonic* A.). Again, the highest point of a melody, when by its position in the bar it does not occur at the same time as the highest point of the dynamic development, must be marked (*melodic* A.). On the other hand, dynamic contrasts of figures not organically connected, such as are produced with striking effect in orchestral works, must be regarded as direct emanations from the composer's creative phantasy, and cannot be subjected to classification and rule. A kind of negative accent is produced when the culminating point of a loud passage is suddenly changed to *piano*, a means from which Beethoven first drew most powerful effects.—(2) An antiquated ornament and similar to our appoggiatura (Ital. *accento*); it was formerly indicated in various ways. It was executed so that the upper or under second (scale note) was placed before the note which had the A. sign.

Played:

In quick movement, and with notes of short value, the note following lost the half of its value; in the case of longer notes, less. Walther (1732) distinguishes, besides, a *double A.* (*accento doppio*), in which the first note was shortened, and the second taken beforehand in portamento, in quite similar fashion to the *port de voix.*

The indication ǁ is, nevertheless, rare; the signs given above for the simple A. are understood sometimes in the one, sometimes in the other sense; and the terms *A.*, *Chute*, *Porte de voix*, are used synonymously. (*Cf. also* ASPIRATION.) (3) Various attempts have been made to understand and interpret *accents* as musical notes, especially the accents of the Hebrew language. (*Cf.* ANTON.) Anyhow, it is almost certain that the accentuation of the Psalms, etc., was a kind of musical notation, but only in the same sense as the oldest neumes (which, indeed, to all appearances, were evolved from the Greek accents), viz. an *approximate* note-indication, a guide to those who had learnt the melody by oral tradition. It is easy to see, from their verbal significance, that the three Greek accents are the elements from which sprang the neumes ('*oxytonon* = raising of the voice = Virga; again, *baÿy tonon* = lowering of the voice = Jacens, Punctus · - -; and ʌ or ∾ *perispomenon*, a waving to and fro of the voice, a flourish = Plica. (*Cf.* NEUMES.)

Accented, Once-, Twice-. (*Cf.* **A.**)

Accentus, as part of the Catholic ritual, is the counterpart of *concentus*. In the old directions for liturgical singing, everything which the whole of the choir had to perform—*i.e.* hymns, psalms, responses, hallelujahs, sequences, etc.—was included under the name *concentus*. On the other hand, the intonation of the collects, epistle, gospel, lessons, in fact, everything which was sung, or rather recited, by the priest and others who served at the altar, was included under A. For the most part, the A. keeps on the same tone, and the interpunction is indicated by risings (question) or fallings (full stop) of the cadence.

Acciaccatûra (Ital., a crushing), an obsolete ornament in organ and pianoforte music, which consisted of the striking of the under second of the note of a chord at the same time as that note, but immediately relinquishing the auxiliary note. The French name of this ornament is *Pincé étouffé*. The A. was a favourite device with organists and cembalists, and was seldom written out: in a single part it was indicated (*a*) by a small note with a stroke through the stem, in a chord (*b*), by means of an oblique stroke.

(a) *(b)*

Played: Played:

Since the last century, however, the latter sign was used also for *arpeggio* (q.v.). The name A. is now used for the short *appoggiatura*.

Accidentals (Ger., *Versetzungszeichen*) are signs for lowering, raising, and restoring the natural notes of the fundamental scale (q.v.), thus ♭, ♯, ♮, ♭♭, ✗, ♮♭, ♮♯, ♮♮. The simple ♭ lowers the note by a semitone, the ♯ raises it by a semitone; in either case the ♮ restores the scale note. The double flat lowers it by two semitones; for ex., [♭♭ ●] is, on the pianoforte, the key *a*, but it is not called *a*, but *b double flat*. Also after a simple ♭, previously marked, or belonging to the signature, *b*-, *e*-, *a*-*double flat*, etc., require the sign ♭♭. ♮♭, or simply ♭ after a note with ♭♭, turns a note lowered by two semitones into one lowered by one; ♮♮, or simply ♮, restores a doubly lowered note to its original position. The double sharp (✗) raises by two semitones: [✗ ●] means on the pianoforte the key *g* (*f double sharp*). Also with previously indicated single sharps, *f*- *c*- *double sharp*, etc., require a ✗; ♮♯, or simply ♯ after a note with ✗, changes a note doubly raised into one singly raised; ♮♮ restores the note to its original position. With regard to the meaning of the A. indicated at the beginning of a piece or section, especially at the beginning of a line, or after a double bar, *cf.* SIGNATURE. ♮ and ♯ were originally identical signs; the ♭♭ and × are of considerably later origin, and first appeared about 1700. The whole system of chromatic signs (*Cantus transpositus transformatus, Musica ficta, falsa*) has been gradually developed from a twofold form of the B, the second letter of the fundamental scale, which, already in the 10th century, was either round (*B rotundum molle*) or square (*B quadratum durum* [♭]), and then in the first case indicated our B flat, in the latter our B natural (the German *h* appeared in letter notation in the 16th century through being confused with the ♭. (*See* TABLATURE.) Already in the 13th century the ♭ had, by hasty writing, assumed the forms ♯ and ♮, and owing to the transference of the B of double meaning, to other degrees (E, A), became the sign for the higher of two notes connected with each other, while ♭ stood for the lower. Thus ♭ became a sign for lowering, and ♮ for raising, so that even ♮ before F indicated our F sharp, and ♭ before F not F flat, but merely F, to distinguish it from F sharp. Right into the 18th century, ♭ revoked a sharp, and ♯ or ♮ revoked a ♭, and care must be taken not to interpret these accidentals in a modern sense. It must also be remembered that only in the first half of the 17th century did it become the custom for a ♯ or ♭ to be valid for the whole bar; they only remained in force if the same note was repeated several times, but, even with one new note intervening, had to be repeated. (*Cf.* Riemann, " Studien zur Geschichte der Notenschrift," pp. 52–63 [*Die Musica ficta*].)

Accolade, a brace which connects two or more staves (in organ, pf. music, scores, etc.).

Accompagnato (Ital., " accompanied "), technical expression for recitative with constant accompaniment, in contradistinction from *Recitativo secco*, in which only the harmonies are briefly struck. (*See* ACCOMPANIMENT.)

Accompaniment (Fr. *accompagnement*, Ital. *accompagnamento*). In pieces written for solo instruments or voice, the instrumental part other than the solo, for ex., the orchestral part in concertos, the pf. part in songs with pianoforte, etc. **To accompany,** to follow. **Accompanist,** player of the accompaniment, esp. the pianoforte player who accompanies a solo singer or instrumentalist, formerly the cembalist or organist, who, from the figured bass, worked out a complete part. (*See* GENERAL BASS, ACCOMPANYING PARTS, and ACCOMPAGNATO.)

Accompanying parts, those parts in modern music which do not bear the melody, but which are subordinate to the melodic (chief) part, and which unfold its harmonies. The older contrapuntists of the 14th to the 16th century were unacquainted with *A . p.* in the real sense of the term. In purely vocal compositions, with strict or free imitations, which they exclusively cultivated, each part contained melody (was a *concerted* part), and generally that part which bore what we now call the theme (the *Cantus firmus*, by preference, in long, sustained notes) was the least melodious. A primitive kind of accompaniment certainly did exist at a much earlier period. The songs of the troubadours were accompanied by the minstrels on the viol or *vielle;* the bards sang to the *crowd*, the Greeks to the cithara, lyre, or flute, the Hebrews to the psaltery. It appears, however, that the instrumental accompaniment only doubled the vocal part in unison, or in octave, and possibly only those notes which fell upon strong beats. Accompaniment, in the modern sense of the term, appears first about 1600, and its cradle was Italy. When solo- had so merged into choral-music that the simple love-song and the duet appeared only in the form of a chorus à 4 or 5 (Madrigal), the necessary reaction took place, restoring to solo singing its natural rights, without, however, sacrificing the now recognised charm of harmony. Thus *instrumental accompaniment* was at first arranged so that in a choral composition the highest part was assigned to a solo voice, whilst the rest were played by instruments (this pseudo-monody was already common in the 16th century), but later on the composers wrote at once for a solo voice with instrumental accompaniment. This transition suggested, so it seems, arrangements of choral pieces for one vocal part with lute, the *salon* instrument of that day. The impossibility of sustaining sounds on that instrument led to the interpolation of ornaments, arpeggios, runs, etc., and this habit led to a reaction, to a thoroughly different mode of writing for the accompanying instrument. The clavicembalo came into use instead of the lute, and for church performances the organ, and thus there was a gradual leading up to those meagre instrumental accompaniments, known under the name of *General Bass* (*Thorough Bass*) or *Continuo*. In these, figures written over a bass part indicated what harmonies the accompanist had to play, though the actual mode of presenting them was left to his skill. The *continuo*, however, was not always figured, as, for example, in some of Handel's and Bach's works; the proper accompaniment in that case could only be discovered from a perusal of the score. Already in the early part of the 17th century, composers began to add to the *continuo* elaborate parts for single instruments (obbligato), and thus the *A . p.* again came to a state of great independence, without, however, contesting the supremacy of the principal part, which, meanwhile, was given not only to the voice, but to single instruments suitable for the purpose (violin, flute, oboe). A similar change had also taken place in *choral music*, and the soprano (the upper part) had become bearer of the melody, while the other parts were treated in a simpler fashion, a justification for the qualifying term "accompanying." With J. S. Bach the *polyphonic style* flourished once more, reached, indeed, its zenith; but his polyphony is so clear in its harmonies, and in so masterly a manner is the ensemble subordinate to the crowning melody, that his style must be regarded as worthy of the highest admiration, and as a master-pattern. To-day, with a period of strongly marked monophony behind us, one in which melody rules over a chord accompaniment of more or less simplicity (especially in clavier composition), we are actually harking back to a more independent contrapuntal treatment of accompaniment, and thus approaching nearer to the manner of J. S. Bach.

Accord à l'ouvert (Fr.), a chord which requires no stopping, but can be played on the open strings.

Accordare (Ital.), to tune; or, to be in tune.

Accordion (Ger. *Ziehharmonika*), the smallest instrument of the organ species, *i.e.* of wind instruments with keyboard and mechanical contrivance for wind; it was invented in 1829 by Damian at Vienna; its prototype was the Chinese *Shêng* and the mouth-harmonica. Accordions are made of various sizes; in the hands of skilful players the largest and best are not entirely devoid of artistic value. Free reeds are placed against the upper and under boards of a bellows with many folds, and these reeds are bent, some inwards, some outwards; the former speak when the bellows is pressed together, the latter (by suction, as in the American organ) when it is drawn out. Small accordions have only a diatonic scale for the right hand, and for the left a few bass harmonies, which render free modulation impossible. On the other hand, large instruments, such as those made by Wheatstone (MELOPHONE, CONCERTINA), have a chromatic scale, through several octaves, for each hand.

Accordo (Ital.), a chord.

Accordo. (*See* LYRE.)

Accordoir, French name for the tuning-key for the pianoforte, and also for the tuning-cone for the metal lip-pipes of organs.

Accrescendo (Ital.), crescendo.

Achard (L é o n), eminent singer (lyric tenor), b. Feb. 16, 1831, Lyons, pupil of Bordogni at the Paris Conservatoire, made his *début* (1854) at the Théâtre Lyrique; was from 1856–62 at the Grand Théâtre, Lyons, at the Opéra Comique, Paris, from 1862–71; and after fresh study at Milan, at the Paris Grand Opéra from 1871.

Achtfüssig (Ger.), of 8-ft. pitch. (*See* FOOT-TONE.)

Ackermann, A. J., b. Apr. 2, 1836, Rotterdam, pupil of J. H. Lübeck, W. F. G. Nicolas,

and Fr. Wietz at the Royal Music School at the Hague; was appointed pf. teacher there in 1865, for organ and theory in 1867. He composed songs (Op. 2, 9) and pf. pieces for two and four hands.

Acoustics (Greek), literally, the science of hearing, *i.e.* the teaching of the nature of sound, the conditions of its origin, the mode and rapidity of its transmission, as well as its ultimate perception by the ear. A distinction is made between physical A. and physiological A.: the latter treats specially of the perception of sounds. Musical A. only concerns that part of A. which deals with available musical tones (sounds), to be distinguished from unmusical noises. Musical sounds are given out (1) by strings struck by bow or hammer, or plucked with the finger; (2) by wind-instruments (including the human voice); (3) by elastic rods (tuning-fork, steel-harmonicon, straw-fiddle); (4) by curved metal disks (cymbals, gong, bells); (5) by stretched membranes (kettledrums, drums). Musical sound, physically considered, consists of a regular, rapid alternation of condensation and rarefaction of elastic bodies (vibrations); the pitch depends upon the rapidity of succession of the vibrations, and the strength (intensity) of the sound on the extent (amplitude) of the deviations from a state of equilibrium. The vibrations of the elastic body producing sound communicate themselves to the surrounding air (or, previously, to firm bodies in contact with it, *see* SOUND-BOARD), and travel in it at a rate of 340 *mètres* per second, at a temperature of 16° C. For acoustical purposes it is usual to take the velocity of sound at 1,056 feet per second, which number stands in relationship with the determination of pitch according to foot-tone (q.v.). As, in fact, the velocity of sound, divided by the vibration number must necessarily give the length of the sound-wave (a double vibration, *i.e.* the sum of condensation and rarefaction), for contra-C with 33 vibrations (1,056 : 33) we have a wave-sound of 32 feet, *i.e.* as the length of an open flue-pipe only corresponds to a simple wave (half a complete wave), contra-C is produced by an open flue-pipe of 16 feet. The number of vibrations which a sound makes in a given time (seconds) is easily obtained by help of the Syren (q.v.), improved by Cagniard de Latour. Other interesting subjects connected with A. are the phenomena of *overtones, sympathy of tones, combination tones,* and *beats.* (*Cf.* the respective articles.)

Act (Ital. *Atto*), the usual term for the chief sections of dramatic works (dramas, operas, ballets), and even for oratorios, for which, however, the expression "part" is more usual. The various acts are separated from one another by the falling of the curtain and an interval of some length. The acts are often subdivided into *tableaux, i.e.* principal scenes with change of decoration, which are divided by short pauses and falling of the drop-scene. The number of acts varies between 1 and 5 : that of the *tableaux* is naturally, for the most part, greater.

Acte de cadence (Fr.), the two chords that form a cadence.

Action (Ger. *Mechanik ;* Fr. *Mécanique*) is the name given to the more or less complicated mechanism of musical instruments, especially the pianoforte, organ, orchestrion, etc. Concerning the action of older kinds of keyboards (clavichord, clavicimbal), also concerning the difference between the English (Silbermann, Christofori) and German (Stein of Vienna) action and Erard's *Double échappement*, etc., *cf.* PIANOFORTE.

Acuta, a mixture stop in the organ : as a rule, it has a tierce and is smaller than the Mixture, *i.e.* begins with higher sounds (3 fold to 5 fold, of 1⅗ and 1 foot).

Acuteness. A musical sound is said to become more acute (*i.e.* higher) in proportion to the increase in the number of vibrations.

Acutus (Lat.), (1) sharp, acute ; (2) the name of one of the *accentus ecclesiastici.*

Adagio, one of the oldest indications of *tempo,* already in use at the commencement of the 17th century. In Italian A. means conveniently, comfortably, but in the course of time has come to mean in music, at a *slow* rate, even *very slow* (though not so slow as *largo*). This is specially the case in Germany ; whereas in Italy, following the meaning of the word, even to-day A. comes nearer to what we understand by *Andante.* The term A. is used either for a short passage, or when placed at the beginning of a movement indicates the *tempo* throughout, so that it has come to mean the entire movement of a sonata, symphony, or quartet, etc. The A. is generally the second movement, yet there are many exceptions (9th Symphony of Beethoven's, and since then frequently) : such a movement is still called an A., even though it contain a more lively section (*andante, più mosso,* etc.). The superlative *adagissimo,* "extremely slow," is rare. The diminutive form *adagietto* means "rather slow," *i.e.* not so slow as A. ; if written above a piece it indicates a slow piece of short duration (small A.). (*Cf.* TEMPO.)

Adam, (1) L o u i s, b. Dec. 3, 1758, Müttersholtz (Alsace), d. April 8, 1848, Paris ; a distinguished musician, who thoroughly studied Bach and Handel ; from 1797–1843 was professor of the pianoforte at the Paris Conservatoire, and the teacher of Kalkbrenner, Hérold, etc. He was the author of a highly esteemed "Méthode Nouvelle pour le Piano " (1802 ; translated by Czerny, 1826), and published also pf. sonatas, variations, etc. (2) A d o l p h e C h a r l e s, son of the former, a well-known opera composer, b. July 24, 1803, Paris, d. May 3, 1856 ; was intended for a literary

career, yet showed little aptitude for it. But though he was received as a music pupil at the Conservatoire in 1817, he worked carelessly and fitfully, until Boieldieu took him for composition, as he discovered his talent for melody ; and rapid progress was now made. After he had made himself known by all kinds of pianoforte pieces (transcriptions, songs), he brought out his first one-act opera, *Pierre et Cathérine,* at the Opéra Comique (1829) ; good success encouraged him, and there soon followed a series of 13 other works, until he made his mark in 1836 with the *Postillon de Longjumeau.* From 1846–49 Adam ceased writing, for he had a dispute with the director of the Opéra Comique, and started an opera-house on his own account (Théâtre National, 1847) ; the Revolution of 1848 utterly ruined him, and then he devoted himself industriously to composition. After his father's death (1848) he became professor of composition at the Conservatoire. Of his 53 stage works, the operas *Le Fidèle Berger, La Rose de Péronne, Le Roi d'Yvetot, Giralda, La Poupée de Nuremberg,* deserve mention ; also the ballets, *Giselle, Le Corsaire,* etc. If none of Adam's works can be called classical, yet their rhythmic grace and melodic wealth will at least ensure for them a long life. A short biography of Adam was published by Pougin in 1876 ; *vide* also " Derniers Souvenirs d'un Musicien " (autobiographical notices and various newspaper articles from the pen of Adam, 1857–59, 2 vols.).—(3) K a r l F e r d i n a n d, favourite composer of part-songs for male voices, b. Dec. 22, 1806 ; d. Dec. 23, 1867, as cantor at Leisnig (Saxony).

Adam de la Hale (or Halle), nicknamed *Le Bossu d'Arras,* b. about 1240, Arras, d. 1287, Naples ; a gifted poet and composer of high importance (a troubadour), of whose works many have been preserved, and were published in 1872 by Coussemaker (" Œuvres complètes du Trouvère Adam de la Hale," etc.). The most important of them is : *Jeu de Robin et de Marion,* a kind of comic opera (operetta) of which the poem and music are both preserved complete ; also a series of other *Jeux (Jeu d'Adam* and *Jeu du Pèlerin), rondeaux, motets,* and *chansons.* The works of Adam de la Hale are of incalculable value for the musical history of his time.

Adam von Fulda, b. 1450, one of the oldest German composers, who was much thought of in his time ; also the author of an interesting treatise on the " Theory of Music," printed by Gerbert in the third volume of the " Scrip tores."

Adamberger, V a l e n t i n (not Joseph), famous tenor singer, b. July 6, 1743, Munich, d. Aug. 24, 1804, Vienna, pupil of Valesi ; gained triumphs in Italy under the name Adamonti ; appeared also in London ; and was engaged in 1780 at the Vienna court opera, and in 1789 as singer in the court band. Mozart wrote the Belmonte, and some concert arias for him. His daughter Antonie was betrothed to Theod. Körner.

Adami da Bolsena, Andrea, b. 1663, Bolsena, d. July 22, 1742, Rome; was papal maestro, and wrote "Osservazioni per ben regolare il coro dei cantori della Capella Pontifica" (1711), a book rich in historical notes.

Adamonti, *vide* ADAMBERGER.

Adams, Thomas, a distinguished English organist and composer for that instrument, b. Sept. 5, 1785, London, d. there, Sept. 15, 1858; superintended, amongst other things, the musical performances on the Apollicon, built by Flight and Robson. His published works are organ fugues, interludes, sets of variations (also for pf.), and sacred music.

Adcock, James, b. 1778, Eton, Bucks, d. Apr. 30, 1860, Cambridge; was chorister at St. George's Chapel, Windsor, and then at Eton; in 1797 became a lay clerk, and afterwards a member of various church choirs in Cambridge, where he finally became choirmaster at King's College. He published "The Rudiments of Singing," and a number of glees of his own composition.

Addison, John, English composer, b. about 1770, d. Jan. 30, 1844, London; led an active life as double-bass player, conductor (Dublin), cotton manufacturer (Manchester), music-seller (with M. Kelly in London), and finally as composer and teacher of singing, and of the doublebass. His wife (Miss Williams) was a highly esteemed opera singer. Addison's operettas were much admired in their day (1805-18).

Addolorāto (Ital.), with expression of grief.

Adelboldus, Bishop of Utrecht, d. Nov. 27, 1027; the author of a treatise on musical theory, printed by Gerbert in the first volume of the "Scriptores."

Adelburg, August, Ritter von, violinist, b. Nov. 1, 1830, Constantinople, d., disordered in intellect, Oct. 20, 1873, Vienna; was intended for the diplomatic career, but studied (1850-4) under Mayseder, who made him a first-rate violinist. In the sixties he created a sensation by the fulness of his tone. He composed sonatas and concertos for violin, stringed quartets, etc.; also 3 operas, *Zrinyi* (1868 at Pesth), *Wallenstein*, and *Martinuzzi*.

Adelung, *vide* ADLUNG.

À demi jeu (Fr.), with half the power of the instrument.

À demi voix (Fr.), with half the power of the voice (*mezza voce*).

À deux (Fr.), for two instruments or voices. This expression is also used for *à deux temps*.

Adgio, Ado, abbreviations for ADAGIO.

Adiaphon (= incapable of getting out of tune), or *Gabelklavier*, an instrument with keyboard invented by Fischer and Fritzsch at Leipzig, patented in 1882, and successfully

produced at the festival of the Allgemeiner Deutscher Musikverein at Leipzig in 1883. Instead of strings it has tuning-forks. The ethereal though somewhat empty sound of the instrument has recently been strengthened by double forks tuned in octave.

Adirāto (Ital.), in an angry manner.

Adjustment *of the registers of the voice.* (*See* REGISTER.)

Adler (1), Georg, Hungarian composer, b. 1806, Ofen; excellent performer on the violin and pianoforte, and teacher; published a series of good chamber-music works, pf. variations, songs, and part-songs.—(2) Guido, b. Nov. 1, 1855, Eibenschütz (Moravia), son of a physician, after whose early death (1856) the mother moved to Iglau. In 1864 A. attended the academic Gymnasium at Vienna, of which he conducted the pupils' choir for a time, and also the Conservatorium, where he became pupil of Bruckner and Dessoff. In 1874, after gaining a prize, he left the Conservatorium, attended the University, and, together with F. Mottl and K. Wolf, founded the academic Wagner Society, which soon became an important body. In 1878 he took the degree of *Dr. juris*, in 1880 that of *Dr. phil.* (Dissertation "Die historischen Grundklassen der christlich abendländischen Musik bis 1600," printed in the *Allg. M. Z.*, 1880, Nos. 44-47), and in 1881 qualified himself at the Vienna University as a private lecturer on the science of music (Thesis: "Studie zur Geschichte der Harmonie," printed in the report of the "Phil. hist. Kl. d. kaiserl. Acad. der Wissensch.," Vienna, 1881, also separately). In 1882 he went as delegate to the International Liturgical Congress at Arezzo, of which he wrote a detailed report. In 1884, together with Chrysander and Spitta, he founded the *Vierteljahrsschrift für Musikwissenschaft*, which he edited for a year, and in 1885 was appointed Professor of the Science of Music at the German University at Prague. Adler on that occasion wrote a monograph on the Fauxbourdon (q.v.), and the treatise of Guilelmus Monachus, in which he clearly shows that counterpoint and harmony were of independent origin, and developed themselves collaterally. In 1892 he was elected president of the Central Committee of the International Exhibition for "Musik u. Theater"—(3) Vincent, composer and pianist, b. 1826, d. Jan. 4, 1871, Geneva.

Adlgasser, Anton Cajetan, b. April 3, 1728, Innzell, near Traunstein (Bavaria), pupil of Eberlin at Salzburg, d. there Dec. 21, 1777, where from 1751 he was principal organist of the cathedral. His church compositions were highly valued, and were even performed at Salzburg after his death.

Adlung (Adelung), Jakob, b. Jan. 14, 1699, Bindersleben, near Erfurt, d. July 5, 1762; studied philology and theology at Erfurt and

Jena, but at the same time pursued his musical studies with such earnestness that in 1727 he was able to be appointed town organist, and in 1741 professor at the Gymnasium at Erfurt, besides which he was active as a private teacher of music. A. wrote three works of importance for the history of music—" Anleitung zur musikalischen Gelahrtheit " (1758, 2nd ed. 1783, revised by Joh. Ad. Hiller) ; " Musica mechanica organoedi " (1768), and " Musikalisches Siebengestirn " (1768, both published by L. Albrecht).

Adolfati, Andrea, b. 1711, Venice, d. about 1760, pupil of Galuppi ; he was maestro di capella at Venice (St. Maria della Salute), and somewhere about 1750 at Genoa (dell' Annunziazione). A. produced six operas, and wrote, besides, a great quantity of church music.

Adornamento (Ital.), an ornament.

Adrastos, Peripatetic philosopher, about 330 B.C., pupil of Aristotle; he wrote a work on music ("Ἁρμονικῶν βίβλια τρία ") of which, however, only extracts have been preserved in the " Harmonica " of Manuel Bryennius.

Adriansen (Hadrianius), Emanuel, b. Antwerp; a distinguished performer on the lute in the 16th century. He published in 1592 " Pratum musicum," etc., a collection of compositions by Cyprian di Rore, Orlando di Lasso, Jachet van Berchem, Hubert Waelrant, and others, freely transcribed for the lute in tabulature (preludes, fantasias, madrigals, motets, canzonets, and dance pieces).

Adrien (really Andrien), Martin Joseph, called La Neuville, also A. *l'aîné*, b. May 26, 1767, Liége ; bass singer at the Paris Opéra, 1785–1804, afterwards chorus-master there. He died Nov. 19, 1824, as teacher of singing at the *École royale de musique ;* he was the composer of the " Hymne à la Liberté " on the occasion of the departure of the Prussians (1792), and the " Hymne à la Victoire " (1795), and the one to the Martyrs to liberty.

Adufe (Sp.), tambourine, timbrel.

A duoi and **a doi** (Ital.). The same as *a due. Duoi* and *doi* are obsolete spellings of *due.*

Aegidius, (1) Aegidius Zamorensis (Johannes), Spanish Franciscan friar of Zamora, about 1270; he was author of a treatise on the theory of music printed by Gerbert (" Scriptores," vol. iii.).—(2) Aegidius de Murino, theorist of the 15th century, whose treatise on measured music was printed by Coussemaker (" Scriptores," vol. iii.).

Æolian Harp (Ger. *Windharfe, Wetterharfe, Geisterharfe*) is a long narrow sound-box with or without sound-holes, on which a number (*ad libitum*) of catgut strings are stretched ; these must vary in thickness, so that a different tension for each will be required to produce the same pitch, but none should be very tightly stretched. If the strings are exposed to a current of air, they begin to sound, and in conse-

quence of difference of tension, would give various kinds of partial vibrations, yet naturally only produce tones which belong to the series of upper tones of the common fundamental tone. The sound is of fairy-like, enchanting effect, as, according to the strength of the air currents, the chords proceed from the most delicate *pianissimo* to a rushing *forte*, and then die away again. The Æ. H. is ancient. St. Dunstan (10th century), Athanasius Kircher (17th century), and Pape (1792) are named, the first as the inventor and the others as improvers. Kircher, in his " Phonurgia " (i. 7), gives a detailed description of such an instrument. It has been materially improved within a recent period, especially by. H. Chr. Koch.

Æolian Key. (*See* CHURCH MODES and GREEK MUSIC.)

Aeoline (Aeolodion, Æolodikon), Klavaeoline, are names for old keyed instruments similar to the present harmonium (free vibrating reeds without tubes). According to Schafhäntl, in his " Biography of Abt Vogler " (p. 36), the organ builder Kissnik at Petersburg was the first who constructed instruments of this kind, about 1280 (in imitation of the human voice).— As a name for organ stops, they indicate such as are of similar construction, *i.e.* free reeds without any tubes, or very small ones, which give a very soft tone, and can be used specially in echo work (mostly with Venetian swell).

Æolomelodicon, or **Choraleon.** This instrument, invented by Professor Hoffmann, and in 1825 constructed by the mechanician Brunner, of Warsaw, was a kind of small organ. Its tone was capable of modification as regards character as well as loudness.

Æqual (Ger., from Lat.). This term signifies " of 8 feet pitch " (*see* FOOT-TONE), *i.e.* of normal pitch ; it is used for organ stops, which on the key C give the sound C ; for ex., *Æqual-principal, i.e.* Open-Diapason 8-ft. (*Cf.* VOCES ÆQUALES.)

Æquisonus (Lat.), unison.

Aerophon. (*Vide* HARMONIUM.)

Aerts, (1) Egide, flautist, b. March 1, 1822, Boom, near Antwerp ; entered the Brussels Conservatoire at the age of twelve, and already in 1837 made a sensation as a flautist at Paris ; became teacher of the flute at the Brussels Conservatoire in 1847, but died on June 9, 1853, of consumption. His compositions (symphonies, flute concertos, etc.) are not printed.—(2) Felix, b. May 4, 1827, St.-Trond, d. Dec., 1888, Nivelles ; was a pupil at the Brussels Conservatoire (C. Hanssen), worked first for some time as violinist at Brussels, then as conductor at Tournay ; lived for some years in Paris, and from 1860 was music teacher at Nivelles. A. published two essays on Gregorian song (plain chant), a book of school songs, litanies, an elementary instruction book, also a series of fantasias for orchestra, violin variations, etc.

Aesthetics. (*See* ESTHETICS.)

Aeusserst (Ger.), extremely; as *äusserst rasch*, extremely quick.

Aevia, or **Ævia, aeuia,** is the oldest mode of noting the abbreviations of the word *Alleluja* (with omission of consonants) in liturgical song.

Affabile (Ital.), in a pleasing, kindly manner.

Affanato (Ital.), in a distressed, sorrowful manner.

Affanosamente (Ital.), anxiously, restlessly.

Affanoso (Ital.), anxious, restless.

Affetto (Ital.), with emotion; *con a.*, *affettuoso*, with tender feeling, with much expression (and free rendering).

Affettuosamente, Affettuoso (Ital.), with passionate and tender feeling.

Affilar (or **filar**) **il tuono** (Ital.), to sustain steadily a sound, similar to *metter la voce, messa di voce* (q.v.), though in the latter term a *Crescendo* and *Diminuendo* are generally understood.

Affilard, Michel d', tenor singer in the chapel of Louis XIV. from 1683 to 1708. He published a method for sight-singing ("Principes très faciles," etc., 1691, 1705, 1710, and 1717).

Afflito (Ital.), cast down, sorrowful.

Affrettando (Ital.), hurrying, like *stringendo*. *Affrettato*, in a hurrying manner, like *più mosso*.

A ♭. A lowered by a flat; *A-flat major* chord = *a flat, c, e flat; A-flat minor* chord = *a flat, c flat, e flat; A-flat major* key, with signature of 4 flats, *A-flat minor* key, with 7 flats. (*See* KEY.)

Afranio, degli Albonesi at Ferrara, b. end of the 15th century at Pavia; he was the inventor of the bassoon (q.v.).

Afzelius, Arvid August, b. May 6, 1785, d. Sept. 25, 1871; pastor at Enköping (Sweden). He published two collections of Swedish folk melodies: "Svenska folkvisor" (1814–1816, three vols.), and "Afsked of svenska folksharpan" (1848).

Agazzari, Agostino, b. Dec. 2, 1578, Siena, d. there April 10, 1640; was first a musician in the service of the Emperor Matthias, then for a time maestro di capella at the German College, the church of St. Apollinaris, and afterwards at the *Seminario Romano*, where he became acquainted with Viadana, and adopted his innovations. In 1630 he became maestro of Siena cathedral. In his time he was held in high esteem as a composer; his works (madrigals, motets, psalms, and other sacred compositions, many of them à 8) were reprinted in Germany and Holland. A. was one of the first to give instructions as to the execution of figured basses

(in the preface to the third book of his motets, 1605).

Agelaos, of Tegea, was the first victor in the musical contest in the Pythian games (559 B.C., 8th Pythiad). He is said to have been the first virtuoso on the cithara without song. (*See* CITHARROEDA.)

Agende (Ger., from Lat. *agenda*, "things which have to be done") are the prescriptions for the order and special arrangement of divine service, particularly in the Reformed Church; in the Catholic Church this is fixed by the *Ritual*.

Agevole, or **con agevolezza** (Ital.), lightly, with ease.

Agilità (Ital.), nimbleness.

Agilmente (Ital.), nimbly.

Agitato (Ital.), agitated, restless.

Agnelli, Salvatore, b. 1817, Palermo, trained at Naples Conservatorio by Furno, Zingarelli, and Donizetti; he first wrote a series of operas for Italian theatres (Naples and Palermo). In 1846, however, he went to Marseilles, and produced the operas *La Jacquerie* (1849), *Léonore de Médicis* (1855), and *Les deux Avares* (1860), also several ballets. He wrote, besides, a Miserere, Stabat Mater, a cantata (Apotheosis of Napoleon I., performed by three orchestras in the Jardin des Tuileries, 1856); and he had in manuscript three operas (*Cromwell, Stefania,* and *Sforza*). He died in 1874.

Agnesi (1), Maria Theresia d', an excellent pianist, b. 1724, Milan, d. about 1780. She composed many works for the pianoforte, and four operas (*Sofonisbe, Ciro in Armenia, Nitocri,* and *Insubria consolata*). — (2) Louis Ferdinand Leopold Agniez, named *Luigi A.*, b. July 17, 1833, Erpent (Namur), d. Feb. 2, 1875, London. He was an excellent bass singer, studied at the Brussels Conservatoire, was for a time maestro at the church of Ste. Catherine, and conductor of several societies at Brussels. The small success of his opera, *Harmold le Normand* (1858), however, induced him to devote himself to singing. He studied afresh under Duprez at Paris, and then fulfilled various engagements, and made concert tours; during his last years he was famed in London as a Handelian singer. He composed songs, motets, etc.

Agniez. (*See* AGNESI 2.)

Agnus Dei (Lat., "Lamb of God"). (*See* MASS.)

Agobardus, Archbishop of Lyons, d. 840, Saintonge. He was the author of three musical treatises: "De divina psalmodia," "De ecclesiæ officiis," and "De correctione Antiphonarii" (printed in "Bibl. Patr.," XIV.).

Agoge is the Greek term for *tempo* (**Rhythmical A.**) (*See* AGOGICS.)

Agogics. This term relates to the small modifications of *tempo* (also called *tempo rubato*), which are necessary to genuine expression. The editor of this dictionary made a first attempt in his "Musikalische Dynamik und Agogik" (1884) to establish a systematic theory of expressive performance. The science of Agogics, speaking generally, works on parallel lines with dynamics, *i.e.* a slight motion is associated with *crescendo*. Notes which form centres of gravity are dwelt upon, and feminine endings return gradually to the normal value (diminuendo). This holds specially good within narrow limits, whereas within wider ones the agogic restraint, the powerful repression of the shock must produce a more intense effect. (*Cf.* DYNAMICS, SCIENCE OF, and "EXPRESSION.")

Agogic Accent is the name given by H. Riemann, in his phrasing-editions, to the slight prolongation of the note-value indicated by ⌢, in rhythms, which are in conflict with the species of time, and which clearly preserves the centre of gravity of the bar motive; more especially, in suspensions, whereby the harmonic value is rendered clearer.

Agon (Gr.), contest ; the musical A. formed an essential part of the festival games of ancient Greeks, especially of the Pythian.

Agostini (1), Ludovico, b. 1534, Ferrara, d. there Sept. 20, 1590, as maestro di capella to Alfonso II., of Este, and at the cathedral. He wrote madrigals, masses, motets, vespers, etc., which were printed partly at Venice (Gardano), and partly at Ancona (Landrini).—(2) Paolo, b. 1593, Vallerano, pupil and son-in-law of Bern. Nanini, d. 1629 as maestro at the Vatican. He was a distinguished contrapuntist, and wrote a great number of sacred compositions (up to 48 parts), which have been in some measure preserved in Roman libraries. Two books of psalms (1619), two books of Magnificats and Antiphones (1620), and five books of masses, were printed.—(3) Pietro Simone, b. 1650, Rome, was ducal maestro at Parma ; an opera of his (*Il ratto delle Sabine*) was produced at Venice.

Agrell, Johann, b. Feb. 1, 1701, Loeth (East Gothland), d. Jan. 19, 1765, Nuremberg. From 1723 to 1746 he was "Hofmusikus" (violinist) at Cassel, where he also made a name as a performer on the harpsichord ; from 1746 he was capellmeister at Nuremberg. A series of his excellent compositions (symphonies, concertos, sonatas, etc.) were engraved at Nuremberg, while many others have come down to us in manuscript.

Agréments (Fr.), ornaments.

Agricŏla, (1) Alexander, one of the most celebrated composers of the 15th century, who, according to the most recent investigations (Van der Straeten), appears to have been a German ; he was for a long time, up to June 10, 1474, singer in the Ducal chapel at Milan, went then to Lower Italy with his family, served (1500)

at Brussels as chaplain, and as chapel singer at the Court of Philip I., the Fair, whom he followed to Spain (1505), where he probably died 1506, at the age of 60 (in that case b. 1446). He was highly esteemed as a composer, so that Petrucci in his three oldest publications (from 1501 to 1503) included 31 of his Songs and Motets, and (1504) printed a volume of his Masses ("Missæ Alexandri Agricolae: Le Serviteur, Je ne demande, Malheur me bat, Primi toni, Secundi toni"). How well known A. was can be gathered from the fact that he was frequently only called "Alexander."—(2) Martin, b. 1486, Sorau, d. June 10, 1556; one of the most important musical writers of the 16th century, together with Seb. Virdung, one of the chief authorities for the history of instruments of his time, a musical automath. From 1510 he was private music teacher at Magdeburg, appointed in 1524 cantor of the Lutheran school ; he lived in somewhat needy circumstances. His most important works are : "Musica figuralis deudsch," "Von den *Proportionibus*" (both without name of year, but reprinted together 1532) ; "Musica instrumentalis deudsch" (1528, 1529, and 1532, the most important work) ; "Rudimenta musices" (1539, 2nd ed. 1543, under the title "Quaestiones vulgariores in Musicam ") ; "Duo libri musices" (1561, "Rudimenta" and "De proportionibus" together) ; "Scholia in musicam planam Wenceslai de Nova Domo" (1540). He also published some collections of pieces ("Ein kurz deudsch Musica," 1528 ; "Musica choralis deudsch," 1533 ; "Deudsche Musica und Gesangbüchlein," 1540; "Ein Sangbüchlein aller Sonntags-Evangelien," 1541), and published Virdung's "Musica getutscht" in verse, with the original illustrations. A., departing from the custom of his time, made use of mensural notation instead of the German tablature in the "Musica instrumentalis."—(3) Johann, b. about 1570, Nuremberg, professor at the Augustine Gymnasium, Erfurt, published, 1601–11, a number of sacred compositions (Motets, Cantiones, etc.).—(4) Wolfgang Christoph, published, in 1651, at Würzburg and Cologne : "Fasciculus musicalis" (eight Masses), and "Fasciculus variarum cantionum " (Motets).—(5) George Ludwig, b. Oct. 25, 1643, Grossfurra, near Sondershausen. 1670 capellmeister at Gotha, d. there Feb. 22, 1676; published at Mühlhausen several collections of sonatas, preludes, and dance movements for stringed instruments, also some Penitential songs and madrigals.— (6) Joh. Friedrich, b. Jan. 4, 1720, Dobitschen, near Altenburg, d., according to Forkel's statement, Nov. 12, 1774, but according to L. Schneider, Dec. 1, 1774, Berlin ; studied law at Leipzig, became pupil of J. S. Bach, and later (1741) of Quanz at Berlin ; 1751 court composer, and in 1759 Graun's successor as director at the royal chapel. He wrote eight operas, (produced from 1750–72 at Potsdam and Berlin, and church compositions, which, however, have remained unpublished. As a writer on music he produced polemical pamphlets against Marpurg (under the pseudonym Olibrio) also a translation of Tosi's "School of Singing," and contributed to Adelung's "Musica mechanica organoedi." His wife, E m i l i a, *née* M o l t e n i (b. 1722, Modena, d. 1780, Berlin), was a distinguished singer, and for a long time member of the Italian Opera at Berlin.

Agthe (1), K a r l C h r i s t i a n, b. 1762, Hettsstädt (Mansfeld), d. Nov. 27, 1797, as Court organist to the Prince v. Bernburg, at Ballenstedt; wrote five operas, a ballet, and some small vocal works.—(2) W i l h e l m J o s e p h A l b r e c h t, son of the former, b. 1790, Ballenstedt; 1810 music teacher and member of the Gewandhaus orchestra at Leipzig, 1823 music teacher at Dresden, 1826 at Posen (where Theodor Kullak was his pupil). He was frightened away by the political disturbances of 1830, and went to Breslau, and in 1832 to Berlin, where up to 1845 he was director of a new music institution. A. published a number of pianoforte compositions of merit; d. 1873.— (3) F r i e d r i c h W i l h e l m, b. 1794, Sangershausen, pupil of Müller and Riemann at Weimar, and of Weinlig at Dresden, 1822–28, cantor at the "Kreuzschule," d. Aug. 19, 1830, disordered in intellect, at Sonnenstein, near Pirna.

Aguado, D i o n i s i o, celebrated guitar player, b. April 8, 1784, Madrid, d. Dec. 29, 1849; he published in 1825 a "Method of playing the Guitar," which passed through three Spanish and one French edition (1827); also *études*, rondos, etc., for his instrument.

Aguilera de Heredia, S e b a s t i a n, monk and maestro di capella at Saragossa at the beginning of the 17th century; published (1618) a collection of Magnificats, which are still sung at Saragossa.

Agujāri, L u c r e z i a, phenomenal singer, b. 1743, Ferrara, d. May 18, 1783, known as *La Bastardella* (she was the natural daughter of a man of high rank, who had her trained by the Abbé Lambertini). She threw into ecstasy, not only Italy (Florence, Milan, etc.), but also London (1775). In 1780 she retired from the stage, and married at Parma the maestro di capella Colla, whose compositions she preferred to all others. The range of her voice upwards was incredibly high; she could shake on f^3, and take the c^4.

Ahle, (1) J o h. R u d o l p h, **b.** Dec. 24, 1625, Mühlhausen in Thuringia, d. there, July 9, 1673; cantor of St. Andreas' church, Göttingen; in 1654 organist of St. Blasius' church, Mühlhausen; in 1656 member of the council, and in 1661 even burgomaster of that town. His principal works are: the "Geistliche Dialoge" (songs in several parts, 1648); "Thüringischer Lustgarten" (1657); also the posthumous "Geistliche Fest und Kommunionandachten;" he also wrote two theoretical works: "Compendium pro

tonellis" (1648; 2nd ed. 1673, "Brevis et perspicua introductio in artem musicam," 3rd and 4th eds., 1690 and 1704, under title "Kurze doch deutliche Anleitung, etc.), and "De progressionibus consonantium."—(2) J o h. G e o r g, son and pupil of the former, b. 1651, d. Dec. 2, 1706, Mühlhausen; was his father's successor as organist, and was promoted later to the town council. He received from the Emperor Leopold I. the poet's wreath (*poeta laureatus*). He was scarcely of less importance than his father, and wrote a number of sacred works which were highly prized, many of which, however, were destroyed by fire. "Musikalische Frühlings-, Sommer-, Herbst-, u. Wintergespräche" form a method of composition in four parts (1695–1701). Besides this are to be mentioned: "Instrumentalische Frühlingsmusik" (1695–96), and "Anmutige zehn vierstimmige Viol-di-gamba-Spiele" (1681).

Ahlström, A. J. N., b. 1756, Sweden; organist at St. James's Church, Stockholm, and court accompanist; published sonatas for pf. and for violin (1783 and 1786), and songs; and he is said to have also composed operas. For two years he edited a musical paper, *Musikalisk Tidsfoerdrife*, also published, jointly with Boman, a collection of Swedish folk-dances and folk-songs. Died **Aug. 11, 1835.**

Ahna. (*Vide* DE AHNA.)

Aibl, J o s e p h, celebrated music publishing firm at Munich (established 1824); the present proprietors are Ed. Spitzweg (since 1836), and his sons, Eugen and Otto.

Aiblinger, J o h a n n K a s p a r, b. Feb. 23, 1779, Wasserberg on Inn, d. May 6, 1867, Munich; studied music at Munich, and in 1802 near S. Mayr, Bergamo, lived from 1803–11 at Vicenza, and in 1819 at Milan as second maestro to the vice-king; he then went to Venice, where he founded the "Odéon" union, and was appointed in 1825 second capellmeister at Munich, and in 1833 was again in Bergamo. His church compositions were very famous (masses, litanies, requiems, psalms, offertoires). He was less successful with his stage works: the opera *Rodrigo e Ximene* (Munich), and three ballets, *La Spada di Kennet* (Venice, 1819), *Bianca*, and *J. Titani* (both at Milan, 1819).

Aichinger, G r e g o r, b. about 1565 (Augsburg?); organist to the Baron Jacob Fugger at Augsburg. He wrote a great number of sacred works: three books, "Sacræ cantiones" (1590 at Augsburg and Venice, 1595 at Venice, and 1597 at Nuremberg), "Tricinia," "Divinae laudes," "Ghirlanda di canzonette spiritale," etc. He died at Augsburg, Jan. 21, 1628, as vicar choral and canon of the cathedral there.

Aigner, E n g e l b e r t, b. Feb. 23, 1798, Vienna, d. about 1852; was for some time ballet director at the Vienna court opera (1835–37); in 1839 he built a large machine factory, but gave it up in 1842 and lived in retirement at Vienna. Many of his comic operas and vaudevilles were produced at Vienna at the "Kärntnerthor" Theatre (1826–29); he also wrote masses, a requiem, choruses for male voices, a quintet with flute, etc.

Aimo. (*Vide* HAYM 2).

Air, song, melody, *Lied* (Ger.); also instrumental melodies, dances (gavotte, musette, etc.), rormerly were regularly called airs. (*See* ARIA.)

Aireton, E d w a r d, celebrated English instrument maker at London during the second half of the 18th century, d. 1807, aged 80; he successfully imitated the violins and 'cellos of Amati.

Ajahli Keman, a Turkish stringed instrument with a foot, somewhat smaller than the 'cello.

Ajolla. (*Vide* LAYOLLE.)

Akeroyde, S a m u e l, popular and prolific English composer of songs at the end of the 17th century. His compositions are to be found in numerous English collections of that time, in "D'Urfey's Third Collection of Songs" (1685), in "The Theatre of Music" (1685–7), "Comes amoris" (1687–92), "Thesaurus musicus" (1693–96), etc.

Al (Ital.) = *a il* ("up to") for ex., *crescendo al forte.*

Ala, Giovanni Battista, organist at the church *dei servitori* in Monza at the beginning of the 17th century; he published canzonets and madrigals (1617, 1625); "Concerti ecclesiastici" (1616–28, four books); also the "Pratum Musicum" (1634) contains some of his motets. He is said to have died at the early age of 32, and according to Gerbert in 1612 (?).

Alard (1), D e l p h i n, violinist, b. March 8, 1815, Bayonne, d. Feb. 22, 1888, Paris; pupil at the Paris Conservatoire (Habeneck), and professor of the violin there (1843–75) as successor to Baillot; he was one of the most famous of French violinists, and an excellent teacher (Sarasate was his pupil); his playing was free and easy, and full of *verve*. A. published a great number of compositions for the violin (fantasias on operatic and original airs, concertos, *études*, duets for pf. and violin, etc.), as well as a highly meritorious "Violin School," which has been translated into Spanish, Italian, and German.—(2) C é s a r, excellent 'cellist, b. May 4,1837,Gosselies (Belgium); pupil of Servais.

Alary, G i u l i o, b. 1814, Mantua, d. April 17, 1891, Paris; pupil at the Milan Conservatorio; was for some years flautist at La Scala, but went in 1833 to Paris as music teacher, and made a name as composer in the shallow style of the period, but produced also nine operas and the oratorio *La Rédemption* (1850).

Alayrac. (*See* DALAYRAC.)

Albanese, b. 1729, Albano, Apulia, d. 1800, Paris; principal singer (*evirato*) in the *Concerts spirituels* from 1752–62; was in his time much in vogue as a composer of romances.

Albani, M a t t h i a s, name of two celebrated violin makers (father and son). The e l d e r, b. 1621, Botzen, pupil of Steiner, d. 1673, Botzen. The s o n worked for several years with the master violin makers at Cremona, and then settled down in Rome. The instruments which he made between 1702–9 are very celebrated, and considered almost equal to those of Amati.

Albani, M a r i e Louise Cécilia Emma L a j e u n e s s e (stage name, A.), famous dramatic soprano singer, b. 1850, Chambly, near Montreal, first sang in public at the cathedral of Albany (State of New York). She then studied at Paris under Duprez, afterwards under Lamperti, and made her *début* at Messina in *Sonnambula* (1870). She then sang for a time at La Pergola (Florence), and at the Italian Opera (Covent Garden) for the first time in 1872. She visited Paris, Petersburg, America, etc., everywhere becoming a centre of attraction. In 1878 she married Ernest Gye, lessee of Covent Garden Theatre. Madame Albani is also an excellent oratorio singer, appears at the principal musical festivals and concerts, and is, in addition, a good pianist.

Albeniz, (1) D o n P e d r o, Spanish monk, b. 1755, Biscay, d. 1821, San Sebastian; was maestro of San Sebastian Cathedral, where he published in 1800 a Method of Music highly prized in Spain. A very large number of masses, motets, villancicos, etc., testify to his diligence as a composer; they brought him, anyhow, fame in his own country.—(2) An early master of modern pianoforte playing in Spain, b. April 14, 1795, Logroño (Old Castile), d. April 12, 1855, Madrid; pupil of H. Herz, for some years organist at San Sebastian, 1830 pianoforte professor at the newly-established Royal Conservatorio at Madrid, 1834 court organist, and loaded with honours of all kinds. A large number of pf. compositions (variations, rondos, fantasies, études, etc.) appeared in print, also a pianoforte Method, introduced into the Madrid Conservatorio.

Albergati, P i r r o C a p a c e l l i, Conte d', was a highly-esteemed composer at the end of the 17th and the beginning of the 18th century (2 operas, 15 oratorios, masses, motets, cantatas, psalms, also sonatas for 2 violins with continuo, dance pieces, etc.). B. 1663, d. 1735

Albert, Prinz von Sachsen-Koburg-Gotha, b. Aug. 26, 1819, from 1840 Prince Consort of the Queen of England, d. Dec. 14, 1861; he was a zealous cultivator and patron of music, and himself composed many vocal works, masses, an operetta, *Les Petits du Premier* (Paris, 1864), an opera, *Jean le Fol* (Bagnieres de Bigone, 1865), songs, etc.

Albert, (1) H e i n r i c h, b. July 8 (old style, June 28), 1604, Lobenstein, Voigtland, d. Oct. 6, 1651, Königsberg. He attended the Gymnasium at Gera, and went in 1622 to his uncle, Heinrich Schütz (q.v.) in Dresden, but at the wish of his parents was compelled to break off the musical studies which he had commenced with Schütz, and to study law at Leipzig. In 1626 he went to Königsberg i. Pr., started with an embassy to Warsaw, but on the road was taken prisoner by the Swedes, and only returned in 1628, after enduring many hardships. In 1632 he was appointed organist at the cathedral, and resumed his musical studies under Stobäus. A. was not only an excellent musician, but also a poet, and wrote the words to the greater number of his songs (others are written by Simon Dach, his contemporary and friend). Chorales, of which he wrote both music and words, are still sung in Prussia. His most important works are: 8 sets of Arias (1638–1650), of which the first seven were frequently reprinted, and the "Kürbshütte" (1645), collections of songs, Lieder and chorales, partly for one, partly for several voices.—(2) M a x, b. Jan. 7, 1833, Munich; performer on the zither, and an improver of this instrument ; he died Sept. 4, 1882, Berlin.—(3) E u g è n e F r a n c i s C h a r l e s d', distinguished pianist and gifted composer, b. April 10, 1864, Glasgow, son of the musician and dancing master, Charles d'A. (b. Feb. 25, 1809, Nienstteten, near Altona, d. May 26, 1866, London). He was elected Newcastle Scholar at the National Training School (E. Pauer, Dr. Stainer, E. Prout, and Sullivan). In 1881, as Mendelssohn Scholar, he went to study on the Continent, under Richter at Vienna and Liszt at Weimar. Already on Feb. 5, 1881, he played Schumann's Concerto at the Crystal Palace (London), and in October of the same year a pianoforte concerto of his own at a Richter Concert. At the present time d'A. stands as a pianist of the first rank (*Tausig redivivus*), and is held in esteem also as a composer (pianoforte concerto in B minor ; overtures, " Hyperion " and " Esther," symphony in F, pianoforte suite, quintet for strings in A minor, charming songs, etc.). For the last few years d'A. has resided in Germany.

Albertazzi, E m m a, *née* Howson, celebrated contralto singer, b. May 1, 1814, London, d. there Sept., 1847, made her *début* in London in 1830, was afterwards engaged at Piacenza, Milan, Madrid, Paris, and London, and again in Italy, after her voice had begun to fail; she sang finally once again in London. Her singing, for the rest, was lifeless and without passion.

Alberti, (1) J o h. F r i e d r i c h, b. Jan. 11, 1642, Tönning (Schleswig), d. June 14, 1710 ; studied first theology, then music under Werner Fabricius at Leipzig; he became cathedral organist at Merseburg, but in consequence of a stroke of apoplexy was compelled to resign the post in 1698. He was held in high esteem as a learned contrapuntist and a composer of sacred music.—(2) G i u s e p p e M a t t e o, b. 1685, Bologna, a celebrated violinist and instrumental composer (concertos, symphonies, etc.).

—(3) D o m e n i c o, b. at the beginning of the 18th century at Venice, was an enthusiastic lover of music, and first appeared as an amateur singer, later also as a pianist, and finally as a composer (sonatas, etc., also three operas), he was admired by his circle of friends. (*Cf.* ALBERTI BASS.)—(4) K a r l E d m u n d R o b e r t, b. July 12, 1801, Danzig, d. in 1874 at Berlin ; studied theology and philosophy at Berlin, but at the same time was a diligent student of music under Zelter. As pastor at Danzig he founded a musico-dramatic union of amateurs, and when in 1854 he became member of the school board at Stettin, was still zealously active in the cause of music. He composed only a few books of songs, but, on the other hand, was active as a writer on music : "Die Musik in Kirche und Staat" (1843); "Andeutungen zur Geschichte der Oper" (1845); " Richard Wagner," etc. (1856) ; "Raphael und Mozart " (1856) ; "Beethoven als dramatischer Tondichter" (1859). From 1866 he lived in private at Berlin, and contributed various interesting articles to the *Neue Berliner Musik-zeitung.*

Alberti Bass, a bass consisting of chords broken in a similar manner, as accompaniment to a melody played with the right hand, a form much in vogue at the present day in easy pianoforte music (*e.g.* Mozart's Sonata in F).

It derives its name from Domenico Albert, who first made extensive use of it.

Albertini, (1) G i o v a c c h i n o, b. 1751, d. April, 1811, Warsaw, royal Polish capellmeister about the year 1784 ; in his time a favourite composer of Italian operas : his *Circe ed Ulisse* was performed at Hamburg (1785) with great success; also *Virginia* in 1786 at Rome.—(2) M i c h a e l, called *Momoletto,* celebrated *evirato* at Cassel at the beginning of the 18th century, where also his sister G i o v a n n a, called R o m a n i n a, distinguished herself as principal singer.

Albicastro, H e n r i c o (really W e i s s e n-b u r g). He was a Swiss by birth, and took part in the war respecting the Spanish Succession (1701–14). He published a series of chamber-music works (sonatas for violin, partly *a tre, i.e.* with 'cello and bass, partly *a due* with only *continuo*).

Albinoni, T o m m a s o, prolific Italian opera composer, b. 1674, Venice, d. there, 1745 ; wrote 49 operas mostly from Venice, but also a number of valuable instrumental works (sonatas, *a tre* and *a due, da camera e da chiesa* symphonies, concertos, etc.). J. S. Bach, who esteemed A.'s music very highly, wrote two fugues (in A major and F minor) on themes of A.'s.

Alboni, M a r i e t t a, celebrated contralto singer, b. Mar. 10, 1823, Cesena (Romagna), pupil of Bertolotti and Rossini at Bologna; made her *début* in 1843 at Milan as Orsini in Donizetti's *Lucrezia Borgia*, threw London and Paris into a state of ecstasy in 1847, and in 1853 made a triumphal tour through North and South America, and married Count Pepoli in 1854. In 1863, though still in full possession of her noble, rich-toned voice, she retired from the stage, and only appeared once again in public (1869) in Rossini's small *Messe solennelle*.

Albrecht, (1) J o h. L o r e n z ("Magister A."), b. Jan. 8, 1732, Görmar, near Mühlhausen (Thuringia), d. 1773, Mühlhausen; studied philology at Leipzig, but devoted himself at the same time so ardently to music that, in 1758, he was appointed both collegiate teacher and organist at the principal church at Mühlhausen. A. is best known as editor of J. Adlung's "Musica mechanica organoedi" and "Musikalisches Siebengestirn," but he also wrote a series of original works: "Gründliche Einleitung in die Anfangslehren der Tonkunst" (1761); "Abhandlung über die Frage: ob die Musik beim Gottesdienst zu dulden sei oder nicht" (1764); besides some essays in Marpurg's *Kritische Beiträge*, etc. A. was arbitrator in the theoretical dispute between Marpurg and Sorge. He published also some compositions (cantatas, a Passion, and harpsichord lessons).— (2) J o h. M a t t h ä u s, b. May 1, 1701, Osterbehringen, near Gotha; organist at St. Catharine's Church, later at the "Barfüsser" Church at Frankfort, where he died in 1769. His highly praised clavier concertos have not been published.—(3) E u g e n M a r i a, b. June 16, 1842, Petersburg, where his father, Karl A. (native of Breslau) was for twelve years capellmeister at the Imperial Russian Opera; 1857–60 pupil of David at the Leipzig Conservatorium, 1860–77 leader of the orchestra at the Petersburg Italian Opera, from 1867–72 director of the instruction in music and singing at the military schools, and from 1877 musical inspector of the Imperial Theatres at Petersburg; founder and president of the union established in 1872 for chamber music; violin teacher to several of the Imperial princes, etc. A. was an excellent violinist; he died Feb. 9, 1894.

Albrechtsberger, J o h. G e o r g, b. Feb. 3, 1736, Klosterneuburg, near Vienna, d. March 7, 1809. He was a distinguished theorist and composer, and the teacher of Beethoven. After he had held several appointments in small towns he became *Regens chori* to the Carmelites at Vienna, court organist in 1772, and in 1792 capellmeister at St. Stephen's. Only a small portion of his compositions appeared in print (organ preludes, pianoforte fugues, quartets, quintets, sextets, and octets for strings, a pianoforte quartet, and a *Concerto léger* for pf., 2 violins, and bass). The following remain in manuscript: 26 masses, 6 oratorios, 4 grand symphonies, 42 stringed quartets, 38 quintets, 28 stringed trios, many hymns, offertories,

graduals, etc. His theoretical works are, however, of the most importance: "Gründliche Anweisung zur Komposition" (1790 and 1818; French, 1814); "Kurzgefasste Methode den Generalbass zu erlernen" (1792); "Klavierschule für Anfänger" (1808), and some smaller treatises. A complete edition of his theoretical works was brought out by J. v. Seyfried.

Albrici, V i n c e n z o, b. June 26, 1631, Rome; about 1660 capellmeister to Queen Christina of Sweden at Stralsund, 1664 electoral capellmeister at Dresden, 1680 organist at St. Thomas's Church, Leipzig; he died in 1696, as director of church music at Prague. His once highly prized works were bought for the Dresden library, but destroyed during the bombardment of 1760. Only a few works were preserved (a Te Deum à 10, the 150th psalm, etc.), but not printed.

Albumblatt (Ger.), album leaf; a title often given to short instrumental pieces.

Alcarrotti, G i o v. F r a n c e s c o, published 2 books of madrigals à 5–6 (1567 and 1569).

Alcock, J o h n, b. Apr. 11, 1715, London; pupil of the blind organist Stanley. Already in 1731 he was organist of two London churches; went later to Plymouth, Reading, and finally to Lichfield as organist of the cathedral, where he died Feb. 23, 1806. In 1761 he took his doctor's degree at Oxford. A. published many anthems, glees, psalms, hymns, etc.; also pianoforte lessons, songs, etc. He also wrote a novel: "The Life of Miss Fanny Brown." His son, of the same name, published several anthems (1773–76).

Alday, French musical family at Perpignan. The father, b. 1737, a performer on the mandoline, taught his sons, of whom the eldest, b. 1763, Paris, first appeared at the *Concerts spirituels* as mandoline player, afterwards as violinist; he published a Violin Method. The younger, b. 1764, a pupil of Viotti, went later to England, settled in Edinburgh as a teacher of music, and published a large number of pleasing compositions for the violin.

Aldovrandini, G i u s e p p e A n t o n i o V i n c e n z o, b. about 1665, Bologna, member of the Philharmonic Academy, president of the same in 1702 (*Principe dei filarmonici*). He wrote (1696–1711) fifteen operas, six oratorios, and some other sacred and instrumental works.

Aldrich, H e n r y, b. 1647, London, d. Jan. 19, 1710, Oxford; was a student at Christ Church, studied theology, and finally became dean. A. was not only a learned theologian and historian, but also an architect and musician. Apart from his other learned works he wrote: "On the Commencement of Greek Music," "Theory of Organ-Building," "Theory of Modern Instruments," etc. His compositions are to be found in various collections (Boyce, Arnold, Page); others have been preserved in manuscript in Oxford churches.

Alembert, J e a n le R o n d d', the famous mathematician, who gave a scientific account of Rameau's musical system; b. Nov. 16, 1717, Paris, d. there, Oct. 29, 1783. His works relating to music are: "Éléments de musique théorique et pratique, suivant les principes de M. Rameau" (1752, passed through many editions; German by Marpurg, 1757). Besides this (in the Mémoires of the Berlin Academy), " Untersuchungen über die Kurve einer schwingenden Saite " (1747 and 1750); " Ueber die Schwingungen tönender Körper " (1761, etc.); and "Ueber die Fortpflanzungs-geschwindigkeit des Tons," etc.

Alessandri, F e l i c e, b. 1747, Rome, trained at Naples; he was at first maestro at Turin, then led a stirring life in Paris, London, Petersburg, and in various Italian cities. From 1789 to 1792 he was second conductor at the Berlin Opera, but was driven out of this post by intrigues, and died at Berlin in 1811. His 25 operas had everywhere only an ephemeral success. He died Oct. 29, 1783, at Paris.

Alessandro Romano, named **della Viola,** was singer in the Pope's Chapel about 1560, afterwards Olivetan monk. He wrote motets, madrigals, etc., and, according to Fétis, also instrumental compositions (for viola). Of his works have been preserved only two books of " Canzoni alla Neapolitana " (1572 and 1575), the second book of his Madrigals (1577), a book of Motets à 5 (1579), and detached pieces in the collection, " Delle muse libri, III., etc." (1555-61).

Alexandre-Orgel. (*See* AMERICAN ORGAN.)

Alfarabi, more correctly, *El Farabi (Alpharabius)*, also named, in abbreviated form, *Farabi*, after his birthplace, Farab, the present Otrar in the land beyond the Oxus. He was the famous Arabian musical theorist, b. about 900 A.D., and died somewhere about 950. His real name was A b u N a s y r M o h a m m e d B e n T a r c h a n. A. possessed a sound knowledge of the Greek writers on music, and attempted, though in vain, to introduce the Greek system of scales into his own country. Anyhow, the Arabians do not seem to have required schooling from the Greeks. (*Cf.* ARABIANS and PERSIANS.)

Alfieri, A b b a t e P i e t r o, at one time Camadulian monk, was professor of singing at the English College, Rome, b. June 29, 1801, Rome, d. there June 12, 1863. He published many treatises on Plain Song (" Accompagnamento coll' organo, etc.," 1840); " Ristabilmente del Canto, etc." (1843); " Saggio storico," etc. (1855); and also a " Prodromo sulla restaurazione," etc. (1857); biographical sketches of Bern, Bittoni, Jomelli, and others, and the well-known " Raccolta di musica sacra," a first reprint of Palestrina's works in seven thick volumes, with a few sets of pieces by other masters (Genet, Goudimel, Festa, Morales in the last volume). This collection preceded any others of smaller extent (" Excerpta ex celebr. de mus. viris," 1840; " Motets of Palestrina, Vittoria, Anerio, etc.," 1841), etc. He also translated into Italian Catel's " Traité d'harmonie " (1840).

Algarotti, F r a n c e s c o, b. Dec. 11, 1712, Venice, d. May 3, 1764, Pisa; a man of wide culture and worldly wisdom; he was drawn to Berlin by Frederick the Great in 1746, where he remained for nine years as chamberlain, and was raised to the dignity of Count. In 1749 he returned to Italy for the sake of his health; a monument was erected to him in Pisa by Frederick the Great. A. wrote, among other things, " Saggio sopra l'opera in musica" (1755, many times republished, and translated into French and German).

Aliquotflügel. (*See* BLÜTHNER.)

Aliquot tones. (*See* OVERTONES.)

À livre ouvert (Fr.), at sight.

Alkan, C h a r l e s H e n r i V a l e n t i n (*Morhange*, called A.), b. Nov. 30, 1813, Paris, d. there March 29, 1888; was admitted to the Conservatoire of Paris in his sixth year, received the first *solfège* prize after a year and a half's study, and, at the age of 10, the first pianoforte prize (pupil of Zimmermann). In 1831 he competed for the *Prix de Rome*, and obtained honourable mention. From that time he devoted himself to composition and to teaching, appearing from time to time as pianist at the Conservatoire concerts and elsewhere. A. was highly esteemed in Paris, and published a number of excellent pianoforte works (Preludes, Études, Marches, a Concerto, a Sonata, etc.).— His brother, Napoléon Morhange A., b. Feb. 2, 1826, Paris, was a sound pianist and published detached piano pieces; d. Mar. 29, 1888.

All', alla (Ital.), to the, at the, in the, in the style of.

Allabreve-Time (named also *alla cappella*) is a 4, or rather ⁴⁄₂ time, in which, not crotchets, but minims are beaten (counted); it is indicated by the sign ₵. The so-called *great A.*, indicated by ₵|₵ (the old ₵ formerly employed to give to the breve the value of 3 O with breve counts), or ⁴⁄₁ is likewise counted in minims, of which it contains four. (*Cf.* BREVIS.)

Alla caccia (Ital.), in the hunting style.

Alla camera (Ital.), in the style of chamber music.

Alla cappella (Ital.), the same as *a cappella*.

Allacci (*Allatius*), Leo, b. 1586, Chios, of Greek parents, d. Rome, Jan. 19, 1669; went as a boy to Calabria, later to Rome, where, after diligent study, he became teacher at the Greek College, and in 1661 " custode " of the Vatican Library. For the history of music, the " Drammaturgia " (1666) of this learned archæologist is an important work; it is a catalogue of all dramas and operas produced in Italy up to his time.

Alla diritta (Ital.), ascending or descending by degrees.

Alla francese (Ital.), in the French style.

Alla hanacca (Ital.), in the style of a *hanacca* (q.v.).

Alla marcia (Ital.), in the style of a march.

Alla mente (Ital.), extemporaneous. (*v.* Contrapunto alla mente.)

Alla militare (Ital.), in the military style.

Alla moderna (Ital.), in the modern style.

All' antico (Ital.), in the ancient style.

Alla Palestrina (Ital.), (1) in the noble, chaste church style of Palestrina. (2) For voices without instrumental accompaniment.

Alla polacca (Ital.), like a polonaise.

Alla quinta (Ital.), at, or in, the fifth.

Allargando (Ital.), becoming broader (slower); specially used in place of *ritardando* (*rallentando*), where the tone is to be increased (agogic restraint).

Alla scozzese (Ital.), in the Scotch style.

Alla siciliana (Ital.), in the style of a *Siciliano* (q.v.).

Alla stretta (Ital.), in the manner of a *stretto* (q.v.).

Alla turca (Ital.), in the Turkish style.

Alla zingara (Ital.), in the style of gipsy music.

Alla zoppa (Ital.), in a limping, lame manner.

Allegramente (Ital.), *Allegro* (*moderato*).

Allegrettino (Ital.), (1) a short *allegretto*. (2) A movement not so fast as *allegretto*.

Allegretto (Ital., abbr. *All^{tto.}*; diminutive of *Allegro*), moderately lively, a time-indication of doubtful meaning; there are *Allegretti* more like to *Allegro* (*e.g.* in Beethoven's Sonata, Op. 14, No. 1), whilst others have altogether an *Andante* character (as in the A-major Symphony).

Allegrezza (Ital.), joyfulness.—*Con allegrezza*, joyfully.

Allegri, (1) G r e g o r i o, b. 1584, Rome, descended from the Coreggio family, a pupil of Giov. M. Nanini, from 1629 singer in the Papal chapel, d. Feb. 18, 1662. He was the composer of the famous "Miserere" for nine voices, which is sung during Holy Week in the Sistine Chapel, and which, formerly, was not allowed to be copied (Mozart, however, once took down the notes during performance (since then it has been often published, among others by Burney and Choron). Besides this Miserere are known of A.: two books of "Concerti" (à 2 to 4), and two books of Motetti (à 2–6), while a great number of manuscripts are preserved in the Archives of Santa Maria in Vallicella, and in those of the Papal chapel.—(2) D o m e n i c o, one of the first composers who wrote a real instrumental accompaniment to vocal music (*i.e.* not in unison); he was maestro di cappella

at Santa Maria Maggiore in Rome from 161o to 1629. Only a few of his works (Motetti) have been preserved.

Allegro (Ital., abbr. *A^{llo.}*), one of the oldest time indications, signifies in Italian, " lively," " gay," but in the course of time has acquired the meaning of "quick," so that it is now used in connections which, with regard to the Italian significance of the word, appear pleonastic, or even void of meaning, *e.g.* A. *giojoso* (" gay-lively "), A. *irato* (" gay-passionate "). The old word-meaning really no longer exists. By *Adagio* is generally understood a slow piece, and so too the word *A.* has the general meaning of a piece moving in quick time. Thus, for example, the first movement of a Symphony is called an A., even though the same may have the superscription *vivace* or *con fuoco*. The superlative *allegrissimo* is rare, but has a meaning somewhat similar to *presto*.

Allegro di bravura (Ital.), a brilliant *allegro*, a quick movement full of executive difficulties.

Allegro furioso (Ital.), quick and impetuous.

Allemande (French, " German Dance ") one of the principal movements of the old French *Suite* (q.v.), a kind of Prelude with skilful workmanship, of moderate, comfortable rate in ⁴⁄₄ time, with an up-beat of a quaver or semiquaver. It was accepted under the same name by German composers at the beginning of last century, and, with *naïve* patriotism, specially cultivated. The A. in ²⁄₄ time, as a real dance, is of later origin; also a more lively dance in ³⁄₄ time, common in Switzerland, is called A.

Allen, H e n r y R o b i n s o n, highly esteemed English stage singer (bass), b. 1809, Cork, d Nov. 27, 1876, Shepherd's Bush, pupil of the Royal Academy of Music.

Allentando (Ital.). (*See* RALLENTANDO.)

All' improvista (Ital.), extemporaneously.

Alliteration (Ger. *stabreim*), the oldest form of rhyming in German poetry. It consisted either of an accordance of vowels on certain important syllables of a verse (assonance), or of consonants at the beginning of the syllables (man, fan; dark, drear), and not, as now, of end-rhymes.

All° abbr. for *Allegro;* **All^{to}** for *Allegretto*.

Almeida, F e r n a n d o d', b. about 1618, Lisbon, d. Mar. 21, 1660, entered the order of Christ, in fact into the monastery at Thobar, and in 1656 became visitor of the order. A. was one of the best scholars of Duarte Lobo, and highly esteemed by King John IV. A folio volume in manuscript (" Lamentações responsorios e misereres dos tres officios da IV., V. e VI. feria da semana santa ") is all that remains of his works.

Almenräder, K a r l, b. Oct. 3, 1786, Ronsdorf, near Düsseldorf, d. Sept. 14, 1843, Biebrich; from needy circumstances he raised himself by industry : he was self-taught, and became an excellent bassoon player ; in 1810, bassoon professor at the Cologne Music-school ; 1812, bassoon player in the theatre orchestra at Frankfort. During the second French campaign (1815) he was bandmaster in the 3rd Militia Regiment, 1816 in the 34th Regiment of the line at Mayence, where he settled permanently and gave up the military career. He held frequent intercourse there with Gottfried Weber. In 1820 he established a manufactory for wind instruments, but gave up the same in 1822, and entered into the Nassau Band at Biebrich, superintending, at the same time, the construction of bassoons in the Schott manufactory of instruments at Mayence. A. materially improved the bassoon, and wrote a pamphlet on the subject ; he also wrote a method for the bassoon, and composed concertos, phantasias, etc., for bassoon with strings, also some vocal pieces, among which the popular ballad, " Des Hauses letzte Stunde."

Alphabet, musical. (*See* LETTER NOTATION.)

Alpharabius. (*See* ALFARABI.)

Alphorn (Alpenhorn), a somewhat primitive, ancient wind instrument used by shepherds in the Alps, from 5 to 6 feet long, with conical tube composed of staff-wood, and provided with a mouthpiece made of hard wood.

Alquen, Peter Cornelius Johann d', b. 1795, Arnsberg, Westphalia, d. Nov. 27, 1863, Mülheim-on-Rhine ; studied medicine in Berlin, and music under Klein and Zelter, but while practising as doctor at Mülheim, turned specially to composition, and became popular through his songs. His younger brother, Friedrich A. E., b. 1810, d. June 18, 1887, London, was destined for the law (Dr. Jur.), but was trained under Ferd. Ries as a violinist, and settled in Brussels in 1827 as a teacher of music. He went to London in 1830, where he published various works for pianoforte and violin.

Alschalabi, Mohammed, Spanish Arabian, wrote a work at the beginning of the 15th century on the musical instruments of his time ; the manuscript is at the Escurial.

Alsleben, Julius, b. March 24, 1832, Berlin, d. there Dec. 8, 1894 ; studied Oriental languages there, took his degree at Kiel, but then devoted himself entirely to music. For his knowledge of pianoforte playing he was indebted to Leuchtenberg and Zech, for theory to S. Dehn. After making successful appearances as pianist in various concerts, he developed great activity as a teacher of the pianoforte, was conductor of various societies, and from 1865 was president of the Berlin " Tonkünstlerverein " and one of the founders and also president of the " Musiklehrerverein " (1879). In 1872 he received the title of Professor. A. was a contributor to several musical papers ; he edited from 1874, for several years, the musical paper "Harmonie," and

published " Zwölf Vorlesungen über Musikgeschichte," " Licht- und Wendepunkte in der Entwickelung der Musik " (1880).

Alstedt, Joh. Heinr., b. 1588, Herborn (Nassau), professor of theology and philology there, and later at Weissenburg (Siebenbürgen), where he died in 1638. He wrote much about music in his " Encyklopädie der gesammten Wissenschaften" (1610), published also an " Elementale mathematicum " (1611), of which the section " Elementale musicum " has been separately translated into English (1644, by J. Birchensha) ; he also touched on music in the 8th part of his " Admiranda mathematica " (1613).

Altenburg, (1) Michael, b. May 27, 1584, Alach, near Erfurt, as the son of a well-to-do blacksmith, from 1600 was active as teacher in various posts ; 1611 pastor in Tröchtelborn, and 1621 in Gross-Sömmerda. He escaped from the dangers of war to Erfurt, became deacon there, and died Feb. 12, 1640. A. was a prolific and esteemed church-composer. Especially worthy of mention are his Church- and Home-Songs, his Festival-Songs, and his Intrade for violin, lute, etc., with a chorale as Cantus firmus.—(2) Joh. Ernst, b. 1734, Weissenfels, d. 1796 as organist in Bitterfeld, a celebrated virtuoso on the trumpet and field trumpeter during the Seven Years' War. He published a kind of instrumental instruction book for trumpets and drums : " Anleitung zur heroisch-musikalischen Trompeter- und Pauken-Kunst " (1795).

Alteration, in mensural notation, a doubling of the time of duration of the second of two notes of the same kind (two *breves* or two *semibreves*), which took place when Ternary Rhythm was indicated by notes of the nearest greater species : the two notes stood either between two such greater ones (*e.g.* two *Breves* between two *Longs*), or were divided by a *punctum divisionis* from the following equal or smaller ones. Thus in Perfect Time (*Tempus perfectum* O) the succession ☐ ◇ ◇ ☐ would mean (in modern notation, with values reduced by one half).

$$ \circ\cdot \,|\, d \; \circ \,|\, \circ\cdot $$

Alterato (Ital.), **Altéré** (Fr.), altered in pitch, raised or lowered a semitone.

Altered Chords are those *dissonances* (q.v.) which arise through the chromatic raising or lowering of a note of a major or minor chord, especially of the *augmented triad* c, e, g♯ produced by raising the fifth of the major chord, or a♭, c, e produced by lowering the fundamental note of the minor chord, and of the *augmented chord of six-four* (g♭, c, e = c, e, g♭) and the *augmented chord of six-three* (c, e, a♯ = a♯, c, e), the former produced by lowering the fifth of the major chord, the latter by raising the fundamental note of the minor chord (the under fifth, *cf.* MINOR CHORD).

Alternamente (Ital.), alternatively.

Alternativo (Ital.), alternate. The term used for small pieces in dance form which alternate with a Trio (*Menuetto, a*); the Trio in such pieces can also be called an *A*.

Altès, Joseph Henri, b. Jan. 18, 1826, Rouen, d. July 24, 1895, Paris; 1840, pupil of the Paris Conservatoire, a celebrated flautist, member of the orchestra of the Grand Opéra; 1868, successor of Dorus at the Conservatoire; he also published compositions for flute.—His brother, Ernest Eugène, b. Mar. 28, 1830, Paris, an able violinist, was second maître de chapelle at the Grand Opéra (1880–87).

Altgeige (Ger.), the tenor violin, the viola.

Althorn, a valve-bugle in E♭, having a compass similar to that of the horn in E♭; it is only used in wind-bands.

Alti naturali (Ital.), "natural altos." (*Vide* ALTO.)

Altissimo (Ital.), the highest; extremely high. (*Vide* IN ALTISSIMO.)

Altnikol, Joh. Christoph, pupil and son-in-law of J. S. Bach (married, Jan. 20, 1749, Elizabeth Juliane Frederica Bach); 1748, organist at Naumburg, d. there, July, 1759; was esteemed in his time as a composer, but nothing appeared in print. Some manuscripts are to be found in the Berlin library.

Alto, (1) *Alto voice* (Ital. *Contr'alto* [*Alto*], French, *Haute-contre;* in the Latin designation of the voices *Altus, Vox alta,* or *Contratenor*), the lower of women's and boys' voices, chiefly in chest register. In the time of complicated mensural music—which could not be performed by boys because it took years to learn the rules —the high parts (*A*. and Discant, *i.e.* soprano) were sung by men with falsetto voices (*Alti naturali*), or indeed by *evirati*, as women were not allowed to sing in the churches ("*mulier taceat in ecclesia*"); for this reason the discant and alto parts of that period have only a very moderate compass upwards, and on the other hand a greater one downwards. The normal compass of the genuine alto voice extends from *a*, in a deep *A*. (contralto) from *f* (exceptionally *e, d*) to *e″, f″* (but in voices of specially wide compass higher still). Viewed historically, the alto part was the one last introduced by composers; for over the normal men's part which took the *Cantus firmus* (tenor), a higher one was first placed, to which was given the name of *Discant*. Afterwards a third lower voice was placed under the tenor, which at once served as a foundation (harmonic support, basis), and, if the tenor descended, as a middle filling-up voice. Finally, this third voice separated into two: the bass became definitely the support of the harmony, while the contra-tenor or alto (*altus*), as a fourth voice, was inter-polated between tenor and discant.—(2) *Alto instruments.* When, in the 15th and 16th centuries it became the custom, owing to the powerful development of polyphonic music, to strengthen the voice parts by instruments in unison, or even to replace them, all kinds of instruments were constructed in three or four different sizes, answering to the four kinds of voices; thus there were: Discant-, Alto-, Tenor-, and Bass-viols, trombones, flutes, krummhorns. Of these the four kinds of trombones have been retained to the present time; also the foundation of our orchestra, the string-quartet, has at least a similar division; only that in consequence of the powerfully extended compass of instrumental music upwards and downwards the original alto instrument, the Alto Viol (Viola da Braccio), has been assigned to the third of the highest parts, and the Bass instrument (the Violoncello still included among the "*Bassi*") to the second of the lowest parts.

Alto clarinet, *Alto Oboe, Alto Trombone,* etc., are instruments of which the middle register answers fairly to the compass of the alto voice. (*See* ALTO.) (*Cf.* CLARINET, OBOE, etc.)

Alto clef, the c′ clef on the middle line

equal to ; it was formerly in general use for the alto voice, but at the present day is only employed for viola music.

Alvsleben, Melitta. (*See* OTTO-ALVSLEBEN.)

Alypios, Greek writer on music about 360 A.D., whose "Introduction to Music" was first printed by Meursius ("Aristoxenus, Nikomaches, *A.*, etc.," 1616), and afterwards by Meibom ("Antiquae musicae auctores septem," 1652). The treatise contains all the transposition scales of the Greeks in Greek vocal and instrumental notation, for the knowledge of which we are principally indebted to A.

Alz (*alzamento,* "a raising"), signifies the opposite of *abb.* (q.v.).

Amabile, *con amabilità* (Ital.), amiably.

Amadé, Ladislaw, Baron von, b. Mar. 12, 1703, Kaschau (Hungary), d. Dec. 22, 1764, Felbar, as Councillor of the Exchequer; he was a favourite national poet and composer of folk-songs, which were published in 1836 by Thaddäus, Graf von A.; the latter b. Jan. 12, 1783, Pressburg, d. May 17, 1845, Vienna, likewise an officer of state, was an excellent pianist, and the discoverer of Liszt's talent, for the training of which he provided means. In 1831 he was named "Hofmusikgraf."

A major Chord = *a, c♯, e; A major key* with signature of 3 sharps. (*See* KEY.)

Amalia, the name of three artists, princesses by birth. (1) Anna A., Princess of Prussia, sister of Frederick the Great, b. Nov. 9, 1723. d. Mar. 30, 1787; composed a series of excellent chorales, and also wrote new music to the text-book of Graun's "Tod Jesu."—(2) Anna A., Duchess of Weimar, mother of the Grand-duke Ernst August, b. Oct. 24, 1739, d. Apr. 10, 1807; composed the operetta *Erwin und Elmire* (text by Goethe).—(3) Marie A. Friedetike, Princess of Saxony, sister of King John of Saxony; b. Aug. 10, 1794, Dresden, d. there, Sept. 18, 1870. As a writer of comedies she was known under the name "Amalie Heiter;" composed also church music and several operas (*Una donna*, *Le tre cinture*, *Die Siegesfahne*, *Der Kanonenschuss*, etc.).

Amarevole, *con amarezza* (Ital.), bitter, sad.

Amarezza (Ital.), bitterness, sadness.

Amateur (Fr.; Ital. *Dilettante*), a lover of music who does not pursue the art professionally. At the present day the word *A.* is used in a somewhat depreciatory sense, but formerly this was by no means the case. In 1768 Boccherini dedicated his first stringed quartets "*ai veri dilettanti e cognoscitori di musica*." The taste of *dilettanti* was not always so thoroughly bad, nor so favourable to shallow, affected, ephemeral music as it is to-day; chamber-music was more cultivated at home by non-professionals, and music was more seriously studied and better played, than at the present day. Dilettantism now means a superficial and mannered study of art, whether as composer or executant. An *A.* is one who has learnt nothing properly; and musicians of this class should strive to obtain for their name more honourable recognition.

Amati, (1) the family of celebrated violin-makers at Cremona of the 16th and 17th centuries, whose instruments are now considered real treasures. The eldest A., who evolved the violin from the viol, was Andrea (*c*. 1530–1611). He still continued to make violins of various sizes; his younger brother and partner, Nicola, made principally bass viols, and of excellent quality, between the years 1568 and 1586. Antonio A. (b. 1555, d. 1635), Andrea's eldest son, devoted himself almost exclusively to violins, the size of which, however, varied much at that period (1589-1627). He was for some time associated with his brother, Girolamo (*c.* 1556 to Nov. 2, 1630), a younger son of Andrea's, but inferior to him in skill, and all of whose violins are somewhat large. The most eminent A. was Nicola, son of Girolamo, b. Dec. 3, 1596, d. April 12, 1684, who had as pupils Andrea Guarneri and Antonio Stradivari. The Amati violins are valued not so much for the fulness as for the softness and purity of their tone. Nicola A. was succeeded by his son Girolamo, b. Feb. 26, 1649, d. Feb. 21, 1740, the last representative of the family, but far inferior to his father. Giuseppe A., who at the beginning of the 17th century made violins and basses at Bologna, which are said to have a fine clear tone, may possibly have belonged to the same family.—(2) Vincenzo (Amatus), doctor of theology and maestro at Palermo Cathedral about 1665; b. Jan. 6, 1629, Cimmina (Sicily), d. July 29, 1670, Palermo. He published sacred compositions and an opera (*L'Isauro*, 1664).—(3) Antonio and Angelo, brothers, organ-builders at Pavia about 1830.

Ambitus (Lat.), compass; the *A.* of a melody is the distance from the lowest to the highest note in it. One speaks also of the *A.* of a Church Mode (whether it be from *A—a* or *C—c*, etc.).

Ambo (Lat.). This was the name in the more ancient Christian Churches of a small reading-desk placed before the railing of the presbytery, in front of, or on the steps of which (*in gradibus ambonis*), the Gradual (*Responsorium graduale* or *gradale*) was sung, and hence its name.

Ambros, August Wilhelm, musical historian, b. Nov. 17, 1816, Mauth, near Prague, d. June 28, 1876, Vienna, a nephew of R. Kiesewetter, who also rendered signal service as an historian of music. A. studied jurisprudence, but, at the same time, worked diligently at music. He, indeed, entered government service, and in 1850 was appointed Prosecuting Attorney at Prague, but he was also active as a musical critic, and produced some compositions of his own. His reputation as a writer on music dates from the publication of his pamphlet, "Die Grenzen der Poesie und Musik" (1856, 2nd ed. 1872), an answer to Hanslick's essay, "Vom Musikalisch-Schönen," which brought him into contact with Liszt and others. In 1860 he received a commission from the publisher Leuckart (C. Sander) at Breslau to write a "History of Music," which task he almost fulfilled, and in the most brilliant manner. Unfortunately, he died before completing the 4th volume, treating of the time of Palestrina and the beginnings of modern music (Vols. 1-4, 1862-78). The 2nd and 3rd volumes are of special value, the former treating of the music of the Middle Ages, the latter of the Netherland School. The new "Westphalized" edition of the first volume, published by B. v. Sokolowski, must be rejected as an impiety towards the author. O. Kade, making use of the materials left behind by Ambros, published in 1882 a fifth volume (a collection of examples to the 3rd volume); W. Bäumker, in the same year, a list of names and table of contents; and W. Langhans (q.v.), a continuation of the work up to the present time, and written in a somewhat lighter style. For the extensive journeys for the purpose of study which his work rendered necessary, A. not only obtained leave of absence, but received a money grant from the Vienna Academy. In 1869 he was appointed Supplementary Professor at Prague University, and at the same time member of the board of directors and teacher of the history of music at the Prague Conservatorium. In 1872 he was called to Vienna, where, together with an appointment in the offices of the Minister of Justice, he became tutor to the Crown Prince Rudolf, and received a professorship at the Conservatorium. As a composer, A. was of a certain importance ; he wrote sacred music (a mass, a Stabat Mater, etc.), pianoforte pieces in the style of Schumann, also a Bohemian national opera, *Brelislaw a Jitka*, overtures, songs, etc. ; yet his chief importance lies in his literary work, which was one of great distinction, if not altogether free from error. His "Kulturhistorische Bilder aus dem Musikleben der Gegenwart " (1860) also deserves mention.

Ambrosian Chant, the ecclesiastical singing introduced by St. Ambrose, Bishop of Milan, into the churches of his diocese. The Ambrosian Chant is one of the most enigmatical chapters in the history of music, for we really know next to nothing about it ; the only certain thing is that Ambrose transplanted the singing of the Halleluja, and the antiphonal singing from Greece into Italy, and that he is also looked upon as the originator of the Responses. As however, he not only introduced into Italy the singing of hymns, but wrote many hymns himself, the Ambrosian Chant seems scarcely to differ from the Gregorian, especially as, according to the trustworthy testimony of St. Augustine, the exclamations of joy formed the kernel of the Ambrosian, as afterwards of the Gregorian Chant. To all appearance the Gregorian Chant did not differ in principle from the Ambrosian, but was only a comprehensive revision, as a pattern for united Catholic Christendom, of Church song, to which, doubtless, much that was new had been added since the death of Ambrosius (397). Anyhow, the liturgy of the Milan diocese (as well as of other districts) appears, in spite of the ecclesiastical prescript for the whole Church, to have retained for a long period certain peculiarities, perhaps even certain melodies, to which certain remarks concerning Ambrosian song by writers of the Middle Ages may refer. (*Cf.* GREGORIAN CHANT.)

Ambrosian Hymn (*Hymnus Ambrosianus*) is the name given to the noble song " *Te Deum laudamus.*" It is by no means certain that Ambrosius was the author ; but more probable that the same was handed down to him from the Greek Church, and that he only translated the text.

Ambrosius, Bishop of Milan from 374 ; b. 333, Trèves, d. April 4, 397, Milan. Great merit must be ascribed to him for the manner in which he developed Christian Church song, in so far as he introduced into Italy various kinds of ritual singing (especially antiphonal and hymn singing as it had been developed in the Eastern Church). (*Cf.* AMBROSIAN CHANT.) It is also more than probable that he took over the four church Tones of the Greek Church (which, afterwards, by division into authentic and plagal were increased to eight). On the

other hand, it is not likely that he was acquainted with the designation of sounds by means of the first seven letters of the alphabet. (*See* LETTER NOTATION.) A. himself composed a great number of hymns. (*Cf.* AMBROSIAN HYMN.)

Âme (Fr.), the sound-post of the violin and other stringed instruments of that class.

Amerbach (Ammerbach), E l i a s N i k o l a u s, an excellent composer of the 16th century, who was organist about 1560 at St. Thomas's Church, Leipzig. He published a work on Tablature, which is of great historical importance, as it contains directions for fingering of instruments, explanations of ornaments, etc., " Orgel- und Instrument-tabulatur " (1571), etc. Fétis, in the 2nd edition of the " Biographie universelle," makes mention of a second Tablature work by Amerbach (spelt thus), " Ein neu künstlich Tabulaturbuch," etc. (1575), which does not seem to be identical with the one mentioned above, and the second edition of which came out in 1583.

American Organ, a peculiar instrument similar to the harmonium ; the reeds are made to speak, not by compressed air forced outwards, but drawn inwards ; there are also other small differences. The invention of the A. O. originated from a workman in the harmonium-factory of Alexandre at Paris, who went to America. These instruments, however, in their present complete form, only came into vogue after 1860, through the firm of Mason and Hamlin at Boston. The " Alexandre " organ, built by Édouard Alexandre (b. 1824, d. March 9, 1888) at Paris in 1874, is an instrument of a similar kind.

A minor Chord $= a, c, e ;$ *A minor key*, without signature (minor fundamental scale). (*See* KEY.)

Amiot, Pater, Jesuit and missionary in China, b. 1718, Toulon ; he translated a work on the theory of Chinese music (by Li-Koang-Ti) into French, which was reprinted with comments by the Abbé Rouffier in the " Mémoires concernant l'histoire des Chinois," as 6th volume.

Ammerbach. (*See* AMERBACH.)

Ammon, B l a s i u s, contrapuntist of the 16th century, born, according to the titles and dedications of his works, in the Tyrol. He was brought up as soprano singer in the service of Archduke Ferdinand of Austria, at whose expense he was sent to Venice. He afterwards became Franciscan monk at Vienna, where he died in June, 1590. His first work, a volume of introits à 5, appeared at Vienna in 1582, and a volume of masses à 4 came out there in 1588. A volume of motets, à 4–6, was published at Munich (a part of the edition announces that A. had died meanwhile). Still another volume of motets appeared at Munich after his death (1591), and a second volume of introits (à 4) was published in 1601 by his brother, Stephen Amon (*sic*). The Munich Library possesses a number of motets by A. in manuscript, written in part in organ tablature. The dates given after Fétis, in the 1st edition of this dictionary, which were generally accepted, are quite untrustworthy.

Amner, John, organist and choirmaster at Ely Cathedral, 1610–41. He took the degree of *Dr. mus.* at Oxford in 1613. He was a good church composer (in 1615 appeared " Sacred Hymns," à 3–6).—His son, Ralph, was bass singer at the Royal Chapel, Windsor (1623–63).

Amon, Joh. Andreas, b. 1763, Bamberg, d. March 29, 1825, Wallerstein; studied singing and various instruments, but devoted himself at last principally to the French horn, and became a pupil of Giov. Punto (Stich), who took him to Paris, and had him instructed in composition by Sacchini. After many concert tours with Punto, he became director of the music at Heilbronn. He died as capellmeister to the Prince of Oettingen-Wallerstein. A. was a prolific composer. Symphonies of his are printed, also concertos for pf., and flute and viola, sonatas for various instruments, trios, quartets, quintets, sets of variations, songs, etc. Two masses, a requiem, and two operettas remain in manuscript.

Amore (Ital.), love, affection.—*Con amore,* with tenderness, with devotion.

Amorevole, *amoroso* (Ital.), tenderly, lovingly.

Amplitude of *vibrations* is the extent of the departure of the vibrating body from a state of rest: the A. of the vibrations determines the strength of the sound: the period, the pitch. A swinging pendulum (of a clock) shows clearly the difference: the excursions of the pendulum (*i.e.* the A.) may be augmented ever so much by strengthening the moving power, the period (time between each tick) remains the same.

Anacker, Aug. Ferdinand, b. Oct. 17, 1790, Freiberg (Saxony), d. there Aug. 21, 1854; worked by himself at Leipzig, whither he went for the purpose of study, and became a sound musician. In 1822 he became cantor, musical director, and teacher in the normal school of his native town; he established there grand performances of sacred music, and also founded a " Singakademie." In 1827 he became, besides, conductor of the miners' wind-band. Of his compositions are to be named the cantatas *Bergmannsgruss, Lebens Blume und Lebens Unbestand,* pf. pieces, songs and part-songs, a chorale book, and seven songs to Döring's vernacular drama *Bergmannstreue* (Dresden).

Anakrusis (Gr.). (*See* UP-BEAT.)

Analysis *of sounds by the ear* is a term of modern acoustics, and implies the distinguishing of the partial tones contained in the single sounds (clangs) of our musical instruments. The ear is capable of analysing the compound vibration form of tones, *i.e.* distinguishing the various partial tones (*see* CLANG), but in a manner not hitherto sufficiently explained; resonators are frequently employed to strengthen the various partial tones, yet for a good musical ear they are, as a rule, unnecessary.

Analysis *of musical works* is an inquiry into their formal construction, both as regards the subdivision of themes into phrases, sections, and motives, and the way in which they are combined and transformed, also period formation, order of modulation, etc. A. of this sort is one of the most important duties of music schools, but it has been made light of, or altogether neglected. In recent times, short analyses of the works to be performed, together with historical remarks, have appeared on concert programmes. This system of *analytical programmes* sprang up in England about the middle of this century.

Anapest is a rhythmical foot consisting of two short and a long, or of two unaccented and one accented notes ♫ | ♩, also ♫ | ♩, or

♫ | ♩., etc., as well as ♩ ♩ | ♩

Anche (Fr.) is the channel over which lies the tongue in organ reed-pipes; *jeux à anches,* reed-stops. The spatula-like reed of the clarinet is also called A., and instruments such as the oboe and bassoon, which have a double reed, are called *instruments à a. double.*

Ancora (Ital.), same as *da capo ;* again.

Ancot, (1) Jean, b. Oct. 22, 1779, Bruges, d. there July 12, 1848; studied from 1799 to 1804 in Paris under Kreutzer and Baillot (violin), and under Catel (harmony), and then settled down as teacher of music in his native town. Only a small portion of his compositions is in print (four violin concertos, sacred compositions, overtures, marches, etc., in part for wind band, etc.). He gave a thorough musical training to his two sons. The elder—(2) Jean, b. July 6, 1799, d. June 5, 1829, Boulogne, received his final training at the Paris Conservatoire under Pradher (pianoforte), and Berton (composition); went in 1823 to London, and became professor at the Athenæum, and pianist to the Duchess of Kent; but he left London already in 1825, made concert tours in Belgium, and returned to Boulogne. His activity as composer was astonishing (225 works before he had reached the age of 30). Specially to be mentioned are his sonatas, a concerto, sets of variations, études, fugues, 4-hand fantasias for pianoforte, etc., besides his violin concertos, vocal *scenas,* with orchestra overtures, etc. The younger—(3) Louis, b. June 3, 1803, d. 1836, Bruges, went for long tours on the Continent, also to London, and became pianist to the Duke of Sussex. He afterwards lived for a time in Boulogne and Tours as music teacher, and finally in his native town. As composer he was certainly not so prolific as his brother, but, nevertheless, made attempts in almost every branch of musical art.

Andacht (Ger.), devoutness. *Mit Andacht*, devoutly.

Andächtig (Ger.), devoutly.

Andamento (Ital., "movement"), the name given to the free episodes in a fugue (although, as a rule, they are formed from motives taken from subject or countersubject) which occur between the various developments (also *Divertimento*).

Andante (Ital.). This is one of the oldest indications of rate of movement. In Italian it means "going" (*i.e.* in moderate movement, somewhat slow), and one must guard against taking it in the sense of "slow," for in that case certain additional indications would be misunderstood. *Più A.* or *un poco a.* means "quicker," and not "slower," as many (and, unfortunately, many composers) imagine. *Meno a.* means "less agitated," *i.e.* "slower." The diminutive form *andantino* indicates a *slower* movement than *a.*, but already in the last century it was falsely taken to mean quicker than *a.* *Andantino* relates mostly to the short duration of a piece. (*Cf.* ADAGIETTO.) By A., as in a similar way by Adagio, is meant, at the present day, a slow movement of a symphony, sonata, etc.

Andantino. (*See* ANDANTE.)

Ander, A l o y s, a famous opera singer (lyric tenor), b. Oct. 13, 1817, Liebititz (Bohemia), d. Dec. 11, 1864, at the baths of Wartemburg (Bohemia). From 1845, until his intellect became disordered and the last years of his life in consequence rendered fruitless, he was a highly-esteemed member of the Vienna opera house.

Anders, G o t t f r i e d E n g e l b e r t, b. 1795, Bonn, d. Sept. 22, 1866, Paris. He was for a long period archivist and superintendent of the musical department of the Bibliothèque at Paris. He wrote monographs on Paganini (1831) and Beethoven (1839).

Anderson, L u c y (*née* Philpot), English pianist, b. Dec., 1790, d. Dec. 24, 1878 ; married (1820) the violinist, G. Fr. Anderson.

Anding, J o h a n n M i c h a e l, b. Aug. 25, 1810, Queienfeld, near Meiningen ; attended the training college at Hildburghausen, and, after occupying the post of teacher in various towns, became (1843) music teacher at Hildburghausen college, where he died, Aug. 9, 1879. Several school song-books, part-songs, and organ pieces appeared in print, as well as a "Vierstimmiges Choralbuch" (1868) and "Handbüchlein für Orgelspieler" (3rd edition, 1872).

André, (1) J o h a n n, the founder of the famous music publishing house at Offenbach, b. March 28, 1741, d. June 18, 1799. He was intended to carry on his father's silk factory business, but this he declined, and adopted the career of music, for which he showed strong inclination and a healthy talent. He made early attempts at composition, and in the beginning of the sixties produced a comic opera, *Der Töpfer* (The Potter), of which he wrote the libretto, and likewise the operetta, *Erwin und Elmire* (Goethe), which was given with success at Frankfort. In 1777 he became capellmeister at the Döbbelin Theatre at Berlin, and during the seven following years composed with great diligence (many operettas, entr'actes, a ballet, songs, etc.). In 1784 he returned to Offenbach, where already in former days he had founded, close to the silk factory, a music-printing office, which he now extended into a large publishing business. Of his compositions the *Rheinweinlied* (Claudius) is the best known ; his operas are now forgotten.—(2) J o h a n n A n t o n, third son of the former, b. Oct. 6, 1775, Offenbach, d. April 6, 1842. From 1793 to 1796 he received a thorough musical training from Vollweiler in Mannheim ; he studied afterwards at Jena, made extensive tours, and on his father's death undertook the publishing business. In that same year he went to Vienna, and acquired from Mozart's widow the musical remains of the master, whereby at one stroke the firm became one of the most important in the world. The art of music-printing received a new impulse by the employment of lithography, which Franz Gleissner introduced on a large scale. But Anton A., both as composer (among other things, two operas) and theorist, was of greater importance than his father. His principal work was the "Lehrbuch der Tonsetzkunst" (1832–43), which, however, he did not complete ; the two volumes which appeared treat of harmony, counterpoint, canon, and fugue (lately revised by H. Henkel). Among his sons who turned their attention to music were :—(3) K a r l A u g u s t, b. June 15, 1806, d. Feb. 15, 1887, proprietor of a piano factory at Frankfort. He wrote "Der Klavierbau und seine Geschichte" (1855).—(4) J u l i u s, b. June 4, 1808, d. April 17, 1880, Frankfort, an excellent organist and pianist, who studied with Aloys Schmitt (himself a pupil of Anton André) ; he composed some good organ pieces.—(5) J o h a n n A u g u s t, b. March 2, 1817, followed Anton André as proprietor of the publishing business at Offenbach ; his sons, C a r l (b. Aug. 24, 1853) and A d o l p h (b. April 10, 1855), entered the business on June 1, 1880, of which they became the sole proprietors at their father's death, Oct. 29, 1887.—(6) J e a n B a p t i s t e, b. March 7, 1823, d. Dec. 9, 1882, Frankfort, pianist, studied under Aloys Schmitt, Taubert (pianoforte), Kessler, and Dehn (theory). He bore the title "Herzoglich bernburgischer Kapellmeister" without holding office, and lived many years in Berlin. He published several pieces for voice and pianoforte.

Andreoli, (1) G i u s e p p e, b. July 7, 1757, Milan, d. there Dec. 20, 1832 ; he was a distinguished contrabassist in the orchestra of La

Scala, and teacher of his instrument at Milan Conservatorio; also a good harpist.—(2) Guglielmo, b. April 22, 1835, d. March 13, 1860, Nice; studied at Milan Conservatorio. He was a distinguished pianist and noted for his neat and expressive playing. From 1856 to 1859 he attracted notice at various concerts in England (Crystal Palace, etc.).—(3) His brother, Carlo, b. Jan. 8, 1840, Mirandola, where his father (Evangelista A., b. 1810, d. June 16, 1875) was organist and teacher. He, too, was an excellent pianist, and from 1875 teacher of his instrument at Milan Conservatorio, where he had been a pupil. Already in 1858 he gave some successful concerts in London.

Andreozzi, Gaetano, b. 1763, Naples, d. Dec. 21, 1826, Paris. A prolific composer, who wrote 34 operas for Rome, Florence, Naples, Venice, etc., also for Petersburg and Madrid, and, besides, three oratorios. He always visited the places where he obtained success, but finally settled down in Naples, where he devoted himself to giving music lessons; but he became poor, and went to Paris to invoke the protection of the Duchesse de Berry, his former pupil. His wife, Anna A., b. 1772, Florence, was engaged at Dresden as *prima donna* (1801-2), but met with a fatal accident June 2, 1802, while on a journey from Pillnitz to Dresden.

Andrevi, Francesco, one of the most distinguished Spanish composers, b. Nov. 16, 1786, Sanabuya, near Lerida (Catalonia), of Italian parents, d. Nov. 23, 1853, Barcelona. He was a priest and successively maestro at the cathedrals of various towns (Barcelona, Valencia, Sevilla, etc.), and finally became conductor of the royal band. During the Carlist war he fled to Bordeaux, where he found an appointment. From 1845 to 1849 he lived at Paris, and afterwards became maestro at Notre Dame Church, Barcelona, which post he held until his death. Specially deserving of mention are his *Last Judgment* (oratorio), a Requiem for Ferdinand VII., and a *Stabat Mater*. A theoretical work of his on harmony and composition appeared at Paris in French translation (1848).

Andrien. (*See* ADRIEN.)

Andries, Jean, b. April 25, 1798, Ghent, d. there Jan. 21, 1872; in 1835 professor of the violin and ensemble classes, in 1851 successor of Mengal as director of Ghent Conservatoire, then until 1855 solo violinist at the theatre, and from 1856 honorary director of the Conservatoire. He published some historical works: "Aperçu historique de tous les instruments de musique, actuellement en usage"; "Précis de l'histoire de la musique depuis les temps les plus reculés, etc." (1862); "Instruments à vent. La flûte" (1866); "Remarques sur les cloches et les carillons" (1868).

And^te., abbr. for *Andante*.

And^tino., abbr. for *Andantino*.

Anemochord (*Animocorde*), a pneumatic stringed instrument, a clever attempt of the pianoforte manufacturer, J. J. Schnell, in Paris (1789), by means of wind artificially produced (by bellows), to give an Æolian-harp effect to really artistic music on an instrument resembling a pianoforte. (*Cf.* "Allgemeine Musikalische Zeitung," 1798, p. 39, f.) The idea was afterwards taken up by Kalkbrenner and Henri Herz, the latter of whom named his instrument, constructed in a similar manner, *Piano éolien* (1851).

Anerio, (1) Felice, one of the most distinguished of Roman composers of the time of Palestrina, b. 1560, Rome, d. Sep. 28, 1614; pupil of G. M. Nanini. On April 3, 1594, he became the successor of Palestrina as composer of the Papal Chapel (Ruggiero Giovanelli receiving the post of maestro). Several of Anerio's compositions passed for a long time as those of Palestrina ("Adoramus te, Christe," and a *Stabat Mater* for three choirs). Printed copies exist of A.'s works of the period 1585-1622: several books of madrigals à 5-6, two books of hymns, *cantica*, and motets, besides canzonets and madrigals à 3-4, *Concerti spirituali* à 4, litanies à 4-8, and separate motets, etc., in collections. Many manuscripts are preserved in Roman libraries.—(2) Giovanni Francesco, according to the scanty information which the titles and dedications of his works afford, was probably a brother of the former, b. about 1567, Rome; from 1575 to 1579 chorister at St. Peter's under Palestrina; about 1609 received an appointment at the Court of Sigismund III. of Poland; in 1610 maestro di cappella at Verona Cathedral; 1611, Prefect at the Jesuit College of St. Ignaz; 1613-20, maestro at the Jesuit Church, St. Maria di Monti, at Rome; and in 1616 (at the age of 49) took holy orders. His first work, a book of madrigals à 5, appeared at Venice in 1599; those which appeared after 1620 were not edited by him, so that he probably died in this year. A. arranged Palestrina's *Missa Papae Marcelli* à 6, for four voices, in which form it passed through an endless number of editions. His own compositions (madrigals, motets, litanies, canzonets, psalms, etc.) are based partly on the traditions of the 16th century, partly on the innovations of the 17th (solo singing, with figured bass).

Anet, Baptiste. (*See* BAPTISTE.)

Anfossi, Pasquale, a once famous opera composer, b. April 25, 1737, Naples, d. Feb., 1797, Rome; pupil of Piccini. He wrote his first opera, *Cajo Mario*, for Venice in 1769, made a name with *l'Incognita perseguitata* in 1773 at Rome, and afterwards won triumphs, so long as his works were specially praised up to the skies in order to depreciate those of his teacher, Piccini. He wrote in all 54 operas (1769-96). In Paris he met with no success (1780). **After**

being conductor for two years at the Italian Opera, London (1781–3), he brought out operas at Prague, Dresden, and Berlin, and then returned to Italy, and in 1791 took the post of maestro at the Lateran. In his last years he was chiefly occupied with sacred compositions (four oratorios, masses, psalms, etc.).

Angelet, Charles François, b. Nov. 18, 1797, Ghent, d. Dec. 20, 1832; pupil of the Paris Conservatoire. He was trained under Zimmerman, became an excellent pianist, and studied composition under Fétis after he had settled down as teacher of music in Brussels. In 1829 he was appointed court pianist to King William of the Netherlands. His compositions consist principally of pianoforte pieces (fantasias, variations, etc.), yet among them are a trio, and a symphony which obtained a prize.

Angelica (*Vox a.*, "Angel's voice"). An organ stop, generally of 4 ft., which, like the *Vox humana* (8 ft.), is constructed in various ways, for the most part with free vibrating reeds and short tubes.

Angeloni, Luigi, b. 1758, Frosinone (States of the Church), d. 1842, London. He was on the committee which issued the proclamation of the Roman Republic in 1799, and was therefore forced to escape. He went to Paris, but in 1801 was implicated in the conspiracy of Ceracchi and Topino-Lebrun, and suffered ten months' imprisonment. In 1823, on account of his relations with Carbonari, he was expelled from Paris, and went to London. A. published an important work : " Sopra la vita, le opere ed il sapere di Guido d'Arezzo " (1811).

Anglaise, "English Dance." This was the old name for the dance now called *Française* (q.v.). Many other English dances (ballads, hornpipes, etc.) were, however, called Anglaises.

Anglebert, Jean Henri d', chamber-musician to Louis XIV., published in 1689 "Pièces de Clavecin," among which were 22 variations on the "Folies d'Espagne," to which Corelli also set variations in 1700. A. belongs to the better class of old writers for the clavier; in the preface to the work mentioned above there are explanations with regard to the manner in which certain ornaments (*Tremblement simple* and *appuyé, Cadence, Double, Pincé, Chute, Port de voix, Coulé, Arpège*) should be performed.

Angoscioso (Ital.), full of anguish ; with fear.

Anhang (Ger.), coda (q.v.).

Anima (Ital.), soul ; *con a., animato, animando,* " with life," with warmth, with fire.

Animoso (Ital.), eager, spirited.

Animuccia, Giovanni, b. at the end of the 15th or beginning of the 16th century, d. 1570, or beginning of 1571, Rome. He was the real predecessor of Palestrina, not only in office (Palestrina became his successor as maestro at St. Peter's), but also in the manner in which, amid contrapuntal devices of every kind, he

strove after harmonic clearness. The name of Animuccia is, however, more frequently associated with the species of composition named *Oratorio* (q.v.), as one of the originators; his "Laudi" composed for Neri's Oratorio were, however, not in any way connected with this form of art, but simple songs of praise, hymn-like in character. A. was appointed maestro at the Vatican in 1555. The following of his compositions appeared in print : A volume of masses (1567), two volumes of Magnificats, a Credo à 4, also several volumes of motets, psalms, sacred madrigals, and hymns ; but many works must have remained in manuscript in the Vatican library.—His brother, Paolo, likewise a contrapuntist of importance, was maestro at the Lateran (1550–52), and died in 1563. Only detached works of his have, however, been preserved in collections.

Ankerts d'. (*See* DANKERS.)

Ankteriasmus (Gr.), infibulation, a mild form of castration (to prevent mutation).

Anna, Amalia. (*See* AMALIA (1).)

Annibale, a contrapuntist of the 16th century, b. Padua (hence called Patavinus or Padovano). In 1552 he became organist of the second organ at St. Mark's, Venice ; his successor was Andreas Gabrieli (1556). The following of his compositions have been preserved : a book of motets à 5, and one à 6 (1567) ; madrigals à 5 (1583) ; and motets à 4 (1592) ; also two masses and a few madrigals in collections (1566 and 1575). Neither the year of his birth nor of his death is known.

Anschlag (Ger.), obsolete term for a particular kind of appoggiatura (q.v.).

Anschütz, (1) Joh. Andreas, b. March 19, 1772, Coblentz ; grandson and pupil of the court organist and Electoral musical director A. at Trèves. He studied jurisprudence at Mayence, and died as State Attorney at Coblentz (1856). In 1808 he established at Coblentz a musical society, together with a school for instrumental and vocal music, which was subsidised by the state. A. was an excellent pianist, and published successful compositions, especially for pianoforte.—(2) Karl, son of the former ; a first-rate conductor, b. 1815, Coblentz, d. Dec., 1870, New York ; a pupil of Fr. Schneider. In 1844 he undertook the direction of the institute of music established by his father, but went in 1848 to England, and in 1857 to America. For several years he was opera conductor under Ullmann at New York, and in 1864 undertook a German opera season on his own account. He appears only to have composed small pianoforte pieces.

Anselm von Parma (Anselmus Georgius Parmensis), a man of wide learning, who flourished in the 15th century, author of the treatise, "De harmonia dialogi," supposed to have been lost, but discovered at Milan in 1824.

Answer, a term used in fugue (q.v.).

Antegnati, an organ-builder, organist, and composer at Brescia; b. about 1550, d. about 1620. He published masses, motets, psalms, *canzoni,* as well as several works in organ tablature.

Anteludium (Lat.), prelude, introduction.

Anthem. A form of art peculiar to England; corresponding somewhat to the German Church-Cantata, but differing from it in the direction of the motet. The word A. is derived from Anti-hymn or Antiphon, and referred originally to alternate singing; but even in the A. of the olden time (Tye, Tallis, Byrd, Gibbons) there is no longer any trace of such meaning. The A. was introduced into the English Church as an essential element of divine service in 1559; it attained to higher importance through the contributions to this branch of musical art by Purcell and Handel. A distinction is made between "full" and "verse" anthems; in the former the chorus predominates, in the latter soli, duets, etc., have the prominent place; in both kinds the orchestra sometimes takes part. The words are Biblical (Psalms, Proverbs, etc.).

Anthologie (Fr. and Ger.), anthology, a collection of choice compositions; lit., "a gathering of flowers."

Anthropoglossa, the *vox humana* stop in the organ.

Anthropophony, science of (Gr.), treats of the nature of the human voice.

Anticipation (Lat. *Anticipatio*), a term used in harmony for the entry in advance of a note or notes belonging to the chord on the next beat, and forming, for the most part, a dissonance with the harmony on which they fall; they must not, however, be understood in that sense, but as entering before their time, thus:

The A. at *b,* in the old masters, almost invariably occurs in full closes; it can, without any alteration of meaning, be extended to all the parts (*c*). It is much more difficult to explain anticipations in the middle of a cadence, entering on unaccented beats, and suggesting new harmonies, thus:

This passage occurs in Bach's two-part Invention, No. 9, and the *d flat* is an entry in advance of sub-dominant harmony, while the under part keeps firmly to the tonic. In any case the sub-dominant is not fully felt until after the bar-stroke.

Antienne (Fr.), antiphony. (*See* ANTIPHON.)

Antiphon (Fr. *Antienne, cf.* also ANTHEM.) This term really implies the alternate singing between two choirs. It is one of the oldest elements of the Catholic Ritual service, and, according to the testimony of Aurelianus Reomensis (9th century), was adopted by St. Ambrosius from the Greek Church, and transplanted into Italy; St. Chrysostom is said to have introduced antiphonal singing into the Greek Church. A. at the present day merely means a verse of a psalm sung first by the priest and afterwards by the choir.

Antiphonical, *antiphonically* ("sounding against"). This was a term applied by the ancient Greeks (already by Aristotle) to the interval of the octave, the only harmony of which they made use. (*Cf.* PARAPHONY.)

Antiphonary, really a collection of the Antiphons of the Catholic Ritual, and then generally a collection of church music for festival days, of Antiphons, and also responses, offertories, communion services, hallelujahs, "tractus" melodies, hymns, and psalms for the various hours of the day.

Antiquis, Johannes de, maestro at the church of St. Nicholas, Bari (Naples) in the second half of the 16th century. He published a collection "Villanelle alla Napoletana" (1574) by local composers, including himself; and a collection of "*canzone*" (1584). A volume of madrigals à 4 of his appeared also in 1584.

Antiquus, Andreas (*de Mondona*), a music-printer at Rome, perhaps the *Andreas de Antiquis* of whom Petrucci printed some *frottole* (1504–8). He published a volume of masses, "Liber XV. missarum," 1516, by the most distinguished masters (Josquin, Brumel, Pipelare, etc.).

Antistrophe. (*See* STROPHE.)

Antithesis (Gr.), countersubject; *antithetically,* by way of contrast.

Anton, Konrad Gottlob, professor of Oriental languages at Wittenberg from 1775; d. July 3, 1814. He wrote on the metrical system of the Hebrews, and attempted to decipher their accents as musical notes; his pamphlets only rank as curiosities in the history of music.

Antony, Franz Joseph, b. Feb. 1, 1790, Münster (Westphalia), d. there 1837. From 1819 he was musical director at the cathedral in that city, and from 1832 cathedral organist as successor to his father. Besides sacred compositions, he published an "Archäologisch-liturgisches Gesangbuch des Gregorianischen Kirchengesangs" (1829), and a "Geschichtliche Darstellung der Entstehung und Vervollkommnung der Orgel" (1832).

Aoidos (Gr.), a singer in ancient Greece. (*Cf.* RHAPSODIST.)

Apel, Joh. August, b. 1771, Leipzig, d. there Aug. 9, 1816; took his degree of *Dr. juris* at

Leipzig, afterwards became member of the council there. He published two interesting works on rhythm in opposition to Gottfried Hermann's "Elementa doctrinae metricae," viz., a series of articles in the *Allgemeine musikalische Zeitung* of 1807 and 1808, and a comprehensive "Metrik" (1814–1816, 2 vols.).

Apell, Joh. David von, b. Feb. 23, 1754, Cassel, d. there 1833, secret member of the board of finance, and theatre intendant; member of the Academies of Stockholm, Bologna (Philharmonic) and Rome (Arcadian). He was a very prolific composer (partly under the pseudonym Capelli) in the department of sacred music (a mass dedicated to Pius VII., for which he received the order of the Golden Spur, etc.), as well as in that of the opera, cantata, and instrumental music. He also wrote "Galerie der vorzüglichsten Tonkünstler und merkwürdigen Musikdilettanten in Cassel vom Anfang des 16 Jahrhunderts bis auf gegenwärtige Zeiten" (1806).

Apertus (Lat.), open. A term applied to organ pipes that are open at the top, to distinguish them from stopped pipes.

Aphony (Gr.), deprived of voice, to be distinguished from *Alaly*, speechlessness, dumbness. This is a sign that the larynx is out of order, and it can proceed from causes of the most varied kind (inflammation, abscesses, paralysis, etc.). A. only takes away tone from the voice, and thus produces thickness of speech.

Apollon (Apollo), the Greek god of light who awakens the lute of Nature and orders the movements of the planets, the harmony of the spheres; hence called the god of poetry and music, in whose train are the muses ("Musagetes"). In honour of A. the Pythian Games were celebrated every four years at Delphi, at which musical contests occupied the foremost place.

Apollonicon, an instrument constructed at London by Flight and Robson (1812–16), and taken to pieces in 1840. It was both a gigantic orchestrion and an organ with five manuals.

Apotome was the name given in ancient Greece to the interval now called a "chromatic semitone;" the diatonic semitone was named *Limma* (a–b flat, Limma; b flat–b natural A.). According to our acoustical calculations, the diatonic semitone (15 : 16) is greater than the chromatic (24 : 25, likewise 128 : 135), but with the ancients it was the reverse, for the Limma consisted of the remainder after two whole tones (both as 8 : 9) had been subtracted from a fourth (3 : 4), *i.e.* $\frac{3}{4} : [\frac{8}{9}]^2 = \frac{243}{256}$, whilst the A. was the remainder after the Limma ($\frac{243}{256}$) had been subtracted from the whole tone (8 : 9), *i.e.* $\frac{2048}{2187}$. (*Cf.* Tone, Determination of.)

Appassionato (Ital.), with passion, *i.e.* in an agitated manner and with emphatic expression.

Appel, Karl, b. March 14, 1812, Dessau,

was known by his quartets for male voices, especially those of a humorous kind. He died Dec. 9, 1895.

Appenato (Ital.). distressed, in a sorrowful manner.

Applicatur (Ger.), fingering.

Appoggiando, Appoggiato (Ital.), leaning and leaned against. These terms are applied to notes which are connected with others—to syncopations and suspensions—and are also synonymous with *col portamento di voce*. (*Vide* Portamento.)

Appoggiatura (Ital., Ger. *Vorschlag*, Fr. *Port de voix*). This term is applied to the ornaments of a melody which, as accessory, are indicated by small notes, and are not counted in the time-value of the bar. There are two kinds of appoggiatura which must be carefully distinguished, the long and the short A. (1) The long A. is only the expression of an harmonic relationship by means of the notation; long appoggiatura notes are holding-back notes, and the term *suspension* ("Vorhalt") would be the most suitable for them. In former times composers preferred to cover and hide suspensions taken without preparation by writing them as small ornamental notes; at the present day such anxiety is unknown, and accordingly the long A. has become quite obsolete. Therefore in new editions of old works (before Beethoven) it should be removed, and the amateur no longer tortured by having to learn the rules for the execution of the same; by this means many faults would be rendered impossible. As appoggiaturas have no time value, the note before which the free suspension occurs (the principal note written as a large one) is marked with the full value which both together have; *but the suspended note with the value which it is actually to have.* Thus the mode of execution is quite simple, if the small note is played as written, and the following note with what remains of the value:

Written

Played

Only in duple ternary time (2 triplets $= \frac{6}{8}, \frac{6}{4}$, etc.) there is sometimes a difficulty, when, instead of the correct mode of writing as at N B, a), the incorrect as at b) is employed; in both cases the execution should be as at N B, c. On the other hand it is better to render the phrase,

(a)   (b)

not as at *a*, but as at *b;* and even here the mode of writing is not altogether free from misconception.—(2) The short A. (at any rate in 19th century publications) is distinguished from the long by means of a cross stroke through the tail (it is never written as a note of larger value than the quaver):

But the short A. offers another problem, viz., whether it should be given at the beginning of the note-value of the principal note, or whether it should take from the value of the previous note. There have been advocates for both modes of executing the ornament, but the best masters have decided that the A. must enter on the beat, the short as well as the long; the other mode was already condemned by Ph. E. Bach (1753) as amateurish:

Not   But

As the short A. is always played very quickly, it would be difficult to distinguish between the two but for the fact that the accentuation in the one case differs entirely from that in the other. *The appoggiatura note has the accent*, but *cf.* NACHSCHLAG. When there are several notes, as in the *Schleifer* (a) and the *Anschlag* (b), the first note is likewise the accented one.

(a)   (b)

Played

Also when an A. occurs before the note of a chord, it is executed in a similar manner. But an exception occurs when an A. in a melody is strengthened by octaves, as for example (Schubert):

Not   But

The first mode of execution would be false, for it would result in two-part writing not intended by the composer.—(3) There are A. notes which hold a middle place between the long and the short A., and by many are reckoned as belong-

ing to the latter. Such are A. notes which have the fourth part of the value, or even less, of the principal note, but yet no cross stroke. These too are performed with the exact value given to them by the composer.

Written

Played

Appun, Georg Aug. Ignaz, b. Sept. 1, 1816, Hanau, d. there, Jan. 14, 1885. He studied under A. André and Schnyder von Wartensee (theory), Suppus and Al. Schmidt (pianoforte), Rink (organ), and Mangold ('cello). He was accomplished in many ways as a musician, and played nearly every kind of instrument. Up to about 1860 he laboured successfully at Frankfort as a teacher of theory, and of instrumental and vocal music. From that time he devoted himself exclusively to investigations in acoustics, and to the construction of delicate acoustical apparatus, and constructed an harmonium with a scale of 53 degrees (pure intonation, *see* TONE, DETERMINATION OF, etc.), which was the means of his entering into close relationship with authorities like Helmholtz, v. Oettingen, etc., acquiring thereby great fame.

À première vue (Fr.), **A prima vista** (Ital.), at sight.

Aprile, Giuseppe, an eminent contraltist and teacher of singing; b. Oct. 29, 1738, Bisceglia, d. 1814, Martina. From 1763 he was for several years an ornament on various operatic stages (Stuttgart, Milan, Florence, Naples), and lived afterwards in Naples as a teacher of singing. A. studied under Avos, and was the teacher of Cimarosa and Manuel Garcia, junior. Up to now there does not seem to be sufficient ground for the attempts which have been made to turn the one A. into two, because in 1809 a tenor singer A. distinguished himself at the Pergola, Florence. Aprile's vocal method with solfeggi, entitled " The Italian Method of Singing, with 36 solfeggi," first appeared in London at Broderip's.

Aptommas, the name of two brothers, distinguished harpists, who have written good music for their instrument. The one was born in 1826, the other in 1829 at Bridgend. Both are teachers in London. *See also* THOMAS (3).

A punta d'arco (Ital.), with the point of the bow.

A punto (Ital.), exact, in accurate time.

À quatre mains (Fr.), **A quattro mani** (Ital.), for four hands; expressions used in speaking of pianoforte and organ duets.

À quatre voix (Fr.), **A quattro voci** (Ital.), for four voices.

Arabians and Persians. The music of the A. and P. has been described in a monograph by R. G. Kiesewetter (1842). According to this writer the Arabians, before Islamism, had no musical culture worthy of the name; but a flourishing period of musical art commenced after the conquest of Persia (7th century), when the old Persian culture passed over to the conquerors, and blossomed afresh. The oldest Arabian writer on music is Chalil (d. 776 after Christ), who wrote a book of rhythms (metre) and a book of tones. In the 10th century Alfarabi (q.v.) attempted to introduce the Greek theory. Persian writers on music first appear in the 14th century, after Persia had escaped from the rule of the Turks and had come under that of the Mongols, under which (especially under Tamerlane) the arts and sciences put forth fresh blossoms. The founder of the new Persian school was Ssaffieddin, an Arabian; his principal work, the " Schereffije," was written in the Arabian tongue. Other distinguished representatives are: Mahmud Schirasi (d. 1315), Mahmud el Amul (d. 1349), and Abdolkadir Ben Isa (in the Persian language). The musical system of these writers is that which arose in Persia whilst under Arabian rule, undoubtedly containing old Arabic elements against which Alfarabi had already fought. The peculiarity of this system is the division of the octave into 17 parts (third-tones); if we take the first note as *c*, then (according to Abdolkadir's monochord) the others are: $2\,d\flat$, $3\,e\flat\flat$, $4\,d$, $5\,e\flat$, $6\,f\flat$, $7\,e$, $8\,f$, $9\,g\flat$, $10\,a\flat\flat$, $11\,g$, $12\,a\flat$, $13\,b\flat\flat$, $14\,a$, $15\,b\flat$, $16\,c\flat$, $17\,d\flat\flat$, $18\,c$, or, if we ignore differences which are absolutely imperceptible (*cf.* TONE, DETERMINATION OF), they may be indicated otherwise (cf. LETTER-NOTATION): c, $c\sharp$, d, d, $d\sharp$, e, e, f, $f\sharp$, g, g, $g\sharp$, a, a, $b\flat$, $b\natural$, c, c. It is not by chance that this system offers a great number of almost absolutely pure thirds, viz., c, e, $d\,f\sharp$, $e\,g\sharp$, $f\,a$, $g\,b\natural$, $a\,c\sharp$, $b\flat\,d$, $b\,d\sharp$. (*Cf.* MESSEL.) In face of this solid practical substratum we may, perhaps, venture to conclude that the twelve principal keys (Makamat) of the theorists are only theory; practical music really makes no keys, but melodies. The keys are as follows (the tone names are given according to the above numbered scheme): *Uschak* $= c$, d, e, f, g, a, $b\flat$, c; *Newa* $= c$, d, $e\flat$, f, g, $a\flat$, $b\flat$ c; *Buselik* $= c$, $d\flat$, $e\flat$, f, $g\flat$, $a\flat$, $b\flat$, c; *Rast* $= c$, d, e, f, g, a, $b\flat$, c; *Irak* $= c$, d, e, f, g, $g\sharp$, a, $b\natural$, c; *Iszfahan* $= c$, d, e, f, g, $a\flat$, $b\flat$, c; *Zirefkend* $= c$, d, $e\flat$ f, $f\sharp$, $g\sharp$, a, b, c; *Busurg* $= c$, d, e, f, $f\sharp$, g, a, $b\natural$, c; *Sengule* $= c$, d, e, f, $f\sharp$, a, $b\flat$, c; *Rehawi* $= c$, $d\flat$, e, f, $g\flat$, $a\flat$, $b\flat$, c; *Husseini* $= c$, $d\flat$, $e\flat$, f, $g\flat$, $a\flat$, $b\flat$, c ($=$ *Buselik*); *Hidschas* $= c$, $d\flat$, $e\flat$, $g\flat$, $a\flat$, $b\flat$, c. Already in the 14th century the

Western tone system of seven fundamental tones and five intermediate tones was known in Persia, and obtained firm footing there, especially in the practical use of music; the theorists, however, stuck to the Messel system (q.v.) even up to recent times. According to Alfarabi, the lute (q.v.) was the chief *musical instrument* of the Arabians. They received it from the Persians, and, indeed, according to information derived from Arabian writers before the period of Islamism the Persians may have got it from the Egyptians (*see* EGYPT) during the period of their rule in Egypt (525–323 B.C.). A degenerate form of the lute was the *Tanbur* (with long neck, small resonance-box, and only three strings tuned in unison). The Persian writers of the 14th century make mention besides of stringed instruments similar to our zither: Kanun (evidently derived from the Greek monochord, canon), Tschenk and Nushet, as well as the *stringed instruments* Kemangeh and Rebab (Rubeb), the origin, according to general belief, of stringed instruments (q.v.) in the West. But against this may be placed the fact that the primitive construction of these instruments (the sounding case of the Kemangeh is a cocoanut shell slit open, and covered with fish-skin, and that of the Rebab a four-cornered chest running upwards to a point), which has remained the same up to the present day, and the striking fact that the *fidula* (*fiedel, viola, viella*) was already known to Western writers in the 9th century, and the oldest representations show a highly developed form, whereas before the 14th century the Orientals make no mention of any instruments of the kind. The *wind instruments* were of two kinds, *Ney* (beaked-flute), and *Arganum* (Organum ? Bagpipe). The number of names used by writers for Arabic-Persian instruments is very great, yet it can be shown that many of the same refer to one and the same instrument. (*Cf.* Kiesewetter's " Die Musik der A. und P.," p. 90, etc.)

Araja, Francesco, Italian opera composer, b. 1700, Naples, d. about 1770, Bologna; produced in 1730 his first opera, *Berenice*, at Florence. He soon acquired fame, and went in 1735 with an Italian Opera company to Petersburg, where he wrote Italian and Russian operas, and with great success. His *Cephalos and Prokris* (1755) is the oldest Russian opera. In 1759 he returned to Italy. A plan for a new journey to Russia (1761) was speedily abandoned, owing to the assassination of Peter III. A. also wrote a Christmas oratorio.

Aranda, (1) Matheus de, Portuguese musician, Professor of Music at Coimbra University (1544), wrote: " Tratado de cantollano y contrapuncto por Matheo de A., maestro de la capilla de la Sé de Lixboa," etc. (1533). —(2) Del Sessa d', an Italian composer of the 16th century, spoken of in high terms by M. Prætorius; a volume of madrigals à

} of his was published in 1571 by Gardano at Venice.

Arauxo (*Araujo*), Francisco Corrêa de, Spanish Dominican monk, d. Jan. 13, 1663, as Bishop of Segovia. He wrote : " Tientos y discursos musicos y facultad organica" (1626), and " Casos morales de la musica " (MS.).

Arbeau, Thoinot, pseudonym of *Jean Tabourot*, an official at Langres towards the end of the 16th century ; he published, " Orchésographie," etc. (1589 and 1596), a literary curiosity, in which dancing, drum and fife playing, are taught in dialogue form, and by means of a kind of tablature. (*Cf.* CHOREOGRAPHY.)

Arbitrio (Ital.), free-will ; *a suo a.*, at one's pleasure.

Arbuthnot, John, English doctor, physician-in-ordinary to Queen Anne (1709), d. Feb. 27, 1735. He was a warm partisan of Handel's in the composer's disputes with the members of his opera company. He gave interesting details about various personages in his " Miscellaneous Works."

Arc., abbr. for *arco* (bow).

Arcadelt, Jacob (also written *Jachet Arkadelt, Archadet, Harcadelt, Arcadet*), celebrated Netherland composer, b. about 1514 ; went to Rome, and became teacher of singing of the boys' choir at the Papal Chapel (1539), then singer there (1540), later on chamberlain to an abbot (1544). He followed the Duc de Guise to Paris about 1555, where we find him with the title of *Regius musicus* (1557). A goodly number of Arcadelt's compositions have come down to us, principally six books of madrigals à 5, in which form of art A. chiefly excelled (1538–56), and a volume of masses à 3–7 (1557 ; his publishers, Gardano and Scoto at Venice, and Le Roy and Ballard at Paris, were the most celebrated of that time). Many motets, *canzoni*, etc., are to be found in collections of the period.

Arcadia (*Accademia degli Arcadi*), a society of artists (poets and musicians), founded at Rome in 1690. The members bore old Greek shepherds' names.

Arcais, Francesco, Marchese d', b. Dec. 15, 1830, Cagliari (Sardinia), d. Aug. 15, 1890, Castelgandolfo, near Rome, was for many years musical critic of the *Opinione*. He had an excellent pen, but his tastes were somewhat antiquated, and he held in horror, not only Wagner, but any departure from Italian opera in the good old sense of the term. He himself made several attempts at composition (three operettas), but met with little success. A. was also a contributor to the Milan *Gazetta musicale*. During the last years of his life he resided in Rome ; he followed the *Opinione* from Turin, passing through Florence.

Arcato (Ital.), played with the bow.

Archadet. (*See* ARCADELT.)

Archambeau, Jean Michel d', Belgian composer, b. March 3, 1823, Hervé, was at the age of 15 teacher of music at the college there. He was afterwards organist at Petit Rechain, and has written masses, litanies, motets, romances, and drawing-room pieces.

Archeggiare (Ital.), to play with the bow.

Archer, Frederick, excellent English organist, b. June 16, 1838, Oxford ; was trained at London and Leipzig. He was at first conductor, but since 1881 has been organist at Brooklyn (New York). He has published works on the organ and organ compositions, and was for some time editor of *The Key-Note*.

Archi.... and **Arci....** as a prefix to the names of old instruments, refers to a specially extensive compass, and to large size, as, for example, *Archicymbal* (*arcicembalo*, an instrument with six keyboards, constructed in the 16th century by Vicentino ; it had special keys and strings for the three ancient genera—the diatonic, chromatic, and enharmonic) ; *Archiliuto* (*arciliuto*, Fr., *archiluth*, Ger., *Erzlaute ; cf.* BASS LUTE, CHITARRONE, and THEORBO), *Archiviola di Lira* (Lirone, Accordo, Lira da Gamba, the largest kind of lyres [viols with many strings]), etc.

Archytas, a Greek statesman and Pythagorean philosopher, at Tarentum circa 400–365 B.C. He was a celebrated mathematician, probably the first whose divisions of the tetrachord fixed the ratio of the third at 5 : 4 (handed down by Ptolemy). Only fragments of his writings have been preserved.

Arco (Ital.), bow ; *coll' arco* (abbr. *arc., c. arc.*), *arcato*, " with the bow." A sign for stringed instruments, after a *pizzicato* passage, that the bow is to be used again.

Ardente (Ital.), with fire and ardour.

Arditi, (1) Michele, Marchese, b. Sept. 29, 1745, Presicca (Naples), d. April 23, 1838 ; a learned archæologist and composer, in 1807 director of the Bourbon Museum, in 1817 chief inspector of excavations in the kingdom of Naples. He wrote one opera, *Olimpiade*, as well as numerous cantatas, arias, and instrumental works.—(2) Luigi, b. July 22, 1822, Crescentino (Vercelli). He studied at the Milan Conservatorio, was a violinist and maestro at Vercelli, Milan, Turin ; he went in a similar capacity to Havannah, New York, Constantinople, and finally to London, where he conducted the Italian Opera for several years, and he has since been living as music teacher and composer. His name has become specially popular through his vocal dances, of which " Il bacio" has made the round of the world. He has also written three operas, as well as instrumental pieces (pianoforte fantasias, scherzo for two violins, etc.). Died May 1, 1903.

Ardito (Ital.), with spirit and boldness.

Aretinian (*Guidonian*) **Syllables,** same as solmisation syllables (*ut, re, mi, fa, sol, la*), which Guido d'Arezzo first employed as tone-names. (*Cf.* SOLMISATION.)

Argine, Constantino dall', b. May 12, 1842, Parma, d. March 15, 1877, Milan. A favourite composer of ballets in Italy; he also produced several operas.

Aria (Ital., Ger. *Arie*) is the name given to solo vocal pieces developed at length, and with orchestral accompaniment, whether taken from an opera, cantata, or oratorio; or it may stand for a detached work (concert aria) intended for concert performance. It differs from the ballad, which also has orchestral accompaniment, in that it is lyrical, *i.e.* expresses feelings in the first person, while the ballad relates (epico-lyric). The expression can rise to a high degree of dramatic power, when speech, passing from simple description and reflection, takes the form of apostrophe; hence there are arias which are monologues set to music, while others appear as parts of a great ensemble scene. A special group is formed by the *sacred arias* (*Church arias, Aria da chiesa*), which are either prayers or devout meditations, and express moods of the most varied kind (contrition, anguish, thankfulness, joy, mourning, etc.). The A. differs from the Lied in that it is laid out altogether on a broader plan, but principally in its exterior condition, for the Lied is only accompanied by one or a few instruments (*Klavierlied*, Lied with violin or 'cello and pf.). Arias of small compass, which closely resemble the Lied, and which, when a pianoforte accompaniment is substituted for the orchestra (as is always the case in drawing-room performances), entirely lack the feature which distinguishes them from the Lied, are called *Cavatinas, Ariettas*, or even actually *Lieder*. (COUPLET, CANZONE.) The French word *Air* has, at the present day, a much more general sense, and fairly answers to the word "melody," *i.e.* it is used as much for vocal pieces of various kinds as for instrumental pieces, provided only that a beautiful melody forms their chief feature. In the 17th and 18th centuries the word *Arie* had the same meaning in Germany, and there was the *Spielarie* (Instrumental A.), as well as the *Gesangsarie* (Vocal A.). The A. was developed into a fixed art-form of high importance in the so-called *grand* or *da capo* A., which consists of two sections, contrasting with each other in mood, movement, and mode of artistic treatment. The first section gives the vocalist an opportunity to display his or her agility of voice: there are many repetitions of words, and the theme is richly developed; while in the second section the vocal part is quieter, and on that account displays richer harmonic and contrapuntal means. This second section is followed by a *da capo, i.e.* the first is faithfully repeated, only with rich ornamentation on the part of the singer. An essential element of the

grand A. is the instrumental *ritornello* at the commencement, containing the principal melody. The ever-increasing demands resulting from the ever-increasing virtuoso capabilities of the singers became of such prime importance in Italian opera, that composers had in the first place to think about writing grateful numbers for the singers; and thus the grand A. became the *coloratura* or *bravura* A. The "da capo" A. arose already in the 17th century (*see* SCARLATTI, 1), and flourished until about the end of the 18th century; it has now gone out of vogue, and has given place to a freer multiform treatment of the A. The literal *da capo* has been given up, as undramatic; the *ritornello* is only to be found exceptionally, and the thematic articulation of the A. is fixed by the demands of the text, so that it is frequently in rondo form, or includes an allegro movement between two movements in slower time, etc. The *æsthetic meaning* of the A. in the musical drama (opera) is a pause in the action in favour of the broader unfolding of a lyrical moment. Wagner and his adherents look upon such as unauthorised and offensive in style, while another strong party looks upon the A. as the finest flower of dramatic music. These are questions of great importance concerning which it is impossible to come to an understanding, but only to take a side. The bravura aria written solely for the virtuoso is æsthetically a reprehensible thing, but between that and the great A. in *Fidelio* there is a difference great enough for the despisers of the former to be admirers of the latter.

Aribo, Scholasticus, about 1078; he was the author of an extremely valuable treatise on the theory of music, giving a commentary on the writings of Guido d'Arezzo. It is printed in Gerbert's "Script," II.

Arienzo, Nicola d', b. Dec. 24, 1842, Naples, pupil of V. Fioravanti, G. Moretti, and Sav. Mercadante; produced, at the age of nineteen, his first opera, *La Fidanzata del Perucchiere*, at Naples, which up to 1880 was followed by seven others, among which, *La Figlia del Diavolo* (1879), attacked by the critics as too realistic and of forced originality. He also wrote several overtures. In 1879 appeared his theoretical work, "Introduction of the Tetrachordal System into Modern Music," in which he advocated pure intonation (in place of equal temperament), and together with the two ruling modes, major and minor, asserts the existence of a third, that of the minor second. (*Cf.* MINOR SCALE.)

Arietta (Ital.; Fr. *Ariette*), same as a small aria (q.v.).

Arion, the fable-encircled singer of Grecian antiquity, who lived about 600 B.C.

Arioso (Ital.) is the term used for a short melodious movement in the middle, or at the conclusion of a recitative. The A. differs from the Aria in that it has no thematic articulation; it is only a start towards an A., a lyrical movement of short duration.

Ariosti, A t t i l i o, b. 1660, Bologna, a once celebrated opera composer; he made his *début* in 1686 at Venice, and died *circa* 1740. At first he closely followed the manner of Lully, but later on imitated that of Alessandro Scarlatti. In 1698 we find A. at Berlin as "Hofkapellmeister." In 1716 he went to London, where, together with Buononcini, he won triumphs until the shining star of Handel threw them both into the shade. In 1728 he published a volume of cantatas by subscription in order to improve his circumstances; in this he succeeded, and thereupon returned to Bologna.

Aristides, Q u i n t i l i a n u s, Greek writer on music of the 1st-2nd century A.D.; his work, "περὶ μουσικῆς" was published in Meibom's "Antiquae Musicae Auctores Septem" (1652).

Aristotle, (1) The Greek philosopher, pupil of Plato, lived from 384 to 322 B.C. His writings contain little about music, but that little is of the highest importance for the investigation of the nature of Greek music, especially the 19th section of his "Problemata," drawn up in the form of question and answer, which treats exclusively of music; besides some chapters of his "Politica," and some passages of his "Poetica."—(2) Pseudonym of a writer on measured music, who flourished between the 12th and 13th centuries; from various indications he is considered identical with the author of the musical treatise erroneously ascribed to the Venerable Bede (7th century), and published in the collection of his works.

Aristoxenus, a pupil of Aristotle, the oldest and most important of the Greek writers on music (apart from single treatises of Plato and Aristotle), born about 354 B.C. Of his numerous writings the "Harmonic Elements" alone have been preserved complete. Only fragments remain of the "Rhythmical Elements." Both works appeared in Greek and German, with critical comments by P. Marquard, in 1868. (*Cf.* WESTPHAL.)

Armbrust, K a r l F., excellent performer on the organ, b. Mar. 20, 1849, Hamburg; pupil of the Stuttgart Conservatorium, especially of Faisst, whose son-in-law he became in 1874. He succeeded his father already in 1869 as organist of St. Peter's Church at Hamburg, and he was also active as pianoforte and organ teacher at the Hamburg Conservatorinm, and as a musical critic. Died July 12, 1896, Hanover.

Armer la clef (Fr.), to indicate the key by means of the signature. *Armure* same as signature.

Armgeige. (*See* VIOLA.)

Armingaud, J u l e s, celebrated violinist, b. May 3, 1820, Bayonne; trained in his native town. In 1839 he wished to perfect himself at the Paris Conservatoire, but was refused on the ground that he was too far advanced. From that time he was active in the orchestra of the Grand Opéra, and he formed a stringed quartet society with Léon Jacquard, E. Lalo, and Mas, which won for itself great fame; later, increased by some wind players, it took the name of *Société classique.* A. also published some compositions for the violin. Died Feb., 1900.

Armonie (*Harmonie*) is said to have been an instrument of the *Ménestriers* from the 12th to the 13th century; probably the same as the *chifonie* (*symphonie*), a name given to the *Vielle* (Organistrum, Hurdy-Gurdy).

Arnaud, (1) Abbé F r a n ç o i s, b. July 27, 1721, Aubignan, near Carpentras, d. Dec. 2, 1784; went to Paris 1752, became (1765) Abbot of Grandchamps, afterwards reader and librarian to the Count of Provence, and member of the Académie. A. wrote a series of musical essays which are mostly to be found in larger works: his collected writings appeared in three vols. at Paris, 1808. He was a zealous partisan of Gluck's: his letters in relation to this matter are to be found in the "Mémoires pour servir à l'histoire de la révolution opérée dans la musique par M. le Chevalier Gluck."—(2) J e a n E t i e n n e Guillaume, b. March 16, 1807, Marseilles, d. there Jan. 1863, favourite composer of romances, known also in Germany (*Zwei Aeuglein so blau*).

Arne, (1) T h o m a s A u g u s t i n e, b. March 12, 1710, London, d. there, March 5, 1778; one of the most eminent English musicians, composer of the melody "Rule Britannia." His wife, Cecilia A., daughter of Young the organist, was a famous opera singer, pupil of Geminiani. A. wrote about thirty operas, and music to Shakesperian and other dramas, two oratorios (*Abel, Judith*), songs, glees, catches, pianoforte sonatas, organ concertos, etc. The University of Oxford conferred on him the degree of Doctor. A set of eight sonatas by Arne have been republished in Pauer's "Old English Composers."—(2) M i c h a e l, son of the former, b. 1741, London, d. about 1806; composed likewise some operas, which he produced with success. In 1770 he attempted the discovery of the philosopher's stone, and built a laboratory at Chelsea. Ruined by the expense, he returned to music, and wrote (1778-83) a number of small pieces for the London theatres.

Arneiro, J o s é A u g u s t o Ferreira V e i g a, Vicomte d', Portuguese composer, b. Nov. 22, 1838, Macao (China); he sprang from a noble Portuguese family (his mother was of Swedish descent); studied law at Coimbra, and from 1859 harmony under Manvel Joaquim Botelho, counterpoint and fugue under Vicente Schira, and pianoforte under Antonio José Soares, and commenced to compose with assiduity. A ballet was produced by him, 1866, at the theatre San Carlos, Lisbon, entitled *Ginn.* His principal work is a Te Deum, which was produced first at St. Paul's Church, Lisbon, in 1871, and afterwards in Paris under the title Symphonie-Cantate (a name of late much in vogue in France). An opera was produced at the Carlos Theatre, Lisbon, *L'Elisire di Giovinezza*, and another, *La Derelitta* (1885). A. ranked among the most eminent modern Portuguese composers. Died July, 1903.

Arnold, (1) G e o r g, church composer of the 17th century, b. Weldsberg (Tyrol); at first organist at Innsbruck, afterwards to the Bishop of Bamberg; he published, 1652–76, motets, psalms, and two books of masses in nine parts.—(2) S a m u e l, b. Aug. 10, 1740, London, d. Oct. 22, 1802; trained as chorister of the Chapel Royal under Gates and Nares. Already, at the age of twenty-three, he received a commission to write an opera for Covent Garden, which was brought out with success—*The Maid of the Mill* (1765). Up to 1802 he wrote no less than 45 works for the stage, and five oratorios. In 1783 he became organist and composer to the Chapel Royal; 1789, conductor of the Academy of Ancient Music; 1793, organist of Westminster Abbey; in 1773 he obtained the degree of Doctor of Music at Oxford. His most memorable work is perhaps the "Cathedral Music," a collection of the best services by English masters (1790, 4 vols.), a continuation of a work of the same name by Boyce, republished in 1847, by E. F. Rimbault. His edition of Handel's works (1786, etc., 36 vols.) is, unfortunately, not free from faults.—(3) J o h a n n G o t t f r i e d, b. Feb. 15, 1773, Niedernhall near Oehringen (Hohenlohe); excellent 'cellist and composer. After prolonged study under the best masters (M. Willmann, B. Romberg), and many concert tours in Switzerland and Germany, he became first 'cellist at the theatre at Frankfort, where he died already, July 26, 1806. His principal works are: five 'cello concertos, six sets of variations for 'cello, a *Symphonie concertante* for two flutes with orchestra, etc.—(4) I g n a z E r n s t F e r d i n a n d, b. April 4, 1774, Erfurt, a lawyer there, d. Oct. 13, 1812. He published (1803, etc.) short biographies of Mozart, Haydn, Cherubini, Cimarosa, Paesiello, Dittersdorf, Zumsteeg, Winter, and Himmel, which were reprinted in 1816 in 2 vols. as "Galerie der berühmtesten Tonkünstler des 18 u. 19 Jahrhunderts." He wrote besides: "Der angehende Musikdirektor oder die Kunst ein Orchester zu bilden, etc." (1806). —(5) K a r l, b. March 6, 1794, Neukirchen near Mergentheim, d. Nov. 11, 1873, Christiania; son of Johann Gottfried A., after whose death he was brought up in Offenbach, where Alois Schmitt, Vollweiler, and Joh. Ant. André were his instructors in music. After an exciting life as pianist, he first settled in Petersburg (1819), where he married the singer, Henriette Kisting; from thence he went (1824) to Berlin, 1835 to Münster, and 1849 to Christiania as conductor of the Philharmonic Society and organist of

the principal church. Of his compositions may be mentioned a series of excellent chamber-music works (pf. sextet, sonatas, fantasias, variations, an opera, *Irene*, produced at Berlin 1832, etc.). His son, Karl, b. 1820, Petersburg, pupil of M. Bohrer, was 'cellist in the royal band at Stockholm.—(6) F r i e d r i c h W i l h e l m, b. March 10, 1810, Sontheim, near Heilbronn, d. Feb. 13, 1864, as music-seller at Elberfeld; he published ten series of "Volkslieder," besides the "Locheimer Liederbuch," Konrad Paumann's "Ars organisandi" (both in Chrysander's "Jahrbücher"), pf. pieces, arrangements of the symphonies of Beethoven for pf. and violin, etc.—(7) Y o u r i j v o n, b. Nov. 13, 1811, Petersburg, where his father was councillor of state, studied political economy at Dorpat, entered the Russian army in 1831, and went through the Polish campaign; but left the military service in 1838 in order to devote himself entirely to music; he composed the Russian operas, *The Gipsy* (1853) and *Swätlana* (1854, gained a prize); and further, overtures, songs, choral songs, etc. He gave lectures on the history of music and acoustics, and became a serious critic. From 1863 to 1868 he lived in Leipzig, showed himself a zealous supporter of new German tendencies, and edited a paper of his own. He was in Moscow from 1870 to 1894, and then at St. Petersburg. He died at Sinferopol July 20, 1898.

Arnulf von St. Gillen (15th century), author of a treatise printed in Gerbert ("Script" iii.), "De Differentiis et Generibus Cantorum."

Arpa (Ital.), Harp; *Arpanetta,* small or "pointed" harp.

Arpeggiando (Ital.), playing the notes of a chord in succession.

Arpeggio (Ital.), or *arpeggiato,* really "after the manner of a harp." This is a term which indicates that the notes of a chord are not to be struck together, but one after the other, as on the harp. The A. is marked by the written word (or in abbreviated form as *arp.*), or by the following signs:

Only the first sign is now in common use, but the fourth is to be found in Mozart's pianoforte sonatas in the Peters edition (but *see* ACCIACA-TURA); the last two signify a breaking up of the minim into quavers. Formerly there were special signs for the A. from below (Ex. I.), and for the one from above (II.); the A. from above has now to be indicated by small notes (III.).

I below.   II above.   III above.

If a long appogiatura stands before a note of an arpeggio chord, that appogiatura note belongs to the A., and the other notes follow as at *a*; short appogiaturas are played as at *b*.

The usual way of playing the A. is to give one quick succession of notes of the series commencing on the beat. Formerly, however, it was usual for the A. sign to serve as an abbreviation for all kinds of chord passages, which naturally had first to be written out once. (*Cf.* ABBREVIATIONS.) In old compositions for the violin (Bach), one often meets with a series of chords, in notes of long value, with the arpeggio sign, and it is usual to play them in the following, or some similar, manner.

Arpeggione (*Guitar Violoncello*), a stringed instrument similar to the Gamba, constructed in 1823 by G. Staufer, of Vienna. Franz Schubert wrote a sonata for it, and Vinc. Schuster published a Method. The six strings were tuned as follows: E, A, *d, g, b, e'*.

Arpichord, same as HARPSICHORD.

Arquier, Joseph, French opera composer, b. 1763, Toulon, d. Oct. 1816, Bordeaux; wrote more than fifteen operas, six of which were produced at Paris, and nine in the provinces. In 1798 A. became conductor at the Paris theatre, "des jeunes élèves," and some years later he went with an opera troupe to New Orleans, but failed, and returned in 1804.

Arrangement, adaptation of pieces for other instruments than those for which they were written by the composer. For example, the pianoforte score of an orchestral work is an A.; in the same way pianoforte duets are "arranged" as solos; also pianoforte works scored for orchestra are called arrangements. The opposite of A. is an "original composition."

Arriaga y Balzola, Juan Crisostomo Jacobo Antonio, Spanish composer, b. Jan. 27, 1806, Bilbao, d. end of February, 1825. He studied at the Paris Conservatoire under Fétis in 1821, and three years later was undermaster there for harmony and counterpoint. A. also was full of promise as a violinist, but the expectations justified by his youthful genius were frustrated by his early death. Of his compositions only three stringed quartets were printed (1824).

Arrieta, Don Juan Emilio, Spanish composer, director of the Madrid Conservatorio, b. Oct. 21, 1823, Puente la Reina (Navarre); he was a pupil at the Milan Conservatorio from 1842 to 1845, in which city he soon afterwards produced his first opera, *Ildegonde*. He returned to Spain in 1848, and produced a number (up to 1883 already 39) of operas and operettas. He was appointed teacher of composition at the Madrid Conservatorio in 1857, and in 1875 successor of Eslavas as councillor in the ministry of public instruction. Died Feb. 12, 1894, Madrid.

Arrigoni, Carlo, b. Florence at the beginning of the 18th century, an excellent lutenist, maestro to Prince de Carignan. In 1732 he was called to London by Handel's enemies, in order, with Porpora's help, to oust him from popular favour, but he soon had to lower his sails before the great genius.

Arrigo Tedesco (Heinrich der Deutsche), the name given to Heinrich Isaac (q.v.) in Italy.

Arsis (Gr.), heaving, the contrary of *Thesis* (sinking); by these terms the Greeks distinguished between the heavy (accented) and light (unaccented) parts of a bar, so that the heavy one was marked as Thesis, and the light as A. (Raising and lowering of the foot in dancing.) The Latin grammarians of the middle ages inverted the meaning, took A. in the sense of raising of the voice (with emphasis), and thesis as lowering (without emphasis); and with these meanings the terms are still used in the art of metre, whereas in that of music the old meaning has again come into vogue: lowering (Thesis) and raising (A.) of the stick or hand. Thus:—

Ancient metre. . . .	Th. *A.* Th. *A.*
Metre of the middle ages and of modern times	*A.* Th. *A.* Th.
Music of the present .	Th. A. Th. A.

Artaria, the well-known house at Vienna for prints and music, established by Carlo A. in 1769 as a print shop, and in 1780 as a music publishing house. Three cousins of the same, Francesco, Ignazio, and Pasquale A. were partners from the beginning. A branch of the business at Mayence was closed already in 1793, and at Mannheim a business was established by two brothers of Pasquale, Domenico and Giovanni, on their own account, trading under the name "Domenico A.," and later on, with the bookseller, Fontaine, as partner, under that of " A. & Fontaine." The Vienna business received two new partners in 1793, Giovanni Cappi and Tranquillo Mollo. Cappi retired from the firm in 1796, and set up a publishing house under his own name (afterwards Tobias Haslinger) ; Mollo did likewise in 1801 (afterwards Diabelli). The inheritor of the business, Domenico A., son-in-law of Carlo, died in 1842; his son, August, d. Dec. 14, 1893, Graz.

Arteaga, Stefano, a Spanish Jesuit, b. Madrid, d. Oct. 30, 1799, Paris. After the order had been suppressed in Spain he went to Italy, and lived for several years in the house of Cardinal Albergati at Bologna, and in friendly intercourse with Padre Martini, who urged him to write the now celebrated history of opera in Italy. Later on A. went to Rome, where he became intimate with the Spanish ambassador, Azara ; he followed the latter to Paris, where he died. His work is entitled " Le Rivoluzioni del Teatro Musicale Italiano " (1783 ; thoroughly revised, 1785). A work on ancient rhythm, left in manuscript, has disappeared.

Articulation in speech refers to the clear utterance of each syllable ; in music to the art of producing and combining sounds, and therefore to the various forms of *legato* and *staccato*. (*Cf.* TOUCH.) The meanings of " Articulation " and " Phrasing " have been confused together, and likewise separated in an unsatisfactory manner ; and this has caused one of the principal hindrances to a proper understanding of the latter term. *Articulation* is in the first instance something purely technical, mechanical, whilst *Phrasing* in the first instance is something ideal, perceptionable. I articulate properly, if in

I connect the sounds under the same slur, and break off the last note within the slur. I phrase when I perceive that just the last note within the slur and the first within the next slur together form one motive.

(*Cf.* PHRASING.)

Artist (Fr. *Artiste*), a word specially used in France for actors and opera-singers.

Artôt, name or surname of a distinguished musical family, whose real name was Montagney. The ancestor of the musical branch was (1) Maurice Montagney, named A., b. Feb. 3, 1772, Gray (Haute Saône), d. Jan. 8, 1829. He was bandmaster of a French regi-

ment during the Revolution, went afterwards as first horn player to the Théâtre de la Monnaie, Brussels, where he was also appointed conductor at the Beguine Monastery. A. was at the same time an excellent performer on the guitar and violin, and a teacher of singing.— (2) Jean Désiré Montagney (A.), son of the former, b. Sept. 23, 1803, Paris, d. March 25, 1887, St. Josse ten Noode ; pupil of his father, and his successor at the Brussels theatre, first horn player in the regiment of the Guides, in 1843 professor of the horn at the Brussels Conservatoire, in 1849 first horn player in the private band of the King of the Belgians ; he received a pension in 1873. He published a number of compositions for horn (fantasias, études, quartets for four chromatic horns or *cornets à piston*). — (3) Alexandre Joseph Montagney (A.), brother of the former, b. Jan. 25, 1815, Brussels, d. July 20, 1845, Ville d'Avray, near Paris ; he studied with his father, then under Snel in Brussels, and from 1824–31 under Rudolf and August Kreutzer at the Paris Conservatoire. He became an excellent violinist, and, holding no appointment, made most extensive artistic tours through Europe and America (1843). He published various compositions for violin (A minor concerto, fantasias, sets of variations, etc.) ; quartets for strings, a pf. quintet, etc., remained in manuscript.—(4) Marguerite Josephine Désirée Montagney (A.), daughter of Désiré A., b. July 21, 1835, Paris, while her parents were on a journey. She studied under Mme. Viardot-Garcia, 1855–1857 ; first appeared at concerts in Brussels in 1857, and on the recommendation of Meyerbeer was engaged at the Paris Grand Opéra in 1858. She met with extraordinary success. After a short time, however, she gave up her engagement, appeared as a " star " at a great number of French, Belgian, and Dutch theatres, and then went to Italy in order to perfect herself in Italian singing. Her triumph reached its zenith when she appeared in Lorini's Italian company at Berlin ; for several years she sang, principally in Germany, especially Berlin. She went to Russia in 1866, paid also visits to London, Copenhagen, etc. In 1869 she married the Spanish baritone, Padilla y Ramos (b. 1842, Murcia, pupil of Mabellini at Florence), who from that time shared her success. Artôt's voice was originally a full mezzo-soprano of passionate expression ; but by steady practice she materially extended her compass upwards, so that she can sing the most important dramatic soprano parts. Even as late as 1886 she was a star of the first magnitude.

Artusi, Giovanni Maria, Canon in Ordinary at San Salvatore, Bologna, d. Aug. 18, 1613. He published " Arte del Contrapunto " (1586–89, 2 parts ; second ed. 1598) ; " L'Artusi, ovvero delle Imperfecioni della Moderna Musica " (1600–1603, 2 parts), as well as some essays

("Considerazione Musicali," 1607, etc.), and a volume of Canzonets à 4 (1598). A. was a thoroughly well trained contrapuntist, but could not enter into the spirit of the innovations of a Monteverde or Gesualdo di Venosa, or even of men like N. Vincentino, Cyprian de Rore, A. Gabrieli ; he was one of those apparitions which are always to be met with in art in times of fermentation and of development of new tendencies.

Asantschewski, Michael Pawlowitsch von, Russian composer, b. 1838, Moscow, d. there Jan. $\frac{12}{24}$, 1881; studied, 1861–62, composition at Leipzig under Hauptmann and Richter ; lived in Paris, 1866–70, where he acquired the valuable musical library of Anders, which, together with his own, of considerable value, he presented to the Petersburg Conservatoire, of which, in 1870, he became the director in place of Zaremba. In 1876, however, his withdrew from this post and devoted himself to composition, but up to now he has published little (pianoforte pieces, a stringed quartet, overtures).

Asas (Ger.), *A* double flat.

Aschenbrenner, Christian Heinrich, b. Dec. 29, 1654, Altstettin, d. Dec. 13, 1732, Jena. He studied first with his father, who had been ducal capellmeister at Wolfenbüttel, and who at the time of his birth was director of music at Altstettin. In 1668 he studied with Theile at Merseburg, and finally with Schmelzer at Vienna. A. was an excellent violinist, and, with interruptions which caused him anxiety with regard to means of living, occupied the post of first violin at Zeitz (1677–1681), Merseburg (1683–1690), musical director to the Duke of Sachsen-Zeitz (1695–1713), and capellmeister to the Duke of Sachsen-Merseburg (1713 to 1719). From that time he lived on a small pension, giving lessons at Jena even when advanced in years. The following is all that has been preserved of his compositions : " Gast- und Hochzeitsfreude, bestehend in Sonaten, Präludien, Allemanden, Couranten, Balletten, Arien, Sarabanden mit drei, vier und fünf Stimmen, nebst dem basso continuo " (1673).

Ascher, Joseph, b. 1831, London, of German parents, d. there June 20, 1869. He enjoyed the instruction of Moscheles, whom he followed to Leipzig in 1846 as pupil at the Conservatorium. In 1849 he went to Paris, where he was afterwards named court pianist to the Empress Eugénie. He was known as the composer of light, so-called *salon*-music.

A sharp (Ger. *Ais*), A. raised a semitone. *A sharp major* chord $=a$ *sharp, c double-sharp, e sharp; A sharp minor* chord $=a$ *sharp, c sharp, e sharp; A sharp minor* key, 7 sharps signature. (*See* KEY.)

Ashdown, Edwin, music publisher, London, succeeded in 1860, in company with Mr. Parry,

to the firm of Wessel and Co., the greater number of whose publications they bought. They have since added a variety of popular works to their catalogue. In the year 1884 Messrs. Ashdown and Parry separated, and the business is now carried on under the title Edwin Ashdown, limited.

Ashton, Algernon, b. Dec. 9, 1859, Durham. He was the son of a cathedral singer, and went, after his father's death, in 1863, to Leipzig, remained as pupil of the Conservatorium there from 1875 to 1879; studied after that with Raff from 1880 to 1881, and then settled down in London, where he was appointed teacher of the pianoforte at the Royal College of Music in 1885. A. is a gifted composer (choral and orchestral works, pf. concerto, chamber music, songs, and pf. pieces, English, Scotch, and Irish Dances, etc.).

Asioli, Bonifacio, b. August 30, 1769, Correggio, d. there May 18, 1832 ; became composer at an inconceivably early age (he is said to have already written, when eight years old, three masses, a series of other sacred works, a violin concerto, pianoforte pieces, etc., and indeed without any previous theoretical instruction). After he had taken regular lessons in composition for some years with Morigi at Parma, he was appointed maestro di capella at Correggio. In 1787 he went to Turin, where, diligently composing, he resided until 1796, and then accompanied the Marquise Gherardini to Venice, and in 1799 settled in Milan. In 1801 he was appointed maestro di capella to the Vice-King of Italy, and in 1808 became the first president of the new Conservatorio at Milan, which offices he held until 1813. He then returned to his native city, composing still up to 1820. A. wrote a great number of cantatas, masses, motets, songs, duets, etc., concertos for various instruments, nocturnes à 3—5, with and without accompaniment, seven operas, one oratorio (*Jacob*), etc., as well as a number of theoretical works, viz., "Principj Elementari di Musica " (a general instruction book, which appeared in 1809, and was frequently republished ; also in French, 1819) ; " L'Allievo al Cembalo " (Piano Method); "Primi Elementi per il Canto " (Vocal Method) ; " Elementi per il Contrabasso" (1823) ; " Trattato d'Armonia e d'Accompagnamento" (Method of Thorough Bass); " Dialoghi sul Trattato d'Armonia " (Question and Answer Book to the Treatise on Harmony, 1814) ; " Osservazioni sul Temperamento proprio degli Stromenti stabili, etc."; and " Disinganno sulle Asservazioni," etc. ; finally, " Il Maestro di Composizione" (a sequel to the Method of Thorough Bass, 1836).

Asola (*Asula*), Giovanni Matteo, prolific sacred composer, b. Verona, d. Oct. 1, 1609, Venice. He was one of the first to make use of *basso continuo* for the accompaniment of sacred vocal music with organ. Besides a number of masses, psalms, etc., two books of madrigals (1587, 1596) have been preserved.

Aspa, M a r i o, prolific Italian opera composer, b. 1806, Messina, d. 1861 (?). He wrote forty-two operas, of which especially *Il muratore di Napoli* won lasting popularity.

Aspiration (Lat.), a now antiquated ornament, answering to the still older *Plica* (q.v.); it indicated a light touching of the upper or under second at the end of the value of a note:

Played :

Rousseau gives this definition for Accent.

Assai (Ital. " enough," " fairly "), a tempo indication, or one of expression, adding intensity, *e.g. Allegro A.*, at a good rapid pace.

Assez (Fr.), enough, rather. *Assez lent*, rather slow.

Assmayer, Ignaz, b. Feb. 11, 1790, Salzburg, d. Aug. 31, 1862, Vienna. He studied under Brunmayr and M. Haydn ; in 1808 was organist of St. Peter's, Salzburg, went to Vienna in 1815, where he received further training from Eybler. In 1824 he became capellmeister at the Scotch church ; was named Imperial organist in 1825 ; in 1838 supernumary vice-, and in 1846 second capellmeister to the Court, as successor to Weigl. Of his fifteen meritorious masses he only published one ; also only a small portion of his Graduals, Offertories, appeared in print. Haslinger published the oratorios *Sauls Tod* and *David und Saul* (Vienna).

Assoluto (Ital.), absolute ; *primo uomo a*, a singer for principal *rôles*.

Assonance (Fr. ; Ger. *Assonanz*), vowel-rhyme, *e.g.* " man " and " sang." (*See* ALLITERATION.)

Astaritta, G e n n a r o, Italian composer of operas, b. about 1750, Naples ; wrote from 1772 to 1793, over twenty operas, mostly for Naples, of which *Circe ed Ulisse* (1777) became universally popular, and was also produced in Germany.

Astorga, E m a n u e l e d', b. Dec. 11, 1681, Palermo, d. Aug. 21, 1736, Prague. He was the son of an insurgent Sicilian nobleman, who was beheaded in 1701. A lady in high position took charge of the boy, and placed him in the Spanish monastery of Astorga, where he had an opportunity of developing his musical talent. Three years later she procured for him the title of Baron d'Astorga, under which name he entered into society, and received from the Spanish Court a diplomatic mission to the Court of Parma. By his songs and his singing he soon became a general favourite, so that for the sake of his daughter, Elizabeth Farnese, the duke held it advisable to send away the dangerous singer on a diplomatic mission to Vienna. A. also, after that, led a life of

adventure ; appeared again in Spain in order to seek out his benefactress, visited Portugal, Italy (with exception of his native place, to which he was forced to remain a stranger), England, then returned to Vienna, and spent his last years in a monastery at Prague. The compositions of A. are distinguished by their originality of invention : their principal traits are charm, simplicity, and warm feeling. Many of his works have been preserved, among which, cantatas (detached Arias with clavier), also duets, an opera, *Dafne*, and, best known of all, a Stabat Mater for four voices, with instrumental accompaniment.

A suo arbitrio (Ital.)   } At the will, at the pleasure, of the
A suo bene placito (Ital.)   } performer. The same as *ad libitum*.

A suo commodo (Ital.), according to the convenience of the performer.

A tre (Ital.), for three voices or instruments.

Attacca (Ital.) [*Attacca subito* (Ital.), attack immediately] is a term frequently used with a change of *tempo*, or at the end of a movement followed by another one, and it indicates that what follows should be suddenly introduced, so that the pause which is made be of only very brief duration.

Attacca-Ansatz (Ger., Attacca-touch) is, in pianoforte-playing, the sudden stiffening of the muscles of the arms and of the hands for specially strong accents, a quick development of power and pressure, close to the keyboard, by which the disagreeable effect of the slashing, banging touch from a distance is avoided.

Attacco (Ital.), a term applied to a short subject of a fugue which, apparently, only consists of a few notes ; in fact in such cases (as, for instance, in the c ♯ major fugue of the second part of the Wohl. Clavier) the *Dux* appears from the outset *in stretto* with the *Comes*. A. is also used as a term for a short motive taken from a theme, and developed in various ways in the middle section of a movement in sonata form.

Attaignant (*Attaingnant, Atteignant*, Latinised *Attingens*), P i e r r e, the oldest Parisian music-printer who adopted movable types. (*Cf.* PETRUCCI.) The types of A., elegant and clear, originated in the workshop of Pierre Hautin (q.v.), who prepared his first punches in 1525. He printed between 1526 and 1550, among other things, no less than 20 books of motets Attaignant's publications consist principally of works by French composers, and are on that account of special interest ; but they have become very rare.

Attenhofer, K a r l, b. May 5, 1837, Wettingen, near Baden, in Switzerland. He was son of an innkeeper, a pupil of Dan. Elster (teacher of music at the seminary at Wettingen), and of Kurz at Neuenburg. From 1857 to 1858 he studied at the Leipzig Conservatorium under Richter,

Papperitz (theory), Dreyschock and Röntgen (violin), and Schleinitz (singing), and in 1859 was appointed teacher of music at a school at Muri (Aargau). In 1863 he accepted the post of conductor of the male choral union at Rapperswyl, and so distinguished himself at the Confederate Musical Festival held there in 1866, that he was entrusted with the direction of three male choral unions in Zurich ("Zurich," "Studentengesangverein," and "Aussersihl"). In 1867 he settled down in Zurich, conducting a number of other societies in various directions (Winterthur, Neumünster, etc.). In 1879 he became organist and choirmaster at the Catholic Church, Zurich (this post he has lately resigned), and, before that, was teacher of music at the school for young ladies ; he has also been for some years teacher of singing at the Zurich School of Music. A. is one of the most famous of Swiss composers, especially in the department of songs for male voices, with and without accompaniment, but he has also written many part songs for female and for mixed voices ("Frühlingsfeier," Op. 51, for mixed chorus and orchestra), also children's songs, pf. Lieder, masses, pf. pieces, and light studies for the violin.

Attrup, Karl, Danish composer and organist, b. March 4, 1848, Copenhagen ; studied with Gade, and in 1869 became his successor as teacher of the organ at Copenhagen Conservatoire, and in 1871 organist of the Friedrichskirche, in 1874 organist of St. Saviour's, and teacher of the organ at the Institute for the Blind in that city. A. has published valuable educational pieces for the organ, also songs.

Attwood, Thomas, b. Nov. 23, 1765, London, d. March 24, 1838, at his residence, Cheyne Walk, Chelsea. At the age of nine he became a chorister in the Chapel Royal, where he had the advantage of studying under Nares and Ayrton ; he soon distinguished himself so much that the Prince of Wales sent him to Italy for further training. From 1783 to 1784 he was at Naples under Filippo Cinque and Gaetano Latilla, and afterwards at Vienna under Mozart, who entertained a favourable opinion of his talents. He returned to England in 1787, and at once received several appointments. In 1796 he became organist of St. Paul's Cathedral, and composer to the Chapel Royal. In 1821 he was nominated organist of George IV.'s private chapel at Brighton, and in 1836 organist of the Chapel Royal. A. was on friendly terms with both Mozart and Mendelssohn, and thus forms a rare link between these two musical natures. His activity as a composer may be divided into two periods ; in the first he devoted himself exclusively to opera, in the second to sacred music. He worked diligently in both branches, and obtained favourable results (19 operas, many anthems, services, and other vocal works,

also pf. sonatas, etc.). He ranks among England's most distinguished composers.

Aubade (from the Provençal, *alba ;* Fr., *aube,* "dawn"), a *morning song* of the Troubadour period, having as subject-matter the parting of lovers at dawn of day, and is thus opposed to the serenade. Like the latter term, so A. became associated with instrumental music, especially in the 17th and 18th centuries.

Auber, Daniel François Esprit, b. Jan. 29, 1782, Caen (Normandie), the home of his parents, who, however, settled in Paris ; d. May 12/13, 1871, during the Commune. (*Cf.* DANIEL.) The father of Auber was *Officier des chasses* of the king, painted, sang, and played the violin ; only after the Revolution does he appear to have started a business in objects of art (prints) ; the grandfather was, indeed, *Peintre du roi.* A. sprang, therefore, from a family connected, not with trade, but with art. Already, at the age of eleven, the boy wrote romances, which became favourites in the *salons* of the Directory. The father determined that he should be a merchant, and sent him to England, but A. returned (1804) more musician than ever. In 1806 he was received as member of the society of the "Enfants d'Apollon," to which his father also belonged, for the former was already at that time distinguished as a composer. A. first entered on the career in which he spent the greater part of an active life—viz. that of dramatic composition—by setting music to an old libretto, *Julie,* for an amateur theatre (1812) which only had an orchestra composed of a few stringed instruments. Cherubini, who attended the performance, in spite of the inadequate representation and the poorness of the means, recognised his important gifts, and induced him to the serious study of composition under his direction. The amiable talent of A. quickly developed, and soon bore the finest fruits. A mass (of which a fragment as prayer has been preserved in the *Muette di Portici*) was followed by his first publicly performed opera, *Le Séjour Militaire* (Théâtre Feydeau, 1813), which, however, like the succeeding one—*Le Testament (Le Billet Doux,* 1819)—met with only a very moderate success. He was first recognised by the critics in 1820 with *La Bergère Châtelaine,* and his fame increased more and more, first with *Emma (La Promesse Imprudente),* and then with a series of operas, for the greater part of which Scribe, with whom he had made friends, wrote the libretti : *Leicester* (1822), *La Neige (Le Nouvel Eginhard,* 1823), *Vendôme en Espagne* (together with Hérold, 1823), *Les Trois Genres* (with Boieldieu, 1824), *Le Concert à la Cour* (1824), *Léocadie* (1824), *Le Maçon* (1825). With the last opera A. made the first impression of lasting importance ; it shows him as the chief representative of comic opera. More than anyone else, Boieldieu excepted, A. combined in himself true French style, grace, amiability, and ease. Once (in *La Neige*) had

A.—thinking probably that only thus he could attain success—imitated Rossini and cultivated *coloratura;* in *Le Maçon* there is no further trace of it, but the melodies flow on in free and happy manner, without any unnecessary, unnational ballast. Two small works—*Le Timide* and *Fiorella* (both 1826) followed, and then, after a year's pause, came A.'s first grand opera, which brought him to the summit of fame, *La Muette di Portici* (1828), the first of those three works which, in quick succession, completely revolutionised the *répertoire* of the Grand Opéra (the two others were, Rossini's *Tell*, 1829, and Meyerbeer's *Roberto*, 1831). The master of comic opera unfolded in this work a grandeur of plot, dramatic impulse, fire and passion, which one had not expected of him, and which, in fact, were the weak points of his talent. The subject of the opera stands in intimate relation to the agitated times in which it appeared; it won historical importance from the fact that its production in 1830 was the signal for the revolution which ended with the separation of Belgium and Holland. After the *Muette* came *La Fiancée* (1829), a homely *genre* piece like *Le Maçon*, and (1830) the more elegant *Fra Diavolo*, A.'s most popular opera at home and abroad. For a stately series of years A.'s fame remained at its full height. There followed: *Le Dieu et la Bayadère* (1830, containing, like the *Muette*, a dumb, but dancing principal character), *La Marquise de Brinvilliers* (1831, together with eight other composers), *Le Philtre* (1831), *Le Serment, ou Les Faux Monnayeurs* (1832), *Gustave III. (Le Bal Masqué*, 1833), *Lestocq* (1834), *Le Cheval de Bronze* (1835; extended into a grand ballet, 1857), *Actéon, Les Chaperons Blancs, L'Ambassadrice* (1836), *Le Domino Noir* (1837), *Le Lac des Fées* (1839), *Les Diamans de la Couronne* (1841), *Le Duc d'Olonne* (1842), *La Part du Diable* (1843), *La Sirène* (1844), *La Barcarolle* (1845), *Haydée* (1847). The last works of A. show a gradual falling off, and traces of the increasing age of their composer. He wrote besides: *L'Enfant Prodigue* (1850), *Zerline, ou ia Corbeille d'Oranges* (1851), *Marco Spada* (1852, extended to a grand ballet, 1857), *Jenny Bell* (1856), *Manon Lescaut* (1855), *La Fiancée* (1859), *La Circassienne* (1861), *La Fiancée du Roi de Garbe* (1864), *Le Premier Jour de Bonheur* (1868), *Rêves d'Amour* (1869), and some cantatas *d'occasion*. In the last days of his life he wrote several quartets for strings, not hitherto published. A. succeeded Gossec as member of the Académie in 1829, and Cherubini as director of the Conservatoire in 1842; further, in 1857 Napoleon named him imperial maître-de-chapelle.

Aubert, Jacques, eminent violinist, b. 1678, d. Belleville, near Paris, May, 1753; member of the orchestra of the Grand Opéra and of the *Concerts spirituels,* 1748 leader of the band there. He published a good number of stylish compositions for the violin, and other chambermusic works.

Aubéry du Boulley, Prudent Louis, French composer, b. Dec. 9, 1796, Verneuil (Eure), d. there, Feb., 1870; pupil of Momigny, Méhul, and Cherubini, at the Paris Conservatoire (until 1815). The number of his compositions is indeed very great (156), among which a whole series of chamber-music works, in which the guitar (for which he seems to have had a special fancy) is combined with pianoforte, violin, flute, viola, etc.). He wrote "Grammaire Musicale" (1830), a method of instruction in musical composition.

Audiphone is the name of an apparatus lately invented in America (by Greydon and Rhodes) which, by conveying molecular vibration to the teeth, allows the teeth nerves to take the place of those of hearing, and hence enables persons completely deaf to hear to a certain extent.

Audran, (1) Marius Pierre, singer, b. Sept. 26, 1816, Aix (Provence), d. Jan. 9, 1887, Marseilles, pupil of E. Arnaud, afterwards at the Paris Conservatoire, where, however, he obtained no scholarship. His parents, unfortunately, had not sufficient means to educate him (Cherubini and Leborne were of opinion that he had no talent); he received, therefore, training to the end from his old teacher, Arnaud. Seven years later A.—who meanwhile had appeared with success at Marseilles, Brussels, Bordeaux, and Lyons —became first tenor at the Opéra Comique, Paris, solo singer at the Conservatoire concerts, and member of the Conservatoire jury. From 1852 he led a restless life, appearing on various stages and making concert tours, until in 1861 he settled in Marseilles, where, in 1863, he became director of the Conservatoire, and likewise professor of singing. He also wrote a number of pleasing songs. His son (2) Edmond, b. April 11, 1842, Lyons, went with his father in 1861 to Marseilles, where he is musical director at St. Joseph's Church. He produced 23 operas and operettas with success at Marseilles and Paris, also a mass, a funeral march for Meyerbeer's death, etc. Of his operettas, the two most in vogue are *Les Noces d'Olivette* (1879) and *La Mascotte* (1880).

Auer, Leopold, b. June 7, 1845, Veszprim, Hungary, was trained by Ridley Kohne at the Prague Conservatorium, and then at the Vienna Conservatorium from 1857 to 1858 by Dont, and lastly by Joachim at Berlin. He ranks among the most distinguished living performers; in 1863 he received his first appointment as leader at Düsseldorf, in 1866 he went in a similar capacity to Hamburg, and since 1868 he has been solo violinist to the Emperor at Petersburg, and professor of the violin at the Conservatoire in that city.

Aufsätze, name given in Germany to the tubes of reed pipes, which are either inverted wood pyramids, or of metal (organ-metal, also zinc), and are then funnel-shaped or cylindrical. A. are not essential to the production of tone in reed pipes, as can be seen from the harmonium, but they give to them a strength and fulness which otherwise they would not possess. The more they widen out at the top the more brilliant and penetrating the tone, and, on the other hand, the latter is more sombre and quieter in proportion as they become narrower. The height of the tube has some influence on the pitch : a cylindrical tube of more than half the height of an open lip-pipe giving the reed note lowers the latter considerably, and one of the whole height lowers it by about an octave, etc. It would be an interesting task for those learned in the science of acoustics to try to find out how far the mysterious phenomenon of undertones (q.v.) is concerned with this matter. An investigation of this kind would naturally include instruments with reed tongues (oboe, clarinet) and membranous tongues (horns, trumpets, etc.).

Augener, George, founder of the music-publishing firm (A. & Co.) which started with the importation of foreign music in the year 1853, at 86, Newgate Street, London. So far back as the year 1855 they introduced the first cheap type edition of the classics, published by L. Holle, of Wolfenbüttel ; later, when Holle's edition was superseded by the superior one of Peters, of Leipzig, they obtained the sole agency for England of the latter. In 1867 Augener's Edition of Classical and Modern Music was commenced, which, while supplementing the foreign Peters Edition with works that have special interest for England, embraces also a large number of volumes of great educational value. This collection now (1907) amounts to over 5,000 volumes, revised by first-rate musicians ; it is well engraved and printed in England on superior English paper. Besides cheap editions, Augener's publish some 10,000 or more works in sheet music form, representing every class of music and including many of the best names of the present day. Important theoretical works by E. Prout, Dr. Riemann, etc., must also be mentioned. In 1871 was started the *Monthly Musical Record* (circulation 6,000). Among its contributors are many writers of note—Ebenezer Prout (B.A.London), Professor F. Niecks, Professor E. Pauer, J. S. Shedlock (B.A.London), etc. In 1896 the firm acquired the business of Robert Cocks & Co., at 6, New Burlington Street, W., with premises at 199, Regent Street, became the principal West End branches, the reserve stock, amounting to over 31,000 feet, being carried at extensive warehouses in Beak Street and Great Pulteney Street. The City branch is now 22, Newgate Street. Nineteen gold medals and diplomas have been awarded to the publications of the firm, including the only gold medal for music printing at the Inventions Exhibition, London, 1885. The printing of the firm, which is of the highest class, is carried on at 6 to 10, Lexington Street, W. In 1904 the combined businesses of Augener & Co. and Robert Cocks & Co. were converted into a company under the style of Augener Ltd., the founder of the firm of A. & Co. being chairman of the company.

Augmentation, (1) The prolongation of the theme in fugue and in other contrapuntal formations. (*See* DIMINUTION.) (2) In measured music the opposite of diminution, *i.e.* as a rule, merely the restoration of the usual note-value. (*Cf.* PROPORTION.)

Augmented intervals, intervals one semitone greater than major or perfect intervals.

Augustinus, Aurelius (St. A.), Father of the Church, b. Nov. 13, 354, Tagaste (Numidia), d. Aug. 28, 430, as Bishop of Hippo (now Bona, in Algeria). The works of St. A. contain important testimony with regard to the state of music in the ancient Christian Church, especially with regard to the so-called Ambrosian Song. A. was baptised by Ambrosia himself, and became one of his most intimate friends. He wrote a work, " De Musica," which, however, only treats of metre.

Auletta, Pietro, maestro to the Prince of Belvedere ; he wrote, between the years 1728 and 1752, eleven Italian operas for Rome, Naples, Venice, Munich, Turin, Bologna, and Paris. A composer named Domenico A. produced an opera at Naples about 1760, entitled *La locandiera di Spirito*.

Aulos, an ancient Greek wind instrument, most probably similar to the now forgotten beak-flute (*see* FLUTE), which was in great vogue up to the middle of last century. The player of the instrument was named *Aulētes*, or the *Aulētik*, *i.e.* the art of flute-playing ; on the other hand, *Aulody* indicates singing with flute accompaniment. The A. was constructed in various sizes, answering to the various kinds of human voice, and in different keys. (*Cf.* FISTULA, CAPISTRUM, and WIND INSTRUMENTS.)

Aurelianus Reomensis, a monk of Réomo (Moutier St. Jean, near Langres) in the 9th century. He wrote a treatise on the theory of music, printed in Gerbert (" Script," I.).

Auspitz-Kolar, Augusta, b. 1843, Prague, daughter of the player and dramatic poet, J. G. Kolar. In 1865 she married H. Auspitz at Prague, and died Aug. 23, 1878. She was an excellent pianist, a pupil of Smetana, afterwards of J. Proksch, and lastly of Madame Clauss-Szarvady at Paris. She also published some pianoforte pieces.

Auteri-Manzocchi, Salvatore, Italian composer, b. Dec. 25, 1845, Palermo ; he wrote the opera *Dolores* (first produced in 1875 at the Pergola, Florence ; this was followed by two more, *Il Negriero* (1878), and *Stella* (1880).

Authentic Mode. (*See* ECCLESIASTICAL MODES.)

Auto (Spanish " Act ") is the name given in

Spain to any public or judicial action (*e.g. A. da Fé, actus fidei,* "religious tribunal"), but especially to dramatic representations of stories from the Bible, Mysteries (*autos sacramentales*) in association with music. The most distinguished Spanish poets (Lope de Vega, Calderon) have written Autos. In 1765 they were forbidden by royal command.

Automatic Musical Machines (mechanical musical instruments) are apparatus which simply by the employment of mechanical means (turning of a handle, or winding up of a spring), and thus without any musical effort on the part of the performer, can be made to play tunes. According to the manner in which they are set in motion, they are classed as—

(*a*) Machines with springs or weights (musical clocks).

(*b*) Machines with a handle to be turned (hurdy-gurdy).

And according to the means for producing sound, as—

(*c*) Machines with bells, small bells, steel rods, or strings.

(*d*) Machines with flute- or reed-work.

All old mechanical musical machines have in common—

(*e*) A barrel pointed with pins, whether set in motion by clock-work (*a*), or by a handle (*b*), and whether the sounds are produced by bells, steel rods, or strings (*c*), or pipes (*d*).

Quite recently, barrels have been replaced by—

(*f*) Plates with perforated holes (the so-called sheets of music ["NOTENBLÄTTER"]).

In the Glockenspiel (Carillon), which is, perhaps, the oldest mechanical instrument, the pins of the barrel produce sounds by the lifting of hammers which strike the bells; but lately the English firm, Gillet & Bland, at Croydon, has so changed the mechanism that the pins only release the hammers which are lifted by separate cam-wheels. In small musical snuff-boxes and musical clocks, the pins rub against teeth, variously tuned, of a metal comb (*i.e.* steel rods). In barrel-organs the pins open the valves of the several pipes. But as after the passing of the pin the valve would at once close, in barrel-organs, instead of pins, there are doubly-bent wires (⌐——⌐), which keep the valves open for the time required. The perforated plates, like the new mechanism of the Carillon, do not lift, but loosen a spring. In the barrel-organ the barrel turns much slower than the handle, which is concerned with the mechanism of both bellows.

The Orchestrion, a fairly large-sized organ, with flute and reed stops, with clock-work and weights (up to now only with pin-barrels), is the largest automatic musical machine. On the other hand, the Ariston, Herophon, and Manopan, have turning-handles and perforated plates (NOTENBLÄTTER). In the Manopan, the latter are fasciated; all three, like the Harmonium, have reed-stops. The Swiss musical snuff-boxes (with handle), and the Swiss musical clocks (with clock-work) have pin-barrels and metal combs. The new German musical snuff-boxes (SYMPHONION) have perforated circular steel-plates (Lochmann's patent).

In the *Dreh-Piano* (organ-clavier) *Orpheus* of Paul Ehrlig, a mechanical keyboard is played in the same manner.

Auxiliary Notes (Ger. *Nebennoten*) are, in the shake, mordent, turn, battement, etc. (*see* ORNAMENTS), the upper and under second of the note to be ornamented, and which is properly called the principal tone. Also in the case of a suspension (q.v.), the note held on before the note of the chord is called an auxiliary note. Passing notes and changing notes can also be classed as A. N. (melodic A. N.), while every note belonging to the chord is a principal note.

Ave (*Ave Maria*), the salutation of the angel Gabriel at the Annunciation, a favourite subject for sacred composition. The salutation of the angel is followed by that of St. Elizabeth, closing with a prayer to the Virgin.

Aventinus, J o h a n n e s, really *Turmair*, but took the name of A. after his native town Abensberg (Bavaria), a Bavarian historiographer, b. July 4, 1477, d. Jan. 9, 1534. He drew up the "Annales Bojorum," which, so far as music is concerned, must be used with caution and compared with more ancient annals. He did not write, but only edited, the "Musicæ rudimenta admodum brevia, etc." (by Nikolaus Faber).

Avison, C h a r l e s, b. 1710, Newcastle-on-Tyne, d. 1770. He studied in Italy and in London under Geminiani, became organist in 1736 in his native town, published a pamphlet of no great value on musical expression, " An Essay on Musical Expression " (1752), which was sharply attacked by W. Hayes. He also wrote works for orchestra and chamber music. In 1757, A., jointly with J. Garth, published Marcello's Psalm-paraphrases, with English words.

A vista (Ital.), at sight. (*v.* À première vue.)

A voce sola (Ital.), for one voice alone.

Ayrton, (1) E d m u n d, b. 1734, Ripon, **d.** 1808; for many years master of the boys at the Chapel Royal, London. He wrote some sacred music (two complete morning and evening services, and various anthems).—(2) W i l l i a m, son of the former, b. 1777, London, d. 1858. He was a musical critic of note to various papers, member of musical societies in London, promoter and member of the Philharmonic Society, more than once musical director at the King's Theatre, and distinguished himself by producing Mozart's operas. From 1823 to 1834, jointly with Clowes, he published the monthly musical periodical, *Harmonicon*, and also two collections of practical music — "Musical Library" (1834, 8 vols.), and "Sacred Minstrelsy" (2 vols.).

Azevedo, Alexis Jacob, French writer on music, b. March 18, 1813, Bordeaux, d. Dec. 21, 1875, Paris. He was at first a contributor to the *France Musicale*, and to the *Siècle*; afterwards editor of a paper of his own, which, however, soon failed; then occasionally to the *Presse*, and finally from 1859 to 1870 *feuilletoniste* to the *Opinion Nationale*. A. was a passionate admirer of Rossini and of the Italian school, and by no means courteous in his criticisms of works of a different order. He also wrote several pamphlets attacking Chevé's endeavours to reform notation (system of figures).

Azione sacra, oratorio.

B.

B, really the second note of the musical alphabet, was, in Germany, through a misunderstanding, replaced by an H, and itself became a chromatic sign (♭). In England and Holland B still stands for the whole tone above A (and as in Germany this note is called H, B is there applied to that note lowered a semitone). (*See* CHROMATIC SIGNS.) In old, also German, theoretical works *B quadratum* (*quadrum, durum;* Fr. *bécarre*) indicates our B, and it is also the sign for a natural (♮). On the other hand, *B rotundum* (*molle,* Fr. *bémol*) answers to B flat, and is used also as a sign for lowering the pitch (hence German "*Moll*-Akkord," "*Moll*tonart," *i.e.* minor chord, minor key, with lowered third). *B cancellatum,* cancelled B = ♯, was originally identical with ♯; but a distinction was made at the beginning of the 16th century.—The old solmisation name of B was *B, fa, mi, i.e.* either *B fa* (= *b♭*) or *B mi* (= *b♮*). In Italy and France B flat is called *si♭* (*si bémol*).

B = *Basso, c.B.* = *col Basso, C.B.* = *Contrabasso, B.C.* = *Basso continuo.* B. is also an abbreviation for Bachelor: *Mus. B.* = *Musicæ Baccalaureus* (M.B., on the other hand, *Medicinæ B.*).

ba. (*See* BOBISATION and SOLMISATION.)

Babbi, Christoph, b. 1748, Cesena, went to Dresden in 1780 as leader of the Electoral band, and d. there in 1814. He composed violin concertos, symphonies, quartets, etc.

Babini, Matteo, one of the most celebrated tenor singers of the last century, b. Feb. 19, 1754, Bologna, d. there, Sept. 22, 1816; was intended for the medical profession, but, as his parents left him without means, he was trained by his relative Cortoni, a teacher of singing, and made his *début* about 1780. His success was so great that he soon received engagements in Berlin, Petersburg, Vienna (1785), and London. In Paris he sang a duet with Marie Antoinette. The Revolution drove him back to Italy, but he was again in Berlin in 1792. He was still singing in 1802, and died a wealthy man

Baboračka and **Baborak,** Bohemian dances with various changes of *tempo.*

Bacchius (*Senior*), Greek writer on music (about 150 A.D.), of whom two theoretical treatises have been handed down to us (published by Meibom, Mersenne, and Fr. Bellermann). C. von Jan wrote an analysis of his "Isagoge" (1891).

Bacfart (*Bacfarre*, really *Graew*), Valentin, a famous performer on the lute, b. 1515, Siebenbürgen; he lived alternately at the Imperial Court at Vienna, and at the Court of Sigismund Augustus of Poland, and d. Aug. 13, 1576, Padua. B. published two works on the tablature of the lute (1564 and 1565).

Bach, name of the Thuringian family in which, as in no other, the pursuit of music was hereditary (during the 17th and 18th centuries), and carefully nourished from childhood. When several members of this family met together musical performances of a serious kind took place, opinions were exchanged concerning new compositions, and there were improvisations; in fact, they so strengthened one another in knowledge and ability that the Bachs were held in the highest esteem throughout the land, and furnished many cantors and organists to the Thuringian towns. So in Erfurt, Eisenach, Arnstadt, Gotha, Mühlhausen, we find Bachs as organists, and still at the end of the 18th century the town-pipers in Erfurt were called "the Bachs," although not one among them was any longer a Bach. Spitta, in his biography of J. S. Bach, has shown that the family sprang from Thuringia, and not, as was formerly supposed, from Hungary. The baker, Veit Bach, who wandered (about 1590) from Hungary to Wechmar, near Gotha, was a native of that very village. Veit B. pursued the art of music for pleasure (he played the cithara); his son, Hans B. (the great grandfather of J. S. Bach) was, on the other hand, a musician by profession, and was trained at Gotha under Nikolaus B. Thus the Bachs were already at that time, apparently, "in the trade." Of the sons of Hans Bach Johann became the ancestor of the Erfurt "Bachs," Heinrich, organist at Arnstadt, the father of Joh. Christoph and Joh. Michael B., and Christoph B. organist and town-musician at Weimar, the grandfather of J. S. Bach. By the sixth decade of the 17th century the Bachs were, so to speak, settled occupants of the music posts at Weimar, Erfurt, and Eisenach; if a place was vacant here or there, one of them came forward and filled the gap. Thus, for example, a son of Christoph B., Ambrosius B. (the father of J. S. Bach), went from Erfurt to Eisenach to take the place of another B. The most important composers of this family are:—

(1) Johann Christoph, son of Heinrich Bach, and thus uncle of J. S. B., b. Dec. 8, 1642, Arnstadt, from 1665 until his death, March 31, 1703, organist at Eisenach, is the most distinguished of the older Bachs, especially in the department of vocal music. A work after the manner of an oratorio, *Es erhob sich ein Streit* (Rev. 12, v. 7-12), also some motets, 44 chorale preludes, and a Sarabande with twelve variations for clavier, have been preserved. His son, Nikolaus, b. 1669, d. Nov. 4, 1753, was for a period of 58 years musical director at the Jena University, and a conspicuous connoiseur in the construction of instruments. Of his compositions have been preserved a " masterly " mass and a comic *Singspiel*, " Der Jenaische Wein- und Bier-Rufer."

(2) Johann Michael, brother of the former, b. Aug. 9, 1648, Arnstadt, from 1673 organist at Gehren, near Arnstadt, where he died, 1694. His youngest daughter, Maria Barbara, became J. S. Bach's first wife, the mother of K. Ph. Emanuel and W. Friedemann Bach. The instrumental works of Johann Michael are of greater importance than those of his brother; unfortunately, only a few chorale preludes have come down to us, but these lead us to form a high opinion of his ability. So far as can be judged from the few motets which have been preserved, his vocal works show technical facility, but are inferior to those of his brother.

(3) Johann Sebastian, b. Mar. 21, 1685, Eisenach, d. July 28, 1750, Leipzig; one of the greatest masters of all times, and one of those who cannot be surpassed, inasmuch as they embody the musical feeling and potency of an epoch (Palestrina, Bach, Handel, Gluck, Haydn, Mozart, Beethoven, Wagner). Bach, however, is of special importance, and his greatness is without parallel, for in him the styles of two different ages attained to a high pitch, so that he stands, as it were, a striking landmark between these two, in each of which he displayed gigantic power. B. belongs with equal right to the period of polyphonic music with its contrapuntal imitative style, which lay behind him, and to the period of harmonic music bearing the stamp of tonality. He lived in a transition period, *i.e.* at a time when the old imitative style had not yet outlived itself, and when the new still stood in the first stage of its development and bore the stamp of immaturity. The genius of Bach united the characteristics of both styles in a manner which must be looked upon as worthy of aspiration for a period extending into the far future. There can therefore be no question of Bach's music becoming antiquated; the most that can be said is that certain accessories—such as cadences, ornaments, and such like, in which Bach showed himself a true child of his time—remind us of the past. On the other hand, his melody is so thoroughly healthy and inexhaustible, his rhythm so manifold and pulsating with life, his harmony so choice, so bold, and yet so clear and intelligible, that his works are not only the object of wonder, but are most zealously studied and imitated by the musicians of the present day, as indeed they will be by musicians in the far future. The outward life of Bach was simple. His father was the town-musician Ambrosius B., b. Feb. 22, 1645, d. June 28, 1695, his mother, Elizabeth, *née* Lämmerhirt, of Erfurt. At the early age of nine years he lost his mother, and a year later his father, and was handed over to the care of his brother, Johann Christoph B. (b. June 16, 1671), organist at Ohrdruf. This brother, a pupil of Pachelbel, now became his teacher. In 1700 he obtained free tuition at St. Michael's school at Lüneburg, from which place he made several excursions (on foot) to Hamburg to hear the famous organists Reinken and Lübeck. In 1703 he received his first appointment, that of violinist in the private band of Prince Johann Ernst, of Saxony, at Weimar, but only remained there a few months, as he was offered the post of organist of the new church at Arnstadt. From that place he made (1705-6) the famous journey on foot to Lübeck, to Dietrich Buxtehude, the celebrated organ-master, and this brought him into conflict with the authorities at Arnstadt, as he considerably outstayed the allotted time. Matters did, not, however, come to a crisis, as they much wished to retain the gifted youth. In 1706, through the death of Joh. G. Ahle, the post of organist of St. Blasius at Mühlhausen became vacant, and Bach obtained it in 1707, having married his cousin, Maria Barbara, daughter of Joh. Michael Bach, at Gehren. Although the musical conditions at Mühlhausen were not unpleasing, and in any case better than those at Arnstadt, B. remained only a year, and went in 1708 as Court organist and "Kammermusicus" to the reigning Duke of Weimar, where, in 1714, he was appointed "Hofkonzertmeister." But already, in 1717, he wandered to Cöthen as capellmeister and "Kammermusikdirector" to Prince Leopold of Anhalt—a post of an entirely different kind from those which he had hitherto occupied, for he had neither an organ to attend to nor a choir to conduct, but had to occupy himself entirely with orchestral and chamber music. As the various posts which he filled always had a marked influence on his activity as a composer, so in Cöthen he wrote almost exclusively

chamber music. But he only developed his full creative power at Leipzig, whither he went in 1723 as Cantor to the St. Thomas's School, and as musical director to the University, as successor to Johann Kuhnau. In this post he died after 27 years active service. He was tormented during the last three years of his life by a malady of the eyes which gradually impaired his sight, till at the last he became completely blind. He was twice married. Maria Barbara died in 1720, and, however happily they had lived together, B. felt compelled to give a new mother to his children, and in 1721 married Anna Magdalena, daughter of the "Kammermusikus" Wülken at Weissenfels, who survived him. B. left six sons and four daughters; five sons and five daughters had died before him.

The works of J. S. Bach are very great in number. First are to be named his church cantatas, of which he wrote a complete series for five years (for all Sundays and festival days), but of these many have not been preserved. Also of five Passions only three remain, viz. the "St. Matthew Passion" (a truly gigantic work), the "St. John Passion," and the dubious "St. Luke Passion." To the two former named immense works the B minor Mass forms a worthy companion, which, together with four short masses, are all that remain of a great number written by B. The "Magnificat" à 5, is also one of his most striking works. The *Christmas*, and also the *Ascension* and *Easter* oratorios are not far behind the Passions. Still more imposing is the number of the instrumental compositions, especially those for clavier, organ, as well as clavier, with other instruments (preludes and fugues, fantasias, sonatas, toccatas, partitas, suites, concertos, variations, chorale preludes, chorales, etc.). Particularly worthy of mention are: "Das wohltemperirte Klavier" (the name strictly belongs only to the first set of 24 preludes and fugues, but is almost universally used for the two sets, making two for each major and each minor key; it is a *vade mecum* which every pianoforte player should possess), and the "Art of Fugue" (15 fugues and 4 canons on one and the same theme). For violin alone three partitas and three sonatas—works which have not their equal; the great Chaconne in the D minor Partita alone suffices to give a conception of Bach's immense power. For instruments no longer in use B. wrote three sonatas for gamba, three partitas for lute, and a suite for viola pomposa—an instrument of his own invention. Only a small part of the works of B. appeared in print during his lifetime ("Klavierübung," "Das musikalische Opfer," the "Goldberg" variations, chorales, etc.); the "Art of Fugue" was published by Ph. E. B. in 1752. When, after about fifty years of neglect, considerable attention was bestowed on the works of B., some were printed or reprinted.

But Mendelssohn had the merit of bringing the composer to light in his full greatness by the performance of the "St. Matthew Passion" in 1829 at Berlin. The ever-increasing cultivation of the works of Bach made it possible for Peters in 1837 to undertake a complete edition of Bach's instrumental works; and later on the same thing was done for the vocal. But the Bach Society (Bach-Gesellschaft), founded at Leipzig in 1850 by Härtel, K. F. Becker, M. Hauptmann, O. Jahn, and R. Schumann, has, since 1851, been preparing a truly monumental critical edition : at least one thick folio volume appears each year. The yearly subscription for the members of the society is fifteen marks, in return for which they receive a copy of the year's publication. Bach societies (Bach-Vereine), specially formed for the cultivation of the composer's music, exist at Berlin, Leipzig, London, Königsberg, and other places. On the 28th of September, 1884, a monument was erected to Bach in his native town, Eisenach—hitherto the only one, with the exception of the small one set up at Leipzig by Mendelssohn.

The history of the life of J. S. Bach has been written by various authors—first by K. Ph. Emanuel Bach and J. Fr. Agricola in Mizler's "Musikalische Bibliothek," vol. iv. 1 (1754), then by Forkel ("Ueber J. S. Bach's Leben, Kunst und Kunstwerke," 1802), Hilgenfeldt (1850), Bitter ("J. S. B.;" 2nd ed., 1881, 4 vols.). Ph. Spitta has recently published an exhaustive biography worthy of the master ("J. S. B.," 1873-80, 2 vols.; English translation by Clara Bell and Fuller Maitland : Novello).

(4) Wilhelm Friedemann (Bach of Halle), eldest son of the former, b. Nov. 22, 1710, Weimar, d. July 1, 1784, Berlin, was exceptionally gifted, and his father's special favourite, but by his disorderly mode of living became incapable of serious work. From 1733-47 he was organist of St. Sophia's church, Dresden, then of St. Mary's, Halle, until 1764. When compelled by his extravagant behaviour to give up this post, he lived, without any fixed employment, now here now there (Leipzig, Berlin, Brunswick, Göttingen, etc.), and died in complete poverty at Berlin, a ruined genius in the true sense of the word. There exists a great number of his compositions in manuscript in the Berlin library. Unfortunately, through his fault, a great part of his father's works were lost; for, of the manuscripts divided between the two eldest sons at Bach's death, so far as is at present known, only those which fell to the share of Ph. E. have been preserved.

(5) Karl Philipp Emanuel (the "Berlin" or "Hamburg" B.), the second of the surviving sons of J. S. Bach, b. March 8, 1714, Weimar, d. Dec. 14, 1788, Hamburg, was intended for the law, and for this reason his father allowed his musical fancy to turn more in the direction of the light "gallant" style; and to this very tendency he owes his

greatness, for by it he became the father of modern instrumental music, the precursor of Haydn, Mozart, and Beethoven in the department of the sonata, symphony, etc., which he clothed in more pleasing modern dress. His career was simple enough. He went to Frankfort on the Oder in order to study jurisprudence, but instead of doing this he founded a choral union. In 1738 he went to Berlin, and in 1740 became chamber cembalist to Frederick the Great, a rare musical *dilettante*, who often sorely plagued B. when the latter had to accompany his flute performances. The Seven Years' War cooled the musical ardour of the king, and therefore in 1767 B. asked for his discharge in order to take the place of Telemann as church musical director at Hamburg. He died, highly esteemed, of a chest complaint. For us his most important work is the "Versuch über die wahre Art das Klavier zu spielen" (1753–62, two parts), the principal source for explaining the ornaments of the previous century. The number of his compositions is very great, especially for clavier (210 solo pieces, 52 concertos, many sonatas, etc.). In the department of church music he was certainly prolific, but less important (22 Passions, many cantatas, two oratorios, etc.). K. H. Bitter wrote the life of the sons of Bach, "K. Ph. Emanuel B. und W. Friedemann B. und deren Brüder," (2 vols., Berlin, 1868). H. v. Bülow has republished six clavier sonatas of K. Ph. E. Bach (Peters), and C. F. Baumgart the complete collection of sonatas "für Kenner und Liebhaber" (Leuckart, six books), E. Pauer, eighteen of his popular pieces (Augener's Edition).—(6) Johann Christoph Friedrich (the "Bückeburg" B.), the third of J. S. Bach's musical sons, b. June 21, 1732, Leipzig; also first studied law, but finally became a musician, and from 1756 was capellmeister to Count Schaumburg at Bückeburg, where he died, Jan. 26, 1795. He was likewise a diligent composer (sacred and chamber music works, cantata *Pygmalion*, opera *Die Amerikanerin*), though not of equal importance with Ph. Emanuel.—(7) Johann Christian (the "Milan" or "English" B.), the youngest son of J. S. Bach, b. 1735 (baptised Sept. 7), Leipzig, d. Jan. 1, 1782, London; like Friedemann, he was endowed with great talent, but almost as light-minded. After his father's death he was trained by Ph. Emanuel B., went in 1754 as organist to Milan, and became there an opera composer *à la node*. In 1759 he came to London and became court composer; he also gained a great but ephemeral success as a composer of Italian operas.—(8) Wilhelm Friedrich Ernst, grandson and last male descendant of J. S. Bach, son of the "Bückeburg" B. (6), b. May 27, 1759, Bückeburg, d. Dec. 25, 1845, Berlin; pupil of his father and of the "English" B. (7), for whose instruction he came to London. He was an excellent performer on the pianoforte

and organ, and much sought after as a teacher in London. When his uncle died he went to Paris, where he gave concerts, and then settled down in Minden. In 1792 he settled in Berlin, where he was appointed cembalist to the queen with the title of capellmeister; later on he became cembalist to Queen Louise, and music-master to the royal princes, but was pensioned off after the death of the queen, and lived in retirement until his own death. Only a few of his compositions (songs and pf. pieces) have been published.

Bach, not belonging to the family of J. S. Bach, but possibly in some way connected with it.—(1) August Wilhelm, b. Oct. 4, 1796, Berlin, d. April 15, 1869, son of Gottfried B., the secretary of the lottery department and organist of the church of the Holy Trinity; he was organist of various Berlin churches; in 1822 teacher at the Royal Institute for church music; 1832 director of the same, as successor to Zelter; member of the Academy, and appointed Professor in 1858. He published sacred compositions, also pf. pieces and songs. B. was Mendelssohn's teacher for the organ.—(2) Otto, b. Feb. 9, 1833, Vienna, where his father was advocate, pupil of Sechter at Vienna, of Marx at Berlin, and of Hauptmann at Leipzig. He was chief capellmeister at various German theatres, and in 1868 became artistic director of the Mozarteum and capellmeister of the cathedral at Salzburg. From April 1, 1880, he was capellmeister at the new great "Votivkirche" at Vienna. He died July 3, 1893. Of his compositions may be mentioned the operas *Die Liebesprobe (Der Löwe von Salamanka*, 1867), *Leonore* (1874), *Die Argonauten, Medea, Sardanapal*, a requiem, four symphonies, the ballad for chorus and orchestra, *Der Blumen Rache*, the overture *Elektra*, chamber music works, partsongs, masses, Te Deum, etc. He showed praiseworthy activity as director of the Mozarteum.—(3) Leonhard Emil, b. March 11, 1849, Posen; pianist, pupil of Kullak (pianoforte), of Wüerst and Kiel (theory); was for many years teacher at Kullak's Academy.

Bache, (1) Francis Edward, b. Sept. 14, 1833, Birmingham, d. there Aug. 24, 1858; studied the violin under A. Mellon, then composition under Bennett. From 1853–55 he was a pupil of Hauptmann and Plaidy at the Leipzig Conservatorium; he was a very talented composer, but, unfortunately, was consumptive. He spent 1855–56 in Algiers and Italy, the summer of 1856 at Leipzig and Vienna, and from the summer of 1857 was in England. A number of pianoforte pieces, songs, a trio, violin romances, are published; a pf. concerto and two operas (*Rübezahl* and *Which is Which*) remain in manuscript.—(2) Walter, brother of the former, b. June 19, 1842, Birmingham, d. March 26, 1888, London; was first a pupil of the organist Stimpson at Birmingham, then at the Leipzig Conservatorium under Plaidy,

Moscheles, Hauptmann, and Richter, together with his fellow-countrymen Sullivan, Dannreuther, C. Rosa, Fr. Taylor, etc. After a short stay in Milan and Florence, he went in 1862 to Rome and studied for three years under Liszt, and was on friendly terms with G. Sgambati. In 1865 he returned to England, and lived from that time as conductor and music teacher in London. B. was a warm admirer of Liszt, and brought out in London nearly all his Symphonic Poems, also *The Legend of St. Elizabeth*, and Psalm XIII., and himself played both Liszt's pf. concertos in E♭ and A.

Bachelor (Ger. *Bakkalaureus;* Fr. *Bachelier*). An academic degree, formerly usual at all universities, but now only granted by English and a few German. It is lower than that of Doctor, and, as a rule, has to precede it. (*Cf.* DOCTOR OF MUSIC.)

Bachmann, (1) A n t o n, court musician and instrument-maker at Berlin, b. 1716, d. March 8, 1800. His son, and heir to the business, K a r l L u d w i g, b. 1743, d. 1809, was a good violist, and as such a member of the royal band. His wife, C h a r l o t t e K a r o l i n e W i l h e l m i n e, *née* S t ö w e, b. Nov. 2, 1757, Berlin, d. Aug. 19, 1817, was an accomplished singer and a worthy member of the " Singakademie " under Fasch.— (2) Pater Sixtus, b. July 18, 1754, Kettershausen (near Babenhausen), d. 1818 ; a monk of the order of White Canons at Marchthal, was a prolific composer both of instrumental and vocal music, of which, however, very little has been printed. At the age of nine he entered into a musical contest with young Mozart, and passed through the ordeal with honour ; at that time he was remarkable for his excellent memory. B. was a contributor to Hofmeister's Collection of music.—(3) G e o r g e C h r i s t i a n, celebrated clarinettist, b. Jan. 7, 1804, Paderborn, d. Aug. 28, 1842, Brussels ; a highly esteemed solo player in the royal band at Brussels and teacher of his instrument at the Conservatoire. He was also well known as a clarinet-maker of the first rank, whose instruments even to-day fetch high prices.

Bachofen, J o h. K a s p a r, sacred composer, b. 1697, Zürich, d. 1755 ; became in 1718 singing master at the Latin School and organist there, and afterwards director of the male choral union. His compositions, at one time very popular in Switzerland, consist, for the most part, of sacred songs : " Musikalisches Halleluja," " Irdisches Vergnügen in Gott " (after Brockes), " Psalmen," the Brockes' " Passion," etc., also an instructive " Musikalisches Notenbüchlein."

Bachrich, S i g i s m u n d, b. Jan. 23, 1841, Zsambokreth (Hungary). He went to the Vienna Conservatorium from 1851–7, and studied under Boehm (violin). After acting for a short time as conductor at a small theatre at Vienna, he went in 1861 to Paris, where, for some years as conductor in an inferior post,

journalist, even apothecary, he fought his way with difficulty ; so he returned to Vienna and joined the Hellmesberger quartet party, to which he has belonged for twelve years. B. has composed chamber music, violin pieces, and songs, the comic operas *Muzzedin* (1883) and *Heini von Steier* (1884), which were favourably received. Already in 1866 these had been preceded in Vienna by two operettas ; a third operetta, *Der Fuchs-Major*, was brought out at Prague in 1889. Also a ballet of his, *Sakuntala*, was produced. B. is teacher at the Vienna Conservatorium and member of the Philharmonic and Opera orchestras, also a member of the Rosé quartet party.

Backer-Gröndahl, A g a t h e, Norwegian pianist and composer, b. Dec. 1, 1847, Holmestrand ; pupil of Kjerulf and Lindemann ; in 1863 at Kullak's Academy, Berlin ; 1871 under Bülow in Florence ; married her teacher of singing, Gröndahl, in Christiania, 1875 (songs, pf. pieces, concert études, Op. 11, etc.).

Backers, A m e r i c u s. (*See* BROADWOOD.)

Backfall, one of the old English graces, an appoggiatura.

Backofen, J o h. G. H e i n r i c h, performer on the harp, clarinet, and other instruments, b. 1768, Durlach, d. 1839, Darmstadt. On his concert tours he attracted notice as a many-sided artist ; in 1806 he was chamber musician at Gotha, and in 1815 an instrument maker at Darmstadt. B. published compositions for harp, a Harp Method, and Methods for the basset-horn and clarinet.

Back-positive (Ger. *Rückpositiv*) is the name given to the set of pipes which stand at the player's back, hiding him from the church. In three-manual organs it belongs usually to the lowest manual, which is connected with the pipes by a mechanism carried under the floor.

Bacon, R i c h a r d M a c k e n z i e, clever musical critic, b. May 1, 1776, Norwich, d. there Nov. 2, 1844 ; he was the editor of the *Quarterly Musical Magazine and Review* (1818–28), also of the " Elements of Vocal Science " (1828). He was also the founder of the triennial musical festivals at Norwich.

Badarczewska, T h e k l a, b. 1838, Warsaw, d. there, 1862 ; became known by her *pièces de salon* (" La prière d'une vierge ").

Bader, K a r l A d a m, celebrated opera singer (tenor), b. Jan. 10, 1789, Bamberg, d. April 14, 1870, Berlin ; received his first musical training from his father, who was cathedral organist at Bamberg, became his successor in 1807, and wished to take holy orders, but on the advice of T. A. Hoffmann (q.v.) went on the stage (1811), and appeared with gradually increasing success at Munich, Bremen, Hamburg, and Brunswick, and in 1820 was finally engaged as leading tenor at the Berlin Court Opera, of which he was a conspicuous ornament for twenty years. In 1845 he gave up singing, but was *régisseur* still up to 1849, and for a long time after that was active as director of the music at the Catholic " Hedwigskirche." B. was a specially famous representative of the hero tenor rôles in Spontini's operas ; he was one of the few tenors who could do something more than sing, and he had an imposing presence.

Badia, (1) Carlo Agostino, b. 1672, Venice, d. Sept. 23, 1738, Vienna ; already on July 1, 1696, he was appointed royal court composer at Vienna, when the office was first established. He wrote seventeen operas and serenatas, and fifteen oratorios, also twelve cantatas for one voice with clavier (*Tributi Armonici*, printed), besides thirty-three à 1–3 (preserved in manuscript). B., for the rest, had only moderate gifts, and wrote in an antiquated style. A singer, Anna Lisi Badia, was a member of the Vienna court company (1711–25).—(2) Luigi, b. 1822, Tirano (Naples), composed four operas, also songs, with which he had good success.

Bagatelle (Fr.), a trifle.

Bagge, Selmar, b. June 30, 1823, Coburg. 1837, d. July 17, 1896, Basel, pupil of the Prague Conservatorium (Dionys Weber), and afterwards of S. Sechter at Vienna ; in 1851 he was teacher of composition at the Vienna Conservatorium ; in 1854 organist at Gumpendorf, near Vienna. In 1855 he resigned his post at the Conservatorium and criticised the organisation of that institution in the *Monatsschrift für Theater und Musik*, also in 1860 in the *Deutsche Musikzeitung*. B. remained for many years musical critic and editor ; in 1863 he undertook the editing of the *Allgemeine Musikalische Zeitung*, which had been established by Breitkopf and Härtel, but discontinued since 1848, and he conducted the same for two years, when (1866) it passed over to the firm of Rieter-Biedermann. (*Cf.* PERIODICALS.) B. was director of the School of Music at Basel from 1868. Besides his journalistic work he published chamber music, a symphony, songs, and a " Lehrbuch der Tonkunst " (1873).

Bagpipe (Ger. *Dudelsack, Sackpfeife ;* Ital. *Cornamusa, Piva ;* Fr. *Musette, Sourdeline ;* Lat. *Tibia utricularis ;* Gr. *Askaulos* (leathern pipe). In the Middle Ages, like the hurdy-gurdy, *Symphonia*, corrupted into *Samponia, Zampugna*, etc., it was made in the 17th century (Prætorius) in various sizes ; *grosser Bock*, (drone ; contra G or great c), *Schaperpfeif* (drones : b♭ f'), *Hümmelchen* (f' c'), and *Dudey* (e♭ flat, b♭ flat, e″ flat). The B. is practically an obsolete instrument, and only found now in the hands of beggars and the indigenous population of England, Scotland, and Ireland. It consists of a leathern wind-bag, which is either filled by the player by means of a tube of pipe-shape (as in those of the older kind and in the Scotch Highland bagpipes) or by means of small bellows worked by the arm. Several pipes are fastened to the leathern skin, by means of which, when pressed by the player's

arm, they are made to speak ; also a chanter with six sound-holes on which melodies are played, and from one to three drones (Ger. *Stimmer ;* Fr. *bourdons, cf.* DRONES), which give out, without interruption, one and the same sound. The bagpipe closely resembles the *Vielle*, and, like it, was a fashionable instrument from the 17th to the 18th centuries. The skin was at that time covered with silk, the little case which received the drone reeds being made of ivory, and ornamented with gold, precious stones, etc. Descouteaux, Philidor, Douet, Dubuisson, Hotteterre, Charpentier, Chediville, etc., were famous as players on the B.

Bahn, Martin. (*See* TRAUTWEIN.)

Bähr (Bär, Beer), Johann, leader of the band of the Duke of Weissenfels, b. 1652, St. Georg a.d. Enns (Austria), d. 1700 of a wound received at a rifle match. He made a reputation by his satirical, polemical, musical pamphlets, in which he latinised his name (Bär, " Bear ") into *Ursus* (" *Ursus murmurat, U. saltat, U. triumphat,*" etc., against the " Gymnasialrektor " Hartnoth at Gotha, 1697, etc.) ; also by his " Bellum Musicum " (1701) and " Musikalische Diskurse " (1719), both posthumous.

Bai, Tommaso, b. about 1650, Crevalcuore, near Bologna ; he was a tenor singer in the Papal Chapel, 1713 maestro, but died already Dec. 22, 1714. B. was the composer of the celebrated Miserere which is sung alternately with those of Allegri and Baini in the Papal Chapel during Holy Week. It is published in the collections of Papal Chapel music for the Holy Week (Burney, Choron, Peters). Many other compositions of B. are to be found in manuscript in Roman libraries.

Baif, Jean Antoine de, poet and musician, b. 1532, Venice, d. Sept. 19, 1589, Paris ; published two lute tablature works, twelve sacred songs, and two books of chansons à 4.

Baillot, (1) Pierre Marie François de Sales, b. Oct. 1, 1771, Passy, near Paris, d. Sept. 15, 1842 ; one of the most celebrated violinists that France has produced. He received his first instruction on the violin from a native of Florence, Polidori by name, at Passy, then in 1780, when his parents settled in Paris, from Sainte-Marie, who laid great stress on exact playing. After the death of his father (1783) he was sent for additional training to Rome, to Pollani, a pupil of Nardini's, who laid stress on big tone. In 1791 he returned to Paris, and played to Viotti, who procured for him the post of first violin at the Théâtre Feydeau. In spite of his high artistic development, he does not yet appear to have taken up music as a profession, for soon afterwards he accepted a subordinate appointment in the *Ministère des Finances*, which he held until 1795, making himself all the while more known by appearances at concerts, until he was appointed professor of the violin at the newly-organised Conservatoire. He now sought to fill up the gaps in his musical knowledge, and studied theory diligently under Catel, Reicha, and Cherubini. Only in 1802 did he undertake his first tour, and indeed, to Russia. This was followed by others through France, the Netherlands, England, and Italy. In 1821 he became first violin at the Grand Opéra, and in 1825 solo player in the royal band. He died highly esteemed, and was mourned by a large number of distinguished pupils. B.'s principal work was his " L'Art du Violon " (1834), which is excellent, and not to be surpassed. He published, jointly with Rode and Kreutzer, the " Méthode du Violon," a work officially recognised by the Paris Conservatoire, repeatedly republished, reprinted, and translated into foreign languages. He edited, besides, the " Méthode de Violoncelle " of the Conservatoire (authors: Levasseur, Catel, and Baudiot). He wrote also " Notice sur Grétry " (1814), " Notice sur Viotti " (1825), and other small essays. His compositions, which, at times, make heavy demands upon the executant, are 10 violin concertos, 30 sets of variations, a *symphonie concertante* for two violins with orchestra, 24 preludes in all keys, capriccios, nocturnes, etc. for violin, 3 stringed quartets, 15 trios for two violins and bass, etc.—His son (2), René Paul, b. Oct. 23, 1813, Paris, d. there, Mar. 28, 1889, was professor of ensemble playing at the Paris Conservatoire.

Baini, Abbate Giuseppe, b. Oct. 21, 1775, Rome, d. there, May 21, 1844; at first pupil of his uncle Lorenzo B. (maestro at the Church of the Twelve Apostles, Rome), a worthy musician of the Roman School who still held fast to the traditions of the Palestrina style. Later on he became the pupil and friend of Jannaconi, maestro of St. Peter's, who procured for him an appointment as singer in the Papal Chapel; he became Jannaconi's successor in 1817, which post he retained up to his death. B. was a strange phenomenon in our century; he lived and moved completely in the music of the 16th century, and understood nothing of the powerful development of the art which had since taken place. In his opinion, music had been going down hill since the death of Palestrina. His own compositions must be looked at and judged from the standpoint of that period. It is well known that during his lifetime (1821) a Miserere of his was included among the regular Holy Week performances at the Sistine Chapel (alternately with the Misereres of Allegri and Bai). B's chief work, and the one to which he devoted the greater part of his life, was the biography and characteristics of Palestrina (" Memorie storico critiche della vita e delle Opere di Giovanni Pierluigi da Palestrina, etc.," 1828), which was translated into German by Kandler (with comments by Kiesewetter, 1834). He wrote, besides, an essay on ancient rhythm (1820), and a sharp

criticism of a prize motet by Santucci written for four choirs.

Bajetti, Giovanni, Italian opera and ballet composer, b. about 1815, Brescia, d. April 28, 1876, Milan (*Gonzalvo*, *L'Assedio di Brescia*, *Uberto da Brescia*, ballet *Faust*, jointly with Costa and Panizza).

Baker, G., famous English composer, b. 1773, Exeter, d. Feb. 19, 1847; pupil of W. Cramer and Dussek in London, afterwards organist at Stafford; in 1801 he took his degree of D.Mus. at Oxford. His chief works are anthems, glees, voluntaries, pf. sonatas, etc.

Balakireff, Mily Alexejewitsch, b. 1836, Nishnij Nowgorod, already, as a boy, took part in concerts, but went to the Gymnasium, and attended the University at Kasan in order to study mathematics and physics; through friendly intercourse with A. v. Ulibischew, he resolved to devote himself to music. In 1855 he appeared at Petersburg as pianist with great success. In 1862, jointly with Lamakin, he founded the " Free School of Music," under the patronage of the Grand Prince, heir to the throne. In 1865 he went to Prague to the Czechish theatre, to put Glinka's *Russlan and Ludmilla* into rehearsal. From 1867 he was sole director of the Free School, conducted the concerts of the Russian Society of Music from 1867 to 1870, but in 1872 retired altogether into private life. B. pays homage to the Berlioz-Liszt tendencies. His principal works are :— Overtures on Russian, Spanish, and Czechish themes, symphonic poem, " Tamara," music to *King Lear*, an Oriental fantasia for pianoforte (" Slamey "), pf. pieces, pf. arrangements of overtures by Glinka and Berlioz, etc., as well as a collection of Russian popular melodies.

Balalaika, a primitive stringed instrument of the guitar family, which is used in the Ukraine to accompany the songs of the people; it is also sometimes found in the hands of gipsies.

Balancement (Fr.), same as BEBUNG (q.v.), a manner of playing peculiar to the clavichord.

Balart, Gabriel, Spanish composer of Zarzuelas (operettas), b. June 8, 1824, Barcelona, d. July 5, 1893.

Balatka, Hans, conductor and 'cellist, b. March 5, 1827, Hoffnungsthal, near Olmütz, pupil of Sechter and Proch at Vienna; went in 1849 to America, and founded at Milwaukee a Musical Union, which soon flourished, and still exists. In 1860 he was called to Chicago as conductor of the Philharmonic Society. After the great fire in that city he went back to Milwaukee, and, for a time, to St. Louis, but returned to, and finally settled down in Chicago. B. enjoys great fame as conductor of male choral unions (Chicago Festival, 1881), and especially deserves credit for his share in the progress of the culture of music in America.

Balbi, (1) Ludovico, church composer,

about 1600 maestro at St. Antonius' Church at Padua, later at the great Franciscan monastery, Venice; edited jointly with Joh. Gabrieli and Orazio Vecchi the Graduals and Antiphons which Gardano published in 1591 at Venice. Of his compositions have been preserved: masses (1584), Cantiones (1576), motets (1578), Ecclesiastici Concentus (1606).—(2) Melchiorre Cavaliere, b. June 4, 1796, Venice, d. June 21, 1879, Padua, theorist and composer, pupil of Antonio Calegari (d. 1828), whose "Sistema Armonico" he published in 1829 with notes; he wrote besides "Grammatica ragionata della musica sotto l'aspetto della lingua" (1845) and "Nuova scuola basata sul sistema semitonato equabile" (1st part, 1872; a "chromatist" therefore). From 1818 to 1853 B. was leader in both theatres at Padua, and afterwards maestro at the basilica St. Antonio. He brought out also three operas (1820–25)

Baldewin. (See BAULDEWIJN.)

Balfe, Michael William, one of the most distinguished of modern English composers, b. May 15, 1808, Dublin, d. Oct. 20, 1870, Rowney Abbey (Hertfordshire). B. was one of the few Englishmen who devoted himself to the composition of operas, but certainly without presenting this art species in any new light, for B. was only an Italian opera composer of English descent. Already at the age of seventeen (1825) B. went with a rich patron to Italy and studied counterpoint under Frederici at Rome, and later on singing under Fillippo Galli at Milan. His first attempt of any note at composition was the ballet La Pérouse, for Milan (1826). In 1828 he appeared at the Italian Opera, Paris, as principal baritone under Rossini, after he had studied for a short time with Bordogni. Up to 1835 he sang at various Italian theatres, produced some Italian operas at Palermo (I Rivali di se Stessi), Pavia (Un Avertimento di Gelosi), and Milan (Enrico IV. al passo della Marno, 1833), and married the German vocalist Fräul. Rosen (d. June 8, 1888, London). On his return to England as composer and singer, he celebrated a double triumph. Then followed in quick succession the operas, Siege of Rochelle, 1835; The Maiden of Artois, 1836; Catharina Grey, 1837; Joan of Arc, 1837; Diadeste, Falstaff, 1838; and Keolanthe, 1841—in the last of which his wife appeared. Falstaff was produced at Her Majesty's Theatre, the others at Drury Lane, with exception of the last-named, which B. brought out at the Lyceum when he was manager of an opera company. The undertaking failed, and soon afterwards B. went to Paris, where he produced with great success, at the Opéra Comique, Le Puits d'Amour, 1843, and Les Quatre Fils d'Aymon, 1844. In 1843 followed at Drury Lane The Bohemian Girl, his most famous opera, which was given at the principal theatres of note throughout Europe; in 1844 The Daughter of St. Mark; in 1845 The Enchantress=L'Etoile

de Seville, written for the Paris Grand Opéra Other operas followed (The Bondman, 1846; The Maid of Honour, The Sicilian Bride, The Devil's In It, The Rose of Castille, Satanella, Bianca, The Puritan's Daughter, The Armourer of Nantes, Blanche of Nevers, The Sleeping Queen, 1864; also two Italian operas—Pittore e Duca, at Trieste, 1854 (=Moro, the Painter of Antwerp), and Il Talismano (=The Knight of the Leopard, London, 1874), but Balfe's fame began gradually to decline. In 1846 he visited Vienna, in 1849 Berlin, Petersburg and Trieste, from 1852 to 1856, producing operas, and coining money. In 1857 his daughter Victoire made her début in Italian opera at the Lyceum. From 1864 B. lived on his estate, Rowney Abbey. In 1874 his statue (by Mallempre) was placed in the vestibule of Drury Lane Theatre. Besides operas, B. also wrote cantatas, ballads, etc. B.'s good points were his extraordinary ease of conception and natural aptitude for melody appealing to the feelings; but his faults were the lack of all self-criticism and serious application to more solid work.

Balgklavis (Ger.). (See CLAVIS.)

Ballad (Ital. Ballata; Fr. Ballade), originally a song accompanied by dancing (from Ital. ballo, "dance"). It was in Scotland and England that B. acquired the meaning of an epico-lyric poem with features of a saga or fantasy kind. Acquaintance with the Scotch ballads prompted the great German poets of the last century to write poems of a similar nature, but they did not thoroughly distinguish between the romance and the B. The musical form of the B. is as indefinite as the poetical. Songs are called ballads if narrative in character; all songs, including ballads, are poems which the poets, without doubt, class among romances. According to present use, the B. is a narrative poem composed for one voice with pianoforte or orchestral accompaniment; but if the musical development be extended so as to include choruses, various soli, etc., then it is no longer called a B. (although in such cases composers have occasionally used the term). In order to make confusion worse confounded, the term B. has been employed in purely instrumental music, and now we have pianoforte, violin, and orchestral ballads, etc., which half belong to programme-music, inasmuch as composers in writing them would seem to have something definite in their mind. It would, however, be extremely difficult to show in what way Chopin's Ballades are entitled to that name. Composers would do well to reserve the name B. for ballad poems set to music (also for those in which choruses are introduced), and extend it, at most, to instrumental works with programme.

Ballad-opera, a term applied in England to an opera composed, for the most part, of popular songs; the first example of the kind was John Gay's The Beggar's Opera (1727).

Ballard, celebrated French family of printers, and, with exception of P. Attaignant, the oldest Paris firm in this particular department. Attaignant appears to have died about the same time that Robert B. began to print; the latter received in 1552 from Henri II. a patent making him " *Seul imprimeur de la musique de la chambre, chapelle, et menus plaisirs du roi,*" and this he held in common with his brother-in-law and *associé Adrien Le Roy.* Trusting to their patent, which had been constantly renewed (Pierre, 1633; Robert, 1639; Ed. Christophe, 1673; Jean Baptiste Christophe, 1695; Christophe Jean François, 1750; Pierre Robert Christophe, 1763), the family took no notice of the progress made in the art of printing, and still in 1750 used the original types, namely, those made by Guillaume le Bé (q.v.) in 1540, whose punches Pierre B. had acquired for the sum of 50,000 livres. For the time at which they were made they are elegant and clear, but even in the last century, by the side of those of J. Breitkopf, appear old-fashioned. The removal of the patent in 1776 put an end to the privileges of the Ballards and to their firm.

Ballet (Ital. *Balletto,* from *ballo,* "dance") is the name now given to the dances introduced (and standing frequently in very loose relationship to the action) into operas, and consisting of most varied *pas seuls* and evolutions of the *corps de ballet;* also to independent stage pieces in which there is little speaking or singing, but rather an action represented by pantomime and dances. Both kinds of B. can be traced back to a remote period, and this without reckoning the measured dance movements of the chorus in old Greek tragedy. Pantomimes with music treating of subjects taken, for the most part, from Greek mythology, with allegorical allusions to royalty present, were frequent already in the 15th century, at the Courts of Italy and France at marriage festivities; these differed in principle scarcely at all from the modern "grand" B. Immense sums of money were spent in "mounting" such pieces. But ballets in opera are also of long date; dances with or without singing, in the middle or at the close of tragedies (in imitation of the ancient choral dances), are already met with in the 15th century. But even in the first period of opera they developed themselves into the rare form of *Intermèdes,* which, when introduced in fragmentary fashion into the action of an opera, formed a second action, standing in no sort of relation to the principal one. The name *balletto* for a complete ballet opera, in which, however, there was singing, is to be found already in 1625 (*La Liberazione di Ruggiero dall' isola d'Alcina,* libretto by Saracinelli, music by Francesca Caccini). Ballets were in special favour at the French Court, where not only the high nobility, but even the kings themselves (Louis XIII., 1625; Louis XIV. very frequently) joined in the dancing; the ballets of the Quinault-Lully opera in the time of Louis XIV. were much admired. Noverre (d. 1810) made essential changes in the B.; he assigned to dancing its proper subordinate place, and brought to the fore pantomime with its wealth of expression he was the real creator of the modern ballet.

Balletto (Ital.) is the frequent title, at the beginning of the 18th century, for what we now call "Partita" or "Suite," a series of dances of various character in the same key (Allemande, Sarabande, Courante, Gigue), written for stringed instruments.

Ballets, light compositions in madrigal style, frequently with a "Fa la" burden. Morley says that these pieces were "commonly called Fa las."

Balli (Ital.), dances; *Balli inglesi,* English dances; *balli ungaresi,* Hungarian dances.

Balthasar-Florence, Henri Mathias (Balthasar called B.-F.), b. Oct. 21, 1844, Arlon (Belgium), pupil of Fétis at the Brussels Conservatoire; he married, in 1863, the daughter of the instrument maker Florence, of whose instruments he has a warehouse at Namur; a diligent and talented composer (operas, symphonies, *Missa Solemnis,* cantatas, a pf. concerto, a violin concerto). His daughter, pupil of the Brussels Conservatoire, is a clever violinist.

Banchieri, Adriano, b. about 1567, Bologna, d. 1634; first of all, organist at Imola, later on "Monaco olivetano" of St. Michael's Monastery, Bologna; he was in his time a famous composer, and many of his works are preserved (masses, madrigals, canzonets, sacred concertos, etc.); but more important for our time are his theoretical pamphlets, "Cartella Musicale sul Canto Figurato" (2nd ed. 1610), "Direttorio Monastico di Canto Fermo" (1615), etc. (*Cf.* also BOBISATION.)

Banck, Karl, b. May 27, 1809, Magdeburg, d. Dec. 28, 1889, Dresden. He studied with B. Klein, L. Berger, and Zelter, in Berlin, and with F. Schneider in Dessau; he made a long journey through Italy (1830–31) with the poet and painter, Karl Alexander Simon, and then lived at Magdeburg, Berlin, and Leipzig, afterwards in Thuringia (Jena, Rudolstadt, etc.), and from 1840 at Dresden. In 1861 he married an American lady, and remained for a year in North America. B. was one of the most esteemed German musical critics, and his *Lieder* are well known; he published, besides, pianoforte pieces, part-songs, etc. He distinguished himself as editor of a series of old and previously unpublished works (sonatas of Scarlatti and Martini, arias of Gluck, etc.).

Band (Ital. *Banda;* Fr. *Bande*), music-band. This was a term formerly used, and by no means in a depreciatory sense, for a body of musicians, especially wind-players; but the twenty-four violins of Louis XIV. were called *bande*, and the twenty-four fiddlers of Charles II. the *King's private band*, etc. In Italian opera orchestras B. is the collective term used for the players of wind and percussion instruments; and an orchestra appearing on the stage is also called a B.

Bandola (Span.), Bandolon, Bandora, Bandura, an instrument of the lute family, with a smaller or larger number of steel or catgut strings, which were plucked with the finger, like the Pandora, Pandura, Pandurina, Mandora, Mandola, Mandoer, Mandura, Mandürchen. In essential points it was identical with the Mandoline (q.v.), still existing at the present day.

Banister, (1) J o h n, excellent violinist, b. 1630, St. Giles-in-the-Fields, London, d. Oct. 3, 1679; he was sent to France by Charles II. to perfect himself, and later on was appointed leader of the king's band. He was afterwards dismissed because he spoke contemptuously of the French violin players patronised by the king (his successor was the Frenchman, Grabu), and lived up to his death as director of a music school, and manager of concerts in London. B. wrote music to Davenant's *Circe*, and, jointly with Pelham Humphrey, music to Shakespeare's *Tempest*, and also songs, lessons for violin, etc.—(2) J o h n, b. about 1663, d. 1735; son of the former, was principal violinist at Drury Lane, wrote some music for the theatre, and was contributor to H. Playford's "Division Violin" (1685).—(3) C h a r l e s W i l l i a m (1768–1831), published a "Collection of Vocal Music." —(4) H e n r y J o s h u a, 1803–1847, an excellent 'cellist.—(5) H e n r y C h a r l e s, son of former, b. 1831, professor of harmony at the Royal Academy of Music and at the Royal Normal College for the Blind. He published "Textbook of Music" (1872), symphonies, pf. music, "Life of Macfarren," "Lectures on Musical Analysis," etc. Died Nov. 20, 1897, London.

Banjo, a favourite instrument among the American negroes, who brought it from Africa, where it is found under the name *Bania.* The B. is a kind of guitar with a long neck, a body like a drum-head (a parchment stretched upon a hoop, and without any back). It has from five to nine strings; the *chanterelle* is played with the thumb, and lies on the bass side of the lowest-tuned string.

Bannelier, C h a r l e s, writer on music, b. March 15, 1840, Paris; pupil of the Paris Conservatoire; he was for many years contributor to the *Revue et Gazette Musicale,* and chief editor during the last years of its existence (the paper ceased to appear in 1880). Besides many excellent articles in the paper just named, he wrote a French translation of Hanslick's "Vom Musikalisch-Schönen" (1877), translated also the text of Bach's "Matthew-Passion," and published a pianoforte duet arrangement of Berlioz's "Symphonie Fantastique."

Banti, B r i g i t t a, *née* G i o r g i, vocalist, b. 1759, Crema (Lombardy), d. Feb. 18, 1806, Bologna. She was discovered as a *chanteuse* in a *café* at Paris, and afterwards attracted much notice by her noble voice both in Paris and London; but she could never make up for the want of musical training, and remained during her whole life a singer with only nature's gifts. In her journeys through Germany, Austria, and Italy, she celebrated great triumphs. From 1799 to 1802 she was engaged in London as *prima donna,* and after that lived in Italy.

Baptiste (really *Baptiste Anet*), famous violinist about 1700, studied with Corelli, attracted notice at Paris, went afterwards to Poland, where he died as capellmeister. He wrote some violin sonatas, and sonatas for two *musettes.*

Bar (Ger. *Taktstrich,* Fr. *barre*) is the name of the perpendicular line crossing the stave, which marks off a metrical foot, but always so that it comes before the principal accent of the same, and in no manner marks its end. (*Cf.* METRE, ART OF.) However indispensable the B. may appear to us, it was not known in measured notation, at any rate not in the part-books for the singers, before the year 1600; for composers it was, if only as a small memorandum (for even after 1600 it is often met with running through only one line), naturally indispensable in writing out a score, and this is confirmed by the few early scores which have been preserved. On the other hand, it had been in use for a long period in organ and lute tablature.

Bar. (*See* STROPHE.)

Barbacola (*Barbarieu, Barberau*). (*See* BARBIREAU.)

Barbarini, M a n f r e d o L u p i, composer about the middle of the 16th century, detached motets of whom are to be found in collections under the simple name Lupi (q.v.), but this cipher was used by many other masters of that period.

Barbedette, H e n r i, b. about 1825, published pianoforte and ensemble works, but became known especially as a musical writer by his biographical works on Beethoven, Chopin, Weber, Schubert, Mendelssohn, and Stephen Heller. For many years B. has contributed biographical articles to the *Ménestrel.*

Barbereau, M a t h u r i n A u g u s t e B a l t h a s a r, b. Nov. 14, 1799, Paris, d. there, July 18, 1879; he was a pupil of Reicha at the Conservatoire, obtained in 1824 the Grand Prix de Rome, was for some time conductor at the Théâtre Français, was occupied for many years with historical studies, and lived as music teacher in Paris. He was appointed in 1872 professor of composition at the Conservatoire, but exchanged this post for that of professor of the history of music; as, however, he had no talent for speaking, he was soon compelled to give up the latter (E. Gautier became his successor). B. published "Traité théorique et pratique de composition musicale" (1845, incomplete), and "Études sur l'Origine du Système Musical" (1852, likewise unfinished).

Barbier, Frédéric Étienne, b. Nov. 15, 1829, Metz, d. Feb. 12, 1889, Paris; pupil of the organist Darondeau at Bourges, where in 1852 he had his first stage success (*Le Mariage de Columbine*). He made his *début* in 1855 at the Théâtre Lyrique, Paris, with *Une Nuit à Séville*, and since then has produced no less than thirty pieces (but written more than sixty), for the most part in one act; he has taken more and more to the style of *opéra bouffe*.

Barbieri, (1) Carlo Emanuele di, b. Oct. 22, 1822, Genoa, d. Sept. 28, 1867, Pesth. He was a pupil of Mercadante at Naples, maestro at various Italian theatres, then in 1845 at the "Kärntnerthor" Theatre, Vienna; in 1847 at the "Königsstadt" Theatre, Berlin; 1851, Hamburg; 1853, Rio Janeiro; lived in private from 1856 to 1862 in Vienna; and then, until his death, became capellmeister at the Pesth National Theatre. B. wrote a number of operas, among which, specially *Perdita, ein Wintermärchen* (1865), was performed at many German theatres.—(2) Francisco Asenio, b. Aug. 3, 1823, Madrid, in modest circumstances, d. Feb., 1894; studied at the Madrid Conservatorio the pianoforte, clarinet, singing, and composition; was at first clarinettist in a military corps, and in a small theatre orchestra, then went as leader of the chorus and *souffleur* in an Italian opera company to North Spain (Pamplona, Bilbao, etc.). One day he took the part of Basilio in the *Barbier* for a singer who was ill, and now became for some time an opera singer. On returning to Madrid in 1847, he was named secretary of the association for the establishment of a Zarzuela (operetta) Theatre, also musical critic to the *Illustracion*, and made a name as teacher of music, composing diligently all the time. In 1850 he produced his first one-act Zarzuela, *Gloria y peluca*, and, especially after the success of the three-act Zarzuela, *Jugar con fuego*, quickly became the hero of the day. B. was not only the most popular "Zarzuelero" in Madrid (during thirty years he wrote more than sixty Zarzuelas), but was member of several artistic societies, an excellent conductor, and a genuine musical *savant*. In 1859 he established the *Concerts spirituels* in the Zarzuela Theatre, which, meanwhile, had been built, arranged in 1866 regular concerts of classical music, from which the Madrid Concert Society was developed (in 1866 he gave fifty concerts); and in 1868 he was appointed professor of harmony and of the history of music at the Conservatorio, and in 1873 member of the Academy of Arts. Notwithstanding this many-sided activity, he also wrote a great number of orchestral works, hymns, motets, chansons, and articles for musical, political, and scientific papers.

Barbireau (*Barbiriau, Barberau, Barbarieu, Barbyrianus, Barbingant, Barbacola*), Jacques, was choir-master at Nôtre Dame, Antwerp, in 1448, and died there, Aug. 8, 1491. He was a highly esteemed contrapuntist, on friendly terms with Rudolf Agricola, and quoted by Tinctoris as an authority. The Vienna Library contains a few of his works in manuscript.

Barbitos (*Barbiton*), an old Greek stringed instrument, a favourite with Alcæus, Sappho, and Anacreon, as an accompaniment to their songs. Nothing, however, more is known of its construction, except that it had a greater number of strings than the cithara and lyre (harp?).

Barcarola or **Barcaruola** (Ital.; Ger. *Barcarolle*, Fr. *Barcarolle*), Italian boatman's song. Gondoletta.

Bards, the name given to the singers (poets) among the ancient Celts in England, Scotland, Ireland, and Wales, where they formed a caste specially favoured, highly honoured, and protected by laws. They soon disappeared from Wales and those parts of Britain which fell under the yoke of the Romans, for they were systematically persecuted by the latter as fosterers of patriotism. Bards existed in Ireland until the Battle of the Boyne (1690), and in Scotland until the abolishment of hereditary jurisdictions (1748). The Germans never had a special class of singers, but the Scandinavians had their Scalds (q.v.). The instrument with which the bards accompanied their songs was the chrotta (Irish cruit).

Bardi, Giovanni, Conte Vernio, a rich and intelligent Florentine nobleman at the end of the 16th century, who assembled in his house the most distinguished artists and scholars of Florence; and the first attempts at dramatic composition (opera), in imitation of ancient tragedy, appear to have been due to his personal influence. A madrigal à 5, of his, which has been preserved, testifies to his ability as a composer.

Bardit, *Bardiet*, a bard's song. The term was introduced into German poetry by Klopstock, and it arose from an incorrect reading of a passage in Tacitus (*barditus* instead of *baritus*); from this it was concluded that the Germans had bards. (*See* BARDS.)

Bardone, *Viola di B.*, is the same as Baryton, of which word it was probably only a corruption. The term *Viola di bordone*, which is also to be met with, refers to the plucked or sympathetically sounding strings below the finger-board. (*Cf.* BORDUN.)

Barem, the name of a specially soft-toned organ stop; as a rule an 8-ft. Gedackt stop.

Barge, Johann Heinrich Wilhelm, distinguished flautist, b. Nov. 23, 1836, Wulfsahl, near Dannenberg (Hanover). He was self-taught; and from his 17th to his 24th year flautist in a Hanoverian royal regiment, then principal flautist in the Court orchestra at Detmold, and since 1867 has occupied a similar position in the Gewandhaus orchestra at Leipzig. B. has published a "Flute Method," four sets of orchestral studies for flute (a collection of the most important passages from operas, symphonies, etc.), and arrangements ("Bearbeitungen") of many classical and modern compositions for flute and piano.

Bargheer, (1) K a r l L o u i s, violinist, b. Dec. 31, 1831, Bückeburg, where his father was member of the court band. He was trained (1848–50) under Spohr at Cassel, as a virtuoso player, and was then appointed to the Detmold court band. He made use of the liberal leave of absence granted for further study with David (Leipzig) and Joachim (then in Hanover). In 1863 he became court capellmeister at Detmold. In numerous concert tours he proved himself an excellent solo and *ensemble* performer. On the change of government in Detmold in 1876 the band was dissolved, and B. accepted the post of leader of the Philharmonic Society and that of teacher at the Hamburg Conservatorium, holding both until 1889. Since then he has been leader of the Neue Abonnement-Concerte under Hans von Bülow.—(2) Adolf, brother of the former, b. Oct. 21, 1840, Bückeburg, Spohr's last pupil (1857–58); received his final training from Joachim. Like his brother, he was for two years "Hofmusikus" at Detmold, then for five years leader at Munich, and afterwards leader and principal teacher at the Basle school of music. Died March 10, 1901.

Bargiel, W o l d e m a r, composer, b. Oct. 3, 1828, Berlin, d. Feb. 23, 1897. His father, who died in 1841, was the teacher of music A d o l f B.; his mother, Marianne, *née* Tromlitz, was Fr. Wieck's first wife. B. was therefore step-brother to Clara Schumann (q.v.). He first received training from his parents, and studied afterwards with Hauptmann, Moscheles, Rietz, and Gade, at the Leipzig Conservatorium. After giving private lessons for some time in Berlin, he became teacher at the Cologne Conservatorium, in 1865 director of the institution of the "Maatschappij tot bevordering van toonkunst" at Amsterdam, in 1874 professor at the "Hochschule für Musik" at Berlin, in 1875 member of the senate of the Academy of Arts in that city, and afterwards one of the heads of the "Meisterschule für Musikalische Composition" in connection with the Academy of Arts. B. was a distinguished instrumental composer, and belonged to the school of Robert Schumann. Several overtures (*Prometheus*, *Medea*, *Zu einem Trauerspiel*), a symphony, sonatas, trios, quartets, an octet, suites, etc., display inventive power and skilled workmanship. B. also published some part-songs, and psalms for chorus and orchestra.

Baribasso (Ital.), a deep bass voice.

Baritenore (Ital.), a low tenor voice.

Barker, C h a r l e s S p a c k m a n n, b. Oct. 10, 1806, Bath, d. Nov. 26, 1879, Maidstone. A famous organ-builder in London. He went to Paris in 1837, and took direction of the business of Daublaine and Callinet. In 1860 he set up a factory of his own under the style of Barker & Verschneider. In 1845 he built an organ for St. Eustache, and also repaired that of the church of St. Sulpice. He returned to England in 1870. He was the inventor of the pneumatic lever (q.v.), and of electric action, which effected a complete revolution in the art of organ playing.

Bärmann, (1) H e i n r i c h J o s e p h, famous clarinet player, b. Feb. 17, 1784, Potsdam, d. June 11, 1847, Munich; was oboe player in a Berlin regiment of the guards, and afterwards "Hofmusikus" at Munich. B. was on friendly terms with Weber (who dedicated three concertos to him), Meyerbeer, and Mendelssohn (who wrote his Op. 113 for him); and on his concert tours his success as a performer on the clarinet was unprecedented. His compositions for clarinet are now held by performers in high esteem.—(2) K a r l, son of the former, b. 1820, Munich, d. there May 24, 1885; accompanied his father on his later concert tours, and also gained great fame as a clarinet player. After his father's death he took his place as first clarinet player in the court band. Besides various compositions for clarinet, he has established a lasting memorial to himself by his "Clarinet Method."

Barnby, J o s e p h, b. Aug. 12, 1838, York, d. Jan. 28, 1896, London; pupil of the Royal Academy of Music, conductor of the Royal Albert Hall Choral Society. In 1875 he was appointed director of musical instruction at Eton College. He became conductor of the Musical Society on its formation. In 1886 he succeeded Mr. Shakespeare as conductor at the Royal Academy of Music. His psalm, *The Lord is King*, was produced with success at the Leeds Festival of 1883. In 1884 he gave two concert performances of Wagner's *Parsifal* at the Albert Hall. In 1892 B. was appointed Principal of the Guildhall School of Music, as successor to Mr. Weist Hill, founder of that institution; and in the same year he received the order of knighthood.

Barnett, (1) J o h n, b. July 1, 1802, Bedford, d. April 17th, 1890, Cheltenham. He was the son of a German jeweller who emigrated to England, and whose real name was B e r n h a r d B e e r. At an early age B. received a thorough musical training, and came forward before the footlights of the Lyceum Theatre with his operetta, *Before Breakfast*, in 1825. He soon became a prolific composer for the stage, and, after writing a number of small pieces, which were produced partly at the Lyceum, partly at the Olympic and Drury Lane theatres, he made his first serious attempt with *The Mountain Sylph* in 1834 ; *Fair Rosamund* followed in 1837, and *Farinelli* in 1838. In 1841 B. settled at Cheltenham as teacher of singing. The number of detached songs which he wrote is said to number about 4,000. He wrote three operas which have never been produced.—(2) J o h n F r a n c i s, nephew of the former, b. Oct. 16, 1837, London; a gifted composer and good pianist, free scholar at the Academy. He played already, in 1853, Mendelssohn's Concerto in D minor under Spohr's direction, at the New Philharmonic. From 1857 to 1860 he was pupil at the Leipzig Conservatorium, and made an appearance at the Gewandhaus in 1860. The following of his compositions deserve mention :—a symphony, symphonic overture, overture to the *Winter's Tale*, stringed quartets and quintets, pf. trios, a pf. sonata, impromptus, an oratorio (*The Raising of Lazarus*), two cantatas for the Birmingham Festivals (*The Ancient Mariner* and *Paradise and the Peri*), and a *Tantum Ergo* à 8. For the Liverpool Festival of 1874 he wrote an orchestral piece, *The Lay of the Last Minstrel*, for the Brighton Festival of 1876 the cantata *The Good Shepherd*, for the Leeds Festival of 1880 *The Building of the Ship*, and for Norwich in 1881 *The Harvest Festival*. Also a scena for contralto, "The Golden Gate," a flute concerto, flute sonata, etc.

Baron, E r n s t G o t t l i e b, famous lutenist and historiographer of the lute, b. Feb. 27, 1696, Breslau, d. April 20, 1760, Berlin. He was appointed court lutenist at Gotha in 1727, and in 1734 theorbist to the Prussian Crown Prince, who afterwards became King Frederick II. His principal work was "Historisch-theoretische und praktische Untersuchung des Instruments der Laute, etc." (1727). He added an appendix on the lute to Marpurg's "Historisch-kritische Beiträge" (2nd vol.), and this was followed by "Abhandlung von dem Notensystem der Laute und der Theorbe." Of less value are the following works : "Abriss einer Abhandlung von der Melodie," "Zufällige Gedanken über verschiedene Materien," "Versuch über das Schöne," and "Von dem uralten Adel und dem Nutzen der Musik."

Baroxyton (Gr. literally "something which sounds low and high"), a brass wind instrument constructed in 1853 by Cerveny at Königgrätz : it is of wide measure, with the respectable compass of contra D to once-accented *a* (, D to *a'*).

Barre de mesure (Fr.), a bar-line.

Barre de répétition (Fr.), a double bar with dots, indicating a repeat.

Barré, (1) L é o n a r d, contrapuntist of the 16th century (also named *Barra*), b. Limoges, studied with Willaert, appointed Papal chapel singer in 1537. He was a member of the special musical commission sent by the Pope to the Council of Trent (1545). Some of his

madrigals and motets have been preserved.— (2) A n t o i n e, a contemporary, and perhaps a relation of the former. He was a composer of madrigals, and proprietor of a printing-press at Rome from 1555 to 1570. He afterwards went to Milan.

Barré (Fr.), in guitar playing the placing of the forefinger of the left hand on several strings. The placing of the forefinger on more than three strings is called *grand barré*.

Barrel organ (Ger. *Drehorgel*), a small portable organ with covered pipes, or even reeds, which, by means of a handle, is not only provided with wind, but also made to play. The handle turns a roller set with pins (or, more recently, plates perforated with holes) which open the valves to the pipes. The B. O. is often provided with a tremolo, which causes the tone to be intermittent. The B. O. is the instrument most in vogue amongst itinerant beggars, and has almost entirely superseded the older hurdy-gurdy.

Barret, A p o l l o n M a r i e R o s e, distinguished oboe player, French by birth, b. 1804, d. March 8, 1879, London. He studied under Vogt at the Paris Conservatoire, was a member of the orchestras of the Odéon Theatre and of the Opéra Comique, and of the Italian Opera, London, up to 1874. He was the author of an excellent "Complete Method for the Oboe," to which a set of sonatas and studies for that instrument is appended.

Barrett, (1) J o h n, music master at Christ's Hospital, and organist at St. Mary-at-Hill, London, about 1710. He composed songs once very popular in England, one of which Gay put into his *Beggar's Opera*, and also overtures and entr'actes.—(2) W i l l i a m A l e x a n d e r, b. Oct. 15, 1836, Hackney, English writer on music, chorister at St. Paul's, London ; 1870, Mus.Bac. (Oxford). He published, with Dr. Stainer, a "Dictionary of Musical Terms" (1875), and wrote monographs on the English glee and madrigal composers, on English Church composers, and on Balfe ; he was musical critic of the *Morning Post*, and formerly edited the *Monthly Musical Record*, also the *Musical Times*. He died suddenly Oct., 1891.

Barrington, D a i n e s, b. 1727, London, d. there March 11, 1800. He was recorder of Bristol, afterwards judge in Wales. He was the author of many small musical essays, and also of a letter on Mozart's appearance in London (1764), and a description of the two old Welsh instruments, the Crewth (*see* CHROTTA) and Pib-corn (Horn-pipe).

Barry, C h a r l e s A i n s l i e, b. June 10, 1830, pupil of Walmisley, afterwards at the Conservatorium of Leipzig and that of Dresden ; from 1875-9 he was editor of the *Monthly Musical Record*, in 1886 Secretary of the Liszt Scholarship. He is an advanced musical writer, also composer ("Festival March," songs, pf. pieces).

Barsanti, Francesco, b. about 1690, Lucca; came in 1714 with Geminiani to England and entered the orchestra of the Italian Opera as flautist, but afterwards took up the oboe. For a long time he held a lucrative post in Scotland, but returned again in 1750 to London, and was engaged as viola-player at the opera and at Vauxhall. B. published a collection of old Scotch songs with bass, twelve violin concertos, six flute solos with bass, six sonatas for two violins with bass, and six antiphons in the "Palestrina" style.

Barsotti, Tommaso Gasparo Fortunato, b. Sept. 4, 1786, Florence, d. April, 1868, Marseilles; founded in 1821, at Marseilles, a free (!) school of music, of which he was director until 1852. His published works are pf. variations, a "Salvum fac Regem," and a "Méthode de Musique" for the free school of music (1828).

Bartay, (1) **Andreas,** b. 1798, Széplak (Hungary), d. Oct. 4, 1856, Mayence. In 1838 he was director of the Hungarian National Theatre; in 1848 he gave concerts in Paris, and afterwards lived at Hamburg. He composed Hungarian operas (*Aurelia, Csel, Die Ungarn in Neapel*), an oratorio, *Die Erstürmung Ofens,* masses, ballets, etc. His son (2) **Ede,** b. Oct. 6, 1825, is director of the National Music Academy at Pesth, founder of the Hungarian "Musiker-Pensions-Anstalt," and likewise a composer (overture *Pericles*).

Barth, (1) **Christian Samuel,** celebrated oboe-player and composer for his instrument, b. 1735, Glauchau (Saxony), d. July 8, 1809, Copenhagen. He was a pupil of J. S. Bach at St. Thomas' School, and was oboist successively in the bands at Rudolstadt, Weimar, Hanover, Cassel, and Copenhagen.—(2) F. **Philipp C. A.,** son of the former and his successor as oboist in the court band at Copenhagen, b. about 1773, Cassel; published collections of Danish and German songs, also a flute concerto, and left behind oboe concertos in manuscript.—(3) **Joseph Joh. Aug.,** b. Dec. 29, 1781, Grosslippen (Bohemia), was in Vienna from about 1810 to 1830, a highly-esteemed concert singer (tenor) and member of the royal band.—(4) **Gustav,** b. Sept. 2, 1811, Vienna, son of the former, pianist and composer of vocal works ; from 1848, and for a long time, conductor of the Vienna Male Vocal Union, and now living in private at Frankfort. He married the celebrated singer Wilhelmine Hasselt.—(5) **Karl Heinrich,** b. July 12, 1847, Pillau, near Königsberg, the son of a teacher ; received his first musical training from his father, 1856–62 from L. Steinman in Potsdam, and after that was a pupil of Bülow at Berlin (1862–64), of Bronsart, and, for a short time, of Tausig. In 1868 he became teacher at the Stern Conservatorium, and in 1871 at the Royal High School, Berlin. B. is an excellent pianist, and, besides, an ensemble player of the first rank : he has made several successful concert tours in Germany and England, some of them with Joseph and Amalie Joachim. The trio party B., de Ahna, Hausmann, enjoyed a high reputation.

Barthel, Johann Christian, b. April 19, 1776, Plauen, d. June 10, 1831; musical director at Greiz, later on court organist at Altenburg (successor of Krebs) ; he wrote a large number of sacred works (104 psalms, Easter cantata), organ pieces, etc. ; but only a few dances for pianoforte were printed.

Barthélémon, François Hippolyte, b. July 27, 1741, Bordeaux; d. July 20, 1808, Dublin ; great violin player, who came to England in 1764, was engaged as leader of the opera band, and had great success in London as an opera composer, *Pelopida* (1766), *Le Fleuve Scamandre* (in French, Paris, 1768), *The Judgment of Paris, The Enchanted Girdle, The Maid of the Oaks, The Election, Belphegor* (1778). In 1770 he became leader at Vauxhall. After long tours in Germany, Italy, and France, he accepted a post in Dublin in 1784. B. also wrote an oratorio, *Jefte* (1776), and published a great number of instrumental works (for violin, organ, and pianoforte). One of his violin sonatas (Op. 10, No. 2), is published in G. Jensen's "Classische Violinmusik berühmter Meister."

Bartöli, (1) Pater **Erasmo,** b. 1606, Gaeta; lived, under the name of Pater Raimo, at Naples, entered, finally, the order of the Oratorians, and died of the plague on July 14, 1656. His compositions (in manuscript) are preserved in the Oratorian Library (masses, psalms, motets, etc.).—(2) **Danielo,** b. 1608, Ferrara, d. Jan. 13, 1685, Rome ; a learned Jesuit, author of a work on acoustics, " Del Suono, de' Tremori, Armonici e dell' Udito " (1681).

Bartholomew, William, b. 1793, d. 1867; a violin-player and excellent flower-painter. He translated into English, or adapted, the texts of most of Mendelssohn's vocal works. In 1853 he married Miss Mounsey, for whom Mendelssohn wrote " Hear my Prayer : " she died June 24, 1891.

Baryton (Ital. *Baritono*), (1) the finest of all the kinds of male voices, combining the dignity and strength of the bass with the brilliancy of the tenor voice, and thus a medium between the two ; and, according as it extends upwards or downwards, is called a tenor-baryton or a bass-baryton. The tenor-baryton can with difficulty, if at all, be distinguished from the dramatic tenor (Heldentenor), for very many dramatic tenors are nothing more than tenor-barytons with the upper register specially cultivated. The term B. really means "deep-toned," and is evidently selected as antithesis to the higher tenor. It is named *basse-taille* by the French, *i.e.* low-tenor, and to this name it fully answers ; or *Concordant* (agreeing with), probably because in position it agrees about as much with the bass as with the tenor ($A—f'\sharp$.

or *G—g'*). Of late, opera composers willingly write principal parts for B., but this is not in the slightest degree the result of the scarcity of good and well-trained tenors.—(2) A *stringed instrument*, now obsolete, but one which in the last century enjoyed great popularity (Ital. *Viola di Bordone* or *Bardone*). It was of the size of the 'cello (likewise of the gamba), and was constructed like the bass instrument called the *Viola d'amour*, in so far as it had seven strings, under which, however (under the finger-board), there lay a number of wire strings (nine to twenty-four), which sounded sympathetically when the instrument was played upon, or were even pinched with the thumb of the left hand. The tuning of the upper strings was as follows : Contra *B*, *E*, *A*, *d*, *g*, *b*, *e'*. Prince Nikolaus Esterhazy, Haydn's patron, was a great amateur player on this instrument, and Haydn, therefore, wrote a great number (175) of pieces for the same (125 divertimenti for B., tenor, and 'cello, six duets for two barytons, twelve sonatas for B. and 'cello, seventeen cassations, etc.). The greater number of these were destroyed by a fire, and not one has been printed. Several other contemporary composers also wrote for the B. (F. Päer, Weigl, Eybler, Pichel, etc.). The instrument was constructed already in the 17th century, for instance, by A. Stainer (1660).— (3) A *brass wind instrument* (*Baryton Horn*) of the family of the bugle-horn, or bass tuba (wide measure). (*Cf.* BUGLE.) It is also called euphonium.—(4) In combination with the names of instruments, B. refers to the compass of the same ; for example, Baryton Horn (*see* above, 3) ; Baryton Clarinet (*see* CLARINET).

Baryton clef is the F clef on the middle line : it is now antiquated. (*Cf.* CHIAVETTE and TRANSPOSITION.)

Bas-dessus (Fr., "low soprano"), mezzo-soprano.

Basevi, Abramo, Italian writer on music, b. Dec. 29, 1818, Livorno, d. Nov., 1885, Florence. He practised first of all as a physician at Florence, but turned to music. His first attempts as an opera composer (*Romilda ed Ezzelino*, 1840 ; *Enrico Howard*, 1847) met with no success. He founded a music paper, *Armonia*, which became extinct in 1859 ; but in that year he established the Beethoven-Matinées, which afterwards developed into the *Società del quartetto*. He also offered a yearly prize for the composition of a stringed quartet. B. was a diligent contributor to the musical paper *Boccherini*, and wrote besides, "Studio sulle opere di G. Verdi" (1859), "Introduzione ad un Nuovo Sistema della Musica" (1862), and "Compendio della Storia della Musica" (1866). Finally he was engaged in philosophical studies.

Basili, Francesco, b. Feb., 1766, Loreto, d. March 25, 1850, Rome. He studied under the Papal maestro Jannaconi at Rome, and

first held small posts as conductor at Foligno, Macerata, and Loreto, while a series of (14) operas of his were given at Milan, Rome, Florence, and Venice. In 1827 he was appointed censor at the Royal Conservatorio, Milan, and finally, in 1837, was called to Rome as maestro of St. Peter's. B. wrote a number of sacred compositions (masses, offertories, magnificats, motets, etc.), also a requiem for Jannaconi's obsequies, and an oratorio, *Samson* (1824).

Basil, St., the Great, b. 329, Cæsarea (Cappadocia), d. there as bishop in 379. He is said to have won great merit in the matter of Church song, and to have introduced antiphons which, according to contemporary writers, Ambrosius had learnt from him and carried to Milan.

Basis (Gr. foundation), an obsolete term for the bass part, especially in the hellenizing of the 16th century, in place of *Bassus*.

Bass (Ital. *Basso*, Fr. *Basse*), (1) The deepest of male voices. A distinction is made between the low (second) B., and the high (first) B. (Bass-baryton, *see* BARYTON.) The compass of the bass is, as a rule, *F—f'* ; the deep bass extends somewhat further downwards, in certain cases to contra B♭ and further, the high bass not so far (to great A) ; while in the other direction the limit in both differs, at most, by 1 to 1½ tones (the low extends to *e'*♭, the high to *f'*♯). With regard to *timbre*, there is the *Basso profondo*, of which the tone is full and powerful, and *Basso buffo*, of a shouting, less noble character, and for which volubility of tongue is essential.—(2) The *instruments* which take the lowest part in instrumental music are called *basses*. In Germany, by B. is, for the most part, understood merely *double bass* (q.v.), but formerly the *violoncello* (q.v.). *Bassi* (basses), on the other hand, includes both 'celli and double basses playing in octaves ; and by "*Harmonie*" *bass* is understood the lowest bass instrument of a wind band (bassoon, trombone, bass-tuba, helikon, etc.).— (3) The lowest part of a piece of music (*cf.* BASIS), which, as support, foundation of the harmonies, requires a particular mode of treatment. (*See* PARTS, PROGRESSION OF.) In the compositions of the great period of the imitative style (*see* NETHERLAND SCHOOL), in which there was no independent instrumental music, even a simple dance piece, a bass part in our sense of the term did not exist, even though certain considerations, which it was impossible to ignore, carried weight (progressions by fourth or fifth in cadences). The inventor of the bass part in a modern sense was *Viadana* (q.v.) ; his *Basso continuo* is a real supporting part. A real difference existed between *Basso continuo* (*General bass*) and *Fundamental bass* (Fr. *basse fondamentale*) ; the latter (also called *Ground bass*), an invention of Rameau's, is no real part, but one theoretically formed in the analysis of a piece

of music to show the succession of the fundamental tones of the harmonies. (*See* CLANG-
SUCCESSION.)—(4) In combination with names
of instruments (for example, bass clarinet, bass
trombone, bass trumpet, *Basse de Viole, Basse de
Cromorne*, etc.), B. indicates the nature of the
compass of the instrument (*cf.* the simple
names). In the organ the addition of B. shows
that the stop belongs to the *pedal* board, for
example, *Gemshorn-bass*, etc.

Bassa (Ital. "low, under- . . ."), when joined
to 8, 8ᵛᴬ (*ottava*), it indicates the *lower-* or *under-*
octave. (*Cf.* ABBREVIATIONS.)

Bassanello, an obsolete wood-wind instrument, related to the bassoon, with double reed
which was placed in a funnel-shaped mouthpiece. It had a bent neck (**S**), and was built in
three different sizes (Bass, Tenor, and Discant).
Bassanelli of 8 and 4 feet are reed stops to be
met with in old organs.

Bassani, (1) G i o v a n n i, teacher of music at
the College of St. Mark's Church, Venice,
about 1600. Two books, "Concerti Ecclesiastici" (1598 and 1599), and a book of canzonets
à 4 (1587) have been preserved.—(2) G i o v a n n i
B a t t i s t a, b. about 1657, Padua, d. 1716, Ferrara; maestro di cappella of Bologna Cathedral, lived at Ferrara from 1685. He was an
excellent violinist (teacher of Corelli), and a
prolific composer whose works were held in
high esteem. Sonatas (suites) for violin (Op. 1
and Op. 5), many solo songs, motets, psalms,
masses, etc., and six operas.—(3) G e r o n i m o,
b. Venice, pupil of Lotti, excellent singer and
teacher of singing; also composer of sacred
music (masses, motets, vespers) and operas
(*Bertoldo*, 1718; *Amor per forza*, 1721, both of
which were produced at Venice).

Bass Clarinet. (*See* CLARINET.)

Bass Clausel, the usual bass progression in a
full close (*clausula finalis*), *i.e.* a fifth downwards
or a fourth upwards, from dominant to tonic.

Bass Clef is the name of the F clef on the

fourth line . In former times both the

G and F clefs, like the C clef at the present
day, were placed on various lines—

Baritone clef.   Deep bass clef.

(*Cf.* F and CLEF.)

Basse (Fr., *see* BASS).

Basse chantante (Fr.), the high bass voice,
or a singer who has such a voice. The more
flexible "singing bass" (*basso cantante*) as distinguished from the "deep bass" (*basso profondo*).

Basse chiffrée (Fr.), figured bass (q.v.).

Basse contrainte (Fr.), same as BASSO OSTI-
NATO. (*See* OSTINATO.)

Basse contre (Fr.), low bass voice, just as
Hautre-contre is the lowest of the high (female)
voices (Alto, Ital. *Contr'alto*).

Basse double (Fr.), double-bass.

Basse taille (Fr.), the name of the male voice
which lies between the *basse* (bass) and *taille*
(tenor)—namely, the barytone. The expression is also used synonymously with *basso cantante*.

Basset-Horn (Ital. *Corno di bassetto*, Fr. *Cor de
basset*), a wood-wind instrument lately gone out of
use, an alto clarinet in F, which has below four
semitones more than the clarinet (q.v.); its
compass is from F to (thrice accented) c‴ᵃ (written c—g‴). The B. H., on account of its considerable length, is curved or bent. The real
sound-tube is generally straight, but the mouthpiece is fixed on at a flat angle, and the small
brass bell at the end turned out in the opposite
direction. Mozart has employed two basset-
horns in his *Requiem*, and has also written *soli*
for the instrument in his *Titus*. Mendelssohn,
again, wrote two concert-pieces for clarinet and
B. H. The quality of tone, as in the bass
clarinet, especially in the lower register, is
sombre, but soft.

Bassett (*Bassettl*, also *Bassl*), old German
name for the violoncello. (*See* L. Mozart's "Violin
School," p. 3.) Joined with names of other
instruments, B. means that they have a middle
compass (tenor compass), for example, *Basset-
horn* (q.v.), Bassettpommer (*see* BOMHART), Bas-
sett-flute, etc. There is also an organ stop
of this name (B. 4-feet, a *pedal* flute-stop).

Bassevi. (*See* CERVETTO.)

Bassflöte (Ger.), a bass flute; the lowest
member of the old family of straight, or direct,
flutes (*Flûtes à bec*).

Bassgeige (Ger.), violoncello.—**Grosse Bassgeige,** double-bass.

Bass Horn, a wood wind-instrument allied to
the serpent, with cupped mouthpiece on an
S-tube, and with brass bell. It had a compass
of four octaves, from C to c‴ but it was of slow
speech, and had a dull tone. It was made at
the beginning of the century, but only remained
in vogue for a few decades.

Bassi, L u i g i, b. 1766, Pesaro, d. 1825, Dresden; distinguished baritone singer, was from
1784 to 1806 at Prague, and then, in consequence of the war, lived at Vienna without any
settled appointment. In 1814 he was again in
Prague (under Weber), and afterwards director
of the Dresden Opera. Mozart wrote the part
of *Don Juan* for B.

Bassiron, P h i l i p p e, a native of the Nether-
lands, composer of the 16th century, of whom
Petrucci has printed some masses in his
"Missæ diversorum" (1508).

Bass Lute, a large kind of lute (q.v.).

Basso (Ital.). (*See* BASS.)

Basso numerato (Ital.), a figured bass. (*See* GENERAL BASS.)

Bassoon (Ital. *Fagotto*, Fr. *Basson*), a symphonic orchestral wood wind-instrument of the present day, and successor to the *Bomhart*, common in the 16th century. The bulky dimensions of the larger kinds of the latter (*Basspommer* and *Doppelquintpommer*), which were over eight and ten feet long, suggested to Afranio degli Albonesi, canon of Ferrara in 1525, the idea of bending the tube and putting it together like a bundle (*fagotto*). The construction of the first bassoons was so imperfect, that the *Bomhart* remained in vogue for over a century. On account of its much softer tone, the B. was called for a long time *Dolcian* (Dulcian). The B. belongs to the double-reed instruments (like the oboe and English horn). The reed is inserted and fixed in the S-shaped neck of the instrument, whereas in the Schalmeys and Bomharts, the reed is free in the kettle-shaped mouthpiece, and is not touched by the player. In the oboe and bassoon there is no mouthpiece whatever, and the player takes the double reed directly between his lips, whereby he has full control over the tone. The B. is thus not merely a bent Bomhart with improved sound holes and key mechanism, but the invention which turned the Schalmey into an oboe must be assumed. Almenräder and Th. Böhm in this century have materially improved the mechanism of the B. The compass of the B. extends from (contra) B flat to (twice-accented) c″, and on the most modern instruments to e″ flat. Virtuoso players can even bring out the e″ and f″, but b″ flat is the usual limit for orchestral use. A soft reed is better for the production of the lower notes, a hard one for the higher; in orchestral music the composer must, therefore, carefully distinguish between the 1st and the 2nd B. The *Double Bassoon* is an octave lower in pitch than the B.; the *Quint-fagott* (Tenor Bassoon), now completely out of use, a 5th higher (lowest note F). There is a scarcity of good methods for the B. (Ozi, "Nouvelle Méthode, etc.," 1787 and 1800, also in a modern German edition; Cugnier, Blasius, Fröhlich, Küffner); as a rule, the help of fingering tables (Almenräder) is sought for, and the rest left to practice.

Basso ostinato, also **basso obbligato** (Ital.). (*See* OSTINATO.)

Basso profondo (Ital.), a deep bass. (*v.* Basso cantante.)

Basso ripieno (Ital.), Lit., "the filling up bass"—namely, the bass played by all the performers in contradistinction to that played only by one or a few. (*v.* Ripieno.)

Basspommer. (*See* BOMHART and BASSOON.)

Bass Trombone. (*See* TROMBONE.)

Bass Tuba. (*See* BUGLE HORN, *Cf.* TUBA.)

Bastardella. (*See* AGUJARI.)

Bastiaans, J. G., b. 1812, Wilp (Geldres), d. Feb. 16, 1875, Haarlem; pupil of F. Schneider in Dessau, and of Mendelssohn in Leipzig; he settled at Amsterdam, where he became organist of the "Zuiderkerk," and teacher of the organ at the Institute for the Blind. In 1868 he was appointed organist of the famous great organ of St. Bavo, Haarlem, and was highly esteemed as player and teacher. B. published some songs, and a "Choralbuch." He was succeeded by his son, Johann B., b. 1854, d. Dec. 7, 1885, Haarlem.

Baston, Josquin, Netherland composer, b. about 1556; his chansons and motets are to be found in several collections printed at Antwerp, Louvain, and Augsburg (1542–61).

Bates, (1) Joah, a well-known and excellent musical amateur, b. March 19, 1741, Halifax, d. June 8, 1799, as director of Greenwich Hospital. He composed the opera *Pharnacis*, operettas, pf. sonatas, etc. In 1776, together with other "amateurs," he established the Concerts of Ancient Music, which must not be confounded with the *Academy of Ancient Music* established by Pepusch, which only lasted until 1792. He was also the instigator of the great musical festivals given in memory of Handel (1784, 1785, 1786, 1787, and 1791), of which he was also the conductor.—(2) William, English composer, b. at the beginning of the 18th century, date of death unknown. He wrote glees, songs, catches, and canons, etc.

Bateson, Thomas, organist at Chester from 1599, and later on "Vicar and Organist" of Christ Church, Dublin. He was probably the first person who took a musical degree at Dublin University. Two books of his madrigals have been preserved.

Bathyphon (Gr., "deep-sounding") was the name of a wood wind-instrument constructed in 1829 by Skorra of Berlin. It extended from (contra) D to (small) b♭. It appears to have been somewhat similar to the Serpent and Basshorn, but it was only used for a time in military bands.

Batiste, Antoine Edouard, b. March 28, 1820, Paris, d. there, Nov. 9, 1876; a distinguished organist, professor at the Paris Conservatoire (choral singing, harmony, and accompaniment). He was organist of St. Nicholas-aux-Champs, and afterwards of St. Eustache. He composed some organ pieces of value, published a "Petit Solfège Harmonique," and the official "Solfèges du Conservatoire."

Batistin. (*See* STRUCK.)

Bâton (Fr.), Rest stroke

etc. Rests of more than two or three bars are now indicated only by figures. (*Cf.* REST.)— (2) B. de mesure, conducting-stick.

Baton, Henri, performer on the musette, while his brother Charles (B. Le Jeune) played on the vielle, or hurdy-gurdy. The latter wrote compositions for vielle and musette, and published a "Mémoire sur la Vielle in D la re" in the *Mercure*, 1757.

Batta, (1) Pierre, b. Aug. 8, 1795, Maastricht, d. Nov. 20, 1876, Brussels, at the Conservatoire, and was professor of the violoncello in that city. His sons were:—(2) Alexandre, b. July 9, 1816, Maastricht, studied first with his father, then with Platel at the Brussels Conservatoire, had his name coupled with that of Demunck for the first 'cello prize in 1834, and after that his merits were acknowledged abroad, and especially at Paris, where he settled down. His playing, calculated for effect, lacks the higher inspiration. He has published romances for 'cello, fantasies, variations, etc.— (3) Jean Laurent, b. Dec. 30, 1817, Maastricht, an excellent pianist; he lived in Paris, afterwards (1848) as teacher of music at Nancy, where he died, Dec. 1879.—(4) Joseph, b. April 24, 1820, Maastricht, a violinist and composer; he received in 1845 the grand prize for composition at Brussels, and since 1846 has been in the orchestra of the Opéra Comique, Paris.

Battaille, Charles Amable, a distinguished bass singer, b. Sept. 30, 1822, Nantes, d. May 2, 1872. He was originally a physician, and from 1848 to 1857 at the Paris Opéra Comique, after which he was obliged to retire from the stage owing to a throat complaint. He only appeared exceptionally at the Théâtre Lyrique and at the Opéra Comique in 1860. From 1851 he was professor of singing at the Conservatoire. He published a great Method of singing, the first part of which contains elaborate physiological investigations.

Battanchon, Félix, b. April 9, 1814, Paris, a distinguished 'cellist and a noteworthy composer for his instrument. He studied with Vaslin and Norblin at the Paris Conservatoire, and from 1840 belonged to the orchestra of the Grand Opéra. From 1846 to 1847 B. tried to make known a kind of smaller 'cello, which he named Baryton, but the interest which it excited was only short-lived. Died July, 1893, Paris.

Battement (Fr.), an ornament, which, strange to say, has become obsolete, viz., the trill with the under-second (commencing with the latter). There was never any special sign for the B.; it was always indicated by small notes:

Played

The B. takes up the whole of notes of small value. There is no reason, indeed, why this ornament, of equal rank with the upper-second

trill, should be allowed to fall into complete oblivion.

Batten, Adrian, appointed vicar-choral of Westminster Abbey in 1614, and from 1624 held the same office, together with that of organist of St. Paul's. He composed some excellent anthems, which are still sung, also a Morning, Communion, and Evening Service, etc. Some of his music is printed in the English collections of Barnard, Boyce. He died, probably, in 1637.

Batterie, a French term to be recommended for general use for figuration of all kinds, when chords are broken up thus:—

According to Rousseau ("Dict. de Mus."), B. is distinguished from *Arpeggio* in that the former is not played *legato*, but *staccáto*.

Battishill, Jonathan, b. May, 1738, London, d. Dec. 10, 1801. He was cembalist at Covent Garden, for which theatre he wrote several operas, the first of which was *Almena* (in conjunction with Arne, 1764). Later on he gave himself up to sacred composition, and devoted the last years of his life to the collecting together of a valuable musical library. Some of his glees, anthems, and fugues are to be found in the collections of Warren and Page; six anthems and ten chants appeared separately in 1804.

Battista, Vincenzo, b. Oct. 5, 1823, Naples, d. there Nov. 14, 1873. He studied at the Naples Conservatorio, and produced eleven operas on various Italian stages with good success for the time, but was quite forgotten before his death.

Battmann, Jacques Louis, b. Aug. 25, 1818, Maasmünster (Alsace), d. July 7, 1886, Dijon. In 1840 he was organist at Belfort, later on at Vesoul. He published many compositions for pianoforte and organ (among which études), a method for pianoforte, a treatise on harmony (for the accompaniment of Gregorian Song), a method for harmonium and many compositions for that instrument; also masses, motets, choral works, etc.

Batton, Désiré Alexandre, b. Jan. 2, 1797, Paris, d. Oct. 15, 1855. He studied at the Conservatoire under Cherubini, and received the Prix de Rome in 1816. He wrote five operas, which met with small success; also in 1831 (jointly with Auber, Carafa, Hérold, Berton, and others) he wrote the *Marquise de Brinvilliers*. After carrying on his father's business (artificial flowers) for a long while, he was appointed inspector of the branch establishments of the Conservatoire in 1842, and, besides, teacher of an *ensemble* class in 1849.

Battu, Pantaléon, b. 1799, Paris, d. Jan. 17, 1870. He studied with R. Kreutzer, was a member of the opera orchestra and the royal band until 1830, and from 1846 second conductor at the opera. He published two violin concertos, some violin romances, variations, and three *duos concertants*.

Battuta (Ital., from *battere*, to beat), time-beat; *a batt.* ("in time"). A prescription for the instruments accompanying a vocal part (in contradistinction to *colla parte*, which means that the instruments are to follow the singer); also an indication for the singer that the passage is to be taken in strict time. The so-called *Arioso*, or *Accompagnato* (q.v.), which sometimes occurs in a recitative, is therefore marked *a batt.* In a more restricted sense B. means *down-beat, i.e.* commencement of a bar; hence *ritmo di tre* or *di quattro battute, i.e.* rhythm of a set of three or of four bars connected with one another (bars forming one bar of higher order. (*Cf.* METRE, ART OF.) In counterpoint B. means a progression forbidden by the old contrapuntists, viz., the passing of the extreme parts from the tenth to the octave on a strong beat, for example :—

Already, about 1725, J. Fux gave up the strict observance of this prohibition.

Baudiot, Charles Nicolas, performer on the 'cello, b. March 29, 1773, Nancy, d. Sept. 26, 1849, Paris. He studied with Janson, and in 1802 became his successor as professor of his instrument at the Paris Conservatoire; and in 1816 first 'cellist in the royal band. He received a pension in 1832. He published many compositions for the 'cello, and, jointly with Levasseur and Baillot, the Méthode for 'cello adopted at the Conservatoire; also, alone, a " Méthode complète de Violoncelle" (Op. 25) and a Guide to composers, showing how they may write and how they ought to write for the 'cello.

Baudoin (Baudouyn). (*See* BAULDEWIJN.)

Bauer, Chrysostomus, Würtemberg organ-builder at the commencement of last century. He introduced the large bellows now used in organs, in place of the former many small ones.

Bauernflöte (Bauernpfeife, Bäuerlein, Feld-flöte; Lat. *Tibia rurestris*), a by no means rare " Gedakt " pedal stop of wide measure in old organs. If of two feet it is generally called B., if of one foot, *Bauernpfeife* (one-foot stops were for the most part called " Pfeifen," *i.e.* pipes).

Bauldewijn (Baldewin, Balduin, Baulduin, Baudoin, Baudouyn), Noël (Natalis), maître de chapelle at Nôtre Dame, Antwerp, from 1513 to 1518; he died there in 1529. Motets of his are to be found in various collections (for example, in Petrucci's " Motetti della Corona "); masses in manuscript at Rome and Munich

(Missa " Mijn Liefkens Bruijn Oghen" and a " Da pacem," formerly attributed to Josquin).

Baumann. (*See* PAUMANN.)

Baumbach, Friedrich August, b. 1753, d. Nov. 30, 1813, Leipzig. He was capellmeister at the Hamburg Opera, 1778–89, and after that lived in Leipzig, devoting himself exclusively to composition. Besides many instrumental and vocal works (for pianoforte, violin, guitar, etc.), he wrote the musical articles in the ' Kurz gefasstes Handwörterbuch über die schönen Künste," which appeared in 1794.

Baumfelder, Friedrich, composer of *salon* music, b. May 28, 1836, Dresden. He studied under Joh. Schneider and at the Leipzig Conservatorium (1851). Besides many brilliant drawing-room pieces, B. wrote études (especially *Tirocinium musicæ*, Op. 300), a pianoforte sonata (Op. 60), and a suite (Op. 101).

Baumgart, E. Friedrich, b. Jan. 13, 1817, Grossglogau, d. Sept. 15, 1871, Warmbrunn. He was *Dr. phil.*, director of the music at the University and teacher at the Royal Institute for church music, Breslau; a distinguished amateur, known in wider circles by his edition of the Clavier Sonatas of Ph. Em. Bach.

Baumgarten, (1) Gotthilf von, b. Jan. 12, 1741, Berlin, d. 1813 as " Landrath " at Gross-strelitz (Silesia). He composed operas which were performed (*Zémire und Azor, Andromeda, Das Grab des Mufti*, the last of which was published in pianoforte score, 1778).—(2) Karl Friedrich, b. in Germany, came as a young man to London, and was for many years leader at the Opera, Covent Garden (1780–1794). His operas, *Robin Hood* and *Blue Beard*, were repeatedly performed there.

Baumgartner, August, b. Nov. 9, 1814, Munich, d. there Sept. 29, 1862; since 1853 Regens chori of St. Anna, at Munich. He published in the *Stenographische Zeitschrift* (1852) suggestions for musical short-hand writing, and a " Kurz gefasste Anleitung zur musikalischen Stenographie oder Tonzeichenkunst " (1853). He also published a " Kurz gefasste Geschichte der musikalischen Notation " (1856).

Bäumker, Wilhelm, b. Oct. 25, 1842, Elberfeld, studied theology and philology at Münster and Bonn, took holy orders in 1867; he has been chaplain since 1869, and school inspector since 1880 at Niederkrüchten. In his leisure hours B. is a zealous writer on music. In 1889 the University of Breslau rewarded him with the title of *Dr. theol. hon. c.* for his researches into the history of music. He wrote: " Palästrina, ein Beitrag," etc. (1877), " Orlandus de Lassus ein historisches Bildnis" (1878), " Zur Geschichte der Tonkunst in Deutschland " (1881), " Der Todtentanz," a study (1881), " Das katholische deutsche Kirchenlied in seinen Singweisen von den frühesten Zeiten bis gegen Ende des 17 Jahrh." (1883–1891), continuation (vols. 2-3) of the work commenced (vol. 1, 1862) by K. S. Meister ; he also brought out a complete revision of the first volume in 1886 ; and besides, in 1888, " Niederländische geistliche Lieder nebst ihre Singweisen aus Handschriften des 15 Jahrh." B. contributes articles to the *Allg. Deutsche Biographie, Monatshefte für Musikgeschichte*, etc.

Bausch, Ludwig Christian August, b. Jan. 15, 1805, Naumburg, d. May 26, 1871, Leipzig ; an instrument - maker in Dresden (1826), Dessau (1828), Leipzig (1839), Wiesbaden (1862), and from 1863 again in Leipzig. He became specially famous as a maker of violin bows and restorer of old violins. During his last years he worked together with his son, Ludwig, b. 1829, who, after a long residence in New York, set up business on his own account in Leipzig, and died shortly before his father (April 7, 1871). His brother Otto, who inherited the business, was born in 1841, and died already, Dec. 30, 1874. The business then passed into the hands of A. Paulus, in Markneukirchen.

Baxoncello, (Span.), Open Diapason (organ stop). *B. de* 13 = Open Diapason 8 feet, *B. de* 26 = Open Diapason 16 feet. But, on the other hand, Open D. 32 feet = *Flauto de* 52, Open D. 4 feet = *Octava*, Open D. 2 feet = *Quincena*, Open D. 1 foot = *Flauto en* 22 (triple octave).

Bazin, François Emanuel Joseph, b. Sept. 4, 1816, Marseilles, d. July, 1878, Paris. He studied at the Paris Conservatoire, received the *Prix de Rome* in 1840, was appointed professor of singing on his return from Italy in 1844, and later on professor of harmony ; in 1871 he became professor of composition, as successor to A. Thomas, who was advanced to the post of director ; and in 1872 he succeeded Carafa as member of the Académie. Of his nine operas, not one remained in the repertoire. He published a " Cours d'Harmonie théorique et pratique."

Bazuin (Dutch), trombone.

Bazzini, Antonio, an eminent violinist and composer, b. March 11, 1818, Brescia, where he studied under maestro Faustino Camisani ; in 1836 he played before Paganini, who advised him to travel. B., after many short journeys (1841-45), went to Germany—making an especially long stay in Leipzig, then at the zenith of its musical fame—and became an enthusiast of German art, and especially of Bach and Beethoven. After a stay of many years in Italy, he went in 1848 to Spain and France, and settled in Paris in 1852. In 1864 he returned to Brescia in order to devote himself entirely to composition, but in 1873 accepted a call to Milan Conservatorio as professor of composition, and in 1880 became director of that institution. As a composer, Bazzini occupies a special position among the Italians ; the freedom and grace of his melodies are thoroughly

Italian, but the careful workmanship and harmonic wealth betray the influence of Germany. Among his works his three quartets and quintet for strings stand highest, yet he made successful ventures in choral and in orchestral composition : *La Resurrezione di Christo*, the symphony-cantata *Senacheribbo*, the 51st and 5th Psalms, overtures to Alfieri's *Saul* and Shakespeare's *King Lear*, and a symphonic poem, *Francesca da Rimini*. On the other hand, he had no success with the opera *Turandot* (produced at La Scala, Milan, in 1867). Died Feb. 10, 1897.

Bazzino, (1) Francesco Maria, eminent theorbist, b. 1593, Lovero (Venetia), d. April 15, 1660, Bergamo. He wrote for the theorbo, but also *canzonette*, an oratorio, etc.—(2) Natale, d. 1639, published masses, motets, psalms, etc.

b b, double-flat. (*See* Chromatic Signs.)

Bearbeitung (Ger.), revision or adaptation.

Beards are small projections placed on both sides of the mouth, or directly under the same, or even on both places, in the lip-pipes of the organ, to promote better speech, especially in the case of pipes of narrow measure. A distinction is made between *side-beards* and *crossbeards*.

Bear-pipe (Ger. *Bärpfeife, Barpip, Bärpipe,* etc.). A reed-pipe stop in old organs, probably named after some instrument now obsolete. The tubes of peculiar construction were almost covered, and they gave out a somewhat growling tone. Prætorius describes the pipes as sounding inwardly (" Sie klingen in sich hinein ").

Beat, (1) a melodic ornament, by some described as a *mordent*, by others as a *battement*.—(2) The movement of the hand or foot in marking the time, and the corresponding division of the bar.

Beating Reeds. (*See* Reed and Reed-pipes.)

Beats (Ger. *Schwebungen, Schläge, Stösse ;* Fr. *Battements*) are those striking reinforcements of intensity at regular intervals which occur when two notes of slightly different pitch are sounded together. For instance, if 436 is the vibration number per second of the one note, and 438 that of the other, the difference per half-second amounts to one vibration, *i.e.*, the first of every 218 vibrations of the former note begins at the same moment as the first of every 217th of the other, or, otherwise expressed, at every 217th and 218th vibration, respectively, the maximum of intensity occurs (the greatest amplitude), producing striking reinforcements of sound (beats). If the number of beats per second reaches the figure which answers to the vibration number of the lowest clearly perceptible sound (about thirty per second), the beats pass from a grating to a low buzzing sound, and generate a *combination tone* (q.v.). The slower B., which can easily be counted (from two to four per second), offers valuable assistance in fixing the temperament of keyed instruments. (*See* Tuning, 3)

Bé, Guillaume le. (*See* Le Bé.)

Beauchamps, Pierre François Godard de, b. 1689, Paris, d. there 1761. He wrote a History of the French theatre since the year 1161 (1735), and "Bibliothèque des Théâtres" (description of dramas, operas, etc., which have been performed, with notices of composers, etc., 1746).

Beaulieu, Marie Désiré Martin, b. April 11, 1791, Paris, d. Dec. 1863, Niort; pupil of Méhul; won the Prix de Rome in 1810, but did not accept it. Soon afterwards he married and withdrew to Niort, where he founded a musical society, and devoted himself to study and to composition. In the course of years he stirred up musical life in other *départements* of the west, so that in 1835 a great central society, under the name "Association Musicale de l'Ouest," sprang into life, and established a grand musical festival every year in alternate towns. B. bequeathed 100,000 francs to this society. The Paris society for classical music was also created by B. The list of his compositions is a stately one, including operas, *Anacréon, Philadelphie;* lyrical scenes, "Jeanne d'Arc," "Psyché et l'Amour;" oratorios, masses, hymns, orchestral pieces, fantasias for violin, songs, etc. But besides these, B. published the following writings : "Du Rhythme, des effets qu'il produit et de leurs causes" (1852) ; "Mémoire sur ce qui reste de la musique de l'ancienne Grèce dans les premiers chants de l'Église"; "Mémoire sur le caractère que doit avoir la musique d'Église, etc." (1858) ; "Mémoire sur quelques airs nationaux qui sont dans la tonalité grégorienne" (1858) ; "Mémoire sur l'origine de la musique" (1859).

Beaumarchais, Pierre Augustin Carron de, b. Jan. 24, 1732, d. May 19, 1799, Paris ; famous French poet, whose two comedies, *The Barber of Seville* and *The Marriage of Figaro,* furnished the two libretti in each of which the genius of Mozart and of Rossini was most fully displayed.

Beauquier, Charles, French writer on music, b. about 1830. He published a "Philosophie de Musique" (1865), a book of doubtful value. B. was for a long period a contributor to the *Revue et Gazette Musicale;* he was also the poet of the libretto of Lalo's *Fiesque.* Since 1870 he has been an administrative officer.

Bebisation. (*See* Bobisation.)

Bebung (Fr. *Balancement*). This was a mode of playing on the clavichord, not possible on the pianoforte (the clavier of our day). It consisted of a light balancing of the finger on the key, which produced a soft rubbing of the tangent against the string. The B. was indicated by ⌣⌣⌣ above the note. Somewhat similar is the trembling of the tone on stringed instruments, also on the zither and the guitar, *i.e.,* a light vacillation of pitch produced by a quick trembling movement of the finger placed on the string. The tremolo of the voice (which singers prefer to call B. or *vibrato*) is a similar kind of effect. Excessive use of such mannerisms produces dulness, and renders the performance effeminate.

Bécarre (Fr.), the natural (♮, *B. quadratum*). (*See* B.)

Beccatelli, Giovanni, Francesco, a native of Florence, maestro at Prato, d. 1734. He wrote several short musical essays, some of which were printed in *Giornale de' letterati d'Italia* (33rd year and third Supplement) ; the rest remained in manuscript.

Becher, (1), Alfred Julius, b. April 27, 1803, Manchester, of German parents ; went as a child to Germany, was for a short time lawyer at Elberfeld, but devoted himself to musical studies and to composition ; was editor of a paper at Cologne, went next to Düsseldorf, the Hague, and finally to London, where he was appointed harmony teacher at the Academy in 1840. From there he moved to Vienna, where in 1848, on account of participation in the Revolution, he was condemned by martial law and shot. A great number of his pf. works and songs were printed, also the pamphlets "Das niederrheinische Musikfest, ästhetisch und historisch betrachtet" (1836), and "Jenny Lind, eine Skizze ihres Lebens" (1847).—(2) Joseph, b. Aug. 1, 1821, Neukirchen (Bavaria), first prefect of the normal school and precentor at Amberg, afterwards minister at Mintraching, near Ratisbon. He wrote a great number of sacred compositions (of masses alone more than sixty).

Bechstein, Fr. W. Karl, pianoforte maker, b. June 1, 1826, Gotha ; worked first in various German pianoforte factories, and from 1848–52 managed the business of G. Peran, at Berlin. He then travelled, for the purpose of study, to London and Paris, where he worked with Pape and Kriegelstein, and in 1856, with modest means, set up business on his own account in Berlin. Within a short space of time the house took such a favourable turn that the greatest pianists began to show an interest in Bechstein's manufactory. His three large factories in Berlin, with two steam-engines of 100 horse-power, at present give employment to 500 workmen, and he turns out yearly over 3,000 instruments, of which 1,200 are grands, and the rest cottage pianos. At the international exhibitions of London (1862), Paris (1868), and at other important exhibitions, his pianos received the highest medals. In London the firm keeps up a branch house. Bechstein's three sons now successfully assist him in the management of his factories, offices, and storehouses.

Beck, (1) David, organ maker, at Halberstadt, about 1590; built the organ at Grüningen, near Magdeburg, 1592–96, which was restored 1705 (*cf.* A. Werckmeister), the organ of St. Martin's

Church, Halberstadt, etc.—(2) R e i c h a r d t
K a r l, published a book of dance pieces (allemandes, ballets, etc.), for two violins and bass,
at Strassburg (1654).—(3) J o h a n n P h i l i p p,
edited a volume of dance pieces for viola
da gamba (1677).—(4) M i c h a e l, professor of
theology and Oriental languages at Ulm, b.
there Jan. 24, 1653; wrote " Über die Musikalische Bedeutung der hebräischen Accente "
(1678 and 1701).—(5) G o t t f r i e d J o s e p h, b.
Nov. 15, 1723, Podiebrad (Bohemia), d. April
8, 1787, Prague; organist at Prague, afterwards
Dominican monk, professor of philosophy at
Prague, and finally provincial of his order; he
wrote much church music, also instrumental
works.—(6) F r a n z, b. 1730, Mannheim; good
violinist, and highly esteemed at the court, but
on account of a duel with fatal result, he was
forced to leave, and went to Bordeaux, where
he became concert director (1780), and died
there, Dec. 31, 1809. He wrote some excellent
instrumental and vocal pieces.—(7) C h r i s t i a n
F r i e d r i c h, lived at Kirchheim, and published
(1789–94) instrumental works (pf. sonatas, concertos, variations, etc.).—(8) F r i e d r i c h A d o l f,
published at Berlin (1825) " Dr. Martin Luther's
Gedanken über die Musik."—(9) K a r l, b.
1814, the first singer in the title-*rôle* of
Lohengrin, d. March 3, 1879, Vienna.—(10)
J o h a n n N e p o m u k, b. May 5, 1828, Pesth;
celebrated baritone singer; was engaged in
succession at Vienna, Hamburg, Bremen,
Cologne, Düsseldorf, Mayence, Würzburg,
Wiesbaden and Frankfort, and from 1853 until
he received his pension (1885) was the pride of
the Vienna Opera.—(11) J o s e p h, son of the
former, b. June 11, 1850; likewise an excellent
baritone vocalist; sang first on various provincial stages in Austria, and was engaged in
1876 at Berlin, and in 1880 at Frankfort.

Becké, J o h. B a p t i s t, b. Aug. 24, 1743,
Nuremburg; first of all adjutant to General v.
Roth, during the Seven Years' War, afterwards
" Hofmusikus " at Munich (1766). He was an
excellent performer on the flute, and published
flute concertos.

Becker, (1) D i e t r i c h, published at Hamburg
in 1668 " Sonaten für eine Violine, eine Viola
di Gamba, und Generalbass über Chorallieder,"
also " Musikalische Frühlingsfrüchte " (instrumental pieces à 3–5 with *basso continuo*).—(2)
J o h a n n, b. Sept. 1, 1726, Helsa, d. 1803; court
organist at Cassel, composer of sacred music, of
which only one chorale book appeared in print.
—(3) K a r l F e r d i n a n d, b. July 17, 1804, Leipzig, d. Oct. 26, 1877; was in 1825 organist of St.
Peter's Church, 1837 of St. Nicholas Church
there, 1843 teacher for organ-playing at the
Conservatorium. He resigned his appointments
in 1856, presented his library to the town
(" Becker's Stiftung," rich in works on theory),
and lived in private at Plagwitz until his death.
B.'s most meritorious work is the revision of

Forkel's " Systematisch-chronologische Darstellung der Musiklitteratur " (1836; supplement in 1839). The following also deserve
mention; " Die Hausmusik in Deutschland im
16., 17., und 18. Jahrhundert " (1840); " Die
Tonwerke des 16. und 17. Jahrhunderts " (1847),
etc. He also published some instrumental
compositions (pf. and organ pieces) and several
chorale books. B. was a diligent collector, but
not a learned scholar.—(4) K o n s t a n t i n
J u l i u s, b. Feb. 3, 1811, Freiberg, d. Feb. 26,
1859; pupil of the above, 1837 editor of the
Neue Zeitschrift für Musik, settled in Dresden in
1843 as teacher of music, and lived from 1846
in Oberlössnitz. He wrote operas, choral and
instrumental works, also a " Männergesang-
schule " (1845), " Harmonielehre für Dilettanten " (1844); also a novel with a purpose, " Der
Neuromantiker " (1840).—(5) V a l e n t i n E d-
u a r d, b. Nov. 20, 1814, Würzburg, d. Jan. 25,
1890, Vienna; 1833, municipal functionary at
Würzburg, lived later on in Vienna; a well-
known composer of songs for male voices (" Das
Kirchlein "), wrote also masses, operas (*Die
Bergknappen* and *Der Deserteur*), songs, and many
instrumental works, of which a quintet for
clarinet and strings gained a prize.—(6) G e o r g,
b. June 24, 1834, Frankenthal (Rheinpfalz),
writer on music and composer; a pupil of Kuhn
and Prudent, lives at Geneva; he has published:
" La Musique en Suisse " (1874), " Aperçu sur
la Chanson Française," " Pygmalion de J. J.
Rousseau," " Eustorg de Beaulieu," " Guillaume de Guéroult," etc., and has other monographs in his portfolio. He has also published
for several years a small musical print, *Ques-
tionnaire de l'Association Internationale des Mu-
siciens-écrivains*, and is contributor to various
newspapers dealing with special subjects, especially the *Monatshefte für Musikgeschichte*. Of
his compositions have appeared pf. pieces and
songs.—(7) A l b e r t E r n s t A n t o n, b. June
13, 1834, Quedlinburg, pupil there of Bönicke,
and of Dehn at Berlin (1853–56); lives as
teacher of music in Berlin; since 1881 teacher
of composition at Scharwenka's Conservatorium; 1881 conductor of the Berlin Dom-
Chor. A symphony in G minor of B.'s gained
a prize from the " Gesellschaft der Musikfreunde " in Vienna. In 1877 his songs from
Wolff's *Rattenfänger* and *Wilder Jäger* first
excited general notice. His great mass in B♭
minor (first produced in 1878 at the twenty-fifth
anniversary of the foundation of the Riedel
Union, printed by Breitkopf and Härtel) is a
work of much importance. Besides the above
must be mentioned *Reformationskantate* (1883, at
the Luther Festival); the oratorio *Selig aus
Gnade*, psalms, motets, and songs for solo
voices or chorus.—(8) J e a n, b. May 11,
1833, Mannheim, d. there Oct. 10, 1884, pupil
of Kettenus and Vincenz Lachner, a celebrated
violinist; was appointed leader of the band at
Mannheim, but already in 1858 gave up this

post and made long tours as a virtuoso, during which he appeared, among other places, at Paris and at London with great success. In 1866 he settled down in Florence and founded the "Florentine Quartett" (2nd violin, Masi; viola, Chiostri; 'cello, Hilpert), which, owing to his special efforts, obtained world-wide reputation, and continued until 1880 (from 1875 with L. Spitzer-Hegyesi as 'cellist in place of Hilpert). During the past years B., when he was not on tour, lived in Mannheim, where it was his intention to found a violin school. His daughter, J e a n n e, b. June 9, 1859, Mannheim, pupil of Reinecke and Bargiel, is an excellent pianist; his son H a n s, b. May 12, 1860, Strassburg, pupil of Singer, an accomplished violaplayer; and H u g o, b. Feb. 13, 1864, Strassburg, pupil of Friedrich Grützmacher, a highly gifted 'cellist. From the time of the dissolution of the "Florentine Quartett" B. made successful concert tours with his children.—(9) R e i n h o l d, b. 1842, Adorf, Saxony; he lived for some time in the south of France as violinist, and gave concerts, but, on account of a hand affection, was obliged to abandon that mode of life, and has since been living in Dresden. He composed a violin concerto, symphonic poem, "Prinz vom Homburg," a work for male chorus, "Waldmorgen," operas *Frauenlob* (1892), *Ratbold* (1898), and songs.

Beckmann, J o h. F r. G o t t l i e b, **b.** 1737, d. April 25, 1792; organist at Celle, was a celebrated pianist, and also famed for his improvisations. He published twelve pf. sonatas, six concertos, and a solo for pf.; in 1782 his opera, *Lukas und Hannchen*, was produced at Hamburg with great success.

Beckwith, J o h n, b. Dec. 25, 1750, Norwich, d. June 3, 1809; became organist of St. Peter Mancroft's there in 1794, and of the Cathedral in 1808. He took the degree of Mus. Doc. at Oxford in 1803. He wrote many anthems, glees, songs, which in their day were popular, and also pianoforte sonatas and an organ concerto. He was succeeded by his son J o h n C h a r l e s, b. 1788, d. Oct. 5, 1828.

Becquié, J. M. (?), b. about 1800, Toulouse, d. Nov. 10, 1825, as flautist of the Opéra Comique; he was a pupil of the Paris Conservatoire. His compositions for the flute (rondos, variations, fantasies) are of great merit. —His brother, J e a n M a r i e, named B. de Peyreville, b. 1797, Toulouse, d. 1876, distinguished himself as violinist (pupil of Rudolf and August Kreutzer); he was for many years member of the orchestra of the Théâtre Italien, and published pieces for the violin.

Bečvařovsky (Beczwarzowsky), A n t o n F e l i x, b. April 9, 1754, Jungbunzlau (Bohemia), d. May 15, 1823, Berlin. In 1777 he became organist of St. James's Church, Prague, and in 1779 of the principal church at Brunswick. In 1796 he resigned, resided in Bamberg up to 1800, and after that in Berlin. He published

sonatas and concertos for pianoforte, as well as songs and important vocal pieces with pf. accompaniment.

Bedon (Fr.), formerly a kind of drum. *B. de Biscaye*, same as *Tambour Basque*. (*Cf.* TAMBOURINE.)

Bedos de Celles, D o m F r a n ç o i s (or simply D o m B e d o s), b. 1706, Caux, near Béziers, became a Benedictine monk at Toulouse in 1726, and died Nov. 25, 1779. B. wrote a work of great importance, "L'art du Facteur d'Orgues," 3 vols. (1766–78); a fourth part containing a brief history of the organ, has been translated into German by Vollbeding (1793). All later works (esp. those of Töpfer) are based upon it, and the excellent drawings are always reprinted. B. also drew up a report of the new organ of St. Martin at Tours (1762, in the *Mercure de France*), which is to be found in Adlung's "Musica Mechanica," etc.

Beecke, I g n a z v o n, b. about 1730, d. Jan 1803, Wallerstein; he was an officer in the Wurtemberg army, and afterwards "Musikintendant" to the Prince of Ötting-Wallerstein. He was an excellent pianist, and a friend of Gluck, Jomelli, and Mozart. He wrote seven operas, instrumental works, songs, and an oratorio (*Auferstehung*).

Beellaerts. (*See* BELLÈRE.)

Beer, (1), J o s e p h, b. May 18, 1744, Grünwald (Bohemia), d. 1811; he was at first fieldtrumpeter in an Austrian regiment, afterwards in the French army. He became one of the best performers of his time on the clarinet. After an exciting life of concert touring, he died at Potsdam, as royal Prussian chamber musician. B. improved the clarinet (by the addition of a fifth key), and wrote various pieces for his instrument (concertos, etc.).—(2) J u l e s, b. about 1835, nephew of Meyerbeer, was a zealous amateur composer (operas, songs, psalm with orchestra, etc.), but neither in Paris, where he resides, nor in Brussels, did he achieve success.— (3) M a x J o s e p h, b. 1851, Vienna, received his first instruction on the pianoforte from his father, and, after obtaining a Government scholarship, studied composition under Dessoff. Beer's compositions are principally lyrical pf. pieces for two and four hands ("Eichendorffiana," "Spielmannsweisen," "Abendfeier," "Heidebilder," "Was sich der Wald erzählt"), and songs. Besides these, are a pf. suite (Op. 9), "Der Wilde Jäger" (soli, chorus, and orchestra), a burlesque operetta, *Das Stelldichein auf der Pfahlbrücke* (which won a prize and was published), and in manuscript the operas, *Otto der Schütz* and *Der Pfeiferkönig*.

Beethoven, L u d w i g v a n, was baptised at Bonn on Dec. 17, 1770, therefore probably b. Dec. 16; d. March 26, 1827, Vienna. His father was tenor singer at the Electoral Chapel, his grandfather bass singer, and finally capellmeister; during several generations, indeed, the family had followed music as a vocation. B. received his first musical instruction from his father, afterwards from the genial oboist Pfeiffer, to whom, later on, B. sent help from Vienna ; and the court organist, van der Eden, and his successor, Chr. Gottl. Neefe, were also his teachers. Already, in 1785, B., thus early developed, was appointed organist of the Electoral Chapel. For this appointment, and for his being sent later on to Vienna, he was indebted to Count Waldstein, his first, and in every respect most important patron. The same was knight of the " Teutonic " order, afterwards commander and chamberlain to the Emperor, and not only held music in high esteem, but himself played the pianoforte remarkably well (B., as is known, dedicated to him the Sonata in c, Op. 53). When Haydn returned from England in 1792, and was entertained by the Bonn orchestra at Godesberg, B. had the opportunity of placing before him a cantata, of which the former thought very highly (probably on this occasion it was arranged that B. should go to Vienna). In October of this year Waldstein wrote as follows : " Dear Beethoven, you are travelling to Vienna in fulfilment of your long-cherished wish. The genius of Mozart is still weeping and bewailing the death of her favourite. With the inexhaustible Haydn she found a refuge, but no occupation, and is now waiting to leave him and join herself to someone else. Labour assiduously, and receive Mozart's spirit from the hands of Haydn.— Your true friend, Waldstein." Already, in 1787, B. (with recommendations from the Elector to his brother, the Emperor Joseph II.) had spent a short time in Vienna, when Mozart is said to have heard him, and to have predicted for him a great future. B. was two-and-twenty years old when he went to Vienna. As he was well recommended, he could not fail to gain access to high art-loving circles (Prince Karl Lichnowski, Count Moritz Lichnowski, Count Rasumowski, etc.). But little came of the proposed lessons of Beethoven with Haydn ; the latter was not born to be a teacher. Beethoven certainly went through a course of instruction in composition with him ; but, behind Haydn's back, B. worked with Schenk, the composer of the *Dorfbarbier*, and went to Haydn with his exercises already corrected by Schenk. This well-meant mystification lasted for two years. B. was a gainer, for he learnt the strict style from Schenk, and profited by Haydn's wider, more artistic mode of looking at things. Further, he studied counterpoint with Albrechtsberger, and dramatic composition with Salieri. To the first period of B.'s artistic career, which is generally considered to extend to 1800, belong the works with the opus numbers 1–18, among which are six pf. trios, nine pf. sonatas, four trios, and one quintet for strings, several sets of variations, the grand aria, " Ah perfido," and the first set of six quartets for strings. The critic of the Leipzig *Allgemeine Musikalische Zeitung* did not doubt the importance of the man, but opposed his bold harmonies and daring rhythms. The circle of distinguished lovers of music which surrounded Beethoven was increased by Count Franz v. Brunswick, Baron v. Gleichenstein, and Stephan v. Breuning, an old friend and patron dating from the Bonn period. The brothers of Beethoven—Karl, who held office in a bank, and Johann, an apothecary, settled in Vienna—represented the hard prose of life to one to whom poetry was indispensable, for they carried on a provokingly petty trade with his manuscripts. B.'s pecuniary position was good : he never accepted a post again, but, from the time of his arrival in Vienna, lived solely by his compositions. His works were well paid, and he received from Prince Lichnowski a yearly allowance of 600 florins; and from 1809 to 1811 a yearly sum of 4,000 florins from Archduke Rudolf and the Princes Lobkowitz and Kinsky. In spite of this manifold relationship to archdukes and princes, B. was by no means a time-serving man and a courtier, but rather remained all through his life a democrat and a republican, and looked upon rulers as tyrants. As is known, he originally dedicated his " Eroica " symphony to Napoleon, because he regarded him as a genuine republican ; but when the latter assumed the title of Emperor, B. tore up the dedication. When, during the Vienna Congress (1814), the foreign monarchs present, together with B., were frequent guests at the house of the Archduke Rudolf, the composer (to quote his own expression) made these high personages pay court to him, and he put on airs. He felt himself, and rightly, a king of art. The saddest period of his life began after the death of his brother Karl (1815), of whose son B. became guardian. This boy caused him much sorrow (concerning him, as well as for all other details of B.'s life, we refer the reader to detailed biographies of the composer). Of quite different, but far deeper, import for the character, and consequently the tendency of his music, was the malady of the ears, which commenced at a very early period, and increased, so that already in 1800, he had great difficulty in hearing, and gradually became quite deaf. He was ashamed of this difficulty of hearing, and attempted to hide it ; his rough, morose, and monosyllabic demeanour was, therefore, in early years at least, to some extent a mask, though, in other respects, it was an inevitable result of the malady. His health, which, for the rest, was robust, began gradually to give way about 1825; in 1826 symptoms of dropsy showed themselves, which threatened his life. A violent cold, which he caught in December of this year, confined him to bed. After a painful operation, his dropsy gradually undermined his health, and he died at six o'clock on the evening of March 26, 1827.

In B. we honour the greatest master of modern instrumental music, but he wrote, at the same time, vocal works of equal importance (*Fidelio* and *Missa solemnis*). If religious feeling found its noblest expression in the works of Bach, on the other hand it is the purely human joy and sorrow which appeals to us with the language of passion in those of Beethoven. Subjectivity, the characteristic agent of our time, coming gradually to the fore, is embodied in B., but turned, through the beauty of form, into classic purity. In detailed figurative development of themes, B. is unequalled—nay, unapproachable. In the last period of his creative power he attained to a degree of refinement, the full comprehension of which is only to-day dawning upon the world at large. This is preeminently true of his art of rhythm. The "last B." dates from about the time (1815) in which he took charge of his nephew, changed his style of living, and set up a household establishment of his own, etc. During this period arose the five pf. sonatas, Op. 101, 106, 109, 110, and 111 ; the great stringed quartets, Op. 127 (E♭), Op. 130 (B♭), Op. 131 (c♯ minor), Op. 132 (A minor), and Op. 135 (F) ; the great quartet-fugue, Op. 133 ; the ninth symphony ; *Missa solemnis* and the overtures, Op. 115 and 124. The number of Beethoven's works, as compared with those of other great masters, is not large. He wrote : two masses (one in c, Op. 86 ; and the *Missa solemnis* in D, Op. 123), one opera (*Fidelio*), one oratorio (*Christus am Oelberge*), nine symphonies (No. 1, c, Op. 21 ; No. 2, D, Op. 36 ; No. 3, E♭ ("Eroica"), Op. 55 ; No. 4, B♭, Op. 60 ; No. 5, c minor, Op. 67 ; No. 6, F, (Pastoral), Op. 68 ; No. 7, Op. 92 ; No. 8, F, Op. 93 ; No. 9, D minor, Op. 125, with chorus (Schiller's "*Hymne an die Freude*"), *Die Schlacht von Vittoria* (fantasia for orchestra), music to *Prometheus* and *Egmont*, *Die Ruinen von Athen* (overture and march with chorus), besides seven overtures (*Coriolan*, three *Leonora* overtures, *König Stephen*, *Namensfeier*, Op. 115, and *Zur Weihe des Hauses*, Op. 124), one violin concerto (D, Op. 61), five pf. concertos (c, Op. 15 ; B♭, Op. 19 ; c minor, Op. 37 ; G, Op. 58 ; E♭, Op. 73 ; besides the arrangement of the violin concerto) ; one triple concerto for pf., violin, 'cello, and orchestra (Op. 56) ; one fantasia for pianoforte, orchestra, and chorus ; one rondo for pf. and orchestra ; two Romances for violin and orchestra, a fragment of a concerto for violin, one Allegretto for orchestra, two marches, twelve minuets, twelve German dances, and twelve *Contertänze* for orchestra ; "Cantata on the death of Joseph II." (1790), and one on the accession of Leopold II. to the throne (1792) ; *Der glorreiche Augenblick* (cantata), *Meeresstille und glückliche Fahrt* (four solo voices and orchestra), "Ah perfido" (soprano solo with orchestra), *Opferlied* (ditto), "Tremate empj" (soprano, tenor, and bass, with orchestra), *Bundeslied* (two solo voices, three-part

chorus, two clarinets, two horns, and two bassoons), *Elegischer Gesang* (quartet with stringed orchestra), sixty-six songs and one duet with pf., eighteen canons for voices, *Gesang der Mönche* (à 3, *a cappella*), seven books of English, Scotch, and Welsh songs, with pf., violin, and 'cello ; thirty-eight pf. sonatas, ten violin sonatas, one rondo and one set of variations for pf. and violin, five 'cello sonatas, three sets of variations for 'cello and pf., seven sets of variations for flute and pf., twenty-one sets of variations for pf. alone, one sonata, two sets of variations, and three marches for pf. for four hands ; four rondos, three books of Bagatelles, three preludes, seven minuets, thirteen Ländler, an Andante (F), Fantasia (G minor), Polonaise—all for pf. ; one sonata for horn and pf. ; eight trios for pf., violin, and 'cello ; two sets of variations for trio ; one trio for pf., clarinet, and 'cello ; arrangements of the second symphony and septet as trios for pf., clarinet, and 'cello ; four pf. quartets (three posthumous juvenile works, and one arrangement of the pf. quintet), one quintet for pf. and wind instruments, two octets and one sextet for wind instruments (Op. 71), one septet and one sextet for stringed and wind instruments, two stringed quintets, one arrangement of the c minor pf. trio for stringed quintet, sixteen stringed quartets (Op. 18, 1-6, belonging to the first period ; Op. 59, 1-3 ; Op. 74, 95, and the great "last," Op. 127, 130, 131, 132, 135), also a fugue for stringed quartet and for quintet, five stringed trios, one trio for two oboes and English horn, three duets for clarinet and bassoon, two *Equali* for trombones.

The first complete edition of B.'s works (by Rietz, Nottebohm, Reinecke, David Hauptmann, etc.) appeared in twenty-four series (1864-7), published by Breitkopf & Härtel, and a Supplement in 1890. *Biographies:* F. G. Wegeler and Ferd. Ries, "Biographische Notizen über Ludwig van B." (1838) ; A. Schindler, "Biographie von Ludwig van B." (1840 ; 3rd ed. 1860) ; W. v. Lenz, "B. et ses trois styles" (1854, 2 vols), "B. eine Kunststudie" (1855-60, 6 vols ; 2nd ed. of vol. i. (Biography) under separate title, 1869) ; L. Nohl's "Beethoven's Leben" (1864-77, 3 vols.) ; "B. nach den Schilderungen seiner Zeitgenossen" (1877) ; Ulibischeff, "B., ses Critiques et Glossateurs" (1857 ; in German, by Bischoff, 1859) ; A. B. Marx, "Ludwig van Beethoven's Leben und Schaffen" (3rd ed. 1875, 2 vols.). A. W. Thayer has written the most exhaustive biography—"Ludwig van Beethoven's Leben" (in German, by H. Deiters, 1866-79, vols. i.-iii. ; the fourth and last volume has not yet appeared) ; "L. van Beethoven," by W. J. v. Wasielewski, 2 vols. ; and "Neue Beethoveniana," by Dr. T. Frimmel. Interesting information is given also in Gerhard v. Breuning's "Aus dem Schwarzspanierhaus" (1874). The published *letters* of Beethoven are : Nohl's

"Briefe Beethovens" (1865, containing 411);
"Neue Briefe Beethovens" (1867, 322 letters);
Köchel, "83 neu aufgefundene Originalbriefe
Beethovens an den Erzherzog Rudolf" (1865);
"Briefe von B. an Gräfin Erdödy und Mag.
Brauchle," edited by Schöne (1867); and there
are other detached letters in the biographies, in Pohl's "Die Gesellschaft der Musikfreunde zu Wien" (1871), and other works.
Of former numerous small and great works
about B. may still be named : Ignaz v. Seyfried's
"Ludwig van Beethoven's Studien im General-
bass, Kontrapunkt und in der Kompositionslehre" (1832, recently revised by Nottebohm,
1873); besides Nottebohm's "Beethoveniana"
(1872), "Neue Beethoveniana" (which appeared
originally in the *Musikalische Wochenblatt*, and
were afterwards republished in a volume, as
2te Beethoveniana (1887), and "Thematisches
Verzeichnis der Werke Beethovens" (1868);
Thayer's "Chronologisches Verzeichnis" (1865),
etc. A monument was erected to B. in Bonn (by
Hähnel, 1845), and another in Vienna (by Zum-
busch, 1880).

Beethoven Foundation. (*See* PFLUGHAUPT.)

Beethoven Prize (500 gulden), offered yearly
since 1875 by the "Gesellschaft der Musikfreunde" in Vienna. Hugo Reinhold was the
first to win it in 1879; only former pupils of the
Vienna Conservatorium can compete for it.

Beffara, Louis François, b. Aug. 23, 1751,
Nonancourt (Eure), d. Feb. 2, 1838, Paris,
where he was *Commissaire de Police* from 1792 to
1816. He wrote the "Dictionnaire de l'Académie Royale de Musique" (seven vols.), and seven
more vols. with rules and regulations in connection with the *Académie* (Grand Opéra), and likewise "Dictionnaire Alphabétique des Acteurs,
etc." (three vols.); "Tableau Chronologique
des Répresentations, etc." (from the year 1671);
"Dictionnaire Alphabétique des Tragédies
Lyriques, etc., non répresentées à l'Académie,
etc." (five vols.); and, finally, "Dramaturgie
Lyrique Étrangère" (seventeen vols.). He bequeathed his rich library, together with his
manuscripts, to the city of Paris; but unfortunately everything was destroyed by fire during
the Commune (1871).

Beffroi (Fr.) tocsin; the Tamtam is sometimes called by this name.

Beffroy de Reigny, Louis Abel, b. Nov. 6,
1757, Laon, d. Dec. 18, 1811, Paris (pseudonym,
Cousin Jacques), was a singular personage, who
wrote abstruse works (libretto and music) for
the stage, which, however, met with little
success. The two, *Nicodème dans la Lune*, 1790,
and *Nicodème aux Enfers*, 1791, certainly made a
sensation, and had to be forbidden, as they
excited the democrats.

Beggar's Opera. (*See* BALLAD OPERA.)

Belcke, Friedrich August, b. May 27,
1795, Lucka (Altenburg), d. there Dec. 10, 1874,

a famous trombone-player and composer for his
instrument. He was chamber musician at
Berlin from 1816–58, and after that retired to
his native town.—His brother, Christian
Gottlieb, b. July 17, 1796, Lucka, d. there
July 8, 1875, was, from 1819 to 1832, a famous
flautist in the Gewandhaus orchestra at Leipzig;
and after some years of rest was again active at
Altenburg from 1834–41. His concertos for
flute, fantasias, etc., are well known.

Beldomandis (Beldemandis, Beldemando),
Prosdocimus de, about 1422, professor of
philosophy in his native city, Padua; an interesting writer on measured music, whose
works have been published by Coussemaker
("Script." III.). B. was an opponent of Marchettus of Padua, on matters relating to musical
esthetics, but even the practical teaching of
each reveals important points of difference.

Belegt (Ger.), hoarse, muffled (of the voice).

Beliczay, Julius von, b. Aug. 10, 1835,
Komorn (Hungary), was originally an engineer,
but took up music and became a pupil of
Joachim, Hoffmann, and Franz Krenn, at
Vienna. He lived alternately at Pressburg and
Vienna, and in 1888 became teacher of theory
at the National Academy of Music at Pesth.
Of his compositions the following deserve mention: a quartet for strings in G minor (Op. 21),
a trio in E♭ (Op. 30), Andante for stringed
orchestra (Op. 25), a serenade for strings (Op.
36), an "Ave Maria" for soprano solo, chorus,
and orchestra (Op. 9), pf. works for two and
four hands, études (Op. 52), songs; and, in
manuscript, a mass often performed, antiphons
to the Virgin, etc. Died April 30, 1893, Pesth.

Belin (Bellin), (1) Guillaume, tenor singer at
the Chapelle Royale, Paris, 1547; *Cantiques à 4*
(Biblical hymns of praise, 1560) and *Chansons*,
of which a number are to be found in Attaignant's collections of 1543 and 1544.—(2)
Julien, b. about 1530, Le Mans, a famous
lutenist, who published in 1556 a book of motets,
chansons and fantasias in lute tablature.

Bell (Ger. *Stürze*), the name of the wide opening of brass wind-instruments at the end opposed to the mouth-piece.

Bella, (1) Domenica della, published in
1705 a 'cello concerto, and in 1704, at Venice,
twelve sonatas with 'cello obbligato and cembalo.—(2) Joh. Leopold, b. 1843, St. Nicolan
(Upper Hungary), priest and canon of the
Neusohl Cathedral, composed sacred music ;
also part-songs of national character, and some
pf. pieces.

Bellasio, Paolo, b. Venice, published a book
of madrigals in 1579, and *Villanelle alla Romana*
in 1595. A collection of 1568, entitled "Dolci
Affetti," contains some of his madrigals.

Bellazzi, Francesco, b. Venice, pupil of
Johannes Gabrieli, published psalms, motets,
litanies, *fauxbourdons*, a mass, *canzone*, etc. (for

the most part à 8) in Venice from 1618 to 1628.

Bellère (Bellerus), J e a n, really B e e l l a e r t s; bookseller at Antwerp, entered into partnership with Pierre Phalèse (fils) ; they published principally works of Italian composers up to about 1600.—His son, B a l t h a s a r, transferred the business, after his father's death, to Douai ; he printed, from 1603 to 1605, a catalogue of his publications, which Coussemaker discovered in the Douai library.

Bellermann, (1), J o h a n n F r i e d r i c h, b. March 8, 1795, Erfurt, d. Feb. 4, 1874, Berlin, where from 1819 he was teacher, and from 1847–1868 director of the Gymnasium "Zum Grauen Kloster." He distinguished himself by his researches in connection with (ancient) Greek music. His principal work, " Die Tonleitern und Musiknoten der Griechen" (1847), gives an exhaustive account of the Greek system of notation, and the two smaller pamphlets, " Die Hymnen des Dionysios und Mesomedes " (1840), and "Anonymi Scriptio de Musica et Bacchii Senioris Introductio, etc." (1841), treat of the few remnants of Old Greek practical music.—(2) J. G o t t f r i e d H e i n r i c h, b. March 10, 1832, son and pupil of the former, attended the " Graues Kloster," afterwards the Royal Institute for church music, and was for a long time a private pupil of E. A. Grell. In 1853 he was appointed teacher of singing at the " Graues Kloster," received in 1861 the title of Royal Musical Director, and in 1866 became Professor of Music at the University, on the death of A. B. Marx. In 1875 he was made member of the Academy of Arts. Bellermann's published compositions are all vocal (motets, psalms, songs, part-songs, a choral work with orchestra, " Gesang der Geister über den Wassern "); larger works (even an opera) are still in manuscript, but selections from them have been given, especially the choruses from Sophocles' *Ajax*, *Œdipus Rex*, and *Œdipus Colonus*. Bellermann's " Die Mensuralnoten und Taktzeichen im 15. und 16. Jahrhundert " (1858) is a work of special merit, and the first which enabled persons to study the theory of measured music, who, through lack of knowledge of Latin, had not been able to examine for themselves the treatises of the mensural theorists. In his book, " Der Kontrapunkt " (1862 ; 2nd ed.1877), B. follows J. J. Fux's " Gradus ad Parnassum," a work already old-fashioned in its day (1725). The pamphlet, " Die Grösse der musikalischen Intervalle als Grundlage der Harmonie " (1873) is a bold attempt to make modern acoustics fit in with his counterpoint. The " Allg. Musikal. Ztg." (1868–74) contains valuable articles by B.

Belleville-Oury, E m i l i e, b. 1808, Munich, d. there, July 22, 1880 ; an excellent pianoforte player, pupil of Czerny, who made great concert tours, and married the violinist Oury in London ; she published pf. pieces.

Bell 'Haver, V i n c e n z o, b. about 1530, Venice, pupil of A. Gabrieli, and his successor as second organist of St. Mark's (1556) ; he appears to have died in 1588, as on Oct. 30 of that year J. Giuseppe Guarni succeeded him. B. was a renowned composer of madrigals, of which several books (1567–75), and some in collections, have been preserved.

Belli, (1) G i r o l a m o, b. at Argenta, chapelsinger to the Duke of Mantua ; published a book of motets à 6 (1586), a book of madrigals à 6 (1587), motets à 8 (Venice, 1589), motets and magnificats à 10 (1594) ; also the collection, "De' Floridi Virtuosi d'Italia" (1586), contains some madrigals à 5.—(2) G i u l i o, b. about 1560, Longiano, was choir-master at St. Antonio, Padua about 1600, finally maestro of Imola Cathedral (about 1620) ; he was a prolific church composer : canzonets à 4 (1586 ; 2nd ed. 1595), masses à 5 (1597), masses à 4 (1599), masses and motets à 8 (new edition, with thorough-bass, 1607), masses à 4–8 (1608), psalms à 8 (1600, 1604, 1615, the last with continuo), motets for double chorus, litanies, etc. (1605, 1607), " Concerti Ecclesiastici " with organ bass à 2–3 (1613 and 1621).—(3) D o m e n i c o, musician at the court of Parma, published : " Arie a 1 e 2 Voci per Sonare con il Chitarrone " (1616), and " Orfeo Dolente " (1616, 5 Intermèdes to Tasso's " Aminta ").

Bellicosamente (Ital.), martially, in a warlike manner.

Bellin. (*See* BELIN.)

Bellini, V i n c e n z o, celebrated opera composer, b. Nov. 3, 1801, Catania (Sicily), d. Sept. 24, 1835, Puteaux, near Paris ; pupil of the Naples Conservatorio under Zingarelli. He first published instrumental and sacred compositions. His first opera, *Adelson e Salvina*, was produced in 1825 at the theatre of the Conservatorio ; in 1826 there followed, at the San Carlo Theatre, *Bianca e Fernando*, with such good success that, in 1827, he was commissioned to write for La Scala, Milan. He wrote *Il Pirata*, which was brilliantly received ; but in the following year the success of *La Straniera* was even greater. After that, *Zaira* came out at Parma, but failed ; *Montechi e Capuleti* at Venice, and *La Sonnambula* at Milan. The critics found fault with Bellini's simple instrumentation and with the meagre forms of his vocal numbers ; B. took the reproach to heart, and displayed more careful work in *Norma* (Milan, 1831), and the opera, especially with Malibran in the title-*rôle*, made quite a furore. *Beatrice di Tenda* did not meet with equal success. In 1833 B. settled definitely in Paris, where he won rich laurels, though only for a short time ; for it was granted to him to write only one more opera, *I Puritani*, produced at the Théâtre des Italiens in 1835. The general mourning over his early death found expression in many notices and memorial pamphlets. A brother of

Bellini, Carmelo B., b. 1802, Catania, d. there Sept. 28, 1884, won for himself a modest name as church composer.

Bellmann, Karl Gottfried, b. Aug. 11, 1760, Schellenberg (Saxony), d. 1816 as instrument-maker in Dresden. He made in his time famous pianofortes, and was also a performer on the bassoon.

Bell metronome, a metronome with a small bell which marks the first beat of every bar or group of beats.

Belloli, (1), Luigi, b. Feb. 2, 1770, Castelfranco (Bologna), d. Nov. 17, 1817; performer on the French horn, and in 1812 teacher of that instrument at the Milan Conservatorio. He wrote several operas, and left behind a Method for horn.—(2) Agostino, b. Bologna, likewise a performer on the horn, published several studies for that instrument, and also produced four operas at Milan (1816–23).

Belloni, (1) Giuseppe, sacred composer, b. Lodi; he published: masses à 5 (1603), psalms à 5 (1605), masses and motets à 6 (1606).—(2) Pietro, of Milan, teacher of singing at the Conservatorio di Sant' Onofrio, Naples; afterwards in Paris, where he wrote many ballets (1801–1804), and published a "Méthode de chant" (1822).

Bellows. The simplest bellows of organs is constructed after the manner of smiths' bellows, *i.e.* pump-work. According to the form and manner of drawing-in the wind, a distinction is made between *diagonal* and *horizontal* B.

Bells (Ger. *Glocken*), are musical instruments only occasionally employed (as, for example, in *Parsifal*), but they were formerly much in vogue as Glockenspiel (*see* CARILLON) on church towers. In consequence of an irregular series of overtones (answering to the squares of the natural series of figures—1, 4, 9, 16, 25, etc.), their pitch is not easy to grasp. Even small carillons differ entirely from the Stahlspiel (*see* LYRE), and cymbals, semi-spherical, with thin edges, are used in opera, instead of the more important (too great and too dear) church-bells.

Belly, (1) the upper part of the sound-box of an instrument; that part over which the strings are stretched.—(2) Also the sound-board of the pianoforte.

Bemetzrieder, theorist, b. 1743, Alsace, entered the order of the Benedictines, but soon left it and went to Paris, where Diderot took him in hand, but without being able to make anything of him; all trace of him in London, after 1816, is lost. B. published several theoretical works: "Leçons de Clavecin et Principes d'Harmonie" (1771; in English, 1778), "Traité de Musique, concernant les Tons, les Harmonies" (1776), "Nouvel Essai sur l'Harmonie" (1779), "New Guide to Singing" (1787), "General Instruction in Music" (1790), "A Complete Treatise of Music" (1800), and several smaller ones, also some non-musical, philosophical writings.

Bémol (Fr.), same as ♭ (a sign indicating lowering); *mi bémol = e ♭*, etc.

Benda, (1), Franz, b. Nov. 25, 1709, Altbenatky (Bohemia), d. March 7, 1786, Potsdam. He was a chorister at St. Nicholas' Church, Prague, then a strolling musician, by which means he became a performer on the violin. He was appointed first at Warsaw, in 1732 at Berlin, and in 1771 he became leader of the royal band. He was especially famous for his expression in playing. He formed many pupils. He only published a few solos for violin, and a flute solo. After his death there appeared studies, etc.—(2) Johann, brother of the former, b. 1713, Altbenatky, d. 1752 as chamber musician at Potsdam. He was an excellent violinist, and left behind in manuscript three violin concertos.—(3) Georg, b. 1721, probably also at Altbenatky, brother of the former, d. Nov. 6, 1795, Koestritz. From 1742 to 1748 he was chamber musician at Berlin, and then occupied a similar position at Gotha. The duke of the latter place sent him to Italy, and in 1750 appointed him *Hofcapellmeister*. From 1774 he attracted notice by his melodramas (*Ariadne auf Naxos*, which he also produced at Paris in 1781, but without success; *Medea, Almansor,* and *Nadine*). He considered himself slighted, and hence resigned his post in 1778. He lived at Hamburg, Vienna, and other places, went to Georgenthal near Gotha, and, having entirely renounced music, returned to Koestritz. His compositions are very numerous, and are, for the most part, in manuscript. They have been preserved in the royal library at Berlin (church cantatas, masses, etc.). He wrote fourteen works for the stage (operas and melodramas).— (4) Joseph, the youngest brother and pupil of Franz B., b. March 7, 1724, Altbenatky; was his brother's successor as leader, and, after being pensioned in 1797, d. Feb. 22, 1804, Berlin.—(5) Friedrich Wilh. Heinr., b. July 15, 1745, Potsdam, d. there, June 19, 1814, eldest son of Franz B.; 1765–1810 royal chamber musician, able performer on the violin, pianoforte, and organ; he composed operas (*Alceste, Orpheus, Das Blumenmädchen*), two oratorios, cantatas, and instrumental pieces.—(6) Friedrich Ludwig, son of Georg B., b. 1746, Gotha, d. March 27, 1793; in 1782 conductor of the opera at Hamburg, afterwards virtuoso at the Schwerin Court, and finally director of concerts at Königsberg. He composed several violin concertos and four operas. —(7) Karl, Herm. Heinr., youngest son of Franz B., b. May 2, 1748, Potsdam, d. March 15, 1836, was for many years leader of the royal opera band. He composed some chamber-music.

Bendall, Wilfred Ellington, composer, b. April 22, 1850, London, pupil of Lucas and

Silas and of the Leipzig Conservatorium from 1872–74. He has written operettas, cantatas, songs, trios, duets, pf. pieces, etc.

Bendel, Franz, b. March 23, 1833, Schönlinde, near Rumburg, d. July 3, 1874, Berlin. He studied under Proksch at Prague and Liszt at Weimar, and was for a time teacher at Kullak's Academy at Berlin. He was an excellent pianist, and composed pleasing highclass, drawing-room pianoforte pieces ; also songs which attained great popularity (" Wie berührt mich wundersam ").

Bendeler, Johann Philipp, b. 1660, Riethnordhausen, near Erfurt, d. 1708 as cantor at Quedlinburg. He wrote " Melopœia practica" (1686), " Aerarium melopoeticum " (1688), " Organopœia " (1690 ; republished in 1739 as " Orgelbaukunst "), " Directorium musicum" (1706), " Collegium musicum de compositione " (in manuscript, quoted in Mattheson's " Ehrenpforte ").

Bender, Valentin, b. Sept. 19, 1801, Bechtheim, near Worms, d. April 14, 1873, as musical director of the Royal House, and of the Guides (Guards) at Brussels. He had previously been bandmaster in the Netherlands, and afterwards conductor of the wind-band at Antwerp, which post he handed over to his brother. He became a distinguished virtuoso on the clarinet, and composed several pieces for his instrument, as well as military music.—His brother Jakob, b. 1798, Bechtheim, formerly bandmaster in the Netherlands. He died as director of the windband at Antwerp; he was a good performer on the clarinet, and composed principally military music.

Bendl, Karl, b. March 16, 1838, Prague, chief conductor at Brussels (1864), afterwards chorus master at the German Opera, Amsterdam, He returned to Prague in 1865 as capellmeister of a male choral union. He wrote Czekish national operas (*Lejla, Bretislaw, Cernahorci, Karel Skreta*), songs, choral works, etc. Died Sept. 16, 1897.

Bene, ben (Ital.), well.

Benedict, Julius, b. Nov. 27, 1804, Stuttgart (son of a Jewish banker), d. June 5, 1885, London. He studied under Abeille, Hummel (Weimar, 1819), and K. M. v. Weber (1820). In 1823 he was capellmeister at the " Kärnthnerthor " Theatre, Vienna, and in 1825 at the San Carlo Theatre, Naples, where he produced his first opera, *Giacinta ed Ernesto ;* this was followed by *I Portoghesi in Goa*, at Stuttgart, in 1830. Neither opera met with much success. In 1835 he went from Naples to Paris, and, still in the same year, to London. From that time he became thoroughly English, so that only very few knew that he was a born German. As conductor of the Opera Buffa at the Lyceum in 1836, he produced a small work, *Un Anno ed un Giorno*, and as conductor at Drury Lane Theatre, under Bunn, in 1838, his first English opera,

The Gypsy's Warning, which was followed by *The Brides of Venice* and *The Crusaders*, In 1850 he went with Jenny Lind to America, and soon after his return became musical conductor to Mr. Mapleson (at Her Majesty's Theatre, and afterwards Drury Lane), when, amongst other things, he produced Weber's *Oberon*, with added recitatives. In 1859 he became conductor at the Monday Popular Concerts. He conducted several Norwich Festivals, and the Philharmonic Society at Liverpool from 1876 to 1880. His merits were fully acknowledged; he received the honour of knighthood in 1871, and was decorated with many foreign orders. Of his compositions may be specially named the opera, *The Lily of Killarney* (produced in Germany in 1862 as *Die Rose von Erin*), and the cantatas, *Undine* (1860), *Richard Cœur de Lion* (1862), and the oratorio, *St. Cecilia* (1866), all produced at Norwich. His oratorio, *St. Peter*, was produced at Birmingham in 1870, and his cantata, *Graziella*, there in 1882. His Symphony No. 1, and a portion of No. 2, were given at the Crystal Palace (1873–5). B. also wrote a short biography of Weber for Hueffer's " Great Musicians."

Benedictine Monks. This order has rendered great service to music, its theory, and its history, especially during the Middle Ages, when the Benedictine monasteries were the chief centres of learning. Commencing with Pope Gregory, nearly all the men who are mentioned as distinguished in the musical history of the Middle Ages were Benedictine monks : Aurelianus Reomensis, Remi d'Auxerre, Regino von Prüm, Notker Balbulus, Hugbald von St. Amand, Odo von Clugny, Guido d'Arezzo, Berno von Reichenau, Hermannus Contractus, Wilhelm von Hirschau, Aribo Scholasticus, Bernhard von Clairvaux, Eberhard von Freising, Adam von Fulda. In more recent times may be specially named Prince-Abbot Martin Gerbert of St. Blaise (d. 1793), Dom Bedos de Celles, Jumilhac, Schubiger. A source of great importance for the history of music in the Middle Ages is the work of the Benedictine monk Mabillon, " Annales ordinis S. Benedicti" (1703–39, six vols), together with Gerbert's " De Cantu, etc." and " Scriptores."

Benedictus (Lat.), a portion of the *Sanctus*. (*See* MASS.)

Benedictus Appenzelders (B. von Appenzell), contrapuntist of the 16th century, master of the boys of the royal chapel at Brussels (1539–55) He must not be confounded with Benedictus *Ducis ;* their names have become unfortunately mixed, as many compositions in the collections of chansons, motets, etc. (1540–69), are only marked " Benedict."

Benelli, (1) Alemanno, pseudonym of Bottrigari (q.v.).—(2) Antonio Peregrino, b. Sept. 5, 1771, Forli (Romagna), d. Aug. 16, 1830, Börnichau, in the Saxon Erzgebirge, whither he had retired in 1829. He was first a tenor singer at San Carlo, Naples, and from 1801–22 in Dresden, and later on was engaged in teaching at the Royal Theatre School for Singing, Berlin; he published a "Method" in 1819, "Solfeggi," and some sacred and chamber-music works, etc.

Benesch (Beneš), Joseph, b. Jan. 11, 1793, Batelow (Moravia), violin-player. He was in the orchestra at Pressburg, and afterwards made concert tours in Italy. He was leader at Laibach (1823), member of the band at Vienna (1832), and he published compositions for the violin.

Benevoli, Orazio, b. 1602, Rome, d. June 17, 1672. He was maestro di cappella at various churches in Rome, and finally at the Vatican (1646). He had previously been "Hofmusikus" to an archduke in Vienna. B. was a distinguished contrapuntist; his works (masses à 12, 16, and 24, also motets and psalms) are lying in manuscript in Roman libraries. A mass for twelve choirs (à 48) was performed in Rome (1650) in Santa Maria sopra Minerva.

Benfey, Theodor, a distinguished orientalist and philologist, b. Jan. 28, 1809, Nörten, near Göttingen, d. there June 26, 1881 ; he was also a musician, and active as a writer on music (in the *Neue Zeitung für Musik*).

Benincori, Angelo Maria, b. March 28, 1779, Brescia ; from 1803 he lived in Paris, and died there Dec. 30, 1821. He was a violinist and composer, and published quartets for strings, and pf. trios. His sacred compositions remained in manuscript. He wrote a march for the first act and the last three acts of the opera *Aladdin, or the Wonderful Lamp* (first two acts by Nicolo Isouard), which made a furore in Paris in 1822, while three earlier operas of his met with only moderate success.

Bennett, (1) William Sterndale, b. April 13, 1816, Sheffield, d. Feb. 1, 1875, London. He came of a family of musicians and organists, at the age of eight was chorister at King's College Chapel, Cambridge, where he so distinguished himself, that in 1826 he was received into the Royal Academy of Music (pupil of Lucas, Crotch, W. H. Holmes, and C. Potter). In 1833 he played a concerto in D minor of his own at a prize concert of the Academy. Mendelssohn was present, and gave him much encouragement. The work was published by the Academy. In 1837, at the expense of the Broadwood firm, he went to Leipzig for a year, and there he entered into friendly relations with Mendelssohn and Schumann; a second visit to Leipzig followed in 1841–42. Though the influence of Mendelssohn on Bennett cannot be denied, yet, on the other hand, it must be acknowledged his natural disposition had something akin to that of Mendelssohn's. In 1849 B. founded the London Bach Society, which, among other works, performed the *St. Matthew*

Passion in 1854. In 1856 he was appointed conductor of the Philharmonic Society, but resigned this post when he became Principal of the Academy in 1866. In 1856 he was elected Professor of Music at Cambridge, and soon after had the degree of Doctor of Music conferred on him. In 1867 the University further conferred on him the degree of M.A., and in 1870 Oxford granted him that of D.C.L. He was knighted in 1871. His principal works are : four pianoforte concertos, four overtures ("Parisina," "The Naiads," "The Woodnymph," and "Paradise and the Peri "), G minor symphony, *The May Queen* (cantata), *The Woman of Samaria* (oratorio), music to *Ajax*, sonatas, capriccios, rondos, etc., for pianoforte, songs, a 'cello sonata, a trio, etc. Most of his piano works and all his overtures have been recently published in the Augener Edition. B. is looked upon in England as the founder of an "English School; " and without doubt he ranks among the important musicians which England has produced.—(2) Théodore. (*See* RITTER).—(3) Joseph, writer on music and librettist (Bennett, Mackenzie, Sullivan, Cowen, etc., are indebted to him for some of their best books), b. Nov., 1831, Berkeley (Gloucestershire). He prepares the programmes of the Philharmonic Society, and of the Monday and Saturday Popular Concerts; he is also one of the chief contributors to the *Musical Times*, etc., and is musical critic of the *Daily Telegraph*.

Bennewitz, (1) Wilhelm, b. April 19, 1832, Berlin, d. there Jan., 1871, as member of the orchestra of the royal theatre. He studied with Fr. Kiel, composed an opera, *Die Rose von Woodstock* (1876), also pieces for pf. and 'cello. —(2) Anton, violinist, b. March 26, 1833, Privat (Bohemia). He was director of Prague Conservatorium 1882 to 1901.

Benois, Marie, an excellent pianist, b. Jan. 1, 1861, Petersburg. She studied with her father, who was a pupil of H. Herz, and afterwards with Leschetitzky at the Petersburg Conservatoire: on leaving which, in 1876, she was presented with a gold medal. After that she made concert tours (Vienna among other places) with great success until 1878, when she married her cousin, the painter, Wassily Benois. She has recently played again in public.

Benoist, François, b. Sept. 10, 1794, Nantes, d. April, 1878. He studied at the Paris Conservatoire in 1811, obtained the Prix de Rome (1815–9) and, after his return from Italy, became royal court organist and professor of the organ at the Conservatoire; in 1840 *chef du chant* at the Grand Opéra, and received a pension in 1872. A collection appeared of his organ works entitled, "Bibliothèque de l'Organiste" (twelve books). He wrote, besides, a mass à 3, with organ *ad lib.*, the operas *Léonore et Félix* (1821, printed), *L'Apparition* (1848), and the ballets *La Gipsy* (1839, with Marliani and A. Thomas), *Le*

Diable Amoureux (1840, with Reber), *Nisida* (*Die Amazonen der Azoren*, 1840), and *Pâquerette* (1851).

Benoit, Peter Léonard Leopold, b. Aug. 17, 1834, Harlebecke (Flanders), was a pupil of the Brussels Conservatoire from 1851 to 1855, and during that period wrote music to several Flemish melodramas, as well as a small opera for the *Parktheater*. In 1856 he became conductor of this theatre, and in 1857 won the great state prize (*Prix de Rome*) with his cantata, *Le meurtre d'Abel*. He used the Government grant in extensive journeys, for the purpose of study, through Germany (Leipzig, Dresden, Munich, Berlin), and sent to the Académie at Brussels an essay, " L'École de Musique Flamande et son Avenir." In 1861 he went to Paris to produce an opera (*Erlkönig, Le roi des aulnes*), which was accepted by the Théatre Lyrique, but not put on the stage ; while waiting, he conducted at the Bouffes-Parisiens. On his return to Brussels, he produced a solemn mass, which made a great impression and excited great hopes. B. was heart and soul Flemish, *i.e.* Germanic, and, as Director of the Conservatoire at Antwerp— which post he held from 1867 to 1898—his desire was to establish spiritual relationship with Germany. The most important compositions of B. besides those named are as follows ; a Te Deum (1863), Requiem (1863), pf. concerto, flute concerto ; *Lucifer,* a Flemish oratorio (1866) ; *Het Dorp int Gebergte* and *Isa,* Flemish operas ; *De Schelde,* Flemish oratorio ; *Drama Christi,* a sacred drama for soli, chorus, organ, 'celli, double-basses, trumpets, and trombones ; *De Oorlog* (" War," cantata for double chorus, soli, and increased orchestra) ; a Children's Oratorio " ; " De Maaiers " (" The Mowers "), a choral symphony ; music to *Charlotte Corday ;* music to E. van Gœthem's drama, *Willem de Zwijger* (1876) ; *Vlaandereus Kunstroem* (Rubens-cantata), for mixed chorus, and children's chorus, and orchestra (1877) ; " Antwerpen," for triple male-chorus (1877) ; " Joncfrou Kathelijne," scena for alto solo and orchestra (1879) ; " Muse der Geschiedenis," for chorus and orchestra (1880) ; " Hucbald," for double chorus, barytone solo, and orchestra with harp (1880) ; " Triomfmarsch," for the Exhibition (1880) ; *De Rhyn,* oratorio (1889) ; " Sagen en Balladen," for pianoforte ; " Liefde int leven " (songs) ; " Liefdedrama " (songs) ; motets with organ ; a mass, etc. In 1880 B. became corresponding member, 1882 member in ordinary, of the Royal Berlin Academy. His writings are : " De Vlaamsche Musickschool van Antwerpen" (1873) ; " Considerations à propos d'un Projet pour l'Institution de Festivals en Belgique" (1874) ; " Verhandeling over de Nationale Toonkunde" (2 vols. 1875–77) ; " De Musicale Opvoeding en Opleiding in Belgie " (no date), " Het Droombeeld eener Musicale Wereldkunst " (no date) ; " De Oorspaong van het

Cosmopolitisme in de Musick " (1876) ; " Over Schijn en Blijk en onze Musikale Vlaamsche Beweging " (no date) ; " Onze Musikale Beweging op. Dramatisch Gebied " (no date) ; " Een Koninkhjh Vlaamsch Conservatorium te Antwerpen " (no date) ; " Onze Nederlandische Musikale Eenheid " (no date) ; " Brieven over Noord-Nederland " (no date). B. wrote besides important articles for the papers, *De Vlaamsche Kunstbode, De Eendracht, Guide Musical,* etc. (*Cf.* the reports of the sittings of the Brussels Académie.) Died March 8, 1901.

Berardi, Angelo, maestro di cappella at Viterbo, afterwards at Spoleto (1681), officiating canon at Viterbo in 1687, and, in 1693, maestro at the La Basilica Santa Maria, Trastevere. He was a distinguished theorist (" Ragionamenti Musicali " (1681), " Documenti Armonici " (1687), " Miscellanea Musicale " (1689), " Arcani Musicali (1690), " Il Perche Musicale Ovvero Stafetta Armonica " (1693). The following of his compositions have been preserved : a Requiem à 5 (1663), motets à 2–4 (1665), psalms (1675), offertories (1680), etc.

Berbiguier, Benoit Tranquille, b. Dec. 21, 1782, Caderousse (Vaucluse), d. Jan. 20, 1838, excellent flute-player, studied under Wunderlich at the Paris Conservatoire. From 1813 to 1815 he served in the army, and after that lived in private as a composer ; he wrote a stately series of works for flute (ten concertos, seven books of sonatas, etc.).

Berceuse (Fr.), a lullaby.

Berchem (Berghem), Jachet de (Jaquet, Jacquet, Giachetto di Mantova), one of the most celebrated contrapuntists of the 16th century ; was maestro to the Duke of Mantua from about 1535 to 1565, and was probably born at Berchem, near Antwerp. The number of his works which have come down to us is great— masses, motets, madrigals (1532–67). (*Cf.* Buus.)

Berens, Hermann, b. 1826, Hamburg, d. May 9, 1880, Stockholm ; son of the bandmaster Karl B. at Hamburg, known as flautist and composer for the flute (b. 1801, d. 1857). He studied first with his father, then under Reissiger at Dresden, and, after a concert tour with Alboni, resided for a time in his native city ; went in 1847 to Stockholm, where he deserved well of the lovers of music by performances which he gave of chamber-music. In 1849 he became musical director at Oerebro, in 1860 conductor at the " Mindre " Theatre, Stockholm, afterwards court conductor ; he was appointed teacher of composition at the Academy, and professor and member in ordinary of the Academy. B. composed a Greek drama, *Kodros,* an opera, *Violetta,* as well as three operettas—*Ein Sommernachtstraum, Lully und Quinault,* and *Riccardo*—all received with approval ; also some successful pianoforte and chamber-music. B. is now best known by his "Neueste Schule der Geläufigkeit " (excellent pianoforte studies, Op. 61).

Beretta, Giovanni Battista, b. Feb. 24, 1819, Verona, d. April 28, 1876, Milan. He commenced life as a wealthy amateur, but later on, after the loss of his fortune, was for some time director of the Conservatorio (Liceo musicale) at Bologna. Finally he worked at Milan at the great musical dictionary commenced by Americo Barberi, which, however, he was only able to bring up to the letter G. (" Dizionario artistico, scientifico storico, tecnologico musicale," Milan, published by Gir. Polani).

Berg, (1) Adam, celebrated music printer at Munich, 1540-99; he gave a striking proof of his extraordinary productive activity by taking up the publishing of the great collection (" Patrocinium musicum," ten vols.) at the Duke's expense, the first five volumes of which were exclusively devoted to the works of Orlandus Lassus.—(2) Johann von, also a celebrated music printer, b. Ghent, settled down in Nuremberg, where he entered into partnership in 1550 with Ulrich Neuber; he always named himself Johannes Montanus on the title-page of his books. As Neuber entered into partnership with Gerlach in 1556, B. would seem to have died about this time.—(3) Konrad Mathias, b. April 27, 1785, Colmar (Alsace), violin pupil of Fränzl, in Mannheim, then (1806-1807) pupil of the Paris Conservatoire, d. Dec. 13, 1852, Strassburg, where he settled in 1808 as pianoforte teacher. He wrote pf. works (three concertos, sonatas, variations, ten pf. trios, etc., pieces for four hands), four quartets for strings, etc.; also " Ideen zu einer rationellen Lehrmethode der Musik mit Anwendung auf das Klavierspiel," in G. Weber's " Cäcilia " (vol. 5), and " Aperçu historique sur l'état de la musique à Strasbourg pendant les 50 dernières années " (1840).

Bergamasca (Bergamask dance), an old Italian dance, deriving its name from Bergamo. In *Midsummer Night's Dream*, Bottom asks the Duke if he would care to see a Bergamask dance; hence the dance was already in vogue in England in the 16th century,

Berger, (1) Ludwig, b. April 18, 1777, Berlin, son of an architect, d. there Feb. 16, 1839; passed his youth in Templin and Frankfort-on-Oder, studied harmony and counterpoint under J. A. Gürrlich at Berlin in 1799, travelled in 1801 to Dresden, in order to become a pupil of J. G. Naumann, but when he arrived found that the latter had just died. He dedicated a funeral cantata to his memory. In 1804 he went with M. Clementi, whose acquaintance he had made in Berlin, to St. Petersburg in order to study with him; he there became intimate with A. Klengel, and found, in addition to his teacher, excellent models in Steibelt and Field. He made a happy marriage with the vocalist Wilhelmina Karges, but soon lost wife and child, and went

in 1812 to Stockholm, and from thence to London, where he joined Clementi, and also made the acquaintance of J. B. Cramer. In 1815 he returned to Berlin, where, until his death, he was highly esteemed as a teacher; and among his many distinguished pupils were Mendelssohn, Taubert, Henselt, Fanny Hensel, H. Küster, etc. B. published many excellent pianoforte works, also songs, quartets for male voices, cantatas, etc. In 1819 he founded with B. Klein, G. Reichart, and L. Rellstab, afterwards his biographer, the junior " Liedertafel."—(2) Francesco, composer and pianist, b. June 10, 1835, London, pupil of Luigi Ricci and C. Lickl, and also of Hauptmann. He was for some years director of the Philharmonic Society, and is now Honorary Secretary. He has composed an opera and a mass, part songs, pf. pieces, etc.

Berggreen, Andreas Peter, b. March 2, 1801, Copenhagen, d. there Nov. 9, 1880. He first studied law, then turned his attention to music, and in 1838 became organist of Trinity Church, in 1843 teacher of singing at the metropolitan school, Copenhagen, and in 1859 inspector of singing at the public schools. In 1829 he wrote music to Öhlenschläger's Bridal-cantata; later on an opera, *Billedet og bustan*, music to several of Öhlenschläger's dramas, also pf. pieces and songs. B. edited a collection (eleven vols.) of popular songs of various nations, and from 1836 a musical paper, *Musikalisk Tidende;* he also wrote the biography of Weyse (1875).

Berghem. (*See* BERCHEM.)

Bergkreyen (Bergreihen), originally secular songs, and, as the name indicates, songs accompanied by dancing, to which, however, in the time of the Reformation, sacred words were composed. Collections of secular and sacred B. (but without the melodies) appeared in 1531, 1533, 1537, and 1547. The name *Bergreihen* probably arose from the fact that these songs—as it appears from the title of the 3rd part of Daubmann's B. (1547)—originated in the Erzgebirge; the title runs as follows: " Etzliche schöne Bergreyen vom Schneeberg, Annaberg, Marienberg, Freiberg, und St. Joachimsthal."

Bergmann, Karl, b. 1821, Ebersbach (Saxony), d, Aug. 10, 1876, New York. He was 'cellist and conductor, a pupil of Zimmermann in Zittau, and of Hesse in Breslau. In 1850 he went to the United States, as member of the strolling orchestra, " Germania," of which he soon became the director, and which post he held until the company broke up in 1854. In 1855 he entered the Philharmonic orchestra in New York, and conducted the concerts alternately with Th. Eisfeld, but alone from 1862 until his death. For several years B. conducted the German male choral union, " New York Arion," and rendered important service in the spreading of musical culture throughout the United States. As a composer he only produced a few orchestral pieces.

Bergner, Wilhelm, organist, b. Nov. 4, 1837, Riga, where his father was organist at the church of St. Peter. He studied with his father, afterwards with the cathedral organist, Agthe, at Riga, and with Kühmstadt at Eisenach. After that he became teacher in a boarding school (Liebau), in 1861 organist of the English church at Riga, in 1868 cathedral organist there. By the establishment of a Bach society and cathedral choir B. raised the musical status of Riga, and it was owing to his influence that the great organ in the cathedral was built by Walcker (1882–3).

Bergonzi, Carlo, celebrated violin-maker at Cremona (1716–55), Stradivari's most distinguished pupil. Of less importance were his son, Michelangelo, and his two grandsons, Niccolò and Carlo B.

Bergreihen. (*See* BERGKREYEN.)

Bergson, Michael, composer and pianist, b. May, 1820, Warsaw. He studied at Dessau with Friedrich Schneider, went to Italy in 1846, and produced the opera *Luisa di Montfort* at La Pergola, Florence, in 1847, with success (it was also given at Livorno and at Hamburg in German in 1849). He lived for several years at Berlin and Leipzig, and then settled down in Paris, where in 1859 he produced at a concert his one-act operetta, *Qui va à la chasse perd sa place;* he also offered a two-act opera to the Théâtre Lyrique, but it was not given. In 1863 he went as principal pianoforte teacher to the Geneva Conservatoire, of which institution he soon became director; a few years later he went to London, where he lived as a private teacher. B. wrote many *études* and characteristic pieces for pianoforte, also a pf. concerto, etc. He died Dec. 12, 1897, London.

Bergt, Christian Gottlob August, b. June 17, 1772, Öderan, near Freiburg; from 1802 until his death, Feb, 10, 1837, he was organist at Bautzen, also music teacher at the college and conductor of the choral union there. B. wrote a Passion oratorio, Te Deum, cantatas, and other sacred works, as well as symphonies, quartets, pf. variations, several operas, duets, ballads, and small songs, of which much ·was published.

Beringer, Oscar, pianist and composer, b. 1844, Baden, studied under Moscheles, Reinecke, Richter at the Leipzig Conservatorium, and under C. Tausig and Weitzmann in Berlin. He has resided in London since 1871: and in 1873 established an " Academy for the Higher Development of Pianoforte Playing." He has composed pf. pieces, two sonatinas, songs, etc. He was recently appointed professor of the pianoforte at the Royal Academy of Music.

Bériot, Charles Auguste de, celebrated violinist, b. Feb. 20, 1802, Louvain, d. April 8, 1870, Brussels. He really never had a teacher of any name, but, for his virtuosity, he was indebted to his happy disposition, to his persevering diligence, and to the solid elementary training of his guardian, Tiby, a music teacher at Louvain. When he played to Viotti in 1821, he was already an independent artist. For a short time he attended the Conservatoire as a pupil of Baillot's, but only to make the discovery that this would be prejudicial to his individuality. His first public appearance in Paris was a victory, and he was at once able to make a successful concert journey to England. On returning home he was appointed solo violinist to the King of the Netherlands, with a stipend of 2,000 florins. The revolution of July, 1830, cut off this source of income, and B. was again compelled to travel, this time with Mme. Garcia-Malibran, whom he married, and whose singing, perhaps, had something to do with his method of producing tone. She bore him a son in 1833, but died already in 1836. During the next few years B. made no appearance in public; it was only in 1840 that he undertook a concert tour through Germany. In 1843 he was appointed professor of the violin at Brussels; but the complete loss of his eyesight, and, in addition, paralysis of the left arm, forced him to retire in 1852. His principal works are: seven violin concertos, a violin school in three parts (1858), several sonatas, sets of variations, and many studies for the violin, as well as some trios.

Berlijn, Anton, b. May 2, 1817, Amsterdam, d. Jan. 16, 1870; pupil of Ludwig Erk. He was musical director at Amsterdam, and composed nine operas, seven ballets, one oratorio (*Moses*), symphonies, etc., and many small pieces; out of Holland, however, he is little known.

Berlin, Joh. Daniel, b. 1710, Memel, went in 1730 to Copenhagen, and as organist to Drontheim (Norway) in 1737, where he died in 1775. He published an Elementary Method (1742), also a Guide to Temperament Calculations.

Berlioz, Hector, b. Dec. 11, 1803, Côte St. André (Isère), d. March 8, 1869, Paris. He was the son of a physician, and intended for the medical profession. Against his parents' wish he left the University and went to the Conservatoire, and, since his father refused to help him, he was compelled to earn a living as chorister at the Théâtre Gymnase. He soon left the Conservatoire, as the dry rules of solid learning were not to his taste, and he then gave free rein to his phantasy. A mass with orchestra, first produced at St. Roch, the overtures *Waverley* and *Les Francs Juges*, and the Fantastic Symphony, *Épisode de la vie à un Artiste*, were already written and produced, when B. in 1830 won the Prix de Rome with his cantata, *Sardanapale*. In order to try for that prize, he had again entered the Conservatoire, and become the pupil of Lesueur. During the period of study in Italy, he wrote the *King Lear* overture, and the symphonic poem with vocal music, *Lélio, ou le Retour à la Vie*, a sequel to the *Symphonie Fantastique*. At the same time he was active with his racy pen, contributing *feuilletons* to the *Revue Européenne*, the *Courrier de l'Europe*, *Journal des Débats*, and, from 1834, to the newly founded *Gazette Musicale de Paris*. By word and deed he sought to establish a style of composition which, even to-day, is opposed and disowned by many—the so-called programme-music. In Germany, Liszt was heart and hand with him, adopting his ideas, though in independent fashion. In 1843 B. visited Germany, in 1845 Austria, and in 1847 Russia, producing his works in the most important cities, and, though often meeting with strong opposition, he everywhere excited lively interest. In vain he longed for an appointment as professor of composition at the Conservatoire; he was only appointed Conservator in 1839, and librarian in 1852, which post he occupied until his death. B. was not successful in Paris during his lifetime; only recently is his importance beginning to be understood, and, perhaps, over-rated; and the concert institutions of Paris vie with one another in Berlioz-worship. B. materially helped to remove many prejudices, but the greatest service which he rendered was to enrich the orchestra with new effects and to suggest entirely new treatment of the same. His "Traité d'Instrumentation" (translated into German by Dörffel in 1864, also by Grünbaum, without year of publication, and into English by Mary Cowden Clarke), in spite of many modern attempts, still holds the first place. Besides the above-named works should still be mentioned the grand "Messe des Morts" (for the burial service of General Damrémont at the Invalides, 1837), "Harold en Italie" (Symphony); "Roméo et Juliette" (Symphony, with soli and chorus); the "Te Deum," for three choirs, orchestra, and organ; the operas, *Benvenuto Cellini*, *Béatrice et Bénedict*, *Les Troyens* (1st part, "La Prise de Troie;" 2nd part, "Les Troyens à Carthage"); the dramatic legend *La Damnation de Faust*; the Biblical trilogy *L'Enfance du Christ* (1, "Le Songe d'Hérode"; 2, "La Fuite en Egypte;" 3, "L'Arrivée à Sais"); the "Grande Symphonie Funèbre et Triomphale," for a large wind-orchestra (strings and chorus *ad lib.*); "Le 5 Mai" (bass solo, chorus, and orchestra), for the anniversary of Napoleon's death; *Le Carneval Romain* (overture), etc. To these must be added his writings: "Voyage Musicale en Allemagne et en Italie" (1844, 2 vols.); "Soirées d'Orchestre" (1853); "Grotesques de la Musique" (1859); "À Travers Chants" (1862), etc., translated into German by R. Pohl (complete edition, 4 vols. 1864). After his death appeared his "Mémoires" (1870), which

also contain the letters written during his travels. These have been translated into English by Rachel and Eleanor Holmes.

Bermudo, J u a n, b. cir. 1510, near Astorga, drew up a description of musical instruments ("Declaracion de Instrumentos"), of which one volume appeared in 1545: the manuscript is in the national library at Madrid.

Bernabeï, (1), G i u s e p p e E r c o l e, b. about 1620, Caprarola, d. 1687 Munich; was a pupil of Benevoli's, and (1662–67) maestro di cappella at the Lateran, then at San Luigi de Francesi. In 1672 he succeeded Benevoli at the Vatican, and in 1674 became court capellmeister and member of the Electoral Council at Munich. As a composer, B. belongs to the Roman School. Besides five operas produced at Munich, he wrote specially sacred works: masses, psalms, offertories à 4–16 are preserved in the archives of the Vatican. The only printed works are, motets (1690), and madrigals (1669, 2 books à 3 and à 5–6).—(2) G i u s e p p e A n t o n i o, son of the former, b. 1659, Rome, d. March 9, 1732, Munich. In 1677 he became vice-capellmeister at Munich, and in 1688, as his father's successor, Bavarian court capellmeister. He wrote fifteen operas for Munich, and published a number of masses.

Bernacchi, A n t o n i o, b. 1690, Bologna, d. March, 1756; was a celebrated *evirato*, pupil of Pistocchi. He sang in London already in 1716-17, then at Munich and Vienna, and in 1729 was engaged by Handel again for London (in place of Senesino), as the most distinguished Italian singer of the time. He became specially famous for a new method of ornamentation in singing. In 1736 he returned to Bologna, and founded there a school for singing. The Paris Conservatoire possesses some of his vocal compositions in manuscript. The "Grosse Gesangschule des B. von Bologna," published by Manstein in 1834, was not written by B., but only attempts to reconstruct his method of teaching, so far as this may have been preserved by tradition.

Bernard, (1) E m e r y, b. Orleans; published a Method of singing (1541, 1561, 1570).—(2) M o r i t z, b. 1794, Courland, d. May 9, 1871, Petersburg. He was a pupil of J. Field and Hässler at Moscow, in 1816 capellmeister to Count Potocki, in 1822 teacher of music at Petersburg: in 1829 he founded a music business in the latter city, which attained to a high degree of prosperity. He published some pf. pieces of his own, and wrote a Russian opera (*Olga*).—(3) P a u l, b. Oct. 4, 1827, Poitiers, d. Feb. 24, 1879, as a private teacher in Paris. He was a pupil of the Paris Conservatoire, and published many pf. pieces, songs, etc., was also active as critic to the Paris musical papers, *Ménestrel* and *Revue et Gazette Musicale*.—(4) D a n i e l, b. 1841, also a writer on music, and principal contributor to the *Ménestrel;* he died at Paris, June, 1883.

Bernardi, (1), S t e f f a n o, canon at Salzburg about 1634. He published a series of books of madrigals, also masses, motets, and psalms 1611–37), as well as a " Lehre vom Kontrapunkt" (1634).—(2) F r a n c e s c o, under the name Senesino, a world-famed *evirato*, b. 1680, Siena. He was first engaged at Dresden, from which place Handel won him in 1720 for London ; in 1729 he quarrelled with Handel and went over to Bononcini. In 1739 he returned to Italy.— (3) E n r i c o, b. March 11, 1838, Milan, was conductor of the theatre in that city ; he wrote, for stages of Upper Italy, a number of operas, operettas, and ballets, but only with moderate success. Died July 17, 1900, Milan.

Bernardini, M a r c e l l o, b. about 1762, Capua (Marcello di Capua), wrote (1784–94) twenty operas, mostly comic, for the Italian stage, which had good success, but were speedily forgotten ; he himself, for the most part, wrote the *libretti.*

Bernasconi, A n d r e a, b. 1712, Marseilles, d. Jan. 24, 1784, Munich, where he became vice-capellmeister in 1753, and court capellmeister in 1755. He wrote twenty operas for Vienna, Rome, and especially Munich ; also some sacred works of his exist in manuscript.

Bernelinus, writer on music at Paris (probably a Benedictine monk) about 1000; his treatise on the division of the monochord is printed in Gerbert, " Script." I.

Berner, F r i e d r i c h W i l h e l m, b. May 16, 1780, Breslau, d. there May 9, 1827. He was organist at St. Elizabeth's Church, music teacher at the college, and later on director of the Royal Academical Institute for Church Music. He was a distinguished organist (teacher of Ernst Köhler and Ad. Hesse) and a fair composer (principally sacred works; much remains in manuscript).

Bernhard, C h r i s t o p h, b. 1627, Danzig, d. Nov. 14, 1692, Dresden, was a pupil of H. Schütz in the latter city. He was twice sent to Italy by the Elector of Saxony to engage singers; in 1655 he became vice-capellmeister at Dresden, was (1664–74) cantor at Hamburg, and then Schütz's successor as capellmeister at Dresden. B. was an excellent contrapuntist. The following of his works were printed: " Geistliche Harmonien" (1665) and " Prudentia Prudentiana," (Hymns 1669); his " Tractatus Compositionis," and a work on counterpoint, remain in manuscript.

Bernhard, v o n C l a i r v a u x, S a i n t, b. 1091, Fontaines (Burgundy), d. Aug. 20, 1153, as Abbot of Clairvaux. He wrote an introductory letter, " De correctione antiphonarii" to the work drawn up under his authority, " Praefatio seu Tractatus in Antiphonarium Cisterciense." " Tonarium " (*Tonale* in dialogue form), known

under his name, is likewise only under his authority. All three works are printed in a collection published at Leipzig, 1517 (*Cf.* Fétis, " Biographie Universelle, article " Bernard "); only the *Tones* are to be found in Gerbert (" Script." II.) ; and only the Letter and the Prologue in Mabillon's edition of the works of St. Bernhard.

Bernhard der Deutsche is said to have been the inventor of organ pedals, but probably only introduced them into Italy. He was organist of St. Mark's, Venice (1445–59), and, according to the register of that church, was called Bernardo di Steffanino Murer.

Bernicat, F i r m i n, b. 1841, d. March, 1883, Paris ; wrote a number (thirteen) of operettas for Paris theatres.

Berno, Abbot of Reichenau monastery (hence named A u g i e n s i s) from 1008, d. June 7, 1048. Besides many works not relating to music, he wrote a " Tonarium " with a Prologue ; also " De Varia Psalmorum Atque Cantuum Modulatione " and " De Consona Tonorum Diversitate " (all printed in Gerbert, " Script." II.). Trithemius mentions, besides, a treatise, " De Instrumentis Musicalibus." W. Brambach wrote a monograph on Berno's system of music (1881).

Bernouilli, J o h a n n, b. July 27, 1667, Basle, d. there, Jan. 2, 1747, as Professor of Sciences; and his son, D a n i e l, b. Feb. 9, 1700, Groningen, d. March 17, 1782, as Professor of Sciences at Basle ; both wrote important treatises on acoustics.

Bernsdorf, E d u a r d, b. March 25, 1825, Dessau; studied there under Fr. Schneider, and under A. B. Marx at Berlin. He was a teacher of music, and musical critic (of the *Signale*) at Leipzig, and completed the " Universal-Lexicon der Tonkunst" (three vols., with appendix, 1855-56), commenced by J. Schladebach. As a composer he produced a few pf. pieces and songs. Died June 27 1901, Leipzig.

Bernuth, J u l i u s v o n, distinguished conductor and teacher, b. Aug. 8, 1830, Rees (Rhine Province). He studied law at Berlin, but enjoyed at the same time musical instruction from Taubert and Dehn ; and, after being referenary at Wesel for two years, went, in 1854, to the Leipzig Conservatorium. In 1857 he founded the *Aufschwung* Union, in 1859 the Amateur Orchestral Union; was conductor for a time of the " Euterpe " (successor to Langer), of the Vocal Academy (successor to Rietz), and of the Male Choral Union. In 1863 he studied singing in London under Garcia. For several years he again conducted the " Euterpe " concerts, and with very great success ; from 1867 he conducted the Philharmonic Concerts and the Singakademie at Hamburg, and from 1873 he was director of a prosperous conservatorium there. The impulse given to musical affairs at Hamburg is mainly owing to the efforts of B. In 1878 he was named " K. Preuss Professor." Died Dec. 24, 1902.

Berr, Friedrich, famous performer on the clarinet and on the bassoon, b. April 17, 1794, Mannheim, d. Sept. 24, 1838. He was at first bandmaster in various French regiments, then (1823) first clarinettist at the Théâtre des Italiens, Paris; in 1831 teacher of the clarinet at the Conservatoire, in 1832 solo clarinet player in the royal band, and in 1836 became director of the newly-established Military School of Music. He published in 1836 a " Traité Complet de la Clarinette à 14 Clefs."

Bertali, Antonio, b. 1605, Verona, d. April 1, 1669, Vienna; from 1637 "Hofmusicus" in the latter city, and from 1649 court capellmeister, as successor to Valentini, which position he occupied with honour until his death. Already, from 1631 to 1646, cantatas of his own composition were produced by him at Vienna, but later the operas, *L'Inganno d'Amore* (1653, with great success), *Teti* (1656), *Il rè Gelidoro* (1659), *Gli Amori di Apollo* (1660), *Il Ciro Crescente* (1661), *L'Alcindo* (1665), *Cibele e Atti* (1666), *La Contesa dell' Aria e dell' Acqua* (1667); and the oratorios, *Maria Magdalena* (1663), *Oratorio Sacro* (1663), and *La Strega dell' Innocenti* (1665).

Bertelmann, Jan Georg, b. Jan. 21, 1782, Amsterdam, d. there Jan. 25, 1854. He was a pupil of the blind organist, D. Brachthuijzer, a highly esteemed teacher (Stumpff and Hol were his pupils), and a composer of importance. He published a requiem, a mass, a quartet for strings, and compositions for violin and pianoforte. Cantatas, violin studies, clarinet concertos, double-bass concertos, etc., as well as a " Harmonielehre," remain in manuscript.

Bertelsmann, Karl August, b. 1811, Gütersloh, d. Nov. 20, 1861; was a pupil of Rinck's at Darmstadt, then teacher of singing at Soest seminary, and went finally to Amsterdam, where, in 1839, he undertook the direction of the newly established society, " Eutonia." In 1853 he conducted the musical festival at Arnheim. He wrote songs for solo voice, part-songs for male chorus, and some pianoforte pieces.

Berthaume, Isidore, b. 1752, Paris, d. March 20, 1802, Petersburg; became first violinist at the Grand Opéra in 1774, in 1783 conductor of the " Concerts Spirituels," travelled and gave concerts during the Revolution, became leader of the ducal band at Eutin in 1793, and afterwards solo violinist in the private band at Petersburg. B. published violin sonatas and also a violin concerto.

Berthold, K. Fr. Theodor, b. Dec. 18, 1815, Dresden, d. there April 28, 1882; studied under Fr. Schneider, and J. Otto. From 1840 to 1864 he lived in Russia, and founded at Petersburg the St. Anne Union (for oratorios). In 1864 he

succeeded Fr. Schneider as court organist at Dresden. B. was a sound composer (*Missa Solemnis;* oratorio *Petrus*, symphonies, etc.). In collaboration with M. Fürstenau, he wrote " Die Fabrikation musikalischer Instrumente im Voigtlande " (1876).

Bertin, Louise Angélique, devoted herself to composition (also poetry and painting), b. Feb. 15, 1805, Roche, near Bièvre, d. April 26, 1877, Paris. She wrote the operas, *Guy Mannering, Le Loup Garou, Faust*, and *Esmeralda* (*Nôtre Dame de Paris*), the last of which was given at Munich. She also composed songs, choral pieces, stringed quartets, a trio, etc., some of which appeared in print.

Bertini, (1) Abbate Giuseppe, b. 1756, Palermo, royal maestro di cappella there, published in 1814 "Dizionario Storico-Critico degli Scrittori di Musica"; he was still living in 1847.—(2) Benoît Auguste, b. June 5, 1780, Lyons; studied with Clementi in London (1793), lived for a time in Paris, Naples, and again in London as teacher of the pianoforte. In 1830 he published " Phonological System for Acquiring Extraordinary Facility on all Musical Instruments as well as in Singing "; and also, at an earlier date, in Paris, " Stigmatographie, ou l'Art d'écrire avec des Points, suivi de la Mélographie," etc.—(3) Henri (the younger), younger brother and pupil of the former, b. Oct. 28, 1798, London, d. Oct. 1, 1876, Grenoble. At the age of six he went to Paris, where—not reckoning his concert tours—he resided for the most part. In 1859 he withdrew to his Villa Meylan, near Grenoble, and died there. His *Études* are educational works universally known; they are of great technical service, and are not only useful, but melodious and harmonically interesting, especially Ops. 100, 29 and 32 (in which order they may be looked upon as preparatory to Czerny's Op. 299). Gius. Buonamici has published a selection of fifty studies, with excellent comments and modern fingering.—(4) Domenico, b. June 26, 1829, Lucca, studied at the music school there, and under Puccini. In 1857 he became maestro di cappella and director at the Massa Carrara music school; went to Florence in 1862, where he also acquired fame as conductor of the Società Cherubini, and as a musical critic. Songs, fragments from two operas which were not produced, and a system of harmony, "Compendio de' Principii di Musica Secondo un Nuovo Sistema" (1866), appeared in print.

Berton, (1) Pierre Montan, b. 1727, Paris, d. there May 14, 1780, as royal maître de chapelle, and chef d'orchestre at the Grand Opéra. He was an excellent conductor, and his services were of value for the performance of Gluck's works. He also wrote several operas, and re-arranged some of Lully's.—(2) Henri Montan, son of the former, b. Sept. 17, 1767, Paris, d. there April 22, 1844; a favourite opera composer. In 1795 he became professor of harmony at the newly established Conservatoire, in 1807 conductor of the *Opera buffa* (Italian Opera), in 1815 member of the Académie, in 1816 professor of composition at the Conservatoire. Besides many operas (forty-eight)—from among which may be mentioned *Montano et Stéphanie* (1799), *Le Délire* (1799), and *Aline* (1803), and four ballets—he also wrote five oratorios, cantatas, etc., which were produced at the "Concerts Spirituels."—(3) Henri, natural son of the former, b. May 3, 1784, Paris, d. July 19, 1842; was professor of singing at the Conservatoire from 1821 to 1827; he likewise wrote some operas.

Bertoni, Ferdinando Giuseppe, b. Aug. 15, 1725, on the island of St. Malo, near Venice, d. Dec. 1, 1813, Desenzano. In 1752 he became first organist at St. Mark's, and in 1757 also choir-master at the Conservatorio "de Mendicanti." In 1784 he succeeded Galuppi as maestro di cappella at St. Mark's, and retired to Desenzano in 1810. B. wrote many sacred works (including five oratorios) and thirty-four operas, as well as some chamber music.

Bertrand, Jean Gustave, b. Dec. 24, 1834, Vaugirard, near Paris, a learned writer, musical critic, and contributor of articles to various Paris papers. He published "Histoire ecclésiastique de l'orgue (1859), "Essai sur la musique dans l'antiquité," "Les origines de l'harmonie" (1866), "De la réforme des études du chant au Conservatoire" (1871), and "Les nationalités musicales étudiées dans le drame lyrique" (1872).

Berwald, (1) Joh. Friedrich, b. 1788 (?), Stockholm, d. 1861; was a youthful prodigy, played the violin in public at the age of five, and produced a symphony at the age of nine, made many concert tours, was for a long time pupil of Abt Vogler, in 1806 was named chamber musician, and in 1834 conductor at Stockholm. Of his compositions, which, for the rest, are not of great value, some appeared before 1800.—(2) Franz, nephew of the former, b. July 23, 1796, Stockholm, d. there April 30, 1868, as director of the Conservatoire, wrote symphonies and chamber-music works, of which only a few appeared in print; also an opera, produced at Stockholm, *Estrella de Soria*.

Berwin, Adolf, b. March 30, 1847, at Schwersenz, near Posen, attended the Gymnasium at Posen, learnt the pianoforte with Lechner and the violin with Fröhlich, then studied counterpoint at Berlin with Rust, and composition with Dessoff at Vienna. B. is academical professor and regular member of the Cecilia Academy at Rome, principal librarian of the same and of the Lyceum of Music; and he was knighted in 1879. By royal decree, in 1882, he became director of the Royal Library and of the St. Cecilia Academy, amalgamated into one. He edited an Italian translation of the Lebert and Stark "Pianoforte School," and is working

at a "Geschichte der dramatischen Musik in Italien während des 18. Jahrhunderts."

Besard, Jean Baptiste, b. Besançon, lutenist and composer for the lute, published: "Thesaurus harmonicus" (1603, arrangements for the lute), "Novus partus" (1617, the same), and "Traité de luth," in a second edition, as "Isagoge in artem testudinariam" (1617).

Beschnitt, Johannes, b. April 30, 1825, Bockau, Silesia, d. July 24, 1880, Stettin; attended the Normal School at Breslau (1842), and from 1844-5 the Royal Institute for Church Music there. In 1848 he was appointed cantor and teacher at the Catholic School at Stettin, directed a male vocal society, and wrote a large number of light, easy choruses for male voices ("Mein Schifflein treibt inmitten," "Ossian," etc.).

Besekirsky, Wasil Wasilewitch, violinist, b. 1836, Moscow, went in 1858 to Brussels, to Léonard, appeared there and at Paris with great success, and in 1860 returned to Moscow, where he had already been member of the theatre orchestra. Since then he has made many concert tours, among others, in 1866 to Madrid, 1869 to Prague, etc.; he has also published much for the violin.

Besler, (1) Samuel, b. Dec. 15, 1574, Brieg; 1599 cantor, and 1605 rector of the Gymnasium "zum Heiligen Geist," at Breslau; d. July 19, 1625, of the plague. A series of compositions for the church, written between 1602-24, have been preserved.—(2) Simon, 1615-28, cantor at St. Maria Magdalena, Breslau, was probably related to the former; only a small number of his songs à 4, printed in score, have been preserved. For the two Beslers cf. E. Bohn's Catalogue of Musical Publications in Breslau up to the year 1700.

Besozzi, Louis Désiré, b. April 3, 1814, Versailles, d. Nov. 11, 1879, as music teacher in Paris; he sprang from a very musical family (many excellent performers on the oboe, bassoon, and flute distinguished themselves at Turin, Parma, Dresden, and Paris from 1750), studied composition under Lesueur at the Paris Conservatoire, received in 1837 the *Prix de Rome*, and wrote besides pianoforte works.

Bessems, Antoine, b. April 6, 1809, Antwerp, d. there Oct. 19, 1868; was in 1826 pupil of Baillot at the Paris Conservatoire, and for some time member of the orchestra of the Italian Opera, but then went on concert tours as violin player, and settled in Antwerp in 1852. B. has written instrumental works and some sacred compositions.

Besson, Gustave Auguste, improver of the mechanism of the valves of wind instruments, b. 1820, Paris, d. there, 1875.

Best, William Thomas, b. Aug. 13, 1826, Carlisle, distinguished organist, first in 1840, of Pembroke Chapel, Liverpool; 1847 of the

Church of the Blind, and 1848 organist of the Philharmonic Society there; in 1852 London, at the famous Panopticon organ, and at St. Martin's Church, 1854 at Lincoln's Inn Chapel, and 1855 at St. George's Hall, Liverpool; he was, besides, organist of the Musical Society and of the Philharmonic Society in that city (1872). In addition to anthems and other compositions for the church, he composed especially fugues, sonatas, and other organ and pf. pieces; also two overtures. But his principal works are: "The Modern School for the Organ" (1853) and "The Art of Organ Playing" (1870, pts. 1 and 2; two more parts are still in manuscript). In recent years Best had been arranging twenty books of Handel's rarely performed instrumental music, and four of his concertos for concert use, editing and revising a series of original organ works by different authors, called "Cecilia," and also editing and thoroughly revising J. S. Bach's organ works. All these later works have appeared in Augener's Edition. He died May 10, 1897.

Betont (Ger.), emphasized.

Bettlerleier. (*See* HURDY-GURDY.)

Betz, Franz, b. March 19, 1835, Mayence, a most distinguished stage singer (baritone); from 1856 to 1859 he was on the stage at Hanover, Altenburg, Gera, Bernburg, Coethen, and Rostock, and since then at the Royal Opera House, Berlin, where he made his *début* as Don Carlos in *Ernani* (1859). B. was one of the best Wagner singers; he died Aug. 11, 1900, at Berlin.

Bevin, Elway, 1589 organist of Bristol Cathedral, 1605 gentleman extraordinary of the Chapel Royal. In 1637 he lost both appointments because he became attached to the Roman Catholic faith. He published Church music (anthems, etc.), and "Brief and Short Introduction to the Art of Music" (1631).

Bexfield, William Richard, b. April 27, 1824, Norwich, d. Oct. 29, 1853, London; was at first organist at Boston (Lincolnshire), from 1848 at St. Helen's in London. He took the degree of Mus. Bac. in 1846, at Oxford; that of Doctor in 1849, at Cambridge. He wrote an oratorio, *Israel Restored;* and a cantata, *Hector's Death;* also organ fugues and anthems.

Beyer, (1) Joh. Samuel, b. 1669, Gotha, d. May 9, 1744, Carlsbad; 1697 cantor at Freiberg i.S., 1722 at Weissenfels, and in 1728 again as musical director at Freiberg; he published: "Primæ lineæ musicæ vocalis" (Elementary Method of Singing, 1703), also "Musikalischer Vorrath neu variirter Festchoralgesänge, etc." (1716) and "Geistlich-musikalische Seelenfreude, bestehend aus 72 Konzertarien, etc." (1724).— (2) Rudolf, b. Feb. 14, 1828, Wilther, near Bautzen, d. Jan. 22, 1853, Dresden, composer and valued private music teacher, 1840 pupil of Weinlig and Hauptmann, later at the Leipzig

Conservatorium. He composed songs, chamber music, music to O. Ludwig's "Maccabäer," etc.

B-flat chord $= b$ *flat, d, f;* B flat *major* key, two flats in the signature. (*See* KEY.)

B-flat minor chord $= b$ *flat, d flat, f;* B flat *minor* key, five flats in the signature. (*See* KEY.)

Bi. (*See* BOBISATION.)

Bial, Rudolph, b. Aug. 26, 1834, Habelschwerdt (Silesia), d. Nov. 13, 1881, New York; he was violinist in the orchestra at Breslau, made a concert tour with his brother, the pianist, Karl B. (b. July 14, 1833), in Africa and Australia, and then settled down in Berlin, and first as conductor of the Kroll orchestra. He became capellmeister in 1864 of the Wallner Theatre, where he brought out his amusing farces and operettas; afterwards director of the Italian Opera in Berlin; finally concert agent in New York. Karl d. Dec. 20, 1892, Steglitz.

Bianca (Ital.), white (note), *i.e.* a minim.

Bianchi, (1) Francesco, b. 1752, Cremona, d. Sept 24, 1811, Bologna. He went to Paris in 1775 as cembalist at the Italian Opera, to Florence in 1780, and to Milan (S. Ambrogio and La Scala) in 1784. In the following year he became second organist of St. Mark's, Venice, but was dismissed in 1791 as unsuitable. In the following year, however, through the favour of patrons, he was reinstated. In 1793 he went to London as conductor at the King's Theatre, and in 1800 married the singer, Miss Lucy Jackson. Up to 1795 he produced at least one new opera every year (altogether, up to 1800, forty-seven operas). A theoretical treatise of his remained in manuscript.—(2) Valentine, celebrated stage-singer (soprano of extensive compass), b. 1839, Wilna, d. Feb 28, 1884, Candau (Courland), was trained at the Paris Conservatoire, made her *début* at Frankfort and Berlin in 1855, and was then engaged at Schwerin (1855–61), Stettin, Petersburg (1862–65), and Moscow (until 1867); and during this period, and for some years afterwards, accepted starring engagements and gave concerts. In 1865 she married the chief-forester, Von Fabian, and in 1870 withdrew into private life.—(3) Bianca (really Schwarz), stage-singer (high soprano), b. June 27, 1858, in a village on the Neckar, was trained at Heidelberg by the musical director, Wilczek, and by Madame Viardot-Garcia, in Paris, at Pollini's expense, who engaged her for ten years. She made her *début* at Carlsruhe in 1873 as Barbarina in *Figaro*. After she had sung for him in London, she accepted an engagement at Mannheim, then at Carlsruhe, and in 1880 at Vienna.

Biber, (1) Heinrich Johann Franz (von), b. 1644, Wartenberg (Bohemia), d. May 3, 1704, Salzburg. He was a violinist, raised by Leopold I. to the rank of a nobleman; he was afterwards at the Bavarian Court, and published six violin sonatas (1681), seven partitas à 3, two sonatas, "Tam Aris Quam Aulis Servientes," and a book of Vespers and Litanies with instrumental accompaniment (1693).—(2) Aloys, b. 1804, Ellingen, d. Dec. 13, 1858, at Munich, an esteemed pianoforte manufacturer.

Bichord, an instrument with two strings, or an instrument the strings of which are tuned in pairs, each pair in unison. A bichord pianoforte is one with two strings to each key.

Bicinium (Lat.), a composition in two parts; a term used specially in vocal music. (*Cf.* TRICINIUM.)

Biedermann, . . . about 1786 official receiver of taxes at Beichlingen (Thuringia), was one of the last performers on the vielle (hurdy-gurdy), which he himself improved.

Bierey, Gottlob Benedikt, b. July 25, 1772, Dresden, d. May 5, 1840, Breslau. He studied under Weinlig, was at first musical director of an itinerant opera company, but, by the successful performance of his opera, *Wladimir* (1807, Vienna), he was called to Breslau as capellmeister in the place of K. M. v. Weber. He became director of the theatre in 1824, retired in 1828, and lived for several years in various German towns, but finally returned to Breslau. Besides many operettas, he also wrote cantatas, masses, as well as orchestral and chamber music, and a "Method of Harmony" which remained in manuscript.

Biese, Wilhelm, b. April 20, 1822, Rathenow, a pianoforte maker (especially pianinos) established at Berlin since 1853; d. Nov. 14, 1902.

Bifara (*Bifra*, or *Piffara*, *Piffaro*, really *Tibia bifaris*, "double-speaking pipe") is an organ stop which replaces the *Tremulant*, and gives a slight trembling to the sound.

Bigaglia, Diogenio, b. Venice; a Benedictine monk there. He published in 1725 twelve sonatas for violin or flute alone; other works remained in manuscript.

Bignio, Louis Von, distinguished opera singer (baritone), b. 1839, Pesth, son of a high functionary. After attending the Gymnasium, he went to the University. He was, however, soon attracted to music, studied at the Pesth Conservatorium, and afterwards was trained under Rossi and Gentiluomo for the stage. He made a favourable *début* at the German theatre, Pesth, in 1858; but, after a few months, was engaged at the Hungarian National Theatre. In 1863 the Vienna Opera succeeded in getting him, and there he specially distinguished himself in lyrical parts. He was universally esteemed, and remained thus until he received his pension in 1883. He then returned to the Pesth National Theatre. B. also appeared with great success as a concert singer (in London, among other places).

Bigot, Marie (*née* Kiene), b. March 3, 1786, Colmar, d. Sept. 16, 1820. She was a distinguished pianist, and was held in high esteem by Beethoven. She lived many years in Vienna, where her husband was librarian to Count Rasumowski. She settled in Paris in 1809, and gave pianoforte lessons from the year 1812.

Bilhon (Billon), Jean De, a singer in the Papal chapel, whose masses, motets, etc., are to be found in collections between 1534 and 1544.

Billert, Karl Fr. August, b. Sept. 14, 1821, Altstettin, d. Dec. 22, 1875, Berlin; was a painter and musician. He studied at the Academy of Painting, and at the class for composition of the Royal Academy at Berlin. He produced some important works of his own at Berlin. He contributed a great number of articles to the Mendel-Reissmann "Musiklexikon."

Billet (Alexandre Philippe), French composer and pianist, b. 1817, Petersburg, lived in London as teacher and composer.

Billeter, Agathon, a favourite composer of male part-songs ("Im Maien"), b. Nov. 21, 1834, Maennedorf (Lake of Zürich). He studied at the Leipzig Conservatorium, and became organist and conductor at Burgdorf (Switzerland).

Billings, William, American composer, b. 1746, Boston, d. there 1800. He wrote, "Music in Miniature" (1779), "The Psalm Singer's Amusement" (1781), etc.

Billington, Elizabeth (*née* Weichsel), b. about 1768, London, d. Aug. 25, 1818. She was the daughter of a German musician, and was the pupil of Joh. Christian Bach. She was a distinguished vocalist and a striking beauty. She married the contrabassist, James B., in 1784, and went with him to Dublin, where she commenced her stage career. She returned in the same year to London, and obtained an engagement at Drury Lane, for which she received a thousand pounds. She left London in 1794, and was a "star" in Italy. Her husband died at Naples, and she soon separated from a second one (Felissent). In 1801 she returned to London, and sang in public up to 1811. In 1817 she became reconciled with her second husband, and retired to a country seat near Venice, where she died.

Billroth, Joh. Gustav Friedrich, b. Feb. 17, 1808, Halle, near Lübeck, d. March 28, 1836, as Professor of Philosophy at Halle. He was a contributor to musical papers, and, jointly with K. F. Becker, published chorales of the 16th and 17th centuries.

Bilse, Benjamin, b. Aug. 17, 1816, Liegnitz, was educated from early youth for a musical career. He was "Stadtmusikus" in his birthplace, and brought the band there to such a high state of perfection, that he ventured to travel with his orchestra to the Paris

Exhibition of 1867, giving concerts on his way thither and homewards in many great cities, and with marked success. Through intrigues he had already lost his appointment, but kept his orchestra together at his own expense, and made concert tours abroad with it. From 1868 he lived in Berlin, and his concerts (in the "Konzerthaus") were thought much of. In 1884 he withdrew from active life. The Emperor bestowed on him the title of "Hofmusikdirector." Died July 13, 1902.

Binchois, Gilles (Aegidius), one of the oldest composers of the first Netherland School, contemporary of Dufay, b. about 1400, Bins (Binche), Hennegau, was in 1452 second chaplain in the Chapel of Philip the Good of Burgundy, and died at Lille in 1460. Of his compositions little has been preserved. Besides those named by Fétis, six rondos and two songs have recently been discovered in the Munich Library, and published by Dr. H. Riemann.

Bind (Ger. *Bindebogen*). (*See* LEGATO and SLUR.)

Binder, (1) K. Wilh. Ferd., b. 1764, Dresden, was a famous harp builder in Weimar about 1797.—(2) Karl, b. Nov. 29, 1816, Vienna, d. there Nov. 5, 1860; was first capellmeister at the Joseph Town Theatre in that city, afterwards at Hamburg, Presburg, and finally returned to Vienna; composed operettas, melodramas, etc.

Bioni, Antonio, b. 1698, Venice, produced first some operas in Italy, went then, in 1726, as musical director of an Italian Opera company to Breslau, where in 1730 he himself became theatre manager, and composed with incredible diligence (in all, twenty-six Italian operas). His *Endimione* (1727) met with special success. He was appointed court composer to the Elector of Mayence in 1731. The Breslau undertaking came to an end in 1733, and no further trace of B. can be found.

Birchall, Robert, English music publisher, one of the first to establish a circulating musical library. He was originally employed by Randall, and his successors were Lonsdale and Mills. He published works by Beethoven, Mozart, Haydn, etc.; he died in 1819.

Birckenstock, Johann Adam, violinist, b. Feb. 19, 1687, Alsfeld (Hesse), d. Feb. 26, 1733, Eisenach. The Landgrave had him carefully trained by Ruggiero Fedeli at Cassel, Volumier at Berlin, Fiorelli at Baireuth, and de Val at Paris. From 1725 to 1730 he was capellmeister at Cassel, and was afterwards employed in a similar capacity at Eisenach. B. published twenty-four violin sonatas with continuo, also twelve concertos for four violins, with tenor, 'cello, and bass.

Bird. (*See* BYRD.)

Birkler, Georg Wilhelm, b. May 23, 1820, Buchau (Würtemberg), d. June 10, 1877, as professor of the Ehingen College. He wrote about old Church music in Roman Catholic musical papers, and himself published masses, psalms, etc.

Birnbach, (1) Karl Joseph, b. 1751, Köpernick, near Neisse, d. May 29, 1805, as capellmeister of the German Theatre, Warsaw. He composed works of all kinds, of which little was published.—(2) Joseph Benjamin Heinrich, son of the former, b. Jan. 8, 1793, Breslau, d. Aug. 24, 1879, as proprietor of a musical institution at Berlin. Towards the close of his life he was completely blind. He composed and published many instrumental works; also edited a book of musical instruction, "Der vollkommene Kapellmeister" (1845).

Birne (Ger. "pear"), the name, owing to its form, given in Germany to the mouthpiece of the clarinet.

Bis (Lat.), twice. (*See* ABBREVIATIONS, I.)

Bischoff, (1) Georg Friedrich, b. Sept. 21, 1780, Ellrich (Harz), d. Sept. 7, 1841, Hildesheim; at first cantor and school teacher at Frankenhausen, 1816 musical director at Hildesheim; he has the merit of having organised the first Thuringian Festival (July 20, 21, 1810, at Frankenhausen, under Spohr's direction and co-operation as soloist). He took an active part in the arrangements for subsequent musical festivals.—(2) Ludwig Friedrich Christian, b. Nov. 27, 1794, Dessau, d. Feb. 24, 1867, Cologne; was from 1823–49 college director at Wesel, founded in 1850, at Cologne, the *Rheinische Musikzeitung*, gave up the same in 1853, and established in its place the *Niederrheinische Musikzeitung*, which he edited until his death; he also translated Ulibischeff's work on Beethoven (1859).—(3) Kasper Jakob, b. April 7, 1823, Ansbach, studied (1842) in Munich, under Ett, Stuntz, and Franz Lachner, gained the Mozart stipend, and went to Leipzig. In 1850 he founded, at Frankfort, an Evangelical Sacred Choral Union, and lived from that time as teacher of singing. B. wrote some sacred compositions, symphonies, etc., and lately a great "Method of Harmony" (1890).—(4) Hans, pianist and writer on music, b. Feb. 17, 1852, Berlin, d. June 12, 1889, Niederschönhausen, near Berlin, pupil of Th. Kullak and Rich. Wüerst; studied, 1868–72, philosophy and modern languages at Berlin, took the degree of Dr.Phil. (dissertation on "Bernard von Ventadorn") in 1873, became teacher of pianoforte playing (1879, also for method of teaching) at Kullak's Academy, later on at the Stern Conservatorium. B. made successful concert tours; recently he has undertaken the conductorship, with Hellmich, of the Monday Concerts of the Berlin "Singakademie." Of his publications should be mentioned: the revision of Ad. Kullak's "Aesthetik des Klavierspiels" (1876), an "Auswahl Händelscher Klavierwerke" (Steingräber), "Kritische Ausgabe von J. Seb. Bach's

Klavierwerken " (six vols., Steingräber), and other editorial work (he had much to do with the Kullak-Chopin edition). He wrote two programme essays, " Ueber die ältere Französische Klavierschule " and "Ueber Joh. Kuhnaus Biblische Geschichten, etc."

Biscroma (Ital.), **Biscrome** (Fr.), a demisemiquaver.

Bisdiapason, the double octave, or fifteenth.

Bishop, Henry Rowley, b. Nov. 18, 1786, London, d. April 30, 1855, pupil of Francesco Bianchi, 1810 composer and conductor at Covent Garden, 1813 conductor of the newly-founded Philharmonic Society, 1819 conductor of oratorios at Covent Garden, 1830 musical director at Vauxhall, 1839 Bachelor of Music of Oxford, 1841 Professor of Music at Edinburgh, which post he resigned in 1843, was knighted in 1842, 1848 succeeded Dr. Crotch as Musical Professor at Oxford, and received the degree of Doctor of Music in 1853. He conducted the Ancient Concerts (1840–8). B. was one of the most distinguished composers England has produced ; his productivity in the department of dramatic composition was extremely great (eighty-two operas and vaudevilles, besides some ballets and revisions of old operas) ; he also wrote an oratorio, *The Fallen Angel ;* a cantata, *The Seventh Day* (of creation), a triumphal ode, etc.; he also published the first volume of " Melodies of Various Nations," and three volumes of national melodies set to Moore's words. His wife, Anna (Rivière), b. 1814, London, d. March 18, 1884, New York, was a highly-esteemed concert-singer, travelled, from 1839, with the harpist Bochsa, went in 1847 to America, in 1855 to Australia, where Bochsa died ; she married, in 1858, an American of the name of Schulz.

Bisogna (Ital.), it is necessary. *Si b. d. c. dal segno =* must be repeated from the sign. (*Cf.* SEGNO.)

Bitter, Karl Hermann, Prussian Minister of Finance, 1879–82, b. Feb. 27, 1813, Schwedt on the Oder, d. Sept. 12, 1885, Berlin. He is distinguished as the author of the following works : " J. S. Bach "(biography, 1865, two vols.; second ed. 1881, four vols), " Mozart's Don Juan und Gluck's Iphigenia in Tauris ; ein Versuch neuer Uebersetzungen " (1866), " K. Ph. E. und W. Friedemann Bach und deren Brüder " (1868 two vols.; his most meritorious work), " Ueber Gervinus' 'Händel und Shakespeare' " (1869), " Beiträge zur Geschichte des Oratoriums " (1872), " Studie zum Stabat Mater " (1883), " Die Reform der Oper durch Gluck und Wagner " (1884). He also published K. Loewe's autobiography (1870).

Bittoni, Bernardo, b. 1755, Fabriano, d. there May 18, 1829. He resided for many years at Rieti, but returned to his native city. He was a diligent musician, and of a genial disposition ; his sacred compositions, preserved in manuscript at Rieti and Fabriano, deserve special mention. Alfieri wrote his biography.

Bizet, Georges (his real names were Alexandre César Léopold B.), a distinguished French composer, b. Oct. 25, 1838, Paris, d. June 3, 1875, Bougival, near Paris. He was the son of a teacher of singing, and, at the age of nine, entered the Conservatoire, where during ten years of study he carried off prize after prize. His teachers were Marmontel (piano), Benoist (organ), Zimmermann (harmony), and Halévy (composition). In 1857 B. received the *Grand Prix de Rome,* shortly before which he had won the victory over Lecocq with his operetta, *Le Docteur Miracle,* in a competition appointed by Offenbach. From Italy B. sent proofs of his use of the stipend, viz. : an opera, " Don Procopio " (produced Monte Carlo in 1906), two symphonic movements, an overture, *La Chasse d'Ossian ;* and a comic opera, *La Guzla de l'Émir.* On his return from Italy he produced a grand opera at the Théâtre Lyrique in 1863, entitled, *Les Pêcheurs de Perles,* which, however, together with *La jolie Fille de Perth,* in 1867, were coldly received by the public ; his endeavours to emulate Wagner bore bad fruit for him. The one-act work, *Djamileh* (1872), increased the ill-feeling. He was more successful with the symphonic movements and the *Patrie* overture produced by Pasdeloup. However, B. was not discouraged by the failure of his operas ; after a long pause, the music to Daudet's drama, *L'Arlésienne,* appeared ; it was played also in Germany, and it gave favourable proofs of Bizet's talent. Lastly, *Carmen,* an opera in four acts, his masterpiece, appeared in 1875 ; it excited great hopes for the composer's future career, but these were frustrated by his death, of heart disease, which quickly followed. B. married Halévy's daughter, Geneviève. (*Cf.* Ch. Pigot's " B. et son Œuvre " [1886].)

Blaes, Arnold Joseph, b. Dec. 1, 1814, Brussels, d. there January, 1892; distinguished performer on the clarinet. He studied under Bachmann, who obtained for him an appointment in the royal band and at the Conservatoire. B. was successor to Bachmann, on the death of the latter in 1842, as solo clarinet and teacher at the Conservatoire.

Blagrove, Henry Gamble, b. Oct., 1811, Nottingham, d. Dec. 15, 1872. He was a distinguished violinist, and the first pupil of the Royal Academy of Music opened in 1823, and especially of François Cramer. From 1833 to 1834 he went to Spohr at Cassel, and from that time up to his death was member of the best London orchestras.

Blahag, Joseph, b. 1779, Raggendorf (Hungary), d. Dec. 15, 1846. In 1802 he became tenor singer at the Leopoldstadt Theatre, Vienna, and in 1824 the successor of Preindl as capellmeister of St. Peter's Church in that city.

He was a prolific composer of sacred music (masses, oratorios, etc.).

Blahetka, Marie Leopoldine, b. Nov. 15, 1811, Guntramsdorf, near Vienna; studied with Czerny, afterwards with Kalkbrenner and Moscheles. She was a distinguished pianist, also a performer on the physharmonika, and a composer of merit (S. Sechter was her teacher). She lived in Boulogne from 1840 until her death, Jan. 17, 1887. Many of her pf. pieces, concert pieces, sonatas and rondos, are printed. An opera of hers, entitled *Die Räuber und die Sänger*, was produced at the " Kärntnerthor " Theatre, Vienna, in 1830.

Blainville, Charles Henri, b. 1711, near Tours, d. 1769 as 'cellist and teacher of music in Paris. He published two symphonies and some small pieces, and also transcribed Tartini's sonatas as grand concertos. He wrote, " L'esprit de l'art musical " (1754; in German in Hiller's " Nachrichten "), " Histoire générale, critique et philologique de la musique " (1767), and " Essai sur un troisième mode " (1751). B. held interesting views in the matter of theory. He looked upon the inversion of the major scale—*i.e.* the pure minor scale—as the basis for a third mode having equal rights with those of the major and minor. A symphony composed in this mode was performed at a " Concert Spirituel," May 30, 1751, and, to Rousseau's astonishment, Sarre attacked B.'s theory. B. defended himself in the *Mercure*, 1751, but without doing himself much good.

Blamont, François Colin de, b. Nov. 22, 1690, Versailles, d. there, Feb. 14, 1760, as Surintendant de la Musique du Roi. He studied composition with Lalande, wrote a number of operas and ballets—partly for the Opera, partly for court festivals; also cantatas, motets, songs, and a treatise, " Essai sur les goûts anciens et modernes de la musique française " (1754).

Blanc, Adolphe, b. June 24, 1828, Manosque (Basses-Alpes); one of the few French composers who turned their attention principally to chamber-music. He went to the Paris Conservatoire in 1841, and afterwards was a special pupil of Halévy for composition. In 1862 he received from the Académie the *Prix Chartier* for his services in the department of chamber-music. He was, for a time, conductor at the Théâtre Lyrique under Carvalho. Besides many sonatas, trios, quartets, quintets, he wrote also songs, two operettas, and a one-act comic opera, *Une aventure sous la ligne*.

Blanchard, Henri Louis, b. Feb. 7, 1778, Bordeaux, d. Dec. 18, 1858, Paris. He studied the violin with R. Kreutzer, harmony with Beck and Walter, composition with Méhul and Reicha. From 1818 to 1829 he was conductor at the Théâtre des Variétés, Paris; and in 1830 at the Molière Theatre. Besides operas, B. wrote chamber-music, the latter containing more solid work than the former. In addition, especially in his later years, he was active as a musical critic, and wrote for newspapers many musical biographies (Fr. Beck, Berton, Cherubini, Garat).

Blanche (Fr.), white (note), *i.e.* a minim.

Blangini, Giuseppe Marco Maria Felice, b. Nov. 18, 1781, Turin, d. Dec., 18, 1841, Paris. At the age of nine he was a chorister boy at Turin Cathedral under Abbate Ottani, and, at the age of twelve, he already composed sacred music, and played well on the 'cello. When the war broke out in 1797, the family moved to the south of France, where B. gave successful concerts. In 1799 he went to Paris, and first made a name as composer of romances, but from 1802 as an opera composer ; he was also soon sought after as a teacher of singing. In 1805 he produced an opera at Munich, and was appointed court capellmeister. In 1806 the Princess Borghese, sister of Napoleon, made him her capellmeister, and he held a similar office at the court of King Jérôme, at Cassel, in 1809. He returned to Paris in 1814, where he became " Surintendant de la Musique du Roi " composer to the court, and professor of singing at the Conservatoire; the last-named post was, however, taken away from him. Fortune, indeed, began to desert him. In 1830 his rich savings commenced rapidly to diminish, his operas no longer drew, and his successes are now forgotten. B. wrote 174 romances for one, and 170 notturnos for two voices, four orchestral masses, thirty operas, etc.

Blankenburg, (1) Quirin van, b. 1654, Gouda, d. about 1740 as organist at the Hague. He wrote, " Elementa musica, etc." (1739), and " Clavicimbel en orgelboek der gereformeerde psalmen en kerkgezangen, etc." (1772).—(2) Christian Friedrich von, b. Jan. 24, 1744, Kolberg, d. May 4, 1796, an officer in the Prussian army; received a captain's pension in 1777. He published additions, treating specially of music, to Sulzer's " Theorie der schönen Künste " which were incorporated in the 2nd edition of this work, 1792-94.

Blaramberg, Paul, Russian composer, b. Sept. 26, 1841, Orenburg. He studied law at Petersburg, and, at the same time, and with diligence, music under Balakireff. He entered the statistical Bureau Central service, but withdrew from this post in 1870, and became journalist (editor of the Moskow *Russische Zeitung*). Of his compositions are to be named the operas, *Maria Tudor* and *Der erste Russische Komiker*, music to Ostroffski's *Der Wojewode*, the cantata *Der Dämon* (after Lermontoff's poem), the Tartar dances of which were much admired. B. belongs to the new Berlioz-Liszt school.

Blasius, Matthieu Frédéric, b. April 23, 1758, Lauterburg (Alsace), d. 1829, Versailles. In 1795 he was professor of wind-instruments at the Paris Conservatoire, in 1802 conductor at the Opéra Comique, and received a pension in 1816. He was an excellent performer on the clarinet and bassoon, also on the violin; his compositions for wind-instruments became popular (Suite for wind-instruments, clarinet concerto, bassoon concerto, "Nouvelle méthode pour la clarinette," 1796, etc.). But he also wrote three concertos for violin, twelve stringed quartets, violin sonatas with bass, etc., and two comic operas.

Blassmann, Adolf Joseph Maria, b. Oct. 27, 1823, Dresden, d. June 30, 1891, Bautzen; an excellent pianist; studied with Charles Mayer and Liszt. He was first of all teacher at the Dresden Conservatorium, from 1862 to 1864 conductor of the Euterpe concerts at Leipzig, then again in Dresden; in 1867 court capellmeister at Sondershausen, and after that again in Dresden. Up to the present he has only published small pieces for the pianoforte.

Blatt, Franz Thaddäus, b. 1793, Prague. He attended first the Academy of Painting in Vienna, but went in 1807 to the Prague Conservatorium under Dionys Weber, where he became an excellent clarinet player, and was appointed assistant teacher in 1818, and regular teacher of his instrument in 1820. He composed especially for the clarinet, and also published a Method for that instrument (1828), and a Method of singing (1830).

Blatt (Ger.), reed. (Cf. REED PIPES and WIND INSTRUMENTS.)

Blauwaert, Emiel, an excellent concert singer (bass), b. June 13, 1845, St. Nikolaas, d. Feb. 2, 1891, Brussels. He studied at the Brussels Conservatoire (Goossens and Warnots), and made his *début* in 1865 in Bénoit's *Lucifer* as the "Spottgeist" (mocking spirit), and soon made a name for himself throughout Europe. He also sang the part of Gurnemanz in Wagner's *Parsifal* at Baireuth with great success. From 1874, until the return of Huberti, he was professor of singing at the music schools of Bruges, Antwerp, and Mons.

Blaze, (1) François Henri Joseph, named Castil-Blaze, b. Dec. 1, 1784, Cavaillon (Vaucluse), d. Dec. 11, 1857, Paris. He received his first instruction in music from his father, H. Sebastien B. (b. 1763, d. May 11, 1833), who, while actively engaged as a notary, was a diligent composer (operas, sonatas) and a poet (Novel: "Julien, ou le prêtre"). The son also became a lawyer, but at the same time studied at the Paris Conservatoire, where he received a thorough musical training. He gave up the law in 1820, and went with wife and child to Paris, where he soon made a name as writer on music and as critic; and then as the author of "L'Opéra en France" (1820, 2nd ed., with a supplement on the lyrical drama and on rhythm), and as musical editor of the *Journal des Débats.*

He published besides: "Dictionnaire de musique moderne" (1821, 2nd ed., 1825; republished in 1828 by Mées, with a sketch of the history of modern music, and a supplement giving biographies of Flemish musicians); "Chapellemusique des rois de France," and "La Danse et les ballets depuis Bacchus jusqu'à Mademoiselle Taglioni" (reprints of articles for the *Revue de Paris*, as well as the two following); "Mémorial du grand opéra" (from Cambert, 1668, up to and including the Restoration); "Histoire de Musique" (not complete in itself); "Molière musicien" (1852), and "Théâtres Lyriques de Paris" (1847 to 1856, three vols.; a history of the Grand Opéra and of Italian Opera). He won great merit by his translations into French of German and Italian opera texts (*Don Juan, Figaro, Freischütz, Barbiere,* etc.).—(2) Henri Baron de Bury, son of the former, b. May 1813, Avignon, d. March 15, 1888, Paris; was for a time *attaché* to an embassy, during which he was made a nobleman. Like his father, he became a *littérateur,* and contributed a series of musicoæsthetic essays and biographical sketches to the *Revue des Deux Mondes,* the first of which was undersigned "Hans Werner" (his other *nom de plume* was "Lagenévais"). The "Musiciens Contemporains" (1856) is a collection of such articles in which a standpoint, now obsolete, is maintained. In his pamphlet, "Musiciens du passé, du présent, etc.," he sought to deal out a certain measure of justice to Wagner, whom, up to that time, he had persecuted without mercy.

Bletzacher, Joseph, b. Aug. 14, 1835, Schwoich (Tyrol), d. June 16, 1895. After attending the Salzburg Gymnasium, he studied jurisprudence for four years in Vienna, then turned to singing, and for the last twenty-two years was principal bass at the Royal Theatre, Hanover, and also an excellent and popular concert singer. He was honorary member of various societies, among others, of the "Maatschappij tot bevordering van toonkunst," in Amsterdam.

Blewitt, Jonathan, b. 1782, London, d. there Sept. 4, 1853. He was the son of the organist, Jonas B. (d. 1805), who published "A Treatise on the Organ," and organ pieces. He held appointments as organist in several churches in London and the provinces, and at last became organist of St. Andrew's Church, Dublin, and composer and conductor at the Theatre Royal in that city, and, likewise, organist to the Masonic body of Ireland, and conductor of the principal concerts in Dublin. In 1825 he returned to London, where he produced a number of operas and pantomimes (*The Man in the Moon,* 1826) at Drury Lane and other places. He won considerable popularity by his ballads.

Blied, Jacob, b. March 16, 1844, Brühl-on-Rhine, d. Jan. 14, 1884. He attended the teachers' college at Brühl, where he afterwards became teacher, and music teacher in 1874. He also became known by clever educational works for pianoforte, violin, and for singing, and composed motets, masses, etc.

Blochflöte (Blockflöte) was a direct flute of small dimensions used in the 16th century. Also an organ stop (flute-stop) of pyramid shape, and covered; of somewhat dull tone, and, according to Walther, of two feet; also four, eight, and sixteen feet.

Blockx, J a n, composer, pianist, and conductor, b. Jan. 25, 1851, Antwerp, pupil of Benoit (composition) and Callaerts (pf.): he was a pupil there of the Flemish Music School, and of L. Brassin at Brussels, and then went to Leipzig. He has been teacher of harmony at the Antwerp Conservatorium since 1886, and musical director of the "Cercle artistique," etc. His works are:— "Vredesang" (for double chorus, solo, and orch.), "Op den spoom" (double chorus, solo, and orch.), *Jets vergeten* (one-act opera), "De Landvestrizers" (madrigal à 8), "Een liedeke in den o de trant" (flute, oboe, bassoon, and four 'celli), *Rubens* (overture for grand orchestra, etc.).

Blodek, (1) P i e r r e A u g u s t e L o u i s, b. Aug. 15, 1784, Paris, d. 1856. He studied at the Paris Conservatoire (Baillot, Gossec, Méhul), received the *Prix de Rome* in 1808 (cantata, *Maria Stuart*), and on his return from Italy was tenor player at the Grand Opéra until 1842. Besides a quantity of chamber music, pf. pieces, songs, he wrote: two grand Te Deums, one mass for double choir, three overtures, one opera, and one ballet, all of which were produced; also theoretical works: a Method of Singing; an Elementary Instruction Book; a Treatise on Harmony, Counterpoint, and Fugue; and a History of Music since the Christian era.— (2) W i l h e l m, flautist and pianist, b. Oct. 3, 1834, Prague, d. there May 1, 1874. He studied at the Conservatorium in that city, and after teaching privately for three years at Lubycz (Poland), he was appointed professor at the Prague Conservatorium in 1860. During the last four years of his life his intellect became disordered, and he died in a lunatic asylum. His Czeckish comic opera, *Im Brunnen*, produced with great success at Prague in 1867, was published; a second, entitled *Zidek*, he left unfinished. He composed, besides, especially quartets for male voices, songs, pf. pieces, but also a grand mass and an overture.

Blow, J o h n, b. 1648, probably in London, d. Oct. 1, 1708. In 1660 he became chorister at the Chapel Royal, under Henry Cooke, and already in 1663 composed anthems. He afterwards studied under J. Hingeston and Ch. Gibbons, and was chosen organist of Westminster Abbey already in 1669; he had to make way for Purcell in 1680, but, on the death of the latter in 1695, was re-appointed. He was sworn-in one of the gentlemen of the Chapel Royal in 1674, and soon after succeeded Humphreys as "Master of the Children"; later on he became organist, and finally composer, to the Chapel. He received the degree of Doctor of Music from Oxford University. The number of Blow's sacred compositions, which have been preserved, is very great (anthems, services, odes for New Year's and for St. Cecilia's Days), but of the anthems few are printed. Organ pieces and "Lessons for Harpsichord" were published, and a collection of his songs, by subscription ("Amphion Anglicus," 1700). A number of his pieces have been republished in Pauer's "Old English Composers."

Blum, K a r l L u d w i g, poet and composer, b. 1786, Berlin, d. July 2, 1844. He was for many years *régisseur* at the opera house, Berlin; he was a thoroughly-trained musician (pupil of Fr. A. Hiller at Königsberg, and Salieri at Vienna), and wrote a great number of works for the stage (operas, ballets, vaudevilles, the last of which he was the first to introduce into Germany); also instrumental compositions, which pleased much in their day, but, through lack of originality, were not long-lived.

Blumenthal, (1) J o s e p h v o n, b. Nov. 1, 1782, Brussels, d. May 9, 1850, Vienna. He studied with Abt Vogler in Prague, followed him to Vienna in 1803, where he found an appointment as violinist in an orchestra, and, later on, became precentor at the "Piaristenkirche." B. was an excellent violinist, and wrote much for his instrument (Violin Method, duets, studies, etc.), and made successful attempts in the department of orchestral and of dramatic composition.—(2) J a c o b, b. Oct. 4, 1829, Hamburg, an excellent pianist, pupil of F. W. Grund at Hamburg, and of Bocklet and S. Sechter at Vienna, after which he went to the Paris Conservatoire under Herz. Since 1848 he has been living in London. B. has written many brilliant *salon* pieces and also some chamber music.—(3) P a u l, b. Aug. 13, 1843, Steinau-on-Oder (Silesia), studied at the Royal Academy, Berlin. Since 1870 he has been organist of the principal churches at Frankfort-on-Oder (royal musical director, 1876). He has composed orchestral works, masses, motets, etc.

Blumner, (1) M a r t i n, composer and conductor, b. Nov. 21, 1827, Fürstenberg (Mecklenburg). In 1845 he commenced studying theology at Berlin, afterwards philosophy and science, but in 1847 he turned entirely to music, and had the advantage of instruction in composition from S. W. Dehn. In 1853 he became vice-conductor, and in 1876 conductor, of the Berlin "Singakademie," of which he was already member in 1845. He also conducted for a long time the Zelter Liedertafel. B., as a vocal composer, is conservative in his tendencies: his oratorios, *Abraham* (1859) and *Der Fall Jerusalems* (1874), a Te Deum à 8, psalms, motets, etc., also songs, duets, and other works display scholarly writing of a high order. In 1875 he was named member in ordinary of the Royal Academy of Arts, and recently, a member of the Senate. The Government also conferred on him the titles of "Kgl. Musikdirector" and "Professor."—(2) Siegismund, b. 1834.

Blüthner, Julius Ferdinand, b. March 11, 1824, Falkenhain, near Merseburg, founder and manager of a pianoforte manufactory at Leipzig (since Nov. 7, 1853). He is "Kgl. Sächs. Kommerzienrath" (Counsellor of Commerce), and in 1856 received a patent for improvements in the construction of the pianoforte, and speedily acquired such fame for his establishment that for many years he has used steam power ; up to Jan. 1, 1880, 15,000 instruments had been made, giving employment to more than 500 workmen. Blüthner's instruments have repeatedly won the highest prizes (Paris, 1867 ; Vienna, 1873; Philadelphia, 1876; Sydney, 1880 ; Amsterdam, 1883 ; Melbourne, 1889). A speciality of Blüthner's are the "Aliquot" pianos, in which the tone is strengthened by a double set of strings (those that lie higher, and are not struck by the hammer, are tuned in the upper octave). In 1872 Blüthner, jointly with Dr. Gretshal, published an instruction book on the making of pianofortes.

Bobisation, a comprehensive term for the different solmisation-syllable names given to the seventh note of the fundamental scale ; various propositions were made in the 16th and 17th centuries by many composers and theorists, until at last the "si" was generally accepted. In order fully to understand the importance which this matter once had, we English, Germans, Dutch, must bear in mind that the designation of sounds by letters, now universally adopted, was formerly employed in Germany and the Netherlands, not exclusively, but together with solmisation (chiefly for instrumental music, and specially for keyed instruments). In Italy and France they were only used in combination with the solmisation names (c solfaut, f faut, etc.). When, however, these were found to be cumbrous, and, what is of greater importance, insufficient (especially as names of the chromatic sounds), and a fixed meaning, once for all, was given to the syllables, ut, re, mi, fa, sol, la, so that they could be changed at pleasure by ♭ and ♯, it was noticed that the sound (answering to b) had no name. By giving a name to this sound solmisation received its death-blow, for in mutation, thus set aside, consisted its very essence. It would certainly have been easier to return to plain letter notation, as clearly seen in our clef signs—F, c, g =

Instead of this, Hubert Waelrant, a Belgian composer and founder of a school at Antwerp about the year 1550, is said to have proposed and introduced the seven syllables, bo, ce, di, ga, lo, ma, ni (BOCEDISATION), and, about the same time, the Bavarian Court musician, Anselm, of Flanders, selected for b the name si, but for b♭, bo (according to the old view, both were fundamental sounds). Henri Van de Putty (Puteanus, Dupuy) in his "Modulata Pallas" (1599), made bi stand for b ; Adriano Banchieri, in the "Cartella Musicale" (1610), on the other hand, chose ba, and Don Pedro d'Urenna, a Spanish monk, about 1620, ni. Daniel Hitzler was in favour of totally different syllables (1628), LA, BE, CE, DE, ME, FE, GE (BEBISATION), answering to our a, b, c, d, e, f, g ; and, again, Graun (1750) thought he was doing something useful in proposing da, me, ni, po, tu, la, be (DAMENISATION). Most of these proposals only had local influence ; a Frenchman, Lemaire, is said to have obtained general recognition for the si in place of b (but without bo for b♭). He can, however, scarcely be credited with this, for Mersenne ("Harm. univers," p. 342) only mentions that a certain Lemaire proposed the name za for the last syllable, while Brossard ascribes to Lemaire a book of which he was not the author ("Le gamme du Si, nouvelle méthode pour apprendre à chanter en musique sans nuances," 1646; author, Nivers). It almost seems as if Anselm of Flanders had gradually succeeded with the si, for Seth Calvis, the most worthy cantor of St. Thomas's, Leipzig, decided in favour of Bocedisation in his "Compendium musicæ practicæ pro incipientibus" (1611), but in his "Exercitatio musicæ tertia, etc.," for the si, which, from the way he mentions it, would appear to have been something universally known; for, with him, it is no longer a question how the seventh note should be named, but whether solmisation with si (therefore without mutation), or with mutation, is the more correct. That si was finally accepted is sufficiently clear from the fact that it was taken, like the other solmisation syllables, from the well-known St. John's Hymn (the first letters of the two words of the concluding line, Sancte Ioannes). (Cf. SOLMISATION.)

Bocca (Ital.), the mouth ; a b. chiusa. (See BOUCHE FERMÉE.)

Boccherini, Luigi, an important Italian composer of chamber-music, b. Feb. 19, 1743, Lucca (all dates differing from these are false), d. May 28, 1805, Madrid. He was the son of a double-bass player, studied with Abbate Vannucci, maestro to the Archbishop of Lucca, and afterwards received additional training in Rome. On his return to Lucca, B., who was an excellent 'cello player, undertook a great concert tour, lasting several years, with the violinist, Filippino Manfredi ; this led them to Paris in 1768, where B. published his first stringed quartets (Op. 1 : "6 sinfonie o sia quartetti per due violini, alto e violoncello dedicati a veri dilettanti e conoscitori di musica") also two books of stringed trios (for two violins and 'cello), which were received with special and lasting favour. In 1769 the two artists (of whom, indeed, the other was more a man of business) went to Madrid, where B. settled down, first as *virtuoso di camera* to the Infante Luis, and, after his death, in a similar capacity to the king. In 1787 he received from Friedrich Wilhelm II. of Prussia, in return for a work dedicated to him, the title of chamber-composer, and from that time he wrote only for this king, who unfortunately died in 1797, when B. lost his salary. B. appears, later on, also to have lost his post of capellmeister, for he spent his last years in great poverty. His works were badly paid, however much they may have been admired by musicians and amateurs. He published not less than 91 stringed quartets and 125 stringed quintets (113 with two 'celli, twelve with two viole), 42 trios, 54 stringed trios, twelve pf. quintets, eighteen quintets for stringed quartet with flute or oboe, sixteen sextets, two octets, violin sonatas, duets, etc., twenty symphonies, an orchestral suite, and a 'cello concerto; he also wrote sacred music (mass, *Stabat Mater*, a Christmas cantata, Vilhancicos, etc.), and an opera. L. Picquot wrote an excellent monograph on the life and works of Boccherini (1851).

Bocedisation. (*See* BOBISATION.)

Bochkoltz-Falconi, A n n a (really B o c k-holtz), a vocalist, b. 1820, Frankfort, d. Dec. 24, 1879, Paris. She made her *début* at a Conservatoire concert at Brussels (1844), then in the following year at Paris in the "Concerts de Musique Ancienne," arranged by Prince de la Mosskva (Joseph Napoléon Ney). When the Revolution broke out in 1848, she went to London, then to Italy, was engaged for a time in Coburg, and at last settled down in Paris as teacher of singing (1856). She published songs and vocal studies.

Bochsa, (1) K a r l, oboe player in the theatre orchestra at Lyons, and afterwards Bordeaux. He went in 1806 to Paris, where he had a music business, and died in 1821. He published quartets for clarinet, violin, viola, and 'cello, six duos concertants for two oboes, likewise a Method for flute and one for clarinet.—(2) Robert Nicolas Charles, harpist, son of the former, b. Aug. 9, 1789, Montmédy (Maise), d. Jan. 6, 1856, Sydney (Australia). He began to compose at an early age, for he wrote an opera when only sixteen. He studied with Franz Beck at Bordeaux, and in 1806 at the Paris Conservatoire under Catel and Méhul. His teachers for harp-playing were Nadermann and Marin; but he soon went his own way. In 1813 he was appointed harpist to the Emperor Napoléon, and remained court-harpist under Louis XVIII.; but in 1817, on account of forgeries, he had to flee the country, and went to London, where he was sought after as a teacher.

Parish-Alvars and Chatterton were his pupils. He arranged Lenten oratorios with Smart in 1822, and in the following year on his own account. When the Academy of Music was established (1822), he was appointed professor of the harp, but was dismissed in 1827 because he could not answer certain charges brought against him. From 1826 to 1832 he was conductor of the Italian opera at the King's Theatre. Finally, in 1839, he ran away with H. Bishop's wife, made extensive tours, and died in Australia. He published a Method and compositions for harp, and produced seven (French) operas at the Opéra-Comique, Paris, between the years 1813 and 1816; an eighth (English) followed in London in 1819, where, up to 1837, he produced four ballets and an oratorio.

Bock. (*See* BOTE UND B.)

Bock (Polish B.; Gross-Bock). (*See* BAGPIPE.)

Böckeler, H e i n r i c h, b. July 11, 1836, Cologne; in 1860 he became priest, 1862 vicar-choral and conductor of the cathedral choir at Aix-la-Chapelle. Since 1876 he has edited the *Gregorius-Blatt*. He has published songs for male chorus (1875), and has also written some sacred works.

Böckh, August, learned philologist and antiquarian, b. Nov. 24, 1785, Carlsruhe, d. Aug. 3, 1867, as professor in Berlin. In his comprehensive introduction to his edition of Pindar (1811, 1819, and 1821), he wrote, under the heading " De metris Pindari," with great knowledge of, and sharp judgment concerning the music of the Greeks (harmony, melopoeïa, symphony, musical instruments, etc.).

Bocklet, K a r l M a r i a v o n, b. 1801, Prague, d July 15, 1881, Vienna. He studied the piano with Zawora, violin with Pixis, and composition with Dionys Weber. In 1820 he was violinist at the "Theater an der Wien," Vienna, but soon devoted himself entirely to pianoforte playing. He made public appearances for a time as pianist, but afterwards confined himself to giving lessons. Beethoven took an interest in him, and Schubert was his friend.

Bockmühl, R o b e r t E m i l, 'cellist and diligent composer for his instrument; b. 1820, Frankfort, d. there, Nov. 3, 1881.

Bockshorn (Capricornus), S a m u e l, b. 1629, was musical director at a church in Pressburg, and, from 1659, capellmeister at Stuttgart, where he died about 1669. B. published sacred music (masses, motets, etc), and some secular songs and instrumental works.

Bockstriller (Ger. " goat-trill "), a faulty shake; the giving out, in a wretched, bleating manner, of one note instead of two alternate notes.

Bocquillon-Wilhem. (*See* WILHEM.)

Bode, J o h a n n J o a c h i m Christoph, b.

Jan. 16, 1730, Barum (Brunswick), d. Dec. 13, 1793, Weimar. He was the son of a poor brick-maker, and gradually trained himself. He began his musical career as a pupil of the "Stadtmusicus" Kroll in Brunswick, in 1755 was oboist at Celle, from 1762 to 1763 music teacher at Hamburg and likewise editor of the *Hamburger Korrespondent;* ten years later, in company with Lessing, printer and publisher there (he brought out the *Hamburgische Dramaturgie*), and from 1778 he lived at Wei-mar. B. wrote many instrumental compositions, and published (symphonies, bassoon concertos, 'cello concertos, violin concertos, soli for viola d'amour, etc.). He was also a clever trans-lator from English, and translated Burney's "Tour in Germany" (1773, which he himself published).

Bödecker, Louis, composer, b. 1845, Ham-burg, pupil of Marxsen, lives in Hamburg as teacher of music and musical critic. He has published songs, pf. pieces: Variations, Op. 6 and 8; Rhapsodies, Op. 9; "Frühlingsidyll," for four hands; a "Phantasie Sonate," for pf. and violin (Op. 15), and a "Trio-Phantasie" (Op. 18), etc.—about thirty works. He has orchestral, vocal, and chamber compositions in manuscript.

Bodenschatz, Erhard, b. 1570, Lichtenberg (Erzgebirge), d. 1638. He studied theology at Leipzig and became master of arts, was cantor at Schulpforta (1600), pastor at Rehhausen (1603), and from 1608 pastor at "Gross-Oster-hausen," near Querfurt. The name of B. is kept alive, not by his own compositions ("Mag-nificat sampt Benedicamus," 1599; "Psalterium Davidis," 1605; "Harmonia Angelica," 1608; "Bicinia," 1615), but by his compilations, above all by the "Florilegium Portense" (two parts: the first in 1603, second edition 1618, printed in eight, the second, 1621, in ten part-books). The work contains 115 and 150 songs à 4 to 10, by ninety-three composers of the time (about 1600). A smaller compilation is the "Flori-legium selectissimorum hymnorum" (for school use, hence repeatedly republished; last of all in 1713).

Boekelmann, Bernardus, excellent pianist, b. June 9, 1838. He studied with his father, the musical director, A. J. Boekelmann, at Utrecht; from 1857 to 1860 he was pupil of the Leipzig Conservatorium, and from 1861 to 1862 in Berlin, a private pupil of Kiel, Weitzmann, and H. von Bülow. In 1864 B. went to Mexico and played several times before the court. Since 1866 he has resided in New York, where he has become known as teacher and pianist, and especially by the chamber-music evenings of the New York Trio Club, which he established. In 1884 he undertook the direction of music at one of the greatest institutions in Farmington.

Boëly, Alexandre Pierre François, b. April 19, 1785, Versailles, d. Dec. 27, 1858, Paris. He was an excellent pianist and violinist, and for a time pupil of the Conservatoire (Ladurner). He was a musician of serious aim and classic taste; he published pf. and violin sonatas, stringed trios, organ pieces, etc.

Boësset, Antoine (Sieur) von Villedieu, music intendant of Louis XIII., b. about 1585, d. 1643; he composed ballets for the court festivities.

Boëtius, Anicius Manlius Torquatus Severinus, b. about 475 B.C. at Rome. He was of noble origin, consul in the year 510, for many years a trusty counsellor of Theodoric, King of the Ostrogoths, who, however, in 524 (526) had him unjustly put to death, because he sus-pected him of a secret and treasonable cor-respondence with the Byzantine Court. B. was a philosopher, a distinguished mathematician, and wrote a work, "De Musicâ" (in five books), a comprehensive revision of the then declining Greek system of music. What the Middle Ages knew about Greek music they had learnt from B., who, for the rest, was a disciple of Pythagoras, *i.e.* opposed to the views of Aris-toxenos. There are manuscripts in many libraries of the "De Musicâ" of B.; it was printed in the collected writings of B. at Venice, 1491–92, and a second edition in 1499 (Gregorii); also Basle, 1570 (Glarean), and in separate form (only with the "Arithmetic") at Leipzig, 1867; also in German by O. Paul (1872). A French translation by Fétis has, up to now, remained in manuscript. The general opinion that B. used Latin letters in place of Greek is an erroneous one; and the term "Notation Boëtienne" false, as applied to the notation in vogue from the 10th to the 12th century with a—p, or A—P.

Bogenflügel, Bogenklaviere (Ger.), bow-piano-fortes. In these instruments attempts have been made to combine the effect of stringed in-struments with a key-board. On Hans Heyden's Nuremberg *Geigenwerk* (*Geigenklavicymbal,* 1610) the catgut strings, which on pressing the keys were drawn down by means of little hooks, were acted on by rosined rollers kept in con-stant motion by means of treadles. (*Cf.* Hurdy-gurdy and Schlüsselfiedel.) In 1709 Georg Gleichmann, organist at Ilmenau, constructed a similar instrument, with certain improve-ments, and named it *Klaviergambe;* in 1741 Le Voirs at Paris followed likewise with a *Gambe-klavier,* and Hohlfeld at Berlin with the *Bogen-klavier,* an improvement on Heyden's instru-ment, inasmuch as the wheels were covered with horsehair. In 1710 Garbrecht, at Königs-berg, brought out a *Bogenklavier* with improve-ments, which proved failures; Mayer one at Görlitz in 1795, which Kunze turned to account at Prague in 1799; and, finally, Röllig, at Vienna, in 1797, with the *Xänorphika,* the most complicated instrument of the kind, having a bow in motion for each key and string. In spite of all the anxious thought devoted to these instruments, not one of them has attained to higher fame than that of being a curiosity. Karl Greiner's *Bogenhammerklavier* (1779) was a combination of the *Bogenflügel* with an ordinary pianoforte.

Bogenhammerklavier and **Bogenklavier**. (*See* BOGENFLÜGEL.)

Bohm, K a r l, pianist and *salon* composer, b. Sept. 11, 1844, Berlin; pupil of Löschhorn, Fl. Geyer, and Reissmann. He lives in Berlin.

Böhm, (1) G e o r g, distinguished performer on the organ and clavier, b. 1661, Goldbach (Thuringia), d. 1734, Lüneburg, where from 1698 he was organist of the St. John's Church. His Suites in E and C minor rank among the best of their time.—(2) T h e o b a l d, b. April 9, 1794, Munich, d. there Nov. 25, 1881, was for many years member of the royal band (Hofmusicus), a performer on the flute, composer for his instrument, in the construction of which he made some clever improvements. The "B. System" created a perfect revolution in the construction of woodwind instruments. Together with the Englishman, Gordon, he started, from the idea that not convenience in the mode of fingering, but the acoustical principles for the best resonance, must determine the position of the sound-holes; so he first fixed the bore of the flute, and then sought after a suitable arrangement of the mechanism. The holes, formerly so small, he made so wide that the tips of the fingers did not completely cover them, etc. The tone of the Böhm flute is certainly very different from that of the old flute; it is much fuller, rounder, diapason-like in quality; the opponents of the system miss in it the speciality of flute tone. Professor v. Schafhäutl was Böhm's scientific adviser.—(3) J o s e p h, b. March 4, 1795, Pesth, d. March 28, 1876, Vienna, an excellent violinist and teacher, pupil of Rode, appeared at Vienna in 1815 with great success, then travelled in Italy, and after his return (1819) was appointed professor of the violin at the Vienna Conservatorium, and in 1821 member of the Imperial band. From 1823 to 1825 he made many concert tours. B. was held in high esteem as a teacher: Ernst, Joachim, Singer, Hellmesberger (sen.), L. Straus, Rappoldi and others were his pupils. In 1848 he gave up his post of teacher at the Conservatorium, and in 1868 retired from the band. He published only a few works for the violin.

Böhme, (1) J o h a n n A u g u s t, established himself at Hamburg, in 1794, as music publisher and seller; in 1839 his successor was his son, J u s t u s E d u a r d B., and in 1885 his grandson, A u g u s t E d u a r d B.—(2) A u g u s t J u l i u s F e r d i n a n d, b. Feb. 4, 1815, Gandersheim (Brunswick), d. there, May 30, 1883. He was a pupil of Spohr, was theatre capellmeister at Berne and Geneva, in 1846 conductor of the "Euterpe" and director of

the music school at Dordrecht; and in 1876, after some years of rest, owing to a disorder of the eyes, he appeared in Leipzig as a composer, with orchestral, chamber, and vocal works.—(3) F r a n z M a g n u s, b. March 11, 1827, Willerstedt, near Weimar. He studied with G. Töpfer, afterwards with Hauptmann and Rietz in Leipzig; for eleven years he was schoolmaster, and then for more than twenty years active in Dresden as teacher of music. He received from the King of Saxony the title of Professor, and in 1878 was appointed teacher of the history of music and of counterpoint at the newly-established Hoch Conservatorium at Frankfort, which post he quitted in 1885. From 1886 B. was again living in Dresden. He has published "Altdeutsches Liederbuch" (1877, a thankworthy, elaborate, although not altogether trustworthy collection of texts and melodies), an "Aufgabenbuch zum Studium der Harmonie" (1880), a "Kursus der Harmonie" (Mayence, 1882), a "Geschichte des Tanzes in Deutschland" (Leipzig: Breitkopf & Härtel, 1886); also several books of songs in parts (sacred partsongs, popular songs for male chorus).

Böhmer, K a r l, excellent violinist and prolific composer for his instrument; b. Nov. 6, 1799, Hague, d. July 20, 1884, Berlin. He wrote also two small operas.

Bohn, E m i l, b. Jan. 14, 1839, Bielau, near Neisse. He attended the Gymnasium there, and studied classical and oriental philology from 1858 to 1862 at Breslau, but already as a student conducted the concerts of the academical musical society, and finally devoted himself exclusively to music as pupil of J. Schäffer (theory), and E. Baumgart (organ). In 1868 he became organist of the "Kreuzkirche," Breslau, and founded in the same year the "Bohn Choral Union," which of late has attracted much notice by its historical concerts. In 1884 the Breslau University conferred on B. the degree of Dr. Phil. Hon. C., and he undertook the direction of the University Choral Society, and the singing at the Mathias-Gymnasium; he gives, likewise, lectures at the University. In 1884, also, he became musical critic of the *Breslauer Zeitung*. In 1887 the Philharmonic Academy at Florence, and in 1891 the "Cecilia" Academy at Rome, named him honorary member. As a composer, B. has only produced songs and part-songs. His "Bibliographie der Musikdruckwerke bis 1700, welche auf der Universitätsbibliothek, Stadtbibliothek, etc., zu Breslau aufbewahrt werden" (1883), and "Die Musikalische Handschriften des 16 und 17 Jahrhunderts in der Stadtbibliothek zu Breslau" (1890), are works of great merit. B. also edited the pianoforte works of Mendelssohn and Chopin. At the present time he is engaged on a monumental work, viz., a complete edition in score of all secular songs in several parts between the years 1550 and 1630.

Böhner, Johann Ludwig, b. Jan. 8, 1787, Töttelstedt, near Gotha, d. March 28, 1860, Gotha. He was a composer of much talent, whose life bore some similarity to that of Friedemann Bach. About 1810 B. was theatre capellmeister in Nuremburg for one year, but otherwise held no fixed appointment; he constantly led a wandering life, giving concerts, and settling down, often for years together, wherever the fancy took him. Unfortunately, he came gradually down in the world, and gave way to drink. His compositions are: pianoforte sonatas and concertos, fantasias, overtures, marches and dances for orchestra, divertissements, etc.; also an opera, *Der Dreiherrnstein.* It is supposed to be B. whom E. T. A. Hoffmann portrayed as Kapellmeister Kreisler.

Bohrer, (1) Anton, b. 1783, Munich. He was a performer on the violin; studied with his father, afterwards with R. Kreutzer in Paris. He and his brother—(2) Max, b. there 1785, performer on the 'cello, pupil of Schwarz—were, at an early age, appointed members of the Bavarian court orchestra, in which their father was double-bass player, and they then made extensive tours together (1810-14) through Austria, Poland, Russia, Scandinavia, and England; in 1815 France, in 1820 Italy, etc. In 1834 Anton B. settled in Hanover as leader of the orchestra, and died there in 1852. Max B. became principal 'cellist and leader at Stuttgart in 1832, and died there Feb. 28, 1867. Both published concertos and solo pieces for their instruments, and also chamber music. Max was more important as a virtuoso; Anton, on the other hand, acquired more note as a composer.

Boieldieu, (1) François Adrien, b. Dec. 15, 1775, Rouen, d. Oct. 8, 1834, on his estate, Jarcy, near Grosbois. His father was secretary to an archbishop, and the boy joined the choir of the metropolitan church, and received further regular instruction in music from the organist Broche, who treated him cruelly, and made him do menial duties, so that once B. ran away from him, and had to be brought back from Paris. When B. was eighteen years old (1793), a small opera of his (*La fille coupable*) for which his father had prepared the libretto, was produced in his native town, Rouen; and, in 1795, followed a second—*Rosalie et Myrza.* The favourable reception given to both these works encouraged him to go to Paris and try his luck there. B. was well received by the house of Erard, and had the opportunity of seeing the most distinguished composers, and of making their acquaintance (Méhul, Cherubini). The singer, Garat, first performed some of his songs, and he soon won fame and found a publisher. In 1796 he brought out at the Opéra-Comique a one-act comic opera, *Les Deux Lettres,* and in 1797 a second, *La Famille Suisse,* which, by reason of their fresh melodies, met with general approval.

Zoraïme et Zulnare, produced in 1798 with success, gave still higher proof of Boieldieu's gifts, after several small and unimportant works had, in the meantime, been coldly received. Another fortunate venture was *Le Calife de Bagdad* (1800). At the same time B. began to make a name as instrumental composer (pf. sonatas, a concerto, pieces for harp). The career of B. is simple enough. His knowledge of composition was obtained in a practical way, and he never troubled much about counterpoint and fugue. He had learnt what was essential from Broche, and he profited by hints from Méhul and Cherubini, but was never actually their pupil. His *naïveté* and naturally fresh invention would, perhaps, have only been spoilt under their influence. In 1802 B. married the dancer, Clotilde Auguste Mafleuroy. The choice was not a fortunate one, and already in 1803, to escape domestic broils, he resolved to go to Petersburg, where he remained until 1810. The operas which he produced there (B. was named court composer) met with no lasting recognition; but, on the other hand, the opera which he produced after his return, *Jean de Paris* (1812), proved a brilliant success. In 1817 he was appointed professor of composition at the Conservatoire, as successor to Méhul; and, in order to justify the choice, he devoted the utmost care to his work (he was, as a rule, conscientious) *Le Chaperon Rouge,* the first performance of which (1818) was a real triumph. After a long interval (during which he was engaged on two works jointly with Cherubini, Kreutzer, Berton, and Paer), there followed at last, in 1825, *La Dame Blanche,* the crown of Boieldieu's creations. He only wrote one more opera, *Les Deux Nuits* (1829); and it was received with just the respect due to the composer of *La Dame Blanche.* B. keenly felt this, and laid aside his pen for ever. After the death of his first wife (1825) he married in the following year the singer, Phillis, sister of Jeanette Phillis. In 1829 he retired from the Conservatoire and received a good pension, which was, however, reduced in 1830. The king, indeed, gave him an extra pension, and the director of the Opéra-Comique did likewise. But he lost both entirely in 1830, so that during his last years he was forced to think seriously about his position. He begged to be reappointed at the Conservatoire, and was actually reinstated, but died soon afterwards of pulmonary disease. His obsequies were celebrated in the Dôme des Invalides, and Cherubini's Requiem was performed. Boieldieu's most celebrated pupils were Fétis, Adam, and Zimmermann. To the list of his works must still be added: *L'heureuse Nouvelle* (1797), *Mombreuil et Merville* (*Le Pari,* 1797), *La dot de Suzette* (1798), *Les Méprises Espagnoles* (1799), *La Prisonnière,* jointly with Cherubini (1799), *Beniowsky* (1800), *Ma Tante Aurore* (1803), *Le Baiser et la Quittance* (1803, jointly with Méhul, Kreutzer, etc). In Petersburg: *Aline Reine de Golconde, La Jeune*

Femme Colère, Amour et Mystère (Vaudeville), *Abderkan, Calypso* (= *Télémaque*), *Les Voitures Versées* (Vaudeville, afterwards arranged as a comic opera for Paris), *Un Tour de Soubrette* (Vaudeville), *La Dame Invisible, Rien de Trop* (*Les Deux Paravents,* Vaudeville), choruses to *Athalie.* Lastly, in Paris, after 1810: *Le Nouveau Seigneur de Village* (1813), *Bayard à Mézières* (jointly with Cherubini, Catel, and Niccolò Isouard—his rivals for many years), *Les Béarnais* (*Henri IV. en Voyage,* 1814, jointly with Kreutzer), *Angéla* (*L'Atelier de Jean Cousin,* 1814, jointly with Madame Gail, pupil of Fétis), *La Fête du Village Voisin, Charles de France* (with Hérold), *La France et l'Espagne* (Intermezzo), *Blanche de Provence* (*La Cour des Fées,* 1821, with Cherubini, Berton, etc.), *Les Trois Genres* (with Auber), *Pharamond* (with Cherubini, Berton, etc.), *La Marquise de Brinvilliers* (with Berton and others). A. Pougin wrote the life of B.—"B., sa Vie et ses Œuvres" (1875).—(2) A d r i e n L. V., son of the former, b. Nov. 3, 1816, d. there July, 1883, also made a name by a series of operas. He wrote a Mass which was performed at Rouen on the hundredth anniversary of his father's birth, 1875.

Boise, Otis Bardwell, b. Aug. 13, 1845, Ohio (North America), a pupil of the Leipzig Conservatorium, 1863-4; after that, for some time under Kullak at Berlin. Since 1868 he has been living at New York, and is held in high esteem both as teacher and composer. He has written a symphony, two overtures, a pf. concerto, trio, songs, and part-songs.

Boito, A r r i g o, b. Feb. 24, 1842, Padua, studied with Mazzucato, at the Milan Conservatorio. He is an opera composer and poet full of talent, visited Paris, Germany, and Poland (the home of his mother, the Countess Josephine Radolinska) in 1862 and 1869, and became enamoured of German music and the musico-dramatic reforms of Wagner. After he had first made himself known by the cantatas, *The 4th of June* (1860) and *Le Sorelle d'Italia* (1862, jointly with F. Faccio), he came forward, in 1868, with the opera, *Mefistofele* (after Goethe's *Faust,* first and second parts); it failed completely at Milan, but since then has been received with increasing favour (revived at Bologna in 1875 with great success, and at Hamburg in 1880). An older opera, *Hero e Leander,* and two more recent ones, *Nerone* and *Orestrade,* have not been produced; neither has the *Ode to Art* (1880). In Italy, B. (pseudonym in anagram form, *Tobia Gorrio*) is held in higher esteem as a poet than as a musician ("Libro dei versi," "Re Orso"; libretti: "Gioconda," "Alessandro Farnese," "Zoroastro," "Iram," "Otello"; many novels). B. lives in Milan. The King of Italy gave him the title of Cavalier, and later on appointed him Ufficial and Commendatore; of these titles, however, B. makes no use.

Bolck, O ş k a r, b. March 4, 1839, Hohenstein (East Prussia), d. May 2, 1888, Bremen. He studied at the Leipzig Conservatorium, and lived alternately as teacher of music in Leipzig and in various capacities at Wiborg (Finland), Liverpool, Würzburg, Aix, and Riga. From 1870 B. was for many years active as chorus-master at the Leipzig theatre, occupied a similar post in 1886 at Hamburg, and finally at Bremen. Besides various small compositions (pf. pieces, songs, etc.), B. wrote three operas (*Gudrun, Pierre Robin,* and *Der Schmied von Gretna Green.*

Bolero, Spanish national dance, mostly in ¾ time, but often with change of time, and of moderately quick movement. The dancer accompanies his steps with castanets. Characteristic is the rhythm—

Bolicius. (*See* WOLLICK.)

Bombardon is the name of a deep brass instrument of wide measure, with valves. (*Cf.* TUBA.)

Bombo (Ital.; Ger. *Schwärmer*), an old term for what is now called *Tremolo,* a quick repetition of a sound.

Bombyx (in German *Brummer?*), an old Greek wind instrument of great length, probably with reed.

Bomhart (Bommert, Pommer, a corruption of the French *Bombarde*) was a wood-wind instrument of fairly large dimensions: the bass instrument of the Schalmey family. But the B. itself was constructed of different sizes—as an ordinary bass instrument (simply called B.), as double-bass instrument (great Bassbomhart, Doppelquintbomhart, Bombardone), and as tenor instrument (Bassetbomhart cr Nicolo), and as alto instrument (Bombardo piccolo). The unwieldy length of both the large kinds led to the introduction of the bassoon, for it occurred to Afranio (q.v.) to bend the tubes. In the organ, a powerful reed-stop with funnel-shaped tubes (16 or 32 feet); the French *Bombarde* is the usual term for the *Posaune,* or Trombone

Bomtempo, J a ã o D o m i n g o s, b. 1775, Lisbon, d. Aug. 13, 1842. He went, in 1806, for further training to Paris, and, after a short visit to London, lived again in Paris up to 1820. He founded subsequently, in Lisbon, a Philharmonic society, which, however, came to an end already in 1823. In 1833 he became director of the Conservatorio in that city. B. was a composer of merit and an excellent pianist. He wrote two pf. concertos, sonatas, variations, several masses, a requiem in memory of Camoens, an opera, and a Method for the pianoforte.

Bona, G i o v a n n i, b. Oct. 12, 1609, Mondovi (Piemont), d. Oct. 25, 1674, as cardinal, at Rome. He wrote "De divina psalmodia"

(1653, and often afterwards), a work giving many explanations with regard to old ecclesiastical music.

Bonawitz (Bonewitz), J o h. H e i n r i c h, b. Dec. 4, 1839, Dürkheim-on-Rhine, a pianist of merit ; he attended the Liège Conservatorium, but already in 1852 migrated with his parents to America, whence he returned to Europe in 1861 in order to obtain further musical training. From 1861 to 1866 he gave concerts in Wiesbaden, Paris, London, etc. From 1872 to 1873 he gave popular symphony concerts in New York, and produced two operas at Philadelphia in 1874 (*The Bride of Messina* and *Ostrolenka*). During several years after that he lived in Vienna, making now and then concert tours. He is at present settled in London as teacher and composer.

Bönicke, H e r m a n n, b. Nov. 26, 1821, Endorf, organist and music teacher at Quedlinburg, d. Dec. 12, 1879, as conductor of the Musical Society at Hermannstadt (Siebenbürgen). He published pleasing part-songs for male voices, a " Method " of choral singing, and " Kunst des freien Orgelspiels."

Boniventi, G i u s e p p e, b. about 1660, Venice; between 1690 and 1727 he wrote eleven operas for his native city and one (*Venceslao*) for Turin.

Bonnet, (1) J a c q u e s, b. 1644, Paris, d. there 1724, as parliamentary paymaster. He published " Histoire de la Musique depuis son origine jusqu'à présent " (1715), and " Histoire de la danse sacrée et profane " (1723).—(2) J e a n B a p t i s t e, b. April 23, 1763, Montauban, in 1802 organist in his native city, performer on the violin, and composer of violin duets and concertantes for two violins.

Bonno, J o s e p h, b. 1710, Vienna, d. there April 15, 1788, was appointed royal court composer in 1739, together with Wagenseil, and from 1732-62 wrote for Vienna twenty operas and serenades and three oratorios. There are also some psalms, à 4, and a Magnificat preserved in manuscript.

Bononcini, (1) G i o v a n n i M a r i a, b. 1640, Modena, d. there Nov. 19, 1678 ; prolific composer of instrumental pieces, chamber sonatas, also some cantatas (solo vocal pieces), and madrigals. He wrote a work on counterpoint, " Musico pratico, etc." (1673). His sons were: (2) G i o v a n n i B a t t i s t a, b. 1660, Modena (usually signed his name " Buononcini "), greatly celebrated as an opera composer in his time; he was a pupil of his father and of Colonna, at Bologna, and at first wrote masses and instrumental works. About 1691 he went to Vienna as 'cellist in the Court band, wrote in 1694, *Tullo Ostilio* and *Serse* for Rome; 1699, *La fede publica*, and 1701, *Affetti più grandi vinti dal più giusto* for Vienna; 1703, *Polifemo* for Berlin, where, until 1705, he was court composer to Queen Sophie Charlotte, who herself

accompanied on the harpsichord at the first performance of *Polifemo*. After the death of the queen he went again to Vienna, and there followed : *Tomiri* (1704), *Endimione* (1706), *L'Etearco* (1707), *Turno Aricino* (1707), *Mario Fugitivo, Il Sacrifizio di Romolo* (1708), *Abdolonimo* (1709), *Muzio Scevola* (1710), etc. In 1716 he was called to London to the newly-established King's Theatre, and there followed the celebrated rivalry between B. and Handel, which, in consequence of the patronage of Handel by the Court, and of Bononcini by the Duke of Marlborough, assumed an almost political character. B. wrote for London: *Astarte* (1720), *Ciro, Crispo, Griselda* (1722), *Farnace, Erminia* (1723), *Calpurnia* (1724), and *Astianatte* (1727). The end was the defeat of Bononcini, which was rendered complete by the discovery that he had given out one of Lotti's madrigals as his own composition. In 1733 he went with an alchemist to Paris, by whom he was thoroughly swindled, so that he was compelled again to think of earning money. He wrote still in 1737 for Vienna (*Alessandro in Sidone;* oratorio, *Ezechia*). The year of his death is unknown, but he probably lived to the age of ninety. His brother (3) M a r c o A n t o n i o, b. about 1675, Modena, maestro there in 1721, d. July 8, 1726, wrote likewise several operas (*Camilla*), of which the greater number exist in manuscript in the Berlin Library, as well as an oratorio, *Die Enthauptung Johannis des Taufers,* and a Christmas cantata. Padre Martini praises him for his refined and noble style, and places him above most of his contemporaries.

Bontempi, G i o v a n n i A n d r e a, really A n g e l i n i (he took the name B. at the wish of his guardian), b. 1620, Perugia, d. about 1697. He lived for a time at the Berlin Court, in 1647 was member of the band of the Electoral Prince at Dresden, and returned to Perugia in 1694. He wrote " Nova quatuor vocibus componendi methodus " (1660), " Tractatus in quo demonstrantur convenientiæ sonorum systematis participati " (1690), and " Istoria musica nella quale si ha piena cognizione della teoria e della pratica antica della musica armonica " (1695). In Berlin he wrote the operas, *Paride* (1662) (dedicated to the Margrave, Christian Ernst, and printed in Dresden), *Apollo und Daphne* (1671), and *Jupiter und Io* (1673). B. was, for the rest, gifted in many ways, and highly cultivated (linguist, singer, conductor, composer, historian, architect, mechanist, etc.).

Bon temps de la mesure (Fr.), the accented part of a bar.

Boom, van, (1) J a n, b. April 17, 1783, Rotterdam; he was a performer on the flute, and a composer for his instrument. He lived in Utrecht. His sons were—(2) J a n, b. Oct. 15, 1807, Utrecht, d. April, 1872, as professor of the pianoforte (since 1849) at the Stockholm Academy, where he settled down, after a concert tour through Denmark, in 1825. He composed a pianoforte concerto, stringed quartets, trios, symphonies, etc.—(3) Hermann M., b. Feb. 9, 1809, Utrecht, d. there Jan. 6, 1883, a distinguished flautist, pupil of Toulou, at Paris; after 1830 he lived for a long time in Amsterdam.

Boosey & Co., an important London publishing firm, founded in 1825 by Thomas Boosey, with copyrights for England, especially of Italian operas (Rossini, Mercadante, Bellini, Donizetti, Verdi) : these, however, were lost in 1854 by a decision of the House of Lords. Since then, the firm has devoted itself specially to popular English music.

Borde, de la. (*See* LABORDE.)

Bordese, Ludovico, b. 1815, Naples, d. March 17, 1886, Paris. He studied at the Conservatoire there, produced an opera at Turin in 1834; then went to Paris, where, in spite of many attempts, he was unable to obtain success on the stage. From about 1850 he turned his back on the theatre, and wrote an immense quantity of small vocal pieces, also a Mass, a Requiem, etc., and a Vocal Method, an Elementary Vocal Method, solfeggi, etc.

Bordier, Louis Charles, b. 1700, Paris, d. there, 1764. He wrote a Method of Singing (1760 and 1781), and a Method of Composition (1779).

Bordogni, Marco, b. 1788, Gazzaniga, near Bergamo, d. July 31, 1856, Paris. He was a distinguished teacher of singing, and studied with Simon Mayr. He was in Milan from 1813 to 1815, and engaged at the Théâtre des Italiens as tenor singer from 1819 to 1833, after which he gave his time entirely to teaching. From 1820, with one interval of several years, he was professor of singing at the Paris Conservatoire. He was the master of Sontag, and of many other celebrities. He published a number of excellent vocalises. Death prevented the carrying out of a great Method of Singing.

Bordoni, Faustina. (*See* HASSE (3).)

Bordun, Bourdon (Fr. ; Ital. *Bordone;* also in corrupt form *Barduen, Perduna, Portunen*), a common term for the 16-feet Gedackt (Grobgedackt) of the organ. The derivation of the word is uncertain. *Bourdon* in French means humming; *Faux bourdon,* drone; but it is a question whether these meanings are not more recent. The word *bordunus* occurs in the 13th century as the term for the bass strings *lying near the finger-board* of the *Viella.* The strings lying both sides of the finger-board of the hurdy-gurdy (*Organistrum*), and which continually sounded sympathetically, were called Bordune (*bourdons*), and from these the name probably passed to the bass fifth of the bagpipes. It seems reasonable to suppose that the word B. comes from *bord* (Ital. *bordo*), "edge."

(For FAUX BOURDON, FALSO BORDONE, *cf.* FAUX BOURDON).

Borghi, Luigi. He was a pupil of the famous violinist Pugnani, settled in London about 1780, acted as leader of the second violins at the Handel Commemoration in 1784, and published a number of sonatas, concertos, symphonies, and Italian canzonets. G. Jensen, who published in " Classische Violinmusik " two of Borghi's violin sonatas, remarks : " Borghi's works combine, in a happy manner, something of classicality with the taste of his time." This is true: we find in them a compromise, as it were, between the measured, restrained, and even severe beauty in form and expression of an earlier age, and the ease, grace, and limpidity of the new era of which Joseph Haydn became the presiding genius.

Borghi-Mamo, Adelaide (*née* Borghi), a remarkable opera singer (contralto), b. 1829, Bologna. She was induced by Pasta to train herself for the stage, made her *début,* 1846, at Urbino, sang with ever increasing success on various Italian stages, married at Malta in 1849, won triumphs in Vienna in 1853, and at the Italian Opera, Paris, from 1854 to 1856, and was engaged in 1856 at the Paris Grand Opéra. In 1860 she returned to the Italian opera, and, after some " star " engagements, withdrew from public life. Pacini, Mercadante, and Rossi, wrote parts for her. Her daughter, Erminia B., soprano singer, with a clear, flexible voice, appeared with great success at Bologna in 1874, and afterwards at the Paris Italian Opéra.

Borodin, Alexander, b. Nov. 12, 1834, Petersburg, d. there Feb. 27, 1887. He studied medicine and chemistry at the medico-surgical school there ; he became military surgeon, and then followed an academical career. He was professor in ordinary at the above named school, academician, active counsellor of state, knight, etc. B. was not only engaged in scientific pursuits, but was a zealous musician, and one of the chief representatives of the new Russian school. He was on friendly terms with Balakireff, at whose suggestion he trained himself to be a musician. He was president of the Society of Amateurs at Petersburg. B. travelled much also in Germany. His principal works are: two symphonies (No. 1, E♭, produced in 1880 at the Wiesbaden gathering of composers), symphonic poem " Mittelasien," pf. pieces, chamber music (stringed quartets), etc. His opera (*Fürst Igor*) was performed in 1890 at Petersburg.

Boroni (Buroni), Antonio, b. 1738, d. 1797, Rome. He studied with Padre Martini, and afterwards with Gir. Abos', from 1770 to 1780 he was court capellmeister at Stuttgart, and finally maestro at St. Peter's, Rome. He wrote four operas for Venice (1760 to 1764), one for Prague (1765), three for Dresden (1769), and eight for Stuttgart (1771-78).

Bortnianski, Dimitri Stefanowitsch, b. 1751, Gluchow (Ukraine), d. Oct., 1825, Petersburg. He studied first at Petersburg under Galuppi; then, under the patronage of Catherine II., continued to work at Venice with the same master; and after that stayed in Bologna, Rome, and Naples for the purpose of study. In 1778 he produced an opera at Modena (*Quinto Fabio*), returned in 1779 to Petersburg, and was appointed Imperial capellmeister. To him belongs the merit of having thoroughly weeded the chapel choir, and thus brought it into high repute. For this reformed choir he wrote thirty-five psalms à 4, and ten à 8, a mass, and a Greek ritual, etc. His compositions take a high rank. Tschaikowsky edited a complete edition of his works in ten volumes.

Bösendorfer, an important pianoforte manufactory at Vienna, founded in 1828 by Ignaz B. (b. July 28, 1796, Vienna, a pupil of J. Brodmann, d. April 14, 1859), and since managed by his son, Ludwig B. (b. April, 1835, Vienna).

Bote und Bock, an important firm of music publishers in Berlin, founded in 1838 by Eduard Bote and Gustav Bock, who bought the music business of Fröhlich and Westphal. E. Bote soon retired. After the death of G. Bock (April 27, 1863) his brother, Emil Bock, became manager, and when he died (March 31, 1871) his place was taken by Hugo Bock, son of Gustav Bock. The last-named edited the *Neue Berliner Musikzeitung*—which came out in 1847—up to his death. To this firm belongs the merit of having first issued cheap editions of classical works.

Bötel, Heinrich, tenor singer, b. May 6, 1858, Hamburg. He was a cab-driver until Pollini discovered his high c; since then he has been principal lyric tenor in the theatre of that city.

Botgorschek, Franz, celebrated flautist, b. May 23, 1812, Vienna, d. May, 1882, Hague. He was trained at the Vienna Conservatorium, and was for many years teacher at the Hague Conservatoire. B. published compositions for flute.

Bott, Jean Joseph, b. March 9, 1826, Cassel, son of the court musician, A. Bott, who was his first teacher; he afterwards became a pupil of Moritz Hauptmann and of Ludwig Spohr. In 1841 he won the Mozart scholarship, in 1846 was solo violinist in the Electoral band, in 1852 under Spohr as second capellmeister, in 1857 court capellmeister at Meiningen, and in 1865 held a similar post at Hanover. He received a pension in 1878, lived for several years in Magdeburg as a teacher of music, went to Hamburg in 1884, and left there for America in 1885. B. was an excellent violinist, and Spohr held him in high esteem. He published violin concertos, solo pieces for violin and piano, songs, a symphony, and two operas, *Der Unbekannte* (1854) and *Aktäa, das Mädchen von Korinth* (1862)

Bottée de Toulmon, Auguste, b. May 15, 1797, Paris, d. March 22, 1850. He studied originally for the law, but never held any appointment, for he preferred a free life, following his own, and especially his musical inclinations, of which 'cello playing was one. When the *Revue Musicale* appeared in 1827, he turned his attention to musical literature. In 1831 he offered himself as librarian to the Conservatoire without salary, and was accepted. From the time of the Revolution in 1848 his mind was disordered. Among other things, B. wrote: "De la Chanson en France au moyenâge" (1836), "Notice Biographique sur les Travaux de Guido d'Arezzo" (1837), "Des Instruments de Musique au moyen-âge (1833 and 1844; all of which are in the "Annuaire Historique;" also separately).

Bottesini, Giovanni, b. Dec. 24, 1823, Crema (Lombardy), d. July 7, 1889, Parma. He studied at the Milan Conservatorio, especially under Rossi (double-bass), Basili and Vaccai (theory). From 1840 to 1846 he gave concerts in Italy as a double-bass virtuoso, went then as conductor to Havannah, from whence he paid visits to the American continent. In 1855 he returned *viâ* England, and ‑was conductor for two years at the Théâtre des Italiens, Paris. After that he continued his wanderings, became maestro at the Bellini Theatre, Palermo in 1861, at Barcelona in 1863, then established at Florence the Società di Quartetto, for the cultivation of German classical music, was opera conductor at the Lyceum, London (1871), returned to Italy, was director of the Parma Conservatorio, and finally produced at Turin the operas, *Ero e Leandro* (1879) and *La Regina del Nepal* (1880). His operas of earlier date were: *Christoforo Colombo* (Havannah, 1847), *L'assedio di Firenze* (1856), *Il Diavolo Della Notte* (1858), *Marion Delorme* (1862), *Vinciguerra* (1870), *Ali Baba* (1871). His oratorio, *The Garden of Olivet*, was produced under his direction at the Norwich Festival of 1887. He wrote, besides, many compositions for doublebass, but none were published.

Bottrigari, Ercole, b. Aug. 1531, Bologna. He came of a good and wealthy family, and died at his castle Sept. 30, 1612. He was a man of distinguished culture, and wrote: "Il Patrizio, ovvero de' tetracordi armonici di Aristosseno, etc." (1593), "Il Desiderio, ovvero de' concerti di varii stromenti musicali, dialogo, etc." (1594, under the *nom de plume* Alemanno Benelli), "Il Melone, discorso armonico, etc." (1602). Besides these, he left some works (principally translations) in manuscript. The titles of the above-named works relate to friends of Bottrigari—Francesco Patrizio, Grazioso Desiderio, and Annibale Melone. The second work appeared under the last name in form of anagram.

Bouche (Fr.), mouth (in organ pipes).

Bouché (Fr.), stopped (of horn notes); *covered* (of organ pipes).

Bouche Fermée (Fr.; Ger. *Brummstimmen*), vocalisation without words, and with closed mouth (*a bocca chiusa*), so that only a humming sound comes through the nose. B. F. is often used in part-songs for male voices.

Boucher, Alexandre Jean, b. April 11, 1778, Paris, d. there, after an agitated life, Dec. 29, 1861. He was a performer on the violin, of great interest and originality. From 1787 to 1805 he was solo violinist to Charles IV. of Spain. He published two violin concertos.

Bourdon (Fr.). (*See* BORDUN.)

Bourgault-Ducoudray, Louis Albert, composer, b. Feb. 2, 1840, Nantes, pupil of the Paris Conservatoire, gained the *Prix de Rome* in 1865, and made further study at Rome. He founded an amateur choral society in Paris. He has composed a *Stabat Mater*, cantatas, fantasia, etc.

Bourgeois, Loys, one of the first who arranged the French psalms (in Clément Marot's translation) for several voices, also the composer of some of the melodies to which they are set. He was born about 1510, Paris, lived from 1545 to 1557 in Geneva, and after that probably in Paris. Three collections of psalms à 4–6 by him appeared at Lyons in 1547, and Paris in 1561. He also published at Geneva, in 1550, "Le droict chemin de musique, etc.," in which he proposed a reform in the naming of sounds, which was generally adopted in France, viz., in place of (reading downwards)—

F	G	A	B	C	D	E
fa	*sol*	*la*	—	—	—	—
ut	*re*	*mi*	*fa*	*sol*	*la*	—
—	*ut*	*re*	*mi*	*fa*	*sol*	*la*
—	—	—	—	*ut*	*re*	*mi*

the more rational method, with *ut* first—

F	G	A	B	C	D	E
ut	*re*	*mi*	*fa*	*sol*	*la*	—
fa	*sol*	*la*	—	*ut*	*re*	*mi*
—	*ut*	*re*	*mi*	*fa*	*sol*	*la*

These names remained in use even after the *si* had been introduced. (*Cf.* BOBISATION.)

Bourges, Jean Maurice, b. Dec. 2, 1812, Bordeaux, d. March, 1881, Paris. He gained a good reputation as musical critic, and especially as co-editor of the *Revue et Gazette Musicale*. An opera of his (*Sultana*) was produced at the Opéra-Comique in 1846. He published a *Stabat Mater*, and many romances.

Bourrée, an old French dance of lively movement in $\frac{4}{4}$ time, beginning on the fourth crotchet, and having frequent syncopations between the second and third crotchets. According to Rousseau, the B. came originally from Auvergne.

Bousquet, Georges, b. March 12, 1818, Perpignan, d. June 15, 1854, St. Cloud. He was a gifted composer, received the *Prix de Rome* in

1838, became conductor of the National Opera (1847), later of the Italian Opera, and was for some time member of the tuition commission of the Conservatoire. He was also esteemed as a critic (of the *Commerce,* the *Illustration,* and *Gazette Musicale de Paris*). He wrote some operas: *L'hôtesse de Lyon* (1844), *Le Mousquetaire* (1844), *Tabarin* (1852).

Boutade, a term for short improvised ballets, also instrumental fantasias and similar pieces.

Bovery, Jules (really Antoine Nicolas Joseph Bovy), b. Oct. 21, 1808, Liège, d. July 17, 1868, Paris. He was at first conductor at Ghent, then at Parisian operetta theatres (Folies Nouvelles, Folies St. Germain), and wrote twelve operas and operettas, also overtures, etc.

Bovy. (*See* LYSBERG.)

Bow (Ger. *Bogen*; Ital. *Arco;* Fr. *Archet*), the instrument by means of which the strings of violins, 'cellos, etc., are set in motion. Bows are made of very hard wood (Brazil, Pernambuco), to which horsehair is attached, the tension of which can be regulated by means of a screw in the nut. The terms, *A punto d'arco* (with the point of the bow), and "from the nut," indicate, the one, very light, the other, very heavy playing.

Bowing, Art of (Ger. *Bogenführung;* Fr. *Coup d'archet*). The handling of the bow (generally with the right hand) in stringed instruments is, for playing, of equal, if not of greater, importance than the art of fingering, *i.e.*, shortening of the strings by means of the other hand. The purity of tone with regard to pitch depends upon the fingering, but everything else—softness or hardness of tone, expression, articulation—depends upon the bowing. A distinction is made in bowing between the *down stroke* and the *up stroke*. In methods for the violin and in studies, the mode of bowing is exactly indicated. ⊓ (nut) stands for the down stroke, and V (point of the bow) for the up stroke (any other use of these signs—viz., ⋀ for the down stroke, in contradistinction to V, also ⊔ for the up stroke in contradistinction to ⊓; or, again, ⊔, together with ⊓, for the down stroke, and ⋀, together with V, for the up stroke— is confusing, and should be strongly opposed).

Bowman, Edward Morris, b. July 18, 1848, America, pupil (1872–74) of Fr. Bendel, Haupt, and Weitzmann. He is organist at Newark (New Jersey), president of various musical unions, etc. B. published Weitzmann's Method of Harmony in English, also his School System.

Boyce, William, b. 1710, London, d. Feb. 7, 1779. He was a chorister of St. Paul's, a pupil of Maurice Greene, and later of Pepusch, in 1736 organist of St. Michael's Cornhill, and soon after composer to the Chapel Royal, as Weldon's successor. In 1737 he became conductor of the festivals of the Three Choirs of Gloucester, Worcester, Hereford. In 1749 he was chosen organist of All Hallows, Thames Street; in 1755 master of the King's band. When appointed organist in 1758 of the Chapel Royal, he resigned his places at St. Michael's and All Hallows, and withdrew to Kensington, to devote himself entirely to the publication of the collection prepared by Greene of "Cathedral Music" (an edition in score of English sacred compositions of the last two centuries). An old ear complaint ended in complete deafness. His principal works are: "Cathedral Music" (1760–78, three vols., containing morning and evening services, anthems, settings of the Sanctus by Aldrich, Batten, Bevin, Bird, Blow, Bull, Child, Clarke, Creighton, Croft, Farrant, Gibbons, Goldwin, King Henry VIII., Humphrey, Lawes, Lock, Morley, Purcell, Rogers, Tallis, Turner, Tye, Weldon, Wise); "Lyra Britannica" (collection, in several books, of songs, duets, cantatas, by B.); "Fifteen Anthems, Te deum, and Jubilate" (published in 1780 by his widow); Masque for *The Tempest*, Dirges for *Cymbeline* and *Romeo and Juliet*, twelve violin sonatas, a violin concerto, symphonies, an oratorio, *Noah*, etc.

Brabançonne, the national air of the Belgians, words by Louis Dechez, surnamed Jenneval, music by Franz v. Campenhout, 1830. It begins thus—

and there follows the refrain, "La Mitraille a brisé l'orange sur l'arbre de la liberté."

Braccio (Ital.), arm. *Viola da b.* (*See* VIOLA.)

Brace, a bracket connecting two or more staves.

Bradsky, Wenzel Theodor, b. Jan. 17, 1833, Rakonitz (Bohemia), d. there Aug. 9–10, 1881. He received his musical training at Prague (Caboun and Pischek), and afterwards became a member of the cathedral choir at Berlin, where he also taught singing and composed diligently. In 1874 he was appointed court composer to Prince George of Prussia, to whose *Iolanthe* he wrote music. B. is best known by his songs and part-songs (also Bohemian); his operas *Roswitha*, Dessau, 1860; *Jarmila*, Prague, 1879; and *Der Rattenfänger von Hameln*, Berlin, 1881, met with only moderate success. Three older works, *Der Heiratszwang*, *Die Braut des Waffenschmieds*, and *Das Krokodil*, were not produced.

Braga, Gaetano, b. June 9, 1829, Giulianova (Abruzzi), studied at the Naples Conservatorio. He lived at Florence, and was esteemed as a performer on the 'cello, and as a composer (songs, and eight operas, of which *La Reginella*, produced at Lecco in 1871, was particularly successful).

Braham (really Abraham), John, b. 1774,

London, of Jewish parents, d. there Feb. 17, 1856. He was a distinguished singer, and appeared at Covent Garden, Drury Lane, Royalty Theatre, etc. He was the first Sir Huon in Weber's *Oberon*, written for London. B. was accustomed to write the music for his own parts, and many numbers achieved considerable popularity. He lost the large fortune which he had amassed by the "Colosseum" speculation in 1831, and that of St. James's Theatre in 1836.

Brähmig, Julius Bernhard, b. Nov. 10, 1822, Hirschfeld, near Elsterwerda, d. Oct. 23, 1872, as teacher of music at the collegiate school at Detmold. He published a "Choralbuch" (1862), "Ratgeber für Musiker bei der Auswahl geeigneter Musikalien" (1865); school song-books, pf. and organ pieces, Methods for pianoforte, violin, and viola.

Brahms, Johannes, the greatest of living musicians, b. May 7, 1833, Hamburg, where his father was double-bass player, and from him he received his first musical instruction, and further training from Edward Marxsen. Schumann's warm recommendation in the *Neue Zeitschrift für Musik* (Oct. 23, 1853) drew the attention of musicians, public, and publishers to the young man, who afterwards, slowly but surely, built up his temple of artistic fame. After working for some time as conductor at the Lippe Court at Detmold, B. retired to his native city, studying the old masters diligently, and maturing his general culture. In 1862 he went to Vienna, which became his second home. For although, after conducting the concerts of the "Singakademie" in 1864, he left Vienna, yet he could find no place (Hamburg, Zürich, Baden-Baden, etc.) in which he could comfortably settle, and returned in 1869 to the city on the Danube. Then, again, after conducting the concerts of the "Gesellschaft der Musikfreunde" (1871–74) until Herbeck, who, meanwhile, had again taken his place as court capellmeister, replaced him, he lived for some time away from Vienna (near Heidelberg), but returned to that city in 1878. The degree of Mus. Doc. was conferred on him by the University of Cambridge in 1877, and that of Dr. Phil. Hon. C. by Breslau in 1881. In 1886 the Prussian Government named him Knight of the *Ordre pour le Mérite*, with voting power, and also member of the Berlin Academy of Arts; and in 1889 he was presented with the freedom of his native city. What gives to Brahms a place among the immortals is the deep, true feeling which is always expressed in the choicest manner. All his works (with the exception of some dating from his storm-and-stress period, which, here and there, are somewhat bombastic and unruly) gain on closer acquaintanceship. He makes many new experiments in harmony, and these, at first, are confusing to the understanding, but, on that very account, all the more conducive to lasting interest. Brahms' art of rhythm can, with good reason, be regarded as a continuation of that of Beethoven, in so far as it has turned from Schumann's characteristic mode of adhering to some marked rhythm, only suitable to small forms, to organic variety and to refinement of figuration in thematic work. The somewhat obtrusive syncopation to which B. was at first partial recedes more and more into the accompanying parts. B. depicts moods in a masterful manner; not only has he at his command, and more so than any of his contemporaries, the strikingly sombre tone, the particular feature of the serious art of to-day, but, equally so, the redeeming euphony, the mild reflection of undying light which fills the soul with peace and devout feeling. Brahms' music comes straight from the heart: it is not made, but felt; and this becomes more and more evident the more it is contrasted and compared with the wanton " picture " music of to-day, with its calculated objectivity. The difference between music which comes from the heart and that which comes from the head may quickly be shown by placing a work of Brahms over against one by Bruckner, whom so many, at the present time, would rank near to, if not above, Brahms. The latter employs all art technique only as a means to an end, and that long, and it may be interesting, spinning out and thematic weaving together of motives only as the subsoil from whence spring the radiating blossoms of overflowing feeling, whereas with Bruckner one is forced to recognise the technique and instrumental apparatus as an aim in itself, if one would not pine away longing after some soul-stirring emotion. Although Schumann's recommendation at once brought B. into note, the recognition of his importance, in wider circles, only dates from the production (1868) of his " Deutsches Requiem " (Op. 45). This noble and yet so charming work has opened the eyes of many, who hitherto had looked upon him as a plodder. Since that time every new work from his pen has been looked forward to with expectation and ever-increasing joy. We give here a complete list of the composer's works which have appeared up to 1892, without, however, noticing the very numerous arrangements of the same : A.—For Orchestra : Two serenades (Op. 11, in D for full, Op. 16, in A for small orchestra) ; four symphonies (Op. 68, C minor ; Op. 73, D ; Op. 90, F ; Op. 98, E minor) ; Variations on a Theme by Haydn (Op. 56) ; " Academic Festival " Overture, Op. 80 (Brahms' thanks for the Breslau Doctor's degree), and " Tragic " overture, Op. 81. B.— Concertos : Two pf. concertos (Op. 15, D minor ; Op. 83, B♭) ; a violin concerto (Op. 77, D) ; a double concerto for violin and 'cello (Op. 102, A minor). C.—Vocal Works with Orchestra : Ave Maria for female chorus and orchestra (or organ), Op. 12 ; Funeral Hymn, for male chorus ‿ nd wind (Op. 13) ; German Requiem, for soli,

chorus, and orchestra (Op. 45) ; " Triumphlied," for chorus à 8 and orch. (Op. 55) ; " Schicksalslied," for chorus and orch. (Op. 54) ; " Gesang der Parzen," for chorus à 6 and orch. (Op. 89) ; " Rinaldo," for tenor solo, male chorus, and orch. (Op. 50) ; " Rhapsodie," for alto solo, male chorus, and orch. (Op. 53) ; " Nänie," for chorus and orch. (Op. 82). D.—Chamber Music : Two sextets for strings (Op. 18, B♭ ; Op. 36, G); two quintets for strings (Op. 88, F ; Op. 111, G) ; a quintet for strings and Clar. (D minor, Op. 115) ; three quartets for strings (Op. 51, C minor and A minor ; Op. 67, B♭) ; a pf. quintet (Op. 34, F minor) ; three pf. quartets (Op. 25, G minor ; Op. 26, A ; Op. 60, C minor) ; five pf. trios (Op. 8, B. minor [completely revised, 1891] ; Op. 40, E♭ [with horn or 'cello ad lib.] ; Op. 87, C ; Op. 101, C minor ; Op. 114, A minor [with clarinet]); two 'cello sonatas (Op. 38, E minor ; Op. 99, F) ; three sonatas, pf. and violin (Op. 78, G ; Op. 100, A ; Op. 108, D minor). E.—Pianoforte Music : (a) For four hands : Variations on a Theme by Schumann (Op. 23), waltzes (Op. 39), Hungarian Dances (four books) ; (b) for two hands : three sonatas (Op. 1, C ; Op. 2, F♯ minor ; Op. 5, F minor) ; four ballads (Op. 10) ; scherzo (Op. 4) ; two rhapsodies (Op. 79) ; eight pieces (Op. 76, Capricci and Intermezzi) ; Variations (Op. 9 [Theme by Schumann] ; Op. 21, Op. 24 [Theme by Handel] ; Op. 35 [Studies on a Theme by Paganini], and Studies [on a theme by Chopin, on the *Perpetuum Mobile* by Weber, a Presto by Bach, E minor], the D minor chaconne by Bach [for left hand alone]). F.— Choral : (a) *Sacred :* " Geistliches Lied " (Op. 30, with organ) ; the 23rd Psalm (Op. 27, for female chorus, with organ) ; " Marienlieder " (Op. 22) ; two motets (Op. 29, à 5) ; two motets (Op. 74); three sacred choruses for female voices (Op. 37) ; three motets à 4 and 8 (Op. 110) ; (b) *Secular :* Part-songs : Op. 31 (three quartets with pf.) ; Op. 42 (three à 5) ; Op. 62 (seven lieder) ; Op. 64 (three quartets with pf.) ; Op. 92 (four quartets with pf.) ; Op. 93a (six lieder and romances à 4) ; Op. 93b (Taffellied à 6) ; Liebeslieder-Walzer, with pf. duet (Op. 52 and 65) ; " Zigeunerlieder " (Op. 103 and 112, à 4, with pf.) ; Op. 17 (four songs for female chorus, two horns, and harp) ; Op. 44 (twelve lieder and romances for female chorus, with pf. *ad lib.*) ; Op. 41 (five songs for male chorus); " Deutsche Fest und Gedenksprüche," for double chorus (Op. 109). G.—Duets : Op. 20 (three for soprano and alto); Op. 28 (four for alto and baritone); Op. 61 (four for soprano and alto) ; Op. 66 (five for soprano and alto); Op. 75 (ballads and romances). H.—Songs : Op. 3, 6, 7, 14, 19, 32, 33 (" Magelone " romances) ; 43, 46, 47, 48, 49, 57, 58, 59, 63, 69, 70, 71, 72, 84, 85, 86, 91 (with viola), 94, 95, 96, 97, 105, 106, 107 (with pf.), 108, 109, and " Mondnacht." I.—For Organ : Prelude and fugue in A minor, fugue in A♭ minor. H. Deiters wrote a special account of B. (1880). (*Cf. also* B. Vogel's biographical sketch " J. B.")

Brah-Müller, Karl Friedrich Gustav, (Müller, as composer B.), b. Oct. 7, 1839, Kritschen, near Oels (Silesia), d. Nov. 1, 1878, Berlin. He attended the normal school at Bromberg-on-Brahe, whence he published his first work (hence the name B.). He was for some time teacher at Pleschen, then at Berlin; he still pursued his musical studies under Geyer and Wüerst, and in 1867 was appointed teacher at the Wandelt Institute of Music. B. composed pf. pieces, songs, some operettas, etc. A quartet of his gained a prize at Milan in 1875.

Brambach, (1) K. Joseph, b. July 14, 1833, Bonn; studied at Cologne Conservatorium from 1851–4, then won the Mozart scholarship and went to Frankfort, and, still holding the scholarship, became private pupil of Ferdinand Hiller at Cologne. From 1858 to 1861 he was teacher at the Cologne Conservatorium, in 1861 musical director at Bonn, gave up this post in 1869, and since then has lived as composer and private teacher. B. had made his name specially known by a series of important choral works: "Trost in Tönen," "Das eleusische Fest" (with soli), "Frühlingshymnus" for mixed chorus with orchestra, "Die Macht des Gesangs," "Velleda," "Alcestis" for male chorus, soli and orchestra. His latest works of this kind were: "Prometheus," which received a prize at the Rhenish "Sängerverein" in 1880, and "Columbus" (1886); also some smaller choral works, among which "Germanischer Siegesgesang," "Das Lied vom Rhein," part-songs, pf. songs, duets, etc.; a sextet for strings, a pf. sextet, two pf. quartets, a pf. concerto, a concert overture (*Tasso*), etc.—all published. Died June, 19 1902.—(2) Wilhelm, a philologist of note, b. Dec. 17, 1841, Bonn; in 1866 ex-assistant professor, in 1868 professor in ordinary of philology at Freiburg, and since 1872 principal librarian of the "Hof- und Landesbibliothek" at Carlsruhe. Besides various works on philology, he wrote: "Das Tonsystem und die Tonarten des christlichen Abendlandes im Mittelalter, etc." (1881), also "Die Musiklitteratur des Mittelalters bis zur Blüte der Reichenauer Sängerschule" (1883), "Hermanni Contracti Musica" (1884), and "Die Reichenauer Sängerschule"(1888), monographs of importance.

Brambilla, (1) Paolo, b. 1786, Milan; produced from 1816–19, in Milan and Turin, four comic operas; and 1819–33, in Milan, nine ballets.—(2) Marietta, b. about 1807, Cassano d'Adda, d. Nov. 6, 1875, Milan, a highly esteemed teacher of singing. She was a pupil at the Conservatorio of her native town, made her *début* in 1827 in London with great success as Arsaces in Rossini's *Semiramis*, and was for some years an ornament to the opera houses of London, Vienna, and Paris. She published also vocalises, songs, etc.

Brancaccio, Antonio, b. 1813, Naples, d. there Feb. 12, 1846, trained at the Naples Conservatorio, made his *début* as dramatic composer

at Naples with *I Panduri* (1843), followed in the same place by *Il Morto ed il Vivo, L'Assedio di Constantina, Il Puntiglio,* and *L'Incognita* ("Dopo 15 anni"). Of five other posthumous operas, *Lilla* (1848) was performed in Venice in 1848.

Brandeis, Friedrich, pianist and composer, b. 1832, Vienna, pupil of Fischhof and Czerny (pianoforte), and Rufinatscha (composition). In 1848 he went to New York, where he occupies a high position as teacher of his instrument. B. has published pf. pieces (including a sonata), and songs, also an Andante for orchestra, and a Ballad for chorus, soli, and orchestra.

Brandes, Emma, b. Jan. 20, 1854, near Schwerin, an able pianist, pupil of Aloys Schmitt, and the court pianist, Goltermann; recently married the philologist, Professor Engelmann, of Utrecht.

Brandl, (1) Johann, b. Nov. 14, 1760, at the Rohr monastery, near Ratisbon, d. May 26, 1837, Carlsruhe, as court musical director; composed masses, oratorios, symphonies, an opera, and some small pieces.—(2) Johann, Viennese operetta composer, since 1869 has produced every other year at Vienna, a dramatic work, but of no artistic value.

Brandstetter. (*See* GARBRECHT.)

Brandt, Marianne (really Marie Bischof), b. Sept. 12, 1842, Vienna, where she became a pupil of Frau Marschner at the Conservatorium; was first engaged in 1867 in Graz, was from 1868–86 a highly esteemed member of the Berlin Opera (contralto); from 1869–70, during the vacation, she studied with Viardot-Garcia in Paris. In 1882 she sang at Baireuth as Kundry in Wagner's *Parsifal.*

Brandus, Dufour & Co., great Paris music-publishing firm, founded (1834) by Moritz Schlesinger (q.v.). In 1846 it was taken up by the brothers, Louis B. (d. Sept. 30, 1887), and Gemmy B. (b. 1823, d. Feb. 12, 1873).

Branle (Bransle), an old French ring-dance of moderate movement and in binary time, as was indeed the case with all old dances accompanied by singing. It had a refrain after each strophe.

Brant, Jobst, or Jodocus, vom, the younger. He was a captain at Waldsachsen, and governor of Liebenstein. His friend, George Forster, speaks of him as a "fein lieblicher Komponist" (1549 and 1556). The fifty-four German songs in harmony, and a Motet à 6, prove that he was not only a sound contrapuntist, but a musician of deep feeling. (*Cf.* Eitner: "Bibliogr. of Collections of Musical Works, etc.," 1877.)

Brassin, (1) Louis, b. June 24, 1840, Aix, d. May 17, 1884, Petersburg. He was a distinguished pianist. He studied with his father, the operatic singer Gerhard B. (b. 1810, d. Sept., 1888, Brühl, near Bonn), and then under

Moscheles at the Leipzig Conservatorium. In 1866 he was at first teacher at the Stern Conservatorium in Berlin, from 1869 to 1879 at the Brussels Conservatoire, after that at the Petersburg Conservatoire. Of his pianoforte compositions the Études deserve special mention. His brothers are—(2) Leopold, b. May 28, 1843, Strassburg, d. 1890, Constantinople; court pianist at Coburg, then teacher at the Berne Music School. He lived also for some time in Petersburg.—(3) Gerhard, b. June 10, 1844, Aix, celebrated violinist; in 1863 teacher at the Berne Music School, then leader at Gothenburg (Sweden), in 1874 teacher at the Stern Conservatorium in Berlin, 1875–80 conductor of the Society of Artists in Breslau, and since then has resided in Petersburg. He has published several pieces for violin alone of great merit and technical interest.

Bratsche (Ger.). (*See* VIOLA.)

Bravo (Ital.), brave, valorous; the usual word for a shout of approval; in the superlative, *bravissimo*. To a man the Italians call *bravo*, *bravissimo* (pl. *bravi*); to a lady, *brava, bravissima* (pl. *brave*).

Bravour (Fr.; Ital. *Bravura*), bravery. *Bravourarie, i.e.* an aria with great technical difficulties; and so also *Bravourstück, Allegro di bravura, Valse de bravour,* etc.

Brawl, an old country dance; a round.

Breath, the air stored up in the lungs, which, during expiration, condensed by muscular contraction, produces the effect of wind, and evokes sounds from the human wind-instrument (the voice), as well as from other wind-instruments into the mouth-piece of which the air is conducted. Proper economy with the breath, and the right time for taking it, are difficult matters both in singing and blowing. For both, *deep breathing* (taking a full B.), where the pause is long enough, is of importance; for with the lungs, thus once well filled with fresh air, there is no necessity to take repeated small gasps of breath (taking a half breath). For the singer it is, besides, of importance that he should not breathe (*see* EMBOUCHURE) before the formation of the note; and, even when the breathed mode of attack is adopted, he should endeavour to make it as short as possible. While a note is being held out, all puffing out of the air must be avoided, especially in *piano* and *mezzoforte,* when the need of air is exceedingly small; only the *forte* demands a stronger pressure, and even then a great waste of breath is possible. The composer has principally to show where a breath should be taken. The wind-instrument player must not break up a tied phrase, and, in addition, the singer must take notice of the words, and breathe in places where, in speaking, short pauses would be made. A special caution must be given against taking breath at the end of a bar, or between article and substantive, etc.

Brebos, Gilles. (*See* GILLES.)

Bree, Jean Bernard van, b. Jan. 29, 1801, Amsterdam, d. there Feb. 14, 1857. He studied with Bertelmann, and, in 1829, was artistic director of the Felix Meritis Union; in 1840 he founded the St. Cecilia Society, which he conducted up to the time of his death, and was director of the music school of the Union for the Advancement of Musical Art. B. was a prolific composer of instrumental and vocal music (opera, *Sapho,* 1834).

Breidenstein, Heinrich Karl, b. Feb. 28, 1796, Steinau (Hesse), d. July 13, 1876, Bonn. He first studied law, but went to Heidelberg, where he made the acquaintance of Thibaut, and turned to philology. He then became private tutor in the house of Count Wintzingerode, in Stuttgart, and afterwards principal teacher at Heidelberg. In 1821 he went to Cologne, where he gave lectures on music, and in 1823 was appointed musical director at Bonn University, qualified himself as lecturer, and afterwards received the title of professor. He was the promoter of the Beethoven monument at Bonn, for the unveiling of which he wrote a festival pamphlet, and produced a cantata. Some of his chorales are particularly well known. The valuable materials which he had collected for a Method for Organ came into the possession of the compiler of this dictionary. His Method of Singing was formerly much in vogue.

Breitkopf und Härtel, renowned firm of music publishers in Leipzig, was founded in 1719 as a printing-office by Bernhard Christoph Breitkopf, from Klausthal (Hartz), b. March 2, 1695. His son, Johann Gottlob Immanuel Breitkopf, b. Nov. 23, 1719, entered, in 1745, the business, which from 1765 traded under the name B. C. Breitkopf und Sohn, and which increased so rapidly that the "Zum goldnen Bären" house was not large enough, and more room had to be obtained by purchasing that of the "Silberner Bär" house. When the father died, March 26, 1777, Immanuel Breitkopf became sole proprietor. This name is of importance in the history of music-printing, for he it was who wisely revived Petrucci's invention of movable types. (*Cf.* MUSIC-PRINTING.) Although this invention, which might justly be regarded as a new one, soon found imitators, he benefited principally by it. The music business, too, prospered greatly under his hands, for he gathered together a comprehensive store of manuscript and printed music and books, and published catalogues. He also wrote: "Ueber die Geschichte und Erfindung der Buchdruckerkunst" (1779); "Versuch, den Ursprung der Spielkarten, die Einführung des Leinenpapiers und den Anfang der Holzschneidekunst in Europa zu erforschen" (1784); "Ueber Schriftgiesserei und Stempelschneiderei;" "Ueber Bibliographie und Bibliophilie" (1793). After his death (Jan. 28, 1794), his son, Christoph Gottlob Breitkopf, b. Sept. 28, 1750, took the business, but soon handed it over entirely to his friend, partner, and heir, G. C. Härtel, and died already April 7, 1800.—Gottfried Christoph Härtel was b. Jan. 27, 1763, Schneeberg, and when he became partner the firm was called B. and H. He increased the business by the addition of a pianoforte manufactory, which soon acquired an immense reputation, began, from Oct. 1798, to publish the *Allgemeine Musikalische Zeitung* (the first musical paper of durable fame), brought out complete editions of the works of Mozart and Haydn, etc., introduced pewter plates, and in 1805 arranged with Senefelder, the inventor of lithography, to introduce lithography for the printing of the titles. He died July 25, 1827. His nephew, Florenz Härtel, continued the business for the heirs, until in 1835 the eldest son of Gottfried, Dr. Hermann Härtel, b. April 27, 1803, became the head (d. Aug. 4, 1875, Leipzig; married the pianist, Luise Hauffe, b. Jan. 2, 1837, Düben, d. March 20, 1882, Leipzig). His brother, the town-councillor, Raimund Härtel (b. June 9, 1810, d. Nov. 10, 1888, Leipzig) shared the management with him. These two men, who for a long period stood at the head of the Leipzig book-trade, were faithful to the good traditions of the house, causing it to be held in still higher esteem. To them we owe monumental, critical, complete editions of the works of Beethoven, Mozart, and Mendelssohn; the Bach Society Edition is engraved and printed by them. Their number of publications extends to 16,000. B. and H. have recently undertaken a cheap edition of the classics (Volksausgabe), which compares favourably with others of the same kind. But the book department under their management has increased in an extraordinary manner. After the death of Hermann Härtel and the withdrawal of his brother Raimund (1880), the sons of their two sisters, Wilhelm Volkmann (b. June 12, 1837, Leipzig, son of the Halle physiologist), and Dr. Oskar Hase (b. Sept. 15, 1846, Jena, son of the Jena Church historian), became the sole managers of the business. The latter published a monograph on the book trade in the 16th century, "Die Koberger" (2nd edition, 1885). The former d. Dec. 24, 1896.

Brendel, Karl Franz, b. Nov. 26, 1811, Stolberg, d. Nov. 25, 1868, Leipzig. He studied philosophy at Leipzig, and, at the same time, the pianoforte under Fr. Wieck, graduated at Berlin, and only in 1843 turned his attention entirely to music. He held lectures on the science of music in Freiberg, and later on in Dresden and Leipzig. In 1844 he undertook the editorship of the *Neue Zeitschrift für Musik* (founded in 1834 by Schumann), which he carried on in the spirit of the "new German" school; the same lines were followed in his monthly pamphlet, *Anregungen für Kunst, Leben, und Wissenschaft* (1856–60). Soon afterwards he became teacher

of the history of music at the Leipzig Conservatorium, which post restrained him from acting logically, and siding with Liszt and Wagner B. was one of the original founders, and for many years president, of the Allgemeiner Deutcher Musikverein (1861). Besides his newspaper articles, he published: "Grundzüge der Geschichte der Musik" (1848; fifth ed. 1861); "Geschichte der Musik in Italien, Deutschland, und Frankreich von den ersten christlichen Zeiten an, etc." (1852, two vols.; sixth ed., published by F. Stade, 1879); "Die Musik der Gegenwart und die Gesamtkunst der Zukunft" (1854); "Franz Liszt als Symphoniker" (1859), and "Geist und Tecknik im Klavierunterricht" (1867).

Brenner, Ludwig von, b. Sept. 19, 1833, Leipzig, pupil of the Leipzig Conservatorium, lived at Petersburg for fifteen years as member of the Imperial band, was conductor (1872–76) of the Berlin "Symphoniekapelle," and afterwards of an orchestra of his own (the "Neue Berliner Symphoniekapelle"). He is now conductor at Breslau, and has written orchestral and vocal works.

Breslaur, Emil, b. May 29, 1836, Kottbus, attended the Gymnasium of his native town, and the training college at Neuzelle, and, after a long probation, became instructor in religion and preacher to the Jewish community of his native town. In 1863 he settled in Berlin for the purpose of devoting his whole attention to music. He studied four years at the Stern Conservatorium, especially under Jean Vogt, H. Ehrlich (pianoforte), Fl. Geyer, Fr. Kiel (composition), H. Schwanzer (organ), and J. Stern (playing from score, conducting). From 1868 to 1879 he was teacher at Kullak's academy for pianoforte playing and theory, and lately for the art of teaching pianoforte playing. Since 1883 B. has been choir-master at the reformed synagogue as Stern's successor. B. was also active as a musical critic (*Spenersche Zeitung*, *Fremdenblatt*). In 1879 he founded a union for music teachers (male and female) at Berlin, which, thanks to his efforts and to the influence of his paper (see below), developed in 1886 into the "Deutscher Musiklehrer-Verband." B. is the founder and director of a college for the training of pianoforte teachers (male and female). For the instructive work, "Die Technische Grundlage des Klavierspiels" (1874), he received the title of Professor. In 1881 the Philharmonic Academy at Bologna named him honorary member. In wider circles, B. is especially known by his pedagogic periodical, *Der Klavierlehrer* (since 1878), also by the "Noten-Schreibhefte" published by Breitkopf & Härtel. He has also written a number of choral pieces, songs, pf. pieces, a "Klavierschule," and a "Führer durch die Klavierunterrichtslitteratur"; also the pamphlets, "Zur Methodischen Uebung des Klavierspiels," "Der Entwickelnde Unterricht in der Harmonielehre," "Ueber die schädlichen Folgen des unrichtigen Uebens." His " Methodik des Klavierunterrichts in Einzelaufsätzen " (1887) is a collection of treatises by various authors.

Breunung, Ferdinand, b. March 2, 1830, Brotterode, below Inselsberg, d. Sept. 22, 1883, Aix-la-Chapelle, pupil of the Leipzig Conservatorium, 1855 Reinecke's successor as pianoforte teacher at the Cologne Conservatorium, and from 1865 " Musikdirektor " at Aix-la-Chapelle.

Breval, Jean Baptiste, b. 1756, Département de l'Aisne, d. 1825, Chamouille, near Laon, 'cello player, principal 'cellist at the Grand Opéra, and 'cello professor at the Paris Conservatoire until 1802, when the institution was reorganised and he received a pension. He wrote a great quantity of instrumental music, especially concertos and chamber-music for stringed instruments; also an opera—*Inès et Léonore* (1788).

Brevis, the third species of note in measured music = $\frac{1}{2}$ or $\frac{1}{3}$ of a *Longa* (according to the measure prescribed; *cf.* MENSURAL NOTE). The B. occurs in our present notation only in the so-called great allabreve time ($\frac{2}{1}$) where, as bar unit, it has the value of two semibreves or whole notes. Concerning breves in ligatures, *cum proprietate* and *sine perfectione, see* LIGATURE, PROPRIETAS, and IMPERFECTION. In reprints of old music the B. is generally represented by ▯.

Briard, Étienne, type-founder at Avignon about 1530. His types, instead of notes of the usual angular shape, gave round ones, and, in place of the complicated ligatures, notes with their proper value. The works of Carpentras (q.v.) were printed with such types by Jean de Channay at Avignon in 1532—a unique undertaking.

Briccialdi, Giulio, b. March 2, 1818, Terni (States of the Church), d. Dec. 17, 1881, Florence, excellent flute-player, made extensive journeys and lived for a long time in London. His compositions for flute are held in esteem.

Bridge (Ger. *Steg*) is, in stringed instruments, the delicately cut block of hard wood over which the strings are stretched. The B. rests with its two feet firmly on the top block. Exactly under one foot, between top and bottom block, is placed the sound-post. This prevents any giving way of the top block, and gives to the B. a firm support on the one side; and this, as soon as the string vibrates, enables the vibrations to be transmitted by jerks from the other foot to the top block. (*Cf.* SOUND-BOARD, TRUMBSCHEIT (2).) The B. is used for a similar purpose in pianofortes. Here, it is a long ledge running parallel with the pinblock. This ledge lies on the sound-board, and the strings are stretched over it.

Bridge, (1) John Frederick, b. Dec. 5,

1844, Oldbury, Worcester, pupil of J. Hopkins and J. Goss, at first in 1865 organist at Trinity Church, Windsor, then in 1869 at Manchester Cathedral, 1875 deputy, and 1882 principal, organist at Westminster Abbey. B. is also Professor of Harmony and Counterpoint at the Royal College of Music, conductor of the Western and the Madrigal Societies, and Examiner of Music at the University of London, etc. (he took his degree of Dr. Mus. at Oxford with his oratorio *Mount Moriah*). B. has written hymns, cantatas, also anthems and orchestral works, and primers on Counterpoint, Double Counterpoint, Canon, and Organ Accompaniment of the Choral Service. B. was decorated by the Queen for his "Jubilee" Service in 1887.— (2) Joseph Cox, brother and pupil of the above, b. Aug. 16, 1853, Rochester; studied also under Hopkins, and is likewise a celebrated organist, since 1877 at Chester Cathedral, where he helped to resuscitate the Chester Triennial Festival, which had not been held for fifty years. He took his degree of Dr. Mus. in 1879 at Oxford. He has also written several important vocal works (*Daniel, Rudel,* 1891).

Briegel, Wolfgang Karl, b. May 21, 1626, 1650 court cantor at Gotha, 1670 capellmeister at Darmstadt, d. there Nov. 19, 1712. He was a very prolific composer of sacred music, instrumental pieces, etc.

Brillante (Ital.), brilliant, sparkling.

Brillenbässe (Ger. "spectacle basses"), a nickname for the figure which has to be resolved into quavers or semiquavers.

Brindisi (Ital.), a drinking song.

Brink, Jules ten, composer, b. Nov., 1838, Amsterdam, d. Feb. 6, 1889, Paris. He studied with Heinze at Amsterdam, with Dupont at Brussels, and with E. F. Richter at Leipzig. He was musical director at Lyons from 1860 to 1868, and then settled in Paris, where he displayed his gifts as a composer in some instrumental compositions, produced partly at a Concert spirituel, partly at a concert given by himself in 1878 (orchestral suite, symphonic poem, symphony, violin concerto, etc.). A one-act comic opera (*Calonice*) was given at the Athénée Theatre in 1870, and favourably received. A grand opera in five acts remained in manuscript.

Brinsmead, John, founder of the celebrated London pianoforte firm, J. B. & Sons, b. Oct. 13, 1814, Wear Giffard (North Devon). He established the business in 1835, and in 1863 took his sons, Thomas (d. 1906) and Edgar, into partnership. The younger, Edgar B., wrote a " History of the Pianoforte " (1868; partly rewritten and republished in 1879).

Brio (Ital.), vivacity; *con b., brioso,* with fire.

Brisé (Fr.), broken, played *arpeggio.*

Brissler, Friedrich Ferdinand, b. June 13, 1818, Insterburg, pupil of the Berlin Academy (Rungenhagen, A. W. Bach, F. Schneider, and R. Schumann); gave concerts from 1838–45 as pianist, and was for a long time teacher at the Stern Conservatorium. B. was especially known through his numerous useful vocal scores (for two and four hands), an opera, symphony, etc. He died Aug. 6, 1893, Berlin.

Bristow, George F., pianist and violinist, b. 1825, New York. He was trained by his father, and is highly esteemed in his native city as teacher, performer, conductor. He has also made a reputation as composer (two symphonies, opera *Rip van Winkle,* oratorios *Daniel* and *St. John,* many pf. pieces, songs, etc.). At present B. is professor of singing at New York Municipal Schools.

Brixi, Franz Xaver, noteworthy Bohemian Church composer, b. 1732, Prague, d. there Oct. 14, 1771. He was an orphan at the age of five, and was brought up at Kosmanos by an ecclesiastic to whom he was related, and afterwards received musical training under Segert at Prague, where he also attended the university. B. was first appointed organist of St. Gallus, and became capellmeister at Prague Cathedral in 1756. B. wrote fifty-two grand festival masses, twenty-four smaller masses, many psalms, litanies, vespers, several oratorios, a Requiem, etc. His masses are still performed in Bohemia.

Broadwood & Sons, the eminent pianoforte makers in London. The firm was established *c.* 1728 by an immigrant Swiss, Burkhard Tschudi (Shudi), whose harpsichords soon became famous (some of his instruments are in Windsor Castle and at Potsdam). John Broadwood, originally a cabinet-maker, became Tschudi's partner, son-in-law, and heir. The so-called "English action," first applied to pianofortes by Americus Backers in 1770— and which, before his death in 1781, he recommended to Broadwood—is only a development of the action invented by Cristofori and developed by Silbermann. (*See* PIANOFORTE.) John Broadwood, b. 1732, d. 1812, was succeeded by his sons, James Shudi and Thomas Broadwood. The late head of the firm, Henry Fowler Broadwood, d. July 8, 1893. The manufacture of pianofortes has increased to a colossal extent. The firm turns out several thousands of instruments every year.

Brod, Henry, b. Aug. 4, 1801, Paris, d. there April 6, 1839. He was a distinguished performer on the oboe, and professor at the Paris Conservatoire.

Broderies (Fr.), Ornaments (q.v.).

Brodsky, Adolf, distinguished violinist, b. March 21, 1851, Taganrog (Russia). He played in public at Odessa when only nine years of age, and excited the interest of a well-to-do citizen there, who had him trained under J. Hellmesberger at Vienna, and finally at the Conservatorium (1862–63). B. then joined the Hellmesberger quartet-party, and from 1868 to 1870 was member of the opera orchestra, making appearances at the same time as soloist. A long artistic tour ended at Moscow in 1873, where B. resumed his studies under Laub. In 1875 he received an appointment at the Conservatoire, and became successor to Hrimaly, who was advanced to the post left vacant by the death of Laub. In 1879 B. left Moscow, conducted the symphony concerts at Kiev, and in 1881 recommenced touring, appearing at Paris, Vienna, London, Moscow with great success until, in the winter (1882–83) he received the violin professorship at Leipzig, which, through the departure of Schradieck, had become vacant. Since 1892 he has been living in New York.

Broer, Ernst, b. April 11, 1809, Ohlau (Silesia), d. March 25, 1886, Tarnopol. He was 'cellist and organist (about 1840 at the "Dachsemkirche," Breslau), 1843–84 teacher of singing at the Matthias Gymnasium there; also a composer of sacred music.

Bromel. (*See* BRUMEL.)

Bronsart von Schellendorf, Hans (Hans von Bronsart), pianist and composer, b. Feb. 11, 1830, Berlin. He was the eldest son of the General Lieutenant v. B.; he studied from 1849 to 1852 at the Berlin University, and, at the same time, studied the theory of music with Dehn. He lived for several years at Weimar, working with Liszt, and gave concerts in Paris, Petersburg, and the principal cities of Germany. From 1860 to 1862 he conducted the "Euterpe" concerts at Leipzig, and the concerts of the "Gesellschaft der Musikfreunde" at Berlin as Bülow's successor. In 1867 he became intendant of the royal theatre at Hanover, and was afterwards named royal chamberlain; and since 1887 he has been "Hofmusikintendant" at Berlin. Of his compositions the Trio in G minor, and the pianoforte concerto in F♯ minor have become known far and wide; and besides, his "Frühlings-phantasie" for orchestra has been repeatedly performed. In addition to many pianoforte works may be named a cantata, *Christnacht* (performed by the Riedel Society at Leipzig), and a sextet for strings. In 1862 B. married the pianist, Ingeborg Starck (b. Aug. 24, 1840, of Swedish parents), a distinguished pianist and pupil of Liszt. Both have won reputation as composers for the pianoforte. Frau v. B. has also written three operas (*Die Göttin zu Saïs, Hjarne, Jery und Baeteli*), also songs, violin pieces, etc.

Bros, Juan, b. 1776, Tortosa (Spain), d. 1852, Oviedo. He was, in turn, maestro at the cathedrals of Malaga, Leon, and Oviedo. He was famed as a composer of sacred music.

Broschi, Cario. (*See* FARINELLI.)

Brosig, Moritz, b. Oct. 15, 1815, Fuchs-winkel (Upper Silesia), d. Jan. 24, 1887, Bres-lau. He attended the Matthias Gymnasium at Leipzig, was then a diligent pupil of the musical director and cathedral organist Franz Wolf, and, when the latter died in 1842, replaced him in his various posts. He became cathedral capellmeister in 1853, was named doctor of philosophy, and became sub-director of the Royal Institute for Catholic Church Music, and lecturer at the University, also a member of the "Cecilia" Academy at Rome. B. was a diligent and prolific composer of sacred music, and published four great, and three small in-strumental masses, seven books of graduals and offertories, twenty books of organ pieces, an "Orgelbuch" in eight parts, a "Choralbuch," a "Modulationstheorie," and a "Harmonie-lehre" (1874).

Brossard, (1) Sébastien de, b. 1660, d. Aug. 10, 1730, Meaux; took holy orders, and was at first prebendary, in 1689 capellmeister at Strassburg Cathedral, and, from 1700 up to his death in 1730, *grand chapelain* and musical director at the Cathedral of Meaux. B. is the author of the oldest musical dictionary (apart from Tinctor's "Definitorium," Naples, cir. 1475; and Janowka's "Clavis ad thesaurum magnæ artis musicæ, etc.," 1701). His work bears the title "Dictionnaire de musique, contenant une explication des termes grecs, italiens et français les plus usités dans la musique, etc." (1703, 2nd ed., 1705; 3rd ed., without year of publication). B. also published some books of church composi-tions.—(2) Nöel Matthieu, b. Dec. 25, 1789, Châlon sur Saône, where he died as magistrate. A clever theorist who, in his work, "Théorie des sons musicaux" (1847), called attention to the various possible acoustical values of sounds, and of these he reckoned forty-eight within the compass of the octave. He also published a table of keys (1843), as well as a Guide how to use them in teaching (1844).

Brouck, Jakob de, also de Prugg, b. in the Low Countries, was alto in the Royal Chapel, Vienna, from 1573 to 1576. He pub-lished a collection of motets at Antwerp (1579), and three are also to be found in Joanellus' Collection of 1568. (*Cf.* BRUCK.)

Brouillon-Lacombe. (*See* LACOMBE.)

Bruch, Max, b. Jan. 6, 1838, Cologne, re-ceived his first musical instruction from his mother (*née* Almenräder), who was an esteemed teacher of music, and who, in her youth, re-peatedly took part in Rhenish musical festivals as soprano singer. Already at the age of eleven, B., at that time pupil of K. Breidenstein, tried his hand at compositions on a large scale, and, at the age of fourteen, produced a symphony at Cologne. In 1853 he gained the scholarship of the Mozart Foundation (q.v.), which he held for four years, and was the special pupil of Ferdinand Hiller for theory and composition,

of Karl Reinecke (until 1854), and of Fer-dinand Breunung for pianoforte. After a short stay in Leipzig, he lived as teacher of music at Cologne from 1858 to 1861, where, already in 1858, he produced his first dramatic composi-tion, Goethe's Singspiel, *Scherz, List und Rache.* After the death of his father, in 1861, he made an extensive tour for the purpose of study, which, after a short stay at Berlin, Leipzig, Vienna, Dresden, Munich, ended at Mannheim, where in 1863 his opera (written to the libretto prepared by Geibel for Mendelssohn), *Loreley,* was produced. In Mannheim (1862–64) he wrote the choral works, *Frithjof, Römischer Triumphgesang, Gesang der heiligen drei Könige, Flucht der heiligen Familie,* etc. From 1864–65 he travelled again (Hamburg, Hanover, Dresden, Breslau, Munich, Brussels, Paris, etc.), and produced his *Frithjof* with extraordinary success at Aix, Leipzig, and Vienna. From 1865–67 he was musical director at Coblenz ; from 1867–70 court capellmeister at Sondershausen. At Coblenz he wrote, among other things, his well-known first violin concerto, and at Son-dershausen two symphonies and portions of a mass, etc. The opera, *Hermione,* produced at Berlin in 1872, where B. resided from 1871–73, only met with a *succès d'estime.* The choral work, *Odysseus,* also belongs to the Berlin period. After devoting five years at Bonn (1873–78) exclusively to composition (*Arminius, Lied von der Glocke,* the 2nd violin concerto), only making two journeys to England for per-formances of his works, he became in 1878, after the departure of Stockhausen, conductor of the Stern Choral Union, and in 1880, as successor to Benedict, conductor of the Philhar-monic Society, Liverpool. In 1881 he married the vocalist, Fräul. Tuczek, from Berlin. In 1883 he resigned his post at Liverpool, in order to undertake the direction of the orchestral society at Breslau, as successor to Bernard Scholz ; he remained here until the end of the year 1890. In 1892 B. succeeded H. v. Her-zogenberg at the Kgl. Hochschule, Berlin. In the department of choral music B. is one of the most distinguished German composers. The great works for mixed chorus, soli, and orchestra, *Odysseus, Arminius, Lied von der Glocke,* and *Achilleus* (1885), as well as the choruses for male voices, *Frithjof, Salamis, Normannenzug,* are his most important crea-tions : his first violin concerto, however, is a favourite with all violinists. The characteristic points of B.'s style of writing are delight in beautiful effects of sound, simplicity, and na-turalness of invention. Further may be men-tioned his 3rd symphony in E (Op. 61) ; the 3rd violin concerto in D minor (Op. 58) ; the Hebrew melody, "Kol Nidrei," for 'cello ; the choral work, *Schön Ellen* (an early work) ; the cantata, *Das Feuer Kreuz* (Op. 52) ; and two choruses for male voices, with orchestra, Op. 53 (*Thermo-pylä, Spartãos*).

Bruck, (Brouck), A r n o l d v o n, probably a German from Switzerland. Already in the year 1534 he was principal capellmeister to the Emperor Ferdinand I., and died in 1545. A medal was struck off in his honour in 1536. He was one of the most distinguished composers of the 16th century, and many of his German songs in parts (secular and sacred), motets, hymns, etc., have been preserved in collections of the 16th century. (*See* BIBLIOGRAPHY OF EITNER. *Cf.* BROUCK.)

Brückler, H u g o, a highly-gifted song composer, who unfortunately died at an early age, b. Feb. 18, 1845, Dresden, d. there Oct. 4, 1871. At the age of ten he was member of the Evangelical chapel boys' choir. He was a pupil of Johann Schneider, and received further training at the Dresden Conservatorium (Schubert for violin, Krebs, Armin, Früh, Rietz). He published (Op. 1 and 2) songs from Scheffel's *Trompeter von Säckingen* (1. Five Songs of Young Werner by the Rhine. 2. Songs of Margaret). After his death, A. Jensen published "Sieben Gesänge" and Rheinhold Becker the ballad, "Der Vogt von Tenneberg."

Bruckner, A n t o n, composer and organist, b. Sept. 4, 1824, Ansfelden (Upper Austria). He was the son of a village schoolmaster, from whom he received his first musical instruction. After the premature death of his father he was received as chorister in the collegiate church of St. Florian. Though in extremely needy circumstances as assistant schoolmaster in Windhag, near Freistadt, and afterwards as teacher and temporary organist at the Church of St. Florian, B. trained himself, and became a distinguished contrapuntist and excellent organist, so that in 1855, at the competition for the post of cathedral organist at Linz, he came off conqueror. B. went frequently to Vienna from Linz, as he had already done from St. Florian, in order to receive further training from Sechter in counterpoint; and from 1861 to 1863 he studied, in addition, composition with Otto Kitzler. After Sechter's death, and on Herbeck's recommendation, B. was appointed successor to the former as court organist, and, at the same time, professor of organ-playing, counterpoint, and composition at the Vienna Conservatorium, to which appointments that of lecturer on music at the University was added in 1875. Up to the present B. has written eight symphonies, of which No. 2 in c minor, the 3rd, in D minor, and the eighth, in c minor, were produced in Vienna (1876, 1877, and 1892), but without creating any special impression. No. 3 appeared in print. It was first by No. 7 (E major, printed in 1885), introduced with great flourish of trumpets, that the name of B. came into everyone's mouth, although his music has never met with general recognition. So far as one can judge from the specimens published, Bruckner's peculiarity is a striking, and often repulsive, harmonic mixture, which

may be explained by his tendency to employ Wagner's stage style for absolute music. His contrapuntal training is undeniable, and so is the cleverness of his instrumentation, but his music lacks warmth, and appears made rather than felt—so to speak, *external* music. Bruckner's art of rhythm, all appearances to the contrary notwithstanding, is exceedingly poor, for it is confined within the limits of never-changing 4-bar rhythm. To the above-named works, for the sake of completeness, we must add : a grand Te Deum, a quintet for strings; "Germanenzug," for male chorus ; some graduals and offertories. Besides the symphony in E flat (of which fragments have been heard), he has also in manuscript three grand masses and works for male chorus of large and of small compass.

Bruhns, N i k o l a u s, b. 1665, Schwabstädt (Schleswig), distinguished violinist, organist, and composer for the organ and pianoforte. He was a pupil of Buxtehude's, at Lübeck, at whose recommendation he was first appointed organist at Copenhagen. From there he afterwards went to Husum, where he died in 1697.

Brüll, I g n a z, b. Nov. 7, 1846, Prossnitz (Moravia). He studied the piano with Epstein at Vienna, composition with Rufinatscha, and afterwards Dessoff. When he had become a competent pianist, he gave concerts in Vienna of his own compositions (pf. concerto, etc.), and, later on, made concert tours as pianist. An orchestral serenade was first produced at Stuttgart in 1864. From 1872 to 1878 he was pianoforte teacher at the Horak Institute, Vienna. The increasing success of *Das Goldene Kreux* induced him to devote himself entirely to composition. Up to now he has written the operas, *Die Bettler von Samarkand* (1864), *Das Goldene Kreuz* (1875, a favourite work, which speedily made its way, and has been translated into other languages and produced abroad ; London, among other places), *Der Landfriede* (1877), *Bianca* (1879), *Königin Mariette* (1883), and *Das steinerne Herz* (1888) ; and, besides, a *Macbeth* overture (Op. 46), two pf. concertos, a violin concerto, a sonata for two pianofortes, a 'cello sonata, two violin sonatas, a trio, suite for pianoforte and violin (Op. 42), pianoforte pieces, songs, etc.

Brumel, A n t o n, distinguished Netherland contrapuntist, contemporary of Josquin and pupil of Okeghem. He lived at the Court of Sigismund Cantelmus, Duke of Sora, and in 1505 went from there to Alfonso I., Duke of Ferrara. Here he appears to have remained until the end of his life (see the documents, "Monatshefte f. Musikg. XVI. 11"). In 1503 Petrucci printed five masses à 4 of Brumel's, another one ("*dringhs*") in the first book of the "Missæ Diversorum" (1508), also portions of masses in the "Fragmenta Missarum," Motets in the "Motetti XXXIII." (1502), the "Canti CL." (1504), "Motetti C." (1504), "Motetti Libro quarto"(1505), and "Motetti della Corona"(1514). There are three masses in the " Liber XV. Missarum " of Andreas Antiquus " (1516), one in the " Missæ XIII." of Grapheus (1539), and two in the " Liber XV. Missarum " of Petrejus (1538). Finally, one mass à 12 (!), and three credos à 4 are in the Munich Library (a copy of the mass by Bottée de Toulmon is in the library of the Paris Conservatoire).

Brummeisen (Ger.). (*See* JEW'S HARP.)

Brunelli, A n t o n i o, cathedral maestro at Prato, afterwards at Florence, where finally he received the title of Maestro to the Grand Duke. He was a composer of sacred music, who published, between 1605 and 1621, motets, *Cantica*, madrigals, etc., and a work on counterpoint— " Regole e dichiarazioni di alcuni contrapunti doppi e maggiormente . . . contrapunti all' improviso, etc." (1610).

Brunetti, G a e t a n o, performer on the violin, and composer, b. 1753, Pisa, d. 1808 through terror at the taking of Madrid by Napoleon. He was a pupil of Nardini's, and was attracted to Madrid by Boccherini in 1766, where, by intercourse with this master, his talents quickly developed. Yet he was ungrateful towards Boccherini, for he carried on intrigues against him, and compelled him to give up his posts of maestro and court composer. Thirty-one of his symphonies for orchestra, and numerous chamber-music works have been preserved, but for the most part in manuscript ; they are in the possession of Picquot, the biographer of Boccherini.

Bruni, A n t o n i o B a r t o l o m m e o, performer on the violin, b. Feb. 2, 1759, Coni (Piedmont), d. there 1823. He studied under Pugnani and Spezziani, went to Paris in 1781, where he was at first violinist at the Comédie Italienne, then *chef d'orchestre* at the Théâtre Montansier, at the Opéra-Comique, and finally at the Italian Opera. Between 1786 and 1815, twenty-one French comic operas of his were produced. In 1801 he retired to Passy, near Paris ; in 1816 he made a somewhat unfortunate stage venture (*Le Mariage par Commission*), and then returned to his native town, Coni. He also published a Method for violin and for viola, likewise duets for violins.

Brunner, C h r i s t i a n T r a u g o t t, b. Dec. 12, 1792, Brünlos, near Stollberg (Erzgebirge), d. April 14, 1874, as organist and conductor of the choral society at Chemnitz. He became known by his educational pianoforte pieces, potpourris, etc., especially for beginners.

Brustwerk (Ger. ; Lower Manual), a term for the second or third manual in the organ, connected with pipes in the centre of the instrument. As a rule, the tone of the Lower Manual is not so strong as that of the Great Organ. (*See* MANUALS.)

Bruyck, K a r l D e b r o i s v a n, writer on music, and composer, b. March 14, 1828, Brünn. He went, already in 1830, with his parents to Vienna, where, after attending the Gymnasium, he studied jurisprudence, and only turned to art when he was twenty-two years of age. He was a pupil of Rufinatscha's for the theory of music, and soon became a diligent contributor to several musical newspapers. Up to 1860 he published about thirty works. His musical activity was interrupted for a long period by philosophical studies ; but he published two excellent monographs, " Technische und ästhetische Analyse des Wohltemperirten Klaviers " (1867 ; 2nd ed. 1889), and " Robert Schumann " (the latter in Kolatschek's " Stimmen der Zeit," 1868), and began again to compose diligently. An essay—" Die Entwickelung der Klaviermusik von J. S. Bach bis R. Schumann " (1880)—was his last publication. B. lived at Waldhofen on the Ybbs. Died Aug. 1, 1902.

Bryennius, M a n u e l (sprung, according to Fétis, from an old French family which settled in Greece at the time of the Crusades), was the last Greek writer on music (about 1320). His " Harmonica," of which many copies exist, is, however, not an independent work, but an arrangement and comprehensive digest of earlier writings on music by the ancient Greeks, and contains extracts of more or less importance from Adrast, Aristoxenos, Euclid, Ptolemy, Nicomachos, Theo of Smyrna, and others. The explanation of the Neo-Grecian Church Modes is taken from Pachymeres (1242 to 1310). B's " Harmonica " is printed in the third volume of Joh. Wallis's " Opera Mathematica " (1699). *Cf.* CHRIST on B.'s system of harmony, and Paranika's " Aids to Byzantine Literature " (Report of a sitting of the Munich Academy, 1870), two treatises of great value.

Buccina (from Gr. *bukane;* or Lat. *bucca,* "cheek," and *canere,* "to sing.") A Roman wind instrument ; probably a straight trumpet or tuba, from which came our trombone (and also its German name " Posaune ").

Buchholz, an old and famous Berlin firm of organ-builders, founded 1799 by J o h. S i m. B., b. Sept. 27, 1758, Schlosswippach, near Erfurt, d. Feb. 24, 1825, Berlin. His son and successor, Karl Aug. B., b. Aug. 13, 1796, Berlin, d. there Aug. 12, 1884. The last representative of the family—his son, Karl Friedrich B. (b. 1821)—followed him to the grave already on Feb. 17, 1885. The Buchholz firm, which built many large organs for Berlin and for other towns, planned many improvements in the mechanism of the organ.

Büchner, E m i l, b. Dec. 25, 1826, Osterfeld, Naumburg, pupil of the Leipzig Conservatorium, 1866 court capellmeister in Meiningen, now director of the Soller Musical Union at Erfurt, a diligent composer (operas—*Launcelot,*

Dame Kobold—overtures, symphonies, chamber-music, etc.).

Buck, (1) Zechariah, b. Sept. 9, 1798, Norwich, d. Aug. 5, 1879, Newport (Essex), for many years organist of Norwich Cathedral. The degree of Mus. D. was conferred upon him by the Archbishop of Canterbury. As a composer he was not remarkable, but he was an excellent teacher.—(2) Dudley, organist and composer, b. March 10, 1839, Hartford (Connecticut). After having been assistant organist in his native town for several years, he studied (1858–59) at Leipzig under Hauptmann, Richter, and especially Rietz, whom he followed to Dresden in 1860, and studied the organ there under Joh. Schneider. He then spent a year in Paris, and in 1862 became organist at Hartford. After the death of his parents he accepted the post of organist of St. James's Church, Chicago; but, after the great fire in that city in 1871, he went to Boston, where he was appointed organist of the Music Hall, and of St. Paul's Church. In 1874 he gave up these posts and became organist of St. Anne's Church, Brooklyn, and assistant conductor of Thomas's orchestra at New York. In 1877 he was appointed organist of the church of the Holy Trinity, Brooklyn. He has composed principally sacred and organ music—Psalm xlvi. for soli, chorus, and orchestra, likewise scenes from Longfellow's " Golden Legend " (which won the prize at Cincinnati), several overtures, songs, part-songs, cantatas, *Don Munio*, *Easter Morning*, *Centennial Meditation of Columbia* (1876), *The Light of Asia*, *Columbus* (for male chorus), overture *Marmion*, a concerto for four horns, two quintets for strings, a symphony, etc.; also a burlesque operetta, etc., and finally an organ Method, " Illustrations in Choir Accompaniment," and Pedal Studies.

Buffo (Ital.), comic. *Opera buffa*, same as comic opera. (*See* OPERA). *Basso buffo*, a bass singer who sings comic parts. (*See* BASS.)

Bugle Horn, signal horn for the infantry ; it is of wide measure, and has no real bell ; hence the tone is full, neither blaring nor noble, but of somewhat coarse quality. Between 1820 and 1835 it was provided with sound-holes and keys, so as to fill the gaps between the open notes of the instrument (*key bugle*, also called *Kent bugle*), with compass from small *c* to twice-accented *g*, or at most thrice-accented *c;* (these are bugles in B♭ and in A). By the addition of three valves, the following modern instruments were formed : piccolo (in E♭), Flügelhorn (in B♭), Althorn (in E♭), and Tenorhorn (in B♭), all of which are only employed in wind bands ; they are despised by the orchestra of the symphony. The so-called cornet-notation (q.v.) is used for all kinds of bugles. The compass of the piccolo is a–b² ; of the Flügelhorn, e–b² ; of the Althorn, A–e²♭ ; of the Tenorhorn, E–b¹♭ (according to the sound). For the buglehorns of larger dimensions, with four or five valves (and with power of producing the real fundamental note), *see* TUBA. The French saxhorns are identical with buglehorns and tubas.

Bühler, Franz (Peter Gregorius), b. April 12, 1760, Schneidheim, near Nördlingen, d. Feb, 4, 1824, Augsburg. He was a Benedictine monk at Donauwörth, in 1801 capellmeister of Augsburg Cathedral. He wrote sacred compositions, small theoretical pamphlets, and also an opera, *Die falschen Verdachte*.

Bull, (1) John, b. 1563, Somersetshire, d. March 12, 1628, Antwerp ; was trained at Queen Elizabeth's Chapel under William Blitheman, became organist of Hereford Cathedral in 1582, and afterwards Master of the children. In 1586 he took his degree of Mus. Bac. of Oxford, and in 1592 that of Mus. Doc. both at Cambridge and Oxford. In 1591 he is said to have become organist of the Chapel Royal, and in 1596 Music Professor at Gresham College, with special permission to lecture in English instead of Latin. He married in 1607, and, in conformity with the statutes, had to resign his post there. He became organist of Antwerp Cathedral in 1617. B. enjoyed the highest fame as an organist, and was a sound contrapuntist ; of his compositions only scholastic pieces and variations for the virginals, an anthem, and some canons have been preserved. A number of his pieces have been republished in Pauer's "Old English Composers."—(2) Ole Bornemann, b. Feb. 5, 1810, Bergen (Norway), d. Aug. 17, 1880, at his country seat, Lysoén, near Bergen. He was a famous, though somewhat eccentric violin virtuoso, whose capricious playing often brought on him the reproach of charlatanism. In 1829 he went to Cassel, against the wish of his parents, in order to become Spohr's pupil, but soon discovered that they were not suited to each other, and was induced to follow Paganini to Paris to appropriate to himself the more sympathetic manner of the latter. In Paris all his goods, even his violin, were stolen, and in despair he threw himself into the Seine, but was soon taken out; a rich lady received and nursed him, and he even had a present made to him of a new violin (a Guarneri). From that time he began his many wanderings through Italy, Germany, Russia, Scandinavia, North America (1844), France, Algeria, and Belgium. In 1848 he returned to Bergen and founded a national theatre, but quarrelled with the town authorities, and went away in 1852, once again to North America, where he purchased large tracts of land in Pennsylvania and founded a Norwegian colony, which, however, failed, and brought him to ruin. On his return to Europe, he travelled once more through France, Spain, Germany, and then retired to Bergen, but afterwards paid several visits to America. As a composer for his instrument, B. wrote much that is interesting and piquant, especially fantasias on Northern themes.

Bülow, H a n s G u i d o v o n, a highly intellectual musician, eminent pianist and conductor, b. Jan. 8, 1830, Dresden, became at the age of nine a pupil of Fr. Wieck for the pianoforte, and of Eberwein for harmony. In 1848 he went to Leipzig University to study jurisprudence, but at the same time worked at counterpoint under Hauptmann. In 1849, excited by the political events, he went to Berlin, and, as contributor to the *Abendpost*, adopted Wagner's theories, whose "Die Kunst und die Revolution" appeared at that time. A performance of *Lohengrin* at Weimar matured his resolve to devote himself entirely to music, and in spite of his parents' opposition, he hastened to Zürich, the place of refuge of the master who had been banished on account of his political convictions, and there, from 1850-51, he received hints in the art of conducting. After B. had won his spurs as theatre conductor in Zürich and St. Gall, he betook himself to Liszt at Weimar, who gave the final touches to his pianoforte playing, which already showed mastery of a high order. In 1853 he made his first concert tour through Germany and Austria; his success was not exactly brilliant, but ever on the increase. A second tour followed in 1855, and ended at Berlin with Bülow's appointment as principal pianoforte teacher at the Stern Conservatorium (in Kullak's place). In 1857 he married Liszt's daughter, Cosima. In 1858 he was named royal court pianist, and in 1863 the degree of Dr. Phil. was conferred on him by the University of Jena. Meanwhile Wagner had found in King Ludwig of Bavaria a distinguished patron, who now drew B. to Munich, and first as court pianist; but in 1867, after a short stay at Basle, giving lessons and concerts, he was appointed court capellmeister and director of the reorganised Royal School of Music. Although active here only for a short period, he exercised great influence on music in Munich. Domestic misunderstandings led in 1869 to a separation, and B. left the city. For several years he settled in Florence, and by establishing regular concerts and performances of chamber music there successfully spread a knowledge of German music in Italy. From 1872, frequently changing his place of residence, he has been recognised as an interpreter of classical pianoforte works, and received everywhere with enthusiasm as a master belonging to the whole of Europe. Even on the Americans he lavished artistic pleasure from his horn of plenty, playing (1875-76) at no less than 139 concerts. On the 1st of January, 1878, he was appointed capellmeister of the court theatre at Hanover (successor to K. L. Fischer), but disputes with the intendancy with regard to the competency of some of the artists, led to a rupture, already at the end of two years. On October 1, 1880, he became "Hofmusik-Intendant" to the Duke

of Meiningen, soon raised the orchestra there into one of the first rank, and undertook concert tours with it through Germany, achieving phenomenal success. The excellence of the orchestra consisted not so much in striking artistic ability of the individual members as in subordination of the players to the authority of the conductor, a subordination without example, and well worthy of imitation; by means of it he was able to display to the full his congenial comprehension of the standard classical works. Unfortunately, B. resigned his post in the autumn of 1885, whereupon the band was reduced, while B. displayed elsewhere his qualities as a conductor—at Petersburg (Philharmonic Concerts), Berlin (Philharmonic Concerts), etc., developing at the same time increased activity as a teacher (at the Raff Conservatorium, at Frankfort-on-Main, and at Klindworth's Conservatorium, Berlin, a month at each institution every year). In August, 1882, and for the second time, B. married; this time with the Meiningen court actress, Fräulein Marie Schanzer. Since 1888 B. has resided at Hamburg, where he established a new concert society (the Subscription Concerts), which naturally was held in the highest consideration. There are many pianists, of high importance too, who go in triumph through the world, but B. is not one of the kind. He not only impresses, but instructs; he is a missionary of true, genuine art, and plays, therefore, from preference, classical music. His *répertoire* is, nevertheless, the most extensive of all pianists, and includes everything of importance which the rising generation has produced. Of new works he is an influential critic—the pieces which he has once played in public have free course. B. always plays by heart, and conducts also without book (he was the first to set the fashion); his memory is without example. The special characteristics of his playing are a finish even to the most minute details, a worthy pattern, but by no means easy to imitate, a thorough entering into the spirit of the work which he has to interpret, technical perfection and smoothness; but he is less imposing in the matters of strength and nobility. He has been active as a composer of pianoforte pieces, songs, and some orchestral works, which all display a well-trained mind and refined feeling. Of high artistic value are the classical works which he has edited (Beethoven's pianoforte works from Op. 53, Cramer's Studies with admirable instructive comments, etc.).

Bulss, P a u l, distinguished opera singer (baritone), b. Dec. 19, 1847, at Birkholz Manor (Priegnitz), pupil of G. Engel; was engaged at Lübeck (1868), Cologne, Cassel, then at Dresden (1876-89), and later at the Berlin Hofoper.

Bungert, A u g u s t, b. March 14, 1846, Mülheim on Ruhr, received there his first instruction on the pianoforte from F. Kufferath, then attended the Cologne Conservatorium, and for further training went to Paris for four years, where Mathias took an interest in him. In 1869 he became musical director at Kreuznach, then at Carlsruhe; and from 1873 to 1881 lived in Berlin (where once again he diligently studied counterpoint under Kiel), and has resided, since 1882, at Pegli near Genoa. B. is a highly talented composer. His pianoforte quartet (Op. 18) won the prize offered by the Florentine Quartet in 1878; besides, he has published pf. pieces, variations (Op. 13), songs (among which many to words by Carmen Sylva from her "Lieder einer Königin), quartets for male voices, overture to *Tasso*, "Hohes Lied der Liebe," symphonic poem "Auf der Wartburg," and in 1884 produced at Leipzig a comic opera—*Die Studenten von Salamanka*. Of his great tetralogy, "Homerische Welt" (1, Circe; 2, Odysseus; 3, Nausikaa; 4, Odysseus-Heimkehr), the third part is printed. A drama (*Hutten und Sickingen*) was produced at Kreuznach and Bonn.

Bunting, Edward, b. Feb. 1773, Armagh, Ireland, d. Dec. 21, 1843, Belfast. B. has the merit of having collected and preserved for posterity the melodies of the immortal Irish bards, and in this he was assisted by then still living harpers of distinction (O'Neill, Hempson, Fanning, and others). His collections appeared in three volumes (1796, 1809, and 1840).

Buonamici, Giuseppe, eminent Italian pianist, b. Feb. 12, 1846, Florence; received his first musical instruction from his uncle, Gius. Ceccherini, and in 1868 studied at the Munich Conservatorium under Bülow and Rheinberger with such success that after two years and a half he was engaged at the same institution as teacher for advanced pianoforte playing. In 1873 B. returned to Florence as conductor of the Florentine Choral Union "Cherubini," and founded afterwards the Florentine Trio Union. While in Munich B. wrote a concert overture, a stringed quartet (which met with Wagner's approval), pf. pieces, and some songs, all of which appeared in print. Specially worthy of mention is B.'s selection of fifty studies from Bertini as a preparation for Bülow's edition of Cramer's Studies.

Buononcini. (*See* BONONCINI, 2.)

Buranello. (*See* GALUPPI.)

Burbure, Léon Philippe Marie Chevalier de B. de Wesembeek, b. Aug. 16, 1812, Termonde (East Flanders), d. Dec. 8, 1889, Antwerp; a wealthy Belgian nobleman, Benedictine monk, first-rate connoisseur and himself an able musician; in 1862 member of the Brussels Academy. B. wrote, and in part published, a number of sacred compositions, also orchestral works, chamber-music, etc., likewise monographs on the old Antwerp community of musicians of St. Jacob and St. Maria Magdalena, on clavier and lute makers at Antwerp

from the 16th century, on Ch. L. Hanssens, C F. M. Bosselet, and Jan van Okeghem, also on the Belgian Cecilian Society. His works are of high value. B. has also drawn up an excellent catalogue of the Antwerp historical museum.

Burck. (*See* BURGK.)

Burci. (*See* BURTIUS.)

Bürde-Ney, Jenny, celebrated stage singer (dramatic soprano), b. Dec. 21, 1826, Grätz, d. May 17, 1886, Dresden; daughter of a singer to whom she owed her first training, made her *début* in 1847 at Olmütz, and sang afterwards at Prague, Lemberg, in 1850 at the *Kärntnerthor theater*, Vienna, 1853 at Dresden, 1855–56 London, and appeared also at Berlin, Hanover, etc. In 1855 she married the actor, E. Bürde, and retired from the stage in 1867.

Burette, Pierre Jean, b. Nov. 21, 1665, Paris, d. May 19, 1747, as Professor of Medicine at the Paris University, member of the Academy, etc.; wrote learned notices of Greek music, all of which are preserved in the memoirs of the "Académie des Inscriptions" (vols. 1–17). B. was of the opinion that polyphonic music was unknown to the ancients: the attempt at the present day (by Westphal) to show the contrary has met with but little success.

Bürgel, Konstantin, b. June 24, 1837, Liebau (Silesia), pupil of M. Brosig at Breslau, and of Fr. Kiel at Berlin; was from 1869 to 1870 pianoforte teacher at Kullak's Academy, Berlin; he lives there now as a private teacher of music. His compositions (chamber-music, overtures, etc.) deserve mention.

Burgk, really Joachim Moller (Müller), named Joachim a B. (Burg, Burck), b. about 1541, Burg, near Magdeburg; about 1566 organist at Mühlhausen (Thuringia), where he d. May 24, 1610. He was one of the most distinguished old Protestant Church composers. His Passions, Nicene Creed, Te Deum à 4, Communion Service, besides Cantiones (of the Villanella kind), German songs, and sacred odes (of the Villanella kind) to poems of the Mühlhausen Superintendent, Helmbold, have been preserved in prints of the years 1550–1626.

Burgmüller, (1) Joh. Friedrich Franz, b. 1806, Ratisbon, d. Feb. 13, 1874, Beaulieu, France (Seine-et-Oise); was a popular composer of light pianoforte music.—(2) Norbert, b. Feb. 8, 1810, Düsseldorf, brother of the former, pupil of Spohr and Hauptmann at Cassel, composed orchestral and chamber works which showed talent; but he died already on May 7, 1836, Aix-la-Chapelle.

Burkhard, Joh. Andr. Christian, a minister and school inspector at Leipheim (Swabia), published in 1832 at Ulm a small musical lexicon, and in 1827 a Method of thorough-bass.

Burla (Ital.), a farce.

Burlesco, m., **Burlesca**, f. (Ital.), burlesque, facetious, comic, merry.

Burletta (Ital.), a burlesque, a whimsical farce.

Burney, Charles, celebrated musical historian, b. April 7, 1726, Shrewsbury, d. April 12, 1814; pupil of Baker at Chester, then of his brother James B. at Shrewsbury, and finally of Arne in London. In 1749 he received a post as organist at London (St. Dionis Backchurch). In 1750 he wrote, for Drury Lane Theatre, music to the three dramas, *Alfred, Robin Hood,* and *Queen Mab;* but his health would not allow of such strained activity, and he therefore took a post as organist at Lynn Regis (Norfolk). In 1760 he returned to London, and brought out some pianoforte concertos of his own composition with great success, and produced a new stage work at Drury Lane Theatre—*The Cunning Man*—music and libretto adapted from Rousseau's *Devin du Village.* In 1769 the University of Oxford conferred on him the degrees of Bachelor and Doctor of Music. His exercise (an Anthem) was often performed afterwards at Oxford, and was produced at Hamburg under the direction of Ph. E. Bach. From the time of his residence at Lynn Regis B. collected materials for a History of Music, and in 1770 he was induced to make a tour of investigation through France and Italy, which was followed by a second in 1772 through the Netherlands, Germany, and Austria. The results of these journeys, in so far as they concerned the music of the time, were published in diary form— "The Present State of Music in France and Italy, etc." (1771), and "The Present State of Music in Germany, the Netherlands, and United Provinces, etc." (1773). In 1776 appeared the first volume of his "General History of Music," at the same time as Hawkins' complete work: the fourth and last volume appeared in 1789. In 1783 he was appointed organist at Chelsea College, and passed the remainder of his life in that institution. Besides the writings named, there are also: "A Plan for a Music School" (1774), "Account of the Musical Performances in Westminster Abbey in Commemoration of Handel" (1785), the musical articles for Rees' "Cyclopedia," and some subordinate non-musical works. B. published also, "La musica che si canta annualmente nelle funzione della settimana santa nella cappella Pontificia, composta da Palestrina, Allegri e Bai" (1784). He also wrote and published sonatas for pf. and for violin, flute duets, violin concertos, cantatas, etc. Miss B., authoress of the novel "Evelina," was his daughter.

Buroni. (*See* BORONI.)

Burtius (Burci Burzio) Nicolaus, b. 1450, Parma, d. there about 1520. He was the author of "Musices Opusculum," printed by Ugone de Rugeriis at Bologna in 1487, the oldest work containing printed measured music (cut on wood-blocks).

Busby, Thomas, b. Dec. 1755, Westminster, d. May 28, 1838. He was organist at various London churches, and took his degree of Mus. Doc. at Cambridge in 1801. He was a diligent and prolific composer of dramatic and other music, but was not gifted with originality. His "History of Music" was compiled from Burney and Hawkins. He wrote, besides, "A Dictionary of Music" (1786); "A Grammar of Music" (1818); "A Musical Manual, or Technical Directory" (1828); "Concert-room and Orchestra Anecdotes" (1825); *The Monthly Musical Journal* (four numbers, 1801), etc.

Busi, (1), Giuseppe, esteemed Italian organist and theorist, b. 1808, Bologna, d. there March 14, 1871. He was trained by Palmerini (harmony) and Tomm. Marchesi (counterpoint), but learnt most by himself, for he copied a large collection of works by composers of Bologna, from 1500 to 1800. In spite of a successful venture, he gave up opera writing, devoted himself to sacred music and to teaching; for many years he was professor of counterpoint at the Liceo Musicale, Bologna. His "Guida allo Studio del Contrappunto Fugato" remained in manuscript. His son—(2) Alessandro, b. Sept. 28, 1833, Bologna, likewise an excellent contrapuntist, succeeded his father as teacher at the Conservatorio. Died July 8, 1895, Bologna.

Busnois, Antoine, really de Busne, important contrapuntist of the first Netherland School, was appointed in 1467 chapel singer to Charles the Bold of Burgundy; he died in 1481. Only a few of his works have come down to us, viz., three chansons in Petrucci's "Canti CL." (1503), and in manuscript two Magnificats, one mass (*Ecce Ancilla*), and a few small pieces at Brussels, several masses in the pontifical chapel at Rome, and detached motets and chansons scattered in various libraries.

Busoni, Ferruccio Benvenuto, highly gifted pianist and composer, b. April 1, 1866, Empoli, near Florence (of a German mother), pupil of W. A. Remy (Dr. Mayer), at Gratz. Already in 1881 he passed the test and became a member of the Philharmonic Academy at Bologna. His technical ability as a pianist is great, and he can improvise on given themes. In 1888 he accepted a post as teacher at the Helsingfors Conservatorium, and exchanged the same in 1890, when he won the Rubinstein prize, for a professorship at the Moscow Conservatoire. The best works of B., which have appeared (two stringed quartets, an orchestral suite, many pianoforte pieces, Variations and Fugue, Op. 22), justify great expectations of his talent as a composer.

Busshop, Jules Auguste Guillaume, b. Sept. 10, 1810, Paris, of Belgian parents, who already returned in 1816 to Bruges, where B. grew up, and by the study of the works of

Albrechtsberger and Reicha became a self-taught composer. His patriotic cantata, *Das belgische Banner*, obtained a prize in 1834. He produced, besides, numerous sacred compositions and choral works with and without orchestra, also symphonies, overtures, etc., and an opera, *La toison d'or*. A grand Te Deum was produced at Brussels in 1860 with great success, and a symphony in F, and several overtures, etc., of his have been given with like results at the Concerts Nationaux lately established at Brussels. He d. Feb. 10, 1896, Bruges.

Bussler, L u d w i g, an esteemed theorist, b. Nov. 26, 1838, Berlin, son of the painter and author, and privy counsellor, Rob. Bussler, and on his mother's side, grandson of C. A. Bader (q.v.). He received his first musical instruction as chorister boy from v. Hertzberg, and afterwards training in theory from Grell, Dehn, and Wieprecht (instrumentation), without, however, appropriating to himself the method of any one of these, but studying in an independent spirit the various methods from Zarlino down to the most recent period, and selecting the best from all. In 1865 B. became teacher of theory at the Ganz School of Music, in Berlin. For some time he was actively engaged as conductor (capellmeister in 1869 at the Memel Theatre), and since 1879 has taught at the Stern Conservatorium. Since 1883 B. has also been one of the musical critics of the *National Zeitung*. The writings of B., on account of their thoroughly practical tendency, are much in vogue. They are as follows : " Musikalische Elementarlehre" (1867; third ed., 1882), "Praktische Harmonielehre in Aufgaben" (1875; second ed. 1885), "Der strenge Satz" (1877), "Harmonische Übungen am Klavier" (without year of publication), "Kontrapunkt und Fuge im freien Tonsatz" (1878), "Musikalische Formenlehre" (1878), "Praktische musikalische Kompositionslehre : I. Lehre vom Tonsatz (1878) ; II. Freie Komposition" (1879), "Instrumentation u. Orchestersatz" (1879), "Elementarmelodik" (1879), "Geschichte der Musik" (six reports, 1882), "Partiturenstudium" (Modulationslehre) (1882), "Lexikon der Harmonie" (1889).

Bussmeyer, (1) H u g o, b. Feb. 26, 1842, Brunswick, pupil of Litolff and Methfessel, went in 1860 to South America, appeared as a pianist at Rio de Janeiro, visited Chili, Peru, etc., and also published some pf. pieces. In 1867 he visited New York and Paris, where he gave concerts with success ; after his return to America he settled down in New York. B. is author of a pamphlet, " Das Heidentum in der Musik " (1871).—(2) H a n s, b. March 29, 1853, Brunswick, brother of the former, pupil at the Royal School of Music at Munich, was for some time with Liszt, made concert tours (1872-74) as a pianist in South America, residing for some length of time in Buenos Ayres. After his return, in 1874, he was appointed teacher

at the Royal School of Music at Munich ; in 1878 he married the singer Math. Wekerlin, and since the autumn of 1879 has been the conductor of the Munich Choral Union, of which he was the founder.

Buths, J u l i u s, distinguished pianist and composer, b. May 7, 1851, Wiesbaden ; he was the son of an oboe player, who gave him his first musical instruction. He attended the Cologne Conservatorium as pupil of Hiller and Gernsheim ; and after conducting the Cecilia Union at Wiesbaden for two years, won the Meyerbeer Scholarship, and continued his studies under Kiel (1872), and journeyed to Italy for the purpose of gaining further musical knowledge. On account of ill health he lived for some time with his parents, and then in Paris, Breslau, and in 1875 became conductor of the musical society at Elberfeld. In 1889 he was appointed successor to Tausch as musical director at Düsseldorf.

Buttstedt, J o h. H e i n r i c h, b. April 25, 1666, Bindersleben, near Erfurt, d. Dec. 1, 1727, as cathedral organist at Erfurt ; an excellent organist, pupil of Pachelbel, composed church music, fugues, preludes for clavier, etc. But he owes his fame to the pamphlet, " Ut re mi fa sol la, tota Musica et Harmonia Æterna," or " Neu Eröffnetes Altes, Wahres, Einziges, und Ewiges Fundamentum Musices " (cir. 1716), which was an attack on Mattheson's "Neu Eröffnetes Orchester," and with some skill sought to uphold solmisation ; but the arguments were thoroughly demolished by Mattheson in his " Beschützes Orchester " (1717).

Buus, J a c q u e s (J a c h e t) d e, Netherland contrapuntist of the 16th century, probably born at Bruges, where the name " de Boes " occurs about the year 1506. In 1541 B. was elected as second organist of St. Mark's, Venice, but owing to the small salary (eighty ducats), he gave up this post and went to Vienna, where he became organist (1553-64) of the court chapel. Two books of "Ricercari" and two of "Canzoni Francesi," and a book of " Motetti " by B. have been preserved (printed 1547-50). The motets to be found in various collections of works, and only marked Jachet, Jacques, Jacches, Giacche, Jaquet, Giachetto, are not by B., but by Berchem (q.v.).

Buxtehude, D i e t r i c h, celebrated organist, b. 1637, Helsingör, where his father, J o h. B. (d. Jan. 22, 1674), who most probably trained him, was organist. Already in 1668 B. obtained the important post of organist at the Marienkirche, Lübeck, which he held until his death, May 9, 1707. In 1673 he established the "Abendmusiken," which soon acquired great fame ; these were grand sacred concerts after the afternoon service of the five Sundays before Christmas, and for these he always wrote new works. It is well known how Bach made the pilgrimage on foot from Arnstadt to Lübeck, in order to hear and to learn of him. The organ works of Buxtehude have recently been published by Ph. Spitta in a complete critical edition. Some "Choral-Bearbeitungen" had already been made known by S. Dehn, Commer, and others; it was, however, not in these, but in his free organ compositions, that B. showed himself to best advantage. Of his vocal works a number of cantatas are to be found in the royal library at Berlin and in the town library at Lübeck, and several of these were printed in the 17th and 18th years of the "Monatshefte für Musikgeschichte." The so-called "Abendmusiken" are said to have been printed from 1673 to 1687, but hitherto have not been found. The only printed works of B. which have been discovered are: five wedding arias, seven sonatas for violin, gamba, and cembalo, "Die Fried-und Freudenreiche Heimfahrt des Alten Simeons" (1674, on the occasion of his father's death), "Die Hochzeit des Lammes" (1681), "Castrum doloris," and "Templum honoris" (1705).

Buzzola, Antonio, b. 1815, Adria, d. March 20, 1871, Venice; son of the director of church music for many years in his native town, from whom B. learnt to play on various instruments, and with whom he also studied composition. He was afterwards a pupil of Donizetti at Naples. B. produced with success some operas (*Faramondo, Mastino, Gli Avventurieri, Amleto,* and *Elisabetta di Valois* or *Don Carlos*) at Venice, and thus became known. After making long journeys for the purpose of widening his knowledge, he became Perotti's successor as chief maestro of St. Mark's, Venice. Besides the operas named (a sixth he left

unfinished), B. wrote several masses (a requiem), also cantatas and many small vocal pieces.

Byrd (also written Bird, Byrde, Byred), William, b. about 1538, London, d. July 4, 1623; was, in 1554, chorister of St. Paul's Cathedral, pupil of Tallis, in 1563 organist at Lincoln, in 1569 Gentleman of the Chapel Royal. In 1575 a patent was granted to B. and his master, Tallis, for twenty-one years, for printing and selling music and music paper; but, after Tallis's death (1585) the patent became the sole property of B. He is, perhaps, the most distinguished of English Church composers. Fétis names him the Palestrina or Orlando Lassus of the English. Of his works printed by himself by virtue of his patent, and also by his assignee, Thomas Easte, a large number have been preserved: "Cantiones (sacræ)" (1575, with some by Tallis); "Psalmæ, etc." (1587); "Songs of Sundrie Natures, etc." (1589); two books, "Sacræ Cantiones" (1589, 1591); two books, "Gradualia ac Sacræ Cantiones" (1607; 2nd ed. 1610); "Psalmes, etc." (1611). He also wrote three masses, all of which were printed, but only a single copy of the third is known to exist. Some English collections of the 16th century contain pieces by B. The so-called "Virginal Book of Queen Elisabeth" in the Fitzwilliam Museum at Cambridge contains seventy organ and clavier pieces by B., and Lady Nevill's "Virginal Book," twenty-six. A number of his pieces have been republished in Pauer's "Old English Composers."

Byzantine Music. (*See* JOHANNES DAMASCENUS, BRYENNIUS, LAMPADARIUS, CHRYSANTHOS.)

C.

C, the name of the third note of the musical alphabet, and indeed one of the notes which, since the invention of staves (10th century), have served as clefs to determine the meaning of the lines. The letters selected for clefs were those under which lay the semitone, *i.e.* *f* and *c* (*e–f*, *b–c*), so as to warn the singer of the difference between the whole and the half tone; this plan was strengthened by drawing coloured lines: *f*, red, *c*, yellow). From the 11th to the 13th century, the meaning of the *f*- and the *c*-clef was not as yet restricted to small *f* and once-accented *c* (*c'*), but indicated equally well once-accented *f* (*f'*) and small *c*; and then the colour occurred in a space. The form of our *c*-clef

has been gradually evolved from a real *c.*:

A vocal part-book marked *C.* means *Cantus* (*Discantus*); *c* 1, *c* 2 are first, and second soprano.

For *c solfaut, c faut, cc solfa, cf.* SOLMISATION. In Italy, Spain, etc., the first note *C* is simply called *do*, in France *ut* (q.v.).

C, C, and in old publications even **Ɔ**, are time-signatures (q.v.); the *c* is really a half circle (C).

C, as abbreviation, means (1), *con* (with); *c. b.* = *col basso*, with the bass; *c.* 8ᵛᴬ = *coll' ottava*, with octaves; (2), *cantus* (*c. f.* = *cantus firmus*); (3), *capo* (*d. c.* = *da capo*, from the beginning).

Cabaletta, really *cavatinetta* (Ital.), small aria.

Caballero, Manuel Fernandez, b. March 14, 1835, Murcia, pupil of Fuertes and Eslava at the Madrid Conservatorio. He is one of the most popular Spanish composers of *zarzuelas* (operettas); and he has also written sacred music.

Cabo, Francisco Javier, b. 1768, Naguera, near Valencia, d. 1832; was in 1810 chapel singer, 1816 organist, and 1830 maestro di capella of the cathedral at Valencia. He was one of the modern Spanish church composers of note (masses, vespers, etc.).

Caccia (Ital.), hunting, hence, *corno di C., oboe di C.* (*See* HORN, OBOE, etc.).

Caccini, Giulio, b. 1558 or 1560 Rome (hence called Giulio Romano); pupil of Scipione della Palla for singing and lute-playing; went in 1565 to Florence, where he died about 1615. C. was one of the founders of the modern style of music, the style of our time, the nature of which is accompanied melody: his " Nuove Musiche " (1602) gave to it its first distinguishing name. At the meetings of artists and literati at the houses of Bardi and Corsi (q.v.) in Florence, the new style was discussed in a sober manner. It was a question of helping to its rights a text overladen with contrapuntal confusion of vocal parts, and of giving to it greater pathos and expression by means of simple musical declamation. Thus arose recitative, from which, by an increase of musical expression, was evolved the aria, and this proved also the germ of the new art form of the opera: the new style made its way at the same time into the church. Caccini's earliest compositions were madrigals, of no special value, in the old polyphonic style; it was only after intercourse with Galilei and Peri, at the houses of Bardi and Corsi, that he was urged into the new path by the following of which he indeed quickly acquired extraordinary fame. His first work in the new style was "Il combattimento d'Apolline col serpente " (1590), the poem by Bardi; then followed " Daphne," poem by Rinuccini, written in collaboration with Peri (1594); Rinuccini's *Eurydice* (" Tragedia per Musica," 1600, published by R. Eitner, with accompaniment from written-out figured bass, 1881); " Il Rapimento di Cafalo" (1597, printed 1600); " Le Nuove Musiche" (madrigals for one voice with bass, 1602); "Nove Arie " (1608) and " Fuggilotio Musicale" (madrigals, sonnets, etc., 1614).

Cachucha, a Spanish dance resembling the *Bolero.*

Cadaux, Justin, b. April 13, 1813, Alby (Tarn), d. Nov. 8, 1874, Paris; composer of comic operas, pupil of the Paris Conservatoire, from which, however, he was dismissed for irregularity. He lived for a long time in Bordeaux, afterwards in Paris, and for a time in London.

Cadeac, Pierre, French contrapuntist of the 16th century, choir-master at Auch. Of his compositions, masses and motets were published separately at Paris, 1555–58 (Le Roy & Ballard), as well as detached works scattered in collections of that period.

Cadence (Ital. *cadenza;* Fr. *cadence*), an harmonic turning-point forming a rest or close. A *perfect* C. is the same as a full close, an *imperfect* C. as a half-close. The plagal C. (subdominant-

tonic) is, however, also named imperfect, and the *great* C. (tonic—under-dominant—upper-dominant—tonic) perfect. (*See* CLOSE.) A *suspended* C. (pause) in concertos with orchestra, sonatas, etc., is a break in the middle of the C., as a rule, on the chord of six-four (q.v.) of the tonic, followed by a more or less extended flourish, in which the virtuoso generally has to grapple with the most formidable difficulties. Formerly (up to the end of last century), at the suspended cadence, artists improvised on themes of the work which they were playing. Beethoven preferred to prescribe to the virtuoso what he should play at this point, and wrote special " cadenzas " (for this was the name given to the insertions themselves) for his earlier concertos. In his E ♭ concerto, the cadenza was, from the outset, organically connected with the whole movement. Nevertheless, pianists nowadays prefer to introduce, at any rate into the other concertos, cadenzas of their own (but no longer improvised ones) instead of those provided by the composer: Moscheles, Reinecke, and others, have published such cadenzas. In Schumann's pianoforte concerto, and other modern works, the C. forms an integrant part of the movement. (*See also* SHAKE.)

Cadence brisée (Fr.), an abrupt shake; it begins with the upper auxiliary note, but is not, like the *cadence pleine,* preceded by it as a long *appoggiatura.*

Cadence évitée (Fr.), lit. " avoided cadence." A dissonant chord followed by another dissonant chord instead of the expected consonant triad.

Cadence imparfaite (Fr.), an imperfect cadence, a half close (tonic-dominant).

Cadence interrompue (Fr.), an " interrupted cadence."

Cadence irregulière (Fr.), the same as CADENCE IMPARFAITE.

Cadence pleine (Fr.), (1) a shake which is preceded by the upper auxiliary note as a long *appoggiatura.* (2) A dissonant chord followed by a consonant chord.

Cadenza d'inganno, or **Cadenza finta** (Ital.), a deceptive cadence.

Cæsura (Lat.), a pause; metrical break.

Cafaro, Pasquale, eminent Italian composer, b. Feb. 8, 1706, San Pietro, Galantina, near Lecce (Naples); pupil of Leonardo Leo at the Conservatorio della Pietà, Naples, where he died Oct. 23, 1787. He wrote oratorios, cantatas, and other church works, as well as operas; his Stabat Mater (Canon à 2 with organ) deserves special mention. (*See* CAFFARELLI.)

Caffarelli, really Gaetano Majorano, famous castrato, b. April 16, 1703, Bari, d. Nov. 30, 1783, Santo Dorato, near Naples; was discovered and trained by Cafaro (q.v.), and, to do the latter honour, called himself **C**. Cafaro afterwards sent him to Porpora, who at the end of five years dismissed him as a singer of the first rank. After he had acquired great renown in Ita.y, he came in 1737 to London, where he did not meet with special success, but celebrated afterwards greater triumphs in Italy, Vienna, and Paris. C. was very covetous, and amassed a large fortune, with which he purchased the dukedom of Santo Dorato (from which time he also bore the title of *Duca*), and built a grand palace with the proud inscription, " Amphion Thebas, ego domum." C. excelled in pathetic song, and possessed also immense skill in coloratura, especially in chromatic runs,

pupil of the Conservatoire, pianist and music teacher in Paris, composed a few operettas, etc.

Caillot, J o s e p h, distinguished French actor and opera singer (tenor-baritone) at the Paris " Comédie Italienne," b. 1732, Paris, d. there Sept. 30, 1816.

Caimo, J o s e f f o, madrigal composer of the second half of the 16th century, published 1568–85, four books of madrigals (à 5), and one book (à 5–8), also two books of canzonets (à 4).

Ça ira, celebrated song (*Carillon national*) of the French Revolution, 1789, words by a streetsinger of the name of Ladré, melody by Bécourt, drummer at the Grand Opéra; begins

Ah! ça　i - ra,　ça　i - ra,　ça　i - ra! Le peuple en　ce　jour sans ces - se　ré - pè - te, etc.

which he seems to have been the first to cultivate.

Caffi, F r a n c e s c o, Italian writer on music, b. 1786, Venice, d. there, 1874; was advocate at the Court of Appeal in Milan until 1827, from which time he lived privately in Venice occupied with the study of the history of music. His principal work is " Storia della Musica Sacra nella già Capella Ducale di San Marco in Venezia dal 1318 al 1797 " (1854–55, 2 vols.). We are also indebted to him for monographs on Zarlino (1836), Bonaventura Furnaletto (1820), Lotti, Benedetto Marcello (in Cicognia's " Veneziani Inscrizioni " and Giammateo Asola, 1862). A " History of the Theatre " remained unfinished.

Caffiaux, D o m P h i l i p p e J o s e p h, Benedictine monk of the congregation of St. Maur, b. 1712, Valenciennes, d. Dec. 26, 1777, at the abbey of St. Germain des Prés, Paris; he was the author of a somewhat voluminous history of music, the publication of which was advertised in 1756, but not carried out. Fétis discovered the manuscript in the Paris " Bibliothèque," and highly extols it.

Cagniard de la Tour, C h a r l e s, B a r o n de, b. May 31, 1777, Paris, d. there, July 5, 1859, celebrated natural philosopher and mechanician, member of the Académie, etc.; was the ingenious improver of the syren (q.v.), which he transformed into an instrument recording with precision the vibration numbers of sounds.

Cagnoni, A n t o n i o, favourite Italian opera composer, b. Feb. 8, 1828, Godiasco (Voghera), pupil of the Milan Conservatorio. His *Don Bucefalo*, written before leaving the Conservatorio (1847), became part of the *répertoire* of the Italian stage. He wrote about twenty operas. In 1886 he became maestro di cappella of Santa Maria Maggiore at Bergamo. He died April 30, 1896, Bergamo.

Cahen, E r n e s t, b. Aug. 18, 1828, Paris,

Caisse roulante (Fr.), long side-drum. (*See* DRUM.)

Calamus (Lat.), also *calamellus*, reed, reedflute; the French *chalumeau* and the German *Schalmei* are derived from this word.

Calando (Ital.), decreasing in loudness, also rapidity. It has also the meanings of *diminuendo* and *ritardando* combined.

Calandrone, an Italian flute used by peasants.

Calascione (*Colascione*, Fr. *colachon*), an instrument with finger-board similar to the mandoline, in use in Lower Italy; it is struck with a plectrum.

Calata, old Italian dance of quiet movement, and in binary time.

Calcando (Ital.), hurrying the time.

Calcant (Ger.), bellows-treader.

Caldara, A n t o n i o, a prolific, and in his time highly appreciated, composer, b. 1670, Venice; became in 1714, after many years' residence at Bologna and Mantua, imperial chamber-composer at Vienna; from Jan. 1, 1716, vice-capellmeister (J. J. Fux was chief capellmeister), and died at Vienna, Dec. 28, 1736, at the age of 66. C. wrote no less than sixty-six operas and serenades, twenty-nine oratorios (nearly all of them at Vienna), besides much church and chamber music.

Calegari, (1), F r a n c e s c o A n t o n i o (Callegari), Franciscan monk, b. at Venice; about 1702 maestro di cappella at the great Minorite monastery at Venice, 1703–1724 maestro at Padua, where G. Rinaldi and Vallotti became his successors in 1729. In addition to various church compositions, C. wrote " Ampia Dimostrazione degli Armoniali Musicali tuoni." Vallotti and Sabbatini knew his manuscript, and made use of it.(—2) A n t o n i o, b. Oct. 18, 1758, Padua, d. there July 22, 1828, brought out (1779–89) four operas at Modena and Venice, lived during the early years of the present century at Paris, wh re he published a French edition of his method of composition for non-musicians, "L'Art de Composer, etc.," 1802; 2nd ed. 1803; previously in Italian (under title "Gioco Pittagorico, 1801). He afterwards returned to Padua, where he became first organist and maestro di cappella of San Antonio. C. wrote six psalms in the style of B. Marcello (but without his genius), a continuation of the latter's "Estro Poetico." After his death, his "Sistema Armonico" was published with notes by Melch. Balbi, 1829, and another posthumous work, a Method of Singing, on Pacchierotti's system, "Modi Generali del Canto," appeared in 1836.

Caletti-Bruni. (*See* CAVALLI.)

Calkin, J. B., esteemed pianist, organist, and composer, b. March 16, 1827.

Callaerts, J o s e p h, famous organist and composer, b. Aug. 22, 1838, Antwerp, pupil of Lemmens at the Brussels Conservatoire, where he received the first prize in 1856; 1851-56 organist of the Jesuit College, afterwards of Antwerp Cathedral; since 1867 teacher of the organ at the Music School. He composed a symphony for the Brussels Académie (1879, which gained a prize), a pf. trio (1882, also a prize work), the comic opera, *Le Retour Imprévu* (Antwerp, 1889), masses, litanies, cantatas, organ and pianoforte works, etc.

Callcott, J o h n W a l l, b. Nov. 20, 1766, Kensington, d. May 15, 1821, Bristol; was organist of various London churches, Bachelor of Arts and Doctor of Music (Oxford), from 1806 lecturer on music at the Royal Institution (successor to Crotch). C. wrote a great number of glees and catches, also anthems, odes, etc. A collection was published in 1824 by his son-in-law, Horsley. C. intended to write a musical dictionary, and had procured the manuscript left behind by Boyce, and collected a quantity of material; but in 1797 he had not got beyond the syllabus. His only theoretical work is a "Musical Grammar" (1806). Callcott's son, W i l l i a m H u t c h i n s C., b. 1807, d. Aug. 4, 1882, London, was highly esteemed as a vocal composer (songs, anthems, etc). He was also a popular arranger of pianoforte pieces.

Callinet. (*See* DAUBLAINE ET C.)

Calmato (Ital.), calmed, quieted.

Calore (Ital.), heat, affection. *Con calore*, with warmth, with passion.

Caloroso (Ital.), with warmth, with passion.

Calvisius, S e t h u s, really S e t h K a l l w i t z, son of a labourer at Gorschleben (Thuringia), b. Feb. 21, 1556, d. Nov. 24, 1615, at Leipzig. By singing in the streets of Magdeburg for alms he was able to attend the Gymnasium, and, by giving private lessons, obtained sufficient for a visit to the Universities of Helmstedt (1579) and Leipzig (1580). In 1581 he became musical director of the Paulinerkirche at Leipzig, in 1582 cantor at the Schulpforta, and

in 1594 cantor at the St. Thomas' School and musical director of the principal churches of Leipzig. This honourable position he retained until his death, refusing all appointments to other places, as, for instance, that of professor of mathematics at Wittenberg. C. had a good theoretical training, and his works are still one of the most important sources for the state of musical instruction in his time: "Melopœia seu Melodiæ Condendæ Ratio" (1582); "Compendium Musicæ Practicæ pro Incipientibus" (1594; 3rd ed., under the title "Musicæ Artis Præcepta Nova et Facillima," 1612); "Exercitationes Musicæ Duæ" (1600); "Exercitatio Musicæ Tertia" (1611). (*Cf.* BOBISATION.) Of his compositions the following have been preserved: "Auserlesene teutsche Lieder" (1603); "Biciniorum Libri Duo" (1612); "Der 150. Psalm" (à 12); besides a collection, "Harmoniæ Cantionum Ecclesiasticarum a M. Luthero et aliis Viris Piis Germaniæ Compositarum" (1596), and an arrangement (à 4) of Cornelius Becker's psalm melodies (1602, 1616, 1618, 1621). Manuscripts of motets, hymns, etc., are still in the library of St. Thomas' School.

Calvœr, C a s p a r, learned theologian, b. 1650, Hildesheim, d. 1725, as general superintendent at Clausthal; wrote "De Musica ac singillatim de Ecclesiastica eoque Spectantibus Organis" (1702), as well as a preface to Sinn's "Temperatura Practica" (1717).

Cambert, R o b e r t, b. about 1628, Paris, d. 1677, London; pupil of Chambonnières, and for some time organist of the collegiate church, St. Honoré; became, in 1666, intendant of music to the queen-mother, Anne of Austria. C. was the true creator of the French opera, but through Lully his merit was afterwards darkened and denied. Excited by the representation of Italian operas brought about by Mazarin in 1647, Perrin sketched out a libretto for a lyrical stage piece, which he called *La Pastorale*, and which was set to music by C. (1659); the representation at the Château d'Issy was successful, and Louis XIV. interested himself in it. In 1661 followed *Ariane; ou, le Mariage de Bacchus*, and in 1662 *Adonis* (which was not produced, and is entirely lost). In 1669 Perrin received a patent for the establishment of regular operatic performances under the name, "Académie Royale de Musique." He associated himself with C., and in 1671 the first real opera, *Pomone*, came out; another one, *Les Peines et les Plaisirs de l'Amour*, was not produced, because in 1672 Lully succeeded in having the patent transferred to himself. Embittered, C. left Paris and came to London, where he was at first a military bandmaster, but became master of the music to Charles II., and died holding that post. Fragments of *Pomone* were printed by Ballard; and in a recent edition *Pomone* and *Les Peines et les Plaisirs de l'Amour* (in "Chefs d'Œuvre

Classiques de l'Opéra Français," published by Breitkopf and Härtel) have been brought out.

Cambiata (Ital.), changing note.

Cambīni, Giovanni Giuseppe, b. Feb. 13, 1746, Leghorn, d. 1825, Paris, pupil of Padre Martini; in 1770 he went, after some strange adventures, to Paris, where he met with success as a composer of ballets, and occupied the post of conductor at various theatres, but finally fell into great poverty, and died in the workhouse at Bicêtre. C. wrote with remarkable facility, and composed in very few years sixty symphonies, some of which were performed through Gossec's influence; besides, several oratorios, 144 quartets for strings, etc. From 1810–1811 he was a contributor to Geraudé's musical paper, *Tablets de Polymnie*.

Camera (Ital.), chamber. *Musica da camera*, chamber music; *sonata da camera*, chamber sonata.

Camidge, (1) John, b. about 1735, d. April 25, 1803, organist of York Cathedral for forty-seven years. He published "Six Easy Lessons for the Harpsichord."—(2) Matthew, son of former, b. 1758, d. 1844, succeeded his father at York Cathedral. He published "A Method of Instruction in Musick by Questions and Answers."—(3) John, son of the former, succeeded his father at York; the present organ was constructed chiefly under his superintendence. He died in 1859.

Campagnoli, Bartolommeo, b. Sept. 10, 1751, Cento, near Bologna, d. Nov. 6, 1827, Neustrelitz; violin pupil of Dall' Ocha (pupil of Lolli at Bologna), of Quastarobba (pupil of Tartini) at Modena; and after many years of activity as violinist in the orchestra at Bologna, he still became a pupil of Nardini's at Florence. After he had made himself known by giving concerts in various towns, he became in 1776 leader of the band belonging to the Abbot of Freising, and afterwards musical director to the Duke of Courland at Dresden, whence he undertook extensive concert tours; from 1797–1818 he was leader at Leipzig, and finally court capell-meister at Neustrelitz. Besides a great deal of chamber music, he wrote concertos for flute and one for violin; also a violin Method.

Campana, Fabio, Italian opera composer, b. Jan. 14, 1819, Leghorn, d. Feb. 2, 1882, London, where he lived for a long time. His *Esmeralda* (*Nostra Dama di Parigi*) was produced with success at St. Petersburg (1869). Besides this, C. brought out in Italy six other operas, as well as a ballet in London.

Campana (Ital.), bell.

Campanella, small bell.

Campanetta (Ital.), a set of bells, a carillon.

Campenhout, François van, b. Feb. 5, 1779, Brussels, d. there April 24, 1848; he was at first violinist at the Théâtre de la Monnaie, after-

wards a much-prized tenor there and on other Belgian, Dutch, and French stages until 1827. He afterwards devoted himself to composition at Brussels, and made a name with a series of operas, masses, Te Deums, a symphony, etc., but is specially remembered as the composer of *La Brabaçonne* (q.v.).

Campion, (1) Thomas, physician, composer and writer on music in London, d. 1619; published "Two Bookes of Ayres" (with lute and viols, 1610; the third and fourth books followed in 1612); a "New Way of Making Fowre Parts in Counterpoint" (1st edition, undated; 2nd edition, 1660. He also wrote many Masques and *pièces d'occasion*.—(2) François, theorbist at the Grand Opéra, Paris (1703–19); published "Nouvelles Découvertes sur la Guitare" (1705); "Traité d'Accompagnements pour la Théorbe" (1710); "Traité de Composition selon les Règles de l'Octave" (1716), and "Additions," etc., to the works named (1739).

Campiōni, Carlo Antonio, b. 1720, Leghorn, d. 1793 as court maestro, Florence. He was much admired as a violinist and as a composer of church music.

Camporese, Violante, b. at Rome, 1785, a soprano singer. She sang at Paris, Milan, etc. Made her *début* at King's Theatre, London, in 1817, and appeared at the Ancient and Philharmonic concerts. She died after 1860.

Campos, João Ribeiro de Almeida de, b. about 1770, Vizen, Portugal; in 1800 maestro at Lamego, also professor and examiner of church singing; published "Elementos de Musica" (1786) and "Elementos de Cantochâo" (Elements of *Cantus Planus*, 1800; many times reprinted).

Campra, André, the most noteworthy French opera composer of the period between Lully and Rameau; b. Dec. 4, 1660, Aix (Provence), d. July 29, 1744, Versailles; was at first maître de chapelle of the cathedrals at Toulon (1679), Arles (1681), and Toulouse (1689 or 1690), then went to Paris as maître de chapelle of the collegiate church of the Jesuits, and soon after of Nôtre Dame. As this appointment, however, prohibited him from bringing out operas, he gave it up after having gained success with two operas which he had had performed under the name of his brother, Joseph C. (viola player at the Opéra). In 1722 he became royal *chef d'orchestre*, and director of the music page-boys. His operas were as follows: *L'Europe Galante* (1697), *Le Carnaval de Venise* (1699), *Hésione* (1700), *Aréthuse* (1701), *Tancrède* (1702), *Les Muses* (1703), *Iphigénie en Tauride* (1704, with Desmarets), *Télémaque, Alcine* (1705), *Le Triomphe de l'Amour, Hippodamie* (1708), *Les Fêtes Vénitiennes* (1710), *Idoménée* (1712), *Les Amours de Mars et Vénus, Télèphe* (1713), *Camille* (1717), *Les Âges* (1718, ballet opera), *Achille et Déidamie* (1735); and to these may be added a number of *divertissements* and smaller operas for court festivities at Versailles, as well as (printed) three books of cantatas (1708, etc.) and five books of motets (1706, etc.). *L'Europe Galante* and *Tancrède* appeared in new editions by Breitkopf and Härtel. (*Cf.* CAMBERT.)

Camps y Soler, O s c a r, b. Nov. 21, 1837, at Alexandria, of Spanish parents; went with them to Florence, where he became a pupil of Döhler, and already in 1850 made his *début* as pianist. He finished his studies under Mercadante at Naples, and, after some extended concert tours, settled in Madrid. Besides various compositions (songs, pf. pieces, and a grand cantata, etc.), he has also published "Teoria Musical Illustrada," "Metodo de Solfeo," "Estudios Filosoficos sobre la Musica," and a Spanish translation of Berlioz's "Traité d'Instrumentation."

Canarie (Fr.), a dance much in vogue in the time of Louis XIV.; a lively kind of gigue in $\frac{3}{8}$ or $\frac{6}{8}$ time, sharply accentuated, and with the dotted note staccatoed.

Cancrizans (Lat.), retrogressive.

Candeille, A m é l i e J u l i e (S i m o n s C.) singer, actress, and composer, b. July 31, 1767, d. Feb. 4, 1834, Paris, daughter of Pierre Joseph Candeille, a somewhat fortunate opera composer (b. Dec. 8, 1744, Estaire, d. April 24, 1827, Chantilly). She made her *début* in 1782 as Iphigénie in Gluck's *Iphigénie en Aulide* with great success at the Paris Grand Opéra, but already in 1783 quitted this stage to go as actress to the Théâtre Français, to which she belonged until 1796. In 1798 she married Simons, the carriage-builder at Brussels, who, however, failed in 1802. She then separated from him and lived as a music-teacher in Paris, and in 1821 married a painter (Piérié, d. 1833), for whom she procured the post of director of the drawing-school at Nîmes. Madame C. brought out, with great success in 1792, at the Théâtre Français, an operetta, *La Belle Fermière*, of which she had written words and music; she played the title-*rôle*, sang and accompanied herself with piano and harp. In 1807 she made a fiasco with a comic opera, *Ida, l'Orpheline de Berlin*. Of her works, the following appeared in print: three pianoforte trios, four sonatas for piano, a sonata for two pianos, the songs out of *La Belle Fermière*, and some romances and piano fantasias.

Cange, D u. (*See* DUCANGE.).

Cannabich, (1) C h r i s t i a n, b. 1731, Mannheim, d. 1798, Frankfort, while on a journey; son of the flautist in the electoral band, Matthias C., pupil of Stamitz. C. studied for many years, at the expense of the Elector, in Italy under Jomelli, and became leader in 1765, and in 1775 capellmeister of the band at Mannheim, which, as is well known, then acquired great fame. The lights and shades, especially the *crescendo* and *diminuendo*, were first brought to perfection

under C. at Mannheim. In 1778 the court of Carl Theodor, and with it the band, removed to Munich. Cannabich's compositions (operas, ballets, symphonies, violin concertos, chamber music, etc.) were held in esteem. (2) C a r l, son of the former, b. 1769, Mannheim; in 1800 succeeded his father as court capellmeister at Munich, d. March 1, 1805; he was also a capable leader, violinist, and composer.

Canniciari, D o n P o m p e o, composer of the Roman school, d. 1744. He wrote masses, motets, magnificats, etc. He was maestro of S. Maria Maggiore, 1709.

Canon, (1) according to present usage the strictest form of musical imitation; it consists of two or more parts progressing in a similar manner, but not simultaneously. In the *C. in the unison*, the parts actually give out the same notes, but the second (imitating) part enters a half or a whole bar, or even later still, after the first. In the *C. in the octave*, the second part gives out the melody in the upper or the lower octave. In the *C. in the fifth below*, the melody is transposed a fifth lower, and here a further distinction is made, according as the imitating part repeats all the intervals exactly, or modifies them in conformity with the ruling scale. There are, likewise, canons in the upper fifth and fourth, in the upper or under second, etc. Further changes arise from lengthening or shortening the value of the notes in the imitating part (*canon per augmentationem* or *diminutionem*), or by inversion of all intervals (*al inverso, per motum contrarium*), so that rising are answered by falling progressions; or so that the second part gives the melody backwards (*canon cancricans*, crab-canon). The Netherland contrapuntists of the 15th and 16th centuries brought the art of C. to its highest stage of development. (*Cf.* Ambros, "History of Music," vol. iii.; also O. Klauwell, "Die historische Entwickelung des Musikalischen Canons," 1877). In Greek the word C. means prescription, indication (rule), and the older contrapuntists were not in the habit of writing out their canons in score or parts, but merely of noting down one part and indicating the entry of the other parts, likewise pointing out the special modes of imitation by enigmatical prescriptions (Riddle C.); this inscription was called a C., the piece itself *Fuga* or *Consequenza*. The terms *Dux* (Subject) and *Comes* (Answer), which are now used for fugue —a strict, though in comparison with C. a very free form of imitation—served also for the C.; the first part was called *Guida, Proposta, Antecedente, Precedente*, and the part which followed *Consequente, Risposta*. If the parts were at the distance of half a semibreve (*Minima*), the C. was named *Fuga ad minimam*. (*Cf.* example in article ENTRY-SIGNS.)—(2) The old name for the Monochord, because by means of it the intervals were measured (octave $= \frac{1}{2}$ of length of string, etc.); hence the followers of

Pythagoras, whose theory of music was based on the C., were named *Canonists* in opposition to the *Harmonists* (Aristoxenos and his school), who did not lay much stress on mathematics in music.

Cantabile (Ital., " in a singing style "), full of expression, synonymous with *con expressione*. In passages marked *c*, the principal melody is always made more prominent than the accompanying parts.

Cantata, a " vocal piece," just as sonata originally meant nothing more than instrumental music. But, as the term sonata gradually acquired a fixed meaning, so was it with the term C., only with this difference, that all old forms, to which in their time the name C. was given, are still so called in spite of the restricted meaning attached to that word, whereas it would occur to no one to call a short simple prelude a sonata. By C. is now understood an important vocal work consisting of solos, duets, etc., and choruses with instrumental accompaniment. The C. differs from the oratorio and the opera by the exclusion of the epic and dramatic elements ; a total exclusion of the latter is indeed impossible, as the purest lyrics occasionally rise to dramatic pathos. The art form is exhibited in the clearest manner in the department of church music (CHURCH CANTATAS). Here J. S. Bach has created types of the highest artistic beauty, and in great number, and from these it is not difficult to form a definition. The C. expresses a feeling, a mood in manifold forms, which are connected in a higher sense by this unity of mood. The solos in the church C. do not introduce various personages speaking for themselves, but in the name of the congregation ; their subjectivity has, it is true, an individual colouring, but still it is a general subjectivity. Thus it happens that the ensemble and choral movements, especially the chorales, form the real core of the church cantata : the various singing characters are not sharply opposed to one another, but exalt one another mutually. If we preserve this definition of the C. for the *secular* C., then very many works, though thus designated by their authors, are not cantatas. We find, on the one hand, works arranged in a completely dramatic fashion, and differing from the opera principally by being shorter, and by the absence of scenery. Of late the title *Lyrical Scenes* has been aptly introduced for such compositions. On the other hand, there are works of a decided epic character in which an action is developed almost entirely in narrative form ; if such pieces are laid out on a grand scale, and if the subjects are Biblical, heroic, or ancient, the name *Oratorio* is more in vogue, and a better one ; also for Biblical, or those in any way religious, the name *Legend*. For romantic subjects, especially if treated briefly, the term is very loose and uncertain : composers are always in a state of perplexity, and, in fact, avoid giving any title at all. A suitable title would be *Ballad*, but this term for important forms has gone quite out of fashion. Apparently, then, there remains little to which the term C. is appropriate ; but, on closer examination, there is still a considerable number of important vocal works to which it may be applied. Thus, Liszt's setting of Schiller's " An die Künstler " is a real C., and so with Brahms's *Triumphlied* and *Schicksalslied*, Beethoven's *Hymnus an die Freude* at the end of the Ninth Symphony, and many others, especially all festival cantatas. Works such as the settings of Schiller's " Glocke " (Romberg, Bruch) are indeed difficult to classify. Strictly speaking, they belong to none of the art forms named, but consist of mixed elements, like Bach's " Passions." The latter are at the same time oratorios and cantatas, and the former, scenes, ballads and cantatas. Historically considered, *Cantata*, after the invention of accompanied monody (1600), was the name for vocal solos developed at length, in which *arioso* singing of a dramatic kind alternated with *recitativo ;* but this alternation was not at first a result connected with the name C., but merely the natural consequence of the extension of the piece ; and in the first half of the 17th century there was no sharp distinction between *aria* and *cantata*. Carissimi introduced the name *Chamber Cantata* (*Cantata di camera*), to mark the difference from the *Church Cantata* (*Cantata di chiesa*), which, in the meanwhile, had sprung up. Yet both remained for a long time within very narrow limits : instead of one, two or three vocal parts with *continuo* were introduced, and one or two obligato accompanying parts, but they lacked entirely the characteristic features of the grand C. of the present day with chorus and orchestra. Even Dietrich Buxtehude (d. 1707) wrote detached cantatas only for one voice. The grand secular C. was at first developed as a festal cantata for marriage festivities, acts of homage, etc. ; but the Church C., under the name of *Church Concerto*. J. S. Bach used that name for the greater number of the cantatas, to which he gave a title other than the first words of the text, *i.e. Conzerte*, thus hinting at the essential part which instruments play in them. (*Cf.* ANTHEM and VILLANCICOS.)

Cantatorium (Lat.), a service-book in the Roman Catholic Church, containing the music of the Antiphonary as well as that of the Gradual.

Cantatrice (Fr.), singer.

Cantica (Lat.), **Cantici** (Ital.), canticles, hymns.

Cantico (Ital.), canticle, hymn.

Canticum (Lat.), canticle. The three so-called " evangelical," *i.e.* New Testament hymns of praise, or *Cantica majora* of the Catholic Church, are the " C. Mariæ " (at the Annunciation),

"Magnificat anima mea" (generally called "Magnificat"), the "C. Zachariæ," "Benedictus Dominus Deus Israel," and the "C. Simeonis," "Nunc dimittis servum tuum." The *Cantica minora* (seven in number) are taken from the Old Testament. All of the canticles are classed under psalm-singing, and the Psalms themselves are called *Cantica* (*Davidis*)—*Cantica graduum*, i.e. Graduals; *C. canticorum*, the Song of Solomon.

Cantilena (Ital.), a song-like composition; a song-like melody.

Cantiones [**Sacrae**] (Lat., "sacred songs;" Ital. *Canzoni spirituali*). This term, from the 15th to the 18th century, was used in the sense of *motets*.

Cantique (Fr.), a canticle.

Canto a cappella (Ital.), vocal church music without instrumental accompaniment.

Canto Ambrosiano (Ital.), Ambrosian chant.

Canto armonico (Ital.), a vocal composition in parts.

Canto cromatico (Ital.), chromatic vocal music.

Canto fermo (Ital.), cantus firmus (q.v.).

Canto figurato (Ital.). (*See* CANTUS FIGURATUS.)

Canto Gregoriano (Ital.), Gregorian chant.

Canto plano (Ital.), plain-chant.

Canto primo (Ital.), first soprano.

Canto recitativo (Ital.), recitative, declamatory singing.

Canto secondo (Ital.), the second soprano.

Cantor (singer), precentor of a congregation in large churches where there is a choir. The teacher and leader (capellmeister) of this choir, especially where there is a school with scholarships for the choristers attached to the church, as at St. Thomas's School, Leipzig (q.v.). The French *maîtrises* were similar to these foundation schools for choristers, and the post of *maître de chapelle* was similar to that of the German Cantor.

Cantus (Lat.; Ital. *canto*), song, melody, hence the part specially bearing the melody, the soprano (*Discantus*). With the contrapuntists of the 15th and 16th centuries the tenor was really the principal part, the one bearing the melody, as the *C. firmus*, a *theme* usually taken from Gregorian song (*C. planus*), was assigned to it, and against it the other parts moved busily in counterpoint (*C. figuratus*). Among these other parts it was undoubtedly the soprano which stood out as the most melodious. Besides, the tenor notes were often of such length that of melody in the proper acceptation of the term there was none.

Cantus, *durus, mollis, naturalis* (Lat.). (*Cf.* MAJOR, MINOR, SOLMISATION, and MUTATION.)

Cantus firmus (Lat.), lit. "fixed chant." (1) plain-chant, plain-song, Gregorian chant. (2) A fragment of plain-song or any other melody to which counterpoint is added.

Cantus planus (Lat.), Plain-Song.

Canzona (Ital. *Canzone* and *Canzonetta;* Fr. *Chanson*), secular songs in several parts, popular in style, of the 15th and 16th centuries, hence known under the names *Canzoni Napoletani, Siciliani, Francesi*, etc. In Germany corresponding compositions at that time were called *Lieder* ("Frische teutsche Liedlein," "Gassenhäwerlin," etc.). To the C. genus belong also *villanellas* and *villotas*, only that in these the style of composition is still simpler (note against note, with little movement in the middle voices). When the strict polyphonic style flourished compositions of this kind stood nearest to the taste of the present day, for they were sharply articulated, and showed period-formation answering to the rhyme positions in the stanzas consisting for the most part of short lines. The C. sprang from the *Volkslied;* in many ways it can be shown that the tenor part of these songs is used by various composers, and thus they are popular melodies arranged in four parts. Skilful masters (for ex., Heinrich Isaak, in "Inspruck, ich muss dich lassen," 1475) have set against the original melody in the tenor part a more beautiful one in the soprano, which afterwards was taken for the principal melody. The French *chansons* can be traced back to the songs of the Trouvères (troubadours), and the Neapolitan and Sicilian C. to fishermen's songs. Again, the French *chanson* is written for one voice with pianoforte accompaniment, but it has retained its fresh character. In its rhythm, answering to the national character, it may be distinguished, and to its advantage, from the *Romance*, the sweet *Lied* after the manner of Abt and Kücken. The modern art song is called in France by the German name, *Lied, Lieder*.

Canzonetta, diminutive of *Canzone*, a little song. (*See* CANZONA.)

Capella, Martianus Minneus Felix, Latin poet and savant at Carthage at the beginning of the 5th century A.D., whose "Satyricon" (9th book) treats of music. Remi d'Auxerre (Remigius Altisiodorensis) wrote a commentary on the same (printed in Gerbert's "Scriptores," I.). The first two books of the "Satyricon," entitled "De nuptiis Philologiæ et Mercurii," contain extracts from Aristides Quintilian (reprinted in Meibom's "Antiquæ Musicæ Auctores," VII., and in the various editions of the "Satyricon," the last by F. Kopp, 1836).

Capellmeister (Ger.; Ital. *Maestro di capella;* Fr. *Maître de chapelle*), master of the children, choir-master; also conductor of an orchestra (Fr. *Chef-d'orchestre*).

Capistrum (Lat.; Gr. *Peristomion, Phorbeia*)

was the name given by the ancients to the bandage which the flute-player put round his cheeks, so as to prevent immoderate stretching of the same when blowing vigorously. Schafhäutl ("Bericht über die Ausstellung zu München," 1854) concludes from the employment of the C., that the flute was not a beak-flute, but a reed instrument with kettle mouthpiece. (*Cf.*, however, WIND-INSTRUMENTS (1) and FISTULA.)

Capo (Ital.), head, beginning. *Da capo* (abbr. *d.c.*), from the beginning, a sign for the repetition of a piece up to the place marked *fine* (end.)

Capocci, Filippo, b. May 11, 1840, Rome, excellent Italian organist, son of Gaëtano Capocci, maestro di cappella at San Giovanni in Laterano, Rome. C. commenced to study the organ at an early age, and, thanks to exceptional gifts and hard work, rose, until in 1875 he became organist of San Giovanni. He is an organ composer of some distinction.

Capotasto (Ital., from *capo* = head, and *tasto* = touch or tie ; *Capodaster*), the upper end of the finger-board in stringed instruments. Also (especially in the guitar) a contrivance, by means of which the first fret is made a C. (the strings shortened by a semitone).

Capoul, Joseph Amédée Victor, tenor singer, b. Feb. 27, 1839, Toulouse. He learnt singing at the Paris Conservatoire under Révial and Mocker. He was at the Opéra Comique from 1861 to 1872, and since then has appeared at New York, London (with Christine Nilsson), and other places with great success.

Cappella (Ital. ; Ger. *Kapelle*), originally the name for the place (recess) set apart for the worshipping of a particular saint, in a large or even in a small church ; then it was applied to the place occupied by the body of singers, and lastly to the body of singers itself. The oldest chapels were wholly vocal chapels, and of these the oldest, which bore, and still bears, the name of C., is the Papal Chapel (*Cappella pontifica*). The Berlin Cathedral choir, the court Chapels of Munich and Vienna, King's Chapel (Chapel Royal) at London, and formerly the *Sainte Chapelle* at Paris, etc., at each of which there is a body of paid singers, are institutions of a similar kind. As in old times sacred compositions were written for voices only without any kind of instrumental accompaniment (up to 1600), the term *a cappella* (*alla Cappella*) received the meaning of polyphonic vocal music without accompaniment. When, after the date mentioned above, instrumental accompaniment was also introduced into sacred music, it became necessary to add instrumental players to the C., and the corporate body also gradually received the name of C. (*Cf.* ORCHESTRA.)

Capriccio (Ital. ; Fr. *Caprice*). This term, when applied to a piece of music, does not imply any particular form, but only indicates that it is piquant in rhythm, and especially rich in original and unexpected turns of thought. The C., therefore, cannot be distinguished from the *Scherzo ;* pieces like Chopin's B♭ minor Scherzo might with equal right be called *capricci. A.c., ad libitum,* at pleasure ; a free characteristic rendering.

Capricornus. (*See* BOCKSHORN.)

Caraccio, Giovanni, b. *circa* 1550, Bergamo, d. 1626, Rome ; employed as singer at the court at Munich, afterwards maestro of the cathedral, Bergamo, and finally of Santa Maria Maggiore, Rome. Of his compositions there exist two books of magnificats, five books of madrigals (the third book is missing), psalms, canzone, requiems, etc.

Carafa (de Colobrano), Michele Enrico, b. Nov. 17, 1787, Naples, d. July 26, 1872 ; second son of Prince Colobrano, Duke of Alvito. He was an officer in the Neapolitan army, from 1806 personal adjutant to Murat, with whom he went through the Russian campaign. When Napoleon fell, he gave up the military career and devoted himself entirely to music, which he had already cultivated with assiduity. Already in 1802 and 1811 he had had small operas performed at Naples. After he had written a great number of operas for Naples, Milan, and Venice, and also brought out a few pieces at the Théâtre Feydeau, Paris, he settled there in 1827 ; in 1837 he became a member of the Académie (successor to Le Sueur), and in 1840 professor of composition at the Conservatoire. Besides thirty-six operas and some cantatas and ballets, he also wrote a few important church works (masses, requiems, Stabat Mater, Ave Verum).

Caramuel de Lobkowitz, Juan, b. May 23, 1606, Madrid, d. Sept, 8, 1682, as Bishop of Vigevano (Lombardy); published, "Arte nueva de Musica, inventada anno 600 por S. Gregorio, desconcertada anno da 1026 por Guidon Aretino restituida a su primera perfeccion anno 1620 por Fr. Pedro de Urenna, etc." (1644). (*Cf.* BOBISATION).

Caressant (Fr.), **Carezzando** (Ital.), **Carezzevole** (Ital.), in a caressing, insinuating manner.

Carestini, Giovanni, evirato, known under the name of Cusanino, which he added to his own in honour of the family of Cusani in Milan, which had taken him under its protection when he was only twelve years of age ; b. about 1705, at Monte Filatrano, near Ancona, d. there about 1760. He sang at Rome, Prague, Mantua, London (1733-35, under Handel, when Farinelli was engaged by his adversaries), afterwards at Venice, Berlin, St. Petersburg (1755-58).

Carey, Henry, b. about 1690, d. Oct. 4, 1743, London ; natural son of George Savile, Marquis of Halifax ; he was a favourite English composer of ballads, operettas, and of so-called ballad-operas. He published in 1737 a collection of 100 ballads under the title, "The Musical Century." According to Chrysander's showing ("Jahrbuch" I.), Carey was the composer of "God Save the King," which Clark (1822) tried to assign to John Bull. It should, however, be stated that the same Clark, in 1814, had written a book to prove that Carey *was* author of the tune. (*Cf.* long and interesting articles on the subject by W. H. Cummings, *Musical Times*, 1878.)

Caricato (Ital.), overloaded with regard to embellishments, dissonances, instrumentation, or any other means of musical expression.

Carillon, set of bells (Ger. *Glockenspiel*). In former centuries carillons were much in vogue. The grandest kind of C. is to be found on church towers, where a number of small bells are played by means of clockwork mechanism with rollers, as in the barrel-organ or the musical-clock. Carillons of this kind are common in Holland and the Netherlands, and were only transplanted to England within modern times, where the mechanism has been brought to a great state of perfection. In 1885 the *Petri-kirche* at Hamburg received a new C. with forty bells. Smaller carillons were played either by means of a keyboard (as those in old organs for the upper half of the keyboard), or struck by small mallets (especially the portable ones, formerly common in military music, now replaced by the lyra with steel rods). The idea of the C. is very ancient, and was realised, particularly by the Chinese, a long time ago ; it is possible that the Dutch may have received them thence. The monks of the early Middle Ages had, however, already constructed bells tuned in different ways (*nolæ, tintinnabula*). A mass of indications how to fit these up for the nine tones of the octave (*C—c*, with *b♭* and *b♮*) have been preserved in manuscripts of the 10th to the 12th century, and, in part, reprinted in Gerbert ("Scriptores," etc.). The cymbalum (miniature drum) appears to have been of equal importance. Carillons is also the name given to musical pieces, especially for pianoforte, which imitate a peal of bells (melody in 3rds with *ostinato* upper and lower notes).

Carissimi, Giacomo, born about 1604 at Marino (Papal States), was at first maestro at Assisi, and from 1628 occupied a similar post at the Church of St. Apollinaris, attached to the German College, Rome, where he died Jan. 12, 1674. C. contributed much towards the development of the monodic style which arose at the beginning of the 17th century ; he rendered essential aid in perfecting recitative and giving greater charm to instrumental accompaniments. He is said to have been the inventor of the chamber cantata, but this statement is misleading, inasmuch as all his cantatas are composed to sacred words. Many of his works have, unfortunately, been lost, for when the Order of the Jesuits

was abolished, the library of the German College was sold. But even of the printed ones (motets à 2–4, 1664 and 1667; "Arie da Camera," 1667) there exist only single copies. The Paris Library possesses a manuscript with ten oratorios by C.; the library of the Conservatoire and that of the British Museum contain also detached works by C. The Fitzwilliam Museum, Cambridge, possesses motets, madrigals of C., some of them autographs. There is, besides, a specially rich collection (made by Dr. Aldrich) in the library of Christ Church, Oxford. A sacred cantata, *Jonah*, has been edited by Henry Leslie (Augener, No. 9,117). A small treatise, "Ars Cantandi," by C., exists only in a German translation, as supplement to the "Vermehrter Wegweiser" (Augsburg, Jak. Knoppmayer, 2nd ed., 1692; 3rd ed., 1696).

Carmagnole, one of the most noted popular songs of the *Terreur* period of the French Revolution, of which both poet and composer are unknown. It commences thus :—

Ma - dame Ve - to a - vait pro - mis, Ma - dame Ve - to a - vait pro - mis, etc.

The name is derived from the C., the jackets worn by the members of the Jacobin Club.

Carnicer. Ramon, b. Oct. 24, 1789, near Tarrega (Catalonia), d. March 17, 1855; from 1818–20 conductor at the Italian Opera, Barcelona, 1828 at the Royal Opera, Madrid, and 1830–54 professor of composition of the Conservatorio of that city. He composed nine operas, many symphonies, church music, songs, etc.

Carol, Carola (Ital.), **Carole** (Fr.), a mediæval dance (ring-dance), which, like all old dances, was accompanied by singing. The name has recently been given in England to songs half-sacred, half-secular, of a popular kind, sung at festival times, especially at Christmas. (CHRISTMAS CAROLS.)

Carolan. (*See* O'CAROLAN.)

Caron, Firmin, distinguished contrapuntist of the 15th century, contemporary of Okeghem, Busnois, etc., pupil of Binchois and Dufay. With the exception of a few masses in the library of the Pope's chapel and a three-part *chanson* in a manuscript in the Paris Bibliothèque, nothing has been preserved.

Carpani, Giuseppe, b. 1752, Brianza (Lombardy), d. Jan. 22, 1825, Milan, as Imperial court poet. C. is principally known by his "Le Haydine, Ovvero Lettere su la Vita e le Opere del Celebre Maestro Giuseppe Haydn" (1812), and "Le Rossiniane, ossia Lettere Musico-teatrali" (1824). He produced several operas at Milan.

Carpentras (Ital. *Il Carpentrasso*, real name *Eleazar Genet*), b. about 1475, Carpentras (Vaucluse) ; became in 1515 principal singer in the Pope's chapel, and soon after maestro di cappella ; he was sent to Avignon (1521) to settle some negotiations connected with the Papal chair, and appears to have died there after 1532. A book of his masses, Lamentations, hymns, and Magnificats was published by Jean de Channay at Avignon (1532) ; it was printed with round notes (!) and without ligatures. (*Cf.* BRIARD.) Single numbers from it have been reprinted in collections of the present day. Some motets of C. are to be found in Petrucci's " Motetti della Corona " in the first and third volumes (1514 and 1519).

Carré, L o u i s, b. 1663, Clofontaine (Brie), d. April 11, 1711 ; mathematician and member of the Paris Académie ; he published several works on acoustics.

Carreño, Teresa, b. Dec. 22, 1853, Caracas (Venezuela), the daughter of a distinguished functionary. She studied with L. Gottschalk, and is a most accomplished pianist. She made her *début* in Europe already in 1865–66, but her fame dates only from the time of her reappearance (1889). C. is also singer, composer ("National Hymn of Venezuela"), and, as manageress of an Italian opera troupe, was sometimes compelled to wield the *bâton*. She married, 1892, the pianist Eugen d'Albert.

Carrodus, J o h n T i p l a d y, b. Jan. 20, 1836, Keighley (Yorkshire), violinist, pupil of Molique in London and in Stuttgart (1848 to 1853). He resided in London from 1854 as solo violinist and leader of some of the principal orchestras. He published several violin solos. Died July 12, 1895.

Carter, T h o m a s, b. about 1735, Dublin, d. Oct. 12, 1804 ; studied music in Italy, and (1775–82) wrote incidental music to several plays produced at Drury Lane Theatre. In 1787 he became musical director of the Royalty Theatre, for which he wrote operas. He composed, besides, concertos and lessons for pianoforte, as well as ballads, some of which became very popular.

Cartier, J e a n B a p t i s t e, violinist, b. May 28, 1765, Avignon, d. 1841, Paris ; pupil of Viotti, afterwards accompanist to Queen Marie Antoinette, 1791–1821 violinist at the Grand Opéra, 1804 member of the imperial, 1815–30 of the royal band, after which he received a pension. Besides variations, *études*, sonatas, duets for violin, he wrote two operas and published an excellent Method, " L'art du violon " (1798 and 1801).

Caruso, L u i g i, b. Sept. 25, 1754, Naples, d. 1822, Perugia ; he was one of the most prolific opera and church composers of his time (sixty-one operas for all the great stages of Italy).

Carvalho, M a r i e C a r o l i n e F é l i x, *née* M i o l a n, b. Dec. 31, 1827, Marseilles, distin-

guished French opera singer (soprano, lyric artist) ; in 1853 she married Léon Carvaille, who was called C. (b. 1825, d. July 10, 1895 ; first of all opera singer [1855], then, until 1869, manager of the Théâtre Lyrique, which flourished under his direction ; from 1876 director of the Opéra Comique). Madame C. was first engaged at the Opéra Comique, then sang at the Lyrique, 1869 at the Grand Opéra, 1872 again at the Opéra Comique, and in 1875 again at the Grand Opéra. She retired in 1885, and d. July 10, 1895.

Cary, A n n i e L o u i s a, a distinguished American contralto vocalist, b. 1846, Wayne (Kennebec, co. Maine), daughter of a physician. She was trained at Boston and, after a journey to Milan for the purpose of study, made her *début* at Stockholm. She then went under Madame Viardot - Garcia (Baden - Baden) for further study, and was engaged first at Hamburg, 1868, and then at Stockholm. After that she sang at Brussels, London, New York (1870), Petersburg (1875), etc. She married at Cincinnati in 1882, where she was engaged as soloist at the Festival in May.

Casali, G i o v a n n i B a t t i s t a, from 1759 to 1792 maestro at the Lateran ; a church composer in the style of the Roman school.

Casamorata, L u i g i F e r n a n d o, b. May 15, 1807, Würzburg, of Italian parents, d. Sept. 24, 1881, Florence. He went with his parents to the latter city in 1813, received at an early age regular musical instruction, but studied law and took his degree ; he assisted in the editing of the *Gazetta Musicale* at Florence, and was a zealous contributor to the Milan paper of like name. C. produced ballet music and an opera, but on the failure of these he turned his attention to sacred vocal, and to instrumental music. In 1859 he was appointed vice-president of the foundation committee of the Royal Institute of Music at Florence, and was afterwards entrusted with the working out of the organisation, and named director of the Institution. Besides many vocal and instrumental works, he published a " Manuale di armonia " (1876), likewise " Origini, storia e ordinamento del R. Istituto Musicale Fiorentino."

Casella, P i e t r o, b. 1769, Pieva (Umbria), d. Dec. 12, 1843, as Professor of the Royal Conservatorio, Naples. He was maestro of several Naples churches, and wrote many masses, vespers, etc., also several operas.

Caserta, P h i l i p p d e, writer of the 15th century at Naples on the theory of measured music ; a treatise of his has been printed by Coussemaker (Script. III.).

Cassa (gran C.). (*See* DRUM.)

Cassation (Ger. *Kassation*, Ital. *Cassazione*), really a " farewell." This was in the last century a serenade (esp. as " Abendmusik ") to be performed in the open air. It consisted of a piece in several movements, of simple character.

and arranged for several instruments. (*Cf.* SERENADE, DIVERTIMENTO.)

Cassiodorus, Magnus Aurelius, b. about 470 (in Lucania), was chancellor of the kings Odoacer and Theodoric, and worked beneficially as consul at Rome (514). Deposed by Vitiges (537), he retired to the monastery at Vivarium (Vivarese, Calabria), where he wrote his work "De artibus ac disciplinis liberalium litterarum," of which the part treating of music ("Institutiones musicæ") was printed by Gerbert (Script. I.).

Castanets (Sp. *Castañuelas*), a simple clapper instrument much in vogue in Spain and Lower Italy. It consists of two pieces of wood, in shape something like the capsule of a chestnut slit through the middle; these are fastened by means of a cord to the thumb, and struck one against the other by means of the other fingers. An effect similar to the C. can be obtained by drawing the fingers quickly from the point to the ball of the thumb, to which movement the name C. is applied. C. are indispensable features of Spanish or Neapolitan dances in our modern ballet. For further details *see* Gevaert's "Nouveau Traité d'Instrumentation."

Castel, Louis Bertrand, Jesuit father, b. Nov. 11, 1688, Montpelier, d. Jan. 11, 1757, Paris; he seized hold of the idea suggested by Newton of colour harmony, and constructed, first in theory, afterwards in practice, a coloured keyboard (*Clavecin oculaire*), the description of which was translated into German by Telemann (1739). He wrote besides "Lettres d'un académicien de Bordeaux sur le fond de la musique" (1754), as well as the reply to it ("Réponse critique d'un académicien de Rouen, etc." (1754). C. was acquainted with Rameau, and it is said that he had a hand in Rameau's theoretical writings, but this has not been proved. C. was a dreamer, but Rameau a musician with a fine sense of harmony.

Castelli, Ignaz Franz, b. March 6, 1781, Vienna, d. there Feb. 5, 1862; author of the libretto of Weigl's *Schweizer Familie* and other favourite operas, also the translation into German of many foreign operas for stage use. He was appointed "Hoftheaterdichter" at the Kärntnerthor Theater; and from 1829–40 was founder and editor of the *Allgemeiner Musikalischer Anzeiger*.

Castration, the emasculation of boys practised for centuries in Italy to prevent the mutation (q.v.) which takes place at the age of puberty, *i.e.* for the sake of preserving the boy's voice, the quality of which, as is known, is more agreeable than that of a woman's. The voice of *evirati* combined with the *timbre* of a boy's voice the developed chest and lungs of a man, so that they could sing passages of enormous length, and could produce wonderful *messa di voce* effects. Castration flourished during the 17th and first half of the 18th century; but cases are to be found far into the 19th century. The origin of C. for the purpose named must be sought for in mutilations through some accident or other; and the most famous *evirati* of the 17th century had always some tale to tell how they had suffered C., for no one willingly submitted to it. In consequence of the enormous success of certain *evirati*, C. became, as it appears, a matter for most reprehensible speculation; a great number of boys were emasculated who never developed into singers of any importance. It has not been proved that the church approved of C., but it certainly tolerated it, and even at the beginning of the present century *evirati* were admitted into the Papal Chapel. The following were specially famous: Farinelli, Senesino, Cusanino, Ferri, Momoletto, Gizziello, Bernacchi, Caffarelli, Crescentini, Pacchierotti, Manzuoli, Marchesi, Salimbeni, Velluti.

Castrucci, Pietro, b. 1689, Rome, d. 1769, London, violinist, pupil of Corelli, came (1715) to London as leader of Handel's opera band. In his playing he showed a straining after effect. He was specially famous as a performer on the *violetta marina*, a stringed instrument of his own invention. Handel used the instrument in *Orlando* and *Sosarme;* in the former an air is accompanied by two *violette marine*, "Per gli Signori Castrucci," *i.e.*, Pietro and his brother Prospero. C. died in great poverty. He published two books of violin sonatas, and twelve violin concertos.

Catalani, Angelica, b. Sinigaglia, May, 1780, d. of cholera, Paris, June 12. 1849, a singer of the first rank at the beginning of last century. Already as a child she made a great sensation, and was looked upon as a prodigy. She was educated at the Santa Lucia convent at Gubbio, near Rome, which derived great pecuniary advantage from her presence. She never became the pupil of a great master, and was never able to shake off certain faulty mannerisms of which Crescentini, later on, complained. Her voice was full, flexible, and of great compass. At first she tried sustained, expressive singing, but for that she lacked inner warmth. She only rose to her true height when she devoted herself to bravura singing. In 1795 she made her *début* at the Fenice, Venice, then sang at La Pergola, Florence, in 1799, and in 1801 at La Scala, Milan, and afterwards at Trieste, Rome, Naples. In 1801 she accepted an engagement at the Italian Opera, Lisbon, where she studied her parts with M. Portugal. She married Valabrègue, of the French embassy, who, as a pure man of business, directed her further career with the sole aim of making as much money as possible. They first went to Paris, where C. only appeared at concerts, but definitely established her fame. She went to London in 1806 to fulfil a brilliant contract, and by 1807 had received no less than £16,700. She remained seven years in London, visiting Scotland and Ireland during the off season. On the fall of Napoleon (1814) she returned to Paris, and King Louis XVIII. gave over to her the management of the Théâtre Italien with a subsidy of 160,000 frs. During the "hundred days" she retired before Napoleon, visited Germany and Scandinavia, and only returned through Holland to Paris after the capture of the emperor. This dread of Napoleon first arose in 1806, when she refused his offer of an engagement for Paris, and gave the preference to London. As directress of a theatre she met with little success. In 1817 she gave up the management, and for the next ten years led a wandering life. In 1827 she sang in Berlin for the last time, and at York Festival in 1828, after which she spent the rest of her life in retirement on her country estate in the neighbourhood of Florence, giving lessons in singing, it is said, to young girls gifted with a voice. C. had not only an extraordinary voice, but, in addition, a handsome figure and a lofty, majestic bearing.

Catalectic. A poetical measure is called thus if the last foot of the verse is incomplete, *i.e.* if there is a pause in place of the last syllable.

Catalini, Alfredo, b. June 19, 1854, Lucca, studied with his father, and afterwards at the Paris Conservatoire and Milan Conservatorio. He produced a one-act opera, *La Falce* (1875), and also *Elda* (Turin, 1880), *Dejanice* (Milan, 1883), *Ero e Leandro* (1885), *Edmea* (1886).

Catch, a species of composition peculiarly English; a kind of vocal fugue with comic words and all sorts of technical difficulties (division of the lines, nay, even of the words among the different voices), rendering the singing of catches a troublesome art. The oldest collections of catches are: "Pammelia" (1609), "Deuteromelia" (1609), and "Melismata" (1611). The words of the catches were often of a highly questionable character. A *Catch Club* has existed in London since 1761 for the preservation and cultivation of this peculiar form of art. The club counts princes and noblemen, together with the best musicians of the country, amongst its members. The prizes offered have been won, amongst others, by Arne, Hayes, Webbe, Cooke, Alcock, Callcott, and, in recent times, Cummings.

Catel, Charles Simon, b. June 10, 1773, L'Aigle (Orne), d. Nov. 29, 1830, Paris; went at an early age to Paris, where Sacchini took interest in him, and obtained admission for him into the École Royale de Chant (afterwards the Conservatoire). Gobert and Gossec were his teachers there. Already in 1787 he was appointed accompanist and "professeur-adjoint" of the institution, in 1790 accompanist at the Opéra and sub-conductor of the band of the Garde Nationale (Gossec was the principal).

On the formation of the Conservatoire in 1795, C. was made professor of harmony, and was commissioned to write a "Traité d'Harmonie," which appeared in 1802. In 1810 he became, jointly with Gossec, Méhul, and Cherubini, one of the inspectors of the Conservatoire, but gave up all his posts in 1814 when Sarrette, who had been friendly to him, was dismissed. In 1815 he was elected member of the Académie. C. wrote much for the stage, but with little success (*Sémiramis, Les Bayadères, Les Aubergistes de Qualité*, etc.) ; also his national festival cantatas and some chamber works, though 'displaying good workmanship, show no inventive power. His chief title to merit is his "Traité d'Harmonie," which for twenty years was a standard work at the Conservatoire. C. also took part in the publication of the "Solfèges du Conservatoire."

Catelani, Angelo, b. March 30, 1811, Guastalla, d. Sept. 5, 1866, Modena; was a pupil of Zingarelli at the Naples Conservatorio in 1831, and private pupil of Donizetti and Crescentini; in 1834 conductor of the opera at Messina, in 1837 town musical director at Correggio; lived in Modena from 1838, where he was appointed, in turn, town, court, and church maestro di cappella, and in 1859 sub-librarian of the Este library. C. wrote several operas, but is more worthy of mention as a musical historian. He wrote biographical notices of Pietro Aaron and Nicola Vincentino (for the Milan *Gazetta Musicale*, 1851), published letters of celebrated old musicians (1852–54), wrote concerning the two oldest Petrucci prints discovered by Gaspari at Bologna (1856), and finally about the life and works of Orazio Vecchi (1858) and Claudio Merulo (1860).

Catena di trilli (Ital.), a chain or succession of trills.

Catrufo, Giuseppe, b. April 19, 1771, Naples, d. Aug. 19, 1855, London. On the outbreak of the Naples revolution he entered the service of France, and remained officer until 1804. He settled in Geneva, but went to Paris in 1810, and from thence to London in 1835. C. was a prolific, but not an original, writer of operas; he produced also arias, sacred pieces, and compositions for pianoforte and other instruments, as well as a "Méthode de Vocalisation" (1830).

Cauda (Lat. "tail"). This is the name given in the terminology of the writers on measured music to the vertical stroke falling from the noteheads of the Maxima ⊨, and the Longa ⊢,

as well as the commencement and close of the *ligatures* (q.v.). C. is, sometimes, though rarely, used to indicate the upper stroke (*sursum C.*) in the Minima ◊ and Semiminima ◆, and the

ligatures *cum opposita proprietate*. The *Plica*
(q.v.) at the close of ligatures is frequently
called C. in old measured music.

Caurroy, François Eustache du, Sieur
de St. Frémin, b. Feb. 1549, Gerberoy, near
Beauvais, d. Aug. 7, 1609, Paris. In 1569 he
became singer in the royal chapel, afterwards
conductor, and in 1598 " surintendant de la
musique du roi." In his time he was highly
esteemed as a composer. His Requiem, two
books of " Preces," besides " Mélanges " (*chansons*, psalms, and Christmas songs) and " Phan-
tasies," have been preserved.

Cavaillé-Col, Aristide, b. 1811, Montpelier,
d. Oct. 12, 1899, sprang from an old family of
organ-builders. He went to Paris in 1833, and
became successful competitor for the construction of an organ at St. Denis. He settled in
Paris ; and besides the St. Denis organ, in
which Barker's pneumatic levers were first
used, built also the celebrated instruments for
St. Sulpice, the Madeleine, and many others in
Paris and the provinces, and for Belgium, Holland, etc., of some of which detailed descriptions have been given (by La Fage, Lamazou,
etc.). C. introduced important improvements
in the construction of organs, as, for example,
the employment of separate wind-chests with
various intensities of wind for the low, middle,
and upper parts of the keyboard, and again the
flûtes octaviantes. He wrote " Études Expéri-
mentales sur les Tuyaux d'Orgue " (Report for
the Académie des Sciences 1849); " De l'Orgue
et de son Architecture " (" Revue Générale de
l'Architecture des Travaux Publics, 1856"), and
" Projet d'Orgue Monumental pour la Basilique
de Saint-Pierre de Rome " (1875).

Cavalieri, Emilio del, b. at Rome, of noble
family, lived there many years, and then was
appointed " Inspector-General of Arts and
Artists " at Florence by Fernando de Medici.
He appears to have died in that city in 1599, as
his most famous work, " Rappresentazione di
Anima e di Corpo," was published in 1600 by
Alessandro Guidotti, together with a preface
and comments. C. was, without doubt, one of
the founders of the modern (homophonic, accompanied) style of music, and of these the
first to die. Hitherto it has not been clearly
established whether he was drawn towards the
new tendency by the esthetic circle in the
houses of Bardi and Corsi (q.v.)—for it is not
even known that he was a member of it—or
whether, on the other hand, he influenced it.
Anyhow, as well as they, he was hostile to
counterpoint, and, if they came together, the
reasons of it are assuredly to be sought for
outside of music. Already, in the work named
above, C. wrote a *Basso continuato* (Continuo)
with figuring, and Guidotti explained the meaning of the same. C. also attached importance
to the formation of melody, to which he, perhaps first, added ornaments (borrowed from

the lute and clavicembalo), the signs of which
were explained by Guidotti in the above-mentioned preface. Cavalieri's compositions appear
dry and monotonous to modern taste, but it
should not be forgotten that they were the first
attempts in an entirely new style. The *Rappresentazione* is looked upon as the first oratorio
(q.v.), just as his *Disperazione di Filene*, his
Satiro (1590), and *Giuoco della Cieca* (1595) must
be considered the beginnings of opera. The
earliest work of C. is a book of over eighty
madrigals, known only by name. Like Caccini,
he first wrote in the *stilo osservato*.

Cavalieri, Katherina, b. Währing (Vienna),
1761, d. 1801, a dramatic singer mentioned by
Mozart in a letter as "a singer of whom Germany might well be proud." It was for her
that he composed the part of Constance in the
Entführung, and the air " Mi tradi " in *Don
Giovanni* on its first representation at Vienna.

Cavalli, Francesco (really Pier Francisco
Caletti-Bruni), b. 1599 or 1600, Crema,
where his father, Giambattista Caletti, named
Bruni, was maestro, d. Jan. 14, 1676, Venice.
On account of his musical talent he was taken
by Federigo C., a Venetian nobleman, for a
time podesta at Crema, to Venice to be trained
as an artist. According to the fashion so
common in Italy he assumed the name of his
patron. In 1617 he became singer at St. Mark's
under the name Bruni, in 1628 as Caletti, and
1640 as second organist under the name Caletti
detto C. He became first organist in 1665, and
maestro of St. Mark's in 1668. His Requiem,
written not long before his death, was performed at his funeral. C. was held in high
esteem as organist, as church composer, but especially as an opera composer (forty-two operas).
The pupil of Monteverde, and heir of his
spiritual gifts, C. in his works advanced a step
beyond ; his detached vocal pieces already
show broader form and more warmth of expression. Rhythmical power and sound melody
invest them with something more than historical value. One can judge of the fame which
C. enjoyed from the fact that it was he who
composed the festival opera (*Serse*) for the marriage ceremony, at the Louvre, of Louis XIV.
(1660), and the *Ercole Amante* on the occasion
of the Peace of the Pyrenees (1662). His *Giasone* was produced with the greatest success on
Italian stages (1649-62) ; it was republished by
Eitner in the twelfth volume of the publications
of the " Gesellschaft für Musikforschung."

Cavata (Ital.), (1) production of tone.—(2) The
word has also been used synonymously with
cavatina.

Cavatina (*Cavata*), a lyrical vocal solo in an
opera, of simpler character than the aria, and
treated more in Lied form—*i.e.* it avoids repetition of words and long coloratura passages,
and has only one *tempo*. Although, as a rule,
the C. is of shorter duration than an aria, it

frequently has a longer text. In modern opera, the C. is generally a separate number, but occurred formerly also as the lyrical close of a recitative.

Cavos, C a t t e r i n o, b. 1775, Venice, d. April 28, 1840, Petersburg, pupil of Bianchi. He went in 1798 to Petersburg, where, after the success of his opera—*Iwan Sussanina,* composed to a Russian text—he was appointed capell-meister to the court, a post which he held until his death. C. wrote thirteen Russian operas, which were favourably received, and won for him many marks of distinction. Besides, he composed a French and several Italian operas, also six ballets (*Zephyr und Flora*).

Caylus, A n n e C l a u d e P h i l i p p e de Tu-b i è r e s, C o m t e, b. Oct. 31, 1692, Paris, d. there Sept. 5, 1765. He wrote much about the music of the ancients in his "Recueil d'Antiquités Égyptiennes, Étrusques, Grecques, Romaines, et Gauloises" (1752, etc., 17 vols.), and on the same in his "Mémoires de l'Académie des Inscriptions" (vol. 21).

C barré (Fr.), the $\large{\math(}$ which indicates *alla breve* time—²₁ and ³₄.

C double sharp (Ger. *Cisis*), the c doubly raised by means of a ×.

Cebell, an old English term for a lively Gavotte (used by Purcell and others).

Cecilia, S a i n t, was a noble Roman lady, who suffered martyrdom for the Christian faith A.D. 177. A later age has adorned the history of her death with legends, and has even attributed to her the invention of the organ. She is the patron saint of music, particularly of church music; her anniversary day is Nov. 22nd, and for this festival many celebrated composers (Purcell, Clark, Handel) have written special sacred pieces (Odes to St. Cecilia). Musical societies without number bear the name of St. Cecilia: the oldest is probably the one founded in Rome by Palestrina, which was at first a kind of order with many privileges from the popes, and which in 1847 was changed into an academy by Pius IX., which maintains the reputation of its church music. The London "Cecilian Society" was founded in 1785, and until 1861 was valued for its performances of oratorios (especially those of Handel and Haydn). The "Cäcilienverein für Länder deutscher Zunge" was founded in 1867 by Franz Wilt, at Ratisbon, for the improvement of Catholic church music. (*See* UNIONS.)

Celere (Ital.), quick, nimble.

Celerità (Ital.), celerity, swiftness. *Con celerità,* with swiftness, quickly, nimbly.

Celestina. (*See* TREMULANT; *cf.* BIFARA.)

Celestino, E l i g i o, b. 1739, Rome, considered by Burney the best Roman violinist of his time. He came to London when sixty years of age,

and published some compositions for violin and 'cello in that city.

Celler, L u d o v i c, pseudonym of Louis Le-clerq, b. Feb. 8, 1828, Paris. Under the name C., he published, together with other non-musical works, "La Semaine Sainte au Vatican " (1867); "Les Origines de l'Opéra et le Ballet de la Reine " (1868), and " Molière-Lully, Le Mariage Forcé (le Ballet du Roi) " (1867).

Cellier, A l f r e d, English composer, of French origin, b. Dec. 1, 1844, Hackney (London), d. Dec. 28, 1891, pupil of Th. Helmore and chorister of St. James's Chapel Royal; in 1862 he received a post of organist, and in 1866 became conductor of the Ulster Hall Concerts and the Philharmonic Society at Belfast. He conducted from 1871–75 at the Prince's Theatre, Manchester; from 1877–79 at the Opéra Comique, London; and, jointly with Sullivan, the Promenade Concerts at Covent Garden. He lived for a long time in America and Australia, but returned to London in 1887. C. wrote a large number of operettas : *Charity Begins at Home* (1870); *The Sultan of Mocha; The Tower of London; Nell Gwynne; Bella Donna; The Foster Brothers; Dora's Dream; The Spectre Knight; After All; In the Sulks* (1880); *The Carp* (1886); *Mrs. Jarramie's Genie* (1888), and also a grand opera, *Pandora* (Boston, 1881), a symphonic suite, etc.

'Cello, abbr. of *violoncello.*

Cembal d'amour, a species of clavicembalo constructed by Gottfried Silbermann with strings of double length divided exactly in the middle by a bridge, so that both halves gave the same note. The strings were raised by means of tangents, each one, according to the strength of the blow, at a different height from the bridge. The attempt to obtain by this means the desired piano and forte was soon abandoned. (*Cf.* PIANOFORTE.)

Cembalo (Ital.). (*See* PIANOFORTE.)

Cento (Ital.), (1) the Antiphonary of Gregory the Great (q.v.), which was a collection of the various chants sung in the churches of Italy.— (2) *Centone,* a patch-work opera, or a composi-tion (*Pasticcio*) consisting of fragments taken from various works. The verb *centonizare,* de-rived from it (Fr. *centoniser*), means, therefore, to join together, and is used mostly in a depreciatory sense.

Cercar la nota (Ital., "to seek for the note ") is a singing term to indicate the sounding quietly beforehand of the note falling on the next syllable, as is done in the so-called *porta-mento :*—

Cernohorsky. (*See* CZERNOHORSKY.)

Cerone, Domenico Pietro, b, 1566, Bergamo; he went to Spain in 1592, and entered the chapel of Philip II.; in 1608, under Philip III., he joined the chapel at Naples, where he was still living in 1613. He wrote "Regole per il Canto Fermo" (1609), and "El Melopeo y Maestro, Tractado de Musica Theorica y Pratica" (1613), which is perhaps founded on a MS. of Zarlino's which has totally disappeared. (*Cf.* FÉTIS, "Biogr. Univ.")

Cerreto, Scipione, b. 1551, Naples, where he appears to have lived and died. He wrote three important theoretical works, of which two appeared in print, "Della Pratica Musica Vocale e Stromentale" (1601), and "Arbore Musicale," etc. (1608, very scarce); the third, in two different versions (1628, 1631), has remained in MS.

Certon, Pierre, choirmaster of the Sainte Chapelle, Paris, was one of the most important French contrapuntists of the first half of the 16th century. His works, consisting of masses, Magnificats, motets, psalms, and a number of *chansons*, are to be found in French and Dutch publications (Attaignant, Susato, Phalèse, etc.) of the years 1527 to 1560.

Ceru, Domenico Agostino, b. Aug. 28, 1817, Lucca, engineer and musical amateur there, published in 1864 a biography of Boccherini, and in 1870 a letter to A. Bernardini, comparing German with Italian music; and in 1871 a valuable historical inquiry respecting music and musicians at Lucca.

Cerveny (Czerveny), V. F., b. 1819, Dubeč (Bohemia), celebrated manufacturer of brass instruments at Königgrätz (from 1842), whose firm, trading since 1876 under the name "V. F. C. u. Söhne," shows great enterprise, and among other things has a bell foundry. C.'s numerous inventions have been universally recognised, and have been awarded prizes in many exhibitions (*see* Schafhäutl's comprehensive report of the musical instruments at the Munich Industrial Exhibition, 1854). His inventions are the "Tonwechsel-" and the "Walzenmaschine," etc., and, besides, the instruments phonikon, baroxyton, kornon, contrabass, contrabassoon, subcontrabass, and subcontrabassoon, and other brass wind-instruments, for the most part of very wide measure (Ganzinstrumente); also drums of modern construction ("Votivkirchen-Tympani," because he presented the earliest specimens to the new "Votivkirche" at Vienna). Turkish cymbals, tamtams, etc., have also been made by C. Died Jan. 19,1896.

Cervēra, Francisco, Spanish theorist of the 16th century; wrote, among other things, "Declaracion de lo Canto Ilano " (1593).

Cervetti. (*See* GELINEK.)

Cervetto, Giacomo (Bassevi, called C.), distinguished 'cellist, b. about 1682, in Italy, came, 1728, to London and entered the orchestra at Drury Lane, of which, after a few years, he became for some time director. He died Jan. 14, 1783, over a hundred years of age, leaving £20,000 to his son. This son, likewise named Giacomo (English, James C.), d. Feb. 5, 1837, was also an excellent 'cellist; he performed for a time at concerts, but after his father's death gave up public life. He published solos for 'cello, and duets and trios for violin and 'cello.

Cesi, Beniamino, b. Nov. 6, 1845, Naples, pupil for composition of Mercadante and Pappalardo at the Naples Conservatorio, and private piano pupil of Thalberg ; he was an excellent pianist, and, besides Italy, played also at Paris, Alexandria, Cairo, etc. He was professor of the pianoforte at the Conservatorio, Naples, from 1886. He published piano pieces and songs ; a pianoforte Method and an opera, *Vittor Pisani*, remain in manuscript. Died Feb., 1907.

Cesti, Marc Antonio, b. about 1620, Arezzo, d. 1669, Venice; pupil of Carissimi at Rome, 1646 maestro di cappella at Florence, 1660 tenor singer in the Pope's chapel, 1666-69 vice-capellmeister at Vienna to the Emperor Leopold I. He was one of the most famous opera composers of the 17th century. C. transferred to the stage the cantata, which had been perfected by Carissimi (mixture of recitative and *arioso* singing). The following operas of his are only known by name : *Orontea* (1649) ; *Cesare Amante* (1651) ; *La Dori* (1661, new edition by Eitner in vol. xii. of the "Publ. der Ges. f. Musikforschung") ; *Il Principe Generoso* (1665) ; *Il Pomo d'Oro* (1666) ; *Nettuno e Fiora festiggianti* (1666) ; *Semiramide* (1667) ; *Le Disgrazie d'Amore* (1667) ; *La Schiava Fortunata* (1667) ; *Argene* (1668) ; *Argia* and *Genserico* (1669). Besides these a few *Arie da Camera* have come down to us. *La Dori* had the greatest success.

Cetera (Ital.). (*See* ZITHER.)

C flat (Ger. *Ces*), c lowered by means of a flat ; $c\flat$ major chord $= c\flat$, $e\flat$, $g\flat$; $c\flat$ minor chord $= c\flat$, $e\flat\flat$, $g\flat$; $c\flat$ major key with signature of seven flats. (*See* KEY.)

Chabrier, Alexis Emmanuel, b. Jan. 18, 1841, Ambert, (Puy de Dôme), studied law, and received an appointment at the Ministère de l'Intérieur. He studied the pianoforte with Ed. Wolff and composition with Ar. Hignard, and produced in 1877 his first operetta, *L'Étoile ;* after which, in 1879, *L'Éducation Manquée ;* 1885, a scene with chorus, "La Sulamite;" 1886, a grand opera, *Gwendoline* (Brussels) ; and 1887, at the Opéra Comique, Paris, *Le Roi malgré Lui.* C. also published pf. pieces, and a Spanish rhapsody. From 1884–85 C. was choir director at the Château d'Eau, and helped Lamoureux with the rehearsals of *Tristan und Isolde.* Died Sept. 13, 1894, Paris.

Chaconne (Ital. *Ciacona*) is an instrumental piece which, like the Passacaglia (q.v.), consists of a series of variations over a *basso ostinato* of, at most, eight bars ($\frac{3}{4}$ time, slow movement).

A grand example is to be found in the noble C. attached to J. S. Bach's Sonata in D minor for violin alone.

Chadwick, George Whitfield, b. Nov. 13, 1854, Lowell (Mass.). He studied at the Leipzig Conservatorium; he is composer (orchestral and choral works), conductor and organist at Boston.

Challier, Ernst, b. July 9, 1843, Berlin, where he has a music business. He is noted for his monographic catalogues (catalogue of songs, 1885 ; also one of duets and trios, etc.).

Chalumeau. (*See* SCHALMEY, OBOE, CLARINET.)

Chamber Music is the name for music suitable for performance in small rooms, as distinguished from church music or theatre music, and, at the present day, especially from concert music. The term C. M. came into use at the beginning of the 17th century, *i.e.* at a time when instrumental music in the modern sense was in its infancy, and was limited to dances, *Toccatas, Ricercari*, etc., in 4 parts; it referred then almost exclusively to vocal music, and especially to accompanied vocal music (chamber cantata, chamber duet). When the more important forms of instrumental music came into existence (chamber concerto, suite, symphony [overture], sonata, etc.), these, and everything which was not church- or theatre-music, received the name of C. M. At the present day only works performed by a few solo instruments—such as trios, quartets, quintets, etc., up to octets and nonets, for strings, or strings and wind, with or without pianoforte, sonatas for the pianoforte and one stringed- or one wind-instrument, solo compositions for one instrument, and even songs, duets, trios for voices with accompaniment of one or a few instruments—are included in the term C. M. Concert music (orchestral and choral) is the real term opposed to C. M. As in C. M. the lack of fulness of sound and variety of instrumentation must be made up for by fine shading and detailed workmanship, it is quite correct to speak of a special *chamber style*. C. M. works in which the parts are treated orchestrally are faulty. (For *chamber-cantata, chamber-sonata, chamber-concerto*, and other compounds, *see* CANTATA, SONATA, CONCERTO, etc. *Cf.* L. Nohl's " Die geschichtliche Entwickelung der Kammermusik," 1885.)

Chamber Pitch or Tone, same as Normal Pitch. As formerly there were no means of counting vibrations, such a thing as an absolute fixed pitch did not exist ; but in the course of time pitch changed repeatedly both upwards and downwards. From the 16th to the 17th century it appears to have been very high, as can be shown from old organs which are about a tone higher than our C. P. But it gradually came down, especially when independent instrumental music (*chamber music*) was developed outside the church, and soon acquired a normal

pitch of its own, which, as C. P., was distinguished from that of the organs according to which the choir sang (*Choir Pitch*). Still higher than the choir pitch was the *Cornett-ton* (a minor third above the C. P.), probably the tuning of the " Stadtpfeifer." Choir Pitch and C. P. have existed side by side for a long time, moving up or down pretty much in parallel lines. Even after choir pitch had become antiquated, C. P. varied for a long time, until the Paris Académie in 1858 (for ever, let it be hoped) adopted the *Diapason normal*, fixed by a commission at 870 simple, or 435 double vibrations per second, for once-accented *a*. (For further details *see* A.)

Chamber Style. (*See* CHAMBER MUSIC.)

Chambonnières, Jacques (Champion de), really Jacques Champion, was, like his father and grandfather, a highly valued organist ; he was principal chamber cembalist to Louis XIV., and teacher of the elder Couperins, d'Anglebert, and Le Bègue. Two books of his clavier pieces (1670) have been preserved.

Champein, Stanislaus, b. Nov. 19, 1753, Marseilles, d. Sept. 19, 1830, Paris ; was, at the early age of thirteen, maître de chapelle of the monastery church at Pignon (Provence), and went in 1770 to Paris, where he first became known through some sacred works, and also two operettas, which were performed at the Théâtre Italien. After 1780 he wrote over forty operettas and operas for the Théâtre Italien, the Théâtre de Monsieur, and the Grand Opéra, of which the most admired were *Mélomanie* (1781), and *Le Nouveau Don Quichotte* (1789). At least sixteen were never produced.

Champion. (*See* CHAMBONNIÈRES.)

Change, Enharmonic. (*See* ENHARMONICS.)

Changing Note is used (1) in the sense of the Ital. *Nota cambiata*, Fr. *Note d'appogiature*, Ger. *Wechselnote ;* but also (2) for a note which takes the place of one belonging to a chord, and which lies a second below or above it ; also for an auxiliary note from which a downward spring of a third is made.

The last kind of C. N. is old (16th century), but there is no reason why analogous formations should be forbidden, such as :

Changing Notes of this kind have been

characteristically described as "passing notes by leap;" they could also appear thus:

Another kind of free contrapuntal formation consists in the laying hold of the neighbouring note, in the opposite direction, to the sound which follows:

Channnay, Jean de, music printer at Avignon in the 16th century. (*Cf.* BRIARD and CARPENTRAS.)

Channels (*Cancellæ*) are the separate portions of the wind-chest by which wind is conveyed to the pipes; and, in the sound-board, only pipes belonging to one and the same key stand over one and the same channel; but in the wind-chest used in Germany and called *Kegellade* (cone-box), all pipes belonging to one and the same stop. The *channel valve*, by means of which the wind gains access from the wind-chest into the channels, is therefore identical in the former with the playing-valves, *i.e.* is ruled by the keys. In the *Kegellade*, on the other hand, the wind is admitted by a register pallet, while each pipe, likewise each set of pipes, has its separate playing-valve.

Chanot, François, b. 1787, Mirecourt, son of an instrument maker. He performed military service as naval engineer; but at the time of the Restoration, in consequence of a satirical lampoon, he was dismissed from the service on half-pay, and placed under police supervision. At this time he laid before the Académie a violin which, in various ways, was a return to older and less complete forms (without side curves and without tail-piece, with straight sound-holes in the direction of the strings, and constructed lengthways of one piece). The Académie exposed itself to ridicule by its very favourable judgment, which placed the violin of Chanot on an equality with those of the Stradivari and Guaneri. C. was again taken into favour; and his brother, an instrument-maker at Paris, worked for some time according to his model, which, however, he was soon compelled to give up.

Chanson (Fr. = song). (*See* CANZONA.)

Chant, a short composition to which the Psalms and Canticles are sung. There are two kinds of chants, Gregorian and Anglican: the latter are either single or double chants. A single chant consists of a strain of three and one of four bars. Double chants consist of four strains, respectively of three and four, and again three and four bars. Quadruple chants

have latterly also been introduced. Apart from tonality and rhythm, the ancient Gregorian chant differs from the modern Anglican chant by certain opening notes called the *intonation*. The several parts of the Gregorian chant are: the intonation, first reciting note, mediation, second reciting note, and termination. The Anglican chant begins at once with the reciting note. Monotone recitation (on the reciting note) followed by melodic modulations (the mediation and termination) in the middle and at the end of each verse are the characteristics of what, in the restricted sense of the word, is called "chanting," the original and wider meaning of the word being "song" or "singing." (*Vide* AMBROSIAN CHANT, GREGORIAN CHANT, and PLAIN CHANT.)

Chant sur le livre (Fr.), an extemporaneous counterpoint added by one or more singers to the *canto fermo* sung by others. It is identical with *contrappunto alla mente.*

Chanter à livre ouvert (Fr.), to sing at sight.

Chanterelle (Fr. "singing string"), the highest string of the instruments of the violin and the lute classes, especially the E string of the violin.

Chantry, an endowed chapel where masses are said for the souls of the donors.

Chapel boys, Chorister boys (Ger. *Kapellknaben,* Fr. *Enfants de chœur*), are the boys who form the choir in churches and cathedrals. In important churches they receive education and special musical training. Many distinguished composers commenced their career as chorister boys.

Chapel Royal, King's Chapel. (*See* CAPPELLA.)

Chappell & Co., celebrated London music publishing firm, founded in 1812 by Samuel C., the famous pianist and composer, Jean Baptist Cramer, and F. T. Latour. Cramer retired from the business in 1819, Latour in 1826. After the death of Samuel C. (1834), his son, William, became principal (b. Nov. 20, 1809, d. Aug. 20, 1888, London). He started the "Musical Antiquarian Society" (1840), for which he published Dowland's songs and a collection of old English airs which, from 1855–59, was enlarged to "Popular Music of the Olden Time" (2 vols.); he also left behind a "History of Music" (incomplete). A younger brother, Thomas C., founded the Monday and Saturday Popular Concerts, which, under the direction of the youngest brother, Arthur C., have become an important factor in London musical life.

Character of Keys. The variety in the character of keys is no vain fancy, but it does not, as one might feel inclined to believe, and as has been asserted by some writers—depend upon unequally tempered sounds (viz., the idea of c major with perfectly just intonation); the effect is an esthetic one, and proceeds, for the most part, from the manner in which our musical system has been built up. This is based on the musical scale of the seven fundamental sounds A–G, and the two keys of c major and A minor, in which prominent use is made of them, appear plain, simple, because they can be presented in the simplest manner. The deviations on the upper-tone side (♯ keys) appear more intense, clearer, more brilliant; those on the under-tone side (♭ keys) relaxing, more sombre, more veiled : the former effect is of a major, the latter of a minor, kind. Then, in addition, there is the difference of the esthetic effect of major and minor keys themselves, which is based on the difference of their consonant element (see CLANG) : major sounds clear, minor sombre. Major keys with sharps have therefore potential brilliancy, and minor keys with flats potential sombreness; the chiaro-oscuro of major keys with flats, and the pale light of minor keys with sharps, offer characteristic mixtures of both effects, which vary in intensity according to the number of sharps or flats. Absolute pitch, as it appears, has the least share in the character of keys.

Charakterstücke (Ger.), characteristic pieces; pieces descriptive of moods, impressions, and events.

Charpentier, M a r c A n t o i n e, b. 1634, Paris, d. March, 1702 ; went at fifteen years of age to Italy to train himself as a painter, but was so drawn to music by Carissimi's compositions that he devoted himself entirely to it, and studied under Carissimi at Rome. After his return, he was appointed maître de chapelle to the dauphin, but through Lully's intrigues he lost his post; hence his aversion to Lully, which went so far that, as an opera composer, he shunned the style of the former, although by so doing he spoilt his own success. He next became maître de chapelle and music teacher to Mademoiselle de Guise, then intendant of the Duke of Orleans, then maître de chapelle to the monastery church and to the religious house of the Jesuits, and finally occupied a similar position at the Sainte-Chapelle. Charpentier was Lully's superior in training and in knowledge, but lacked his genius. Besides fifteen operas, he wrote some *tragédies spirituelles* for the Jesuit monastery, as well as some pastorales, drinking songs, and sacred music (masses, motets, etc.).

Chauvet, C h a r l e s A l e x i s, a prominent organist, who unfortunately died young, b. June 7, 1837, Marnes (Seine-et-Oise), d. Jan. 28, 1871, Argentan (Orne) ; in 1850 he entered the Paris Conservatoire as organ pupil of Benoist and composition pupil of Ambroise Thomas, and in 1860 was awarded the first prize in the organ class. He then became organist of some of the smaller Paris churches, but in 1869 of the newly-built large Eglise de la Ste.-Trinité. A chest affection put an early end to his fame.

A series of excellent organ compositions of his were printed.

Chavenne, I r e n e v o n, famous stage singer (alto), b. about 1867, Gratz ; 1882–85 pupil of Joh. Resz, at the Vienna Conservatorium, since 1885 at the Dresden Court Opera.

Check (Ger. *Fänger*), a cross of silk thread, in old pianofortes, which caught the hammer rebounding from the string, and prevented it from striking against the hard wood and bounding upwards again. A ledge covered with cloth now takes the place of the above C.

Chef d'attaque (Fr.), he or she who leads the singers of a chorus part—the sopranos, altos, tenors, or basses. This term is also applied to orchestral leaders.

Chef d'orchestre (Fr.), the conductor of an orchestra.

Chelard, H i p p o l y t e A n d r é Jean Baptiste, b. Feb, 1, 1789, Paris, where his father was clarinet player at the Grand Opéra, d. Feb. 12, 1861, Weimar ; pupil of Fétis, then only sixteen years of age, at the Hix Pension. In 1803 he was admitted to the Conservatoire, where Dourlen and Gossec became his teachers. In 1811 he obtained the *Prix de Rome*, studied the Palestrina style under Baini, under Zingarelli the accompanied church style, and, for a time, opera composition under Paisiello at Naples. In 1815 his first opera was performed at Naples (*La Casa a Vendere*). In 1816 he returned to Paris and entered the Opéra orchestra as violinist. Not until 1827 was he able to bring out an opera, *Macbeth* (libretto by Rouget de l'Isle), but this effort met with such small encouragement that he went to Germany, and in 1828 this opera, thoroughly revised, was performed at Munich with brilliant success, whereupon he was engaged as court capellmeister. In 1829, however, he returned to Paris, came to grief with *La Table et le Logement*, and founded a music warehouse, which the revolution of 1830 ruined. He thereupon returned to Munich, and with new operas (*Der Student, Mitternacht*) and a mass gained renewed success. From 1832–33 he was conductor of the German Opera in London ; but the undertaking proved a failure, and he once more returned to Munich, where in 1835 he brought out his best work, *Die Hermannsschlacht*. In 1836 he was appointed court capellmeister at Weimar, and brought out there his comic operas, *Der Scheibentoni* (1842) and *Der Seekadett* (1844). He remained here, when Liszt had been drawn to Weimar in a similar capacity, up to about 1850. From 1852–54 he again lived in Paris. He left behind an opera, *L'Aquila Romana*, which was performed at Milan in 1864.

Chelleri, F o r t u n a t o, b. 1686, Parma, d. 1757, Cassel, of German descent (Keller), was trained by his uncle, Fr. Mar. Bassani, maestro di cappella of Piacenza Cathedral ; he wrote with good success from 1707 (*Griselda*) to 1722 (*Zenobia e Radamisto*) sixteen operas for the stages of North Italy, especially for Venice. In 1725 he went to Cassel as court capellmeister, but on the death of Carl I. was attracted to Stockholm by Friedrich I., who was at the same time King of Sweden; he was not, however able to stand the climate, and so returned to Cassel. He does not appear to have written any operas after leaving Italy; but in 1726 he published in London a volume of cantatas and arias, and in 1729, at Cassel, a volume of sonatas and fugues for organ and clavier. He also wrote masses, psalms, oratorios, and chamber pieces.

Cheri, Victor (Cizos, called C.), b. March 14, 1830, Auxerre, d., by his own hand, Nov. 11, 1882, Paris. He was a pupil of the Paris Conservatoire, was an excellent conductor, first at the Théâtre des Variétés, then at the Châtelet, and for some years at the Gymnase; composed charming ballet-music and a comic opera, *Une Aventure sous la Ligue* (Bordeaux, 1857).

Cherubini, Maria Luigi Zenobio Carlo Salvatore, b. (according to Choron) the 8th (but according to his own statement) 14th Sept., 1760, Florence, d. March 15th, 1842, Paris. His father, who was accompanist at the Pergola theatre, was his first teacher, then Bartolomeo Felici and A. Felici, and after their deaths, Bizarri and Castrucci. In 1778 the Grand Duke, afterwards the Emperor Leopold II., sent him to Sarti, at Bologna, under whom he studied the Palestrina style for a few years; without doubt C. had to thank Sarti for his perfect mastery of the polyphonic style. Until 1779 he only wrote church music (for Florence); but in 1780 he entered the domain of opera with *Quinto Fabio* (produced at Alexandria). There soon followed *Armida* (Florence, 1782); *Adriano in Siria*, *Il Messenzio*, *Lo Sposo di tre* (Venice, 1783), *Idalide*, *Alessandro nell' Indie* (Mantua, 1784). In the last-named year he was attracted to London, where he wrote *La Finta Principessa* and *Giulio Sabino*, and received the appointment of royal court composer. His reputation was already made; and also in Paris, where he first went in 1787, his talents received full recognition. In the winter of 1787–88 he wrote, at Brescia, *Didone Abbandonata*, and at Turin *Ifigenia in Aulide*. In the year 1788 he settled down in Paris. The opposition between the Gluckists and the Piccinists was well calculated to lead a man of Cherubini's gifts to earnest thought. Up to this time he had written his operas in the light Italian style, but from the time of his removal to Paris he became a new man. It would be misleading to say that he followed Gluck; he searched deeply among the stores of his knowledge, and thus gave depth to his musical ideas. His works, therefore, appeared to the Gluckists, as well as to the Piccinists, as something new. His first Paris

creations were, *Démophon* (1788), *Lodoïska* (1791), *Éliza* (1794), *Il Perruchiere* (1796), *Médée* (1797), *L'Hôtellerie Portugaise* (1798), *La Punition* (1799), *Emma* (*La Prisonnière*, 1799), *Les Deux Journées* (1800), *Épicure* (1800), *Anacréon* (1803), and the ballet, *Achille à Scyros* (1804). All these works, with the exception of *Démophon* (which was written for the Grand Opéra, but produced no effect), were brought out at the Théâtre de la Foire St. Germain; C. himself conducted, 1789–92, at this little theatre founded by Léonard, Marie Antoinette's hairdresser. In 1795, at the organisation of the Conservatoire, he was named one of the inspectors of the institution. Other marks of recognition were denied, and the doors of the Grand Opéra remained closed to him because Bonaparte, who was rising higher and higher, disliked Cherubini. C. was no flatterer, and had found fault with the general's musical judgment; this the emperor had never forgotten. In 1805 Cherubini was commissioned to write an opera for Vienna, which was all the pleasanter to him as his income in Paris had been very meagre. He therefore went to Vienna, and after *Lodoïska* had been put on the stage, *Faniska* followed in Feb., 1806 (Kärntnerthor-Theater); Haydn and Beethoven were full of enthusiasm for this work. The events of 1806 led him to Vienna at the same time as Bonaparte, who commanded him to take the conductorship of his court concerts at Schönbrunn, but C. still remained in disfavour. On his return to Paris with *Pigmalion* he made his last attempt to win the emperor's favour, but again to no purpose. Disheartened, he then gave himself up for a length of time to inactivity. From 1806–1808 he wrote next to nothing; he drew pictures and studied botany. A chance circumstance turned him to other thoughts: at Chimay a church was to be consecrated, and C., who had been staying for some time at the castle of the Prince de Chimay for his health, was invited to write a mass for the occasion. The noble mass in F was the result; C. therein displayed his pure and perfect mastery over the severe style, and with it returned to a path which he had abandoned eighteen years previously. For the rest, he did not as yet quite give up writing for the stage; there still followed *Crescendo* (1810), *Les Abencerrages* (1813, at the Grand Opéra, but an entire failure), two occasional works in collaboration with other opera composers; *Bayard à Mezières* (1814) and *Blanche de Provence* (1821), finally his last important work, *Ali Baba* (1833), worked up from *Koukourgi*, an early opera, which had remained in manuscript. The success, however, of his mass at home and abroad, strengthened his determination to concentrate his energies more in other directions. In 1815 he spent some months in London, and wrote for the Philharmonic Society a symphony, an overture, and a four-part hymn to Spring, with orchestra. The suppression of the Conservatoire at the beginning of the Restoration deprived him of his post of inspector; but in 1816 he became professor of composition, and was named royal superintendent of music, and from that time diligently wrote masses and motets for the royal chapel. In 1821 he was appointed director of the Conservatoire, and quickly restored that somewhat declining institution to its former splendour. A year before his death he had withdrawn from all his appointments. A catalogue of Cherubini's works, drawn up by himself, was published in 1843 by Bottée de Toulmon; in it are mentioned eleven grand masses (five printed), two requiems, many fragments of masses (a part of them printed), one credo (à 8) with organ, two Dixits; one magnificat, miserere, Te deum, each with orchestra; four litanies, two Lamentations, one oratorio, thirty-eight motets, graduals, hymns, etc., with orchestra; twenty antiphons, fifteen Italian and fourteen French operas; many arias, duets, etc., introduced into Italian and French operas; one ballet, seventeen grand cantatas and other occasional compositions with orchestra, seventy-seven romances, Italian songs, nocturnes, etc.; eight hymns and republican songs with orchestra, many canons, solfeggi, etc.; one overture and one symphony, several marches, country dances, etc.; six quartets for strings, one quintet, six pf. sonatas, one sonata for two organs, one grand fantasia for piano, etc. His life was written (anonymously, in German) 1809, by Loménie (under pseudonym "Homme de Rien"), 1841; Miel, 1842; Place, 1842; Picchianti (Italian, 1844); Rochette, 1843; Gamucci (Italian, 1869); Bellasis (English, 1876). In 1869 a memorial was erected to him at Florence. The well-known "Theory of Counterpoint and Fugue" was not written by C., but by his pupil Halévy (q.v.).

Chest of Viols, a set of viols. A good chest of viols consisted of two trebles, two tenors, and two basses.

Chest Voice. (*See* REGISTER (2), and FALSETTO.)

Chevalet (Fr.), bridge (of stringed instruments).

Chevé, Émile Joseph Maurice, b. 1804, Douarnenez (Finistère), d. Aug. 26, 1864; originally a physician, married Nanine Paris (d. June 28, 1868), and published, in collaboration with her, a series of articles on P. Galin's method of notation and of teaching music (Méloplast). He also founded a music school, in which he employed this method, and tried repeatedly, but in vain, to provoke the Conservatoire into a discussion of methods.

Chiara, f. (Ital), clear, pure.

Chiaramente (Ital.), clearly, distinctly.

Chiarezza (Ital.), brightness, clearness.

Chiarina (Ital.), a species of trumpet, a clarion.

Chiaro, m. (Ital.), clear, pure.

Chiaromonte, Francesco, b. July 20, 1809, Castrogiovanni (Sicily), d. Oct. 15, 1886, Brussels, choir singer at Palermo, pupil of Donizetti at Naples, composed operas and church music; he was afterwards professor of singing at the Conservatorio there, but was compromised in the disturbances of 1848 and imprisoned for two years; and in 1850, while his new opera, *Caterina di Cleves,* was being performed with success, he was banished. He first went to Genoa, where he brought out operas with diminishing success; then to Paris, as *répétiteur* at the Théâtre Italien. He came afterwards to London, as chorus director at the Italian Opera, and finally settled in Brussels as teacher of singing, receiving in 1871 an appointment at the Conservatoire. Here he brought out important sacred compositions, also a *Méthode de Chant.* At Brussels, in 1884, his Biblical opera, *Job,* was performed at the Conservatoire.

Chiave (Ital.), (1) clef; (2) key of an instrument; (3) tuning-key.

Chiavette (*Chiavi trasportate*) was the name given at a later period to the transposing clefs used in the 16th century. Instead of the usual clefs—

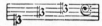

either those raising the sound-meaning of the lineal system by a third (high Ch.)—

or those lowering the same by a third (low Ch.)—

were employed. By these the composer intended the composition to be performed so much higher or so much lower. Or, expressed in modern language, the high Ch. stood for the ordinary clefs, only with three flats or four sharps (E♭ or E major, instead of C major; C minor or C♯ minor, instead of A minor; the low Ch. (rare) stood for the ordinary clefs with three sharps or four flats (A major or A♭ major, instead of C major; or F♯ minor or F minor instead of A minor). Thus the music was sung at about the pitch which the notation would have had if the ordinary clefs had been given in place of the Ch.,

i.e., and as

but the Ch. governed the shifting of the relations of the tone and semitone to the key into which transposition was made, just as the key-signature does now. As, besides, *real transposition* to the lower fifth (by the signature of the ♭ before *b*) was in general use, and the ♭ could be employed with both kinds of Ch., it was possible, notwithstanding appearances to the contrary, to sing in pretty well any key, and to indicate the transposition by means of clef and ♭. For the simple discant-clef, without ♭ answered to our c major, with ♭ = F major, high Ch., without ♭ = E major (E♭ major), with ♭ = A major (A♭ major), low Ch. without ♭ = A major (A♭ major), with ♭ = D major (D♭ major). The theory of the Ch. however simple it may thus appear, was in reality highly complicated, because the choice of another clef, other than the usual one, did not always indicate the Ch., but was frequently used when the compass of the vocal part would necessitate ledger lines. The g-clef

also was frequently used in the highest part to indicate a transposition to the upper fifth answering to the transposition to the lower fifth with the ♭ signature. Then f♯ instead of f would be self-evident, and a ♭ would have to be placed before F, if the violin clef were only chosen for the sake of avoiding ledger lines.

Chica, a Spanish dance much in favour with the descendants of the Spanish settlers in South America.

Chickering & Sons, celebrated pianoforte manufacturers at Boston and New York, founded in 1823 by Jonas C. (b. 1800, d. 1853, Boston), a rival of Steinway's, of New York, in the magnificence of the tone of their instruments. In 1867 the firm added to its fame by gaining the first prize at the Paris Exhibition, the head of the firm being named *Chevalier de la légion d'honneur;* he died in 1891.

Chiesa (Ital.), church. *Concerto da chiesa,* a sacred concerto.

Chiffré (Fr.), figured. *Basse chiffrée,* figured bass.

Chifonie (*Cyfonie*), a corrupt Old French form of *Symphonia,* name for the *Hurdy-Gurdy* (q.v.), to be met with even in the 15th century.

Child, William, noted organist, Mus. Doc. (Oxford), b. 1606, Bristol, d. March 23, 1697, Windsor; organist and chanter of the Chapel Royal, as well as royal private musician; he published psalms (1639; 3rd ed., 1656); and single anthems, catches, etc., of his composition are to be found in collections (Hilton, Playford, Boyce, Arnold, Smith).

Chipp, Edmund Thomas, b. Dec. 25, 1823, London, d. Dec. 17, 1886, Nice, celebrated organist; from 1866 organist at Edinburgh, and from 1867 of Ely Cathedral; he composed an oratorio, *Job,* a Biblical idyll, *Naomi;* published a book of organ pieces and other smaller compositions.

Chiroplast (Gr., "hand-former"), an apparatus first invented at London by J. Bernhard Logier, and patented in 1814; it prevented the

wrist from falling, and the fingers from striking in any but a vertical direction. The C. made much sensation, was imitated by Stöpel, and simplified by Kalkbrenner under the name of the "Bohrer Hand-guide." It has been improved and revived in recent times, but, whatever the form in which it has been presented, quickly laid aside; for a pupil, once the mechanical help withdrawn, will always fall back into the old faults. The best C. is a good teacher. An invention of more value is Seeber's finger-former, which only forces the nail-member to draw in, *i.e.* prevents a bending backwards of the end joint at the moment of striking; for the rest the whole hand has complete freedom, as only a separate and small pressure is put upon each finger. The advantage of this apparatus consists in this, that the faulty bending backwards of the separate fingers can be removed by employing separate restraints. As the joint is not thereby rendered completely inactive, a strengthening of the same, by practising with the restraining apparatus, is the wholesome result.

Chitarra. (*See* GUITAR and ZITHER.)

Chitarrone (Ital., " Great Chitarra," "Bass Chitarra"), one of the large bass instruments of the lute kind of the 17th and 18th centuries. It was used for the general bass. It was a kind of large guitar with steel strings struck with a plectrum. (*Cf.* THEORBO.)

Chiuso (Ital.), close. *Canone chiuso* (q.v.).

Chladni, Ernst Florens Friedrich, b. Nov. 30, 1756, Wittenberg, d. April 3, 1827 Breslau; studied jurisprudence in his native town and at Leipzig. He graduated in 1780, and taught at Wittenberg; and after the death of his father (professor of law), turned to the study of physical science, to which, as an amateur, he had already diligently applied himself. To his unwearying investigations science owes great and important discoveries, above all, in acoustics. He turned his attention specially to the vibrations of glass plates; the *sound-figures, i.e.* the peculiar, regular, star-shaped forms into which sand scattered on a plate shapes itself when a bow is drawn along the edge of the plate, still bear his name. Amongst his discoveries are also the *Euphon* (glass-rod harmonica) and the *Clavicylinder* (glass-rod keyboard). C. travelled a great deal, introducing his inventions and giving scientific lectures. His most important writings on acoustics are " Die Akustik " (1802; French ed. 1809); " Neue Beiträge zur Akustik " (1817); " Beiträge zur praktischen Akustik " (1821); " Kurze Übersicht der Schall- und Klanglehre " (1827), besides the smaller works which appeared earlier: " Entdeckungen über die Theorie des Klanges " (1787), and " Ueber die Longitudinalschwingungen der Saiten und Stäbe " (1796); also articles in periodicals; in Reichardt's *Musikalische Monatsschrift* (1792), in the *Neue Schriften der*

Berliner Naturforscher (1797), Voigt's *Magasin*, etc.; Guilbert's *Annalen* (1800), and in the Leipzig *Allgemeine Musikalische Zeitung* (1800 to 1801).

Chœur (Fr.), choir, chorus.

Choir, that part of the church in which the singers are placed, generally in front of the organ, opposite the altar.

Choir Organ was originally the name given to the small organ with stops of small tone, used to accompany the vocal choir. In modern three-manual organs, the so-called third manual.

Chopin, Frédéric François, highly celebrated, epoch-making pianist, and a delicate and original composer, especially for the pianoforte; b. Feb. 22, 1810, Zelazowa Wola, near Warsaw, d. Oct. 17, 1849, Paris. He was the son of an emigrant Frenchman (Nicolas C., from Nancy, at first private tutor, afterwards teacher at the Warsaw Lyceum); his mother was a Pole, Justine Kryzanowska. Already at the age of nine C. played in public, and excited wonder. His teachers were a Bohemian, Zwyny by name, and Joseph Elsner, director of the Warsaw music school. In 1830 he left his native town as a perfect piano virtuoso, and went to Paris, giving concerts on the way at Vienna and Munich. He appeared like a meteor in the heavens, sending out luminous splendour, but only for a brief time. He came fully equipped to Paris, and had already a great number of compositions in his portfolio, and amongst them his two pianoforte concertos. His first publication, variations on a theme from *Don Juan* (Op. 2), inspired Schumann with great enthusiasm, and it was a true *fête* day when C. arrived in Leipzig. In Paris he soon found a most delightful circle of friends— Liszt, Berlioz, Heine, Balzac, Ernst, Meyerbeer —men who understood him, and in whom he himself found something more than insipid admirers. After having introduced himself both as pianist and composer, Chopin soon became much sought after as a teacher, and in the best circles. Unfortunately, dark shadows soon began to steal over his sensitive, though not naturally melancholy soul. Symptoms of a dangerous chest affection set in, and in 1838 he went by way of cure to Majorca. George Sand, the novelist, whom he enthusiastically honoured, accompanied and nursed him, but during the last years of his life left him in the lurch. The malady was not to be removed, but made startling progress. Early in 1849 there appeared to be a slight improvement, and he carried out a long-cherished wish when he visited England and gave several concerts; careless of the state of his health, he went into society, also visited Scotland, and returned quite worn-out to Paris. He died in the autumn of the same year. At his funeral, in accordance with his expressed desire, Mozart's Requiem was performed; his grave lies between those of Cherubini and Bellini. C. was of a rare, poetic nature; as Heine in words, so did he compose, in full, free tones, untrammelled by tradition and recognised forms. But not only in the main, but also in detail was he entirely new and original; he was the founder of something unknown up to that time, a perfectly new *genre*, a new pianoforte style, which Liszt took up and propagated, but without really developing it further; of that it is not capable, however little C. may have done in that direction after his twentieth or twenty-second year. Schumann copied him once or twice in small pieces; the anecdote is also known how Liszt imitated his mode of improvisation so as completely to deceive even his friends—also in imitations, Chopin can be recognised; but, for all that, they remain imitations. Chopin's music is not of a stereotype kind; he is not limited to a few original turns and graces; on the contrary, it is just in the very wealth of such that the key to this mystery of his nature is to be sought. His works, exclusively pianoforte works, or works with pianoforte, are : two concertos (E minor, Op. 11; F minor, Op. 21); Krakoviak, Op. 14 (with orchestra); "Don Juan" Fantasia, Op. 2 (with orchestra); E♭ Polonaise, Op. 22 (with orchestra); Fantasia on Polish Airs (with orchestra); Duo Concertante, for pf. and 'cello (themes from *Robert le Diable*); Introduction et Polonaise, for pf. and 'cello, Op. 3; a pf. and 'cello sonata, Op. 65; a trio (G minor, Op. 8); a rondo (c, Op. 73) for two pianofortes. Further, for pf. solo, three sonatas (c minor, B♭ minor, B minor), four ballades, one fantasia, twelve polonaises, a polonaise-fantasie (Op. 61), fifty-six mazurkas, twenty-five preludes, nineteen nocturnes, fifteen waltzes, four impromptus, three écossaises, bolero, tarantella, barcarolle, berceuse, three rondos, four scherzi, three sets of variations, one funeral march, concert allegro, twenty-seven concert études, and seventeen Polish songs; in all seventy-four works with Op. number and twelve works without Op. number. His life has been described in an imaginative way by Liszt (2nd ed. of the original French, 1879; in German by La Mara, 1880), and with critical conscientiousness by Karasowski (2nd ed. 1878). Two volumes also, by Frederick Niecks, entitled "Frederick Chopin as a Man and Musician," were published in 1888 (Ger. ed. 1889). In 1880 a tablet to his memory was erected in the Church of the Holy Trinity at Warsaw.

Choragus (Lat.), the leader of the ancient dramatic chorus.

Choralbearbeitung (Ger., "working up of chorales"), the contrapuntal treatment of the chorale, either as a simple composition in four or more parts, *note against note*, or with rhythmical ornamentation in several, or in all parts, with the chorale as *Cantus firmus* (" figurierter Choral "); or with canonic developments, whether of the chorale melody itself, or of the free parts (Chorale Canon), or lastly in the form of a fugue (chorale fugue, fugued chorale), which likewise can appear in two different forms, viz., as fugue over a chorale as chorale fugue, or as a fugal working of the chorale theme itself. All forms of the C. are found both for voices and instruments. The fugued C. with *Cantus firmus* is suitable as an organ accompaniment for congregational singing, but was more frequently employed as a chorale prelude. The greatest master in C. was John Sebastian Bach.

Choralbuch (Ger.), chorale book; a collection of chorales arranged, for the most part, in plain four-part harmony, or only melody with figured bass, for the use of organists in accompanying the singing of the congregation in the Protestant Church. The name C. first appears before 1692, but J. Walther's "Geystlich Gesangk-Buchleyn" (1524) must be regarded as a C. Until after the middle of the 18th century the hymn-book served as a C., for it contained the melodies with figured bass. The most comprehensive C. of the 18th century was the "Harmonische Liederschatz" of Joh. Balthazar König (1st ed. 1738; 2nd ed. 1776: 2,000 chorales for 9,000 hymns). Of importance are also the chorale books of Doles (1785), J. Chr. Kühnau (1786), J. Ad. Hiller (1793), G. Umbreit (1811), Schicht (1819), F. Chr. H. Rinck (1829), F. Becker (1844), Eck (1863), Kade (1869), Jakob and Richter (1873), and I. Faisst (1876).

Chorale (Ger. *Choral*), (1) the plain song (*Cantus choralis, Cantus planus*) of the Catholic Church which sprang from the so-called *Gregorian song* (q.v.) of the early Christian centuries. G r e g o r y t h e G r e a t certainly only flourished about 600, but the songs which bear his name were of earlier date, and not essentially different from *Ambrosian song* (q.v.). There was the chorale song (*Concentus*), which differed from the reciting *Accentus* of an officiating priest. The chorale song has no rhythm. As used to-day, in spite of renewed attempts at reform, it consists of a series of sounds of equal length of a wearisome monotony, which only dogmatic credulity can deny. This, however, came about in the course of time, especially from the period when counterpoint flourished. Formerly it was full of life, and most like to the shouting, jubilant exclamations of the Hallelujah- and Psalm-singing. The never-ending extensions of syllables consisted formerly of ornaments and *colorature* beyond the powers of German and French singers. Unfortunately, the key to the rhythmic system of the old notation (neumes) has been lost, and there appears no hope of a complete restoration of chorale song in its original form. When music in several parts came into existence, together with the chorale song, called *Cantus firmus* or *Tenor*, which remained unchanged, was associated a part (*Organum*), moving in parallel octaves or fifths (fourths), which later on proceeded, according to

rule, by contrary motion (*Discantus*); this soon, however, acquired greater freedom, and formed an ornamental melody above the C. So gradually it became the custom to treat the C. as a rigid skeleton, which the contrapuntist clothed with parts alive with flesh and blood. The greatest portion of the rich musical literature of the 12th to the 16th century is built on *Cantus planus;* and still to-day church composers frequently base their works on chorale motives. (*Cf.* CHURCH MUSIC.)

(2) The *Protestant* C. has a history quite similar to that of the *Catholic*. When it was a question of obtaining fresh songs for the young reformed church, and not such as recalled the stiffness of the Roman creed, Luther laid hold of the Volkslied and the popular songs in several parts—compositions which at that time enjoyed great prosperity ("Frische Liedlein," etc.), and boldly adopted them by setting to them sacred words. Many chorales—for example, "Ein' feste Burg"—were certainly composed expressly for the church, but in the same form, and, so far as the hymns were concerned, similar to the simple Strophenlied of two short stanzas (Stollen), and after-song (Abgesang). Also Catholic hymns of similar character were employed. All these chorales were pregnant with rhythm, but, like the Gregorian song, were stiffened into notes of equal length. All attempts to revive the rhythmical chorale have, as yet, failed. It appears that again here the contrapuntists are guilty of the destruction of the rhythm, and this time the German organists who, as formerly, were the chapel singers, were the chief representatives of musical composition. The circumstance also—that already in the course of the 16th century the congregation began to take part in the C., especially in churches which had no trained choir—may have had much to do with the shaping of the melody, so that it might be suitable for a congregation. In proportion as the melody grew slower and the rhythm disappeared, a more lively accompaniment became a matter of necessity, and the figuration of chorales (*see* CHORALBEARBEITUNG), already in the 17th century, was developed with great show of art. Concerning the origin of the Protestant C. and its development, *cf.* v. Winterfeld, " Der evangelische Kirchengesang " (1843-47, 3 vols.). Of Protestant Church composers who enriched the treasury of church songs (chorales) may be mentioned Johann Walther, Georg Rhau, Martin Agricola, Nikolaus Selneccer, Johann Eccard, Ehrhardt Bodenschatz, Melchior Franck, Heinrich Albert, Thomas Selle, Johann Rosenmüller, Johann Crüger, Georg Neumark, Andreas Hammerschmidt, Joh. Rud. Ahle, Joh. Herm. Schein, and Johann Sebastian Bach. (*Cf.* Tucher, " Schatz des evangelischen Kirchengesangs im ersten Jahrhundert der Reformation " (1848, 2 vols). The reformed church received chorale song much later than the Lutheran, and, first

of all, indeed, in Switzerland, where fifty psalms translated by Marot were provided with melodies by Wilhelm Franck (1545), which were arranged for four voices by Claude Goudimel (q.v.) in 1562; Bourgeois and Claudin Lejeune followed his example. In the course of the 16th century the English Church introduced chorale singing (psalms sung in unison).

Choraliter (Lat.), **Choralmässig** (Ger.), in the style of Plain-Song.

Choralnote (Ger.) is a term applied to the notation of Gregorian song (by which, not rhythm but only changes of pitch were expressed). All the notes of *Musica plana* (*Cantus planus*)—as, on account of the absence of rhythm, Gregorian song was afterwards named—are black, and are square shaped (■), and have hence been named *nota quadrata* or *quadriquarta*. The only exception is a note-shape which occurs in certain figures, such as ■♦ or ♦ ♦ ■. These signs have nothing in common with the values of Long, Breve, and Semibreve in mensurable music, notwithstanding the similarity of shape. The measured music which came into vogue in the 12th century, merely used the note signs of the C., and gave to them fixed rhythmical meaning; this is the reason why occasionally for the C. use was not made of the signs ■ and ♦, but merely of ■. The C. is really nothing more than *Neumæ* (q.v.) *placed on lines*, with the required pitch more sharply determined by the body of the note: ▮ is the old Virga (■), and ♦ the Point. The direct descent from neume notation is especially seen in the so-called *Figura obliqua* in compound figures—oblique strokes which indicate a note both in their beginning and end, for ex., ◖▚. Such figures were termed Ligatures (q.v.), and they were introduced into measured music.

Chord (Lat. *chorda*), the combination of several sounds of different pitch; and a special distinction is made between consonant and dissonant chords. (*Cf.* MAJOR CHORD, MINOR CHORD, and DISSONANCE.)

Chordæ essentiales (Lat.), the tonic, third, and fifth of any key.

Chordometer (Gr. "chord measurer"), a simple instrument for gauging the strength of strings. (*See* SET.)

Chord Passage, arpeggio, a chord in figuration, *i.e.* a quick passing through the sounds of a chord, as distinguished from scale passages proceeding by degrees.

Chords *proper to the scale* are such as consist only of notes which belong to the scale of the ruling key. (*Cf.* KEY.)

Choreographie (Gr. literally "dance writing"). The notation of dances by means of conventional signs for steps and evolutions. The

system was first employed by Arbeau (q.v.), who named it "Orchésographie." The term C. was introduced by Lefeuillet and Beauchamp.

Choriambus, a metrical foot consisting of two short syllables between two long ones: — ⌣ ⌣ —.

Chorley, Henry Fothergill, b. Dec. 15, 1808, Blackley Hurst (Lancashire), d. Feb. 16, 1872; was from 1830 to 1868 musical critic of the *Athenæum*, also dramatic poet, novelist, and author of libretti for English composers (Wallace, Bennett, Benedict, Sullivan, etc.). He was highly esteemed as a man of impartial, though somewhat one-sided judgment (he could not endure Schumann). His works which specially belong to musical literature are: "Music and Manners in France and North Germany" (1841, 3 vols.), "Modern German Music" (1854, 2 vols.), "Thirty Years' Musical Recollections" (1862, 2 vols.). After his death there appeared his interesting "Autobiography and Letters" (published by Hewlett, 1873, 2 vols.) and "National Music of the World" (1879).

Choron, Alexandre Étienne, b. Oct. 21, 1772, Caen, d. June 29, 1834, Paris; learned theorist: he studied languages, and afterwards mathematics. He was stirred up by Rameau's theory of music based on acoustic phenomena, and, though against his father's wish, diligently pursued his theoretical musical studies. Only at the age of twenty-five did he devote himself entirely to music: he studied the Italian and German theorists, and became "the most thoroughly trained theorist France ever possessed" (Fétis). A great number of publications of old practical and theoretical works, besides numerous works of his own, show the untiring industry of this man. In 1811 he became corresponding member of the Académie des Arts, and was entrusted by the ministry with the reorganisation and regulation of church choirs (*maîtrises*). He was also appointed conductor of religious and other festivals: it is true that his practical knowledge as such was not great, but he managed to get on. In 1816 he was appointed director of the Grand Opéra, and then brought about the reopening of the Conservatoire (closed in 1815) as "École Royale de chant et de déclamation." In 1817, dismissed without pension because he experimented too much with novelties, he founded the "Institution royale," also named the "Conservatoire de musique classique et religieuse," which acquired great fame, and existed until the Revolution of July. (*See* NIEDERMEYER.) Its fall was his deathblow. From among the great number of C.'s writings may be noted: "Dictionnaire historique" (with Fayolle, 1810–11, 2 vols.), "Principes d'accompagnement des écoles d'Italie," 1804; "Principes de composition des écoles d'Italie" (1808, 3 vols; 2nd ed., 1816, 6 vols.), "Méthode élémentaire de musique et de plain-chant" (1811), Francœur's "Traité général des voix et des instruments d'orchestre"

(revised and augmented, 1813), French translations from Albrechtsberger's " Gründliche Anweisung zur Komposition " and " Generalbassschule " (1814, 1815; new complete edition,
1830), and Azopardi's " Musico Prattico " (1816),
" Méthode concertante de musique à plusieurs
parties " (1817; on this method his Conservatoire was founded), " Méthode de plain-chant "
(1818), " Liber choralis tribus vocibus ad usum
collegii Sancti Ludovici " (1824), and finally, in
collaboration with Le Fage, " Manuel complet
de musique vocale et instrumentale, ou Encyclopédie musicale " (1836–38, 8 vols.).

Chor-Ton, also **Kapellton** (Ger.; choir-pitch).
C. was formerly the normal absolute pitch for
church choirs in opposition to that of instrumental music (chamber-tone). Both changed
repeatedly, and M. Praetorius is quite wrong
in naming the high pitch *chamber tone*, and the
low *choir tone*. Praetorius puts the latter at
424, and the *chamber tone* (which, however, was
the tuning of the church organs at that time)
at 567 (double vibrations). (*Cf.* Ellis's " History of Musical Pitch " (1880–81).

Chorus, Choir (Gr. *Choros*). (1) This was the
name given to the body of singers (12–15) in
the Greek tragedy of the classical period, and
to the body of 24 in comedy, which performed
dances in measured movement around the
Thymele (altar) on the portion of the stage
(orchestra) set apart for that purpose, and
which was led by the *choragos*, who struck his
shoes against the ground; the rhythmical song
accompanying the dance, likewise called C.,
was throughout in unison, and without instrumental accompaniment. The principal kinds
of choruses were the *entrance chorus* (Paro-
dos), *the singing while standing on the orchestra*
(Stasima), and the *departure chorus* (Aphodos).
The C. took no part in the action, but moved
around it generally, only passing reflections on
the resolutions of the actors.—(2) In quite a
general sense, a union of singers for artistic
purposes. The oldest choirs of the Christian
Church sang, like those of ancient times, in
unison, or, if boys' voices were used together
with men's voices, in the octave. From the
10th to the 12th century the various kinds of
voices (high and low voices both of men and
boys) were distinguished by the various parts
of the *Organum* (q.v.). Composers of measured
music at the close of the 12th century already
wrote Tripla and Quadrupla, *i.e.* pieces in
three and four independent parts. The introduction of female voices into choirs appears to
have come into vogue only in the 17th century;
for a long period the Catholic Church forbade
the singing of women in church (*mulier taceat
in ecclesia*). Concerning the different kinds of
voices, *cf.* SOPRANO, ALTO, TENOR, BASS. According to the combination, one speaks of a
male C., female C. (C. of boys' voices), or a
mixed C. A double choir (q.v.) consists, for
the most part, of two four-part choirs.

Chouquet, Adolphe Gustave, b. April 16,
1819, Havre, d. Jan. 30, 1886, Paris; lived from
1840 to 1860 as a teacher of music in America,
after that in Paris engaged in historical work.
In 1864 he received the *Prix Bordin* for a history of music from the 14th to the 18th century,
and in 1868 the same prize for a work on
dramatic music in France, which he published
in 1873, " Histoire de la musique dramatique
en France depuis ses origines jusqu'à nos
jours." From 1871 C. was keeper of the collection of instruments at the Conservatoire, and
in 1875 published a catalogue of the same. C.
also wrote the words of several cantatas, which
became well known (amongst others " Hymne de
la Paix," the prize cantata for the Exhibition of
1867).

Christiani, (1) Lise B., b. 1827, Paris, d. 1853,
Tobolsk, was in the forties a highly esteemed
'cellist; Mendelssohn wrote for her the well-
known Lied ohne Worte for 'cello.—(2)
Adolf Friedrich, pianist and teacher, b.
March 8, 1836, Cassel, d. Feb. 10, 1885, Elizabeth, near New York; went already in 1855 to
London as a teacher of music, afterwards to
America, and, after stays of longer or shorter
duration at Poughkeepsie, Pittsburg, and Cincinnati, settled down in New York in 1877.
During the last five years of his life he was
director of a music school at Elizabeth. C.
was the author of an interesting work (" The
Principles of Musical Expression in Pianoforte
Playing," New York, 1886; German ed., Leipzig, 1886, " Das Verständniss im Klavierspiel "),
but died before the book came out.

Christmann, (1) Franz Xavier, excellent
Austrian organ-builder, d. May 20, 1795, during
the construction of an organ at Rottenmann
(Styria). — (2) Joh. Friedrich, b. 1752,
Ludwigsburg, d. 1817, Heutingsheim; an evangelical minister; composer of church songs and
chamber-music; he published " Elementarbuch
der Tonkunst " (1782; 2nd part, 1790).

Chroma (Gr., " colour "), (1) same as *chromatic semitone*, *i.e.* the interval which a note of
the fundamental scale (note without an acci-
dental) forms with that same degree raised by
a ♯ or lowered by a ♭; likewise the interval
which a sharpened note forms with that same
degree doubly sharpened (by means of a ×), or
a flattened note with that same note doubly
flattened (by means of a ♭♭):

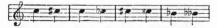

In the mathematical determination of intervals
(*cf.* TONE, DETERMINATION OF) a distinction is
made between a major and a minor C.; the
major C. (128 : 135) occurs between notes which
stand to each other in the relationship of the
triple step of a fifth and the step of a third, as
$f : f\sharp$ $(f–c–g–d–f\sharp)$; the small one (24 : 25)

between those which stand to each other in the relationship of the double step of a third and the step of a fifth in the opposite direction, as $g : g\sharp$ $(g\text{-}c\text{-}e\text{-}g\,\sharp)$, for example:

Major.   Minor.

By the enharmonic identification of d with $\underline{d}$ (by the mediation of the $\underline{a}$), the distinction has, in fact, no practical meaning; but the acoustical formulæ remain as the equivalents of different harmonic conceptions, which determine not the absolute sound but the connection. *Chromatic notes* in a chord are only such as can be conceived as raisings or lowerings of a note belonging to a clang (fundamental note, third, fifth of the major or minor chord), for example, $g\sharp$ as raised fifth of $c.e.g'$, $a\flat$ as lowered fundamental note of $a.c.e$, likewise also g in the chord of c *sharp major*, and a in the chord of D *flat major*, etc. (*See* ALTERED CHORDS.) For the chromatic mode of the Greeks *see* GREEK MUSIC ; for the chromatics of the 16th century *cf.* VICENTINO and GESUALDO.—(2) A society lately established, the aim of which is to reform our system of music, *i.e.* to set aside the fundamental scale (q.v.), and establish a division of the octave into twelve equal parts (*Zwölfhalbtonsystem*), so that, for example, on the keyboard, each black key should have its independent name, and not be derived from the lower key. (*Cf.* VINCENT (2), HAHN (2), SACHS (2), and JANKÓ.)

Chroma duplex (Lat.), a double sharp (×).

Chroma simplex (Lat.), a single sharp ($\sharp$).

Chromatic Instruments are such as have at command all the notes of the chromatic scale, *i.e.* which can produce all the twelve semitones within the octave of the tempered system. The term is used specially in connection with brass wind-instruments with valves (likewise, formerly, keys), and in contradistinction to *natural* instruments, which have only the series of overtones of the lowest note of the tube. (*Cf.* HORN, TRUMPET, CORNET.)

Chromatic Scales are those which run through the twelve semitones of equal temperament. The notation of a chromatic scale differs according to the key in which it occurs, and according to the harmony with which it is connected. If the diatonic scale is to be regarded as a major or minor chord with passing-notes (*cf.* SCALES), and if the choice of passing-notes—especially from the third to the fifth, and from the fifth to the octave—differs according to the key in which a chord occurs (*cf.* Riemann : " Neue Schule der Melodik," 1883), so must the C. S.—which, after all, is only a filling out of the diatonic scale by chromatic intermediate notes—be regarded from a similar point

of view. The rising C. S. has sharpened, the falling, flattened notes. So, for example, in c major, the D *minor* chord generally gives the diatonic scale :—d, e, f, g, a, b, c, d ; the D *major* chord in A—$d, e, \sharp f, \sharp g, a, b, \sharp c, d$; and the D *flat* major chord falling in G flat—$\flat d, \flat c, \flat b, \flat a, \flat g, f, \flat e, \flat d$. The chromatic scales in these three cases will appear thus :—

It is to be noticed that some old composers (Mozart), in the ascending chromatic scales, are fond of replacing the augmented second, fifth, and sixth by the enharmonic intervals of the minor third, sixth, and seventh, whereby the harmonic meaning is often deeply concealed.

Chronometer (Gr., " time-measurer "). (*See* METRONOME.)

Chronos protos (Gr., " the first time "), *i.e.* the smallest time-unit ; in ancient metre, the duration of the simple Short, which served as measurement for the long-syllable values. Thus, for example, the simple Long = two *chronoi protoi*. R. Westphal (" Allgem. Theorie der musikal. Rhythmik ") made an unfortunate attempt to show the existence of an indivisible *C. p.* in modern music.

Chrotta, one of the oldest, if not the oldest, of European stringed instruments, already mentioned by Venantius Fortunatus (609) in the verse " Romanusque Lyra plaudat tibi, Barbarus harpa, Græcus achilliaca, chrotta Britanna canit." It seems that the C. (*crwth, crowd, crowth*) was originally a British instrument, and that for a long period it preserved its peculiar shape only in Great Britain and in Brittany, whereas it was quickly transformed in France and Germany. From the instruments in use since the 9th century (Lyra, Rebeca, Rubeba, Viella) it is distinguished by the absence of a neck. The four-cornered sound-box is really prolonged in hoop-form, and at the top, in the centre, the string-pegs are fixed ; the strings (five) pass, partly over, partly near to a narrow finger-board (without frets), which extends from the hoop-end to the middle of the sound-box. It has also sound-holes and a bridge. The most ancient kind of C. had only three strings (no *Bourdons*). As soon as the hoop was done away with, and replaced by a solid continuation in the middle (under the finger-board), the instrument became a Vielle. This transformation appears to have taken place at an early date. The C. must not be confused with the

Rotta (q.v.). The C. in its ancient form existed among the natives of Ireland, Wales, and Bretagne still at the end of the former and the beginning of the present century. J. F. Wewerten wrote a comprehensive and learned treatise on the Chrotta and Rotta, " Zwei veraltete Musikinstrumente " (*Monatsh. für Mus. Geschichte*, 1881, Nos. 7–12).

Chrysander, Friedrich, b. July 8, 1826, Lübtheen (Mecklenburg), studied philosophy at Rostock and graduated there. After he had several times changed his place of residence, and lived for a long time in England, he settled permanently at Bergedorf, near Hamburg. C. is one of our most meritorious writers on music. His still unfinished biography of Handel (1858–67, extending to the first half of the third volume) is a work showing great industry, historical knowledge, and a warm admiration for the master ; but the most important period of Handel's life, that of his great oratorios, has still to be written. C. is one of the founders of the Handel Society, and superintends the monumental Handel edition, In 1863 and 1867 appeared, under C.'s name, two " Jahrbücher für musikalische Wissenschaft," with valuable contributions from different writers (among other things the " Locheimer Liederbuch " and Paumann's "Ars organisandi," edited by F. W. Arnold). From 1868–71, and again from 1875 until it ceased to exist (end of 1882), he edited the *Allgemeine Musikalische Zeitung*, in which have appeared numerous interesting articles from his pen, among others a sketch of the history of music-printing (1879), investigations with regard to the Hamburg opera under Keiser, Kusser, etc. (1878–79). Since the beginning of 1885, in conjunction with Spitta and C. Adler, he has edited a " Vierteljahrschrift für Musikwissenschaft." Two little pamphlets, " Über die Molltonart in Volksgesängen " and " Über das Oratorium," appeared in 1853. Finally, he has also published Bach's " Klavierwerke " (1856) and " Denkmäler der Tonkunst," oratorios by Carissimi, sonatas by Corelli (Joachim), pièces de clavecin by Couperin (Brahms).

Chrysanthos, von Madyton, Archbishop of Durazzo (Dyrrhachium), in Albania, formerly teacher of church singing at Constantinople ; one of those who of late years have simplified the liturgical notation of the Byzantine Church by the removal of many superfluous signs. His two works are, " Introduction to the Theory and Practice of Church Music " (" Isagoge," etc.), 1821, edited by Anastasios Thamyris, and " Great Theory of Music " (" Theoretikon mega," 1832).

Church Cantata (*Cantata da chiesa*) is the name given to the grand sacred cantata with soli, chorus, and orchestra, in contradistinction to the *chamber cantata*, with simple accompaniment and for few solo voices ; and also to the secular *festive cantata*, of similar plan, but different contents (for marriage and coronation festivals, birthdays, etc.). The form of the C. C. reached its highest point of development in J. S. Bach. (*Cf.* CANTATA.)

Church Modes are the various possible species of octaves of the musical alphabet (q.v.), which during the period of one-part (homophonic) music, and also during that in which counterpoint (polyphonic music) flourished, were regarded as special keys or modes, somewhat similar to our major and minor. The development of harmony, the recognition of the importance of consonant chords (triads), and their position in the key (tonic, dominant) caused the C. M. to be set aside, and led finally to the two modes, major and minor. The different species of octaves received the name of C. M. because the chants of the Gregorian Antiphonary (q.v.) were written so as to be within the compass (*ambitus*) of one of the same, without using any other chromatic notes except the semitone b♭, in addition to the whole tone, b, above the a of the middle position (small *a*). By that means a strict diatonic style was, so to speak, sanctioned by the church, when the Greek system of music, from which, after all, the C. M. were derived, had degenerated into chromatics and enharmonics. The oldest Western writers who make mention of C.M. (Flaccus Alcuin in the 8th century, Aurelianus Reomensis in the 9th) knew nothing of their connection with Greek music, and simply numbered them as modes 1–8, or as authentic 1–4, and plagal 1–4 (see below). On the other hand, in the old Byzantine writers on music (especially Bryennius, q.v.), traces are found of the transformation of the ancient system into that of the Middle Ages. The old Byzantine Church also distinguished four C.M. (ἤχοι), but arranged them from top to bottom, thus :—

    1st mode (*a*) $= g-g'$ (without chromatic signs).
    2nd mode (*β*) $= f-f'$,,   ,,
    3rd mode (*γ*) $= e-e'$,,   ,,
    4th mode (*δ*) $= d-d'$,,   ,,

The plagals of these principal C. M. lay, however, like the ancient hypo-keys, a fifth (not a fourth) lower than the authentic :—

    1st plagal $= c-c'$
    2nd plagal $= B-b$
    3rd plagal $= A-a$
    4th plagal $= G-g$.

The fourth plagal mode of that old Byzantine system was then based on the note, which the West from the time of Odo of Clugny designated by Gamma (Γ), and looked upon as an indispensable lowest note, notwithstanding the fact that the lowest Western plagal mode (see below), only reached to A (in ancient *Codices* before the Γ was used, the note was called *Quintus primo* [!]). The compiler of this dictionary, in his treatise " Die Μαρτυρ.αι der Byzantischen

Liturgischen Notation" (report of a sitting of the Munich Akademie d. Wiss., 1882, ii. 1), has shown that probably the old Byzantine system of C. M. was evolved from the mode system of the ancient Greeks, and, first of all, in entirely setting aside chromatic and enharmonic notes, and forming from the fundamental notes of the most essential transposition scales (the Dorian, Phrygian, Lydian, Mixolydian, Hypodorian, Hypophrygian, and Hypolydian) a fixed diatonic fundamental scale. The initial letters of the old names were probably used at first as memoranda (Μαρτυριαι) for the new designation of modes by means of the first letters of the Greek alphabet (said to have been introduced by St. Ambrosius), and still retained with the new Byzantine notation. In the West there appeared a new notation, first in the 10th century, so far as we know (and thus a long time after Ambrosius), which used the first letters of the Latin alphabet in a similar manner (*cf.* LETTER-NOTATION), viz. :—

A B C ♯ D E F G ♯ A, in the sense of our *c d e f g a b c'*. (♩ shows the semitone steps.) The older Byzantine notation was—

α β γ ♯ δ ε ξ ♩ η,

likewise with solfeggio syllables, πα βου γε δι κε ζω νη. In the West the pitch-meaning of the letters was afterwards lowered a third ; but in Byzantium the pitch rose one degree, so that the α was equal to our *d.*, *i.e.* the key-note of the first church mode of the later order formed from the Western mode. Bryennius has also handed down a nomenclature of the Byzantine church modes of the older order, together with the names of the ancient Greek modes ; in it the church mode answers, as the intervals show, to the ancient transposition scale on which it is based (*c–c'* Dorian, *d–d'* Phrygian, *e–e'* Lydian, *f–f'* Mixolydian, etc.). A similar, but less reasonable, shifting of the meaning of names took place also in the West (by [pseudo-] Notker and [pseudo-] Hucbald) through a misunderstanding of a passage in Ptolemy, and what he wrote about different positions of pitch was erroneously made to refer to the different species of octaves. The C.M. of the West are :—(1) The first church or authentic mode (*Authentus protus*) D E F G a ♮ c d (our *d e f g a b c' d'*), named the *Dorian* mode (*Dorius*) since the time of Hucbald.—(2) The second, or first plagal (*Plagius proti, plagis proti, plaga proti ; lateralis, subjugalis proti*), A B C D E F G a (= A B *c d e f g a*), the *Hypodorian* (*Hypodorius*).—(3) The third, or second authentic (*Authentus deuterus*), E F G a ♮ c d e (= *e f g a b c' d' e'*), the *Phrygian* (*Phrygius*).—(4) The fourth, or second plagal (*Plagius*, etc., *deuteri*), B C D E F G a ♮ (= B *c d e f g a b*), the *Hypophrygian* (*Hypophrygius*).—(5) The fifth, or third authentic (*Authentus tritus*), F G a ♮ c d e f (= *f g a b c' d' e' f'*), the *Lydian* (*Lydius*).—(6) The sixth, or third plagal (*Plagius triti*), C D E F G a ♮ c (= *c d e f g a b c'*), the *Hypo-*

lydian (*Hypolydius*).—(7) The seventh, or fourth authentic (*Authentus tetartus*), G a ♮ c' d' e' f' g' (= *g a b c' d' e' f' g'*), the *Mixolydian* (*Mixolydius*).—(8) The eighth, or fourth plagal (*Plagius tetarti*), D E F G a ♮ c d (= *d e f g a b c' d'*), the *Hypomixolydian* (*Hypomixolydius* since the 11th century). The plagal modes (2, 4, 6, 8) were merely shiftings of the authentic ; the principal note (*Finalis*) was not the limiting note of the octave, but occurred in the middle as fourth note. The *Final* of the first and second modes was therefore D, of the third and fourth E, of the fifth and sixth F, of the seventh and eighth G. The eighth and first are therefore by no means identical. Not one of the four authentic modes has C or A as Final ; hence the two modes (C) major and (A) minor, the only ones used in modern music, were wanting. In the 16th century, which first perceived the principles of harmony (*cf.* ZARLINO), and opened up the way to modern tonality, two new authentic modes with their plagals were added : the fifth authentic, *Ionian*, *c d e f g a b c'*, and the sixth authentic, *Æolian*, *a b c' d' e' f' g' a'* (also named *modos peregrinus*), and the plagal fifth, or *Hypoionian*, G A B c d e f g, and the plagal sixth, or *Hypoæolian*, *e f g a b c' d' e'*, so that then there existed twelve church modes (*cf.* GLAREAN, "Dodekachordon"). The seventh authentic mode, the Locrian (q.v.) was never of much importance. *Cf.* the following synopsis :—

Dorian mode.   Hypodorian mode.

Phrygian mode.   Hypophrygian mode.

Lydian mode.   Hypolydian mode.

Mixolydian mode.   Hypomixolydian mode.

Ionian mode.   Hypoiorian mode.

Æolian mode.   Hypoæolian mode.

Church Music, Cathedral Music (*Musica ecclesiastica, sacra, divina ;* Ital. *Musica da chiesa ;* Fr. *Musique d'église*). C. M. is nearly as old as the church itself. The oldest C. M. was only vocal music, yet already in the early middle ages instruments appear to have been introduced to reinforce the voices; but, according to the statement of the Abbot Engelbert of Admont (13th century), these, the organ excepted, were banished. In the course of the 16th century it again became general to strengthen, likewise partly to replace, the vocal parts; and, with the introduction of the continuo about 1600, the first step was taken towards regularly accompanied C. M. Instrumental music also, in the first place as solo organ-playing, was introduced into the church about the end of the 16th century, and probably for the first time at Venice, by Merulo and the two Gabrielis. The *Ritual music* of the Catholic Church is old—probably handed down in part from the Jews; possibly also certain pagan melodies may have been adapted to Christian words. *Antiphonal singing* also was developed in the Byzantine Church, and was transplanted into Italy by St. Ambrosius (d. 397); *Gradual singing* arose in Italy; *singing of hymns*, specially cultivated by Ambrosius, probably had its origin in pagan worship. Pope Gregory the Great (d. 604) established uniform Ritual music for the whole Western Church; this, under the name of *Gregorian song*, has remained up to the present day, and unchanged, so far as was possible with the imperfect neume notation—almost the only one used in the 12th century. Yet the melodies seem to have been preserved fairly intact, while the whole ancient art of rhythm has completely disappeared. From the jubilant exclamations of the time of Ambrosius and Augustine was gradually evolved up to the 12th century the psalmody void of rhythm in use at the present day. Gregorian song was entirely in one part; only from the 9th to the 10th century does singing in several parts (*Organum*)—though scarcely differing from that in one part—make its appearance. The principle of real polyphony only came to light in the 12th century, *i.e.* contrary movement (*Discantus*), and from that time was gradually developed complicated polyphonic writing, but always based on the Gregorian chant (*Cantus Firmus*).

The names of the oldest *forms* of church compositions (in the 13th century) in several parts are: *Organum, Discantus, Conductus, Copula, Ochetus, Motetus, Triplum* (three-part), *Quadruplum* (four-part). The following were distinguished masters at that early period: Leoninus, Perotinus, Robert of Sabilon, Petrus de Cruce, Johannes de Garlandia, the two Francos, Philipp of Vitry (14th century), Johannes de Muris, Marchettus of Padua, etc. Thus, already about the middle of the 15th century, we find *counterpoint* brought to a high state of perfection. Forms of importance, more or less independent of the Gregorian chant, were developed (Motet, Mass, Magnificat), and a long list of names of great importance indicates a long period in which an art, now fast passing away, flourished, but which finally degenerated into subtleties (Busnois, Dufay, Okeghem, Hobrecht, Josquin, de la Rue, Brumel, Clemens *non Papa*, Mouton, Fevin Pipelare, de Orto, Willaert, de Rore, Goudimel, Orlando Lasso, Paul Hofhaimer, Heinrich Isaac, Senfl, Hasler, Gallus, Morales). All these masters wove their parts together with art, and in obedience to the laws of strict imitation. In sharp contrast to this music laden with artifices, stood out the popular (four-part) *Lied*, from which was evolved the Protestant *Chorale*, and it was probably on this account that the Council of Trent resolved to banish polyphonic music from the church, unless a plainer, more suitable style of C. M. could be provided. Thus, by an impulse from without, arose the noble and simple Palestrina style, whose representatives, in addition to Palestrina, were the Naninis, Vittoria, and the two Anerios. (*Cf.* ROMAN SCHOOL.) In so far as the forms of accompanied C. M. (Church concerto, Cantata), directly evolved from the musical drama and oratorio which arose about the year 1600, were transplanted into their native country by Germans trained in Italy (Schütz), the Italians can be looked upon as participating in the grand development of Protestant C. M., which reached its zenith in the Cantatas and Passions of Bach. C. M., since his time, breathes a modern spirit: the display of instrumental means is more brilliant, the melodies are weaker, sentimental (operatic), the harmonies are more piquant; but in grandeur of the total effect and earnestness of conception they only rarely approach Bach. The most distinguished representatives of modern C. M. are Mozart (Requiem), Beethoven (*Missa Solemnis*), Fr. Liszt, and Fr. Kiel.

Chute (Fr.), obsolete *ornament* (q.v.), from which was evolved the long appoggiatura expressed by small notes. When the old French clavier masters wanted the C., they placed a little hook before the note, (♪ (d'Anglebert, 1689), or an oblique stroke, ♪, likewise ♪. The upper- and under-second took from the real note half its value.

Chwatal, (1) F r a n z X a v e r, b. June 19, 1808, Rumburg (Bohemia), d. June 24, 1879, Soolbad Elmen; went in 1822 as teacher of music to Merseburg, whence in 1835 he removed to Magdeburg; wrote much pianoforte music, especially *pièces de salon* and some instructive works, amongst others two Methods of the pianoforte, as well as quartets for male voices, etc. (2) J o s e p h, brother of the above, b. Jan. 12, 1811, Rumburg. He (with his son) is organ-builder at Merseburg, and has made many valuable small improvements in the mechanism of the organ.

Ciacona (Ital.). (*See* CHACONNE.)

Cifra, Antonio, b. 1575, Papal States, d. 1638, Loreto; pupil of Palestrina and Nanini; at first maestro at the German College at Rome, then at Loreto; in 1620 at the Lateran, 1622 in the service of the Archduke Carl of Austria, from 1629 again at Loreto. C. was one of the best composers of the Roman school, to which a goodly series of printed volumes which have been handed down bear witness (five books of masses, seven books of motets [à 2 et à 4] with organ accompaniment, motets and psalms[à 12], scherzi and Arie with cembalo or chitarrone, madrigals, ricercari, canzone, *concerti ecclesiastici*, etc., in publications from 1600–1638).

Cimarŏsa, Domenico, b. Dec. 17, 1749, Aversa, Naples, d. Jan. 11, 1801, Venice; was the son of a mason, and an orphan at an early age. He attended the school for poor children of the Minorites at Naples, and, when his musical talent showed itself, was taught by Pater Polcano, organist of the Minorite monastery. In 1761 he was placed in the Conservatorio Santa Maria di Loreto, where Manna, Sacchini, Fenaroli, and Piccini successively became his teachers. In 1772 he began his career as a dramatic composer with *Le Stravaganze del Conte* for the Teatro de' Florentini at Naples, and, although Paisiello was then at the height of his fame, C. was soon able to take rank beside him. With unexampled rapidity his works followed one another. In 1779 he wrote for Rome *L'Italiana in Londra*, and lived alternately in Naples or Rome according to the custom of the time of always writing an opera in the very place in which it was to be performed. In 1781 he wrote for each of the cities of Rome, Venice, Turin, and Vicenza a new opera, and thus he continued. In 1789 he was offered brilliant terms to go to Petersburg, where from 1776–85 Paisiello had supplied the Italian Opera with novelties. He travelled by way of Florence and Vienna, and was everywhere received with the greatest honour. But he was not able to bear for any length of time the Russian climate, and left in 1792 for Vienna, where they would willingly have kept him. He there wrote his most famous work, *Il Matrimonio Segreto*, the success of which not only surpassed that of all his previous operas, but was unexampled. C. had then already written seventy operas in less than twenty years. *Il Matrimonio Segreto* was also played at Naples in 1793, and repeated sixty-seven times. Other operas followed, of which the most noteworthy was *Astuzie Feminili* (1794). He took part in the Neapolitan insurrection, was arrested and sentenced to death, but was pardoned by King Ferdinand and set at liberty, and, with the intention of going to Russia, went to Venice; but was taken ill and died there, it was said, of poison. Public opinion blamed the Government, and it needed an official proclamation of the physician of Pius VII., who resided in Venice, to dissipate the rumour and to certify a natural death (abscess in the abdomen). Besides over eighty operas, C. composed several masses (two requiems), oratorios (*Judith* and *Triumph of Religion*), cantatas, and 105 detached vocal pieces for the court at Petersburg. C.'s *Il Matrimonio Segreto* still appears from time to time on the best stages. According to our present ideas, his music is simple, but fresh and full of humour. A splendid bust of C. by Canova, who was commissioned by Cardinal Consalvi, is to be seen in the Pantheon at Rome.

Cimbal, Cimbalon, Cinelli. (*See* CYMBAL and CYMBALUM.)

Circle. (*See* FIFTHS, CIRCLE OF.)

Circular Canon (Lat. *Canon perpetuus*), a canon without end, which, as it returns to its commencement, is frequently set out in circular form; it can be repeated at pleasure. If it is to have a coda it cannot be presented in circular form, but has a repetition sign with coda added. Canons set out in circular form have a pause marked over the end note.

Cistole, Cistre, Citole, Cither. (*See* ZITHER.)

Cizos. (*See* CHERI.)

Cl., abbreviation for *Clarinetto.*

Clairon, French name for the Buglehorn.

Clang, Sound is the name given to audible vibrations of elastic bodies, *i.e.* C. or S. is the scientific word for the lay term *tone.* In acoustics a distinction is made between sound and noise; by the latter is understood the impression produced on the ear by irregular, and by the former that produced by regular *vibrations.* Regular vibrations are those which follow one another at equal intervals of time, like those of the pendulum of a clock; and, as the rapidity of succession (period) of the separate vibrations determines the height of the sound heard, it follows that vibrations of like period produce sounds or clangs of constant *pitch.* Since it has been known that the sounds of our musical instruments are not simple tones, but compounded of a series of simple tones which can be distinguished by a most attentive listener (but commonly are not thus distinguished), the term S., in scientific works, has been replaced by the more general, comprehensive one, C., whilst sound is applied to the simple sounds as part of the C. The height of the C. is determined by the pitch of the lowest, and, as a rule, the strongest of its compound tones, which are also called *Partial tones, Aliquot tones, Scale of nature.* As all the other partial tones lie higher than the *ground tone, fundamental tone, principal tone,* which gives to the C. its name, they are usually called *overtones,* but, let it be understood, the second overtone is not the third tone of the series, but the second. In so far as the remaining tones above the ground tone usually escape notice, they are also called *secondary tones,* and so far as they stand in close (harmonic) relationship to the former, also *harmonic* tones (*sons harmoniques*). For example, for the tone *c* the series of the first sixteen partial tones is as follows :—

The tones written in minims are all component elements of the major chord of the ground tone (*c major* chord), and it cannot be doubted that the *consonance* of the *major chord* (major consonance) must be referred to the series of overtones, *i.e.* a major chord, whatever the arrangement of notes, must be regarded as a C., in which certain overtones (those answering to the notes of the chord independently produced) are reinforced. The following examples may make this clearer; the low note placed after the chord is the ground tone of the C., of which the chord must be regarded as the representative :—

The ground tone of the C. here indicated is indeed always present as a combination tone. The series of partial tones, however, is not only completed by the combination tones down to the ground tone of the C., but continues upwards through the series of upper tones of the chord tones. For this reason it is quite natural that far higher overtones than those which can be distinguished in any particular C. (note of an instrument) play an important *rôle* in musical hearing; for in modern harmony very high overtones are produced with unusual strength, to which still higher ones, the immediate overtones of the same, are added. The monophonic music of ancient times and of the early middle ages was necessarily forced to move within very narrow harmonic limits, since it was concerned only with the nearest overtones. The overtones indicated above by means of a * do not quite agree in pitch with the notes by which they are represented; if they are produced as independent notes in the chord they will no longer have the meaning of the series of overtones, but must be regarded rather as approximations, tones related in a minor sense (see further, below); this is the case with the overtones from the seventh, whose cardinal numbers are prime numbers. But those whose cardinal numbers are the result of multiplication (9 = 3 × 3, 15 = 3 × 5, 25 = 5 × 5, etc.) are

understood as overtones of overtones, in fact secondary overtones, *i.e.* as integral elements of the primary ones (the 9th as 3rd of the 3rd, the 15th as 5th of the 3rd, etc.). If these are represented in the chord, *i.e.* produced in equal strength with the primary ones, they give the effect of dissonance; the primary overtone of which they are the overtones itself appears as a C. ground tone, so that *two clangs are represented at the same time.* The simplest ratio (2 : 1), that of the octave, forms an exception; no power to which it may be raised ever yields a dissonance; and indeed all other intervals can be extended or contracted one or several octaves without changing their harmonic meaning. If we then strike out all octave tones from the series of overtones there remain as dissimilar elements of the major consonance of the *upper clang* only the ground tone (1), the twelfth (3), and seventeenth (5); the original form of the major chord is therefore not actually the triad in a narrow position. 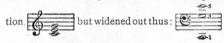 but widened out thus :

The cardinal numbers of the partial tones represent at the same time the *relative number of vibrations* of the intervals formed by them. For example, the vibration ratio of the fifteenth to the sixteenth overtone (leading-note ratio *b* : *c*) = 15 : 16. (*Cf.* INTERVAL.) It should not be forgotten that the pleasing effect of certain dissonances which of late have come much into vogue (Wagner) must be explained by their approximative agreement with higher overtones (for example, *c, e, b♭, f♯* = 4 : 5 : 7 : 11).

The *consonance of the minor chord* cannot be explained by the series of overtones, and all attempts, nevertheless, to do this (Helmholtz) must lead to results unsatisfactory to musicians. On the other hand, if looked at from a reverse point of view, the result desired will be obtained. Long before the discovery of overtones the major consonance was referred to the string division, 1—⅙, *i.e.* 1 is the string length of the ground tone, ½ that of the octave, ⅓ that of the 12th, and so on up to the 6th partial tone. The minor consonance, on the other hand, was referred to the inversion of the series, *i.e.* to the string lengths 1—6; 1 was the principal tone, 2 the under octave, 3 the under twelfth, etc. This conception of the minor consonance as the *opposite pole* of the major consonance is first to be found, so far as is known, in the thirtieth chapter of Zarlino's "Istitutioni armoniche" (1558). It has also been maintained with more or less consistency by Tartini, one of the most learned and intelligent theorists; and within recent years since M. Hauptmann (1853) by a number of young theorists (O. Kraushaar, O. Tiersch, O. Hoftinsky), and with great acuteness and consistency by A. v. Öttingen, and by the compiler of this dictionary. The minor consonance is related to a series of undertones in precisely the same way as the major consonance to the series of overtones: the phenomena in acoustics which justify the acceptation of this undertone series are those of *sympathetic* and *combination tones*. A sounding tone sets bodies capable of producing sound into sympathetic vibration, whose own tone answers to one of its undertones, or, which is the same thing, of whose ground tone it is an upper tone. In any case, bodies sounding by sympathetic vibration make, first of all, strong partial vibrations (with so many nodes that the causal tone is produced), but they also make total vibrations (weaker, and therefore more difficult to detect). The lowest combination tone of an interval is always the first undertone common to both intervals; for example, for *e′ g′*, c : for *c″, d″*, likewise c, and even for *e′ d″*, c, and so on. The series of the first sixteen undertones, taking *c‴* as starting tone (principal tone), is as follows :—

of the upper clang. They cannot, any more than the latter, be directly referred to the principal tone, but only through the mediation of primary partial tones, of which they, in their turn, are primary partial tones, *i.e.* represent the clangs of the same; and thus their introduction, together with primary undertones, into a chord, forms a dissonance resulting from the simultaneous presentation of two clangs. (*Cf.* CLANG SUCCESSION and DISSONANCE.)

Clang Colour (*Timbre*). The difference of C. C. in the tones of our musical instruments, according to the investigations of Helmholtz (" Lehre von den Tonempfindungen "), is mainly caused by the varied composition of the sounds or clangs. Many (such as those of bells, rods) have secondary tones other than those of stringed and wind instruments, which are employed for real musical purposes; but in these latter, the different kinds of intensity, likewise the absence of certain tones of the overtone series, bring about a similar change. The varied clang colours of the human voice depend partly on the formation of the vocal chords, partly on the resonant qualities of mouth and nasal cavities. The numerous vowel gradations also produce varieties of C. C. Professor v.

| 1 | 2 | 3 | 4 | 5 | 6 | 7 | 8 | 9 | 10 | 11 | 12 | 13 | 14 | 15 | 16 |

The ordinal figures of the undertones represent the relative string-lengths for the same; the ratios of vibration are expressed by the series of simple fractions, 1, ½, ⅓, etc., just as, with reversed meaning, the ratios of string-lengths for the tones of the overtone series are represented by the series of simple fractions. For instance, if *c* = 1, then the octave *c : c′* in an overtone series sense is expressed by 1 : 2 with regard to the relative number of vibrations; but by 1 : ½, with regard to length of string. On the other hand, in an undertone series sense (taking *c′* = 1), the vibration ratio is expressed by 1 : ½, but that of the string length by 1 : 2. The 1st, 2nd, 3rd, 4th, 5th, 6th, 8th, 10th, 12th, 16th, etc., in fact all tones of the undertone series, which answer to the lower octaves of the 1st, 3rd, and 5th undertones, are component parts *of the minor chord under c, i.e. of the c underclang*, just as the same numbers of the overtone series give the major chord above the ground tone, *i.e.* the upper clang (in above example the chord of *c major*). The 7th, 11th, 13th undertones, in fact all answering to prime numbers from the 7th, are of as little use for chord formation as the primary overtones from the 7th. But the figures obtained by multiplication (9 = 3 × 3, 15 = 3 × 5, etc.) are, as secondary undertones, as much dissonant against the principal tone of the under clang as the secondary overtones against the principal tone

Schafhäutl (*Allgem. Musik. Zeitung*, 1879) is right in insisting on the fact that the material of which a musical instrument is constructed has great influence on the C. C.; that, for example, a trumpet made of wood or pasteboard sounds quite differently from one made of metal. The difference of C. C. is called *timbre*. Here the molecular vibrations of the body of the instrument play an important *rôle*, as is sufficiently evident from the sound-board of stringed instruments. Organ-builders have long known that it is something more than a matter of price or outward beauty whether the diapason pipes are made of tin or lead, or whether the tubes of reed-pipes are made of zinc or metal.

Clang Figures. (*See* CHLADNI.).

Clang-relationship (*Chord-relationship*). (*See* KEY-RELATIONSHIP.)

Clang Succession is the succession of two chords with regard to their clang-meaning. In order to be able to speak about C. S., all chords, even the dissonant, must be conceived and classed according to a clang-meaning; and —to look at the matter from a general point of view—a terminology is necessary: one which will be suitable, not to a special case, but to a large number of cases. The beginnings of such a terminology are common property. Within recent times the triads of the various degrees of a scale have been provided with cardinal numbers—large ones for the major chords, small ones for the minor—with a small nought added for diminished, and a stroke for augmented triads (Richter):

(a) Major

I   II   III   IV   V   VI   VII⁰

(b) Minor

I   II⁰   III′   IV   V   VI   VII⁰

V–I indicates, then, a succession of two major chords, of which the first is upper-dominant of the second; V–I, on the other hand, the transition from a major to a minor chord, of which the former is upper-dominant, etc. But, in a free system of harmony, this mode of indicating the chords is insufficient. The series of chords —c major, A♭ major, D major, G major, c major —which forms a perfectly intelligible little period—could not be made clear according to above system of figuring; for, although it in no way implies modulation, one would have to look upon the A♭ major chord as connected with F minor or c minor, and the D major chord, with G major.

C: I   V⁷   I
f: V   III
    c: VI
     G: V⁷

For such a C. S., figuring in the sense of one *scale* is not possible: it belongs to the free *tonality* (q.v.) which has only recently been recognised, and whose limits extend far beyond those of a scale-established system of harmony. This tonality recognises neither chords true nor foreign to the scale, but only a *principal clang* and *related clangs*. In the above example, the c *major* chord is, and remains, principal clang to which the others are referred: the chord of A♭ *major* is its under-third clang, the D *major* chord the clang of its second upper-fifth, the G *major* chord that of its first upper-fifth. The first step (c *major*—A♭ *major*) inclines towards the undertone side, the second proceeds by leap to the overtone side (A♭ *major*—D *major*), while the third and fourth steps lead back to the principal clang. The succession A♭ *major*—D *major* does not appear incomprehensible, because, from the relation which it bears to the principal clang (A♭–c–[G]–D), it consists of the step of a third and a double fifth step (or step of a whole tone). The terminology demanded by

considerations of this sort must proceed from the degree of relationship to the principal note; this therefore causes a distinction to be made between steps of a fifth, of a third, whole tone steps, steps of a minor third, leading tone, and tritone steps. Further, it must be seen whether both clangs belong to the same mode (major or minor), or whether there is a change. If successions of chords of like kind be simply called *steps*, and those of unlike kind, *changes*, then there are four kinds of chord succession in which the principal notes stand in fifth relationship. In the matter of tonality it makes a great difference whether a step from the tonic takes place on the upper-, or on the under-tone side. (*Cf.* CLANG.) From a major chord, the latter would prove a contradiction to the clang principle; and, in the former case, there would be a similar objection to a minor chord. Hence, the steps and changes to clangs in an opposite direction are appropriately distinguished by the prefix "Contra." The succession c *major*— G *major*, and likewise A *minor*—D *minor* (E-*under-clang*—A-*underclang*), is therefore a (*plain*) *fifth-step*; and c *major*—F *major*, likewise A *minor*— E *minor* (E-*underclang*—B-*underclang*, or briefly, under-E—under-B, indicated according to explanations given in article "Klangschlüssel" as ⁰e—⁰b), a *contra-fifth-step* (Gegenquintschritte). Again, c *major*—c *minor* (⁰g), likewise A *minor* (⁰e)— A *major*, is a (plain) *fifth change*; but c *major*— B♭ *minor* (⁰f), likewise A *minor* (⁰e)—B *major*, a *contra-fifth change*. In all kinds of clang succession the plain changes, as here, are easily understood, but the *contra*-changes cause very great difficulty. The third successions are, for example: (plain) third-step (c *major*—E *major*, likewise A *minor*—F *minor* (⁰e—⁰c); *contra-third-step* c *major*—A♭ *major*, likewise A *minor*—c♯ *minor* (⁰e—⁰g♯); (plain) *third-change* c *major*— A *minor* (⁰e), likewise A *minor* (⁰e)—c *major*; lastly the *contra-third-change*, c *major*—D♭ *minor* (⁰a♭). Every step towards a clang which lies at a distance creates a desire to spring to a middle one, which has been omitted, and to such a one it is easy to *modulate*, *i.e.* to assign to it the meaning of a principal clang. (*Cf.* MODULATION.) In his "Skizze einer neuen Methode der Harmonielehre" (1880), "Neue Schule der Melodik" (1883), and "Systematische Modulationslehre" (1887), Herr Riemann has systematically developed this terminology; and also in his "Musikalische Syntaxis" (1877), but in too complicated a manner, so that it was replaced in the above-mentioned works by a more suitable one. (*Cf.* CLANG, KLANGVERTRETUNG, and KLANGSCHLÜSSEL.)

Clapisson, Antoine Louis, b. Sept. 15, 1808, Naples, d. March 19, 1866, Paris, as member of the Académie, and keeper of the collection of musical instruments of the Conservatoire, the greater number of which he had gathered together and sold to the state; he was also a composer (twenty-one operas, many romances, etc.).

Clarabella, a soft, sweet-toned organ-stop invented by Bishop, usually of 8-feet pitch.

Clari, Giovanni Carlo Maria, b. 1669, Pisa, d. about 1745, pupil of Colonna at Bologna, maestro at Pistoja ; he composed an opera for Bologna (*Il Savio Delirante*). He is also of importance as a composer of sacred music (masses, psalms, a requiem, etc.), but became famous by his various chamber duets and trios with continuo (1720), which may worthily be set side by side with those of Steffani.

Claribel flute, an organ-stop similar to the Clarabella, but generally of 4-feet pitch.

Clarichord. (*Vide* CLAVICHORD.)

Clarinet or **Clarionet** (*Clarinetto*, diminutive form of *Clarino* [q.v.], Ger. *Klarinette*), (1) the well-known *wood-wind-instrument* used in the symphonic orchestra and in wind bands ; it has a cylindrical tube, and is blown by means of a single reed, which closes the under-side of the beak-shaped mouth-piece, and acts as a beating reed. (*See* WIND-INSTRUMENTS.) The C. in over-blowing, gives out first, not the octave, but the twelfth (fifth of the octave) ; all the partial tones represented by even numbers in the overtone series are, in fact, missing (*see* CLANG) ; the sound-hole and key mechanism is therefore much more complicated than in the flute and oboe, which only need the intermediate space of an octave to be filled up by shortenings of the tube. Over-blowing in the twelfth is facilitated by the help of a small hole covered with a key (at the spot where lies the nodal point for the division of the column of air into three equal parts). This was the invention of Gustav Denner of Nuremberg (about 1690), who, by that means, transformed the old French *Chalumeau*, which was limited to the low register, into the present clarinet. The *Chalumeau* had nine sound-holes, was in F, and extended (diatonic notes) from *f* to *a'*. The clarinet of to-day has eighteen sound-holes (since there are eighteen semitone steps between the fundamental note and the twelfth), of which thirteen are covered by keys. The art of playing on this complicated instrument is indeed a difficult one. The compass of the C. extends (with chromatic notes) from *e* to *c'''*, but the highest notes (above *g'''*) are dangerous, and of shrill tone, whereas the lowest ones are always good. To avoid blowing in keys which lie at a remote distance from the natural key of the instrument, clarinets are constructed of various pitch, viz., in c, B♭, and A, formerly also in B—great clarinets used only in the symphonic orchestra. But for all kinds the natural key is noted as c, *i.e. e* (the lowest note of the C.) sounds on a c clarinet as *e*, on a B♭ C. as *d*, on an A C. as *c♯*, on an E♭ C. as *g*, and on a D C. as *f*. The *small*

clarinets higher than c—*i.e.* in D, E♭, F (obsolete), and A♭, of shrill sound—are only used in military music, especially wind-bands, in which they take the place of violins. It almost seems, however, as if the B♭ C. would supplant the others in the symphonic orchestra. The extraordinary state of perfection which this instrument has reached through the efforts of Stadler, Iwan Müller, and Klosé, by means of partial application of the Böhm flute-mechanism, has made pure playing possible in all keys ; and the best clarinet orchestral players have not only mastered the difficulties of fingering, but can transpose at sight, and play what has been written for the A or c clarinet on the one in B♭. It would be a matter for regret were the A clarinet, with its mild tone, to disappear from the orchestra ; conductors may therefore be advised to insist that the B♭ C. should not be used when the one in A is prescribed. To the family of the C. belong also the *a*) *Alto Clarinets* (*Barytone* C.) in F and E♭, sounding a fifth lower than those in c and B♭. The Alto C. was never popular, as was the *Basset-horn* (q.v.), from which it differed but little ; *b*) *Bass Clarinet*, sounding an octave lower than the C., generally in B♭, seldom in c ; in Wagner also in A. The Bass Clarinet has the full soft tone of the C., and therefore is distinguished, much to its advantage, from the bassoon. The following are the names of distinguished clarinetists :—Beer, Tausch, Yost, Lefèvre, Blasius, Blatt, Bärmann (father and son), Berr, Val. Bender, Iwan Müller, Klosé, Blaes ; Blatt, Bärmann (junior), Berr, Iwan Müller, and Klosé wrote Methods for the C. which have become famous. (2) *Organ stop ;* the C. is a reed-pipe of eight feet, and of somewhat soft intonation ; *Clarionet-flute,* on the other hand, a kind of reed flute (covered flue-work with holes in stopper).

Clarinetto (Ital.). (*See* CLARINET.)

Clarino, (1) Ital., same as Trumpet, a name used formerly in Germany for the high solo trumpet, which only differed from the lower (Prinzipal Trompete) in having a narrower mouthpiece. To blow the clarino ("Clarin blasen"), in the trumpeter's art of the last century, meant to blow the high solo trumpet ; to blow the "Principal" ("Prinzipal blasen"), the low trumpet. The bass part (which really belonged to the drum) of a choir of trumpets was called Toccato. The compass of the trumpet was formerly considerably higher than at present (up to *d³*) ; we should now take little pleasure in its thin, pointed highest notes. (*Cf.* EICHBORN, "Die Trompete alter und neuer Zeit" (1881).—(2) Name of the middle register of the clarinet (*b¹–c³*), produced by overblowing the notes of the shawm register in the twelfth. When the *Clarin* passed away, the new reed instrument took its name and *rôle.*—(3) A 4-ft. trumpet stop in the organ, octave trumpet (Fr. *Clairon, Clarin ;* Eng. *Clarion*) ; in the

London Panopticon organ there was a 4-ft. *Clarion*, and also a 2-ft. *Octave Clarion;* at the Marien-Kirche, at Lübeck, there is a 4-ft. C., a flute-stop (a half-stop from *f'*).

Clarion, a shrill - toned trumpet. (*Vide* CLARINO.)

Clark, (1) J e r e m i a h, old English composer, in 1704 joint organist with Croft at the Chapel Royal; he shot himself December 1, 1707, owing to an unfortunate attachment to a lady in high position. C. was the first composer of music for Dryden's Ode to St.Cecilia("Alexander's Feast"), 1697; he also wrote anthems, cantatas, and, in conjunction with Purcell (Daniel) and Leveridge, music for operas and plays.—(2) R i c h a r d, b. April 5, 1780, Datchet (Bucks), d. Oct. 5, 1856; lay clerk at St. George's and Eton College, afterwards lay vicar of Westminster Abbey and vicar choral at St. Paul's; he made himself known by his glees, anthems, etc., also by some pamphlets on Handel's *Messiah* and " Harmonious Blacksmith," on " God Save the King," and on the etymology of the word " Madrigal," and by a collection of the words of favourite glees, madrigals, rounds, and catches (1814).—(3) R e v. S c o t s o n, organist and composer, b. Nov. 1840, d. July, 1883. He was a pupil of the Royal Academy, studied under Bennett, Goss, and Lucas, the organ under Hopkins, and harmonium under Léfébure-Wély. He afterwards devoted himself to the church, and studied both at Cambridge and Oxford, in the latter city filling the post of organist at Exeter College. In 1873 he returned to London, and established the London Organ School. Clark was a talented performer, more especially on the organ and harmonium. His most successful compositions were his marches, and a number of voluntaries. His organ works contain fifteen marches, forty-eight voluntaries, communions, improvisations, etc., and are published in three vols. For harmonium he wrote five vols. of original pieces and arrangements, while of pianoforte pieces he left more than one hundred, mostly of a brilliant character (London, Augener).

Clarke, J o h n (C. W h i t f i e l d), b. Dec. 13, 1770, Gloucester, d. Feb. 22, 1836, Holmer, near Hereford; pupil of Hayes, at Oxford, organist in succession at Ludlow, Armagh, and Dublin (St. Patrick's Cathedral and Christ Church); he left Ireland in consequence of the disturbances in 1798, and became organist and choirmaster of Trinity and St. John's Colleges, Cambridge, but changed his appointment (1820) for a similar one at Hereford. He retired from active life in 1833. In 1799 the degree of Mus. Doc. was conferred on him by the University of Cambridge, and in 1810 by Oxford; and in 1821 he was appointed professor of music at Cambridge. In 1805 he published four volumes of " Cathedral Services," and anthems, and a collection of church compositions by various masters; besides which he wrote an oratorio,

The Crucifixion and the Resurrection, as well as glees, songs, etc., and arranged Handel's oratorios and other works for voice with piano accompaniment.

Clasing, J o h a n n H e i n r i c h, b. 1799, Hamburg, d. there Feb. 22, 1836, composed operas (*Micheli und sein Sohn; Welcher ist der Rechte*), oratorios (*Belsazar ; Jephtha*), choral works (" Vater unser "), etc.

Classical, a term applied to a work of art against which the destroying hand of time has proved powerless. Since only in the course of time a work can be shown to possess this power of resistance, there are no living classics; also every classic writer is considered romantic by his contemporaries, *i.e.* a mind striving to escape from ordinary routine.

Claudin. (*See* SERMISY.)

Claudin le Jeune. (*See* LEJEUNE.)

Claudius, O t t o, b. Dec. 6, 1793, Camenz, d. Aug. 3, 1877, Naumburg, as cantor of the cathedral ; he composed much church music, and several operas (*Der Gang nach dem Eisenhammer*), songs, etc.

Claussen, W i l h e l m, a celebrated composer, who died young (the first recipient of the Meyerbeer scholarship, q.v.), b. 1844, d. Dec. 22, 1869, Schwerin; he was a pupil of A. Schäffer.

Clausula (Lat.), cadence (q.v.), or close. *Clausula bassizans* is the name given to the usual progression of the bass in a full close (Dominant-Tonic). The terms *Clausula cantizans, altizans, tenorizans,* are also met with, but, being interchangeable, are of no value.

Clauss-Szarvady, W i l h e l m i n e, b. Dec. 13, 1834, Prague, distinguished pianist, pupil of the Procksch Institute; she has lived in Paris since 1852, married in 1857 Fr. Szarvady (d. March 1, 1882, Paris). She is one of the classical interpreters who think more of the intention of the composer than of effect.

Claveoline, same as ÆOLINE.

Clavecin, Clavicembalo, Clavichord. (*See* PIANOFORTE.)

Claviatur (Ger.), the keyboard of a pianoforte, organ, harmonium, etc.

Clavicylinder, a keyboard instrument constructed by Chladni in 1799, consisting of a cylinder made to rotate by means of a treadle; steel rods pressed down by keys produced the notes of a scale. (*Cf.* EUPHONIUM.)

Clavicytherium. (*See* PIANOFORTE.)

Clavis (Lat., pl. *Claves ;* Ger. *Schlüssel*). This was the name first given to the keys of the organ, which, in fact, exercise the function of a key in that they open a way for the wind to the pipes. It was customary (already, as can be shown, in the 10th century) to write the names of the sounds on the keys of the organ, and, hence, the name C. passed over to the letters which stood for the sounds. When, in the 11th century, letter notation was abbreviated by means of the staff system, by using only some of the letters as signs before the lines (*Claves signatæ*), these specially retained the name of C. (the "clef" of to-day). At the same time the name C. remained for the keys of the organ, and from thence passed to the harpsichord and all similar instruments. The keys of wind-instruments are also called *claves*. The bellows-handle in an organ is called in Germany *Balgclavis*.

Clay, Frédéric, b. Aug. 3, 1840, Paris, of English parents, d. Nov. 24, 1889, Oxford House, Great Marlow, near London, received his musical training under Molique, at Paris, and also studied for a short time at Leipzig, under Hauptmann. Between 1859–60 he came out privately as an opera composer in London with two little pieces, but afterwards brought out a whole series of operas and operettas at Covent Garden: *Court and Cottage* (1862), *Constance* (1865), *Ages Ago* (1869), *The Gentleman in Black* (1870), *Happy Arcadia* (**1872**), *The Black Crook* (1872), *Babil and Bijou* (1872, of the last two C. only wrote a part), *Cattarina* (1874), *Princess Toto* and *Don Quichote* (both 1875), *The Merry Duchess* (1883), *The Golden Ring* (1883). Besides these operas he wrote incidental music to dramas, and the cantatas *The Knights of the Cross* and *Lalla Rookh*.

Cleemann (Kleemann), Fr. Joseph Christoph, b. Sept. 16, 1771, Kriwitz, Mecklenburg, d. Dec. 25, 1827, Parchim; he wrote a "Handbuch der Tonkunst" (1797), as well as a book of songs.

Clef (Lat. *Clavis*, Ger. *Schlüssel*) is a note-letter at the beginning of a stave, so called, because only by means of it do the notes receive a definite pitch-meaning :—

F, or bass-clef ;	Soprano-clef ;	Alto-clef ;	Tenor clef ;	G-clef, or Violin-clef.
f	c'	c'	c'	g'

With regard to the separate clefs, compare the respective articles. Those letters were first (10th to 11th century) selected as clefs (*Claves signatæ*) which marked the place of the semitone degrees in the fundamental scale, *i.e.* f (e : f) and c (b : c'); and in order to impress this step of a semitone more forcibly upon the memory, the clef lines were coloured (f red, c yellow). The ☉, Γ (Gamma, for our capital G), g and dd (g' and d') also used as *Claves signatæ* (already in the 13th century) did not really assume practical importance. Only from the 15th to the 16th century did the g clef become more frequent, and, indeed, in connection with the old meaning of the C. as sign of the transposition

of the Church Modes into the upper fifth, with raising of f to f♯, so that even the 𝄞 marked the semitone (though in another sense, *cf.* CHIAVETTE). In the Tablature (q.v.) notation of the *Cantus*, the g clef, on the other hand, had, already in the 16th century, become quite common without transposition meaning. (With regard to the transformation of the clef letters to their present shape, *cf.* the articles C, F, and G, C.)

Clemann (Kleemann), Balthasar, writer on music about 1680; he wrote a work on counterpoint, and "Ex musica didactica temperiertes Monochordum."

Clemens non Papa ("C., not the Pope"), really Jacob Clemens, Netherland contrapuntist of the 16th century. He was, at first, capellmeister to the Emperor Charles V., and ranks as one of the most famous composers of the epoch between Josquin and Palestrina. Eleven masses, and a great number of motets, chansons, etc., were published in special editions by Peter Phalèse at Louvain (1555–80), as well as four books, "Souter Lidekens" (psalm-songs), *i.e.* psalms based on popular Netherland melodies, printed 1556–57 by Tylmann Susato at Antwerp, besides many separate pieces in collections by different printers and publishers since 1543. According to the ingenious, but risky conclusions of Fétis, C. was born about 1475 and died 1558; but it is probably more accurate to place him altogether in the 16th century.

Clement, Franz, violin virtuoso, b. Nov. 19, 1784, Vienna, d. there Nov. 3, 1842; he came out as a boy, with great success, at London and Amsterdam; was from 1802–11 conductor at the Theater an der Wien, afterwards leader under C. M. v. Weber at Prague; from 1818 to 1821 again at the Theater an der Wien, and then travelled for many years with Catalani. C. wrote six concertos, and twenty-five concertinos for violin, pf. concertos, overtures, quartets, and some small pieces for the stage.

Clément, (1), Charles François, b. 1720 in Provence, afterwards lived in Paris as teacher of the pianoforte. He published "Essai sur l'Accompagnement du Clavecin" (1758), "Essai sur la Basse Fondamentale" (1762); both these works were united under the former title. He also brought out at Paris two small operas, a book of harpsichord pieces with violin, and a "Journal de clavecin" (1762–65). (2) Félix, b. Jan. 13, 1822, Paris, d. there Jan. 23, 1885. With the fixed determination to become a teacher, unknown to his parents he devoted himself at an early age to musical studies; was then for some years private tutor in Normandy and at Paris, until in 1843 he resolved to devote himself entirely to music, and at that time busied himself especially with the study of the history of music. In that same year he became music teacher and organist at Stanislas College, and then, in succession, maître de chapelle of the churches St. Augustine and St. André d'Antin, and finally organist and choir-master of the church of the Sorbonne. In 1849 he conducted the church festivals in the Sainte-Chapelle, on which occasions he performed, and also published in score, a series of compositions of the 13th century under the title "Chants de la Sainte-Chapelle" (1849). It was principally at his suggestion that the Institute for Church Music was founded, the direction of which was given over to Niedermeyer. Of his numerous writings the most celebrated are: "Méthode Complète de Plain-chant" (2nd ed., 1872); "Méthode de Musique Vocale et Concertante," "Histoire Générale de la Musique religieuse" (1861), "Les Musiciens Célèbres depuis le XVI Siècle, etc." (1868; 3rd ed., 1879), "Dictionnaire lyrique, ou Histoire des Opéras" (1869, with four supplements up to 1897), the last-named enumerating "all" (?) dramatic musical works produced since the birth of opera; and "Méthode d'Orgue, d'Harmonie et d'Accompagnement" (1874).

Clementi, Muzio, b. 1752, Rome, d. March 10, 1832, at his country estate, Evesham, Worcestershire. The son of a goldsmith, he received, as soon as his musical talent showed itself, regular instruction in music, first in piano-playing and thorough-bass from a relative, the organist Buroni, afterwards from Carpani and Santarelli in counterpoint and singing. In addition, he had already filled a post as organist since 1761. When fourteen years of age, he caused excitement at Rome by his musical knowledge and skill, and attracted attention by his compositions. An Englishman, Bedford (Beckford) by name, obtained from his father permission to take the boy to England, and undertook to provide for his further training. C. lived in the house of his patron until 1770, and distinguished himself as a performer on the pianoforte. Introduced by Bedford, he quickly succeeded in gaining great renown as master and teacher of his instrument. He officiated (1777–80) as cembalist (conductor) at the Italian Opera, and in 1781 made his first tour on the continent, travelling through Strassburg and Munich to Vienna, where he gained honour in a musical contest with Mozart. In 1785 followed a concert tour to Paris. Between these two tours, and afterwards, until 1802, he worked in London with ever-increasing repute, taking a share in the music-publishing department, and in the pianoforte factory of Longman and Broderip; and, after their failure, founding a similar business on his own account, in company with Collard, under whose name it still exists. In addition to his mechanico-technical studies for the construction of pianos, he found time to write a series of high-class pianoforte works, and to train celebrated pupils (J. B. Cramer and John Field).

In 1802 he went with Field, by way of Paris and Vienna, to Petersburg, and was everywhere received with enthusiasm. Field remained behind, obtaining a lucrative post, but he was replaced by Zeuner. In Berlin and Dresden Ludwig Berger and Alexander Klengel—men who afterwards acquired high fame—associated with them. Moscheles and Kalkbrenner studied for a time under C. in Berlin. C. married in that city, but lost his young wife before a year had expired, and, deeply distressed, travelled with his pupils, Berger and Klengel, to Petersburg; but he returned in 1810, and went to Vienna, Italy, and afterwards England. With the exception of a winter (1820–21) spent in Leipzig, he remained, for the future, in London, and married for the second time in 1811. He left a large fortune. His principal works are: 106 pf. sonatas (of which forty-six with violin, 'cello, flute), also the "Gradus ad Parnassum," considered, still at the present day, an educational work of the highest importance: it is everywhere used, and has appeared in many editions. Also symphonies, overtures, 2 duets for two pianofortes, caprices, characteristic pieces, etc., as well as an anthology of the clavier works of old masters.

Clement y Cavedo, b. Jan. 1, 1810, Gandia, near Valencia. He was, at first, organist at Algamesi, afterwards at Valencia, and lived from 1840–52 as teacher of music at Guéret (France), and afterwards Madrid, where he published an elementary musical instruction book, "Grammatica musical." By order of Espartero (1855), he elaborated a plan for the reorganisation of the School of Music, and contributed articles to the papers *El Rubi* and *El Artista*. He also gave instruction in the French language, and in music. He became known as a composer by a magic opera and a farce (*Zarzuela*), as well as by romances and ballads.

Clicquot, François Henri, b. 1728, Paris, d. there 1791. He was one of the most important French organ-builders of the last century, and worked in partnership with Pierre Dallery from 1765. From this establishment many excellent organs were turned out for Paris and the provinces.

Clifford, James, b. 1622, Oxford, d. Sept., 1698, as senior cardinal of St. Paul's Cathedral. He published in 1663 the words of anthems usually sung in cathedrals (2nd ed. 1664).

Clifton, John Charles, b. 1781, London, d. Nov. 18, 1841, Hammersmith. He was first conductor at Bath, then produced a musical piece at Dublin, and, from 1816, taught music in London on Logier's system. He composed glees, songs, also an opera (*Edwin*), and invented a kind of melograph (q.v.), named "Eidomusicon," of which, however, owing to the expense, he was not able to make practical use. He wrote a simplified system of harmony, which, however, was not printed, and published a collection of British melodies.

Cloche (Fr.), a bell.

Clochette (Fr.), a little bell.

Close. The feeling of a close in music depends upon two things—rhythmical symmetry and harmonic consequence. The nature of the former is explained under METRE, THE ART OF; the latter depends upon the necessity for clear tonality, *i.e.* the uniform relation of an harmonic series to one principal clang, the tonic. Every deviation from the tonic is, in the strictest sense, a conflict which can only be settled by a return to the same; within the key this conflict is most sharply expressed by the under-dominant which appears in real opposition to the tonic, whereas the upper-dominant leads back to the tonic. (For more on this matter see Riemann's " Musikalische Syntaxis," 1875, and his " Systematische Modulationslehre," 1887.) The basis of logical tonal progression is to be found in tonic—under-dominant—upper-dominant—tonic. The effect of a perfect close depends, harmonically, on the succession, upper-dominant to tonic (at least in a major key), the so-called *authentic* C.; the return from the under-dominant to the tonic is not a real solution of the conflict, but only, as it were, a retractation, a renunciation of further formation—the so-called *plagal* C. Apart from this distinction, which, as already said, does not exactly apply to the minor key, the effect of a close, generally speaking, depends, harmonically, on the *return from some related clang to the principal clang* (that related clang may even be, for example, *a third* clang. *Cf.* CLANG SUCCESSION.) A real effect of close is felt, however, only when the concluding tonic enters on a beat which has rhythmical cadential power, *i.e.* one on which the symmetry can come to a proper conclusion. (*Cf.* METRE, THE ART OF.) A cadence-like effect arises also when the upper-dominant enters on a beat capable, in a marked manner, of close; this is called a *half* C. The half close produces decided articulation; it forms a strong cæsura, but in no way disturbs the symmetry, *i.e.* the construction proceeds undisturbed, and in symmetrical fashion. The reason of this is that the upper-dominant, as cadence member before the final tonic, leads one to expect the latter; but, though it may afterwards reappear, it is not as an end, but as a new commencement. The under-dominant at a moment of such rhythmical cadential power produces quite a different effect; as a real conflicting chord it presses forward to a near termination, and disturbs the symmetry in proportion to the closing power of the beat on which it enters. The under-dominant at the fourth or eighth bar leads almost invariably to a disturbance of the symmetrical construction, since, as a rule, a close follows it two bars later. It entirely takes away the effect of a close, and always produces a double

relationship (double phrasing). The so-called *deceptive* C. produces a specially important modification of cadence-effect; for in it all the parts carry out the cadence according to rule, but the bass moves one degree upwards, instead of proceeding from the fundamental tone of the dominant to that of the tonic. The deceptive cadence is then a *real* C., but one *disturbed* by a *foreign* note. This foreign sound naturally gives impulse to further formation, but does not obliterate the feeling of a principal section; it demands, as it were, a rectification, a fresh cadence, without the unwelcome disturbance. To the pure forms here explained many mixed ones can be added, above all the borrowing of the deceptive C. from the tonic minor, *i.e.* for c major the one belonging to c minor, and *vice versâ;* and again the change of the under-dominant occurring on a cadence-beat, into the second upper-dominant by the raising of its fundamental note, whereby, for the rest, its effect of pressing to a close is not altered. Purely rhythmical changes of the C. are obtained by delaying the entry of the concluding tonic by means of suspensions; the effect of these is enhanced if directly before the close-beat the under-dominant enters, so that the upper-dominant only enters on the close-beat, producing altogether the effect of a suspension of the tonic, for example :—

(8th bar.)

All cadences which, owing to suspensions, have to be brought to an end on the following unaccented beat (no matter the order) are called *feminine* (*weibliche*), to distinguish them from the perfect, or *masculine.* The syncopated anticipation of the closing chord is itself only a rhythmical modification.

In the polyphonic style of the 15th and 16th centuries, especially in the old music built on the church modes, a knowledge of cadences was of great importance, because the indefinite system of harmony in the closes of the several sections and subsections must have required particular management if a real cadence effect was to be obtained. Only now, when we are beginning to understand the principles of the harmonic formation of movements, do we become aware of the difficulties which polyphonic writing in the church modes must have cost. To-day we know that the effect of a close is only possible by means of the return from a few directly-related sounds to the tonic, and that to bear the stamp of definite tonality there must be relationships, not only from the overtone, but also from the undertone series. Now in the Phrygian mode (*e—e'*, natural notes), taking the E minor as tonic chord (which is not, indeed, correct, but was for a long period taken thus), the upper relationships are entirely wanting :—

Phrygian: *d f a c e g b*
Tonic

and, on the other hand, in the Dorian mode (*d–d'*) those below :—

Dorian : *d f a c e g b*
Tonic

so in the Lydian the relationships below, and in the Mixolydian, those above are wanting—

Lydian: *f a c e g b d*
Tonic

Mixolydian : *f a c e g b d*
Tonic

Nevertheless, with an imperfect comprehension of the original meaning of the church modes (q.v.), for centuries there was a struggle to harmonise these four systems. This, of course, led to all sorts of concessions, *i.e.* departures from the kind of harmony actually belonging to these scales, especially in the closes; whereas, with the exception of the closes, pieces keeping strictly to the modes were of necessity indefinite in tonality. The concessions were : introduction of the sub-semitone (of the major seventh), *c♯* for the Dorian and *f♯* for the Mixolydian, and introduction of the minor sixth for the Dorian (*b flat*), and of the perfect fourth for the Lydian (*b flat*). Hence arose quite different systems, viz. :—

Dorian : *g b♭ d f a c♯ e* (Min.)
Tonic

Lydian : *b♭ d f a c e g* (Maj.)
Tonic

Mixolydian : *c e g b d f♯ a* (Maj.)
Tonic

i.e. in the cadences the church modes changed into our modern keys. Nothing, however, could be done with the Phrygian, as the change of *d* into *d♯* lay beyond the sphere of that period, and without a simultaneous change of *f* into *f♯* would not even have produced a satisfactory result. Hence the great difficulty with regard to the *Phrygian Cadence* (q.v.).

Close Position of chords, in contradistinction to " wide position " or " scattered harmony," *e.g.* :—

Close position. Wide position.

Clotz. (*See* KLOTZ.)

Cluer, John, English music printer during the first half of the 18th century, probably the inventor of engraving on tin plates. (*Cf.* Chrysander's treatise in the *Allgemeine Musikalische Zeitung*, 1879, No. 16). C. published several works of Handel, and after his death the copyright was bought by Walsh.

C Major Chord = *c, e, g ;* c *major* key, without signature (major fundamental scale). (*Cf.* KEY.)

C Minor Chord = *c, e♭, g ;* c *minor* key with signature of three flats. (*See* KEY.)

Cocchi, Gioacchino, b. 1720, Padua, d. 1804, Venice; a prolific composer of operas, who, from 1743 to 1752, wrote a series of operas for Rome and Naples, and afterwards for Venice, where he became maestro at the Conservatorio degli Incurabili. In 1757 he went to London, where, up to 1763, he produced more works, and returned in 1773 to Venice. Although C. cultivated the serious as well as the buffo style, it was in the latter that he met with most success.

Coccia, Carlo, b. April 14, 1782, Naples, d. April 13, 1873, as maestro of the cathedral at Novara. He was an exceedingly prolific composer, and wrote forty operas, *Maria Stuarda, Eduardo Stuard in Iscozia, L'Orfana della Selva, Caterina di Guisa, La Solitaria delle Asturie,* 1831 ; *La Clotilde,* etc., a series of cantatas, twenty-five masses, and other sacred music.

Coccon, Nicolò, b. Aug. 10, 1826, Venice, pupil of E. Fabio, published his first compositions (motets) at the age of fifteen, became in 1856 principal organist and in 1873 maestro of St. Mark's Church. C. was one of the most esteemed musicians of Italy, and a very prolific composer, especially of sacred music (over 400 works, among which eight requiems, thirty masses, etc.) ; he also wrote an oratorio (*Saul*), two operas, etc. He died Aug. 4, 1903.

Cochläus, Johannes, b. 1479, Wendelstein, near Nuremberg (hence he also published some works under the name Wendelstein), d. Jan. 10, 1552, as canon at Breslau. He published : " Tractatus de Musicæ Definitione et Inventione, etc." (1507, under the name Joh. Wendelstein) ; " Tetrachordum musices Joannis Coclæi Norici, etc." (1511 ; republished 1513 and 1526).

Cocks & Co., Robert, celebrated London music publishing firm, founded in 1827 by Robert C. ; in 1868 he took his sons, Arthur Lincoln and Stroud Lincoln C., into partnership. In 1898 the business was acquired by Augener & Co., now Augener Ltd.

Coclicus, or **Coclico,** Adrian Petit, b. about 1500, Hennegau. He studied with Josquin Deprès, lived an unsteady life, and was for a time singer in the Pope's Chapel, and confessor to his Holiness. He was imprisoned on account of his sinful course of life, and, on recovering his liberty, went, in 1545, to Wittenberg, and embraced the new teaching. He went to Frankfort-on-the-Oder in 1546, then to Königsberg, and, finally, to Nuremberg, where he probably died ; there are two letters of his in the *Monatsh. f. M.-G.*, vii., 168. He published "Compendium Musices" (1552) ; a book of psalms à 4 (" Consolationes," etc., 1552).

Coda (Ital., from Lat. *cauda*, "tail"), a closing section in movements with repeats. The term C. is employed, especially, when on taking the repeat a skip has to be made ; as, for example, in scherzi, where after the trio the scherzo has to be repeated, and then the C. played (*Scherzo da capo epoi la c*). The free ending in canons is also called C.

Codetta (Ital.), A short coda. (*Vide* FUGUE.)

Cœnen, (1) Johannes Meinardus, b. Jan. 28, 1824, the Hague, was trained at the Conservatoire there under Ch. H. Lübeck. He was a performer on the bassoon, was chef d'orchestre, in 1864, of the grand Dutch Theatre at Amsterdam, then capellmeister of the Palais d'Industrie, and town musical director. He composed cantatas (a festival cantata for the 600th anniversary of the foundation of Amsterdam, 1875), music to Dutch dramas, ballet music, overtures, two symphonies, a clarinet concerto, flute concerto, quintet for pf. and wind, sonata for bassoon or 'cello, clarinet and pf., fantasias for orchestra, etc.—(2) Franz, b. Dec. 26, 1826, Rotterdam, died at Leyden, Jan. 24, 1904. He studied first with his father, then with Molique and Vieuxtemps, made concert tours as violinist with H. Herz, and afterwards with E. Lübeck in America, and then settled in Amsterdam. C was director and professor of the violin and of composition at the Amsterdam Conservatoire, one of the branches of the *Maatschappy tot bevordering van toonkunst*, also chamber musician (solo violinist) to the King of the Netherlands, etc. The string quartet-party which he organised enjoyed great fame. C. was also highly esteemed as composer (32nd Psalm, symphony, cantatas, quartets, etc.).—(3) Cornelius, b. 1838, the Hague, a violin soloist who travelled much, composed overtures, songs for chorus and orchestra, etc., became in 1859 conductor of the theatre orchestra at Amsterdam, and in 1860 bandmaster of the Garde Nationale at Utrecht.

Cohen, (1) Henri, b. 1808, Amsterdam, d. May 17, 1880, Brie-sur-Marne. He went, as a child, with his parents to Paris, where he studied theory with Reicha, and singing with Lays and Pellegrini. After somewhat fruitless attempts to make a name in Naples as dramatic composer (1832–34, 1838, and 1839), C. settled in Paris as teacher of music, and was also, for a time, principal of the branch of the Paris Conservatoire at Lille. As his numismatic knowledge was great, he was appointed Conservator of the cabinet of medals of the National Library. Besides some operas and small pieces, C. wrote various elementary works on theory, and contributed criticisms to various musical papers.—(2) Léonce, b. Feb. 12, 1829, Paris, pupil of Leborne at the Conservatoire, received the *Prix de Rome* in 1851, became violinist at the Théâtre Italien, composed some operettas, and published the exceedingly comprehensive " École du Musicien."—(3) Jules, b, Nov. 2, 1830, Marseilles, a pupil of Zimmermann, Marmontel, Benoist, and Halévy at the Paris Conservatoire. As his parents were well off, he withdrew from the competition for the *Prix de Rome*, and received first a post as assistant-teacher, and, in 1870, one as regular teacher of the ensemble-singing-class at the Conservatoire. In spite of repeated attempts, C., as a dramatic composer, has met with no success ; his numerous sacred compositions (masses, etc.), instrumental works (symphonies, overtures, etc.), and cantatas, appear to be of greater value.

Col (Ital.) = *con il*, " with the."

Colasse, Pascal, contemporary and pupil of Lully, b. about 1640, Rheims, d. Dec., 1709, Paris, became chorister at the church of St. Paul, Paris, and was trained by Lully, who entrusted to him the writing out of the accompaniment parts of his operas from the figured bass. In 1683 C. received one of the four posts of master of the music, and in 1696 the appointment of royal chamber musician. Louis XIV. granted to him the privilege of performing operas at Lille ; but he was unfortunate, for the opera-house was burned down with all its contents. The king granted him compensation, and restored to him his post of master of the music ; but C. set his mind on discovering the philosopher's stone, completely ruined himself, and died an imbecile. Of his operas only *Les Noces de Thétys et de Pelée* (1689) had real success. He also wrote many sacred and secular songs.

Colin (Colinus, Colinäus, also with the sobriquet Chamault), Pierre Gilbert, 1532–36, chapel-singer at Paris under François I., afterwards chorus-master at Autun Cathedral, was one of the best French contrapuntists. Numerous masses and chansons, also some motets in original publications up to 1567, have been preserved.

Coll' (Ital.), before vowels, for *colla* (for *con la*) or *collo* (for *con lo*), " with the " ; *coll' arco*. (*See* ARCO.)

Colla (Ital.), same as *con la*, " with the " ; *c. parte*, " with the principal part," a term used in connection with accompanying parts to show that in the matters of time and expression, they must follow the principal part.

Collard, celebrated London piano manufactory, originally Longman & Broderip (1767), transferred in 1798 to Muzio Clementi (q.v.), who had F. W. C. as a partner, to whom, before his death, he handed over the sole management of the business. (*See* KIRKMAN.)

Collins, Isaak, celebrated English violinist, b. 1797, d. 1871, London. His sons are Viotti C. (violinist) and George ('cellist).

Collo (Ital.), same as *con lo*. (*See* COLL'.)

Colonna, Giovanni Paolo, b. 1640, Brescia, d. Dec. 4, 1695, as maestro of San Petronio, at Bologna, one of the founders, and several times president of the Accademia Filarmonica; he was one of the most celebrated Italian church composers of the 17th century. A great number of his works have been preserved : three books of psalms à 8 with organ (1681, 1686, 1694); "Motetti a Voce Sola con 2 Violini e Bassetto de Viola" (1691); motets à 2–3 (1698); litanies and antiphons to the Virgin à 8 (1682); masses à 8 (1684); eight masses, psalms. etc. (1685); complines and sequences à 8 (1687); Lamentations à 8 (1689); "Messe e Salmi Concertati" à 3–5 (1691); vesper psalms with instrumental accompaniments à 3–5 (1694); and an oratorio, *La Profezia d'Eliseo*" (1688); also many other works in manuscript (Vienna, Bologna).

Colonne, Édouard (his real Christian name was Judas), b. July 23, 1838, Bordeaux, pupil at the Paris Conservatoire, especially of Girard and Sauzay (violin), Elwart and A. Thomas (composition); founder and conductor of the Concerts du Chatêlet (from 1874). He is famous as a conductor, and has won merit by the performances of the works of Berlioz (*Requiem, Roméo et Juliette, La Damnation de Faust, L'Enfance du Christ, La Prise de Troie*). In 1878 he conducted the official concerts at the Exhibition.

Colophonium (resin), a very hard gum (named after the city Colophon, in Asia Minor), with which the bows, stretched with horsehair, of stringed instruments are rubbed. Resin is what is left after turpentine oil has been extracted from turpentine.

Color (Lat.), was the general designation in measured music for notes of different colour; hence both for the *red* note (*notula rubra*) which was used in the 14th century, and for the *white* note (*notula alba, dealbata, cavata*), also in the 14th century, in contradistinction to the black, which was then general. When the white note became common (15th century) the term C. was employed for the *black* (*notula nigra, denigrata*) in opposition to the former. Originally C. (red colour) employed instead of a time signature, indicated a change of measure (q.v.) : thus, in perfect time, the introduction of red indicated imperfect time, and in the latter, with reversed meaning, a change to perfect. This last method was, however, soon given up, and this much was settled, viz., that the C. should indicate imperfect time. The white note of the 14th century was therefore always imperfect, and so with the black note of the 15th and 16th centuries. C. was given up

at the commencement of the 17th century. (*Cf.* HEMIOLIA.)

Coloratura (Ital.), ornamental passage. *C. aria*. (*See* ARIA.)

Combinaison de Pédales, a clever invention of Cavaillé-Col's (q.v.); by means of a treadle it is possible to set into action the stops of an organ in groups, instead of drawing them out singly.

Combination Tone is the name given to a note produced by two notes sounding simultaneously. The cause of the origin of combination tones is probably the same as that of beats. It is well known that two strings not tuned in perfect unison give out reinforcements of sound at regularly recurring intervals, and this phenomenon is known under the name of shocks or beats. Each beat must be looked upon as the occurrence of a maximum of condensation of the sound-waves of both tones. If the number of beats reaches somewhere about thirty in the second, the single beats are no longer separated, but there arises the sensation of a low humming, *i.e.* a low note is heard, the C. T. The recurring beats account for the origin of this note. Combination tones are of considerable strength, and with some practice can be heard without the assistance of resonators. Tartini, the discoverer of combination tones, first of all (in the *Trattato*) fixed their pitch generally as corresponding to the second tone of the overtone series in which the given interval occurs with the smallest possible ordinal figures ; but later on he corrected himself (in the pamphlet "Dei Principi, etc."), stating that the C. T. is always the fundamental tone of the series in question. This definition has been changed by most physicists, who assert that the vibration number of the combination tone always answers to the difference of the vibration numbers of the generators (*differential tone*); but it cannot be disputed that, under all circumstances, the note answering to the fundamental tone of the harmonic series is audible (unless of a pitch imperceptible to the ear), whether it be defined as a C. T. of the first or of the second order. On closer investigation, it becomes apparent that the whole harmonic series to which the given interval belongs is audible; not only lower, but also higher tones. According to Helmholtz, the combination tones of the interval $g : e'$ are as follows :

1st   2nd   3rd Order.

but, according to Tartini,

1st   2nd Order

i.e. every interval produces the note of which both tones of the interval are the nearest overtones (here third and fifth); and in the second place the full overtone series of this note. Helmholtz makes mention of another kind of combination tones, which he names *Summation Tones, i.e.* those which answer to the sum of the vibration numbers of the tones of the interval, *i.e.* for $g : e'$ $(3 + 5 = 8) = c''$. It is not, however, right to say that this tone would be the more prominent one of the series; for the first overtone common to both intervals, *i.e.* $(3 \times 5 = 15)$, the fifteenth overtone b'', is very prominent (the *phonic* overtone of v. Oettingen, named *multiplication tone* by the compiler of this dictionary; *cf.* the result of his investigations respecting combination tones in the pamphlet "Die objektive Existenz der Untertöne in der Schallwelle," 1875).

Come (Ital. "as"); *C. sopra* ("as above"), an abbreviation of notation when a passage is repeated.

Comes (Lat.). (*See* FUGUE.)

Come stã (Ital.), as it stands, as it is written.

Comettant, Oscar, b. April 18, 1819, pupil of Elwart and Carafa at the Paris Conservatoire, lived from 1852–55 in America, after that in Paris, and made a name, not so much by his compositions (choruses for male voices, pf. fantasias, études, some sacred songs), as by his activity as a writer. C. was musical *feuilletoniste* of the *Siècle*, and contributor to many other papers (especially musical papers). He also published: "Histoire d'un inventeur au XIX. siècle, Adolphe Sax" (1860); "Portefeuille d'un Musicien," "Musique et Musiciens" (1862); "La Musique, les Musiciens et les Instruments de Musique chez les Différents Peuples du Monde" (1869, in connection with the Paris Exhibition, 1867), etc. Died Jan. 24, 1898.

Comma is the name given to the differences which result from the comparison of mathematical determinations of notes of nearly the same pitch; these differences are (1) the C. *of Pythagoras,* 531441 : 524288, by which six whole tones, with the ratio 9 : 8, exceed the octave $\left(\frac{9^6}{8^6} : \frac{2}{1}\right)$; (2) the C. of Didymus, or C. *syntonum,* 81 : 80, the difference between a major and a minor tone $\left(\frac{9}{8} : \frac{10}{9}\right)$. (For further information respecting the C. and also the schisma, *see* the table given under TONE, DETERMINATION OF.)

Commer, Franz, b. Jan. 23, 1813, Cologne, d. Aug. 17, 1887, Berlin. He was first a pupil of Leibl and Jos. Klein at Cologne, and, already in 1828, organist of the Carmelite church, and cathedral chorister there. In 1832 he went for further training to Berlin, and studied under Rungenhagen, A. B. Marx, and A. W. Bach. He was commissioned to set in order the library of the Royal Institute for Church Music, and this led him into the path of history, and the result, the following collections of old works :—

"Collectio operum musicorum Batavorum sæculi XVI." (12 vols.), "Musica sacra XVI., XVII. sæculorum" (26 vols.), "Collection de Compositions pour l'Orgue des XVI., XVII., XVIII. Siècles" (6 parts), and "Cantica Sacra" (16–18th centuries, 2 vols.). In addition to the work of editing and revising these publications, he occupied the posts of *regens chori* at the Catholic Church of St. Hedwig, of teacher of singing at the "Elisabeth" School, at the theatre school of singing, and at the French College, etc. In 1844, in conjunction with H. Küster and Th. Kullak, he founded the Berlin "Tonkünstlerverein," and, in the same year, became Royal Musical Director, also member of the Akademie, Royal Professor, and, finally, was named member of the senate of the Akademie. C. wrote masses, cantatas, choral works, music to the "Frogs" of Aristophanes and the "Electra" of Sophocles. He was also president of the "Gesellschaft für Musikforschung."

Commodo (Ital.), in a comfortable manner; *a suo c.,* at pleasure.

Compenius, Heinrich, b. 1540, Nordhausen, organ-builder, also composer, perhaps a brother of Esajas C., who, about 1600, was a celebrated organ-builder in Brunswick, and, according to Prætorius ("Syntagma," II.), is said to have written on the construction of organpipes. Esajas C. invented the double flute (Duiflöte).

Compère, Loyset, celebrated Netherland contrapuntist, d. Aug. 16, 1518, as canon of St. Quentin Cathedral. Unfortunately, only few of his motets have been preserved (21), and in very scarce books, viz., in Petrucci's "Odhecaton." (*Cf.* PETRUCCI.) To the works mentioned by Fétis must be added a Magnificat, which is in the Munich Library.

Compiacevole (Ital.), in an agreeable, pleasant manner.

Compline (Lat. *Completorium*), the last (before going to bed) of the *horæ canonicæ;* likewise the songs prescribed by the Romish Church (psalms, hymns, etc.).

Composition, generally speaking, is the mode of constructing musical works of art—musical gift, "talent for composition," being assumed. The art of composition can regulate, forward talent, but not act as a substitute for it. The study of composition begins with learning the elements of our system of music (general instruction-book), and then exercises in several parts, with prescribed harmonies, must be written out (*see* PART-WRITING, GENERAL-BASS), and with this is carried on, as a rule, the study of the relationship of notes. (HARMONY, METHOD OF.) Real musical productivity receives richer nourishment from exercises in *counterpoint* (q.v.), and, by submitting to the fetters of the imitative style (*see* CANON and FUGUE), becomes worthy of full freedom. At length the fledged bird can venture to fly : it reaches the last rung of the usual educational ladder, free C. (*Cf.* FORM.) That, at least, is the general plan and order of study, and in it, the *creation of melody* and the study of the nature of *rhythm* are left out of consideration. These two (inseparable) modes of discipline should never be lugged in, but rather proceed apart, together with the study of harmony. Youthful and impulsive talent has little respect for study planned according to certain divisions, and with certain gradations, and often attempts composition of the freest kind before working at harmony and counterpoint ; many a one, indeed, never studies the elements on which music is based, but, on that very account, remains, all through life, an unruly talent. The great masters studied earnestly, though perhaps not strictly according to the present system in force. By instruction in composition is generally understood all branches of musical writing, *i.e.* the arts of harmony, melody, rhythm, counterpoint, and form. But, in a narrower sense, the art of composition—as opposed to the various branches of theory belonging to the earlier stages of musical development—is the highest and last course of study, and concerns the creation of works of art, with the study of musical form as a starting-point. The rules for composition are not so much of a technical, as of a general esthetic nature. A distinction is properly made between the grammar of composition and musical esthetics. To the former belong harmony and counterpoint, whilst the art of composition consists, in a narrower sense, of applied esthetics. (*Cf.* FORM, ESTHETICS, HARMONY, COUNTERPOINT, RHYTHM, etc.) The great treatises of C. by Reicha, Fétis, Marx, Lobe, and others, discuss all the branches named in separate sections.

Compound times are those in which several simple times are grouped together : $\frac{3}{4}$ time, for instance, is simple time; $\frac{6}{8}$ time, compound time.

Con (Ital.), with.

Con alcuna licenza (Ital.), with a certain degree of licence.

Concentus. (*See* ACCENTUS.)

Concert (Ger. *Konzert*), a public musical performance (Symphony concert, Sacred concert, Military concert, Garden concert, etc.).

Concertante (*Duo* [*Trio*] *concertant*), a composition for two (three) principal instruments with accompaniment. (*See* CONCERTO—3.)

Concertina. (*See* ACCORDION.)

Concertino. (*See* CONCERTO.)

Concerto (Ger. *Konzert*), (1) an important instrumental piece for a solo instrument, as a rule, with orchestral accompaniment, which offers great difficulties to the executant, and enables him to display his virtuosity (piano concerto, violin concerto, etc.). The form of

the concerto is that of the sonata and symphony, with modifications resulting from the aim of the composition.—(2) A form of composition, no longer in vogue at the present day, in which several voices or instruments vie with one another (hence the name C., "contest "). The oldest form of the concerto in this sense is to be found in the *sacred concertos* (*Concerti ecclesiastici* or *da chiesa*), first introduced by Viadana (1602), motets for one (!), two, three, and four voices, with organ bass. These reached their highest stage of development in the cantatas of J. S. Bach, who himself always named them *concerti*; and taking into consideration their concertante style (apart from the chorales introduced into them), they can lay full claim to that title. The *chamber concerto* (*concerto da camera*) arose considerably later ; Giuseppe Torelli was the first to introduce the name, and he also wrote double concertos : the first (1686) as *concerto da camera*, others (1709) as *concerti grossi*—the former for two violins with bass, the latter for two concertante, and two *ripieni* violins, viola, and continuo. The *concerto grosso* was extended by Corelli, already in 1712, to three concertante instruments (*di concertino*), and this number remained the usual one. On the other hand, the orchestra (*concerto grosso*) became more and more strengthened. The chamber concerto passed into our present C. (*see* above). Corelli, Vivaldi, J. S. Bach brought these forms to perfection.

Concert piece (Ger. *Konzertstück*), a concerto in one movement of somewhat free form, for the most part with change of *tempo* and measure. The term is also applied to small solo pieces intended for concert performance.

Concerts du Conservatoire (Fr.), one of the most esteemed concert institutions of Paris, and one of the best in the world, founded in 1828 under the direction of Habeneck, whose successors up to the present have been : Girard (1849), Tilmant (1860), Hainl (1864), Deldevez (1872). The number of concerts during the year was at first six, and is now nine ; but since 1866 each concert is given twice for two sets of subscribers. The orchestra consists of seventy-four ordinary, and ten extra members ; while thirty-six members form the ordinary standing choir.

Concerts spirituels (Fr., "spiritual concerts "), the name given in the last century in Paris to concerts given on church festival days when the theatres were closed. They were established by Philidor (1725), and were held on twenty-four days in the year in the Salle des Suisses at the Tuileries. They were continued by Mouret, Thuret, Royer, Mondonville, d'Auvergne, Gaviniés, Le Gros, up to 1791. The Revolution put an end to them. The C.s were the fashion then, as are now the *Concerts du Conservatoire* (q.v.). The Paris C.s of to-day are only held in Holy Week, and are limited to religious music ; they were revived in this form in 1805

From 1770 there was great rivalry between the C.s. and the *Concerts des Amateurs* under the direction of Gossec, which from 1780 took the name of *Concerts de la Loge Olympique*, for which Haydn wrote six symphonies. The *Concerts de la Rue de Cléry* (from 1789) and the *Concerts Feydeau* (1794) also gained repute for a time.

Concitato (Ital.), in an agitated manner.

Concône, Giuseppe, b. 1810, Turin, d. there June 1, 1861, as organist of the royal chapel; before that he lived for ten years in Paris as teacher of singing (up to 1848). Of his compositions—among which are to be found two operas, aria, scenas, etc.—*vocalizzi* (five books) came into high repute, and are prized by teachers of singing.

Concussion-bellows is a small bellows in the organ, placed near the wind-chest, over an opening in the wind-trunk, the top plate of which is kept half raised by means of a spring. When the air is suddenly condensed, or rarefied (through inattention on the part of the bellows-blower, or through excessive use of the wind by the playing of full chords), by the taking in of superfluous air, or drawing it out, the concussion bellows regulates and steadies the wind in the wind-chest.

Con desiderio (Ital.), with an expression of longing.

Con desperazione (Ital.), in a despairing manner.

Con dolce maniera (Ital.), in a sweet manner.

Conducting, Art of. A musical work, even within the limits prescribed by the composer, can be presented in various ways, according to the particular conception of the interpreter. In the performance of an opera, symphony, etc., not one, but many take part, and their individual conception has to give place to one of a more general character; for then the conductor is really the performing artist. The means by which he can give effect to his conception are very limited, at any rate, during the actual performance. At rehearsal he can explain by word of mouth, can sing over passages to the executants, or play them over on their instruments, or hammer out the rhythms with his stick, etc.; but nothing of the sort can be done at performance; and only noiseless movements of the marshal's *bâton* in his hand can be the interpreters of his intentions. A glance cast at a singer or player may occasionally prove of priceless service, and an occasional movement of the left hand may be found useful; but still, the conducting-stick remains the most important factor, and its movements have therefore a fixed conventional meaning. As its German name—*Taktstock* ("time-stick")—shows, its chief province is to mark the time clearly, *i.e.* to give the *tempo*, and mark the primary accents. The principal movements are as follows:—the first part of a bar is, as a rule, indicated by a down

beat; the middle beats are neither high nor low, and the last goes upwards. It is of no importance whether the second beat be taken from right to left, or *vice versâ;* it can be indicated in various ways. The usual and most important kinds of time-beating are:—binary time ($\frac{2}{8}$, $\frac{2}{4}$, $\mathbb{C}$ $\frac{2}{1}$, but also $\frac{6}{16}$, $\frac{6}{8}$, $\frac{6}{4}$ in fast time [when only two is counted]); ternary time ($\frac{3}{8}$, $\frac{3}{4}$, $\frac{3}{2}$, but also $\frac{9}{16}$, $\frac{9}{8}$, $\frac{9}{4}$ [when only three is counted]); quadruple time ($\mathbf{C}$, $\frac{4}{2}$, $\frac{4}{8}$, also $\frac{12}{16}$, $\frac{12}{8}$, etc.), and sextuple time ($\frac{6}{4}$, $\frac{6}{8}$). They are beaten in the following manner:—

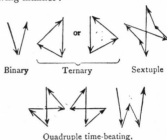

Binary   Ternary   Sextuple

Quadruple time-beating.

Compound triple time is taken as three times three, compound quadruple as four times three; but, always, so that the beginning of the bar is made clear by a beat from a greater height. A crescendo is generally indicated by beats of greater sweep, and a diminuendo in the reverse way; sharp accents (*sforzati*, etc.) are marked by short, jerky movements, changes of *tempo* (*stringendo*, *ritardando*) with the assistance of the left hand; but already here, individual characteristics come into play. The length of a pause is shown by a raised and motionless stick, and the end of the same, by a short curved movement. For further information consult the appendix to Berlioz's "Treatise on Instrumentation" ("The Orchestral Conductor"), also Prof. C. Schroeder's "Handbook of Conducting." A good conductor is only formed by practice; only the elements can be learned from books. (*Cf.* Richard Wagner, "Ueber das Dirigieren," 1869.)

Conductor, in German *Capellmeister* (q.v.).

Conductus (Lat.), one of the oldest forms of composition in several parts (12th century); it differed from Organum and Discantus in that counterpoint was not added to a Cantus Gregorianus in the tenor part, but this part was also invented by the composer. A distinction was made between C. *simplex* (in two parts) and *duplex* (in three parts, hence also *triplum*), etc.

Con facilità (Ital.), with facility.

Con fermezza (Ital.), with firmness, with decision.

Con festività (Ital.), in a festive manner.

Con fiducia (Ital.), with confidence.

Con fierezza (Ital.), fiercely.

Confinal. (*See* FINAL.)

Con fiochezza (Ital.), hoarsely.

Con forza (Ital.), with force.

Confrèrie (Fr.), "brotherhood." (*See* GUILDS.)

Con fretta (Ital.), hurriedly.

Con fuoco (Ital.), with fire.

Con furore (Ital.), with fury, with vehemence.

Con garbo (Ital.), with elegance, gracefully.

Con giustezza (Ital.), with precision.

Con grandezza (Ital.), with dignity, with majesty.

Con grazia (Ital.), with grace.

Con gusto (Ital.), with taste.

Con impeto (Ital.), impetuously.

Coninck, (1) J a c q u e s F é l i x de, b. May 18, 1791, Antwerp, d. April 25, 1866, pupil of the Paris Conservatoire, excellent pianist; he lived for many years in America, where he travelled, among others, with Malibran, was then for some years in Paris, and finally in Antwerp as conductor of the *Société d'Harmonie* which he founded. His compositions are: concertos, sonatas, sets of variations for pianoforte.—(2) F r a n ç o i s, b. Feb. 20, 1810, Lebbeke (East Flanders); he first studied at Ghent, afterwards at Paris under Pixis and Kalkbrenner, and then settled in Brussels as teacher of music in 1832. He published a Method of the Pianoforte, and various pf. pieces.—(3) J o s e p h B e r n a r d, b. March 10, 1827, Ostend; he went when young with his parents to Antwerp, where he received a thorough musical training under the guidance of Leun, maître de chapelle of St. Andrew's Church. His "Essai sur l'Histoire des Arts et Sciences en Belgique" gained a prize in 1845 from the "Verein zur Beförderung der Tonkunst." In 1851 he went to Paris, studied at the Conservatoire under Leborne, and settled in Paris as teacher of music, and as musical critic to various papers. C. has written several operas, besides small vocal and pf. pieces.

Con ira (Ital.), with an expression of anger.

Con leggerezza (Ital.), with lightness, airily.

Con lenezza (Ital.), in a gentle, quiet manner.

Con lentezza (Ital.), slowly.

Con mano destra (Ital.), with the right hand.

Conradi, A u g u s t, b. June 27, 1821, Berlin, d. there May 26, 1873; pupil of Rungenhagen at the Academie, 1843 organist of the "Invalidenhaus" at Berlin, 1849 theatre capellmeister at Stettin, 1851 at the old "Königsstadt" theatre, Berlin, then at Düsseldorf and Cologne; and, from 1856, again in Berlin, where he worked alternately as capellmeister at the Kroll, new Königsstadt, Wallner, and Victoria theatres. He left his property to musical institutions. C. is at present chiefly known by his potpourris, arrangements, etc., for garden concerts. He

had formerly some success with his operas, farces, and likewise with a symphony.

Con sdegno (Ital.), scornfully, angrily.

Conseguente (Ital.), the "following after" (*i.e.* imitating) part in a canon.

Conseguenza, same as CANON.

Conservatorium (Ital. *Conservatorio*, Fr. *Conservatoire*), the name of the great schools of music at which scholars receive a great number of lessons in music free of charge, or at a moderate cost; and where they are trained to become composers, teachers, virtuosi, or merely orchestral players. The name C. comes from the Italian, but is by no means chosen because these institutions are considered to "conserve" true art; in Italian, indeed, *conservatorio* means "hospital," "orphan-asylum." The first were, in fact, nothing else but orphan-asylums, in which talented children received a musical training; as in the *Conservatorio Santa Maria di Loreto*, founded at Naples in 1537, and also in the three *Della pietà de' Turchini*, *Dei poveri di Giesù Christo*, and *Di Sant' Onofrio*, founded at Naples, likewise in the 16th century. By command of King Murat these four were amalgamated into the *Collegio reale di musica*. The pupils of this institution are divided into interns and externs: the interns are pensioners (private scholars), *i.e.* receive board and lodging. The institution is wealthy enough to give away seventy scholarships. The age limits for scholars are from twelve to twenty-three; exceptions are, however, permitted. In 1885 the number of teachers was thirty-five; of scholars, about two thousand. The oldest music schools of Venice were not named *Conservatorio* but *Ospedale* ("hospital"), and further, *Della pietà*, *Dei mendicanti*, *Degl' incurabili*, and *San Giovanni e Paolo* (*Ospedaletto*, only for girls). At present the principal C. of Venice is the *Liceo Benedetto Marcello*, with (since 1877) subsidies from city and state. Its organisation is similar to that of German schools (no board, and few scholarships). The number of teachers is 13; of pupils 135 (1885). An old C. is also that of the *Regio conservatorio di musica* at Palermo, opened in 1615 as *Conservatorio buon pastore;* by a change of statute, rechristened (1737) *Collegio di musica;* and in 1863, by confiscation of its property, changed into a state institution (twenty-six teachers, fifty-six pupils). Many other Conservatoria have arisen in Italy within recent years, of which the most important are: the *Liceo musicale* at Bologna (founded 1864, town institution; only scholarships, but without board), twenty-two teachers, 313 pupils (1885), and a library of great importance (works bequeathed by Padre Martini and Gaet. Gaspari); the *Regio conservatorio di musica* at Milan, founded by Eugène Beauharnais (1807), with twenty-four scholarships (maintenance scholars): reorganised in 1850 (maintenance withdrawn), thirty-six teachers, about two hundred pupils, and directors up to the present:

Lauro Rossi, Mazzucato, Ronchetti-Monteviti; the *Civico instituto di musica* at Genoa, founded 1829, subsidised by the city since 1838 (nineteen teachers); the *Regio instituto musicale* at Florence, founded 1860, state institution, richly endowed (twenty-six teachers, 216 pupils); the *Liceo musicale* at Turin, developed from a humble beginning in 1865, city institution, free instruction (eighteen teachers, 155 pupils [1884]); and the *Liceo musicale Rossini*, founded by a legacy of 2,300,000 lire from Rossini, established 1883: twenty-six teachers, seventy-four pupils (only scholarships).

Older than these, and, indeed, the oldest C. out of Italy, is the *Paris Conservatoire de Musique*, founded 1784 under the name *École royale de chant et de déclamation* for the purpose of training opera-singers, enlarged 1793 to the *Institut national de musique;* it has existed since 1795 under its present name, only resuming that of *École royale de chant et de déclamation* during the period of the Restoration. This C. is one of the greatest of all existing institutions of the kind, and enjoys a distinguished reputation. The most renowned musicians of France esteem it an honour to act as professors at the C. The directors since the foundation have been as follows: Sarette, Cherubini, Auber, Ambroise Thomas. Besides A. Thomas, the most prominent professors for theory and composition are: J. Massenet, Bourgault-Ducoudray, Dubois, Pessard, Lenepveu, Barthe; for singing: Masset, Saint Yves Bax, Boulanger, R. Bussine, Barbot, Crosti, Bonnehée; for elementary instruction: Danhauser, Heyberger, Mouzin, Hommey, N. Alkan, Lavignac (dictation), and the ladies: Mercié-Porte, Doumie-Saint-Ange, Devrainne, Donne; choral singing: J. Cohen; declamation: Obin, Mocker, Ponchard, Got, Delaunay, Worms, Maubant; history of dramatic literature: de Lapommeraye; mimic art: Petipa, Mlle. Marquet; conducting: Deldevez; ensemble-playing: R. Baillot; pianoforte: Marmontel, Mathias, Le Couppey, Delaborde; harp: Hasselmans; violin: Dancla, Sauzay, Maurin, Garcin, Chaîne; violoncello: Delsart; for other instruments, nine more teachers. A committee of tuition (*Comité des Études*), composed of the most important professors and special members (among others, also Gounod, Saint-Saëns, Legouvé, Alex. Dumas), regulates the course of study, and for each department has issued a carefully-prepared method. For pupils who distinguish themselves there are prizes in the several classes. The highest prize for composition offered by the state, the *Grand Prix de Rome*, a three years' stipend (two in Rome and one in Germany), the stipendiary having, during that period, to send in compositions, from time to time, to the Académie, as proofs of diligent study. In the chief provincial towns of France so-called Succursales (branches, affiliated institutions) of the C. are established (at Marseilles, Toulouse, Nantes, Dijon, Lyons, Rouen).

Another important musical institution at Paris is the *École Niedermeyer*, which sprang from Choron's Church-music Institution (1817); present director Gust. Lefévre (School of Organists).

The *C. at Prague* is another excellent establishment, and of old date; it was opened May 1, 1811, under the direction of Dionys Weber, whose successors were Kittl, Joseph Krejei, and Bennewitz, the present director (instrumental and vocal music: practical and theoretical); also religion (Catholic), German grammar, geography, history, arithmetic, and calligraphy; and, besides, in the higher section, style and literature, mythology, art of metre, esthetics, history of music, and the French and Italian languages are taught. The instruction in instrumental music includes all orchestral instruments. (*Cf.* Ambros, "Das K. in Prag," 1858.) The *Vienna C.* (*K. der Gesellschaft der Musikfreunde*) was opened Aug. 1, 1817, under Salieri, as a vocal school; instruction on the violin was added in 1819; and in 1821 the institution was so far developed as to become a real C. G. Preyer (1844–48) was the first actual director (up to that time the institution had been under the management of a committee); his successor was J. Hellmesberger, who is still at the head; and from among many distinguished teachers may be named: J. Böhm, J. Merk, S. Sechter, Frau Marchesi, Herbeck, A. Brückner. The institution is in high repute and well attended (52 teachers and 758 pupils [1883]; 104 scholarships; *cf.* K. F. Pohl, "Die Gesellschaft der Musikfreunde, etc.," 1871). From among all German Conservatoria, the one founded by Mendelssohn at *Leipzig* (opened April 2, 1843) occupied, for several decades, the foremost place; since 1876 it has been called "Kgl. Konservatorium." The first teachers there were men of eminence:—Mendelssohn, Schumann, Ferd. David, M. Hauptmann, L. Plaidy, E. F. Wenzel, E. F. Richter, K. F. Becker, and K. A. Pohlenz; and, afterwards, F. Hiller, Niels Gade, I. Moscheles, J. Rietz, C. Reinecke, Fr. Brendel, K. Fr. Götze, etc.; but of these only Reinecke remains. The institution counts at present over 450 pupils; among the teaching-staff are to be found the names of C. Reinecke, S. Jadassohn, R. Papperitz, Jul. Klengel, O. Paul, Coccius. From the long list of pupils who have made a name may be mentioned Th. Kirchner (the first whose name was entered), W. Bargiel, L. Meinardus, L. Brassin, S. Jadassohn, Rob. Radecke, F. v. Holstein, E. Grieg, A. Sullivan, A. Wilhelmj, J. S. Svendsen. (*Cf.* the "Jubiläumsschrift" of E. Kneschke, 1868.)

The oldest C. in Berlin is the one founded Nov. 1, 1850, by A. B. Marx, Th. Kullak, and J. Stern; Kullak withdrew (1855) and Marx (1857), and the institution, which was carried on by Stern alone, still flourishes; in addition to the founders, the following were teachers there:— Hans von Bülow, G. Brassin, Barth, A. Kullak,

A. Krug, O. Tiersch, B. Scholz, R. Wüerst, etc. After twenty-five years the school list showed over three thousand names, among which J. Huber, H. G. Götz, and M. Moszkowski. The *Neue Akademie der Tonkunst*, opened by Th. Kullak, April 1, 1855, assumed still larger dimensions; at one time there were over one thousand pupils, and over a hundred teachers. Training in pianoforte-playing was the speciality of the institute, which was closed by Dr. F. Kullak in 1890. The *Königliche Hochschule für Musik* is undoubtedly the most important, though, at the present moment, not the best attended, musical training institution in Berlin; it forms a branch of the Royal Academy of Arts, and consists of three sections. Of these the oldest is the *Königliches Institut für Kirchenmusik*, opened in 1822; principals, A. Haupt (1869–91), Rob. Radecke; admissible number of pupils, twenty (gratuitous instruction). The section for *musical composition (akademische Meisterschulen)* was opened in 1833; the teachers at present are Bargiel, Blumner and Max Bruch; the instruction is also gratuitous. Finally, the section for *executive art* was opened on Oct. 1, 1869, under the direction of J. Joachim. It included, at first, only classes for violin, 'cello, and pianoforte; on Oct. 1, 1871, an organ class was added; on April 1, 1872, classes for singing, wind-instruments, and double-bass were established; and, further, in April, 1873, a " Chor schule," and in 1874, a choir. This section is now divided into four branches, each of which has its own director: strings (Joachim), theory (Bargiel), pianoforte (Rudorff), singing (Schulze). Ph. Spitta is, at present, administrative director of the " Hochschule." In addition to Joachim, there are the following teachers: Ph. Spitta, Bargiel, Wirth, Rudorff, Ad. Schulze, G. Engel, Hausmann, A. Dorn, Barth, Raif, Wieprecht, Succo, and others. *The Cologne C.*, of good fame *(Rheinische Musikschule)*, was founded by the city of Cologne in 1850, and the organisation and management were entrusted to F. Hiller. Among the present teachers, besides Hiller's successor, Fr. Wüllner, are: I. Seiss, M. Pauer, Klauwell, G. Jensen, E. Mertke, G. Holländer. The Royal C. at *Dresden* was established Feb. 1, 1856, by the chamber musician Tröstler, and taken up by F. Pudor in 1859; it was formerly under the artistic direction of F. Wüllner, and is now under a directorship composed of the principal teachers: Eugen Krantz (the present proprietor of the institute), F. Dräseke, Rappoldi, and F. Grützmacher; and of pupils may be named—Stägemann, Frau Otto-Alvsleben, Fides Keller, Anna Lankow, etc. The institution consists of schools for instrumental music, opera, drama, and a college for music teachers; in 1883 there were over seven hundred pupils. The *C. at Stuttgart*, founded (1856–57) by Stark, Faiszt, Lebert, Laiblin, Brachmann, and Speidel (directors: Faiszt and Scholl), is also an excellent school of music, and specially famous for

its pianoforte teaching. It consists of two distinct schools—the one for artists, the other for amateurs (forty-three teachers, and over six hundred pupils). The Royal Music School at *Munich*, founded in 1867, reorganised in 1874, is a public institution; at the head stood, until 1893, the court musical intendant, K. v. Perfall, while J. Rheinberger superintends the instrumental and theory classes. The organisation is excellent, and worthy of the municipality; and, as at the Prague C., general culture is not neglected for the sake of musical culture. By means of the performances of the " Kgl. Hofkapelle " (a *cappella*-choir), accessible to the students, the history of music is illustrated in a vivid manner; (there are thirty-three teachers, and about two hundred pupils). There is also a Royal School of Music at *Würzburg*, founded in 1801, town-(1820), state-institution (1875), which is well attended (Kliebert is the director; there are seventeen teachers, and over five hundred and fifty pupils). The " Hoch " C. at *Frankfort* is still young, but well endowed, and provided with a good teaching staff; it was founded in 1878, under the direction of J. Raff, with the help of a legacy left by the late Dr. Hoch. The institution is well attended, and has a future before it; of this there is proof in the fact that the Mozart-foundation (q.v.), taking into consideration the prosperity of the " Hoch " C., definitely abandoned its intention of establishing a C. of its own. (The administration of the Mozart fund was recently amalgamated with that of the " Hoch " C.) The principal teachers are: Bernhard Scholz (director), J. Kwast, B. Cossmann, Dr. Krückl, H. Heermann, Hugo Becker (attendance about two hundred pupils; only those showing talent are received). Of other German schools of music, of which nearly every town has several, may be still mentioned the " Königliche Institut für Kirchenmusik " (J. Schäffer, M. Brosig), at *Breslau;* the C., under the direction of v. Bernuth (teachers: J. v. Bernuth, K. Bargheer, K. v. Holten, Arn. Krug, K. Armbrust, A. Gowa, W. Marstrand, Max Fiedler, E. Krause, and others), at *Hamburg;* the " Kirchliche Musikschule " (Haberl) at *Ratisbon;* the municipal C. at *Strassburg-i.-E.* (director, Franz Stockhausen, founded 1855, reorganised 1873; eighteen teachers and about three hundred pupils); the " Grossherzogliche Orchester und Musikschule " (director, Müller-Hartung, opened 1872) at *Weimar;* the " Frankfurter Musikschule," founded in 1860 by H. Henkel, Hilliger, Hauff, Oppel, at *Frankfort* (the original founders are, in turn, directors [Hilliger died 1865]) ; and the " Raff Conservatorium " founded by teachers who left the " Hoch " C. when Bernh. Scholz assumed the management of the latter (1883; founders: Roth, Schwarz, and Fleisch) ; the " Grossherzogliche Conservatorium " (founded 1884 by Heinr. Ordenstein) at *Carlsruhe;* the C. (founded in 1872 by V. Freudenberg), present director, Albert Fuchs, teachers—Dr. Hugo Riemann, Ed. Uhl, Oskar Brückner, Max Reger, and others, at *Wiesbaden;* the Scharwenka, Schwanzer, Luisenstadt Conservatoria, the music schools of Klindworth, W. Freudenberg and others at *Berlin.* At Vienna the brothers Eduard and Adolf Horak have a flourishing pianoforte institute in three branches (the Wieden, Mariahilf, and Leopoldstadt); at *Ofen-Pest* there are the "Landes Musikakademie," of which Fr. Liszt was honorary director, the National Conservatorium (director, E. Bartay), and the "Ofener Musikakademie" (Szantzner); at *Graz* the music training-school of J. Buwa; at *Innsbruck* the "Musikschule des Musikvereins" (founded in 1818; director, J. Pembaur); at *Lemberg* the "Musikschule des Galizischen Musikvereins" (Mikuli); at *Salzburg* the "Musikschule des Mozarteums" (since 1880; already over three hundred pupils). The most important Swiss schools of music are those at *Geneva, Basle* (director, Bagge), *Berne* (Reichel), and *Zürich* (Fr. Hegar). One of the largest institutions in existence is at *Brussels,* founded (1813) as a municipal school of music, reorganised (1832) and changed into a government institution. The first director was Fr. J. Fétis, and, since his death, Fr. A. Gevaert (forty-eight teachers, 539 pupils; instruction gratuitous, but foreigners are only received by consent of the minister and the director). The school at *Liège* (founded 1827 as " Kgl. Musikschule," reorganised in 1832) is a worthy rival of the former, and is still better attended (one thousand pupils; director, Th. Radoux). Both institutions are supported by the state; and, likewise, the *C. at Ghent* (founded 1833, state institution since 1879; first director, Mengal; since 1871 Ad. Samuel); the *C. at Antwerp,* " Antwerpens Vlaamsche Muzickschool," is an institution subsidised by the state, and it was founded in 1867 by its present head, the far-famed Peter Benoit (thirty-eight teachers). This last-named institution, thanks to its director, Benoit, cultivates specially German music, and, besides, nourishes, and in a manner not to be despised, the political sympathy of Antwerp for the German Empire. Of Dutch conservatoria must be named the one at *Amsterdam,* C. of the " Maatschappij tot bevordering van toonkunst," opened in 1862, reorganised in 1884; in 1883, sixteen teachers and 560 pupils; and the one at *Rotterdam,* founded in 1845 (present director,᎐ R. v. Perger; fifteen teachers, over six hundred pupils). At *The Hague* there exists since 1826 a flourishing Royal School of Music (first director, J. H. Lübeck, and at present H. Viotta; instruction gratuitous, three hundred pupils). Also the C. founded at *Luxemburg* in 1864 is not without importance. *Russia* has a C. at Warsaw (1821), one at Petersburg (1865), and one at Moscow (1864; there are at present forty-eight teachers and over 340 pupils). In *London* there are five :—the Royal Academy of Music,

founded in 1822 : principal, Dr. A. C. Mackenzie, about eighty teachers and about four hundred pupils; the London Academy of Music, founded in 1861; Trinity College, 1872, which grants diplomas; the Guildhall School of Music, 1880, over one hundred teachers and over two thousand pupils : principal, Sir J. Barnby; and the Royal College of Music, 1883 (which sprang from the National Training School of Music founded in 1876, under Sullivan's direction) : principal, Sir George Grove (over sixty teachers; a richly endowed institution, and one full of promise for the future); also one in Edinburgh, and one in Dublin. *Scandinavian* schools have been established at Copenhagen (1867, but, in accordance with the intentions of the founder [P. W. Moldenhauer], receives only fifty pupils), at Christiania (1865) and at Stockholm (1771); the last-named is a state institution, with instruction gratis, twenty teachers and about 150 pupils. *Spain* has a C. at Madrid (1830, twenty-eight teachers, thirty-four assistant teachers, and over two thousand pupils), at Saragossa and Valencia; and *Portugal,* one at Lisbon (since 1836; fifteen teachers, over 350 pupils); *Greece* one at Athens; and lastly *America,* which, thanks to the industrial feeling of the nation, possesses many in the more important cities (New York, Boston, Baltimore, Cincinnati (1880; 283 pupils).

Opinions are divided respecting the value of a Conservatorium; the collegiate intercourse of young musicians with one another is, without doubt, uncommonly stimulating; but to many a fresh talent, full of danger. The greater number of unprejudiced thinkers are, nevertheless, agreed that most of the Conservatoria produce unsatisfactory results, inasmuch as their aim is a purely musical one. What is exceptional at Prague and Munich should be the rule in all institutions, viz., compulsory teaching of the most necessary branches of general culture.

Consolante (Ital.), consoling.

Consonance (Lat. *Consonantia,* " sounding together "). The coalescence of two or more tones forming clang-unity. Tones are consonant which belong to the same clang, whether it be as fundamental note, fifth, or third. (*See* Clang.) It is, however, necessary for tones which can be regarded as elements of one and the same clang to be made really intelligible in this sense by their context, otherwise they are not consonant but dissonant. A striking illustration of this is offered by the *chord of six-four,* for although it contains only tones (g : c : e ; g : c : e♭) which can be understood in the sense of one and the same clang (c-*major* chord or c-*minor* chord), yet for the most part it is a dissonance, and treated as such, *i.e.* it is resolved by progression of a second. When it appears in its characteristic form as a preparation for a cadence, it is regarded as a G-*major* chord with double appoggiatura, with the fourth in place of the third, and the sixth (major or minor) in place of the fifth. For this reason neither the fourth nor the sixth of the chord of six-four is doubled in four-part writing (*as a rule dissonant tones are not doubled*), but the bass-note; for this is really the fundamental tone, and the only one representing the clang. The old dispute about the C. or dissonance of the fourth is, from this, easy to understand, and to settle. *g* : *c*, taken in the sense of the c-major or c-minor chord, is consonant; but in the sense of the chord of G-major, or G-minor, or also F-minor, F-major, or A♭, is dissonant. The sense of the clang presentation—which depends on the tonality of the previous harmonies, and often indeed on rhythmical position—decides the question of C. or dissonance. (For consonant intervals *cf.* INTERVAL.) Of consonant *chords* there are only two kinds—*major chords* and *minor chords* (q.v.). The major consonance is the sounding together of a fundamental tone with its upper fifth and upper third, and the minor consonance the sounding together of a fundamental tone with its under fifth and under third. This is established with further detail under CLANG.

Con sonorità (Ital.), sonorously.

Con sordino (Ital.), with the mute. This indicates: (1) in pianoforte-playing that soft pedal is to be used; (2) in violin-, viola-, etc., playing, that a mute is to be placed on the bridge; (3) in horn-, trumpet-, etc., playing, that a mute is to be inserted into the bell. *Sordini* is the plural of *sordino*. (*See* SORDINO.)

Constantin, Titus Charles, famous conductor, b. Jan. 7, 1835, Marseilles, pupil of Ambroise Thomas at the Paris Conservatoire; in 1866, conductor at the Fantaisies Parisiennes, also after their removal to the Athenæum, 1871 conductor of the Concerts du Casino, 1872 at the "Renaissance" Theatre, 1875 at the Opéra Comique. C. has written some operas, overtures, etc.

Con strepito (Ital.), noisily.

Contano (Ital., abbr. *cont.*, "they count," *i.e.* pause). An indication in scores at the beginning of a movement, not that the instruments against which the C. is marked are to be silent (otherwise *tacet* or *tacent* would be marked), but that they enter later on; to save room, however, and for convenience of reading, no stave is marked for those instruments until they enter. This term is also used in the middle of a movement when certain instruments are silent for a long time; it is intended, of course, for the copyist writing out the parts from the score.

Conti (1), Francesco Bartolommeo, b. Jan. 20, 1681, Florence; he was court theorbist at Vienna in 1701, court composer in 1713, d. there July 20, 1732. He was highly esteemed as an opera composer, and as a performer on the theorbo. His most important work was *Don Chisciotte in Sierra Morena* (1719). He wrote

in all sixteen operas, thirteen serenades, nine oratorios, and many (more than fifty) cantatas. —(2) Ignazio (Contini), son of the former, b. 1699, d. March 28, 1759, Vienna. He wrote there a number of serenades and oratorios, but was less talented than his father, light-minded, and died in great poverty.—(3) Gioacchino, named Gizziello (after his teacher Gizzi), one of the most famous *evirati* of the last century, b. Feb. 28, 1714, Arpino (Naples), d. Oct. 25, 1761, Rome. He made his *début* in this city in 1729 with very great success, sang there up to 1731, then at Naples, and from 1736 to 1737 in London, afterwards in Lisbon, Madrid, and again Lisbon. In 1753 he retired from public life, and went to Arpino.—(4) Carlo, opera composer, b. Oct. 14, 1797, Arpino, d. July 10, 1868, Naples. He was a member of the Academy of Arts of that city, and in 1846 professor of counterpoint at the Conservatorio, and in 1862 director in place of Mercadante, who had become blind. Of his eleven operas *Olimpia* (1829), obtained the greatest success. C. wrote also six masses, two requiems, and other sacred compositions. Florimo, Marchetti, etc., were his pupils.

Continuo, Giovanni, Italian contrapuntist, teacher of Luca Marenzio; he became maestro to the Gonzaga family in Mantua, and d. in 1565 (his successor was Giaches de Wert).

Continuo (Ital.), really *Basso c.* or *Continuato*, a "continuous bass." This was the name given to the figured instrumental bass part which came into vogue in Italy about 1600, and from which was gradually evolved the modern style of accompaniment. (*See* ACCOMPANYING PARTS and ACCOMPANIMENT.) Caccini, Cavalieri, Viadana, and others began about the same time to use the C., so that it is difficult to say who was actually the first—probably Cavalieri. It is worthy of note that an Englishman, Richard Deering, coming from Rome, published already in 1597 at Antwerp, "Cantiones à 5 cum basso c."

Contra (Lat. and Ital.), over, against, facing, opposite to.

Contrabasso (Ital.). (*See* DOUBLE-BASS.)

Contrainte (Fr.). (*See* OSTINATO.)

Contr'alto (Ital.; Fr. *Haute-contre*). Alto voice. (*See* ALTO.)

Contra octave, the notes ͵C to ͵B:—

(*Cf.* "Synopsis of notes," p. 1 of this Dictionary.)

Contrapunctus (Lat.), counterpoint (q.v.); *C. æqualis*, equal counterpoint; *C. inæqualis*, unequal counterpoint; *C. floridus, diminutus*, ornamental, florid (*i.e.* unequal) counterpoint (two or more notes against one, in equal values or rhythmical motives).

Contrapunto (Ital.), counterpoint (q.v.), *C. alla zoppa*, "limping," syncopated counterpoint (*C. sincopato*); *C. sopra (sotto) il soggetto*, counterpoint above (below) the *Cantus firmus; C. alla mente*, improvised counterpoint (Fr. *Chant sur le livre*), the oldest kind of counterpoint ; for discant (*see* DISCANTUS), *i.e.* placing a different part over against the tenor of the Gregorian chant, was at first (12th century) entirely an improvisation. The rules for discant, which have been preserved, were not intended for compositions to be written out, but as instructions for the singers (who, in fact, were at that time the chief composers). The inevitable bad effects of discant in more than two parts naturally led to rules and regulations for counterpoint, which had to be worked out in writing. *C. alla mente* (*al improviso*) was, however, kept up until the 16th century.

Contr'arco (Ital.), bowing (on the violin, etc.) in a manner contrary to rule.

Contrary Motion is the opposite of Parallel Motion (*cf.* MOVEMENT, KINDS OF, 3). Concerning the prohibition of many parallel progressions, and the way in which they can be avoided by Contrary Motion, *see* PARALLELS and PART-WRITING. Concerning C. M. in another sense, viz., as inversion of a theme (theme in C. M.), which plays an important *rôle* in the imitative style, *cf.* INVERSION.

Contratempo (Ital.), Fr. *Contretemps*, accenting of a note on an unaccented part of a bar; syncopation (q.v.).

Contratenor (Lat.), countertenor. (*See* ALTO.)

Contredanse (Fr.), a dance of English origin (*Anglaise*), which was introduced into France at the beginning of the last century, and quickly became popular. The name C. refers to a characteristic feature of the dance—viz., that the couples are opposite to each other, and do not follow one another as in round dances. The derivation of the word from "country dance" is a false one, although Türk gives it in his " Klavierschule" (1789).

Contre-sujet (Fr.), countersubject.

Converse, C h a r l e s C r o z a t, American composer, b. 1832, Massachusetts, pupil of the Leipzig Conservatorium; he lives, as a lawyer, at Erie (Pennsylvania).

Conversio (Lat.), inversion.

Conveyances are tubes in the organ which carry the wind from the wind-chest to special rows of very great pipes which are not placed over the chest. C. are generally tin tubes of narrow measure.

Cooke, (1) B e n j a m i n, b. 1734, London, d. Sept. 14, 1793. In 1752 he became the successor of Pepusch as conductor at the Academy of Ancient Music; in 1757, after the retirement of

Gates, choir-master, in 1758 lay vicar, and in 1762 organist of Westminster Abbey. He handed over the conductorship of the Academy, in 1789, to Arnold. In 1775 he took his degree of Mus.Doc. at Cambridge, and in 1782 likewise at Oxford. C. is specially famed in England as a composer of glees, canons, and catches, for which he frequently received prizes from the Catch Club. He wrote, besides, anthems and other sacred pieces, also odes for the Academy of Ancient Music, and various instrumental works; and he was, at the same time, highly esteemed as a theorist.—(2) T h o m a s S i m p s o n (Tom C.), b. 1782, Dublin, d. Feb. 26, 1848, London ; he was at first leader of the band at Dublin, then, for many years, opera singer (tenor) at London (Drury Lane), and, finally, conductor again at Drury Lane, Covent Garden, also assistant-conductor of the Philharmonic Society, and from 1846 leader of the *Concerts of Ancient Music*. C., like the above, was a composer who received many prizes for glees, catches, etc. ; but above all he was a very prolific opera composer (for Drury Lane), and a celebrated teacher of singing ; he also published a vocal Method.

Cooper, G e o r g e, b. July 7, 1820, London, d. Oct. 2, 1876; from a boy he occupied various posts as organist, and was afterwards singing-master and organist of Christ's Hospital, and in 1856, organist of the Chapel Royal. C. rendered meritorious service by the cultivation of Bach's organ works; he also edited a number of instructive organ pieces.

Coperario (really C o o p e r), J o h n, English lutenist and lute composer, and music teacher to the children of James I.; Henry and William Lawes were his pupils. Some *pièces d'occasion* (funeral odes and masques) appeared from 1606–14. He died in 1627.

Coppola, Pier A n t o n i o, b. Dec. 11, 1793, Castrogiovanni (Sicily), d. Nov. 13, 1877, Catania; a talented opera composer, who had the misfortune to be a contemporary of Rossini. After repeated attempts, crowned with only moderate success, he made a fortunate venture with *Nina Pazza per Amore* (1835), frequently performed not only on all Italian stages, but also at Vienna, Berlin, Madrid, Lisbon, and Mexico. It was given at Paris in 1839, in revised form, under the title *Eva*. About the same time C. undertook an engagement as maestro at the Royal Opera, Lisbon, and, later on, brought out new operas in Italy. Besides *Nina*, he had most success with *Enrichetta di Baienfeld* (Vienna, 1836) and *Gli Illinesi* (Turin).

Copula (Lat.), coupler ; also a term applied to flue stops; (*a*) for 8-ft. Open Diapason, probably because this stop is suitable for coupling with any others; (*b*) for the 8-ft. Hohlflöte (Koppelflöte), which, on the other hand, needs coupling with other stops.

Copyright, the exclusive right which an

author has of publishing his works for a number of years; a right which he may sell absolutely, or conditionally, to a publisher or any other person.

Cor (Fr.), horn; *C. anglais*, English horn (Altoboe, *see* OBOE).

Coranto (Ital.), a courante (q.v.).

Corbett, W illi a m, an English violin virtuoso, member of the Queen's band; he lived from 1711 to 1740 in Italy (Rome). He occasionally gave concerts in most of the large towns, and collected musical books and instruments. After his return to London, he resumed his position in the band, and died in 1748. He bequeathed his collection of instruments to Gresham College, with a stipend for someone to look after them. C. published various instrumental works, especially for violin.

Corda (Ital.) string; *una c.* (" on one string ") indicates in pianoforte music that the left-hand (shifting) pedal is to be used; *due corde* (" with two strings "), with half shifting; *tutte le corde* (" all strings "), *i.e.* without soft pedal.

Cordans, B a r t o l o m e o, b. 1700, Venice, d. May 14, 1757, Udine; an extremely prolific composer; he entered, when young, the Franciscan order, but obtained a dispensation from the Pope, and withdrew from it. C. afterwards brought out a number of operas at Venice with moderate success. In 1735 he accepted the post of maestro at Udine Cathedral, and then wrote an immense amount of sacred music; for—although he handed over a large number of manuscript volumes to a firework manufacturer for the purpose of making rockets—over sixty masses, over a hundred psalms, including some for double choir, and motets, have been preserved.

Cor de chasse (Fr.), a hunting-horn.

Cordella, G i a c o m o, prolific Italian opera composer, b. July 25, 1786, Naples, d. there Aug. 8, 1846, pupil of Fenaroli and Paesiello, theatre maestro, sub-conductor of the royal band, and teacher at Naples Conservatorio; he wrote seventeen operas for Naples, also some cantatas, and sacred music.

Corder, F r e d e r i c k, gifted English composer, b. Jan. 26, 1852, London; he first went into business, but afterwards became a pupil of the Royal Academy of Music, won the Mendelssohn Scholarship, and studied under Ferd. Hiller at Cologne. On his return he became conductor at the Brighton Aquarium, and brought the concerts there into high repute. Of his works the following deserve mention: Overture *Prospero* (1885), *The Bridal of Triermain* (cantata, 1886), the opera *Nordisa* (1887), "Roumanian Suite" (1887), *The Minstrel's Curse*, ballad for declamation with orchestra (1888), "Roumanian Dances" for pf. and violin(1883), etc.

Corelli, A r c a n g e l o, one of the first real virtuosi on the violin, and a classical composer for this instrument. He was b. Feb., 1653,

Fusignano, near Imola, d. Jan. 18, 1713, Rome; he studied counterpoint with Matteo Simonelli, and the violin with Giov. B. Bassani. Little is known of his early life, but he seems to have held an appointment about 1680 at the court of Munich. In 1681 he settled in Rome, where he found in Cardinal Ottoboni a friend and patron. C. lived in the cardinal's palace until his death. Attempts were made to draw him away to Naples, and, after repeated invitations, C. was induced to go there and play before the king. During the performance, however, he made several slips, and imagined that he had failed, and, in great excitement, travelled back to Rome. Here, thrown for a time into the shade by the performances of Valentini, a violinist of ordinary ability, he fell a prey to melancholy. His epoch-making works, which at the present day are highly esteemed by all violinists, are as follows: four sets of twelve sonatas in three parts for two violins (1683-94); as a third part Op. 1 has an organ bass, Op. 2 'cello and bass viol or cembalo, Op. 3 bass lute (Theorbo, Arciliuto) and organ bass, Op. 4 bass viol or cembalo; further, twelve two-part sonatas, Op. 5, for violin and bass viol or cembalo (1700), republished five times up to 1799, arranged as " Concerti grossi " by Geminiani (they also appeared at Amsterdam arranged for two flutes and bass), and also for violin and piano by Gustav Jensen; also nine sonatas for two violins and cembalo (1695 at Rome, and reprinted later at Amsterdam); a set of posthumous sonatas for two violins with organ bass; and his last and greatest work (Op. 6)—twelve " Concerti grossi " for two violins and 'cello as solo instruments (" Concertino obligato "), and also two violins, viola, and bass as accompanying instruments, which may also be doubled (" Concerto grosso "). The forty-eight sonatas (Op. 1–4) and the " Concerti grossi " (Op. 6) were published by Walsh at London in two volumes, and revised by Pepusch. The only complete modern edition of Corelli's works is that (in score) by Dr. Chrysander (London : Augener & Co.). Some numbers from Op. 5 were edited by Alard and David (" Folies d'Espagne "). " All Corelli's compositions succeeded in gaining popularity, and were thus circulated far and wide, and served as models to the musicians of his time; but the 'Opera Quinta' was in this respect the most successful. It was taken up as a school-work in all countries " (Chrysander).

Cormorne (Fr.). (*See* CROMORNE.)

Cornamusa (Ital., Fr. *cornemuse*), an old Italian kind of schalmey, but closed at the lower end, so that the sound-waves were transmitted through the sound-holes. (*Cf.* BASSANELLO.) Also similar to the word Bagpipe.

Cornelius, P e t e r, b. Dec. 24, 1824, Mayence, d. there Oct. 26, 1874, a near relation of the painter of that name. He originally decided to become an actor, but, after an unfortunate *début* on the stage, turned to music; and from 1845 to 1850 studied counterpoint with Dehn at Berlin. In 1852 he went to Weimar, where he joined company with Liszt, and in the *Neue Zeitschrift für Musik* became one of the most zealous champions of the new German school. His comic opera, *Der Barbier von Bagdad*, was given at Weimar in 1858, but it did not take with the public; and Liszt, who held the work in high esteem, was so annoyed, that he left Weimar. C. now went to Wagner at Vienna, and followed him in 1865 to Munich, where he received an appointment at the Royal School of Music. A new opera (*Cid*) was produced at Weimar in 1865. A third (*Gunlöd*, text from the "Edda") remained unfinished. His smaller works (songs, duets, part-songs for mixed and for male chorus) have become best-known; although even these—on account of the uncomfortable voice-parts, and harshness of the harmonies—are only enjoyed by the few. C. wrote the books of his operas, and the words for most of his songs; and he also published a volume of lyric poetry ("Lyrische Poesien," 1861). The *Barbier von Bagdad* has recently been performed with success at Coburg, Hamburg, etc. It was also given twice in London (1891) by the pupils of the Royal College of Music.

Cornet, Julius, opera singer and stage manager, b. 1793, Santa Candida (Italian Tyrol), d. Oct. 2, 1860, Berlin. He studied with Salieri at Vienna, and afterwards received further training in Italy. He at first made *furore* as tenor singer, then, jointly with Mühling, undertook the direction of the Hamburg Theatre, which, however, came to an end after the great fire of 1842. Some time afterwards he was called to Vienna as director of the "Hofoper," but could not endure any interference from higher authorities, and had to give up the post. He was engaged as director of the Berlin Victoria Theatre, but died before it was completed. C. wrote an excellent work—"Die Oper in Deutschland," and skilfully translated the libretti of *La Muette di Portici, Zampa*, and the *Brasseur de Preston* into German.

Cornet (Ger. *Kornett*, Ital. *Cornetto*), (1) same as Zink (q.v.).—(2) In the organ (*a*) a now obsolete reed-stop imitating the tone of the Zinken (8 ft., or as *Cornettino* 4 and 2 ft., and *Grand Cornet* 16 ft.). Its tone was of a bleating character, and it is now found only as a pedal stop of 2 or 4 ft. (*b*) A stop of 3, 4, and 5 ranks, as a rule, 8 ft., seldom 4 ft. The C. is distinguished by the third (fifth overtone), which is the characteristic feature of the C. In the C. the overtones always occur in close series, and indeed commence when it is of 5 ranks from the fundamental tone, when of 4 from the octave, when of 3 from the twelfth, always ending with the seventeenth. At Heilbronn there is one of 6 ranks, but it commences with the double octave ($c = c^1$, e^1, g^1, c^a, e^a, g^a).

Cornet-à-pistons, valve cornet, a brass wind instrument of still higher compass than the trumpet; it was evolved from the old posthorn by the application of valves. The harmonic scale of horns, trumpets, and cornets in c begins from below thus (the lowest C. with tubes of narrow bore does not readily speak):

Cornet:
Trumpet:
Horn:

i.e. if the cornet notation were on the same principle as that of the horn and trumpet, the notes would sound an octave higher than those written, just as the horn in (low) c sounds an octave lower, the c-trumpet, on the other hand, in unison with the notation. But instead of that, the harmonic scale of the cornet is written an octave higher, *i.e.* the following notes sound alike on all of the three instruments named—

Horn   Trumpet   Cornet
in (low) B flat.   in B flat.   in B flat.

But this *b'* flat (according to the clang) is the sixteenth harmonic of the horn, the eighth of the trumpet, the fourth of the cornet. The compass of the C., however, apart from notes obtainable by virtuosi, does not extend upwards higher than that of the trumpet. The valve cornet is still constructed in B♭ (with an A crook). Owing to the want of nobility of its tone, the C. has not found a place in the symphonic orchestra. Arban and Legendre in Paris, Wurm in Petersburg, and J. Kosleck and his associates ("Kaiser-Kornett quartet") in Berlin are virtuosi on the C.

Cornetta (Ital.), (1) a small horn.—(2) A cornet.

Cornettino (Ital.), a small cornetto.

Cornetto (Ital.), (1) a cornet (q.v.).—(2) An obsolete wood wind instrument. *Cornetto muto*, a mute—*i.e.* soft-toned—horn; *cornetto torto*, or *storto*, a crooked horn.

Corno (Ital.), horn. *C. da caccia*, French horn. *C. di bassetto*, basset horn.

Corno Inglese (Ital.), the English horn. (See Cor Anglais.)

Cornon, a large kind of curved *Zink* (q.v.); also a new brass instrument, of wide measure, constructed in 1844 by Cerveny.

Cornopean, a name formerly given to the cornet-à-pistons (q.v.).

Cor omnitonique (Fr.), a horn invented by Sax of Paris, on which, by means of valves, all the tones and semitones of the scale can be produced.

Coro (Ital.), a choir, a chorus.

Corona (Ital.), a pause ⌒.

Corps de voix (Fr.), quality or volume of the voice.

Correctorium (Lat.), tuning-cone, used in tuning an organ.

Corrente (Ital.; Fr. *courante*), an old dance form in triple time, incorporated into the Suite; its characteristic feature is the lively movement of notes of equal value. So, at least, does it appear among the Italians (Corelli), whereas in German and French compositions it was of a more passionate character.

Corrépétiteur (Fr.), **Correpetitor** (Ger.), the musician who teaches the singers their parts; also the musician who makes the ballet-dancers acquainted with the accompanying music.

Corri, Domenico, b. Oct. 4, 1744, Rome, d. May 22, 1825, London. He studied with Porpora, came to London in 1774, where he wrote the operas *Alessandro nell' Indie* and *The Travellers*. His daughter married Dussek, with whom C. established (1797) a music business, which, however, failed. Besides many songs, rondos, arias, sonatas, etc., C. wrote "The Singer's Preceptor" (1798); "The Art of Fingering" (1799); "Musical Grammar," and a "Musical Dictionary."

Corsi, Jacopo, a Florentine nobleman, about 1600, one of the men with whose name the early history of the opera is associated. He was a warm friend of art; and in his house, and in that of his friend, Count Bardi, the founders of the new style—Peri, Caccini, Cavalieri, Galilei, etc.—were frequent guests. C. himself played the gravicembalo (cembalo) at most of the performances of the first attempts at music drama.

Corteccia, Francesco Bernardo di, b. Arezzo, d. June 7, 1571, as court maestro and canon of the Lorenzo Church at Florence. Madrigals (one book, 1544); *Cantica*, festival music for the marriage of Cosimo I. de' Medici have been preserved in print, and a Hymnary in manuscript; many other compositions have been lost.

Coryphæus (Lat.), **Coryphée** (Fr.), **Corypheus,** the leader of the dramatic chorus.

Cossmann, Bernhard, performer of the first rank on the 'cello, b. May 17, 1822, Dessau, studied with Theodor Müller and Kummer; he was in the orchestra of the Grand Opéra, Paris, in 1840; London in 1841; Gewandhaus orchestra, Leipzig, in 1847; at Weimar, under Liszt, in 1852, professor of the 'cello at Moscow Conservatoire in 1866, and from 1870 to 1878 at Baden-Baden, without appointment. Since then he has been professor of the 'cello at Frankfort. C. is as good a quartet- as solo-player.

Costa, (1) Michele, an opera composer of note, b. Feb. 4, 1810, Naples, d. April 29, 1884, Brighton. He studied music with his father,

Pasquale C., his grandfather, Tritto, and Zingarelli, and won his spurs as composer at the Naples theatres. In 1829 he was called to England by Zingarelli in order to conduct an important work by the latter (*Super Flumina Babylon*) at a Birmingham Musical Festival; but instead of so doing he appeared as a tenor singer. From that time he became a naturalised Englishman, and from 1830 was active in London as opera conductor. He himself wrote several operas (*Malek Adel, Don Carlo*), undertook in 1846 the conductorship of the Philharmonic Society, and in 1848 that of the Sacred Harmonic Society. From 1849 he was regular conductor of the Birmingham Musical Festivals, and from 1857 of the Handel Festivals. At the Philharmonic Society, Wagner, for one season, (1855), was his successor. He received the order of knighthood in 1869. In 1871 he was conductor at Her Majesty's Theatre. C. wrote several oratorios for the musical festivals. His half-brother (2), Carlo, b. 1826, d. Jan., 1888, Naples, was teacher of theory at the Conservatorio in that city.

Cotillon (Fr.), lit., "petticoat." "A social game in form of a dance." The cotillon has no characteristic music; a waltz, galop, or any other dance tune is used for the purpose.

Cotta, Johann, b. May 24, 1794, Ruhla (Thuringia), d. March 18, 1868, as pastor at Willerstedt, near Weimar. He was the composer of the Volkslied, "Was ist des Deutschen Vaterland?"

Cotto (Cottonius), Johannes, a writer on music (11th to 12th century), whose treatise, "Epistola ad Fulgentium," contains important notices concerning the beginnings of notation and solmisation (reprinted in Gerbert, "Scriptores," II.).

Cottrau, Guglielmo Louis, a popular composer of *Canzoni* in the Neapolitan dialect, b. Aug. 9, 1797, Paris, d. Oct. 31, 1847, Naples, where he had lived since 1806. His sons, Theodore (b. Nov. 7, 1827, Naples) and Jules (b. 1831, Naples), followed in their father's footsteps, and also acquired great popularity. A third, Filice, b. 1830, Naples, died there Jan., 1887.

Couac (Fr.), the "quack" of the clarinet, oboe, and bassoon, caused by a bad reed or reeds, deranged keys, wearied lips, etc.; in English it is called the "goose."

Coucy, Regnault Châtelain de, troubadour of the 12th century, followed Richard Cœur de Lion in the third crusade, and fell in 1192. When dying, he ordered that his heart should be sent to the lady whom he loved; the jealous husband received it, had the heart roasted and served up before his spouse, who died heart-broken when she learned what she had eaten. So runs the tale in the "Roman vom Chastelain de C. und der Dame de Fayel."

A number (twenty-four) of *Chansons* by Châtelain de C. are preserved in the Paris Library, and are some of the oldest memorials of the music of the West. They have been carefully revised, collated with different manuscripts, and published with the melodies in old notation by Francisque Michel (1830).

Coulé (Fr.). (*See* SCHLEIFER.)

Counterpoint, according to the present common use of the term, is, first of all, a special part of musical technology (theory with a view to practice), in contradistinction to harmony which is concerned with figured basses; polyphonic writing without figures, *i.e.* the polyphonic exposition of a given melody without further support of any kind. Yet by contrapuntal treatment of the parts is understood, in a more restricted sense, *concertante* treatment (a most suitable term, and one which ought to be in general use), in which the parts vie with one another, and do not merely consist of one bearing the melody, and the rest mere harmonic stuffing, as in Italian operas the stereotyped—

Here the harmony suggested by the melodic phrase is expressed in the most primitive manner. In the concertante style, all the parts are melodic, so that there is the effect of a struggle (*concertatio*) for pre-eminence. A good contrapuntal (polyphonic) conduct of the parts is therefore one in which they show themselves independent. To this independency there is naturally a limit; just as we can only understand several simultaneous, or quickly succeeding sounds if we can connect them with one sound, and thus obtain unity of meaning (*see* DISSONANCE and SCALE), so the independent movement of several parts will only be intelligible, if they can be conceived in the sense of the same harmony. It is, of course, self-evident that one part cannot be in the scale of A♭, and another in G; it is not, however, sufficient that both parts progress in the sense of the same clang, but the connection of this clang with others in the two parts must be clear. The teaching of this branch of counterpoint is, as yet, somewhat confused. There are two methods opposed to each other, and it is only by the fusion of the two, that the right one can be found; of these two, the one is based upon the Church Modes, and the other, the modern, on the major and minor scales. The compiler of this Dictionary has shown, in his "Neue Schule der Melodik" (1883), how these apparently irreconcilable elements may be united. (*Cf.* SCALES.)

When the name *Contrapunctus* came into use (in the 14th century), the art of writing in parts was already developed to a high degree. The theoretical treatises of a Johannes de Muris, Philipp

v. Vitry, and others, which appeared as "Regulæ de Contrapuncto," introduced therefore really nothing new; but they are treatises on the mode of writing previously called *Discantus*, with changed terminology. They start from note against note (*punctus contra punctum*, or *nota contra notam*), which Muris expressly called *fundamentum discantus* (Coussemaker, "Script." III. 60). Vitry gives the definition: "Contrapunctus, *i.e.* nota contra notam" (in above work, 23). Muris calls unequal counterpoint *Diminutio contrapuncti*, a term still valid at the present day. Here is one of the examples which he gives—

The imitative forms of counterpoint extend back to the 13th century. Walter Odington (Bishop of Canterbury, 1228) gives this definition of the Rondellus: " Si quod unus cantat, omnes per ordinem recitent " (Coussemaker, "Script." I. 245). In the hands of the contrapuntists of the 15th and 16th centuries these imitations developed into subtleties (*see* NETHERLAND SCHOOL), but in the two following centuries they became simplified, and moulded into the art form of the fugue. Strict canon (q.v.) with close entry of voices, is, indeed, only an artifice, a playing with art. Of far different importance for composition is the so-called double C., which is so arranged that the parts can exchange places, the higher becoming the lower, or *vice versâ*. Double C. is in the octave, the tenth or the twelfth, according as the intervals are to be inverted in the eighth, tenth, or twelfth. Already in 1558, Zarlino, in his "Istitutioni Armoniche," gives a clear exposition of the different kinds of double counterpoint and of canon. The treatises on counterpoint of Martini, Albrechtsberger, Cherubini, Fétis, Bellermann, Bussler, and others, are in the old style (*i.e.* based on the Church Modes). For these writers harmony is only an accident; the rules, in the main, are the same as those which were in force when Discant flourished, and when there was no clear conception of harmony (intervals, rather than harmony, were taught). On the other hand, the works of Dehn, Richter, Tiersch, Jadassohn, and others abound in instruction in harmony, or, more correctly, their aim is to teach harmony by means of counterpoint; the pupil learns instinctively to handle the former by means of the latter. It is already shown above that a deep study of harmony on the lines of counterpoint, *i.e.* a union of both methods, will result in a satisfactory method of instruction. Two important English works have recently been published: E. Prout's "Counterpoint, Strict and Free," and "Double Counterpoint and Canon."

Countersubject is the counterpoint in a fugue

with which the first voice continues, when the second voice enters with the answer. The C. is frequently turned to account in the further course of the fugue, and treated as a second subject, which in a *double fugue* it really is.

Counter-tenor, male alto voice. (*See* ALTO.)

Coup d'archet (Fr.), a stroke of the bow in violin, violoncello, etc., playing.

Couperin is the name of a series of distinguished organists of St. Gervais, Paris. The family sprang originally from Chaume (Brie), and first the three brothers:—(1) L o u i s, b. 1630, d. 1665 as organist of St. Gervais, and *Dessus de Viole* (violinist) to Louis XIII. He left clavier pieces in manuscript.—(2) C h a r l e s, b. April 9, 1638, excellent performer on the organ, died already in 1669 as organist of St. Gervais.—(3) F r a n ç o i s (Sieur de Crouilly), b. 1631, studied the clavier under Chambonnières, d. 1698 as organist of St. Gervais. He wrote "Pièces d'Orgue consistantes en Deux Messes, etc."—(4) F r a n ç o i s (le Grand), son of Charles C., b. Nov. 10, 1668, Paris, d. 1733; he was one year old when his father died. Jacques Thomelin, a friend of the latter and his successor at St. Gervais, became C.'s teacher. In 1698 François succeeded his uncle as organist of St. Gervais, and in 1701 was appointed *Claveciniste de la chambre du roi et organiste de sa chapelle.* His two daughters were excellent performers on the organ ; M a r i a n n e, who entered a convent, and became organist of Montbuisson Abbey, and M a r g u e r i t e A n t o i n-e t t e, who was claveciniste to the king. The works of C. occupy an important place in the history of music ; and in his younger days J. S. Bach followed C., especially in the treatment of French dance forms (above all, of the Courante). C. wrote four books of "Pièces de Clavecin" (1713, 1716, 1722, 1730 ; to the third book of which are appended four concertos) ; "L'Art de Toucher le Clavecin" (1717) ; "Les Goûts Réunis" (new concertos, with a trio, "Apothéose de Corelli" 1724) ; "Apothéose de L'Incomparable L." (Lully) ; "Trios pour Deux Dessus de Violon, Basse d'Archet et Basse Chiffrée ;" "Leçons des Ténèbres." Dr. Chrysander, together with Joh. Brahms, has edited a new complete edition of Couperin's clavier works (London : Augener & Co.). "C. is the first great composer for the harpsichord known in the history of music. The eminent masters who preceded him—Merulo, Frescobaldi, and many others—applied their art quite as much to the organ as to the harpsichord ; whereas Couperin, though he played both instruments, wrote for the latter only. He stands, therefore, at the commencement of the modern period, and must be regarded as clearing the way for a new art. Among his younger contemporaries, and, in part, his pupils, were Scarlatti, Handel, and Bach. Couperin's mode of writing music was very peculiar. It was his constant aim to set down the music with the

greatest possible fulness, exactly as he played it on his instrument. Even the manifold embellishments are most accurately indicated. All this gives to his music a more technical appearance than to that of any other master of the period." (Chrysander.)—(5) N i c o l a s, b. Dec. 20, 1680, Paris, son of the elder François, b. 1748 as organist of St. Gervais.—(6) A r m a n d L o u i s, son of the former, b. Feb. 25, 1725, Paris, d. 1789 ; a distinguished performer on the organ, but of less importance as a composer. He, also, was organist of St. Gervais, and at the same time court organist of the Ste. Chapelle, of St. Barthélemy, Ste. Marguerite ; and was also one of the four organists of Notre Dame, and an authority at the trial of new organs. His wife, Elizabeth Antoinette (*née* Blanchet), was likewise a distinguished performer on the clavecin and organ.—(7) P i e r r e L o u i s, son of the former, assisted his father in his many posts of organist, but died already in the same year as his father (1789).—(8) F r a n ç o i s G e r v a i s, likewise a son of Armand Louis C., the last of the Couperin organists of St. Gervais, and inheritor of all his father's posts, was unworthy of the distinctions conferred on him, for he was an organist of only moderate ability, and a composer of no importance. He was still living in 1823.

Coupler (Ger. *Koppel;* Lat. *Copula*), (1) An organ mechanism, by which playing on one keyboard presses down the keys of one or more other keyboards, so that the pipes belonging to the latter sound together with those of the former. A distinction is made between *Manual couplers* and *Pedal couplers.* The former unite two or three manuals, and, as a rule, in such a manner that with the Great Manual, two or three others may be played at the same time ; yet in large organs the other manuals are united amongst themselves by couplers. The Pedal C. is either constructed in a similar way (Anhängekoppel), or it acts directly on certain valves in the channels belonging to the wind-chest of the Great Manual, without drawing down the keys of the latter. According to the mode of construction a distinction is made between those pedal couplers, which press, from above, down on the keys of a lower keyboard, or draw down those of a higher keyboard.—(2) The *Octave Coupler* unites with every key that of the upper- or under-octave, or both (in the latter case called Double-octave coupler), producing an exceedingly full tone.

Couplet, text-strophe (or several strophes sung to the same melody). In old music same as word *variation,* varied repetitions of the principal theme (as in the rondos and passacailles of Couperin). The term, which really means "little pair," is probably to be referred to the old dances accompanied by singing, in which solo-singing and tutti (refrains) alternated.

Couppey. (*See* LE COUPPEY.)

Courante (Fr.). (*See* CORRENTE.)

Couronne (Fr.), a pause.

Courtois, J e a n, French contrapuntist, about 1539 maître de chapelle to the Archbishop of Cambrai. Of the eight masses in the Munich Library ascribed to him by Gerber and Fétis, only one, *Domine quis Habitabit*, is by C. Besides this, only motets and psalms by C. have been preserved in print.

Courvoisier, K a r l, violinist and composer, b. Nov. 12, 1846, Basle, was originally destined for the career of a merchant, but attended the Leipzig Conservatorium, 1867, as pupil of David and Röntgen, and pursued his studies, from 1869 to 1870 at Berlin, under Joachim. After a short engagement in the orchestra of the Thalia Theatre at Frankfort (1871), he worked in this city as teacher and conductor, studying, all the while, singing under Gust. Barth. In 1875 he became conductor of the Düsseldorf Orchestra, but already in 1876 returned to teaching, devoting himself also to the conductorship of choral societies. In 1885 he went to Liverpool, where he is especially occupied as a teacher of singing. C. published an essay, "Die Violintechnik" (translated into English by H. E. Krehbiel), which has become widely known, and a Violin School, "École de la Vélocité" (a large work containing violin exercises and studies; London, Augener). Of his compositions, which have been produced with success, may be mentioned, a symphony and two concert overtures; a violin concerto is still in manuscript. Only small pieces have appeared in print.

Coussemaker, C h a r l e s E d m o n d H e n r i de, b. April 19, 1805, Bailleul (Nord), d. Jan. 10, 1876, Bourbourg. He studied law at Paris, and, at the same time, took private lessons in singing with Pellegrini, and in harmony with Payer and Reicha. At Douai, where he commenced his career as a lawyer, he still studied counterpoint under Victor Lefebvre. He gave practical proofs of the musical knowledge which he had acquired, in compositions of the most varied kind (masses, fragments of operas, *Ave, Salve regina*, etc.; but, with the exception of a book of romances, everything remained in manuscript). Excited by the *Revue Musicale*, edited by Fétis, he now commenced to study the history of music, and to devote his attention to the study, especially, of the Middle Ages; by unwearying investigations he became one of the most distinguished musical historians of our day. At the same time he pursued his career as a jurist, and became justice of the peace at Bergues, tribunal judge at Hazebrouck, administrative officer at Cambrai, judge at Dunkirk and Lille. His musico-historical works are: " Mémoire sur Hucbald" (1841); "Histoire de l'Harmonie au Moyen-Âge" (1852); "Drames Liturgiques du Moyen-Âge" (1860); "Les Harmonistes des XII. et XIII. Siècles" (1864); "L'Art harmonique au XII. et XIII. Siècles" (1865); "Œuvres complètes d'Adam de la Halle" (1872); further, a magnificent collection in four stout quarto volumes, "Scriptores de Musica medii Ævi" (continuation of the Gerbert "Scriptores," 1866–76). Of smaller pamphlets there are the following: "Notices sur les Collections Musicales de la Bibliothèque de Cambrai et d'autres Villes du Département du Nord" (1843); "Essai sur les Instruments de Musique au Moyen-Âge" (in Didron's "Archäologische Annalen," with many illustrations); "Chants Populaires des Flamands de France" (1856), etc. C. was corresponding member of the French Académie.

Cousser. (*See* KUSSER.)

Coward, J a m e s, distinguished English organist, b. Jan. 25, 1824, London, d. there Jan. 22, 1880. He was organist at the Crystal Palace from the beginning, conductor of the Western Madrigal Society from 1864 to 1872. He was also conductor of the Abbey and City Glee Clubs; and, besides, organist of the Sacred Harmonic Society, and the Grand Lodge of Freemasons. He himself composed anthems, glees, madrigals, pf. pieces, etc.

Cowen, F r e d e r i c H y m e n, b. Jan. 29, 1852, Kingston, Jamaica, was brought to England by his parents when four years old; he showed decided taste for music, and they wished him to be trained by Benedict and Goss. From 1865–68 he continued his studies at Leipzig and Berlin. In 1882 he was appointed director of the Academy of Music at Edinburgh. He has written an operetta, *Garibaldi;* two operas, *Pauline* (produced with success at the Lyceum in 1876); *Thorgrim* (produced at Drury Lane in 1890); the choral works, *The Rose Maiden* (1870); *The Corsair* (1876); *Saint Ursula* (Norwich, 1881); *The Sleeping Beauty* (Birmingham Festival, 1885); *Ruth* (1887). Also five symphonies (a "Scandinavian," No. 3; a "Welsh," No. 4; No. 5 is in F); and an overture, an orchestral suite, "The Language of Flowers," several chamber works, songs, etc.

Cracovienne (Fr.). (*See* KRAKOWIAK.)

Cramer, (1) K a r l F r i e d r i c h, b. March 7, 1752, Quedlinburg, d. Dec. 8, 1807, Paris. He was at first professor at Kiel, but lost his post in 1794, because he openly showed sympathy with the French Revolution. C. published several collections with critical introductions ("Flora," pianoforte pieces and songs; "Polyhymnia," operas in pianoforte score; *Magazin für Musik*, 1783–89). He translated Rousseau's works into German, and wrote a "Kurze Übersicht der Geschichte der Französischen Musik" (1786).—(2) W i l h e l m, a distinguished violinist, b. 1745 (1743), Mannheim, d. Oct. 5, 1799, London. He studied with Stamitz and Cannabich, was in the Mannheim band up to 1772, and, after that, in London as conductor of the king's band, and at the same time leader at the

Opera, Pantheon, Ancient Concerts, and the Professional Concerts; he was also leader at the Handel Festivals of 1784 and 1787. He was highly esteemed as a solo player.—(3) Franz, b. 1786, Munich, nephew of the former, lived at Munich as principal flautist in the band. Flute concertos, variations, etc., of his appeared in print.—(4) Johann Baptist, one of the most distinguished pianists and teachers of any age, b. Feb. 24, 1771, Mannheim, the eldest son of Wilhelm C. (*see* 2), d. April 16, 1858, London. He studied with Schröter and Clementi, who imparted to him a knowledge of the classical composers; but in the matter of theory, he was, for the most part, self-taught. He began his concert tours in 1788, which quickly spread his fame as a pianist. He always regarded London as his home and resting place; he resided in Paris from 1832 to 1845, but then returned to London. In 1828, jointly with Addison, he established a music-publishing house, which brought out, specially, classical works, and which he himself conducted up to 1842; the firm still flourishes under the title " C. & Co." Cramer's compositions (105 pf. sonatas, seven concertos, a pf. quintet and pf. quartet, variations, rondos, etc.) are well-nigh forgotten at the present day; only his " Grosse Pianoforte - Schule," and especially the fifth part, the eighty-four Studies (also separately as Op. 50, with sixteen new Studies; a selection, sixty, has been edited by Bülow, with remarks and certain alterations; and another selection, with a second pianoforte accompaniment, by Ad. Henselt) have, as material for instruction, achieved immortality. A noble, poetical spirit breathes through these studies; and this renders them agreeable both to pupils and teachers. The " Schule der Fingerfertigkeit," Op. 100 (100 daily studies, the second part of the " Grosse Pianoforte-Schule "), also enjoys a certain name, but not to the extent which it deserves.

Cranz, August, a music-publishing house in Hamburg, founded in 1813 by August Heinrich C. (b. 1789, d. 1870). The present proprietor, his son, Alwin C. (b. 1834), came into the business in 1857, bought, besides, in 1876, the important publishing business of C. A. Spina (*cf.* Schreiber), at Vienna, and set up a branch establishment (A. Cranz) at Brussels in 1883, and at London, 1892.

Craywinckel, Ferdinand Manuel de, b. Aug. 24, 1820, Madrid, has been living in Bordeaux since 1825, where he was trained by Bellon, one of Reicha's pupils. C. is a composer of note (six grand masses, a Stabat, motets, *Cantica*, etc.).

Create, to, to perform a musical work, to impersonate a *rôle* for the first time in public.

Credo (Lat.), the third part of the Mass (q.v.).

Cremonese Violins, a term applied to those instruments made by the Amati, Stradivari, and Guarneri; also to those of Bergonzi, Guadagnini, Montagnana, Ruggieri, Storione, and Testore.

Crequillon (Crecquillon), Thomas, contrapuntist of the 16th century, maestro to Charles V. at Madrid about 1544. He was afterwards canon at Namur, Terbonde, and finally at Béthune, where he died in 1557. He was one of the best masters during the period between Josquin and Orlando di Lasso. A great number of his works (masses, cantatas, etc.) have been preserved, partly in special editions, partly in collections.

Crescendo (Ital., " growing "), increasing in loudness. A C. is brought about in the orchestra in two ways; either by the gradual addition of instruments, or by louder playing on the various instruments. The human voice, wind and string instruments, have full power over the C., as they can swell out any particular tone; on the pianoforte this is not possible, and the C. must be produced by a stronger touch. Formerly the organ entirely lacked the C. ; by gradually pulling out stops, an increase of sound was brought about, but the effect was naturally a jerky one. Within recent times, attempts have been made in two ways to remedy this evil :— (1) one or two soft stops have been enclosed in a box with movable shutter, worked by means of a pedal (Swell, *Dachschweller, Jalousieschweller*);— (2) a clever mechanical apparatus, worked by a pedal, effects a gradual entry of the stops in a definite succession. But, even now, the organ cannot produce a real C., such as one hears in the orchestra; and this, perhaps, is not to be desired, as it would rob the organ tone of its majestic passionlessness, and tend to a sentimental or pathetic mode of playing. (*Cf.* Expression, Dynamics, Phrasing, art of.)

Crescent (Ger. *Halbmond, Schellenbaum, Mohammedsfahne*), a Turkish rattle- or bell-instrument introduced into the German regimental bands at the time of the Turkish wars.

Crescentini, Girolamo, one of the last and most distinguished Italian sopranists (*evirati*), b. 1766, Urbania, near Urbino (Papal States), d. 1846. He made his *début* at Rome in 1783, and was then engaged at Livorno, Padua, Venice, Turin, London (1786), Milan, Naples (1788-89), and other places. Napoleon heard him in 1805, gave him the decoration of the Iron Crown, and attracted him to Paris in 1806 In 1812 he withdrew definitely from the stage. In 1816 he settled in Naples, and for many years was teacher of singing at the *Real Collegio di Musica*. Fétis speaks of him as the last great singer that Italy produced. To a voice of marvellously beautiful quality he united virtuosity of the highest order, and overpowering dramatic warmth. C. also composed several interesting vocal pieces; and he published a collection of *vocalises* with introductory remarks on the art of singing.

Cressent, A n a t o l e, b. April 24, 1824, Argenteuil (Seine-et-Oise), d. May 28, 1870, as jurist in Paris ; he was a thoroughly well-trained musical amateur. In his will he left a legacy of 100,000 francs (to which his heirs added 20,000) for the purpose of establishing a double competition for the writers of libretti, and for the composers of operas (*Concours C.*). The prize, consisting of the interest of the capital, is given away every three years. The first to obtain it was William Chaumet, with a comic opera, *Bathylle* (1875).

Cristofori (falsely called Cristofali, Cristofani), B a r t o l o m m e o, Latinised *Bartholomæus de Christophoris*, the inventor of the Hammerclavier, or, as he named it, and as it is still called, pianoforte. He was born May 4, 1655, Padua, d. March 17, 1731, Florence ; he became principal clavier-maker in his native town, and later on (about 1690) at Florence, where, in 1716, Ferdinand of Medici placed under his charge his collection of instruments. C.'s invention was announced and described by Marchese Scipione Maffei in *Giornale dei Letterati d'Italia* in 1711 ; but, notwithstanding this description—translated by König, given in Mattheson's " Critica Musica " (1725), and in Adlung's " Musica Mechanica Organœdi " (1767), and the attention called to all these proofs by Schafhäutl in his well-known " Sachverständigenbericht über die Münchener Ausstellung, 1854 "—O. Paul, in his " Geschichte des Claviers " (1869), attributed the honour of the invention to the organist Schröter, of Nordhausen. (*Cf.* SCHRÖTER.) Apart from clever improvements of certain details, the mechanism employed by C. was the same as that employed by Gottfried Silbermann, Streicher, Broadwood, etc., the so-called English action. (*Cf.* PIANOFORTE.) In honour of C., a grand festival was held at Florence in 1876, and a memorial tablet erected in the cloisters of Santa Croce.

Crivelli, (1) A r c a n g e l o, b. Bergamo, chapel-singer (tenor) to the Pope about 1583, d. 1610. He composed masses, psalms, and motets, but these, with the exception of a few motets, remained in manuscript.—(2) G i o v a n n i B a t t i s t a, b. Scandiano (Modena) ; from 1629 to 1634 he was capellmeister at the Electoral Court, Munich, and engaged in a similar capacity to Franz I. of Modena (1651), and became maestro of S. Maria Maggiore, Bergamo, in 1654. He composed " Motetti concertati " (1626) and " Madrigali concertati " (1633),—(3) G a e t a n o, distinguished tenor singer, b. 1774, Bergamo, d. July 10, 1836, Brescia. He first sang on all the great stages of Italy, from 1811 to 1817 at the Théâtre Italien, Paris, the following year at London, and after that, again in Italy. He sang up to 1829, although his voice had long been worn-out. His son, D o m e n i c o, b. 1794, Brescia, wrote an opera for London, was for some years teacher of singing at the *Real*

Collegio di Musica, Naples, and, after that, lived as teacher of singing in London. He published a Method, " The Art of Singing " (Augener, 9998).

Croce, G i o v a n n i d a l l a, b. about 1560, Chioggia, near Venice (hence called " Il C h i o z o t t o), d. May 15, 1609. He studied with Zarlino, who placed him in the choir of St. Mark's, and in 1603 he became successor of Donato as maestro at that Cathedral. C. was not only a contemporary, but also of kindred mind with the younger Gabrieli, and one of the most important composers of the Venetian school. Those of his works which have been handed down to us are : —sonatas à 5 (1580), two books of motets à 8 (1589-90) ; the second book republished in 1605 with organ bass, and the whole in 1607), two books of madrigals à 5 (1585-88), " Triacca Musicale " (1595, " Musikalische Arznei," humorous songs [*Capricci*] à 4-7 ; among others, the contest between the cuckoo and the nightingale, with the parrot as umpire), six madrigals à 6 (1590), a fourth book of madrigals (à 5-6, 1607), " Cantiones sacra " à 8 with continuo, canzonets à 4 (2nd ed. 1595), masses à 8 (1596), Lamentations à 4 and à 6, Improperia à 4, Psalms à 3 and à 6, motets à 4, Magnificats à 6, vesper Psalms à 8, and many detached pieces in collections.

Croche (Fr.), quaver ; *Double c.*, semiquaver.

Crocheta, (Lat.), crotchet.

Croes, H e n r i J a c q u e s d e, baptised Sept. 19, 1705, Antwerp, d. Aug. 16, 1786, Brussels. He was, at first, violinist and deputy-conductor at St. James's, Antwerp, was appointed (probably capellmeister) at the Thurn and Taxis Court at Ratisbon, Sept. 4, 1729. He went in 1749 to Brussels, and became royal maître de chapelle (1755). C. wrote many sacred and instrumental works. The complete catalogue of his works is in Fétis's " Biographie Universelle."

Croft (Crofts), W i l l i a m, b. 1678, Nether Eatington (Warwickshire), d. Aug. 14, 1727, London. He was one of the children of the Chapel Royal, and sworn in as a gentleman (1700) ; in 1704, jointly with Clark, organist of the same, and after the death of the latter (1707), sole organist. In 1708 he succeeded Blow as organist of Westminster Abbey, and master of the children, and composer to the Chapel Royal. His principal works are : " Musica Sacra " (2 vols., forty anthems, and a Burial Service), the first English work engraved in score (1724) ; " Musicus apparatus academicus " (the exercise for his Doctor's degree), two odes for the Peace of Utrecht, violin sonatas, flute sonatas, etc.

Crooks (Ger. *Bogen*, *Krummbogen*), accessory pieces of tubing applied to the mouthpiece of the natural horn, by which means a c-horn can be changed into a B♭-horn, etc. In the few orchestras in which natural horns are found, crooks are still used.

Crosdill, John, an excellent performer on the 'cello, b. 1751, London, d. Oct. 1825, Escrick (Yorkshire). From 1769 to 1787 he was principal 'cellist of the Festivals of the Three Choirs, and in 1776 of the " Concerts of Ancient Music," in 1777 violist of the Chapel Royal, in 1782 chamber-musician to Queen Charlotte, and teacher to the Prince of Wales (George IV.). In 1788 he married a lady of fortune, and retired from public life.

Cross-flute (Ger. *Querflöte*). (*See* FLUTE.)

Crossing of parts takes place in a musical composition when, for example, the tenor occasionally goes above the alto, or the alto above the soprano, or the bass above the tenor, and so on. Crossing of parts in elementary exercises in four voices is forbidden; but afterwards (when the pupil can write *currente calamo*), in order to make use of the full compass of a voice, also to make the parts move freely and melodiously, it becomes necessary for the teacher to point out the advantages of crossing of parts.

Crotch, William, b. July 5, 1775, Norwich, d. Dec. 29, 1847, Taunton. He was an extraordinary youthful prodigy, for at the age of 2½ he began to play on a small organ built by his father, who was a carpenter. An account by Burney of this rare phenomenon was printed in the *Philosophical Transactions* of 1779. C. did not become a Mozart; he did not, however, as most wonder children, remain in the stage of early development, but became an accomplished musician and teacher. In 1786 he went to Cambridge as assistant to Professor Randall, studied for the church at Oxford from 1788, but was appointed organist of Christ Church there in 1790. He took his degree of Mus. Bac. in 1794, and in 1797 succeeded Hayes as Professor of Music at the University, and as organist of St. John's College. He received his Doctor's degree in 1799, and from 1800 to 1804 delivered lectures in the Music School. About 1820 he was appointed lecturer at the Royal Institution, London, and in 1822 was named Principal of the newly-established Royal Academy of Music, and remained in this post until his death. C. composed several oratorios (of which *Palestine* is the best), anthems, glees, cantatas for special occasions (odes), three organ concertos, etc. He also wrote; " Practical Thorough Bass," " Questions in Harmony" (Catechism, 1812), " Elements of Musical Composition " (1833).

Crotchet, the name for the quarter-note ($\downarrow$). It is confusing to find that the French term for $\downarrow$ is *croche*. The simple explanation is as follows :—*Crocheta* was the old name for the *semiminima*, when it was represented by a white note with a hook (Fr. *croc, crochet*), thus, . When the black *semi-minima* became general, the English retained the name for the value, but the French, for the figure.

Crout (Crowd, Crwth). (*See* CHROTTA.)

Crucifixus (Lat.), a part of the *Credo* in the mass.

Crüger, (1) Pankraz, b. 1546, Finsterwalde (Niederlausitz), rector at Lübeck, d. 1614 as professor at Frankfort-on-the-Oder. According to Mattheson, he was an opponent of solmisation, and was in favour of letter names for the notes; and for this reason was dismissed from his post at Lübeck.—(2) Johannes, b. April 9, 1589, Grossbreesen, near Guben, d. Feb. 23, 1662, Berlin. He was trained for a schoolmaster, and was private tutor at Berlin in 1615, but went in 1620 to Wittenberg to study divinity. According to his own statement (1646) he acquired, at the same time, sound musical knowledge, especially under Paulus Homberger at Ratisbon, who was a pupil of Joh. Gabrieli; and in 1622 he became organist of St. Nicholas' Church at Berlin, which post he retained until his death. C. was one of the best composers of church song, and his chorales are still sung at the present day ("Nun danket alle Gott," " Jesus meine Zuversicht," " Schmücke dich, o liebe Seele," " Jesus, meine Freude "). His collections of sacred melodies bear the titles : " Neues vollkömliches Gesangbuch Augspurgischer Konfession, etc." (1640); " Praxis pietatis melica, etc." (1644); " Geistliche Kirchenmelodeyen, etc." (1649); " Dr. M. Luthers wie auch andrer gottseliger christlicher Leute Geistliche Lieder und Psalmen " (1657); " Psalmodia sacra, etc." (1658). Langbecker wrote a monograph on Crüger's chorales (1835). C. composed besides: " Meditationum musicarum Paradisus primus" (1622) and "secundus" (1626); " Hymni selecti " (without year of publication); " Recreationes musicæ " (1651). The following works on theory are of the highest interest for a knowledge of musical art of that period : " Synopsis musica " [" musices "] (1624 ?, 1630, and enlarged in 1634); " Praecepta musicae figuralis " (1625); " Quaestiones musicae practicae " (1650).

Cruvelli, two sisters gifted with splendid voices (contralto), whose real name was Crüwell. The elder, (1) Friederike Marie, b. Aug. 29, 1824, Bielefeld (Westphalia), appeared in London in 1851, and created great astonishment by her singing; but her success was not lasting, for she lacked solid training. She soon withdrew from the stage, and died of grief, owing to her unfortunate career, at Bielefeld, July 26, 1868. The younger—(2) Johanne Sophie Charlotte, b. March 12, 1826, Bielefeld, met with better—indeed great success. She made her *début* at Venice in 1847, and celebrated brilliant triumphs. In 1848 she appeared in London as the Countess (*Figaro*), but, as Jenny Lind played the part of Susanna, her merits were not fully recognised. Her passionate disposition, as well as her imperfect training, led her more and more to modern Italian Opera. She went in 1851 to Paris, appeared at the Italian Opera, and obtained a brilliant success in Verdi's *Ernani*. Her Paris reputation assisted her in obtaining the recognition which she so desired in London. She sang here for several seasons, and in 1854 received an engagement at the Paris Opera-house with a yearly stipend of 100,000 francs. The enthusiasm of the public over her impersonation of Valentine in *Les Huguenots* knew no bounds, but it was not of long duration. Even in Paris her faults began to attract notice; but once more the public warmed towards her in Verdi's *Vêpres Siciliennes*. In 1856 she married Count Vigier (d. Oct. 20, 1882), and withdrew from the stage. She resides alternately at Paris and at Bielefeld.

Crystal Palace Concerts, Sydenham, London, were started Sept. 22, 1855, under the direction of August Manns, and their fame is not surpassed by any other similar institution. A concert takes place every Saturday from the beginning of October to the end of April, with a break at Christmas. There are sixty-one strings in the orchestra, which is therefore greater than that of the Paris Conservatoire. The programmes are arranged on the same plan as those of the Gewandhaus, Leipzig (one symphony, two overtures, one concerto, solos and songs).

C sharp (Ger. *Cis*), c raised by a sharp. c♯ *major* chord = c♯, e♯, g♯; c♯ *minor* chord = c♯, e, g♯; c♯ *major* key with signature of 7 ♯; c♯ *minor* key with signature of 4 ♯. (*See* KEY.)

Cui, Cesar Antonowitsch, b. Jan. 6, 1835, Wilna; he first attended the Gymnasium there, then the School of Engineering, and the Engineering Academy in Petersburg; and, when his studies were ended, was appointed first under-master, then successively teacher, assistant-professor, and finally professor of fortification at the same Academy. In connection with that special branch he wrote " Lehrbuch der Feldbefestigungen " (3rd ed. 1880), and a brief sketch of the history of fortification. From early youth C. busied himself with music, received regular theoretical instruction from Moniuzsko, and, together with Balakireff, studied the scores of the best masters. From 1864 to 1868 he contributed musical articles to the *St. Petersburger Zeitung*, and warmly advocated the cause of Schumann, Berlioz, and Liszt. From 1878 to 1879 he published in the Paris *Revue et Gazette Musicale* a series of articles—" La musique en Russie." As a composer C. belongs to the " innovators " (young Russian school: Rimski-Korsakoff, Mussorgski, Dargomyzski), *i.e.* programme-musicians; yet with the intelligent reservation that all programme-music shall be good music, even without the programme. His principal works are: four operas (*Der Gefangene im Kaukasus, Der Sohn des Mandarins, William Ratcliff, Angelo*—the last two appeared with Russian and German words), two scherzi and a tarantelle for orchestra, a suite for pf. and violin, and over fifty songs. An " Esquisse

Critique " on the composer and his works was written by Countess de Mercy-Argenteau.

Cummings, William Hayman, an esteemed English oratorio singer (tenor), b. 1831, Sidbury (Devon); he was, at first, in the choir of St. Paul's and afterwards in that of the Temple Church. Later on he became tenor-singer at the Temple, Westminster Abbey, and the Chapels Royal, but resigned all these posts. He was appointed conductor of the Sacred Harmonic Society in 1882. He edits the publications of the Purcell Society, and has also written a Purcell biography (for the " Great Musicians " series), and a " Primer of the Rudiments of Music " (Novello); he has also composed a cantata, *The Fairy Ring*, and sacred music. Elected Principal Guildhall School of Music, 1896.

Curci, Giuseppe, b. June 15, 1808, Barletta, d. there Aug. 5, 1877. He was a pupil of the Naples Conservatorio (Furno, Zingarelli, Crescentini) and first became known in Italy as an operatic composer. He lived as a teacher of singing at Vienna, Paris, London, and finally returned to Barletta. C. published many sacred works, four organ sonatas, also cantatas, songs, and solfeggi.

Curschmann, Karl Friedrich, b. June 21, 1805, Berlin, d. Aug. 24, 1841, Langfuhr, near Danzig. He first studied jurisprudence, but, already in 1824, changed in favour of music, and became a pupil of Hauptmann and Spohr at Cassel. In 1828 his one-act opera *Abdul und Erinnieh* was produced at Cassel. From that time C. lived in Berlin as a composer of songs and also as an excellent singer. His songs (of which a complete edition was published in 1871) stand about on the same level with those of Abt, perhaps somewhat higher; and they are exceedingly popular.

Curti, Franz, an opera composer, b. Nov. 16, 1854, Cassel. He first studied medicine at Berlin and Geneva, then became the pupil of Ed. Kretschmer and Schulz-Beuthen at Dresden, where he afterwards resided. He wrote the operas *Hertha* (Altenburg, 1887), and *Reinhard von Ufenau* (Altenburg, 1889), and music to W. E. Kirchbach's stage stories, " Die letzten Menschen " (Dresden, 1891, at a concert); also a choral work, " Die Gletscherjungfrau," songs, orchestral works, etc. Died Feb. 6, 1898.

Curwen, John, founder of the Tonic Sol-fa Method (q.v.), b. Nov. 14, 1816, Heckmondwike (Yorkshire), d. June 26, 1880, Manchester, was trained for the profession of his father, a Nonconformist minister. It was at a conference of teachers at Hull that he was first led towards the great object of his life. His " Grammar of Vocal Music " appeared in 1843, and ten years later he founded the Tonic Sol-fa Association, and in 1879 the Tonic Sol-fa College. Of his educational works may be named: " The Standard Course of Lessons and Exercises on the Tonic Sol-fa Method " (1861; 2nd ed. 1872);

"The Teacher's Manual, etc." (1875); "How to Observe Harmony" (1861; 2nd ed. 1872); "A Tonic Sol-fa Primer" (Novello); "Musical Theory" (1879); "Musical Statics" (1874). He also published the *Tonic Sol-fa Reporter* from 1851, various hymn- and tune-books, collections of part-music, etc.

Cusanino. (*See* CARESTINI.)

Cusins, William George, b. Oct. 14, 1833, London, was one of the Chapel Royal boys, became a pupil of Fétis at the Brussels Conservatoire in 1844, was King's scholar at the R. A. M., London, in 1847, under Potter, Bennett, Lucas, and Sainton. In 1849 he was appointed organist to the Queen, and became, at the same time, violinist in the orchestra of the Royal Italian Opera. In 1867 he became assistant professor, and later on professor, at the R. A. M. In 1867 he succeeded Bennett as conductor of the Philharmonic Society, and as examining professor at Queen's College. In 1870 he was appointed Master of the Music to the Queen, and was knighted 1892. In 1876 he became, jointly with Hullah and Goldschmidt, examiner for the granting of scholarships for the National Training School of Music. C. has also appeared at concerts in Germany (Leipzig and Berlin) as violinist. As composer he has written a serenade for the wedding of the Prince of Wales (1863), an oratorio, *Gideon*, some overtures, a pf. concerto, etc. D. Aug. 31, 1893, at Remonchamps.

Custos (Lat.), a direct, the sign 𝕎 placed at the end of a line or page.

Cuzzoni, Francesca, distinguished vocalist, b. 1700, Parma, d. 1770. She studied with Lanzi, sang from 1722 to 1726 under Handel, at London, with enormous success, but fell out with the composer, and was replaced by Faustina Bordoni, who afterwards became the wife of Hasse (q.v.). For a whole year the two vocalists were bitter rivals, C. singing at the theatre set up in opposition to Handel. In 1727 she married the pianist and composer Sandoni, and accepted an engagement at Vienna, went afterwards to Italy, but failed, and was imprisoned in Holland for debt. In 1748 she reappeared in London, but made no impression, and died in complete poverty in Italy, where during her last years she earned a living by making silk buttons.

Cyclic Forms. (*See* FORM.)

Cylinder (valves of horns, etc.). (*See* PISTONS.)

Cymbal (Ger.), (1) *Dulcimer* (q.v.), the predecessor of the clavier, which itself is only a dulcimer struck by means of a keyboard. (KLAVICYMBAL.) The name C. in its Italian form, "Cembalo," was used for the harpsichord, and was a common term until the end of the last century. The C. is now only to be found in gipsy bands (Zimbalon) with a compass of four octaves (chromatic), from E to e'''.—(2) A mixture stop in the organ, of small scale, like the *Scharf*. (*See* ACUTA.)

Cymbals (Ger. *Becken;* Fr. *Cymbales;* Ital. *Piatti*), percussion instruments of unchangeable and indefinite pitch, which produce a stirring, loud, sharp, rumbling, and long-reverberating sound. If they are intended to give only short beats, immediately after being struck, the player deadens the sound by pressing the instrument against his chest. C. are plates of metal with broad, flat edges, which latter are really the sounding portions, while the middle concave perforated part, to which straps are fastened for the hand to lay hold of, does not vibrate; two such plates are struck together (forte), or the edges are made to jingle slowly against each other (piano). Originally C. were undoubtedly instruments belonging to military music, and even now they are most frequently to be found in military bands (Janissaries' music), yet they have been introduced with good effect into operatic and symphonic music. C. are often played by the performer who has charge of the big drum, and one of the C. is fastened loosely to the big drum, so that the player can work both instruments at the same time; with one hand he wields the drum-stick, with the other the second cymbal. This can be done when C. and drum have only, with rough strokes, to mark one rhythm; but artistic treatment of the C. requires the musician to hold one in each hand.

Cymbalum, (1) a kind of cymbal (instrument of percussion) used by the Romans; hence, probably, the present Italian name for cymbals (*Cinelli*).—(2) A kind of small bell, of which the monks (10th to 12th century) had a set cast with different pitch (a scale of from eight to nine notes), and this was worked after the manner of a Glockenspiel. Many hints as to the mode of preparing them have been handed down to us in Gerbert, "Scriptores, etc."

Cymbelstern, a kind of toy; a visible star with small bells, found on the pipes "in prospect" of old organs; it was set in motion by a current of air acted on by a special draw-stop; the tinkle which resulted was of no real artistic value.

Czardas, a wild Hungarian dance with changes of *tempo*.

Czartoryska, Marcelline (*née* Princess Radziwill), b. 1826, Vienna, a pupil of Czerny's, and a distinguished pianist. She lived in Paris from 1848; d. June 8, 1894, at her castle near Cracow.

Czernohorsky, Bohuslaw, b. about 1690, Nimburg (Bohemia), d. 1720, whilst travelling to Italy. He entered the order of the Minorites, was Regens chori at St. Antonio at Padua, afterwards (about 1715) organist of the monastery church at Assisi (where Tartini was his pupil), about 1735 director of the music of St. James's Church, Prague (where Gluck was his pupil). C. was a distinguished composer of sacred music; unfortunately nearly all his works were lost in the fire which destroyed the monastery of the Minorites in 1754.

Czerny, Karl, b. Feb. 20, 1791, Vienna, d. there July 15, 1857. He was the son and pupil of an excellent pianist and teacher, Wenzel C., and had, for some time, the privilege of lessons from Beethoven. His development was so rapid that already at the age of fifteen he was much sought after as a teacher. With the exception of some short journeys to Leipzig, Paris, London, etc., he lived in Vienna, teaching, and composing, for the most part, educational works. Wonderful was the result of his activity as a teacher. Liszt, Döhler, Thalberg, Frau v. Belleville-Oury, Jaell, and others were his pupils. The number of Czerny's compositions exceeds one thousand, among which are many sacred (masses, offertoria, etc.), orchestral, and chamber-music works. Only his studies, however, have won lasting importance, especially " Schule der Geläufigkeit" (Op. 299), "Schule der Fingerfertigkeit" (Op. 740), forty " Tägliche Studien" (Op. 337), " Schule des Legato und Stakkato (Op. 335); Schule der Verzierungen" (Op. 355), " Schule des Fugenspiels" (Op. 400), "Schule des Virtuosen" (Op. 365), " Schule der linken Hand " (Op. 399), and the Toccata in c (Op. 92). C. understood better than anyone else the simple primitive forms from which all pianoforte-passage writing is evolved ; his studies, therefore, are of immense help in the earlier stages of development. In contrast to many modern studies, they are written in an uncommonly clear style, and are organic in structure.

Czersky. (*See* TSCHIRCH.)

Czerveny. (*See* CERVENY.)

Cziak. (*See* SCHACK.)

Czibulka, Alphons, b. May 14, 1842, Szepes-Várallya (Hungary), bandmaster at Vienna, a prolific composer of dance music (also an operetta, *Pfingsten in Florenz*, 1884); d. Oct. 27, 1894.

D.

D, the letter name of the fourth note of the musical alphabet (q.v.); the *d* of the twice-accented octave belonged, from the 13th century, to the *Claves signatæ* (clefs), but was scarcely ever employed. Only in the Tablature notation of the 16th century, when the melody is placed on a stave, do we find the *dd*-clef combined with the *gg*-clef :

(For the solmisation names of D, *cf.* MUTATION.) In France, Italy, etc., D is now simply called RE.—As abbreviation, *d* means the right hand (*droite, dextra, destra, sc. main, manus, mano,* hence *d. m.* or *m. d.*), or the Italian *da, dal,* which, however, it is better not to abbreviate (*d. c. = da capo, d. s. = dal segno*). As a label on vocal-part books, D (*Discantus, Dessus*) has the same meaning as C (*Cantus*) and S (*Sopranus, Superius*).

Da (Ital.), " from," *Da Capo.* (*See* CAPO.)

D'accord (Fr.), in tune.

Dach (Ger. ; lit., " roof "), the upper part of the sound-box of a string-instrument ; the belly of a violin, etc.

Dachs, Joseph, b. Sept. 30, 1825, Ratisbon ; studied from 1844 at Vienna, under Halm and Czerny, then an esteemed teacher of the pianoforte at the Conservatorium "der Musikfreunde."

Dachschweller. (*See* CRESCENDO.)

Dactyl, a metrical foot consisting of three syllables, the first long, the other two short : — ‿ ‿.

Dactylion (Gr., " finger-trainer "), an apparatus of the Chiroplast kind (q.v.), constructed by H. Herz in 1835, and, like all similar attempts, soon forgotten.

Dal (Ital.), for *da il* (" from the ").

Dalayrac, Nicolas (d'Alayrac), b. June 13, 1753, Muret (Hte. Garonne), d. Nov. 27, 1809, Paris ; in his time he was a favourite French composer of operettas, of extraordinary fertility and rapidity of production (sixty-one operas in twenty-eight years, 1781–1809). His works, however, even during his lifetime, were not known beyond Paris.

Dalberg, Johann Friedrich Hugo, Reichsfreiherr von, b. May 17, 1752, Aschaffenburg, d. there July 26, 1812 ; member of the cathedral chapter at Trèves and Worms ; he was an excellent pianist, fair composer, and thoughtful writer on music. He composed chamber-works, sonatas, variations, *Evas Klage* and *Der sterbende Christ an seine Seele* (both cantatas after Klopstock), etc., and wrote: " Blick eines Tonkünstlers in die Musik der Geister " (1777), " Vom Erkennen und Erfinden " (1791), " Untersuchungen über den Ursprung der Harmonie " (1801), " Die Äolsharfe, ein allegorischer Traum " (1801), " Ueber griechische Instrumentalmusik und ihre Wirkung," and translated Jones' " The Musical Modes of the Hindus " (1802).

D'Albert. (*See* ALBERT.)

Dall, Roderick, the last Scotch " wandering harpist " ; he was still alive about 1740 at Athol, wandering from one nobleman's seat to another. (*Cf.* BARDS.)

Dalla (Ital), same as *da la* (" from the ").

Dall' Argine. (*See* ARGINE,)

Dalvimare, Martin Pierre, harpist of note, and composer for his instrument, b. 1770, Dreux (Eure-et-Loire). He first took up music as an amateur, but by the revolution of 1789 was compelled to depend upon his skill for support. In 1806 he became harpist to the court, but gave up this post in 1812, as the inheritance of an estate placed him in easy circumstances. He was still living in 1837. His works are: sonatas for harp and violin, duets for two harps, for harp and pf., harp and horn, variations, etc.

Damcke, Berthold, b. Feb. 6, 1812, Hanover, d. Feb. 15, 1875, Paris; pupil of Aloys Schmitt and F. Ries at Frankfort; from 1837 conductor of the Philharmonic Society at Potsdam, and of the Choral Union for operatic music, with which he arranged grand concerts (1839–40). In 1845 D. went to Petersburg, where he obtained an honourable and lucrative post as teacher. In 1855 he moved to Brussels, and from 1859 lived in Paris. He was an ardent worshipper of Berlioz, and one of his most intimate friends (one of his executors). Damcke's own compositions (oratorios, part-songs, pf. pieces) show a practised hand, but little originality. The last years of his life were worthily employed in revising Mlle. Pelletan's edition of the scores of Gluck's operas.

Damenisation. (*See* BOBISATION.)

Damm, (1) Friedrich, b. March 7, 1831, Dresden, pupil of Jul. Otto, Krägen and Reichel, lived for many years in America, and is now music teacher at Dresden. He has published many brilliant pianoforte pieces; works of a more serious character remain in manuscript.—(2) G. (*See* STEINGRÄBER.)

Damoreau, Laure Cinthie, *née* Montalant, distinguished opera singer, b. Feb. 6, 1801, Paris, d. there Feb. 25, 1863; she studied at the Conservatoire, first sang at the Italian Opera, under the name Mlle. Cinti, in London (1822), then again in Paris; from 1826–35 was a "star" at the Grand Opéra (Rossini wrote several *rôles* for her), then, until 1843, at the Opéra Comique, where, amongst other works, Auber wrote the *Domino Noir* for her. After retiring from the stage, she appeared for several years at concerts in Belgium, Holland, Russia, also in America. In 1834 she was appointed teacher of singing at the Conservatoire, in which capacity she published a " Méthode de Chant " and romances of her own. In 1856 she retired to Chantilly.

Damper. (*See* SORDINO.)

Dämpfer (Ger.), a damper; a mute.

Dämpfung (Ger.), (1) damping, muffling.—(2) The part of the pianoforte action which stops the vibrations of the strings.

Damrosch, Leopold, b. Oct. 22, 1832, Posen, d. Feb. 15, 1885, New York, showed musical talent at an early age, and predilection for a musical vocation; but in obedience to the wishes of his parents he studied medicine, and

in 1854 took his degree of Dr.Med. His professional studies at an end, he devoted himself entirely to music, though against his parents' wish; and, as they withdrew all support, he was compelled to earn his living, and in a miserable way. He first travelled about as a violinist, visiting small towns and watering-places; then he obtained engagements as conductor at small theatres, until at last he received a fixed appointment in the court band at Weimar. Here he entered into personal intercourse with Liszt and his most distinguished pupils, Bülow, Tausig, Cornelius, Lassen, and also into friendly relationship with Raff. D. married at Weimar Helene v. Heimburg, an excellent *Lieder*-singer, who had appeared on the stage there. In 1858 he accepted the post of conductor of the Breslau Philharmonic Society, and gained merit by making known the works of Wagner, Liszt, and Berlioz. In 1860 he gave up this post, in order to make several concert-tours with Bülow and Tausig, but resided at Breslau, where he established Quartet *soirées*. In 1862 he founded the Breslau Orchestral Society (seventy members; present conductor Maszkowsky); the new enterprise was everywhere recognised, and the best artists appeared at its concerts. He established, besides, a choral union, conducted the society for classical music, was for two years capellmeister at the theatre, and appeared, besides, as soloist at Leipzig, Hamburg, etc. In 1871 he was invited by the Arion Male Choral Union at New York to be their conductor, and this he accepted all the more willingly as his enthusiasm for new German tendencies had created many difficulties for him at Breslau. In New York he now developed his organising talent, raised the society to a state of extraordinary prosperity, founded in 1873 the Oratorio Society—a choral union which now counts hundreds of members, and produced the most important choral works from Handel, Haydn, Bach ("Matthew Passion"), Beethoven (every year the 9th Symphony) to Brahms, Berlioz, and Liszt—and in 1878 the New York Symphony Society, both institutions of the highest importance for musical life in New York. His Symphony concerts at the Steinway Hall took the place of the Thomas Orchestra Concerts when the latter had been given up. The University of Columbia conferred on him the degree of Mus.Doc. Liszt dedicated to him his " Triomphe funèbre du Tasse." D. himself composed twelve sets of songs, several works for violin (concerto in D minor, serenades, romances, impromptus), a Festival Overture, some vocal works with orchestra ("Brautgesang" for male choir; " Ruth und Naomi," and " Sulamith," Biblical idylls with soli and chorus; "Siegfrieds Schwert," tenor solo), duets etc. D. distinguished himself as conductor of the first great musical festival held at New York in 1881 (over 1,200 singers and 250 instrumentalists). He established German Opera at

New York (1884), in the direction of which his son W a l t e r has succeeded him.

Dances. The older dances were originally accompanied by singing, like the German "Ringelreihen" and "Springtänze"; the Spanish Sarabandes; the French Branles, Gavottes, Courantes, Gigues, Rigaudons, Musettes, Bourrées, Passepieds, Loures, etc.; the Italian Paduane, Gagliarde, Ciacone, Passamezzi, etc. The players of instruments spread abroad the melodies, and, even before the 16th century, they may often have been played by instruments only, without singing. Anyhow, they were artistically worked out with polyphonic accompaniment, at latest, at the beginning of the 16th century, of which period many printed collections have been preserved. Dances passed through a new phase of development, when several of them were united in a cycle, the unity of key forming, first of all, the bond of union. Hence resulted the form of the *Partita* (Partie) or *Suite* (q.v.), specially cultivated, from the 17th to the 18th century, for harpsichord or violin alone, or the latter with harpsichord. Thus D. became considerably extended, and consisted, not merely of short (repeated) sections of eight bars, but of theme, counter-theme, and developments.

Danckerts (*See* DANKERS.)

Dancla, J e a n B a p t i s t e C h a r l e s, b. Dec. 19, 1818, Bagnères de Bigorre (Htes.-Pyrénées), pupil of Baillot (violin), Halévy, and Berton at the Conservatoire, Paris. Already in 1834 he entered the orchestra of the Opéra-Comique as second solo violinist, soon made for himself a name at the *Société des Concerts*, and in 1857 was appointed professor of the violin at the Conservatoire. His quartet *soirées* enjoyed a high reputation; in these two of his brothers took part:—A r n a u d, b. Jan. 1, 1820, d. Feb., 1862, Bagnères de Bigorre, an excellent 'cellist and author of a 'cello Method; and L é o p o l d, b. June 1, 1823, who is likewise a good violinist, and has published studies, fantasias, etc. D. has written about 150 works, mostly for violin, or ensemble chamber music (violin concertos, quartets for strings, trios, etc.), and has repeatedly received prizes of high honour, among others, the *Prix Chartier* for chamber music (1861, jointly with Farrenc). Among his educational works are: a " Méthode élémentaire et progressive de Violon," " École de l'Expression," " École de la Mélodie," " Art de moduler sur le Violon," etc.

Danel, L o u i s A l b e r t J o s e p h, b. March 2, 1787, Lille, d. there April 12, 1875. He was a printer, but retired in 1854, and devoted the last twenty years of his life to benevolent aims. D. invented an original notation for elementary musical instruction, the " Langue des Sons," as he called it, which expressed by letters, not only the name, but the duration of the notes, also the $\sharp$, $\flat$, etc.; so that a syllable answered to each note. For example, *bel* = (b = b, e =ρ, 1 =$\flat$). For further details see his " Méthode simplifiée pour l'enseignement populaire de la Musique Vocale " (4th edition, 1859). D., at great cost, established free courses of his method in various towns and villages of the Département du Nord. His efforts for the public good were rewarded with the *Croix de la Légion d'Honneur*.

Danican. (*See* PHILIDOR.)

Daniel, S a l v a d o r, during the Commune of 1871 was, for a few days, director of the Paris Conservatoire, as successor to Auber, but died on the 23rd of May of the same year in an engagement with the regular troops. However little qualified he may seem to have been for the post of Director of the Conservatoire, still he was not without merit, for he had been engaged for several years as music teacher in an Arab school at Algiers. In 1863 he published a monograph, " La Musique Arabe," together with a supplement on the origin of musical instruments; also an album of Arabian, Moorish, and cabalistic songs, and a treatise in letter form on the French *chanson*. He was for some time a contributor to Rochefort's *Marseillaise*.

Danjou, J e a n L o u i s F é l i x, b. June 21, 1812, Paris, d. March 4, 1866, Montpelier; organist of various Paris churches, and, in 1840, of Notre-Dame. He was the first to start the question of the reform of Gregorian song in his pamphlet, " De l'État et de l'Avenir du Chant Ecclésiastique " (1844), and made a deep study of the history of Church song, the results of which he made known in his " Revue de la Musique Religieuse, Populaire et Classique " (1845-49). In a journey undertaken with Morelot through the south of France and Italy, in 1847, he discovered a number of musical manuscripts of the Middle Ages, among them the celebrated Antiphonary of Montpelier (with neumes and so-called *Notation Boétienne; cf.* LETTER NOTATION). For the sake of improving French church organs, D. made a deep study of the art of organ-building in Germany, Holland, and Belgium, and became associated with the Paris firm, Daublaine and Callinet (q.v.); but, by so doing, lost his fortune; and, besides, his efforts at reform in the department of church music raised up many enemies against him. Embittered, he entirely renounced music in 1849, and lived first at Marseilles, then at Montpelier, as a political journalist.

Dankers (Danckerts), G h i s e l i n, Dutch contrapuntist of the 16th century, b. Tholen (Zeeland), singer in the Papal Chapel, 1538-65; in the latter year he received a pension. Two books of motets, à 4-6, of his have been preserved (1559); detached motets exist in the

Augsburg collections of 1540 and 1545. He also wrote an autograph treatise on the ancient scales, the judgment in a controversy between Vicentino (q.v.) and Lusitano; this autograph is in the Vallicellan library, Rome.

Danneley, John Feltham, b. 1786, Oakingham, d. 1836 as music teacher in London. He published an elementary instruction book, "Musical Grammar" (1826), and in 1825 a small "Encyclopedia, or Dictionary of Music."

Dannreuther, Edward, b. Nov. 4, 1844, Strassburg. At the age of five he went with his parents to Cincinnati, where he received his first musical training from F. L. Ritter. From 1859 to 1863 he attended the Leipzig Conservatorium, and since then has resided in London. He is esteemed as pianist, teacher, and *littérateur*. D. is an enthusiastic champion of Wagner. In 1872 he founded the London Wagner Society, whose concerts he conducted from 1873 to 1874. He was one of the chief promoters of the Wagner Festival in 1877, and translated into English Wagner's "Briefe an einen französischen Freund," "Beethoven" (1880)—the latter with an appendix on Schopenhauer's philosophy—and "Ueber das Dirigiren" (1887). He is, besides, the author of "Richard Wagner, his Tendencies and Theories," "Musical Ornamentation," as well as articles in musical papers on Beethoven, Chopin, Wagner's *Nibelungen*. He was a contributor to Grove's "Dictionary of Music and Musicians," and has given lectures on Mozart, Beethoven, and Chopin. D. is one of the most esteemed musicians in London.

Danzi, (1) Franz, b. May 15, 1763, Mannheim, d. April 13, 1826, Carlsruhe, was the son of the 'cellist of the Electoral band, Innocenz D. He was a pupil of his father for the 'cello, and of Abbé Vogler for composition; and in 1778, when the band was removed to Munich, he became a member of it. In 1780 his first opera (*Azakia*) was produced, and was followed, up to 1807, by seven others; two more remained in manuscript. In 1790 he married the singer, Margarete Marchand, daughter of the Munich theatre director. He received unlimited leave of absence, went with her to Leipzig, Prague, and travelled through Italy. After the death of his wife (1799), he retired for several years into private life. In 1798 he was appointed vice-capellmeister. From 1807-8 we find him again capellmeister at Stuttgart, and, finally, occupying a similar post at Carlsruhe. Besides the ten operas, D. wrote a number of cantatas, masses, Te Deums, magnificats, symphonies, 'cello concertos, sonatas, quartets, trios, songs, etc.—(2) Franziska. (*See* LEBRUN.)

Dargomyzski, Alexander Sergiewitsch, b. Feb. 2, 1813, on his father's estate in the Russian Government of Tula, d. Jan. 29, 1869, Petersburg. At an early age he made attempts at composition, and appeared with success as a pianist. From 1835 he lived at Petersburg. He won his first success as a composer with the opera *Esmeralda*, written in 1839, produced at Moscow in 1847, and at the "Alexandra" theatre, Petersburg, in 1851. His *Bacchusfest* (vocal ballet written in 1845) was first produced at Moscow in 1867. From 1845 to 1850 he published a great number of songs and duets, which soon became popular. In *Esmeralda* he adopted the form of the operas most in vogue (Rossini, Auber); but in his *Russalka* (*Die Nymphe* after A. Puschkin), written in 1855, and first performed in 1856, a more important *rôle* was assigned to recitative. He only sketched a few scenes of a fantastic comic opera, *Rogdana*. In 1867 he was elected president of the Russian Musical Society; and his house became the meeting-place of the young Russian school which pays homage to Schumann, Berlioz, Wagner, and Liszt. D. adopted more and more the principles of Wagner, until at last (and not to his advantage) he went further than the master. In his posthumous opera (*Kamennoi góst* ["The Stone Guest"], scored by Rimsky-Korsakoff, and given, with an after-piece by Cui, at the "Maria" theatre in 1872), in which A. Puschkin's poem, "Don Juan," has been faithfully adhered to, D. entirely does away with musical forms, and only recognises musical recitative. The orchestral compositions of D.—the "Finnish Fantasia," the "Kozaczek" (Cossack Dance), "Baba-Jaza," etc.—and his songs, ballads, etc., have achieved great popularity.

Darmsaiten (Ger.), catgut strings.

Daser, Ludwig, important German contrapuntist of the second half of the 16th century. He was, at first, capellmeister at Würtemberg, and then at Munich (predecessor of Orlando Lasso). A Passion à 4 of his is printed in the Patrocinium, and a motet in the "Orgel Tabulaturbuch" of J. Paix; but the Munich Library possesses masses of his (13 à 4, 7 à 5, and 1 à 6), also a series of mass-services and motets.

Daube, Joh. Friedrich, b. about 1730 (Cassel, Augsburg?), d. Sept. 19, 1797, Augsburg, court musician at Stuttgart, afterwards secretary to the Augsburg Academy of Sciences. He published sonatas for lute, and the following works: "Generalbass in drei Akkorden" (1756, attacked by Marpurg in the *Beiträge*); "Der musikalische Dilettant" (1773, Art of Composition), "Anleitung zum Selbstunterricht in der Komposition" (1788, two parts). The "Generalbass in drei Akkorden" is of special importance: the three chords are—the tonic triad, the chord of the under-dominant with added sixth, and the chord of the upper-dominant with seventh.

Daublaine et Callinet, Paris organ-builders. The firm was established in 1838 as Daublaine et Cie. Danjou (q.v.) was the intelligent mind directing the business, and Callinet the skilled craftsman (b. 1797, Ruffach, Alsatia, joined the firm in 1839), while D a u b l a i n e was the merchant. Callinet, in 1843, quarrelled with his partner, destroyed what had been constructed for the St. Sulpice organ, left the firm, and entered Cavaillé's factory. The name of the firm, which has repeatedly changed hands, became, in 1845, *Ducrocquet et Cie*, in 1855, *Merklin, Schütze et Cie*. The business is now carried on by Merklin (q.v.) alone, and the principal factory is at Lyons.

Daumenaufsatz (Ger.), thumb position.

Dauprat, L o u i s F r a n ç o i s, famous hornplayer and composer for his instrument, b. May 24, 1781, Paris, d. there July 16, 1868. He studied under Kenn at the Conservatoire, then became a member of the military band of the "Garde Nationale," afterwards of the "Musique des Consuls." From 1801 to 1805 he again went through a course of theory at the Conservatoire under Catel and Gossec; from 1806 to 1808 he was principal horn-player at the Bordeaux Theatre, and afterwards succeeded Kenn and Duvernoy at the Paris Opéra. He was, besides, chamber musician to Napoleon and to Louis XVIII. In 1802 he was appointed assistant-teacher, and in 1816 professor of the horn at the Conservatoire; in 1831 he retired from the Opéra, and in 1842 from the Conservatoire. His published works are : "Méthode pour cor alto et cor basse " (*i.e.* for first, and second horn), concertos for horn and *ensemble* chamber works with horn. Symphonies, a Method of harmony, a " Théorie analytique de la Musique," etc., remained in manuscript.

Daussoine-Méhul, L o u i s J o s e p h, nephew and foster-son of Méhul, b. June 24, 1790, Givet (Ardennes), d. March 10, 1875, Liège. He was a pupil of Catel and Méhul at the Conservatoire, received in 1809 the *Grand Prix de Rome*, and after his return from Italy, tried his luck as an opera composer; but he met with great difficulties, and after some moderate successes, renounced the stage. In 1827 he was appointed director of the Conservatoire at Liège, in which post he remained until 1862, raising the institution to a high degree of prosperity. That he had a sound talent is proved by the fact that in the posthumous works of his uncle which he completed, the critics could not distinguish between what was his and what was his uncle's. As member of the Brussels Académie, B. published a series of musical treatises on the reports of the meetings of this institution.

Davenport, Francis William, b. 1847, Wilderslowe, near Derby, pupil, and afterwards son-in-law of G. Macfarren; he became professor of the Royal Academy of Music in 1879, and of the Guildhall School of Music in 1882. He has written two symphonies—one in D minor (first prize at the Alexandra Palace Competition, 1876), and the other in C major, an overture (*Twelfth Night*), prelude and fugue for orchestra,

a pf. trio (B♭), pieces for pf. and 'cello, partsongs and songs; and likewise the theoretical works—" Elements of Music" (1884), and " Elements of Harmony and Counterpoint " (1886).

David, (1) F e r d i n a n d, an important violinist and one of the best teachers that ever lived, b. Jan. 19, 1810, Hamburg, d. July 18, 1873, on a journey, at Klosters in Switzerland. He studied under Spohr and Hauptmann at Cassel (1823–24), and, already in 1825, appeared as a finished artist in the Gewandhaus, Leipzig (with his sister Luise, afterwards Frau Dulcken). In 1827 he joined the orchestra of the "Königsstadt " Theatre at Berlin, and in 1829 became leader of a quartet party in the house of a wealthy amateur (von Liphardt) at Dorpat, whose daughter he married, and made himself a name as violinist in concerts at Petersburg, Moscow, Riga, etc. In 1836 Mendelssohn, who had made his acquaintance in Berlin, drew him to Leipzig as leader of the Gewandhaus orchestra. The eminently musical nature of David now found a rich field of activity, especially after the establishment of the Conservatorium in 1843 ; and, through his efforts, Leipzig was for a long period the high school of violin-playing, even after the prestige of Mendelssohn, Schumann, and Gade had declined. The manner in which he kept the Gewandhaus orchestra together will never be forgotten ; the *ensemble* movements of the bows of the violin-players made almost a military impression ; and D. who, as leader, had to conduct solo performances with orchestral accompaniment, was an object of terror to the *virtuosi* who made their *début* there. His powers as a teacher may be measured by his pupils. The best German violinists of the later decades before his death studied under him (among them, Joachim and Wilhelmj). Mendelssohn held D. in high esteem, and, during the period of their collaboration in Leipzig, frequently sought his advice. The violin concerto of the former sprang into existence under David's eyes, and in its creation he lent a helping hand. David's compositions are : five violin concertos, sets of variations, solo pieces, an opera (*Hans Wacht*), two symphonies, and, above all, a violin Method which ranks among the best, and the " Hohe Schule des Violinspiels " (a collection of old compositions for the violin, especially of French and Italian masters of the 17th and 18th centuries. His son, P e t e r P a u l, b. Aug. 1, 1840, Leipzig, leader at Carlsruhe from 1862 to 1865, is now teacher of the violin at Uppingham.

(2) F é l i c i e n C é s a r, distinguished French composer, b. April 13, 1810, Cadenet (Vaucluse), d. Aug. 29, 1876, St. Germain en Laye. On account of his beautiful voice he went as chorister to Saint Sauveur, Aix, and obtained a scholarship at the Jesuit College ; but, after three years, ran away from the school in order to devote himself entirely to music, and

supported himself as clerk in a lawyer's office until he was appointed second chef d'orchestre at the Aix Theatre. In 1829 he was named choir-master of Saint Sauveur's; but he soon longed to acquire more knowledge, so as to be able to give expression, with technical correctness, to the musical thoughts which sprang up within him; and, with a meagre support of fifty francs a month, he wandered to Paris. Cherubini, before whom he placed some of his attempts at composition, obtained for him admission into the Conservatoire, and D. became a pupil of Fétis (composition) and Bénoist (organ), receiving, in addition, private lessons from Réber. When at last his uncle withdrew his small support, D. maintained himself by giving private lessons. Saint-Simonism, for which he became enthusiastic, proved the turning-point in his life. At first he wrote part-songs for the concerts of the apostles of Saint-Simonism, of whom he was one; and, after the sect was abolished by law in 1833, he went, with some of the other apostles, to the East, as a missionary of the new doctrine. Meeting with all kinds of adventures, they went *viâ* Marseilles to Constantinople, Smyrna, Egypt; later on, D. passed alone through Upper Egypt to the Red Sea, but was driven away by the plague, and returned to Paris in 1838. His journey resulted in a thorough acquaintance with the music of the East, in a collection of original Oriental melodies, and powerful impressions exercising a lasting influence on his imagination. The collection of Oriental airs which he published in 1835 did not produce the expected effect, and D., out of humour, withdrew to a friend's house in the country, where he wrote a large number of instrumental works, some of which were produced at Paris. In 1844 he succeeded in getting his ode-symphonie, "Le Désert," performed at a Conservatoire concert—a work in which the noble impressions of his Oriental journey are musically recorded. It met with extraordinary success, and D. was at once recognised as a musician of importance. He was not able, in 1845, to excite the same ecstasy in Germany; yet his reputation was firmly established, and attention was now bestowed on his former, likewise on all his future works. His oratorio, *Moïse au Sinaï* (1846), certainly only met with a quiet reception, and the mystery, "Eden," and the ode-symphony, "Columbus," did not awaken the same enthusiastic applause as the "Désert." During the year 1848 the Parisians had no leisure to pay proper homage to works of art; but D. had free course, and even found the doors of opera-houses open to his works. In 1857 he produced *La Perle du Brésil* at the Théâtre Lyrique. His *La Fin du Monde*, by reason of the strange subject, was refused at the Grand Opéra, but put into rehearsal at the Théâtre Lyrique, though not produced. First in 1859 the Grand Opéra gave it under the title —*Herculanum;* in 1862 followed *Lalla Rookh*, and

in 1865 *Le Saphir*. His "Désert," however, was, and remained, his master-work; the *Saphir* was somewhat of a falling-off, whilst *Lalla Rookh* met with great success. A fifth opera, *La Captive*, D. himself withdrew, and wrote no more for the stage. Of his other works, the twenty-four stringed quintets ("Les Quatre Saisons"), two nonets for wind-instruments, a symphony in F, songs, etc., deserve special mention. In 1867 D. received from the Académie the great State Prize of 20,000 francs; in 1869 he became Academician in Berlioz's place, and was appointed successor to the latter as librarian at the Conservatoire.

(3) S a m u e l, b. Nov. 12, 1836, Paris; he was pupil of Bazin and Halévy at the Conservatoire, and from 1872 musical director of the Jewish Synagogue, Paris. In 1858 he received the *Prix de Rome* (cantata, *Jephtha*), and in 1859 a prize for a work for male chorus and orchestra ("Le génie de la terre"), which was performed by six thousand singers. He wrote several comic operas and operettas—*La Peau de l'Ours*, 1858; *Les Chevaliers du Poignard* (rehearsed, but not performed); *Mademoiselle Sylvia*, 1868; *Tu l'as voulu*, 1869; *Le bien d'autrui*, 1869; *Un Caprice de Ninon*, 1871; *La Fée des Bruyères*, 1878. The following remain in manuscript: *La Gageure, Une Dragonnade, L'Éducation d'un Prince, Absalom, Les Chargeurs*, and *I Maccabei* (Italian); also four symphonies, many small songs, and a pamphlet—"L'Art de jouer en Mesure." Died Oct. 3, 1895, Paris.

(4) E r n e s t, meritorious writer on music, b. July 4, 1844, Nancy, d. June 3, 1886, Paris. In spite of a lively inclination towards music, he at first resolved to become a merchant; and only in 1862, when paralysis of both legs compelled him to lead a retired life, did he devote himself to the study of the history of music under Fétis, with whom he corresponded. At first he contributed to the *Revue et Gazette Musicale*, the *Ménéstrel*, and the *Bibliographe Musicale*. In 1873 he published a study, "La Musique chez les Juifs," and with M. Lussy (q.v.) the "Histoire de la Notation Musicale depuis ses Origines"—a work which, although it received a prize, is not altogether original. D. also wrote a Bach biography ("La Vie et les Œuvres de J. S. Bach").

Davidoff, C a r l, distinguished 'cellist, b. March 15, 1838, Goldingen (Courland), d. Feb. 26, 1889, Moscow. He went, as a boy, to Moscow, became a pupil of H. Schmidt for the 'cello, received further training from C. Schuberth at Petersburg, and then went to Leipzig, where he studied composition under Hauptmann. In 1859 he appeared at the Gewandhaus with extraordinary success, was engaged as solo 'cellist, and entered the Conservatorium as teacher in the place of F. Grützmacher. After some concert tours, however, he returned to Petersburg, where he became solo 'cellist in the Imperial orchestra, teacher at the Conservatoire (1862), and, later on, conductor of the Russian Musical Society, and director of the Conservatoire; the last-named post he resigned in 1887. His compositions consist principally of concertos, solo pieces, etc., for 'cello; he published, however, some excellent chamber works (pianoforte quintet, etc.).

Davies, F a n n y, excellent pianist, b. Guernsey, was a pupil (pianoforte) of the Leipzig Conservatorium in 1882, and from 1883 to 1885 at the Hoch Conservatorium at Frankfort (Clara Schumann); she made her *début* at the Crystal Palace in 1885, and has since appeared in England, Germany (Berlin, Leipzig) and Italy, and with great success.

Davison. (*See* GODDARD.)

Davison, James William, b. Oct. 5, 1813, London, d. March 24, 1885, Margate. He was a pupil of Holmes (pianoforte), and of G. A. Macfarren (theory). He first attempted composition, but soon devoted himself entirely to musical criticism. He edited the *Musical Examiner* from 1842 to 1844, and the *Musical World* from 1844 down to his death; and wrote, likewise, for the *Saturday Review, Pall Mall Gazette,* and *Graphic.* He was musical critic of *The Times* from 1846 to 1879, in which post he exercised great influence. D. suggested, and wrote the analytic programme-books for the Popular Concerts until his death; he wrote similar books for the "Hallé" recitals. In 1859 he married Arabella Goddard, who had been his pupil since 1850.

Davy (1), John, b. near Exeter, 1765, d. Feb. 22, 1824, London, a favourite opera composer in London from 1800 to 1820. His songs, of which "The Bay of Biscay" was one, gained great popularity.—(2) Richard, an English composer of the early part of the 16th century.

Day, Alfred, b. Jan., 1810, London, d. there Feb. 11, 1849. He studied for the medical profession in London and Paris, took his degree of Dr.Med. at Heidelberg, and practised as an homœopathist in London. He is the author of an interesting "Treatise on Harmony" (1845), in which, with great intelligence, he strives after suitable reforms in the method of teaching. He replaces thorough bass figuring by a new bass figuring (and from this, unfortunately, he could not rid himself); in this figuring the identity of the harmonic meaning in the various positions of the same chord was to be made clear. The sore point of his system is the putting forward of the monstrous chord of the thirteenth as a formation of chief importance.

D. c., abbreviation for *da capo.* (*See* CAPO)

D double-sharp, D doubly raised by a ×.

De Ahna, (1) Heinrich Karl Hermann, b. June 22, 1835, Vienna, d. Nov. 1, 1892, pupil of Mayseder at Vienna, and afterwards of Mildner at the Prague Conservatorium; he appeared, already at the age of twelve, at

Vienna, London, etc., as a violinist, and in 1849 was appointed chamber-virtuoso to the Duke of Coburg-Gotha. In spite, however, of good success, he gave up music, and entered the Austrian army as cadet on October 1, 1851; he became lieutenant in 1853, and went through the Italian campaign of 1859. When peace was concluded, his love for an artistic vocation revived; he left the army, made concert tours through Germany and Holland, and in 1862 settled in Berlin, and, first of all, as member of the royal band. In 1868 he was appointed leader, and in 1869 teacher, at the Royal High School of Music. D. was not only a good virtuoso, but also an excellent quartet player.—(2) E l e o-n o r e, sister of the former, b. Jan. 8. 1838, Vienna, studied under E. Mantius; she was an excellent singer (mezzo-soprano), and was engaged at the court Opera, but died already May 10, 1865, at Berlin.

Debain, Alexander François, the inventor of the harmonium, b. 1809, Paris, d. there Dec. 3, 1877. He worked first with Ad. Sax, and afterwards set up a pianoforte factory of his own in 1834. In August, 1840, he took out a patent for the harmonium, which speedily made his name known. D. was a thoroughly skilled mechanician, and constructed all kinds of automatic musical works; later on he improved the harmonium by means of *prolongement*, and also perfected the accordion (concertina), etc.

Debile, or **Debole** (Ital.), feeble, weak.

Debillemont, Jean Jacques, b. Dec. 12, 1824, Dijon, d. Feb. 14, 1879, Paris. He studied at the Paris Conservatoire under Alard (violin), Leborne, and Carafa, produced some operas in his native town, then (1859) settled in Paris, where he became known by his operettas, *féeries,* and by some comic operas (*Astaroth,* produced at the Théâtre Lyrique, 1861), cantatas, etc. D. was formerly conductor of the concerts of the "Société des Beaux-Arts," and afterwards held a similar post at the Porte St. Martin theatre.

Debois, Ferdinand, b. Nov. 24, 1834, Brünn, where he lived as bank director and conductor of a male choral union of which he was the founder. He wrote part-songs for male voices, which have become popular; also songs, duets, pf. pieces, etc. Died May 10, 1893, Brünn.

Debrois van Bruyck. (*See* BRUYCK.)

Début (Fr.), a first appearance.

Decachord (Ger.), **Décacorde** (Fr.), an instrument of the guitar family, with ten strings.

Déchant (Fr.). (*See* DISCANTUS.)

Decima (Lat.), the tenth degree of the scale, practically the same as the third. A mutation stop in the organ (Tenth, Tierce, Double Tierce), which gives the tenth of the 8-feet pipes, *i.e.* the fifth overtone of the 16-feet pipes, identical with the Tierce of $3\frac{1}{5}$-feet.

Deciso (Ital.), in a decided manner.

Decker, Konstantin, b. Dec. 29, 1810, Fürstenau, Brandenburg, d. Jan. 28, 1878, Stolp (Pomerania), pupil of Dehn at Berlin, an able teacher, pianist, also composer. He lived for some years at Petersburg, and then Königsberg, where his opera *Isolde* was performed in 1852; and from 1859 at Stolp.

Declamando (Ital.), declaiming, speaking rather than singing. (*Cf.* DECLAMATION.)

Declamation is the name in vocal composition for the transformation of poetical, into musical rhythm. The declamation of a song is bad if a weak syllable receives a strong musical accent, or is placed on a long note; or if an accented syllable, or a word of special emphasis, has a short note, or occurs on the unaccented part of a bar. The metrical accent and the musical stress must, generally speaking, coincide, and for that, the melody need not be capable of regular scansion. The simple, popular song, as a rule, follows strictly the course of the metre, while the art-song moulds it in freer fashion, now lengthening, now shortening the periods—by extending the syllables, by the succession of a number of short notes, etc. (*Cf.* Riemann, "Katechismus der Vocalmusik," 1891.)

Decrescendo (Ital.), abbr. *decresc.*, *decr.*, decreasing in loudness, becoming weaker.

Dedekind, (1) Henning, cantor at Langensalza about 1590, afterwards minister there, and in 1622 at Gebesee; he died in 1628. D. published "Dodekatonon musicum Trinciniorum" (without year of publication; 2nd edition as "Neue auserlesene *Tricinia*," 1588); "Eine Kindermusik" (1589, an elementary instruction-book of music arranged in the form of questions and answers); "Præcursor metricus musicæ artis" (1590); and "Dodekas musicarum deliciarum, Soldatenleben, darinnen allerlei Kriegshändel, etc." (1628). The play upon the Greek word δωδεκα is probably a hint at the author's name.—(2) Konstantin Christian, b. April 2, 1628, Reindorf (Anhalt-Dessau), tax-collector, poet-laureate, and "Hofmusikus" at Meissen, speaks of himself in 1672 as "churfürstl. sächs. deutscher Konzertmeister" (he was still living about 1694). He composed sacred songs with instrumental accompaniment, which were much admired in their time: for example, "Musikalischer Jahrgang und Vespérgesang" (120 concertos), 1674; "Davidischer Harfenschall;" "Singende Sonn- und Festtagsandachten," 1683; "Musikalischer Jahrgang, etc." (à 2 with organ, 1694), and other works.

Dedler, Rochus, b. Jan. 15, 1779, Oberammergau, d. Oct. 15, 1822, Vienna, composer of the music for the Passion Play, which is still in use.

Deering (Dering), Richard, sprang from an old Kentish family, received his first musical education in Italy, probably at Rome (Cavalieri, Viadana?), or at Florence, for he is the author of the oldest known work with continuo

(continued instrumental bass). On his journey home from Italy he published at Antwerp—three years before Caccini's *Euridice* and Cavalieri's "Anima e corpo" (1600)—"Cantiones sacræ quinque vocum cum basso continuo ad organum" (1597; 2nd book 1617, third book 1619). In 1610 he took his degree of Mus. Bac. at Oxford, and in 1617, after much entreaty, became organist at the English nuns' convent at Brussels. In 1625 he became court organist to Queen Henrietta Maria, and died already in 1630. He published besides: "Cantica sacra ad melodiam madrigalium elaborata senis vocibus" (1618); two books of canzonets (Antwerp, 1620); "Cantica sacra ad duas et tres voces cum basso continuo ad organum" (1662, probably a selection of the first named). Some of his pieces are to be found in Playford's "Cantica sacra" (1674), and some manuscripts in the library of the Sacred Harmonic Society (now belonging to the Royal College of Music).

Deferrari. (*See* FERRARI.)

Deffès, Louis Pierre, b. July 25, 1819, Toulouse; he went in 1839 from the branch establishment of his native town to the Paris Conservatoire, became a pupil of Halévy, and in 1847 received the *Prix de Rome*. Elegant structure and fine musical feeling are praiseworthy features in his compositions; but they lack originality.

Deficiendo (Ital.), decreasing in tone and movement, like *mancando* and *calando*.

Degele, Eugen, stage-singer (baritone), b. July 4, 1834, Munich, d. July 26, 1866, Dresden, a grandson of Valesi on his mother's side. He attended the Munich Conservatorium, first as a violin pupil, and soon afterwards for singing. He was first trained by A. Bayer and Fr. Dietz. After an unsuccessful *début* at Munich he received further instruction from W. Rauscher, and then made a successful appearance in Hanover as "Nevers" (1856); he was engaged, and remained up to 1861, and then went to Dresden, where he belonged to the court opera up to his death. Marschner held D. in high esteem, as representative of the chief *rôles* in his operas. D. also obtained fair success as a song composer.

Degrees are the several divisions of the scale (tone-steps, "scala"). In counting them a start is generally made from the tonic; so one speaks of the triad, chord of the seventh, etc., of the second, fifth, etc., degree of the scale. A distinction is also made between the various enharmonic tones; it is said that *c* and *d♭* are placed on different degrees, *c*, *c♯* on the same degree of the fundamental scale (q.v.).

Dehaan (de Haan), Willem, composer and conductor, b. 1849, Rotterdam, was trained at the music school there by Nicolai, de Lange and Bargiel. He was subsequently (1870–71) pupil of the Leipzig Conservatorium, and, after visits to Berlin and Vienna, etc. (1872), became musical director at Bingen (1873), in 1876 conductor of the Mozart Verein at Darmstadt, and in 1878 court capellmeister. His most noteworthy compositions are, for chorus with orchestra: " Der Königssohn," " Das Grab im Busento " (both for male voices), and " Harpa" (for mixed chorus); also an opera (*Die Kaiserstochter*), songs, duets, pf. pieces, etc.

Dehn, Siegfried Wilhelm, b. Feb. 25, 1799, Altona, d. April 12, 1858, Berlin. He was the son of a wealthy banker, studied law at Leipzig from 1819 to 1823, but, at the same time, took lessons in harmony with the organist Dröbs, and perfected himself in 'cello playing. In 1823 he received an appointment at the Swedish Embassy, Berlin. In 1829 he lost the fortune which he had inherited, and adopted music as a vocation. He became a pupil of B. Klein, and was soon an accomplished theorist. In 1842 Meyerbeer procured for him the post of librarian of the musical section of the royal library; this he put into complete order, and drew up a catalogue. D. also enriched it, for he made search in all the libraries of Prussia, and added to the royal library such treasures as he discovered. He also wrote out a great number of old works in score. In 1849 he received the title of Royal Professor. From 1842 to 1848 he edited the musical paper *Caecilia*, founded by Gottfried Weber, and also wrote valuable articles for the same. But his chief work is the "Theoretisch-praktische Harmonielehre " (1840), the preface of which contains valuable historical notes; he also published " Analyse dreier Fugen aus J. S. Bach's Wohltemperiertem Klavier und einer Vokaldoppelfuge G. M. Buononcinis " (1858), a " Sammlung älterer Musik aus dem 16. und 17. Jahrhundert" (twelve books), a translation of Delmotte's notice on Orlando Lasso, etc. B. Scholz published (1859), from documents left by D., a " Lehre vom Kontrapunkt, dem Kanon und der Fuge " (2nd ed., 1883). D. was one of the most remarkable teachers of theory. Among his pupils were: Glinka, Kiel, A. Rubinstein, Th. Kullak, H. Hofmann, etc.

Dei (Ital.), same as *di i* (" from the ").

Deiters, Hermann, writer on music, b. June 27, 1833, Bonn; he studied there, first law, and afterwards philology, took his degrees of Dr.Jur. and Dr.Phil. (1858), and was successively active as collegiate teacher at Bonn (1858), Düren (1869), collegiate director at Konitz, West Prussia (1874), Posen (1878), and Bonn (1883). In 1885 he was appointed " Provinzialschulrath " at Coblenz, and in 1890 assistant in the ministry of public worship at Berlin. In addition to his active work as teacher, D. has appeared with great success as a writer on music. Valuable articles from his pen are to be found in Bagge's *Deutsche Musikzeitung* (1860–62), and, besides, in the *Allgemeine Musikalische Zeitung*, among which " Beethoven's

Dramatische Kompositionen " (1865), " R. Schumann als Schriftsteller " (1865), " Otto Jahn " (1870), " Beethoven's Säkularfeier in Bonn " (1871), " Max Bruch's *Odysseus* " (1873), and a series of articles on Brahms; also the *Ergänzungsblätter zur Kenntniss der Gegenwart*, the *Deutsche Warte*, and the *Münchener Propyläen* contain articles of his; also a number of musical biographies in the third edition of " Meyer's Konversations-Lexikon " were written by him. A special study on Brahms appeared in the *Sammlung Musikalischer Vorträge* (1880), translated into English by Rosa Newmarch. But D.'s chief work is the translation of A. W. Thayer's " Beethoven-Biographie " from the original English (not printed) manuscript (up to now 3 vols., 1866–79). A treatise on the sources of the " Harmonica " of Aristides Quintilianus appeared in 1870 as a " Programm " of the Düren Gymnasium. The following are also worthy of mention : " Über das Verhältniss der Matianus Capelle zu Aristides Quintilianus (1881), and " Über die Verehrung der Musen bei den Griechen " (1868). D. is a thorough follower of Otto Jahn.

De Koven, Reginald, b. 1859, Middletown (Connecticut), trained at Oxford, Stuttgart, and Frankfort (under Hauff), and Florence. Composer in light style (songs, operettas, etc.).

Del (Ital.), same as *di il* (" from the ").

Delaborde. (*See* LABORDE.)

Delâtre (Delattre), (1) Olivier, Netherland contrapuntist; his chansons and motets are preserved in old Paris, Lyons, and Antwerp publications (1539–55).—(2) Claude Petit-Jan, *maître de chapelle* at Verdun Cathedral, was engaged in 1555 in a similar capacity to the Bishop of Liège. He was also a composer of chansons and motets, a large number of which are to be found in publications by Phalèse (Louvain), Susato, Bellère (Antwerp), 1546–74.— (3) A mistaken French form of the name of Orlando Lasso (Roland Delattre), which had its origin in a supposed discovery of Delmotte's. (*See* LASSO.)

De l'Aulnaye, François Henri Stanislas, b. July 7, 1739, Madrid, of French parents, d. 1830, Chaillot; he went at an early age to Versailles, and was appointed secretary of the Paris museum at the time of its establishment. When the Revolution broke out, he wrote against it in pamphlets, lost his place, and was forced to hide. After he had squandered the money which he had inherited from his father, he earned a pitiful living as proofreader, and died in the workhouse. D. published several pamphlets on the theory and history of music, among which " De la Saltation Théâtrale " (concerning the origin of pantomime, 1790).

Deldevez, Édouard Marie Ernest, b. May 31, 1817, Paris, pupil of Habeneck (violin),

Halévy, and Berton at the Conservatoire. In 1840 he arranged a concert at the Conservatoire of his own compositions, which proved highly successful. In 1859 he became second conductor at the Grand Opéra and at the Conservatoire concerts, in 1872 principal conductor of the latter, and in 1873, after the death of Hainl, principal conductor at the Grand Opéra ; and in the following year professor of the orchestral class at the Conservatoire. D. is a fairly good composer of symphonic and chamber-music, ballets, lyric scenas, cantatas, sacred works, etc. He has published old violin and other instrumental compositions (" Trilogie "), and has also written two interesting monographs—" Curiosités Musicales " (investigation of certain difficult and doubtful passages in classical works, 1873), and " La Notation de la Musique Classique comparée à la Notation de la Musique Moderne " (concerning the nature of ornaments).

Delezenne, Charles Édouard Joseph, b. Oct. 4, 1776, Lille, d. there Aug. 20, 1866. He was professor of mathematics and natural philosophy in that city, wrote for the session reports of the scientific society at Lille (of which he was member from 1806) very many musical articles (acoustics, intonation, scales, etc.) of the highest scientific value (Vols. i.–xxxv.).

Delibes, Léo, a French composer of great fame, b. Feb. 21, 1836, St. Germain du Val (Sarthe), d. Jan. 16, 1891, Paris ; he became in 1848 a pupil of the Paris Conservatoire (especially of Le Couppey, Bazin, Adam, and Benoist), in 1853 accompanist at the Théâtre Lyrique, and organist of the church of St. Jean et St. François. In 1855 appeared his first one-act operetta, *Deux Sous de Charbon*, at the Théâtre Folies Nouvelles, which was followed by others at the Bouffes Parisiens. The Théâtre Lyrique brought out the one-act comic operas, *Maître Griffard* in 1857, and *Le Jardinier et son Seigneur*, 1863. D. displayed ever-increasing talent for lively, refined, and graceful music. In 1865 he became second chorus-master at the Grand Opéra, where, in 1866, the ballet *La Source* (in Vienna given as *Naila, die Quellenfee*), which D. composed in collaboration with a Pole Minkus, was produced. In 1870 followed the ballet *Coppélia*, which firmly established his reputation, and in 1876, the ballet *Sylvia*. Between the two last-named appeared (1873) the comic opera, *Le Roi l'a dit*, with the best success ; and, since then, it has also been produced in Germany. The later comic operas, *Jean de Nivelles* (1880), and *Lakmé* (1883) were, however, unable to gain a firm footing. To complete the list must be named ballet music interpolated in Adam's *Le Corsaire* (1867), incidental music to *Le Roi s'amuse* (1882), the dramatic scena, *La Mort d'Orphée* (1878), and a number of pleasing romances. His best work was *Coppélia ;* in the others a faulty libretto interferes with the

success of the music. He gave up his post as chorus-master, and in 1881 succeeded Reber as professor of composition at the Conservatoire. In 1884 he was elected member of the Académie, in place of Massé.

Delicato (Ital. *delicatamente, con delicatezza*), in a delicate, refined manner.

Delioux, Charles (D. de Savignac), b. April, 1830, Lorient, made an early appearance as pianist, became a pupil at Paris of Barbereau for theory, and from 1845 to 1849 studied under Halévy at the Conservatoire. In 1854 he brought out his one-act comic opera, *Yvonne et Loic*, at the Gymnase. He wrote, besides, principally pf. pieces and pf. studies, and a " Cours complet d'Exercices," which was adopted by the Conservatoire.

Della Maria, Dominique, b. 1768, Marseilles, d. March 9, 1800, Paris, son of an Italian performer on the mandolin ; he showed early talent for composition, and at eighteen years of age brought out a grand opera at Marseilles. After this he went to Italy, where for ten years he studied seriously at composition, the latter part of the time under Paisiello. In 1796 he went to Paris, received from Duval a libretto, which in eight days he had set to music, so that in a few weeks the opera *Le Prisonnier* was put on the stage (1798) ; the result was excellent, and D. had a won game. He quickly brought out six more operas, and became a great favourite with the Parisians. Sacred music, etc., remained in manuscript.

Dellinger, Rudolf, b. July 8, 1857, Graslitz (Bohemia), 1883 capellmeister at the Karl Schulze Theatre, Hamburg; composer of the operettas *Don Cäsar* and *Lorraine*.

Dello (Ital.), same as *di lo* (" from the ").

Delmotte, Henri Florent, b. 1799, Mons, d. there March 9, 1836, as jurist, son of the writer, Philibert D. He was a zealous bibliophilist, and discovered in the Mons Library important bibliographical material concerning Orlando Lasso, which after his death was published as " Notice Biographique sur Roland Delattre " (1836), and which was translated into German by S. Dehn (1837).

Delprat, Charles, b. 1803, d. Feb., 1888, Pau (Pyrénées), teacher of singing at Paris, pupil of the elder Ponchard ; he wrote " L'Art du Chant et l'École Actuelle " (2nd ed. 1870), and " Le Conservatoire de Musique de Paris et la Commission du Ministère des Beaux-Arts " (1872 ; 3rd ed. 1885 as " La Question Vocale ").

Del Valle de Paz, Edgar, Italian pianist and composer, b. Oct. 18, 1861, Alexandria ; he studied at Naples under Beniamino Cesi and Paolo Serras and, at the age of sixteen, started on concert tours through Italy and Egypt. He is now settled at Florence, and devotes himself to composition and teaching. Besides many pianoforte works, he has composed concerted music, orchestral suites, etc.

Démancher (Fr.) is an expression used in connection with stringed instruments; it signifies a change from one position to another—a gliding up and down with the left hand to or from the neck (*manche*) of the instrument.

Demantius, Christoph, b. 1567, Reichenberg; 1597 cantor at Zittau, 1604 was engaged in a similar capacity at Freiberg (Saxony), where he died, April 20, 1643. Besides sacred works, the following are still known: St. John Passion, à 6 (1631), "Trias precum Vespertinarum" (magnificats, psalms, etc., à 4-6, 1602); "Corona Harmonica" (motets à 6, 1610); "Triades Sioniæ" (introits, masses, proses, à 5-8, 1619); "Weltliche Lieder" (1595); "Timpanum Militare," à 6 (songs of battle and victory, 1600); "Convivalium concentuum farrago" (German canzonets and villanelle, à 6, 1609; "Neue teutsche Lieder" (two parts, 1615); "72 Auserlesene liebliche Polnischer und Teutscher Art Tänze mit und ohne Text, etc." (1601); "Conviviorum Deliciæ, newe liebliche Intraden u. Ausszüge nebst künstlichen Galliarden, und fröhlichen Polnischen Tänzen" (1609); "Threnodiæ" (funeral songs, 1611 and 1620); "Fasciculus Chorodiarum" (à 4 and à 5, Polish and German dances and Galliards "vocaliter" and "instrumentaliter," à 4 and à 5, 1613); also, finally, an "Isagoge Artis Musicæ, etc." ("Kurtze Anleitung recht und leicht Singen zu lernen, nebst Erklärung der griechischen Wörtlein, so bei neuen Musicis im Gebrauch sind," 1605).

Demelius, Christian, b. April 1, 1643, Schlettau, near Annaberg (Saxony), d. Nov. 1, 1711, as cantor at Nordhausen, composed motets and arias (1700), and wrote a "Tirocinium Musicum" (an elementary instruction book on music, without date).

Demeur, Anne Arsène (*née* Charton, married the flautist D., 1847), celebrated stage and concert singer (soprano), b. May 5, 1827, Sanjon (Charente), pupil of Bizot at Bordeaux, where she made her *début* in 1842. She sang first at Toulouse and Brussels (1846), then at London (in French comic opera). Afterwards she sang in Italian opera, and also in 1853 with great success at St. Petersburg, Vienna, Paris (in Berlioz's *Beatrice and Benedict,* and in *Les Troyens à Carthage* (Dido), likewise in America. Her last public appearance was in 1879 as Cassandra in Berlioz's *Prise de Troie.* She died Nov. 30, 1892.

Demol (de Mol), (1) Pierre, b. Nov. 7, 1825, Brussels, pupil of the Brussels Conservatoire, where he was honoured with the *Grand Prix de Rome* for composition (1855). He was principal 'cellist at the Besançon theatre, and 'cello teacher at the Conservatoire there. His compositions which have been performed are the cantatas, *Les Prem'ers Martyrs (Grand Prix de Rome), Dernier*

Jour d'Herculanum; nothing appears to have been printed.—(2) François Marie, nephew of the former, b. March 3, 1844, Brussels, d. Nov. 3, 1883, Ostend, as director of the *Académie de Musique* there. He was trained at the Brussels Conservatoire, and obtained the first prize for counterpoint and fugue and organ playing. He was, at first, organist at the Beguine monastery at Brussels; then, on Fétis' recommendation, was called to Marseilles as organist of the St. Charles Church; while from 1872 to 1875 he conducted the Popular Concerts in that city, and in 1875 became professor of harmony at the Conservatoire. In 1876 he returned to Brussels as conductor at the National Theatre. As a composer, he has only occupied himself with small works. •

Demunck (de Munck), (1) François, celebrated performer on the 'cello, b. Oct. 6, 1815, Brussels, d. there Feb. 28, 1854, son of a teacher of music, and pupil of Platel at the Brussels Conservatoire (1834). He had his name coupled with that of Alexandre Batta for the first prize for 'cello-playing, and, as early as 1835, became assistant-teacher, and, after Platel's death in the same year, principal 'cello professor at the Conservatoire. After a disorderly course of life for some years, his talent and his health were threatened. In 1845 he made long concert tours through Germany; in 1848 he accepted an appointment as 'cellist at Her Majesty's Theatre, London, where his health gradually became worse. In 1853 he returned to Brussels. Only one work of his has been printed—Fantasie and Variations on Russian Themes.—(2) Ernest, son of the above, b. Dec. 21, 1840, Brussels, pupil of his father and of Servais; he travelled for some time in England, Scotland, and Ireland as 'cello virtuoso, settled in London, migrated in 1868 to Paris, where he took part in the Maurin quartet society, and in 1870 was called to Weimar as first 'cellist in the court band. He entirely got rid of a nervous affection of the hand, which for some years had hindered his powers as an executant. In 1879 D. married Carlotta Patti, and from that time lived in Paris.

Dengremont, Maurice, violinist, b. March 19, 1866, Rio de Janeiro, appeared in public as a youthful prodigy, d. Aug. 1893, Buenos Ayres.

Denner, Johann Christoph, b. Aug. 13, 1655, Leipzig, d. April 20, 1707, Nuremberg, son of a horn-turner. D. soon settled in Nuremberg, and acquired great skill in the manufacture of wood-wind instruments. Attempts to improve the construction of the Schalmei led him, in 1700, to the *invention of the clarinet,* which soon became an instrument of importance in all orchestras. The instrumental factory founded by D. was carried on by his sons, and greatly prospered.

Deppe, Ludwig, b. Nov. 7, 1828, Alverdissen (Lippe), d. Sept. 5, 1890, at the Pyrmont baths, a pupil of Marxen's at Hamburg in 1849; he afterwards studied at Leipzig under Lobe, and settled in Hamburg (1860) as music-teacher. He founded a singing academy, which he conducted until 1868, gave concerts, and produced his own compositions. From 1874 he lived at Berlin, where, in 1886, he became court capellmeister, but soon resigned this post. D. conducted the Silesian Musical Festivals established by Count Hochberg (1876). (Cf. Amy Fay's "Music-Study in Germany" ["Deppe as Teacher"].)

Deprès (de Prés), Josquin, also Despres, Depret, Deprez, Dupré, usually only with the Christian name Josquin (diminutive of Joseph); also Latinised, Josquinus and Jodocus (Glarean); in Italian, through error, Jacobo; the family name ("from the meadow") in Latin, *a Prato, a Pratis, Pratensis;* Ital. *del Prato* —the most eminent master of the Netherland school. He was called by his contemporaries the "Prince of Music," and his fame shone with undiminished brilliancy until a new period, with entirely new tastes and style, arrived, one in which his works were not understood. To-day, the greater number of them are only known to historians of music, and, of these, only few are able to throw themselves mentally into a former period, so as to perceive the true grandeur of the master. Yet it is hardly to be doubted that, with further development of the present historical tendency, a great number of D.'s compositions will be brought to light, and performed; only the revival, through singing, can disclose their full beauty. D. shares the fate of so many other eminent men, that next to nothing is known concerning his life. As with Homer, so with D., lands and cities contend for the honour of having given him birth. According to the latest investigations of historians, it appears, nevertheless, pretty certain that D. was born in Hainault; but whether it was precisely at Condé—as Fétis takes for granted, because D. died there, Aug. 27, 1521, as a house-owner, and prior of the cathedral chapter —is still far from proved. The year of his birth may be placed about 1450—not earlier, for Johannes Tinctor in his treatise on counterpoint (written 1477) makes no mention of him; and not later, for he was singer in the Sistine Chapel under Pope Sixtus IV. (1471-84). According to other notices and discoveries, D. was chorister, and afterwards chorus-master at St. Quentin, perhaps also, for a short time, maître de chapelle of Cambrai Cathedral (which town, moreover, and not without probability, has been mentioned as the place of his birth). And further, according to the unanimous statement of several writers, D. had the benefit of Okeghem as a teacher, who, according to Tinctor's testimony, was, about 1476, *premier chantre* at the court of Louis XI. at Paris. Without doubt, all this belongs to a time prior to D.'s sojourn in Rome. That he held an appoint-

ment in Florence is not yet proved, but he was in Ferrara with Isaack probably about 1488 (*see Monatsh. f. M.-G.*, XVII., 24), and expected to receive an appointment (more than this is not known).

A pupil of D.'s, Petit Adrian Coclicus, in his "Compendium Musicale" (1532), has noted down the teaching of his master: *Regula contrapuncti secundum doctrinam Josquini de Pratis.* The compositions of Josquin which have come down to us are: thirty-two masses (the greater part preserved in print), three books, à 5–6, and six masses printed under the title "Misse Josquin," by Petrucci, 1502 [1514], 1515, and 1516; all three books were reprinted together in Junta's edition at Rome, 1526; some of these masses, separately, in the "Liber XV. Missarum" of A. Antiquus [1516] and the "Liber XV. Missarum" of Petrejus; on the other hand, the "Missæ XIII." of Graphäus [1539] contain the masses *Pange Lingua, Da Pacem, Sub Tuum Præsidium,* which are not to be found in Petrucci's three books. Masses in manuscript are to be found in the archives of the Pope's chapel at Rome, as well as in the libraries of Munich and Cambrai. Petrucci printed portions of masses in the "Fragmenta Missarum" (*Cf.* Glarean's "Dodecachordon," S. Heyden's "De Arte Canendi," etc.). Motets by Josquin are to be found in Petrucci's "Odhecaton" (1501–5), and in his books (1, 3, 4, 5) of motets, à 5 (1503–5); further in Konrad Peutinger's "Liber Selectarum Cantionum" (1520), and in many other collections of the 16th century. Special editions of Josquin's motets were brought out by Pierre Attaignant (1533–39 and 1549), Tylman Susato (1544), and Le Roy and Ballard (1555). Finally, a series of French chansons have been preserved, partly in special editions, by Tylman Susato (1545), Attaignant (1549), Du Chemin (1553), partly in collections by the same and by others (also in "Odhecaton"). Fragments of masses, motets, chansons, etc., are to be found in modern notation in Commer's "Collectio Operum Musicorum Batavorum"; in the historical works of Forkel, Burney, Hawkins, Busby, Kiesewetter, Ambros; in Rochlitz' "Sammlung, etc.," in Choron's "Collection, etc."; and in the "Bibliothek für Kirchenmusik" (1844), etc.

Deprosse, Anton, composer, b. May 18, 1838, Munich, d. June 23, 1878, Berlin; until 1855 a pupil of the Munich Royal Music School, and after that, a private pupil of Stunz and Herzog. He was appointed, in 1861, pianoforte teacher at the Royal Music School; in 1864, however, he already gave up this appointment, lived for some time in Frankfort, then as teacher at a musical institution at Gotha, which, however, broke up in 1868. In 1871 he returned to Munich, and went in 1875 to Berlin. Of his works the best-known and the most important is the oratorio *Die Salbung Davids,* besides which, he published many songs and pf. pieces

(Op. 17, Romantic Studies) ; some operas remained in manuscript.

De Reszke, two distinguished operatic singers. The elder, J e a n (b. Jan. 14, 1852, Warsaw), a lyric tenor of the first rank, has been engaged at the Paris Grand Opéra since 1885. The younger, E d u a r d (b. Dec. 23, 1855), an equally important bass singer, has also been at the Paris Opéra since 1885. A sister, J o s e p h i n e, likewise an esteemed stage singer (soprano), appeared at Paris, Madrid, Lisbon, and London. In 1884 she married Herr von Kronenburg of Warsaw, when she retired from the stage. She died March, 1891.

Dering. (*See* DEERING.)

Desaugiers, M a r c A n t o i n e, b. 1742, Fréjus, d. Sept. 10, 1793, Paris. He studied music by himself, went to Paris 1774, and first made himself known by the translation of Mancini's work on "Cantus Figuralis " (1776). He brought out small operas at various Paris theatres (Opéra, Théâtre Italien, Feydeau, etc.) which pleased by reason of their naturalness. D. was full of enthusiasm for the Revolution, and celebrated the storming of the Bastille in a festival cantata entitled *Hiérodrame.* He was on friendly terms with Gluck and Sacchini, and composed a requiem for the funeral obsequies of the latter.

Descant. (*See* DISCANT.)

Deshayes, Prosper Didier, b. about 1760, composed for Paris theatres a number of operettas, ballet divertissements, and two oratorios (*Les Maccabées, Le Sacrifice de Jephte*), as well as a symphony, and smaller instrumental pieces.

Desmarets, H e n r i, b. 1662, Paris, d. Sept. 7, 1741, chamber musician to Louis XIV. ; he married in secret the daughter of a high official, and, through the father's complaint, was condemned to death for rape and abduction ; but he fled to Spain and became maestro to Philip V., which appointment he afterwards exchanged, on account of the climate, for that of music intendant to the Duke of Lorraine at Lunéville. In 1722 his sentence was revoked, and his marriage declared valid ; he nevertheless remained at Lunéville. His operas once found great favour. A number of his motets appeared under the name of Goupilliers, the Versailles maître de chapelle.

Des Près. (*See* DEPRÈS.)

Dessauer, J o s e p h, b. May 28, 1798, Prague, d. July 8, 1876, Mödling, near Vienna, pupil of Tomaczek and Dionys Weber. He was an admired song composer, and also wrote overtures, quartets for strings, pf. pieces, and the operas—*Lidwina* (1836), *Ein Besuch in St. Cyr* (1838), *Paquita* (1851), *Domingo* (1860), *Oberon* (not performed).

Dessoff, F e l i x O t t o, b. Jan. 14, 1835, Leipzig, d. Oct. 28, 1892, Frankfort, pupil of the Leipzig Conservatorium, specially of Moscheles, Hauptmann, and Rietz. He was (1854–60) theatre capellmeister at Chemnitz, Altenburg, Düsseldorf, Aix, Magdeburg, 1860–75 court capellmeister at Vienna, teacher at the Conservatorium of the " Gesellschaft der Musikfreunde," and conductor of the Philharmonic Concerts. In 1875 he became capellmeister at Carlsruhe, and from 1881, at Frankfort. D. has published chamber-music (pf. sonatas, pf. quartet, quintet, etc.).

Dessus (Fr. " above "), upper part, discant, soprano ; hence also an old name for the violin (*D. de Viole*).

Destouches, (1) A n d r é C a r d i n a l, opera composer, b. 1672, Paris, d. there 1749 ; he was (1713–31) " surintendant de la musique du roi et inspecteur de l'Opéra," and had the greatest success with *Issé,* which opera he wrote without any theoretical knowledge ; later on, when he had learned more, he lacked good ideas, and his success was not so great. Louis XIV., however, valued him very highly, and declared that he was the only one who made him forget Lully. —(2) F r a n z S e r a p h v o n, opera composer, b. Jan. 21, 1772, Munich, d. there Dec. 10, 1844, pupil of J. Haydn at Vienna, in 1797 musical director at Erlangen, in 1799 leader of the band at Vienna, in 1810 professor of the theory of music at Landshut, in 1826 capellmeister at Homburg, and from 1842 lived in retirement at Munich. D. composed one opera, *Die Thomasnacht* (1791, libretto by his brother Joseph), an operetta, *Das Missverständnis,* and (his last work) a comic opera, *Der Teufel und der Schneider* (libretto by his nephew, Ulrich v. D.), much incidental music (to Schiller's *Tell, Jungfrau von Orleans, Wallensteins Lager, Braut von Messina,* Werner's *Wanda,* Kotzebue's *Hussiten vor Naumburg*), etc. There appeared in print some pf. sonatas, fantasias, variations, etc., for pf., a concerto for pf., a trio, etc.

Destra (Ital.), right (hand).

Desvignes, V i c t o r F r a n ç o i s, b. June 5, 1805, Trèves, d. Dec. 30, 1853, Metz ; he was for many years conductor at theatres in various French provincial towns, and in 1835 founded at Metz a Conservatoire, which soon reached such a stage of perfection that in 1841 it was taken over by the Government as a branch establishment of the Paris Conservatoire. He published a quantity of chamber music, also sacred choruses and many larger works ; likewise two operas which remained in manuscript.

Deswert (de Swert), J u l e s, b. Aug. 15, 1843, Louvain, d. Feb. 24, 1891, Ostend, pupil of Servais at Brussels. He was a famous performer on the violoncello, was appointed leader at Düsseldorf in 1865, after having spent many years in concert tours which had brought him much fame. From Düsseldorf he went, in 1868, to Weimar as principal 'cello in the court band, and in 1869 was called to Berlin as royal leader, solo 'cellist, and teacher at the "Hochschule." In 1873 he gave up this appointment and undertook new concert tours, then moved to Wiesbaden, and in 1888 became director of the music school at Ostend, and teacher at the Ghent and Bruges Conservatoires. He composed three concertos for the 'cello, a great number of smaller pieces, and arrangements for pf. and 'cello, also a symphony—"Nordseefahrt." His opera, *Die Albigenser*, was brought out with success at Wiesbaden (1878), and a second one, *Graf Hammerstein* (1884), at Mayence.

Détaché (Fr.), staccato. In connection with string-instruments *grand D.* = grand staccato; *d. sec.* = short staccato.

Determinato (Ital.), determined; in a resolute manner.

Detonieren (Ger.; Fr. *détonner*), to sing out of tune; to drag down the pitch—an exceedingly common fault amongst imperfectly trained singers. D. is often the result of a certain natural indolence, in which case it can easily be cured; but impure intonation, caused by a faulty musical ear, is a more serious matter. That *a-cappella* choirs easily fall in pitch—*i.e.* end lower than they commenced—is, as a rule, the fault of D. The changing acoustic relations of tones, which in modern times have often been held responsible for this, would be just as likely to cause the pitch to rise; this happens but rarely, and is, in most cases, the result of intentional effort on the part of particular singers.

Dettmer, Wilhelm, distinguished stage singer (bass), b. June 29, 1808, Breinum, near Hildesheim. He was the son of a peasant, attended the Gymnasium at Hildesheim and the seminary for school teachers at Alfeld, but ran away, and joined a troupe of strolling players. After he had been engaged for some time in subordinate positions at Hanover, Brunswick, Breslau, and Cassel, he appeared in 1842, at Dresden, as a singer of the first rank; but he still studied under Mieksch. When he exchanged Dresden for Frankfort, a lifelong pension was assured to him. In 1874 he withdrew from the stage. D. was equally good in comic and in tragic *rôles*.

Detto (Ital.), said, named.

Deuterus (*Authentus D.*). (*See* CHURCH MODES.)

Deutsche Tabulatur. (*See* TABLATURE (2).)

Deutsche Tänze, or simply **Deutsche** (Ger.), lit., "German dances." A name for the old slow waltzes.

Deutz. (*See* MAGNUS.)

Devienne, François, b. Jan. 31, 1759, Joinville (Haute-Marne), d. Sept. 5, 1803, in the lunatic asylum at Charenton; performer on the flute and bassoon, member of the band of the " Musique des Gardes-Suisses " at Paris, bassoon-player in the orchestra of the Théâtre de Monsieur (1788), later on professor at the Conservatoire, and, when it was re-organised in 1802, received a pension. He wrote eleven operas and operettas, many concertante pieces for wind-instruments with orchestra, flute and bassoon concertos, quartets, trios, and sonatas for wind- and string-instruments, twelve suites for wind-instruments (à 8 and à 12), and an important flute Method (1795).

Devozione (Ital.), devotion. *Con devozione,* with devotion.

Dextra (Lat.), right (hand).

Dezède (also Desaides), b. about 1740, Lyons, d. 1792, Paris, a much-admired French operetta composer, who, from 1772, brought out in Paris eighteen pieces (1–3 acts), which were also, in part, given in Germany (*Julie*). Four operas remained unperformed.

Di (Ital.) indicates, like the French *de*, the genitive; *tempo di marcia*, march-time.

Diabelli, Antonio, b. Sept. 6, 1781, Mattsee, near Salzburg, d. April 7, 1858, Vienna; he received his first musical training as a chorister at the monastery of Michaelbeurn, and afterwards at the cathedral of Salzburg; he studied at the "Lateinschule," Munich, and in 1800 entered the monastery of Raichenhaslach. Michael Haydn superintended his attempts at composition. When in 1803 the monasteries in Bavaria were secularised, he went to Vienna, where he first lived as teacher of the pianoforte and guitar, then entered into partnership with the music publisher Cappi, and in 1824 took over the publishing business on his own account (D. & Co.). In 1854 he sold his business to C. A. Spina. D. was a very prolific and ready composer, but of his works only the instructive piano pieces (sonatinas, sonata duets, etc.) have lived, while his operas, masses, cantatas, chamber music, etc., were soon forgotten. D. was Schubert's principal publisher: he paid the composer badly, and, in addition, reproached him for writing too much.

Diapason, (1) Greek name for the octave.—(2) With the French, the expression, in a metaphorical sense, stands for the *measure* of instruments, *e.g.* for flutes, oboes—the determination of the exact distance of the sound-holes. *D. normal :* the normal octave with regard to absolute pitch. Hence D., even without any addition, means pitch, "chamber-pitch," "Paris pitch," and finally is used for the *tuning-fork*.—(3) It is also the name of the principal foundation stops of the organ.

Diapente, Greek name for the fifth.

Diaphonia, (1) Greek term for dissonance, opposed to symphony, or consonance.—(2) In the early Middle Ages (9th to 12th cent.) the term D. was identical with *Organum* (q.v.), *i.e.* the most primitive kind of polyphony— continued parallel motion in fourths or fifths, only broken, in exceptional cases, by thirds, seconds, or unisons.

Diaschisma. (*See* SCHISMA.)

Diastema, Greek term for *Interval.*

Diastolik (Gr.), punctuation, the name given by the older theorists to the teaching of divisions in music, *i.e.* of the right articulation of the musical thoughts, or of phrasing.

Diatessaron, Greek name for the fourth.

Diatonic (Gr.) is the name given to a succession of notes in which whole tones predominate, in contradistinction to chromatic and enharmonic. The ancient diatonic tetrachord (*e, f, g, a*) consisted of a semitone and two whole tones ; the chromatic (*e, f, f♯, a*) of two half-tones and a minor third ; and the enharmonic (*e, e♯, f, a*) of two quarter-tones and a major third. In our modern system of sounds, the term D. is connected with the *fundamental scale*, *i.e.* the whole-tone or semitone progression from one degree of the fundamental scale to the next, whether by means of a ♯, ♭, ×, ♭♭, or not, are called diatonic. The passings from one tone to another on the same degree of the scale, and differing by a ♯, ♭, etc., are chromatic ; tones, finally, are enharmonic which are derived from two tones of the fundamental scale near to one another, or at the distance of a third, which differ only slightly in pitch, and which, in the system of equal temperament of twelve degrees, are identical.

Diatonic.   Chromatic.   Enharmonic.

Diaulos, double *aulos* (q.v.), two flute pipes meeting at a sharp angle, and blown by means of a common mouthpiece. This is all that is known about them.

Diazeuxis (Gr.), in the Greek system the separation of two tetrachords by the interval of a tone.

Dibdin, C h a r l e s, b. March 15, 1745, Southampton, d. July 25, 1814, London. He was first an opera singer at Covent Garden and Drury Lane, and composed, later on, a large number of operettas and other dramatic works, mostly of a lively character ; of the greater number he was also the librettist. A projected tour to India led him to travel through England, giving concerts to raise the necessary funds ; the impressions of this tour he recorded in the book, "The Musical Tour of Mr. Dibdin" (1788). However, in the end, he completely gave up the Indian journey. In 1796 he built a little theatre of his own in Leicester Place, which he sold in 1805. In his latter days he opened a music school, but the speculation failed, and he became bankrupt. A subscription

was made for him, with part of which an annuity was bought, and, subsequently, his pension of £200 from the Government was restored to him. He wrote a number of "Table-entertainments" (solo vocal scenas), an elementary Method ("Music Epitomised"), and a "History of the English Stage" (1795, five vols.).

Dichord, (1) a two-stringed instrument. (2) An instrument the strings of which are tuned in pairs.

Dictionaries, Musical. Works of this class consist of (1), explanations of technical expressions commonly used in music, descriptions of instruments, and presentation of the rules of musical composition in more or less condensed form (*technological* D.) ; or (2), biographies of musicians in alphabetical order (*biographical* and *bibliographical* D.); or, finally (3), a combination of both kinds (*universal* dictionaries of music, musical encyclopædia). The oldest musical D. were of the first kind : Tinctoris' "Terminorum Musicæ Diffinitorium" (1474) ; Janowka's "Clavis ad Thesaurum magnæ Artis Musicæ" (1701) ; Brossard's "Dictionnaire de Musique" (1703) ; Grassineau's "Musical Dictionary" (1740) ; Rousseau's "Dictionnaire de Musique" (1767) ; and of more recent ones, especially Koch's "Musikalisches Lexikon" (1802 ; 2nd edit., by Arrey v. Dommer, 1865). Of *biographical* D. there are : Gerber's "Historisch biographisches Lexikon der Tonkünstler" (1790–92, two vols.), "Neues historisch-biographisches Lexikon der Tonkünstler" (1812–13, four vols.) ; the "Dictionnaire Historique des Musiciens," by Choron and Fayolle (1810 and 1811), and Fétis' "Biographie Universelle des Musiciens" (1835–44 ; 2nd ed., 1860–65, eight vols. ; supplement by Pougin, 1878–81, two vols.). The oldest dictionary of the mixed kind is Walther's "Musikalisches Lexikon" (1732), followed by Lichtenthal's "Dizionario e Bibliografia della Musica" (1826, four vols.) ; Castil-Blaze's "Dictionnaire de Musique Moderne (1821) ; Schilling's "Universallexikon der Tonkunst" (1835–42, seven vols.); Gathy's "Musikalisches Konversationslexikon" (1835 : 3rd edit. 1873) ; the "Dictionnaire de Musique" of the brothers Escudier (1844) : Gassner's "Universallexikon der Tonkunst" (1845) ; the "Neues Universallexikon der Tonkunst," by Schladebach (continued by Bernsdorf, 1856–61 ; three vols. and supplement) ; Mendel's "Musikalisches Konversationslexikon" (continued by Reissmann ; 1870–79, eleven vols. and supplement) ; Aug. Reissmann's "Handlexikon der Tonkunst" (1882), and the present Riemann dictionary (3rd German edition 1887, 4th ed. 1893; English ed. do). Of English dictionaries may be named : "Dictionary of Musicians" (two vols., 1822–27) ; Sir George Grove's excellent "Dictionary of Music and Musicians" (1879–90, four vols. ; also appendix and index), and Brown's "Biographical Dictionary of Musicians" (1886).

Diderot, D e n i s, the chief editor of, and most diligent contributor to the celebrated "Encyclopédie" (1751–65), b. Oct. 5, 1713, Langres, d. July 30, 1784, Paris. He wrote, among other things, "Principes d'Acoustique" (1748), and "Mémoires sur Differents Sujets de Mathématique" (1748).

Didymos, Greek grammarian, b. 63 B.C., Alexandria, wrote, in addition to many essays on subjects not relating to music, a work on harmony, which is only known to us by the epitome of Porphyry, and by quotations in Ptolemy. The divisions of the tetrachord according to D. are:

$$\text{diatonic} \quad \frac{16}{15} \cdot \frac{10}{9} \cdot \frac{9}{8} \quad \text{(for ex.—\underline{b} \underline{c} \underline{d} \underline{e})};$$

$$\text{chromatic} \quad \frac{16}{15} \cdot \frac{25}{24} \cdot \frac{6}{5} \quad \text{(for ex.—\underline{b} \underline{c} \underline{c\sharp} e)};$$

$$\text{enharmonic} \quad \frac{32}{31} \cdot \frac{31}{30} \cdot \frac{5}{4} \quad \text{(for ex.—\underline{b} x c e)}.$$

(*Cf.* the tables under TONE, DETERMINATION OF.) It almost seems as if D. grasped the meaning of the third 5 : 4, as he adheres to it in all three genera (c e). The difference between the major and minor whole tone ($\frac{9}{8} : \frac{10}{9}$) is rightly called after him, the comma of Didymus; also the *comma syntonum* (81 : 80).

Dienel, Otto, b. Jan. 11, 1839, Tiefenfurth (Silesia), pupil of the Görlitz Gymnasium, of the seminary at Bunzlau, and of the Royal Institute for Church Music, and of the Royal Akademie at Berlin (1863). He was a performer on the organ, organist of the "Marienkirche," and teacher of music at the seminary, Berlin ; and, since 1881, he is Royal "Musikdirektor."

Diener, F r a n z, distinguished opera singer (dramatic tenor), b. Feb. 19, 1849, Dessau, d. there May 15, 1879 ; he was at first violinist in the Dessau court orchestra, and, later on, at the Luisenstadt Theatre, Berlin, where he also made his *début* as a singer. D. was likewise engaged as principal tenor at Cologne (1872–73), Berlin, Nuremberg, again at Cologne (1876), Hamburg, Dresden (1878).

Diës, A l b e r t K., landscape-painter, b. 1755, Hanover, d. Dec. 28, 1822, Vienna ; he was the author of the earliest biography of Haydn : "Biographische Nachrichten von Joseph Haydn" (Vienna, 1810).

Dies Iræ (Lat.), the sequence (q.v.) of the *Missa pro defunctis*, of which the author is unknown. It forms the second section of the Requiem, and gives to the composer a grand opportunity for tone-painting. (*See* the powerful D. I. in Berlioz's Requiem.)

Diesis (Gr. ; Ital. *Diesi;* Fr. *Dièse, Dièze*), a term for a sharp ($\sharp$). Pythagoras named the excess of a fourth over two whole tones a D.,

i.e. the Pythagorean semitone 256 : 243, afterwards named Limma ; and this name was given to the *pykna* (small intervals) of the enharmonic genus. The 15th century, with its *renaissance* efforts, put life again into the ancient, and long extinct theory of music, and in its own peculiar way. The D. was revived as a quarter-tone, and an attempt was made—by means of it —to discover the secret of the wonderful effect of ancient music, by the introduction of various differences of pitch into instruments constructed with special keys for the quarter-tones, etc. When the illusion had passed away, the name D. remained to express the $\sharp$. It is, however, false to suppose that the $\sharp$ dates from this period. The $\sharp$ with its present form and meaning is already to be met with in the 13th century ; it was called, however, *B quadratum*, whether it revoked a preceding $\flat$, or raised a natural note. In the 15th century the term D. was only used for the $\sharp$ as a sign for raising pitch : the $\sharp$ as a sign of revocation ($\natural$) retained the name *b quadratum* (Ger. *quadrat*, Fr. *bécarre*). The strict difference of shape for the two meanings is not yet two hundred years old.

Dieter (Dietter), C h r i s t i a n L u d w i g, violinist, b. June 13, 1757, Ludwigsburg, d. 1822, as chamber musician at Stuttgart, for which town he wrote the *vaudevilles :—Der Schulze im Dorf; Der Irrwisch ; Das Freischiessen ; Der Rekrutenaushub ; Glücklich zusammengelogen ; Die Dorfdeputierten ; Der Luftballon ; Elisinde ;* and the comic operas *Belmont und Konstanze ; Des Teufels Lustschloss ;* and the grand opera, *Laura Rosetti.* His concertos for violin, horn, flute, oboe, and bassoon, violin solos, concertantes for flutes, for oboes, etc., remained in manuscript.

Dietger. (*See* THEOGERUS.)

Dietrich, (1) S i x t u s (also Dieterich, Xistus Theodoricus), German contrapuntist of the 16th century, said to have been born between 1490 and 1495 at Augsburg, spent his youth at Freiburg (Breisgau), went in 1517 to Strassburg in the service of the Rudolfinger house, and in 1518 was appointed schoolmaster at Constance. D. had a deeply sensitive musical nature, but, not having made a professional study of music, the higher musical appointments of that time were closed to him. At a later period, when he was in more comfortable circumstances, he went to Wittenberg and attended the lectures there (1540). It was not, however, for this reason that he gave up his appointment at Constance, but, as he wrote, as early as 1540, to Ambrose Amerbach at Basle, principally because he suffered from gout ; and, for the same reason also, during the siege of Constance by Charles V., was conveyed to St. Gallen, where he died Oct. 21 of the same year. Of his works in separate editions there are only known up to the present one book of magnificats (1535), a collection of antiphons, à 4 (1541), and a large collection of antiphons, à 4 (1545). Single motets, songs, etc., are to be found in different collections printed in Germany between 1538 and 1545.—(2) Albert Hermann, noteworthy composer of our time, b. Aug. 28, 1829, in the forester's house at Golk, near Meissen, the son of a chief forester; he attended the "Kreuz-schule," Dresden, and received there the best theoretical teaching from Julius Otto, continued his musical studies (1847–51) under Rietz and Moscheles, and, at the same time, attended the University. In 1851 he went to Robert Schumann at Düsseldorf, and stayed with him as a faithful pupil until the outbreak of the composer's mental malady (1854). From 1855 he held the post of conductor of the subscription concerts at Bonn (from 1859, that of town musical director), until, in 1861, he was called to his present appointment of court capell-meister at Oldenburg. D. is a thoughful composer, and certainly one of the most distinguished of Schumann's pupils. His symphony in D minor, Op. 20, is a widely known, and much admired work; his overture, "Norman-nenfahrt," the choral works with orchestra, "Morgenhymne," "Rheinmorgen," and "Alt-christlicher Bittgesang" have won considerable success; and the same may also be said with regard to his violin concerto, 'cello concerto, his piano trios, 'cello sonata, his pf. duet sonata, his romance for horn with orchestra, besides songs, duets, choruses, pf. pieces, too numerous to mention. His three-act opera, *Robin Hood*, was brought out with success at Frankfort in 1879.

Dietter. (*See* DIETER.)

Dieupart, Charles, French clavier player and composer; he went in 1707 to London, officiated under Handel as cembalist at the opera, and died 1740 in needy circumstances. Of his compositions there been preserved, "Six Suites de Clavecin . . . . mises en Concert pour un Violon et une Flûte, avec Basse de Viole et un Archiluth," and other clavier suites.

Diez, Sophie, *née* Hartmann, excellent stage singer (soprano), b. Sept. 1, 1820, Munich, d. there May 3, 1887, pupil of Fr. Lachner; she was engaged at the Munich court opera, 1837–78. In 1841 she married the tenor singer, Friedrich D. (1837–49 at the Munich court theatre), and retired from the stage in 1878.

Dïezeugmenon. (*See* GREEK MUSIC (1).)

Differentiæ tonorum (Lat.; Ger. *Differenzen*), term given in the Gregorian Psalm-singing of the Middle Ages to the different possible cadences (now called Finals) of the *Seculorum Amen* (*EVOVAE*), of which each psalm-tone had, and to a certain extent still has, several; they formed a link to the antiphon which followed.

Difficile (Ital. and Fr.), difficult.

Dilettante, a lover, and admirer of one of the fine arts. One who more or less occupies himself with an art, but does not follow it either professionally or seriously.

Dilliger, Johann, b. 1590, at Eisfeld, d. 1647, deacon at Coburg; he published (1612–42) sacred compositions ("Prodromi Triciniorum Sacrorum;" "Medulla ex Psalmo LXVIII. de-prompta et harmonica, 6 voc.;" "Exercitatio Musica I., continens XIII. Selectissimos Concentus Musicos variorum Autorum cum Basso Generali;" "Trauerlied auf den Tod eines Kindes," à 4; "Gespräch Dr. Luthers und eines kranken Studiosi," à 4; "Musica Votiva;" "Musica Christiana Cordialis Domestica;" "Musica Concertativa," or "Schatzkämmerlein neuer Geistlicher auserlesener Konzerte;" "Jeremias Pœnitentiarius," etc.).

Diludium (Lat.), interlude.

Diluendo (Ital.), dying away, same as *morendo*.

Diminished intervals (q.v.) are those which are smaller than minor or perfect ones, by a chromatic semitone. By inversion, diminished intervals become augmented.

Diminuendo (Ital.), abbr. *dim., dimin.*, diminishing in loudness; becoming weaker.

Diminution, in mensural music, was a shortening of the note value, and, as a rule, by one half. The oldest sign for diminution is a vertical stroke through the time-signature, ($\)), ($\mathbb{C}$; it had somewhat of the meaning of our *Allegro*, *i.e.* it indicated lively time. We still have the sign $\mathbb{C}$ with similar meaning. (*See* ALLABREVE TIME.) The D., instead of being indicated by the stroke (which was also called *medium*, *per medium, medietas*), was often marked by the figure 2 or 3 after the time-signature, O_2, O_3, and also by $\frac{2}{4}$ or $\frac{3}{1}$, $\frac{4}{1}$, $\frac{6}{1}$ in the middle of a piece of music; in that case, however, it was not called D., but *Proportion* (q.v.). D. was revoked by the sign of the *integer valor*, the ordinary note-value (C, O); but the sign for proportion, on the other hand, was revoked by inversion, $\frac{1}{3}$, $\frac{2}{4}$, $\frac{1}{6}$, etc.

Dingelstedt, Jenny, *née* Lutzer, became the wife of the poet, Franz D. (1843), b. March 4, 1816, Prague, d. Oct. 3, 1877, Vienna; she was a famous opera singer (soprano) at Prague (1832) and Vienna (until 1845).

Dionysia, Rural, were Roman festivals at which boys and youths performed mimic dances.

Dioxia, a somewhat rare Greek term, instead of *Diapente*, for the fifth.

Diritta or *dritta* (*mano*), Ital. for right hand.

Diruta, (1) Girolamo, b. about 1560, Perugia, studied under Claudio Merulo, who was proud of his pupil (*see* the preface to his "Canzoni a la Francese in Tavolatura," 1598). About 1580, D. was lay brother at Correggio (Minorite), 1593 organist at Gebbio (Papal States), where he remained until 1609, then organist of the cathedral of Chioggia (the year of his death is unknown). He published a highly-interesting work—" Il Transilvano " (dedicated to Sigismondo Batori, Prince of Transylvania) ; " O dialogo sopra il vero modo di sonar organi e stromenti da penna " (1st part, 1593, 2nd ed., 1612 ; 2nd part, 1609, 2nd ed., 1622, with the separate title, " Sopra il vero modo di intavolare chiaschedun canto ").—(2) A g o s t i n o, also b. at Perugia, Augustine monk, maestro at Asola, was afterwards engaged in a similar capacity to his own order at Rome, finally chorus director of the same order at Perugia ; he composed masses, litanies, vespers, psalms, and " Poesie Heroiche " (printed 1622–47).

Di salto (Ital.), by leaps or skips.

Discant, soprano ; in old German organs a term for stops extending through only the upper half of the keyboard ; for example, if the oboe is a discant stop, the bassoon generally forms the bass (the lower half). As a prefix to the names of instruments (Discantposaune, Discantpommer, etc.), the term indicates a high register.

Discant Clef, the name given to the C-clef on the lowest line of the stave.

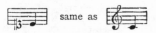

same as

Discant-Stimmen (Ger.), or **Discant-Register** (Ger.), the organ stops which comprise only the treble, not the bass notes. They are also called *Halbe-stimmen,* half-stops. (*See* DISCANT.)

Discantus, (1) soprano, *Cantus* (Fr. *Dessus*).—(2) The French " Déchant," the polyphony of the 12th century—as opposed to the usual parallel motion of the *Organum* (q.v.)—based on the principle of contrary motion, and strictly carried out. From the amalgamation of these two opposite styles of writing real counterpoint was evolved. At the beginning, D. was throughout in two parts. Over against the melody of the *Cantus planus,* note against note, was set a different and higher (!) melody—one not noted down, but improvised by the singers (*contrappunto alla mente, chant sur le livre*). Later on discant was in two or three parts, and then it became indispensable to work it out by writing, so as to prevent hopeless confusion. According to the oldest *Regulæ discantandi,* the octave, fifth, and unison were the only intervals allowed.

Discord, (1) A dissonant interval ; an interval that does not satisfy the ear but causes unrest. The opposite of a *discord* is a *concord.*—(2) A chord which contains one or more dissonant intervals, and which, on account of its unsatisfying and disquieting effect, requires to be resolved into a consonant chord.

Discordance (Lat. *Discordantia*), musical inconsistency, impossible (incomprehensible) combination of tones.

Discreto (Ital.), discreet, in a discreet manner.

Disdiapason, interval of two octaves.

Disharmonie, dissonance.

Disis (Ger.), D double-sharp ; D doubly raised by a ×.

Disperato (Ital.), desperate, hopeless.

Disposition of an Organ is really the estimate of cost before building ; likewise the designation of stops, number of key-boards, mechanism, bellows, etc., which the organ is to have ; but, in organs already built, the term is used for a summary description of the work—viz., number of stops, couplers, draw-stop action, etc.

Dissonance (Lat. *Dissonantia*), interference with the uniform conception (consonance) of the tones belonging to one clang, by one or more tones which are representative of another clang. *Musically* speaking, there are not really dissonant intervals, but only dissonant notes. Which note is dissonant in an interval physically (acoustically) dissonant, depends on the clang to which that interval has to be referred (in *c : d,* as c *major* chord, *d* is the dissonant note ; as G *major,* the note *c*). But, musically, even acoustic consonances can be dissonant (for example, in *c : g* as A♭ *chord, g* is a suspension). It is important to notice that the clang represented by the dissonant notes is not at once fully perceived, but only becomes clear by the progression ; so that it seems justifiable to set out all dissonant chords in relation to one ruling clang. The most important *dissonant chords* are as follows :—I. Those consisting of four notes (1) the major chord with minor seventh (dominant seventh chord), the most important and frequent of all dissonances, for example, *g : b : d : f.*

(2) The minor chord with minor under-seventh (chord of seventh of the second degree of the minor key), for example, *b : d : f : a,* next to the chord of dominant seventh, the most important dissonance, and its exact counterpart. (3) The major chord with major sixth, for example, *f : a : c : d.* Identical in its composition with (3), but different in conception (and in music everything depends upon this), is (4), the minor chord with major under-sixth, for example, *c : d : f : a.* (5) The major chord with major seventh, for example, *c : e : g : b,* from which (6) the minor chord with major under-seventh, for example, *c : e : g : b,* only differs in conception. (7) The major chord with minor sixth, likewise major under-third, for example, *c : e : g : a♭.* (8) The minor chord with minor under-sixth, for example, *c♯ : d : f : a.* All these eight four-note dissonant chords arise *from a note being added to a major or minor chord,* disturbing the consonance of the same. The first two kinds frequently occur in an elliptical manner ; in (1), for instance, the principal note of the major

chord is omitted ([g] b : d : f), and in (2), the upper note of the minor chord (the actual principal note of minor chord, cf. CLANG), for example, b : d : f : (a) ; in both cases there remains the so-called *diminished triad*.—II. Dissonant chords of quite a different kind arise when a note of a major or minor chord is left out, and another neighbouring note is taken in its place : these are the so-called chords of suspension—(1) when, instead of the principal note, the second is introduced, for example, d : e : g in place of c : e : g; (2) when the second takes the place of the third, for example, c : d : g; (3) when the fourth takes the place of the third, for example, c : f : g; (4) when the fourth takes the place of the fifth, for example, c : e : f (the same formations are also possible for the minor chord). In place of the major second and perfect fourth, the minor, or augmented second and the augmented fourth, can be employed as suspensions; also the minor or major sixth can represent the fifth, so that for the chord of c major the following formations arise : d♭ : e : g, c : d♯ : g, c : e : f♯, c : e : a♭; c : e : a. Interesting formations are obtained by the introduction of such suspensions into the chords of 1 to 3 under Section I.

The combination of the suspension of the fourth with that of the sixth results in the chord of six-four (q.v.).—III. Other dissonant forms arise from the raising or lowering of the fifth of the major chord, likewise of the fundamental note of the minor chord, viz., the *augmented triads* (c : e : g♯, likewise ♭a : c : e) which generally appear in a position indicating the interval of the augmented sixth (♭g : c : e, likewise c : e : a♯). Also in the major and minor chords with seventh (I., 1 and 2) these chromatic changes frequently appear (b♭ : c : e : g♯; ♭a : c : e : f♯; ♭g : b♭ : c : e; c : e : f♯ : a♯).—Chords of this kind are named *altered* chords.—IV. The chords of the ninth are dissonant chords composed of five notes, especially the major chord, with minor seventh and major or minor ninth—for instance, g : b : d : f : a♭, or g : b : d : f : a; both also with omission

of the fundamental note, whereby the first becomes the chord known in figured bass as the chord of diminished seventh. If the minor tenth be suspended over the minor ninth, a formation occurs containing the interval of the diminished octave, (g) : b : d : f : b♭. It is seldom necessary to consider the chord of diminished seventh as derived from the minor chord, i.e. d♯ : f♯ : a : c : (e). According to the definition given above, it is easy in all these formations to see which are the dissonant notes. By thus distinguishing dissonant (contradictory to a clang, disturbing to its consonance) notes in place of the old system of intervals and chords, a much clearer view of chords is obtained. *Every note is dissonant which is not a fundamental note* (unchanged), *neither third nor fifth of the major or minor chord forming the essential elements of a clang.* There is one rather complicated case, viz., that of the organ-point—*i.e.* the holding out of the note of a harmony in which it is an essential note of the chord (especially the fundamental note) through foreign harmonies, to a new harmony, to which again it belongs as a chord note. This consists, so to speak, in holding fast to a harmony (avoiding absolute dissonance), and bringing it into association alternately with other related and complete harmonies. It is therefore a simultaneous presentation of two harmonies, one of which, however (the one represented by the held note), is the ruling one, and it affords an illustration of a compound conception of tonality. (*Cf.* RESOLUTION.)

Distinctio (Lat.) (1) is a term used for the breaks in Gregorian song answering to interpunction, which, as a rule, are made prominent by a longer group of neumæ ; in the older neume notation of the Graduals a psalm verse generally shows three *distinctions*, for example : *Domine—libera animam meam—a labiis iniquis—et a lingua dolosa.* At the present day, on the contrary, the verse is sung in one breath to the middle cadence (mediatio), and, thence, straight to the closing cadence.—(2) The same as DIFFERENTIÆ TONORUM.

Distinto (Ital.), distinct, clear.

Distonare, or **Stonare** (Ital.), to sing or play out of tune.

Dithyrambus (Gr.), a hymn in honour of Bacchus.

Ditonus, the Greek name for the major third

Ditson, Oliver, b. Oct. 30, 1811, d. Dec. 21, 1888, the founder of the oldest and most important music-publishing firm in America. The head-quarters of the firm (the catalogue of which contains 50,000 musical works and 2,000 books) are at Boston, with branches at New York and Philadelphia.

Ditters (von Dittersdorf), Karl, celebrated composer, b. Nov. 2, 1739, Vienna, d. Oct. 31.

1799, at Castle Rothlhotta, near Neuhaus. While yet a boy he received good instruction on the violin, and played in the orchestra of the Benedictine Church; he then became page to the master-general of the ordnance, Prince Joseph von Hildburghausen, who provided entirely for his training, and in 1760 procured for him a situation in the court orchestra. After many years of activity, D. became capellmeister to the Bishop of Grosswardein (Hungary), as successor to Michael Haydn. Industry in composition was the order of the day there, and D. wrote a large quantity of orchestral and chamber music, likewise several oratorios. When, in 1769, the bishop dissolved his band, D. journeyed for a short time, and then received an appointment from Count Schaffgotsch, Prince-Bishop of Breslau; in addition to the post of band leader, he also occupied that of ranger to Neisse's princely domain, and rose in 1773 to the position of captain-general of the Freienwalde province. In 1770 D. received the order of the Golden Spur from the Pope, and in 1773, also through the medium of the Graf von Schaffgotsch, letters of nobility from the Emperor (henceforth D. von Dittersdorf). D. had a small theatre erected at Johannisberg, for which he composed industriously, yet without neglecting oratorio, orchestral, or chamber music. His most celebrated works, however, were written during occasional sojourns in Vienna (1770, 1776, 1786), namely, the oratorios *Esther, Isaac,* and *Hiob,* as well as the comic operas, *Doktor und Apotheker* (1786); *Betrug durch Aberglauben; Liebe im Narrenhaus; Hieronymus Knicker;* and *Rotkäppchen.* He fell into distress on the death of the Prince-Bishop (1795), but found shelter with Ignaz von Stillfried, at whose castle, Rothlhotta, he died. D.'s operas were thrown into the shade at Vienna by those of Mozart, especially after the death of the latter, yet his *Doktor und Apotheker* has survived up to the present; healthy humour, fresh and natural invention, and a correct and flowing style are the characteristics of his music. Besides twenty-eight operas, several oratorios and cantatas, D. wrote a " Concerto Grosso," for eleven (concertante) instruments and orchestra; fifteen orchestral symphonies on Ovid's " Metamorphoses " (1785), forty-one unpublished symphonies, twelve violin concertos, six quartets for strings, twelve divertissements for two violins and 'cello, twelve pianoforte duet-sonatas, etc., as well as the treatises: " Brief über die Grenzen des Komischen und Heroischen in der Musik; " " Brief über die Behandlung Italienischer Texte bei der Komposition," etc. (in the *Leipziger Allgemeine Musikalische Zeitung,* 1799); and, finally, his autobiography (published in 1801 by Spazier).

Div. (*See* DIVISI.)

Divertimento (Ital.; Fr. *Divertissement,* " entertainment "), (1) a term formerly used (more especially in France) for the dances interpolated into operas.—(2) A somewhat loose combination of several pieces of chamber music, similar to the *Suite* or Sonata; the D. generally has five, six, or even more movements. There are divertimenti for wind instruments, for wind and strings, for pianoforte with other instruments, and for pianoforte alone. From the older concerto the D. is distinguished by greater simplicity of structure and part-writing, and by shorter length.—(3) In the sense of Potpourri.-(4) A free episode in a fugue. (*See* ANDAMENTO.)

Divisi (Ital. abbr. *div.,* "divided"), a term used in orchestral parts of stringed instruments in passages where there are two or more parts; it indicates that they are not to be played by double-stopping, but to be divided between the instruments.

Divisio modi (Lat.) = *Punctum divisionis.* (*See* POINT.)

Division, (1) a variation of a simple theme.—(2) A long note divided into short notes. A series of notes forming a chain of sounds, and, in vocal music, sung to one syllable. *To run a division* is to execute such a series of notes.

Divitis, Antonius (Antoine le Riche), chapel singer to Louis XII., and about the time of the death of the latter (1515), one of the most celebrated French contrapuntists of that period. A few motets and chansons of his have been preserved in collections (" Motetti de la Corona," 1514; also in publications of Attaignant, Petrejus, Rhaw, and Duchemin up to 1551), a manuscript mass at Cambrai, and a Credo and a *Salve Regina* à 5 at Munich.

Divoto, divotamente, in a devout, religious manner.

D'Ivry. (*See* IVRY.)

Dizi, François Joseph, excellent performer on the harp (self-taught), b. Jan. 14, 1780, Namur. He came, at the age of sixteen, to London, but on the way hither, while in a Dutch harbour, jumped overboard to save a drowning man; as he himself could not swim, he had, in his turn, to be rescued. The ship sailed away with his harp and all his other possessions. His effects were not recovered, but D. came to London, and to Erard, who gave him a harp, introduced him to pupils; and he soon gained great renown. He also made ingenious improvements in the mechanism of the harp, invented the perpendicular harp, and established, with Pleyel, a harp factory at Paris, which, however, did not prosper; shortly after his arrival in Paris he became harp teacher to the royal princesses. The year of his death is not known (1840 ?). D. composed a great deal for the harp (romances, variations, etc.).

Dlabacz, Gottfried Johann, b. about 1760, Böhmisch-Brod, d. Jan. 4, 1820, Prague, as chorus-master and librarian of the Premonstratensian convent there; he published

" Allgemeines historisches Künstlerlexikon für Böhmen " (1815-18, three vols.), and also wrote several treatises for Riegger's " Statistics of Bohemia, etc.''

D-major chord $= d, f\sharp, a$; *D-major* key, with signature of 2 sharps. (*Cf.* KEY.)

D-minor chord $= d, f, a$; *D-minor* key, with signature of one flat. (*Cf.* KEY.)

Do was the later Italian solmisation name, in place of *ut,* for our *c.* It is said to have been first used by Bononcini (" Musico Pratico," 1673).

Dobrzynski, Ignaz Felix, distinguished Polish pianist, b. Feb. 25, 1807, Romanoff, Volhynia, d. Oct. 18, 1867, Warsaw, where his father was maître de chapelle to Prince Ilinski ; he received his first training from his father, but, after the removal of the latter to Warsaw, from Elsner, as fellow pupil with Chopin, with whom he became united in ties of the closest friendship. D. made several concert trips to Germany, and at Dresden, Berlin, and Leipzig met with a very favourable reception. His compositions are well worthy of notice, and ought not to be neglected ; they consist of a symphony, a sextet for strings, two quintets and two quartets for strings, a trio for strings, a violin sonata, notturno for pf. and 'cello. D. also wrote an opera (*Die Filibustier,* Warsaw, 1861). His wife, Johanna, *née* Miller, was a gifted singer, but only appeared at intervals ; she was chiefly engaged as teacher in the Warsaw theatre school.

Doctor of Music, the academical degree of *Dr. Mus.* exists only in Great Britain, and only the Universities of Oxford, Cambridge, London, Dublin, and St. Andrews have the power to confer it ; a like power, curiously, vests in the Archbishop of Canterbury. As a rule, the Doctor's degree is preceded by that of *Bachelor.* Famous Oxford doctors of music were and are : John Bull, Arne, Burney, Callcott, Haydn, Crotch, Wesley, Bishop, Parry ; and of Cambridge : Greene, Boyce, Cooke, Bennett, Macfarren, Sullivan, Stanford, Joachim, Brahms, Dvořák, Boïto, Tschaïkowsky, and Saint-Saëns. For the *Mus. Doc.* degree, an exercise in eight parts, with fugue, and accompaniment for full orchestra, must be sent in before the *vivâ voce* examination is held. The Archbishop of Canterbury simply grants the degree by diploma. The title of Doctor, obtained by musicians in Germany, is, for the most part, that of *Dr. Phil.;* but in the great body of the faculty of philosophy music has found a small corner. To pass in it an essay on history, theory, or acoustics must be written ; and the examiners lay emphasis on the sciences (philosophy, physics, literature, etc.) related to music. The title of *Dr. Phil. honoris causa* is bestowed on musicians of eminence.

Dodecuplet, a group of notes formed by the

division of a bar, or part of a bar, into twelve portions of equal length.

Döhler, Theodor, pianist, b. April 20, 1814, Naples, d. Feb. 21, 1856, Florence ; he was a pupil of Julius Benedict at Naples, and afterwards of Czerny, and of S. Sechter at Vienna, where he soon appeared as a pianist, and with great success. The following years he spent at Naples, often playing at the court. He then (1837-45) travelled through Germany, Austria, France, England, Holland, Denmark, Russia, finally settling in Petersburg, giving up concert-playing, and devoting himself entirely to composition. After the Duke of Lucca—his patron from youth—had raised him to the rank of a nobleman, he married, in 1846, a Russian countess, and then lived successively at Moscow, Paris, and, after 1848, at Florence. He suffered from a spinal disease during the last ten years of his life, which gradually became worse, and of which he died. D. was an elegant pianoforte-player, and his compositions are also elegant, but without depth (nocturnes, variations, transcriptions, fantaisies, etc., for piano ; and one opera [*Tancreda,* performed at Florence, 1880]).

Doigter (Fr.), fingering.

Dolcan (Dulcan, Dulzain, Dolce), a term, in the organ, for soft flute stops, wider at the top than at the bottom (4- and 8-ft., requiring little wind); of still softer intonation is the *Dolcissimo,* 8-ft.

Dolce (Ital.) ; *con dolcezza,* soft, sweet ; *dolcissimo,* very soft and sweet.

Dolcian (Dulcian), (1) old name for the Fagotto, or Bassoon (in the 16th and 17th centuries).—(2) In the organ, a reed-stop, of 8- or 16-ft. (FAGOTTO.)

Dolendo (Ital. ; also *dolente*), plaintive, sad.

Doles, Johann Friedrich, b. April 21, 1716, Steinbach (Meiningen), d. Oct. 8, 1797, Leipzig. He was a pupil of J. S. Bach, was appointed (1744) cantor at Freiberg, in 1756, as successor to G. Harrer, cantor of the Thomas Schule, Leipzig. After thirty-three years of active work in this honourable post, he took his farewell in 1789. As a composer he was lively and pleasant ; his mode of writing is easy to understand ; truly it strikes one as strange that D., the pupil and successor of Bach, should have pleaded for the banishment of fugue from church music (see the preface to his cantata, *Ich komme vor dein Angesicht,* dedicated to Mozart and J. G. Naumann, 1790). D. published the following works : cantatas, chorales, chorale-preludes, " Anfangsgründe zum Singen "; there remained in manuscript :—Passions, masses, a German magnificat, etc.

Dolore (Ital., " grief ") ; *con d., doloroso,* with an expression of grief.

Dolzflöte (Ger. ; Ital. *Flauto dolce;* Fr. *Flûte douce*), (1) an obsolete kind of cross-flute, with a plugged mouthpiece.—(2) In the organ, an open flute stop of somewhat narrow measure.

Dom Bedos. (*See* BEDOS DES CELLES.)

Domchor (Ger.), cathedral choir, body of singers in a cathedral.

Dominant (*Upper-dominant*) is the name of the fifth degree of the scale; *Under-dominant* is the name of the note lying under the D. These terms were determined purely by the position of the notes in the scale. In the key of c major—

a is called *Superdominant.*
g „ „ *Dominant.*
f „ „ *Subdominant.*
e „ „ *Mediant.*
d „ „ *Submediant or Supertonic.*
c „ „ *Tonic.*
b „ „ *Subsemitonium.*

In recent systems, however, the harmonic relationship is taken into account; G major is the clang of the upper fifth, F major that of the lower fifth of the tonic; while the remaining notes form part of these three chords:

Under-dominant   Upper-dominant

f a c e g b d

Tonic

(*Cf.* MAJOR and MINOR KEYS.)

Dominiceti, Cesare, b. July 12, 1821, Desenzano, Lake Garda, d. June 20, 1888, Sesto di Monza, Italian opera composer (*I Begli usi di Citta*, 1841; *Due Mogli in Una*, 1853; *La Maschera*, 1854; *Morovico*, 1873; *Il Lago dalle Fate*, 1878; *L'Ereditaria*, 1881).

Dommer, Arrey von, b. Feb. 9, 1828, Danzig, was destined for a theologian, and attended the Gymnasium there; but in 1851 he went to Leipzig in order to devote himself to music, and studied composition under Richter and Lobe, and organ-playing under Schellenberg. From 1854 he studied literature for several years at the University there. After he had spent some years as a music-teacher in Leipzig, and drawn attention to himself by his literary activity, he removed (1863) to Hamburg, gave lectures, was for seven years musical critic to the *Correspondent*, from 1873–89, secretary of the city of Hamburg library; after that he retired from public life. Dommer's principal works are: "Elemente der Musik" (1862); "Musikalisches Lexikon" (1865, based on Koch's work; an exceedingly good book); "Handbuch der Musikgeschichte" (1867; 2nd edition 1878), likewise an excellent work touching on matters of recent investigation. D. has also published a psalm *a cappella* (à 8), and arranged, in four parts, melodies by Joh. Wolfg. Franck.

Donati, (1) Baldassaro, Italian contrapuntist of the 16th century; about 1562, maestro of the "small choir" of St. Mark's, Venice, which had been established during the last years of Willaert for his relief (the singers for the great choir were trained in it); and later on, after Zarlino had been appointed (1565), and the small choir disbanded, he again became simply a singer in the choir. But after Zarlino's death (1590), he was appointed his successor, as principal maestro, and died at Venice in 1603. He was one of the most distinguished composers of madrigals and motets of his time. Of his works have been preserved, "Canzonetti Villanesche alla Napoletana (1551 and 1555), several books of madrigals, à 4, 5, and 6 (1559–68), and a book of motets, à 5–8 (1569).—(2) Ignazio, b. Casalmaggiore, near Cremona, church maestro at Ferrara, and at Casalmaggiore, also, from 1633, of Milan Cathedral. He published a book of motets à 1–5 (1612), two books of "Concerti Ecclesiastici," à 2–5 (1617, 1619); two books of masses à 4–6 (1618), "Le Fanfalage" (madrigals à 3–5), two books of "Motetti Concertati" à 5–6 (1626, 1627), a book of "Motetti a Voce Sola," with continuo (1628), and "Salmi Bosarecci à 6" (1629).

Doni, (1) Antonio Francesco, b. 1519, Florence, d. Sept. 1574, Monselice, near Padua. He entered at an early age into the Servite monastery of his native town, but left it in 1539, and led a wandering life. Besides many non-musical essays, he wrote a "Dialogue on Music" (Lat. 1534; Ital. 1541 and 1544). His "Libreria" (1550, 1551, and 1560) is, for the historian, a valuable catalogue of the works of his time.—(2) Giovanni Battista, b. 1593, Florence, d. there, 1647; he gained, at Bologna and Rome, a deep knowledge of ancient literature, but was intended for the career of a lawyer. When Cardinal Corsini went as Papal Legate to Paris in 1621, D. joined him, eagerly visiting the Paris libraries; he made friends with Mersenne, and moved in the best literary circles. The death of a brother summoned him back to Florence in 1622, and, soon after, Cardinal Barberini, nephew of Urban VIII., a great amateur of music, drew him to Rome; D. also travelled with the Cardinal to Paris, Madrid, etc., and back again to Rome. In his society D. made a deep study of ancient music, which had long been one of his favourite pursuits; he also constructed a kind of double lyre, which he dedicated to the Pope (*Lyra Barberina*, Amphichord). Fresh deaths in his family called him back to Florence in 1640; this time he remained there, married, and received from Ferdinand II. of Medici a professorship of elocution. His works relating to music were: "Compendio del Trattato dei Generi e Modi della Musica, etc." (1635, epitome of a larger, unpublished work); "Annotazioni sopra il Compendio, etc." (1640, supplement to above); "De Præstantia Musicæ veteris libri tres, etc." (1647). Fétis discovered three pamphlets by D., written in French, in the Paris library. In 1773 Gori and Passeri published at Florence a description of the *Lyra Barberina*, and a series of small essays which

D. had left in manuscript; while many others remained unpublished.

Donizetti, Gaetano, b. Nov. 29, 1797, Bergamo, d. there April 8, 1848. He was first a pupil of Simon Mayer at Bergamo, and then of Pilotti and Mattei at Bologna (1815). He produced at Venice his first opera, *Enrico Conte di Borgogna* (1818), the success of which gave him great encouragement. Rossini, who at that time ruled the stage, was his model. He imitated his forms with skill and success, and a natural gift for creating melody was of service to him. From 1822 to 1836 D. wrote every year from three to four operas, and, naturally, did not trouble much about details of workmanship. With Bellini as a rival, he felt compelled sometimes to make more earnest efforts. Bellini's *Sonnambula* he answered by *Anna Bolena* at Milan in 1831; and when his *Marino Falieri* at Paris, in 1835, was outdone by Bellini's *Puritani*, he wrote—putting forth all his power—*Lucia di Lammermoor*, his best work, for Naples. The death of Bellini, which happened in the following year, left him undisputed master of the Italian stage. The success of *Lucia* procured for him the post of professor of counterpoint at the Naples Conservatorio. When, in 1839, the censorship at Naples forbade the production of his *Poliuto*, written for Adolphe Nourrit (*Polyeucte*, called afterwards in Paris *Les Martyrs*), he was indignant, and travelled to Paris, where he undertook the direction of a newly established opera company in the Salle Ventadour (Théâtre de la Renaissance), and produced new works there, and also at the Grand Opéra and Opéra Comique, among which the French operas, *La Fille du Régiment* and *La Favorite;* but these operas, which afterwards became so popular, obtained, at first, only moderate success, and D. went off to Rome, Milan, and Venice, and for the last city wrote, in 1842, *Linda di Chamounix,* which procured for him the title of Imperial Court Composer and Maestro. During the next two years he lived alternately in Paris, Vienna, and Naples. His last work was *Catarina Cornaro,* written for Naples in 1844. On his return journey from that city to Vienna, the first symptoms of mental disorder showed themselves; and when he arrived in Paris he had a severe attack of paralysis, which totally disabled him. During his last years he was subject to fits of deep melancholy, for which no cure could be found; from 1847 he lived in his native town (Bergamo), and died there. In all, D. wrote about seventy operas (also some cantatas), of which *La Fille du Regiment* and *Lucia di Lammermoor* are still in the *répertoire* of Italian opera; while *Elisire d'Amore, La Favorite, Lucrezia Borgia, Linda di Chamounix,* and others, only live, through some of their favourite melodies, in *potpourris.*

Dont, Jakob, celebrated teacher of the violin, and composer, b. March 2, 1815, Vienna,

d. there Nov. 18, 1888, son of the 'cellist, Joseph Valentin D. (b. April 15, 1776, Georgenthal, Bohemia, d. Dec. 14, 1833, Vienna). He studied at the Vienna Conservatorium under Böhm and Hellmesberger (senior), and became member of the orchestra of the " Hofburg " theatre (1831), and in 1834, of the court band. He wrote a large number of works for his instrument, of which the studies (published in a collection as " Gradus ad Parnassum ") enjoy a high reputation. D. first taught, for a short time, at the " Akademie der Tonkunst," then at the St. Anna grammar-school, and, from 1873, at the Conservatorium.

Door, Anton, celebrated pianist, b. June 20, 1833, Vienna, pupil of Czerny and S. Sechter. He gave concerts with great success (1850) at Baden-Baden and Wiesbaden, then, with Ludwig Strauss, in Italy; he travelled from 1856 to 1857 through Scandinavia, and was appointed court pianist, and member of the Royal Academy, at Stockholm. In 1877 he made a tour with Sarasate through East Hungary, and appeared with great success at Leipzig, Berlin, Amsterdam, etc. D. also made himself known by introducing novelties (Brahms, Raff, Saint-Saëns, etc.). After teaching for ten years at the Imperial Conservatoire, Moscow, he accepted the post of professor at the " Conservatorium der Gesellschaft der Musikfreunde," Vienna (1869), which he still occupies.

Dopo (Ital.), after.

Doppelflöte (Ger., also *Duiflöte;* Ital. *flauto doppio*), a covered organ-stop (8-ft.), with double mouth, double lips, etc., on opposite sides (behind and before) like the *Bifara* (see TREMULANT), but exactly the same height, so that the tone does not undulate, but is very full. The pipe cross-section is a rectangular figure twice as deep as it is broad. The D. was invented by Esajas Compenius (q.v.).

Doppelquintpommer. (*See* BASSOON.)

Doppio (Ital.), double; *d. movimento,* twice as fast; *d. valore* (*d. note*), double-note value, *i.e.* twice as slow. In names of instruments (*Lira d.,* etc.), *d.* indicates double size, and, therefore, lower compass (bass instruments). *Contrabasso d.,* a double-bass (q.v.) of huge dimensions, which lies an octave lower than the usual double-bass.

Doppler, (1) Albert Franz, flautist, b. Oct. 16, 1821, Lemberg, d. July 27, 1883, Baden, near Vienna. He received his musical training from his father, who was afterwards oboist at the theatre at Warsaw, and later on at Vienna, where D. soon made his *début* as flautist. After he had undertaken several concert tours with his younger brother Karl (*see* below), he obtained the post of principal flautist at the Pesth Theatre, for which he composed his first opera, *Benjowski* (1847); then followed in 1849 *Ilka, Die beiden Husaren,* also *Afanasia, Wanda,* and *Erzébeth* (jointly with his brother and Erkel). In 1858 he became first flautist and second ballet conductor at the Vienna Opera; he was promoted afterwards to the post of first ballet conductor, and, from 1865, became teacher of the flute at the Conservatorium. Besides the already named operas, he wrote, in 1870, a German opera (*Judith*) for Vienna, also overtures, ballet pieces, flute concertos, etc.—(2) Karl, brother of the former, b. 1826, Lemberg, likewise a flautist, gave concerts with his brother at Paris, Brussels, London, etc., with great success; he is musical director at the "Landestheater," Pesth, and has written, besides, several pieces for flute, etc., also several Hungarian operas.

Dörffel, Alfred, b. Jan. 24, 1821, Waldenburg (Saxony); he was thoroughly trained at Leipzig under G. Fink, K. G. Müller, Mendelssohn, etc. He established a valuable lending library of musical literature containing many rare old theoretical and historical works, complete collections of nearly all musical papers, and also scores of great modern orchestral works. This library passed into the hands of his son. D. succeeded K. F. Becker as custodian of the musical section of the town library (Becker's foundation). For many years he has been editor of the classical editions, remarkable for their correctness, published by Breitkopf & Härtel, and C. F. Peters. He has published a "Führer durch die musikalische Welt," thematic catalogues of the works of J. S. Bach and Schumann, a translation of Berlioz's "Treatise on Instrumentation," with appendix; also as musical critic he has won an honourable position. He wrote the festival pamphlet for the hundredth anniversary of the "Gewandhaus" Concerts. In 1885 the degree of *Dr. Phil. honoris causa* was bestowed on him by the University of Leipzig.

Dorian, the name of the first church mode of the Middle Ages—the most important, as being the one most in vogue; also the name in ancient Greece for the key held in highest honour. The Dorian key of the Greeks (*see* GREEK MUSIC), and the Church Mode named D. from about the 9th century, are, however, not identical. (*Cf.* CHURCH MODES.)

Döring, (1) Gottfried, b. May 9, 1801, Pomerendorf, near Elbing, d. June 20, 1869, Elbing, trained by Zelter at the Institute for Church Music in Berlin, from 1828 cantor of the "Marienkirche" at Elbing. D. wrote a "Choralkunde" (1865), also "Zur Geschichte der Musik in Preussen" (1852), and two chorale books.—(2) Karl Heinrich, pianoforte teacher, b. July 4, 1834, Dresden, pupil of the Leipzig Conservatorium (1852-55), studied privately under Hauptmann and Lobe, since 1858 teacher at the Dresden Conservatorium. D. wrote a number of excellent studies, of which Ops. 8, 24, 25, and 38, but especially the "Rhythmische Studien" (Op. 30), have been widely circulated.

Dorn, (1), Heinrich Ludwig Egmont, b. Nov. 14, 1804, Königsberg. From an early age he received a good musical education; but studied law at the same time, although he had already chosen his vocation in life. After a long tour, he settled in Berlin, and became a pupil of Ludwig Berger (pianoforte), Zelter, and Bernhard Klein. His career was that of a practical capellmeister. After occupying, for a brief period, the post of teacher of music at a musical institute at Frankfort, he went to Königsberg, in 1828, in a similar capacity: from there, in 1829, to Leipzig, and in 1832 replaced Krebs at Hamburg. But he soon went to Riga, where he accepted a post as church musical director, and, besides, was active as teacher. In 1843 he was called to Cologne as capellmeister at the Theatre, and municipal musical director. In 1845 he founded a school of music, the nucleus from which sprang (1850) the Conservatorium. He conducted the Lower Rhenish Musical Festivals from 1844 to 1847, received the title of Royal Musical Director, finally, in 1849, succeeded Nicolai as capellmeister at the Opera House, Berlin, and, later on, became member of the Academy of Arts. In 1869 he received his pension at the same time as Taubert, and the title of Professor; and from that time lived in Berlin, highly esteemed as teacher and musical critic. As a composer D. occupied an honourable position; he wrote the operas *Die Rolandsknappen* (produced at the "Königsstadt" theatre, Berlin, in 1826; his maiden attempt at the close of his studies); *Die Bettlerin* (Königsberg, 1828), *Abu Kara* (Leipzig, 1831), *Der Schöffe von Paris* and *Das Banner von England* (Riga, 1838 and 1842), *Die Nibelungen* (produced at Berlin, 1854, also at Weimar and Breslau, etc.), *Ein Tag in Russland* (1856), *Der Botenläufer von Pirna* (1865); the operetta *Gewitter bei Sonnenschein* (1869), and the ballet *Amors Macht* (Leipzig, 1830). His songs are widely known, especially the humorous ones; he also wrote pianoforte pieces, "Siegesfestklänge" for orchestra (1866), etc. He contributed excellent articles to the *Neue Berliner Musikzeitung*, and brilliant critical notices to the *Post*; also a pamphlet, "Ostrakismus, ein Gericht Scherben" (1875), etc. His autobiography ("Aus meinem Leben") appeared in six parts (1870-79). He died Jan. 10, 1892.— (2) Alexander Julius Paul, b. June 8, 1833, Riga, son of the former; he was trained exclusively by his father, was for some time private music teacher at a manor in Russian Poland; lived from 1855-65, for the sake of his health, at Cairo and Alexandria, as teacher of music, and conductor of German male choral societies; became, from 1865-68, conductor of the "Liedertafel" at Crefeld; and since 1869, he has been pianoforte teacher at the Royal High School, Berlin. More than four hundred works from his pen have appeared (operettas for female voices, pianoforte pieces, songs). Works of greater importance (three masses for male chorus and orchestra; " Der Blumen Rache," for soli, chorus and orchestra; pianoforte pieces, etc.) are still unpublished, but have been performed.—(3) O t t o, gifted composer, b. Sept. 7, 1848, Cologne, likewise son and pupil of Heinrich Dorn, attended for a while the Stern Conservatorium, and in 1873 received the first prize of the Meyerbeer scholarship. Of his compositions the following deserve mention: the overtures " Hermannsschlacht " and " Sappho," a symphony, " Prometheus;" an opera, *Afraja* (Gotha, 1891); many songs, pianoforte pieces, etc. He lives at Wiesbaden.—(4) E d u a r d, writer of a great number of light and popular pieces and transcriptions.

Dörner, A r m i n W., b. June 22, 1852, Marietta (Ohio), went in 1859 to Cincinnati ; he studied from 1871–79 at Berlin (under Kullak, Bendel, Weitzmann), Stuttgart, and Paris, and was appointed teacher of the pianoforte at the newly opened college of music at Cincinnati. D. excelled especially in ensemble playing (duets, with H. G. Andrews, for two pianofortes). Of his compositions may be named the Technical Exercises.

Dornheckter, R o b e r t, b. Nov. 4, 1839, Franzburg (Pomerania), d. 1890, Stralsund, as organist, teacher of singing at the Gymnasium, and conductor of the " Dornheckter " choral union, and royal musical director. He was a pupil of the Royal Institute for Church Music, and of Fl. Geyer and H. Ries in Berlin. He composed organ and pianoforte pieces, also songs, part-songs, etc.

Doss, A d o l f v o n, b. Sept. 10, 1825, Pfarrkirchen (Lower Bavaria), d. Aug. 13, 1886, Rome ; he studied at Munich, entered the order of the Jesuits (Nov. 11, 1843), and laboured in Bonn, Münster, Mayence, Liége, and Rome. At the age of twenty-five he wrote the opera *Baudouin du Bourg,* frequently performed in Belgium and France. His great Mass in E gained a prize from the Academy of Fine Arts at Brussels in 1876. Six operas, two operettas, eleven oratorios and cantatas, together with three symphonies, are among the musical archives of St. Servais College, Liége, some printed, some in manuscript (*Johann ohne Land, Das Gastmahl des Baltassar, Die Sündfluth, Die Löwengrube, St. Cäcilia, Mauritius, Wittekind, Percival,* etc.). His musical works are about 350 in number, among which there are three great collections : " Melodiæ Sacræ," Münster, 1862 ; " Mélodies Religieuses," and " Collection de Musique d'Église," published by L. Muraille, Liége.

Dötsch, A u g u s t, talented 'cellist, pupil of De Swert, b, 1858, d. already Nov. 19, 1882, Wiesbaden.

Dotzauer, J u s t u s J o h a n n F r i e d r i c h, celebrated 'cellist, b. Jan. 20, 1783, Häselrieth,

near Hildburghausen, d. March 6, 1860, Dresden, pupil of Kriegck, Meiningen ; from 1801–5 he was member of the court band there, studied B. Romberg's style of playing, from 1806, at Berlin, and was engaged in 1811 in the court band, Dresden. In 1821 he became first 'cellist, worked zealously there until 1852, and resided there, after receiving his pension, up to his death ; his pupils were K. Schuberth, K. Drechsler, L. Dotzauer, etc. The literature of the 'cello is indebted to him for concertos, variations, duets, etc. ; he also wrote symphonies, overtures, masses, an opera (*Graziosa*), and a 'cello Method.—His sons are J u s t u s B e r n h a r d F r i e d r i c h, b. May 12, 1808, Leipzig, d. Nov. 30, 1874, Hamburg, esteemed as a teacher of music, and K a r l L u d w i g (L o u i s), b. Dec. 7, 1811, Dresden, pupil of his father, excellent 'cellist ; from 1830 he was appointed principal 'cellist in the court band at Cassel.

Douay, G e o r g e s, b. Jan. 7, 1840, Paris, composer of a large number of French operettas, for the most part in one act.

Doublé (Fr.), turn (q.v.).

Double bar, two thick lines drawn vertically through the stave, showing the end of a part or piece.

Double-bass, (1) the largest of the *stringed instruments* in use at the present day (Ital. *contrabasso,* Fr. *contrebasse*), belongs to the violin family, and, like the violoncello, only came into existence after the violin had beaten the viol entirely off the field, *i.e.* at the commencement of the 17th century. (*Cf.* INSTRUMENTS, STRINGED.) The deep bass stringed instruments of the previous period—which, naturally, only disappeared gradually—were the bass viols belonging to the viol family (Bassgeige, *Archiviola da Lyra,* viola da gamba). In the 17th century, even the D.-B. was surpassed by the construction of gigantic instruments twice the size. The most recent experiment of that kind was the octobass of Vuillaume, produced at the Paris Exhibition of 1855, now in the museum of instruments at the Conservatoire. Originally, as to-day, the D.-B. was provided (like all instruments belonging to the family), with four strings, and these, it appears, were tuned to C, G, D, A (an octave lower than the violoncello), but sometimes it was preferred to mount it with only three strings, tuned G, D, A (Italian), or A, D, G (English). The only rational tuning at the present day is

The notes for the D.-B. are written an octave higher than the sounds. For orchestral music

the usual compass is from contra E (formerly, up to about the year 1830, frequently from the contra c) to small *a*, — or, at most, to once accented *c*, thus :

Notation.

Sound.

Celebrated D.-B. *virtuosi* of old and modern times are—Dragonetti, Andreoli, Wach, August Müller, Bottesini. (2) Brass wind-instrument, D.-B. of the wind-band (*Bombardon*), was constructed in circular form by Cerveny (1845), and frequently imitated (Sax-horn D. B., Helicon, Pelliton) in c, B♭, F, and E♭. In 1873 Cerveny constructed a Subcontrabass going down to double contra c.—(3) In the organ, a 16- or 32-ft. gamba stop, and sometimes a 16-ft. reed-stop (*e.g. Basse contre*, Paris, St. Vincent de Paul).

Double-bassoon, an instrument an octave lower in pitch than the bassoon ; its compass extends from the double contra D to the small *f ;* it has recently been made of brass, and named *Tritonikon.* The mode of notation (as with the double-bass) is an octave higher than the sound.

Double canon, contrapuntal combination of two canons.

Double choir is a choir divided into two half-choirs. As a rule each choir is for the four kinds of voices, and the D. C., therefore, eight-part. Yet music written for D. C. is not, on that account, always in eight parts, as the two choirs frequently alternate, or can enter without the full number of parts. As a rule, one of the two choirs is treated as first—*i.e.* is higher than the second—so that the soprano of the second choir appears as a second soprano, etc. In a mixed D. C., combinations of the most varied kind can be obtained from sets of four voices :—

(1) Soprano, Alto, Tenor, Bass.
(2) Two Soprani, two Alti (chorus of boys or women in four parts).
(3) Two Tenori and two Bassi (male chorus in four parts).
(4) Two Soprani and two Tenori (bright tone).
(5) Two Alti and two Bassi (sombre tone).
(6) Two Alti and two Tenori, etc.

There can also be various groupings of five and six voices ; but if each of the two choirs is placed in a different part of the church or hall, such groupings are scarcely practicable. Some of the great contrapuntists have, in certain cases, greatly increased the number of parts.

Double corde, the French technical term for double-stopping on stringed instruments.

Double counterpoint. (*See* COUNTERPOINT.)

Double-croche (Fr.), semiquaver.

Double diapason, an organ stop of 16-ft. pitch.

Double dot after a note increases its value by one half, and half of that half, for example :—

$$\text{♩.. = ♩ ♪ ♬}$$

The D. D. was not known in old notation, but the single dot or point was also used as a D. D., for example :—

$$\text{◌. ♩ = ◌ ..♫}$$

Double-flat (♭♭). (*See* LOWERING OF PITCH OF A NOTE.)

Double fugue, a fugue on two subjects ; fugues with three or more subjects are likewise called double fugues. In the real D. F. a theme is first treated fugally in the ordinary manner, then a second theme ; and, finally, both are combined. Fugues in which the so-called countersubject is simply adhered to, always appearing simultaneously with the principal subject, are likewise named double fugues.

Double pedal-point, the sustaining of the tonic and dominant by two parts, whilst other parts above them move on in varying harmonies. (*See* PEDAL-POINT and SUSTAINED NOTES.)

Doubles (Fr.) is the old name for " variations ;" thus, we find D. in Handel, Bach, Couperin, etc. These old variations, however, change neither harmony nor mode, nor key of the theme, but rather continue to add embellishments to the same, and ever-increasing movement in the figuration of the accompanying parts.

Double shake, a concurrence of two shakes :

It is executed in the same way as the single shake, but when played with one hand the technical difficulty is, naturally, much greater. On the pianoforte double shakes (like the one above in thirds) are generally played with the fingering $\frac{4}{2}\frac{5}{1}$ or $\frac{3}{2}\frac{4}{1}$; only specially-trained hands can perform a D. S. without disturbing the relative position of thumb and second finger, *i.e.* with $\frac{3}{1}\frac{4}{2}$, also $\frac{4}{2}\frac{5}{3}$. The D. S. in *fourths* forms, as a rule, a portion of the *triple shake (shake or chord of six-three) :*

On the pianoforte it is played with $\frac{4}{2}\frac{5}{1}$ or even with $\frac{4}{1}\frac{5}{2}$. The D. S. in *octaves* is played with $\frac{1}{1}\frac{5}{1}$.

the thumb moving swiftly to and fro; this should only be attempted by virtuosi. Also the *shake in sixths* is difficult, and can only be played comfortably by large hands ($\frac{4}{5}$). A well-known substitute for the shake in thirds is the following:

Double sharp is the sign for the double raising of a note, now generally **X** or ⁑; formerly also ♯♯ ♯♯ or ✳. (*See* RAISING OF THE PITCH OF A NOTE.)

Double - stopping (Ger. *Doppelgriffe*), simultaneous sounding of two or more notes on the same instrument.

Double-tongueing is a term used for a method of blowing on the flute, by means of which figures similar to

can be executed in rapid time. The separation of the two notes of like pitch is effected by articulating the letter T, and thus interrupting for a moment the current of air (hutuhutu, etc.). In a similar manner, by articulation of consonants, the same note can be rapidly repeated on the trumpet.

Double trumpet, a 16-ft. organ reed-stop.

Doublette (Fr.), a 2-ft. organ stop.

Dourlen, Victor Charles Paul, b. Nov. 3, 1780, Dunkirk, d. Jan. 8, 1864, Batignolles, near Paris. He studied at the Paris Conservatoire, carried off the *Prix de Rome* in 1805, after having already been under-master of an elementary singing-class (1800). In 1812 he was appointed assistant professor of harmony, and in 1816 professor in ordinary, which post he held until he received a pension in 1842. D. wrote several small operas for the "Feydeau" theatre, published some chamber works (pianoforte-, violin-, flute-sonatas, trios, etc.), and expounded his method of teaching harmony, based on that of Catel, in a "Tableau Synoptique des Accords" and in a "Traité d'Harmonie" (1834).

Dowland, John, famous lutenist, b. 1562, Westminster (London), d. 1626. From 1584 he made a tour of several years' duration through France, Germany, and Italy; took the degree of *Mus.Bac.* in 1588 at Oxford and Cambridge; lived from 1600-9 as royal chamber-lutenist in Denmark, then in London as lutenist to Lord Walden; and, about 1625, became one of the six royal lutenists. The Psalms à 4, published by Thomas Este in 1592, are partly arranged by him, but his chief work is a large lute tablature book, of which the first part appeared in 1597

("The First Booke of Songs or Ayres, etc."), republished in 1600, 1603, 1608, and 1613; and in 1844, published in modern notation by the Musical Antiquarian Society. The second part appeared in 1600, the third in 1602. In 1605 he published "Lachrymæ, or Seven Teares Figured in Seven Passionate Pavanes, etc." (à 5, for lute and viols, or violins). He translated Onithoparcus's "Micrologus" into English.—His son R o b e r t, likewise a distinguished performer on the lute, and his father's successor at court, published in 1610 two works on the lute—"A Musical Banquet" and "Varieties of Lessons"; to the latter work are added instructive remarks concerning lute-playing by Jean Baptiste Besard and John D.

Down-beat, the conductor's beat marking the beginning of a fresh bar. (*See* ARSIS, and CONDUCTING, ART OF.)

Down-bow (Ger. *Herunterstrich*) is, in violin-playing, the movement during which the bow touches the strings first with the head (nut), and lastly with the point (in 'cello and double-bass the German word *Herstrich*—"hither-stroke"—is used). The opposite is *Up-bow* (Ger. *Hinaufstrich, Hinstrich*—"thither-stroke"). For strong accents the D. is to be preferred to the up-bow; for chords—when the bow crosses from the lower to the higher strings—this is self-evident (for example, g, d', b', g'').

Doxology (Gr.), the Gloria. The great D. is the "Gloria in Excelsis Deo" ("Hymnus angelicus," the song of the angels on Christmas night); the small D.—"Gloria patri et filio et spiritui sancto" ("sicut erat in principio et nunc et semper in sæculorum, amen"). The former was introduced into the mass; the latter appended to the singing of psalms. (*See* EVOVÆ.)

Draghi, (1) A n t o n i o, an exceedingly prolific Italian opera and oratorio composer, b. 1635, Ferrara, d. Jan. 18, 1700, Vienna. He wrote (almost exclusively for Vienna, where in 1674 he became "Hoftheaterintendant" to Leopold I., and Capellmeister to the Empress Leonore), from 1661 to 1699, not less than eighty-seven operas, eighty-eight festival pieces, and serenades and oratorios—some jointly with the Emperor himself. He also wrote some libretti (among others "Apollo delusio" for Leopold I.).—(2) G i o v a n n i B a t t i s t a, contemporary, and probably brother of the former, lived in London about 1667-1706, eminent harpsichord-player, music-master to Queen Anne, and, probably, Mary. He published instructive harpsichord lessons, also wrote music to various stage pieces (Shadwell's *Psyche;* jointly with Lock, D'Urfey's *Wonders in the Sun*, etc.).

Dragonetti, D o m e n i c o, b. April 7, 1763, Venice, d. April 16, 1846, London, one of the most famous performers on the double-bass. He studied principally by himself, and only received a few lessons from Berini, the double-bass player at St. Mark's, whose successor he became in 1787, after he had already played under him in Venetian opera orchestras during a period of six years. His skill in handling the gigantic instrument is said to have been unsurpassed. He frequently played on it the 'cello part of quartets, and his own compositions were studded with difficulties, which he alone knew how to overcome. In 1794 he obtained leave of absence for a visit to London, where, on his first appearance, he was at once definitely engaged for the King's Theatre, and for the concerts there. With the exception of several journeys to Italy, Vienna, etc., he lived in London until his death, and for a space of fifty-two years was the inseparable companion of the 'cellist Lindley. As late as 1845 he was in full possession of his powers as an executant, and took part at the Bonn Festival on the occasion of the unveiling of the Beethoven monument, when he was the principal of thirteen double-basses in the c minor Symphony. He bequeathed to the British Museum his rich collection of scores, old instruments, engravings; and his favourite instrument (a Gaspero da Salò), on which he had played for a period of nearly sixty years, to St. Mark's, Venice. His biography by F. Caffi was published in 1846. Besides concertos, sonatas, etc., for double-bass, he wrote some vocal music (canzonette).

Dramatic music is music connected with poetry, and stage action, and it would be one-sided to consider it only from a formal, musical point of view. The esthetic law of unity of conception requires that in absolute music there should be a certain regular organisation: repetition of themes, agreement, or inner relationship of keys, etc. (*Cf.* FORMS, MUSICAL.) This restriction does not exist in the case of D. M., and it is therefore a question whether Wagner—whom one is accustomed to regard as an anti-formalist—did not go too far in his latest music-dramas, in seeking to preserve thematic unity in D. M. Such an aim was alien to the old opera, in which there was no unity pervading the whole work; for it was divided into series of numbers (scenes) following one another, but each self-contained—art-productions too complete and too numerous to be able to resolve themselves thoroughly into a higher unity; often, indeed, they were a drag on the dramatic development. The reaction brought about by Gluck in the last, and by Wagner in the present century, against the overgrowth of music beautiful and satisfactory *per se*, was thoroughly necessary—and, so far as concerned style, just. It is merely a question whether Wagner's *Leitmotive* are not a formalism equally reprehensible; on this matter the further development of art will pronounce sentence. If natures less gifted, and of less creative power than Wagner, are able to develop themselves successfully within his art-form, the voice of history will be a favourable one; in the other case, it will have to be acknowledged, that only the rich imagination and technical mastery of Wagner were able to ward off the dangers of rigid schematism. The task of D. M. is, in the first place, to intensify the inflections of the voice so as to produce singing. Recitative, therefore, is not in any way the essential element of dramatic singing, but only its lowest foundation. It would be acting contrary to sense to exclude the final intensification, *i.e.* real melody. On an equally weak footing rest the objections brought against *ensemble* singing in the music-drama. The task of the accompanying instruments in a music-drama is to create and continue a mood, to bind together the singing of the various personages, to accentuate the sense of their words; it is really the atmosphere in which the singers live; and, if the illusion of the intensified poetical situation is to be preserved, indispensable. As every sound, every movement, takes musical form, it is altogether natural to sing, and not to speak. Declamation with illustrative music is therefore an unsatisfactory bastard species. Recitation appears an altogether too everyday, dry element, and weakens the impression of music, instead of the latter strengthening the former. In spoken drama, only mute scenes are suitable for music. According to this, the *Ballet* stands much higher than the melodrama; it is a pure species of art. The pantomimic ballet intensifies gestures in quite the same way in which song intensifies speech. Concerning programme-music, which must be considered from the stand-point of dramatic music, *cf.* PROGRAMME-MUSIC and ABSOLUTE MUSIC.

Dramma per musica, the usual Italian term for opera, was used by the Florentine inventors of the *Stilo rappresentativo* to designate their works. The expression *opera, opera in musica,* generally signifies in Italian "work" (*opus*); only with the addition *seria* or *buffa,* does it convey the meaning generally attached to that word. (*See* OPERA.)

Drammaticamente (Ital.), dramatically.

Drammatico (Ital.), dramatic.

Dräseke, Felix August Bernhard, b. Oct. 7, 1835, Coburg, where his father (son of bishop D.) was court preacher. He studied at the Leipzig Conservatorium, especially under Rietz (composition), then lived at Weimar, an enthusiastic partisan of Liszt, and of the new German school generally. He became a friend of Bülow's, went later to Dresden, was teacher at the Lausanne Conservatoire from 1864 to 1874, with a break of one year (1868–69), in which Bülow drew him to Munich, as teacher at the Royal School of Music. After he had lived for some time in Geneva he went to Dresden, and settled there. His early compositions, which he wrote while under Liszt's influence, are eccentric, and show a doubtful originality at the expense of charm ; his literary activity, also, was devoted to the Extreme Left—as, for instance, his articles in the *Neue Zeitschrift für Musik*, and his " Anregungen für Kunst und Wissenschaft " (1857–59). In later years his relationship to Wagner and Liszt cooled down, and his style became somewhat classic. Of his more important compositions may be named : sonata for pf. (Op. 6), first symphony in G (Op. 12), Ghaselen, pf. pieces (Op. 13), six fugues for pf. (Op. 15) ; Requiem in B minor (Op. 22), second symphony in F (Op. 25), first quartet for strings in C minor (Op. 27), Adventlied for soli, chorus, and orchestra (Op. 30), second quartet for strings in E minor (Op. 35), pf. concerto (Op. 36), eighteen canons, à 6, 7, and 8 (Op. 37), sonata for clarinet and pf. (Op. 38), " Osterscene " from *Faust*, for baritone solo, mixed chorus, and orchestra (Op. 39), third symphony (" Tragica," Op. 40), "Canonic Riddles " à 6, for four hands (Op. 42), quintet for pf., violin, viola, 'cello, and horn (Op. 48), serenade in D for orchestra (Op. 49). An opera (*Herrat*), a violin concerto, Concertstück for 'cello and orchestra, Concertic preludes to Calderon's *Life is a Dream* and Kleist's *Penthesilea* remain unpublished. In 1884 D. succeeded Wüllner as teacher of composition at the Dresden Conservatorium. The opinion expressed with regard to his earlier compositions is, possibly, too hard. His theoretical works are : " Anweisung zum kunstgerechten Modulieren " (1876), " Die Beseitigung des Tritonus " (1876), and an amusing Method of Harmony in verse (1884).

Drath, Theodor, b. June 13, 1828, Winzig (Silesia), pupil of Marx, cantor of Münsterberg, afterwards teacher at the Seminary at Poelitz, then teacher of music of the Seminary at Bunzlau (royal musical director). He is a composer, also the author of a " Musiktheorie."

Draud (Draudius), Georg, celebrated bibliographer, b. Jan. 9, 1573, Davernheim (Hesse), pastor successively at Grosskabern, Ortenburg, and Davernheim, d. about 1636, Butzbach, whither he had fled from the horrors of war. He published three works of the highest importance to general, and especially to musical, bibliography : " Bibliotheca classica " (1611), " Bibliotheca exotica " (1625), and Bibliotheca librorum germanicorum classica " (1625), to which only the Latin translation of the titles is prejudicial.

Draw-action (Ger. *Zugwerk*) is the action in an organ, or in one of its keyboards, when the keyboard is connected with the rest of the mechanism by means of trackers : pressure on the key produces draw-action.

Drechsler, (1) Joseph, b. May 26, 1782, Wällisch-Birken (Bohemia), d. Feb. 27, 1852, Vienna. He was at first chorus-master at the court theatre, Vienna, then conductor at the theatre at Baden (near Vienna) and at

Pressburg, later on organist of the Servite Church, Vienna, in 1816 precentor at St. Ann's, in 1823 capellmeister at the University and " Hofpfarr " churches, from 1822 to 1830 capellmeister at the Leopoldstadt Theatre, and, in 1844, capellmeister at St. Stephen's. He was devoted to stage and church, not only in his practical career, but also as a composer. In addition to six operas and twenty-five operettas, local farces, etc, he wrote many masses, offertories, a Requiem, etc. ; also sonatas, quartets, songs, etc., a Method for organ, and a treatise on harmony ; he also prepared a new edition of Pleyel's Piano School, and was the author of a theoretico-practical guide to the art of preluding.—(2) Karl, b. May 27, 1800, Kamenz, d. Dec. 1, 1873, Dresden, distinguished player on the 'cello ; he was appointed to the Dessau court band in 1820, continued his studies from 1824 to 1826 under Dotzauer at Dresden, and was then appointed leader of the ducal band at Dessau ; in 1871 he retired into private life. Cossmann, F. Grützmacher, August Lindner, K. Schröder, and others, were his pupils.

Dregert, Alfred, b. Sept. 26, 1836, Frankfort-on-the-Oder, d. 1893, pupil of Marx at the Stern Conservatorium, Berlin. He was at first capellmeister at various theatres, and then conductor of the Male Choral Union at Stralsund, Cologne, Elberfeld (Liedertafel and Teachers' Vocal Union, royal musical director). D. composed part-songs for male voices. Died March 14, 1893.

Dresel, Otto, b. 1826, Andernach, pupil of Hiller and Mendelssohn, d. July 26, 1890, Beverley, near Boston ; he went in 1848 to America, where he distinguished himself as pianist and composer, first in New York, and from 1852 in Boston. Of his compositions some chamber-music, songs, pf. pieces, etc., appeared in print. D. did much to make German music (for example, the songs of Robert Franz) known in America.

Dreszer, Anastasius, W., b. April 28, 1845, Kalisch (Poland). He was, from 1859 to 1861, a pupil of the Dresden Conservatorium, lived for several years at Leipzig, occasionally going to Paris and Berlin. Since 1868 he has been director of a music school of his own, and musical director at Halle-a.-S. He has published two symphonies, also pf. sonatas, songs ; an opera (*Vilnoda*, libretto by Peter Lohmann) is still in manuscript.

Dreyschock, (1) Alexander, distinguished pianist, b. Oct. 15, 1818, Zack (Bohemia), d. April 1, 1869, Venice, pupil of Tomaschek at Prague. For many years he made that city his headquarters, but gave concerts throughout Europe, and obtained many distinctions, and titles of honour—among others that of Imperial Austrian " Kammervirtuoso." In 1862 he was appointed professor of the pianoforte at the Royal Conservatoire, Petersburg, founded by A. Rubinstein, and, at the same time, was chosen director of the

Imperial Theatre School there. His health was never very robust, and was not improved by the Russian climate; and, after having taken leave of absence several times for the sake of his health, he spent the winter of 1868 at Venice, where he died of consumption. His numerous pf. compositions are brilliant, but not deep.—(2) R a i m u n d, brother of the former, b. Aug. 30, 1824, Zack; he devoted himself to the violin (pupil of Pixis at Prague), and from 1850 until his death (1869), he was a successful under-leader of the Gewandhaus orchestra, Leipzig, and active as a teacher of the violin at the Leipzig Conservatorium. His wife, E l i z a b e t h (Nose), b. 1832, Cologne, was formerly a well-known concert-singer (contralto). She settled, after her husband's death, in Berlin, with her Vocal Academy, founded at Leipzig, which institution still flourishes under her management. —(3) F e l i x, son of Raimund D., b. Dec. 27, 1860, Leipzig; in 1875 pupil of the Royal High School for Music. For his higher training in pianoforte-playing he was indebted to H. Ehrlich. From 1883 he gave concerts with success; he also published pf. pieces, songs, and a violin sonata (Op. 16).

Drieberg, F r i e d r i c h v o n, b. Dec. 10, 1780, Charlottenburg. He was, at first, officer in the Prussian army, then lived at Paris, Berlin, etc., and on his estate in Pomerania, and died, as Royal Chamberlain, at Charlottenburg, May 21, 1856. In the Mendel-Reissmann " Musiklexikon " he is represented as a writer of merit on ancient Greek music. This is quite incorrect, for his writings on this subject are in the highest degree amateurish, and are full of incorrect, arbitrary statements, and untenable opinions. That these writings could seriously attract the attention of the German musical world is a sufficient justification for a harsh and unfavourable conclusion respecting the historic and linguistic acquirements of German musicians. D. not only identifies the theoretical system of the Greeks with that of the present day, but also their practice of the art of music. It is scarcely conceivable, after the appearance of Böckh's Pindar-edition, that his fantastic works could have obtained any credit. It was only by the writings of Bellermann that an end was put to that credit. D. wrote, after he had first expounded his views in 1817, in the Leipzig *Allgemeine Musikalische Zeitung,* " Die mathematische Intervallenlehre der Griechen " (1818) ; " Aufschlüsse über die Musik der Griechen " (1819), " Die praktische Musik der Griechen " (1821), " Die pneumatischen Erfindungen der Griechen " (1822), " Wörterbuch der griechischen Musik " (1835), " Die griechische Musik, auf ihre Grundsätze zurückgeführt " (1841), "Die Kunst der musikalischen Komposition . . . nach griechischen Grundsätzen bearbeitet " (1858). D. also wrote several operas, of which one (not, however,

produced) is said to have been composed on Greek principles.

Drobisch, (1) M o r i t z W i l h e l m, b. Aug. 16, 1802, Leipzig; from 1826, professor in ordinary of mathematics, and from 1842, of philosophy, in that city. In addition to many purely mathematical and philosophical works of great merit, he issued many clever treatises on the mathematical determination of pitch-relationships—for the most part reports of the class of mathematics and physics of the Royal Saxon " Gesellschaft der Wissenschaften ; " but they have also been issued separately. They are as follows: " Über die mathematische Bestimmung der musikalischen Intervalle " (1846), " Über musikalische Tonbestimmung und Temperatur " (1852), " Nachträge zur Theorie der musikalischen Tonverhältnisse " (1855), " Über ein zwischen Altem und Neuem vermittelndes Tonsystem " (*Allgemeine Musikal. Zeitung,* 1871), "Über reine Stimmung und Temperatur der Töne " (1877). D., formerly the principal champion of the twelve-half-tones system, has, in the last-named pamphlet, adopted the views of Helmholtz. His works are of great value.— (2) K a r l L u d w i g, brother of the former, b. Dec. 24, 1803, Leipzig, pupil of Dröbs and Weinlig, settled in 1826 as teacher of music at Munich, and in 1837 became capellmeister of the evangelical church at Augsburg, where he d. Aug. 20, 1854. D. wrote a large number of sacred works (many masses, three requiems, graduals, etc.), also the oratorios *Bonifacius, Des Heilands letzte Stunden,* and *Moses auf Sinai.* His son, Theodor, b. 1838, Augsburg, is also an able musician—since 1867 musical director at Minden.

Droite (Fr.), right (hand).

Drones, the two or three pipes of the bagpipes which furnish the fixed and unvarying accompaniment to the melody of the *chanter,* the third or fourth pipe. A drone bass is often found in orchestral and other instrumental works. (*See* BAGPIPE.)

Drouet, L o u i s, eminent flautist, b. 1792, Amsterdam, d. Sept. 30, 1873, Berne, pupil of the Paris Conservatoire, was, in 1808, solo flautist to the king of Holland (Ludwig Bonaparte), in 1811, in a similar post, at the court of Napoleon I., and, in 1814, first flautist in the court band of Louis XVIII. He came in 1815 to London, where he set up a flute manufactory (which, however, only lasted until 1819), then travelled as a concert-player through Europe with great success, and in 1836 was appointed court capellmeister at Coburg. He went in 1854 to New York, and lived after that, for a long time, at Frankfort, finally at Berne. He composed much for the flute (ten concertos, fantasias, ensemble sonatas, etc.).

Druckwerk (Ger. " pressure action ") is the action of an organ, or of one of its keyboards, when the keys act on the rest of the mechanism by means of stickers. (*Cf.* DRAW-ACTION.)

Drum (Ital. *Tamburo, Cassa;* Fr. *Tambour, Caisse*), the well-known instrument of percussion, consisting of a cylinder of wood or brass, over both open ends of which is stretched calf-skin, kept firm by means of wooden hoops. The hoops are connected by a cord stretched in zigzag fashion, and by tightening this by means of braces—each of which passes over two pieces of the cord—the tone of the drum can be made clearer. One of the skins of the D. is struck with sticks (drum-sticks; for the big drum a mallet covered with leather is used); over the other skin a cat-gut chord is tightly drawn. If the one membrane is set in vibration, the other vibrates sympathetically, and, by coming into repeated contact with the cat-gut chord, produces a grating effect. Without this chord (snares) the tone is short and dull. The D. is not tuned, and, like the other instruments of percussion, with exception of the kettle-drum, only marks the rhythm. The roll of the drum is indicated, as in the kettle-drum, by a shake or *tremolo* sign :

The different kinds of drums are : (1) bass-drum (*Grosse Trommel, Gran tamburo, Grosse Caisse*) generally combined with the cymbals ; (2) the long side-drum (*Caisse roulante*), smaller than the former, but not so big as the (3) military drum, of which the tone is clear and penetrating. As compared with former times, the cylinders of drums are much shortened, especially in the military drum.

Drum-bass, a nickname for the continued repetition of one note in quick succession in the bass.

Dryden, J o h n, English poet, b. Aug. 9, 1631, Northampton, d. May 1, 1700. He wrote the famous Cecilian Ode, which Purcell, Handel, and other composers set to music. He was also writer of the libretti of several of Purcell's operas.

D sharp (Ger. *Dis*), D raised by a sharp. D *sharp major chord* $=d\sharp, f\times, a\sharp$; D *sharp minor chord* $=d\sharp, f\sharp, a\sharp$. D *sharp minor* key, with signature of six sharps. (*See* KEY.).

Dualism, harmonic. (*See* HARMONY and MINOR KEY.)

Dubois, François Clément Théodore, b. Aug. 24, 1837, Rosnay (Marne), received his first instruction at Rheims, was then a pupil of the Paris Conservatoire, especially of Marmontel (pianoforte), Bazin (harmony), Benoist (organ), and A. Thomas (fugue and composition). In 1861 he obtained the *Grand Prix de*

Rome, became, after his return from Italy, first, maître de chapelle of Ste. Clotilde, then of the Madeleine. In 1871 he was appointed professor of harmony at the Conservatoire. D. is also a member of the Committee of Tuition for the classes for composition and organ-playing, as well as deputy member of the *Prix de Rome* commission. As a composer he is highly esteemed, and has produced orchestral and choral works; he has also attempted operas, and not without success. The following oratorios well deserve mention : *Les Sept Paroles du Christ* and *Paradis Perdu* (the latter gained the prize in 1878 offered by the city of Paris); the lyric scena *L'Enlèvement de Proserpine;* the comic operas *La Guzla de l'émir* and *Le pain bis* (also entitled *La Lilloise*); the grand opera *Aben Hamet* (1884), the ballet *La Farandole* (1883), several orchestral suites, a pf. concerto, a symphonic overture (*Frithjof*), also many motets, masses, pf. pieces, songs, etc.

Ducange (du Cange), C h a r l e s D u s f r e s n e S i e u r, b. Dec. 18, 1610, Amiens, d. Oct. 23, 1688, Paris. He published in 1678 "Glossarium ad scriptores mediæ et infirmæ latinitatis" (3 vols.), republished by the Benedictine monks of St. Maux, 1733-36 (6 vols.), and, more recently, 1840-50 (7 vols.), which, for the musical antiquarian, contains very valuable explanations of musical instruments and musical terms of the Middle Ages.

Ducis, B e n e d i c t, Netherland contrapuntist of the 15-16th centuries, pupil of Josquin, for whose death he composed a funeral ode ; probably b. about 1480, Bruges. About 1510 he was superintendent of the guild of musicians at Antwerp, and organist of the Notre-Dame Church there. In 1515 he is said to have paid a visit to England, but on that matter there is no authentic information. It appears, rather, that he lived later on in Germany, for in 1539 he published at Ulm "Harmonien über alle Oden des Horaz für drei und vier Stimmen, der Ulmer Jugend zu Gefallen in Druck gegeben," and various German publications contain motets, psalms, songs, etc., of his; but, unfortunately, the custom of that time was for the composer to sign only with his Christian name, which frequently renders it impossible to distinguish his compositions from those of Benedictus Appenzelder (q.v.).

Ducrocquet, organ-builder. (*See* DAUBLAINE.)

Ductus (Lat.), melodic movement, or order of successive notes, which may be : (1) *rectus,* direct—*i.e.* ascending; (2) *reversus* or *revertens,* reversed—*i.e.* descending ; or (3) *circumcurrens,* circumcurrent—*i.e.* ascending and descending.

Due (Ital.), two ; *a due,* for two. In orchestral scores this term indicates that two instruments written on the same stave (for example, the two flutes, oboes, clarinets, etc.) have to play the same notes; in that case, it is superfluous to write the notes with double stems.

Due corde (Ital.), two strings.

Duet (Ital. *Duetto*, diminutive form for *Duo*) is, especially at the present day, a vocal composition for two voices of the same, or different kind, with accompaniment of one or several instruments. The D. occupies an important place in opera (*dramatic D.*), but without any definite form, as its development differs according to the situation. It consists of speech and rejoinder, sections of aria-like form for one or the other, or both voices; or it appears as a real double song, interrupted by recitative, etc. The *church* D. has a more definite form: it is either in *aria* form, and has a *Da capo*, or is in concertante style with fugal working. Duets of the latter kind are to be found, for instance, in Viadana's church concertos. For duets without bass (or continuo), one must hark back to the *Bicinia* of the 16th century. The so-called *chamber* D. attained to great importance towards the close of the 17th century, and in the second half of the last century, through Agostino Steffani and G. C. M. Clari; in form it does not differ from the *church D.* Of the latter kind Pergolesi's *Stabat Mater* offers a famous example. Duets like those of Mendelssohn are in song form. Modern composers, contrary to good taste, have frequently written songs which, from the sense of the words, are only suitable to one voice (male or female), as duets for soprano and tenor, etc. An instrumental composition for two different obbligato instruments, with, or without accompaniment, is generally named—not *duet*, but *duo* or *concerto* (chamber-concerto), *sonata*, etc., and only *duet* when written for two instruments of the same kind (violin duet, flute duet); but for two pianofortes the term *duo*, not *duet*, is employed. It would be more exact to make the difference one of extent—*duo* for works of large, *duet* for works of small compass.

Due volte (Ital.), twice.

Dufay, Guillaume (Du Fay). According to the most recent investigations of Fr. X. Haberl, Van der Straeten, and Jules Houdoy in the archives at Rome and Cambrai, the period at which this old French master lived has been fixed. It was not from 1380–1432 (as Baini, through a misunderstanding, supposed), but from 1400 to 1474; so that he can no longer be accounted the earliest, but was the latest of the three old masters, Dunstable, Binchois, and Dufay. Thus all contradictions, which hitherto have so puzzled learned heads, are explained. (*See* the "Vierteljahrsschrift f. Mus. Wiss., 1885, 4th book.) D. entered the Pope's Chapel as youngest singer in 1428; in 1437 he went to the court of Philippe le Bon, Duke of Burgundy, took holy orders in Paris, spent seven years in Savoy, and ended his life, as canon, at Cambrai on Nov. 27, 1474. In the archives at Rome, Bologna, and Triest (now at Vienna), Haberl discovered 150 compositions, of which he makes mention in

his work (among these are masses and numerous portions of masses, a magnificat, motets, etc., and some French chansons). Besides these, the following have been preserved: some masses in the Brussels Library, a mass and portions of masses at Cambrai, some motets and chansons in the Paris Library, and a motet à 4 at Munich. D. is said to have introduced white notes in place of the earlier usual black ones; anyhow, the former were adopted in the 15th century. According to the testimony of Adam von Fulda (1490), D. introduced many novelties into notation.

Duhamel, Jean Marie Constant, b. Feb. 5, 1797, St. Malo, d. April 29, 1872, Paris, professor and head of the educational board of the Polytechnique and the *École normale* at Paris. He made a name by rearranging Dom Bedos de Celles' great work on the organ, "Nouveau manuel complet du facteur d'orgues" (1849).

Duiffoprugcar (Tieffenbrucker), Caspar, the oldest known violin-maker, hence looked upon as the inventor of the violin (*cf.* for this STREICH-INSTRUMENTE and VIOLIN); he came originally from the Tyrol, and settled in Bologna (1510). According to Wasielewski ("Die Violine im 17. Jahrhundert") there exist some genuine D. violins of the years 1511 to 1519, and Fétis names one of 1539. François I. of France drew him to Paris in 1515, and he afterwards settled in Lyons, where he died.—A certain Magno Duiffopruckhar was instrument-maker at Venice about 1607.

Dulcan, Dulcian. (*See* DOLCAN, DOLCIAN.)

Dulcimer (Ger. *Hackbrett*, cimbal; Ital. *Cembalo;* Fr. *Tympanon*), an old stringed instrument, apparently of German origin, as it was called for a time in Italy by the name *Salterio tedesco;* this shows, at the same time, that the Psalterium of the early Middle Ages (*Saltirsanch, Rotta*) was probably played in the same way as the D. Virdung and M. Agricola (q.v.) already at the beginning of the 16th century, make mention of the instrument under its present name, and, indeed, ascribe as little importance to it as did Prætorius a hundred years later. The D., a flat, trapezium-shaped soundboard on which steel strings are set, which are struck with two little hammers (one for each hand), was the precursor of the present pianoforte (q.v.). The D. (cimbalon, *cf.* CYMBAL) is now only to be met with in gipsy bands. The Pantaleon (q.v.) of Hebenstreit was an attempt to improve the D. The insufficient muffling of the sound is the chief fault of the instrument. The sound is always confused and noisy, but in *forte* (in the orchestra) is of excellent effect.

Dulcken, Luise, *née* David, pianist, b. Mar. 20, 1811, Hamburg, d. April 12, 1850, London, sister of Ferdinand David, pupil of Grund. She came with her husband in 1828 to London, where she attracted extraordinary notice as a concert-player and teacher, and among her pupils was Queen Victoria.

Dulon, Friedrich Ludwig, blind flautist, b. Aug. 14, 1769, Oranienburg, d. July 7, 1826, Würzburg, made important concert tours, held an appointment, from 1796 to 1800, at the court, Petersburg; he lived then in Stendal, and, finally (from 1823), in Würzburg. D. became blind shortly after his birth. Chr. M. Wieland published his autobiography written at Stendal ("Dulons des blinden Flötenspielers Leben und Meinungen, von ihm selbst bearbeitet," 1804–8, 2 vols.). D. published nine duets and variations for flute and violin, a flute concerto, flute duets, and caprices for the flute.

Duni, Egidio Romoaldo, b. Feb. 9, 1709, Matera (Naples), d. June 11, 1775, Paris, pupil of Durante, and a prolific opera composer. He wrote first for Rome, *Nerone*, with which he beat Pergolesi's *Olimpiade* off the field.; and, besides, operas for Naples, Venice, London; and received a post at the Parma court. As this court was entirely French, D. commenced to write French operas, and was induced, in 1757, to go to Paris, where he produced a stately series of operettas with great success; so that he may be regarded as the real founder of Opéra Comique.

Dunoyer. (*See* GAUCQUIER.)

Dunstable (Dunstaple), John, distinguished English contrapuntist of the first half of the 15th century. According to the testimony of Tinctor, he was one of the fathers of real counterpoint, and an early contemporary of Binchois and Dufay. D. died Dec. 24, 1453, and was buried at St. Stephen's, Walbrook. A chanson à 3 (discovered by Danjou in 1847) is in the Vatican Library: there is another copy at Dijon. A riddle-canon, which has not yet been deciphered, exists in two copies: one in the British Museum, and another in Lambeth Palace; the British Museum has, besides, a long composition, à 3, without words; the *Liceo filarmonico* at Bologna, "Patrem," "Regina cœli lætare," "Sub tua protectione," and "Quam pulchra es"; the University Library of Bologna, 2 Et in terra à 3, 1 Ave maris stella à 2; and many compositions sacred and secular, formerly at Trient, are now transferred to Vienna.

Dunstede. (*See* TUNSTEDE.)

Duo is the term specially used for two (different) obbligato instruments with, or without accompaniment. As a rule, a D. is treated in a polyphonic style, so that both parts are concertante. There are, however, some pieces to which the name D. is given, in which the one part dominates, and the other merely accompanies. Compositions for two voices with accompaniment, also compositions for two instruments of the same kind, are called, not *duos* but *duets* (q.v.). It would be more correct to distinguish between these two terms according to the length of the piece, for *duet* really means a little D.

Duodecima (*duodecima sc. vox*), the twelfth degree of the scale, which also bears the same name as the fifth. (*See* INTERVAL.)

Duodrama, a stage-piece (with or without music) for no more than two persons.

Duole, a figure of two notes, taking the place of, and having the same value as, one of three notes:

Duolo (Ital.), grief.

Dupla (*proportio dupla*), a term in mensural music to indicate the doubling of the *tempo*, the sign for which was $\frac{2}{1}$ or (|), ¢, etc. (*Cf.* DIMINUTION.)

Dupont, (1) Pierre, b. April 23, 1821, Lyons, d. there July 24, 1870, a poet and a favourite composer of romances; he lived for many years at Paris, but, owing to his socialistic-political songs, was banished by Napoleon III. to Lambessa in 1852. Of music he was quite ignorant. —(2) Joseph (the elder), b. Aug. 21, 1821, Liége, d. Feb. 13, 1861, as professor of the violin at the Conservatoire there, an able violinist, pupil of Wanson and Prume at the Liége Conservatoire. He wrote two operas (*Ribeiro Pinto* and *L'île d'or*), also violin, vocal, and ensemble pieces; but of these few were published. His brother (3) Alexander, b. 1833, Liége, d. there April 4, 1888, wrote a "Répertoire dramatique Belge."—(4) Auguste, b. Feb. 9, 1828, Ensival (near Liége), d. Dec. 17, 1890, Brussels, distinguished pianist; he attended the Liége Conservatoire in 1838, where Jalheau (pupil of Herz and Kalkbrenner) was his teacher; afterwards he travelled for several years in England and Germany, until he was appointed, in 1850, professor of the pianoforte at the Brussels Conservatoire. D. was a prolific composer for his instrument, and wrote concertos, studies, fantasias, etc., also some ensemble works.—(5) Joseph (the younger), brother of the former, b. Jan. 3, 1838, Ensival, eminent teacher and conductor, was trained at the Liége and Brussels Conservatoires, received at the latter the *Grand Prix de Rome*, and, at the conclusion of the four years' stipend, became (1867) conductor at Warsaw, and, in 1871, at the Imperial Theatre at Moscow. Already in 1872 he was called back to Brussels as professor of harmony at the Conservatoire, became conductor of the Théâtre de la Monnaie, and of the Society of Musicians; and to these functions he was soon added that of conductor of the Popular Concerts, as successor to Vieuxtemps. A third brother (6) Joseph D., d. June 26, 1867, The Hague, was, finally, director of the German Opera at Amsterdam.—(7) J. Franz, b. 1822, Rotterdam,

d. March 21, 1875, Nuremberg, pupil of Mendelssohn and David, was from 1858–74 theatre capellmeister at Nuremberg (opera, *Bianca Siffredi*).

Duport, two brothers, celebrated 'cellists:— (1) J e a n P i e r r e, b. Nov. 27, 1741, Paris, d. Dec. 31, 1818, Berlin, where he was appointed principal 'cello in the court band (1773), afterwards director of the court concerts; he was pensioned in 1811.—(2) J e a n L o u i s, the more eminent of the two, b. Oct. 4, 1749, Paris, d. there Sept. 7, 1819. He made his *début* at the *Concerts Spirituels* in 1768, and, on the breaking out of the French Revolution, went to his brother at Berlin, but returned to Paris in 1806, and received a post in the service of the ex-King of Spain (Charles IV.) at Marseilles, and in 1812 also one from the Empress Marie Louise; he finally became solo 'cellist in the royal band, and teacher at the Conservatoire. He indeed lost the latter post in 1815, through the suppression of the Conservatoire, but remained solo 'cellist in the royal band. His 'cello (Stradivari) was purchased by Franchomme for the sum of 25,000 frs. D. wrote sonatas, variations, duets, fantasias, etc., for 'cello, also a Method, " Essai sur le doigté du violoncelle et la conduite de l'archet, etc."

Duprato, J u l e s L a u r e n t, b. Aug. 20, 1827, Nîmes, d. 1892, pupil of Leborne at the Paris Conservatoire, gained in 1848 the *Prix de Rome*. He composed songs, cantatas, and operettas; but for an energetic development of his talent, he met with too little encouragement, and too few offers of assistance, from the directors. In 1866 he was appointed assistant teacher, and, in 1871, professor of harmony at the Conservatoire.

Duprez, G i l b e r t L o u i s, b. Dec. 6, 1806, Paris, d. Sept. 22, 1896, a highly-distinguished singer; already as a boy he had a fine voice, for which reason Choron (q.v.) placed him in his musical institute. During the period of mutation D. studied diligently at theory and composition, and as soon as he was in possession of a fine tenor voice he continued his vocal studies. He made his *début* in 1825 at the Odéon Théâtre; but his fame only dates from 1836, when, after studying for several years in Italy, he received an engagement as principal tenor, as successor to Adolphe Nourrit, at the Paris Grand Opéra. From 1842–50 he was likewise professor of singing at the Conservatoire, but retired from that post, and founded a vocal academy of his own which gained great prosperity. In 1855 he retired from the stage, and now appeared, on a large scale, as a composer, but with little success (operas, mass, a requiem, an oratorio, songs). His vocal Methods—" L'art du chant " (1845, German 1846), and " La mélodie, études complémentaires, etc."—enjoy a great, and well-deserved reputation. His wife, *née* D u p e r r o n, was a highly-esteemed vocalist; his daughter, C a r o l i n e (b. 1832, Florence, d. April 17, 1875),

also became, under his training, an excellent vocalist. From 1850 to 1858 she distinguished herself on Paris stages (Théâtre Lyrique, Opéra Comique, Opéra), but had to give up the stage in 1859, and withdrew with her husband, Vandenheuvel (whom she married in 1856), to Pau.

Dupuy. (*See* PUTEANUS.)

Dur (Ger.). (*See* MAJOR.)

Duramente (Ital.), in a harsh manner.

Durand, (1) A u g u s t e F r é d é r i c (really Duranowski), violinist, b. 1770, Warsaw, where his father was court musician. He was sent in 1787, by a Polish nobleman, to Paris, to Viotti, in order to perfect himself in violin-playing. After making concert tours for several years as a violinist, he entered the French army as an officer; but, after a time, was forced to leave the service, and reappeared as a violin virtuoso. Finally he settled in Strassburg as conductor and teacher, where he was still living in 1834.— (2) É m i l e, b. Feb. 16, 1830, St. Brieuc (Côtes du Nord), studied at the Paris Conservatoire, and, whilst still (1850) a pupil for composition, was appointed teacher of an elementary singing-class, and in 1871 became professor of harmony. D. has written songs, and some operettas, also a Method of harmony and accompaniment.—(3) M a r i e A u g u s t e, b. July 18, 1830, Paris, pupil of Benoist for the organ, from 1849 successively organist of St. Ambroise, Ste. Geneviève, St. Roch, and St. Vincent de Paul (1862 to 1874), was also active as a musical critic, became a partner of Schönewerk in 1870, and bought the music-publishing business from Flaxland. The name of the firm (" D. et Schönewerk," now " D. et fils ") is also well known in Germany and England, for it has brought out a large number of the best French novelties (Massenet, Saint-Saëns, L+lo, Widor, Joncières, etc.). D. himself has composed and published many works (masses, songs, dance pieces in old style, etc., pieces for harmonium—his favourite instrument, and one in the making known of which he has taken an active part).

Durante, F r a n c e s c o, b. March 15, 1684, Fratta Maggiore (Naples), d. there Aug. 13, 1755. He was at first a pupil of Gaetano Greco at the Conservatorio dei Poveri di Gesù Christo, and when this institution was abolished, continued his studies under Alessandro Scarlatti at the Conservatorio Sant' Onofrio. Besides receiving instruction from these masters, D. diligently studied the works of the Roman School. In 1718 he became director of Sant' Onofrio, which post he exchanged for that at Santa Maria di Loreto, rendered vacant by the departure of Porpora for London in 1742. D. ranks among the most important representatives of the so-called Neapolitan School; but how greatly he was influenced by the Roman School is seen from the fact that he wrote almost exclusively sacred music; whilst Scarlatti, Leo, and the later composers (Jomelli, Piccini, etc.), all wrote for the stage. His style happily combines Neapolitan melodiousness with solid Roman counterpoint. The Paris Conservatoire possesses an almost complete collection of his works (thirteen masses, and portions of masses, sixteen psalms, sixteen motets, some antiphons, hymns, etc., also twelve madrigals, six clavier sonatas, etc.). Some other works ("Lamentations") are to be found in the Vienna Library. Nothing appears to have been printed during his lifetime, and recent publications (collections of Commer, Rochlitz, etc.) contain only a few specimens of his compositions.

Durchführung (Ger.), working out, development of a subject or subjects.

Durchkomponirt (Ger., "through-composed"), a term applied to a song, when the different strophes of the poem have each their own melody, and are not, as in the volk-song and simple art-song, sung to one and the same melody. The D. song can, naturally, closely follow the contents of the various stanzas, whereas the strophe-song can only express the mood in a general way.

Durezza (Ital.), hardness.

Duro (Ital.), hard, harsh.

Dürrner, Ruprecht Johannes Jul., favourite composer of songs for male voices, b. July 15, 1810, Ansbach, d. June 10, 1859, Edinburgh, attended the National Seminary at Altdorf, and studied under Fr. Schneider at Dessau. From 1831 to 1842 he was cantor at Ansbach, but still received further training at Leipzig under Mendelssohn and Hauptmann, and was then, from 1844 until his death, active as a teacher of singing and musical director in Edinburgh. D. composed some quartets for mixed, and male voices.

Durutte, François Camille Antoine Comte, b. Oct. 15, 1803, Yprès (East Flanders), d. Sept 24, 1881, Paris. He was originally intended for an engineer, but gave himself up to music, and settled in Metz. He was much talked about in France as the author of a new system of theory, which he first expounded in his "Esthétique musicale: Technie ou Lois générales du système harmonique" (1855). He afterwards completed the same in his "Résumé élémentaire de la Technie harmonique et complément, etc." (1876). For practical purposes, however, his system is unproductive, and, in its mathematical speculations, erroneous. D. wrote several operas, and sacred and chamber-music.

Dussek, (1) Franz, b. Dec. 8, 1736, Czotinbor (Bohemia), d. Feb. 12, 1799, Prague, pupil of Habermann, a refined pianist and an able pianoforte teacher, also a composer (pf. sonatas for four hands, and chamber music, symphonies, concertos, etc.).—(2) Johann Ladislaus, distinguished pianist and composer, b.

Feb. 9, 1761, Tschaslau (Bohemia), d. March 20, 1812, St. Germain-en-Laye, near Paris. He studied the dead languages at the Jesuit College at Iglau, and then, theology at Prague, where he took his bachelor's degree. At the same time, however, he had so trained himself in music that his patron (Count Männer) procured for him an organist's post at Mechlin; and from there he went, in a similar capacity, to Bergen-op-Zoom, and in 1782, to Amsterdam. Later on he became tutor to the sons of the "Statthalter" at The Hague. He paid a visit to Ph. E. Bach at Hamburg, was kindly received, and found his confidence in his own powers strengthened. Soon afterwards he went to Berlin and Petersburg as performer on the pianoforte and harmonica, and afterwards spent two years with Count Radziwill in Lithuania. In 1786 he played at Paris before Marie Antoinette, went to Italy, returned to Paris, was driven by the Revolution to London, where, with his father-in-law, Corri, he founded, in 1792, a music-publishing house; the business, however, failed, and plunged him into debt, so that in 1800 he was compelled to go to Hamburg. There he became enamoured of a lady of title, and lived with her for two years on an estate near the Danish frontier. In 1802 he visited his old father in Bohemia, attached himself to Prince Louis Ferdinand of Prussia, and, after the death of the latter, to the Prince of Isenburg; and at last, in 1808, entered the service of Prince Talleyrand at Paris. D. was one of the first, if not the first, to make the pianoforte "sing." His tone was rich and full, and with this new style of playing he produced great effect. His pianoforte compositions have life in them still, and are distinguished by their noble, pleasant character; they are numerous (twelve concertos, one double-concerto, eighty violin sonatas, fifty-three piano sonatas for two, and nine for four hands, ten trios, a pf. quartet and pf. quintet, and many small pieces). He also wrote a Pianoforte Method, which appeared in English, German, and French editions.

Dustmann, Marie Luise, *née* Meyer, famous stage singer (dramatic soprano parts), b. Aug. 22, 1831, Aix-la-Chapelle, daughter of a singer. She made her *début* in 1849 at Breslau, and was then engaged at Cassel (under Spohr), Dresden (1853), Prague (1854), and, from 1857, at Vienna, and appeared as a "star" on all important German stages, and also at London and Stockholm. In 1858 she married the bookseller, D. In 1860 she was appointed "Kammersängerin."

Duval, Edmond, b. Aug. 22, 1809, Enghien (Hainault), pupil of the Paris Conservatoire, from which, however, he was dismissed on account of his irregular work. He returned to his native town, and earnestly devoted himself to Catholic Church song, moved thereto by the "Vrais principes du chant grégorien" of the Abbé Janssen. In consequence of this interest the Bishop of

Mechlin gave him the commission to revise the church ritual of the diocese, and to re-edit it on the basis of his historical investigations. He travelled for this purpose to Rome, and, on his return, "Graduale" (1848), "Vesperale" (1848), "Processionale" (1851), "Rituale" (1854), etc., were brought out, based on some publications of the 15th–17th centuries, for the Mechlin diocese. In addition, there appeared studies on these various song-books, also a treatise on the organ accompaniment of Gregorian song, etc. These publications were all violently attacked by connoisseurs, who declare that Duval's works are not improvements, but, in part, grievous misconceptions (Fétis).

Duvernoy (Duvernois), (1) F r é d é r i c, b. Oct. 16, 1765, Montbéliard, d. July 19, 1838, Paris; he was principal horn-player at the Grand Opéra, and, until the temporary suspension of the Conservatoire (1815), also professor of the horn at that institution. He wrote many horn concertos, and chamber pieces with horn.—(2) C h a r l e s, brother of the former, b. 1766, Montbéliard, d. Feb. 28, 1845, was a clarinettist and a member of the orchestras of the "Théâtre de Monsieur" and "Feydeau" at Paris, professor of the clarinet at the Conservatoire (pensioned in 1802); he wrote clarinet sonatas.—(3) H e n r i Louis Charles, son of Charles D., b. Nov. 16, 1820, Paris, pupil of Zimmermann and Halévy at the Conservatoire; from 1838 he was assistant, and from 1848, titular professor of singing there. He published several instructive vocal works, and some light pf. music.—(4) C h a r l e s F r a nçois, b. April 16, 1796, Paris, d. Nov., 1872, was for a long time opera-singer at Toulouse, Havre, at The Hague, and also at Paris at the Opéra Comique (made his *début* in 1830, and appeared again in 1843), of which he was also, for some time, *régisseur*. In 1851 he became teacher of operatic singing at the Conservatoire, and in 1856, superintendent of the *Pensionnat des élèves du chant*.—(5) V i c t o r Alphonse, b. Aug. 30, 1842, Paris, pupil of Marmontel and Bazin at the Conservatoire, an able pianist and gifted composer; in 1869 he founded regular chamber-music *soirées*, with Léonard as first violinist.

Dux (Lat., "leader") is the subject in a fugue (q.v.), as it is given out at first by the part (or voice) which commences the fugue.

Duysen, J e s L e w e, b. Aug. 1, 1820, Flensburg, founded in 1860, at Berlin, a pianoforte manufactory, which enjoys distinguished fame, and carries on an important trade.

Dvořák, A n t o n, b. Sept. 8, 1841, Mühlhausen (Nehalozeves), near Kralup, Bohemia, son of an innkeeper. He was to have been a butcher, but preferred playing the violin with his schoolmaster, and, in 1857, wandered away to Prague in search of sound musical training, and there entered the school for organ-playing (under Pitzsch). He supported himself with difficulty by playing the violin in a small band. In 1862 he was appointed viola-player at the "National Theatre," and in 1873 he succeeded in having a hymn for male chorus and orchestra performed; the success was a brilliant one, and D. left his post in the orchestra, for he now received a stipend, for several years, from the state. He soon made a name for himself, even beyond Bohemia, and, in this matter, the patronage of Liszt was of great service to him. D. was a national composer, and produced effects by means of Bohemian rhythms and melodies, which often border on the commonplace, and even the vulgar. We name "Slavische Tänze" for pf., four hands, and for orch. (four books); "Slavische Rhapsodien" for orch.; "Legenden" for pf., four hands, arranged also for orch.; a Serenade for wind instruments with 'cello and double-bass (Op. 44); "Dumka" (Elegy), for pf.; "Furiante," Bohemian national dances; "Klänge aus Mähren" (duets); a pf. concerto (Op. 35); a violin concerto (Op. 53); Mazurek for violin and orch. (Op. 49); Trio (Op. 65, F minor); Notturno for strings (Op. 40); Scherzo capriccioso for orch. (Op. 66); overtures, "Mein Heim" (Op. 62) and "Husitská"; four symphonies (D, Op. 60, 1882; D minor, Op. 70, 1885; F, Op. 76, 1888; and G, 1890); an oratorio, *Saint Ludmila* (for the Leeds Musical Festival of 1886); and a cantata, *The Spectre's Bride* (for the Birmingham Musical Festival of 1885). His *Stabat Mater* was first heard at London in 1883. He also wrote the 149th Psalm (chorus and orch.), symphonic variations for orch. (Ops. 40 and 78), four stringed quartets, a stringed sextet (Op. 48), a stringed trio (two violins and viola, Op. 74), a stringed quintet, a pf. quintet, pf. quartet, two trios, violin sonata (Op. 57), etc., and the Czeckish operas: *Der König und der Köhler* (Prague, 1874), *Wanda* (1876), *Selma Se lák* (1878), *Twrdé Palice* (1881), and *Dimitry* (1882). D. also wrote many vocal pieces (songs, duets, part-songs, etc.). His "Requiem" (soli, chorus, and orch.) was produced at the Birmingham Festival of 1891. The degree of Mus.Doc. was conferred on him by the University of Cambridge in the same year. D. was for some time principal of the National Conservatoire at New York. He died May 1, 1904, at Prague.

Dwight, J o h n S u l l i v a n, b. May 13, 1813, Boston, received his scientific training at Harvard College there, and at the Training School, Cambridge; in 1840 he was ordained pastor of a Unitarian chapel in Northampton (Massachusetts), but gave up that sacred post, and devoted himself entirely to literary work. In 1852 he set up a musical paper, *Dwight's Journal of Music*, which is not only the oldest and best American musical newspaper, but, amongst other things, has also issued historical essays from the pen of Thayer. (*Cf.* HARVARD ASSOCIATION.) Died Sept., 1893, Boston.

Dyck. (*See* VAN DYCK.)

Dynamics, originally the science of powers, and motions originated by them ; in music, D. refers to the gradations of sound. The different intensity of sound is one of the chief means of producing effect in musical art ; it occurs either as alternate *forte* and *piano,* by way of contrast, or as a gradual increase and decrease (*crescendo* and *decrescendo*). D. of various kinds have elementary power from which there is no escape. The effect of the *fortissimo* is one of strength, massiveness, dignity ; it exalts, or (if the esthetic impression is prejudicially influenced by other factors) ħ

oppresses, causes anxiety, terrifies. On the other hand, the *pianissimo* resembles a glance at nature through a microscope, in which life in its manifold art-forms is presented in the smallest dimensions. *Pianissimo* is an emblem of everything which is apt to escape the notice of man ; *pianissimo* is therefore the essence of spectral music, and only, when the illusion is assured, can *forte* effects be summoned to its aid. *Forte,* like major, is an image of day ; *piano,* like minor, an image of night ; the foundation-tone of all nocturnes is *piano*

E.

E, letter name of the fifth note of our musical alphabet (q.v.). (For its solmisation names *see* MUTATION.) In Italy and France the note is now called *mi.*

e (Ital.), before vowels *ed,* "and " ; *è* (Ital.), " is."

Ear. The human ear, like that of the higher animals, is an extremely complicated piece of mechanism. The outer bell, the concha, together with the auditory canal, ends with the drum or tympanum—a stiffly stretched membrane which shuts in the drum or tympanic cavity. In this lie the three small bones, the first of which, the hammer (*malleus*), holds the drum drawn inwards after the manner of a navel ; the second, the anvil (*incus*) is fastened by means of a joint to the hammer, and, likewise, the stirrup-bone to the anvil. This stirrup-bone, bordered by a thin membrane on the side lying opposite to the drum of the tympanic cavity, closes an opening (the oval window, vestibule window, *fenestra vestibuli*) in the direction of the inner ear —the labyrinth. The whole labyrinth, filled with water, consists of a belly-shaped cavity (vestibule), three arched or semicircular canals with bottle-shaped prolongations, and the *cochlea,* the name of which indicates its shape. In the vestibule, partly floating, partly attached to the osseous walls, is the membranous labyrinth, which, on a smaller scale, imitates the form of the osseous labyrinth. Again, the innermost ear (the cochlea) is divided into two passages by a partition-wall, the first of which (the *scala vestibuli*) opens into the vestibule, and, at the apex of the cochlea, where the partition-wall falls away, communicates with the second (*scala tympani*), which, in its turn, quite closed in, returns to the tympanic cavity, whence it is separated by a delicate membrane—the oval window (*fenestra cochleæ*). If the tympanum be thrown into vibration by sound-waves, the first of the small bones connected by joints is set in motion, and by these the impulse—the stirrup-bone pressing down deeper against the round window—is communicated to the labyrinth water, which can only yield at one place—viz., by means of the membrane of

the round window, *i.e.* after the movement has traversed the whole of the inner ear. The air in the tympanic cavity, by the pressure on it of the oval window, passes down the Eustachian tube (*tuba Eustachii*), a small trumpet-shaped passage which opens into the cavity of the jaws, and thus the tympanum is not set in motion again by it. The auditory nerve (*acusticus*) passes through the apex of the cochlea into the ear, and sends out innumerable offshoots into the wall dividing the *scala tympani* from the *scala vestibuli,* as well as into the membranous labyrinth. Respecting the further transformation of sound-movement into tone-perception only conjectures are possible. For further details consult Helmholtz, "Lehre von den Tonempfindungen" (4th ed., pp. 225f and 649f. ; Eng. translation by A. J. Ellis). From the brief description of the ear just given it may be seen how easily the function of hearing may be interfered with without the nerve being affected.

Eastcott, Richard, Anglican clergyman, d. end of 1828, as chaplain at Livery Dale, Devonshire ; he published "Sketches of the Origin, Progress, and Effects of Music, with an Account of the Ancient Bards and Minstrels " (1793).

Ebeling, (1) Johann Georg, born 1637, Lüneberg, d. 1676, Stettin. In 1662 he became musical director at the principal Church, and teacher at St. Nicolas, Berlin ; and in 1668, professor at the Gymnasium Carolinum, Stettin. His chief work, "Pauli Gerhardi geistliche Andachten, bestehend in 120 Liedern auf alle Sonntage, etc." (à 4, with two violins and bass), appeared first (in folio) in two parts at Berlin (1666–67) in clavier score, 1669 ; then (in octavo), at Nuremberg, in 1682, with a preface by Feuerlein (preacher at the "Liebfrauenkirche " there), and this misled Fétis into the supposition that there were two persons named E., one of whom he placed at the Gymnasium Carolinum, Nuremberg, which did not exist. Of E.'s other works are known—"Archæologiæ orphicæ sive antiquitates musicæ" (1676, unimportant), and a concerto for several instruments

—(2) Christoph Daniel, b. 1741, Garmissen, near Hildesheim, d. June 30, 1817; he studied theology at Göttingen, also *belles-lettres*, was in 1769 teacher at the "Handelsakademie," Hamburg, translated Burney's "Musical Tour," Chastelaux' "Sur l'Union de la Musique et de la Poésie," also, with Klopstock, Handel's *Messiah*; and, in 1784, became professor at the Hamburg Gymnasium, and town librarian. He contributed valuable biographical and historical articles to Hamburg papers, and to the Hanover *Magazin* ("Über die Oper," "Versuch einer auserlesenen musikalischen Bibliothek").

Ebell, Heinrich Karl, b. Dec. 30, 1775, Neuruppin, d. March 12, 1824, as councillor in Oppeln; he was also an able musician, and interrupted his career as jurist (1801–4) to fulfil the duties of capellmeister at Breslau. He composed ten operas and vaudevilles, also an oratorio, arias, songs, and many instrumental works.

Eberhard, Johann August, b. Aug. 31, 1739, Halberstadt, d. Jan. 6, 1809, as professor of philosophy at Halle; in addition to many works not relating to music, he wrote a "Theorie der schönen Künste" (1783, 3rd ed. 1790), "Handbuch der Aesthetik" (1803–5, 4 vols.), and some smaller treatises (in his "Gemischte Schriften," 1784–88, and in the Berlin *Musikalisches Wochenblatt*, 1805).

Eberhard von Freisingen, Benedictine monk of the 11th century, the author of two treatises on the measurement of organ pipes, and on the manufacture of bells (*Nolæ*, *see* TINTINNABULA).

Eberl, Anton, b. June 13, 1766, Vienna, d. there March 11, 1807, an able pianist and gifted composer. He was at St. Petersburg from 1796 to 1800, lived, for the rest, mostly in Vienna, whence he made many concert tours. He was on intimate terms with Mozart, and, as a boy, attracted the notice of Gluck. Besides five operas, he wrote principally instrumental works (symphonies, concertos, chamber ensembles, pf. variations, etc.). Some of his variations were originally published under Mozart's name.

Eberlin, (1) **Daniel**, b. about 1630, Nuremberg, d 1692, after a varied and adventurous life, as captain of the provincial militia in Cassel; he was, in his time, a renowned composer, but only his sonatas for three violins are known (1675).—(2) **Johann Ernst** (Eberle), b. March 27, 1702, Jettingen (Swabia), d. June 21, 1762, as capellmeister to the Archbishop of Salzburg. He was an exceedingly prolific composer, but, all the same, his works occupy an honourable position in the literature of music. Few of his pieces have been printed:—"IX Toccate e fughe per l'organo," of which one fugue, for a long time, was considered a composition of Bach's (Ed. Griepenkerl, Book 9, No. 13), some sonatas, motets, and organ pieces; and, lately,

some fugues and toccatas in Commer's "Musica sacra." Proske's library at Ratisbon contains the autographs of thirteen oratorios, the Berlin Library an offertory and miserere, and the Royal Institute for Church Music in Berlin, a volume of organ pieces.

Ebers, Karl Friedrich, b. March 25, 1770, Cassel, d., in embarrassed circumstances, Sept. 9, 1836, Berlin. He was theatre capellmeister at Schwerin, Pesth, Magdeburg, and became known by his pianoforte transcriptions. His own compositions (four operas, marches, dances, rondos, sonatas, variations, etc.) are not of importance.

Eberwein, (1) **Traugott Maximilian**, b. Oct. 27, 1775, Weimar, d. Dec. 2, 1831, as capellmeister to Prince of Rudolstadt. He was, in his time, an esteemed composer (eleven operas; sacred, orchestral, and chamber music). Of his works, however, none have shown any signs of prolonged life.—(2) His brother, **Karl**, b. Nov. 10, 1786, Weimar, d. there March 2, 1868, as chamber-virtuoso (violin), was often mentioned by Goethe in his books (music to *Faust*). Of his works the best known is the music to Holtei's *Leonore*. He wrote three operas, cantatas, a flute concerto, string quartets, etc.

Eccard, Johannes, b. 1553, Mühlhausen (Thuringia), d. 1611, Berlin; from about 1571–74 he was a pupil of Orlando Lasso at Munich, received (1578) an appointment, first from Jacob Fugger at Augsburg; and, about 1579, became vice-capellmeister (under Riccio). In 1588 he was capellmeister to the Duke of Prussia at Königsberg, and in 1608 went to Berlin as electoral capellmeister. E. is one of the most important composers of this period, and to his merits K. v. Winterfeld first called special attention in his "Der evangelische Kirchengesang, etc." Since then his chorales have again been revived by Mosewius, Teschner, Neithardt, and by the Riedel Union at Leipzig. C. published, first jointly with Joachim von Burck, "Odæ sacræ," twenty sacred songs (1574), "Crepundia sacra, christl. Liedlein mit 4 Stimmen" (two parts, 1578, 1589, 1596), the words of both by Deacon Helmbold of Mühlhausen. Also, by himself: "Neue deutsche Lieder mit 4 und 5 Stimmen," dedicated to Fugger (1578, twenty-four numbers); "Newe Lieder mit 5 und 4 Stimmen" (1589, fourteen numbers with the quodlibet "Zanni et Magnifico," which Winterfeld regards as the scene in the market-place at Venice); "Geistliche Lieder auf den Choral mit 5 Stimmen (1597, two parts, with fifty-one songs; new edition by Teschner. Stobæus published the Lieder in 1634, and added six of Eccard's, and forty-four arranged by himself). After Eccard's death, Stobæus still published "Preuss. Festlieder auf das ganze Jahr für 5–8 Stimmen" (1642; two parts, 1644), which Teschner republished, in 1858, in modern score.

(*Cf.* STOBÆUS.) In addition, E. composed many occasional songs.

Eccles, J o h n, b. about 1650, London, d. Jan., 1735. He was the pupil of his father, S a l o m o n E., who was a famous teacher of virginals and viols. He wrote music for a great number (forty-six) of dramatic pieces, among which *Don Quixote,* jointly with Purcell (1694). In 1710 he published a collection of songs, including many which he had written for the stage.— His two brothers, H e n r y and T h o m a s, were performers on the violin. The former entered the king's band at Paris. He wrote twelve solos for the violin in the style of Corelli. Thomas, whom Handel engaged in 1733, gave way to drink, and was brought very low.

Ecclesiasticus (Lat.), belonging to the church.

Échappement (Fr.), *double échappement, double action,* double escapement; an invention introduced into pianoforte mechanism by S. Erard at Paris in 1823. (*Cf.* PIANOFORTE.)

Échelle (Fr.), scale.

Echo, a sound reverberated. As sound-waves are propagated in a rectilineal manner, and are reflected from surfaces at the same angle at which they fall on them, so, under conditions which can easily be fixed mathematically, a great part of the sound rays proceeding from a sounding body (for example, from a singing, or speaking human voice) can be drawn back to the same; and thus, close to it, may be perceived the echo of the original sound. The E. is, naturally, not so strong as the original call. —In the technical terminology of musical composition, E. means the repetition of a short phrase, with diminished intensity of tone. The E. frequently appears in the upper or lower octave. In several places Beethoven produces an original effect with repetitions of an echo kind (sonatas Op. 81*a* and 90). In the orchestra, by means of varied instrumentation, the effect of an echo can be easily produced; in great organs there exists for that purpose a special manual (echo-work).

Eck, J o h a n n F r i e d r i c h, b. 1766, Mannheim, d. 1809 or 1810, Bamberg. He was the son of a horn-player of the famous band in the above-named city, which was removed to Munich in 1778. He was a distinguished violinplayer, "Hofmusikus" at Munich in 1780, leader of the band in 1788; and, finally, capellmeister at the Opera. In 1801 he married, resigned his appointment, and went to France. Six violin concertos and a concertante for two violins of his are known.—His brother F r a n z, one of his pupils, was born 1774, Mannheim, d. 1804. He was also an excellent violinplayer, and for several years member of the Munich band. On account of a love adventure, however, he was compelled to leave Munich; he went to Russia, was appointed solo-violinist in the band at Petersburg; but he became a bigot,

and melancholy, and appears to have died in a lunatic asylum at Strassburg. E. was Spohr's last teacher.

Eckelt, J o h a n n V a l e n t i n, b. about 1680, Werningshausen, near Erfurt, d. 1732. He was an organist, first, in 1696, at Wernigerode, and afterwards, in 1703, at Sondershausen. He left organ works, a Passion, and cantatas in manuscript. He published "Experimenta musicæ geometrica" (1715); "Unterricht, eine Fuge zu formieren" (1722); "Unterricht, was ein Organist wissen soll" (without year of publication).

Ecker, K a r l, b. March 13, 1813, Freiburg-i.-Br., d. there Aug. 31, 1879. He was the son of a surgeon, studied law at Freiburg and Vienna, but, contrary to his parents' wish, devoted himself to music, and studied composition under S. Sechter. In 1864 he returned to Freiburg, where he remained, a highly-esteemed composer, until his death. His quartets for male voices and songs became the most popular of his works; his orchestral compositions were only produced in his native town.

Eckert, K a r l A n t o n F l o r i a n, b. Dec. 7, 1820, Potsdam, d. Oct. 14, 1879, Berlin. He was the son of a sergeant-major, but, at an early age, found a patron in the poet F. Förster, who had him trained by good teachers (Greulich, Hubert Ries, Rungenhagen). In 1826 he excited wonder as a musical prodigy, and, already in 1830, wrote an opera, *Das Fischermädchen,* and in 1833 an oratorio, *Ruth.* High patronage enabled him to make long journeys for the purpose of study, after which, in 1851, he became accompanist at the Théâtre Italien at Paris, and, after a journey to America with Henriette Sontag, conductor at the same theatre. In 1853 he went to Vienna, where he became capellmeister, and afterwards technical director at the court Opera; but in 1860 he exchanged this post for that of capellmeister at Stuttgart, whence he was suddenly dismissed in 1867. He lived some time without employment at Baden-Baden, and, in 1869, was called to Berlin as principal "Hofcapellmeister" (in the place of Taubert and Dorn, who had been pensioned). Of his compositions (three more operas, two oratorios, sacred works, chamber music, etc.) only a few songs met with approbation.

Églogue, a pastoral.

Écossaise, a *Scottish* round dance in $\frac{3}{2}$ or $\frac{3}{4}$ time. The dance now called É. is, however, a kind of lively *contredanse* in $\frac{2}{4}$ time; the old meaning of the É. is preserved in the *Schottische* (Polka).

Eddy, C l a r e n c e H., organist, b. Jan. 30, 1851 (Greenfield, Massachusetts), pupil of Haupt in Berlin (1871), became, on his return home, organist of a church at Chicago, in 1879 of the principal church; and in 1877 director of the

"Hérshy" school of music. E. gives a series of organ concerts every year. He translated Haupt's " Kontrapunkt und Fuge " (1876), and published a collection, " The Church and Concert Organist " (1882 and 1885).

Edgcumbe, Richard, Earl of Mount-E., b. Sept. 13, 1764, London, d. there Sept. 26, 1839. He was a zealous lover of music, and in 1800 produced an opera, *Zenobia*, at the King's Theatre, and published in 1825 " Musical Reminiscences of an Amateur," chiefly respecting the Italian Opera in England for fifty years, 1773 to 1823 (4th ed. 1834), which contains many interesting anecdotes about Catalani, Grassini, Billington, and other male and female vocalists.

Éditeur, Édition (Fr.), editor, edition.

Eeden, (1) *see* VAN DEN E.—(2) Johann van der, b. Dec. 21, 1844, Ghent, pupil of the Conservatoire there, and of the Brussels Conservatoire under Fétis, where he received several prizes for composition. He lived for a long time at Assisi, and is now director of the Mons Conservatoire (Hainault). He has written the oratorios *Brutus* and *Jaquelino de Bavière*.

E flat, E lowered by a flat. E♭ chord = e♭, g, b♭ ; E♭ min. chord = e♭, g♭, b♭ ; E♭ key, with three flats in signature ; E♭ minor key, with six flats. (*See* KEY.)

Egenolff (Egenolph), Christian, one of the older German music-printers at Frankfort ; but he was famed, to his disadvantage, for his very bad printing. He was also one of the first who made a living by piracy, and that is why most of the compositions in his collections of works bear no author's name. Thus the Odes of Horace by P. Tritonius, which Œglin already published in 1507, appeared in 1532 without name ; and, misled by this, these compositions were attributed to Egenolff in former editions of this dictionary. In 1550 he republished these Odes with others. The most valuable legacies from his printing-house are the two song-books à 4 " Gassenhawerlin " and " Reuterliedlein," of 1535 (in complete form, Zwickau). He is probably also the reprinter of the song-books described in Eitner's Bibliography, p. 35, and G. 41, and which are there spoken of as pirated.

Eggeling, Eduard, b. July 30, 1813, Brunswick, d. April 8, 1885, Harzburg, pianist, composer, and didactic writer.

Egghard, Jules, pseudonym of Count Hardegg, b. April 24, 1834, Vienna, d. there March 22, 1867, an excellent pianist ; he was a pupil of Czerny, and composer of favourite *salon* pieces.

Egli, Johann Heinrich, b. March 4, 1742, Seegraben, Wetzicon (Zürich), d. there Dec. 19, 1810, a composer highly esteemed in his fatherland ; he wrote principally sacred music (sacred odes of Klopstock, Gellert, Lavater, Cramer, two New Year cantatas, etc.), Swiss songs, March of the Swiss and German troops, etc.

Eguale (Ital.), equal ; *egualmente*, equally, smoothly flowing ; *voci eguali* (Lat. *voces æquales*), equal voices, *i.e.* only men's, or only women's voices.

Egypt, the land of an ancient civilisation, extending back far beyond the period of old Grecian culture, appears also to have been far advanced in the domain of musical art while Europe was, as yet, in a state of complete barbarism. It is indeed true that neither a scrap of Egyptian music, nor a single theoretical treatise, has come down to us ; but the most ancient tombs in the rocks show representations of musical instruments which excite the greatest astonishment. There, by the side of instruments similar to the Grecian lyre, and ornamented after Egyptian fashion, we meet with harps : some, of the most primitive, others, of the most elaborate construction and of the most tasteful workmanship ; these instruments are very high (over man's height), and they have a great number of strings. Harps of similar construction were used in ancient times by no other people, except by the Israelites, who, most probably, became acquainted with them in Egypt. Still more striking is the occurrence, in these representations, of instruments of the lute kind, instruments with long necks (fingerboards), and round or arched sound-bodies, with or without sound-holes. Instruments of this kind, from which sounds of different pitch were obtained by shortening the strings, were utterly unknown to the Greeks, and are first met with among the Persians, likewise among the Arabs after the conquest of Persia (7th century). The old Egyptian name for the harp was *Tebuni*, and that of the lute, *Nabla*. (*Cf.* NABLUM.) The wind-instruments of the Egyptians were principally straight flutes (Mam or Mem), also double flutes, and straight trumpets. They had, besides, many instruments of percussion, and rattles ; the oft-mentioned *Sistrum* was really not a musical instrument, but was employed at the sacred services to attract the attention of the worshippers. (*Cf.* Kiesewetter : " Die Musik der Neuern Griechen, etc.," from page 41, etc. [1838]; Ambros' " Geschichte der Musik," Vol. I., from page 137 [1862].)

Ehlert, Louis, writer on music and composer, b. Jan. 13, 1825, Königsberg, d. Jan. 4, 1884, Wiesbaden (from a stroke of apoplexy during a " Kurhaus " concert). In 1845 he studied at the Leipzig Conservatorium under Mendelssohn and Schumann, continued his studies at Vienna and Berlin, and, in 1850, settled in the latter city as teacher of music and musical critic. He frequently visited Italy for periods of several years, conducted at Florence the " Società Cherubini," afterwards (1869) taken up by H. v. Bülow, taught, from 1869 to 1871, at Tausig's " Schule des höheren

Klavierspiels," Berlin, lived for some years in Meiningen as teacher of music to the Ducal Princes, and, finally, at Wiesbaden. In 1875 he received the title of Professor. Of his compositions have been published principally : pianoforte pieces, songs and part-songs ; also an overture, " Hafis." A " Frühlingssymphonie " and a " Wintermärchen " overture have been produced at Berlin at the " Symphoniesoiréen " of the royal band, but not printed; likewise the " Requiem für ein Kind," produced by the Stern Vocal Union, and in 1879 by the " Tonkünstlerversammlung " at Wiesbaden. In addition to many contributions to the *Neue Berliner Musikzeitung*, the *Deutsche Rundschau*, etc., he wrote : "Briefe über Musik an eine Freundin " (3rd ed. 1879, translated into French and English), and " Aus der Tonwelt," essays (1877–84, two vols.).

Ehnn (E.-Sand), B e r t h a, celebrated stage vocalist, b. 1848, Pesth, pupil of Frau Andriessen of Vienna, made her *début* in 1864 at Linz, sang then at Graz, Hanover, Nuremberg, Stuttgart, etc., as a " star," and was appointed in 1867 at Vienna. In 1873 she sang at Berlin with great success in Lucca's principal *rôles*.

Ehrlich, (1) F r i e d r i c h C h r i s t i a n, b. May 7, 1807, Magdeburg, d. there May 31, 1887, as teacher of singing at the Cloister College, " Königl. Musikdirector," pianist (pupil of Hummel), and composer of the operas *Die Rosenmädchen* and *König Georg*.—(2) H e i n r i c h, pianist and writer on music, b. Oct. 5, 1822, Vienna, became an accomplished player (worked under Henselt, Bocklet, and Thalberg), and studied theory with S. Sechter. He was, for several years, court pianist to king Georg V. of Hanover, was at Wiesbaden from 1855 to 1857, then in England, Frankfort, and in 1862 went to Berlin. From 1864 to 1872 he was teacher of the pianoforte at the Stern Conservatorium in that city, and was active, at the same time, as a writer and private teacher. (He was musical critic of the *Berliner Tageblatt*, the *Gegenwart*, as well as of the *Neue Berliner Musikzeitung*.) In 1875 he received the title of Professor. E. composed a pianoforte concerto, and "Lebensbilder." He edited Tausig's "Technische Studien," also the pamphlets " Schlaglichter und Schlagschatten " (1872), " Aus allen Tonarten," " Für den Ring des Nibelungen gegen Bayreuth," " Wie übt man am Klavier " (1879 ; 2nd edition 1884), as well as a brief " Musik-Aesthetik von Kant bis auf die Gegenwart " (1881) ; further, " Musikstudium und Klavierspiel " (" Esthetic considerations with regard to performing "), well worthy of perusal, and " Dreissig Jahre Künstlerleben ' (1893). He wrote several novels. Died Dec. 30, 1899.

Eibenschütz, I l o n a, excellent pianist, b. May 8, 1872, Pesth.

Eichberg, (1) J u l i u s, excellent violinist, b. June 13, 1824, Düsseldorf, d. Jan. 18, 1893,

Boston, U.S., pupil of J. Rietz at Düsseldorf. He attended the Brussels Conservatoire from 1843 to 1845, and, in 1846, became violin teacher at the Conservatoire at Geneva. In 1857 he went to New York, and in 1859 to Boston as conductor of the Museum Concerts (1859–66), and founded there a Conservatorium (1867), which, under his direction, was brought into high esteem. E. wrote a large number of compositions for violin (études, duets, characteristic pieces, etc.), also four English operettas, *The Doctor of Alcandra, The Rose of Tyrol, The Two Cadis, A Night in Rome*.—(2) O s k a r, b. Jan. 21, 1845, Berlin, pupil of Löschhorn and Fr. Kiel, teacher of music at Berlin, published from 1879–89 a serviceable " Music Calender," and directed for one year and a half the *Neue Berliner Musikzeitung*. Since 1888 he has been president of the Berlin Music Teachers' Union. During fifteen years he conducted a mixed choral union, and is at the present time musical critic of the *Berliner Börsen Courier*. As composer, he has only produced pf. pieces, songs, and part-songs. His brother R i c h a r d, b. May 13, 1825, Berlin, lives there likewise as music teacher.

Eichborn, H e r m a n n L u d w i g, writer on music and composer, b. Oct. 30, 1847, Breslau, studied law, and obtained a doctor's degree ; he, however, withdrew from courts of justice, and devoted himself entirely to music. His teacher was E. Bohn (q.v.). Besides pf. pieces and songs, he wrote several comic operas and vaudevilles (*Drei auf einen Schlag, Zopf und Krummstab, Blaue Kinder,* etc.). The following monographs are of importance : " Die Trompete alter und neuer Zeit ; ein Beitrag zur Musikgeschichte und Instrumentationslehre " (1881) and " Zur Geschichte der Instrumentalmusik ; eine produktive Kritik " (1885). E. is himself a performer on the French horn and the trumpet, and, jointly with the instrument-maker, E. G. Heidrich, invented a new kind of Waldhorn, which is especially rich in the upper and lower notes (the " Oktav-Waldhorn," which has been especially accepted in Silesian military bands). Since 1883 E. has edited a paper on hygiene, *Das zwanzigste Jahrhundert*, in which are to be found many articles on art ; he is also a diligent contributor to the *Zeitschrift für Instrumentenbau* (De Wit).

Eichhorn, the brothers J o h a n n G o t t f r i e d E r n s t (b. April 30, 1822, d. June 16, 1844) and J o h a n n K a r l E d u a r d (b. Oct. 17, 1823), sons of the Coburg court musician, J o h a n n P a u l E. (b. Feb. 22, 1787, d. Oct. 17, 1823), attracted attention as musical prodigies (aged six and seven, respectively), and performed on the violin in grand concert tours up to 1835. They afterwards received appointments in the Coburg band.

Eis (Ger.), E sharp.

Eisfeld, T h e o d o r, b. April 11, 1816, Wolfenbüttel, d. Sept. 2, 1882, Wiesbaden, pupil of

Karl Müller at Brunswick (violin), and of K. G. Reissiger at Dresden (composition), from 1839–43 court theatre capellmeister at Wiesbaden. In 1843 he became conductor of the "Concerts Viviennes" at Paris, in which post he obtained great merit by encouraging high-class music, studying, between whiles, singing under Rossini at Bologna. He was appointed honorary member of the Academy of St. Cecilia. After a short stay in Germany, he went to New York as conductor of the Philharmonic Concerts. In 1865, being on a journey to visit Germany, the ship *Austria*, on which he was a passenger, was destroyed by fire while on the high seas ; he was saved, but a severe nervous complaint almost entirely prevented him from exercising his profession. He lived, last of all, at Wiesbaden.

Eissler M a r i a n n e, violin-player, b. Nov. 18, 1865, Brünn, pupil of Heissler. Her eldest sister, E m m a, is a pianist.

Eisteddfod (Welsh). The triennial assemblies of the Welsh bards from a very early period were known by this name. *Eisteddfodau* of special importance were held in the years 1450, 1567, 1681, and 1819. The modern Eisteddfodau are held annually ; but they retain little more than the name of the great gatherings of former times.

Eitner, R o b e r t, a musical historian of merit, b. Oct. 22, 1832, Breslau, was for five years a pupil of M. Brosig ; he went to Berlin in 1853 as teacher of music, established, in 1863, a music school of his own, and has recorded his experiences as teacher in his " Hilfsbuch beim Klavierunterricht " (1871). Some of his compositions have also appeared in print. His historical and bibliographical labours, relating especially to works of the 16th and 17th centuries, occupied much of his time, and form his chief title to merit. In a competition appointed by the Amsterdam Society for the Advancement of Art he won the prize (1867) for his dictionary of Dutch composers (manuscript). He also edited for the society a new edition of the organ works of Sweelinck. E. was chiefly instrumental in starting and organising the " Gesellschaft für Musikforschung" ; the organ of this society, the *Monatshefte für Musikgeschichte*, has been edited by E. since 1869. He edits likewise the *Publication älterer praktischer u. theoretischer Musikwerke, etc.* Of Eitner's other writings the following are specially deserving of mention : " Verzeichnis neuer Ausgaben alter Musikwerke aus der frühesten Zeit bis zum Jahr 1800 " (*Monatshefte*, 1871) ; " Bibliographie der Musiksammelwerke des 16. und 17. Jahrhunderts " (with Haberl, Lagerberg, and Pohl) ; " Verzeichnis der gedruckten Werke von Hans Leo Hassler und Orlandus de Lassus" (*Monatshefte*, 1873–74), and S. G. Staden's " Seelewig " (*Monatshefte*, 1881). E. has lived for some time at Templin-i.-d., Uckermark. He has rendered valuable assistance in preparing the new editions of this dictionary.

Elegante (Ital.), with refinement.

Elegia (Ital.), composition expressive of sorrow.

Elegiaco (Ital.), in a sorrowful manner.

Electricity has of late been employed in the construction of organs, by conducting electricity from the keys to their respective pipes. An electro-magnet opens the valves, as soon as, by pressing down the keys, the connecting current is established. The electrical apparatus is a welcome improvement for very large organs, as, by means of it, the uncertain or tardy speaking of distant pipes is done away with. It renders the pneumatic lever superfluous, and the touch of the instrument can surpass that of the pianoforte in lightness. To English organbuilders (Barker, Bryceson) we are indebted for this introduction of electricity. Quite recently an attempt has been made to make strings sound by means of intermittent electric currents (electric pianoforte).

Elers (Elerus), F r a n z, cantor and music director at Hamburg, b. about 1500, Uelzen ; about 1530 cantor and teacher at Hamburg. He died Feb. 22, 1590, as musical director of the cathedral ; he published (1588) a great Singing-book in two parts : the first part contains collects and responses (*Cantica Sacra*, etc.) ; the second the chorales (Psalmi, Dr. Martin Luther, etc.), with intonation of the Church Modes according to Glarean's system.

Elevatio (Lat.), elevation. (1) The up beat in beating time.—(2) The unaccented part of a bar.—(3) The rising of a melody beyond the *ambitus* (compass) of the mode.—(4) A motet or any other vocal or instrumental composition performed during the elevation of the Host.

Elevation. To the four meanings given in the preceding article is to be added : (5) The obsolete English name of two ornaments. As one of the " smooth graces," it is synonymous with an ascending double appoggiatura ; as one of the " shaked graces," it is more complicated

Elewyck, X a v i e r V i c t o r (Chevalier) v a n, writer on music, b. April 24, 1825, Ixelles lez Bruxelles. d. April 28, 1888, in a lunatic asylum at Zickemont, maître de chapelle of the Louvain Cathedral (without salary, as an amateur). He arranged sacred concerts with orchestra every Sunday and on festival days ; and also published motets and orchestral works of his own. E. became known by a series of monographs : " Discours sur la musique religieuse en Belgique" (1861) ; "Mathias van den Gheyn, le plus grand organiste et carilloneur belge du xviii. siècle" (1862) ; "De la musique religieuse, les congrès de Malines (1863 and 1864), et de Paris (1860), et la législation de l'église en cette matière " (1866), and " De l'état actuel de la musique en Italie " (1875). He also published a collection of old clavier pieces by Netherland composers.

El Farabi. (*See* ALFARABI.)

Elias Salomonis, priest of St. Astère (Perigord) about 1274, the author of a treatise, "Scientia artis musicæ," printed by Gerbert (" Script." III.). This work contains directions for improvised counterpoint (Chap. 30), as well as very characteristic advice respecting the use of clefs (p. 56), which, however, was not adopted.

Ella, J o h n, b. Dec. 19, 1802, Thirsk (Yorks), d. Oct. 2, 1888, London, violinist, and an excellent conductor, pupil of Fémy for the violin. He was, from 1822, member of the orchestra at the King's Theatre, also, afterwards, of the Concerts of Ancient Music and of the Philharmonic Society, London. In 1826 he was still a pupil of Attwood's for harmony, and only studied counterpoint and composition under Fétis in 1845. On his return to London, he established in 1845 " The Musical Union " (chamber-music matinées), which existed up to 1880, when he retired from active life ; and, at the same time, the " Musical Winter Evenings," which, however, were discontinued in 1859. For these concerts E. introduced so-called " analytical programmes " (with remarks on the structure of the works to be performed, as well as on the period at which the composers lived, their importance, etc.), which soon became the fashion. In 1855 E. was appointed lecturer on music at the London Institution. Some of his lectures are published. He also wrote, occasionally, musical articles for the London papers, a biographical notice of Meyerbeer, and published " Musical Sketches Abroad and at Home" (1869 ; 3rd edition 1878).

Eller, L o u i s, celebrated violinist, b. 1819, Graz, d. July 12, 1862, Pau (Pyrénées), published études and fantasias for violin.

Ellerton, J o h n L o d g e, an extraordinarily prolific composer, b. Jan. 11, 1801, Cheshire, d. Jan. 3, 1873, London. He wrote seven Italian, one German, and three English operas, besides one oratorio (*Paradise Lost*), six masses, five symphonies, four concert overtures, forty-four stringed quartets, three quintets, eleven trios, thirteen sonatas, sixty-one glees, six anthems, seventeen motets, eighty-three vocal duets— truly an astonishing record for an amateur even taking into account that he had studied counterpoint at Rome for two years.

Ellig (Ger.), a somewhat obsolete expression for 2-feet, used in connection with organ-stops. (*See* FOOT-TONE.)

Ellis, A l e x a n d e r J o h n (formerly Sharpe), a meritorious writer on acoustics, b. June 14, 1814, Hoxton, d. Oct. 28, 1890. He first studied jurisprudence, but soon (1843) turned to acoustics, and studied music under Donaldson of Edinburgh. At the suggestion of Max Müller, he devoted all his attention, in 1863, to Helm-holtz's " Lehre von den Tonempfindungen " (of which he published an English translation in 1875 ; 2nd ed. 1885) ; as early as 1868 he had published Ohm's " Geist der mathematischen Analyse " in English, and, in the " Proceedings " of the Musical Association (1876–77), Preyer's " Über die Grenzen der Tonwahrnehmung " in rearranged form. All these publications contain comments and additions, the valuable results of independent investigation. The additions to Helmholtz first appeared separately in the publications of the Royal Society—"On the Conditions . . . of a Perfect Musical Scale on Instruments with Fixed Tones " (1864), " On the Physical Constitutions and Relations of Musical Chords " (1864), " On the Temperament of Instruments with Fixed Tones " (1864), and " On Musical Duodenes ; or, the Theory of Constructing Instruments with Fixed Tones in Just or Practically Just Intonation " (1874). Papers containing new theories, etc., for the Musical Association are as follows : " The Basis of Music " (1877), " Pronunciation for Singers " (1877), and " Speech in Song " (1878). He wrote in detail on Musical Pitch for the " Proceedings " of the Society of Arts (1877, 1880, and 1881; also separately, 1880–81, and a summary in the appendix to the second edition of his translation of Helmholtz's work), for which he received silver medals; also the " Tonometrical Observations, or Some Existing Non-harmonic scales " (Royal Society, 1884), and " On the Musical Scales of Various Nations " (Society of Arts, 1885).

Elsner, J o s e p h X a v e r, b. June 29, 1769, Grottkau (Silesia), d. April 18, 1854, Warsaw. After studying for the medical profession, he entered the theatre band at Brünn as violinist, and in the following year became capellmeister at the Lemberg, and in 1799, at the Warsaw theatre, in which latter city he established a school for organists, which proved the germ of the Warsaw Conservatoire, of which he became director. The troubles of 1830 led to the closing of the establishment, which was reopened in 1834, with Soliva as director, and is still flourishing at the present day. His compositions are numerous (nineteen operas, several ballets, duodramas, incidental music to plays, symphonies, concertos, cantatas, sacred music, etc.), but his works excited no general and lasting interest. He was also the author of two treatises on the suitableness of the Polish language to composition. E. was Chopin's teacher at Warsaw.

Elterlein, E r n s t v o n, pseudonym of Ernst Gottschald, b. Oct. 19, 1826, Elterlein (Saxony), jurist, author of a popular esthetic analysis of Beethoven's pianoforte sonatas (1st ed. 1857; 3rd ed. 1883).

Elvey, S t e p h e n, b. June 27, 1805, Canterbury, d. Oct. 6, 1860; he became, in 1830, organist of New College, Oxford, took his degree of Mus.Bac. in 1831, and from 1840 was choragus at the university. He composed a few songs and some sacred music.—His brother and pupil, George Job, b. March 27, 1816, became, in 1835, organist of St. George's Chapel, Windsor, took his degrees of *Mus.Bac.* and of *Doc.Mus.* in 1838 and 1846, and was knighted in 1871. He was also a composer of sacred works (hymns, anthems, etc.). Died Dec. 9, 1893, Windsor.

Elwart, Antoine Aimable Élie, b. Nov. 18, 1808, Paris, d. there Oct. 14, 1877, was, at the age of ten, chorister at St. Eustace. He was sent by his father as apprentice to a packing-case maker, but ran away from the latter, and joined the orchestra of a suburban theatre as violinist. He was received into the Conservatoire in 1825, and studied under Fétis and Le Sueur. In 1828 he and several of his fellow-scholars started the *Concerts d'émulation* in the small hall of the Conservatoire. In 1834 he received the *Grand Prix de Rome*, after he had already been for two years assistant-master in Reicha's composition class. On his return from Italy he resumed his post as assistant-master, and in 1840, was appointed professor of a new, second harmony class organised by Cherubini. After thirty years of successful activity (Th. Gouvy, A. Grisar, Weckerlin, etc., were his pupils), he resigned his post in 1871. He wrote a series of important works (masses, oratorios, Te Deum, cantatas, lyric scenas, an oratorio-symphony (*Le Déluge*), several operas (of which, however, only one—*Les Catalans*—was performed, at Rouen); but his position as theorist and writer was a distinguished one. He wrote: "Duprez, sa vie artistique, avec une biographie authentique de son maître A. Choron" (1838), "Théorie Musicale" ("Solfège progressif, etc.," 1840), "Feuille Harmonique" ("Theory of Chords," 1841), "Le chanteur accompagnateur" (General-bass, ornaments, organ-point, etc., 1844), "Traité du contrepoint et de la fugue," "Essai sur la Transposition," "Études élémentaires de Musique" (1845), "L'art de chanter en chœur," "L'art de jouer impromptu de l'altoviola," "Solfège du jeune âge," "Le Contrepoint et la fugue appliqués au style idéal," "Lutrin et Orphéon" (theoretical and practical vocal studies), "Histoire de la Société des concerts du Conservatoire" (1860; 2nd ed. 1863), "Manuel des aspirants aux grades de chef et de souschef de musique dans l'armée française" (1862), "Petit manuel d'instrumentation" (1864), "Histoire des concerts populaires" (1864). From 1867 to 1870 he undertook a complete edition of his own compositions, which, however, only reached the third volume.

E-major chord $= e, g\sharp, b;$ E-major key with signature of four sharps. (*See* KEY.)

Embouchure (Ger. *Ansatz*), (1) is the term used for the position of the lips in blowing wind-instruments, the mouthpiece of which is placed not in, but only before the mouth. E. in flute-playing differs altogether from that for brass wind-instruments, in which the edges of the lips represent reeds; and hence E. must differ greatly according as high or low sounds have to be produced. The player says that he has no E. when he is not fully master of his lips, *i.e.* when he is excited or languid.—(2) In *singing*, it refers to the manner in which a sound beginning a phrase is produced. A distinction is made between (*a*) E. *with closed glottis*, on the opening of which, a peculiar guttural sound (the Hebraic *Aleph*) precedes the note; and (*b*) the *breathed* E., when the glottis is slowly opened, and the note is preceded by a soft breathing (*spiritus lenis*). E. again is the term applied to the position of the larynx, palate, and mouth, all of which are concerned in tone-formation and resonance, and one speaks of a "palatal E.," etc. Although so many learned works have already been written on voice-formation, yet scientific results beyond dispute, and useful aids for practice, are still lacking. The best teacher of singing is, after all, the best singer, *i.e.* the one who shows how everything should be done. The works of Helmholtz ("Lehre von den Tonempfindungen," 1862), of Merkel ("Anthropophonik," 1856), and others, treat, in the most detailed manner possible, of the functions of the vocal cords, of the connection of vowels with overtones, etc., but almost entirely overlook the fact that the form of the E. *tube*—*i.e.* the hollow space from the larynx to the lips which produces the sounds produced by the vocal cords, even for the same vowel (*e.g.* for the pure A)—differs greatly according to the position of the soft parts of the palate, etc. The singer knows that he can sing his A in front from the teeth, or right at the back from the palate, and that the former gives a "flat," the latter a "crushed" tone (the genuine palatal tone); and that the best tones are those which he feels in the middle of the mouth. The singer knows too that it is extremely difficult to give this kind of resonance to a U, or to a bright-toned E., etc., and that for the sake of roundness and fulness of tone something of the strict characteristic of a vowel must be sacrificed (U takes an O colouring, E an OE, I a U). These are hints which the singer at once understands, and which are of more service to him than any, or all, hypotheses concerning the action of the vocal cords. The human voice is a reed-pipe; but organ-builders know that tone-colour, tone-fulness, etc., depend far less on the form of the tongue and force of wind, than on the form of the tube.

Emery, Stephen A., b. Oct. 4, 1841, Paris, Oxford Co. (State of Maine, North America), pupil of the Leipzig Conservatorium; he lives at Boston highly esteemed as a teacher. He also composes.

E-minor chord = *e, g, b;* ᴇ *minor key,* with signature of one ♯. (*See* KEY.)

Emmerich, R o b e r t, composer, b. July 23, 1836, Hanau, where his father was counsellor, d. July 11, 1891. He studied law at Bonn, but, at the same time, studied music diligently under Dietrich. He entered the army in 1859, but in 1873 left the service, as captain, to devote himself to music. From 1873–78 he lived in Darmstadt, and produced there the operas *Der Schwedensee, Van Dyck,* and *Ascanio,* and also wrote two symphonies, a cantata (*Huldigung dem Genius der Töne*), songs, etc. From 1878–79 E. was capellmeister at Magdeburg Theatre; after that he lived at Stuttgart, and in 1889 was appointed conductor of the Male Choral Union.

Encke, H e i n r i c h, b. 1811, Neustadt, Bavaria, d. Dec. 31, 1859, Leipzig; he was a distinguished pianist, pupil of Hummel, composed many instructive pf. pieces, and arranged standard classical works as pianoforte duets.

Enckhausen, H e i n r i c h F r i e d r i c h, b. Aug. 28, 1799, Celle, d. Jan. 15, 1885, Hanover, as court pianist and castle organist, pupil of Aloys Schmitt. He published instructive pf. pieces, also orchestral and sacred compositions, an opera (*Der Savoyarde,* 1832), and an excellent chorale-book.

Encore (Fr.), again, yet, also.

Energico (Ital.), in an energetic manner (with power, decision).

Engel, (1) J o h a n n J a k o b, b. Sept. 11, 1741, Parchim, Mecklenburg, d. there June 28, 1802; he was professor at the Gymnasium, Berlin, later on, tutor to the crown prince (Friedrich Wilhelm II.), after whose accession to the throne he became theatre director, which post he, however, resigned. He wrote "Über die musikalische Mahlerey, an den königlichen Kapellmeister Herrn Reichardt" (1780), and his collected writings contain various articles relating to music.—(2) D a v i d H e r m a n n, b. Jan. 22, 1816, Neuruppin, d. May 3, 1877, Merseburg, excellent organ-player and composer, pupil of Fr. Schneider at Dessau, and of A. Hesse at Breslau; he lived first as music teacher at Berlin, and was appointed in 1848 cathedral organist, and teacher at the cathedral Gymnasium, Merseburg. E. composed organ pieces, psalms, an oratorio, *Winfried,* etc., and wrote "Beitrag zur Geschichte des Orgelbauwesens" (1855); "Über Chor und instruktive Chormusik"; "Der Schulgesang" (1870).—(3) G u s t a v E d- u a r d, celebrated teacher of singing, and clever writer on music, b. Oct. 29, 1823, Königsberg, studied philology, attended lectures at Berlin by Marx on the science of music, took part as singer in the Singakademie, and in the cathedral choir; and in 1848, when his year of probation

as collegiate teacher at the "Graues Kloster" had expired, devoted himself entirely to the teaching of music, especially of singing. In 1862 he became teacher of singing at Kullak's Academy, and in 1874 was appointed to the Royal High School for Music, receiving at the same time the title of professor. Krolop, Bulss, and others rank among his pupils. Besides various philosophical writings, he has published: "Sängerbrevier" (daily vocal exercises, 1860), "Übersetzungen und Vortragsbezeichnungen," and for the classical albums published by Gumprecht, "Die Vokaltheorie von Helmholtz und die Kopfstimme" (1867), "Das mathematische Harmonium" (1881), and a clever "Aesthetik der Tonkunst" (1884). In 1853 he became musical reporter to the *Spenersche,* and, in 1861, to the *Vossische* newspaper, and was an influential member of the Berlin musical press. D. July 19, 1895.—(4) K a r l, a musical historian of merit, b. July 6, 1818, Thiedenwiese, near Hanover, d. Nov. 17, 1882, Kensington, London; he received his musical training from the organist Enckhausen at Hanover, and from Hummel and Lobe at Weimar. He lived, first at Hamburg, Warsaw, and Berlin, then went, in 1846, to England, first to Manchester, but afterwards (1850) to London, where he became active as a writer, and was universally recognised as an authority on matters relating to the history of musical instruments, and to the music of various nations, ancient and modern. He published: "The Music of the Most Ancient Nations" (1864; 2nd ed. 1870); "An Introduction to the Study of National Music" (1866); "A Descriptive Catalogue of the Musical Instruments in the South Kensington Museum" (1874); "Catalogue of the Special Exhibition of Ancient Musical Instruments" (2nd ed. 1873); "Musical Myths and Facts" (1876, two vols.); "The Literature of National Music" (1879); besides "The Pianist's Handbook" (1853), and "Reflections on Churchmusic for Church-goers" (1856). E. was a diligent contributor to the *Musical Times,* and other papers devoted to special subjects.

Engelstimme. (*See* ANGELICA.)

Englisches Horn (Ger.), English horn, *cor anglais* (q.v.).

Enharmonic (Gr.), a term relating to sounds, which, according to the mathematical determinations of pitch, and also the notation, are different, but in musical practice are identical: for example, *f* and *e sharp, b* and *c flat,* etc. The ancient Greeks, in addition to the diatonic and chromatic genera, had an *enharmonic* genus in which the two middle notes of the tetrachord, by lowering the upper one, were brought to the same pitch (*e, f, f, a*); this, at any rate, was the oldest form of E. (*Olympos*). A later E. separated these two identical notes, placed the third in the tetrachord at the distance of half a tone from the lowest, and gave to the second a middle pitch—

(*See* GREEK MUSIC.) The 16th century, with its mania for everything Greek, revived the enharmonic genus, and explanations of various kinds were attempted with regard to the same. To these very small differences of pitch was given the name of *enharmonic diesis* (*cf.* DIESIS). The practical result of these endeavours—useless so far as their special aim was concerned—was the recognition that various mathematical values could be applied to one and the same note of our system of music, but that in practice only approximative values are and can be given to them. Thus theory gradually apprehended equal temperament which in practice had long been adopted, and which equalises these approximative values (enharmonically identified). The table given under *Tone, determination of*, gives for each upper key of our pianoforte, eight, and for each lower key, thirteen; for these the mean value of equal temperament stands in the place, *i.e.* they are, for us, enharmonically identical. By *enharmonic change* is understood the exchange of these really different values. This exchange is either for facility of reading, *i.e.* a key with flats is chosen, for a time, instead of one with sharps; or (especially if only the meaning of one note is changed) it indicates really a new conception.

Enigmatical Canon. (*See* CANON.)

Enoch & Co., music publishing firm, established in London 1869. They are agents for the Litolff edition. Their vocal catalogue includes many works by English composers, Cellier, Clay, Pinsuti, etc.

Ensemble (Fr.) signifies the working together of several persons on the stage, especially in an opera, and especially when more than two are taking part in the scene; terzets, quartets, quintets, etc., with or without chorus, are the real ensemble numbers of an opera. In instrumental music, ensemble works are compositions for several instruments, especially for pianoforte with strings, or with wind-instruments (*ensemble music*).

Entr'acte (Fr.), between the acts of a dramatic performance.

Entrée (Fr.; Ital. *Entrata*; Sp. *Entrada*), entry, introduction, prelude; especially a pompous instrumental introduction to old theatre pieces (operas, festival plays). As a piece of dance music (mostly in $\frac{4}{4}$ time), the E. meant the same as our present Polonaise; it is frequently met with as the first part of a serenade.

Entry Signs are the marks in a canon (of which only one part is written out; *cf.* CANON)

for the entry of the imitating parts; for example (Zarlino)—

the .ℒ. are E.S. which show at what distance the parts follow one another. The above canon would be performed thus—

The form of these signs is of no importance; they are written in many ways, for example: § or cross (†), or a small star (*), etc. The sign which a conductor gives to a player or singer to come in after a long pause is also called an Entry Sign.

Enunciation of words in singing. Within recent times special importance has been attached to clear enunciation, since, according to the modern tendency of vocal compositions, from the simple song to the opera, the delivery of the words is speech intensified rather than singing; and, as a rule, there is only one note to each syllable. In Italian opera, in which the words often seem a mere pretext for employing the voice, clear E. is of far less importance than beauty of tone, and therefore frequently gives way in favour of the latter. It must, however, be acknowledged that the various vowels, in consequence of their different natural resonance (in speech), can easily give rise to a difference in the production of sounds, and this cannot be altogether neglected (*see* EMBOUCHURE) without prejudice to the purity of many vowel sounds. In the interest, therefore, of beautiful, smooth singing it is not by any means objectionable to take from the *i*, *e*, *ae* (ä) somewhat of their sharpness, and from *u* and *o* somewhat of their dulness; and that can be managed without the vocalisation falling into a kind of *oe* (ö) sound, and the singing becoming altogether of an instrumental character. The enunciation of the consonants *l* and *r*, especially before *a*, causes special difficulty to the singer; the strongly-bent tongue in the former case is apt to remain in its position and affect the resonance, while, in the latter case, there is a tendency to make the *a* resound close to the palate. By conscientious practice, both may easily be avoided, especially if care be taken to give the consonant quickly and sharply, and then to set aside all trace of it in the position of the mouth. The palate-*r* can also be replaced by the tongue-*r*. Beginners often make the mistake of passing too quickly from the vowel to the following consonant, so that either a gap, a break, or a shortening of the time-value takes place ; still worse is it, if with *w, v, f, l, m, n, r, s*, the remainder of the note-value is sung with the position of the mouth required for the consonant, *i.e.* the effect produced is as follows : *ww–w, vv–v, ff–f, ll–l, m–m, n–n, rr–r, ss–s*. Also in the singing of double vowels (diphthongs) untrained singers or beginners frequently err. It is not proper to sing *eī, aū, eū*, but only *ăĭ, ăŭ, ŏĭ*, or *aĭ* (aj), *aŭ* (aw), *ōĭ* (oj) ; the former is false, the latter correct. With regard to the different degrees of resonance of the vowels in the hollow of the mouth, *cf.* EMBOUCHURE. With regard to the consonants within a word on which a note can be held (semi-vowels, *j, r, l, m, n, w, v*), the question as to whether they are to be taken with the note of the preceding or of the following vowel, must be decided by the division of the word according to the sense, *i.e.* compound words must be separated into their respective elements ; for instance, "for-lorn" (the "r" must be sung on the *o* note, and the "l" on the *o* which follows it ; and in a similar manner "un-less," "Al-mighty") ; even in the case of consonants of little or no tone (*b, p, d, t, g, k, z, ch, s, sch, h*), when they appear next to consonants capable of being held on a note, this distinction is of importance ; for instance, "help-less" (not "hel-pless"). Where the sense does not admit of the breaking up of a word, the intermediate sounding consonants, on the other hand, must all be sung on the next note helping the meaning ; *ll, mm, nn, rr* are to be clearly enunciated as double consonants ; the first to be sung on the preceding, the second on the following note, hal-loo, har-row, ham-mer.

Epicède (Fr.), **Epicedio** (Ital.), **Epicedium** (Lat.), an epicede—*i.e.* a funeral song, an elegy.

Epigonos (Gr.), born after. The sons of the chiefs that fell in the first war against Thebes were called *epigonoi*, after-born. The expression is not unfrequently applied to composers who do not open new paths, but follow in the tracks of their predecessors.

Epilogue (Gr.), a concluding word ; postlude.

Epinette (Fr.), a spinet.

Epinicion (Gr.), a song of victory.

Epiodion (Gr.), a funeral.

Episode (Gr.), (1) a term used in ancient tragedy for the return of the players after the marching up of the chorus (the Pavidos) ; hence similar to the word Intermezzo.—(2) An incidental, accessory part of a composition.

Epistrophe (Gr.), a return to the first theme.

Epithalamion (Gr.), a nuptial song.

Epode. (*See* STROPHE.)

Epstein, Julius, b. Aug. 14, 1832, Agram, studied under A. Joh. Rufinatscha and A. Halm

at Vienna, devoted himself to the pianoforte, and since 1867 has been teacher at the Conservatorium there.—His two daughters, Rudolfine and Eugenie, since 1876, have become favourably known—the one as 'cellist, the other as violinist.

Equalisation of the registers of the voice. (*See* REGISTER.)

Erard, Sébastian, celebrated pianoforte-maker, b. April 5, 1752, Strassburg, d. Aug. 5, 1831, at his château near Passy. Sprung from a German family (Erhard), and son of a cabinet-maker, E. placed himself under a harpsichord-maker, but soon knew more than his principal, and, therefore, was dismissed. A clever piece of work, however, drew upon the young man the notice of his new employer. His *clavecin mécanique* created a great sensation. It was a complicated instrument, in which, among other things, the strings could be shortened by one-half (transposition in the upper octave) ; and this was accomplished by means of a bridge worked by a pedal. At the age of twenty he had already won considerable fame, and a lady with a taste for the fine arts—the Duchess of Villeroi—gave him room in her château for the erection of a workshop. Here E. constructed his first pianoforte, the first really made in France (*see*, however, SILBERMANN, 5). About this time his brother, Jean Baptiste, came to Paris, and the two brothers founded an establishment of their own in the Rue de Bourbon. Rival establishments complained of him because he did not belong to the Fanmakers' Guild, but a lawsuit was settled by the king specially in Erard's favour, and this made him the talk of Paris. The instrument-makers put fancy work, mother-of-pearl mosaic on their instruments, and, at that time, had to belong to that guild. (*See* GUILDS.) He next constructed the *piano organisé* (organ-piano, a pianoforte combined with a small two-manual organ), and the harp *à fourchette*. E. went to London in 1786, where he set up a branch establishment, took out a patent, and brought his new instruments into great fame. In 1811 he constructed the harp with double action (*à double mouvement*), which, at one stroke, removed all the deficiencies of the instrument. The success was enormous, and in one year he sold harps to the amount of £25,000. But in 1823 he surpassed all his previous inventions by that of the repetition action (*double échappement*) for the pianoforte. (*See* ESCAPEMENT.) His last work was the ingenious construction of the *Orgue Expressif* for the Tuileries. After the death of Sebastian Erard, the business passed into the hands of his nephew, Pierre E. (b. 1796, d. Aug. 18, 1855). The latter published " The Harp in its Present Improved State Compared with the Original Pedal Harp " (1821), and " Perfectionnements apportés dans le mécanisme du piano par les Erard depuis l'origine de cet instrument jusqu'à l'exposition de 1834 " (1834).

He was succeeded by the nephew of his widow, Pierre Schäffer (d. Dec. 13, 1878).

Erato, the muse of amorous, lyrical poetry.

Eratosthenes, Alexandrian mathematician, b. 276 B.C., Cyrene, d. 195, as custodian of the celebrated library at Alexandria. In his " Catasterismoi " (translated into German by Schaubach, 1795, original text published by Bernhardy, 1822) he has given detached notices of Greek music and instruments. His division of the tetrachord (given in one of his works which has been lost) has been preserved to us by Ptolemy.

Erbach, Christian, b. about 1560, Algesheim in the Palatinate, was organist (1600) at Augsburg, and afterwards " Ratsherr " of that city. He was one of the most important German composers of his time, and his sacred works (motets à 4-8) appeared from 1600 to 1611 (Augsburg library). Of these several are included in Bodenschatz's " Florilegium Portense." There are MS. motets of E. in the Berlin library.

Erdmannsdörffer, Max, b. June 14, 1848, Nuremberg, pupil of the Leipzig Conservatorium, and of Rietz in Dresden. From 1871 to 1880 he was court capellmeister at Sondershausen; he distinguished himself by producing numerous works of modern tendency (Liszt, Berlioz, Brahms, Raff, Saint-Saëns, etc.) at the " Loh " concerts, formerly the nursery of the new German school, to which, indeed, he gave a new impulse. For some time E. lived at Leipzig, and in 1882 undertook the direction of the Imperial Russian Musical Society at Moscow, where, in 1885, he established an Orchestral Union of Students. Up to now his compositions (choral works, " Prinzessin Ilse," " Schneewittchen," " Traumkönig und sein Lieb," " Selinde; " overture, " Narziss; " songs, pf. pieces) have had no lasting success.—His wife, Pauline, née Oprawik, named, after her adopted father, Fichtner, b. June 28, 1847, Vienna, is an excellent pianoforte player (pianist to the courts of Weimar and Darmstadt). She was the pupil of Liszt from 1870 to 1871, and married E. in 1874.

Erhard (Erhardi), Laurentius, b. April 5, 1598, Hagenau (Alsatia), " Magister " at Saarbrücken, Strassburg, and Hanau, cantor at Frankfurt-a.-Main (1640). He wrote : " Compendium musices " (1640; 2nd ed. 1660; revised and enlarged in 1669), likewise a " Harmonisches Choral- und Figural-Gesangbuch " (1659).

Erk, (1) Adam Wilhelm, b. March 10, 1779, Herpf, near Meiningen, was organist at Wetzlar (1802), Worms (1803), Frankfurt-a.-Main (1812), Dreieichenhain, near Darmstadt (1813), and died in the last-named city Jan. 31, 1820. He published pieces for organ, and school-songs written for the collections of his son Ludwig.—(2) Ludwig Christian, son of the former, b. Jan. 6, 1807, Wetzlar, d. Nov.

25, 1883, Berlin, was teacher of music at Moers seminary from 1826 to 1835, then at the municipal seminary at Berlin. In 1836 he became conductor of the liturgical choral singing of the cathedral (the cathedral choir in its present form did not exist at that time), which post, however, he resigned in 1838, and founded in 1843 the Erk Male Choral Union, and in 1852 the Erk Choral Union for mixed voices; in 1857 he was appointed Königlicher Musikdirektor, and later named Professor. The name of Erk has become distinguished and popular by his numerous, and many times republished, school song-books (" Liederkranz," " Singvögelein," " Deutscher Liedergarten," " Musikalischer Jugendfreund," " Sängerhain," " Siona," " Turnerliederbuch," " Frische Lieder," etc.), many of which were written jointly with his brother Friedrich and his brother-in-law, Greef. He published besides :—" Die deutschen Volkslieder mit ihren Singweisen " (1838 to 1845), " Volkslieder, alte und neue, für Männerstimmen " (1845–46), " Deutscher Liederhort " (Volkslieder, 1856), " Mehrstimmige Gesänge für Männerstimmen " (1833–35), " Volksklänge " (for male chorus, 1851–60), " Deutscher Liederschatz " (for male chorus, 1859–72), " Vierstimmige Choralgesänge der vornehmsten Meister des 16. und 17. Jahrhunderts " (1845), " J. S. Bach's mehrstimmige Choralgesänge und geistliche Arien " (1850–65), " Vierstimmiges Choralbuch für evangelische Kirchen " (1863), " Choräle für Männerstimmen " (1866), as well as exercisepieces for pianoforte, and a " Methodischer Leitfaden für den Gesangunterricht in Volksschulen " (1834, part 1). His valuable library fell into the possession of the Royal School of Music.—(3) Friedrich Albrecht, brother of the former, b. June 8, 1809, Wetzlar, d. Nov. 7, 1879, as teacher of the high school, Düsseldorf. Besides his contributions to his brother's school song-books, he published the well-known and frequently reprinted " Kommersbuch " (with Silcher), the " Allgemeine deutsche Turnliederbuch " (with Schauenburg), and a " Freimaurer-Liederbuch."

Erkel, Franz, national Hungarian composer, b. Nov. 7, 1810, Gyula, d. June 15, 1893, Pesth, from 1838 capellmeister of the national theatre, Pesth, honorary conductor of the Male Choral Unions of Hungary. He composed a series (nine) of Hungarian operas, of which Hunyady Laszlò (1844) and Bank Bán (1861) were received with enthusiasm; also some popular songs.— His son Alexander, b. 1846, Pesth, d. Békés-Gyula Oct. 14, 1900, made his début as an opera composer at Pesth in 1883 with Tempefœi.

Erler, Hermann, b. June 3, 1844, Radeberg, near Dresden, was for a long time manager of the firm of Bote and Bock at Berlin. He edited the Neue Berliner Musikzeitung, and was musical critic of the Berliner Fremdenblatt. In 1873 he established a publishing business in Berlin (now

Ries and Erler). E. has published letters of Schumann (" R. Schumanns Leben und Werke aus seinen Briefen geschildert," two vols.).

Ernst, (1) F r a n z Anton, b. 1745, Georgenthal (Bohemia), d. 1805. In 1778 he was leader of the orchestra at Gotha, and in his day was famous as a performer on the violin ; he also composed for his instrument (concerto in E♭), and wrote, amongst other things, " Über den Bau der Geige" in the Leipzig *Allgemeine Musikalische Zeitung* (1805).—(2) H e i n r i c h Wilhelm, b. May 6, 1814, Brünn, d. Oct. 8, 1865, Nice, likewise a violinist, and of still greater fame. He held no fixed appointment, but made, for the most part, concert tours ; and he spent several years in Paris. His " Elegy," "Otello" fantasia, etc., are still favourite concert pieces.—(3) H e i n r i c h, singer, b. Sept. 19, 1846, Dresden, son of the far-famed dramatic singer, Josephine E. Kayser, connected with the Pesth Hungarian Theatre from 1851 to 1861, nephew of H. W. E., pupil of the Pesth Conservatorium. He was engaged at the Leipzig Theatre as baritone singer in 1872, but was soon trained by F. Rebling to take dramatic tenor *rôles*, and since 1875 has been a highly esteemed member of the Royal Opera Company at Berlin.

Ernst II. (IV.), Duke of Saxe-Coburg-Gotha, b. June 21, 1818, Coburg, d. Aug. 22, 1893, Reinhardsbrunn, was occupied with music from his youth, and composed songs, cantatas, hymns, likewise the operas *Zaire, Toni, Casilda, Santa Chiara* (1853), *Diana von Solange* (1858), and the operettas *Der Schuster von Strassburg* (Vienna, 1871 ; pseud. Otto Wernhard), and *Alpenrosen* (Hamburg, 1873 ; pseud. N.v.K.), which have been performed with success on several stages.

Eroico (Ital.), heroic.

Erotica (Gr.), love-songs.

Escapement, a contrivance in the mechanism of the pianoforte whereby the hammer, immediately after touching the string, falls back to its former position. (*See* PIANOFORTE.)

Eschmann, J u l i u s Karl, b. 1825, Winterthur, d. Oct. 27, 1882, Zürich, an excellent teacher of the pianoforte, first in Cassel, and from 1852 in Zürich. He published numerous educational works (studies, a Piano Method [1st part, for first year's instruction ; 2nd part, for the second and third years], "One Hundred Aphorisms" from the Method) ; also characteristic pieces, songs, violin pieces with pianoforte, etc.

Escudier, two brothers, M a r i e (b. June 29, 1819, d. April 17, 1880) and L é o n (b. Sept. 17, 1821, d. June, 1881), natives of Castelnaudary (Aude), went as young men to Paris, and displayed brilliant journalistic activity. They founded in 1838 the music paper, *La France Musicale*, established a music business (works of

Verdi), were contributors to various political papers, edited (from 1850 to 1858) *Le Pays* (*Journal de l'empire*), and together wrote the following :—" Études biographiques sur les Chanteurs Contemporains " (1840), " Dictionnaire de Musique d'après les Théoriciens, Historiens et Critiques les plus célèbres (1844, 2 vols. ; 2nd ed. under the title " Dictionnaire de Musique Théorique et Historique," 1854), " Rossini, sa vie et ses œuvres (1854), " Vie et aventures des cantatrices célèbres, précédées des musiciens de l'empire et suivies de la vie anecdotique de Paganini " (1856). In 1862 the brothers separated, and Léon, who kept the publishing business, brought out a new newspaper (*L'Art Musical*) which still appears, whilst the *France Musicale* continued by Marie collapsed in 1870. In 1876 Léon had the direction of the Théâtre Italien for a short period.

Esercizio (Ital.), exercise, étude.

Eses (Ger.), the E lowered by the sign ♭♭. Chord of E *double flat = e double flat, g flat, b double flat.*

Eslava, D o n M i g u e l Hilarion, b. Oct. 21, 1807, Burlada (Navara), d. July 23, 1878, Madrid ; probably the most important of modern Spanish composers and theorists. In 1828 he became cathedral maestro at Ossuña, took priest's orders, and in 1832 became maestro of the metropolitan church in Seville, and (1844) court maestro to Queen Isabella. E. wrote a great number of sacred works, besides three operas (*Il Solitario, La Tregua di Ptolemaide, Pedro el Cruel*), an elementary Method of Music much in vogue (" Metodo de Solfeo," 1846), and a composition Method (" Escuela de Armonia y Composicion" ; 2nd ed. 1861). From 1855–56 he published a musical paper (*Gaceta musical de Madrid*). His best works are the collections " Museo organico español," which also contain some organ compositions from his own pen, and especially the " Lira sacro-hispaña " (1869, 5 vols. in 10 half-volumes), containing sacred compositions of Spanish masters of the 16th to the 19th century ; the 8th half-volume contains only his own compositions.

Espagne, F r a n z, b. 1828, Münster (Westphalia), d. May 24, 1878, Berlin, pupil of Dehn there ; in 1858 he was, for a short time, musical director at Bielefeld, and, in the same year, Dehn's successor as keeper of the musical section of the Royal Library, Berlin ; also choirmaster of the " Hedwig " church. In addition to his zealous activity as librarian, he made a name as editor of various new editions of old works, especially those of Palestrina (jointly with Witt, for Breitkopf u. Härtel ; now continued by Haberl).

Espirando (Ital.), expiring, dying away ; similar to *morendo.*

Espressione (Ital.), expression ; *con espr., c. espr., espressivo, espr.,* with expression ; frequently used for solo passages in orchestral parts.

Espringale, spring dance.

Essential Discords. This term is applied by many theorists to harmonic formations in which dissonant notes appear with harmonic meaning, in contradistinction to chance discords, which arise from changing or passing notes. This distinction has a practical value, and the term is especially applicable to the major and minor chords of the seventh, and to the major chord of the sixth. (*Cf.* DISSONANCE.)

Esser, Heinrich, b. July 15, 1818, Mannheim, d. June 3, 1872, Salzburg. He was leader of the band in 1838, afterwards theatre capellmeister at Mannheim; and was for some years conductor of the "Liedertafel" at Mayence, 1847 capellmeister at the "Kärntnerthor-Theater," Vienna, 1857 court opera capellmeister there, also for some years conductor of the Philharmonic Concerts; and, after receiving a pension, he resided at Salzburg. E. was, if not an inspired, still a gifted composer; his quartets for male voices, and songs, are highly popular—less so his orchestral and chamber compositions. In his earlier years he also wrote some operas (*Silas*, 1839, Mannheim; *Riquiqui*, 1843, Aix-la-Chapelle; *Die beiden Prinzen*, 1844, Munich).

Essipoff, Annette, celebrated pianist, b. Feb. 1, 1851, Petersburg, daughter of a high official, pupil of Wielhorski and Leschetitzki (at the Conservatoire), and, since 1880, wife of the latter. She made her *début* as pianist in her own country in 1874, appeared in London and Paris in 1875 and America in 1876 with great success. She lives in Vienna with her husband. Passion and poetry are the chief characteristics of her playing.

Este (Est, East, Easte), Thomas, noted English music-printer (16th to 17th century). His first publication was Byrd's "Psalmes, Sonets, and Songs of Sadnes and Pietie" (1588); this was followed by works of Orlando Gibbons, Th. Morley, Weelkes, etc. A collection of special interest entitled "The Whole Book of Psalmes, with their wonted Tunes in foure Parts," contains psalms harmonised by Alison, Blancks, Cavendish, Cobbold, Dowland, Farmer, Farnaby, Hooper, Johnson, and Kirbye (1592; new editions, 1594, 1604).

Esthetics, Musical, the speculative theory of music in opposition both to the mere theory of music with a practical aim (harmony, counterpoint, composition), and to the philosophical investigation of the phenomena of sound and the sensation of hearing (acoustics and the physiology of hearing). Musical esthetics form a portion of esthetics and art-philosophy generally, and seek to fathom the specific nature of musical impressions, *i.e.* (1) to investigate the nature of the elementary force of melody, dynamics, agogics, which acts on our soul (music as expression, as communication, as will); (2) to define the beautiful in music, *i.e.* to point out the laws of order and unity through which music receives shape and form (harmony and rhythm), likewise their relationship to mental working (music as perception); and (3) the power of music to awaken worthy, and definite associations, and—whether alone, or supported by the other arts—to characterise, to illustrate, to describe, *i.e.* to transfer the feelings of the composer, while listening or playing, to a special object (music as manifestation of will). (*Cf.* Riemann, "Wie hören wir Musik," 1888.) The basis for a system of musical esthetics, in the sense here sketched out, has been laid by Schopenhauer, Lotze, Fechner, Hanslick, G. Engel, Helmholtz, Stumpff, Hostinsky, Fr. von Hausegger, Arthur Seidl.

Estinto (Ital.), a term used for the utmost degree of *pianissimo* (Liszt).

Ett, Kaspar, b. Jan. 5, 1788, Erringen, near Landsberg, Bavaria, d. May 16, 1847, Munich. He studied with J. Schlett and J. Gratz at the Electoral College, Munich, and from 1816 was court organist of St. Michael's Church there. E. rendered valuable service in reviving and producing old sacred musical works of the 16th to the 18th century, which he took as a model for his own compositions (masses with and without orchestra, requiem, miserere, Stabat Mater, etc.); of these, only a few appeared in print (Graduals and *Cantica sacra*). Also a Method of composition remained unpublished, and is preserved, together with all his other manuscripts, in the Munich library.

Étude (Fr.), really identical with "study"; but now the idea of a technical exercise piece—whether for the first beginnings in learning an instrument, or for the highest development of virtuosity—is specially attached to the term E. Certainly a branch of étude literature is intended for public performance, and hence the contents are of considerable importance (concert-study); yet even here the principal feature consists in a heaping-up of technical difficulties. Generally a technical motive is worked through the É. (scales, arpeggio-passages, leaps, staccato, polyphonic syncopations, etc.), or there are a small number of motives related to one another. There are also many études in which several themes are developed; thus to one of passage-like character may be added, by way of relief, a second, more melodious one.

Euclid, Greek mathematician, flourished in Alexandria about 300 B.C. Two treatises on music, under his name, have been preserved: "Katatomè Kánonos" ("Sectio canonis") and "Eisagogè harmoniké" ("Introductio harmonica"). Perhaps he wrote neither; anyhow he was not the author of both, for the first follows the views of Pythagoras, the second, those of Aristoxenos. Some manuscripts mention Cleonides as author of both treatises.

Eulenburg, Philipp Graf zu, b. Feb. 12, 1847, Königsberg, i. Pr., Royal Prussian ambassador at Stuttgart. He composed songs (" Skalden-gesänge," " Nordlandslieder," " Seemärchen," " Rosenlieder " (all to words of his own).

Euler, Leonhardt, important mathematician and physicist, b. April 15, 1707, Basle, d. Sept. 3, 1783, Petersburg. He studied under Bernouilli, was professor of mathematics at Petersburg (1730), went to Berlin in 1740, where in 1754 he became director of the mathematical classes at the Akademie; he returned to Peters-burg in 1766, and shortly afterwards lost his eyesight. He wrote (apart from his other works) a large number of treatises on acoustics for the reports of the Berlin and Petersburg Academies, but his chief work in relation to music is, " Tentamen novæ theoriæ musicæ " (1729), the negative results of which show that mathematics, as the base of a musical system, will not suffice; for, since, according to mathe-matical theory, an interval is more difficult of comprehension, i.e. becomes more dissonant, the greater the figures by which it is repre-sented, the fourth octave (16), according to E., with regard to its degree of consonance, must be classed between the fifteenth and seventeenth overtones; therefore $c : c'''$ is less consonant than $c : \underline{b''}$ (!). E. was, moreover, the first to in-troduce logarithms in order the better to show pitch differences.

Euphonium, *Euphonion, Euphon,* (1) an instru-ment invented by Chladni in 1790, consisting of glass rods of different pitch which were rubbed with moistened fingers. These rods vibrated longitudinally, but produced trans-verse vibrations in rods of metal with which they were in communication. (*Cf.* Chladni's description of the Clavicylinder, etc., 1821.)— (2) (*Baritone horn*) a brass wind-instrument of wide measure introduced into German military bands. (*See* BARYTON, 3.)

Euphony (Gr.), agreeable sound.

Eustachian Trumpet. (*See* EAR.)

Euterpe, the Muse of stringed instruments.

Evacuatio, a term used in the 15th and 16th centuries to indicate the substitution of a "void" (*i.e.* open-headed) note for a full (*i.e.* closed) one; as, for instance, a minim for a crotchet.

Evers, Karl, b. April 8, 1819, Hamburg, d. Dec. 31, 1875, Vienna, an excellent pianist and elegant composer. He studied at Hamburg under Krebs, and at Leipzig under Mendelssohn, made extensive concert tours through the whole of Europe, lived at Paris, Vienna, established himself as music-seller at Gratz in 1858, but returned to Vienna in 1872. He composed four pianoforte sonatas, "Chansons d'amour" (twelve songs without words) characteristic of various nationalities (Provence, Germany, Italy, etc.), songs, etc.

Evesham, Monk of. (*See* ODINGTON.)

Evirato (Ital.), castrato.

Evovæ = *seculorum amen.* Close of the *Gloria Patri* generally added to the singing of the psalms in the Roman Catholic Church. (*See* TROPI.)

Ewer & Co., a London firm of music publishers founded by John J. Ewer in 1820. Later on the business passed into the hands of E. Buxton, who, by the acquisition of the copy-right of the greater number of Mendelssohn's works for England, brought it to a high state of prosperity. In 1860 it was sold to William Witt, and in 1867 united to the firm of Novello & Co. (Novello, Ewer & Co.).

Exequiæ (Lat.), Exequies, funeral rites.

Eximeno, Antonio, Spanish Jesuit, b. 1732, Balbastro (Aragon), professor of mathematics at the military school at Segovia, went, when the order to which he belonged was suppressed, to Rome, where he died in 1798. He wrote " Dell' origine della musica colla storia del suo progresso, decadenza e rinovazione " (1774), a work directed against " gray theory; " it was violently opposed, amongst others by Padre Martini, whose principal work E. then specially attacked in " Dubbio di D. Antonio E. sopra il saggio fondamentale, etc." (1775). E. warded off further attacks in the " Risposte al giudizio delle efemeridi di Roma, etc." The first two works were translated into Spanish by Guturiez.

Exposition, a " putting out " of the subject or subjects of a piece. In a fugue the term is employed to denote the introduction of the subject in the several parts or voices. In a movement in sonata-form it refers to the first section, separated, as a rule, from what follows, by double bars. This E. contains the subject-matter on which the whole movement is based.

Expression (Ital. *Espressione*), (1) is the term used to indicate the finer shading in the performance of musical works which it is not possible to express in the notation, i.e. all the slight draw-ings back, hurryings on, also the dynamic grada-tions, accentuations and tone-colouring of various kinds by means of touch (pianoforte), bowing (violin, etc.), embouchure (wind-instru-ments, human voice), etc., which in their totality make up what is called *expressive playing.* If an attempt were made to indicate all the small accents by means of a $\wedge$ > or *sf.*, etc.—accents indispensable to the correct artistic performance of a work—the notation would be overladen; and, at the same time, the artist would be so occupied with the marks as to be quite in-capable of genuine feeling for the music. It is scarcely possible, when many are performing together, as in the orchestra, to give much play to subjectivity; the *expressivo* must be limited to solo passages played by single instruments, whilst the *tutti* must keep to the prescribed signs, or to modifications indicated by the conductor: the latter, in a *tutti*, is really the performing artist. It is not easy to give definite rules for expression, but still it is possible; otherwise all good artists would not, in the main, make the same deviations from the rigid uniformity which a mere rendering of the written music would give. Attempts have been made by several writers to lay down general maxims. The best contribution of earlier times is the article written by J. P. A. Schulz, " Vortrag," in Sulzer's " Theorie der schönen Künste" (1772). Among recent works on this subject are to be named A. Kullak's " Ästhetik des Klavierspiels " (1861), Mathis Lussy's " Traité de l'expression musicale" (1873; in German by Vogt, 1886; in English by Miss M. E. von Glehn, 1885), Otto Klauwell's " Der Vortrag in der Musik" (1883), H. Riemann's " Musikalische Dynamik und Agogik" (1884), and A. J. Christiani's " Das Verständnis im Klavierspiel " (1886). The very varied results of these works show how much has still to be done ; only a few general points can be considered as fixed. First of all, in the matter of small changes of *tempo*, it may be remarked that hurrying implies intensification, and drawing back, the reverse; hence, as a rule, a slight urging, pressing forward is in place when the musical development becomes more intense, when it is positive; and, on the other hand, a tarrying, when it approaches the close. These changes must naturally be exceedingly minute in detached musical phrases, but can already become more important in a theme of a certain length ; while for whole movements they are of such extent as to be seldom ignored in the notation. The swelling of tone is likewise an intensification, the decreasing of the same, a giving way ; the natural dynamic shading of a musical phrase is therefore *crescendo* up to the point of climax, and *diminuendo* from there to the end. Generally speaking, melodic movement goes hand in hand with dynamic shading, so that phrases growing in intensity have rising melodies, and those which show a decrease, fall ing. Of course dynamic and agogic shadings must be used with economy ; the difference of increase of tone and of movement must be less for a short phrase than for a whole theme, or for the working up of a development section. A composer indicates, for the most part, any deviation from these very general rules ; for example, a *diminuendo* combined with a rising melody, or with a *stringendo;* or a *ritardando* with a rising melody and *crescendo;* he surely commits a sin of omission if he does not point out what is irregular. Further, the rule holds good, that anything specially striking in the course of a passage of simple melody, rhythm, and harmony, should be made prominent, accentuated ; especially, from harmonic considerations, chords which are foreign to the tonic, or detached, and sharply dissonant sounds. A modulation to a new key is generally accom-

panied by a *crescendo;* the chords or notes by which it is introduced receive stronger accents than those to which, by reason of their metrical and rhythmical position, they are entitled. To soften a sharp dissonance by playing without emphasis is to hush it up, to draw attention away from it ; it would cause it to be imperfectly understood, or rather misunderstood, and produce a bad effect similar to that of false relation (q.v.). The composer is, however, at liberty, with full artistic consciousness, to demand quite contrary modes of performance ; he can bring about quixotic modulations with *diminuendo*, or the roughest dissonances with a *pianissimo:* his aim will be to give the impression of something strange, wonderful, legendary, uncanny, etc., and therefore the avoidance of what is perfectly clear will be intentional. But even here the abnormal, the deviation from simple modes of performance, must be specially indicated.— (2) A stop in the harmonium, which makes the swelling or diminishing of tone dependent on the pressure of the feet.

Extempore Playing, improvisation, playing without premeditation.

Extraneous Sharps and **Flats** are such as do not belong to the key.

Extreme, (1) augmented, in speaking of intervals.—(2) The lowest, or the highest part, in speaking of part-writing or part-music.

Eybler, Joseph (from 1834 Edler von), b. Feb. 8, 1765, Schwechat, near Vienna, where his father was schoolmaster, d. July 24, 1846, Schönbrunn. He received his musical training at Vienna, at the boys' seminary, under Albrechtsberger (1777–79), was intended for the law, and only adopted music as a profession when his parents, through misfortune, were no longer in a position to assist him. Friendly relations with Haydn and Mozart were now of service to him, for they recommended him to the publisher Artaria, and helped to make known his musical capacity. E. nursed Mozart during his last illness, and the composer's widow entrusted to him the task of completing the Requiem. (He began the work, but soon gave it up.) In 1792 he became choirmaster of the Carmelite church, in 1794 also to the " Schottenstift," in 1804 vice " Hofcapellmeister," in 1810 music-master to the Imperial princes, and in 1824, on the retirement of Salieri, principal capellmeister. In 1833, while conducting a performance of Mozart's Requiem, he was seized with a stroke of apoplexy, and from that time was forced to give up all activity, both as conductor and composer. As a sacred composer he occupies an honourable position (thirty-two masses, of which seven are printed, one requiem, two oratorios, seven Te Deums, thirty offertories, of which seven are printed, etc.); many of his works are still performed at Vienna. His symphonies, quartets, sonatas, concertos, songs, etc., are now forgotten.

Eyken, (1) (Eycken, Du Chesne) S i m o n v a n. (*See* QUERCU.)—(2) (Eijken), J a n A l b e r t v a n, b. April 26, 1822, Amersfoort (Holland), d. Sept. 24, 1868, Elberfeld. He was the son of an organist, studied organ-playing and composition, from 1845 to 1846, at the Leipzig Conservatorium, and, on Mendelssohn's advice, for some time also with Joh. Schneider at Dresden, and gave concerts with great success in Holland. In 1848 he became organist of the "Remonstrantenkirche," Amsterdam, in 1853 of the "Zuyderkirche," and teacher at the Rotterdam school of music, and from 1854 until his death, was organist of the Reformed Church at Elberfeld. As a composer, E. has become specially known by his organ pieces (three sonatas, 150 chorals with introductions, twenty-five preludes, toccata and fugue on the name *BACH*, variations, transcriptions, arrangements of clavier fugues of Bach for organ, etc.); he also wrote ballads, songs, quartets for mixed voices, a violin sonata, music to the tragedy *Lucifer*.—His brother G e r a r d I s a a k, b. May 5, 1832, is also an organist, and, since 1855, has been music teacher at Utrecht.

F.

F, (1) Letter name of the sixth note of our musical alphabet (q.v.), the oldest one of our musical system, which was placed as a clef (*clavis signata*) before a stave. The use of the F-*clef* extends back to the 10th century. From the 11th to the 13th century the F-line was generally coloured red (*minium*), and the c-line, on the other hand, yellow (*crocum*), so that they might be more prominent. The clef was originally, and for centuries, a real F or *f*, and only gradually assumed its present form:—

In Italy, France, etc., our F is called *fa* (for the compound solmisation names, *cf.* MUTATION).—(2) Abbreviation of *forte; ff = fortissimo; fff = fortissimo possibile.*—(3) The holes in the belly of the violin, tenor, 'cello, and double-bass, from their shape, are often called the *f, ff* holes.

Fa, in Italy, France, Belgium, Spain, etc., is the name of the sound called *f* in Germany, England, Holland, Sweden, etc. (*Cf.* SOLMISATION, *also* MUTATION.)

Faber, (1) N i k o l a u s, by name, the oldest known German organ-builder. He built (1359-61) the organ in Halberstadt Cathedral, which was described by Prætorius ("Syntagma" II).—(2) N i k o l a u s, published in 1516 "Rudimenta Musicæ" (2nd ed. revised by Aventinus).—(3) "Magister" H e i n r i c h, b. Lichtenfels, d. Feb. 26, 1552, Oelsnitz i.V.; he was rector in 1538 of the St. George Monastic School near Naumburg, whence he was expelled in 1545 on account of some satirical songs against the Pope, and afterwards became rector at Brunswick. He was the author of "Compendiolum musicæ pro incipientibus" (1548, many times republished; in German by Christoff Rid, 1572, and by Joh. Gothart 1605, both repeatedly republished; in Latin and in German by M. Vulpius, 1610 [with additions, seven editions]. The translation by Rid was revised by A. Gumpeltzhaimer 1591, 1600, 1611, etc.), as well as "Ad musicam practicam introductio" (1550, 1558, 1563, 1568, 1571, etc.), of which the "Compendiolum" is only an abstract. The rector, Heinrich F., who died at Quedlinburg in 1598, has nothing to do with these two works, and his name ought to be struck out of musical dictionaries. (*Cf.* Eitner's reference to the matter in the *Monatshefte für Musikgeschichte*, 1870, No. 2.) — (4) B e n e d i k t (1602-31), who held an appointment at Coburg, was composer of psalms à 8, "Cantiones sacræ," à 4-8, of an Easter cantata, Congratulation cantata, etc. (all of which appeared at Coburg).

Fabio. (*See* URSILLO).

Fabri, (1) S t e f f a n o, maestro di cappella at the Vatican, 1599 to 1601, and at the Lateran, 1603 to 1607. He wrote two books of "Tricinia" (1602 and 1607).—(2) S t e f f a n o (the younger), b. 1606, Rome, d. Aug. 27, 1658. He was a pupil of Nanini, about 1648 maestro di cappella at the French church of St. Louis, and in 1657 at Santa Maria Maggiore. He wrote motets à 2-5 (1650), and *Salmi concertati* à 5 (1660).

Fabricius, (1) W e r n e r, b. April 10, 1633, Itzehoe, d. Jan. 9, 1679. He studied music at Hamburg with Sellius and Scheidemann, and also law at Leipzig, and became a lawyer there; but at the same time he filled the post of organist at St. Thomas's Church, and that of musical director at St. Paul's Church. He wrote: "Deliciæ harmonicæ" (65 Pavanes, Allemandes, etc., à 5, 1657), sacred Arias à 4-8, dialogues and concertos (1662).—(2) J o h a n n Albert, son of the former, b. Nov. 11, 1668, Leipzig, d. April 30, 1736, as professor of elocution at Hamburg. He was a distinguished bibliographer, and published "Thesaurus antiquitatum hebraicarum" (1713, 7 vols.), "Bibliotheca græca sive notitia scriptorum veterum græcorum" (1705-28, 14 vols.), all three important works of reference in connection with the history of music.

Façade (Fr.), in an organ the front-board with pipes " in prospect."

Faccio, F r a n c o, b. March 8, 1841, Verona, d. July 23, 1891, Monza, in a private asylum; he studied with Ronchetti and Mazzucato at Milan Conservatorio, and became a friend of Arrigo Boïto's, wandering with him away from the broad high road of Italian operatic music. Of his two operas—*I profughi Fiamminghi* (1863) and *Amleto* (1865)—the latter (libretto written by Boïto) especially gained for him the laudable reproach that it was *à la* Wagner. It was well received at Florence, but hissed at La Scala, Milan. In 1866 F. and Boïto served in the campaign under Garibaldi. In 1867-68 they visited Scandinavia together, about which time the former wrote his symphony in F. From 1868 F. was professor at the Milan Conservatorio (at first for harmony, afterwards for counterpoint and composition), and at the same time conductor at the Teatro Carcano, and later on at La Scala. He enjoyed the fame of being, after Mariani's death, the best conductor in Italy. Besides operas, F. wrote some sets of songs, and (jointly with Boïto) the cantata *Le sorelle d'Italie* (1862).

Facilemente (Ital.), easily, fluently.

Fackeltanz (Ger.), a dance with torches; a kind of polonaise.

Facture (Fr.), the style in which a composition is written.

Fa feint (Fr.), **Fa fictum** (Lat), lit. " feigned Fa." Notes lowered a semitone by a flat were called thus in the old theory of music. If, for instance, you flatten the note B, this B♭ will, as regards pitch, be in the same relation to A as F (Fa) to E (Mi).

Fag., abbr. of **Fagott** (Ger.), *fagotto* (Ital.).

Fage. (*Vide* LAFAGE.)

Fago, N i c o l a, b. 1674, Tarento (hence called *il Tarentino*); was at first a pupil of A. Scarlatti at the Conservatorio dei Poveri, then of Provenzale at the Conservatorio de' Turchini. After his studies were completed he became assistant teacher to Provenzale, and, finally, his successor. The year of his death is not known, but he was still living in 1729. Leonardo Leo was one of his pupils. He was a prolific composer for the church, and wrote also an oratorio (*Faraone sommerso*), cantatas, and several operas. His works are to be found in manuscript in various libraries in Italy, as well as in that of the Paris Conservatoire.

Fagott (Ger.), the bassoon.

Fahrbach, (1) J o s e f, b. Aug. 25, 1804, Vienna, d. there June 7, 1883, an important flautist and guitar player; he wrote many flute concertos. His son was—(2) W i l h e l m, b. 1838, Vienna, d. there 1866, conductor of an orchestra of his own, and dance composer.—(3) P h i l i p p, favourite dance composer and conductor, b. Oct. 25, 1815, Vienna, d. there March 31, 1885, pupil of Lanner; he also tried his hand at opera (*Der Liebe Opfer*, 1844 ; *Das Schwert des Königs*, 1845). His son is—(4) P h i l i p p, b. 1843, a favourite dance composer and bandmaster at Pesth, d. Feb. 15, 1894, Vienna.

Faignient, N o ë, Dutch contrapuntist about 1570; he lived at Antwerp, and wrote in the style of Orlando Lasso (three-part arias, motets, madrigals, 1567 ; chansons, madrigals, and motets, four to six parts, 1568; motets and madrigals, four to six parts, 1569; madrigals, five to eight parts, 1595 ; and, besides, separate ones in collections).

Faisst, I m m a n u e l G o t t l o b F r i e d r i c h, distinguished organist, b. Oct. 13, 1823, Esslingen (Württemberg), studied theology at Tübingen, but, meanwhile, had so far trained himself as a musician, that Mendelssohn, to whom he submitted some compositions at Berlin in 1844, advised him to continue his studies without the aid of a teacher. He held intercourse with Haupt, Dehn, Thiele, but without receiving instruction from them. After he had made concert tours as organist in various towns (1846), he settled in Stuttgart, founded, in 1847, a union for classical church music, with others, in 1849, the " Schwäbischer Sängerbund," and in 1857, with Lebert and others, the Conservatorium, in which he became principal teacher of the organ and of composition. In 1859 he undertook the direction of the institution, which has developed into one of the most important music schools of Germany. He was, besides, organist of the Stiftskirche, and member of the committee of the " Allgemeiner deutscher Sängerbund." From the university of Tübingen he received the degree of doctor for his " Beiträge zur Geschichte der Klaviersonate " (in Dehn's " Caecilia," vol. xxv., 1846), and the King of Württemberg named him professor. Among his compositions are organ pieces, a double fugue for pf. (in Lebert-Stark's Pianoforte School), songs, choruses, motets, cantatas, etc. In conjunction with S. Lebert he brought out the far-famed edition of classical pf. works published by Cotta (Beethoven, from Op. 53, edited by Bülow); and with Stark he published an " Elementar- und Chorgesangschule " (two parts, Instruction- and Exercise-book). Several works for male voices gained prizes (" Die Macht des Gesanges," " Gesang im Grünen "). D. June 5, 1894, Stuttgart.

Fa la, the burden and name of songs that came into favour in the latter part of the 16th century. (*Vide* BALLET.)

Falsa (Lat. and Ital.), False; *quinta falsa,*

diminished fifth; *musica falsa*, the same as *musica ficta*. (*Vide* FICTA.)

False Fifth, the same as DIMINISHED FIFTH. (*See* FIFTH.)

False relation (Ger. *Querstand*) is the conspicuous appearance, and one the effect of which is unpleasant to the ear, of a chromatically changed note in a part other than the one in which it could have been reached by the step of a semitone. The unpleasant effect of false relation merely proceeds from an insufficient comprehension of the harmonic relationship; and of this, one can easily become convinced, since by the frequent repetition of an harmonic progression involving false relation, the unpleasantness almost entirely disappears. An effect of false relation will always happen when a progression of parts, not otherwise modulating, cannot possibly be explained as a case of impure intonation. Mozart and Schubert, in their pianoforte works, are extremely fond of playing with effects of false relation; the performer, however, need only make the note producing false relation a little more prominent than the rest in order to remove all unpleasantness. The most risky kind of false relation occurs in passing from a major chord to a minor chord of the same fundamental tone (*a*); but it is of no moment when the second fundamental tone is a major third above or below the first (*b*), or a minor third above or below the first (*c*):

Falsetto (Ital.). (1) The head-voice as distinguished from the chest-voice.—(2) A singer who sings soprano or alto parts with such a voice. *Falsetti* must not be confounded with *castrati*. (*See* REGISTER.)

Falso bordone (Ital.). *See* FAUX BOURDON.

Faltin, Richard Friedrich, b. Jan. 5, 1835, Danzig, pupil there of Markull, of Fr. Schneider (Dessau), and of the Leipzig Conservatorium; in 1856 music teacher at an institute in Wiborg, from 1869 at Helsingfors, as conductor of the Symphony Concerts, 1870 organist and University musical director, from 1872 also director of a choral union, 1873–83 capellmeister of the Finnish Opera. He has published Finnish National Songs, and a Finnish Book of Songs.

Fa mi. In the old solmisation the name of the semitone progression—in the first place of V—E, then of B♭—A, E♭—D, etc.

Faminzin, Alexander Sergiewitch, b. Oct. 24 (Nov. 5), 1841, Kaluga (Russia), pupil of Jean Vogt at Petersburg; of Hauptmann, Richter, and Riedel at Leipzig; and of Seifriz at Löwenberg; he became, in 1865, professor of the history of music at the Petersburg Conservatoire, and in 1870 secretary of the Russian Musical Society. F. commands high respect for his compositions (Russian rhapsody for violin with orchestra, stringed quartets, operas —*Sardanapal* [1875] and *Uriel Acosta* [1883], pf. works, etc.) and also for his writings. He is a contributor to various newspapers, musical critic to the Russian *St. Petersburger Zeitung*, and has translated E. F. Richter's "Harmonielehre," Marx's "Allgemeine Musiklehre," etc., into Russian.

Fandango (Rondeña, Malagueña), a Spanish dance in $\frac{3}{8}$ time, of moderate movement (*allegretto*), with accompaniment of guitar, and castanets, with the castanet rhythm:

It is performed between rhymed verses, during the singing of which the dance stops.

Fanfare, a stately festive trumpet signal, of greater or less extent, in which the triad only is used, and which, as a rule, ends on the fifth. A celebrated example (concluding, however, on the tonic) is the F. in the second act of *Fidelio*, which announces the approach of the governor.

Fanfare (Fr.), same as HORN-MUSIC (q.v.).

Faning, Eaton, English composer, b. May 20, 1851, Helston, Cornwall. He studied at the Royal Academy of Music, and won the Mendelssohn Scholarship in 1873. He is director of the music at Harrow School. He has written two operettas, a symphony, two quartets, anthems, songs, part-songs (the "Song of the Vikings" has attained wide popularity).

Fantasia (Ger. *Phantasiestück*). As a name for instrumental pieces, F. indicates no definite form, but, on the contrary, free production, having no relation to fixed forms. Thus, many of the pieces first composed expressly for instruments (those of G. Gabrieli, H. Vecchi, etc.) appear under the name *Fantasia*, although it is not possible to distinguish them formally from *Ricercar, Sonata, Toccata*, etc. The common characteristic of these indefinite compositions consisted of the development of a musical thought by means of free imitation, or fugal working, though not, as in the fugue at the fifth, according to a fixed scheme. When a definite fugue form had been evolved, the name F. came to have the meaning of something quite opposed to fugue (*cf.* J. S. Bach's Fantasia and Fugue in A minor); it also differed from the sonata in its departure from strict cyclic form (*cf.* Mozart's

Fantasia and Sonata in c minor). The liberation of the sonata from the schematism of three- or four-fold division, and from the stereotyped sonata-form (q.v.) of the first movement, drew sonata and F. once more closer to each other (*cf.* Beethoven, "Sonata quasi Fantasia," Op. 27, I. and II.; he might have also given this inscription to Ops. 78, 90, and to the "last five"). Many arrangements of operatic melodies, or folk-songs of the pot-pourri type, are now called fantasias; it would be better to style them paraphrases (pieces ornamented with tinsel-finery) of certain melodies. A F. is produced when anyone improvises, preludes, or extemporises.

Fantastico (Ital.), fantastic, in free form.

Fantasy is the creative activity of the mind, the *power of imagination*, the real mother of all art, in so far as art is something more than mere imitation of nature—a spontaneous generation. In any case, the creative faculty of man depends on the impressions which he receives; the material with which he works is bestowed on him by nature. This faculty is the reproduction of impressions received, yet not a direct, unchanged reproduction, but a free transformation of the same according to laws implanted in the human mind. The freedom of the fantasy-faculty is nowhere so evident as in music; and, again, it is here that the laws by which it is ruled, and which prevent it from degenerating into mere caprice, are most clearly made manifest. The painter, the sculptor, is confined within much narrower limits, in so far as he must imitate forms given to him by nature; and even the poet, in imagination, evokes pictures from surrounding nature. It is otherwise with the musician, for whom nature only provides elements of the most primitive kind, but, at the same time, inexorable laws, according to which he must create, out of the raw material, works of art. Nature produces landscapes, figures, situations, which often the painter has only slavishly to copy in order to create a perfect work of art; but she makes no music, she sings no melodies—she only gives tones to the musician, and his tone-pictures are his own work; he has no model for them, only laws in his mind which will point out the right road to his imagination. These laws are valid for mental activity of all kinds. They enforce unity in variety, *i.e.* unity clearly set forth in its various embodiments of contrast, conflict, and esthetic reconciliation. (*Cf.* ESTHETICS.) The laws respecting musical creation, on close investigation, can be particularised down to minute technical details, and it is seen that music has no projection in nature, but exists in the inner life of man; that it is a picture of the movement of the soul in its various states. Thus the F. of the composer is not, indeed, an imitation of nature, but still a creation according to natural laws from which no departure

can be made without producing the effect of imperfection or ugliness.

Farabi. (*See* ALFARABI.)

Farandole, a Provençal dance in $\frac{6}{8}$ time, similar to the gigue (for instance, in Gounod's *Mireille*, and Bizet's *L'Arlésienne*).

Farce (Fr., *Farsa* Ital.), a farce.

Fargas y Soler, A n t o n i o, Spanish writer on music, published as a supplement to the Madrid musical paper *La España Musical*, and from 1866, in sections, a biographical Dictionary of Music—"Biografias de los Musicos, etc." (extracts from Fétis); he has also published a "Diccionario de Musica."

Farinelli, (1) celebrated singer (evirato), b. June 24, 1705, Naples, d. July 15, 1782, Bologna. His real name was Carlo Broschi, and he sprang from a noble Neapolitan family. He received an artistic training from Porpora, and already as a half-grown lad became famous in Italy under the name *Il Ragazzo* (the boy). In 1722 he gained an unprecedented triumph at Rome in Porpora's opera, *Eumene*. His *messa di voce* is said to have been unusually fine, both as regards duration and production of tone. He received the final polishing touch as late as 1727 from Bernacchi in Bologna, after the latter had beaten him in a competition. He repeatedly went to Vienna, exciting his audience there, as everywhere, to a high pitch of enthusiasm by his astonishing "divisions" and his faultless shake. He then, at the personal request of the Emperor Charles VI., also studied sustained and expressive singing, and became, in consequence, as important a dramatic singer (in the noble sense of the word) as he had previously been a coloratura virtuoso. In 1734 he was drawn to London, on the advice of Porpora, by Handel's enemies, and met with such success that Handel was forced to give up his opera undertaking at the Haymarket, and from that time to devote all his powers to oratorio. Laden with gold, F. turned his steps towards Spain (1736), where an extraordinary fate detained him; for his singing cured the melancholy of Philip V., and F. did not venture to leave; and he remained, indeed, after the death of Philip, for many years as the favourite of Ferdinand VI., exerting immense influence on the important policy of this king. Only at the accession to power of Charles III. (1759) was he driven from Spain. In 1761 he built himself a magnificent palace at Bologna, and died there, in perfect retirement, at the age of 77.— (2) G i u s e p p e, b. May 7, 1769, Este, d. Dec. 12, 1836, Trieste, pupil of the Conservatorio della Pietà at Naples (Barbiello, Fago, Sala, Tritto), a prolific opera-composer in the style of Cimarosa, whose *Matrimonio Segreto* was repeatedly performed with a duet by F., without any difference in the style being noticed. He composed fifty-eight operas (mostly comic), several oratorios and cantatas, also a number of sacred works (five grand masses, two Te Deums, Stabat Mater, etc.). F. lived from 1810–17 as maestro at Turin, then Venice, and in 1819 became maestro at Trieste.

Farmer, John, b. Aug. 16, 1836, Nottingham, pupil of the Leipzig Conservatorium and of A. Späth at Coburg ; he was teacher at a music school in Zürich, 1862 music-teacher at Harrow School, in 1885 organist of Balliol College, where he instituted regular concerts. F. has composed an oratorio (*Christ and His Soldiers*, 1878), a Requiem, a fairy opera (*Cinderella*), choral songs with orchestra, and has also published several collections of school songs.

Farrenc, Jacques Hippolyte Aristide, b. April 9, 1794, Marseilles, d. Jan. 31, 1865, Paris ; he was second flute at the Théâtre Italien, Paris, in 1815, and in the following year studied at the Conservatoire. After that he was active as a teacher of music and as composer, especially for the flute. He established a music business, but gave it up in 1841, and, inspired by Fétis' *Revue musicale* and " Biographie Universelle," devoted himself to historical studies in connection with music, so that when Fétis was preparing the second edition of his great work, Farrenc was able to render him valuable aid. He was also for many years a contributor to the *France musicale*, and other newspapers.—His wife, Jeanne Louise, daughter of the sculptor Jacques Edme. Dumont, sister of the sculptor Auguste Dumont, b. May 31, 1804, Paris, d. there Sept. 15, 1875, was a distinguished pianist and highly esteemed composer. She was a pupil of Reicha, and appointed professor of the pianoforte at the Conservatoire in 1842, receiving a pension in 1873. She composed symphonies, variations, sonatas, trios, quartets, quintets, a sextet, a nonet, etc., twice received a prize (*Prix Chartier*) from the Académie for distinguishing herself in the department of chamber-music, and wrote historical notes and comments to her husband's publications of classical works for the pianoforte (" Trésor du Pianiste ").

Farsa. (*See* FARCE.)

Fasch, (1) Johann Friedrich, b. April 15, 1688, Buttelstädt, near Weimar, a pupil of Kuhnau at Leipzig, d. 1758 (1759) as court capellmeister at Zerbst : he composed masses, motets, concertos, an opera, etc.—(2) Karl Friedrich Christian, son of the former, founder of the " Singakademie " at Berlin, b. Nov. 18, 1736, Zerbst, d. Aug. 3, 1800, Berlin. In spite of weakness of constitution, and without any instruction, he developed considerable musical talent, and, taking the greatest care of his health, trained himself for the musical profession. In 1756 he was called to Berlin as second cembalist to Frederick the Great, Ph.

Em. Bach being his coadjutor ; but, through the Seven Years' War, he soon lost this appointment. From 1774 to 1776 he was, *ad interim*, capellmeister at the opera, but afterwards had once again to depend on private teaching. He made use of his free time for zealous study of composition, and developed masterly contrapuntal skill (among other things, a combination of five canons for twenty-five voices). Lastly, in 1792, he found a praiseworthy field for activity in the " Singakademie," which he founded at Berlin, an institution which quickly developed to a state of great prosperity, and which to-day enjoys the highest fame. Of this, F. was conductor up to the time of his death. Zelter was his successor, and, in memory of him, wrote a short biography (1801). Only a few compositions of F. have been preserved (among which a Mass à 16 published by the " Singakademie") ; the greater number of his works were burnt, by his order, shortly before his death.

Fassade. (*See* FAÇADE.)

Fastoso (Ital.), pompous, stately.

Faugues, Vincent, Dutch contrapuntist of the 15th century, manuscripts by whom have been preserved in the Pope's Chapel. Tinctor makes mention of a composer named Guillaume F.

Faure, Jean Baptiste, b. Jan. 15, 1830, Moulins (Allier), son of a church singer. He lost his father at an early age, and soon, by means of his attractive boy's voice, supported his mother and brothers and sisters. He entered the Paris Conservatoire, became chorister boy at St. Nicolas des Champs, and afterwards at the Madeleine, where, in *maître* Trévaux, he found an excellent teacher. During the period of mutation he played the double-bass in a suburban orchestra. When his voice returned to him as a baritone, full and pleasing in quality, he was soon successful. After further study at the Conservatoire, for the space of two years, under Ponchard and Moreau-Sainti, he received the first prize in the Opéra Comique singing-class. In 1852 he was engaged at the Opéra Comique with Bataille and Bussine. His first successes were not phenomenal, but good, and he advanced *crescendo*. He sang for a long time as principal baritone at the Opéra Comique after the retirement of the singers named above ; he then went to the Grand Opéra, and achieved a success such as had not been witnessed since the time of Duprez. In 1857 he was appointed professor of singing at the Conservatoire, but soon resigned. He has published some books of songs.

Fauré, Gabriel Urbain, noteworthy composer, b. May 13, 1845, Pamiers (Ariège), pupil of Niedermeyer, Dietsch, and Saint-Saëns, 1866 organist at Rennes, 1870 accompanying organist of St. Sulpice, Paris, afterwards principal organist of St. Honoré, and finally maître de chapelle of the Madeleine. He has written, besides various vocal pieces (songs, duets, etc.), a well-known violin sonata (1878), a Berceuse and Romance for violin and orchestra, an Élégie for 'cello, two pf. quartets, a violin concerto, an orchestral suite, symphony in D minor, a Requiem (1888), a choral work (" La Naissance de Vénus"), the "Chœur des Djinns," etc. In 1885 he received the *Prix Chartier* (for the best chamber composition).

Faust, Carl, German composer and bandmaster, b. Feb. 18, 1825, Neisse, Silesia, d. Sept. 12, 1892, Bad Cudowa. Bandmaster from 1853–63; capellmeister at Holstein (1863–69), Waldenburg (1869–80). He has written a quantity of light, pleasing dance music.

Faustina. (*See* HASSE, 3.)

Faux-bourdon (Fr.; Ital. *Falso bordone;* Eng. *Fa-burden*), (1) is one of the oldest forms of vocal harmony. It arose in England, but its age has not hitherto been established. Gulielmus Monachus (14th to 15th century), whose treatise, " De præceptis artis musicæ," etc., was printed by Coussemaker (" Script." III., 273, f.), gives a detailed description of F. (*Faulx bordon*), mentions it as "*apud Anglicos communis,*" *i.e.* as something well known in England. F. was in three parts; to the Gregorian *Cantus firmus* (tenor) was added a part (contra-tenor) in parallel movement in the upper third, beginning and closing, however, on the fifth; and one in the under third, beginning and closing on the unison. The latter part was sung an octave higher than written, so that it fell to the soprano—

Notation.

Effect.

Dr. Guido Adler (q.v.) has written a valuable monograph on the F.—(2) At a later date F. came to mean a simple harmonisation of the *Cantus firmus,* not, indeed, as formerly, in parallel movement, but chiefly, or even exclusively, note against note in consonant chords, similar to the improvised counterpoint. In the 17th century the term was equivalent to *Contrapunto alla mente,* improvised according to similar rules, but ornamented with shakes and coloratura. Lastly, the term *Falso bordone* was also used for the reciting-note of the Psalms, which remains throughout at the same pitch.

Favarger, Réné, French pianist and composer, b. 1815, d. Étretat, near Havre, Aug. 3, 1868. He wrote a great many pianoforte pieces of a light, graceful character.

Fawcett, John, b. 1789, Bolton-le-Moors (Lancashire), d. there Oct. 26, 1867. He was originally a shoemaker, but afterwards devoted himself to music, and made a name as a sacred composer. He published collections of psalms and hymns : " The Voice of Harmony," " The Harp of Zion," " Miriam's Timbrel," and an oratorio, *Paradise.* He arranged the accompaniments to a collection (" Melodia divina ") of psalms published by Hart, etc. His son John, b. 1824, d. July 1, 1857, Manchester, Mus.Bac. (Oxford), was held in esteem as an organist.

Fay, (1). (*See* DUFAY.)—(2) Amy, pianist, b. May 21,1844, Bayon Goula (Mississippi), studied with Tausig, Kullak, Liszt, and also Deppe, and became known by her book, " Music Study in Germany." She lives at Chicago.

Fayolle, François Joseph Marie, b. Aug. 15, 1774, Paris, lived in London from 1815 to 1829, then in Paris, where he died Dec. 2, 1852, He published in 1810–11, jointly with Choron (q.v.), a " Dictionnaire historique des musiciens" (two vols.), to which, however, Choron only contributed a few articles and the introduction, while F. made use, for the most part, of Gerbert's old dictionary, making many errors in translation. He published besides : " Notices sur Corelli, Tartini, Gaviniés, Pugnani et Viotti, extraits d'une histoire du violon" (1810); " Sur les drames lyriques et leur exécution " (1813); " Paganini et Bériot " (1830).

F double sharp, the note F raised by a ×.

Fechner, Gustav Theodor, physicist and philosopher, also a clever poet (pseudonym, Dr. Mises), b. April 19, 1801, Gross-Särchen (Niederlausitz), d. Nov. 18, 1887, Leipzig. He was, from 1834, professor in ordinary of physics, and distinguished not only on account of his works on physics, which treat thoroughly of many matters relating to music (" Repertorium der Experimentalphysik "), but also for his philosophical writings, especially the " Elemente der Psychophysik " (1860, two vols.), and the " Vorschule der Ästhetik " (1876, two vols), of essential importance in establishing the first principles of a rational system of musical esthetics.

Fedele. (*See* TREU.)

Federclavier (Ger.), a spinet.

Federici, Vincenzo, Italian opera composer, b. 1764, Pesaro, d. Sept. 26, 1826, Milan, wrote fourteen serious operas, and one comic opera, *La Locandiera Scaltra* (Paris, 1812), also several cantatas. He was professor of counterpoint, and, from 1812, censor at the Milan Conservatorio.

Feldflöte (Ger.). (*See* BAUERNFLÖTE.)

Felstein, Sebastian von (Felstinensis), bachelor of music and director of church music at Cracow about 1530, wrote a small treatise on Gregorian Chant: "Opusculum musicæ" (several times republished; 2nd ed. 1515), also one on mensural music, "Opusculum musicæ mensuralis"; both were published together in 1519. In 1536 he prepared an edition of the text of St. Augustine's "Dialogi de musica," and also published a volume of hymns of his own composition.

Feltre, Alphonse Clarke, Comte de, b. June 27, 1806, Paris, d. Dec. 3, 1850, son of the marshal, Duke of F. He was an officer in the French army, but resigned already in 1829, and devoted himself entirely to music; he composed several operas, pianoforte pieces, songs, ensembles, etc.

Fenaroli, Fedele, b. April 15, 1730, Lanciano (Abruzzi), d. Jan. 1, 1818, Naples; he was a pupil of Durante at the Conservatorio di Loreto there (1742), and, after his course of study was ended, teacher at the Conservatorio della Pietà until his death. A large number of famous composers (Cimarosa, Zingarelli, etc.) studied under him. He composed in a plain, unostentatious style (motets, masses, hymns, etc.); he also published studies on counterpoint and a Method of general-bass (" Regole per principianti di cembalo ").

Feo, Francesco, eminent teacher of singing and composer at Naples, pupil of Gizzi, and his successor in his post as teacher. He wrote his first opera, *Zenobia (L'amor tirannico)* in 1713, which was followed by a series of others, an oratorio, masses, etc. The year of his death is not known.

Fermamente (Ital.), firmly.

Fermāta (Ital.), pause sign (⌢). The F. lengthens the value of a note or rest for an indefinite time; it is sometimes written over the bar-stroke, and then a pause is made. The F. over rests of long value (for ex. ⌢〓▬〓) does not lengthen their value, but only renders them indefinite; in some cases they are actually made shorter. (*Cf.* "L. Mozart, Violinschule," p. 45.) By raising his bâton and holding it still, a conductor indicates the length of the F. In the complicated canonic notation of the 15th to the 16th century the conclusions of voice-parts are shown by means of an F. (*corona*), which then gives to the note in question the value of the concluding Longa. Of especial importance is the F. in concertos, etc., which defers (interrupted cadence) the final cadence, and which gives an opportunity to interpolate a last, and extended solo; as a rule, this F. is on the second inversion of the tonic chord. (*See* CADENZA.)

Feroce (Ital.), fierce, violent.

Ferrabosco (Ferabosco), (1) Alfonso, Italian composer of madrigals, in the service of the Duke of Savoy (madrigals à 4, 1542; à 5, 1587;

some in Pierre Phalèse's "Harmonie céleste," 1593).—(2) Domenico, papal chapel-singer about the same time, madrigals by whom are to be found in various collections.—(3) Constantino, for several years in the imperial service at Vienna, published a book of Canzonette (1591). —(4) Alfonso, b. about 1580, Greenwich, of Italian parents (the above-mentioned Alfonso F. was considered his father), d. 1652; about 1605 he became teacher of music to Prince Henry, to whom, in 1609, he dedicated a volume of " Ayres." He was a contributor to Leighton's *Teares* (Lamentations, 1614), composer of " Fancies" (Fantasias) for viols.

Ferranti. (*See* ZANI DE FERRANTI.)

Ferrari, (1) Benedetto, poet and composer, b. 1597, Reggio, d. Oct. 22, 1681, Modena; he received his musical training at Rome, and distinguished himself, first as performer on the theorbo, and for this reason he received the nickname "Della Tiorba." After he had lived for some time in Venice, and written libretti, and composed operas for the theatres there, he received in 1645 an appointment in the court band at Modena, but exchanged it in 1651 for a better one at Vienna, and brought out operas there, and also at Ratisbon. He was recalled in 1653, as maestro di cappella, to Modena, but on the change of government in 1662, he was dismissed, and only in 1671, when Franz II. reassumed the reins of government, was he reappointed maestro. The libretto of *Andromeda*, written by F., was set to music by Manelli, and the work was produced at the Teatro San Cassiano, Venice (1637). It was the first opera performed in a public theatre (F. undertook to defray the costs of the undertaking); before that, all performances of opera were of a private nature. The first opera F. composed (to his own libretto) was *Armida* (1639). The music of his operas is lost. Six opera libretti appeared in 1644 (and 1651); and the instrumental introduction to a ballet (*Dafne*) is preserved in manuscript at Modena. There also still exists in print " Musiche varie a voce sola " (1638).—(2) Domenico, distinguished violinist, b. at Piacenza, d. 1780, Paris, pupil of Tartini, lived first of all at Cremona; he appeared in 1754 with great success at Paris, and was for some years leader of the band at Stuttgart. Six of his violin-sonatas with bass exist. His brother— (3) Carlo, an eminent 'cellist, b. 1730, Piacenza, d. 1789, as member of the court band at Parma, is said to have been the first who introduced into Italy the use of the thumb as a nut. He published soli for the 'cello.—(4) Jacopo Gotifredo, b. 1759, Roveredo (South Tyrol), d. Dec. 1842, London; he received his first musical education at the Mariaberg monastery, near Chur, studied afterwards under Latilla at Naples, whither he went as the travelling companion of Prince Liechtenstein. Campan, Marie Antoinette's master of the household, took him to Paris, where he received the post of accompanist to the queen, and afterwards occupied a similar post at the Théâtre Feydeau. The Revolution frightened him away, and, after several years of tour-making, he settled in London as a teacher of music. Besides many works for the voice, pf., harp, and flute, four operas, two ballets, etc., he published a Vocal Method (" A Treatise of Singing," 2 vols), " Studio di musica praticae teorica," and Reminiscences of his life (" Anedotti, etc.," 1830, 5 vols.).—(5) S e r a f i n o A m a d e o d e (Deferrari), b. 1824, Genoa, d. there March 31, 1885, as director of the Conservatorio. He was a composer of Italian operas (*Don Carlo* [1853], *Pipelè* [1856], *Il Menestrello*, etc.).—(6) F r a n c i s c a, b. 1800, Christiania, d. Oct. 5, 1828, Gross-Salzbrunn (Silesia); she was a celebrated performer on the harp.—(7) C a r l o t t a, b. Jan. 27, 1837, Lodi, pupil of Mazzucato at the Milan Conservatorio; she acquired great fame as a composer in Italy with several operas (*Ugo*, 1857; *Sofia*, 1866; *Elenore d'Arbocea*, 1871), a grand festival mass (1868), a Requiem (1868), and many songs. She was at the same time a very prolific poetess (she also wrote the libretti for her operas, and the words for her songs).

Ferreira da Costa, R o d r i g o, Portuguese theorist, doctor of jurisprudence and mathematics, and member of the Lisbon Academia, d. 1834 (or 1837) ; he wrote " Principios de musica " (1820–24, 2 vols.).

Ferretti, G i o v a n n i, b. about 1540, Venice, published five books (à 5) and two books (à 6) of *Canzoni alla napoletana*, also a book of madrigals à 5 (1567–91).

Ferri, B a l d a s s a r e, famous evirato, b. Dec. 9, 1610, Perugia, d. there Sept. 8, 1680 ; he was, at the age of eleven, chorister to Cardinal Crescenzio at Orvieto. In 1625 the Prince (afterwards king) Wladislaus (IV.) of Poland won him for the court of Sigismund III. at Warsaw. In 1655, when Johann Kasimir V. broke up the court at Warsaw, F. entered the Imperial service at Vienna. In 1675 he returned to his native country. F. was one of the most distinguished vocal artists of any age. His virtuosity was almost incredible, and his length of breath almost inexhaustible; but to these qualities he united that of quiet, expressive singing.

Ferté. (*See* P A P I L L O N D E L A F.).

Fervente (Ital.), fervent, ardent, passionate.

Fesca, (1) F r i e d r i c h E r n s t, violinist and composer, b. Feb. 15, 1789, Magdeburg, d. May 24, 1826, Carlsruhe, received his first musical instruction in his native town, where he also appeared at concerts ; he studied in 1805 under A. E. Müller at Leipzig, and played at the same desk with him in the theatre and Gewandhaus orchestras. In 1806 he

received an appointment in the Oldenburg court band, and, in 1808, became solo violinist in the band of King Jérôme at Cassel. After the fall of Napoleon and the suppression of the kingdom of Westphalia, he lived for a short time at Vienna, and in 1815 became violinist in the court band at Carlsruhe, where he was soon advanced to the post of leader. As a composer he is highly esteemed for his chamber-music works (twenty quartets and five quintets, first published separately, afterwards together, at Paris) ; he wrote besides, three symphonies, four overtures, two operas (*Cantemira*, *Omar und Leila*), psalms, songs, etc.—(2) A l e x a n d e r E r n s t, son of the former, b. May 22, 1820, Carlsruhe, d. Feb. 22, 1849, Brunswick. He received his training in Berlin from the best teachers (Rungenhagen, J. Schneider, and Taubert), made concert tours as a pianist with success, but soon succumbed to the effects of a disorderly life. Four operas (*Marietta*, *Die Franzosen in Spanien*, *Der Troubadour*, *Ulrich von Hutten* (1849) were produced at Carlsruhe and Brunswick ; they were light in style, but gave evidence of great talent. His songs (forty-eight of them appeared under the title " F. Album ") are exceedingly popular.

Festa, (1) C o n s t a n t i o, distinguished contrapuntist, was appointed singer in the Pope's chapel (1517), d. April 10, 1545. He can be looked upon as a predecessor of Palestrina, with whose style his music has many points of similarity. He was the first Italian contrapuntist of importance, and gives a foretaste of the beauties which were to spring from the union of Netherland art with Italian feeling for euphony and melody. Of his works have been preserved : motets à 3 (1543), madrigals à 3 (1556), and Litanies (1583) ; also many motets and madrigals in collections, first in Petrucci's " Motetti della Corona " (1519), and a Te Deum à 4 and a Credo à 5 in manuscript (Abb. Santini). The Te Deum is still sung in the Vatican on grand festival occasions.—(2) G i u s e p p e M a r i a, b. 1771, Trani (Naples), d. April 7, 1839, as maestro at the Teatro San Carlo, and royal maestro at Naples ; he was a distinguished violinist, who also appeared in Paris. He wrote some compositions for the violin (quartets). His sister—(3) F r a n c e s c a, b. 1778, Naples, d. 1836, Petersburg, pupil of Aprile, was a well-known singer, first in Italy, 1809–11, Paris, then after her marriage, as Signora F.-Maffei again in Italy, and from 1829 at Petersburg.

Festing, M i c h a e l C h r i s t i a n, famous violinist, b. London, d. July 24, 1752 ; son of the equally famous flautist F. who played under Handel (1727), pupil of R. Jones and Geminiani, royal chamber musician, 1742 conductor and leader at Ranelagh Gardens, founder (with Greene) of the Society of Musicians (for the maintenance of decayed musicians and their families). His compositions are pieces for the violin (soli, sonatas, concertos), also some odes and cantatas.

Festivo (Ital.), festive.

Fétis, François Joseph, famous musical *littérateur*, b. March 25, 1784, Mons (Belgium), d. March 26, 1871, Brussels. He was a man of distinguished musical gifts, enormous diligence, and of almost unexampled working power; and very much is owing to him for his investigations concerning the history, theory, and philosophy of music. Son of an organist, already at the age of ten he began to write works of large dimensions; he became organist in his native town, and soon excited astonishment by his zest for learning, and by his attempts at composition. When his professional training at the Paris Conservatoire (where, from 1800 to 1803, Rey, Boieldieu, and Pradher were his teachers) came, nominally, to an end, he entered the field in which he gathered the finest laurels, that of the investigation of history. His first great work was a history of Gregorian Song; he was induced thereto by a Paris publisher (Ballard), who, on the re-establishment of Catholic worship, interrupted by the Revolution, had an idea of bringing out a new Ritual service-book, and commissioned F. to prepare one; the preparatory studies for that purpose increased gradually in dimension, yet, after all, the book was never published. Another path into which F. was soon led was that of the study of harmony: he already commenced at the Conservatoire, when Catel attacked Rameau's system. F., who had diligently studied ancient and modern languages, compared the works of Sabbatini and Kirnberger, and tried hard to form independent opinions. To his meditations we are indebted for the modern conception of tonality (q.v.). The works of Cimarosa, Paisiello, Guglielmi, which then ruled the stage; the reputation, ever growing brighter, of the German masters (Haydn, Mozart, Beethoven); the severe tendency of Cherubini to point back to the old Italian masters (Palestrina)—all this led him to the study of practical musical literature, and matured his mode of viewing things. He found himself emancipated from the spirit of any particular age, and able to render justice to all the various styles of music. In 1806 he married a rich lady (*see below*), but, after a few years, lost the whole of his fortune through the breaking of a Paris bank, and withdrew to the Ardennes in 1811, composing all the more diligently, and occupying himself with philosophical considerations concerning music. In 1813 he became organist of St. Peter's, Douai, and teacher of harmony and singing at the music school there. From that period dates the working out of an elementary Method of singing, which appeared later, and of a system of harmony which he presented to the Académie. In 1818 he settled again in Paris, and in 1821 was appointed professor of composition at the Conservatoire. In 1826 he founded the *Revue Musicale*, a musical paper of scientific tendency such as had not previously existed, neither has there since been one of a similar kind; he conducted this paper all by himself for five years, until he received a call to Brussels. At the same time he was musical critic to the *Temps* and the *National*. In 1827 he became librarian at the Conservatoire, and arranged, in 1832, historical concerts and historical lectures; but already in 1833, he undertook the direction of the Brussels Conservatoire, which post he retained until his death (for thirty-nine years). At the same time he exercised the functions of conductor, and was an active member of the Brussels Académie. The great merit of F. does not, indeed, lie in his compositions, although he himself entertained a high opinion with regard to them. He published pf. works (variations, fantasias, sonatas, etc., for two and four hands), a violin sonata, three quintets for pf. and strings, a sextet for pf. (four hands), and stringed quartet, two symphonies, a symphonic fantasia for orchestra and organ, a concert overture, requiem, songs, etc. Six operas were given from 1820 to 1832; a seventh (*Phidias*) remained in manuscript, as well as many sacred works (masses, Te Deums, etc.). Of his writings the following are the most important: "Méthode élémentaire et abrégée d'harmonie et d'accompagnement" (1824, practical method of harmony, many times republished, and much used in Belgium and France; also translated into Italian and English); "Traité de la fugue et du contrepoint" (1825, 1846; a celebrated work); "Traité de l'accompagnement de la partition" (1829; playing from score); "Solfèges progressifs" (1827; elementary method of singing, many times republished); a "Mémoire" on the merits of the Netherland composers (1829; cf. KIESEWETTER); "La musique mise à la portée de tout le monde" (1830, many times published and translated; German by Blum, 1833); "Biographie universelle des musiciens et bibliographie générale de la musique" (1835–44, eight vols., 2nd ed. 1860–65; A. Pougin wrote a supplement of two volumes, 1878–80, the most comprehensive work of its kind, and containing, by reason of its enormous size, unavoidable faults; but even now, especially for the musical history of the Middle Ages, and for modern Italian, French, and Netherland music, it is the best source, and is constantly quoted; "Manuel des principes de musique" (1837); "Traité du chant en chœur" (1837; "Manuel des jeunes compositeurs, des chefs de musique militaire, et des directeurs d'orchestre" (1837); "Méthode des méthodes de piano" (1837, analysis of the best pianoforte methods; published twice in Italian, 1841); "Méthode des méthodes de chant;" "Esquisse de l'histoire de l'harmonie" (1840, now only fifty copies); "Méthode élémentaire du plain-chant" (1843); "Traité complet de la théorie et de la pratique de l'harmonie" (1844, several times republished—in Italian, twice, by Mazzucato and Gambale, 1849; in Spanish by Gil, etc.); unfortunately, F. as theorist was a dictator, and brooked no reply; "Notice biographique de Nicolo Paganini" (1851, with a short history of the violin); "Antoine Stradivari" (1856, with investigations concerning the development of bowed instruments); "Exposition universelle de Paris en 1855 (1856, report of musical instruments); "Exposition universelle de Paris en 1867" (the same); a number of important essays in his *Revue Musicale* and its continuation, the *Revue et Gazette Musicale de Paris;* also in the reports of the Brussels Académie (commencing from the 11th vol.), and "Histoire générale de la musique" (1869–75, five vols.; extends only up to the 15th century). Several important works remain unfinished in manuscript.

F.'s wife, Adélaide Louise Cathérine, b. Sept. 23, 1792, Paris, d. June 3, 1866, Brussels, was the daughter of the editor of the *Mercure National*, P. F. J. Robert (friend of Danton's), and of the well-known Mademoiselle Céralio, a friend of Robespierre's. Madame F. translated Stafford's "History of Music" into French (1832). The two sons of F. likewise became musicians: Édouard Louis François, b. May 16, 1812, Bouvignes, near Dinant; he took part in the editorship of his father's *Revue Musicale*, and conducted it himself from 1833–35. He then followed his father to Brussels, and undertook the direction of the musical, afterwards of the art fueilleton of the *Indé-† ndant* (now *Indépendance Belge*), and next became subordinate officer in the Brussels Library; and for a long time has been librarian in ordinary, and member of the Académie etc. He published: "Les musiciens belges" (1848, two vols.). The younger son, Adolphe Louis Eugène, b. Aug. 20, 1820, Paris, d. there March 20, 1873, pupil of his father, and in pianoforte playing of Henri Herz; he composed many pieces for pf., harmonium, etc., also an opera, but without any special success. He lived at Brussels, Antwerp, and from 1856 was music teacher in Paris.

Feurich, Julius, pianoforte-maker, b. March 19, 1821, Leipzig, established himself in 1851 in his native town, after working under good masters (Pleyel, Wolff & Co. among others) in Paris. He has become specially famous for his pianinos.

Fevin, (1) Antonius de, distinguished (probably Netherland) contrapuntist, contemporary and rival of Josquin; nothing positive is known about his life (the Spaniards look upon him as a Spaniard, the French as a Frenchman). Of his works are preserved: three masses in Petrucci's "Missæ Antonii de F." (1515), three

others in Antiquis's "Liber XV. missarum" (1516), masses in manuscript at Munich and Vienna, motets in Petrucci's "Motetti della corona" (1514), and in several later collections. —(2) Robertus, b. Cambrai, was maestro to the Duke of Savoy, In Petrucci's masses "Antonii de F." is preserved a mass by Robertus de F. on "Le vilain jaloux;" another on "La sol fa re mi" is to be found in manuscript in the Munich library. As the two masses are side by side in Petrucci and in the Munich manuscript, the two F.'s were possibly related to each other.

Fèvre, le. (*See* LEFÈVRE.)

Fiacco (Ital.), weak, languishing.

Fiasco, failure.

Fibich, Zdenko, composer, b. Dec. 21, 1850, Seborschitz, near Tschaslau. He received his first instruction at Prague, then at the Leipzig Conservatorium (1865), and under Vincenz Lachner; he became, in 1876, second capellmeister of the National Theatre at Prague, and in 1878, director of the choir of the Russian church. F. is one of the most famous of the young Czeckish composers, and among his works deserving mention are the symphonic poems *Othello*, *Zaboj und Slavoj*, *Toman und die Nymphe*, two symphonies without programme, several overtures, two stringed quartets, choral ballad, "Die Windsbraut"; and, besides, a "Frühlingsromanze" for chorus and orchestra, and a symphonic tone-picture, "Vesna"; the Czeckish operas *Bukowin*, *Blanik* (1877), and *Die Braut von Messina* (1883); and melodramas, part-songs, a pf. quartet in E minor, Op. 11, songs, and pf. pieces, etc. He has also published a pianoforte Method.

Fiby, Heinrich, b. May 15, 1834, Vienna, pupil of the Conservatorium there, was at first conductor and violin soloist at the Laibach Theatre, and in 1857 became Stadtmusikdirector at Znaim, where he founded a music school and a musical union, both of which flourished under his direction. F. became specially known by his songs for male voices (also three operettas).

Fichtner, Pauline. (*See* ERDMANNSDÖRFFER.)

Ficta (Lat.), feigned; *Musica ficta*, feigned music, was the name formerly given to music in a transposed key, which, of course, required accidentals.

Fiddle (Lat. *Fidula*, Ger. *Fidel*), equivalent to viol, a comprehensive term for the older stringed instruments (8th to 14th century). The German *Fidel* preserved, for a longer period than the *viole* of the French, the arched and pear-shaped form of the sound-box; and, to distinguish it from the former, it was called in the 12th century *gigue(ham)* by the French. The German word *Geige* is derived from *gigue*.

Fides (Lat.), (1) a catgut string.—(2) a string-instrument.

Fidicen (Lat.), a lyre, harp, or lute-player; indeed, a player on any stringed instrument.

Fiedler, A u g. M a x, pianist and composer, b. Dec. 31, 1859, Zittau, studied the pianoforte with his father (Karl August F., teacher of music there), and theory and organ-playing with G. Albrecht; from 1877 to 1880 he studied at the Leipzig Conservatorium, where he gained the Holstein scholarship; and since 1882 he has been teacher at the Hamburg Conservatorium. He appeared with success as a concert player, and has published a piano quintet and pf. pieces; songs, a stringed quartet, a symphony in D minor (produced in 1886, Hamburg) are in manuscript.

Field, J o h n, one of the most original pian-istic phenomena, b. July 16, 1782, Dublin, d. Jan. 11, 1837, Moscow; he sprang from a family of able musicians, but was of a tender, weak con-stitution. At an early age he became a pupil of Clementi's, with whom he went in 1802 to Paris, and from there to Petersburg. He settled in the latter city as teacher, and became extra-ordinarily famous. After a long residence there, he returned to London in 1832, where he gave concerts with the greatest success, and travelled through Belgium, France, Italy, etc. His con-stitution, undermined by his irregular course of living, broke down at Naples; a Russian family took him back to Moscow. Field's highest achievement was displayed in his Nocturnes, which became models for Chopin (of the twenty now so-called Nocturnes, only twelve had that name given to them by F.). He wrote, besides, for the pianoforte, seven concertos, four son-atas, one quintet, two divertissements (piano-forte, two violins, flute, viola, and bass), varia-tions for 2–4 hands, rondos, etc.

Fiero (Ital.), proud.

Fife, a simple cross-flute (*See* FLUTE), gener-ally either in the key of F or B♭, and chiefly used in military music in combination with the side-drum, in what are called drum-and-fife bands.

Fifre (Fr.), a fife.

Fifths, *circle of*, is the rotation through the twelve fifths of the tempered system—*c* (*b♯*)—*g* (*f×, a♭♭*)—*d* (*c×, e♭♭*)—*a* (*g×, b♭♭*)—*e* (*f♭*)— *b* (*c♭*)—*f♯* (*g♭*)—*c♯* (*d♭*)—*g♯* (*a♭*)—*d♯* (*e♭*), *a♯* (*b♭*)—*e♯* (*f*)—*b♯* (*c*). When the circle of F. has to return to the starting-note, there must be an enharmonic change somewhere. Modula-tions through the whole circle of F., or a part of the same, are convenient, but from an artistic point of view, objectionable.

Fifths (*Parallel Fifths*). (*See* PARALLELS.)

Figuralmusik (Ger.), unequal counterpoint (q.v.; *cf.* FIGURATION).

Figura muta (Lat. and Ital.), a rest.

Figura obliqua (Lat.), in mensural music, was the joining together of two note-bodies into one slanting stroke. The F. O. of mensural music had no special meaning within the liga-tures, but at the close it meant *Imperfectio* for the last note. (*See* LIGATURE.)

Figuration (Ger. *Figurierung*) is the working out of more lively melodico-rhythmical motives (figures) in the contrapuntal parts accompany-ing a given part (figured counterpoint, figured chorale, etc.). Also the term F. is applied to the variation of a theme by the introduc-tion of accompanying figures ever increasing in liveliness, which, to a larger or smaller extent, twine round, and conceal the theme.

Figurato (Ital.), figurate or figurative.

Figured Bass. (*See* GENERAL BASS.)

Filar il tuono (Ital.). (*See* AFFILAR IL TUONO.)

Filippi, (1) G i u s e p p e d e, b. May 12, 1825, Milan, d. June 23, 1887, Neuilly, near Paris, son of the physician of like name who died 1856 (author of a " Saggio sull' estetica musicale," 1847). He lived from 1846 at Paris as a writer, was contributor to Pougin's supplement to Fétis's " Biographie universelle," and published " Guide dans les théâtres " (1857, jointly with the architect Chaudet) and " Parallèle des théâtres modernes de l'Europe " (1860).—(2) F i l i p p o, b. Jan. 13, 1833, Vicenza, d. June 25, 1887, Milan, studied law and took his degree at Padua, but soon devoted himself entirely to musical criticism. He undertook in 1858 (after having been on the staff for several years) the editing of the Milan *Gazetta Musicale*, and later on became musical critic to the *Persever-anza*. He published, separately, a series of musical articles under the title of " Musica e musicisti " (1876). F. is a follower of Wagner. His pamphlet on Richard Wagner was trans-lated into German, 1876 (" Richard Wagner: Eine musikalische Reise in das Reich der Zukunft ").

Filling-up Parts, (1) are those, in a composition of several parts, which are not treated melodic-ally, but which only, according to need, com-plete the harmony (in contradistinction to melody part, fundamental part [bass], con-certante parts). For instance, the chords in old pieces played by the accompanying organist, cembalist, likewise theorbist, gambist, etc., from the figuring above the continuo were F. P. (a good accompanist was not content with adding plain chords and ornamental runs, but could introduce figuration based on motives). In works in the concertante style (fugue, canon, trio, quartet, etc.) extra notes appear in cadenzas, or in the final cadence, and these must be regarded as filling-up, since, for the moment, they increase the number of parts; though in such a case it is better to speak of them as filling-up notes.— (2) In the organ the mutation stops (quint-, tierce-, mixture-stops) are F. P.; and in a similar sense the expression is employed for orchestral parts which enter in unison with other parts to mark accents, or to intensify the sound in *forte* passages, as, for instance, is frequently the case with the trombones.

Filling-up Stops. (*See* MUTATION STOPS.)

Fillmore, John Comfort, b. Feb. 4, 1843, New London County (Connecticut), pupil of the Leipzig Conservatorium (1866), a gifted teacher of music in America, now director of a music school of his own at Milwaukee. He has written: "History of Pianoforte Music" (1883), "Lessons on Musical History," "New Lessons of Harmony," "On the Value of Certain Modern Theories" (on von Oettingen's and Riemann's systems), and translated into English Riemann's "Klavierschule" and "Natur der Harmonik."

Filtsch, Karl, b. July 8, 1830, Hermannstadt, Siebenbürgen, an extraordinarily precocious pianist, in 1842 pupil of Chopin and Liszt at Paris; he made concert tours, in 1843, to London, Paris, etc., but died already on March 11, 1845, Vienna.

Fin'al, or *fino al* (Ital.), up to.

Final. The final is in the Church modes what the tonic is in our modern musical system. In the authentic modes the final is on the first degree, in the plagal modes on the fourth degree of the scale. Besides the *regular* finals (*i.e.* "concluding notes") there are also *irregular* ones (*confinals*), which occur frequently in the endings of the Psalms and in the sections of the Responsories, Graduals, and Tracts.

Finale (Ital., "closing movement") is the name given to the last part of compositions in several movements, especially in the case of sonatas, and works of like form (trios, quartets, etc.); and more especially when it has not the lively character of the rondo, but the more serious, passionate mood of a first movement, and is similar to it in structure. The last movement of a symphony is always called F. In opera by F. is understood the closing scene of an act, in which there is generally a grand *ensemble* (mostly with chorus). (*Cf.* OPERA.)

Finck, (1) **Heinrich,** one of the most important of German contrapuntists, received, according to the testimony of his grand-nephew, Hermann F., his training in Poland (Cracow), and was afterwards at the royal court of Poland under Johann I. (1492), Alexander (1501), and Sigismund (1506). The years of his birth and death are unknown. Of his works are still known: "Schöne auserlesene Lieder des hochberühmten Heinrich Finckens, etc." (1536), also some in Salblinger's "Concentus 8, 6, 5 et 4 vocum" (1545), and in Rhaw's "Sacrorum hymnorum liber I" (1542). A collection of songs, hymns, and motets has recently been published in vol. viii. of the *Publik. der Ges. f. Musikforschung* (Breitkopf &

Härtel). Two manuscript copies of a four-part "Missa dominicalis" signed "H. F." have been preserved in the Munich Library; the initials probably refer to Heinrich F.—(2) Hermann, b. March 21, 1527, Pirna (Saxony), grand-nephew of Heinrich F., studied in 1545 at Wittenberg, and then occupied the post of organist there, but died already on Dec. 28, 1558, Wittenberg, and, indeed, as a contemporary says, "er kam plötzlich elendiglich ums Leben" (he suddenly and miserably lost his life). His theoretical work, "Practica musica" (1556) ranks him amongst the first writers of that period, and, in the few compositions which he left he shows talent of a deep and prominent kind. (*See* the above-mentioned work, p. 84 f.)

Fincke, Fritz, pianist, violinist, and teacher of singing, b. May 1, 1836, Wismar, pupil of the Leipzig Conservatorium, was for a short time violinist at the Frankfort Theatre, then organist at Wismar, and in 1879 became teacher of singing at the Peabody Conservatoire at Baltimore. He published, besides a pf. compositions, a small instructive treatise, "Anschlagselemente" (1871).

Fine (Ital. "end"). The word is met with at the end of a composition, but is specially employed in works with a D.C. (*da capo*), to show how far the repeat extends, *i.e.* it marks the end right in the middle of the music.

Finger-board (Ger. *Griffbrett*). This is the name, in stringed instruments, lutes, guitars, etc., of the black-stained or ebony board placed over the smooth surface of the neck, on which the player presses his finger in shortening the strings. In instruments plucked by the fingers, as well as in the old viols (Gamba, etc.), the F. (the "collar") was divided into frets (q.v.), which made it easier to find the correct pitch.

Fingering (Ger. *Fingersatz*, *Applikatur*; Fr. *Doigter*). For all instruments on which the various sounds are produced by means of the fingers, the employment of suitable fingering is indispensable for technical treatment. (With regard to the fingering of stringed instruments, *see* POSITION.) F. appears in its simplest form in brass wind-instruments, which have so few keys (pistons, valves, etc.) that they can be managed with the fingers of one hand, without any change of position. More difficult is the F. of wood-wind instruments, in which the number of round holes and keys exceeds in number the fingers of both hands, so that various functions are assigned to the same finger; and, under certain circumstances, the same keys are acted on by different fingers. The F., however, is most complicated in instruments with key-boards (pianoforte, organ, harmonium, etc.); in this case it has a precise history, and a comprehensive literature: every pianoforte method, in fact, half consists of a school of F. The old style of playing (before

Bach) almost entirely excluded the thumb and little finger; during the following period, right up to the early decades of this century, the use of the two short fingers was generally limited to the lower keys. The Liszt-Tausig-Bülow, the most recent phase, takes no note whatever of the unevenness of the key-board (upper and lower keys), and removes all restrictions to the employment of the short fingers. Such free considerations are, however, only of service to the virtuoso: a player with less developed technique will derive comfort from respecting the black keys, and not putting the thumb or little finger on them. The system of F. in England differs from that of other countries: the forefinger is called the first finger, and the thumb is indicated by means of a +. The English method is the old German one, as it is to be found in Amerbach's "Orgel- und Instrument-Tabulatur" (1571); only there the thumb is indicated by a nought (0) instead of a + :—

Amerbach . . 0 1 2 3 4
English . . . + 1 2 3 4

Finger Trainer. (*See* DACTYLION.)

Fink, (1), Gottfried Wilhelm, b. March 7, 1783, Sulza (Thuringia), d. Aug. 27, 1846. From 1804 he studied theology at Leipzig, and acted there as assistant preacher; from 1812 to 1827 he was at the head of a training institution of which he was the founder. From a child he had taken great interest in music; in Leipzig he extended his knowledge, and composed much. In 1818 his first work "Über Takt, Taktarten, etc.") appeared in the *Allg. Mus. Zeitung,* to which he afterwards became a zealous contributor. In 1827 he himself became editor, and continued in this post until 1841. In 1842 he was named musical director of the University, gave lectures, and received the title of Doctor of Philosophy *honoris causâ.* Death overtook him in Halle whilst on a pleasure excursion. His compositions are: pieces for pianoforte and violin, songs, terzets and quartets for male voices, "Häusliche Andachten." He also published a collection of a thousand songs, "Musikalischer Hausschatz der Deutschen" (1843). His writings are: "Erste Wanderung der ältesten Tonkunst" (1821); "Musikalische Grammatik" (1836); "Wesen und Geschichte der Oper" (1838); "Der neumusikalische Lehrjammer" (1842); "System der musikalischen Harmonielehre" (1842); "Der musikalische Hauslehrer" (1846). After his death appeared his "Musikalische Kompositionslehre" (1847). F. was, besides, contributor to Schilling's "Universallexikon der Tonkunst," Ersch & Gruber's "Encyclopädie," and to the 8th edition of Brockhaus' "Conversationslexikon." A "Handbuch der allgemeinen Geschichte der Tonkunst, etc.," remained in manuscript. F. was a diligent worker, but not an original thinker.—(2) Christian, b. Aug. 9, 1831, Dettingen (Württemberg), attended

the seminary at Esslingen (under Frech), and then became elementary teacher at Stuttgart, and in 1849 assistant music-teacher at the seminary at Esslingen. From 1853-55 he studied at the Leipzig Conservatorium, besides taking lessons at Dresden with Joh. Schneider in organ-playing and composition. He then resided up to 1860 at Leipzig, highly esteemed as a performer on the organ and as teacher; after this, he was appointed principal teacher of music at the Esslingen seminary, and musical director and organist of the principal church there. In 1862 he received the title of professor. F. has published a great number of excellent organ works (sonatas, fugues, trios, exercises, preludes, etc.), as well as sacred compositions (psalms, motets, etc.) ; also pianoforte pieces (four sonatas) and songs.

Fino. (*See* FIN'AL.)

Finto, Finta (Ital.), feigned.—*Cadenza finta,* a deceptive cadence; *Fa finto,* the same as FA FEINT (q.v.).

Fioravanti, (1) Valentino, b. Sept. 11, 1769, Rome, d. June 16, 1837, whilst on a journey to Capua; he studied privately with Sala at Naples, made his *début* as opera-composer with *Gli inganni fortunati* (Naples, 1788), and *Con i matti il savio la perde* (Florence, 1791): these were followed by a series of comic operas for Turin, Milan, Naples, Lisbon, and one for Paris (*I virtuosi ambulanti,* 1807). In 1816 he was appointed successor to Jannaconi as papal maestro at St. Peter's, and, while in office, wrote a number of sacred compositions—inferior, however, to his forty-nine operas, which, at least, were not lacking in humour and freshness.—(2) Vincenzo, son of the former, b. April 5, 1799, Rome, d. March 28, 1877, Naples. In 1833 he became maestro of a church at Naples, and afterwards musical director of the *Albergo dei poveri* in that city. He was also highly esteemed in his native land as a composer of comic operas; he made his *début* in 1819 with *Pulcinella molinaro* at the small Carlo Theatre at Naples, and wrote about forty operas, mostly for the *Teatro nuovo* at Naples.

Fiorillo, (1) Ignazio, b. May 11, 1715, Naples, d. June, 1787, Fritzlar; he studied under Leo and Durante, made his *début* as an opera-composer at Venice in 1736 with the serious opera *Mandane,* which was followed by several others. He was appointed "Hofkapellmeister" at Brunswick in 1754, and called to Cassel in 1762; he received a pension in 1780, and withdrew to Fritzlar. Besides eight serious operas he wrote a requiem, three Te Deums, an oratorio (*Isacco*), etc.—(2) Federigo, son of the former, b. 1753, Brunswick, an excellent violinist and composer; he became capellmeister at Riga in 1783, went to Paris in 1785 and to London in 1788, where he appears to have turned his attention to the viola, as he played this instrument in Salomon's quartet-party, and performed a concerto at the Ancient Concerts. The year of his death is unknown. Many of his compositions for violin, and ensemble works have been preserved, of which the "Thirty-six Caprices" were edited by Spohr (with a second violin part), and again, recently, by Ferd. David : they rank as classical studies.

Fioriture (Ital.), ornaments (q.v.).

Fiqué, Carl, b. 1861, Bremen, pupil of the Leipzig Conservatorium, lives at Brooklyn (New York) ; he is an able pianist and composer (stringed quartet, E minor ; pf. pieces).

Fis (Ger.), F sharp.

Fischel, Adolf, b. 1810, Königsberg, an excellent violinist, pupil of Spohr. He composed several works for the violin, also stringed quartets which display a healthy talent. For many years he has been proprietor of a cigar business at Berlin.

Fischer, (1) Christian Friedrich, b. Oct. 23, 1698, Lübeck, d. 1752 as cantor at Kiel ; he was member of the Mizler Society, and highly spoken of by Mattheson ; also author of a four-part chorale book with an introduction on church music, and an essay, "Zufällige Gedanken von der Komposition," both of which, however, only exist in manuscript-copies.

(2) **Johann Christian,** celebrated oboist and composer for his instrument, b. 1733, Freiburg (Baden), was in 1760 member of the Dresden court band, made great tours in Italy for the purpose of study ; he also gave concerts, and was appointed, in 1780, court musician at London. He died April 29, 1800, from a stroke of apoplexy whilst performing an oboe solo. Besides ten oboe concertos (some of which are still played) he wrote flute solos, duets for two flutes, quartets for flute and stringed instruments, etc.

(3) **Christian Wilhelm,** stage singer (*basso buffo*), b. Sept. 17, 1789, Konradsdorf, near Freiberg, d. Nov. 3, 1859, Dresden ; he made his *début* in 1810 under Seconda in Dresden, was (1817–28) *basso buffo* and director of the chorus at Leipzig, 1828–29 at Magdeburg, 1829–32 opera *régisseur* and chorus-master at Leipzig ; then in a similar post at Dresden, where he staged works of Wagner. Marschner wrote for F. the part of Toms Blunt (*Vampyr*) and Friar Tuck (*Templer und Jüdin*).

(4) **Ludwig,** highly esteemed bass-singer, with voice of enormous compass (D–a'), b. Aug. 18, 1745, Mayence, d. July 10, 1825, Berlin : he was first of all singer at the Electoral Chapel, Mayence, then was engaged at Mannheim (Munich) and Vienna, appeared with extraordinary success in 1783 at Paris, and afterwards in Italy ; and in 1788 was engaged for life at Berlin, and pensioned in 1815. The Osmin in Mozart's *Entführung* was written for F.

(5) **Michael Gotthard,** music-teacher at the seminary and concert-director, b. June 3, 1773, Alach, near Erfurt, d. Jan. 12, 1829, Erfurt, as organist. He was a celebrated organ-player (pupil of Kittel), and composed organ-works (which are still in use)—motets, stringed quartets, a stringed quintet, bassoon concerto, clarinet concerto, symphonies, etc.

(6) **Anton,** b. 1777, Ried (Swabia), d. Dec. 1, 1808, Vienna. He was Capellmeister at the Josephstadt Theatre, Vienna, later (1800), at the Theater an der Wien (under Schikaneder), composed numerous vaudevilles, a pantomime, a children's operetta, and revised Grétry's *Raoul, Barbe-Bleue*, and *Les deux Avares* for the stage at Vienna.

(7) **Gottfried Emil,** b. Nov. 28, 1791, Berlin, d. Feb. 14, 1841, son of a teacher of natural philosophy at the Graues Kloster, Professor Ernst Gottfried F. (b. July 17, 1754, Hoheneiche near Saalfeld, d. Jan. 21, 1831, Berlin, author of a treatise on the vibrations of stretched strings). In 1817–25 he became mathematical teacher at the Royal Military School, and in 1818, until his death, singing teacher at the Graues Kloster, Berlin. He composed motets, chorales, songs, school-songs, melodies to v. d. Hagen's *Minnesänger*, was contributor to the *Allgemeine Musikalische Zeitung*, and wrote "Über Gesang und Gesangunterricht" (1831).

(8) **Karl Ludwig,** excellent violinist and conductor, b. 1816, Kaiserslautern, d. Aug. 15, 1877, Hanover, was theatre capellmeister at Trèves, Cologne, Aix-la-Chapelle, Nuremberg, Würzburg, 1847–52 at Mayence, 1852 second capellmeister (jointly with Marschner) at Hanover, 1859 first court capellmeister ; he composed vocal works, choruses for male voices, etc.

(9) **Adolf,** b. June 23, 1827, Uckermünde, in 1845 pupil of the Royal Institute for Church Music at Berlin (A. W. Bach, Grell), 1848 organist of St. John's Church, Berlin ; he became a pupil of Grell and Rungenhagen at the Akademie, in 1851 cantor and organist at the Gr. Friedrichs-Waisenhaus, 1853 organist of the two principal churches at Frankfort-a.-O., and director of the Singakademie, 1864 royal musical director, 1870 principal organist of St. Elizabeth's, Breslau, where in 1880 he founded the "Schlesisches Conservatorium." D. Dec. 7, 1893.

(10) **Karl August,** b. July 25, 1828, Ebersdorf, near Chemnitz, d. Dec. 25, 1892, at Dresden, was first of all organist at the English, and at St. Ann's Church, next at the Dreikönigskirche, Dresden ; he was a celebrated organ-player. Of his compositions are to be mentioned four organ symphonies with orchestra, three organ concertos ("Weihnachten," "Ostern," and "Pfingsten"), a grand festival mass, an opera (*Loreley*, libretto by Geibel), two orchestral suites, also pieces for violin and organ, and 'cello and organ.

(11) **Franz,** 'cellist and conductor, b. July 29, 1849, Munich, pupil of Hippolyt Müller, 1870, solo 'cellist at the Pesth National

Theatre under Hans Richter, then at Munich and Bayreuth under Wagner, 1876 chorus-director at Bayreuth, 1877–79 first Hof-kapellmeister at Mannheim, and, later on, occupied the same post at Munich.

(12) P a u l, b. Dec. 7, 1834, Zwickau, from 1862 cantor at Zittau, contributor to the *Neue Zeitschrift für Musik*, editor of a " Liedersammlung für höhere Lehranstalten." Died Mar. 3, 1894.

(13) A d o l f, excellent 'cellist, b. Nov. 22, 1847, Brussels, d. March 18, 1891, in a lunatic asylum near Brussels. He received his musical training from his father, who was highly esteemed as conductor of choral societies and of orchestral music, and afterwards from Servais at the Brussels Conservatoire. From 1868 he lived at Paris, whence he repeatedly made concert tours.

(14) I g n a z, b. 1828, d. July 7, 1877, Vienna, was for some time court opera capellmeister there.

(15) J o s e f, b. 1828, composer of the song, " Hoch Deutschland, herrliche Siegesbraut," was chamber musician at Stuttgart, where he died Sept. 27, 1885.

Fischhof, J o s e p h, b. April 4, 1804, Butschowitz (Moravia), d. June 28, 1857; he studied medicine at Vienna, but was, at the same time, a diligent student of music (composition under J. v. Seyfried). Later on he devoted himself entirely to music, and, after several years' activity as a private teacher of music, was appointed music-teacher at the Conservatorium of the " Gesellschaft der Musikfreunde." Besides several pianoforte pieces and ensemble works, he published, " Versuch einer Geschichte des Klavierbaus " (1853).

Fisis (Ger.), F double-sharp; a doubly-raised F.

Fistel (Ger.), Falsetto. (*See* REGISTER.)

Fistula (Lat.), reed, hence pipe; the common term used by the Latin writers of the Middle Ages for organ pipes (*fistulæ organicæ*); hence it is scarcely probable that the F. of the Romans was a reed instrument (the *calamus*, on the other hand, certainly was). *Cf.* WIND-INSTRUMENTS.

Fistulieren (Ger.), to speak or sing with head-voice.

Fitzenhagen, W i l h e l m K a r l F r i e d r i c h, 'cellist, b. Sept. 15, 1848, Seesen (Brunswick), d. Feb. 14, 1890, Petersburg; he made a name as virtuoso by concert tours, and published many pieces for his instrument. F. was leader of the Imperial Russian Society of Music at Moscow, and professor at the Conservatoire.

Fitzwilliam Collection, The. A valuable collection of books, engravings, manuscript music, etc., left by Viscount Fitzwilliam to the University of Cambridge, of which he was a member. The manuscript music contains, among other treasures, the so-called " Virginall-book of Queen Elizabeth," a volume of anthems in the handwriting of Purcell, Handel Sketches, etc. A valuable catalogue has been drawn up

by Mr. J. A. Fuller-Maitland, M.A., and Dr. A. H. Mann (1893).

Fl., abbreviation for flute (Ital. *Flauto*, Fr. *Flûte*, Ger. *Flöte*).

Flageolet, (1) A small wind-instrument, the last representative of the *flûte à bec* (*see* FLUTE), still used in subordinate orchestras in Belgium and France. Like the piccolo flute, it is an octave higher in pitch than the ordinary cross-flute.—(2) A small organ stop (2-ft. and 1-foot), a flute stop of somewhat narrow measure.—(3) Term used for the tones produced by the partial vibrations of strings of stringed instruments (flageolet tones), which have a peculiar piping, but soft, ethereal sound, free from the rasping noise of the other tones of these instruments. The F. tone is produced by touching gently with the tip of the finger the point of the string which corresponds to the half, third, or fourth of the string; the latter does not then vibrate through its whole length, but in two, three, four, etc., sections, each one of which produces independently the overtone in question. Other overtones than the natural ones can be produced by firmly pressing upon, and shortening the string (*cf.* NUT) so that the tone desired may be in the overtone series of the changed sound of the string, *e.g.*, $c''\sharp$ on the *g*-string by pressing upon *a*, and touching lightly the place of $c'\sharp$ ($\frac{1}{5}$). Further details may be found in any treatise on instrumentation. Flageolet tones speak on thick strings (double-bass, 'cello) more easily than on thin ones, but not so well on covered as on plain ones.

Flammenorgel (Ger.). (*See* PYROPHONE.)

Flat, the character ($\flat$) by which the normal pitch of a note is lowered a semitone.

Flautato, *flautando* (flute-like), an expression used with stringed instruments, indicating that the bow should be kept near the finger-board (somewhere about the middle of the string), whereby the formation of the even-numbered overtones is prevented, and the tone receives indeed a clang-tint more like the clarinet than the flute. F. is sometimes used for flageolet-playing.

Flautino, small flute (piccolo-flute) or flageolet.

Flauto (Ital.), flute.

Flauto amabile (Ital.), a sweet-toned organ stop, most frequently of 4-feet pitch.

Flaxland, G u s t a v A l e x a n d r e, b. 1821, Strassburg, studied at the Paris Conservatoire, and was a music-teacher for several years; he founded in 1847 a music-publishing business, which soon became one of the most famous in Paris, especially after F. had obtained the copyright of works by Schumann and Wagner—a somewhat risky undertaking at that time. In 1870 he sold his business to Durand and Schönewerk, and, jointly with his son, opened a pianoforte manufactory. He died Nov. 11, 1895.

Flebile (Ital. " weeping "), doleful, mournful.

Fleischer, Reinhold, lecturer on music at the Berlin University, custos of the royal collection of ancient instruments, b. April 12, 1842, Dahsau (Silesia), pupil of the Royal Institute for Church Music, and of the Royal Akademie at Berlin; he became, in 1870, organist of the principal church and conductor of the "Singakademie" at Görlitz, 1885 royal musical director; composer of organ pieces, songs, motets, and the cantata *Holda*.

Flemming, Friedrich Ferdinand, b. Feb. 28, 1778, Neuhausen in Saxony, d. May 27, 1813, as practical physician at Berlin; member of the Zelter Liedertafel, composer of Horace's " Integer vitæ " for male chorus.

Flessibile (Ital., " pliant "), smooth, flowing.

Florentine Quartet. (*See* BECKER, 3.)

Florentine Reformation of Music, the theoretical exposition, and first practical exercise of a new style which took place about 1600, and which, in opposition to the over-artificialities of counterpoint of the preceding epoch, placed chief value on plain declamation and on the natural pathos of solo-singing with instrumental accompaniment. Opera, oratorio, cantata, the chief aims of modern music, are to be traced to the esthetic circle in the houses of the Florentine noblemen Bardi and Corsi. (*Cf.* OPERA, CACCINI, CAVALIERI, etc.)

Florimo, Francesco, one of the most meritorious of Italian investigators of music, b. Oct. 12, 1800, San Giorgio Morgeto, near Reggio, d. Dec. 18, 1888, Naples. He became (1817) a pupil of the Real Colleggio di Musica at Naples, where Furno, Elia, Zingarelli, and Trito were his teachers. From 1826 he was librarian of that institution. The principal work of F. is " Cenno storico sulla scuola musicale di Napoli " (1869–71, two vols.; 2nd ed., in four stout vols., 1880–1884, under title " La scuolo musicale di Napoli e i suoi conservatorii," a history of the Neapolitan schools of music, of the professors connected with them, and of the pupils trained by them). He wrote, besides, the pamphlets " Riccardo Wagner ed i Wagneristi " (1876), and " Trasporto delle ceneri di Bellini a Catania " (F. himself escorted the body of Bellini from Paris to Catania). As a composer he is represented by sacred and orchestral works, cantatas, and some books of songs in Neapolitan dialect, with added Italian version. His " Metodo di canto " is used at the Naples Conservatorio.

Flotow, Friedrich Freiherr von, composer, b. April 27, 1812, on the Teutendorf estate (Mecklenburg), d. Jan. 24, 1883, Darmstadt. He studied composition under Reicha at Paris (1827–30), returned to Mecklenburg on the outbreak of the July Revolution, but went again to Paris after a few years, where his first musico-dramatic attempts were produced on small stages (1836). He obtained his first noteworthy success in 1839 with *Le Naufrage de la Méduse* (jointly with Piloti and Grisar); this piece was to have been given at Hamburg, but the great fire put a stop to it, and F. rewrote it under the title *Die Matrosen* and produced it there in 1845. His next operas were *L'âme en peine* (known in England as *Leoline*), *L'esclave de Camoëns*, produced at the Opéra Comique in 1843. But his most fortunate ventures were the operas *Alessandro Stradella* (Hamburg, 1844) and *Martha* (Vienna, 1847). The March Revolution once more drove F. from Paris. In 1850 he produced *Die Grossfürstin* at the Berlin Opera, but without much success; he was more fortunate with *Indra* in 1853, but the following fell flat: *Rübezahl* (1854), *Hilda* (1855), *Albin* (*Der Müller von Meran*), 1856. F. was appointed intendant of the court music of the Grand Duke of Mecklenburg in 1856. In 1863 he returned once more to Paris, and produced the operettas *Veuve Grapin* (1859) and *Pianella* (1860), also the comic operas : *Zilda* (1866) and *L'Ombre* (*The Phantom*, 1870). *Zilda* met with no success, but it was very different with *L'Ombre*. In 1868 F. settled permanently on an estate near Vienna, spending the season sometimes in Vienna, sometimes in Paris, or making a stay in Italy. The Court Opera at Vienna produced the following novelty from his pen : *Die Libelle* (ballet, 1866); the Darmstadt Opera, the ballet *Tannkönig* (1867); and Prague, the opera *Am Runenstein* (1868, jointly with Genée). Revisions of older operas not produced are *Naïda* (1873) and *Il fior d'Harlem* (1876). His last works were *L'incanteresse* (Ital. *Alma l'incantatrice;* Ger. *Die Hexe*, 1878, a revision of *Indra*) and *Rosellana* (posthumous). Flotow's music is French rather than German; the rhythm is graceful and piquant, while the plain, easily comprehensible melodies form its most essential feature. *Martha* and *Stradella* are truly popular. Besides operas, F. wrote some chamber-music works and small vocal pieces, but none of them in any way striking.

Flue-pipes, those organ pipes (metal as well as wooden) which are made to sound by forcing the wind through a slit (the wind-way) at the top of the foot, and against a sharp edge (the upper-lip), which divides the wind, part of which only enters the body of the pipe. A *flue-work* is the aggregate of such pipes.

Flue-work (Ital. *Organo di legno*), a small organ, containing only lip-stops, in contradistinction to reed-work (Schnarrwerk), Regal, which had only reed-stops.

Flügel, since centuries, the German name for Claviers, not the square ones in table form, but those in the shape of a right-angled triangle with the acute angle rounded off. Their strings ran in the direction of the keys; and not, as in the table claviers, crossways. Before the invention of the hammer-mechanism the F. was called *Clavicembalo* (*Cembalo*) by the Italians, *Clavecin* by the French, and *Harpsichord* by the English.

Flügel, (1), G u s t a v, organist and composer b. July 2, 1812, Nienburg-on-the-Saale, attended the Gymnasium at Bernburg, and received his first instruction in pianoforte playing and theory from the Cantor Thiele, in the neighbouring village of Altenburg; he was then, from 1827 to 1829, a private pupil of Fr. Schneider in Dessau, and attended his school for music there until 1830. F. lived and taught successively at Nienburg, Bernburg, Cöthen, Magdeburg, Schönebeck, and, from 1840 to 1850, at Stettin. In 1850 he took a post as teacher of music at the seminary at Neuwied, where in 1856 he received the title of "Königlicher Musik Direktor." In 1859 he returned to Stettin as cantor and organist of the "Schlosskirche." Of F.'s compositions for the organ must be specially named his book of preludes (112 Choralvorspiele); he wrote, besides, many organ pieces, pf. works of all kinds (five sonatas), sacred and secular vocal part-songs for mixed and male chorus, some of them for schools, songs with pianoforte accompaniment, etc.

(2) E r n e s t P a u l, son of the former, b. Aug. 31, 1844, Stettin, received his musical training from his father, and from 1862 to 1863 was a pupil of the Royal Institution for Church Music at Berlin, and of the School for Composition of the Akademie. He enjoyed also private instruction from Bülow, Fl. Geyer, and Kiel, and then lived chiefly as a teacher of music at Treptow-a.-T., and Greifswald, became organist at Prenzlau, and teacher of singing at the Gymnasium there in 1867, and in 1879 Cantor at the "Bernhardinkirche," Breslau; he founded a society bearing his name, and was also active as a musical critic Among his published compositions the following deserve mention: the 121st Psalm (Op. 22), and "Mahomet's Song" (Op. 24), and a pf. trio (Op. 25); also pieces for pianoforte, organ, and songs.

Flügelharfe (Ger.). (*See* SPITZHARFE.)

Flügelhorn (Ger.). (*See* BUGLE HORN.)

Flute (Ital. *Flauto;* Fr. *Flûte*), one of the oldest wood wind-instruments in which the tone is produced, not by means of vibrating tongues (as in the oboe, bassoon, clarinet, etc.), but by directing a thin stream of air against a sharp edge. (*Cf.* WIND-INSTRUMENTS.) The instrument is blown either by means of a mouthpiece, which conducts the wind (exactly as in the flue-pipes of an organ) through a narrow fissure against the upper edge of the opening situate above (straight-flute, *flûte à bec, flûte droite, Schnabelflöte, Plockflöte, Blockflöte;* (*cf.* SCHWEGEL); or (as in the only kind of flute in present use) the player points his lips so that a narrow, band-like stream of air is formed, which he directs against the sharp edge of a round blow-hole of the instrument held

obliquely (German- or cross-flute, *Querflöte, Flûte traversière, Flûte allemande, Flauto traverso*). The flute in its present form is a German instrument: its oldest name is "Schweizerpfeiff." The different notes of the c (not D) instrument are produced partly by the shortening of the tube by opening the sound-holes, partly by overblowing (the overtones of the tube produced by overblowing). The modern F. (system of Boehm, q.v.) has fourteen sound-holes, which are closed by means of keys. The compass of the F. extends from (small) b to c^4 (chromatic). Of all orchestral instruments the F. is the most agile; immense leaps in rapid *tempo* can easily be taken on it. From the 15th to the 17th century the F., like all other instruments, was constructed of different sizes (*Discant-, Alto-,* and *Bass-flutes*). At the present day, besides the "large" F., there is only used the "small" F. (*Pickelflöte, Flauto piccolo*) an octave higher in pitch; and in France and Belgium, the *Flageolet* (q.v.). In military bands there are also the small flutes, respectively a semitone and a minor third higher in pitch than the piccolo in D♭ (erroneously said to be in E♭) and the one in E♭ (erroneously said to be in F). The *tierce flute* (in E♭ [erroneously said to be in F]), the *quart flute* (in F [erroneously said to be in G]), and the *Flûte d'amour* (in A) are obsolete. F. Weingartner recently proposed the re-institution of the *alto flute*. Of Flute Methods specially worthy of mention there are the following:—Berbiguier: "Grande méthode de la flûte" (three parts); Hugot and Wunderlich: A complete Flute Method, accepted by the Conservatoire, Paris (also in German editions); A. B. Fürstenau: "Flötenschule," Op. 42, and "Die Kunst des Flötenspiels," Op. 138; Fahrbach: "Wiener Flötenschule"; Soussmann: "Praktische Flötenschule," Op. 54 (five books); Tulou: "Méthode de Flûte," Op. 100; W. Popp: "Neue praktische und vollständige Schule des Flötenspiels"; Terschak: Op. 131, a collection of valuable *études;* Barge, orchestral studies for flute (four books), besides exercises and solo pieces by Drouet, Doppler, Briccialdi, Böhm, etc. There are also to be mentioned the works of Böhm, "Über den Flötenbau" (1847), and "Die F. und das Flötenspiel" (no date). The works of Quantz, Tromlitz, Devienne, etc., are obsolete.—(2) The term *flute-work* is applied to all lip-pipes; and *flute* (or its German equivalent, *Flöte*) appears as a part of compound names denoting special stops, such as: Cross-flute (Querflöte), Swiss-flute, Zartflöte, Fernflöte, Stillflöte, Dulcet-flute, Hellflöte, Hohlflöte, Tubalflöte, Rustic-flute (Feldflöte), Waldflöte, Spindle-flute (Spillflöte), Blockflöte, Pyramidflöte, Double-flute, Reed-flute, etc. Most of the flute stops are of 4- or 8-ft.; those of 2-ft. and 1 foot are generally called "fifes," such as Cross-fife (Schweizerpfeife), Rustic-fife (Feldpfeife), etc.

Flûte (Fr.), flute. *F. à bec* (Schnabelflöte).

F-minor-chord = F. *a♭*, *c*; *F-minor*-key, with signature of 4 ♭s. (*See* KEY.)

Foco. (*See* FUOCO.)

Fogliani, Ludovico, a noteworthy theorist, b. Modena, d. there about 1539. He published "Musica theorica" (1529), the work in which the ratio of the major-third was first fixed at 4 : 5, and the difference made between the major and the minor tone, *i.e.* our modern determination of intervals. It was not Zarlino, but already F. who restored to the light of day the principle set forth by Didymos and Ptolemy, and obtained for it a meaning which it could not have had in antiquity. Some compositions of F. are to be found in Petrucci's "Frottole" (1504–8).

Foglietto (Ital.), a "cue"; in parts written out from a score; especially the first violin part, in small notes, written in when long pauses occur.

Foignet, (1) Charles Gabriel, b. 1750, Lyons, d. 1823, Paris, teacher of singing and composition; he wrote twenty-five comic operas for small Paris theatres (1791–99).

His son (2) François, b. about 1780, Paris, d. July 22, 1845, Strassburg, followed in his father's footsteps, and wrote, between 1799 and 1819, comic operas and fairy pieces, in some of which he appeared himself as a singer.

Foli, A. J., Irish bass singer, b. 1835, Cahir; d. 1899. He had a big voice and one of great compass; his style was highly artistic, and he was very popular. He sang in Great Britain, Ireland, America, South Africa and Australia.

Folias (Sp.), **Folies d'Espagnes** (Fr.), **Follia** (Ital.), a Spanish dance in $\frac{3}{4}$ time.

Folk Song (Ger. *Volkslied*) is either a song sprung from the people (*i.e.* whose poet and composer are unknown), or one that has become popular; or, finally, one of a popular kind, *i.e.* one with melody and harmony simple and easily comprehensible.

Fondamental (Fr.), forming the basis. (*See* FUNDAMENTAL BASS.)

Fonds d'orgue (Fr.), the series of foundation stops (8′) especially the lip-pipes of the organ.

Foote, Arthur, b. March 5, 1853, Salem (Massachusetts), trained in America. He lives in Boston as a teacher of music, and composer of light pieces.

Foot-tone, a term for pitch (8 ft., 16 ft., 4 ft., etc.) connected with organ-building. An open lip-stop of medium measure (Open Diapason) tuned to (great) *C*, has a height of about 8 feet. All those organ stops then, which, when the key *C* is struck, sound *C* are called 8-ft. stops (the real normal, or foundation stops of the organ). On the other hand, a stop is described as of 4 ft. when the *C* key gives a sound such as would be produced by an open lip-pipe 4 feet high, *i.e.* small *c*; and it is said to be of 16 feet when the *C* key gives the contra *C* instead of great *C*. In the same way there are stops of 32-, 2-ft., and 1 foot; Quint stops of $10\frac{2}{3}$, $5\frac{1}{3}$, $2\frac{2}{3}$, $1\frac{1}{3}$ feet, or $\frac{2}{3}$ of a foot; Tierce stops of $6\frac{2}{5}$, $3\frac{1}{5}$, $1\frac{3}{5}$ feet, or $\frac{4}{5}$, $\frac{2}{5}$, $\frac{1}{5}$ of a foot; Seventh stops of $4\frac{4}{7}$ or $2\frac{2}{7}$ feet, etc. Quint stops give always the third, Tierce the fifth, Seventh the seventh partial tone of a fundamental stop ($10\frac{2}{3}$ as $\frac{32}{3}$ is a mutation stop belonging to a 32-ft. stop, etc.). The word F. is used, with transferred meaning, when one speaks quite generally, not only of an 8-ft *C*, but also of *D*, *E*, *F*, etc., and likewise of 4-ft. sounds other than *c*. The notes of a whole octave are thus named according to the *c* from which they start: the great octave, the 8-ft.; the small, the 4-ft.; the once-accented, the 2-ft., etc. The usual abbreviation for foot-tone is an ′ placed near to the figure; for example, 4′, 8′, etc. Recently it has become the fashion to replace foot-tone determination of pitch by that of mètre measurement. If the velocity of sound (*see* ACOUSTICS) be 340 mètres, 34 instead of 33 vibrations must be taken for *C* as normal, in order to obtain a sound-wave of 5 m. ($\frac{340}{34 \cdot 2}$). Thus Diapason $16' = 5$ m., $32' = 10$ m., $8' = \frac{5}{2}$ m., $4' = \frac{5}{4}$ m., $2' = \frac{5}{8}$ m.; Quint $10\frac{2}{3}' = \frac{10}{3}$ m., $5\frac{1}{3}' = \frac{5}{3}$ m., $2\frac{2}{3}' = \frac{5}{6}$ m., $1\frac{1}{3}' = \frac{5}{12}$ m., $\frac{2}{3}' = \frac{5}{24}$ m.; Tierce $6\frac{2}{5}' = \frac{10}{5}$ m. (2 m.), $3\frac{1}{5}' = \frac{5}{5}$ m. (1 m.), $1\frac{3}{5}' = \frac{5}{10}$ m. ($\frac{1}{2}$ m.), $\frac{4}{5}$ m. $= \frac{5}{20}$ m. ($\frac{1}{4}$ m.), etc. It is, however, thoroughly unpractical to substitute decimal fractions, as the overtone ratios cannot then be recognised.

Forberg, Robert, b. May 18, 1833, Lützen, d. Oct. 10, 1880, Leipzig; in 1862 he opened a music-publishing house there, which quickly won a good name, and issued works by Rheinberger, Reinecke, Raff, Jensen, etc.

Forchhammer, Theodor, b. July 29, 1847, Schiers (Graubünden), pupil of the Stuttgart Conservatorium, became in 1885 G. A. Ritter's successor as organist at Magdeburg Cathedral, and in 1888 royal musical director. He published with Brosig a Guide through Organ Literature (1890), composed an organ concerto (with orchestra), and other organ works, pf. pieces, songs, etc.

Forkel, Johann Nikolaus, the celebrated historian of music, b. Feb. 22, 1749, Meeder, near Coburg, d. March 17, 1818, Göttingen. He was the son of a shoemaker, and received his first musical instruction from the Cantor of his native place, and then became chorister of the principal church at Lüneburg; he attended the college there, and, in 1766, became "Chorpräfect" at Schwerin. At the same time he found opportunity to perfect himself in organ- and harp-playing; and from Mattheson's "Vollkommener Kapellmeister" he extracted further knowledge of the art of music. In 1769 he went to Göttingen, really for the purpose of studying law, for which he obtained the necessary means by giving lessons in music; but he became more and more absorbed in musical history, was appointed, first of all, organist, and in 1778 Universitäts-Musikdirektor, and in 1780 received the title of Doctor *honoris causâ*. F. applied for the post at Hamburg, as successor to Ph. E. Bach, but did not succeed in obtaining it, and he remained for the rest of his life in Göttingen. F. rendered important services to musical history and bibliography; he was the first in Germany to labour in that special department on a large scale, though in England Hawkins and Burney were his predecessors. His works are: "Über die Theorie der Musik, sofern sie Liebhabern und Kennern derselben notwendig und nützlich ist" (1774); "Musikalisch-kritische Bibliothek" (1778-79, three vols.); "Ueber die beste Einrichtung öffentlicher Konzerte" (1779); "Genauere Bestimmung einiger musikalischer Begriffe" (1780); "Musikalischer Almanach für Deutschland" (for the years 1782, 1783, 1784, and 1789); "Allgemeine Geschichte der Musik" (1788 to 1801, two vols.; unfortunately the work does not extend beyond the year 1550, or thereabouts. He left materials for the remaining period, which passed into the hands of the publisher Schwickert); "Allgemeine Litteratur der Musik oder Anleitung zur Kenntnis musikalischer Bücher" (1792, an epoch-making work, the first of its kind); "Über Johann Sebastian Bachs Leben, Kunst und Kunstwerke" (1803; English, 1820). A work of F.'s, unique of its kind, is a transcription of Graphäus' "Missæ XIII." of 1539, and of the "Liber XV. missarum" of Petrejus (1538) in modern score (masses of Okeghem, Obrecht, Josquin, H. Isaac, Brumel, Pierre de la Rue, etc.). It was intended to publish the latter, and it was, in fact, engraved, and a proof in F.'s hands for correction; but after the battle of Jena the French, who had marched into Leipzig, melted down the plates for cannon balls. The proof, carefully corrected by F., is in the Berlin Library. His compositions are now forgotten (pf. sonatas, variations, songs of Gleim were printed); the following remained in manuscript: an oratorio, *Hiskias;* cantatas, *Die Macht des Gesangs* and *Die Hirten an der Krippe zu Bethlehem*, trios, symphonies, part-songs, etc.

Forlana, an obsolete, exceedingly lively dance in $\frac{6}{4}$ or $\frac{6}{8}$ time (originated in Friuli).

Form, Musical. In art there must be form, which is merely a placing together of the parts of a work of art so as to form a uniform whole; but such placing together is only possible if the various elements are intimately related one to another. If this condition be not fulfilled the result is merely proximity, juxtaposition. The first condition for form of all kinds, also musical, is therefore unity; yet this can only fully unfold its esthetic effect by means of antithesis, as contrast, and as contradiction (conflict).

Formation, specially of a musical kind, tending to unity, is exhibited in the consonant chord, in clearly establishing a key, in holding fast to a particular measure or rhythm, in the return of rhythmic-melodic motives, in the framing and repetition of well-rounded themes; contrast and conflict are exhibited in changes of harmony, rhythm, dissonance, and modulation, and in opposing to each other themes of contrary character. Contrast must be subject to, conflict resolved into, a higher unity, *i.e.* the succession of chords must bear the stamp of definite tonality; modulation must move around a principal key, and lead back to it; dissonance must be resolved; the themes must disentangle themselves from the development section, etc. Thus laws for specific musical formation can be deduced from general esthetic laws; yet within certain prescribed lines, formations of various kinds are possible. For instrumental music the most usual forms with regard to the grouping of themes are as follows:—

(1) Pieces with only one theme (rare; generally in études, bagatelles, album-leaves, songs without words).

(2) Pieces with two themes (A = 1st theme, B = 2nd theme):

    (I.) A — B — A.

    (II.) A — B — A — B (B the second time in the key of A).

    (III.) A — B — $\frac{B}{A}$ — A — B (that is, a development section in the middle).

    (IV.) ‖: A – B :‖ — $\frac{B}{A}$ — A — B (B at the close in the key of A).

    (V.) ‖: A — B :‖ — $\frac{B}{A}$ — B — A.

    (VI.) A — B — A ‚in the key of B) — B (in the key of A) — A.

(3) Pieces with three themes:

    (I.) A — B — C — A — B (in the key of A).

    (II.) A — B — C — B — A.

    (III.) A — B — A — C — A — B — A (both of the middle A's in other keys).

    (IV.) A — B — C — B — C — A (the second C in the key of A), etc.

The form 2, I. is generally called song-form, 2 IV.—V. sonata-form, 2, VI. (3, III.) rondo-form; but the setting-up of these three forms only is an unjustifiable limitation in contradiction with practice. All the other forms given above, and many others besides, are permissible, and, from an esthetic point of view, justifiable for a detached movement, or for a movement of a work in which there are several movements. Works consisting of several movements (*cyclic* forms) are in similar manner compounded of movements of different character, key, and measure; for example (S = slow, Q = quick):

(1) S — Q.
(2) Q — S — Q.
(3) S — Q — S — Q.

(4) Q — S — Q — Q.
(5) Q — Q — S — Q.
(6) Q — S — Q — S — Q.

It is not usual to end with a slow movement;

Beethoven, however, in his sonata in E (Op. 109) has obtained by that means a magnificent effect.

(7) S — Q — S.
(8) Q — S — Q — S, etc.

By using these one-movement and cyclic *abstract* forms in music, differing according to the number and character of instruments employed, and according to the aim and style, there arise many *concrete* forms, of which the name already awakens a different conception, viz. : A. for purely *instrumental music :* Études, prelude, fantasia, song without words, air, theme with variations, etc., dances (allemande, bourrée, branle, chaconne, czardas, gaillarde, galop, gavotte, gigue, hornpipe, loure, mazurka, minuet, passacaglia, passamezzo, passepied, pavana, polka, polonaise, rigaudon, sarabande, schottisch, siciliana, tambourin, waltz, etc.), march (funeral march, etc.), fugue, toccata, suite, partita, sonata, fantasia, duo, trio, quatuor (quartet), quintuor (quintet), sextuor (sextet), septuor (septet), octet, nonet, divertissement, serenade, cassation, concerto, overture, symphony. B. for *vocal music :* Song, part-song, canzone (chanson), romance, ballad, bicinium, tricinium, duet, terzet, quartet, etc., antiphon, psalmody, sequence, hymn, chorale, motet, madrigal, ode, mass, requiem, etc. C. for *accompanied vocal music* for stage or otherwise : recitative, arioso, cavatina, aria, concerto, cantata, oratorio, opera, Passion, romance, ballad, legend, etc. (*Cf.* articles under respective names.)

Formes, the name of two brothers, celebrated opera-singers—(1) K a r l J o s e p h (bass), b. Aug. 7, 1816, Mühlheim, on the Rhine, d. Dec. 15, 1889, New York ; he made his *début* in 1841 as Sarastro at Cologne, and was engaged in 1843 at Mannheim, where he was very popular ; but in 1848 he took part in the revolution, and was forced to flee. From 1852 to 1857 he was engaged at the Royal Italian Opera in London, and afterwards divided his time between America and Europe. As late as 1874 he met with great success in Berlin.
(2) T h e o d o r (tenor), b. June 24, 1826, Mühlheim, d. Oct. 15, 1874, Endenich, near Bonn ; made his *début* in 1846 at Ofen, was then engaged at Vienna, Mannheim (1848), and at the Berlin Court Opera (1851–66), and travelled with his brother through America. After a temporary loss of voice, he appeared once again at Berlin, and with brilliant success, but lost his reason, and had to be placed in an asylum. Taubert and Dorn wrote *rôles* for him.
Another, belonging to the same family, was the baritone singer, W i l h e l m F., b. Jan. 31, 1834, at Mühlheim, d. March 12, 1884, New York.

Formschneider. (*See* GRAPHÄUS.)

Förner, C h r i s t i a n, b. 1610, Wettin, d. there, 1678, was a famous organ-builder, whose instruments at Halle-a.-S. (Ulrichskirche) and Weissenfels (Augustusburg) still exist. He was the inventor of the " Windgänge " (q.v.).

Forster, (1) G e o r g, physician at Nuremberg, and editor of collections of songs and motets, b. Amberg, and entered the University of Wittenberg on Oct. 15, 1534, practised first in Amberg, then in Würzburg ; he was appointed by the Duke of Bavaria physician at Heidelberg, and went through the French campaigns. After 1544 he settled in Nuremberg, and d. there Nov. 12, 1568. The principal service which he rendered to music was the collecting and editing of secular songs with harmonies (five parts) ; they appeared at Nuremberg between 1539 and 1556, and form a real treasury of choice melodies entitled " Volkslieder."
(2) G e o r g, for a short time, deputy capellmeister at the Saxon court at Dresden, was, according to Walther, cantor in Zwickau (1556), and in Annaberg (1564). In 1568 he went as performer of the double-bass to Dresden, became vice-capellmeister in 1581, principal capellmeister in 1585, after the departure of Pinelli, and d. Oct. 16, 1587. He has hitherto only found a place in dictionaries by being confounded with the physician (1) (*see Monatshefte für Musik-Geschichte*, I. 1, etc.)
(3) N i k o l a u s (F o r t i u s), celebrated contrapuntist of the 16th century at the court of Joachim I. of Brandenburg, but only a mass à 16 of his is known by name.
(4) K a s p a r (also written F ö r s t e r), b. 1617, Danzig, d. March, 1673, at the Olivan monastery, near Danzig ; he was for many years capellmeister at Copenhagen, lived for a time also at Venice, and was famous as a composer and theorist. His works, however, have completely disappeared.

Forster, (1) W i l l i a m, English violin-maker, b. May 4, 1739, Brampton, Cumberland, d. 1808 ; he was also the publisher of many of Haydn's works (eighty-three symphonies, twenty-four quartets, etc.).
(2) W i l l i a m, English violin-maker, son of the above, b. Jan., 1764, London, d. July 24, 1824 ; some of his instruments are of a high order of merit.

Förster, (1), C h r i s t o p h, b. Nov. 30, 1693, Bebra (Thuringia), d. Dec. 6, 1745 ; for many years he was ducal Saxon capellmeister at Merseburg, in 1745 capellmeister at Rudolstadt, and was a very prolific composer (symphonies, organ pieces, pf. pieces, cantatas, etc.).
(2) E m a n u e l A l o y s, b. 1757, Neurath (Austrian Silesia), d. Nov. 19, 1823, Vienna, where he lived for many years as a teacher of music. He published many instrumental works (pf. sonatas, variations, stringed quintet, stringed quartets, pf. quartets, a pf. sextet, *Notturno concertante* for strings and wind), some songs, a " Huldigungskantate," and published an " Anleitung zum Generalbass " (1805).
(3) A d o l p h M., a well-known American

composer and conductor, b. Feb. 2, 1854, Pittsburg (Pennsylvania), pupil of the Leipzig Conservatorium; he lives at Pittsburg.

Forsyth Brothers, English music-publishing firm, established at London and Manchester. They publish, besides many works by various composers, Charles Hallé's arrangements for the pianoforte.

Fort (Fr.), strong; an organ term used in connection with mixture stops; it is equivalent to "fold," for example: fourniture 4 tuyaux fort = 4-fold mixture.

Forte (Ital.), abbr. *f*, loud; *fortissimo* (*ff*), very loud; *mezzoforte* (*mf*), moderately loud; *fortepiano* (*fp*), loud, and directly afterwards, soft; *poco forte* (*pf*), rather loud; *più forte* (*pf*), louder—(*pf*) must not be understood as meaning *piano forte*. (*Cf.* SFORZATO.)

Fortepiano, pianoforte. (*See* PIANOFORTE.)

Fortlage, Karl, writer on esthetics, b. June 12, 1806, Osnabrück, d. Nov. 8, 1881, Jena; in 1829 he was a private teacher of philosophy at Heidelberg, 1845 at Berlin, from 1846 professor of philosophy at Jena. He published, besides several important philosophical works: "Das musikalische System der Griechen in seiner Urgestalt" (1847), an investigation of the old Greek system of notes and theory of scales, etc.—the best work on the subject; yet, as F. Bellermann's monograph ("Die Tonleitern und Musiknoten der Griechen"), arriving at nearly the same conclusions, appeared at the same time, it was almost entirely overlooked.

Förtsch, Johann Philipp, b. May 14, 1652, Wertheim (Franconia), d. Dec. 14, 1732, as Aulic counsellor at Eutin, studied medicine, but turned to music, and in 1671 was tenor singer at the "Rathskapelle," Hamburg. In 1680 he became successor of Theile as capellmeister to the Duke of Schleswig at Gottorp, but, owing to the political events, he soon lost the post, whereupon he returned to medicine, and in 1694 became body physician to the Bishop of Eutin. F. wrote, during his musical career, twelve operas, clavier concertos, etc. Mattheson praises him highly in his "Musikalischer Patriot."

Forza (Ital.), force, vigour.

Forzato, same as SFORZATO.

Foundation Stop is a stop in the organ which on the key c also gives the note c or one of its octaves. The term is used specially for the 8-ft. and for pedal 16-ft., from which the smaller octave stops are distinguished as secondary stops (Seitenstimmen). In a further sense the foundation stops are opposed to the mutation stops, *i.e.* the quint-, tierce-stops, mixtures, etc.

Fouqué, Pierre Octave, b. Nov. 12, 1844, Pau (Lower Pyrénées), d. there April 21-22, 1883; he went, when young, to Paris. became a pupil

of Reinhold Becker (harmony) and Chauvet (counterpoint), and was received in 1869 into A. Thomas's composition class at the Conservatoire. F. was active as a composer of pf. pieces and songs, also of some small operettas. He was still more important as a writer. He published the following: "On Music in England before Handel," "J. F. Lesueur, the Predecessor of Berlioz," and "M. J. Glinka" (biography), "Histoire du Théâtre Ventadour" (1881). F. was librarian of the Conservatoire, musical critic of the *République Française*, and wrote for the *Ménestrel* and the *Revue et Gazette Musicale*.

Fournier, Pierre Simon, type-founder, b. Sept. 15, 1712, Paris, d. there Oct. 8, 1768. In place of the note types of Pierre Hautin (q.v.), which the Ballards, by virtue of their patent, had used for 225 years, F. introduced types more suitable to his day, *i.e.* of a shape (round heads) agreeing with written and engraved notes. (*Cf.* BREITKOPF.) F. described his improvements in his "Essai d'un nouveau caractère de fonte pour l'impression de la musique" (1756); he also published a "Traité historique et critique sur l'origine et les progrès des caractères de fonte pour l'impression de la musique" (1765).

Fourniture (Fr.), same as mixture in the disposition of a French organ.

Française (Fr.), (1) a lively dance in $\frac{6}{8}$ time. —(2) Instead of *Contredanse française*, the former word being understood.

Francesco cieco (Ital. "the blind"), also called *degli organi*. (*See* LANDINO.)

Franchinus. (*See* GAFORI.)

Franchi-Verney, Giuseppe Ippolito, Conte della Valetta, b. Feb. 17, 1848, Turin, writer on music, and critic; he studied law at Turin, passed his examination in 1867, and entered state service. But in 1874, after suffering from severe pains in the head, he gave up jurisprudence and devoted himself to musicoliterary pursuits, receiving at the same time further musical training from good teachers (Marchisio, Stefano Tempia). Already in 1872 he had taken great interest in the establishment of the "Popular Concerts" at Turin. In 1875 he and several friends started a Quartet Society for the performance of comparatively unknown works, and in 1876, jointly with his teacher Tempia, the "Accademia di canto corale." F. is an active and distinguished musical critic (from 1875 to 1877 of the *Gazetta del Popolo*, under the name Ippolito Valetta, and since then of the *Risorgimento*, etc.). F. is favourable to Wagner's musico-dramatic reforms. Some years since he married Teresina Tua.

Franchomme, Auguste, b. April 10, 1808, Lille, d. Jan. 21, 1884, Paris; in 1825 he was pupil of the Paris Conservatoire (Levasseur and Norblin), received, already in 1826, the first prize of the 'cello class, and appeared as 'cellist in the orchestra of the Ambigu Comique, in 1827 at the Théâtre Italien ; together with D. Alard and Ch Hallé he established chamber-music *soirées*, and was an intimate friend of Chopin's. In 1846 he was appointed teacher of his instrument at the Conservatoire. After Duport's death he bought his Stradivari 'cello for 25,000 francs. F. was known as one of the most distinguished 'cellists of this century. He composed a few solo pieces for 'cello (a concerto, Adagios, sets of variations, etc.).

Franck, Melchior, (1) an exceedingly prolific composer of church music, b. about 1573, Zittau, d. June 1, 1639, as court capellmeister at Coburg. He published : " Melodiæ sacræ " (à 4—12, 1600-7, three parts) ; " Musikalische Bergreyen" (1602) ; " Contrapuncti compositi " (1602) ; " Teutsche Psalmen und Kirchenge-sänge" (1602) ; " Neue Paduanen, Galliarden, etc." (1603) ; " Opusculum eticher newer und alter Reuterliedlein " (1603) ; " Neues Quodlibet " (1604) ; " Farrago 4 voc." (1604) ; " Teutsche (weltliche) Gesänge und Täntze " (1605) ; " Geist-liche Gesänge und Melodien " (1608) ; " Newes Echo " (1608) ; " Cantica gratulatoria " (and some other *pièces d'occasion*, 1608-9) ; " Neue musikalische Intraden " (1608) ; " Flores music-ales " (1610) ; " Musikalische Fröhlichkeit " (1610) ; " Tricinia nova " (1611) ; " Vincula natalitia " (1611) ; " Sechs deutsche Konzerte von acht Stimmen " (1611) ; " Suspiria musica " (1612) ; " Opusculum etlicher geistlicher Ge-sänge " (1612) ; " Viridarium musicum " (à 6—10, 1613) ; " Recreationes musicæ " (1614) ; " Zween Grabgesänge " (1614) ; " Zwey newe Hochzeitsgesänge " (1614) ; " Threnodiæ Davi-dicæ " (1615) ; " Die trostreichen Worte aus dem 54. Kapitel Esaiä " (à 7—15, 1615) ; " Deli-ciæ amoris " (1615) ; " Fasciculus quodlibeti-cus " (1615) ; " Geistlicher musikalischer Lust-garten " (à 4—9, 1616) ; " Lilia musicalia " (1616) ; " Teutsches musikalisches fröhliches Konvivium " (1621) ; " Laudes dei vespertinæ " (1622) ; " Newe teutsche Magnificat " (à 2—8, 1622, four parts) ; " Gemmulæ evangeliorum musicæ" (1623 and 1624, two parts) ; " Newes liebliches musikalisches Lustgärtlein " (à 5—8, 1623) ; " 40 Teutsche lustige musikalische Täntze " (1624) ; " Newes musikalisches Opus-culum " (1624) ; " Sacri convivii musica sacra " (1628) ; " Rosetulum musicum " (1628) ; " Ci-thara ecclesiastica et scholastica " (without date) ; " Psalmodia sacra " (1631) ; " Dulces mundani exilii deliciæ " (1631) ; " Der 51. Psalm für vier Stimmen " (1634) ; " Paradisus musicus " (1636) ; " 2 neue Epicedia " (1639). A careful description of his printed works, also of those preserved in public libraries, is to be found in vol. xvii. of the *Monatshefte für Musik-Ge-schichte.*

(2) Johann Wolfgang, b. 1641, Ham-burg, physician, and opera capellmeister there ; he published sonatas for two violins and bass ; he also produced a series (fourteen) of operas at Hamburg (1679–86). Of his sacred compositions there are preserved " Geistliche Melodien " with general bass (1681, also 1685, 1700), with new text by Osterwald, lately published by D. H. Engel (1857). In 1688 he went to Spain, found favour at court, but is said to have died of poison.

(3) César August, b. Dec. 10, 1822, Liége, d. Nov. 8, 1890, Paris ; he attended, at first, the Liége Conservatoire, and then the one at Paris, where he was a pupil of Zimmermann (piano-forte), Leborne (counterpoint), and Benoist (organ). After Benoist's retirement (1872), he became his successor as professor of the organ at the Conservatoire, and organist of Ste.-Clotilde. Of his compositions F. published an oratorio (*Ruth*), a symphonic poem with chorus (" Les béatitudes "), pf. works, chamber-music, songs, etc.

His brother, (4) Joseph, teacher of music at Paris, has published masses, cantatas, motets, songs, instructive pianoforte pieces, also " Manuel de la transposition et de l'ac-compagnement du plain chant," " Traité d'har-monie," " L'art d'accompagner le plain chant," " Nouvelle méthode de piano facile," etc.

(5) Eduard, b. Dec. 5, 1817, Breslau, was at first teacher of pianoforte-playing at Cologne Conservatorium, 1859 at the Berne School of Music, from 1867 at the Stern Conservatorium at Berlin, and since 1886 taught at Emil Bres-laur's Klavierlehrer-Seminar. F. published a large number of instrumental compositions (symphony, Op. 47 ; pf. quintet, Op. 45 ; sextet, Op. 41 ; 'cello sonata, Op. 42 ; duets for two pianos, Op. 46 ; six sonatas, Op. 49 ; three ditto, Op. 44, etc.). Died Dec. 1, 1893, Berlin.

Francke, Augustus Hermann, founded in 1865 at Leipzig a pianoforte manufactory, which has gained great prosperity.

Franco, a name which has a distinguished sound in the history of measured music, for under it have been handed down to us several of the most famous treatises on Discant ; yet a great uncertainty prevails respecting the period at which F. flourished, the place of his birth, and his position. He has been set down as a scholastic of Liége in the 11th century ; but this is a thoroughly untenable supposition, since his theory of measured music is too far de-veloped for this period. A passage in an anony-mous treatise belonging to the first half of the 13th century, printed in Coussemaker's " Script." I. (Anonymous 4), brings bright light into what had hitherto been dark-ness. In it is written : " Mark, that Magister Leoninus was distinguished as a composer (*organista*), and had written a great work in Organum style based on the *Graduale* and *Anti-phonarium* to obtain variety in Divine service ; and that this work was in use up to the time of the great Perotinus, who himself made an epitome of it, and added many new and better compositions, inasmuch as he had an excellent knowledge of Discant, and in that matter surpassed Leoninus. Magister Perotinus himself wrote some fine compositions in four and three parts (on a *Cantus planus*) and also threefold, twofold, and single *Conductus*. The book, or the books, of Magister Perotinus were in use in the choir of Notre-Dame Cathedral at Paris, and, indeed, up to the time of Robert of Sabilon, and from him, in like manner, up to recent times, when men arose such as Petrus, a distinguished composer (*notator*), and Johannes the Great (*Primarius*), and, in the main, up to the time of Magister *Franco the Elder*, and of the other Magister *Franco of Cologne*, who, partly in their works, introduced a changed notation, and, on that account, established rules applying specially to their works." From that passage it is evident that there were *two Francos*, viz., *F. of Paris* and *F. of Cologne*, and that the former was older than the latter; but they were, approximately, contemporaries, and, as it appears, both acted as maître de chapelle at Notre-Dame, Paris. Anyhow, it is quite possible that the Cologne F. did not live at Paris, but, during his lifetime, was celebrated there. Then it could be assumed that the F. born at Dortmund, who in 1190 was prior of the Benedictine Abbey at Cologne, wrote the treatise commencing " Ego Franco de Colonia " (in Gerbert, " Script." II., and Coussemaker, " Script." I.); for the monks were not named after their place of birth, but after their cloister. On the other hand, F. of Paris wrote the treatise which Johann Ballox has given in condensed form. (*Cf.* Coussemaker, " Histoire de l'harmonie," etc., No. V., and " Script." I., p. 292.)

Francœur, (1) F r a n ç o i s, b. Sept., 1698, Paris, d. there Aug. 6, 1787, violinist ; he became a member of the Opéra orchestra in 1710, where he made the acquaintance of Franç. Rebel, with whom he stood during his whole life on terms of the closest friendship. Gradually he rose to be chamber musician (member of the 24 violons du roi, chamber composer, opera inspector, director of the Opéra, and finally (1760) royal principal intendant. F. wrote two books of violin sonatas, and, jointly with Fr. Rebel, ten operas.

(2) L o u i s J o s e p h, nephew of the former, b. Oct. 8, 1738, Paris, d. there March 10, 1804, likewise violinist ; he pursued the same career as his uncle, but, owing to the Revolution, lost his appointments of director of the Opéra and chief music intendant. He also wrote several operas (only one produced); likewise a good treatise on wind-instruments.

Frank, E r n s t, an eminent conductor and composer, b. Feb. 7, 1847, Munich, d. Aug. 17, 1889, Oberdöbling, near Vienna (of unsound mind). He attended the Gymnasium at the Metten Cloister, and also the Munich University,

but the study of the pianoforte under Mortier de Fontaine and of composition under Franz Lachner soon became his chief occupations; and, as court organist and conductor of the rehearsals at the Opera, F. made a firm start as conductor. In 1868 he was capellmeister at Würzburg, 1869 chorus-master at the Vienna Opera, and afterwards conductor of the " Singverein " and of the " Akademischer Gesangverein "; he ably discharged the duties of court capellmeister at Mannheim from 1872–77, where, among other things he produced in 1874 Götz's *Der Widerspenstigen Zähmung* (*The Taming of the Shrew*), and in 1877 *Francesca da Rimini*, the opera which the composer left unfinished (completed by F.). In 1877 he received a call to the Frankfort Theatre as principal capellmeister, where, under Otto Devrient as intendant, a new era for the encouragement of true art was expected to begin. Unfortunately, the good resolutions did not last; when Devrient, who, owing to his earnest efforts, proved inconvenient, was removed, F. resigned. At the end of 1879 he was richly compensated by being called to Hanover as Bülow's successor. Of F.'s compositions his songs and partsongs have become especially well known (Duettinos for two female voices from Kate Greenaway's " At the Window," and " Rattenfängerlieder," from Wolff's " Singuf," with violin obbligato). F. wrote the operas *Adam de la Halle* (Carlsruhe, 1880) and *Hero* (Berlin, 1884), and translated into German Stanford's *The Veiled Prophet*, and *Savonarola*, also Mackenzie's *Colomba*.

Frankenberger, H e i n r i c h, b. Aug. 20, 1824, Wümbach, Schwarzburg-Sondershausen, d. Nov. 22, 1885, Sondershausen, was trained by the Stadtmusikus Bartel (orchestral instruments), and his son Ernst (instrumentation and theory), the organist Birnstein (organ), and capellmeister G. Hermann (pianoforte) at Sondershausen, also, afterwards, by L. Plaidy, K. F. Becker, and M. Hauptmann at Leipzig. He was appointed in 1847 violinist in the ducal band at Sondershausen, in 1852 teacher of music at a seminary, and later on, sub-conductor of the court band. F. was a distinguished performer on the harp. During the yearly leave of absence he worked as opera-conductor at Erfurt, Halle, Frankfort-on-the-Oder, etc. F. was an able composer and teacher. Three operas, *Die Hochzeit zu Venedig*, *Vineta*, and *Der Günstling*, were produced with success, and some numbers printed. He wrote also: an " Anleitung zur Instrumentierung," a " Harmonielehre," an " Orgelschule," a " Choralbuch," preludes and postludes, a Vocal Method, pf. pieces, songs, etc.

Franko. (*See* FRANCO.)

Franz, (1) R o b e r t (von K n a u t h), b. June 28, 1815, Halle-a.-S., died there Oct. 24, 1892; one of the most thoughtful song-composers and, generally, one of the best musicians of our time. His parents were at first opposed to his leaning towards music, but finally allowed him to go to Dessau to complete his musical knowledge under Friedrich Schneider (1835). He remained there for two years, making a thorough study of counterpoint, although the dry lessons of Schneider were by no means to his taste. In 1837 he returned to Halle, and, as he could not obtain any post nor find a publisher for his compositions, he devoted all his time to the study of Bach and Handel, whose works, by masterly revision of the instrumental portion, he rendered more accessible to our time. After many years of waiting, he at last became organist of the Ulrichskirche (organ by Förner), then conductor of the "Singakademie," and, finally, "Musikdirektor" of the University. In 1843 his first set of songs appeared; at first their merit was acknowledged by a few only; but, among these were the important names of Schumann and Liszt. Further sets quickly followed, and F. became one of the most distinguished lyrical writers, combining Schumann's romanticism with a contrapuntal method of composition reminding one of Bach. In all he published over 250 songs. Already in 1841 his sense of hearing began materially to decline, and this, aggravated by a general disorder of the nerves, reached such a pitch that he was compelled to resign his posts in 1868. His anxiety with regard to the maintenance of his family was removed by a magnanimous gift from Freiherr Senfft von Pilsach, J. Schäffer, Otto Dresel, Frau Magnus, Liszt, and Joachim, the profit resulting from a concert tour undertaken in 1872 for Franz's benefit. Among the most meritorious achievements of F. are his revisions of Bach's and Handel's works, especially of the former: the St. Matthew Passion, Magnificat, Funeral Ode, ten cantatas, as well as many arias and duets; and of Handel: the Messiah, Jubilate, "L'Allegro, il Penseroso ed il Moderato," operatic airs and duets. Of F.'s compositions may be mentioned, in addition, the 117th Psalm for double choir, a Kyrie for soli and chorus, and part-songs for male, and for mixed choir. Essays on F. have been written by Ambros, Liszt, A. Saran, J. Schäffer, and H. M. Schuster.

(2) J. H., Pseudonym of Count Bolko von Hochberg (q.v.).

Fränzl, (1) Ignaz, distinguished violinist, b. June 3, 1734, Mannheim, d. 1803; he became, in 1750, a member of the famous court band of the Elector Karl Theodor, afterwards leader, finally capellmeister at Munich (after the band had been removed to that city in 1778). He travelled with his son, from 1784, for several years, and in 1790 undertook the direction of the Mannheim Theatre band. Of his compositions there appeared in print violin concertos, trios, quartets, etc.

(2) Ferdinand, son of the former, b. May 24, 1770, Schwetzingen (Palatinate), d.

Nov. 1833, Mannheim, pupil of his father, whom he surpassed both as a violinist and a composer; he made concert tours with him to Munich, Vienna, and Italy, studied composition under Padre Martini at Bologna, in 1792 became leader at Frankfort, in 1794 private capellmeister of Bernard at Offenbach, travelled in 1803 in Russia; and in 1806 became Cannabich's successor as court capellmeister and director of the German Opera, Munich, but frequently went on concert tours. On receiving his pension in 1827, he first retired to Geneva, afterwards to Mannheim. He composed nine violin concertos, a double concerto for two violins, duets and trios for violin, overtures, a symphony, several operettas, "Das Reich der Töne" (vocal solos, violin solo, chorus and orchestra), etc.

Frederic II., the Great, King of Prussia, b. Jan. 24, 1712, Berlin, d. Aug. 17, 1786, Sans-Souci. He was not only a zealous dilettante, and a fairly accomplished flautist (*cf.* QUANZ, GRAUN, PH. E. BACH), but also a composer (flute solos, arias, marches, opera, *Il re pastore*, an overture to *Acis und Galatea*). His musical biography was written by K. F. Müller (1847) and W. Kothe. Breitkopf & Härtel have published a selection of his compositions.

Fredon (Fr.), a short run, shake.

Freiberg, Otto, b. April 26, 1846, Naumburg, where his father was Musikdirektor; from 1860–63 a pupil of the Leipzig Conservatorium, in 1865 violinist in the court orchestra at Carlsruhe. He studied afterwards under V. Lachner, in 1880 became Universitäts-Musikdirektor at Marburg, and in 1887 Musikdirektor and assistant professor at Göttingen University.

French horn, natural horn (Waldhorn).

French sixth, the chord of the augmented sixth, with fourth and third *e.g.* A♭, C, D, and F♯.

French violin clef, the G clef on the first line.

Freschi, Giovanni Domenico, b. 1640, Vicenza, d. there 1690, wrote masses and psalms à 3–6, an oratorio (*Judith*), and twelve operas (for Venice, 1677 to 1685).

Fresco (Ital.), fresh.

Frescobaldi, Girolamo, according to the latest investigations by Haberl (1886), was baptised Sept. 9, 1583, Ferrara (therefore probably born a few days previously), and buried at Rome, March 2, 1644. His teacher was Luzzasco Luzzaschi at Ferrara. F. is said to have been organist at Mecklin in 1607. In any case he seems to have lived about this time in the Netherlands, for P. Phalèse published his first work at Antwerp (madrigals à 5, 1608). In 1608 he was elected organist of St. Peter's, Rome (successor of Erc. Pasquini), and held this post until shortly before his death (during the last years of his life he played the organ of St. Lorenzo *in montibus*). From 1628–33 F. obtained leave of absence, and was represented by a deputy, and during this period lived at Florence as organist to the Duke; but, finally, probably fled from the ravages caused by the plague and by war. That F. was held in high esteem is evident from the fact that Joh. Jac. Froberger, who was court organist at Vienna, obtained leave of absence, from 1637–41, in order to study under Frescobaldi at Rome. According to the testimony of contemporaries, F. created a new style of playing, which was generally adopted. As an organist he had no rival; but also as composer he was held in the highest esteem, and, in fact, was a musician of very great importance. He helped materially in the development of fugue. Besides the madrigals named, he published: "Fantasie a quattro" (1608); "Ricercari e canzoni francese" (1615); "Toccate e partite d'intavolutura di cembalo" (1615–16, which, while they were being engraved, were given out in copies of various compass [from fifty-eight to ninty-four pages]; new ed. 1637); "Capricci et arie" reprinted together with the "Ricercari" at Venice, 1626); "Il II. Libro di Toccate, Canzone," etc. (1627); "Canzoni a 1–4 voci" (1628); "Arie musicali" (1630, two books); "Fiori musicali di toccate, etc." (1635, containing some compositions printed in 1627). From the manuscripts left by F., Vincenti also published a (fourth) book, "Canzoni alla Francese" (1645). Single pieces are to be found in collections between 1618–25. Only a Maundy Thursday Lamentation, and an "In te domine speravi" for double choir, remained in manuscript. The second and third books of the "Canzone" have hitherto not been discovered. (*Cf.* Haberl's monograph which preceded his edition of F.'s organ compositions [selected].)

Frets (Ger. *Bünde;* Fr. *Touches;* Ital. *Tasti*), small strips of wood or metal fixed transversely on the finger-board of stringed-instruments; when the finger presses down the string over them they become bridges and definitely fix the length of string which is to vibrate—*i.e.* if the distances between the F. are correctly calculated, pure intonation is rendered easy. F. are specially used for instruments of the lute kind, and appear to have been introduced into the West by the Arabians. (*Cf.* INSTRUMENTS, STRINGED.).

Fretta (Ital.), haste; *con f., frettando,* same as STRINGENDO.

Freudenberg, Wilhelm, b. March 11, 1838, Raubacher Hütte, near Neuwied, was for a long time theatre capellmeister in various towns; he went, in 1865, to occupy a post as director of the Cecilia Union and the "Synagogenverein" at Wiesbaden, where, in 1870, he founded a Conservatorium, which still flourishes; and he was, at the same time, director of the "Singakademie." In 1886 he moved to Berlin, where, jointly with K. Mengewein, he opened a school for music, but soon gave over the directorship to

Mengewein, and went to Augsburg and Ratisbon as theatre capellmeister. He has published: pf. works, songs, music to *Romeo und Juliet,* an overture (*Durch Dunkel zum Licht*), a symphonic poem ("Ein Tag in Sorrento"), and produced the operas *Die Pfahlbauer* (1877), *Die Nebenbuhler* (1879), *Kleopatra* (1882), *Die Mühle im Wisperthale* (1883); *Der St. Katharinentag* (Augsburg, 1889), and *Marino Faliero* (Ratisbon, 1889).

Friberth, Karl, b. June 7, 1736, Wullersdorf (Lower Austria), d. Aug. 6, 1816; in 1759 tenor singer to Prince Esterhazy at Eisenstadt, in 1776 capellmeister at the Jesuit and Minorite churches, Vienna. He wrote sacred compositions (masses, offertories, graduals, etc.).

Fricassé (French), a jocular, and common term in the 16th century for compositions in several parts, with different words for each part.

Frick (Frike), Philipp Joseph, b. May 27, 1740, Würzburg, d. June 15, 1798; he was court organist at Baden-Baden, afterwards travelled as a performer on Franklin's glass-harmonica, and, in 1780, settled in London as a teacher of music, and made fruitless efforts to improve the harmonica. Besides some pf. works, he published "The Art of Musical Modulation," 1780; (in French, "L'art de moduler en musique," without date); "A Treatise on Thorough Bass" (1786); and "A Guide in Harmony" (1793).

Fricke, August Gottfried Ludwig, distinguished stage-singer (bass), b. March 24, 1829, Brunswick, pupil of the baritone Meinhardt there; he made his *début* in 1851 as Sarastro at Brunswick, sang afterwards at Bremen, Königsberg, and Stettin, and from 1856–86 was principal bass at the Royal Court Opera, Berlin.

Frickenhaus, Fanny (*née* Evans), b. June 7, 1849, Cheltenham, an able pianist. She studied under Mr. G. Mount, M. Aug. Dupont, and later, under Mr. W. Bohrer. She appears at the principal London concerts. She played the pianoforte concerto of Goetz for the first time in London.

Friedheim, Arthur, pianist, b. Oct. 26, 1859, Petersburg, of German parents. He developed into a virtuoso at an early age, but attended the Gymnasium; and, after conducting small theatre orchestras for several years, was taken up by Liszt. F. is more especially an interpreter of Liszt.

Friedländer, Max, distinguished concert-singer (bass) and writer on music, b. Oct. 12, 1852, Brieg (Silesia), pupil of Manuel Garcia at London, and of J. Stockhausen at Frankfort. He made his *début* in 1880 at the London Monday Popular Concerts, and quickly obtained great fame. From 1881–83 he resided in Frankfort, and since then has lived in Berlin. In 1882 the university of Breslau conferred on him the degree of *Dr. Phil. hon. causá.* F. edited for Peters a new and complete edition of the songs of Schubert, wrote a biography of this master; and, in his preliminary work for the latter, proved himself an excellent musical investigator, and made a number of highly interesting discoveries. Besides a series of hitherto unpublished songs, he has published varied readings of the words of the songs of Schubert, Schumann, and Mendelssohn, and also rendered assistance in Stockhausen's "Gesangstechnik."

Frike. (*See* FRICK.)

Frimmel, Theodor, b. Dec. 15, 1853, Amstetten (Lower Austria), studied medicine, and took his doctor's degree at Vienna in 1879; but occupied himself at the same time with the plastic arts and music. He made extensive journeys for the sake of the history of art. F. is "Custos-Adjunkt" of the Royal Library at Vienna, and "Dozent" of the Society of Arts. He has written studies on the painters, K. F. Lessing (1881) and Jos. Ant. Koch (1884). His first musico-historical pamphlet was "Beethoven und Göthe (1883), and his most interesting, the "Neue Beethoveniana" (1887, with an authentic likeness of Beethoven; a faithful representation of the man Beethoven). A second and enlarged edition appeared in 1889.

Friska (Fris), the principal section, in lively time, of the czarda.

Fritze, Wilhelm, gifted, but short-lived pianist and composer, b. Feb. 17, 1842, Bremen, d. Oct. 7, 1881, Stuttgart, attended the Gymnasium at Bremen, and was then a pupil of E. Sobolewski for music. In 1858 he attended the Leipzig Conservatorium, and, on Liszt's advice, studied again in Berlin under Hans von Bülow and Weitzmann. After several concert tours in Italy and France, F. settled in Glogau, and in 1867 in Liegnitz, where he directed the "Singakademie" from 1867–77, and then went to Berlin, and recommenced studying under Kiel. In 1879 he went (without, however, any fixed appointment) to Stuttgart. F. wrote works of all kinds (symphony, "Die Jahreszeiten"; oratorios, *Fingal* and *David;* violin concerto, pf. concerto, music to *Faust,* etc.), and also published much music (pf. sonatas, Op. 2, Sanctus, Benedictus, and Agnus for mixed chorus, soli, and orchestra; pf. pieces à 2 et à 4; songs, vocal pieces) which bear favourable testimony to his talent.

Fritzsch, Ernst Wilhelm, b. Aug. 24, 1840, Lützen, pupil of the Leipzig Conservatorium, founded in 1866 a music-publishing firm (works of Rheinberger, Svendsen, Grieg, Herzogenberg, Cornelius; Wagner's "Gesammelte Schriften," etc.), and edited *Musikalisches Wochenblatt,* which he had started in 1870. From 1883, for several years, F. managed a pianoforte manufactory, jointly with Fischer, the inventor of the *Adiaphon* (q.v.).

Froberger, Johann Jakob, eminent organist and composer, whose date and place of birth are unknown. F. studied, from 1637–41, under Frescobaldi in Rome, but was already before that (Sept., 1637), and afterwards again (from 1641–45 and 1653–57), court organist at Vienna, and received from the court two hundred gulden towards the expenses of his journey to Italy for the purpose of study. He also appears to have been in Vienna in 1649. He died, May 7, 1667, at Héricourt, near Montbéliard, in the castle of the Duchess Dowager Sibylla of Württemberg, where he had gone in 1657. (*Cf. Monatshefte für Musikgeschichte,* XVIII., 10.) Of his works the following have been preserved: "Diverse ingegnosissime e rarissime partite di toccate, canzoni, ricercari, capricci, etc." (1693 and 1696, two parts; the first part reprinted without any alteration, 1695 and 1714); "Suites de clavecin" (without date). Manuscripts of his works are to be found in the libraries of Berlin (autographs of 1549 and 1656) and Vienna. E. Schebek published two letters from the Duchess Sibylla to Chr. Huygens concerning F. (1874). F. is a phenomenon of high importance in the history of organ and clavier music. In power of invention he was German, but in workmanship he showed the influence of his Italian training. Franz Beier wrote a monograph on F. (Waldersee's "Samml. mus. Vorträge," Nos. 59, 60).

Frölich, Joseph, b. May 28, 1780, Würzburg, d. there Jan. 5, 1862; he attended the Gymnasium and University of that city, became, in 1801, member of the Electoral court band, founded a vocal and instrumental union among the students ("Akademische Bande"), which was acknowledged in 1804 as the "Akademisches Musikinstitut"; at the same time he became private teacher of music, and Musikdirektor at the University. Gradually, by the admission of pupils of the Gymnasium and other young men musically disposed, the Institute was enlarged: the seminarists were also obliged to attend, and by that means the present Royal School of Music sprang into existence. F. was appointed occasional professor of esthetics, and, later on, of pedagogics and didactics. In 1820 a general school of singing was incorporated with the Institute. In 1844 F. gave up conducting the orchestral rehearsals and performances, and in 1854 resigned his post as professor at the University, and finally, in 1858, the direction of the Institute. F. was active as a composer: masses, a requiem, symphonies, an opera (*Scipio*), sonatas, part- and other songs; and he was known as a writer of serious articles in *Cäcilia,* in Erk and Gruber's Encyclopædia, and in *Mnemosyne* (supplement to the *N. Würzburger Ztg.*), and as the biographer of Abbé Vogler. Besides these, he wrote a "Musiklehre mit Anweisungen für's Spiel aller gebräuchlichen Instrumente" (in four parts), also separate methods for the various instruments, from the violin to the serpent, and a Vocal Method.

Fromm, E m i l, b. Jan. 29, 1835, Spremberg (Niederlausitz), pupil of Grell, Bach, and Schneider, Berlin, in 1859 cantor at Cottbus, from 1869 organist at Flensburg; in 1866 he was named royal musical director, founder of a mixed choral society; he is also a composer (Passion-cantatas, organ pieces, choruses for male voices).

Froschauer, J o h a n n, book printer in Augsburg at the end of the 15th century, also, so far as is known, the first who printed music notes (examples) with types, namely, in Michael Keinspeck's " Lilium musicæ planæ " (1498, coarse chorale notes). In all earlier works (Missals, etc.) the lines were printed, and the notes written in by hand. (*Cf. also* BURTIUS.)

Frost, H e n r y F r e d e r i c k, English musician and able musical critic (*Standard, Athenæum,* etc.). He wrote the " Schubert " for the " Great Musicians " series. He was for many years organist of the Chapel Royal, Savoy.

Frottole (Ital.), a species of dignified Italian popular song of the 16th century, midway between the complicated Madrigal and the simple note-against-note harmonized villanelle and villote, and, having for the most part, words of an erotic character. The poem has a four-line refrain, in rhyme order, *a b b a;* of which the first, or second half returns after each of the five-line strophes (rhyme order of the strophes, *a b a c c*). The verse measure consists of four trochees in each line. From 1504 to 1509 Petrucci published nine books of F., and Junta one book of the same in 1526. Rud. Schwartz wrote a study on the F. in the 4th volume of the " Vierteljahrsschrift f. Musikwissenschaft " for 1886.

F sharp (Ger. *Fis*), F raised by a $\sharp$; F$\sharp$ *major* chord $=f\sharp$ a$\sharp$ c$\sharp$; F$\sharp$ *minor* chord $=f\sharp$ a c$\sharp$; F$\sharp$ *major* key, with signature of six sharps; F$\sharp$ *minor* key, with signature of three sharps. (*See* KEY.)

Fuchs, (1) G e o r g F r i e d r i c h, b. Dec. 3, 1752, Mayence, d. Oct. 9, 1821, Paris; he studied under Cannabich at Mannheim. He was at first military musician at Zweibrücken, went to Paris in 1784, and, when the Conservatoire was established in 1795, he was appointed teacher of the clarinet; he composed many works for wind-instruments.

(2) A l o y s, b. June 6, 1799, Raase (Austrian Silesia), d. March 20, 1853, as assistant-draughtsman in the court council of war; he was a distinguished connoisseur of music, and an enthusiastic collector of musical manuscripts and portraits of artists. He communicated the results of his investigations to Vienna and Berlin periodicals dealing with special branches of musical art. His collections, unique of their kind, were scattered by sales after his death.

(3) K a r l D o r i u s J o h a n n, genially-disposed pianist and intelligent writer on music, b. Oct. 22, 1838, Potsdam, as second son of the teacher of music and organist to the cadet corps G.L.D.F., by whom the youth's talent was strictly guided. At an early age F. lost his mother, and, as collegian (Gymnasiast), was forced to give private lessons on the pianoforte. In 1859 he attended the University at Berlin as student of theology, but at the same time studied privately under Hans von Bülow, who, when, after a year, F.'s pecuniary means did not admit of his paying for further instruction, generously gave him lessons during a space of four years. After long halting between theology and philosophy, F. gave himself up entirely to music, and, amid a constant struggle for mere existence, studied thorough-bass with K. Fr. Weitzmann, and composition with F. Kiel. For two years he was private tutor at Osdorf Manor, near Berlin, and for half a year at the house of Steffeck the painter, working, at the same time, all the more earnestly on his own account. His first literary work was " Betrachtungen mit und gegen Arthur Schopenhauer," in the *N. Berl. Musikzeitung.* In 1868 he entered into the teachers' college of Kullak's " Akademie," but married in 1869, and took an organist's post at the St. Nicholas' Church, Stralsund. In 1868 he published " Ungleiche Verwandte unter den Neudeutschen " (in defence of Tappert), and " Hellas " (pf. pieces on modern Greek themes), in 1869 " Virtuos und Dilettant " (thoughts respecting pianoforte-teaching), a small pamphlet which attracted attention. In 1870 he took his degree of Dr.Phil. at Greifswald (thesis : " Präliminarien zu einer Kritik der Tonkunst," a serious philosophical analysis of art enjoyment in music, the ultra-philosophical conception of which proved a barrier to a wide circulation; and that such was the case could easily be shown if the work were rewritten in plainer language. In 1871 he returned to Berlin, appeared frequently in public as pianist, and wrote various articles for the *Mus. Wochenblatt.* A great work on technique, written at that time, has remained in manuscript. In 1875, while on a concert tour, he went to Hirschberg (Silesia), where he founded a musical society, and proved successful as conductor. In 1879 he exchanged Hirschberg for Danzig, conducted the choral union there (1882–83), became teacher of music at the Victoria College, and, in 1886, organist of St. Peter's Church. F. proved of material assistance to H. Riemann in his efforts to improve musical notation by means of phrase marks, for he wrote " Die Zukunft des musikal. Vortrags " (1884, two parts ; a third still in hand), and " Die Freiheit des musikalischen Vortrags " (1885), and, jointly with H. Riemann, he published " Praktische Anleitung zum Phrasieren " (1886). As a pianist F. possesses a quality rarely to be met with, viz., a faculty

of expression of imposing intensity: he really "phrases." F. was also the first who attempted phrasing in orchestral performances.

(4) J o h a n n N e p o m u k, b. May 5, 1842, Frauenthal (Styria), son of a teacher, studied philosophy and music (Sechter) at Vienna, became opera capellmeister at Pressburg in 1864, and was engaged in a similar capacity at various theatres, finally at Cologne, Hamburg, Leipzig (Carola Theatre), and, from 1880, at the Vienna Opera. An opera, *Zingara*, was produced at Brünn in 1872; F. also arranged Handel's *Almira* for the new staging of the work at Hamburg, Schubert's *Alfonso und Estrella*, and Gluck's *Der betrogene Cadi* for Vienna.

(5) R o b e r t, brother of the former, b. Feb. 15, 1847, Frauenthal, pupil of the Vienna Conservatorium, at present teacher of harmony at that institution. He has published a pf. sonata, two violin sonatas, three serenades, a symphony (Op. 37, in c), a trio, quartet, several sets of variations, etc.

(6) A l b e r t, b. Aug. 6, 1858, Basle, pupil of the Leipzig Conservatorium (1876–79), Musik-direktor at Trèves (1880); he lived at Ober-lössnitz, near Dresden from 1883 to 1889, when he became owner of the Wiesbaden Conservatorium, which, founded by Freudenberg, had been brought low by W. Taubmann, but soon flourished again under F.'s management. He is a talented composer (songs, duets, a 'cello-sonata, pf. pieces, sonata in F minor, Hungarian suite for orchestra).

Fuentes, (1) D o n P a s q u a l e, b. Albaida (Valencia) at the beginning of the 18th century, was maestro, in 1757, of Valencia Cathedral, d. April 26, 1768. He was one of the most eminent of Spanish church composers (masses, Te Deums, motets à 6–12, villancicos, etc.).

(2) Francisco de Santa Maria de, Franciscan monk at Madrid. He published a theoretical work: "Dialectos Musicos" (1778).

Fuertes, M a r i á n o S o r i a n o. (*See* SORI-ANO-F.)

Fuga. (*See* FUGUE.)

Fuga ad octavam (Lat.), a fugue at the octave.

Fuga ad quintam (Lat.), a fugue at the fifth.

Fuga æqualis motus (Lat.), "a fugue of similar motion"—*i.e.* a fugue in which the answer ascends and descends in the same way as the subject. It is synonymous with *fuga recta*.

Fuga al contrario, or *al riverso*, or *al rovescio* (Ital). (*See* FUGA CONTRARIA.)

Fuga authentica (Lat.), a fugue with an ascending subject.

Fuga canonica (Lat.), a canon.

Fuga composita (Lat.), a fugue the subject of which proceeds by degrees, not by leaps.

Fuga contraria (Ger. *Gegenfuge*), a fugue in which the answer is the inversion of the subject, and, indeed, so that the tonic and dominant, for the most part, answer each other. (*Cf.* IN-VERSION.) Fugae contrariae are to be found *e.g.*, in J. S. Bach's "Kunst der Fuge" (Nos 5, 6, 7, 14).

Fuga del tuono (Ital.), a tonal fugue. (*See* FUGUE.)

Fuga doppia (Lat.), a double fugue; a fugue with two subjects.

Fuga homophona (Lat.), a fugue with the answer at the unison.

Fuga impropria (Lat.), the same as *fuga irregularis* (q.v.).

Fuga inæqualis (Lat.), the same as *fuga contraria* (q.v.).

Fuga incomposita (Lat.), a fugue the subject of which proceeds by leaps, not by degrees.

Fuga in consequenza (Ital.), a canon.

Fuga in contrario tempore (Lat.), a fugue in which the accentuation of the answer differs from that of the subject, the accented notes of the one being unaccented in the other, and *vice versâ*.

Fuga inversa (Lat.), a fugue throughout in double counterpoint and contrary motion.

Fuga irregularis (Lat.), an irregular fugue; a fugue which lacks one or more of the features that characterise the form.

Fuga libera (Lat.), a fugue with free episodes.

Fuga ligata (Lat. and Ital.), a fugue without free episodes, entirely developed out of the subject and the countersubject.

Fuga mixta (Lat.), a fugue in which several kinds of answer occur—by augmentation, by diminution, by contrary motion, etc.

Fuga obligata (Lat. and Ital.), the same as *fuga ligata* (q.v.).

Fuga partialis, or **Fuga periodica** (Lat.), a fugue with partial, or periodic, imitation, in contradistinction to a fugue with canonic or uninterrupted (perpetual) imitation; in short, what we call a *fugue*, in contradistinction to a *canon*.

Fuga per arsin et thesin (Lat.), the same as *fuga in contrario tempo*, the accents of the subject being reversed in the answer.

Fuga per augmentationem (Lat.), a fugue in which the answer is by augmentation.

Fuga per diminutionem (Lat.), a fugue in which the answer is by diminution.

Fuga per motum contrarium (Lat.), a fugue in which the answer is by contrary motion.

Fuga perpetua (Lat.), a canon.

Fuga plagalis (Lat.), a fugue with a descending subject.

Fuga propria (Lat), the same as *fuga regularis* (q.v.).

Fugara (*Vogar*), an open lip-stop in the organ of 8 and 4 feet of very narrow measure, with a low narrow slit, and of string-tone. The F. sometimes occurs with Gamba measurement.

Fuga reale (Ital.), a real fugue. (*See* FUGUE.)

Fuga recta (Lat.), the same as *fuga æqualis motus* (q.v.).

Fuga reditta (Ital.), a fugue in the middle or at the end of which two or more parts are treated canonically.

Fuga regularis (Lat.), a regular fugue; a fugue which has all the features that characterise the form.

Fuga retrograda (Lat.), a fugue in which the answer is by retrograde motion.

Fuga retrograda per motum contrarium (Lat.), a fugue in which the answer is both by retrograde and contrary motion.

Fuga ricercata (Ital.), an elaborate fugue; one in which the rarer devices of contrapuntal craftsmanship are employed, such as canonic imitation, and imitation by augmentation, diminution, and by contrary and retrograde motion.

Fuga sciolta (Ital.), the same as *fuga libera* (q.v.).

Fuga soluta (Lat.), the same as *fuga libera* (q.v.).

Fugato (Ital.), worked after the manner of a fugue, yet no actual fugue. In the development sections of sonatas, symphonies, concertos, etc., fragments of themes are often treated in imitation, after the manner of a fugue; also a whole composition, worked in a similar manner, is styled a F.

Fuga totalis (Lat.), a canon.

Fughetta (Ital.), a small fugue.

Fugue is the most highly-developed art-form of concertante style, in which the equalisation of the various parts is brought to the highest pitch, in that a short pregnant theme runs through them alternately, making now the one, now the other prominent. The F. is therefore at least in two parts. Our present Quint-fugue (F. at the fifth) was gradually developed, in the course of the 17th century, from the canonic subtleties of the Netherland school (15th and 16th centuries). At that period, what we now call canon was named *Fugue*, while, from the end of the 16th century, the freer forms, which often resemble our F., were called Ricercar, Toccata, Fantasia, Sonata. The most important names in the earlier history of F. are: Andrea and Giovanni Gabrieli, Frescobaldi, Froberger, J. P. Sweelinck, Scheidt, Pachelbel, Buxtehude. F. received its highest art-development through Johann Sebastian Bach (in his instrumental music) and Handel (in his vocal music). The most essential parts and *termini techni* of F. are: the *theme* (*Führer*, subject, *Dux*, *Guida*, *Proposta*), given out alone by the part or voice which first begins, whereupon a second enters with the *answer* (*Gefährte*, *Comes*, *Risposta*, *Consequente*), to which the first supplies a counterpoint (countersubject) pregnant with rhythm and melody. If the F. is in more than two parts, the third voice introduces the subject again, the fourth the answer, etc. The appearance of the theme once in all the parts is termed *Exposition* (Repercussion). The greater the number of parts in a F. the greater the number of possible repercussions, for with increase of the former is a corresponding increase of permutations. For example: (D = Dux, C = Comes; 1, 2, 3 = 1st, 2nd, 3rd voice counting from above downwards:

I. (two-part): 1 D 2 C — 2 D 1 C.

II. (three-part): 1 D 2 C 3 D — 1 D 3 C 2 D —2 D 1 C 3 D—2 D 3 C 1 D — 3 D 2 C 1 D —3 D 1 C 2 D.

III. (four-part): 1 D 2 C 3 D 4 C — 1 D 2 C 4 D 3 C — 1 D 3 C 2 D 4 C — 1 D 3 C 4 D 2 C — 1 D 4 C 3 D 2 C — 1 D 4 C 2 D 3 C —2 D 3 C 4 D 1 C — 2 D 3 C 1 D 4 C — 2 D 4 C 3 D 1 C — 2 D 4 C 1 D 3 C — 2 C 1 C 3 D 4 C — 2 D 1 C 4 D 3 C, etc.;

in all twenty-four different successions of voices, which commence with Dux and, as a rule, alternate with Dux-Comes. A F. in five parts admits, however, of 120 different entries of voices. Then there are further possibilities in the developments which enter later on in the course of the F., and which can commence with the *Comes* (the second carrying through of the parts begins, as a rule, with the *Comes*); there is also the licence that two parts can have successively Dux or Comes. The variety of means in a F., in spite of the apparent schematism, is evident from the fact that only a small portion of the possibilities can be employed. The answer is a transposition of the subject in the 5th (under-fourth, upper-twelfth, under-eleventh), and, indeed, either quite a faithful transposition (Real Fugue), or one modified so as to preserve the tonality (*Tonal Fugue*, *Fuga de tona*). The principal rule for the tonal answer of a F. subject is that Tonic and Dominant (Prime and Quint of the key) should answer each other mutually, for example:

real

tonal

Examples of both kinds are frequent in Bach. (*Cf.* Hauptmann's "Erläuterungen zu Bachs Kunst der F.," and the articles relating to the same in the "Wiener Rezensionen. The first development (Exposition) of a F. is followed, for the most part, by a short interlude (*divertimento*, *andamento*), with a free working of the motive of the theme or counter-theme, and a smooth modulation to some related key, but a quick return; in fugues of considerable extent the interludes (*Episodes*) must be of an interesting character, otherwise the constant repetition of the theme becomes wearisome. In a third or fourth working-out more freedom is permitted; the theme is presented in other keys: the answer can appear at other intervals than the fifth, and indeed in fresh keys. Special freedom is allowed when a theme is answered in *Inversion, Diminution*, or *Augmentation*, and with certain rhythmical changes. As a rule the last working out is a contrapuntal display, viz., a repeated drawing closer (*Stretto*) of Dux and Comes (in quick succession, so that parts of both sound simultaneously). When the countersubject is worked out jointly with the principal subject, the F. is a *Double Fugue* (q.v.). Dr. Hugo Riemann has published a valuable analysis of Bach's *Well-tempered Clavier* (" Katechismus der Fugen-Komposition," two parts, 1891). Two recent and important English works on F. are E. Prout's " Fugue " and " Fugal Analysis: A Companion to ' Fugue.' "

Führer. (*See* DUX and FUGUE.)

Führer, R o b e r t, Bohemian church composer and teacher of theory, b. June 2, 1807, Prague, d. Nov. 28, 1861, Vienna; he was a pupil of Vitásek, and, first of all, organist at Strahow, in 1830 principal teacher at the School for Organists at Prague, and in 1839 successor of Vitásek as cathedral capellmeister at Prague. In 1845 he gave up this post, and lived later on in Salzburg and Vienna. F. wrote twenty masses, and many other sacred vocal pieces and works for the organ ; also theoretical works on the organ.

Fuhrmann, (1) G e o r g L e o p o l d, published " Testudo Gallo-Germanica " (Nuremberg, 1615), a work on the lute, translated in French and German Tablature (a copy is in the " Landesbibliothek " at Cassel).
(2) M a r t i n H e i n r i c h, 1704 appointed Lutheran cantor at the Friedrich-Werder Gymnasium, one of the best theorists and critics of his time; he published the greater number of his writings in pseudonymic form under the initial letters of his name. They are: (1) " Musikalischer Trichter der edlen Singekunst " (Frankfort-on-the-Spree [*i.e.* Berlin] 1706, with preface signed *Meines Herzens Freude*) ; (2) " Musica vocalis in nuce " (according to Walther, printed in 1728, according to Reimann [*Allg. M. Ztg.*, 1890] before the first-named work), title with the full name, preface as undersigned in (1) ; (3) " Gerechte Wag Schal " (in the contest between J. Meyer and Mattheson),.Brandenburg, 1728 (signed Innocentius Franckenberg) ; (4) " Das in unserm Opera Theater siechende Christenthum und siegende Heidenthum von Liebhold und Leuthold " (Canterbury [*i.e.* in the place of residence of the cantor] in the Musikalisches Hauptquartier, thirty-six miles

from Hamburg, 1728); (5) " Die an der Kirchen Gottes gebaute Satanskapelle " of Marco Hilario *Frischmuth* (Cologne on the Rhine, " bei der heiligen drei Könige Erben M. H. F. G. T. C.," 1729) ; (6) " Musikalische Striegel (Ulm, 1727, or Berlin, 1728) ; (7) " Die von der Pforte der Hölle bestürmte Himmelskirche " (Berlin, 1730, with full name).

Full Organ (Ger. *Volles Werk ;* Ital. *Organo pieno ;* Fr. *Grand chœur*). This is a term used in organ compositions, indicating that in a passage or piece there is to be a powerful combination of stops, *i.e.* a great number, or indeed all; but especially the 16- and 32-ft. diapasons and the mixtures. In modern organs a suitable selection of stops can be quickly drawn out by means of combination-pedals.

Fumagalli, (1) A d o l f, b. Oct. 19, 1828, Inzago, d. May 3, 1856, Florence, pianist and composer.
(2) P o l i b i o, brother of the above, b. Oct. 26, 1830, Inzago, pianist and composer (organ sonatas, Augener's Edition, 5844 and 8733).

Fumi, V i n c e s l a o, Italian composer and conductor, b. Oct. 20, 1823, Montepulciano (Tuscany), d. Nov. 20, 1880, Florence, pupil of Giorgetti there ; he became opera maestro at various Italian theatres, also at Constantinople, Rio de Janeiro, Montevideo, and Buenos Ayres. In the last named town he produced an opera, *Atala* (1862). He spent his last years at Florence, and wrote several orchestral works, and left an incomplete collection of popular songs of all nations and periods.

Fundamental Bass (Rameau's *Basse fondamentale*) is the indication of chords by means of their principal note, for example:—

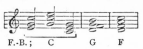

F.-B.; C G F

By thus setting them out, Rameau was led to recognise *that all chords must be understood in the sense either of a major or a minor chord*, the natural bass note of which he termed F. B., and thus he evolved the theory of the inversion of chords which Vallotti, Kirnberger, Abbé Vogler, etc., adopted. Unfortunately not one of them developed the fundamental thought of Rameau, who, for example, describes *d.f.a.c.* as an F major chord with sixth (*accord de la sixte ajoutée*), and *b.d.f.* as a G major chord with seventh, and with omission of fundamental note. Only Gottfried Weber made an attempt to go beyond him, but he could no more free himself from Kirnberger's arrangement of numerous root chords than the other theorists of his time. The editor of this Dictionary, in his " Harmonielehre " (1880), has worked on Rameau's fundamental thought, and in connection with the modern progress of theory, has

developed a new system of figuring chords. (*See* KLANGSCHLÜSSEL.)

Fundamental Chord (Ger. *Stammakkord*), a term in the theory of harmony indicating the contrary of a derived chord. By a F. C. is understood one built up simply in thirds: thus triad, chord of the 7th, or chord of the 9th; the inversions of these chords (derived chords), in which the 3rd, 5th, or 7th is the lowest note, are the chords of six-five, of six-four-three, and of six-four-two, etc. But the term F. C. is frequently employed to denote pure harmonies in contradistinction to those changed by alterations or suspensions.

Fundamental Note is the name given in thoroughbass to that note which, in a building up of the chord by thirds, is the lowest; for example, *c* in *c. e. g*, or *g* in *g. b. d. f.* When the F. N. is bass note the chord is in its *fundamental position;* when it is in some other part or voice, the chord is *inverted.* (*See* MAJOR CHORD, MINOR CHORD, etc.) According, however, to the modern conception of a minor triad, the fundamental note is its highest note. (*See* CLANG.)

Fundamental Position of a chord is in thoroughbass that distribution of notes which shows the fundamental note as the bass note. Thus we have, at *a*, chords in F. P.; at *b*, on the other hand, in *inverted* form (third, also fifth as bass note):

(*Cf.* MAJOR AND MINOR CHORD and SEVENTH, CHORD OF.)

Fundamental Scale (Ger. *Grundscala*) is the succession by degrees of the notes on which a system of music is based, and opposed to which, other notes, received into the system, appear derived. The F. S. of our European western system of music is limited to seven notes; the eighth (the octave) refers to the first, is derived from it, bears the same name; the seven notes originally bore the names of the first seven letters of the alphabet—A, B, C, D, E, F, G—but, by a peculiar complication of relationships, H in Germany took the place of B. (Concerning the various kinds of octave division of the alphabet scale, *see* LETTER NOTATION, B, and CHROMATIC SIGNS.) Our present notation is only a disguise, not a displacement of tone-writing by means of letters; for instead of writing before every line and every space a letter to indicate the names of the notes falling on the same, we are satisfied with the signature of a single clef-letter for each system of five lines. (*See* CLEF.) The F. S. is, and was, already in ancient times, the succession of two whole tones, one half-tone, three whole tones,

one half-tone, which is repeated in like manner in higher and lower octaves.

The octave species of the Greeks (*see* GREEK MUSIC, II.), as well as the Church Modes (q.v.) of the Middle Ages, are nothing more than sections of the compass of an octave taken from this F. S. Of the seven possible kinds (*c–c', d–d', e–e', f–f', g–g', a–a', b–b'*, without signature), only two are of typical importance for the general experience of our day, viz.:

i.e. the major scale without signature (*the major fundamental scale*) and:

i.e. the minor scale without signature (*the minor fundamental scale*). As is shown at greater length under MINOR SCALE, the minor scale, if it is to be regarded as a type, must be noted down from the minor key-note, in which case it appears as the exact contrary of the major scale:

If the relationships of the major fundamental scale (2, ½, 3, ½) are to be established from any other note than *c* (transposed to some other degree), then changes of certain notes of the F. S. will become necessary, *e.g.* for *d—d'* :

Without the sharps the succession would be: 1, ½, 3, ½, 1. The various transpositions of the F. S. are given in notes under KEY.

Funebre (Ital.), funereal, mournful.

Funzioni (Ital.), functions, offices, services— for instance, in the Roman Catholic Church.

Fuoco (Ital.), *foco*, fire; *con fuoco, fuocoso*, in a fiery manner.

Furia (Ital.), rage, fury; *furioso, furibondo*, furious.

Furiant, a lively Bohemian dance with sharp

accents, and alternating time. Türk (" Klavier-schule," 1789) calls it *Furie*.

Furlana. (*See* FORLANA.)

Furlanetto, B o n a v e n t u r a, with the surname M u s i n, b. March 27, 1738, Venice, d. there April 6, 1817. He was at an early age teacher of singing, and conducted performances at the Ospedale della Pietà (a conservatorio in which only girls were trained), and attracted consider-able attention as conductor, player on the organ, and as a composer of masses for per-formance by the scholars (the orchestra was also composed solely of girls). He failed in obtain-ing a post as organist of San Marco; on the other hand, in 1794, he became deputy maestro, and in 1797 actual second maestro at San Marco, and, afterwards, Bertoni's successor as principal maestro; also, in 1811, teacher for fugue and counterpoint at the Philharmonic Institute. His works, mostly sacred, show him as an ex-perienced contrapuntist, but they remained in manuscript.

Furno, G i o v a n n i, b. Jan. 1, 1748, Capua, d. June 20, 1837, Naples, trained at the Con-servatorio di Sant' Onofrio in the latter city, was for a long time teacher of composition at the Neapolitan Conservatorii of Sant' Onofrio and della Pietà; also, in 1808, at the Real Collegio di Musica, with which the institutes above named were connected. Among his pupils were Mercadante, Bellini, Costa, Lauro, Rossi, the brothers Ricci, etc.

Fürstenau, (1) K a s p a r, b. Feb. 26, 1772, Mün-ster (Westphalia), d. May 11, 1819, Oldenburg, as chamber virtuoso; he was a distinguished flute-player.

(2) A n t o n B e r n h a r d, son of the former, b. Oct. 20, 1792, Münster, d. Nov. 18, 1852, as chamber musician at Dresden; he followed worthily in his father's footsteps as flautist, and composer for that instrument.

(3) M o r i t z, son of the former, b. July 26, 1824, Dresden, d. there March 25, 1889; in 1842 member of the court band at Dresden (likewise an excellent flautist); in 1852 keeper of the king's private collection of music, and, from 1858, teacher of the flute at the Dresden Conserva-torium. F. possessed great knowledge of history, and wrote " Beiträge zur Geschichte der könig-lich sächsischen musikalischen Kapelle" (1849), " Zur Geschichte der Musik und des Theaters am Hof zu Dresden " (1861–62, two vols.), " Die Fabrikation musikalischer Instrumente im

sächsischen Vogtland " (1870, jointly with Th. Berthold) ; also many treatises in musical papers, in the *Mitteilungen* of the " Königlich sächsischer Altertumsverein," in Mendel's *Musikalisches Konversationslexikon*, etc. F. was also a contri-butor to v. Lilienkron's " Allgem. Deutsche Bio-graphie."

Fürstner, A d o l f, b. Jan. 2, 1835, Berlin, where he founded in 1868 a publishing-house bearing his name, and purchased (1872), in addition, the publishing business of C. F. Meser in Dresden (Wagner's *Rienzi, The Flying Dutch-man*, and *Tannhäuser*).

Fusa (Lat.), a quaver.

Fuss (Ger.), foot. *Füssig* is the correspond-ing adjective, both words being used in connec-tion with organ pipes and stops :. 8-*füssig*, or *achtfüssig*, of 8-feet pitch.

Fux, J o h a n n J o s e p h, b. 1660, Hirtenfeld, near St. Marein, Styria, d. Feb. 14, 1741 ; he became (1698) organist at the ecclesiastical foundation, " Zu den Schotten," Vienna, in 1698 court composer to the emperor, in 1704 capell-meister at St. Stephen's Cathedral, in 1713 vice-capellmeister to the court, and in 1715 principal capellmeister (successor to Ziani), and then, from 1713–15, capellmeister to the Dowager Empress Amalie. F. wrote a large number of sacred works (no less than fifty masses, three requiems, fifty-seven vespers and psalms, etc.) ; and, besides ten oratorios, eighteen operas, twenty-nine partitas, etc., of which only a small portion appeared in print : the festival opera *Elisa*, " Concentus musico-instrumentalis " (à 7), " Missa canonica " (a contrapuntal show-piece), thirty-eight sonatas à 3 (which, up to the present, have not been discovered), and, above all, his theoretical masterpiece, the " Gradus ad Parnassum " (Latin, 1725 ; German, by Mitzler, 1742 ; Italian, by Manfredi, 1761 ; French, by Denis, 1773 ; English, 1791), which still serves as a guide to many a teacher of counterpoint ; yet, already when it appeared, it was unsuitable to the times, for the system was based, not on modern tonality, but on the Church Modes. L. v. Köchel published a de-tailed biography of F., together with a thematic catalogue of his works (1872).

Fz (*Forzato*), *ffz* (*forzatissimo*), identical with *sf, sff* (*see* SFORZATO), indicates a strong accent, but only refers to one single note.

G.

G, letter-name of the seventh note of the musical alphabet scale, and, indeed, one (violin clef) of those which, as a guide to pitch, are drawn in front of the stave as keys or clefs (*Claves signatæ*). The clef-G is the once-accented note placed a fifth above clef-C. (*Cf.* A and CLEF.) The G-clef was originally a real *g* or *G*, and has gradually assumed its present form :

The French, Italians, etc., call the note *G* "*sol*" ; concerning the compound solmisation names *cf.* MUTATION.—As an abbreviation, *g.* means *gauche* (left-hand) ; *m. g., main gauche* (the same).

Gabelclavier. (*See* ADIAPHON.)

Gabelgriffe, a German term for the artificial system of fingering on the early imperfect flutes, by means of which the sounds which were wanting to the chromatic scale of the instrument were obtained. For example : if the sound-hole for *f'♯* was opened and the one for *e'* closed, a sound of somewhat impure quality was obtained which had to represent *f'*.

Gabrieli, name of two most celebrated Italian composers and masters of the organ. (1) A n d r e a, b. about 1510 in the quarter of Venice called Canareggio, hence named G. da Canareio, d. there 1586. He was pupil of Adrian Willaert, the founder of the Venetian school, in 1536 chapel singer at St. Mark's, in 1566 successor of Claudio Merulo as second organist. His most distinguished pupils were : his nephew, John (Giovanni) G., Hans Leo Hassler, and (?) Jan Pieter Swee-linck, the founder of the North German School of organists. Of his numerous works the following have been preserved : " Sacræ cantiones " a 5 (1565 ; 2nd ed. 1584) ; " Cantiones ecclesiasticæ " à 4 (1576 ; 2nd ed. 1589) ; " Cantiones sacræ " à 6–16 (1578) ; masses à 6 (1570) ; two books of madrigals à 5–6 (1572 and 1587–88) ; three books of madrigals à 3–6 (1575, 1582, 1583) ; two books of madrigals à 6 (1574, 1580 ; 2nd ed. 1586) ; " Psalmi poenitentiales 6 vocum " (1583) ; " Canzoni alla francese per l'organo " (1571 and 1605) ; sonatas à 5 (1586). Joh. G. published a great number of his organ pieces in the " Intonazioni d'organo " (1593), " Ricercari per l'organo " (1595, three vols.) ; in like manner, vocal works in the " Canti concerti " à 6–16 (1587, *cf.* GIOVANNI G.). Detached pieces are to be found in P. Phalèse's " Harmonia celeste " (1593), " Symphonia angelica " (1594), and " Musica divina " (1595), and a sonnet in Zuccarini's " Corona di dodeci sonetti " (1586). His festival songs for double chorus for the reception of Henri III. of France (1574) are in Gardane's " Gemme musicali " (1587).

(2) G i o v a n n i, b. 1557, Venice, pupil and nephew of the above ; in 1585, successor of Claudio Merulo as principal organist of St. Mark's, d. Aug. 12, 1612 (on this day his post was newly occupied by Savii), or Aug. 12, 1613 (according to the memorial stone on his grave). His most celebrated pupil was Heinrich Schütz. The following of his works have been preserved in original editions : " Madrigali a 6 voci o istromenti " (1585) ; " Madrigali e ricercari a 4 voci " (1587) ; " Ecclesiasticæ cantiones 4–6 vocum " (1589) ; " Sacræ symphoniæ " (à 6–16, for voices or instruments, 1597 [2nd ed. ?]) ; " Symphoniæ sacræ, lib. II. 6–19 voc." (1615) ; " Canzoni e sonate a 3–22 voc. (1615). He included ten pieces of his own composition in the edition of the " Canti concerti (di Andrea e di Giovanni G., etc)" ; the " Intonazioni " and " Ricercari per l'organo " (1593–95), named undei Andrea G., contain likewise many pieces by Giovanni G. Single pieces are to be found in nearly all collections of that period up to 1620, first in the " Secondo libro de' madrigali a 5 voci, etc." (1575). After his death a friend of Gabrieli's published some of his motets, together with others by Hassler (à 6–19, 1615). Giovanni G. wrote, with special predilection and noble effect, choruses for two, and for three choirs, and indeed for divided choirs (*Cori spezzati*) ; and to this he was probably prompted, as Willaert had already been, by the fact that St. Mark's had two great organs facing each other, before each of which could be placed a body of singers. (*Cf.* K. v. Winterfeld, " Johannes G. und sein Zeitalter," 1834, 2 vols., and a vol. of music supplements.)

(3) D o m e n i c o (Menghino del Violoncello), b. about 1640, Bologna, d. there about 1690 ; he was a first-rate 'cello-player, and wrote a series of operas (nine) for Bologna and Venice (1683–88). After his death appeared : " Cantate a voce sola " (1691) ; " Vexillum pacis " (motets for alto solo with instrumental accompaniment, 1695), and " Balletti, gighe, correnti e sarabande a due violini e violoncello con basso continuo " (2nd ed. 1703).

(4) ·C a t t e r i n a (Gabrielli), famous coloratura singer, b. Nov. 12, 1730, Rome, d. there April, 1796, daughter of Prince G.'s cook ; when she became famous, out of gratitude, she assumed the Prince's name. A pupil of Padre Garcia (*Lo Spagnoletto*) and of Porpora, she made her *début* in 1747 at Lucca in Galuppi's *Sofonisbe*, shone on various Italian stages, sang 1751–65 at Vienna, then at Parma, from 1768 at Petersburg, 1777 at Venice, 1780 at Milan ; from 1781 she lived in retirement at Rome.

(5) Francesca (Gabrielli), who, in order to be distinguished from Catterina G., was called "La Ferrarese" or "La Gabriellina," b. 1755, Ferrara, d. 1795, Venice, pupil of Sacchini at Venice; she appeared at Florence, Naples, and London (1786 with Mara) as *prima donna buffa*.

(6) Nicolò, Conte (Gabrielli), b. Feb. 21, 1814, Naples, d. there June 14, 1891, pupil of Zingarelli and Donizetti, was a prolific, but unimportant composer of operas and ballets (twenty-two operas and sixty ballets); from 1854 he lived in Paris. His works were produced partly at Naples, partly at Paris, Lyons, Vienna, etc., but only with ephemeral success.

Gabrielli. (*See* GABRIELI, 4-6.)

Gabrielsk, Johann Wilhelm, b. May 27, 1791, Berlin, d. there Sept. 18, 1846, son of an artillery under-officer; he became a distinguished flautist, received (1814) an appointment at the theatre at Stettin, and became (1816) royal chamber-musician at Berlin. He made great concert-tours as a flute virtuoso. He wrote solo and ensemble pieces for flute.—His brother, Julius, b. Dec. 4, 1806, Berlin, d. there May 16, 1878, was also an esteemed flautist, and his son Adolf is at present principal flautist in the royal band.

Gade, Niels Wilhelm, b. Feb. 22 (not Oct.), 1817, Copenhagen, d. there Dec. 21, 1890, the most important of Danish composers, son of an instrument-maker. He grew up, half self-taught, without any real methodical instruction in the theory of music; but on the violin (under Wexschall) he attained to great proficiency, and also received regular instruction on the guitar and pianoforte. Later on, in Weyse and Berggreen, he met with teachers who understood how to develop his talent. As a member of the court band at Copenhagen he listened carefully to the scores of the classics, and by tentative methods became a master of instrumentation. At first he drew the attention of the world to himself by his overture, *Nachklänge aus Ossian* (Op. 1), which gained the first prize at the competition appointed by the Musical Union of Copenhagen in 1841 (Schneider and Spohr were the judges). A royal stipend now enabled him to climb the ladder of fame, encouraged by distinguished masters, and by a thoroughly musical atmosphere. In 1843 G. went to Leipzig, where Mendelssohn, by a previous performance of the above-named overture, and of the first symphony (c minor), had secured for him a good reception. Mendelssohn and Schumann became his friends. He took to himself much of the individuality of both, without on that account sacrificing his own. After a short stay in Italy he returned to Leipzig in 1844, and was entrusted by Mendelssohn, during his absence, with the direction of the Gewandhaus concerts; he remained also through the winter of 1845-46 with Mendelssohn

as sub-conductor, and after the death of the latter (Nov. 4, 1847) became capellmeister, but only for a short time. Already in the spring of 1848, at the outbreak of the Schleswig-Holstein war, he hastened back to his native city in order to undertake the direction of the concerts of the Copenhagen Musical Union, and to accept a post as organist. The concerts of the Musical Union prospered so greatly under his direction that, like those of the Paris Conservatoire, they have now to be given in two series—*i.e.* every week two concerts with the same programme. In 1861, after the death of Gläser, he became for a time royal Danish court capellmeister. G. was honoured with the title of professor; and, on the occasion of the four hundredth anniversary of the Copenhagen University, was made *Dr. Phil. hon. causâ*, and from that time up to the day of his death he was active as composer, teacher, and conductor. G. was chief representative of the romantic school amongst Scandinavian composers; but his Scandinavianism is nothing more than an interesting colouring, a special poetical spirit; the harmonic, melodic, and rhythmical peculiarities of the folk-music of the North are not strongly featured in him. G.'s works are: eight symphonies—I., c minor, Op. 5; II., E, Op. 10; III., A minor, Op. 15; IV., B♭, Op. 20; V., D minor, Op. 25 (with pianoforte); VI., G minor, Op. 32; VII., F, Op. 45; VIII., B minor, Op. 47; five overtures (*Nachklänge aus Ossian*, Op. 1, *Im Hochland*, Op. 7; one in c, Op. 14; *Hamlet*, Op. 37; *Michelangelo*, Op. 39) ; Novelettes for orchestra, Op. 53; also a quintet, a sextet, and an octet for strings, two violin concertos, a pf. trio (in F), trio novelettes, three violin sonatas (A, D minor, and B); many pf. solo works (a sonata, "Aquarellen," "Volkstänze," "Nordische Tonbilder," etc.); nine cantatas (*Comala*, Op. 12; *Frühlingsphantasie*, Op. 23; *Erlkönigs Tochter*, Op. 30; *Die heilige Nacht*, Op. 40; *Frühlingsbotschaft*, Op. 35; *Die Kreuzfahrer*, Op. 50; *Calanus, Zion, Psyche*); songs (German, Scandinavian, etc.); part-songs with orchestra ("Beim Sonnenuntergang"), vocal works for male chorus and for mixed chorus, sacred songs (130th Psalm, etc.). He conducted his cantatas *Zion* and *Crusaders* at the Birmingham Festival of 1876.

Gadsby, Henry, b. Dec. 15, 1842, London, from 1849-58 chorister at St. Paul's, pupil of Bayley; he developed himself, however, for the most part, without the help of a teacher. G. is one of the most important of modern English composers, and has produced the 130*th Psalm*, "Festival Service" (à 8), overture *Andromeda*, cantatas (*Alice Brand, The Lord of the Isles, Columbus, The Cyclops*—the last two for male chorus), a quartet for strings, music to *Alcestis*, pieces for flute and pf. He has also a number of more important works in manuscript, among which there are: three symphonies (portions of which have been performed at the Crystal Palace), several overtures, songs, anthems, services, etc.

Gafori, Franchino (Franchinus Gafurius), often called merely "Franchinus," distinguished theorist, b. Jan. 14, 1451, Lodi, d. July 24, 1522, Milan. He was intended for the church, and studied both theology and music. He lived first in Mantua and Verona, and in the latter city joined the fugitive Doge Prospero Adorno, followed him back to Genoa, and fled with him to Naples. In this city he met distinguished musicians—Johannes Tinctoris, Garnier, and Bernard Hycaert—and held public discussions on music with Philipp von Caserta (Filippo Bononio). After a residence of some years, plague and war drove him back to Lodi. He received first the post of choir-master at Monticello, and finally, in 1484, that of cantor and master of the boys at Milan Cathedral, and likewise that of principal singer in the chapel of Duke Ludovico Sforza at Monticello. His writings, to which the highest value was attached during his lifetime and afterwards, are of great importance for the history of theory: "Theoricum opus musicæ disciplinæ" (1480, 2nd ed. 1492 as "Theorica Musicæ"; it treats of ancient instruction in music according to Boëtius, and of solmisation); "Practica musicæ sive musicæ actiones in IV. libris" (1496, his principal work, with examples in mensural notation in block-print; 2–4 ed. 1497, 1502, and 1512); "Angelicum ac divinum opus musicæ, etc." (1508, Italian; a short sketch of musical theory); "De harmonia musicorum instrumentorum opus" (1518, with a biography of Gafori); "Apologia Franchini Gafurii adversus Joannem Spatarium et complices musicos Bononienses" (1520).

Gagliano, Marco Zanobi da, one of the oldest opera-composers, and a noteworthy composer for the church, a native of Florence; in 1602 maestro at the Lorenzo Church in that city, d. Feb. 24, 1642. In 1607 he wrote an opera, *Dafne*, for the wedding festivities of a prince at Mantua; it was published in 1608 by Marescotti at Florence, and was republished, with the *continuo* written out, by R. Eitner ("Publikationen," 10th vol.). A second one, of 1624, is entitled *La Regina Sant' Orsolo;* his other publications were: masses à 5 (1579), "Responsori della settimana santa a 4 voci" (1580), six books of madrigals à 5 (up to 1617), and "Musiche a 1, 2, e 3 voci" (1615, with continuo).

Gährich, Wenzel, b. Sept. 16, 1794, Zerchowitz (Bohemia), d. Sept. 15, 1864, Berlin; he at first studied law at Leipzig, but adopted music as a vocation, became in 1825 member of the royal band at Berlin (violinist), and after having obtained success with his music to ballets of Taglioni and others (*Don Quichotte*, *Aladdin*, *Der Seeräuber*, etc.), became balletmaster at the Opera (1845–60). Besides ballets

and two operas not produced, he composed symphonies and instrumental and vocal works of various kinds, of which only a few appeared in print.

Gail, Edmée Sophie, *née* Garre, b. Aug. 28, 1775, Paris, d. July 24, 1819, a highly talented lady composer, and singer of great taste; she married the Greek professor, Jean Baptiste G., but lived only a short time with him. She composed songs, romances, nocturnes (for voice), also five small operas (*Angéla* [with Boieldieu], *La Sérénade*).

Gaîment (Fr., also *gaiement*), in a lively manner.

Galandia. (*See* GARLANDIA.)

Galant Style, the free style in clavier music of the last century, which, in opposition to the strict, does not confine itself to a fixed number of real parts, but contains now more, now less; it is for the most part homophonic, in fact, equivalent to our modern style. Ph. E. Bach's clavier sonatas were considered as belonging to the galant style.

Galeazzi, Francesco, b. 1758 (or 1738), Turin, for many years leader of the concerts at the Teatro de la Valle at Rome, d. there 1819. He published: "Elementi teorico-pratici di musica con un saggio sopra l'arte di suonare il violino" (1791 and 1796, two parts; the 1st vol. in a 2nd ed. 1817), one of the oldest violin Methods.

Galilei, Vincenzo, b. about 1533, Florence d. there about 1600, father of the celebrated Galileo G. He was an excellent performer on the lute and violin, skilled in the mathematical theory of the musical determination of intervals of the Greeks, and one of the most distinguished members of the esthetic circle in the house of Count Bardi, from which sprang the musical drama. His enthusiasm for antiquity led him to attack the masters and teachers of elaborate counterpoint (Zarlino), which appeared to him something unnatural, even ridiculous. His highly interesting writings on the history of music are: "Discorso della musica antica e della moderna" (1581; 2nd ed. 1602, increased by a polemical pamphlet against Zarlino, which first appeared in 1589: "Discorso intorno alle opere di messer Gioseffo Zarlino di Chioggia"), "Il Fronimo, dialogo sopra l'arte del bene intavolare e rettamente suonare la musica" (1583).

Galin, Pierre, b. 1786, Samatan (Gers), d. Aug. 31, 1821, as teacher of mathematics at the Bordeaux Lyceum; he commenced in 1817 a course for learning music on a simplified method (*see* MELOPLAST), which he expounded in a treatise, "Exposition d'une nouvelle méthode pour l'enseignement de la musique" (1818). The Meloplast was much talked about, found zealous champions (Chevé, Paris, Geslin, Lemoine), and even ten years after the death of Galin, his pupil Lemoine prepared a 3rd ed. of Galin's

Instruction book (2nd and 3rd ed., with title : "Méthode du Méloplaste," 1824 and 1831).

Galitzin, N i k o l a u s B o r i s s o w i t c h, Prince, d. 1866, Kurski (Russia), is known in the musical world inasmuch as Beethoven dedicated to him his overture, Op. 124, and three of his last quartets for strings, and, up to his death, corresponded with him. He was an ardent friend of music and an able 'cellist, and his wife a capital pianist.—His son G e o r g e, Prince G., b. 1823, Petersburg, d. there Sept., 1872. He was for a time musician by profession, and made concert tours with a large band of his own, in England, France, and America, as a propagandist of Russian music (especially of Glinka's and of his own); he composed masses, orchestral works, instrumental solos, songs, etc. In Moscow he kept up a choir of seventy boys. G. was Imperial chamberlain.

Gallay, J a c q u e s F r a n ç o i s, b. Dec. 8, 1795, Perpignan, d. Oct. 1864, celebrated horn-player ; he became, at the age of twenty-five, pupil of Dauprat at the Paris Conservatoire ; in 1825 member of the royal chapel, and also of the orchestra of the Opéra Italien and of the Odéon Théâtre ; in 1832 chamber musician to Louis Philippe ; and in 1842 professor of his instrument at the Conservatoire. G. composed a series of solos and concerted works for horn (concertos, nocturnes, études, duets, trios, quartets, etc., for horns), and published a " Méthode complète de cor."

Gallenberg, W e n z e l R o b e r t, G r a f v o n, b. Dec. 28, 1783, Vienna, d. March 13, 1839, Rome ; he studied under Albrechtsberger, married in 1803 the Countess Julia Guicciardi, with whom Beethoven was in love, and to whom the " Moonlight " sonata is dedicated. In 1805, at Naples, he wrote festival music in honour of Joseph Bonaparte, and was in partnership (1821-23) with Barbaja when the latter was director of the court theatre, Vienna. He undertook in 1829, on his own account, the Kärntnerthor Theatre, but the enterprise soon brought him to financial ruin, and he was again associated with Barbaja at Naples as composer and director. He wrote about fifty ballets, also some easy pf. music. Beethoven wrote a set of variations on a theme of G.'s.

Galletius, Franciscus (François Gallet), contrapuntist of the second half of the 16th century, b. Mons (Hainault), lived at Douai. He wrote: " Sacræ cantiones à 5, 6 et plurium vocum " (1586), and " Hymni communes Sanctorum," together with some faux-bourdons (1596).

Galliard (Fr. *Gaillarde;* Ital. *Gagliarda*) is nothing more than a Paduana (Pavan) ; as a rule, a quick " after-song " (Nachtanz and Springtanz) in triple time (*Proportio*) ; in Italy it is generally called Saltarello.

Galliard, J o h a n n E r n s t, b. 1687, Celle, son of a French *perruquier,* pupil of Agostino Steffani

at Hanover, came in 1706 to London as chamber musician (oboist) to Prince George of Denmark, was successor of Giov. Batt. Draghi as chapelmaster to the Queen-Dowager Catherine of England, and died at the beginning of 1749. G. composed operas, pantomimes, incidental music to plays, cantatas, flute and 'cello solos Morning Hymn of Adam and Eve, from Milton's " Paradise Lost," a Te Deum, Jubilate, anthems, etc. He translated Tosi's " Opinioni de' cantori, antichi e moderni," into English (" Observations on the Florid Song," 1742) and, according to Hawkins, is the author of the anonymous pamphlet, " A Comparison between the French and Italian Music and Operas " (1709, from the French of Abbé Raguenet), and " A Critical Discourse upon Operas in England."

Galliculus, J o h a n n e s, contrapuntist and theorist at Leipzig about 1520-50, published a small compendium, " Isagoge de compositione cantus " (1520 ; 2nd and 3rd ed., under title " Libellus de compositione cantus," 1538 and 1546 ; the 4th edition, under the title of the first, 1548, etc., with musical examples in wood-type). His motets, psalms, etc., are to be found in Graphäus' " Novum et insigne opus musicum " (1537), in Petrejus' " Psalmi selecti " (one vol., 1538), also in Rhaw's " Harmoniæ selectæ, etc." (1538), and " Vesperarum precum officia, etc." (1540).

Galli-Marié, C é l e s t i n e (Marié de L'Isle ; by marriage, Galli), b. Nov. 1840, Paris, daughter of an opera singer. In 1859 she made her *début* at Strassburg, and was engaged from 1862 at the Opéra Comique, Paris, and became especially famous in the *rôles* of Mignon and Carmen. In 1886 she appeared, with much success, in London.

Gallus, (1) J a c o b u s (really Jakob H ä n d l or H a n d l, H ä h n e l, etc.), b. about 1550, in Carniola, d. July 18, 1591, Prague, one of the most distinguished German contemporaries of Palestrina and Orlando Lasso, was first capellmeister to the Bishop of Olmütz, afterwards Imperial capellmeister at Prague. The Emperor Rudolf II. granted him for ten years the privilege of publication of his works. The following are known : " Missæ selectiores " (1580, à 5-8, four books), " Musici operis harmoniarum, 4, 5, 6, 8, et plurium vocum " (1st part 1586 ; 2nd, 3rd, 1587 ; 4th, 1590), " Moralia 5, 6 et 8 vocibus concinnata " (1586) ; " Epicedion harmonicum . . . Caspari Abb. Zabrdovicensis " (1589), " Harmoniæ variæ 4 vocum (1591), " Harmoniarum moralium (4 voc.) " (1589-90, three parts), " Sacræ cantiones de præcipuis festis 4-8 et plurium vocum " (1597), " Motettæ quæ præstant omnes " (1610). Handel borrowed G.'s well-known motet, " Ecce quomodo moritur justus," for his Funeral Anthem. Bodenschatz's " Florilegium Portense " contains nineteen of his pieces ; single numbers are to be found in Proske's " Musica divina," also in the collections of Schöberlein, Zahn, Becker, Rochlitz, etc.

(2) Johannes (in France usually called Jean le Cocq, Maître Jean, Mestre Jhan, etc.), Dutch contrapuntist, maestro di capella to the Duke Ercole of Ferrara, d. before 1543. Many pieces of his have been preserved in collections and in a volume of motets printed by Scotto (1543). G. was for a long time mistaken for Gero (q.v.).

(3) (*See* MEDERITSCH.)

Galop (*Galoppade*), modern round dance of quick, springing movement in ⅔ time, with the step—

r = right, *l* left foot.

Galoubet, a small kind of flute formerly used in France.

Galuppi, Baldassare, with the surname Buranello, from the island Burano, near Venice, on which he was born, Oct. 6, 1706, d. Jan. 3, 1784, Venice. Son of a musical barber, he studied under Lotti in Venice, and became one of the most popular composers in the department of opera buffa. Between 1722-72 seventy-four of his operas were produced at Venice (some at Vienna, Petersburg, and London). From 1762-64 G. was maestro di capella at St. Mark's, and director of the Conservatorio degl' Incurabili. He accepted, in 1765, a call to Petersburg as imperial maître de chapelle, where he became celebrated, and returned to Venice in 1768. Besides his operas, he composed numerous sacred works, also a number of oratorios; a pf. sonata is included in Haffner's "Raccolta, etc.," and in Pauer's "Alte Klaviermusik" (Vol. I.).

Gamba. *See* VIOLA. (*Viola da gamba*.)

Gamba stops in the organ are open lip pipes of narrow measure and low mouth, with side- and cross-beards, and, accompanied by a pretty strong bellows-murmur, they have a string tone, similar, in fact, to that of stringed instruments; they speak slowly, and easily get sharp. The pipes, on account of the narrow measure, are longer than those of diapason work. To the G. belong all stops which bear the name of stringed instruments : violino, viola, violoncello, violone, contrabasso, quintviola (a quint stop of gamba measure), gambetta, spitzgamba (narrowed at the top), etc. ; the G. have a tone very like the Geigen-Principal (Violin-Diapason, of less narrow measure).

Gamba work. (*See* BOGENFLÜGEL.)

Gambale, Emanuele, music-teacher at Milan, became known through his ideas respecting a reform of our notation in the sense of a fundamental scale of twelve semitones. (*Cf.* CHROMA.) He expounded his system in "La riforma musicale, etc." (1840, translated into

German by Häser, 1843). He made detailed attempts to show its practical use in "La prima parte della riforma musicale," etc. (1846, with études written out in his notation). G. translated Fétis's great work on harmony into Italian.

Gambini, Carlo Andrea, b. Oct. 22, 1819, Genoa, d. there Feb. 14, 1865 ; he composed operas, masses, cantatas, and a dramatic symphony, "Christoforo Colombo," etc.

Gamma (Γ), the Greek letter answering to our G. As the name of the note answering to our great G. [image] it first occurs in Odo of Clugny (d. 942), and therefore was not invented by Guido. As at that time the letters were not arranged, as now, from C to B, but from A to G (*cf.* LETTER-NOTATION), a distinguishing sign was wanted for the lowest note (our great G) of the system of that day ; and hence the Greek letter was used. As, until the 14th century, this note remained the limit downwards, it is easy to understand that the tone steps (scale), the series of tones from the lowest to the highest (*e''*) were called after it ; and in French, *gamme* at the present day means "scale." The Γ was also a clef sign (*Claves signatæ*), and appears in the old notation in company with the F-clef [image]. The solmisation name of the Γ is *Gamma ut*. (*See* MUTATION.) For the reason why great G was the lowest note of the system of church modes, see CHURCH MODES.

Gamucci, Baldassare, b. Dec. 14, 1822, Florence, established there in 1849 a musical union, "Del Carmine," which was later amalgamated with the Royal Musical Institute, of which G. became director. G. composed masses, a requiem, cantatas, psalms, motets, etc., and wrote, "Intorno alla vita ed alle opere di Luigi Cherubini" (1869) ; an elementary Method, ("Rudimenti di lettura musicale"), which passed through many editions ; and various treatises for the reports of the Royal Musical Institute (among others, on the reason why polyphony was unknown to the Greeks).

Ganassi, Silvestro (named del Fontego, after his birthplace near Venice), was the author of two works as important as they are rare—viz., a Method of playing the flûte-a-bec with seven sound-holes, "La Fontegara, la quale insegna di suonare il flauto, etc." (1535, contains instructions concerning ornaments) ; and a Method of playing the viola and the contrabass viola (1542–43), in two parts. Both works were printed by G. himself, and are only known from the one copy in the Liceo Filarmonico at Bologna.

Gandini, Alessandro Cavaliere, b. 1807, Modena, d. there Dec. 17, 1871, pupil and successor of his father (Antonio G., b. Aug. 20,

1786, d. Sept. 10, 1842), as maestro di capella at the Modena court. G. was the author of a history of the theatres at Modena from 1539–1871, published after his death, and augmented by Valdrighi and Ferrari-Moreni ("Cronistoria dei teatri di Modena, etc.," 1873); he also, like his father, wrote several operas for Modena.

Gänsbacher, Johann, b. May 8, 1778, Sterzing (Tyrol), d. July 13, 1844, Vienna, pupil of the Abbé Vogler and Albrechtsberger at Vienna. He lived first as a music-teacher there, and afterwards at Prague, Dresden, Leipzig, returned in 1809 to the Abbé Vogler, who now lived in Darmstadt, and became the fellow-pupil and friend of C. M. v. Weber and Meyerbeer. After he had followed Weber to Mannheim and Heidelberg, he lived for a time at Vienna and Prague, and in 1813 took part in the war (as he had already done in 1796) ; at last, in 1823, he found a settled and satisfactory post as capellmeister at the St. Stephen's Cathedral (successor to Preindl). G. was a prolific composer, but of little originality; he wrote specially sacred works (seventeen masses, four requiems, etc.), of which, however, only a small part appeared in print; and, besides, serenades, marches, a symphony, pf. works, chamber music, songs, a vaudeville, music to Kotzebue's *Kreuzfahrer,* etc.

Ganz, name of three brothers who were distinguished musicians : (1) A d o l f, b. Oct. 14, 1796, Mayence, d. Jan. 11, 1870, London, was capellmeister to the Grand Duke of Hesse Darmstadt. His son E d w a r d, b. Mayence, pianist (pupil of Thalberg), d. 1869. Another son, W i l h e l m, b. 1830, is well known in London as teacher, conductor, and accompanist. He conducted the "Ganz" orchestral concerts from 1879 to 1882.

(2) M o r i t z, b. Sept. 13, 1806, Mayence, d. Jan. 22, 1868, Berlin, leader of the royal band, was a 'cellist of considerable importance.

(3) L e o p o l d, b. Nov. 28, 1810, Mayence, d. June 15, 1869, Berlin, leader of the royal band, was a distinguished violinist.

Ganzinstrumente (Ger., "whole instruments"). This term is applied in Germany to those brass wind-instruments in which the lowest sound proper to the tube speaks, *i.e.* (great) *C ;* this is, however, only possible with instruments of wide measure ; narrow ones give out at once the octave above. Formerly only instruments of narrow measure were constructed (*Halbinstrumente,* "half-instruments"), those whose lowest tone was an octave higher than that of an open organ pipe of equal length, *i.e.* whose lowest natural note did not speak (trumpets, horns, trombones). When about the middle of this century the need was felt of strengthening the double-bass by brass instruments, and also the double-bass was replaced in wind bands, it led to the construction of G. (*cf.* WIEPRECHT, SAX, CERVENY) ; in these the tube from mouth-

piece to bell was much wider than that of half-instruments (*Halbinstrumente*). The diameter ratio of the latter from 1 : 4 to 1 : 8 increases in G. (whole instruments) to 1 : 20 ; the terms G. and *Halbinstrumente* were introduced by Schafhäutl (Report on the musical instruments of the Munich Industrial Exhibition of 1854)

Garat, Pierre Jean, b. April 26, 1762, Ustaritz (Lower Pyrenees), d. March 1, 1823, Paris, a highly celebrated French concert singer and teacher of singing, pupil of Franz Beck at Bordeaux. He was intended for the career of an advocate, and attended the Paris University to study jurisprudence, but fell into serious disagreement with his father, as he attended more to the training of his voice than to perfecting himself in knowledge of the law. The difficulties of this situation were, however, removed by his obtaining the post of private secretary to the Count of Artois; also Marie Antoinette often played or sang with him, and paid his debts several times. Later on his father became reconciled with him. When the Revolution compelled him to seek a living as concert-singer, he went with Rode to Hamburg, where they obtained great triumphs. In 1794, however, they returned to Paris, and G. first appeared, in 1795, at the Feydeau Concerts, with such success that in the same year he was appointed professor of singing at the newly established Conservatoire. A series of distinguished pupils (Nourrit, Levasseur, Ponchard, etc.) testify to his remarkable talent as teacher. Up to his fiftieth year he was universally admired for his noble voice (tenor-baritone of enormous compass), his rare virtuosity in *coloratura* singing, and his stupendous memory. G. was gifted by nature, although he lacked thorough musical elementary training ; yet, as singer and teacher, his equal was scarcely to be found.

Garaudé, Alexis de, b. March 21, 1779, Nancy, d. March 23, 1852, Paris ; he was a pupil of Cambini, Reicha, Crescentini, and Garat at Paris, and in 1808 imperial chapel singer. He remained in the royal chapel after the restoration of the Bourbons, was named professor of singing at the Conservatoire in 1816, and in 1841 received a pension. He wrote : "Méthode du chant " (1809) ; "Solfège, ou méthode de musique ; " "Méthode complète de piano ; " "L'harmonie rendue facile" (1835), and "L'Espagne en 1851 " (description of journeys). He published besides, solfeggi, songs, duets, arias, etc., pf. sonatas and variations, ensemble works for violin, flute, clarinet, 'cello, three quintets for strings, etc.

Garbo (Ital.), *con g.,* with elegance (used in Hummel).

Garbrecht, Fr. F. W., founded in 1862 an important music engraving and printing establishment at Leipzig, which was bought in 1880 by Oskar Brandstätter, who considerably enlarged it. G. died in 1874.

Garcia, (1) D o n Francisco Saverio, Padre G., b. 1731, Nalda (Spain), d. Feb. 26, 1809, Saragossa, of the plague; he lived in Rome as a teacher of singing (*cf.* GABRIELLI) with the surname "lo Spagnoletto," and in 1756 became maestro di cappella of Saragossa Cathedral. G. influenced church music in Spain, for, in place of the fugal style, which had been in vogue up to his time, he introduced a plainer mode of composition.

(2) Manuel del Popolo Vicente, b. Jan. 22, 1775, Seville, d. June 2, 1832, Paris, a singer (tenor) of great name, and a teacher of singing, as well as a prolific composer of operas; he received his first training from Antonio Ripa and Juan Almarcha in Seville, and was already famous at the age of seventeen, so that he was drawn to Cadiz to make his *début* there in opera both as singer and composer. After further successful appearances at Madrid and Malaga, he went in 1808 to Paris, and by his success at the Théâtre Italien laid the foundation of his worldwide fame. After he had distinguished himself on various stages in Italy (1811–16), and essentially improved his style of singing (Murat appointed him chamber-singer at Naples in 1812), he returned to Paris, where he was again received with extraordinary enthusiasm at the Théâtre Italien; but he quarrelled with Catalani, the proprietress of this theatre, and went to London. The following years (1819–24) constitute his most brilliant period, when, after the failure of Catalani, he sang again at the Théâtre Italien; during this time he developed great and remarkable activity as a teacher of singing. In 1824 he returned to London as first tenor at the Royal Opera, was engaged in 1825 by the *impresario* Price, also his two daughters, his son, the younger Crivelli, Angrisani, Rosich, and Berbieri for New York, where they were enthusiastically received. After spending eighteen months with his family in Mexico (1827–28), he returned to Europe, but on his way to Vera Cruz was robbed of all his possessions. On his return to Paris he devoted himself entirely to teaching and to composition. G. wrote no less than seventeen Spanish, eighteen Italian, and eight French operas, also many ballets, of which, however, none have survived. His most famous pupils were his two daughters, Marie (Malibran) and Pauline (Viardot), also his son Manuel (*see* next name).

(3) Manuel, b. March 17, 1805, Madrid, son of the former, accompanied his father to America, but in 1829 retired from the stage (his bass voice was of inferior quality), devoted himself exclusively to teaching singing, and was highly esteemed by his pupils in Paris. He is the inventor of the laryngoscope, and for this invention was named *Dr. Med. hon. c.* by the Königsberg University. Among his pupils were Jenny Lind

and Jul. Stockhausen. In 1840 he sent to the French Académie a "Mémoire sur la voix humaine," one which contained no discoveries, but which was a clever *résumé* of investigations concerning the functions of the vocal organs; for this he was recognised by the Académie, and later on (1847) was appointed professor of singing at the Conservatoire. In connection with this post he drew up his "Traité complet du chant" (1847, German by Wirth). In 1850 he went to London, where he became teacher of singing at the Royal Academy of Music. His pupil and wife, Eugénie (*née* Mayer), b. 1818, Paris, for many years on Italian stages, in 1840 at the Opéra Comique, Paris, 1842 at London, lived (separated from her husband) as teacher of singing at Paris, where she died Aug. 12, 1880.

(4) Mariano, b. July 26, 1809, Aviz (Navarra), a noted Spanish composer of sacred music.

Garcin, Jules Auguste, b. July 11, 1830, Bourges, sprung from a family of artists, pupil of the Paris Conservatoire (Clavel and Alard); in 1856 member, 1871 first solo violin and third conductor in the orchestra of the Grand Opéra; in 1881 second conductor of the Concerts du Conservatoire (successor of Altés), and in 1885 first conductor (successor of Deldevez). G. is also a composer (pupil of Bazin, Adam, and Thomas), especially for the violin (a concerto).

Gardano, Antonio (or Gardane, as he signed himself up to 1557), one of the most distinguished of old Italian music printers, who reprinted many works which had appeared elsewhere, and likewise brought out excellent novelties; and, among other things, also pieces of his own composition in the "Motetti del frutto" (1539) and the "Canzoni francese" (1564). A print bearing the date 1537 is probably his first; he died, as it appears, in 1571, for in this year his two sons, Angelo and Alessandro, took his place; they issued publications up to 1575, but then separated. About 1584 Alexander dates from Rome, whilst Angelo printed up to his death (1610) in Venice, and brought his publishing house into high repute. His heirs traded under his name up to 1650.

Garlandia, (1) Johannes de, French theorist of *Cantus mensurabilis* (c. 1210–32), whose treatise has been printed in two versions by Coussemaker.("Script." I.). There is a dictionary of his which contains valuable explanations concerning ancient instruments. (*See* the "Documents inédits de l'histoire de France," p. 611.)

(2) A writer of the 13th–14th century (Galandia), of whom a treatise on *Cantus planus* has been printed in the above-named work.

Garnier, François Joseph, celebrated oboist, b. 1759, Lauris (Vaucluse), d. there 1825, a pupil of Sallantin; in 1778 second, in 1786 first oboist at the Grand Opéra, Paris. He published concertos for oboe, concertantes for two oboes, for flute, oboe and bassoon, duets for oboe and violin, also an excellent Method for oboe (recently republished in German by P. Wieprecht).

Garrett, George Mursell, b. June, 1834, Winchester, pupil of Elvey and Wesley; from 1854–56 organist of Madras Cathedral, in 1857 organist of St. John's College, Cambridge; he took his degrees of Mus.Bac. and Mus.Doc. in 1857 and 1867; in 1875 he became organist at the University (successor of Hopkins), and in 1878 received the degree of M.A. *propter merita.* He was member of the Examination Commission, etc. G. was a gifted composer (cantata, *The Shunammite* [1882], besides many sacred works and organ pieces). He died April 8, 1897.

Gärtner, Joseph, Bohemian organ-builder, b. 1796, Tachau, d. May 30, 1863, Prague, where are to be found many organs built by him and his forefathers. He published: "Kurze Belehrung über die innere Einrichtung der Orgeln, etc." (1832).

Gaspar van Werbecke, b. about 1440, Oudenarde (Flanders), master of singing at the court of Sforza, Milan, up to 1490, when he returned to his native town. He was a distinguished contrapuntist whose works have been preserved in various publications of Petrucci; five masses, "Misse Gaspar" à 4 (1509), portions of masses in "Fragmenta missarum" (1509), a mass in "Missæ diversorum" (1508), motets in the fourth book of motets (1505), in the "Motetti trenta tre" (1502), in the second book of motets à 5 (1505), Lamentations in the second book of Lamentations (1506). The Papal library contains masses by G. in manuscript.

Gaspari, Gaetano, b. March 14, 1807, Bologna, d. there March 31, 1881; he became in 1820 a pupil at the Liceo Musicale, and specially of Benedetto Donelli, under whose direction he made such progress that in 1827 he received the first prize for composition, and in 1828 was named honorary master of the Academy. After being eight years maestro di cappella at Cento, he went in 1836 in the same capacity to Imola Cathedral: but, at the wish of his master Donelli, who was growing old, he gave up this post in order to help him in his vocation as teacher. His hopes were frustrated by Donelli's death (1839), and he was compelled to accept a meagre appointment as professor of singing at the Lyceum (1840). Only gradually did he gain ground against the jealous academicians, and procure for himself a settled income. In 1855 he became Conservator of the Lyceum library (one of the richest musical libraries), and in 1857 maestro di cappella at the church of San Petronio. G., in the course of time, became one of the most important musical authorities of Italy. In 1866 he was elected member of the royal deputation for inquiry into the history of Romagna, and it fell to his lot to draw up the report concerning the musicians of Bologna. From that time he gave up his appointment as maestro di cappella, and

composed no more (he wrote a number of sacred compositions dignified in style), but devoted all his leisure moments to historical and bibliographical studies, the result of which was recorded in the "Catalogo della biblioteca de Liceo Musicale di Bologna," the first volume of which was published in 1890 by his successor, Federico Parisini (material of great value). The fruits of G.'s investigations with regard to the musicians of Bologna from the 14th to 17th century were published in the annual reports of the above-named deputation from 1867–79 (also separately).

Gasparini (1), Francesco (Guasparini), b. March 5, 1668, Camajore, near Lucca, d. March, 1727, Rome, pupil of Corelli and Pasquini at Rome, music teacher at the Ospedale della Pietà at Venice, in 1735 maestro di cappella at the Lateran, in which post, however, on account of his advanced age, he was assisted by a deputy. G. was, in his time, highly esteemed as a composer for the stage and the church; he wrote from 1702–30 for Venice, Rome, and Vienna, about forty operas, an oratorio (*Moses*), many masses, psalms, motets, cantatas, as well as a thorough-bass Method—"L'armonico pratico al cembalo" (1683, 7th ed. 1802)—which was in use in Italy up to the middle of the present century. Benedetto Marcello was one of his pupils.

(2) Michel Angelo, b. Lucca, pupil of Lotti, established a school for singing in Venice, from which sprang, amongst others, Faustina Hasse-Bordoni. He was himself a distinguished singer (altist), and composed many operas for Venice. He died about 1732.

(3) Quirino, maestro di cappella at the Turin court 1749–70, 'cello player and composer (Stabat mater, motets, trios for strings).

Gasparo da Salò, from Salo, Lake Garda, celebrated instrument-maker at Brescia about 1565–1615, who constructed, specially, first-rate viols, bass and double-bass viols (the predecessors of our double-bass); his violins, of which but few still exist, appear to have been less admired. The favourite instrument of the celebrated contrabassist, Dragonetti, was a double-bass viol of G.'s, but the former had it changed into a double-bass. Fétis, in his Dragonetti article, errs in naming G. as teacher of Andreas Amati, who, in fact, flourished between 1546–77.

Gassenhauer (Ger. "street-song"), a term for the popular songs (*Gassenhawerlin*) of the 16th century. At the present day the term implies something trivial, secondary—and, finally, commonplace, not worthy of art.

Gassier, Édouard, excellent stage-singer (baritone), pupil of the Paris Conservatoire; he made his *début* in 1845 at the Opéra Comique, sang for several years in Italy, married in 1848 the Spanish singer, Josefa Fernandez; and from 1849–52 they both achieved triumphs at Madrid, Barcelona, and Seville. They were afterwards both engaged at the Théâtre Italien, Paris

(1854), London, and Moscow. The wife died Oct. 8, 1866, Madrid; G. on Dec. 18, 1871, Havannah.

Gassmann, Florian Leopold, b. May 3, 1729, Brüx (Bohemia), d. Jan. 21, 1774, Vienna; in his twelfth year he ran away from his father, who wished to bring him up as a merchant, and made a pilgrimage as harpist to Bologna, to Padre Martini, who for two years became his teacher. After fulfilling for some time an appointment with Count Leonardi Veneri at Venice, he went to Vienna (1762) as ballet composer and court capellmeister (as Reutter's successor), 1771; still in the same year he founded the "Tonkünstler" Society (now the Haydn Society in aid of the widows and orphans of Viennese musicians). His compositions (nineteen Italian operas, much sacred music, etc.) were once esteemed. His daughters—Maria Anna and Maria Theresia (Rosenbaum), trained by G.'s most distinguished pupil, Salieri—were celebrated in Vienna as opera-singers.

Gassner, Ferdinand Simon, b. Jan. 6, 1798, Vienna, d. Feb. 25, 1851, Darmstadt; he went there at an early age, where his father was painter at the court theatre, and was at first engaged as supernumerary in the court band, became violinist, 1816, afterwards chorus-master at the Mayence National Theatre, 1818 musical director of the Giessen University. He received (1819) the title of doctor and the *facultas legendi* for music, but in 1826 returned to the court band at Darmstadt, and became, later on, teacher of singing and chorus-master at the court theatre. He wrote: "Partiturenkenntnis, ein Leitfaden zum Selbstunterricht, etc." (1838; in French, 1851, "Traité de la partition"); and "Dirigent und Ripienist" (1846). He published, from 1822–35 at Mayence, the "Musikalischer Hausfreund" (Musicians' Calendar); edited, from 1841–45, a newspaper entitled *Zeitschrift für Deutschlands Musikvereine und Dilettanten;* he made additions in 1842 to the supplement of Schilling's "Universallexikon der Tonkunst"; and, finally, himself compiled a "Universallexikon der Tonkunst" (1849). As a composer he was active, and wrote operas, ballets, cantatas, etc.

Gast, Peter. (*See* Köselitz.)

Gastinel, Léon Gustave Cyprien, b. Aug. 15, 1823, Villers les Pots (Côte d'Or), pupil (for composition) of Halévy. He received in 1846 the *Grand Prix de Rome* for the cantata *Velasquez,* and turned his attention especially to choral and orchestral composition, and produced the following important works: three grand masses (1st, "Messe Romaine," the 3rd with female chorus only), two symphonies, four oratorios (*Le dernier jour, Les sept Paroles, Saül, La fée des eaux*), a Concertante for two violins with orchestra, two overtures, numerous sets of chamber works, the comic operas—*Le Miroir* (one-act, 1854); *L'Opéra aux Fenêtres*

(1857); *Titus et Bérénice* (1860); *Le buisson vert* (1861); *La kermesse, La dame des prés, La tulipe bleue,* and *Le roi barbe* (the last four have not been produced).

Gastoldi, Giovanni Giacomo, a famous contrapuntist of the second half of the 16th century, b. about 1556, Caravaggio, maestro at Mantua, afterwards at Milan (1592), d. 1622. A large number of his works have come down to us: "Canzone à 5" (1581); three books of canzonets à 4 (1581, 1582, 1588); three books of madrigals à 5 (1588, 1589, 1599); madrigals à 5–9 (1602); four books of canzonets à 3 (1592–96, etc.); masses à 5–8 (1600); masses à 8 (1607); masses à 4 (1611); "Completorium ad usum Romanæ ecclesiæ" (1589); vesper psalms à 4 (1588); psalms à 4 (1590–1601); vespers à 5 (1600–2); vespers à 6 (1607); "Balletti" à 5 (dance pieces, 1591, etc.); "Balletti" à 3 (1593, etc.); "Concerti" à 8 (double chorus, 1598, 1610); "Tricinìa" (1600). Single pieces are still to be found in collections of Pierre Phalèse, etc.

Gatayes, (1) Guillaume Pierre Antoine, b. Dec. 20, 1774, Paris, d. there Oct., 1846, performer on the guitar and harp. He wrote trios for the guitar, flute, and violin, duets for two guitars, guitar and pianoforte, guitar and violin or flute, for harp and horn, harp and guitar, and guitar solos and harp sonatas; also a "Méthode de guitare," "Nouvelle méthode de guitare," "Petite méthode de guitare," and "Méthode de harpe." His sons are—

(2) Joseph Léon, b. Dec. 25, 1805, Paris, d. there Feb. 1, 1877, likewise an important performer on the harp; he composed many solo pieces, duets and studies for the harp. He was active for several years as musical critic to various Parisian papers, and was also sporting critic to the *Siècle.*

(3) Félix, b. 1809, Paris, an able pianist and composer of orchestral works; he spent a restless life, made concert tours in America and Australia, and for pecuniary reasons devoted himself especially to the composition of military music.

Gathy, August, b. May 14, 1800, Liége, d April 8, 1858, Paris; he was at first a bookseller at Hamburg; from 1828–30 pupil of F. Schneider in Dessau, 1830–41 in Hamburg, where he edited a "Musikalisches Konversationsblatt," and published in 1835 a "Musikalisches Konversationslexikon" (2nd ed. 1840; 3rd ed. revised by Reissmann, 1873), a small work, but one of great value. From 1841 he lived again in Paris as teacher of music. He was of a weakly constitution and could not display much activity. G. published small vocal pieces.

Gauche (Fr.), left. *Main gauche,* left hand.

Gaucquier, Alard (Dunoyer, named du G., also Latinised Nuceus), b. Lille (hence Insulanus), capellmeister to King Ferdinand I. and Maximilian II., then capellmeister to the Archduke, subsequently Kaiser Matthias ; G. was a famous contrapuntist (Magnificat 4–6 voc. [1547], and "Quatuor missæ 5, 6, et 8 vocum" [1581]).

Gaudentios, "the philosopher," Greek writer on music, probably older than Ptolemy (2nd century A.D.). His "Introductio harmonica" ('Αρμονιχὴ εἰσαγωγή), based on Aristoxenos, was published with Latin translation in the "Antiquæ musicæ auctores septum " (1662).

Gaultier, (1) Jacques (Gautier), named Sieur de Neüe, le vieux ou l'ancien (G. sen.), b. about 1600, Lyons ; from 1617–47 royal lutenist in London ; d. about 1670, Paris, whither he went in 1647. He was a performer on the lute.

(2) Denis (G. le jeune ou l'illustre), b. between 1600 and 1610, Marseilles, cousin of the former, d., not after 1664, Paris, famous lutenist, of whom are preserved two printed collections of pieces for the lute ("Pièces de luth," 1660, and "Livre de tablature," the latter of which was published by his widow and Jacques Gaultier [1]), also a work in manuscript ("Codex Hamilton "). Among the pupils of Jacques and Deniş G. were : Monton, Du Faux, Gallot, Du But. For various persons named Gaultier in the 17th century, cf. the monograph of Oskar Fleischer ("Vierteljahrschrift f. Mus.-Wiss.," 1886, 1st and 2nd books).

(3) Pierre, native of Orleans, likewise a composer for the lute, but probably not related to either of the above. He published (1638) suites for the lute, but of little importance.

(4) Ennémond, son of Jacques, b., according to Fétis, 1635, Vienne (Dauphiné) ; in 1669 royal chamber lutenist at Paris, published two books of pieces for lute in tablature. He died before 1680.

(5) Pierre, b. 1642, Cioutat (Provence), and lost his life by shipwreck in the harbour of Cette in 1697. He bought from Lully, in 1685, the patent of an opera enterprise for Marseilles, and started in 1687 with the production of his opera, Le Triomphe de la paix.

(6) Abbé Aloysius Édouard Camille, b. about 1755 in Italy, d. Sept. 19, 1818, Paris ; he compiled a new method for the instruction of the elements of music, which he described as "Éléments de musique propres à faciliter aux enfants la connaissance des notes, des mesures et des tons, au moyen de la méthode des jeux instructifs " (1789).

Gauthier, Gabriel, b. 1808 in the department of Saône-et-Loire, became blind when he was a year old ; in 1818 he was pupil, and afterwards teacher, at the Institution for the Blind at Paris, and also organist of St. Étienne du Mont. He published : "Répertoire des maitres de chapelle " (1842–45, five vols.) ; "Considérations sur la question de la réforme du plainchant et sur l'emploi de la musique ordinaire

dans les églises " (1843) ; and "Le mécanisme de la composition instrumentale " (1845).

Gautier, (1) Jean François Eugène, b Feb. 27, 1822, Vaugirard, near Paris, d. April 3, 1878, Paris, pupil of Habeneck (violin) and Halévy (composition) at the Conservatoire ; in 1848 second conductor at the Théâtre National, subsequently, at the Théâtre Lyrique ; in 1864 he became professor of harmony at the Conservatoire, which post he exchanged in 1872 for that of professor of history ; he was musical critic of various Parisian papers, from 1874 of the Journal Officiel, and for several years maître de chapelle at St Eugène. He composed a number (fourteen) of comic operas, mostly of one act, which were produced at the Théâtre Lyrique and the Opéra Comique, besides an oratorio (La Mort de Jésu), an "Ave Maria," a cantata (Le 15 Août), and prepared Don Juan, Figaro, and Freischütz for the Théâtre Lyrique.

(2) Théophile. b. Aug. 31, 1811, Tarbes, d. Oct. 23, 1872, Paris, a noteworthy writer, author of the novel "Mademoiselle de Maupin " ; for a long time he was editor of the dramatic feuilleton of the Presse and of the Moniteur Universelle. He published : "Histoire de l'art dramatique en France depuis vingt-cinq ans " (1859, six small vols.). These, and the works which he also left—"Histoire du romantisme " and "Portraits contemporains "—contain interesting details concerning singers, composers, etc

Gaveaux, Pierre, b. Aug., 1761, Béziers (Hérault), d. Feb. 5, 1825, Paris, a tenor singer at the collegiate church of St. Severin, Bordeaux, where he was pupil for composition of Franz Beck, he then became opera-singer at Bordeaux, Montpelier, and from 1789, at the Opéra Comique, Paris (Théâtre de Monsieur, Théâtre Feydeau). G. composed a large number (thirty-three) of operas, mostly for the Théâtre Feydeau (among which, Léonore, ou l'amour conjugal, identical in subject with Beethoven's Fidelio). In 1812 he lost his reason for a time, and from 1819 became an incurable lunatic.

Gaviniés, Pierre, b. May 26, 1726, Bordeaux, from which city his father (violin-maker) afterwards went to Paris, d. there Sept. 9, 1800; one of the most important of French violinists of the last century, whom Viotti distinguished by the title "the French Tartini." He was, for the most part, self-taught. In 1741 he made his début at a Concert Spirituel, and created a great impression by his expressive and noble style of playing. From 1796 until his death he was professor of the violin at the Conservatoire. G. composed : "Les 24 matinées " (études in all keys), six violin concertos, and three violin sonatas ; the heaped-up difficulties, some of them doing violence to the nature of the instrument, cause one to entertain a high opinion of his powers as a virtuoso. An opera (Le prétendu) was produced in 1760. (Cf. Fayolle,

" Notices sur Corelli, Tartini, G. et Viotti" [1810].)

Gavotte, an old French dance in allabreve time ($\frac{4}{2}$), with an up-beat of a minim or two crotchets, and two-bar phrasing. It always closes on an accented beat, is of moderately rapid movement, and has no notes of smaller value than quavers. The G. is one of the usual movements of a Suite (q.v.), and, for the most part, follows the Sarabande. A Musette (q.v.) generally serves as a trio, after which the G. is repeated.

Gaztambide, Joaquin, b. Feb. 7, 1822, Tudela (Navarra), d. March 18, 1870, Madrid, pupil of the Conservatorio there, conductor of the "Pensions" concerts at the Conservatorio, one of the original founders of the Concert Society, and honorary professor at the Conservatorio. G. composed a large number (forty) of Zarzuelas (Spanish operettas), which made him very popular and brought him distinctions of all kinds. A younger relation, Xavier G., is also a composer of operettas.

Gazzaniga, Giuseppe, b. Oct., 1743, Verona, d. at the beginning of 1819, Crema, pupil of Porpora and Piccini; he was a friend of Sacchini, who helped him to produce his first opera (*Il finto cieco*) at Vienna (1770). He wrote a large number (thirty-three) of operas for Vienna, Naples, Venice, Bergamo, Ferrara, Dresden, among which were: *Il convitato di pietra* (Bergamo, 1788) and *Don Giovanni Tenorio* (Lucca, 1792). G. became, in 1791, maestro of Cremona Cathedral, and from that time wrote nothing but sacred music (Stabat Mater, Te Deum), some cantatas, etc.

Gebauer, (1) Michel Joseph, b. 1763, La Fère (Aisne), distinguished oboist, violinist, and violist; but he was forced to give up violin-playing, as he lost tne use of the little finger of the left hand. In 1791 he was oboist in the Garde Nationale, from 1794 to the reorganisation, in 1802 professor at the Conservatoire, then bandmaster of the Garde de Consuls, oboist in the royal band, but succumbed Dec., 1812, to the hardships of the Russian campaign. He wrote many duets for two violins, and for violin and viola, for two flutes, for flute and horn, flute and bassoon, etc.; quartets for flute, clarinet, horn, and bassoon; over two hundred military marches, and many potpourris, etc. The three following were his brothers—

(2) François Réné, b. 1773, Versailles, d. July, 1845; from 1796 to 1802 he was professor of the bassoon at the Conservatoire, and again from 1825; 1801–26 bassoon-player at the Grand Opéra; he wrote also many sonatas, études, duets (108), trios, quartets, quintets, *Symphonies concertantes*, etc., for wind—especially wood-wind instruments—military marches, potpourris, overtures, and a bassoon Method.

(3) Étienne François, b. 1777, Versailles, from 1801-22 flautist at the Opéra Comique,

d. 1823. He wrote flute duets, violin duets, sonatas for flute and bass, solos for flute and clarinet, and exercises for flute.

(4) Pierre Paul, b. 1775, Versailles, died young, and published only twenty horn duets.

(5) Franz Xaver, not related to the former, b. 1784, Eckersdorf, near Glatz, d. Dec. 13, 1822, Vienna; in 1804 organist at Frankenstein, in 1810 teacher of music at Vienna, in 1816 choir-master of St. Augustine Church; a most active member of the "Gesellschaft der Musikfreunde," and the founder (1819) and first conductor of the Concerts Spirituels. G. published a few *Lieder* and part-songs. He was on intimate terms with Beethoven.

Gebel, (1) Georg (father), b. 1685, Breslau. He was apprenticed to a tailor, but ran away from his master and became a musician; in 1709 organist at Brieg, in 1713 at Breslau, where he died in 1750. He made attempts to improve the keyboard (pedal clavier, keyboard with quarter-tones), and composed clavier pieces, canons (up to thirty parts), psalms, masses, cantatas, a Passion oratorio, twenty-four concertos, figured chorales, and organ preludes, all which works remained in manuscript.

(2) Georg (son), b. Oct. 25, 1709, Brieg, d. Sept. 24, 1753, Rudolstadt, pupil of his father; in 1729 second organist at St. Maria Magdalena. He was distinguished by the title of capellmeister to the Duke of Öls, became in 1735 member of Count Brühl's band at Dresden, where he learned to play the pantaleon from Hebenstreit, the inventor of that instrument, and in 1747 became leader and conductor to Prince Rudolstadt. His productiveness was very great. At Breslau he wrote for the Duke of Öls two sets of cantatas for the whole year, a mass, many chamber pieces, a symphony, trios, duets, concertos for flute, lute, gamba, clavier, violin, etc.; but in Rudolstadt, in six years, over a hundred orchestral symphonies, partitas, concertos, two Christmas cantatas, complete set of cantatas for several years, two Passions, twelve operas, and other compositions.

(3) Georg Sigismund, younger brother of the former, organist of the Elizabeth Church, Breslau, d. 1775; he composed fugues and preludes for organ.

(4) Franz Xaver, b. 1787, Fürstenau, near Breslau, d. 1843, Moscow, a pupil of Abbé Vogler and Albrechtsberger, in 1810 capellmeister at the Leopoldstadt Theatre, Vienna, then theatre capellmeister at Pesth and Lemberg; he lived from 1817 as teacher of music at Moscow. He composed several operas, many pf. pieces, a mass, four symphonies, several overtures, stringed quartets and quintets, etc.

Gebhard, Martin Anton, b. 1770, Bavaria, monk at Benediktbeurn; after the suppression of the order, he became priest at Steinsdorf, near Augsburg, where he was still living in 1831. He wrote two philosophical works: "Versuch zur Begründung einer Wissenschaft, Chronometrie genannt" (1808), and "Harmonie," an exposition, in three books, of this idea, and its application to mankind generally (1817). The ideas of G. are brilliant, but he made use of unprofitable symbolism.

Gebhardi, Ludwig Ernst, b. 1787, Nottleben (Thuringia), d. Sept. 4, 1862, as organist and teacher of music at the seminary at Erfurt. He published school songs, organ pieces, a "Choralbuch," an organ Method, and a Method of thorough-bass (1828-35, four vols., several times reprinted).

Gebrochene Akkorde (Ger.), broken chords.

Gedackt (Ger., "covered" or "stopped"), general term for the covered lip-pipe stops of the organ (Fr. *Jeux bouchés*). The G. of 32 ft. is generally called Untersatz, Majorbass, Grosssubbass, Infrabass, Subkontrabass, Lat. *Pileata maxima*, Fr. *sous-bourdon*, Eng. *Great bourdon*, Sp. *Tapada de* 52; the 16-ft. G., also Grobgedackt, Grossgedackt, Bourdon, Bordun, Perduna, Subbass, double-stopped diapason, Lat. *Pileata magna*, Sp. *Tapada de* 26; the 8-ft. G., Mittelgedackt, Fr. *grosse flûte*, Eng. stopped diapason, unison covered, Sp. *Tapada de* 13, Lat. *Pileata major;* the 4-ft. G. Kleingedackt, *Pileata minor*, flûte, etc. Still smaller covered stops are to be found only in old organs (Bauernflöte, Feldflöte à 2'and 1'). Also the Doppelflöte (Duiflöte) and Quintatön (Quintadena) are Gedackte. The covered stops give (approximately) a note about an octave lower than open flutes of equal length, and thus, from motives of economy, they are much used for low registers. Their tone is somewhat dull, and altogether inferior to that of the open diapason. (*Cf.* WIND-INSTRUMENTS.)

Gedämpft (Ger.), muted, muffled.

Gedehnt (Ger.), distended, sustained, drawn out.

Gedicht (Ger.), a poem.

Gegenharmonie (Ger.), countersubject; whatever is opposed to, or accompanies, the subject and answer of a fugue.

Gegensatz (Ger.), countersubject.

Gehalten (Ger.), sustained. *Gut gehalten*, well sustained.

Gehring, Franz, b. 1838, d. Jan. 4. 1884, Penzing, near Vienna, contributor to Grove's "Dictionary of Music," author of Mozart's biography for Hueffer's "Great Musicians"; the lecturer on mathematics at the Vienna University.

Geige (Ger.). (*See* STRINGED-INSTRUMENTS; VIOLIN.)

Geigenklavicimbal. (*See* BOGENFLÜGEL.)

Geijer, Erik Gustaf, b. Jan. 12, 1783, Ransätter (Wermland), d. April 23, 1847, as professor of history at Upsala University; he composed and edited tasteful songs of Swedish national colour, published in 1824, with Lindblad, a collection of modern Swedish songs, and was chief editor of the musical part of the old Swedish Popular Songs (" Svenska Folkvisor," 1814-16, three vols.; 2nd ed. 1846), which he published jointly with Afzelius.

Geisler, (1) Johann Gottfried, lived at Zittau, and died there Feb. 13, 1827. He was the author of "Beschreibung und Geschichte der neuesten und vorzüglichsten Instrumente und Kunstwerke für Liebhaber und Künstler" (1792–1800, twelve parts; in which, among other things, some information was given about the Bogenklavier).

(2) Paul, gifted composer, b. Aug. 10, 1856, Stolp (Pomerania), pupil of his grandfather (musical director at Marienburg), and, for some time, of Konstantin Decker, 1881-82, chorus-master at the Leipzig Stadttheater, afterwards with Angelo Neumann's Wagner company. From 1883 to 1885 he was capellmeister at Bremen (under Anton Seidl), and since then has lived mostly in Leipzig. G. has composed four operas, *Ingeborg* (libretto based on Peter Lohmann's "Frithjof"), *Hertha*, *Die Ritter von Marienburg*, and *Gestrandet* songs and pf. pieces (monologues and episodes). His symphonic poem, "Der Rattenfänger von Hameln," was produced in 1880 at the musical festival of the "Allgemeiner deutscher Musikverein" at Magdeburg (the score is published). He has written besides the symphonic poems "Till Eulenspiegel," "Mira," "Maria Magdalena," "Heinrich von Ofterdingen," "Eckehard," "Beowulf," "Der Hidalgo," "Walpurgisnacht," "Am Meere," "Der wilde Jäger," "Der neue Tannhäuser," and the "Cyklen" for soli, chorus, and orchestra, "Sansara" and "Golgatha." In spite of his great productiveness, G. has not, hitherto, won favour and a firm position among musicians.

Geist (Ger.), spirit, soul, mind, genius.

Geisterharfe (Ger.). (*See* ÆOLIAN HARP.)

Geistlich (Ger.), spiritual, sacred. *Geistliche Lieder*, spiritual or sacred songs; hymns.

Gelassen (Ger.), calm, placid.

Geläufig (Ger.), fluent, voluble.

Geläufigkeit (Ger.), fluency, volubility, ease.

Gelinek, (1) Hermann Anton, named Cervetti, b. Aug. 8, 1709, Horzeniowecs (Bohemia), d. Dec. 5, 1779, Milan. He was a Premonstratensian monk at Seelau, but escaped from the cloister and made a name as violinist; in order not to be discovered, he adopted, when in Italy, the name of Cervetti. He afterwards returned to his monastery, but only to escape for the second time. Violin concertos and sonatas of his composition appeared in print; pieces for organ and sacred music remained in manuscript.

(2) Joseph, Abbé, b. Dec. 3, 1758, Selcz (Bohemia), d. April 13, 1825, Vienna, a composer of empty fantasias and of variations on familiar themes, much in vogue between 1800 and 1810 ; compositions were not only fabricated by himself in great number, but publishers ordered many others to be written under his name. G. was on friendly terms with Mozart, who recommended him as private tutor to Prince Kinsky. G. wrote, besides, a quantity of chamber music (trios, violin sonatas, pianoforte sonatas), which is, however, only on a level with his variations.

Geltung (Ger.), value—for instance, of a note or a rest.

Gemächlich (Ger.), slow, gentle, comfortable, commodious.

Gemässigt (Ger.), moderate.

Geminiani, Francesco, b. 1680, Lucca, d. Dec. 17, 1762, Dublin. He was a distinguished violin virtuoso, composer, and writer on music, and pupil of Lunati ("il Gobbo") and Corelli. He came to London in 1714, where he gained a high position as teacher, but was seldom heard at public concerts. He remained in England, only making occasional flying visits to Paris on the occasions of new works of his being published; it is, however, stated that he lived in Paris from 1748 to 1755. In 1761 he visited his friend and pupil Dubourg, conductor of the Viceroy's band at Dublin, and from that journey he never returned. To G., together with Veracini, belongs the merit of having raised the standard of violin-playing in England. His most valuable work is his "Art of Playing the Violin" (1740; 2nd edition as "The Entire and Compleat Tutor for the Violin"; also in French and German), the oldest of all violin methods (*cf.* MOZART, LEOP.). His violin compositions also take a high rank : xii. solos, Op. 1 (1716) ; twelve solos (Op. 4) ; six concertos, Op. 6 ; xii. sonatas, Op. 11 ; also twelve concertos à 7 (Op. 2-3 ; in parts 1732, in score, 1755) ; six concertos à 8 ; twelve trios. A set of six other trios and 'cello solos are transcriptions from Op. 1. Of less importance are his "Lessons for the Harpsichord," his Guitar Method, also his theoretical works, "Guida Harmonica" (1742, in English; but also in French and Dutch); "Supplement to the Guida Harmonica," "The Art of Accompaniement" (1755, Method of Thorough-bass) ; "Rules for Playing in Taste" (1739) ; "Treatise on Good Taste" (1747) ; "Treatise on Memory"; "The Harmonical Miscellany" (1755, lessons). His Sonatas I., II., and VIII., and also selected movements from others, have been arranged for violin and pianoforte by G. Jensen, and are published in Augener's Edition, which contains also a selection of sonata movements, an allegro in A and giga in A for piano solo.

Gemshorn (Ger.), "chamois horn," the name of a pleasing organ stop, often of 8-ft. pitch, sometimes of 4 or 2 ft., and in the pedal organ of 16 ft.

Gemüth (Ger.), mind, soul, heart.

Genast, Eduard Franz, singer and actor, b. July 15, 1797, Weimar, d. Aug. 4, 1866, Wiesbaden, son of the actor Anton G., made his *début* in 1814 at Weimar as Osmin in Mozart's *Entführung;* in 1828 he was theatre director at Magdeburg, and was engaged in 1829 for life at the Court Theatre, Weimar. When he was young he was as good a singer (baritone) as actor, but afterwards only appeared as an actor. G. composed many songs and two operas, *Die Sonnenmänner* and *Die Verräter auf den Alpen;* he also published his *mémoires*, "Aus dem Tagebuch eines alten Schauspielers" (1862–66, four vols.).

Genée, Franz Fr. Richard, b. Feb. 7, 1823 (not 1824), Danzig, son of the bass singer, Friedrich G. (b. 1795, d. 1856), who was for a long time director of the Danzig Theatre. G attended the Gymnasium at Berlin (Graue Kloster) and at Danzig, studied first medicine, but took up music, and studied composition under Ad. Stahlknecht at Berlin. From 1848–67 he was theatre capellmeister at Reval, Riga, Cologne, Aix-la-Chapelle, Düsseldorf, Danzig, Mayence, Schwerin, Prague, and from 1868, capellmeister at the theatre An-der-Wien ; he now lives at his villa at Pressbaum, near Vienna, entirely engaged in composition and literary work. G. is known as a composer of comic operas and operettas, for some of which he himself wrote the libretti (many, jointly with F. Zell), and he also prepared libretti for J. Strauss, Suppé, and Millöcker. His best-known operas are, *Der Geiger aus Tivol* (1857), *Der Musikfeind, Die Generalprobe, Rosita, Der schwarze Prinz, Am Runenstein* (with Fr. von Flotow, 1868), *Der Seekadett* (1876), *Nanon, Im Wunderlande der Pyramiden, Die letzten Mohikaner, Nisida, Rosina, Zwillinge, Die Piraten, Die Dreizehn* (1887). G.'s talent as a humorist is also shown in numerous songs for male chorus, pf. songs, duets, etc.

Genera (Lat.), the plural of *genus*, kind. The ancient Greeks distinguished three musical G., the diatonic, chromatic, and enharmonic.

Generalbass is a species of chord writing which arose in Italy towards the end of the 16th century, and soon came into general use ; it consists of figures written above or below the notes of a bass part. This had formerly the same meaning which the pianoforte score now has ; in order that the accompanying cembalist or organist might not have the trouble of seeking out from the score of an elaborate vocal composition the harmonies required to support the chorus at rehearsal, or at performance (scores similar to those of the present day were not then in use. *Cf.* SCORE and TABLATURE), figures, reckoned from the bass note and answering to the degrees (according to the signature of the key) on which the required notes would be found, were written over the lowest part, and, at a later period, on a special bass part (Basso continuo) accompanying the other parts from beginning to end. A 3 indicated the third note (interval of the third) from the bass note, a 6 the sixth (SIXTH); if a note was to be taken different from that indicated by the signature, a chromatic sign had to be placed near the figure. Many of the abbreviations now used in generalbass figuring, and mentioned below, were invented in old times. Playing from figured bass was an art which required a thorough knowledge of musical composition, for the chords were not taken literally, as indicated by the figures; the third was not a real third, but, according to circumstances, one or two octaves higher; the figures only indicated the notes, but not the octave position. The chords were connected according to the rules for part-writing; but a skilful player understood how to ornament his part with additional runs, shakes, appoggiaturas, etc. The writing of figured bass in composition is no longer in use; neither, consequently, is playing from the same practised. The figured basses in the works of the old masters have, for the most part, been reduced by some skilful hand (R. Franz and others) to a good organ or pianoforte accompaniment, and G. only exists now as a means in common use for teaching harmony. The exercises in our harmony books are generally given with figured bass, and the following signs are used. The absence of any sign indicates third or fifth, according to the signature, *i.e.* the *triad* (q.v.); a chromatic sign ($\sharp$ $\flat$ $\natural$) above a note changes the third of the triad. If the fifth is to be changed, the chromatic sign must be placed before the figure 5; the raising of the 5th a semitone is, however, often indicated by a stroke through the 5 ($\not5$). A 3 or 5 written down without any chromatic sign before it indicates that the 3rd or 5th (also 8ve) is to be in the highest part. But in marking resolutions of suspensions—for example, 4 3, 6 5, 9 8—the figure does not specially indicate the highest part; in such cases the 10th, instead of the 3rd, can be taken, as for example, when the 7th and 9th proceed together to the 8ve and 10th. A 6 indicates 3rd and 6th, the so-called *chord of six-three;* a chromatic sign *under* the 6 relates to the third; and a stroke through the 6 signifies the raising of it a semitone ($\natural$), though the raising, and likewise lowering, can be indicated equally well by means of a chromatic sign before the 6. ⁶₄ indicates 4th and 6th, the *chord of six-four;* the raising of the 4th or 6th can be effected by means of the stroke, or, like that of lowering, by means of a chromatic sign; for

example, after each of the following signatures the chord of c major is to be played—

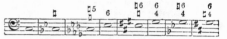

A 7 indicates 3rd, 5th, and 7th, *i.e.* the *chord of the 7th,* according to the signature. Chords of various meaning can be indicated by the simple figure seven—

1.   2.   3.   4.   5.   6.

(1) is the *G major* chord with minor 7th; (2) the *D minor* chord with minor under-7th; (3) the *C major* chord with added major 6th; (4) the *C major* chord with major 7th; (5) a chord of diminished 7th; (6) the *E major* chord with added minor 6th. The figuring shows nothing of the widely differing meaning of these chords, just as little as the above signs of the most varied kind placed together showed that they all referred to the chord of *C major.* The changes of 3rd and 5th in the chords of the 7th are indicated in the same way as in the triads; for example (chord of the 7th, *g, b, d, f*):—

⁶₅, likewise ⁶₅₃, indicates 3rd, 5th, and 6th from the bass note, *i.e.* the first inversion of the chord of the 7th, named, from the figuring, chord of six-five—the signs indicating change will be clear after explanations given above; ⁴₃, or ⁶₄₃, indicates the second inversion of the chord of 7th, the *chord of four-three;* 2, likewise ⁶₄₂, indicates the 2nd, 4th, and 6th, the *chord of six-four-two,* or simply *chord of two,* the third inversion of the chord of the 7th. In generalbass no other figure-signs of abbreviation are used; on the contrary, every other figure refers to the note indicated by it; for example, ⁵₄, 4th and 5th without 3rd; ⁹₇ indicates the 9th added to the chord of the 7th (*chord of the 9th*), and so on. Horizontal lines over bass notes indicate the retention of the previous harmony, or, if the bass note is repeated, a repetition of the same harmony. A nought (0) indicates no upper parts (*Tasto solo*). The oldest explanations of generalbass signs are to be found in Cavalieri (1600), Viadana (1603), Agazzari (1606), Michael Prætorius (1619), and others; of more recent methods of general or thorough bass may be mentioned those of Heinichen (1711), Mattheson (1751), Ph. E. Bach (1752), Marpurg (1755), Kirnberger (1781), Türk (1781), Choron (1801), Fr. Schneider (1820), Fétis (1824), Dehn (1840),

E. F. Richter (1860), Macfarren (1860), S. Jadassohn (1883), Prout (1889). The exclusive use of the thorough-bass figuring would lead a harmony pupil never to attempt, and consequently never to learn, how to write a good bass part ; and so to remedy this fault, quite another kind of chord designation was introduced by Gottfr. Weber (q.v.), improved by E. F. Richter, and further developed by the compiler of this Dictionary. (*Cf.* KLANGSCHLÜSSEL.)

Generali, Pietro, opera composer, b. Oct. 4, 1783, Masserano (Piedmont), d. Nov. 3, 1832, near Novara ; he went at an early age to Rome with his father, who changed his real name, Mercandetti. G. produced his first opera, *Gli amanti ridicoli,* at Rome already in 1800, and afterwards wrote a stately series (fifty-two) of operas for Rome, Venice, Milan, Naples, Bologna, Turin, Florence, Lisbon, etc., of which one, *I Baccanali di Roma* (Venice, 1815), was specially successful. The dazzling lustre, however, of Rossini soon threw him into the shade. In 1817 he went as theatre maestro to Barcelona, where he produced his works which had met with the greatest success, and prepared others more in the style of Rossini. In 1821 he reappeared in Italy, but was unable again to obtain favour. He died as maestro of Novara Cathedral. According to Fétis, Rossini is said to have borrowed certain harmonic progressions and modulations from him. At the commencement and close of his career as a composer G. also wrote many sacred works (an oratorio, *Il voto di Jefte,* masses, psalms, etc.). An irregular course of life prevented him from doing serious work.

Generalpause (Ger.) is a term used in works for several instruments, especially in orchestral works, for a cessation of all the instruments. The name, however, is usually given only to long rests (of, at least, one bar), especially to such as break the flow of a composition in a sudden and striking manner. If a fermata is placed over a G., it does not (according to Leop. Mozart) lengthen the value unconditionally, but renders its duration indefinite, or even shortens it considerably. The rest then loses its rhythmical value—is not counted—but, while it lasts, the feeling of time-beats is, as it were, suspended.

Generalprobe (Ger.), a general, or principal, rehearsal.

Générateur (Fr.), **Generator,** fundamental note, root.

Genere (Ital.), genus, kind.

Generoso (Ital.), generous, noble, magnanimous.

Genet, Eleazar. (*See* CARPENTRAS.)

Gengenbach, Nicolaus, cantor at Zeitz, b. Koiditz (Saxony). He wrote " Musica nova,

newe Singekunst, sowohl nach der alten Solmisation als auch neuen Bobisation oder Bebisation " (1626).

Genial (Ger.), pertaining to genius, clever, ingenious, spirited.

Genre (Fr.), genus, kind, sort, style.

Genss, Hermann, b. Jan. 6, 1856, Tilsit, studied under L. Köhler, Alb. Hahn, and the wife of the latter ; a talented pianist, who after attending the Gymnasium received instruction from Kiel, Grell, and Taubert at the Royal School of Music, Berlin. In 1877 he settled in Lübeck as teacher of music, but in 1880 moved to Hamburg. In 1890 he became teacher of the pianoforte and theory at the Conservatorium at Sondershausen, in 1891 director of the Schumacher Conservatorium, Mayence, and in 1893 one of the directors of the Scharwenka-Klindworth Conservatorium, Berlin. In 1892 G. was named honorary member of the Philosopical Academy at Bologna. G. is a diligent composer (chamber music, orchestral and vocal works).

Gentil, m., **Gentille,** f. (Fr.), **Gentile** (Ital.), pretty, tender, delicate.

Gentillement (Fr.), **Gentilmente** (Ital.), prettily, tenderly, delicately.

Genus *diatonicum, chromaticum, enharmonicum,* the three genera of the ancients. (*See* GREEK MUSIC—V., and the articles CHROMA, DIATONIC, ENHARMONICS.)

Gerade Bewegung (Ger.), similar motion.

Gerade Taktart (Ger.), binary time.

Gerard, Henri Philippe, b. 1763, Liége, d. 1848, Versailles ; he studied under Gregorio Ballabene at the Liége College at Rome ; was in 1788 teacher of singing at Paris, in 1795 professor of singing at the newly established Conservatoire, which post he held for over thirty years. He published : " Méthode de chant " (two parts), " Considérations sur la musique en général et particulièrement sur tout ce qui a rapport à la vocale, etc." (1819), and "Traité méthodique d'harmonie " (1833, based on Rameau).

Gerber, (1) Heinrich Nikolaus, b. Sept. 6, 1702, Wenigen-Ehrich, near Sondershausen, d. Aug. 6, 1775, Sondershausen ; from 1724–27 he studied law in Leipzig, and was a pupil there for music of J. S. Bach ; in 1728 organist at Heringen, and, from 1731, organist to the court at Sondershausen. He composed numerous clavier works (concertos, suites, minuets) and organ works (trios, figured chorales, preludes and fugues, concertos, inventions), which, however, remained in manuscript. He also busied himself with improvements for the organ, and constructed a " Strohfiedel " with keyboard. His son was the famous lexicographer.

(2) Ernst Ludwig, son of the former, b. Sept. 29, 1746, Sondershausen, d. there June 30,

1819; he was first trained by his father, and then went for some time to Leipzig to study jurisprudence, but in the musical atmosphere of this city his taste for music only grew stronger. As an able 'cellist he was frequently engaged both in private and in public. The uncertain health of his father caused G. to return to Sondershausen as his representative, and in 1775 he became his successor; he died after forty-three years of active service. His pecuniary means were limited, and he was unable to make great journeys for the dictionary work on which he had for a long time been engaged; and, as a matter of fact, he had to rely upon the resources of his own library, and on the collections of music and works which his publisher, Breitkopf, placed at his disposal. Thus arose, under circumstances of exceeding great difficulty, and in a small town lying far from intercourse with the world, his "Historisch-biographisches Lexikon der Tonkünstler" (1791 and 1792, two vols.), which was intended to be nothing more than a continuation of the biographical section of Walther's dictionary, and which can only lay any claim to completeness in connection with that work. The book was evolved from short biographical notices for a collection of portraits of musicians which gradually grew to dimensions of immense size; and therefore, in a special supplement to his dictionary, G. gave a catalogue of the pictures, wood-cuts, engravings, silhouettes, paintings, medals, busts, statues, with which he was acquainted. Another supplement contains descriptions of famous organs, of which sketches or drawings exist, as well as a catalogue of the most important modern inventions connected with the construction of instruments, with references to the biographies. As soon as G., by this (now so-called "old") dictionary of musicians, had drawn towards himself the attention of the world, an ever-increasing wealth of material flowed in on him for additions, or for a second edition. Forkel's "Litteratur" (1792) supplied him with a mass of additional information. So, instead of a new edition, he published a supplementary work, one, however, considerably more extensive than the one which required completing, viz., his "Neues historisch-biographisches Lexikon der Tonkünstler" (1812–14, four vols.); to this also is added a catalogue of pictures and a record of instruments. G.'s dictionaries are highly valued even to-day, as they have been only unsatisfactorily reproduced by modern works of the kind. Even the Mendel-Reissmann "Musikalisches Konversationslexikon" keeps bibliographical interest in the background in favour of biographical; and, besides, is far too unequally balanced for it to be considered a substitute for those older books. In this respect there is no German work of equal value with Fétis's "Biographie universelle." Besides the two dictionaries, the following have still to be mentioned: some articles in the

Allgemeine Musikalische Zeitung (years 2–9), in the *Litterarischer Anzeiger* (1797), and the *Deutsche Jahrbücher* (1794). As a composer G. only attempted pieces for clavier and organ, and music for wind band. He sold his extensive library to the "Gesellschaft der Musikfreunde" at Vienna for two hundred louis d'or, reserving to himself the use of it up to his death, and, generously, making additions to it.

Gerbert (von Hornau), M a r t i n, Prince-Abbot of St. Blaise, b. Aug. 11, 1720, Horb on the Neckar, d. May 13, 1793, St. Blaise, where, in 1736, he entered the Benedictine monastery, and from 1764 was Prince-Abbot. As he was then entrusted with the management of the rich library, he devoted himself to the history of the church, but especially to the study of the history of music. The main object of his researches was the history of church song in the Middle Ages. In 1760 he undertook a long journey, for the purpose of study, through Germany, France, and Italy, and made special search in the monastery libraries, and returned with ample spoil of copies of treatises on music of the Middle Ages. At Bologna he entered into friendly relations with Padre Martini, and both learned historians exchanged their rich experiences. The first fruit of his studies was an account of his tours: "Iter Allemannicum, accedit Italicum et Gallicum" (1765, 2nd ed. 1773; German by Köhler, 1767). In 1774 he brought out his most celebrated work, "De cantu et musica sacra, a prima ecclesiæ ætate usque ad præsens tempus" (two vols.), and in 1784 "Scriptores ecclesiastici de musica sacra potissimum" (three vols.). The appearance of the latter work caused an extraordinary sensation, and was of the highest value for the study of the history of music during the Middle Ages; for it enabled those, who were unable to make use of great libraries and to undertake journeys, to study in a convenient manner many works of ancient writers. The collection contains treatises of — Isidorus Hispalensis, Flaccus Alcuin, Aurelianus Romensis, Remi of Auxerre, Notker, Hucbald, Regino of Prüm, Odo of Clugny, Adelboldus, Bernelinus, Guido di Arezzo, Berno of Reichenau, Hermannus Contractus, Wilhelm von Hirschau, Theogerus of Metz, Aribo Scholasticus, Johannes Cotto, Bernhard of Clairvaux, Gerlandus, Eberhard of·Freisingen, Engelbert of Admont, Ægidius of Zamora, Franco of Cologne, Elias Salomonis, Marchettus of Padua, John Muris, Arnulf of St. Gille, Keck of Giengen, Adam of Fulda, likewise many small anonymous treatises, especially concerning the scale of organ-pipes. (*Cf.* the names quoted above.) G. did not clear the treatises from clerical errors, but gave them as he found them, adding thereby to the value of the edition. E. de Coussemaker (q.v.) has recently prepared a magnificent continuation of this valuable publication.

Gerlach, (1) D i e t r i c h, celebrated music-printer at Nuremberg, was in partnership with Ulrich Neuber from 1566–71, carried on the business alone until his death in 1575, when it was continued by his widow up to 1592. A catalogue of his publications appeared at Frankfort, 1609.

(2) T h e o d o r, b. June 25, 1861, Dresden, pupil of Wüllner, composer of songs, chamber-music, etc. He was theatre capellmeister at Sondershausen, Posen, etc., and now lives at Dresden.

Gerle, (1) K o n r a d, a lute-maker at Nüremberg, already famous in 1469, d. Dec. 4, 1521.

(2) H a n s, probably son of the former, was already famous in 1523 as a maker of violins and lutes, and also as a performer on the latter instrument, d. 1570, at an advanced age (a portrait of him taken in 1532 has been preserved). He was the author of tablature works of great historic value : " Lautenpartien in der Tabulatur " (1530) ; " Musica Teusch auf die Instrument der grossen und kleynen Geygen auch Lautten " (1532, contains a guide to violin-playing ; 2nd ed. as " Musica und Tabulatur auff die Instrument, etc.," 1546, " gemert mit 9 teutschen und 38 welschen, auch frantzösischen Liedern unnd 2 Mudeten ") ; likewise " Musica Teusch ander Teil " (1533, only discovered in 1886), and " Ein newes sehr künstliches Lautenbuch, darinnen etliche Preamel unnd Welsche Tentz, etc." (1552).

German flute, the cross-flute. (*See* FLUTE.)

German sixth, the chord of the German sixth consists of a major triad and an augmented sixth—for instance, *f a c d'♯*.   (*Cf.* FRENCH SIXTH and NEAPOLITAN SIXTH.)

Germer, H e i n r i c h, an esteemed teacher of the pianoforte, b. Dec. 30, 1837, Sommersdorf (Provinz Sachsen), attended the teachers' college, Halberstadt, and was for some time teacher, but in 1857 became a pupil in the composition class of the Berlin Akademie. After he had been private tutor in Poland for two years, he settled in Dresden, where he became an active and useful teacher of music. G. became favourably known by his small educational works—" Die Technik des Klavierspiels " (1877), " Die musikalische Ornamentik," " Rhythmische Probleme," " Wie spielt man Klavier ? " He also wrote a pianoforte Method, and prepared instructive editions of classical sonatas and études, among others a clever selection of Czerny's studies.

Gernsheim, F r i e d r i c h, b. July 17, 1839, Worms, was pupil of the Leipzig Conservatorium in 1852, went to Paris for further training in 1855, was appointed musical director at Saarbrück in 1861, teacher of the pianoforte and composition at Cologne in 1865, was named professor by the Duke of Gotha in 1872, became director of Rotterdam Conservatorium in 1874,

and in 1890 teacher at the Stern Conservatorium, and conductor of the Stern Choral Society, Berlin. He is well known as a composer in the department of chamber-music (three pf. quartets ; a pf. quintet, Op. 35 ; trios, Op. 28, 37 ; Introduction and Allegro for pf. and violin, Op. 38 ; two violin sonatas, Op. 50 ; two stringed quartets ; a stringed quintet, etc. He has also written two symphonies, overtures (*Waldmeisters Brautfahrt*), a concerto for pianoforte, and one for violin, choral works (" Salamis," for male chorus, baritone solo, and orchestra ; " Hafis," for soli, chorus, and orchestra ; " Wächterlied a. d. Neujahresnacht 1200," for male chorus and orchestra), " Agrippina " (scena for alto solo with chorus and orchestra, 1883), etc.

Gero, J h a n (J o h a n n), was for a long time erroneously confused with Joannes Gallus (q.v.). According to Fétis, he was maestro of Orvieto Cathedral during the first half of the 16th century. Some of his motets are to be found in Petrucci's " Motetti della Corona " (1519). In addition, the following of his works are known : two books of madrigals à 3 (1541 [1546] and 1555 [1559]) ; two books of madrigals à 2, and French canzonets (1543 [1552, 1572] and 1552 [1572 ; both vols. in one, 1582]) ; also many pieces in collections (Petrejus' " Trium vocum cantiones centum," 1541, alone, contains 32).

Gersbach, (1) J o s e p h, b. Dec. 22, 1787, Säckingen, d. Dec. 3, 1830, as teacher of music at the seminary, Carlsruhe. He published books of school songs—" Singvöglein " (thirty songs in two parts), " Wandervöglein " (sixty four-part songs). His brother published after his death : " Reihenlehre oder Begründung des musikalischen Rhythmus aus der allgemeinen Zahlenlehre " (1832), and " Liedernachlass."

(2) A n t o n, b. Feb. 21, 1801, Säckingen, d. Aug. 17, 1848, brother of the former, and his successor as music teacher at the seminary at Carlsruhe. He published instructive pianoforte works, a pianoforte Method, school songs, quartets for male and for mixed voices, a supplement to his brother's " Singvöglein," and a " Tonlehre oder System der elementarischen Harmonielehre."

Gerson, J e a n C h a r l i e r de, b. Dec. 14, 1363, at Gerson, near Rethel, chancellor of the Paris University, d. July 12, 1429, Lyons ; a learned theologian (*Doctor christianissimus*), among whose works (1706) are to be found the treatises " De laude musices," " De canticorum originali ratione," and " Disciplina puerorum."

Gerster, E t e l k a (Frau Gardini G.), distinguished stage vocalist (high soprano), b. 1855, Kaschau (Hungary), studied under Frau Marchesi at the Vienna Conservatorium (1874–75), made her *début* at Venice in 1876 as Gilda (*Rigoletto*) and Ophelia (*Hamlet*), and then appeared at Marseilles, Genoa, Berlin (at Kroll's.

1877), London, etc. In 1877 she married her impresario Gardini, who then accompanied her on her tours (1878, 1883, and 1887 in America, etc.).

Gervasoni, C a r l o, b. Nov. 4, 1762, Milan, d. there June 4, 1819; he was for many years church musical director at Borgo Taro, member of the Italian Academy of Sciences and Arts. He published the theoretical works, "Scuola della musica" (general Method of music, 1800), "Corteggio musicale" (letters concerning the former work, 1804), "Nuova teoria di musica ricercata dall' odierna pratica" (1812).

Gervinus, G e o r g G o t t f r i e d, the celebrated *littérateur* and historian, b. May 20, 1805, Darmstadt, d. March 18, 1871, as professor at Heidelberg He was a warm admirer of Handel, and was of material assistance in the erection of the Handel memorial at Halle, and in the establishment of the Handel Society at Leipzig. From his enthusiasm for the great masters sprang the work "Händel und Shakespeare. Zur Ästhetik der Tonkunst " (1868). His widow, V i c t o r i a, published a selection of songs from operas and oratorios of Handel, as "Naturgemässe Ausbildung in Gesang u. Klavierspiel " (1892).

Ges (Ger., "g flat"), G lowered by a flat; G *flat major* chord $=g$ *flat, b flat, d flat*; G *flat minor* chord $=g$ *flat, b double-flat, d flat*; G *flat major* key with signature of six flats; G *flat minor* key with signature of five flats and two double-flats. (*See* KEY.)

Gesangbuch (Ger.), a song-book, a hymn-book.

Gesangsgruppe (Ger.), the second subject of a first sonata movement.

Gesangverein (Ger.), a choral society.

Geschlecht (Ger.), genus.

Geschleift (Ger.), slurred.

Gesellschaft für Musikforschung (Society for the Investigation of Music), founded in Berlin in 1868 by Franz Commer (president), and Rob. Eitner (secretary). It has won specially great merit by researches in connection with music of the 15th–17th centuries. The organ of the society, the *Monatshefte für Musikgeschichte* (edited by Rob. Eitner, and founded 1868), arranged in proper order a mass of biographical material, which proved of much service in the compilation of this Dictionary. The "Publikation älterer praktischer und theoretischer Musikwerke," also edited by Eitner, has brought out new editions of: Joh. Otts' 115 Lieder of 1544; Virdung's "Musica getutscht" (1511); Pretorius' "Syntagma musicum," two vols. (1519); H. L. Hassler's "Lustgarten" (1601); Oglin's "Liederbuch " of 1512; selected songs of Heinrich Finck, and Hermann Finck; Joh. Walter's "Wittenbergisch Gesangbuch" (1524); selected compositions of Josquin de Près; a

series of old operas (Caccini's *Euridice*, Gagliano's *Dafne*, Monteverde's *Orfeo*, Cavalli's *Giasone*, Cesti's *Dori*, Lully's *Armide*, and Scarlatti's *Rosaura*). The *Monatshefte* have given translations of Guido's " Micrologus," Hucbald's " Musica Enchiriadis," etc., and reprints of Arnold Schlick's " Spiegel der Orgelmacher und Organisten "(1511), and "Orgel-und Lauten tabulatur" (1512), Staden's "Seelewig" (1644), Prætorius' " Syntagma musicum," two vols., (1618), etc.

Gesius (really Göss), B a r t h o l o m ä u s, b. about 1555, Müncheberg, near Frankfort-on-Oder (his father d. 1557); he studied theology, and, from about 1595 to 1613 (in which year he died), was cantor at Frankfort-on-Oder. (*Cf. Monatsh. M.-G.*, XVI., 105). G. was an esteemed composer and theorist. He published: " The Passion of St. John," à 2–5 (1588); "Teutsche geistliche Lieder " (à 4, 1594); "Hymni 5 vocum" (1595); "Hymni scholastici" (1597, 2nd augmented ed. as "Melodiæ scholasticæ," 1609) ; " Psalmus C." (1603); " Enchiridium etlicher deutscher und lateinischer Gesengen," etc. (à 4, 1603); 108th Psalm à 10 (1606); 90th Psalm, à 5 (1607); " Melodiæ 5 voc." (1598); " Psalmodia choralis" (1600); " Geistliche deutsche Lieder Dr. Lutheri und andrer frommer Christen " (à 4, 1601 [1607, 1608, 1616]; two parts [in two vols.] 1605); "Hymni patrum cum cantu" (1603); "Christliche Musica " (songs of supplication, 1605); " Christliche Choral- und Figuralgesänge" (1611); " Cantiones ecclesiasticæ" (two parts, 1613); " Cantiones nuptiales 5, 6, **7** et plurium vocum " (1614); " Motettæ latino-germanicæ" (1615); " Fasciculus etlicher deutscher und lateinischer Motetten auf Hochzeiten und Ehrentage" (à 4–8, 1616); "Missæ 5, 6, et plurium vocum "(1621) ; " Vierstimmiges Handbüchlein " (1621); " Teutsche und lateinische Hochzeitsgesänge " (à 5–8, and even more parts, 1624). His once widely known theoretical compendium bears the title, " Synopsis musicæ practicæ " (1609 [1615, 1618]).

Gesualdo, D o n C a r l o, Prince of Venosa, one of the most intelligent musicians of the time of the " Nuove musiche," of the time of the pains of labour which preceded the birth of modern music. He was a man superior to the pig-tail theories of his age, and one who moved in a rich sphere of harmony of which the preceding age had no presentiment. There was no place for it in the then prevailing Church Modes, nor even in the major and minor tonality of the succeeding period; only in modern free tonality can it find full expression. G. belongs to the so-called " Chromatists " (*cf.* RORE, BANCHIERI, VICENTINO), and came to his new ideas by way of antiquity; for he wished to revive the chromatic and enharmonic genera of the Greeks. His compositions which have been preserved are six books of madrigals à 5, of which five books were published in parts in 1585, but all six, in 1613, in score, by Simon Molinara.

Getheilt (Ger.), divided. *Getheilte Violinen*, the same as *violini divisi*.

Getragen (Ger.), lit., "carried." Sustained and well connected. *Sostenuto e legato.*

Gevaërt, François Auguste, most distinguished musical *savant* and composer, b. July 31, 1828, Huysse, near Oudenarde. He was, in 1841, a pupil of the Ghent Conservatoire, and at the age of fifteen, organist of the Jesuits' Church there. In 1847 he gained a prize for his Flemish cantata (*Belgie*), and received in the same year the State prize—the *Grand Prix de Rome*—for composition; but, owing to his youth, the compulsory residence for three years abroad for the purpose of study was deferred until 1849, and this was done with consent of the Government. During this period, however, he composed diligently (operas, *Hugues de Somerghen* and *La Comédie à la ville :* the first produced with moderate, the latter with greater, success at Brussels). In 1849 he went to Paris, which city he left, in 1850, with a commission to write an opera for the Théâtre Lyrique. He then lived for a year in Spain (*cf.* his "Rapport sur la situation de la musique en Espagne," printed in the reports of the sessions of the Brussels Académie, 1851), and returned, after a short residence in Italy and Germany, to Ghent in the spring of 1852, intending shortly to settle in Paris. The Théâtre Lyrique brought out his one-act comic opera, *Georgette* (1853), his three-act opera, *Le billet de Marguerite* (1854), which was produced on nearly every French stage, and with the best success, also *Les Lavandières de Santarem* (1855). The Opéra Comique produced *Quentin Durward* (1858), *Le Diable au moulin* (1859), *Le Château-trompette* (1860), *La Poularde de Caux* (1861, jointly with Bazille, Clapisson, Gautier, Mangeant, and Poise), and *Le capitaine Henriot* (1864), finally *Les deux Amours* (1861) at the Baden-Baden Theatre. A work offered to the Grand Opéra was not accepted, although G. became director of music there in 1867. He turned his attention, however, more and more to the study of the history of music and of theory. He has published : "Leerboek van den Gregoriaenschen zang" (1856), "Traité d'instrumentation" (1863), completely revised and augmented as "Nouveau traité de l'instrumentation," Paris, 1885, German by H. Riemann, Leipzig, 1887 (a work which will soon take the place of that of Berlioz). The first half of the second part—"Orchestration"—appeared in 1890, "Les Origines du chant liturgique" (1890; German by H. Riemann; a complete revolution of the traditions respecting the merits of Gregory in the matter of Church Song); "Les Gloires de l'Italie" (a collection of songs from operas, cantatas, etc, by composers of the 17th and 18th centuries, with pianoforte accompaniment, 1868) ; "Chansons du XV. siècle"

(in modern notation, 1875) ; "Vade-mecum de l'organiste ; " "Transcriptions classiques pour petit orchestre ; " also separate articles in papers (attack on Fétis's system of harmony in the Paris *Revue et Gazette Musicale*). In 1870 the siege of Paris drove G. back to his home. After Fétis's death, in 1871, G. was appointed his successor as director of the Brussels Conservatoire. Since that time his most important work has been "Histoire et théorie de la musique de l'antiquité" (1875–81, vols. 1 and 2), in which he adopts the views of Westphal concerning polyphony in Greek music. As a composer G. occupies a distinguished position in his native country. Besides the works already named may still be mentioned : "Super flumina Babylonis," for male chorus and orchestra ; "Fantasia sobre motivos españoles," for orchestra ; "Missa pro defunctis," for male chorus and orchestra ; the festival cantata, *De nationale verjaerdag* (1857) ; cantatas : *Le Retour de l'armée* (1859 ; produced at the Grand Opéra, Paris) and *Jacques van Artevelde ;* ballads (*Philipp van Artevelde*), songs, part-songs, etc.

Gewandhaus Concerts at Leipzig, so called because the old concert-hall was situated in the former "Gewandhaus." They have existed in their present form since 1781. They were established by the burgomaster, K. W. Müller, who first appointed a board of directors selected from the members. A series of twenty-four concerts was started and entrusted to the direction of Joh. Ad. Hiller. At present the number of concerts (including two benefit ones) is twenty-two, taking place every Thursday evening from the beginning of October to the end of March. The conductors, up to the present, have been : J. A. Hiller, J. G. Schicht, J. P. C. Schulz, C. A. Pohlenz, Mendelssohn, Ferd. Hiller, Gade, Rietz, Reinecke, Nikisch. (*Cf.* these names.) Already, from 1743 to 1756, Doles had held subscription concerts in the "Drei Schwanen am Brühl," and J. A. Hiller from 1763–78 in the "Königshaus" ("Liebhaberkonzerte"). These undertakings can be looked upon as forerunners of the G.C. On the occasion of the hundredth anniversary of the foundation of the G. C. (1881), Alfr. Dörffel wrote a festival pamphlet (with chronicle of events), and in 1893 appeared "Die hundertfünfzigjährige Geschichte der Gewandhausconcerte," from the pen of Dr. Emil Kneschke. A magnificent new building —the "Neues Gewandhaus"—was inaugurated Dec. 11–13, 1884.

Geyer, Flodoard, b. March 1, 1811, Berlin, d. there April 30, 1872. At first he studied theology, then composition under Marx, founded in 1842 and conducted the male choral union of the University, was one of the original founders of the Berlin "Tonkünstlerverein," and was held in high esteem as a teacher of music and as musical critic (of the *Spenersche Zeitung, Neue Berliner Musikzeitung,* and the

Deutscher Reichsanzeiger). In 1851 he was appointed teacher of theory at the Kullak-Stern Conservatorium, and remained with Stern, after Kullak's withdrawal, until 1866. In 1856 he received the title of professor. He published a "Compositionslehre" (first part, 1862). G. composed several operas, a lyrical melodrama —*Maria Stuart* (alto solo, chorus, and orchestra), symphonies, symphoniettas, sacred and chamber-music, songs, etc.; but most remained in manuscript (catalogue in the Berlin musical paper, *Echo*, 1872, 23-24).

Gheyn, Matthias van den, b. April 7, 1721, Tirlemont (Brabant), d. June 22, 1785, Louvain. He was for many years organist of St. Peter's Church, and town carilloneur at Louvain. He published: "Fondements de la basse continue" (two lessons and twelve small sonatas for organ or clavier with violin, the latter also in separate form), and six Divertissements for clavier (*c.* 1760), also pieces for organ and carillon (Glockenspiel), while many other works remained in manuscript. G. was most famous in Belgium both as organist and carillon-player. (*Cf.* ELEWYCK.)

Ghiribizzo (Ital.), whim, fancy, humour. *Ghiribizzi* is the plural form of the word.

Ghiribizzoso (Ital.), whimsical, capricious, fantastical.

Ghiselin (Ghiseling, Ghiselinus), Jean, Netherland contrapuntist (15th to 16th century). Van der Straeten supposes him to be identical with Verbonnet; in any case, he was not Ghiseling Dankers. Petrucci printed five masses of his in the "Missæ diversorum" (1503), and five motets in the fourth volume of the "Motetti della corona" (1505). Glarean (Dod. 218) quotes a composition of G. as an instance of joining together bars of various kinds of time.

Ghislanzoni, Antonio, b. Nov. 25, 1824, Lecco, d. July 16, 1893, Caprino Bergamasco, was first an opera singer (baritone), but afterwards devoted himself to literary pursuits; he edited the Milan *Gazetta Musicale*, and wrote a series of excellent opera libretti (Verdi's *Aïda*, Ponchielli's *Lituani*, etc.), also novels, etc.

Ghizeghem. (*See* HEYNE.)

Ghizzolo, Giovanni, Franciscan monk, native of Brescia, cathedral maestro at Ravenna, Milan, and Venice, published: two books of madrigals à 5 (1608 and 1619), four books of motets à 4, three books of canzonets à 3, vesperpsalms à 8 (1609), vespers à 4 and a mass, concerti à 4 (1611), psalms à 5 with bass (1618), mass, psalms, litanies, fauxbourdons, etc., à 5-9 (1619), a mass à 5, complines, and antiphons (1619), psalms à 4, masses, and fauxbourdons (1624), and complines à 5, antiphons, and litanies.

Ghymers, Jules Eugène, b. May 16, 1835, Liége, studied under Ledent (pianoforte) and Daussoigne-Méhul (composition) at the Liége

Conservatoire. He is an excellent musician and teacher, professor of the pianoforte at Liége Conservatoire, musical critic of the *Gazette de Liége*, and for many years was contributor to the *Guide Musical*. Pianoforte works and a "Geschichte des Klaviers" remain in manuscript

Ghys, Joseph, violin-virtuoso, b. 1801, Ghent, d. Aug. 22, 1848, Petersburg. He studied under Lafont, lived as teacher of the violin at Amiens and Nantes, made concert tours in France (1832, and later), Belgium (1835), Germany and Austria (1837), and died while on a grand concert tour through Northern Europe. He wrote violin variations with pianoforte or orchestral accompaniment; étude, "L'orage," for violin alone; caprice, "Le mouvement perpétuel," with stringed quartet; solo pieces, violin concerto (in D), romances, etc.

Giacche, Giachetto. (*See* BERCHEM and BUUS.)

Giacomelli, Geminiano, b. 1686, Parma, d. there Jan. 19, 1743; ducal musical director. After his opera *Ipermnestra* had been favourably received at Parma (1704), he still studied, at the duke's expense, under Scarlatti at Naples, and afterwards became one of the most popular operatic composers of Italy. He was capellmeister for several years at the Imperial court, Vienna, and then wrote again for Naples, Venice, and Turin. *Cesare in Egitto* (1735, Turin) was looked upon as his best work. He also wrote some concert arias with continuo, and the 8th Psalm for two tenors and bass.

Gianelli, Abbate Pietro, b. about 1770, Friaul, lived at Venice, and died probably in 1822. He wrote: "Dizionario della musica sacra e profana, etc." (1801, three vols.; 2nd ed. 1820), the oldest Italian musical dictionary (also biography); and besides, "Grammatica ragionata della musica" (1801; 2nd ed. 1820), and "Biografia degli uomini illustri della musica" (with portraits; only one number, 1822).

Gianettini (Zanettini), Antonio, b. 1649, Venice, d. end of Aug., 1721, Modena, as court maestro. He wrote several operas for Venice, Bologna, and Modena, of which *Medea* and *Hermione* were also given in German at Hamburg (1695). The opera *La schiava fortunata*, ascribed to him, was composed by Cesti and P. A. Ziani. Several oratorios (among others, *La morte di Cristo*, Vienna, 1704) and cantatas of G. have been preserved in manuscript; psalms à 4 with instrumental accompaniment appeared in 1717.

Gianotti, Pietro, b. Lucca, double-bass player at the Grand Opéra, Paris, d. June 19, 1765; he wrote violin sonatas, duos, trios, 'cello sonatas, duos for musettes or vielles, etc.; likewise a "Guide du compositeur" (1759), a theory of fundamental bass on Rameau's system.

Giardini, Felice de, eminent violinist and

composer for his instrument, b. 1716, Turin, d. Dec. 17, 1796, Moscow. He studied under Paladini at Milan (harpsichord, singing, composition) and Somis at Turin (violin), became a member of opera orchestras at Rome, and, later on, of San Carlo, Naples. A box on the ear from Jomelli cured him of his habit of interpolating ornaments in his part. About 1750 he settled in London, where he met with a brilliant reception, and was master of the situation until the arrival of the violinists Salomon and Cramer; he also played with great success at Paris in 1748–49. Brilliancy and absolute purity of intonation were the characteristic features of his playing. In 1752 he succeeded Festing as leader at the London Italian Opera, and in 1756 he undertook the management himself; and, although he suffered great losses, he undertook the management again from 1763 to 1765, but after that he devoted his attention to playing, and acted as leader at the Pantheon concerts and at the Italian Opera. In 1784 he went to Italy, but returned to London in 1790, when he started comic opera at the Haymarket; but he met with no success, and went with his company to Moscow, where he died. Besides five operas (1756–64, London), which were only moderately successful, G. wrote an oratorio, *Ruth*, solos for violin, duets, stringed trios, twelve stringed quartets, six pf. quintets, six violin sonatas (with pianoforte), and eleven violin concertos.

Gibbons, (1) E d w a r d, b. about 1570, Cambridge, took the degree of Mus.Bac. there, and at Oxford; organist of Bristol Cathedral, afterwards at Exeter. When an old man over eighty, he was banished by Cromwell for assisting Charles I. with £1,000. Manuscripts of his compositions have been preserved at Oxford and at the British Museum.

(2) O r l a n d o, one of the most important of English composers, brother of the former, b. 1583, Cambridge, d. June 5, 1625; became in 1604 organist of the Chapel Royal. He accumulated the degrees of Mus.Bac. and Dr.Mus. in 1622, at Oxford; in 1623 he was organist at Westminster Abbey. He died of the smallpox at Canterbury, whither he had gone to conduct his festival composition for the marriage of Charles I. His printed works are: "Fantasies" à 3 for viols (1610, the oldest engraved musical work in England; *cf.* VEROVIO); pieces for the Virginal in the "Parthenia" collection (1611, jointly with Byrd and Blow; both works were reprinted by the Musical Antiquarian Society from 1843–44); madrigals and motets à 5 (1612), church compositions (anthems, hymns, preces, services, etc.) in Leighton's "Teares or Lamentations of a Sorrowfull Soule" (1614), in Wither's "Hymns and Songs of the Church," Barnard's "Church Music" and Boyce's "Cathedral Music." Ouseley published others, which had been preserved in manuscript (1873); a selection of pieces for piano solo appeared in Augener's Edition.

(3) His son C h r i s t o p h e r, b. 1615, London, d. Oct. 20, 1676. He was organist in 1640 at Winchester, in 1644 joined the army of the Royalists; he became, in 1660, organist of the Chapel Royal, private organist to Charles II. and organist of Westminster Abbey; and in 1664 Dr.Mus., Oxford, by royal command. Only a few of his motets exist in manuscript, and in Dering's and Playford's "Cantica sacra" (1674).

Gibel (Gibelius), O t t o, b. 1612, on Femern Island, was taken, when quite young, by his relations to Brunswick to escape the plague, and there he received musical training from H. Grimm. In 1634 he became cantor at Stadthagen (Lippe), and in 1642 at Minden, where he died, in 1682, as school rector. He wrote: "Seminarium modulatoriæ vocalis, das ist ein Pflanz-Garten der Singkunst" (1645, 1657), "Kurtzer jedoch gründlicher Bericht von den vocibus musicalibus (1659, Solmisation and Bobisation), "Introductio musicæ theoriæ didacticæ" (1660), "Propositiones mathematicomusicæ" (1666), "Geistliche Harmonien von 1–5 Stimmen teils ohne teils mit Instrumenten" (1671).

Gibellini, E l i s e o, b. about 1520, Osimo (Ancona), maestro at Ancona until 1581. He published at Venice (Scotto & Gardano) "Motetta super plano cantu" à 5 (1546), other motets à 5 (1548), madrigals à 3 (1552), "Introitus missarum de festis" à 5 (1565), madrigals à 5 (1581).

Gibert, (1) P a u l C é s a r, b. 1717, Versailles, received his musical training at Naples, lived as a teacher of music in Paris, where he died in 1787. He published: "Solfèges ou leçons de musique" (1783) and "Mélange musical" (various vocal pieces, duets, terzets, etc.). He also wrote several operas.

(2) F r a n c i s c o X a v i e r (Gisbert, Gispert), Spanish priest, born at Granadella, in 1800 maestro at Taracena, in 1804 at Madrid, where he died Feb. 27, 1848. He was held in high esteem as composer of sacred music.

Gide, C a s i m i r, b. July 4, 1804, Paris, d. there Feb. 18, 1868, son of a bookseller, and from 1847 partner in his father's business. He wrote, and not without success, a series of operas: *Le roi de Sicile* (1830), *Les trois Cathérine*, *Les jumeaux de La Réole*, *L'Angelus*, *Belphégor* (1858), *Françoise de Rimini* (not produced), and seven ballets.

Giga. (*See* GIGUE.)

Gigelira (Ital.), a Xylophone, or *Strohfiedel* (q.v.).

Gigue, Giga, (1) originally a French nickname for the older form of the viols (Vielle, Fiedel), which was not unlike a ham (*gigue*), to distinguish it from the more modern flat one with carved-out sides. The name first appears in Johannes de Garlandia's dictionary (1210–32).

In Germany the older form remained for a long time the favourite one ; already the troubadour Adenès (" Romans di Cléomadès ") speaks of the *gigéours d'Allemagne* (German fiddlers). In Germany itself the term G. (*Geige*) afterwards came into general use ; the word *giga* appears also in Middle High German at the beginning of the 13th century together with Fidel, but it is not of German origin.—(2) An old dance form in triple time ($\frac{3}{8}$ $\frac{3}{4}$, or in compound time, $\frac{6}{8}$, $\frac{6}{4}$, $\frac{9}{8}$, $\frac{9}{4}$, $\frac{12}{8}$, $\frac{12}{16}$, etc.) ; it appears quite exceptionally, and irregularly, in $\frac{4}{4}$ time (several examples in Bach). As real dance music, the G. consisted of two repeated sections of eight bars ; in suites (partitas), however, these were of much greater extent.

Gil, (1) (y Llagostera) C a y t a n, b. Jan. 6, 1807, Barcelona, principal flautist at the theatre and cathedral there. He composed many works for flute; also symphonies, masses, a requiem, dances for orchestra, etc.

(2) F r a n c i s c o A s s i s, b. 1829, Cadiz, professor of harmony at the Madrid Conservatorio : he studied at Paris with Fétis, whose harmony Method he translated into Spanish (1850), and he himself wrote a " Tratado elemental teorico-pratico de armonia " (1856). He also produced some operas at Madrid, and from 1855–56 was a contributor to Eslava's *Gaceta musical de Madrid*.

Gilchrist, W. W., American composer, b. Jan. 18, 1846, Jersey City (New Jersey), studied with H. A. Clark at Philadelphia, where he lives as organist of Christ Church and conductor of several choral societies. Few of his compositions have been printed, but his choral works have received prizes from societies at New York and Philadelphia; and a prize was awarded to him by the Cincinnati Musical Festival Commission in 1882 for his setting of the 46th Psalm.

Giles, N a t h a n i e l, b. Worcester, d. Jan. 24, 1633, was chorister of Magdalen College, Oxford in 1559, graduated as Bachelor of Music in 1585, became organist and choir-master of St. George's Chapel, Windsor, in 1597, succeeded Hunnis as master of the children of the Chapel Royal ; he became Doctor of Music in 1622. Some of his pieces are to be found in Leighton's " Teares, etc.," Barnard's " Church Music," and in Hawkins' " History of Music." Some of his anthems have been preserved in manuscript.

Gilles (Maitre G., " Masegiles," really Gilles Brebos), famous Netherland organ-builder of the 16th century at Louvain and Antwerp, d. June 6, 1584. G. built, among others, four organs for the two choirs of the Escurial.

Gillet, E r n s t, b. Sept. 13, 1856, Paris, a pupil of Niedermeyer, and also of the Paris Conservatoire. He was afterwards solo 'cellist at the Grand Opéra there. G. now lives in London. He is a composer of *salon* music (" Loin du bal," etc.).

Gillmore, P a t r i c k S a r s f i e l d, a popular American conductor, especially of wind bands, b. Dec. 25, 1829, near Dublin. He went first to Canada, and from there to the United States. He became widely known through his organisation of the Monster Musical Festivals at Boston in 1869 (orchestra 1,000, choir 10,000), and in 1872 (orchestra 2,000, choir 20,000). He undertakes tours with his band, even to Europe.

Gilson, P a u l, b. 1869, Brussels, was self-taught, but won, nevertheless, the first prize for composition (*Prix de Rome*) with his cantata *Sinaï* (1892). Since then he has attracted notice by other works (septet and scherzo for wind instruments, symphonic sketches " La Mer," 1892).

Ginguené, P i e r r e L o u i s, well-known historian of literature, b. April 25, 1748, Rennes, d. Nov. 16, 1816, Paris, as academician, chief of a department in the Ministry of the Interior, etc. He wrote on subjects relating to music : "Lettres et articles sur la musique " (1783, a collection of his articles contributed to various papers from 1780 to 1783 in the Piccini-Gluck war) ; " Dictionnaire de musique de l'Encyclopédie méthodique " (one vol., 1791, jointly with Framery ; Framery wrote the second volume by himself, 1818) ; " Notice sur la vie et les ouvrages de Piccini" (1800) ; " Rapport . . . sur une nouvelle exposition de la notation musicale des Grecs " (1815). Also his great " Histoire littéraire de l'Italie " (1811–35, fourteen vols. ; completed by Salfi), contains much that is interesting (on Guido, the Troubadours, etc.) in connection with the history of music.

Giochevole (Ital.), playful, merry.

Giocondamente (Ital.), playfully, joyously.

Giocondo (Ital.), playful, joyous, gay.

Giocoso (Ital.), jocose, merry.

Gioja (Ital.), joy, mirth, delight.

Giojante (Ital.), mirthful.

Giojoso (Ital.), humorous, mirthful.

Giordani, (1) T o m m a s o, b. *c.* 1740, Naples (his real family name was Carmine). He appeared in 1762 at the Haymarket Theatre as a buffo singer, and then settled in London as a teacher of music. In 1779 he undertook, together with Leoni, the management of an Italian Opera company at Dublin, and, on its failure, remained in Dublin as teacher, where he was still living in 1816. He composed an opera, *Perseverance ;* an oratorio, *Isaac ;* five books of flute duos, trios for flutes and bass, 'cello duos, pf. pieces, and songs.

(2) G i u s e p p e, named G i o r d a n i e l l o, b. 1744, Naples, d. Jan. 4, 1798, Fermo, wrote many (in all twenty-nine) operas (also two oratorios) for Pisa, London, Rome, Venice, Milan,

Mantua, Genoa, Bergamo, Turin up to 1793, and died as maestro of Fermo Cathedral, whither he had been called in 1791. G. published six pf. quintets, three pf. quartets, thirty trios, six stringed quartets, six violin concertos, pf. sonatas for two and four hands, preludes, exercises, soprano duets, five books of canzonets for one voice. A great deal of other music, mostly sacred, remained in manuscript.

Giornovichi. (*See* JARNOVIC.)

Giosa, Nicola de, b. May 5, 1820, Bari, d. there July 7, 1885. He studied under Ruggi, Zingarelli, and Donizetti at Naples, was a prolific composer of Italian operas; but of his twenty-four operas only *Don Checco* (1850, Naples) met with any real success. G. was more fortunate with songs of a popular character (romances, canzonets, etc.); his sacred works remained in manuscript. G. was for a time maestro of the San Carlo theatre, Naples, of the Fenice Theatre, Venice, and of the Italian theatres at Buenos Ayres, Cairo, etc.

Giovanelli, Ruggiero, b. about 1560, Velletri; in 1587 maestro of San Luigi de' Francesci, Rome, afterwards of the German Collegiate Church, in 1594 successor of Palestrina as maestro of St. Peter's, in 1599 Papal chapel-singer. He was still living in 1615. G. is one of the best masters of the Roman School. Of his works are preserved: three books of madrigals à 5 (1586, 1587 [1607], 1589 [1599]); two books of " Madrigali sdruccioli " à 4 (1587); two books of motets à 5–8 ([1594] 1592); canzonets à 3 with arrangement for lute (1592); villanelle à 3 (1593 [1624]). Many of his sacred works are preserved in manuscript in the Archives of the Vatican (masses, psalms, motets). Madrigals are still to be found in collections by Gier. Scotto, and Pierre Phalèse from 1585–1614. G. prepared, by command of Pope Paul V., a new revised edition of Graduals (1614–15, two vols.).

Gioviale (Ital.), jovial, pleasant.

Gique, gigue.

Giraffe (Ger.) is the name for the old upright pianofortes (*Flügel*), of which specimens are still to be found here and there; the strings ran in a vertical direction, as in the clavicytherium and the pianino of the present day.

Girard, Narcisse, b. Jan. 27, 1797, Mantes, d. Jan. 16, 1860. He was a pupil of Baillot's at the Paris Conservatoire; from 1830–32 maître de chapelle at the Opéra Italien, in 1837, in the same capacity, at the Opéra Comique, and in 1846 at the Grand Opéra as Habeneck's successor, in 1847 violin professor at the Conservatoire, and conductor of the concerts there; and in 1856 general musical director at the Grand Opéra. He died of a stroke of apoplexy whilst conducting the *Huguenots*.

Giro (Ital.), turn.

Gisis (Ger., " G double sharp "), G doubly raised by a ×.

Giubilio, Giubilo, or **Giubilazione** (Ital.), jubilation, rejoicing.

Giubiloso (Ital.), jubilant.

Giuocante (Ital.), playful.

Giuochevole (Ital.), playful, gay, merry.

Giusto (Ital.), exact, precise; *allegro g.*, the same as *allegro assai* (a decided *allegro*).

Gizziello. (*See* CONTI, 3.)

Gladstone, Dr. Francis Edward, excellent organist, b. March 2, 1845, Summertown, near Oxford, pupil of Wesley; he has held posts as organist at Weston-super-Mare, Llandaff, Chichester, Brighton, Norwich, and London (Christ Church, 1881–86). He was then received into the Catholic Church, and became director of the choir of St. Mary of the Angels, Bayswater (London). In 1876 and in 1879 he took his degrees of Mus.Bac. and Doc.Mus.; and he is an honorary member of the Royal Academy of Music. G. is also a diligent church composer.

Glarean, really Heinrich Loris (Henricus Loritus), of Glarus, b. 1488, d. March 28, 1563 He attended the Latin School at Berne, studied theology at Cologne, and music under Cochläus. In 1512 he was crowned *poetà laureatus* by the Emperor Maximilian I., in that city, opened in 1517 a training institute at Paris, but, already in 1518, settled in Basle, where he gave lectures until 1529; owing, however, to the outbreak of the religious agitation, in which he was careful not to take part, he went to Freiburg-i.-Br. There he lectured on history and literature, living at last, embittered by many a misfortune, in complete retirement. G. was a man of general culture and great learning, was a friend of Erasmus of Rotterdam, of Justus Lipsius, and other *savants ;* and he was an especially famous authority on the theory of music. His earliest work was, " Isagoge in musicen " (1516, a small compendium); his chief work, " Δωδεκαχορδον " (1547, a treatise on the old eight Church Modes, showing that there ought to be twelve; a development of the system of measured music, with many very interesting illustrations of the complicated contrapuntal formations of the 15th and 16th centuries, from the works of the most important masters). Joh. Ludwig Wonegger published an epitome of it: " Musicæ epitome ex Glareani Dodekachordo " (1557, 2nd ed., 1559; Ger. " Uss Glareani Musik ein Usszug zc," 1557). Martianus Rota published (1570), after G.'s death (with a commentary by Marmelius and R. Agricola), his carefully revised edition of the complete works of Boëtius. H. Schreiber (Freiburg-i.-Br., 1837) and O. F. Fritsche (Frauenfeld, 1890) wrote biographies of G.

Glasenapp, Karl Friedrich, b. Oct. 3, 1847, Riga, studied philology at Dorpat, and has lived since 1875 as head-master at Riga. He wrote: "Richard Wagner's Leben und Wirken" (two vols., 2nd ed., 1882). G. is a zealous Wagnerian, and is also a contributor to the *Bayreuther Blätter*.

Gläser, (1) Karl Gotthelf, b. May 4, 1784, Weissenfels, d. April 16, 1829, Bremen, attended St. Thomas's School, Leipzig, was trained by J. A. Hiller, A. E. Müller, and Campagnoli, became musical director in 1814, and afterwards, music-publisher at Barmen. He published pf. works, chorales, school song-books, also : " Neue praktische Klavierschule" (1817) ; " Kurze Anweisung zum Choralspiel" (1824) ; " Vereinfachter und kurz gefasster Unterricht in der Theorie der Tonsetzkunst mittels eines musikalischen Kompasses" (1828).

(2) Franz, b. April 19, 1799, Obergeorgenthal (Bohemia), d. Aug. 29, 1861, Copenhagen. He studied the violin under Pixis at the Prague Conservatorium, became capellmeister in 1817 at the " Josephstadt Theater," Vienna, in 1830 at the " Königsstädtisches Theater," Berlin, and from 1842 was capellmeister at Copenhagen. Of his numerous works (operas, vaudevilles, farces, incidental music to plays, notturnos, etc.) only the opera *Des Adlers Horst* (Berlin, 1832) met with any success, and it made the round of the German theatres.

Glasharmonica, formerly named simply " Harmonica," was an instrument from which sounds were produced by glass bells, rods, or tubes thrown into vibration by rubbing. The G. of Franklin (1763) became widely known. All the glass bells were fastened to a common axis set in motion by a treadle. This G. was played on by touching with the fingers the glasses previously moistened. Dussek was a celebrated performer on the G. A keyboard was also fitted to it (Hessel, Wagner, Röllig, Klein), and then the instrument was called " Klavierharmonika." Chladni's " Euphon " and " Klavicylinder," as well as Quandt's " Harmonika," are varied forms of the G. (*Cf.* C. F. Pohl, " Zur Geschichte der Glasharmonika," Vienna, 1862.)

Gleason, Frederic Grant, b. Dec. 17, 1848, Middletown (Connecticut), studied at Leipzig and Berlin. G. is esteemed in America as the composer of several romantic operas, also of orchestral and chamber music. He lives at Chicago.

Glee, a form of composition peculiar to England, for at least three (solo) voices (usually those of men), *a cappella*. The name G. does not come from the English *glee* (*i.e.* joy), but from the Anglo-Saxon *gligg* = music. The style of the G. is not contrapuntal, but it has sharply-marked cadences, and the writing is frequently plain note against note. Arne and Boyce wrote the first glees. S. Webb (d. 1816) was the greatest master in this particular branch of art, and it was also cultivated by Attwood, Battishill,

Callcott, Cooke, Horsley, Mornington. From 1787 to 1857 there existed in London a Glee Club similar in organisation to the Catch Club (*Cf.* Catch.)

Gleich (Ger.), equal.—*Gleicher Contrapunkt* " equal counterpoint "—*i.e.* note against note.

Gleich, Ferdinand, b. Dec. 17, 1816, Erfurt studied philology at Leipzig, and music under Fink. He was for some time private tutor in Courland, and, after long journeys, lived in Leipzig, went in 1864 as theatre secretary to Prague, and in 1866 established a theatre-bureau in Dresden. G. has offered only wares of a light character : " Wegweiser für Opernfreunde" (1857) ; " Handbuch der modernen Instrumentierung für Orchester u. Militärmusikkorps " (1860, several times reprinted) ; " Die Hauptformen der Musik, populär dargestellt " (1862) " Characterbilder aus der neuern Geschichte der Tonkunst " (1863) ; " Aus der Bühnenwelt ' (1866).

Gleichmann, Johann Georg, b. Dec. 22 1685, Steltzen, near Eisfeld ; in 1706 organist at Schalkau, near Coburg, in 1717 teacher and organist at Ilmenau, where he died in 1770 as burgomaster. He occupied himself with the construction of instruments, improved the " Geigenwerk " (" Bogenklavier "), and constructed " Lautenklavicimbals."

Gleichschwebende Temperatur (Ger.), equa temperament. (*See* Temperament.)

Gleissner, Franz, b. 1760, Neustadt on the Waldnab, composed numerous instrumenta works, also some operas ; but he is better known through having introduced lithography into music-printing. For Breitkopf, at Leipzig who had entered into business relations with Senefelder, the inventor, printed only the titles of pieces by lithography, but G., on the other hand, in partnership with Falter at Munich, the music itself. The first musical work which was lithographed was a set of songs by G. (1798) In 1799 he established, for Joh. Anton André, of Offenbach, a large lithographic printing-establishment, travelled afterwards to Vienna to make known his invention, and finally went to Munich, where he was still living in 1815.

Glinka, Michail Iwanowitsch, b. June 1, 1803, Nowospask, near Selna (Smolensk), d. Feb. 15, 1857, Berlin. He entered, in 1817 an institution for the nobility at Petersburg, where he devoted himself especially to the study of languages, and frequently distinguished himself. Then he began serious musical study under Böhm (violin) and Charles Mayer (pianoforte and theory). A set of pf. variations on an Italian theme was his first printed work (1825). For the sake of his health he travelled in 1829 to the Caucasus, but with such bad result, that, in 1830, he was forced to seek the milder climate of Italy. For four years he lived in Milan, Rome, and Naples, always in the doctor's hands; but he was diligently composing, and worked so as further to improve himself in theory, by taking lessons of the best Italian masters. The result did not satisfy him, and only in 1834, when, seized with home-sickness, he was wandering back to Russia, did he find a teacher—S. Dehn at Berlin—who understood him and whom he understood. Dehn had recognised his national originality, and encouraged him in the idea of writing "Russian" music. His first attempt was a triumph—the opera, *Life for the Czar* (*Zarskaja skisu*, also as *Iwan Sussanina*), which was first produced in Petersburg on Dec. 9, 1836. The subject was national; the contrast of the Polish and Russian elements was faithfully reflected in his music, while original Russian popular melodies, or reminiscences of such, gave to the whole a thoroughly national colouring. The opera is, up to this day, a favourite piece in the *répertoire* of all Russian theatres. Encouraged by this success, G. at once set to work on the composition of a new opera. Puschkin offered to arrange his fantastic poem, "Ruslan und Ludmilla," into an opera-book; but he unfortunately died in 1837, and G. saw himself left in less capable hands. After many attempts, he at last set to work and made out of the text what there was to be made. On Nov. 27, 1842, the first performance took place, and this was followed in the same season by thirty more. Liszt, who happened to be in Petersburg, was enthusiastically in favour of the work, which still holds a place on the Russian stage. In 1844 G. was compelled, out of consideration for his health, to travel once again southwards. This time he first went to Paris, where Berlioz received him warmly, and, by performances of works of Glinka in the "Cirque," and by an enthusiastic article in the *Journal des Débats*, became a propagandist for the Russian master. From 1845–47 G. lived at Madrid and Seville, where he wrote his "Jota Aragonese" and "Souvenirs d'une nuit d'été à Madrid," the first of which, especially, is well known in Germany. After that, he lived for some time at Warsaw, then again at Petersburg, and undertook in 1851 a second journey to Spain, but was compelled, when at the Pyrenees, to return to Paris; while from 1854–55 he lived in the country, not far from Petersburg, where he wrote his autobiography and formed plans for new opera, which were, however, never to be carried out. For a long time, and in vain, G. sought after a key to the natural harmonisation of Russian national melodies, which he had instinctively discovered, and hastened finally, in 1856, to his old teacher Dehn at Berlin, in order to solve, with his help, the difficult problem. Here he died a year later. His body was taken back to Petersburg. The following have written about G.'s life and works: Serow in the "Theater und Musikboten" (1857), and in his journal "Musik und Theater" (1868);

also Stassoff in "Russischer Bote" (1858); Laroche (ditto, 1867–68); and Solowieff in "Musikalny Listok" (1872). (*Cf.* also C. Cui, "La Musique en Russie" [*Revue et Gazette Musicale de Paris*, 1878–79], and Fouqué, "Étude sur G.") The chronological catalogue of his works contains, besides the works above-named, two unfinished symphonies, some sets of variations, waltzes, rondos for pf., two quartets for strings, a septet, a trio for pf., clarinet, and oboe, many songs (romances), a waltz, and two polonaises for orchestra, tarantella for orchestra with singing and dancing, "La Kamarinskaïa," the Russian National Hymn (words by Schukowski), several dramatic scenas, vocal quartets with accompaniment, etc. G. is the Berlioz of the Russians, the man who attempted something new with definite meaning; but to his countrymen he is still more, namely, the creator of a national musical tendency striving towards independence.

Glissando (Ital.), sliding, also *glissato*, *glissicato*, *glissicando*, indicates—(1) in stringed-instruments, a smooth performance without accentuation (in passages); (2) on the pianoforte, a virtuose effect of little value, viz., a scale passage played on white keys, in rapid *tempo*, by passing one finger (nail side) over them. This was easy on instruments with Viennese action, but is hardly practicable on modern pianos. The G. in 3rds, 6ths, or 8ves is more difficult than that with single notes. New and surprising *glissando*-effects (chromatic *glissando* in one and more parts, in 3rds, 6ths, 8ves, even in chords of the diminished seventh, etc.) are easily executed on P. von Janko's new keyboard ("Terrassen-Klaviatur").

Glissé (Fr.). (*Cf.* GLISSANDO.)

Glöckchen (Ger.), a little bell.

Glocke (Ger.), a bell.

Glockenspiel. (*See* CARILLON and LYRE, 3.)

Glöggl, (1) Franz Xaver, b. Feb. 21, 1764, Linz, theatre capellmeister there, afterwards also proprietor of a music business, and publisher of several short-lived periodicals and writings devoted to music; likewise manager of the theatres at Linz and Salzburg; in 1790 cathedral capellmeister and town musical director at Linz. He lived to celebrate the fiftieth anniversary of his artistic career (1832). G. wrote "Erklärung des musikalischen Hauptzirkels" (1810); "Allgemeines musikalisches Lexikon" (1822, unfinished; only 248 pages); "Der musikalische Gottesdienst" (1822). He left behind in manuscript a collection of drawings and descriptions of musical instruments. His collection of instruments was purchased by the Gesellschaft der Musikfreunde (1824).

(2) Franz, son of the former, b. 1797, Linz, d. Jan. 23, 1872, established a music business in 1843 at Vienna, which he afterwards sold to Bösendorfer, published (1850–62) the *Neue Wiener*

Musikzeitung, was for several years archivist to the Gesellschaft der Musikfreunde, founded in 1849 the Akademie der Tonkunst, which ceased to exist in 1853, likewise, at a later period, a school for singing ("Polyhymnia").

Gloria. (*See* DOXOLOGY.)

Glottis (Gr.), in singing, when a note is produced without any previous breathing (*spiritus lenis*), and with a gentle cracking noise similar to a guttural sound (such as that marked א [Aleph] in Hebrew), the production of tone is termed *coup de la glotte* (blow of the glottis).

Glover, Stephen, popular English drawing-room composer of songs, duets, and pf. pieces of light character, b. 1812, London, d. there Dec. 7, 1870.

Gluck, Christoph Wilibald (afterwards Ritter von), b. July 2, 1714, Weidenwang, near Berching (Middle Franconia), near to the Bohemian border (not March 25, 1700, at Neustadt), d. Nov. 15, 1787, Vienna, son of a gamekeeper of Prince Lobkowitz of Eisenberg. He attended the elementary school at Eisenberg, was chorister, from 1726–32, at the Jesuit church at Komotau, and, as such, was taught singing, clavier, organ, and the violin. He then went to Prague in order to earn a living by singing in churches and fiddling in dancing-rooms. He was trained under the guidance of the Bohemian Czernohorsky, and became an able 'cello player. Encouraged, perhaps, by his father's employer, he ventured in 1736 to Vienna, which even then was an important centre of musical culture. There the Lombardian Prince Melzi, who had heard him play one evening at the house of Prince Lobkowitz, was attracted by his great talent, took him with him to Milan, and placed him under Sammartini for further training; the latter was maestro at Santa Magdalena, and well known as one of the originators of the stringed quartet. After four years' study, G. appeared as an opera composer, first in 1741 with *Artaserse* (Milan); then speedily followed *Ipermnestra* and *Demetrio* (*Cleonice*, Venice, 1742), *Demofoonte* (Milan, 1742), *Artamene* (Cremona, 1743), *Siface* (Milan, 1743), *Alessandro nell' Indie* (= *Poro*) (Turin, 1744), and *Fedra* (Milan, 1744). These works, genuine Italian operas, such as were written by Sacchini, Guglielmi, Jomelli, Piccini, soon made him famous, so that in 1745 he was called to London, in order to write operas for the Haymarket. He produced *La caduta dei Giganti* (1746), revived *Artamene*, and attempted a special *coup* with a pasticcio, *Pivamo et Tisbe*, which he made up from the best arias of his earlier operas; but the experiment was a total failure. The London journey forms a turning-point in his career as a composer; this was in part probably the result of reflection on the fiasco of his pasticcio, partly the consequence of the powerful impression made on him by Handel's music; and also by that of Rameau, with which he became

acquainted about this time in Paris, and which induced him to intensify his style on the side of dramatic expression, and to give to poetry higher rights in connection with music. The complete revolution in his style of writing was a very gradual one, yet there are already some signs of it in his next opera, *La Semiramide riconosciuta*, which he wrote in 1748 for Vienna, whither he had betaken himself to London, and where from 1754–64 he was capellmeister at the court opera. In 1749 he was called to Copenhagen in order to write a small festival opera, *Tetide*. Then followed: *Telemacco* (Rome, 1750), *La clemenza di Tito* (Naples, 1751), *L'eroe cinese* (Vienna, 1755), *Il trionfo di Camillo* and *Antigono* (Rome, 1755), *La Danza* (1755, for court festivities at the Palace of Laxenburg), *L'innocenza giustificata* and *Il re pastore* (Vienna, 1756), *Don Juan* (ballet, Vienna, 1761), *Il trionfo di Clelia* (Bologna, 1762), and a great number of new arias for the re-staging of old operas by other composers at Vienna and Schönbrunn. G. also composed a series of French vaudevilles, so much in vogue about this time in Paris (libretti by Favart, Anseaume, Sedaine, Dancourt), for the court (*Les amours champêtres,* 1755: *Le Chinois poli en France,* 1756; *Le déguisement pastoral,* 1756; *La fausse esclave,* 1758; *L'île de Merlin,* 1758; *L'ivrogne corrigé,* 1760; *Le cadi dupé,* 1761; *On ne s'avise jamais de tout,* 1762; and *La rencontre imprévue,* 1764, in German as *Die Pilgrimme von Mekka*). The year 1762 marks the beginning of a second epoch, the end of years of wandering, of seeking —the attainment to masterhood. G. gave to the world his *Orpheus* (*Orfeo ed Euridice,* Vienna). He found in this year what hitherto he had lacked—viz:, a poet who, like himself, perceived the faults of Italian Opera, and who filled his scenes with action and passion, instead of poetical similes and sentences. This poet was Calsabigi, the creator of the libretti of *Orpheus,* of *Alceste* (Vienna, 1767), and of *Paride ed Elena* (Vienna, 1770). With respect to his aims, G. expressed himself clearly in the two prefaces to the scores of *Alceste* and *Paris and Helena* (published in 1769 and 1770). The less important operas of this epoch have words, and of a feebler kind, by Metastasio (formerly Gluck's principal poet): they were *Ezio* (Vienna, 1763), *Il Parnasso confuso* (Schönbrunn, 1765, for the wedding of Joseph II., performed by members of the imperial family), *La Corona* (1765, likewise performed by the princesses), and 1769 *Intermèdes* for the court of Parma, *Le feste d'Apollo, Bauci e Filemone,* and *Aristeo.* In 1772 G. made in Vienna the acquaintance of the Bailli du Rollet, attaché of the French Embassy, who was enthusiastic for the composer's still bolder ideas of reform, arranged for him, in libretto form, Racine's "Iphigénie," and was the means of his new opera (*Iphigénie en Aulide*), which he had finished in this year, being accepted by the Grand Opéra at Paris; it certainly needed the good offices of the dauphiness, Marie Antoinette, Gluck's former pupil, in order to overcome the violent opposition which at once manifested itself. G. himself (sixty years old) hastened to Paris to conduct the rehearsals; the first performance followed, April 19, 1774, and created an extraordinary stir. Also *Orpheus* and *Alceste* were staged with considerable alterations, and attracted such crowds that, for the first time, tickets were issued for the full rehearsal, which Gluck conducted without surtout and wig, and with his nightcap on his head. Paris was divided into two camps: the admirers of Lully and Rameau were on the side of Gluck, who was also protected by the court; but the great party of the friends of Italian Opera insisted that a libretto, *Roland*, which had been given to G. to set to music, should also be given to Piccini, who, as the composer of sixty operas, had become famous in Italy. G., after he had produced two small, unimportant operas, *Cythère assiégée* and *L'Arbre enchanté* (1775), returned to Vienna and wrote his *Armide*, but was so annoyed at this artifice that he gave up the composition of *Roland* and burnt his sketches. The warfare between the Gluckists (Abbé Arnaud, Suard, etc.) and the Piccinists (Marmontel, La Harpe, Ginguené, d'Alembert) is famous; a number of pamphlets and newspaper articles were published by both parties. (*Cf.* Leblond, " Mémoire pour servir à l'histoire de la révolution opérée dans la musique par M. le chevalier G.," 1781. The supplement to Fétis's " Biographie universelle" under G. gives a catalogue of the different pamphlets, etc.) *Armide* (Sept. 25, 1777) at first met with little success; but, on the other hand, *Iphigénie en Tauride* (May 18, 1779, libretto by Guillard) completely routed the Piccinists. The small impression made by Gluck's last opera, *Écho et Narcisse* (1779), could not diminish his fame. The aged master, warned by a slight stroke of apoplexy of the decrease of his powers, returned, covered with glory, to Vienna in 1780, where he spent his last years in peace; another stroke of apoplexy put an end to his life. Apart from the stage, Gluck wrote only a few works; they are as follows: six symphonies (the older kind, *i.e.* overtures), seven odes of Klopstock, for one voice, with pf.; a " De profundis " for chorus and orchestra, and the 8th Psalm *a cappella*; a cantata, *Das Jüngste Gericht*, remained unfinished (Salieri completed it). *Cf.* A. Schmid, " Chr. W. Ritter von G." (1854); Desnoiresterres, " G. et Piccini" (1872); Siegmeyer, " Über den Ritter G. und seine Werke " (1825); Miel, " Notice sur Christophe G." (1840); Marx, "Gluck und die Oper " (1863), etc. (*Cf. also* OPERA and PICCINI.)

G major chord=*g, b, d*; G *Major key*, signified by one ♯. (*See* KEY.)

G minor chord =*g, b♭, d*; G *minor key*, signified by two flats.

Gnaccare (Ital.), castanets.

Gnecco, F r a n c e s c o, b. 1769, Genoa, d. 1816, Milan, a prolific opera composer, but of little originality; he wrote for Milan, Genoa, Padua, etc., and also had success with the comic opera *La prova d'una opera seria* (Milan, 1805; also under title, *La prova degli Orazzi e Curiazi*).

Gobbaerts, J e a n L o u i s, b. Sept. 28, 1835, Antwerp, d. May 5, 1886, Saint-Gilles, near Brussels, famous pianist, a pupil of the Brussels Conservatoire. Of his compositions for pianoforte, mostly of a light *genre*, there appeared 1,200 numbers, also a piano Method. The greater number of his pieces were published under the pseudonym Streabbog (G. spelt backwards), but others under those of Ludovic and Lévy.

Gobbi, (1) H e n r i, b. June 7, 1842, Pesth, pupil of R. Volkmann and Liszt, published various pf. works of national Hungarian colouring, also male choruses. On the occasion of Liszt's fiftieth anniversary of his public career, G. produced a festival cantata at Pesth, where he lives as teacher of music and musical critic.
    (2) His brother A l o y s, b. Dec. 20, 1844, Pesth, lives there esteemed as violinist.

Göbel, K a r l, b. March 11, 1815, Berlin, d. Oct. 26, 1879, Bromberg, as conductor of the Vocal Union, etc. He was formerly theatre capellmeister in Danzig, wrote several operas (*Chrysalide, Frithjof*), also smaller pieces and a " Kompendium der Klavierlitteratur."

Godard, Benjamin Louis Paul, famous French composer, b. Aug. 18, 1849, Paris, pupil of Reber (composition) and Vieuxtemps (violin) at the Conservatoire; he accompanied the latter twice to Germany, where he met with real encouragement to develop his talent as composer. G. published, first in 1865, a violin sonata, and after that a series of chamber works (violin sonatas, a trio, stringed quartets), for which he was honoured with the *Prix Chartier* by the Institut de France (for merit in the department of chamber music); and, besides pf. pieces, études, over one hundred songs, a " Concerto Romantique " for violin, a pf. concerto, an orchestral suite: " Scènes poétiques," a " Symphonie-ballet " (1882), " Ouverture dramatique " (1883), " Symphonie Gothique " (1883), " Symphonie Orientale " (1884), " Symphonie Légendaire " (soli and chorus, 1886), a lyric scena, " Diane et Actéon," " Le Tasse " (" Tasso," dramatic symphony with soli and chorus, gained the prize of the city of Paris, 1878), and the operas *Pedro de Zalaméa* (Antwerp, 1884), *Jocelyn* (Brussels, 1888), and the music to *Much Ado about Nothing* (Paris, 1887). Two other operas, *Les Guelfes* and *Ruy Blas*, have as yet not been produced. Died Jan. 10, 1895, Cannes.

Goddard, A r a b e l l a, distinguished English pianist, b. Jan. 12, 1838, St. Servans, near St. Malo, pupil of Kalkbrenner in Paris, and of Mrs.

Anderson and Thalberg in London; she played first in 1850, at a concert under Balfe, at Her Majesty's Theatre, and then studied the works of the great masters under J. W. Davison (q.v.), whom she married in 1860. Madame G. was at one time recognised as one of the best lady pianists ; from 1873–76 she made a concert tour round the world (America, Australia, India).

Godebrye. (*See* JACOTIN.)

Godefroid, name of two excellent performers on the harp. (1) J u l e s J o s e p h, b, Feb. 23, 1811, Namur, d. Feb. 27, 1840, Paris (comic operas, *Le diadesté* and *La chasse royale*) ; and (2) F é l i x, b. July 24, 1818, Namur, d. July 12, 1897, brother of the above, lived first at Paris, then at Brussels. He has composed various pieces for harp, and pianoforte pieces of the better kind of drawing-room music ; also three operas (*La harpe d'or, La dernière bataille*, and *La fille de Saül*).

God Save the King, the English National Anthem, the melody of which has been set to "Heil Dir im Siegerkranz," so that now it is also the German National Hymn. It was composed by Henry Carey, and first sung at a dinner given in 1740 to celebrate the capture of Portobello. The German poem, "Heil Dir im Siegerkranz," is by B. G. Schumacher (*Speier-ische Zeitung*, Dec. 17, 1793). (*Cf.* Chrysander's article in the *Jahrb. f. Mus.-Wiss.*)

Goepfart, (1) C h r i s t i a n H e i n r i c h, b. Nov. 27, 1835, Weimar, d. June 6, 1890, Baltimore ; studied under J. G. Töpfer. He was organist and composer, and from 1873 was active in North America as conductor. His sons are :—
(2) K a r l E d u a r d, b. March 8, 1859, Weimar, a diligent composer (operas, choral works, or-chestral works, etc.) ; since 1891, conductor of the Baden-Baden "Verein."
(3) O t t o E r n s t, b. July 31, 1864, Weimar, likewise a composer (of vocal music) ; since 1888, town cantor at Weimar.

Goering, T h e o d o r, b. Oct. 2, 1844, Frank-fort, received instruction in music at an early age, studied physical science at Munich, but turned more and more towards musical criticism (in the Augsburg *Abendzeitung*). From 1880–83 he lived in Paris, and, afterwards, Munich. Among other things he wrote: "Der Messias von Bayreuth" (1881), and was correspondent from Paris of Goldstein's *Musikwelt*. He is at present musical correspondent of the *Köln. Zeitung*.

Goes, D a m i ã o d e, b. 1501, Alemquer (Portu-gal), d. 1553, Lisbon. He was Portuguese am-bassador at various European courts, and lived for a time in private at Louvain engaged in historical pursuits. He was an able musician, of whom motets à 3-6 (manuscript) are pre-served in the royal library at Lisbon. There is a motet à 6 in M. Kriesstein's "Cantiones 7–5 voc." (1545). G. also wrote a "Tratado theorico da musica."

Goethe, (1) W o l f g a n g v o n, the great prince of poets, was not so ignorant of music as is generally supposed. Friedländer, Frimmel, and others, but particularly Ferdinand Hiller, have lately shown this, the latter in his "Goethes musikalisches Leben" (1883). G. was, in fact, an harmonic dualist, and thoroughly disapproved of the current explanation of the minor key. (*See* p. 70 of the above-named work.) His taste, however, allowed him no appreciation beyond Mozart.
His grandson—(2) W a l t e r v o n, b. 1817, Weimar, d. there April 15, 1885, as chamberlain to the Grand Duke. He wrote three vaude-villes : *Anselmo Lancia* (*Das Fischermädchen*, 1839, text by Körner), *Der Gefangene von Bologna* (1846), and *Elfriede* (1853), also ten books of songs and four of pianoforte pieces.

Gogavinus, A n t o n H e r m a n n, Dutch by birth. He lived as physician at Venice, and was on friendly terms with Zarlino. G. was the first to publish a Latin translation of the "Harmonica" of Aristoxenos and of Ptolemy, as well as some fragments of Aristotle and Porphyry (1552). A hundred years passed away before Wallis and Meibom followed his example.

Goldberg, (1) J o h a n n T h e o p h i l u s (Gott-lieb), clavier-player, b. *cir.* 1730, Königsberg (*cf.* Reichardt's "Musikal. Almanach"), went, at an early age, with Freiherr v. Kayserling to Dresden, had the advantage there of instruction from Friedemann Bach, and, later on (1741), from J. S. Bach (who wrote for him the variations which bear his name) ; he then became "Kam-mermusikus" to Count Brühl, and died at an early age. G. is said to have been a very eminent performer on the clavier (also impro-visator), and as composer ranks among the best men of his day (preludes and fugues, twenty-four polonaises, two clavier concertos, one sonata, six trios for flute, violin, and bass, menuet with variations, a motet and a cantata have been preserved, but not printed).
(2) J o s e p h P a s q u a l e, an esteemed teacher of singing, b. Jan. 1, 1825, Vienna, d. there Dec. 20, 1890, studied first under Mayseder and Seyfried, travelled for several years as a violin prodigy, and then was trained by Rubini, Bordogni, and Lamperti, and became a bass singer. He made his *début* already in 1843 at Genoa in Donizetti's *La Regina di Golconda*, and sang for several years in Italy, but then settled in Paris as con-cert singer and teacher of singing. After further concert tours, he took up his abode in London in 1861. G. composed some vocal pieces, also "La marcia trionfale," as an entry march for the army of Victor Emmanuel into Rome. The vocal-ists Fanny G.-Marini and Catherine G.-Strossi are his sisters, the latter was also his pupil.

Golde, A d o l f, b. Aug. 22, 1830, Erfurt, d. there March 20, 1880. He was highly respected as a pianoforte teacher, and as a pianoforte composer of popular pieces.

Goldmark, Karl, b. May 18, 1830, Keszthely (Hungary); he studied the violin under Jansa at Vienna, entered the Conservatorium in 1847, which, however, closed its doors in 1848 for three years. G. then studied privately, and attracted the attention of the musical world by his overture " Sakuntala " and a " Scherzo " for orchestra (Op. 19). The opera *Die Königin von Saba* (Vienna, 1875, and other places ; also Bologna) established his fame, so that since then his works are looked forward to with interest. Of his later publications the most important are : two symphonies, " Ländliche Hochzeit " and one in E flat (1887); the overtures " Penthesilea," " Im Frühling," " Der entfesselte Prometheus," two violin concertos, a pf. quintet, a quartet for strings, a suite for pianoforte and violin, some important pf. solo works (Op. 5, Sturm u. Drang ; Op. 29, Novelletten, Präludium u. Fuga), and " Frühlingsnetz " (for male chorus, pf., and four horns). The long-announced opera *Der Fremdling* has not, up to now, been given ; on the other hand, his *Merlin* was successfully produced at Vienna in 1886.

Goldner, Wilhelm, pianist and *salon* composer, b. June 30, 1839, Hamburg, pupil of the Leipzig Conservatorium ; he lives in Paris.

Goldschmidt, (1) Sigmund, distinguished pianist, b. Sept. 28, 1815, Prague, d. Sept. 26, 1877,Vienna. He studied in the latter city under Tomaschek, attracted notice in Paris from 1845–49 by his sterling playing, and also published a considerable number of excellent compositions (pianoforte and orchestral works), but preferred to manage the mercantile business of his father (banker), and to exchange the *rôle* of artist for that of amateur.

(2) Otto, likewise an excellent pianist, b. Aug. 21, 1829, Hamburg, studied under Jacob Schmitt and F. W. Grund, was with H. v. Bülow at the Leipzig Conservatorium (pupil of Mendelssohn), and, besides, in 1848 under Chopin in Paris. He then went to London, where he first appeared at a concert given by Jenny Lind in 1849; in 1851 he accompanied her to America, and married her in 1852. From 1852–55 they both lived in Dresden, and from 1858 in London. G. conducted the musical festival at Düsseldorf in 1863, and at Hamburg in 1866, and in 1863 became vice-principal of the Royal Academy of Music; in 1875 he founded the Bach Choir, which he brought to a state of great prosperity. G. published, jointly with Benedict, the " Choral-Book for England." Of his compositions are to be named the oratorio *Ruth*, a pianoforte concerto, a trio, etc. Died Feb. 24, 1907.

(3) Adalbert von, gifted composer, b. 1853, Vienna, pupil of the Conservatorium there ; he wrote music to the *Sieben Todsünden*, prepared for him by Rob. Hammerling, as well as an opera, *Helianthus* (Leipzig, 1884), the trilogy *Gaea* (1889), and many songs. Died Dec. 21, 1906.

(4) Hugo, b. Sept. 19, 1859, Breslau, where he attended school, studied jurisprudence, took his degree of Dr.jur. in 1884, but in the same year withdrew from public service, married, and managed his father's estates. The study of music, carried on incidentally under Hirschberg and Schäffer at Breslau, now became a matter of chief importance, and from 1887 to 1890 we find G. a pupil for singing of Stockhausen's at Frankfort. He was then engaged in musico-historical pursuits under the direction of E. Bohn at Breslau, and, finally, in 1893, became one of the directors of the Scharwenka-Klindworth Conservatorium, Berlin. G. has written : " Die italienische Gesangsmethode des 17. Jahrh." (1890, with explanations concerning the ornamental performance of vocal works of the 16th century, about 1600), " Der Vokalismus des neu-hoch-deutschen Kunstgesangs und der Bühnensprache " (1892) ; also some valuable articles for musical papers.

Golinelli, Stefano, b. Oct. 26, 1818, Bologna, pupil of Benedetto Donelli (piano) and Vaccai (composition); from 1840–70 teacher at the Music Lyceum of his native town, during which time he undertook concert tours with success in Germany, England, and France, but afterwards lived in retirement. G. has written about two hundred works, exclusively for pianoforte (five sonatas, three toccatas, forty-eight preludes, etc.), esteemed, indeed, in Italy, yet without special value. Died July 3, 1891.

Gollmick, (1), Karl, b. March 19, 1796, Dessau, d. Oct. 3, 1866, Frankfort, son of the once celebrated tenor singer, Frederick Karl G. (b. Sept. 27, 1774, Berlin, d. July 2, 1852, Frankfort). He studied theology at Strassburg, but, at the same time, made a diligent study of music under the direction of capellmeister Spindler. At an early age he earned a livelihood by teaching music and languages, and settled in Frankfort in 1817 as teacher of the French language. Spohr, at that time capellmeister at Frankfort, engaged him as drummer for the Stadttheater, in which position, acting likewise, later on, as chorus master, he remained until 1858, when he received a pension. Besides many pianoforte works for two and four hands (variations, rondos, potpourris), songs, etc., G. wrote a vocal Method, " Praktische Gesangschule," a " Leitfaden für junge Musiklehrer," " Kritische Terminologie für Musiker und Musikfreunde " (1833 ; 2nd ed. 1839), " Musikalische Novellen und Silhouetten " (1842), " Karl Guhr " (obituary, 1848), " Herr Fétis . . . als Mensch, Kritiker, Theoretiker und Komponist " (1852), " Handlexikon der Tonkunst " (1858), " Autobiographie " (1866) ; also many articles in musical papers.

(2) Adolf, son of the former, b. Feb. 5, 1825, Frankfort, d. March 7, 1883, London. He studied with his father, and learnt the violin under Riefstahl and H. Wolf. In 1844 he

settled in London, where he was esteemed as pianist and violinist. He composed operas, cantatas, orchestral and chamber music.

Goltermann, (1) G e o r g E d u a r d, b. Aug. 19, 1824, Hanover, where his father was organist, pupil of Prell (jun.) for 'cello-playing, and from 1847-49 of Menter at Munich. He studied composition with Lachner, made concert tours as 'cello virtuoso from 1850-52, produced a symphony at Leipzig in 1851, became musical director at Würzburg in 1852, in 1853 second. and in 1874, chief capellmeister at the Stadt theater at Frankfort. He died Dec. 29, 1898. G. was specially famed as performer on the 'cello and composer for his instrument (concertos, sonatas, etc.); but he also published a number of other fairly good works.

(2) J o h. A u g. J u l i u s, b. July 15, 1825, Hamburg, d. April 4, 1876, Stuttgart ; likewise an excellent 'cellist. From 1850-62 he was teacher of the 'cello at the Prague Conservatorium, became in 1862 principal 'cellist of the court band at Stuttgart, and retired in 1870.

(3) A u g u s t, b. 1826, d. Nov. 2, 1890, Schwerin, where he was court pianist.

Gombert, N i k o l a u s, Netherland contrapuntist, b. Bruges, one of the most important, if not the most important, of the pupils of Josquin. He was in 1530 master of the boys at the Imperial Chapel, Madrid ; afterwards (1543) probably maestro of the same chapel. G.'s compositions are distinguished from those of his predecessors by greater fulness ; according to the testimony of Hermann Finck (q.v.), he avoided the use of rests, which in the case of his predecessors often considerably reduced the polyphony. Finck named him " Author musices plane diversæ." G. was an extremely prolific master, and a large number of his ingenious works have been preserved, and in special editions : two books of motets à 4 (Book I. no date, 2nd ed. 1540 ; Book II. 1541 ; both several times republished) ; two books of motets à 5 (Book I. 1541 [1551], Book II. 1541 [1552], also both together, 1552) ; one book of masses à 5 (1549), a book of chansons à 5-6 (1544, the fifth book of the edition of chansons prepared by Tilman Susato of Antwerp). Numerous motets of G.'s are likewise to be found in Gardano's " Motetti del frutto " and " Motetti del fiore," also many others in collections of the 16th century. (Cf. Fétis's catalogue, and the supplement connected with it, in Ambros' " Musikgeschichte," vol iii., p. 293. In addition, there are still some motets and chansons in manuscript in the Munich Library, cf. J. J. Maier's catalogue).

Gomez, A n t o n i o C a r l o s, b. July 11, 1839, Campinos (Brazil), of Portuguese parents, was sent for a musical training to the Milan Conservatorio (under Lauro Rossi), and remained from that time in Italy. G. was an opera composer, but not one of those quick Italian writers,

although his works frequently recall Verdi. After a Portuguese maiden work, *A noite de castello* (Rio de Janeiro, 1861), he made his *début* in 1867 with a *pièce d'occasion, Se sa minga (New Year's Jest)*, at a small theatre in Milan, and the " Song of the Needle-gun " soon made him popular, so that the doors of the Scala were open to him. His principal works are : the ballet opera *Guarany* (Scala, 1870), *Fosca* (Scala, 1873), which was a failure, and yet even this is a good sign, *Salvator Rosa* (Fenice Theatre, Genoa, 1874, with great success, and from that time produced on most Italian stages), and *Maria Tudor* (Milan, 1879). G. wrote, at the request of the Emperor of Brazil, a hymn, " Il salute del Bresile," for the celebration of the declaration of Independence of America, which was performed at the Philadelphia Exhibition of 1876. He died Sept. 17, 1896.

Gondellied (Ital.), gondola song.

Gondoliera, barcarole.

Gong (Tamtam), an oriental (Chinese, Indian) instrument of percussion, consisting of a metal plate made (hammered), for the most part, of precious metal. The centre portion of the G. is quite concave, with a broad, round rim. The G. has a groaning sound, and one which reverberates for a long time ; both in *forte* and in *piano* it inspires terror, anguish. The G. is employed in modern opera orchestras ; but, on account of the great expense in procuring it (good gongs come from China), it is somewhat rare : as a rule, it is replaced by a cymbal (q.v.), suspended like a G., and struck with a stick.

Goovaerts, A l p h o n s e J e a n M a r i e A n d r é, b. May 25, 1847, Antwerp; he sprang from a family of artists, was trained at first for a mercantile career, but afterwards displayed zeal for music ; and, in 1866, when he became assistant librarian at Antwerp, already motets of his composition began to be known. There followed Flemish songs in three parts (for schools), a mass à 4 with organ ; and in 1869, a *Messe solennelle* for chorus, orchestra, and organ, and many short, sacred works (*Adoramus, O salutaris*, etc.). He then made deep historical studies, and in 1874 began to reform the church music of his native town by giving performances of the works of the Old Netherland School, also of Palestrina, for which purpose he established a cathedral choir. In 1887 he became royal archivist at Brussels, and is member of the Gregorian Society in Holland. The historical works of G. are his " Histoire et bibliographie de la typographie musicale, etc." (1800), which gained a prize ; also his monographs on Pierre Phalèse, on some painters of the Netherlands, on the origin of newspapers (" Abraham Verhoeven ") and " La Musique d'église " (also in Flemish, " De Kerkmuzieck," 1876).

Göpfert, K a r l A n d r e a s, b. Jan. 16, 1768,

Rimpar, near Würzburg, d. April 11, 1818, as "Hofmusikus" at Meiningen. He was a performer on the clarinet and a composer, especially for wind-instruments. He wrote four concertos for clarinet, one *symphonie concertante* for clarinet and bassoon; one concerto for horn; duets for two clarinets, for two horns, for guitar and flute, and for guitar and bassoon; five quartets for clarinet, violin, tenor, and bass; quintets and octets for wind, etc.

Gordigiani, (1) Giovanni Battista, b. July, 1795, Mantua, d. March 2, 1871, Prague, was first opera, and then concert singer, and from 1822 teacher of singing at the Prague Conservatorium. G. wrote much sacred music, also canzonets and songs, and two operas (*Pygmalion* and *Consuelo*, Prague, 1845 and 1846).

(2) Luigi, brother of the former, b. June 12, 1806, Florence, d. there April 30, 1860, wrote from 1830–51 seven operas (*Un' eredità in Corsica,* 1847). He was specially successful with his small vocal pieces (duets with pianoforte), and he also published three books of Tuscan popular songs.

Gorgheggiamento (Ital.), the art of performing florid passages, trills, etc.

Gorgheggiare (Ital.), to perform florid passages, trills, etc.

Gorgheggio (Ital.), a florid passage; *Gorgheggi* is the plural.

Goria, Adolf, b. Jan. 21, 1823, Paris, d. there July 6, 1860, for a time a favourite composer of drawing-room pianoforte music.

Göroldt, Johann Heinrich, b. Dec. 13, 1773, Stempeda, near Stolberg (Hartz); in 1803 musical director at Quedlinburg, where he was still living in 1835. He composed pianoforte pieces, chorales for male voices with organ, and left, in manuscript, cantatas, hymns, motets, etc. He is better known by his writings: "Leitfaden zum Unterricht im Generalbass und der Komposition" (1815–16, 2 vols., 2nd ed. 1828); "Die Kunst, nach Noten zu singen" (2nd ed. 1832); "Die Orgel und deren zweckmässiger Gebrauch" (1835); "Gedanken und Bemerkungen über Kirchenmusik" (in "Eutonia," 1830). He also wrote an "Ausführliche theoretisch-praktische Hornschule" (1830).

Goss, John, b. 1800, Fareham, Hants, d. May 10, 1880, Brixton. He was a chorister of the Chapel Royal under Smith, then a private pupil of Attwood. In 1824 he became organist of the new church of St. Luke's, Chelsea, in 1838 succeeded Attwood as organist of St. Paul's Cathedral (till 1872), and in 1856, on the death of Knyvett, became composer to the Chapel Royal. He was knighted in 1872, and took the degree of Doctor of Music at Cambridge in 1876. He composed anthems, psalms, Te Deums, also glees, songs, orchestral pieces, and wrote: "Introduction to Harmony and Thorough-Bass"

(1833, a work well known in England, and many times republished). G. published "Chants, Ancient and Modern" (1841, conjointly with W. Mercer), and "The Organist's Companion" (pieces for organ).

Gossec (really Gossé), François Joseph, b. Jan. 17, 1734, Vergnies (Hainault), d. Feb. 16, 1829, Passy, near Paris (ninety-five years old). He received his first musical training as chorister at the cathedral at Antwerp. He went, in 1751, to Paris with good introductions to Rameau, who procured for him the post of conductor to the private band of La Popelinière, Fermier-général. For him he wrote his first symphony (1754), five years before Haydn's first (*cf.*, however, Sammartini), and in 1759, his first stringed quartets. La Popelinière died in 1762, and G., when the band was dispersed, undertook the direction of that of Prince Conti at Chantilly, and achieved considerable fame. In 1770 he founded and conducted the celebrated *Concerts des Amateurs,* reorganised in 1773 the *Concerts Spirituels,* and conducted them jointly with Gaviniés and A. Leduc, sen., and also for some years alone, but was driven from this post by intrigues (1777). From 1780–82 he acted as sub-director of the Grand Opéra (Académie de Musique), and remained a member of the executive committee up to 1784, when he undertook the organisation and general direction of the École Royale de Chant. When this institution was enlarged under the Republic, and became the Conservatoire de Musique, G. was appointed inspector, jointly with Cherubini and Lesueur, and at the same time became a member of the Institut de France founded in the same year. From 1799 to 1804 and 1809–15 he was member of the commission appointed to examine the operas sent in to the Grand Opéra. From 1815 he lived in retirement at Passy, near Paris. G., as a composer, occupies a prominent position. His symphonies (twenty-six, and three for wind-instruments) were not favourably received at first, but already in 1777 one was encored at a *concert spirituel.* On the other hand, his stringed quartets were, from the first, enthusiastically received, and were repeatedly reprinted in foreign countries. His Requiem (1760), in which there are important instrumental effects, made a deep impression. He also wrote a "Symphonie concertante" for eleven instruments, serenades, overtures, stringed trios, violin duets, quartets for flute and stringed instruments, several masses with orchestra, two Te Deums, motets, several oratorios (*Saül, La Nativité, L'arche d'alliance*), choruses to Racine's *Athalie* and Rochefort's *Electre,* and a series of operas which caused him to be regarded as one of the most important composers in this branch of musical art: the first was the small unimportant *Le faux lord* (1764), but this was followed by the completely successful *Les pêcheurs* (1766); *Le double déguisement* (1767); *Toinon et Toinette* (1767);

Rosine (1786); and *Les sabots et le cerisier* (1803) —all at the Opéra Comique. The following were produced at the Grand Opéra :—*Sabinus* (1774); *Alexis et Daphné* (1775); *Philémon et Baucis* (1775); *Hylas et Sylvie* (1776); *La fête du village* (1778); *Thésée* (1782); *Les visitandines* (jointly with Trial); *La reprise de Toulon* (1796); and finally, at the Brussels Opéra, *Berthe* (1775); to these may be added *Le Périgourdin* (private performance) and *Nitocris* (not produced). G. was enthusiastic for the Republic, and composed a great number of songs, hymns, etc., for patriotic festivals connected with the time of the Revolution; thus, first, the "Chant du 14 Juillet" (for the anniversary of the storming of the Bastille), the hymns—"A la divinité," "A l'être suprême," "A la nature," "A la liberté," "A l'humanité," "A l'égalité," "Serment républicain," "Marche religieuse," "Marche victorieuse," transcription for orchestra of the "Marseillaise," chorus for the apotheosis of Rousseau ; also stage festival pieces, *Offrande à la patrie* (1792) and *Le camp de Grand-Pré* (1793, [The Tambourin will be found in Augener's Edition No. 8299]). G. was, so to speak, official composer to the Republic. (*Cf.* Gregoir, " Notice sur G." (1878), and Hedouin, "G., sa vie et ses œuvres" (1852).

Gottschalg, Alexander Wilhelm, b. Feb. 14, 1827, Mechelrode, near Weimar, received his musical training from G. Töpfer at Weimar as pupil at the training-school, had also the benefit of instruction from Liszt, and in 1847 became teacher at Tiefurt, near Weimar. In 1870 he succeeded Töpfer at the training-school (up to 1881) and became court organist, in 1874 also teacher of the history of music to the "Grossherzogliche Musik und Orchesterschule." From 1865 he was editor of the musical paper *Urania* (for organ), from 1872 musical critic of Dittes's *Pädagogischer Jahresbericht*, from 1885 also editor of the musical paper *Chorgesang;* he published besides, " Repertorium für die Orgel " (jointly with Liszt), and " Kleines Handlexikon der Tonkunst " (1867).

Gottschalk, Louis Moreau, American pianist, b. May 8, 1829, New Orleans, d. Dec. 18, 1869, Rio de Janeiro, studied under Stamaty at Paris ; he commenced his career as a concert-player at Paris in 1845, then travelled through Switzerland, Spain, and France, and in 1853 returned to America, giving concerts, especially in North America. In 1865 he went to San Francisco, and from there to South America, played at Rio de Janeiro in 1869, and fell ill there and died. G. played almost exclusively his own compositions, which belong to the better class of drawing-room music (characteristic pieces of marked Spanish national colour, brilliant, often somewhat sentimental).

Götz, (1) Franz, b. 1755, Straschitz (Bohemia), studied Catholic theology and took his bachelor's degree, but later on gave himself up entirely to music, played the violin in the theatre orchestra at Brünn, became leader at Johannis-berg, afterwards theatre capellmeister at Brünn, and finally capellmeister to the Archbishop of Olmütz, where he was still living in 1799. He wrote symphonies, concertos, chamber-music, etc., all of which remain in manuscript.

(2) Hermann, b. Dec. 7, 1840, Königsberg-i.-Pr., d. Dec. 3, 1876, Hottingen, near Zürich. He received his first musical instruction from Louis Köhler, attended the Stern Conservatorium at Berlin in 1860, where Stern, Bülow, and H. Ulrich were his teachers. In 1863 he undertook the post of organist at Winterthur as successor to Th. Kirchner, settled in Zürich in 1867, resigned, on account of bad health, his post of organist at Winterthur in 1870, and, until his death, was engaged in composition. A vigorous, fine talent went with him, all too early, to the grave. G.'s opera—*Der Widerspenstigen Zähmung* (*Taming of the Shrew*)—ranks amongst the best modern works for the stage, and, soon after its production at Mannheim in 1874, it made the round of the German theatres ; it has also been translated into English and played in England. His second opera (*Francesca von Rimini*) he did not complete. The sketch which he left of the third act was scored by Ernst Frank at Mannheim, where the work was produced on Sept. 30, 1877. Besides these, G. wrote a symphony (in F), Schiller's "Nänie" (" Auch das Schöne muss sterben ") for chorus and orchestra, a " Frühlingsouvertüre," a violin concerto, pf. concerto, the 137th psalm for chorus, soprano solo, and orchestra; a pf. quintet (c minor, with double-bass), a pianoforte sonata for four hands, a pf. trio, a quartet, pf. pieces, two books of Lieder (Op. 4 and Op. 12), " Es liegt so abendstill der See," tenor solo with chorus of male voices and orchestra.

Götze, (1) Joh. Nikolaus Konrad, b. Feb. 11, 1791, Weimar, was musical director to the Grand Duke 1826-48, and chorus-master at the Opera there; he d. Feb. 5, 1861. G. was trained in violin-playing by Spohr (Gotha), A. E. Müller (Weimar), and Kreutzer (Paris, 1813), at the cost of the hereditary Grand Duchess. He was also active as a composer (operas, vaudevilles, melodramas, quartets, and a trio for strings, etc.), but he lacked inspiration.

(2) Franz, b. May 10, 1814, Neustadt-a.-d.-Orla, d. April 2, 1888, Leipzig, violin pupil of Spohr at Cassel. In 1831 he became member of the court band at Weimar, but then studied operatic singing, and from 1836-52 was engaged at the theatre there as principal tenor ; afterwards he was teacher of singing at the Leipzig Conservatorium, which post he, however, resigned in 1867 for reasons clearly set forth in his pamphlet " Fünfzehn Jahre meiner Lehrthätigkeit " (1868). From that time G. lived at Leipzig, highly esteemed as a private teacher of singing. The Grand Duke

of Weimar appointed him professor already in 1855. His daughter and pupil, A u g u s t e, b. Feb. 24, 1840, Weimar, in 1870 teacher at the Dresden Conservatorium, established in 1875 a school of singing of her own (Frau Moran-Olden was her pupil), and in 1891 became teacher at the Leipzig Conservatorium. She has written " Über den Verfall der Gesangskunst " (1884), and, under the pseudonym " Auguste Weimar," some stage poems (" Vittoria Accorimboni," " Magdalena," " Alpenstürme," etc.

(3) K a r l, b. 1836, Weimar, d. Jan. 14, 1887, Magdeburg, pupil of Töpfer and Gebhardi, afterwards of Liszt, was chorus-master at the Weimar opera in 1855, then theatre capellmeister at Magdeburg, Berlin (1869 at the " Residenztheater," then called the " Nowacktheater ; " in 1870 at the " Friedrich-Wilhelmstadt " theatre), Breslau (1872), and Chemnitz (from 1875). G. was an excellent conductor, and also esteemed as a composer (operas : *Eine Abschiedsrolle, Die Korsen, Gustav Wasa,* symphonic poem " Die Sommernacht," pf. pieces, etc).

(4) H e i n r i c h, teacher of music and composer, b. April 7, 1836, Wartha in Silesia, son of a schoolmaster, attended the teachers' training college at Breslau, and had the advantage of instruction in music from Mosewius and Baumgart. After fulfilling the duties of teacher for three years, he became a pupil of the Leipzig Conservatorium, studied singing under Franz Götze, but lost his voice, and then devoted himself entirely to teaching and composition. He first went as private teacher of music to Russia, lived afterwards as private teacher at Breslau, and, in 1871, was appointed teacher of music at the college at Liebenthal-i.-Schl. In 1885 he went in a similar capacity to Ziegenhals (Silesia), and was appointed royal musical director in 1889. Of his compositions the following deserve mention : two serenades (for strings), six sketches (ditto), a pf. trio ; also a mass à 4 with orchestra, many valuable pieces for organ and pianoforte, songs, part-songs, etc. He displayed his merits as a teacher in " Populäre Abhandlungen über Klavierspiel " (1879), and especially in " Musikalische Schreibübungen " ; the latter is the first German work on the important subject of Musical Dictation (q.v.), one to which, as yet, but little attention has been paid.

(5) E m i l, celebrated tenor singer, b. July 19, 1856, Leipzig, was first intended for a mercantile career, but was trained in singing by Prof. Gust. Scharfe at Dresden, and first engaged at the court theatre, Dresden (1878-81), then at the Cologne theatre, whence he made the round of all the important theatres, and with phenomenal success. Unfortunately, acute inflammation of the throat compelled this artist, distinguished both as actor and singer, to discontinue, for a long period, his public career.

Goudimel, C l a u d e, b. about 1505, Besançon, the founder of the Roman School ; he went to Rome about 1535, where Palestrina, G. Animuccia, G. M. Nanini and others became his pupils ; but afterwards to Paris, where for a short time he was in partnership with the music-printer Du Chemin (1555). Whether he left Rome because he was in sympathy with the Reformation is not known. His later conversion to Protestantism has been often called in question. It is a fact that he set to music, in four parts, note against note (!), the complete translated version of the Psalms by Marot and de Bèze (so far as they were not already provided with independent melodies—perhaps even these he may have provided), and that in the night of August 28/29, 1572, he was killed at Lyons as a Huguenot (real or pretended), and his body thrown into the Rhone. The style of G. has something in it akin to that of Palestrina : his writing was rich and full, without canonic artificialities, but always in imitative style, and of extraordinary correctness. It is remarkable that, of a teacher at Rome so famous, nothing was brought out by the Italian printers of that time (Gardano, Scoto, etc.). The works (masses and motets à 5-12), considered to be his oldest, are in manuscript in the Vatican Archives and in the Oratory of Santo Maria, Vallicella. The published ones, without exception, appeared in France and the Netherlands : first some motets in T. Susato's fourth book of motets (1554), then in the special edition of " Q. Horatii Flacci . . . odæ . . . ad rhythmos musicos redactæ " (1555) ; " Chansons spirituelles de Marc Antoine de Muret " (à 4, 1555) ; " Magnificat ex octo modis (à 5, 1557) ; " Missæ tres a Claudio G. . . . item missæ tres a Claudio de Sermisy, Joanne Maillard, Claudio G." (1558) ; " Les psaumes de David mis en musique . . . en forme de motets " (1562, 16 psalms à 4) ; " Les psaumes mis en rime français par Clément Marot et Théodore de Bèze " (1565) ; " La fleur des chansons des deux plus excellents musiciens de notre temps, à savoir de Orlande de Lassus et de D. Claude G." (1574) ; and some chansons in the sixth and eighth books of the collection of chansons of Le Roy and Ballard (1556 and 1557).

Gounod, C h a r l e s F r a n ç o i s, b. June 17, 1818, Paris, d. there Oct. 17, 1893, incontestably one of the most important of French composers, received his first musical stimulus from his mother, who was an accomplished pianist. From 1836–38 he studied, at the Conservatoire, counterpoint under Halévy and composition under Paër and Lesueur. In 1837 he won the second prize, in 1839 the *Grand Prix de Rome,* for his cantata *Fernand ;* and during his residence of three years in Rome he studied the style of Palestrina. In 1841 he produced a mass à 3, with orchestra, at the church of San Luigi dei Francesi, and in 1842, at Vienna, a requiem ; after his return to Paris, he undertook

the post of organist and maître de chapelle of
the Missions Étrangères, attended lectures on
theology, was guest in the Séminaire, and was
on the point of taking holy orders. However,
about this time a change came over him in his
musical efforts. In Germany he had learnt to
know the works of Schumann, and now drew
closer to them and to those of Berlioz; he found
his poetical gifts mightily stirred by both, and
turned from the church to the stage. Nevertheless, it was a sacred work which first attracted
the attention of the world to him; in a concert of
Hullah's at London (Jan., 1851), fragments of
his *Messe Solennelle* were produced, to which the
critics unanimously ascribed high importance.
In the same year G. made his *début* at the Grand
Opéra as an opera composer with *Sapho*, but,
through imperfect knowledge of stage technique,
gained small success (the work even as revised in 1884 was a failure), both with this and
with his next opera, *La nonne sanglante* (1854).
He also failed to make an impression with his
antique choruses to Ponsard's *Ulysse;* but, in
spite of the poor results, he felt his powers
strengthened, and recognised more and more
his vocation as a dramatic composer. Meanwhile, 1852, he had been appointed director of
the Orphéon, the great union of the Paris male
choral societies and schools of singing, which
office he held for eight years. He wrote for
the Orphéonistes two masses and various part-
songs, and made an essay in instrumental music
with two symphonies; but his chief activity
was concentrated on opera. His next attempt
—*Le Médecin malgré lui*, produced at the Opéra
Comique (1858), given in England as *The Mock
Doctor*, and also performed by the pupils of the
Royal College of Music in 1890—showed that
at the Opéra Comique he was not in his right
element. At last, in 1859, he made a decided
hit with *Faust* (Théâtre Lyrique, March 19).
Here he was in his element. The fantastic and
the purely lyrical were admirably expressed by
him. That G.'s *Faust*, so despised by the Germans, is not a caricature of Goethe's *Faust*, is
clear from the fact—which is worth more than
many arguments—that Wagner did not set it
to music; the latter, in fact, pays him a com-
pliment in recalling the church scene in the
address of Walter to Evchen in the *Meistersinger*. The Kermesse and the Garden scene
form two pictures of the first rank. G.'s
style is very sympathetic to the Germans,
for it is really more German than French,
and often reminds one of Weber or Wagner.
But it is not quite a pure style, and sometimes falls into the sentimental or the chanson
type. *Faust* has remained G.'s master-work;
it has carried his name through all countries
of Europe, and was the first French opera
which at Paris made its way from another
stage to that of the Grand Opéra. The works
which followed did not come up to the high
expectations excited by *Faust: Philémon et*

Baucis (Grand Opéra, 1860; London, 1890);
La Reine de Saba (Grand Opéra, 1862; in English
version as *Irene*, in London); *Mireille* (Théâtre
Lyrique, 1864); *La Colombe* (Opéra Comique,
1866; previously at Baden-Baden; in London
as *Pet Dove*). His *Roméo et Juliette* was, again, a
fortunate draw (Théâtre Lyrique, 1867)—in
France it is placed above *Faust;* in Germany,
not far below. Again G. was in complete
sympathy with the subject. In structure he
approaches nearer to Wagner, lays special
stress on the music in the orchestra, and makes
continual use of dissonances by suspension.
After that, he produced other operas of less
value—*Cinq-Mars* (Opéra Comique, 1877), and
Polyeucte (Grand Opéra, 1878); he also wrote
entr'actes to Legouvé's *Les deux Reines*, and
Barbier's *Jeanne d'Arc*. His last opera—*Le
Tribut de Zamora* (1881)—likewise did not fulfil
the hopes which it had excited. The war
of 1870 drove G. from Paris. He went to
London, and founded there a mixed choral
union (Gounod's Choir), with which he arranged
large concerts, and in 1871, for the opening
of the Exhibition, produced his elegiac cantata, *Gallia* (words from the Lamentations
of Jeremiah; a pendant, in fact, to Brahms's
Triumphlied). In 1875 he returned to Paris.
Of his works are still to be named: two masses,
Angeli Custodes and *Messe Solennelle Ste.-Cécile*
(1882), *Messe à Jeanne d'Arc* (1887), a fourth
Messe (1888), and a Te Deum, "Les Sept
Paroles de Jésus," a "Pater Noster," "Ave
Verum," and "O Salutaris," a Te Deum, "Jésus
sur le lac de Tibériade," "Stabat Mater" with
orchestra, the oratorios *Tobie*, *The Redemption*
(Birmingham, 1882), and *Mors et Vita* (Birming-
ham, 1885), symphony, "La Reine des Apôtres,"
"Marche Romaine," "Chant de bataille Arra-
gonais" (1882), "Marche Funèbre d'une Marionette." Cantatas: *A la Frontière* (1870, Grand
Opéra), and *Le Vin des Gaulois et la Danse de
l'épée*, many smaller vocal works, French and
English songs, the widely known "Méditation"
on Bach's first Prelude from the *Well-tempered
Clavier* (for soprano solo, violin, pianoforte, and
harmonium), pf. pieces for two and four hands,
and a "Méthode de cor à pistons." G. was a
member of the Institut de France and *com-
mandeur de la légion d'honneur*.

Gouvy, Ludwig Théodore, b. July 21,
1819, Gaffontaine, near Saarbrück, d. April 21,
1898, Leipzig, attended the college at Metz, and
went to Paris in 1840 to study law, which, however, he soon gave up again, in order to devote
himself entirely to music; he studied counterpoint with Elwart, and took lessons on the pianoforte from a pupil of Herz. He did not attend
the Conservatoire. Possessed of means, he was
able to study German musical life in Germany
itself. He spent the year of 1843 in Berlin, was
on friendly terms with K. Eckert, with whom he
made a journey to Italy in the following year
for the purpose of study. On his return to

Paris he produced, at a concert arranged by himself, his first important works—the symphony in F, two overtures, etc.—which were favourably received. The first symphony was followed by five more, also by a sinfonietta (in D), two concert-overtures, songs, part-songs, concert scenas ("The Last Song of Ossian," for baritone and orchestra), and a considerable number of chamber-music works, a pf. quintet, five trios, sonatas and pieces for violin and 'cello, quartets for strings, a quintet for strings, a serenade for five stringed-instruments, octet for flute, oboe, two clarinets, two horns, and two bassoons (Op. 71), pf. sonatas, variations, characteristic pieces, etc., for two and four hands, etc. But the most important works of G. are the choral ones: "Messe de Requiem," "Stabat Mater," Golgotha (cantata), "Asléga" (lyrico-dramatic scena), "Electra" (dramatic scena for solo, chorus, and orchestra; Duisburg, 1888), and "Frühlings Erwachen" (male chorus, soprano solo, and orchestra, Op. 73). An opera (Cid) was accepted at Dresden, but not given. The influence of Mendelssohn on G. is unmistakable. His music is full of melody, easy to understand, but somewhat effeminate. G. lived at Paris, yet held no appointment.

Graan, Jean de, b. Sept. 9, 1852, Amsterdam, d. Jan. 8, 1874, at the Hague, a pupil of Joachim, and a highly gifted violinist (cf. Kneppelhout: "Een beroemde Knaap").

Graben-Hoffmann (Hoffmann, named G. H.), Gustav, b. March 7, 1820, Bnin, near Posen, attended the teachers' college at Bromberg, was for some time teacher at Posen, but went to Berlin in 1843, and was trained for a singer and teacher of singing. He first taught at Potsdam, studied still for some time under Hauptmann at Leipzig, and in 1858 went to Dresden, in 1868 to Schwerin, and since 1869 has been living in Berlin, a highly esteemed teacher of singing. Besides a great number of songs (of which "500,000 Teufel" became popular), duets, part-songs, and some pianoforte pieces, he has written: "Die Pflege der Singstimne, etc." (1865); "Das Studium des Gesangs" (1872); "Practische Methode als Grundlage für den Kunstgesang, etc." (1874), etc. Died May 20, 1900, Potsdam.

Graces, ornaments, notes of melodic embellishment, such as the appoggiature, turns, shakes, etc.

Gracile (Ital.), small, thin, delicate.

Grad (Ger.), degree.

Grädener, (1), Karl G. P., b. Jan. 14, 1812, Rostock, d. June 10, 1883, Hamburg, composer and theorist, attended the Gymnasium in Altona and in Lübeck, and studied at Halle and Göttingen, but soon devoted himself entirely to music. He then played for three years as 'cellist in a quartet party and as soloist at Helsingfors, and was afterwards, for ten years, university musical director and conductor of the society at Kiel. He founded at Hamburg in 1851 a vocal academy, which he directed for ten years, and, from 1862–65, was teacher of singing and theory at the Vienna Conservatorium, in 1863 capellmeister of the Evangelical Choral Union, and again lived in Hamburg as teacher at the Conservatorium. As a composer G. is of importance, and displays originality; his wealth of melody is not remarkable, but his harmony is refined and his part-writing interesting. Besides many songs, duets, part-songs, etc., he has published: one pf. concerto, two pf. quintets, two trios, one sonata, variations, fantastic étude, "Fliegende Blätter," "Blättchen," and "Träumereien" for pf., three violin sonatas, one 'cello sonata, three quartets, one trio, and one octet for strings, one violin romance with orchestra, two symphonies, one overture ("Fiesco"), etc. He has also published a clever "Harmonielehre" (1877; of which Max Zoder made an epitome), and various articles on art, particularly on music (1872), etc.

(2) His son Hermann, b. May 8, 1844, Kiel, pupil of his father and of the Vienna Conservatorium; in 1862 organist at Gumpendorf, in 1864 member of the Vienna court orchestra (violin), in 1873 teacher of harmony at Horak's Pianoforte School, and for some years at the Conservatorium der Musikfreunde. He is also a diligent and gifted composer (capriccio and sinfonietta for orchestra, octet for strings, pf. quintet, trio, pieces as trios, pieces for piano and violin, sonata for two pianos, pf. pieces, songs, etc.).

Gradevole (Ital.), pleasing, grateful.

Gradevolmente (Ital.), pleasingly, gratefully.

Grado (Ital.), a degree, step.—Grado ascendente, ascending step; grado descendente, descending step.

Graduale (Lat. Responsorium graduale, or gradale), the response sung after the lesson; it was called G. because the priest who chanted it stood on the steps (in gradibus) of the ambo (q.v.). G. is of Roman origin, but old, as already in the Gregorian Antiphonarium the graduals are prominent features. Originally the G. consisted of a whole psalm, which was chanted by the precentors and answered by the congregation; however, Pope Gelasius I. (d. 496) introduced in its place Versus selecti. The graduals of the Gregorian Antiphonarium consist of two verses, of which the first is sung again after the second; afterwards this repetition was done away with.

Graew. (See BACFART.)

Gräfinger. (See GREFINGER.)

Grammann, Karl, b. June 3, 1844, Lübeck, d. Jan. 30, 1897, Dresden, in 1867 pupil of the Leipzig Conservatorium; he lived in Vienna from 1871, and after 1885 in Dresden. He was entirely devoted to composition, for which he showed gifts of no common order. G. made himself known by three operas, *Melusine* (Wiesbaden, 1875, a work which he afterwards revised), *Thusnelda und der Triumphzug des Germanicus* (Dresden, 1881), and *Das Andreasfest* (Dresden, 1882), two symphonies (II. " Aventiure "), an elegiac cantata for chorus, soli, and orchestra, likewise several chamber works. He had completed a fourth opera, *Neutraler Boden* (*Neutral Ground*).

Gran, *grande* (Ital.), great ; *grandezza*, grandeur, dignity.

Gran cassa (Ital.), the big, or bass, drum.

Grand chœur (Fr. ; Ger. *Volles Werk*), full organ.

Grandezza (Ital.), grandeur, dignity.

Grandi, Alessandro, important Italian church composer of the Venetian School, a pupil of Giovanni Gabrieli ; in 1617 chapel singer at San Marco, Venice, 1620 vice-maestro there ; 1627 maestro at Santa Maria Maggiore, Bergamo, where in 1630 he died of the plague. He wrote " Madrigali concertati " (3rd ed. 1619) ; vesper psalms, litanies, Te Deum, and " Tantum ergo " (1607) ; six books of motets à 2–8 (1619–40) ; " Messe concertate 8 voc.," " Missa e salmi à 2, 3, e 4 voci con basso e ripieni " ; " Salmi brevi a 8 voci " (1623) ; " Celesti fiori," à 1–4, three books, " Motetti à 1–4 voci con 2 violini," " Motetti à 1 e 2 voci per cantare e sonare nel chitarrone " (1621) ; " Missa e salmi concertati à 3 voci " (1630) ; " Motetti concertati à 2, 3, e 4 voci " (1632, posthumous).

Grandioso (Ital.), splendid, majestic.

Grand jeu (Fr.), the name of an harmonium stop which brings into play the full power of the instrument.

Grand orgue (Fr.), the principal manual, the keyboard of the great organ.

Grandval. (*See* REISET.)

Granjon, Robert, a famous French type-founder and music printer at Avignon (1532), afterwards at Rome (1582 !).

Graphäus, Hieronymus, important Nuremberg type-founder and music-printer (from 1533), d. May 7, 1556. His real name was Resch (according to other statements Andreä), but on account of his handicraft he took the name Formschneider, which he afterwards changed into one derived from the Greek.

Grappa (Ital.), the brace which connects two or more staves.

Grasseyement (Fr.), a faulty (guttural) pronunciation.

Grasseyer (Fr.), to pronounce gutturally.

Gratiani. (*See* GRAZIANI.)

Graumann, Mathilde. (*See* MARCHESI, 3.)

Graun, (1) Karl Heinrich, b. May 7, 1701, Wahrenbrück (Provinz Sachsen), d. Aug. 8, 1759, Berlin. He attended the Kreuzschule in Dresden (1713–20), and was soon appointed treble-singer to the Rathskapelle. During the period of mutation he applied himself zealously to composition under capellmeister J. K. Schmidt, and specially trained himself by attending the opera performances at Dresden ; he became possessed of an agreeable tenor voice, and was engaged as opera singer at Brunswick. He soon, however, burst forth as an opera-composer, and was appointed vice-capellmeister. Frederick the Great, then Crown Prince, made his acquaintance in Brunswick, and begged the duke to let G. join his company of musicians at Rheinsberg (1735), when opera composing stopped for a while ; on the other hand, G. composed a large number of cantatas to words written by the talented prince. When his patron had ascended the throne G. was appointed capellmeister, and commissioned to establish an opera company of Italian singers at Berlin ; for a considerable time G. himself and Hasse were the only maestri who wrote for the Berlin opera. However closely connected with the opera the simple outward life of G. may appear, the centre of his importance as composer, at least for our time, lies in the works which he wrote for the church. Before all must be mentioned his Passion oratorio, *Der Tod Jesu* (1755), which still, in consequence of a bequest, is annually performed at Berlin ; and by the side of that stands his Te Deum (1756) in commemoration of the battle of Prague ; further, two Passion cantatas, many other cantatas and motets, and the funeral music for the Duke August Wilhelm of Brunswick (1738), and for King Friedrich Wilhelm I. of Prussia (1740). For the Crown Prince he wrote some flute concertos, which were not published. His instrumental compositions (pf. concertos, a concerto for flute, violin, gamba, and 'cello [for the royal family], trios, organ fugues, etc.) were of small value, and remained in manuscript. The names of the operas which he wrote for Brunswick are : *Polydor* (1726), *Sancio und Sinilde* (1727), *Iphigenia in Aulis, Scipio Africanus, Timareta* (Italian, 1733), *Pharao* (with Italian arias), *Lo specchio della fedelta* (Potsdam, 1733) ; those for Berlin (Italian), *Rodelinda* (1741), *Cleopatra* (1742), *Artaserse* (1743), *Catone in Utica* (1744), *Alessandro nell' Indie, Lucio Papirio* (1745), *Adriano in Siria, Demofoonte* (1746), *Cajo Fabrizio* (1747), *Le feste galante, Galatea* (a pastoral play in collaboration with Friedrich II., Quanz, and Nichelmann), *Cinna* (1748), *Europa galante, Ifigenia in Aulide* (1749, v. supra), *Angelica e Medoro, Coriolano* (1750), *Fetonte, Mitridate* (1751), *Armida, Britannico* (1752), *Orfeo, Il giudizio di Paride, Silla* (1753 ; libretto by Friedrich II.), *Semiramide* (1754), *Montezuma* (1755), *Ezio* (1755), *I fratelli nemici* (1756), *Merope* (1756).

(2) Johann Gottlieb, brother of the former, b. about 1698, Wahrenbrück, a violin virtuoso, up to 1726 in the Dresden band, afterwards leader at Merseburg, where Friedemann Bach

was his pupil, d. Oct. 27, 1771, as leader at Berlin. He was, as it were, the complement of Karl Heinrich Graun, for he occupied himself chiefly with instrumental music (forty symphonies, twenty violin concertos, twenty-four stringed quartets, stringed trios, etc.).

Graupner, Christoph, b. Jan., 1687, Kirchberg, Erzgebirge (Saxony), d. May 10, 1760, Darmstadt; he studied under Kuhnau at St. Thomas's School, Leipzig; in 1706 he became accompanist at the Hamburg opera under Keiser, 1709 vice-court-capellmeister at Darmstadt, afterwards principal capellmeister. He was blind during the last ten years of his life. Among his works are to be named the operas which he wrote for Hamburg: *Dido* (1707), *Die lustige Hochzeit* (1708, jointly with Keiser), *Hercules und Theseus* (1708), *Antiochus und Stratonice, Bellerophon, Simson* (1709), and *Berenice und Lucio* (1710), written for Darmstadt, *Telemach* (1711), and *Beständigkeit besiegt Betrug* (1719); further, the clavier works, which he himself engraved, " Acht Parthien für Klavier " (1718), "Monatliche Klavierfrüchte" (1722), "Acht Parthien für das Klavier " (1726), "Die vier Jahreszeiten" (1733), and a " Hessen-darmstädtisches Choralbuch." A large number of instrumental works remain in manuscript.

Grave (Ital.), grave, earnest. It is frequently marked over introductory movements of pathetic character before first movements of symphonies and sonatas. It is also an indication of *tempo*, having a meaning similar to *largo* (very slow).

Graves (*sc. voces* : the " low " [notes]). Already Hucbald, and afterwards Guido and others, named thus the lowest notes of the system of sounds of their day : viz., our (great) G to (small) *c—i.e.* the notes below the four finals (*finales d–g*) of the Ecclesiastical Modes.

Gravicembalo (Ital.), of similar meaning to *Clavicembalo,* and probably only one of those transformations of name which were so common in the 16th century. Since, however, the G., together with the theorbo, archiviola da lyra, and violone, played bass, the reference to *grave,* *i.e.* low, appears by no means irrational.

Gravis (Lat.), heavy, ponderous. The name of one of the *accentus ecclesiastici.*

Grazia (Ital.), grace, elegance, comeliness.— *Con grazia,* with grace.

Graziani, (1) Padre Tommaso, b. Bagnacavallo (Church States), maestro at the Franciscan cloister, Milan. He published: masses à 5 (1569), vesper psalms à 4 (1587), madrigals à 5 (1588), complines à 8 (1601), " Sinfonie, partenici, litanie à 4, 5, 6, e 8 voci " (1617), "Responses to St. Franciscus with Salve " (1627).

(2) (Gratiani) Bonifazio, b. 1605, Marino (Papal States), maestro at the Jesuit church, Rome, d. June 15, 1664; a prolific and, in his time, highly esteemed church composer, whose works were in part published by his brother

after his death : seven books of motets à 2-6, six books of motets for one solo voice, one book of psalms with organ *ad lib.* à 5, one book of *Salmi concertati* à 5, two books of masses à 4-6, and one book for double chorus of concertante vesper psalms, responses à 4 for the Holy Week, litanies à 3-8, salve and antiphons to the Virgin à 4-6, festival antiphons à 2-4, church concertos à 2-5, vesper hymns à 2-5, *Musiche sacre e morali* with organ bass à 1-4, and motets à 2-3, transcriptions from above-named à 2-6. A number of other works remain in manuscript.

(3) Ludovico, distinguished stage singer (tenor), b. Aug., 1823, Fermo, d. there May, 1885 ; he sang principally on Italian stages, but also with great success in Paris (1858), London, and Vienna (1860).

(4) Francesco, brother of the former (baritone), b. April 16, 1829, Fermo; sang with success on the Italian stage, at Paris (1854, and 1856-61 at the Théâtre Italien), New York (1855), London, Petersburg (1861-64).

Grazioso (Ital.), *con grazia,* gracefully.

Grazzini, Reginaldo, b. Oct. 15, 1848, Florence, pupil of Teodulo Mabellini at the royal Conservatorio there. He was at first theatre maestro at Florence, etc., and in 1881 was appointed principal at the Conservatorio and maestro of the theatre at Reggio d'Emilia; already in 1882 he undertook the professorship of theory of music and the artistic direction of the Liceo Benedetto Marcello at Venice. G. is a refined and cultured musician, and has also made a good name as composer (*Cantata Biblica,* 1875 ; a mass à 3, 1882; symphonies, pf. pieces, an opera [manuscript]).

Great octave (C, D, E, etc.).

(*Cf.* ONCE-ACCENTED and A.)

Great organ, a part of the organ which is distinguished from the choir and swell organ by more numerous and more powerful stops. Each of these divisions of the organ has a separate keyboard.

Greco (Grecco), b. about 1680, Naples, pupil of Alessandro Scarlatti at the Conservatorio dei Poveri ; he succeeded his master as teacher, went later on to the Conservatorio di Sant' Onofrio, and became the teacher of Pergolesi and Da Vinci. Litanies with instrumental accompaniment and organ pieces of his have been preserved in manuscript (Rome).

Greef, Wilhelm, b. Oct. 18, 1809, Kettwig, a.d. Ruhr; in 1833, organist and teacher of singing at Mörs, d. Sept. 12, 1875. He is known as colleague of his brother-in-law, L. Erk, in the publication of school song-books, and in the new editions of Rinck's preludes, postludes, and of the same composer's " Choralbuch."

Greek music. The only real information which we have respecting the music of the ancient Greeks is derived from the writings of the theorists, and these have been preserved for us in somewhat considerable number. It is well known that in antiquity the art of music, like the other arts, was held in the highest respect, and not, as in the Middle Ages, as something fit only for vagabonds and outlaws. In the great festival games of the Greeks (the Olympian, Pythian, Nemean, and Isthmian), competitions of the muses (musical and poetical) played an important *rôle*. Originally, the Pythian festivals were merely musical ones in honour of Apollo at Delphi. The conqueror was crowned with a laurel wreath, for which the branches were fetched in solemn procession from the vale of Tempe. The ancient history of Greek music is so mixed up with sagas and myths that the historical kernel can only with difficulty be recognised. The invention of musical instruments, as indeed of music itself, is ascribed to the gods (Apollo, Hermes, Athene, Pan). Amphion, Orpheus, who infused life into stones and tamed wild beasts; Linos and Marsyas, who were put to death by the jealous Apollo—the one on account of his beautiful singing, the other on account of his excellent flute-playing—all these are merely legendary personages. A system of harmony, in the modern sense of the term, was foreign to the Greeks because polyphony was unknown to them: instruments accompanied singing in unison or in the octave. It may perchance have happened that, while the voice sustained a note, the accompanying instrument sounded a different one, after the manner of our changing- or passing-note, or executed an ornamental figure; or perhaps the instrumental accompaniment did not play all, but only the accented notes. Nevertheless, the Greek theory of music is very developed, and has spared much intellectual labour to the theorists of western lands; but has also, for many centuries, loaded their heads with quite superfluous ballast. The most essential part of it will be here briefly presented.

(1) *The system.*—Whilst our whole modern system of music is conceived in a major sense—*i.e.* in the sense of the major scale and the major chord, and in such a manner that the most intellectual theorist of modern times, Moritz Hauptmann (and with him the crowd of his disciples), looks upon the minor chord as a negative major chord—the Greeks regarded the very reverse method as the more natural one. A scale, which throughout was the very opposite of our major scale, formed the central point of their system. The Greeks imagined their scale passing from above downwards, while we are accustomed to think of ours as moving upwards (this is shown in both cases by the order of the letters representing the notes). In spite of many clever attempts, it has not been possible to ascertain the precise

pitch, but the middle octave may be regarded as corresponding to our *e′—e* :

which, as shown by the slurs over the semitones, is the reverse of our major scale c—c′ :

This scale was called the *Dorian*. The Greeks were strangers to the conception of chords (clangs, triads; [*see* SOUND, SUBSTITUTION OF]); hence all their theorems only concerned melody. They regarded this scale, therefore, when analysed, as composed of two similar tetrachords (sections of four tones) :

To a tetrachord of this kind, proceeding downwards by two whole-tone steps and one of half a tone, was given the name *Dorian*. The so-called complete system (*Systema teleion*) extended through two octaves—*i.e.* to the above scale was added a similar tetrachord above and below, but so that the last note of the one formed the first note of the next (conjunct tetrachords); and below, a note was added (*Proslambanomenos*), which was the lower octave of the middle, and the double lower octave of the highest note of the whole system. By this limitation (*A—a′*), as well as by the central position of the *a* (*cf.* also below, I., last paragraph), it is clearly shown that the scale was looked upon as an A minor scale. The tetrachords received the following names:

Extreme tetrachord
(*Tetrachordon hyperbolaeon*).

Disjunct tetrachord
(*Tetrachordon diezeugmenon*).

(*Diazeuxis* = Separation).

Middle tetrachord
(*Tetrachordon meson*).

Lowest tetrachord
(*Tetrachordon hypaton*).

A Proslambanomenos.

The two middle tetrachords were then separated. For modulations to the key of the fifth below (with the Greeks the one nearest related, as with us that of the fifth above), the semitone above the highest note of the middle tetrachord was used; and hence was formed a special conjunct tetrachord (synemmenon), a, $b\flat$, c, d, in apposition to the disjunct one. The full names of all the degrees were:

a' The highest of the extreme ... ... = *Nete*	} Hyper-bolaeon.	
g' The second highest of the extreme = *Paranete*		
f' The third of the extreme ... ... = *Trite*		
e' The highest of the dis-junct ... ... = *Nete*	} Diezeugmenon.	
d' The second highest of the disjunct ... ... = *Paranete*		
(Also the highest of the conjunct)	*Nete*	} Synemmenon. Meson. Hypa-ton.
c' The third of the disjunct = *Trite*		
(Also the second highest of the conjunct	*Paranete*	
b One next to the middle = *Paramese*		
[$b\flat$ The third of the conjunct]	*Trite*	
a The middle note ... ... = *Mese*		
g The forefinger note of the middle = *Lichanos*		
f The last but one of the middle ... = *Parhypate*		
e The lowest of the middle ... ... = *Hypate*		
d The forefinger note of the low... = *Lichanos*		
c The last but one of the low ... = *Parhypate*		
B The lowest of the low ... ... = *Hypate*		
A The added note .. .. = *Proslambanomenos.*		

The theorists attached special importance to the highest note of the middle tetrachord, which was specially called the central one (mese), and had *tonic* meaning. On this system were based not only the theoretical speculations of the Greeks, but also those of the learned musicians of the Middle Ages. Everywhere we meet with these terms; and even the compass, as given, was, for a long time, not exceeded. (*Cf.* GAMMA.) The church song of the early Middle Ages moved entirely within these limits, and the notation by means of Roman letters, which sprang up from the 9th to the 10th century, is strictly related to this scale of two octaves; the agreement extends, indeed, even to the adoption of the chromatic progression in the middle of the system (*Trite synemmenon-Paramese; Cf.* LETTER NOTATION). In its complete form, as here, the system was called either perfect (*Systema teleion*), or changeable, *i.e.* capable of modulation (*Systema metabolon*), in so far as the use of the conjunct tetrachord signified a modulation to the under-dominant; without the conjunct it was called unchangeable (*ametabolon*).

II. *Species of octaves* (Modes).—As the Greeks did not know harmony in our modern sense, their conceptions of key, mode, etc., have a purely melodic meaning; and their so-called keys are therefore nothing more than octave sections (species of octaves) from the same scale, viz., the one of two octaves, as given above; and in this the conjunct tetrachord is not taken into consideration. As middle point of the system there was the octave species e'—e (Dorian); the octave d'—d was called Phrygian, c'—c Lydian, and h—B Mixo-Lydian. These four were the four principal modes of the Greeks, just as the four church modes (q.v.) of the same name (but of different meaning) were the four authentic. In the subordinate modes belonging to them, and distinguished by the prefix "hypo," the

position of the fourth and fifth, of which the octave is composed, is inverted. Thus e' . . a . . e is Dorian; if the fifth e' a be placed an octave lower, or the fourth a e an octave higher, then A . . e . . a, also a . . e' . . a'' are Hypo-Dorian. (The conception of the Church Modes is radically different, *e.g.* the Phrygian (e—e') is composed of the fifth e b and the fourth b e'; if these be inverted, then is B . . . e . . . b = Hypo-Phrygian. Thus, whilst the Greek secondary modes lay a fifth below the principal modes, the plagal Church Modes lie only a fourth below the authentic. Again, the Church Modes are thought of as ascending, and already, harmonic conceptions enter into them.) The seven octave species of the Greeks are:

1. Dorian (e'—e).
2. Phrygian (d'—d).
3. Lydian (c'—c).
4. Mixo-Lydian (b—B).
5. Hypo-Dorian (Æolian, a—A).
6. Hypo-Phrygian (g'—g).
7. Hypo-Lydian (f'—f).
8. Hypo-Mixolydian (= Dorian, e'—e).

The often-mentioned difference between the *Thesis* (position) and *Dynamis* (meaning) of the notes (Ptolemy's "Harmonics," II., 5-11) is thus to be understood: *Thesis* relates to absolute pitch, so that a melody, by a change of *thesis*, only appears transposed, but in other respects preserves its character. *Dynamis*, on the other hand, is, as it were, a tonal function; the *dynamis* of the notes is changed, for example, when the tetrachord synemmenon is employed, whereby the mese a becomes more closely related to d' than to e', for then d' itself becomes mese (Modulation). Ptolemy, therefore, speaks quite logically of a "thesis" change of dynamis, *i.e.* of a totally different position of notes of the instrument (for example, through two octaves in E minor instead of A minor, e—e^2 instead of A—a'). It would, however, be a great mistake to imagine mese, paramese, etc., movable in the sense of the octave species having a mese other than the Dorian. In this respect Ptolemy's Ch. II. of second book—which, if carefully examined, is clear as daylight—has been thoroughly misinterpreted (by Westphal, O. Paul, etc.). On a cithara tuned in the Dorian mode (in A minor), the mese κατὰ θέσιν is at the same time mese κατὰ δύναμιν of the Dorian scale; the paramese κατὰ θέσιν (*i.e.* in the tuning as above, *b*) is the mese κατὰ δύναμιν of the Phrygian, *i.e.* the degree on which rests the Phrygian transposition scale (B minor); the mese κατὰ δύναμιν of the Lydian (*c♯*) takes the place of the *Trite diezeugmenon* κατὰ δέσιν; as Ptolemy, indeed, prudently adds, if the middle section (*E—e*) is tuned in the second octave species (Lydian), it is not *c*, but *c♯*. The notes κατὰ θέσιν, which it is desirable to keep at their absolute pitch and not to re-tune, are—as indeed logically follows if, in accordance with Ptolemy's wish, the flat keys are avoided—

A B e a b e' a',

i.e. mese, paramese, and hypate meson and their octaves, the very same which are unchangeable for the three tone-genera. (*See* below, V.)

III. *Transposition scales* (really modes in a modern sense).—If for the octave species *d'—d*, the tetrachord synemmenon is used instead of the diezeugmenon—*i.e.* *b♭* instead of *b*—it is no longer the Phrygian but the Hypo-Dorian; for the characteristic of the various octave species is the varied position of the semitone-step. (*See* the table under II.) But as the Hypo-Dorian octave species is to be regarded as extending from the Dorian mese to Proslambenomenos, *d'—d* with *b♭* belongs to a transposed Dorian system whose Proslambanomenos is not *A* but *d*. Greek music, as a matter of fact, was not confined to the diatonic scale *A—a'* without signature as in the old Church Modes, but used all the chromatic intermittent degrees, and also a number of higher and lower notes. As we have our major and minor keys on twelve or more different degrees, so had the Greeks their transpositions of the system described in I., and indeed, at a later period, fifteen, of which the oldest had the same names as those of the seven octave species. As may be seen from the tables of Greek notation given below, the fundamental scale of the Greeks was the Dorian: *e'd'c'b a g f e*. The system *A—a'*, without signature, was therefore called the Dorian. The transposed scales are each named according to the octave species which the section *e'—e* gives, for example, *e'd'c'b♭a g f e* is a Mixo-Lydian octave, and the

system *d—d''* with a *♮* is therefore called the Mixo-Lydian. Thus the octave *e'—e* belongs—

without signature to the system *A—a'* = Dorian.

with 1 ♯	,,	,,	*e—e*	= Hypo-Dorian.
,, 2 ♯	,,	,,	*B—b'*	= Phrygian.
,, 3 ♯	,,	,,	*F♯—f♯*	= Hypo-Phrygian.
,, 4 ♯	,,	,,	*c♯—c♯*	= Lydian.
,, 5 ♯	,,	,,	*G♯—g♯*	= Hypo-Lydian.
,, 6 ♯	,,	,,	*d♯—d♯*	= (high) Mixo-Lydian.
,, 1 ♮	,,	,,	*d—d'*	= (low) Mixo-Lydian.

But the Greek notation shows that the Dorian scale was imagined to begin above with *f*, upper leading-note, (A B Γ for *f' e'*), and the nine-stringed cithara had therefore, besides the Dorian (*e'—e*), also a Hypo-Lydian octave species (*f' e' d' c' b a g f*), without re-tuning, at its disposal (wherefore Bellermann and Fortlage regarded it as the fundamental scale of the Greeks). But, by using Trite synemmenon, it became Lydian (*f—f''* with one flat = high-Lydian; *cf.* *e—e''* with four sharps). Further transpositions of the synaphe (in spite of the contradiction of the older theorists) gave for the octave *f—f'* the (later) keys with flats :—

with 2 ♭ in the system of	*G—g'*	= Hypo-Æolian (high Hypo-Phrygian).
,, 3 ♭ ,, ,,	*c—c''*	= Æolian (high Phrygian).
,, 4 ♭ ,, ,,	*f—f''*	= Hypo-Iastian (high Hypo-Dorian).
,, 5 ♭ ,, ,,	*B♭—b♭'*	= Iastian (high Dorian).
,, 6 ♭ ,, ,,	*e♭—e♭''*	= Hyper-Iastian (high Mixo-Lydian).

The system *e♭—e♭''* with six flats is enharmonically identical with *d♯—d♯''* with six sharps. Both were called high Mixo-Lydian. Here ends the circle of fifths. (The names introduced for the six keys [undoubtedly more modern], are also to be met with again as the names of Church Modes, of which the number, in the 16th century, was increased to twelve [*see* GLAREAN], namely, as Ionian [= Iastian] and Hypo-Ionian, Æolian and Hypo-Æolian.)

(IV.) *Greek notation* (τὰ σήματα).—The Greeks possessed two kinds of notation—an older one, originally diatonic, which was still used at a later time for the notation of instrumental music, when the later one, equally adapted for enharmonic or chromatic, was introduced for vocal music. The complete table of both is as follows:

Octave Notes: Intermediate Part:

Middle Part (Enneachord):

Lower Part:

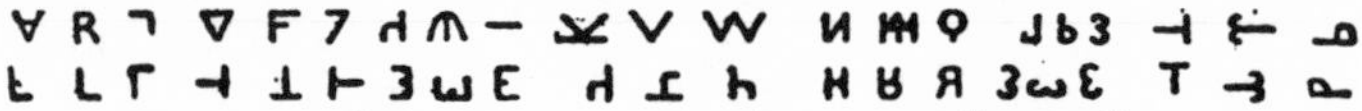

Ⅴ R ⅂ ▽ F ⅂ ⊢⌒ — ⅀ V W   Ⅿ ⋈ Ꝺ ꓕϧϨ ⊣ ⸦ ᴎ

Ⳑ Ⳑⵔ ⊣ ⊥ ⊢ Ӡ ⲱ Ɛ   ⊣ ⸢ ꜧ   Ⲏ Ꞵ Я Ӡⲱ Ɛ   T ⇥ ᴖ

d♯ d   c♯c   B   A♯   A   G♯G F♯   F .E

Not used:

Ⴆ � ꓮⴕ-ⵝⵝ

ꓛ -Ɛ⁘

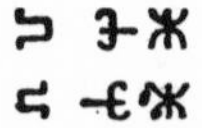

d♯

The upper series contains the (more modern) vocal notation, the lower (the older) the in-strumental. Every third sign of the latter is a fundamental sign of the original diatonic nota-tion: the other two are different positions or modifications of the same. For the practical use of these signs the following simple rules must be taken into account: (1) the half-tone (leading-note) relationship was expressed by two signs immediately following one another; (2) the *Pyknon* (*see* below, V.) of the enharmonic and chromatic tone relationship was expressed by three signs immediately following one another; (3) the middle signs of the above groups of three were only used for Parhypate and Trite (as leading-notes downwards to the funda-mental tones required by the signs given in the third place). From the following synopsis of the Pykna of the oldest scales (Dorian, Phry-gian, Lydian, with their Hypo- keys) the char-acter and spirit of the notation will be per-ceived (in vocal notation after Alypius).

Dorian (A min.).

$A\ B\ \Gamma$ $K\ \Delta\ M$ $N\ O\ \Pi$ $X\ \Psi\ \Omega$

f′   e′   c′   b   b♩   a   f   e

Hypo-Dorian (E min.).

$K\ \Lambda\ M$ $T\ \underline{Y}\ \Phi$ $X\ \Psi\ \mathcal{S}\mathcal{B}$ —   ⊣⌒ —

c′   b   g   f♯   f   e   c   b

Phrygian (B min.).

$X\ \Lambda\ \mathcal{U}$ $H\ \Theta\ I$ $K\ \Lambda\ M$ $T\ Y\ \Phi$

g′   f♯′   d′   c♯′   c′   b   g   f♯

Hypo-Phrygian (F♯ min.).

$H\ \Theta\ I$ $\Pi\ P\ C$ $T\ Y\ \Phi$ $\nabla\ F\ 7$

d′   c♯′   a   g♯   g   f♯   d   c♯

Lydian (c♯ min.).

$\perp\!\perp\ \Theta$ $\Delta\ E\ Z$ $H\ \Theta\ I$ $\Pi\ P\ C$

a′   g♯′   e′   d♯′   d′   c♯′   a   g♯

Hypo-Lydian (G♯ min.).

$\Delta\ E\ Z$ $N\ \Xi\ O$ $\Pi\ P\ C$ $\mathsf{V}\ R\ ⅂$

e′   d♯″   b   a♯   a   g♯   e   d♯

This exposition of the sound-meaning of the Greek note-signs has this advantage over that of Bellermann and Fortlage in that—as is possible in no other—the Dorian remains as fundamental scale (= A min.), whereas, with the above-named theorists, the Hypo-Lydian is taken as such, and the *simple* Dorian can only be represented with five flats or seven sharps

The same is to be found in C. von Jan's specification in Gevaert's " Histoire, etc.," in Leutsch's " Philologischer Anzeiger " (1878), but already evolved by Baron Stiles in the " Philosophical Transactions."

The value of the note was not indicated for singing, but was shown by the metre of the text. For instrumental music there were the signs — (two beats), ⌐ (three beats), ⌐⌐ (four beats, ⊔ (five beats) ; the absence of a sign indicated one beat (short). The general pause sign was ∧, the duration of the pause was shown by combining the ∧ with the signs of duration, ∧̄, ∧̄, etc. Unfortunately, only a very few unimportant fragments of old Greek music have been handed down to us, so that the knowledge of the meaning of the notes has hitherto been of little practical value.

(V.) *The tonal genera*, or modes of the Greeks, were not harmonic differences like ours (major and minor), but melodic. The Greeks divided —as already mentioned—the scale into tetrachords ; the normal tetrachord was the Dorian, consisting of two whole tone-steps and a half tone-step—for example, *e′ d′ c′ b* = ΓΗΛΜ. This *diatonic* genus was the oldest. Next to it arose, in hoary antiquity (according to tradition, an invention of Olympus) the (older) *Enharmonic*, in which the Lichanos, likewise the Paranete, was left out—for example, *e′ . . c̄′ b*. (*Cf.* SCALES OF FIVE DEGREES.) To that was added as third genus the *Chromatic*, which did not leave out the Lichanos or Paranete, but lowered it by a half-tone, so that there were two consecutive half-tone steps as in chromatic terminology of the present day, ♯c c′ b′. Lastly, the (newer) Enharmonic divided the half-tone of the diatonic tetrachord, or, more correctly, it introduced the Pythagorean third together with the pure third : *e′ . . c̄′ c′ b*. (*Cf.* QUINT-TONES.) The notation expresses the succession of the three closely connected tones (the so-called *Pyknon*) by three note-signs following one another directly (*see* IV.) ; *e′ . . c̄′ c′ b* = Γ . . . ΚΛΜ. The chromatic, *e′ . . ♯c′ c′ b*, was expressed by the same signs, only the Κ had a stroke through it, whereby it was understood to be raised by a half-tone. With regard to the various tonal genera, which changed the Paranete and Trite, likewise the Lichanos and Parhypate, the Greeks distinguished these tones as changeable (κινούμενοι), while the extreme tones of the tetrachords (Nete and Hypate, likewise Mese, Paramese, and Proslambanomenos) were unchangeable (ἑστῶτες). (*Cf.* above II., *Close*.) Besides these three tonal genera, the theorists established a great number of other divisions of the tetrachords, which were named colourings (*chroai*), but were not represented in the notation. Some of these were of the most extraordinary kind, and it was, perhaps, no mere chance that among them were to be found determinations

answering exactly to those of the present day viz., the ratio 15 : 16 for the half-tone, and that of 4 : 5 for the major third (as in Didymos and Ptolemy). It is known that Ramos, Fogliano, and Zarlino, who first definitely established these ratios, refer to Ptolemy. For further information respecting the system of scales and divisions of the tetrachord, *see* O. Paul, " Die absolute Harmonik der Griechen " (1866). The following writers give the complete development of the system : F. Bellermann, " Die Tonleitern und Musiknoten der Griechen " (1847) ; K. Fortlage, " Das musikalische System der Griechen in seiner Urgestalt " (1847), and F. A. Gevaert, " Histoire et théorie de la musique de l'antiquité " (1875 to 1881), in which also the Greek notation is presented in detail. In the highest degree interesting, but in many ways dangerous, are the writings of R. Westphal. (*Cf.* the articles relating to this matter by K. von Jan in the *Philologischer Anzeiger*.)

(VI.) The *practical exercise of music* among the Greeks consisted either of plain singing, or singing with accompaniment of stringed-instruments (Citharoedic), or of wind-instruments (Auloedic) ; or of simple playing on strings (Citharistic), or flute-playing (Auletic). The most important instruments, and those for the most part concerned with music of an artistic character, were the lyre, the cithara, and the flute. The *lyre* had an arched, the *cithara* a flat, sound-box. For a long time the number of strings on each was seven, but afterwards they became more numerous. The *magadis* was a larger stringed-instrument with twenty strings, on which it was possible to play in octaves. All the stringed instruments of the Greeks, even the older many-stringed *barbiton* and *pectis*, were plucked with the fingers ; the *plectrum* came into use later on. The aulos was a kind of *flûte-à-bec* constructed of various sizes. The *syrinx* (shepherd's pipe, Pandean pipe) was an instrument of an inferior kind (like that of Papageno in the *Magic Flute*). The melodies invented by composers received fixed names, like those of the Meistersingers : the general name was Nomos (" law," " setting "). Most famous was, for instance, the Pithian Nomos of the flute-player *Sacadas* (585 B.C.), who first insisted that the flute should be allowed as well as the cithara at the Pythian Games. In the matter of Citharoedic, the veteran *Terpander* (676, ninety years earlier) rendered special service. To him must probably be ascribed the establishment of the real musical art-forms of the Greeks. Among those who advanced the art of composition may still be named : *Clonas*, who flourished before Sacadas and, after Terpander, the inventor of important forms in Auletic ; and the still older *Archilochus* (688), who established, in place of the dactylic hexameters which alone were employed, the more popular lyric rhythms ambics); further, the lyric poet *Alcaos* and ie poetess *Sappho*, etc. Plutarch, in his history (music in dialogue form, dates the period of iodern music from *Thaletas* (670), the founder (the Spartan choral dances ("Gymnopädien"), nd Sacadas. The modern enharmonic sys-m seems to have been introduced about this me. (*See* V.). Greek music received its highest evelopment in tragedy, which, in a sense simi-r to that of the modern musical drama, was a nion of the arts of poetry, music, and mimetics. he choruses, at any rate, were sung through-ut, and also many monologues were set to iusic. Unfortunately, no music belonging to ie tragedies has been discovered, so that there , no concrete presentation of it.

(VII.) *Writers on music.*—A great number of reatises on the theory of music by Greek riters have been handed down to us. The ldest, and at the same time one of the most iteresting, is the nineteenth chapter of *Aris-tle's* "Problems" (d. 322 B.C.), also the fifth hapter of the eighth book of the same author's Republic." In *Plato* (d. 347) are only to be und scattered notices relating to music. Of he greatest importance are the writings of *ristoxenos* (pupil of Aristotle) which have ome down to us, and which treat of harmony nd rhythm. Unfortunately, many works of his most important of all Greek theorists have een lost. An epitome of the writings of Aris-xenos by *Euclid* has been preserved, while treatise on intervals (division of a string) is robably to be ascribed to the mathema-ician Euclid (3rd century). The already-named reatise of *Plutarch* on music belongs to the st century A.D.; to the 2nd century belong he writings of the Pythagorean *Claudius Pto-my*, of *Aristides Quintilianus, Gaudentios, Bac-ios, Theo von Smyrna*, and *Nichomachos;* and to he 3rd century the commentary of *Porphyry* n Ptolemy, as well as the table of scales of *lypius.* Also the fourteenth book of *Athenæus* nd the twenty-sixth chapter of *Iamblichus* con-ain notices of music. The "Syntagmo" of *sellus* belongs to the 11th century; the "Har-1onik" of *Bryennius*, as well as the supple-1entary chapter to Ptolemy by *Nicephoros* *regoras*, together with the commentary of *arlaam*, to the 14th century. The work of *Joëtius* (d. 524), "De musica," is a classical -atin revision of the G. system of music. It as recently been translated into German by). Paul (1872), but in a by no means trust-vorthy manner. P. Marquard published the ext of Aristoxenos, carefully revised, in 1868. or the rest, the collections of *Meibom* (1652) nd *Wallis* (1682) are to be found in most reat libraries. *Fr. Bellermann* published, in 840, a few small pamphlets on Greek music Anonymous, and a second essay by Bac-hios), but these attracted little notice. A few ragments of Greek hymns, belonging probably o the 2nd century A.D., are noticed in the same author's "Hymnen des Dionysios und Mesomedes" (1840). (*Cf.* also the important works of K. von Jan.)

Green, Samuel, b. 1730, London, d. Sept. 14, 1796, Isleworth. He was the most famous organ-builder of his time, and made organs not only for his own country, but also for Peters-burg, Jamaica, etc. G. transferred the Venetian shutters from the pianoforte to the organ. (*Cf.* also, GRENIÉ.)

Greene, Maurice, b. about 1696, London, d. there Sept. 1, 1755, chorister of St. Paul's Cathedral under King; he received further train-ing from Richard Brind, became organist of St. Dunstan's, and in 1717 of St. Andrew's, Holborn. In 1718 he succeeded Brind as organist of St. Paul's, and, in 1727, Croft as organist and composer of the Chapel Royal. On the death of Tudway he was elected pro-fessor of music at Cambridge, with the degree of Doctor of Music (1730), and in 1735 was appointed master of the king's band. An estate was bequeathed to him in 1750, and he planned a comprehensive collection of old English sacred music, the publication of which was entrusted to Boyce ("Cathedral Music"). G.'s principal works are: "Forty Select Anthems" (1743), which rank among the better sacred com-positions of the last century (two are contained in Augener's Edition No. 9120; the oratorio· *Jephthah* (1737), *The Force of Truth* (1744); several pieces for the stage (pastoral, *Florimel;* masque, *The Judgment of Hercules;* pastoral opera, *Phœbe*); likewise catches, canons, son-nets, cantatas, preludes, lessons. G. was one of the founders of the Society of Musicians, a friend and admirer of Handel, but a cool-ness sprang up in their friendship when the latter discovered he paid like court to Buonon-cini.

Grefinger (Gräfinger), Joh. Wolfgang (Wolf), Austrian composer of the 16th cen-tury, pupil of Hofhaimer; he lived in Vienna. He wrote: "Aurelii Prudentii Cathemerinon" (1515, odes set à 4); single motets in the second part of Grapheus's "Novum opus musicum" (1538), and in G. Rhaw's "Sacrorum hymn-orum liber I." (1542). G. was also editor of the very scarce "Psalterium Pataviense cum antiphonis, responsoriis, hymnisque in notis musicalibus" (1512).

Gregoir, (1) Jacques Mathieu Joseph, b. Jan. 18, 1817, Antwerp, d. Oct. 29, 1876, Brussels, where, from 1848, he lived engaged in teaching and composition. He was an excellent pianist, a pupil of Henri Herz and Rummel, and pub-lished a great number of pianoforte works, among which a concerto (Op. 100), a set of études; also many fantasias and duets for violin and 'cello, written jointly with Vieuxtemps, Léonard, and Servais.

(2) Édouard Georges Jacques, brother of the former, b. Nov. 7, 1822, Turnhout, near

Antwerp, d. June 28, 1890, Wyneghem, near Antwerp; he appeared likewise in 1837, as a pianist, together with his brother. He studied with Chr. Rummel at Biebrich, travelled also with the sisters Milanollo (1842), but devoted himself more to composition and to the study of musical history, and, after a short but active period as teacher at the normal school, Lierre (1850), settled for good at Antwerp. G. wrote several works for the stage: *La Vie* (Antwerp, 1848); *De Belgen en 1848* (Brussels, 1851); *La dernière nuit d'Egmont* (Brussels); *Leicester* (Brussels, 1854); *Willem Beukels* (Flemish one-act opera, Brussels, 1856); *La Belle Bourbonnaise* and *Marguerite d'Autriche*; also an historical symphony in four sections: "Les croisades," a symphonic oratorio, *Le déluge*, an overture, *Hommage à Henri Conscience*, an overture in c, a "Méthode théorique" of the organ, a "Méthode de Musique," songs for male chorus, pieces for pf., organ, violin, harmonium, songs, etc. His historical and bibliographical works (apart from many articles in the Paris and Belgian musical papers) are: "Études sur la nécessité d'introduire le chant dans les écoles primaires de la Belgique;" "Essai historique sur la musique et les musiciens dans les Pays-Bas" (1861); "Histoire de l'orgue" (1865, with biographical notices of Belgian and Dutch organists and organ-builders); "Galerie biographique des artistes-musiciens belges du XVIII. et du XIX. siècle" (1862, republished 1885); "Notice sur l'origine du celèbre compositeur Louis van Beethoven" (1863); "Les artistes-musiciens néerlandais" (1864); "Du chant choral et des festivals en Belgique" (1865); "Schetsen van nederlandsche toonkunstenaars meest allen wenig of tot hiertoe niet gekend;" "Notice historique sur les sociétés et écoles de musique d'Anvers" (1869); "Recherches historiques concernant les journaux de musique depuis les temps les plus reculés jusqu'à nos jours" (1872); "Notice biographique d'Adrian Willaert;" "Réflexions sur la régénération de l'ancienne école de musique flamande et sur le théâtre flamand;" "Les artistes-musiciens belges au XIX. siècle; réponse à un critique de Paris" (1874); "Documents historiques relatifs à l'art musical et aux artistes musiciens" (1872 to 1876, four vols.); "Phantéon musical populaire" (1877–79, three vols.); "Notice biographique sur F. J. Gossé dit Gossec" (1878); "1830–80: l'art musical en Belgique sous les règnes de Léopold I. et Léopold II." (1879); "Des gloires de l'Opéra et la musique à Paris" (three vols.; the first, 1880, treats of the period 1392–1750). All these works contain a quantity of new notices, especially concerning Belgian and Dutch artists, and the state of music in those countries, which must be noted as of great value (though not absolutely trustworthy) for the history of music. G. bequeathed his library to the Music School at Antwerp.

Gregorian Song, the ritual song of the Christian Church revised by Gregory the Great and hence bearing his name, which, up to the present day, has formed the basis of Catholic Church song (the traditions respecting it have, however, of late, been rudely disturbed by Gevaert). In history, a distinction is made between Ambrosian and Gregorian song, yet the actual difference between the two is far from clear. The tradition that Ambrosian song was full of rhythmical life, and that Gregorian song introduced, in its place, stately movement in notes of equal length, is a great chronological error, for church song only became *Cantus Planus* (in notes of equal value) after measured music had sprung up; and this is clearly shown in many passages in the works of writers of the early Middle Ages. Antiphonal singing, which forms the most essential part of the Gregorian Antiphonarium, is certainly of Ambrosian origin; anyhow, the performance of G. S., especially the singing of the Alleluia as described by writers, so thoroughly agrees with what pre-Gregorian fathers of the church (Augustine) have related respecting the church music of their day, that one is justified in supposing that there was no real difference between Ambrosian and G. S., but that the ritual service specially named Gregorian was nothing more than a general revision of ritual song by one of the first popes bearing the name of Gregory. The Ambrosian singing of hymns was not lively but dignified, quieter than the singing of Antiphons and of Alleluias with their jubilations. The notation of the Antiphonarium bearing the name of Gregory was not, as was formerly falsely supposed, that of Latin letter notation (so that the expression *Gregorian Letters* for A B C D E F G as names for the notes is to be rejected as an historical error), but that of neumes (q.v.). A copy of the original Antiphonarium (which no longer exists) is to be found in the monastery of St. Gallen. Since the invention of lines and clefs (11th century) G. S. is usually written in the so-called Choral note (q.v.). (*Cf.* the works on G. S. of Anton Maslon, Haberl, Kienle, Dom Pothier.)

Gregory I., the Great, Pope from 590 to 604, a name of high distinction in the history of music, for it is borne by the ritual music still in use, of the Catholic Church. (*See* GREGORIAN SONG.) G., however, did not compose the numerous antiphons, responses, offertories, communions, alleluias, tractus, etc., nor did he even introduce them into the Roman Church. The service which he—or indeed some one of the first popes bearing the name of Gregory (according to the opinion of Gevaert, who for strong reasons, refuses to accept the rôle assigned to Gregory I. by tradition—*cf.* his pamphlet "Les origines du chant liturgique, 1890—probably Gregory II. [715–731] or, indeed, his successor, Gregory III. [d. 741])—rendered is rather that of having collected rms of song which had come into use in various stricts during the previous centuries, and ving portioned them out for the ecclesiastal year, and thus framed the canon of the sole of Roman Catholic Christendom, so that ace his time no other changes have been made an those brought about—and against the intion of the church—by time (the transformaon of the original rhythmical life into the stiff ain-Chant in notes of equal length). The stem of four Church Modes, each with their agal, may have originated with G., or about s time, for Cassiodorus (6th century) does not ention them ; yet they are, however, known Flaccus Alcuin (8th century). On the other and, it is falsely asserted that G. introduced ster notation (A—G). The Antiphonarium of . was more probably written in neumes (q.v.). *f.* LETTER NOTATION.)

Grell, Eduard August, b. Nov. 6, 1800, erlin, d. Aug. 10, 1886, Steglitz, near Berlin, n of an organist, attended the college of the raues Kloster, received his musical training om his father, from the organist J. C. Kaufann, from his assistant (afterwards bishop), itschl, and lastly from Zelter. Already in s17 he was appointed organist of the St. icholas Church, entered the Singakademie 1817, became vice-director of the same ogether with Rungenhagen) in 1832, court-thedral organist in 1839, member of the cademy of Arts in 1841, choir-master at the .thedral from 1843–45, after the death of ungenhagen (1851), teacher of composition at se Akademie, member of the senate of the kademie, and principal conductor of the " Singademie," Berlin. In 1858 he received the tle of professor (twenty years previously he ad been named royal musical director), and in 64, as highest distinction, the order *pour le érite*. He retired from the directorship of se " Singakademie " in 1876, but continued is functions at the Akademie until his death. a 1883 he received the title of *Doctor of Theogy hon. c.* from the university of Berlin. He as a worthy contrapuntist, and learned on se subject of ancient music. His merit as a acher and conductor was great, and as a comoser he has made his name respected. With se exception of an overture and pieces for the rgan, he wrote only vocal music; particularly orthy of mention are a grand mass à 16, salms à 8 and 11, a Te Deum, many motets, antatas, hymns, Christmas songs, an oratorio *Die Israeliten in der Wüste*), songs, duets, and a our-part arrangement of the " Choralmelodien umtlicher Lieder des Gesangbuchs zum gottesienstlichen Gebrauch für evangelische Geseinden " (1883, for male chorus). G. was an xtreme representative of the view that vocal ausic is the only real music, and that the se of instrumental music indicates a desdence in pure art. (*Cf.* his " Aufsätze und utachten," published by Bellermann, 1887.)

Grenié, Gabriel Joseph, b. 1757, Bordeaux, d. Sept. 3, 1837, Paris, an administrative functionary who occupied himself in leisure hours with experiments in acoustics ; he was the inventor of the *orgue expressif, i.e.* of a reed-instrument with free vibrating reeds and varying intensities of sound, regulated by treadles acting as bellows-boards. The *orgue expressif* of G. is nothing else than the now universally used harmonium, and the latter differs from the former only by the introduction of several stops. The *orgue expressif* constructed by Erard (q.v.) was an essential development of the instrument, as in it the various intensities of sound depended upon the pressure of the finger ; thus one note could be played loud, whilst the others sounded softer. (*See* HARMONIUM.)

Gresnick, Antoine Frédéric, b. March 2, 1752, Liége, d. Oct. 16, 1799, Paris ; he was trained at the Liége college at Rome, concluded his musical studies at Naples under Sala, and was already known in 1780 as a dramatic composer. His opera (*Il Francese bizarro*) was given at Sarzana in 1784 ; from 1785–91 he lived in London, where already before 1784 he had made his *début* as an opera composer ; he wrote there *Demetrio, Alessandro nell' Indie, La donna di cattiva umore* (which procured for him the post of master of the music to the Prince of Wales), and *Alceste* (for the vocalist Mara). In 1793 he had a great success at the Grand Théâtre, Lyons, with *L'amour exilé de Cythère*, and in consequence found the Paris theatres open for his works. He wrote first some operas for the Théâtre de la Rue du Louvois, then a series for the Théâtre Favart and the Théâtre Montansier. In 1799 the Grand Opéra brought out *Léonidas, ou les Spartiates* (by G. and Persuis), which was not successful, whilst *La forêt de Brahma* was returned to him for revision. He died through sorrow caused by this failure. Besides the operas, G. wrote some small vocal works, and a concertante for clarinet and bassoon, which appeared in print.

Grétry, André Erneste Modeste, b. Feb. 8 (not 11), 1741, at Liége, d. Sept. 24, 1813, Montmorency, near Paris, son of a poor musician, received his first instruction as chorister, and then from different teachers of his native town. When, however, regular instruction in theory began, he was already too impatient to study seriously. But he had tried his hand at composition, and felt the need of understanding form. A Mass, which was produced at Liége, procured for him maintenance from the cathedral chapter, and enabled him, in 1759, to go to Rome for further training, and there he was for five years pupil of Casali, without even then being able to settle down to serious contrapuntal studies. He soon perceived that the field of his glory was not the church, but the theatre. After his first fortunate attempt with an intermezzo (*Le vendem-miatrice*) for a small Roman theatre, he went in 1767 to Voltaire, at Geneva, to ask him for a libretto for a comic opera. He did not succeed in obtaining it, but re-arranged for Geneva an old libretto (*Isabelle et Gertrude*) and met with much success. On the advice of Voltaire he went to Paris, where he at first encountered great difficulties, and did not get further with his first work (*Les mariages Samnites*) than the first orchestral rehearsal ; but already the second (*Le Huron*) met with pleasing success (Opéra Comique, 1768). There quickly followed *Lucile* (1769) and one of his best operas, *Le tableau parlant* (1769), which made him truly popular. He now developed extraordinary fertility. There followed, 1770, *Sylvain*, *Les deux avares*, and *L'amitié à l'épreuve* ; 1771, *Zémire et Azor* and *L'ami de la maison* ; 1773, *Le magnifique* ; 1774, *La rosière de Salency* ; 1775, *Céphale et Procris* (Grand opéra) and *La fausse magie* ; 1776, *Les mariages Samnites* (revised) ; 1777, *Matroco* and *Les événements imprévus* ; 1778, *Le jugement de Midas* and *L'amant jaloux* ; 1779, *Aucassin et Nicolette* ; 1780, *Andromaque* (Grand opéra) ; 1781, *Émilie* (*La belle esclave*, at the Grand Opéra as the fifth act of a ballet, *La fête de Mirza*) ; 1782, *La double épreuve* (*Colinette à la cour*) and *L'embarras des richesses* (both at the Grand Opéra) ; 1784, *Théodore et Pauline* (*L'épreuve villageoise*), *Richard Cœur-de-Lion*, and *La caravane du Caïre* (Grand Opéra), the words by the Comte de Provence, afterwards Louis XVIII. (performed 506 times) ; 1785, *Panurge dans l'île des lanternes* ; 1786, *Les méprises par ressemblance* ; 1787, *Le comte d'Albert*, *La suite du comte d'Albert*, and *Le prisonnier anglais* (*Clarice et Belton*) ; 1788, *Amphitryon* (Grand Opéra) ; 1789, *Le rival confident*, *Raoul Barbe-Bleue*, and *Aspasie* (Grand Opéra) ; 1790, *Pierre le Grand* ; 1791, *Guillaume Tell* ; 1792, *Basile* (*A trompeur, trompeur et demi*), and *Les deux couvents* (*Cécile et Dermancé*) ; 1793, *La rosière républicaine* ; 1794, *Joseph Barra*, *Callias, Denys le tyran* (Grand Opéra), *La fête de la raison* (all pieces connected with the Revolution) ; 1797, *Lisbeth*, *Le barbier de village*, and *Anacréon chez Polycrate* ; 1799, *Elisca* ; 1801, *La casque et les colombes* ; and finally, 1803, *Delphis et Mopsa* and *Le ménage*. G. is an epoch-making personage in the history of comic opera. In his "Mémoires, ou essais sur la musique" (1789, three vols.; in German by Spazier with annotations), he clearly and forcibly lays down the principles by which dramatic composition should be guided. They are closely allied to those of Gluck, only G. goes still further, cares little for actual singing, and would have only recitation. His influence on the further development of comic opera was of lasting importance. Isouard, Boieldieu, Auber, Adam, were the heirs of Grétry. His *Barbe-Bleue* and *Richard Cœur-de-Lion* had a fairly long lease of life in Germany ; the latter opera is still in the Paris *répertoire*. He never really occupied any official post ; he was inspector at th newly established Conservatoire in 1795 on for a few months. He desired to be fre so as to give his whole attention to h dramatic works. On the other hand, honou of all kinds were bestowed on him. Alread in 1785, one of the streets in the neigl bourhood of the Théâtre Italien was calle by his name, and his bust was placed in th *foyer* of the Grand Opéra. A statue in marb was set up in the vestibule of the Opéra Comiqu by Comte Livry in 1809 ; the Prince-Bishop c Liége named him privy councillor in 1783 ; i 1796, on the establishment of the Institut d France he was appointed member of the music section, and was elected among the first knigh of the *Légion d'honneur* by Napoleon in 1802. Fc a time the Revolution diminished his fortur and his pensions, and Cherubini and Méh caused his operas to be forgotten ; but th famous vocalist Elleviou revived his reputatio (1801), and Napoleon bestowed on him a hanc some pension. The last ten years of his lif were spent at Rousseau's "Eremitage," whic he had bought. A murder with theft, whic took place in the neighbourhood, really drov him back to Paris in 1811 ; but, when he fe his end approaching, he was carried back to hi country house to die there. Besides his opera G. wrote a Requiem, *De Profundis, Confiteor*, som motets, six symphonies (1758), two quartets fo pf., flute, violin, and bass, six stringed quartet and six pf. sonatas, some prologues and ep logues (for the opening or closing of Pari theatres), and some *divertissements* for the court He left the following operas, which, however, wer never produced : *Alcindor et Zaïde*, *Ziméo*, *Ze mar*, *Electre*, *Diogène et Alexandre*, and *Les Maure en Espagne*. A statue was erected to G. in hi native town (Liége) in 1842. An exhausti biography of G. has not yet been written ; on the other hand, a number of short notices A. J. Grétry (nephew), "G. en famille" (1815) Livry, "Recueil de lettres écrites à G." (1809) L. D. S. (Saegher), "Notice biographique su A. G." (1869) ; Éd. Gregoir (1883) ; Brune (1884), etc. The commission for the publica tion of the works of old Belgian musicians ha been lately (since 1883) preparing a complet edition of his works. (Breitkopf u. Härtel.)

Greulich, (1) Karl Wilhelm, b. Feb. 13 1796, Kunzendorf, near Löwenberg (Silesia), d 1837 as teacher of music at Berlin. He com posed and published pianoforte works an songs.

(2) Adolf, b. 1819, Posen, d. 1868 as teache of music at the St. Catherine Institute, Mos cow ; he also published pianoforte pieces.

(3) Adolf, successor of Brosig as cathedra capellmeister at Breslau (1884), b. 1836, Schmie deberg, Silesia (where his father was cantor) d. July 20, 1890, Breslau. He studied witl Brosig, Mosewius, Baumgart, and Peter Lüstner

1857 singer in the choir and solo bass of the thedral, in 1870 cathedral organist. He has mposed much sacred music.

Grieg, Edvard Hagerup, b. June 15, 1843, ergen (Norway), received, at an early age, s first musical instruction from his mother, musically gifted lady and a pianist. In 1858, the advice of Ole Bull, he was sent, for rther training, to the Leipzig Conservatorium, nere he became the pupil of Moscheles, auptmann, Richter, Reinecke, and Wenzel. 1863 he went to Copenhagen to continue s studies under Gade, who, together with Hartmann, exercised a certain influence over e development of his talent as composer. A ort but momentous meeting with Rikard Nordak, a young and gifted Norwegian tone-poet, o died shortly afterwards, proved of decisive nsequence. G. himself thus refers to it :— The scales fell from my eyes; through him I st learned to know the feelings of the people d my own nature. We conspired against the eminate Scandinavianism of Gade mixed with endelssohn, and with enthusiasm entered the w path, along which the Northern school is w travelling." In 1867 he founded a choral ciety at Christiania, which he conducted until 8o. In 1865 and 1870 he visited Italy, and d intercourse with Liszt in Rome; he also peatedly made long visits to Germany, and rticularly Leipzig, and produced his comsitions; among others he himself played the noforte concerto (Op. 16) at a Gewandhaus ncert (1879). Since 1880 he has resided mostly Bergen. G. is undeniably a composer gifted th a healthy originality, and he has written rks of a highly poetical nature (especially s three violin sonatas: in F, Op. 8; G minor, o. 13; and c minor, Op. 45). Further may named "Vor der Klosterpforte," for soprano lo, female chorus, and orchestra (Op. 20); anderkennung," for baritone, male chorus, d orchestra (Op. 31); "Der Bergentrückte," baritone with stringed orchestra and two rns (Op. 46); scenes from *Olav Trygvason;* isic to Ibsen's *Peer Gynt* (Op. 23); orchestral rings) suite, "Aus Holbergs Zeit"; concert erture, "Im Herbst"; pianoforte concerto A minor; 'cello sonata (Op. 36); also, and ove all, his pianoforte pieces (Op. 1, 3, 6 Humoresken"], 7 [Sonata], 9, 11, 12, 14, 15, , 19 ["Aus dem Volksleben"], 22 [" Sigurd rsalfar," for four hands], 24 [Ballade], 28, 29, [Norwegian Dances], 37, 38), the romance th variations for two pianofortes, and songs p. 2, 4, 5, 10, 18, 44, 48, 49; the greater number which are included in the Peters' "Griegbums"). *See* E. Closson, "E. G. et la isique scandinave," republished from the Guide musical." G. and his wife visited ndon in 1888 and 1889, also in 1894 and 1897.

Griepenkerl, (1) Friedrich Konrad, b. 82, Peine (Brunswick), was for a long time

(until 1816) teacher at the Fellenberg Institute, Hofwyl (Switzerland), d. April 6, 1849, as professor at the Carolinum, Brunswick. He published a "Lehrbuch der Aesthetik" (1827, based on Herbart), and also, jointly with Roitzsch, J. S. Bach's instrumental compositions.

(2) Wolfgang Robert, son of the former, b. May 4, 1810, Hofwyl; in 1839 teacher of the history of art at the Carolinum, and in 1840 teacher of literature at the military school, Brunswick (until 1847), d. there (1868) in needy circumstances. He proved himself an advanced thinker in some articles in the *Neue Zeitschrift für Musik* and in "Das Musikfest oder die Beethovener" (novel), "Ritter Berlioz in Braunschweig" (1843), and "Die Oper der Gegenwart."

Griesinger, Georg August, "Legationssekretär" to the Saxon Embassy at Vienna, d. April 27, 1828, Leipzig. He was on intimate terms with Haydn, and was the author of the oldest Haydn biography (1810), which served as a basis to Framery for his "Notice sur Haydn" (1810).

Griffbrett (Ger.), the finger-board of stringed instruments, such as the violin, guitar, lute, etc.; the black-stained, or ebony board, glued on to the upper smooth portion of the neck, on which, in order to shorten the strings, the player presses firmly. With instruments whose strings are plucked, also in old viols (gambas, etc.), the finger-board (the neck) is divided into frets (q.v.), whereby the finding of the right pitch is made easier.

Grill, (1) Franz, d. about 1795, Oldenburg, published twelve sonatas for pf. and violin (written in the style of Haydn), twelve quartets, and a caprice for piano.

(2) Leo, b. Feb. 24, 1846, Pesth, studied under Franz Lachner at Munich, since 1871 teacher of choral singing and theory at the Leipzig Conservatorium; also composer.

Grimm, (1) Friedrich Melchior, Baron von, b. Dec. 26, 1723, Ratisbon, d. Dec. 18, 1807, Gotha, went to Paris 1747, where he became acquainted with Rousseau, D'Alembert, Diderot, etc., and afterwards took part in the publication of the great "Eycyclopédie." G. possessed good judgment in music, and took part in the fierce strife between the adherents of the old French serious opera and those who supported the Italian Opera buffa established in Paris in 1752. He sided with the latter (Buffonists), and wrote some pamphlets in their favour (the warfare commenced with his "Lettre sur Omphale," 1752). In 1753 he was appointed correspondent to the Duchess of Gotha, and wrote to her a great number of letters, giving minute details with respect to literary and musical events in Paris; these were published 1812-14 ("Correspondance littéraire, philosophique et critique," seventeen vols.), and contain much that is interesting concerning the operas of Monsigny, Philidor, Grétry, Gluck, etc. The Revolution drove him from Paris.

(2) Karl, b. April 28, 1819, Hildburghausen, d. Jan. 9, 1888, Freiburg (Silesia), is known as the composer of many grateful pieces for 'cello; he was principal 'cellist for about fifty years at the court theatre, Wiesbaden.

(3) Karl Konstantin Ludwig, a distinguished performer on the harp, b. Feb. 17, 1820, Berlin, d. there May 23, 1882, as royal Kammervirtuos, leader and member of the court band.

(4) Julius Otto, b. March 6, 1827, Pernau (Livonia), studied philology at Dorpat, but, after passing the higher teachers' examination, became a pupil of the Leipzig Conservatorium, and lived for some time at Göttingen, where he founded a vocal society. From 1860 he was conductor of the "Cäcilienverein," Münster (Westphalia); from 1878, also, royal musical director at the academy there. Of his compositions the following have obtained warm recognition: "Suiten in Kanonform" (for stringed orchestra), a symphony (in D minor), pf. pieces, songs, etc.

Grimmer, Christian Friedrich, b. Feb. 6, 1800, Mulda, near Freiberg (Saxony), d. June, 1850; he studied theology at Leipzig, but turned to music, and became known as a composer of songs and ballads, which Robert Franz, in 1878, honoured by preparing a new edition of them.

Grisar, Albert, b. Dec. 26, 1808, Antwerp, d. June 15, 1869, Asnières, near Paris; he was originally intended for the career of a merchant, but ran away from his employer at Liverpool and put himself under Reicha at Paris, in 1830, for composition, but was soon obliged to give this up and return to his parents at Antwerp. In 1833 he made his *début* at Brussels as a dramatic composer with *Le mariage impossible,* which procured for him a government subsidy, enabling him to continue his studies in Paris. In 1836 his *Sarah* was brought out at the Opéra Comique, and there followed *L'an 1000* (1837), *La Suisse à Trianon* (Variétés, 1838), *Lady Melvil* (Renaissance, 1838), *L'eau merveilleuse* (Renaissance, 1839), *Les travestissements* (Opéra Comique, 1839), and *L'opéra à la cour* (1840, jointly with Boieldieu). In spite of good success, he resolved to make further serious study, and in 1840 went to Mercadante at Naples. He returned to Paris in 1848, and produced *Gilles ravisseur* (1848), *Les porcherons* (1850), *Bon soir, Monsieur Pantalon* (1841), *Le carillonneur de Bruges* (1852, all at the Opéra Comique); *Les amours du diable* (Théâtre Lyrique, 1853), *Le chien du jardinier* (Opéra Comique, 1855), *Voyage autour de ma chambre* (1859), *Le joaillier de St. James* (Opéra Comique, a revision of *Lady Melvil*), *La chatte merveilleuse* (Théâtre Lyrique, 1862), *Bégaiements d'amour* (also there, 1864), and *Douze innocentes* (Bouffes Parisiens, 1865).

Besides these, he left eleven operas, so[m]e partly sketched out, some almost finished. 1870 a statue (modelled by Brackeleer) w[as] erected to his memory in the vestibule of t[he] Antwerp theatre. G. also published ma[ny] romances and other small vocal pieces.

Grisi, (1) Giuditta, b. July 28, 1805, Mila[n,] d. May 1, 1840, at the villa belonging to h[er] husband (Count Barni) near Cremona. S[he] was a distinguished dramatic vocalist (mez[zo]-soprano), and shone up to 1834 on Ital[ian] stages, and at Paris. Bellini wrote for her t[he] Romeo, and for her sister the Julia, in *M[ontecchi e Capuletti.*

(2) Giulia, sister of the former, b. July [28?] 1811, Milan, d. Nov. 29, 1869, while on a journ[ey] at Berlin. She studied under Giacomelli [and] Bologna, and received further training fr[om] Marliani at Milan. She was a singer of t[he] first rank, was a "star" at Paris from 18[33?] and from 1834–49 was engaged as *prima do[nna]* both at Paris and London. In 1836 she marr[ied] Count Melcy, and afterwards contracted [a] second marriage with the tenor Mario, w[ith] whom she visited America in 1854.

Groningen, S. van, pianist, b. June 23, 18[51?] Deventer, was, first of all, technologist, b[ut] then studied music under Raif and Kiel at t[he] Berlin Hochschule. He settled as teacher, fi[rst] at Zwolle, and afterwards at the Hague, f[re]-quently giving concerts in his native coun[try] and abroad. He now lives at Leyden. [He] is also composer (pianoforte quartet, suite [for] two pianofortes, etc.).

Grosheim, Georg Christoph, b. July [18?] 1764, Cassel, lived there with varying fortu[ne] and died 1847. His compositions are, for t[he] most part, unpublished; only organ prelud[es,] pf. fantasias, variations, etc., school songs, [a] collection of popular melodies, two ope[ras] (*Titania* and *Das heilige Kleeblatt*), "Hect[ors] Abschied" (two solo voices with orchestr[a]) and "Die zehn Gebote" à 1-4 with org[an] appeared in print. He published also a "[D]e-formiertes hessisches Choralbuch," a musi[cal] paper, *Euterpe* (1797 to 1798), a pf. score [of] Gluck's *Iphigenia in Aulis*, with German tra[ns]-lation, and the following pamphlets: "I[m] Leben der Künstlerin Mara" (1823); "Ue[ber] Pflege und Anwendung der Stimme" (183[?]) "Chronologisches Verzeichnis vorzüglic[her] Beförderer und Meister der Tonkunst" (183[?] "Fragmente aus der Geschichte der Musi[k]" (1832); "Ueber den Verfall der Tonkunst" (1835); and "Generalbass-Katechismus." [He] was also a contributor to *Elegante Zeitu[ng,] Freimütige, Amphion* (Dutch), *Cecilia,* and Schilling's "Universallexikon der Tonkunst."

Grosjean, (1) Jean Romary, b. Jan. [?] 1815, Rochesson (Vosges), d. Feb. 13, 1888, Dié. In 1837 he was organist at Remiremo[nt,] in 1839 at St. Dié Cathedral; he was a d[is]-tinguished organist, and his collection of or[gan] ces by good masters is one for which he reserves the gratitude of organists.

(2) E r n s t, nephew of the former, b. Dec. 18, 844, Vagney, organist at Verdun, published many compositions for organ and for pianoforte, and a " Théorie et pratique de l'accompagnement du plain chant."

Gross, J o h a n n B e n j a m i n, b. Sept. 12, 809, Elbing, excellent 'cellist, was from 1834– in the private quartet party of Von Liphardt Dorpat (*See* DAVID, 1). He died Sept. 1, 848, as principal 'cellist in the Imperial orchestra at Petersburg. He published a 'cello nata with bass and another with pianoforte, concertino, duets, and many soli for 'cello, ur quartets for strings, songs, etc.

Gross-, German prefix. For the names of instruments compounded with G.- (*Grosspommer*, c.), and of organ stops, etc. (*Grossnasat, Grossdackt*, etc.), *see* the simple names.

Grosse caisse (Fr.), the big, or bass, drum.

Grossi, (1) G. F. (*See* SIFACE.) (2) C a r l o t t a (Charlotte G r o s s m u c k), stinguished coloratura singer, b. Dec. 23, 849, Vienna, pupil at the Conservatorium ere, was engaged at Vienna in 1868, and, om 1869–78 at the Berlin court opera-house. he returned to Vienna in 1878.

Ground-bass, a bass passage of a few bars hich is again and again repeated, whilst the her parts are varied at every repetition.

Grove, S i r G e o r g e, b. Aug. 13, 1820, lapham (Surrey), celebrated English writer n music, was originally an engineer, and, as ch, made a good career; he built lighthouses, ridges, etc. In 1850 he succeeded Scott Russel secretary of the Society of Arts, and in 1852 came secretary of the Crystal Palace Comny, and in 1873 director of the latter. From at time he has been active also as editor, nerally, to the publishing house of Macmiln & Co., first of *Macmillan's Magazine*, and om 1879 of the excellent " Dictionary of usic and Musicians," which contains many oroughly original studies, some by G. himlf (for example, Schubert). When the Royal ollege of Music was established in 1883, G. came director, and was knighted. G. was so chief contributor to W. Smith's " Dicnary of the Bible," travelled twice to Palesne, and was personally concerned with the tablishment of the Palestine Exploration und. G. was a friend of the famous theologian, tanley, and went with him in 1878 to America, d became his literary executor. " Grove's usical Dictionary," which counts the most lebrated musical savants of various nationities among its contributors, is also specially be valued for its large number of excellent ustrations of old instruments. Through the rsonal influence of Sir George, a society has been formed for the purpose of photographing the MS. scores of Beethoven (1891).

Grua, P a u l, b. Feb. 2, 1754, Mannheim, d. July 5, 1833, Munich, was trained, at the expense of the Elector Karl Theodor, at Bologna by Padre Martini and under Traetta at Venice; he returned in 1779 to Munich, whither, meanwhile, Karl Theodor had transferred his court. G. succeeded his father as court capellmeister, and as member of the duke's councilboard. In addition to an opera (*Telemacco*), G. wrote only sacred and orchestral works (thirtyone orchestral masses, six vespers, twenty-nine offertories and motets, six misereres, three Stabat Maters, three Te Deums, three requiems, psalms, responses, etc., and concertos for pf., clarinet, flute, etc.

Gruber, J o h a n n S i g i s m u n d, b. Dec. 4, 1759, Nuremberg, d. there Dec. 3, 1805, as lawyer. He published: " Litteratur der Musik " (1783, a work greatly inferior to the one of similar title by Forkel), " Beiträge zur Litteratur der Musik " (1785), and " Biographien einiger Tonkünstler " (1786).

Grün, F r i e d e r i k e, excellent stage-singer (soprano), b. June 14, 1836, Mannheim, commenced her stage career there as chorus-girl, first took solo parts at Frankfort, and was then engaged at Cassel (1863) and Berlin (1866–69), and was highly esteemed. In 1869 she married a Russian, Baron v. Sadler. After further successful training under Lamperti at Milan, she sang " Elsa " (*Lohengrin*) at Bologna, and appeared on various stages with marked success.

Grünberg, P a u l E m i l M a x, distinguished violinist, b. Dec. 5, 1852, Berlin, was member of the court band at Meiningen, then leader at Sondershausen, and later on at the Landestheater, Prague; he now lives in Berlin as teacher.

Grünberger, L u d w i g, b. April 24, 1839, Prague, d. Dec. 12, 1896, pianist and composer, studied first under Franz Skroup and Jos. Kisch, then in 1855 at Dresden, under Reichel and Rietz. He published numerous pf. pieces, for two and four hands, songs and choruses, two quartets for strings, a suite for violin and 'cello, and "Nordische Suite u. Humoreske " for orchestra.

Grund, F r i e d r i c h W i l h e l m, b. Oct. 7, 1791, Hamburg, d. there Nov. 24, 1874. He was an excellent musician, and much sought after as a teacher. In 1819 he established the " Singakademie" at Hamburg, and conducted the Philharmonic Concerts (1828–62). G. wrote symphonies, quartets, pf., 'cello, and violin sonatas, a quartet for pf. and wind-instruments, a mass à 8, several operas, and pf. studies (commended by Schumann), etc.

Grundakkord (Ger.), a chord with its fundamental note in the bass ; a chord which is not inverted.

Grundbass (Ger.), a fundamental bass.

Grundstimme (Ger.), the lowest, fundamental, part.

Grünfeld, (1) **Alfred**, important pianist, b. July 4, 1852, Prague, pupil of the Conservatorium there and of Kullak at Berlin; he lives in Vienna as "Kammervirtuos."

(2) **Heinrich**, brother of the former, excellent 'cellist, b. April 21, 1855, Prague, pupil of the Conservatorium there, lives, since 1876, at Berlin, where for eight years he was teacher at Kullak's Academy, and, jointly with X. Scharwenka and G. Holländer (afterwards with Sauret), arranged concerts. In 1886 G. was appointed violoncellist to the Emperor.

Gruppetto (Gruppo, Groppetto, Groppo), Ital. "knot," same as "turn," both when it is written out in full-sized notes, and when it is indicated in small notes, or by ∾ S.

Grützmacher, (1) **Friedrich Wilhelm Ludwig**, b. March 1, 1832, Dessau, where his father was chamber musician. From him he received his first musical instruction, and was trained by Karl Drechsler in 'cello-playing, while Fr. Schneider instructed him in theory. In 1848 he went to Leipzig as member of a small orchestra, was "discovered" by David, and in 1849 appointed Cossmann's successor as principal 'cellist of the Gewandhaus orchestra, and at the same time teacher of his instrument at the Conservatorium. He occupied the post until 1860, when Rietz attracted him to Dresden. He is still there, one of the chief ornaments of the court orchestra; he bears the title "Königlicher Kammervirtuos." G. is not only one of the most remarkable performers on the 'cello, but also a highly prized and prolific composer for his instrument and an exceptionally good teacher. Among others, his younger brother Leopold (q.v.), F. Hilpert, E. Hegar, W. Fitzenhagen, and O. Brückner, have studied under him. Besides concertos, concert pieces, and exercises for 'cello, G. has also written orchestral and chamber music, pf. pieces and songs.

(2) **Leopold**, brother of the former, b. Sept. 4, 1835, Dessau, likewise received instruction from K. Drechsler in 'cello playing, and from Fr. Schneider in theory. He afterwards received further training from his brother, was for a time member of the theatre and Gewandhaus orchestra at Leipzig, later on principal 'cellist in the court band, Schwerin, and after that at the "Landestheater," Prague, whence, on the departure of the younger brothers Müller from Meiningen, he was appointed member of the court band there. Since 1876 he has been principal 'cellist at Weimar with the title of "Kammervirtuos." Leopold G. is also a diligent composer for his instrument.

(3) **Friedrich**, jun., son of Leopold G., a talented 'cellist. He studied with his father and uncle, was, for some years, principal 'cellist in the court band at Sondershausen, whence he went in 1890 to Budapest, and became a

member of the theatre orchestra and teacher a the Conservatorium of that city.

Guaracha (Sp.), a graceful, gay, Spanis national dance, one part of which is in $\frac{3}{8}$ (or $\frac{3}{4}$ and the other in $\frac{2}{4}$ time.

Guaranita, Guarana, or **Garanita** (Sp.), variety of the Spanish guitar.

Guarnerius (Guarneri), name of one of th three most famous families of violin-makers o Cremona. (*See* AMATI and STRADIVARI.) (1 **Andrea**, pupil of Niccolò Amati, worked abou 1650–95. His instruments are vastly inferio to those of his nephew. (*See* below.)

(2) **Giuseppe**, son of the former, worke between 1690 and 1730; his instruments—im tated partly from those of Stradivari, part! from those of his cousin of like name—ar highly esteemed.

(3) **Pietro**, brother of the former, worke between 1690 and 1725, first of all at Cremon afterwards at Mantua; his instruments, thoug prized, lack brilliancy.

(4) **Pietro**, son of Giuseppe G., grandso of Andrea G., worked between 1725–40, an adopted his father's measurements.

(5) **Giuseppe Antonio**, nephew of Andre G., called G. del Gesu, because his labels wer frequently marked "I H S," b. June 8, 168 Cremona, the most celebrated of the famil The instruments made during the middle pa of his creative epoch vie with the best o Stradivarius (he worked from 1725–45), whi! his last are of less value—to explain which a kinds of legends are related. It is said that h led a somewhat dissipated life, at last dran heavily, and died in prison; and that while the he made his inferior instruments, not having a his command the best material.

Gudehus, **Heinrich**, distinguished stag singer (tenor), b. March 30, 1845, Altenhage near Celle (Hanover), as son of a village schoo master. He also chose the vocation of a teache and was appointed successively at the "Mäd chenschule" at Kleinlehnen and the "Höhe Töchterschule" at Celle and Goslar, and becam likewise organist of the "Marktkirche" in th latter town. G. took lessons in singing fro Frau Schnorr von Karolsfeld at Brunswick she soon discovered that he had a fine voic and sent him to Berlin to Von Hülsen, who once engaged him from Sept. 1, 1870, for thre years for the court opera. In January, 1871, h made a successful *début* as Nadori (Jessonda but, after a year and a half left the stage to stud further under Louise Ress at Dresden. H did not reappear on the boards until 1875, an sang successively at Riga, Lübeck, Freibur i.-B., Bremen (1878), was a member of th court opera at Dresden (1880–90), and has bee since then a highly esteemed member of th court opera at Berlin. From 1890–91 he san in German opera at New York. In 1882 C created the *rôle* of Parsifal at Baireuth, an since then has taken part in the festivals there.

Gudok, a Russian stringed-instrument, a kind of violin with only one string on the finger-board, and two drones; the tone of the G. recalls that of the Drehleier (hurdy-gurdy).

Guénin, Marie Alexandre, b. Feb. 20, 1744, Maubeuge (Nord), d. 1814; went to Paris in 1760, where he became a pupil of Capron (violin) and Gossec (composition), in 1777 musical intendant to Prince Condé, 1778 member of the royal band, 1780 to 1800 solo violinist at the Grand Opéra, and after that lived in needy circumstances. G. composed a great number of instrumental works, which on their appearance were compared to those of Haydn —an error of which the public soon became aware, as G. possessed talent and routine, but no genius. He wrote fourteen symphonies, (two violins, alto, bass, two oboes, two horns; the first appeared in 1770), six stringed quartets, eighteen violin duets, six sonatas for a first and an accompanying violin, one concerto for viola, three duets for 'cello, and three sonatas for clavecin and violin.

Guérin, Emmanuel, b. 1779, Versailles, for many years 'cellist at the Théâtre Feydeau, received a pension in 1824. He published sonatas, duets, variations, etc., for 'cello.

Guerrero, Francisco, b. 1528, Seville, for a brief period pupil of the famous Morales, 1546 maestro of Jaen Cathedral, in 1550 chapel singer at Seville Cathedral, d. there about 1600. He published: "Psalmorum 4 voc. liber I. accedit missa defunctorum 4 voc." (1559, 2nd ed. with Ital. title, 1584); "Canticum beatæ Mariæ quod magnificat nuncupatur, per octo musicæ modos variatum" (1563); "Liber I. missarum" (1566): "Libro di motti (!) a 4, 5, 6 e 8 voc." Eslava in the "Lira Sacro-Hispana" has two Passions à 5 by G. G. made, in 1588, a pilgrimage to Jerusalem, which he has described in "El viage de Jerusalem que hiza Francisco G., etc." (1611).

Guerriero (Ital.), warlike.

Gueymard, (1) Louis, an excellent stagesinger (dramatic tenor), b. Aug. 17, 1822, Chapponay (Isère), d. July, 1880, Corbeil, near Paris. After attending the Conservatoire at Paris, he was engaged at the Grand Opéra (1848–68).

(2) Pauline (née Lauters), wife of the former, b. Dec. 1, 1834, Brussels; she was the daughter of a painter and professor at the Brussels Académie. She was trained at the Conservatoire in that city, made her début at the Théâtre Lyrique, Paris, in 1855, and appeared in the following year at the Grand Opéra, to which she still belongs. Her voice is a rich mezzo-soprano, and she is able to take the parts both of Fides and Valentine. Madame G. was first married to M. Deligne.

Guglielmi, (1) Pietro, b. May, 1727, Massa-

Carrara, d. Nov. 19, 1804, Rome. He studied first with his father (maestro to the Duke of Modena), and afterwards with Durante at the Conservatorio of San Loreto, Naples (in the Royal Archives of that city is preserved the text-book of an opera, *Chichibio*, which he composed already in 1739, from which the date of his birth appears questionable). He was for a time the most celebrated operatic composer of Italy, made his *début* at Turin in 1755, won success after success on all the great stages of Italy, went in 1762 to Dresden, where he remained for some years as royal capellmeister, then to Brunswick, in 1772 to London, returned to Italy in 1777, where, meanwhile, two stars —Cimarosa and Paisiello—had arisen; but, by strenuous efforts, he managed to obtain, side by side with them, the favour of the public. In 1793 he was appointed maestro of St. Peter's, Rome, and in this highest post of honour turned his attention entirely to sacred composition. Of his eighty-five operas of which the titles are known (*cf.* the article "Guglielmi" in Riemann's "Opern-Handbuch"), the following are the most important: *I due gemelli, I Viaggatori, La serva inamorata, I fratelli Pappa Mosca, La pastorella nobile, La bella pescatrice, La Didone, Enea e Lavinio*. He wrote besides, the oratorios *La morte d'Abele, La Betulia liberata, La distruzzione di Gerusalemme, Debora e Sisara*, and *Le Lagrime di San Pietro*, an orchestral mass à 5, a psalm à 8, a miserere à 5, motets, six divertissements for pianoforte, violin, and 'cello, pf. pieces, etc.

(2) Pietro Carlo, son of the former, b. 1763, Naples, d. Feb. 28, 1827, Massa-Carrara, pupil of the Conservatorio S. Maria di Loreto, was likewise a famous composer of operas (for Naples and Milan), and finally maestro to the Duchess of Massa-Carrara.

Guida (Ger. *Führer*). (*See* FUGUE.)

Guide (Fr.), subject of a fugue and antecedent of a canon.

Gui de Châlis (Guido, abbot of the Cistercian monastery, Châlis, Burgundy), writer on music at the end of the 12th century, of whom have been preserved a treatise "Cantus planus" ("De cantu ecclesiastico") and a guide to discant ("Discantus ascendit duas voces"). Both have been made accessible to students by Coussemaker, the former in "Scriptores" (II. 163), and the latter in "Histoire de l'harmonie au moyen-âge" (p. 225).

Guidetti, Giovanni, b. 1532, Bologna, d. Nov. 30, 1592, Rome, pupil of Palestrina there, and in 1575 Papal singer and beneficiary. He was engaged jointly with Palestrina, by order of Gregory XIII., to prepare a new edition of the "Leichtenstein Gradual and Antiphonarium," which appeared at Venice in 1580. His career in consequence took a new direction, and he made use of the experience gained by publishing "Directorium chori ad usum sacro-sanctæ basilicæ Vaticanæ " (1582) ; "Cantus ecclesiasticus passionis Domini nostri Jesu Christi secundum Matthæum, Marcum, Lucam, et Johannem " (1586) ; " Cantus ecclesiasticus officii majoris hebdomadæ " (1587) ; and " Præfationes in cantu firmo " (1588).

Guido (of Arezzo, G. Aretinus), b. about 995, as is commonly supposed, at Arezzo (Tuscany), but, according to recent investigations (Dom Germain Morin in the *Revue de l'Art Chrétien*, 1888, III.), he was born near Paris, educated at the monastery St. Maur des Fossés, near Paris (hence his writings are frequently cited under the name of G. de Sancto Mauro ; *cf. Viertelsjahrschr. f. M.-W.*, 1889, p. 490), first went to Pomposa, near Ferrara, and afterwards to Arezzo. G. was a Benedictine monk who rendered great service to the theory and practice of music, but who, by his superior knowledge, excited the envy of his fellow brethren, so that at length he thought it wise to leave the Pomposa cloister. He appears to have withdrawn to the Benedictine monastery at Arezzo, whence the reputation of his learning and of his inventions to facilitate the teaching of singing were so talked about that he was summoned to Rome in 1026 (1028 ?) by Pope John XIX. to expound to him his method. G. completely convinced him of its advantages, and there is little doubt that his improvements in notation were then recommended to the Church generally. Although the abbot of Pomposa, who was in Rome, became reconciled with him, and begged him to return to his monastery, C. appears not to have complied with his wish, since, according to the notice of various annalists, G. became, in 1029, prior of the Camaldulensian monastery at Avellano (d. May 17, 1050 [?]). G.'s great title to merit, and one of importance such as is rarely to be met with in the history of music, was the invention of the stave as it is generally used up to the present time. Certainly, the complete system was not discovered in a moment : the elements of it were already to hand, and much was left for future generations to work out. The use of one and of two lines (the *f*-line and the *c*-line) reaches back to the 10th century, to the time before G.'s birth ; the uncertainty of meaning of the neumes (q.v.) with regard to pitch ceased to exist when G. introduced four lines. He kept the red *f*-line and the yellow *c*-line, but placed between them a black one for *a*, while the other sounds fell on the intermediate spaces ; and, according to the compass of the song to be noted down, another line was added above or below :—

—(e)—	c————		
c————		f.........	f————
	—(a)—		
—(a)—	f————	c————	c........
f————	—(d)—		

The inserted *f*-line indicated small *f*, the *c*-line once-accented *c*. For some time historians have taken pleasure in denying that G. invented anything, just as formerly everything was ascribed to him, even the invention of the clavier—yea, of music itself. His improvement of notation is beyond question : the mensural note (q.v.) he certainly did not invent, but placed on his stave either the old letter notes (as in his treatises), or neumes. The invention of solmisation (q.v.) is likewise refused to him ; but in his letter to Monk Michael it is shown that he made use of the *Versus memorialis*, " Ut queant laxis," etc., in order to make clear the relationship of the intervals of any song which had to be studied. There is no reason to doubt that he used the same for the transposed scale from *f* (with *b♭*). An invention of such importance as the system of transposition (mutation) would have made the discoverer as celebrated as G. already was, had he not been that inventor himself. Already Johannes Cotto, writing not more than half a century after G., ascribes to him both mutation and the " Harmonic Hand." (*See* GUIDONIAN HAND.) On the other hand, G. never thought of *substituting* for the letter names of the notes the syllables *ut, re, mi,* etc. That was, without doubt, a result of the general use of mutation. Guido's writings are : " Micrologus de disciplina artis musicæ," with the letter sent to the Bishop of Arezzo by way of preface (in German by Raym. Schlecht, in the *Monatsh. f. M.-G.*, V. 135, and by Hermesdorff) ; " Regulæ de ignoto cantu " (Prologue to Guido's Antiphonarium with line notation) ; " Epistola Michæli Monacho de ignoto cantu directa " (all printed in Gerbert, " Script." II., 2-50). The " Musicæ Guidonis regulæ rhythmicæ," the " Tractatus correctorius multorum errorum, qui fiunt in cantu Gregoriano," and " Quomodo de arithmetica procedit musica " (also in Gerbert) are not genuine, but probably only a little later than Guido's time. Angeloni, Ristori, Kiesewetter, etc., have written monographs on G. ; also, within recent years, M. Falchi, " Studi su Guido Monaco " (1882), an important work, and J. A. Lans, " Der Kongress von Arezzo " (1882). A monument by Salvini was uncovered at Arezzo, Sept. 2, 1882.

Guidon (Fr.), a direct.

Guidonian Hand (*Harmonic Hand*) was a mechanical help in teaching solmisation (q.v.). It consisted in giving to each finger-joint, and also to the tips of the fingers, the meaning of one of the twenty sounds of the former system, from Γ (gamma, our great *G*) to $\frac{e}{e}$ (our *e″*, *cf.* LETTER NOTATION), and of these the 20th $\left(\frac{e}{e}\right)$ was imagined (for it seldom occurred) above the tip of the middle finger. Thus if the pupils thoroughly understood the " Hand," they could, in the full sense of the term, count off the intervals and scales on their fingers.

Guido von Châlis (*de Caroli loco*). (*See* GUI DE CHÂLIS.)

Guilds. In the exercise of music during the Middle Ages a distinction must be made between secular and sacred music : the latter was almost exclusively vocal music ; the former, on the other hand, principally instrumental music. Sacred songs were performed by priests and monks, who received training for that purpose in singing schools ; instruments had been admitted into the church, but, the organ excepted, were banished in the 13th century, "propter abusum histrionum" (Engelbert v. Admont, in Gerbert, "Script." III.). The *histriones, joculatores (jugleors, jongleurs)* were those very instrumental players, the itinerant musicians (*Spielleute*), fiddlers and pipers, merry folk who carried on buffoonery and jugglery of all kinds, jesters, the fools of the people. That the mode of life of these homeless, vagabond musicians was often not in conformity with strict morality, but loose, and frequently giving rise to scandal of all kinds, is scarcely to be wondered at. The result, however, was that the "itinerant folk" came more and more into disrepute, and, by law, were placed on a level with the rabble who had no means of subsistence. According to the "Sachsenspiegel" and the "Schwabenspiegel," they were outlaws and destitute of honour, and were even excluded from church communities. Under such circumstances, it naturally happened that something was done, on the one hand, by the musicians themselves, and, on the other hand, by the state, to hold together somewhat this loose folk, and to guide them to better manners. The musicians, therefore, who lived in towns formed themselves into *brotherhoods*, and sought to obtain privileges securing to them the legal exercise of their profession within certain districts, and granting to them the protection of the law and the dispensations of the church. Thus arose in 1288, at Vienna, the "Nikolaibrüderschaft," which was afterwards placed under an inspector (1354–76, the hereditary chamberlain Peter von Eberstorff) and a Board of Control, the highest court of appeal in any dispute between the musicians. In Paris Philip le Bel (1295) nominated Jean Charmillon *roi des ménétriers*, and in 1330 arose the "Confrérie de St. Julien des Ménétriers," which received royal privileges, and which held sway over the instrumental players throughout a large district. The last *roi des ménétriers* (or *roi des violons*) was Jean Pierre Guignon. In 1773 the guild was entirely abolished, when it had gone so far as to require organists and teachers of music to belong to it. In 1355 the Emperor Carl IV. nominated Johann the Fiddler, *rex omnium histrionum*, to the Archbishopric of Mayence ; in 1385 the piper Brachte became his successor as *Künig der farenden Lüte*. The Uznach "Brüderschaft zum heiligen Kreuz" and the Strassburg "Brüderschaft der Kronen" were among the oldest guilds of musicians ; the latter was under the jurisdiction

of the "Herren von Rappolzstein," who granted executive powers to a "Pfeiferkönig." In London from 1472–73 the "Musicians' Company of the City of London" was legalised by Edward IV., and had a marshal (for life) and two wardens (*custodes ad fraternitatem*) elected every year ; this company, in reorganised form, and with reformed privileges suitable to the times, still exists. Altogether the organisations and powers of these guilds and of their principals were probably of a similar kind : a piper-king, king of fiddlers, *roi des ménétriers*, marshal, etc., were everywhere the same office. In a district over which a guild exercised authority, no one dared play or sing who did not belong to the guild, *i.e.* who did not pay his share.

Worse off than the musicians were the makers of instruments. The lute- and "fiedel-" makers (luthiers), the flute- and shawm-makers, and the makers of brass instruments were in frequent conflict with the guilds on whose trade theirs appeared to trench, namely those of the coopers, turners, and coppersmiths. The goldsmiths protested against the ornamenting of instruments with precious metals and stones, the cabinet-makers against the inlaying of wood ornaments, the fan-makers against ornamental painting, etc. In 1297 the Paris trumpet-makers actually joined the guild of the coppersmiths. In Rouen, in 1454, we meet with the first "Corporation des joueurs, faiseurs d'instruments de musique et maîtres de danse" ; here, at least, the instrument-makers found themselves in fitting society. In Paris, in 1599, they at length acquired special corporation rights, which they held until the abolishment of G. in 1791. In 1557 the Belgian instrument-makers joined the "Corporation de Saint Luc,' the union of sculptors and painters. For further details concerning itinerant folk, the nature of G., etc., *see* Wasielewski, "Geschichte der Instrumentalmusik im 16 Jahrh." (1878) ; H. Lavoix, "Histoire de l'instrumentation" (1878) ; Sittard, "Jongleurs und Menestrels" (1885) ; Schubiger, "Musikalische Spicilegien" (1873) ; E. Baron, "Die Brüderschaft der Pfeifer im Elsass" (1873) ; Scheid, "De jure in musicos singulari" (Jena, 1738) ; Fries, "Vom sogenannten Pfeifergericht" (Frankfort, 1752), etc.

Guilmant, Alexandre, French organist and composer, b. March 12, 1837, Boulogne. He first studied with his father (Jean Baptiste G., b. 1793 at Boulogne, d. there May, 1890 ; he had been organist at Boulogne for fifty years), then with Carulli, and afterwards with the Belgian organist, Lemmens, became organist already at the age of sixteen, and was appointed when twenty years of age maître de chapelle, and teacher at the Conservatoire of his native town. At the inauguration of the organs of St. Sulpice and Notre Dame at Paris his playing excited such attention that in 1871 he was appointed organist of Ste. Trinité. He achieved extraordinary success by his concert tours in England, Italy, and Russia (Riga), and also by his concerts at the Trocadéro during the Paris Exhibition of 1878. G. has opened up new paths to organ-players in his compositions (symphony for organ and orchestra ; four sonatas, and many concert pieces, etc., for organ ; a choral work, " Belsazar," etc.). His works are clever, and he obtains hitherto unknown sound effects from modern organs.

Guimbarde (Fr.), a Jew's-harp.

Guiraud, Ernest, b. June 23, 1837, New Orleans, d. Paris, May 6, 1892, studied with his father (Jean Baptiste G., *Prix de Rome* at the Paris Conservatoire, 1827, lived as a teacher of music at New Orleans), came to Europe at the age of fifteen, and studied at the Paris Conservatoire under Marmontel (pianoforte), Barbereau (harmony), and Halévy (composition). In 1859 he received the *Grand Prix de Rome* for the cantata, *Bajazet et le joueur de flûte*. After his return from Italy he produced several operas : *Sylvie* (1864, Opéra Comique) ; *En prison* (1869, Théâtre Lyrique) ; and *Le Kobold* (1870, Opéra Comique). After he had served as a volunteer in the Franco-German war, he brought out *Madame Turlupin* (Opéra Comique, 1872) ; the ballet *Gretna-Green* (1873, Grand Opéra) ; *Piccolino* (Opéra Comique, 1876) ; and *La galante aventure* (ditto, 1882). He has also written an orchestral suite, a concert overture, and some smaller pieces. G. became in 1876 professor of harmony at the Conservatoire, and in 1880 professor of composition in the place of V. Massé, who was retiring.

Guitar (Ger. *Guitarre*, Fr. *Guitare*, formerly *Guiterne*, Ital. *Chitarra*, Span. *Guitarra*), a stringed-instrument, played with the fingers, of the lute family, but smaller, and in modern times of a different shape. Virdung (1511) speaks of an instrument (" Quintern ") which answers in every way to the lute, except that it is of smaller dimensions and has only five strings. Pretorius (1618), on the other hand, gives a flat sound-box to the " Quinterna " or " Chiterna " (" kaum zween oder drey Fingerhoch "), and four or five strings. The original history of the G. is therefore that of the lute ; it came, through the Moors, to Spain, and from there to Lower Italy, where different kinds were evolved. (*See* BANDOLA.) It does not appear to have been much in vogue in Germany, as it sprang up there at the end of the last century as something quite new. The G. is now tuned E A d g b e', but the notation is an octave higher in the treble clef ; and, by a so-called Capotasto, all the strings can at once be raised a semitone.

Guitar-violoncello. (*See* ARPEGGIONE.)

Gumbert, Ferdinand, b. April 21, 1818, Berlin, attended the Gymnasium of the " Graues

Kloster " there, and studied music under E. Fischer and Cläpius. He was to have become a bookseller, but in 1839 went on the stage, and was first engaged as tenor singer at Sondershausen, but from 1840–42 as baritonist at Cologne. On the advice of K. Kreutzer, he renounced the stage, devoted himself exclusively to composition and to the teaching of singing, and, by hundreds of songs of a popular character, achieved extraordinary popularity. He also wrote some vaudevilles : " Die schöne Schusterin," " Die Kunst geliebt zu werden," " Der kleine Ziegenhirt," " Bis der rechte kommt," " Karolina," etc. ; he made a skilful translation into German of various French operas, was contributor to musical papers, and published " Musik. Gelesenes und Gesammeltes " (1860). Died 1896.

Gumpeltzhaimer, Adam, b. 1559, Trossberg (Bavaria), 1581 cantor at Augsburg, d. there 1625, was a distinguished composer and theorist. He wrote a theoretical compendium, a revision of the Rid translation of the compendium of Heinrich Faber. The title of the little work shows slight differences in the various editions, and this may have led the bibliographers to suppose that, besides the revision of Faber, there was a special Gumpeltzhaimer compendium (Fétis). The identity of both was established by Eitner (*Monatshefte*, 1870 and 1873). The title of the first edition of 1591 is as follows : " Compendium musicæ, pro illius artis tironibus a M. Heinrico Fabro latine conscriptum et a Christophoro Rid in vernaculum sermonem conversum nunc præceptis et exemplis auctum studio et opera Adami Gumpeltzhaimeri T." [*Trossbergensis*] (1591, and often). Of G.'s compositions the following have been preserved : " Erster," also " Zweiter teil des Lustgärtleins teutsch und lateinischer Lieder von 3 Stimmen " (1591 and 1611, several times republished) ; " Erster (zweiter) Teil des Würtzgärtlein 4 stimmiger geistlicher Lieder " (1594 [1619] and 1619) ; " Psalmus L. octo vocum " (1604) ; " Partitio sacrorum concentuum octonis vocibus modulandorum cum duplici basso in organorum usum " (1614 and 1619, two parts) ; " 10 geistliche Lieder mit 4 Stimmen " (1617) ; " 2 geistliche Lieder mit 4 Stimmen ; " " 5 geistliche Lieder mit 4 Stimmen von der Himmelfahrt Jesu Christi ; " " Newe teutsche geistliche Lieder mit 3 und mit 4 Stimmen " (1591 and 1592). Bodenschatz's " Florilegium Portense " contains a number of G.'s motets.

Gumpert, Friedrich Adolf, horn-player, b. April 27, 1841, Lichtenau (Thuringia), was trained by the town musician, Hammann, at Jena, then was engaged as horn-player at Bad Nauheim, St. Gallen, and, after the termination of his military duties at Eisenach (1862–64), at Halle, whence he was drawn by Reinecke in 1864 to the Gewandhaus orchestra, to which he has since belonged as principal horn-player. G. published a " Praktische Hornschule," which met with great approval, besides a number of transcriptions for horn and a "Solobuch" for horn (important passages from symphonies, operas, etc.), orchestral studies for the clarinet, oboe, bassoon, trumpet, and 'cello, "Hornquartette" (two books), and "Hornstudien."

Gumprecht, Otto, b. April 4, 1823, Erfurt, studied law at Breslau, Halle, and Berlin, and received the degree of *Dr.jur.*, but undertook, in 1849, the editing of the musical feuilleton for the *Nationalzeitung;* he now ranks as one of the best German musical critics. He published in book-form a series of his works under the titles, "Musikalische Charakterbilder" (1869); "Neue Charakterbilder" (1876); "Richard Wagner und der Ring des Nibelungen" (1873); "Unsere klassischen Meister "(2 vols., 1883–85); and "Neuere Meister" (2 vols., 1883); the two last-named being continuations of the "Charakterbilder." For many years G. has been blind.

Gungl, (1) Joseph, b. Dec. 1, 1810, Zsàmbèk (Hungary), d. Jan. 31, 1889, Weimar, where he spent his last days. He was at first oboist, and then band-master in the 4th Austrian regiment of the artillery, and made long concert tours with his band, during which he produced principally dances and marches of his own composition. He established in Berlin an orchestra of his own in 1843, with which, during his travels, he visited America in 1849, was named in 1850 royal musical director, and in 1858 accepted the post of band-master to the 23rd infantry regiment at Brünn, lived from 1864 in Munich, and in 1876 settled in Frankfort. The dances of G. enjoy a popularity equal to those of the Strauss family.

(2) Virginia, daughter of the former, is an opera-singer of merit; she made her *début* in 1871 at the Court Opera, Berlin, and is now engaged at Frankfort.

(3) Johann, b. March 5, 1828, Zsàmbèk, d. Nov. 27, 1883, Pecs (Hungary), likewise a favourite composer of dance music; he gave concerts in Petersburg, Berlin, etc., and from 1862 lived in retirement at Fünfkirchen in Hungary.

Gunn, John, b. about 1763, Edinburgh, from 1790–95 teacher of music in London, then again in Edinburgh. He published: "Forty Scotch Airs arranged as Trios for Flute, Violin, and Violoncello" (1793, with a dissertation on stringed-instruments); "The Art of Playing the German Flute on New Principles" (1794); "Essay, Theoretical and Practical, on the Application of Harmony, Thorough-Bass, and Modulation to the Violoncello" (1801); and "An Historical Inquiry respecting the Performance on the Harp in the Highlands of Scotland" (1807).

Günther, (1) Hermann. (*See* HERTHER.)

(2) Otto, brother of the former, b. Nov. 4, 1822, Leipzig, d. Sept. 12, 1897, studied jurisprudence, practised as a lawyer, and later on as patrimonial director of justice at Lützschena and Lösnig. From 1867–72, however, he was a paid member of the town council at Leipzig, and soon became member of the executive Gewandhaus committee and director of the Leipzig Conservatorium; and, after the death of Schleinitz (1881), president of both institutions. He latterly resigned the presidentship of the Gewandhaus committee in order to devote himself entirely to the Conservatorium, which, under him, received a new impulse by the introduction of classes for all kinds of orchestral instruments, and by the establishment of an operatic school; also, through the efforts of G., a new and magnificent "Schulhaus" was erected in 1887 (in the Grassi Strasse).

Günther - Bachmann, Karoline, excellent singer and actress, b. Feb. 13, 1816, Düsseldorf, d. Jan. 17, 1874, Leipzig, daughter of the bassobuffo and comic actor, Günther, who afterwards distinguished himself in Brunswick. She was associated from early years with the stage, and belonged to the Leipzig Theatre from 1834 up to the time of her death. After 1859 she took comic elderly parts, while in her younger days she excelled in *soubrette* parts and in comedy, and was a popular favourite. In 1844 she married Dr.jur. Bachmann.

Gunz, Gustav, b. Jan. 26, 1831, Gaunersdorf (Lower Austria), pupil of Ed. Hollub at Vienna, Fr. Delsarte, and Jenny Lind, was for many years member of the Opera at Hanover (tenor), from 1864–70 at the Italian Opera, London; then teacher of singing at Dr. Hoch's Conservatorium at Frankfort. D. Dec. 12, 1894, Frankfort.

Gura, Eugen, b. Nov. 8, 1842, Pressern, near Saatz (Bohemia), originally intended for a scientific career, attended the Polytechnic, and afterwards the "Akademie," at Vienna, then Anschütz' School of Painting and the Munich Conservatorium. In 1865 he made his first appearance on the Munich stage as Count Liebenau, in *Waffenschmied,* whereupon he was at once engaged. Afterwards he was successively an ornament of the opera-houses at Breslau (1867–70), Leipzig (1870–76), Hamburg (1876–83), and since then at Munich. G. was one of the most intelligent stage singers of the present, and was likewise distinguished as a concert singer (baritone). Died Aug. 26, 1906.

Gurlitt, Cornelius, b. 1820, Altona, d. there June 17, 1901. He studied under Reinecke (sen.), also under Weyse at Copenhagen, and was organist of the Hauptkirche, Altona, 1864. He was "Armeemusikdirektor" during the Schleswig-Holstein campaign. He published orchestral and chamber-music works (one stringed quartet, three violin sonatas, one 'cello sonata, two 'cello sonatinas, two- and four-hand piano sonatas, etc.), many educational pf. pieces, songs, etc. He composed also two operettas, *Die Römische Mauer* and *Rafael Sanzio,* and a four-act opera.

Scheik Hassan. In 1874 he was appointed royal musical director.

Gürrlich, Joseph Augustin, b. 1761, Münsterberg (Silesia), d. June 27, 1817, Berlin; in 1781 organist of the Catholic "Hedwigskirche," Berlin; in 1790 double-bass player in the court orchestra, in 1811 sub-conductor at the opera, 1816 court capellmeister. He composed operas, ballets, and incidental music to plays, an oratorio (*L'obedienza di Gionata* "), variations, etc., for piano, and songs.

Gusla, Servian stringed-instrument, with arched sound-box, with a skin for sound-board, and one string of horse-hair.

Gusli (*Gussel*), Russian stringed-instrument, a kind of zither.

Gusto (Ital.), taste.—*Con gusto*, with taste; *di buon gusto*, tasteful.

Guter Taktteil (Ger.), the good, *i.e.* accented part of the bar. (*Cf.* METRE, ART OF.)

Gutmann, Adolf, b. Jan. 12, 1819, Heidelberg, d. Oct. 27, 1882, Spezia; eminent pianist and a prolific composer, pupil and friend of Chopin.

Guttural, formed in the throat. A guttural sound is produced in singing when respiration is obstructed in the throat.

Gyrowetz, Adalbert, b. Feb. 19, 1763, Budweis (Bohemia), d. March 19, 1850, Vienna; he went, as secretary of Count Fünfkirchen, to Vienna, where his symphonies met with great approval. After that he studied for two years in Naples under Sala, went through Milan to Paris, then lived for three years in London, where he produced an opera, *Semiramide* (1792), and returned at length, after seven years' absence, to Vienna. As G. spoke six languages, and was well versed in jurisprudence, he held the appointment of secretary of legation for some years at several German courts, and became in 1804 court capellmeister and conductor at the Opera, which office he held until 1831. G. outlived his works; in 1843 his friends arranged a benefit concert for him, in which his cantata, *Die Dorfschule*, was produced. The productiveness of G. exceeds that of Haydn: he wrote not less than thirty operas and operettas and forty ballets, nineteen masses, sixty symphonies, over sixty quartets for strings, two stringed quintets, thirty works for pf., violin, and 'cello, forty pf. sonatas, also many serenades, overtures, marches, dances, nocturnes, cantatas, part-songs, etc. Of his operas the following were the most successful: *Agnes Sorel, Der Augenarzt* (1811, Vienna), and *Die Prüfung;* the *Augenarzt* retained its popularity longest. G. wrote his own life: "Biographie des Adalbert G." (1848).

H.

H is the name given in Germany to B, the second note of the musical alphabet (q.v.). The explanation of this disturbance of the alphabetical order by putting H between A and c will be found under "B." In full scores, pianoforte scores, etc., H. is an abbreviation for Horn.

Haan. (*See* DEHAAN.)

Habeneck, François Antoine, b. June 1 (or Jan. 23, according to Elwart's "Histoire de la Société des Concerts"), 1781, Mezières (Ardennes), d. Feb. 8, 1849, Paris, son of a native of Mannheim, who, however, served in the band of a French regiment. H. learnt the violin from his father, and, when young, composed works of large compass without having received any instruction in theory. He was over twenty years of age when he entered the Paris Conservatoire as a pupil of Baillot, and he received in 1804 the first violin-prize. He then became a member of the Opéra Comique orchestra, and soon obtained a place among the first violins of the Opéra orchestra, and, when Kreutzer undertook the direction, was advanced to the post of leader. From 1806 until the temporary closing of the Conservatoire (1815), the concerts were conducted almost entirely by H.; when the Conservatoire was re-established in 1828 he definitely undertook the direction, and to him these concerts are indebted for their world-wide fame. It was H.'s great merit, by excellent renderings, first to have brought into honour Beethoven's orchestral works at Paris. From 1821–24 he acted as director at the Grand Opéra, was appointed professor of the violin and general inspector of the Conservatoire, and, when Kreutzer received his pension, became conductor at the Grand Opéra, which post he held until 1846. H. was distinguished both as teacher and conductor: among others, Alard and Léonard were his pupils. He published only a few compositions: two violin concertos, three duos concertants for two violins, a set of variations for stringed quartet and one for orchestra, one nocturne for two violins on motives from *La Gazza Ladra*, three caprices for violin solo with bass, polonaises for violin and orchestra, and fantasias for pf. and violin.

Haberbier, Ernst, distinguished pianist, b. Oct. 5, 1813, Königsberg, d. March 12, 1869, Bergen (Norway), whilst playing at a concert. He went in 1832 to Petersburg, where he was successful as a concert-player and teacher (among others, of the Grand Princess Alexandra), undertook, from 1850, important concert tours, during which he attracted attention by a technical peculiarity, in which he had many imitators ; this was the dividing of passages and figures between the two hands. In 1852 he returned to Russia, where he lived alternately at Petersburg and Moscow. Among his compositions deserving of mention are the " Études poésies."

Haberl, Franz Xaver, b. April 12, 1840, Oberellenbach (Lower Bavaria), where his father was teacher, attended the Episcopal training school for boys at Passau, took priest's orders in 1862, was from 1862–67 cathedral capellmeister and musical director at the Passau training school, 1867–70 organist of St. Maria dell' Anima, Rome, from 1871–82 cathedral capellmeister and inspector of the cathedral officiating canons at Ratisbon, where in 1875 he founded a school for church music, which attracts pupils from all parts of the world. H. is one of the best living authorities on matters connected with Catholic church music and its history, and has taken advantage of his frequent visits to Italy to make elaborate literary and bibliographical studies. He has published : " Anweisung zum harmonischen Kirchengesang " (1864) ; " Magister Choralis " (theory and practice of choral singing, of which there have been, since 1865, nine editions, besides translations into Italian, French, English, and Spanish) ; " Lieder-Rosenkranz " (1866) ; "Caecilien-Kalender" (1876–85), and in enlarged form as " Kirchenmusikalisches Jahrbuch," containing valuable information ; " Bertalotti's Solfeggien" (1880) ; " Wilhelm Dufay" (1885); "Officium hebdomadæ sanctæ" (1887, German); "Die römische *schola cantorum* und die päpstlichen Kapellsänger bis zur Mitte des 16. Jahrhunderts " (1887) ; " Psalterium vespertinum" (1888) ; "Bibliographischer und thematischer Musikkatalog des päpstlichen Kapellarchivs im Vatikan zu Rom " (1888). After the death of the cathedral capellmeister Schrems, H. undertook the continuation of the publication of the collection, " Musica Divina," and, after Witt's death (1888), edited the church music paper, *Musica Sacra.* He wrote, jointly with the cathedral organist Hanisch, an accompaniment for organ to " Ordinarium Missæ," Graduale and Vesperale. (H. is a member of the church commission for the authentic revision of official choral books.) In 1879 H. founded a Palestrina Society, and, from Vol. IX., has superintended the edition of Palestrina's works, commenced in 1862 by Th. de Witt, F. N. Rauch, Fr. Espagne, and Fr. Commer (Breitkopf u. Härtel). As H. has collected works of Palestrina hitherto unknown, this is a complete and monumental edition: it was completed in thirty-two vols., 1894 (three hundred years after Palestrina's death). H. was named *Dr. Theol. hon. c.* by the University of Würzburg in 1889, and is honorary member of many learned societies.

Habermann, Franz Johann, b. 1706, Königswart, Bohemia, d. April 7, 1783, Eger, as precentor at the Dekanatkirche, was, previously, maître de chapelle to Prince Condé in Paris (1731), Grand Ducal maestro at Florence, and then precentor at various churches in Prague. Among his compositions which appeared in print are twelve masses and six litanies ; symphonies, oratorios, sonatas, etc., remained in manuscript.

Habert, Johann Evangelista, b. Oct. 18, 1833, Oberplan, Bohemia, d. Sept. 1, 1896 ; from 1861 organist at Gmunden, writer on music and composer (masses, offertories, organ pieces, etc.)

Hadrianius. (*See* ADRIANSEN.)

Häffner, Johann Christian Friedrich, b. March 2, 1759, Oberschönau, near Schmalkalden, d. May 28, 1833, Upsala, pupil of Vierling in Schmalkalden ; in 1776 proof-reader for Breitkopf at Leipzig, afterwards conductor of an itinerant theatre company, settled in Stockholm in 1780, received first a post as organist, was then accompanist, and, after the marked success of his operas (*Elèktra, Alkides,* and *Rinaldo*), written in the style of Gluck, was appointed capellmeister at the court theatre. In 1808 he withdrew to Upsala, where he held a post as organist up to 1820. H. rendered service to Swedish national music: he published Swedish songs with accompaniment, revised the melodies of the Geijer-Afzelius collection of " Volkslieder," published a Swedish " Choralbuch " (" Svensk Choralbok "), restoring the old " Choral " melodies of the 17th century (1819 and 1821 ; two parts), and adding preludes (1822), a Swedish mass in old style (1817) ; and finally an arrangement in four parts of old Swedish songs (1832–33), of which only two books were completed before his death.

Hagemann, (1) François Wilhelm, b. Sept. 10, 1827, Zütphen, in 1846 royal organist at Appeldoorn, in 1848 capellmeister at Nijkerk. H. studied still in 1852 for some time at the Brussels Conservatoire, lived as a teacher of music in Wageningen, became in 1859 organist at Leeuwarden, in 1860 town musical director at Leyden, and has been for some years organist of the " Willemskerk," Batavia. He has also published pf. works.

(2) Mauritz Leonard, brother of the former, b. Sept. 23, 1829, Zütphen, pupil of the Hague and Brussels Conservatoires (Fétis, Michelot, de Bériot), at the latter, laureate in 1852, was musical director at Gröningen from 1853–65, and from 1865–75 director of the Philharmonic Society and Conservatoire at Batavia; and since then he has been musical director at Leeuwarden and founder and director of the municipal Conservatoire there. He is one of the best living Dutch musicians, and has published pf. pieces, songs, several vocal works with orchestra (*Trost der Nacht, Wandervöglein, Abendgesang,* and a festival cantata for female chorus) ; an oratorio (*Daniel*) is in manuscript.

Hagen, (1) Friedrich Heinrich von der, b. Feb. 19, 1780, Schmiedeberg (Ukraine), d. June 11, 1856, as professor in ordinary of German literature at Berlin. His "Minnesinger" (1838-56, five vols.) contains, in the third volume, records of the *Minne* songs, according to the Jenens Codex, etc.; also a treatise on the music of the Minnesingers. He also published "Melodien zu der Sammlung deutscher, vlämischer und französischer Volkslieder" (1807, jointly with Büsching).

(2) Johann Baptist, b. 1818, Mayence, from 1836-41 theatre capellmeister at Detmold, 1841-56 at Bremen, 1856-65 at Wiesbaden, 1865-67 at Riga; then he returned to Wiesbaden, where he died in 1870.

His son (3) Adolf, b. Sept. 4, 1851, Bremen, entered in 1866 as violinist into the royal theatre band, Wiesbaden; from 1871-76 he was musical director at Danzig and Bremen, 1877-79 capellmeister at the town theatre, Freiburg-i.-Br., from 1879-82 with Sucher at the Hamburg Theatre, then, for one season, at the Riga theatre, and went in 1883 as court capellmeister to Dresden, where in 1884 he succeeded Wüllner as artistic director of the Conservatorium. H. has written a comic opera (*Zwei Komponisten*, produced in Hamburg), and a one-act operetta (*Schwarznäschen*).

(4) Theodor, b. April 15, 1823, Hamburg, d. Dec. 21, 1871, New York; he was compromised by the Revolution of 1848, lived after that, first in Switzerland, then in London, and from 1854 in New York as teacher of music and critic; finally, as editor of the *New York Weekly Review*. He published songs, pf. pieces, and wrote (pseudonym, Joachim Fels): "Zivilisation und Musik" (1845), and "Musikalische Novellen" (1848).

Hager, Johannes, pseudonym of the "Hofrath" Joh. v. Hasslinger-Hassingen, of Vienna, b. there Feb. 24, 1822, and under that name published a series of excellent chamber works, also the opera *Iolantha* (Vienna, 1849), *Marfa* (ditto, 1886, but written long before), and produced an oratorio, *John the Baptist*. Died Jan. 9, 1898.

Hahn, (1) Bernhard, b. Dec. 17, 1780, Leubus (Silesia), d. 1852 as cathedral capellmeister at Breslau; he composed sacred vocal works and school songs, and published "Handbuch zum Unterricht im Gesang für Schüler auf Gymnasien und Bürgerschulen" (1829, and other editions), and "Gesänge zum Gebrauch beim sonn- und wochentägigen Gottesdienst auf katholischen Gymnasien" (1820).

(2) Albert, b. Sept. 29, 1828, Thorn, d. July 14, 1880, Lindenau (near Leipzig); from 1867-70 he directed the Musical Union and "Liedertafel" at Bielefeld, lived then alternately in Berlin and Königsberg, and founded in 1876 a musical paper, *Die Tonkunst*, in which he advocated the so-called "chromatic movement."

Hähnel. (*See* GALLUS—1.)

Hainl, François George, b. Nov. 19, 1807, Issoire (Puy de Dôme), d. June 2, 1873, Paris. In 1829 he became a pupil of the Paris Conservatoire (Norblin), undertook in 1840, after having travelled for several years as 'cellist, the post of maître de chapelle at the Grand Théâtre, Lyons, in 1863 that of principal conductor at the Grand Opéra, Paris (with Gevaert as second maître de chapelle), conducted also for a time the concerts of the Conservatoire, and, with the title of maître de chapelle impérial, those of the court, likewise the festival performances at the Paris Exhibition of 1867. H. wrote some pieces for 'cello, also a treatise—"De la musique à Lyon depuis 1713 jusqu'à 1852" (1852).

Haizinger, Anton, celebrated stage-singer (tenor), b. March 14, 1796, Wilfersdorf (Lichtenstein), d. Dec. 31, 1869, Vienna; he was at first teacher there, then engaged in 1821 by Count Palffy at the "An-der-Wien" Theatre, and, after some years, was appointed for life at the Court Theatre, Carlsruhe, whence he paid very successful visits to Paris and London. He received his artistic training, during his Vienna engagement, from Salieri. In 1850 he returned to Vienna.

Halb, a German prefix meaning "half," which (similar to the Latin *semi-*, or Greek *hemi-* in the terminology of the 16th to the 18th century; for instance, *semidiapente* = diminished fifth) often has, not the meaning of smaller by the half, but generally smaller. Thus the *Halbvioline*, the *Halbcello*, are smaller instruments suitable for children, but far beyond the half of the usual sized instruments. Also the term *Halbbass*, *Halbviclon* (German bass) is to be understood in a similar manner, although this instrument was not intended for children, but in small orchestras represented both 'cello and double-bass. A *halbe Orgel* (half organ) is one which lacks a 16-ft. stop—an essential element, in any case, for the pedals of a *whole* (proper) organ. A *Viertelorgel* (quarter organ) was the name given to such as had no 8-ft. stop—an absurdity which does not occur now. In England the term *half-stops* ("halbe Stimmen") is given in the organ to such as run through only the upper or the lower half of the keyboard, for instance, the Oboe and Fagott, which in most organs complement each other. Lastly, *Halbinstrumente* (half-instruments) are those of such narrow measure that their lowest, or fundamental, tone does not speak. (*See* GANZINSTRUMENTE.)

Hâle (Halle). (*See* ADAM DE LA H.)

Halévy, Jacques Fromental Élie, b. May 27, 1799, Paris, d. there March 17, 1862. He was a pupil of Cazot at the Paris Conservatoire (in elementary class, 1809), Lambert (pianoforte, 1810), Berton (harmony, 1811), and Cherubini (composition). Already in 1816 he was admitted to the competition for the *Grand*

Prix de Rome, which he won in 1819 (cantata, *Herminie*), and, according to prescription, spent about three years in Rome. Already before that he had been commissioned to set to music the Hebrew text of "De Profundis" for the obsequies of the Duc de Berry. After his return from Italy he tried to get a work produced on the stage. His first three operas— *Les Bohémiennes, Pygmalion*, and *Les deux Pavillons*—were refused. Finally, in 1827, a one-act comic opera (*L'artisan*) appeared before the lights (Théâtre Feydeau); in 1828 there followed (at the same theatre) the *pièce d'occasion, Le roi et le bâtelier* (in honour of Charles X., in collaboration with Rifaut). His *Clari* was the first to meet with success worthy of the name (Théâtre Italien, 1829); still in the same year followed *Le dilettante d'Avignon* (Opéra Comique), which kept a place in the *répertoire*, and in 1830 *Attendre et courir;* also at the Grand Opéra the ballet *Manon Lescaut. Yelva*, written for the Opéra Comique, was set aside owing to the insolvency of the manager. Then there followed: *La langue musicale* (Opéra Comique, 1831); *La tentation* (ballet-opera, 1832, at the Opéra, jointly with Gide); *Les Souvenirs de Lafleur* (Opéra Comique, 1834), *pièce d'occasion;* the comic opera *Ludovic* (1834), which had been left incomplete by Hérold and was finished by H., and finally *La Juive*, H.'s *chef-d'œuvre* (Grand Opéra, Feb. 23, 1835). H.'s individuality inclines to the serious, the severe. He is also fond of sharp contrasts, passionate outbreaks. In *La Juive* he showed himself thoroughly true to his nature. All the more astonishing was it, that within the same year he produced a work of a totally different kind—a fresh, bright, and elegant comic opera, *L'éclair*. The esteem in which he was held as composer was increased in an extraordinary manner by these two works; and in the following year he was elected member of the Académie in place of Reicha, deceased. He was not only an active writer for the stage, but for some years past had also distinguished himself as teacher at the Conservatoire. Already, in 1816, when still a pupil, he acted as assistant-teacher. In 1827 he became *maestro al cembalo* at the Théâtre Italien, and succeeded Daussoignes as teacher of harmony and accompaniment at the Conservatoire. From 1830–45 he acted as *chef du chant* at the Grand Opéra, and in 1833, on the departure of Fétis to Brussels, he received the professorship of counterpoint and fugue, and in 1840 that of composition at the Conservatoire. In 1854 he exchanged the post of member of the Académie des Arts for that of perpetual secretary of the same institution. The growing success of Meyerbeer, who produced *Les Huguenots* in the following year (1836), caused the operas which followed *L'éclair* to be less favourably received by the public than the two works named. H. himself could not resist the temptation of imitating Meyerbeer. He wrote, besides, a whole series of new works, but, with the exception of *La Reine de Chypre*, not one met with a success at all to be compared with that of *La Juive*:—*Guido et Ginevra*, or *La Peste de Florence* (Grand Opéra, 1838); *Le Shériff* (ditto, 1839); *Les Treize* (Opéra Comique, 1839); *Le Drapier* (Grand Opéra, 1840); *La Reine de Chypre* (ditto, 1841); *Le Guitarero* (Opéra Comique, 1841); *Charles VI.* (Grand Opéra, 1843); *Le Lazzarone* (ditto, 1844); *Les mousquétaires de la reine* (Opéra Comique, 1846); *Les premiers pas* (for the inauguration of the Opéra National (1847), jointly with Adam, Auber, Carafa); *Le Val d'Andorre* (Opéra Comique, 1848); *La Fée aux roses* (ditto, 1849); *La dame de pique* (ditto, 1850); *La Tempesta* (Italian opera for London, 1850); *Le Juif errant* (Grand Opéra, 1852); *Le Nabab* (Opéra Comique, 1853); *Jaquarita* (Théâtre Lyrique, 1855); *L'Inconsolable* (ditto, 1855, under pseudonym Alberti); *Valentine d'Aubigny* (Opéra Comique, 1856); and *La Magicienne* (Grand Opéra, 1857). H. left two operas almost complete—*Vanina d'Ornano* (finished by Bizet), and *Noé* (*Le Déluge*). Besides, are still to be named: scenes from "Prometheus Unbound" (1849, at a Conservatoire concert); the cantatas *Les plages du Nil* and *Italie* (Opéra Comique, 1859); also part-songs for male voices, romances, nocturnes, a pf. sonata for four hands, etc. His "Leçons de lecture musicale" was adopted at the Paris schools for the teaching of singing. As secretary of the Académie, he had repeatedly to read the usual *éloge* of deceased members (Onslow, Adam, etc.): these were collected as *Souvenirs et portraits* (1861) and *Derniers souvenirs et portraits* (1863). H.'s brother, Léon (1862), E. Monnais (1863), and A. Pougin (1865), published biographical notices of H.

Half-close. (*See* CLOSE.)

Half-stopped (half-covered pipes), are, in the organ, certain flute-work pipes, and also the English stop, the clarinet flute (q.v.).

Halir, Karl, distinguished violinist, b. Feb. 1, 1859, Hohenelbe (Bohemia), pupil of the Prague Conservatorium (Bennewitz), and from 1874–76 of Joachim. He then played for some time as first violin in Bilse's orchestra, and after short engagements (at Königsberg and Mannheim), was appointed in 1884 leader of the court band at Weimar, where he still resides. His wife, Theresa (*née* Zerbst), b. Nov. 6, 1859, Berlin, married in 1888, is an excellent singer (soprano), and was a pupil of Otto Eichberg.

Halle, (1) Johann Samuel, b. 1730, Bartenstein (Prussia), d. Jan. 9, 1810, as professor of history at the military school, Berlin; besides many works not relating to music, he wrote: "Theoretische und praktische Kunst des Orgelbaus" (1779; also in the sixth vol. of his "Werkstätte der Künste" 1799).

(2) Karl (Charles Hallé), b. April 11,

1819, Hagen, Westphalia, distinguished pianist and conductor, was first trained by his father, who was capellmeister, then in 1835 by Rinck at Darmstadt, went in 1836 to Paris, where he enjoyed intercourse with Cherubini, Chopin, Liszt, Berton, Kalkbrenner, etc., and was much sought after there as a teacher of music. In 1846, jointly with Alard and Franchomme, he inaugurated chamber concerts in the small room of the Conservatoire, and these were held in high esteem. On the outbreak of the Revolution in 1848 H. came to London, and already in May, 1848, attracted notice by his performance of Beethoven's E♭ concerto at a concert at Covent Garden. He made here also a name as teacher, and undertook, in 1853, the direction of the "Gentlemen's Concerts" at Manchester. In 1857 he established subscription concerts at Manchester with an orchestra of his own (Charles Hallé's orchestra), which ranked amongst the best in the world. In 1884 he was named LL.D. by the university of Edinburgh, and he was knighted in 1888. In the same year he married Madame Néruda (q.v.). His notable activity in Manchester notwithstanding, H. was one of the most important musical forces of London. For many years he gave Beethoven Recitals at St. James's Hall, then recitals with mixed programmes. He had given orchestral concerts in London since 1880, and in that year produced Berlioz's *Faust*, given for the first time in complete form in London. Sir Charles and Lady Hallé visited Australia in 1890, and again in 1891. Died Oct. 25, 1895, Manchester.

Hallé. (*See* HALLE, 2.)

Hallelujah (*Alleluia*; abbr. *Aeuia*), an exclamation of praise to God, which passed from the temple music of the Hebrews into the Christian Church. (In Hebrew H. means "Praise the Lord.") The psalms of praise conclude with it, and it is also introduced at the beginning of, or between, the single verses. According to the testimony of St. Augustine, the H. was introduced into Italy already in the 5th century. When the rhythm of church song, pulsating with life, began to change into the torpid *Cantus planus*, the long melodic phrases on the vowels of the H., especially on the concluding syllable, appeared unintelligible appendages; and hence, already in the 9th century, it became the custom to place words under the closing neumes of the H. (*See* SEQUENCE.)

Hallén, Andreas, gifted Swedish composer, b. Dec. 22, 1846, Gotenburg, was a pupil of Reinecke at Leipzig (1866–68), and of Rheinberger at Munich (1869), and Rietz at Dresden. From 1872–78, and again from 1883, he was conductor of the Musical Union Concerts at Gotenburg; in the intervals he resided mostly at Berlin. He has published up to now: an opera (*Harald der Wiking*, libretto by H. Herrig, produced in 1881 at Leipzig, 1884 at Stockholm); two "Schwedische Rhapsodien" (Op. 17 and 23);

Ballad Cyclus, "Vom Pagen und der Königstochter" (chorus, solo, and orchestra); "Traumkönig und sein Lied (ditto); "Das Aehrenfeld" (female chorus with pianoforte, libretto by Hoffmann von Fallersleben); "Vineta" (choral rhapsody with piano); a violin romance with orchestra, and several books of German and Swedish songs.

Haller, Michael, b. Jan. 13, 1840, Neusaat (Upper Palatinate), was educated at the gymnasium of Metten monastery, where at the same time he studied music, and then attended the priests' seminary at Ratisbon. In 1864 he took holy orders, and became prefect of the Cathedral Institution for chorister boys, and, under Schrems, made serious studies in sacred music. In 1866 he succeeded Wesselack at the "Realinstitut," and became capellmeister of the old chapel. At the same time he was teacher of counterpoint and vocal composition at the school of church music. H. is esteemed as a sacred composer. He completed, amongst other things, and with the greatest skill, six compositions à 12 of Palestrina's, of which the third-choir parts had been lost (Vol. XXVI. of the complete edition). He himself has written fourteen masses (à 2–6, with and without instruments and organ), several volumes of motets à 3–8, psalms, litanies, a Te Deum; also melodramas, stringed quartets, etc. He has also been active as an historical and pedagogic writer, contributing articles to Haberl's "Kirchenmusikalische Jahrbücher," a "Kompositionslehre für den polyphonen Kirchengesang," and "Modulationen in den Kirchentonarten."

Halling, Norwegian popular dance in $\frac{2}{4}$ time, of moderate rate, and usually accompanied by the Hardanger Fiddle (a kind of viola d'amore, with four ordinary, and four sympathetic strings).

Hallström, Ivar, b. June 5, 1826, Stockholm; he studied law, was private librarian to the Crown Prince (now King) of Sweden, and undertook in 1861 the direction of the music school which, up to then, had been in the hands of Lindblad. H. follows national tendencies in his compositions, not only in the subject-matter, but in harmonic and rhythmic treatment. His first opera —*Herzog Magnus* (Stockholm, 1867)—certainly only met with a cool reception, also *Die bezauberte Katze* (1869) made little sensation; but, on the other hand, *Der Bergkönig* (1874) obtained a decided success, and those which followed afterwards were equally fortunate—*Die Gnomenbraut* (1875), *Die Wikingfahrt* (1877), *Nyaga* (1885), and *Per Swinaherde* (1887). An Idyll for soli, chorus, and orchestra ("Die Blumen"), gained a prize in 1860 from the Musical Union at Stockholm.

Halm, Anton, excellent German pianist and worthy teacher of music, b. June 4, 1789, Altenmarkt, Styria, d. April, 1872, Vienna. He resided for many years in the latter city, and became acquainted with Beethoven, with whom he was on very friendly terms. H. wrote a mass, pianoforte trios, sonatas, etc., most of which were published.

Hamel, (1) M a r i e P i e r r e, b. Feb. 24, 1786, Auneuil (Oise), d. after 1870, town councillor at Beauvais, afterwards member of the *Commission des Arts et Monuments*, in which capacity it was his business to send reports to the Minister of Public Worship of all organs newly built, or restored at the expense of the state. In the art of organ-building he was self-taught. Already, in his fourteenth year, he had restored the organ of his native village, and later on he reconstructed the great organ of Beauvais Cathedral (sixty-four stops). He was never an organ-builder by profession. His "Nouveau manuel complet du facteur d'orgues" (1849, three vols., with a history of the organ by way of introduction, and an appendix containing biographies of the most distinguished organ-builders) is an independent and excellent book, which corrects many faults in Dom Bedos' well-known work. H. was also the founder of a philharmonic society at Beauvais, one of the first which introduced Beethoven's symphonies into France.

(2) E d u a r d, b. 1811, Hamburg, was for a long time violin-player in the orchestra of the Grand Opéra at Paris, since 1846 an esteemed teacher of music and critic at Hamburg. He has published chamber-music, pf. pieces, and songs. He has also written an opera (*Malvina*). His daughter, J u l i e, is a gifted composer (songs, "Symphonische Improvisationen" on an original theme, etc.).

(3) M a r g a r e t h e. (*See* SCHICK.)

Hamerik, A s g e r, b. April 8, 1843, Copenhagen, son of a professor of theology, who at first did not approve of the boy's musical inclinations. By self-study, however, the lad made such progress that at the age of fifteen he wrote a cantata, which drew the attention of Gade and Hartmann to his gifts, whereupon he received instruction from Matthison-Hansen, Gade, and Haberbier. In 1862 he went to Berlin to perfect himself in pianoforte-playing under H. v. Bülow, and here made musical studies of the most comprehensive kind; he went in 1864 to Paris to Berlioz, who received him in a friendly manner, travelled with him to Vienna (1866–67), and was instrumental in obtaining H.'s appointment as member of the musical jury of the Paris Exhibition. At that time H. received a gold medal for his "Friedenshymne," which, richly scored for chorus and orchestra, two organs, fourteen harps, and four bells (!), was successfully produced. He wrote besides, in Paris, the operas—*Tovelille* and *Hjalmar et Ingeborg*, as well as the better known choral work, *Trilogie judaique*, and, during a brief residence in Stockholm about this time, a festival cantata in honour of the new constitution of Sweden

(1866). In 1869 H. went to Italy, and in the following year produced at Milan an Italian opera (*La Vendetta*). Since 1871 H. has been director of the musical section of the Peabody Institute at Baltimore, and has rendered great service to the musical life of that city. The Peabody concerts, of which he is conductor, are noteworthy for their catholic programmes, in which justice is rendered to the classical masters and to the romantic writers of various nationalities. Of H.'s chief works there are still to be mentioned: the opera *Der Wanderer* (1872); five symphonies—(1), F, "S. poétique," Op. 29 (1880); (2), C min., "S. tragique," Op. 32; (3), E, "S. lyrique," Op. 33; (4), C, "S. majestueuse," Op. 35; (5), G min., "S. sérieuse," Op. 36 (1891); and "Christliche Trilogie" (choral work, a pendant to the "Trilogie judaïque"); a pf. quartet (Op. 61); five "Nordische Suiten" for orchestra; a fantasia for 'cello and pf.; a concert romance for 'cello and orchestra; several cantatas, vocal pieces, an "Oper ohne Worte" (1883). In 1890 he was knighted by the King of Denmark.

Hamilton, J a m e s A l e x a n d e r, b. 1785, London, d. Aug. 2, 1845, son of a dealer in old books, an able theorist whose writings have passed through many editions. He wrote; "Modern Instruction for the Pianoforte" (frequently republished); "Catechism of Singing;" "Catechism of the Organ;" "Catechism of the Rudiments of Harmony and Thoroughbass;" "Catechism of Counterpoint, Melody, and Composition;" "Catechism of Double Counterpoint and Fugue;" "Catechism on Art of Writing for an Orchestra and of Playing from Score" (instrumentation and score-playing); "Catechism of the Invention, Exposition, Development, and Concatenation of Musical Ideas;" "A New Theoretical Musical Grammar;" "Dictionary comprising an Explication of 3,500 Italian, French, etc., Terms" (3rd ed., 1848). He also translated: H. Cherubini's "Counterpoint and Fugue," Baillot's "Violin School," Frölich's "Kontrabassschule," Vierling's "Anleitung zum Präludieren," etc.

Hamma, (1), B e n j a m i n, b. Oct. 10, 1831, Friedingen (on the Danube), pupil of Lindpaintner, lived for some time in Paris and Rome, and then settled in Königsberg as a teacher of music; he is now director of a school of music at Stuttgart. H. has also written many male choruses, mixed choruses and songs, pf. pieces; also an opera, *Zarrisko*.

(2) F r a n z X a v e r, b. Dec. 3, 1835, Wehingen (Würtemberg), teacher of music at Metz, composer of vocal music; also compiler of singing books for schools.

Hammerklavier, an old German term for our present pianoforte, invented at the beginning of the 18th century (in which the strings were struck by small hammers), in contradistinction to the clavichord and clavicembalo. (*Cf.* PIANO-FORTE.)

Hammerschmidt, A n d r e a s, b. 1611, Brix (Bohemia), in 1635 organist at Freiberg (Saxony), from 1639 in the same capacity at Zittau, where he d. Oct. 29, 1675. His artistic career was one of the most important phenomena in the department of sacred composition in Germany during the 17th century, in that he was not a dexterous copyist, but a conscious creator of new artforms. The Handel oratorio, the Bach passion, have their deepest roots in his Dialogues. In many respects H. may be looked upon as the successor of H. Schütz, but is far too independent to figure only as his follower. The works of H. which have been handed down to us are: "Instrumentalischer erster Fleiss" (1636); "Musikalischer Andachten, 1. Teil, das ist: Geistliche Concerten, mit 2, 3, und 4 Stimmen mit Generalbass" (1638); ditto, part 2, "Geistliche Madrigalien, mit 4, 5, und 6 Stimmen mit Generalbass" (1641); ditto, part 3, "Geistliche Symphonien," for two voices with instruments (1642); ditto, part 4, "Geistliche Motetten und Konzerte, von 5, 12, und mehr Stimmen mit doppeltem Generalbass" (1646); "Dialogi oder Gespräche zwischen Gott und einer gläubigen Seele" (Vol. I., à 2–4, with continuo, 1645 [1652]; Vol. II., Opitz's translation of "The Song of Solomon," à 1–2, with two violins and continuo, 1645 [1658]); "XVII Missæ Sacræ," à 5–12 (1633); "Paduanen, Gaillarden, Balletten &c" (1648 and 1650, two parts); "Weltliche Oden" (1650, two parts); "Lob und Danklied aus dem 84. Psalm," à 9 (1652); "Chormusik, fünfter Teil" (1652): "Motettæ unius et duarum vocum" (1646); "Musikalisches Bethaus" (Fol.); "Musikalische (part 2, "Geistliche") Gespräche über die Evangelia," à 4–7, with continuo (1655–56, two parts); "Fest-, Buss-, und Danklieder" (five vocal and five instrumental parts and continuo, 1659); "Kirchen- und Tafelmusik" (sacred concertos, 1662); and "Fest- und Zeitandachten" (à 6, 1671).

Hampel, H a n s, noteworthy composer and pianist, b. Oct. 5, 1822, Prague, d. there March 30, 1884, pupil of Tomaczek, was organist at Prague. Of his works there have appeared pf. pieces (Op. 10, "Lieb Aennchen;" Op. 16, three rhapsodies; Op. 26, variations for the left hand only; concert waltzes, etc.).

Hanboys (Hamboys), English musical theorist about 1470. His treatise, "Summa super musicam continuam et discretam," is printed in Coussemaker's "Scriptores" (I).

Hand, F e r d i n a n d G o t t h e l f, b. Feb. 15, 1786, Plauen (Voigtland), d. March 14, 1851, Jena, as privy councillor and professor of Greek literature; he published, among other things, an "Aesthetik der Tonkunst" (from 1837 to 1841, two vols.).

Handbassl, stringed instrument smaller than the 'cello, but larger than the viola.

Handel (Händel, Handl). (*See* GALLUS.)

Handel (also Händel, Hendel), G e o r g F r i e d r i c h, b. Feb. 23, 1685 (thus not quite a month before J. S. Bach), at Halle-a.-S., d. April 14 (not 13), 1759, London. His father was a surgeon (*i.e.* barber), but managed to acquire the title of valet-de-chambre and surgeon-in-ordinary to the Prince of Saxony and Elector of Brandenburg; he was already sixty-three years old when he married Dorothea, daughter of Pastor Georg Taust at Giebichenstein. Handel's eminently musically gifted nature soon showed itself, but met with resistance on the father's part; and this was only overcome when the Duke of Saxe-Weissenfels, who had listened in astonishment to the playing of the eight-year-old boy, interposed. H. now received regular musical instruction from the organist, F. W. Zachau. Already in 1696, Handel's father made an excursion with the little eleven-year-old composer to Berlin, and introduced him at the court, where, by his skill in improvisation and in playing from figured bass, he made an impression on Giovanni Bononcini and Attilio Ariosti. The Elector (afterwards King Friedrich I.) offered to send the boy~ to Italy to be trained; but Handel's father preferred to keep him at home, so that he might study law at the same time as music. In the following year the father died (1697); but H. honoured the wish of his departed parent, and actually entered his name (1702) as *Stud. jur.*, receiving at the same time the appointment of organist at the "Schloss-" and "Domkirche" for a year, as reward for his frequent services as deputy for the organist Leporin, who had given way to drink and had been dismissed. When the year had expired he went forth into the world, and indeed to Hamburg, at that time the most musical city of Germany, where, on Jan. 2, 1678, a permanent German Opera had opened with Theile's *Adam und Eva* (with exception of Heinrich Schütz's *Daphne* and Staden's *Seelewig*, actually the first German opera). Certainly at the time when H. came to Hamburg (1703), the opera was already going down hill; for Keiser (q.v.) —up to then one of the most prolific and important of Hamburg opera composers—was co-lessee of the undertaking, and accommodated himself in reprehensible fashion to public taste: on the other hand, the fame of Hamburg was still exceptionally great. H. did not go for the purpose of seeking out a famous teacher, but soon found in Mattheson a mentor who recognised his genius, and who, under such circumstances, was only too willing to be of service. The friendship, however, came to a sudden end when H. on one occasion wounded Mattheson's vanity. A duel which nearly cost H. his life was the result. H. wrote for Hamburg four German operas (but, according to the custom of the time, with Italian interpolations) : *Almira* (1705, recently arranged for the stage by Fuchs, 1878) ; *Nero* (1705) ; *Daphne* (1708), and *Florindo* (1708). The scores of the last three have disappeared. *Almira* had the greatest success. Keiser, jealous of H., set music to the libretti of *Almira* and *Nero*, somewhat modified, and withdrew H.'s operas from the répertoire. In 1706, however, he became bankrupt, and his successor (Saurbrey) commissioned H. to write *Daphne* and *Florindo* (really one work, but, on account of its length, divided into two parts). By the time they were produced H. had already been for some time in Italy. Early in 1707, mainly through the influence of Prince Giovanni Gaston de' Medici (who was present at the production of *Almira*), he sought the birthplace of opera, and the home in which it was principally fostered. His stay in Italy lasted over three years, and he went first to Florence, from April to June to Rome, back again to Florence for the production of his opera *Rodrigo* (with Tesi as prima donna), and at the new year (1708), to Venice, where his second Italian opera (*Agrippina*) was put on the stage. There he formed connections with influential rich Hanoverians and English, forming part of the suite of Prince Ernst August of Hanover, who had a box at the Venice Opera. From Venice H. returned in March to Rome, and this time was received with distinction. He frequented the Academy "Arcadia," became the guest of the Marchese Ruspoli (Prince Cerveteri), and wrote two oratorios (*La Resurrezione* and *Il trionfo del tempo e del disinganno*), the former produced in the "Arcadia," the latter in the palace of Cardinal Ottoboni. In Venice H. had made the acquaintance of Antonio Lotti ; in Rome he was on friendly terms with the two Scarlattis and Corelli. He accompanied the two Scarlattis in July, 1708, to Naples, where he remained until the autumn of 1709, and became imbued with the style of A. Scarlatti in the composition of cantatas. On his journey homewards, he tarried once again in Venice for the carnival of 1710, renewed acquaintance with the friends already named, and followed Abbate Steffani to Hanover. Steffani begged to be dismissed from the post of court capellmeister, and proposed H. to the Elector as his successor. H. himself, however, sought for leave of absence in order to make a journey to England, where, after a short visit to his family at Halle, he arrived towards the close of 1710. In London, under Purcell (d. 1695), it had seemed, for the moment, as if a national opera were about to become established, but Italian opera soon appeared. H., who had become famous in Italy, met, therefore, with a splendid reception, and broke out into enthusiasm when his opera *Rinaldo*, written in fourteen days (and made up of earlier arias), was produced. His duties called him, early in 1711, to Hanover, where he wrote some chamber duets in the style of

Steffani, and some concertos for oboe. But already at the new year (1712) he was again on his way to London. His opera (*Il Pastor Fido*) only met, it is true, with moderate success ; neither was that of *Teseo* brilliant. On the other hand, by the "Utrecht Te Deum" (1713) in celebration of the peace, H. won the hearts of the English ; for they saw, as it were, Purcell living again in him. Queen Anne rewarded him with a pension of £200 per annum ; but H. had now fallen into disfavour with the Elector, for relations were strained between the latter, the legal heir to the English throne, and the queen. The queen died in 1714, and the Elector came to London, at first completely ignoring H., but, by means of a serenade composed in his honour (the so-called "Water-Music"), became reconciled with him. In 1716 H. accompanied him, now king (George I.), to Hanover, and from there paid a visit to his home and to his mother. In Hanover he wrote his last German work—the *Passion*—to words by Brockes, which had been set to music before him by Keiser and Telemann ; another oratorio (*Passion*, to words by Postel) he had already written in Hamburg in 1704. On his return to London, he accepted an invitation from the Duke of Chandos to his mansion Cannons, at Edgware, near London. H. wrote there, during the three following years, the two Chandos "Te Deums," the secular oratorio *Acis and Galatea* (of which he had already made one setting at Naples), and his first grand oratorio—*Esther* (English). A new phase of his life begins in 1719 with the establishment of the Royal Academy of Music for Opera—that great undertaking which sprang from private speculation among the nobility, and which was supported by the king to the amount of £1,000. H. was commissioned to engage artists, and hastened to Dresden, where, for the marriage of the Elector-Prince, special court festivities were being held ; hence the best vocal talent was concentrated there, and he had good choice. In 1720 the Academy performances commenced with Porta's *Numitore*, and the second opera was Handel's *Radamisto ;* in 1721 he wrote the third act of *Muzio Scevola*, *Floridante ;* in 1723, *Ottone, Flavio ;* in 1724, *Giulio Cesare, Tamerlano ;* in 1725, *Rodelinda ;* in 1726, *Scipione, Alessandro ;* in 1727, *Admeto, Riccardo I.;* and in 1728, *Siroe, Tolemeo*. These operas soon spread over the whole of Europe ; even France did not entirely ignore them. Next to H. it was principally Bononcini who wrote for the Academy, and he was a rival in success ; the latter, however, in 1728, made himself impossible in London. (*See* BONONCINI.) In the year 1727 was written the Coronation Anthem for the accession to the throne of George II. In 1728 the Academy was broken up through money difficulties ; the quizzing *Beggar's Opera* of Gay had made it ridiculous to the public, and brought it into ridicule and discredit. The manager, Heidegger, bought the house and the properties, and entrusted H. with the engagement of new vocalists and with the sole direction. H. hastened to Italy, visited for the last time his blind mother in Halle, studied at Naples the school of Scarlatti, in the full tide of its prosperity, and returned to London at the end of September, 1729, with a new company. During this second operatic undertaking, H. wrote: *Lotario* (1729); *Partenope* (1730); *Poro* (1731); *Ezio* (1731); *Sosarme* (1732); and *Orlando* (1732). In 1732 this undertaking came to an end. The dismissal by H. of the famous *evirato*, Senesino, caused the secession of other members of the company, and in 1733, a rival company—"The Opera of the Nobility" —was started by H.'s enemies, with Porpora, and afterwards Hasse, as conductor and composer. Once more H. hastened to Italy to seek for fresh talent. The first year was tolerably successful for H. *Arianna* and *Pastor fido* (revised) were produced in 1734. But when his enemies appeared in the field with Senesino and Farinelli, Heidegger lost courage. H. took Covent Garden, and carried on the undertaking on his own account, while Heidegger let the Haymarket to the opposition company. By feverish efforts H. endeavoured to ward off ruin. The new operas produced were: *Terpsichore* (1734); *Ariodante* (1735); *Alcina* (1735); *Atalanta* (1736); *Arminio, Giustino,* and *Berenice* (1737). H. also produced new oratorios. Already in 1732 his *Acis and Galatea* and *Esther* (both revised) had excited considerable attention; and in 1733, on the occasion of the "Public Act" of the University of Oxford, a kind of festivity to celebrate the reconciliation of the University with the new dynasty, H. produced there: *Acis and Galatea, Esther, Deborah,* the "Utrecht Te Deum," and *Athalia,* and for the marriage of Princess Anna, a wedding anthem. H. produced *Alexander's Feast* at Covent Garden in 1736, and during Lent of 1737 he brought forward *Esther* and *Il Trionfo del tempo e della verità,* revised. Even the giant strength of H. could not stand the strain of such excessive exertion. A stroke of apoplexy paralysed his right side, and disturbed, for a time, his mind. The opera season had to be given up, the singers dismissed with half-salaries, and H. went to take the sulphur waters at Aix-la-Chapelle; he, however, returned after a few months, partly recovered in health. It was then that he wrote the deeply moving "Funeral Anthem" for Queen Caroline, who had just died. Meanwhile, the operatic scheme of his rivals had suffered shipwreck. The never-to-be-beaten Heidegger collected together the remnants of both companies, and in the autumn of 1737 opened again with H.'s *Faramondo* and *Serse,* but then found himself at the end of his tether. H. himself (1739-40) arranged some performances without a regularly engaged company, and with such resources as he found to hand, and produced the new operas—

Imeneo and *Deidamia;* also the oratorios *Saul* and *Israel,* and *L'Allegro, Il Pensieroso ed Il Moderato.* A great number, also, of H.'s instrumental works belong to the period before 1740, thus: twelve sonatas for violin (or flute) with a thorough-bass (several of these have been arranged for violin and pf. by Gustav Jensen); thirteen sonatas for two hautboys (or flute) with bass; six *concerti grossi* (the so-called Hautboy Concertos; five other orchestral works; twenty organ concertos; twelve grand concertos for strings, and a great number of suites, fantasias, and fugues for harpsichord and organ. From 1741 dates, finally, the universal recognition of H.'s genius, after he, so shortly before, had been opposed by fate. In that year he wrote his *Messiah* in three weeks, and it was produced for the first time at Dublin in the following year. It was not given in London until 1743. From 1750 he had it performed every year for the benefit of the Foundling Hospital (and in twenty-eight performances it brought in more than £10,000). From that time H. turned his attention definitely to the composition of oratorios; there followed *Samson* in 1741–42; *Semele* (1743); *Joseph* (1743); *Hercules* and *Belshazzar* (1744); the so-called *Occasional Oratorio* (1745 or 1746; last played on autograph score very indistinct); *Judas Maccabæus* (1746); *Joshua* and *Alexander Balus* (1747); *Solomon and Susanna* (1748); *Theodora* (1749); and *Jephtha* (1751). He thus created his greatest works between the age of 56–66. Already in 1751, threatening blindness hindered him from work, but he continued to give concerts and to play the organ at the performances of his oratorios. The last concert under his direction (*The Messiah*) took place a week before his death. The English rightly regard H. as *their* greatest composer. His Germanism no one can take from him; and even had he come to England as a boy, the specially German element in his musical creative power would scarcely have become completely wiped out. But it must not be forgotten that the direction and mode of development of his musical activity was, in great measure, determined by his outward life, his surroundings, and by the desires and taste of the public. His real training-school was, however, not England, but Hamburg and Italy. Then the influence of the works of Purcell on him must not be ignored; for, in so far as he is lighter, more pleasing, more directly comprehensible than Bach, it is owing to that school. Had he pursued, after the manner of Bach, the hermit-like career of an organist, he might also have devoted himself to writing learned compositions, and the enjoyment of his works might have been tied up with the same difficulties as those which we meet with in the works of Bach. These two most powerful masters, although of the same age, never saw, nor even corresponded with each other. (*Cf.* J. S. BACH.) Busts of H. were prepared already during his lifetime by Roubilliac, the same who provided one in 1762 for his monument in Westminster Abbey. A noble colossal statue (by Heidel) was erected to his memory in his native town, Halle-a.-S., in 1859: but the finest memorial is the monumental edition of his works (under the editorship of Dr. Chrysander), which was undertaken by the German Handel Society in 1856, and of which the first volume appeared in 1859; it is expected to be completed shortly with its 100th volume. An incomplete edition, brought out already in 1786 by S. Arnold at the command of King George III. (thirty-six vols.), is very incorrect. In 1843 a Handel Society in London undertook a new complete edition, but did not carry it through; besides, it is not free from faults, so that the old original editions of Walsh, Meare, and Cluer are to be preferred. On H.'s life and works the following have appeared: Mattheson in the "Ehrenpforte" (1740); Mainwaring: "Memoirs of the Life of the late G. F. Haendel" (1760; German, with comments by Mattheson, 1761; French, by Arnauld and Suard, 1778); J. A. Hiller, in the "Wöchentliche Nachrichten" (1770), and the "Lebensbeschreibungen" (1784); Hawkins, in his "History of Music" (1788), etc. More recent, independent works are: Förstemann: "G. F. Händel's Stammbaum" (1844); Schölcher: "The Life of H." (one vol., 1857); Chrysander: "G. F. H.," not yet completed (1858-67, only up to the first half of the third volume has appeared, extending to 1740); Gervinus: "H. and Shakespeare" (1868); and Rockstro's "Life of G. F. H." (1883).

Handel and Haydn Society, at Boston, is the greatest musical society in America, established 1815, since which regular concerts have been held (1815 to 1887). In 1857 the first great musical festival of the society was held, and similar ones have been given every three years since 1865. The usual subscription concerts are given in the Music Hall every Sunday evening from October to April. The present conductor is C. Zerrahn.

Hand-guide. (*See* CHIROPLAST.)

Handl (Handl, Hähnel). (*See* GALLUS.)

Handlo, R o b e r t d e, English writer on music about 1326; he wrote "Regulæ cum maximis magistri Franconis cum additionibus aliorum musicorum," printed in Coussemaker, "Scriptores."

Handrock, J u l i u s, b. June 22, 1830, Naumburg, an able teacher of music, and composer of numerous, especially instructive, pf. works; he lives at Halle-a.-S.

Handtrommel (Ger.). (*Cf.* TAMBOURINE.)

Hänel v o n C h r o n e n t h a l, J u l i a, married the Marquis D'Héricourt de Valincourt, b. 1839, Graz, was trained in Paris, and became

an esteemed composer. She wrote four symphonies, twenty-two pf. sonatas, a quartet for strings, nocturnes, songs without words, dances, marches, arrangements of Chinese melodies for orchestra, etc. (for the latter she received a medal at the Paris Exhibition of 1867).

Hanfstängel, M a r i e (S c h r ö d e r, married H.), distinguished stage singer, b. April 30, 1848, Breslau, pupil of Mme. Viardot-Garcia at Baden-Baden. She was engaged in 1866 at the Théâtre Lyrique, Paris, but went, when the war broke out in 1870, to Germany, and in 1871 was engaged at the Court Opera, Stuttgart. In 1873 she married the photographer H., and in 1878 made further vocal studies under Vannucini at Florence, and was engaged at the "Stadt" Theatre, Frankfort, in 1882.

Hanisch, J o s e p h, b. 1812, Ratisbon, d. there October 9, 1892, where he was trained by his father, organist of the old chapel, and also by Proske, who took him to Italy, 1834-36, as assistant and fellow-worker; in 1839 he was appointed organist of Ratisbon Cathedral, which post he held up to the last with almost the freshness of youth. He became, in addition, organist and choir-master of the "Niedermünsterkirche," and in 1875 teacher at the School of Sacred Music. H. was a master-performer of sacred music, and of improvisation. He wrote masses, motets, psalms, organ-preludes, and an organ accompaniment to the *Graduale* and *Vesperale Romanum.*

Hanke, K a r l, b. 1754, Rosswalde (Schleswig), d. 1835, Hamburg, in 1777 capellmeister to Count Haditz; he married the vocalist Stormkin, whom he accompanied to various theatres as musical director and operatic composer. He was court capellmeister at Schleswig in 1786, cantor and musical director at Flensburg in 1791, finally, musical director at Hamburg. He composed operas, ballets, incidental music to plays, symphonies, sacred music, duets for horns, etc.

Hanslick, E d u a r d, one of the most distinguished musical critics of the present day, b. Sept. 11, 1825, Prague, son of the Bohemian bibliographer Joseph Adolf H. (d. Feb. 2, 1859), received his first training in music under Tomaschek at Prague, but studied jurisprudence there and at Vienna; took his degree of *Dr.jur.* in 1849, and entered into government service. Already in 1848, however, he began his activity as a writer, first (until 1849) as musical critic of the *Wiener Zeitung,* and as contributor to several musical papers. He very soon felt that he had found his true vocation, and his notices, giving proofs of rare intellectual ability, and a warm feeling for the beautiful, were esteemed at their proper value. He became generally known by his book, "Vom Musikalisch-Schönen, ein Beitrag zur Revision der Aesthetik der

Tonkunst" (1854, 7th ed. 1885; French, 1877; Spanish, 1879; English, 1891); the book, of small compass, is of weighty importance in the matter of modern musical esthetics. Although H., in denying that music is capable of representing anything, went too far; yet, at one blow, he put an end to former sentimental fantastic notions respecting the effect and aim of music. In 1855 H. undertook the editorship of the musical portion of the *Presse*, qualified himself as private teacher of the esthetics and history of music at the Vienna University, and in 1861 was appointed assistant, and in 1870 professor of music in ordinary. In 1886 he received the title of "K. K. Hofrat." In 1864 he exchanged his work on the *Presse* for similar work on the *Neue Freie Presse*, the "feuilleton" of which has since played an important *rôle* in the musical world. At the two Paris Exhibitions in 1867 and 1878, and the one at Vienna in 1873, H. was a juror for the musical department. His "Vom Musikalisch-Schönen" was followed by a number of interesting writings: "Geschichte des Konzertwesens in Wien" (1869), "Aus dem Konzertsaal" (1870, 2nd ed. 1897), "Die moderne Oper" (1875, 8th ed. 1885), "Musikalische Stationen" (1880), "Aus dem Opernleben der Gegenwart" (3rd ed. 1885), "Suite. Aufsätze über Musik und Musiker" (1885). He also wrote the letterpress for the illustrative works, "Galerie deutscher Tondichter" (1873) and "Galerie französischer und italienischer Tondichter" (1874).

Hanssens, (1) Charles Louis Joseph (the elder), b. May 4, 1777, Ghent, d. May 6, 1852, Brussels; he received his first musical training at Ghent, then passed through a course of harmony under Berton at Paris, and commenced his career as theatre capellmeister at an amateur theatre at Ghent. He went from there to the joint opera companies of Amsterdam, Rotterdam, and Utrecht, then in 1804 to Antwerp and Ghent, and in 1827 to Brussels, to the Théâtre de la Monnaie, and was entrusted at the same time with the direction of the Conservatoire. Through the political events of 1830 he lost both posts, acted once more (1835–38) as theatre capellmeister (the direction of the Conservatoire was given over to Fétis in 1833), and, for the third time, in 1840, when he had a share in the speculation, and was financially ruined. H. composed several operas, six masses, and some sacred vocal works.

(2) Charles Louis (the younger), b. July 12, 1802, Ghent, d. April 8, 1871, Brussels; one of the most distinguished of modern Belgian composers, entered already in 1812 (at the age of ten) as 'cellist into the orchestra of the National Theatre at Amsterdam, became second capellmeister in 1822, was engaged in a similar capacity at Brussels in 1824, and was appointed professor of harmony at the Conservatoire in 1827. Like the elder H., he lost both posts in 1830, lived then in Holland, and became second conductor at

the Théâtre Ventadour, Paris, in 1834. He was in 1835 at the French Opera at the Hague, again in Paris and Ghent, and finally, in 1848, appointed conductor at the Théâtre de la Monnaie, Brussels, which post he held until 1869; also from 1851–54 he was director of the Opéra. The number of his works is exceedingly great: he wrote some operas, many ballets, symphonies, overtures, orchestral fantasias, concertos for 'cello, for violin, and for pianoforte, two concertos for clarinet, a "Symphonie Concertante" for clarinet and violin, masses, a requiem, etc.

Harcadelt. (*See* ARCADELT.)

Harfenett. (*See* SPITZHARFE.)

Harknes. (*See* SENKRAH.)

Harmonica, a child's toy, consisting of a row of reed-pipes, blown with the mouth (Mouthharmonica). (*Cf.* ACCORDION and STROHFIEDEL.)

Harmonic Hand. (*See* GUIDONIAN HAND.)

Harmonic stops, organ stops whose pipes, owing to greater pressure of wind, do not produce their fundamental tones, but the first harmonic—*i.e.* the tone an octave above the fundamental tone. Such stops are the *Flûte octaviante* and *Flûte harmonique*.

Harmonie, (1) German and French term for music played by wind-instruments ("Harmoniemusik").—(2) A name given in the Middle Ages to the *Drehleier* (hurdy-gurdy).

Harmonie-musik. (*See* HARMONIE.)

Harmonietrompete, an instrument between a horn and a trumpet, constructed at the beginning of this century, on which stopped notes were employed with success. David Buhl wrote a Method for the H.

Harmoniphon (Fr.), a keyboard wind-instrument, invented in 1837 by Pâris of Dijon. The music produced from it resembles a combination of oboes, *cors anglais*, and bassoons.

Harmonists, a name given to those theorists who were guided directly by musical practice, and not by mathematical determinations of intervals, as opposed to the canonists, who did just the reverse. Among the Greeks the first method was represented by the school of Aristoxenos, the latter by that of Pythagoras. The terms Aristoxenists and H. are therefore identical; likewise those of Pythagorists and Canonists.

Harmonium is now the name in general use for the keyed instruments of the organ kind, with free-vibrating reeds without tubes, which came into vogue only in this century. They differ from the older *Regal* (q.v.) in that they have not striking, but free vibrating reeds, and are capable of tone of a more expressive kind (*crescendo*). The first inventor of the organ stops with free vibrating reeds was, according to the report of Schafhäutl, the Petersburg organ-builder, Kirsnik, about 1780, whose pupil, the

Swede Racknitz, introduced similar ones into Abt Vogler's " Orchestrion." Grenié, the first builder of an instrument which had only such reeds (1810), called it *Orgue expressif;* others gave the names *Æoline* (Clavæoline), *Æolodicon, Phys-harmonica* (Häckel, 1818), *Ærophone, Melophone,* etc., to instruments of similar construction, or to the improved form of those already invented. A. Debain of Paris gave the name H. to the in-struments which he patented in 1840, the first with several stops. Of minor importance are : the introduction of Percussion (striking by means of hammers) of the reeds in order to obtain readier speech; " Prolongement " (keeping separate keys in their pressed-down position); the *Double touche, i.e.* various intensities of sound, according to the depth at which the keys are pressed down, etc. On the other hand, a com-plete revolution in the construction of the har-monium has been effected by the Americans, in that the wind is drawn inwards instead of being forced outwards through the reeds. (*Cf.* AME-RICAN ORGANS.) The circumstance that in reeds the overtones, combination tones, beats, etc., are loud and clearly perceptible, has, on the one hand, made the H. a favourite instrument for acoustical investigations, but, on the other hand, has been distinctly prejudicial to it as a household instrument ; dissonances such as the chord of diminished seventh have a really dis-agreeable effect on the H. It is therefore not by chance that attempts to introduce pure in-tonation were first practically made on the H., and approved of. Without doubt, an H. which gives fifty-three notes of different pitch within the octave can produce milder effects of sound than the tempered system with only twelve. (*See* Helmholtz, " Lehre von Tonempfindungen," 4th ed., p. 669 [Bosanquet's H.]; also Engel, " Das mathematische H." (1881) ; S. Tanaka, " Studien auf dem Gebiete der reinen Stim-mung (1890) ; Riemann, " Katechismus der Musikwissenschaft " (1891) ; *cf.* also the tables under TONE, DETERMINATION OF, and TEMPERA-MENT.) But the grand idea of obtaining only pure music in this manner is not only imprac-ticable, but, on esthetical grounds, not accept-able. (*Cf.* TUNING [JUST], ENHARMONICS AND TEMPERAMENT, ALEXANDRE-ORGUE.)

Harmonometer (Ger.), **Harmonomètre** (Fr.), an instrument for measuring the relative pitch of sounds.

Harmony (Gr.) means " structure," hence (1) used by the Greeks in the meaning of scale, ordered succession of sounds.—(2) In the music of the Middle Ages and of modern times H. has the meaning of chord, a uniting together of sounds mutually intelligible, as a compound sound or clang.—(3) In a narrower sense, H. has then the same meaning as Triad (*consonant chord*), for instance, when one speaks of sounds *foreign to the harmony,* and belonging to that harmony.

Harmony, System of, is one which explains the meaning of harmonies (chords), *i.e.* the definition of the mental processes in listening to music. While a system of H. classifies the various possible combinations of sounds, investi-gates their relations one to another, endeavours to evolve the natural laws of musical, and especially harmonic, formation, *it exercises musical imagination in a systematic manner,* and develops the mental faculties both for the quicker under-standing of musical works, and for the self-pro-duction of thought in sounds. In so far as musical thought (the presentation or compre-hension of sounds) is subject to the same laws as thought in general, and seeing that a casual connection, more or less strong, must be estab-lished between the sound-producing vibrations and the sensations of tone, and, further, between these sensations of tone and musical presenta-tion, thus far is an exact theory of the *nature of harmony,* to a certain extent, possible. The expo-sition of a so-called *system of harmony* is therefore only dependent on caprice in outward matters— in terminology, order of the various branches, etc. In proportion, however, as a knowledge of the nature of harmony becomes greater and deeper, a system of H. must change its aspect; and the real object in view, the practical exercise of music, must always be considered in its con-stantly changing relationship to more compli-cated formations. The science of *musical com-position,* one entirely practical in its tendencies, and also called H.S., must be distinguished from the (speculative) H.S. here defined, and which belongs to philosophy and natural philosophy. Most harmony methods, in the former sense, give little or no explanation respecting the nature of harmony; and their sole aim is to transmit in empirical fashion the art of connecting chords and of the conduct of parts. (*Cf.* GENERAL-BASS and COUNTERPOINT.) The chief problem of a speculative system of H. is the definition and explanation of consonance and dissonance ; here the ground was already prepared by classic antiquity, and the determinations forming the basis of mathematical acoustics already re-vealed. (*See* INTERVAL.) Contrapuntal and har-monic music led gradually to a knowledge of the meaning of the consonant triad. Zarlino (1558) already understood the opposed meaning of the major chord and the minor chord, but does not assert that he had discovered it. Rameau (1722) first noticed that the separate sounds are conceived in the sense of chords ; also that, by a reverse process, chords are uniformly regarded in their relationship to one sound. The prin-ciple in Rameau's " System of Thorough Bass," still somewhat confused, has, within recent times, been expounded with all clearness (Helm-holtz's " Auffassung im Sinn der Klangvertre-tung"). It is only a small step further to the knowledge that all combinations of sound are to be understood in the sense of consonant chords, so that the dissonant ones appear, not as independent formations, but as modifications of consonant chords. (*See* DISSONANCE.) Finally, scale passages must also be taken in a chord sense. (*See* SCALES; *cf.* also CLANG; TONE, RELATIONSHIP OF; KLANGSCHLÜSSEL; CLANGS, SUCCESSION OF; TONALITY, MODULATION, CADENCE.) Real systems of harmony in the sense here sketched are:—Fétis's "Traité de l'harmonie" (11th ed. 1875), Hauptmann's "Natur der Harmonik und der Metrik" (2nd ed. 1873), A. v. Oettingen's "Harmoniesystem in dualer Entwickelung" (1866), Tiersch's "System und Methode der H." (1868), Hostinsky's "Lehre von den musikalischen Klängen" (1879), Riemann's "Musikalische Syntaxis" (1875), "Harmonielehre" (1880), "Systematische Modulationslehre" (1887), "Katechismus der Harmonielehre" (1890), and "Vereinfachte Harmonielehre oder die Lehre von den tonalen Funktionen der Akkorde" (1893).

Harmston, Joh. William, b. 1823, London, d. Aug. 26, 1881, Lübeck, pupil of S. Bennett; he settled in Lübeck as teacher of music in 1848. H. wrote many pieces for pianoforte, violin, and 'cello; also songs.

Harp (Ital. *Arpa;* Fr. *Harpe;* Ger. *Harfe*), one of the oldest stringed instruments, which, already in a form similar to that of the present day, appears to have been in use in Egypt thousands of years ago. Among the instruments whose strings are plucked by the fingers, or struck with the plectrum, the harp is the largest. Up to the beginning of the last century the H. was an instrument on which passages containing modulations to other keys could only be performed with difficulty, as the strings were not tuned chromatically, but diatonically; and to obtain the chromatic intermediate tones every single string had to be retuned by means of a crook which shortened the string. This crook was already a sign of progress (in the Tyrol, at the end of the 17th century). Only in 1720, Hochbrucker introduced the system of retuning all notes of the same name by pedal action, so that the hands of the performer remained free. (*Cf.,* however, OGINSKI.) At last Erard, in 1820, invented the *Double-action Harp,* which allowed of each string being raised twice to the extent of a semitone. This now perfected kind of H. is tuned in c♭, with a compass from contra c♭ to four times accented g♯. By the first action of the seven pedals all the seven flats are set aside, so that the tuning is in c; the second shortening changes the key c into c♯. Rapid chromatic passages, likewise chords which together with the fundamental note contain some octave of the same note chromatically changed, are impossible on the harp even now. The following are special kinds of H., ancient and modern: the old *Gaelish* H. (*Clairseach, Clàrsach, Claasagh*) and the *Cymbrian* H. (*Telyn, Telein, Télen*), which were used by the bards of Great Britain; the

Double Harps, with upright sounding-board and strings placed on both sides; the *Spitzharfe,* or Pointed Harps (*Arpanetta, Harfenett*), similar, but of smaller dimensions; Pfranger's chromatic H. (unpractical on account of the excessive number of strings); and Edward Light's (1798) Harp-lute (*Dital harp*), a noteworthy combination of the harp and lute.

Harpeggio. (*See* ARPEGGIO.)

Harper, Thomas, an eminent performer on the trumpet, b. May 3, 1787, Worcester, d. Jan. 20, 1853, London, where from 1821 he held all the principal appointments (ancient concerts, Italian Opera, musical festivals, etc.). His successor was his son Thomas; two younger sons, Charles and Edward, are esteemed performers on the horn.

Harpicordo (Ital.), a harpsichord.

Harp Instruments, a comprehensive term for those stringed instruments of which the strings are not played with the bow, but with the fingers, or struck with a plectrum, or by means of a hammer; hence a tone is produced of quickly decreasing strength, and one which soon dies away (Fr. *Instruments à cordes pincées;* the German terms *Kneif-* or *Zupf-Instrumente* ["pinched" or "pulled"] are scarcely improvements on H. I.). They are further divided into instruments *without finger-board* (of which the separate strings only give one sound; for the moment no notice is taken of exceptions, such as the pedal harp), and those *with finger-board.* To the first kind (H. I. in a narrower sense) belong all the stringed instruments of Greek antiquity (*Lyre, Cithara, Phorminx, Magadis, Barbitos,* etc.), the instruments of the Egyptians of the lyre and harp kind, the Chē and Kin of the Chinese, Galempung of the Indians, Kanun and Santir of the Turks, and the Western: *Rotta (Zither, Psalterium), Harp, Dulcimer,* and the H. I. with key-board (Monochord, Clavichord, Clavicytherium, Clavicymbal [*Kielflügel*], Spinet, Pianoforte, etc.). To the H. I. with finger-board, which might also be called *Lute Instruments,* belong the instruments of the lute kind of the Egyptians (*Nabla*), known only from their tomb representations; the *Vina* of the Indians; the *Kanon* of the Greeks; the *Lute* in its numerous forms, introduced into the West by the Arabians; *Guitar (Quinterna), Mandoline, Pandora,* etc., *Theorbo, Chitarrone,* great bass-lute, and the modern *Zither (Schlagzither*).

Harpsichord. (*See* PIANOFORTE.)

Harriers-Wippern, Luise (*née* Wippern), famous operatic singer, b. 1837, Hildesheim, d. Oct. 5, 1878, Gröbersdorf (Silesia); she made her *début* in 1857 at the Royal Opera, Berlin (as Agathe), and until she retired with a pension in 1868, in consequence of a throat complaint, she was engaged on that stage only, displaying extraordinary power both in dramatic and in lyrical parts.

Hart (Ger.), hard. This term is also used in the sense of "major."

Hart, (1) J a m e s, was, up to 1670, bass singer at York Minster, and afterwards, until his death, May 6, 1718, member of the Chapel Royal. He wrote songs published in collections of that period ("Choice Ayres, Songs and Dialogues," 1676-84; "The Theater of Music," 1685-87; "Banquet of Music," 1688-92). His son is probably

(2) P h i l i p, organist of several London churches, d. about 1749, published a collection of organ fugues, likewise music to the Morning Hymn from Milton's "Paradise Lost."

(3) J o h n T h o m a s, English violin-maker, b. Dec. 17, 1805, d. Jan. 1, 1874, London, carried on a brisk trade with old Italian instruments, of which he was one of the most famed connoisseurs. His son and heir

(4) G e o r g e, b. March 28, 1829, London, d. there April 25, 1891, was the compiler of one of the most important works relating to the construction of violins : "The Violin, its Famous Makers and their Imitators" (London, 1875).

Härtel, (1) publisher. (See BREITKOPF U. H.)

(2) G u s t a v A d o l f, b. Dec. 7, 1836, Leipzig, d. Aug. 28, 1876, as capellmeister at Homburg v. d. Höhe, violinist and composer. In 1857 he became capellmeister at Bremen, in 1863 at Rostock, and in 1873 at Homburg. H. wrote a "Trio burlesque" for three violins with pf., variations and fantasias for violin, an opera (*Die Carabiners*), and three operettas, etc.

(3) B e n n o, b. May 1, 1846, Jauer (Silesia), pupil of Fr. Kiel, from 1870 teacher of theory at the Royal High School for Music at Berlin. He has published pf. pieces and songs.

(4) L u i s e. (See BREITKOPF U. HÄRTEL.)

Hartmann, (1) J o h a n n P e t e r E m i l, one of the most distinguished of Danish composers, b, May 14, 1805, Copenhagen. He sprang from a German family, but his grandfather (J o h a n n H., b. Grossglogau) died already in 1763 as royal chamber musician at Copenhagen. H. received his first musical instruction from his father, who was organist of the garrison church, Copenhagen, from 1800-50, but he studied law at the same time as music, and pursued for a time the career of jurisprudence ; his talent, however, as composer—which at an early period attracted the attention of Weyse—drew him more and more towards a musical vocation. In 1832 he made his *début* at Copenhagen as an opera composer with *Ravnen (The Raven)* ; in 1834 there followed *Die goldnen Hörner*, and in 1835, *Die Korsen.* In 1836 he undertook a journey to Germany for the purpose of studying music, and produced, amongst other things, at Cassel in 1838, a symphony (No. 1, G minor ; dedicated to Spohr). In 1840 he was appointed director of the Conservatorium at Copenhagen. In 1874 a great concert was given in honour of his artistic jubilee,

the profits of which were devoted to the foundation of a H. scholarship. On this occasion the king bestowed on him the order of the "Danebrog." In 1879 the University of Copenhagen, on the occasion of its jubilee, named him *Dr. Phil. hon. causâ.* H. was the father-in-law of Gade. His works were the first to show a national colouring (northern music). His first operas date ten years before Gade. He has written the opera *Liden Kirsten (Die Kleine Christine*, 1846), incidental music to plays, overtures, symphonies, cantatas (among others, one for the obsequies of Thorwaldsen, 1848), a violin concerto, songs (cycles, "Salomon und Sulamith," "Hjortens Flugt," etc.), pf. pieces (Noveletten, etc.).

(2) E m i l, son of the former, likewise a composer of note, b. Feb. 21, 1836, Copenhagen, pupil of his father and of Gade (his brother-in-law), was appointed organist of a church at Copenhagen in 1861, and court organist in 1871 ; he withdrew, however, in 1873, out of consideration for his health, to Sölleröd, near Copenhagen, where he devotes himself to composition. Of his compositions which have been successful also in Germany the following may be named : "Nordische Volkstänze," for orchestra ; "Lieder und Weisen im nordischen Volkston "; overture, *Eine nordische Heerfahrt ;* three symphonies (in E♭, A minor ["Aus der Ritterzeit," Op. 34], and in D); an orchestral suite, "Scandinavische Volksmusik "; a choral work, "Winter und Lenz ;" several operas (*Die Erlenmädchen,* 1867; *Die Nixe ; Die Corsikaner) ;* a ballet (*Fjeldstuen*), a violin concerto, a 'cello concerto, a pf. trio, a serenade for pf., 'cello, and clarinet, etc.

(3) L u d w i g, b. 1836, Neuss, pupil of the Leipzig Conservatorium, and 1856–57 of Liszt at Weimar, pianist, composer, and esteemed musical critic at Dresden.

Hartog, (1) É d o u a r d de, b. Aug. 15, 1828, Amsterdam, was first a pupil of Bertelmann and Litolff, but enjoyed instruction for a short time in Paris under Eckert, and finally studied from 1849–52 under Heinze and Damcke. In 1852 he settled in Paris, devoting himself to composition, and became known in the same year, as also in 1857 and 1859, by works of his own performed at orchestral concerts specially arranged by himself. Of late he has been engaged in teaching. From among his compositions are to be named : the one-act comic operas, *Le Mariage de Don Lope* (1868, Théâtre Lyrique), and *L'Amour et son Hôte* (Brussels, 1873); the forty-third Psalm, for soli, chorus, and orchestra ; two stringed quartets ; a suite for strings ; several meditations for (violin), 'cello, organ (harp), and pf. ; songs, pf. pieces, etc. A number of other important works remain in manuscript (operas : *Lorenzo Aldini* and *Portici ;* Symphonic Preludes : "Macbeth," "Pompée," "Jungfrau von Orléans ;" six orchestral sketches etc.). H. was a contributor to Pougin's supplement to Fétis's "Biographie Universelle."

(2) Jacques, b. Oct. 24, 1837, Zalt-Bommel (Holland), pupil of Carl Wilhelm at Crefeld, and of Ferd. Hiller at Cologne, etc. He lives as composer and writer on music in Amsterdam, where he is teacher of the history of music at the School of Music. H. translated Lebert and Stark's " Klavierschule," and Langhans' "History of Music," also Breslauer's "Methodik des Klavierunterrichts," into Dutch; he writes notices for the *Centralblatt* (Leipzig), the *Neue Zeitschrift für Musik*, and the *Musikwelt* (Bonn). His compositions (concert-overture, violin concertino, mass, operetta, etc.) are, hitherto, but little known.

Hartvigson, Frits, b. May 31, 1841, Grenaa (Jutland), studied under Gade, Gebauer, and A. Rée, and from 1859-61 at Berlin under Bülow. He has lived in London since 1864 (with the exception of two years [1873-75] at Petersburg), esteemed as a pianist. He was appointed pianist to the Princess of Wales in 1873, professor of music at the College for the Blind at Norwood in 1875, and, in 1887, professor at the Crystal Palace. From 1879-88 a nervous affection of his left arm prevented him from playing in public. His brother, Anton, b. Oct. 16, 1845, Aarhus, studied under Tausig and Edmund Neupert. He has settled in London as pianist and teacher.

Harvard Association, at Boston; one of the oldest and most important of American musical societies (established 1837). It possesses a rich musical library, and gave, up to 1882, a yearly series of concerts in the far-famed Music Hall (with a great organ built by Walcker). Dwight (q.v.) was for many years president of the society; the conductor was Karl Zerrahn (q.v.).

Hase, Oskar, Dr. (*See* BREITKOPF U. HÄRTEL.)

Häser, (1) August Ferdinand, b. Oct. 15, 1779, Leipzig, d. Nov., 1844, as theatre capellmeister; church musical director, and teacher of music at the Training School at Weimar, where he became in 1817 chorus-master at the court Opera. He composed numerous sacred and orchestral works (requiems, Te Deums, Paternosters, misereres, masses, an oratorio—*Die Kraft des Glaubens*—[produced at Weimar 1828, and at Birmingham, 1837], three operas, overtures, etc.), pf. pieces, songs, etc.; he also wrote "Versuch einer systematischen Uebersicht der Gesanglehre" (1820), and a "Chorgesangschule" (1831).

(2) Charlotte Henriette, sister of the former, b. Jan. 24, 1784, Leipzig, was a distinguished vocalist. She sang first at the Dresden Opera, afterwards at Vienna and in Italy, and married the lawyer Vera, in 1813, at Rome. The year of her death is unknown.

(3) Heinrich, brother of the former, b. Oct. 15, 1811, Rome, professor of medicine at Jena. He wrote "Die menschliche Stimme,

ihre Organe, ihre Ausbildung, Pflege und Erhaltung" (1839).

Hasert, Rudolf, pianist, b. Feb. 4, 1826, Greifswald. He first devoted himself to law, became, however, inspired with love for music through Robert Franz at Halle-a.-S., and studied, from 1848-50, under Dehn and Kullak, theory and pianoforte-playing; but he injured one of his hands by overwork, and returned to jurisprudence. The love of art soon came back, and H. made concert tours with success in Sweden and Denmark, and went to Berlin, where he settled in 1861 as teacher of the pianoforte. From 1865 he devoted himself to a theological career, and passed his government examination in 1870. He first took a small post as minister at the Strausberg penitentiary, and, since 1873, has been pastor at Gristow (near Greifswald), which living has long been in the family.

Hasler (Hassler), Hans Leo (von), b. 1564, Nuremberg, d. June 8, 1612, Frankfort, the first German master who sought his musical training in Italy (before that, for nearly two centuries, the Netherlands, the high school of composition, furnished Italy, Germany, Spain, and France with musicians). About 1585 H. became organist to Count Octavianus Fugger at Augsburg, but he studied for several years at Venice under Andreas Gabrieli as fellow-pupil of the great Giovanni Gabrieli. His style bears, therefore, great resemblance to that of the two Venetians; in his canzonets and madrigals with their detailed work he recalls Andrea, but in his great works for double choir, Giovanni Gabrieli. H., however, is something more than an imitator, and was held in high esteem by his contemporaries. He lived for many years at Prague at the court of the Emperor Rudolf II., and was raised to the rank of a nobleman. From 1601-8 he was at Nuremberg, and in the latter year entered the service of the Elector of Saxony, and died, while on a journey, at Frankfort. The works of H. which have been preserved are : "Canzonette à 4 voci" (1590); "Cantiones sacræ . . . 4, 8 et plur. voc." (1591, 1597, 1607); "Madrigali à 5-8 voci" (1596); "Newe teutsche Gesang nach Art der welschen Madrigalien u. Canzonetten" (à 4-8; 1596, 1604, 1609); "Missæ 4-8 vocum" (1599); "Lustgarten newer deutscher Gesäng, Balletti, Galliarden und Intraden mit 4-8 Stimmen" (1601, 1605, 1610); "Sacri concentus, 5-12 voc." (1601, 1612); "Psalmen und christliche Gesänge" (à 4 "fugal," 1607; new score ed. 1777); "Kirchengesänge, Psalmen und geistliche Lieder" (à 4 "simpliciter," 1608, 1637); "Litaney deutsch Herrn Dr. Martini Lutheri" (à 7, for double chorus, 1619); "Venusgarten oder neue lustige liebliche Täntze teutscher und polnischer Art" (1615). H. also published a collection of works—"Sacræ symphoniæ diversorum" (1601, two parts), which contain several of his motets; a large number are to be found in Bodenschatz's "Florilegium Portense" and Schad's "Promptuarium musicum." (Cf. Rob. Eitner's chronological catalogue of the printed works of H. L. von H., and Orlandus de Lassus, *Monatshefte f. Mus.-Gesch.*, 1874, Supplement).—Also his brothers, Jakob (b. about 1601, organist at Hechingen), and Kaspar (b. 1570, d. 1618 as organist at Nuremberg), by worthy compositions, have handed down their names to posterity.

Haslinger, Tobias, b. March 1, 1787, Zell (Upper Austria), d. June 18, 1842. He went to Vienna 1810, entered as book-keeper into the Steiner music business, and afterwards became partner; when Steiner withdrew in 1826, he became sole possessor, trading under his own name. After his death his son, Karl (b. June 11, 1816, Vienna, d. Dec. 26, 1868), prolific composer (more than one hundred operas), undertook the business, trading as "Karl H., *quondam* Tobias," which firm still exists : it passed into the hands of Schlesinger (Lienau) of Berlin in 1875.

Hasse, (1) Nikolaus, organist of the Marienkirche, Rostock, about 1650. He published "Deliciæ Musicæ" (Allemandes, Courantes, and Sarabandes, for stringed instruments and clavicymbal, or theorbo, 1656; 2nd part and "Appendix," 1658).

(2) Johann Adolf, b. May 25, 1699, Bergedorf (near Hamburg), d. Dec. 16, 1783, Venice; one of the most prolific composers of the last century, who was specially famous for his dramatic compositions. He began his career as a stage singer (tenor) at Hamburg (1718), Brussels (1722; on the recommendation of Ulrich König), and Brunswick; in the last town he produced his first opera, *Antigonus,* 1723. He understood, however, only too well, that much was wanting to him as an opera composer, and went therefore in 1724 to Italy, where he studied in Naples, first under Porpora, then under Alessandro Scarlatti, and obtained his first success as a dramatic composer with *Il Sesostrate* at Naples in 1726. H. soon became famous in Italy under the surname *il Sassone* ("the Saxon"). Already at Venice in 1727 he had met the famous Faustina Bordoni, whom he married in 1730 (*see below*), and with whose fate his own was henceforth bound up. In 1731 he was appointed royal "concertmeister" of the Italian Opera, which had been renewed at Dresden, and, at the same time, Faustina was engaged as *prima donna.* Yet, after the production of H.'s *Cleofide* (Sept. 13, 1731), both went to Italy, where, until 1734, they celebrated fresh triumphs. Only after the death of Augustus the Strong was opera revived at Dresden, when both returned to that city. During the following years H. received repeated leave of absence for Italy, where he wrote new operas for all kinds of theatres, and, for a long time, ruled their *répertoires.* Once he was induced to go to London to put his *Artaserse*

(first produced at Venice, 1730) on the stage, but he soon made way for Handel, who was his superior. In Dresden he held, for the most part, a difficult position towards Porpora, his old teacher, with whom he had long quarrelled; it is possible that after the death of Augustus the Strong (1733), this misunderstanding may have been the cause of his almost continual absence from Dresden. After 1740 he appears, on the other hand, to have remained constantly in Dresden, and to have exercised his functions as capellmeister. In 1750 he was appointed principal capellmeister. In 1751 Faustina retired from the stage, possessor of titles and a pension. By the bombardment of Dresden in 1760 the library of H., and a quantity of manuscripts of his operas, etc., became a prey to the flames. In 1763, he, together with Faustina, were dismissed, from motives of economy, without pension. They both went to Vienna, where H. still composed for the court opera, and later on to Venice, where he died. He wrote over a hundred operas, also ten oratorios, five Te Deums with orchestra, many masses, a requiem (for Augustus the Strong) ; further, portions of masses, magnificats, misereres (the one written in 1728 for two sopranos and two altos with accompaniment for strings is one of his finest works), litanies, motets, psalms, cantatas, clavier sonatas, flute concertos, clavier concertos, etc. (The Dresden Library possesses nine masses, twenty-two motets, eleven oratorios, forty-two operas, six clavier sonatas, etc.) (Cf. Riehl's "Mus. Charakterköpfe.")

(3) Faustina (*née* Bordoni), b. 1693, Venice, of noble family; she received her training from Gasparini, made her *début* in 1716 with phenomenal success, and was soon one of the most distinguished singers of Italy. Engaged in 1724 at Vienna for 15,000 fl., she was soon won for London by Handel (£2,000), and was a victorious rival there, 1726-28, of Cuzzoni; they fell out to such an extent, that blood flowed. (Cf. ARBUTHNOT.) On her return to Venice she made the acquaintance of J. A. Hasse, who at that time enjoyed great fame; she married him, and at the same time that he received his engagement as court capellmeister she was called to Dresden as *prima donna* (1731, *see above*). Faustina was esteemed as an artist of the first rank until 1751, then retired from the stage, receiving her full salary until 1763, when both she and her husband were dismissed without pension, and removed to Vienna; the year of her death is unknown. (Cf. A. Niggli, "Faustina Bordoni H.," 1880.)

(4) Gustav, b. Sept. 4, 1834, Peitz (Brandenburg), pupil of the Leipzig Conservatorium, and afterwards of Kiel and F. Kroll at Berlin ; he lives there as teacher of music, and is advantageously known as a composer of songs.

Hasselt-Barth, Anna Maria Wilhelmine (*née* van Hasselt), a famous vocalist (soprano),

b. July 15, 1813, Amsterdam, trained at Frankfort and Carlsruhe (Jos. Fischer), in 1829 under Romani at Florence, made her *début* in 1831 at Trieste. She sang first on various Italian stages, and from 1833–38 at Munich, and was then engaged at the "Kärnthnerthor" Theatre, Vienna, until she received her pension.

Hassler. (*See* HASLER.)

Hässler, Johann Wilhelm, one of the most interesting composers for the pianoforte during the period between Bach and Beethoven ; b. March 29, 1747, Erfurt, d. March 29, 1822, Moscow. He was son of a cap-maker, and followed, for a long time, his father's trade, after he had become advantageously known as a musician ; he was nephew and pupil of Kittel, was already at the age of fourteen organist of the "Barfüsserkirche," Erfurt ; he gave concerts, as an itinerant journeyman, in the most important German towns, and with such success that in 1780 he founded at Erfurt yearly series of concerts, and also a music business. He travelled to England, Russia, etc., and in 1792 was appointed Imperial capellmeister at Petersburg. In 1794 he resigned this post and went to Moscow, where he was highly esteemed as teacher. A pupil erected a monument in granite to him there. H. belongs to the better composers of his time in the department of organ and clavier composition, but was certainly thrown into the shade by Haydn, Mozart, and Beethoven, and soon forgotten beyond his due. His slow movements are, it is true, pigtailed, but strong in expression, and full of minute detail ; his rondos are full of life and humour. His works which have appeared are pianoforte sonatas, concertos, fantasias, variations, and organ pieces and songs. In recent editions there exist of his, besides the well-known great D minor gigue, six sonatinas (1780), and some fantasias, rondos, variations, etc. (*Cf.* L. Meinardus, articles on H. in the *Allgem. M.-Zeitung*, 1865.)

Hasslinger-Hassingen. (*See* HAGER.)

Hastreiter, Helene, an esteemed American opera singer, b. Nov. 14, 1858, Louisville (Kentucky), studied with Lamperti at Milan. She lately married the Italian physician, Dr. Burgunzio.

Hatton, John Liptrot, b. Oct. 20, 1809, Liverpool, d. Sept. 20, 1886, Margate ; from 1832 he settled in London, and in 1842 became conductor at Drury Lane Theatre, where he produced his first operetta, *The Queen of the Thames*. In 1844 he brought out an opera, *Pascal Bruno*, at Vienna ; in 1848 he visited America. From 1853–58 he was musical director at the Princess's Theatre, for which he composed a large amount of incidental music. Other works of his are : *Rose : or, Love's Ransom* (opera, Covent Garden, 1864), *Robin Hood* (cantata, Bradford Musical Festival, 1856), *Hezekiah* (sacred drama, Crystal Palace, 1877), also many songs, several of which he published under the pseudonym "Czapek."

Hauck, Minnie, b. Nov. 16, 1852, New York, an eminent stage singer (soprano), made her *début* at New York and at London in 1868, and in 1869 was engaged for three years at the Grand Opera, Vienna. From that time she made for herself a far-famed name on the most important stages of Berlin, where she was engaged for two years, Paris, Brussels, Moscow, Petersburg, etc. Her *répertoire* is varied, but she has specially cultivated lyric parts.

Hauer, Karl Heinrich Ernst, b. Oct. 28, 1828, Halberstadt, where his father was cantor and teacher, d. March 16, 1892, Berlin; from 1844 he attended the Gymnasium at Halberstadt, was then for two years a private pupil of Marx at Berlin, and again for three years a pupil of the "Kgl. Akademie" (Rungenhagen, Bach, Grell), and distinguished himself in composition. In 1856 he became teacher of music at the Andreas Gymnasium, in 1866 organist of the "Markuskirche." H. has composed many songs, quartets for male and mixed voices, and sacred songs, motets, Ave Maria à 6 *a cappella*, paternoster for solo and chorus, "Luther hymnus," etc. A psalm à 8 with orchestra, his last student-exercise, won for him a silver medal (1853).

Hauff, Johann Christian, b. Sept. 8, 1811, Frankfort, d. there April 30, 1891, an able musical theorist, joint-founder of the Frankfort School of Music. He composed orchestral and chamber music, and published a "Theorie der Tonsetzkunst" (1863–69; three vols. in five parts).

Hauffe, Luise. (*See* BREITKOPF U. HÄRTEL.)

Haupt, Karl August, b. Aug. 25, 1810, Kunern (Silesia), d. July 4, 1891, Berlin, from 1827–30 a pupil of A. W. Bach, B. Klein, and S. Dehn at Berlin, was successively organist of various churches in Berlin, from 1849 at the Parochialkirche. He won the reputation of being an organist of the first rank, so that in 1854 he was entrusted, jointly with Donaldson, Ouseley, and Willis, with the disposition of the great organ for the Crystal Palace, London. In 1869 he succeeded A. W. Bach as director of the Royal Institute for Church Music, at which he had already acted for some years as teacher of theory and of organ-playing; he received at the same time the title of professor, and, by his position, became member of the musical section of the senate of the Akademie. The only published compositions of H. are songs and a "Choralbuch" (1869).

Hauptmann, Moritz, one of the most distinguished theorists, b. Oct. 13, 1792, Dresden, d. Jan. 3, 1868, Leipzig. He was the son of the chief state architect, H. of Dresden, and was originally intended to follow the same profession, but received at an early age thorough musical training under Scholz (violin), Grosse (pianoforte and harmony), and Morlacchi (composition). As his decided gifts for music showed themselves more and more, his father consented to the choice of music as a profession. In 1811 he went to Gotha to Spohr, under whose guidance he zealously studied the violin and composition, entered the Dresden court band as violinist in 1812, made many concert tours, and in 1815 took the post of private teacher of music in the house of the Russian prince Repnin, whom he followed to Petersburg, Moscow, and Pultawa. After five years, devoted to deep study of theory, he returned to Dresden, and in 1822 entered the court band at Cassel under his old teacher Spohr. His fame as theorist and composer gradually increased, and thus in 1842, on the special recommendation of Spohr and Mendelssohn, he succeeded Weinlig in the honourable post of cantor of St. Thomas's School, Leipzig, and, in the following year, was appointed teacher of theory at the newly established Conservatorium. A great number of musicians who have become famous are indebted to him for their theoretical training. The compositions of Hauptmann are distinguished for the remarkable symmetry of their architectonic structure, for the purity of the writing, and the melodiousness of the various parts. His motets, familiar to every church choir in Germany, take first rank; further, two masses, part-songs for mixed voices, canons à 3 for soprano voices; finally, duets and songs for single voice, which belong to the second half of his creative period ("Gretchen vor dem Bilde der Mater dolorosa"). In his younger days he wrote violin sonatas, duets for violins, string quartets, and an opera, *Mathilde* (Cassel, 1826). His works of greatest importance were, however, those connected with theory. He expounded his system in a complete and philosophical form in the "Natur der Harmonik und der Metrik" (1853, 2nd ed. 1873; English, 1888); his other writings are only completions and practical applications of the same, viz., "Erläuterungen zu J. S. Bach's Kunst der Fuge" (Peters), "Ueber die Beantwortung des Fugenthemas" (in the *Wiener Rezensionen*), and other treatises in musical papers. A posthumous work, "Die Lehre von der Harmonik," was published in 1868 by O. Paul, and a number of collected articles, "Opuscula" (1874), were published by Hauptmann's son. Besides, there appeared: Hauptmann's "Briefe an Franz Hauser" (edited by A. Schöne, 1871, two vols.), and "Briefe an Ludwig Spohr, u.a." (edited by F. Hiller, 1876). The polar opposition between the major consonance and the minor consonance forms the key to Hauptmann's system of theory. The thought expressed already three hundred years earlier by Zarlino, 1558 (and possibly handed down from still older theorists), that the minor consonance shows the relationships of the major consonance in inverted form (*see* CLANG), was revived by H., who, however, did not venture on the step necessary to make it fruitful, viz., that of naming as fundamental

note the highest note of the minor triad. Not one of Hauptmann's personal pupils, perhaps from an exaggerated feeling of respect, ventured to take this step which Hauptmann's own reasoning rendered necessary; it had, however, to be taken, and this was done from a theoretical point of view by A. v. Oettingen ("Harmoniesystem in dualer Entwickelung," 1866), and from a practical point of view, by the compiler of this Dictionary (*see* RIEMANN, 3), who worked out a new system of figuring and of terminology.

Hauptner, Thuiskon, b. 1825, Berlin, d. there Feb. 9, 1889, pupil of the composition class of the Akademie there, then for a long time theatre capellmeister. He wrote many vaudevilles, operettas, farces, etc. From 1854–58 he was occupied in Paris studying a method of teaching singing, then returned to Berlin, where he published a a "Deutsche Gesangschule" (1861). In 1863 he became teacher of singing at the Basle school of music, and was, for some years, teacher of singing and conductor at Potsdam.

Hauptsatz (Ger.), (1) The principal part, or division, of a composition.—(2) The first subject of a double fugue.

Hauptwerk (Ger.), the great organ.

Hauschka, Vinzenz, b. Jan. 21, 1766, Mies, in Bohemia, d. 1840 as member of the board of accounts in the administration of the estates of the imperial family at Vienna. He was a distinguished 'cellist and barytone player, and made many concert tours. Of his numerous compositions (for 'cello, barytone, etc.) only nine sonatas for 'cello and bass, and a book of vocal canons à 3, were published.

Hause, Wenzel, professor of the double-bass at the Prague Conservatorium, published at Dresden in 1828 an excellent Double-bass Method (which appeared at Mayence in 1829, both in French and German); also, as continuation, a series of books of admirable exercises for the double-bass.

Hausegger, Friedrich von, b. April 26, 1837, Vienna, where he received musical training under Salzmann and Otto Dessoff. He studied jurisprudence, and was already barrister at Graz, when in 1872 he qualified himself at the University there as teacher of the history and theory of music. His pamphlet, "Musik als Ausdruck" (Vienna, 1885), is one of the most important modern contributions to the department of musical esthetics. He has written besides, "Richard Wagner und Schopenhauer," and contributes articles to musical papers.

Hauser, (1) Franz, b. Jan. 12, 1794, Crasowitz, near Prague, d. Aug. 14, 1870, Freiburg-i.-Br., pupil of Tomaczek, was for many years a highly esteemed opera-singer (bass-baritone) at Prague (1817), Cassel, Dresden, Vienna (1828), London (1832, together with Schröder-Devrient, etc.), Berlin (1835), and Breslau (1836). He retired from the stage in 1837, and, after a prolonged journey through Italy, lived at Vienna as teacher of singing, and in 1846 was appointed director of the Conservatorium which was being organised at Munich, conducted the same up to 1864, acting all the time as teacher of singing, and forming numerous pupils. In 1865, at the reorganisation of the Munich Conservatorium (which, since then, has been known as "Königliche Musikschule"), he received a pension, retired to Carlsruhe, and from 1867 lived in Freiburg. He has related his experiences as a teacher of singing in his excellent "Gesanglehre für Lehrende und Lernende" (1866). He was an enthusiastic admirer of J. S. Bach, and possessed a remarkably complete collection of his works, amongst which, many autographs. He was, besides, a man of exceptional culture, and was either personally acquainted, or corresponded with, a great number of important men. (*Cf.* HAUPTMANN.)

(2) Miska (Michael), b. 1822, Pressburg, d. Dec. 9, 1887, Vienna; he studied under K. Kreutzer, Mayseder, and Sechter in Vienna, then after 1840 made numerous and extensive tours as violin virtuoso, and visited not only all European countries, but also North and South America, Australia, Turkey, etc.; and, by his effective technique and virtuoso tricks of all kinds, he everywhere won great triumphs. His compositions are not of importance. The letters which he first published in the *Ostdeutsche Post* (Vienna) about his great American journey were republished in book form under the title "Wanderbuch eines österreichischen Virtuosen" (1858–59, two vols.).

Häuser, Johann Ernst, b. 1803, Dittchenroda, near Quedlinburg, teacher at the Gymnasium there. He wrote: "Musikalisches Lexikon" (1828, two vols.; 2nd ed. 1833; only Terminology); "Der Musikalische Gesellschafter" (1830, Anecdotes); "Elementarbuch für die allerersten Anfänge des Pianofortespiels" (1832; 1836 as "Neue Pianoforteschule"); "Musikalisches Jahrbüchlein (1833); "Geschichte des christlichen, insbesondere des evangelischen Kirchengesangs" (1834).

Hausmann, (1) Valentin, is the name belonging to five musicians in direct descent, of whom, however, none accomplished anything of special importance. The eldest, b. 1484, Nuremberg, was a friend of Luther and Joh. Walter (composer of chorales); his son, organist at Gerbstädt, composed motets, canzonets, and dances (intrade, paduane, etc.); and his grandson, organist at Löbejün, father, and grandfather of, probably, the two most important of the family: one of them rose to be musical director at the Cöthen court, and also, for a time, cathedral organist at Alsleben (1680); while the other, Valentin Bartholomäus, b. 1678, was cathedral organist at Merseburg and Halle, and died as organist and burgomaster at Lauchstädt. The

last two, according to Gerber, likewise Mattheson, wrote treatises on the theory of music.

(2) Robert, 'cellist, b. Aug. 13, 1852, Rottleberode, in the Harz, studied while at the Gymnasium, Brunswick, up to 1869; as a pupil of Theodor Müller ('cello player in the old Müller quartet party), he studied from 1869–71 at the Berlin "Hochschule," and, finally, under Piatti in London. From 1872–76 he was 'cellist of the "Hochberg" quartet party at Dresden, and, after that, teacher at the Royal "Hochschule," at Berlin, also from 1879 a member of the Joachim quartet party.

Hausse (French), the nut of a bow.

Haut (French, high; *haut-dessus*, high soprano; *haute-taille*, high tenor; *haute-contre*, contralto (alto).

Hautbois (French). (*See* OBOE.)

Hautboistes. (*See* MILITARY MUSIC.)

Hautin (Haultin), Pierre, the oldest French founder of musical types, d. 1580, Paris, at an advanced age; he prepared his first punches (for Attaignant in 1525), and these were intended for single printing. (*Cf.* OEGLIN.)

Hawes, William, b. 1785, London, d. Feb. 18, 1846; in 1814 master of the choristers of St. Paul's Cathedral, in 1817 master of the children of the Chapel Royal, afterwards director of English Opera in London. The production of the operas *Freischütz* (1824), *Cosi fan tutte* (1828), *Vampyr* (1829), was owing to his influence. He wrote English comic operas, and published glees and madrigals, also a new edition of Morley's "The Triumphs of Oriana," etc.

Hawkins, John, b. March 30, 1719, London, d. May 21, 1789; he studied jurisprudence and became a lawyer; but, having married a lady of wealth, and thus become independent, he plunged into the study of the history of music, and the fruits of his sixteen years' work were displayed in his "General History of the Science and Practice of Music" (1776; five vols., with fifty-eight portraits of musicians). The work—at first considered inferior to that of Burney, although the latter made use of H.'s work for the 2–4 vols. of his "General History of Music" (Burney's first volume appeared at the same time as H.'s complete work)—was republished in 1875. H. was not a musician, although he was one of the founders of the Madrigal Society (1741); he was obliged to entrust the really musical part of his work to professional musicians. Thus, Boyce selected the numerous musical illustrations which were inserted, and Cooke transcribed the old notation, etc. H.'s real merit, however, was the conscientious and diligent compilations of quotations, which render his work valuable as a rich collection of material for a history of music. Besides, must be mentioned a monograph on Corelli (in the *Universal Magazine of*

Knowledge and Pleasure, April, 1777). H. was knighted in 1772.

Haydn, (1) F r a n z J o s e p h, b. in the night before April 1, 1732, Rohrau an der Leitha, d. May 31, 1809, Vienna. He was the second of twelve children of a wheelwright of small means who was himself musically disposed. H. showed extraordinary musical talent at a very early age, and was first trained in vocal and instrumental music by his cousin Frankh, the teacher, a man of austere manners, at Hainburg. In 1740 Reutter, capellmeister of St. Stephen's and court composer, discovering the youth to be not only talented, but, moreover, gifted with a beautiful soprano voice, took him away to Vienna to be a chorister at St. Stephen's; and there, besides instruction in singing, clavier, and the violin, he received also a good school education, but, strange to say, no training in theory. Only a few times did Reutter send for him and explain something to him. Nevertheless, the boy composed diligently, and set himself tasks of no ordinary difficulty. In 1745 his brother Michael (*see below*) also joined the choir at Vienna, and Joseph was appointed to instruct him in the elements. The brother proved a worthy deputy as solo soprano singer, and H., therefore, when his voice began to break, was simply dismissed at the first suitable opportunity. A few private lessons enabled the youth of scarcely eighteen to hire a small attic, and now he devoted himself with more diligence than ever to study and to composition. For a time he acted as accompanist to Porpora, when the latter gave lessons in singing. He was treated quite like a menial, but received some instruction in composition, and, through Porpora, made the acquaintance of Wagenseil, Gluck, and Dittersdorf. H.'s compositions now commenced to be known, especially his pianoforte sonatas in manuscript. The first impulse towards the writing of stringed quartets came from K. J. v. Fürnberg, who arranged small musical performances at his estate at Weinzierl. H wrote his first quartet (B♭) in 1750. In 1759 Baron Fürnberg procured for him the post of musical director of the private band of Count Morzin at Lukavec, near Pilsen, and H., now with a salary of two hundred florins, could venture to think of setting up a house of his own. His choice was an unfortunate one, for his wife— Maria Anna, daughter of the wig-maker Keller, of Vienna—was domineering, quarrelsome, bigoted, and utterly void of musical intelligence. For forty years H. bore the hard lot of this marriage, which was, moreover, childless (1760–1800). In Lukavec he wrote his first symphony (in D, 1759). Though H. may not actually have been the first to write symphonies and stringed quartets, yet not one of his predecessors— Sammartini, Gossec, Grétry (q.v.)—treated that particular form of art in an equally comprehensive manner: in any case, they did not create works of such undying, youthful freshness. The Count, unfortunately, was soon compelled to disband his company. For some months H. was without an appointment; but already, in 1761, Prince Paul Anton Esterhazy (d. 1762) named him second capellmeister (under Werner) at Eisenstadt, where the Prince had a private chapel consisting of sixteen members, who, however, under Prince Nikolaus Joseph, were increased to thirty in number (not counting the singers). Werner died in 1766, and H. became sole conductor. In 1769 the chapel was moved to the newly built and luxuriously fitted-up palace of Esterház on the Neusiedler Lake. H. had bought for himself a small house in Eisenstadt, which had been burnt down twice, but both times rebuilt by the Prince. This Prince, Nikolaus Joseph, died on Sept. 28, 1790, and his son and heir, Prince Anton, disbanded the chapel, left, however, to H., the title of capellmeister, and added to the yearly pension of a thousand florins left to him by the deceased four hundred more. H. sold his house at Eisenstadt and went to Vienna. He was now a man fairly independent, since Prince Anton granted to him free leave of absence, and H. therefore finally yielded to repeated invitations from London. Both his journeys to England (1790–92 and 1794) are remarkable events in the history of his life; except for these he, indeed, never left Austria. After the management of the Professional Concerts (W. Cramer) had already in 1787 vainly attempted to persuade H. to visit London, Salomon the violinist, who gave subscription concerts in London, succeeded in talking him over in a personal interview, and carrying him off with him (Dec. 15, 1790). He guaranteed £700 to H., for which H. had to undertake to conduct six new symphonies in person in London. The result fully justified expectations. H. was made a lion of; he concluded advantageous arrangements with publishers, and consented to accept a new contract with Salomon, under still more favourable conditions, for 1792. He passed the summer and autumn on the estates of the English nobility, who vied with one another in attentions and costly presents. Neither did he escape the honorary degree of doctor at Oxford (July 8, 1791). During the ceremony the "Oxford Symphony" was played, and so-called on that account. The second season also passed off with unusual brilliancy. It should be mentioned that this enthusiastic Haydn-worship extended also to the Professional Concerts, for there were performed works of the master accessible to them—in fact, those already published—and the management rivalled, as best it could, the Salomon Concerts. Indeed, in 1792 the directors of the former attracted to London Pleyel, H.'s pupil, who was to play the part of rival to his master; but they never came into conflict. At the end of June, 1792, pressed by Prince Esterhazy and by his wife, who wished to buy a house and settle in Vienna, H. at length turned his steps homewards. In Bonn, where the Electoral band gave him a lunch, he made the acquaintance of the young Beethoven, who soon afterwards became his pupil. From Bonn H. travelled to Frankfort, whither his Prince had summoned him for the coronation of Emperor Franz II., and he returned with the former to Vienna at the end of July. In that city, meanwhile, Mozart, who had been on friendly terms with H., had died (Dec. 5, 1791). Beethoven arrived in November, 1792, and enjoyed lessons in composition from H. until the second English journey. H., so celebrated abroad, was now loaded with honours in his native country. On the 19th of January he started, once again persuaded by Salomon, on his second journey to London, and again passed two concert seasons in the English capital, spending the intermediate time at country estates, etc., and in 1795 travelled back to Vienna by way of Hamburg, Berlin, and Dresden. During his absence, Count Harrach had caused a memorial with the composer's bust to be erected in his native place, Rohrau. Haydn's return, for the rest, was hastened by Prince Nikolaus Esterhazy (Prince Paul Anton d. Jan. 22, 1794), who had re-established the chapel, and had again assigned to H. the functions of capellmeister. But the composer had not yet reached the zenith of his fame. When over sixty-five years of age he wrote *The Creation* and *The Seasons*, his two greatest works. Both were composed to translations of English poems—*The Creation* after a poem of Lidley's, with passages adapted from Milton's "Paradise Lost," and written for Handel, and *The Seasons* after a poem by Thomson: they were both translated by Van Swieten. *The Creation* was first produced April 29 and 30, 1798, *The Seasons* on April 24, 1801 (in the palace of Prince Schwarzenberg). Gradually H. suffered from the infirmities of old age; his strength for work gave way, and during the last years of his life he was seldom able to leave his room. He died a few days after the entry of the French troops into Vienna. Faithfully disposed as he was to the Emperor and to his fatherland, the occupation of the city by the enemy was a bitter grief to him. H.'s immense importance in the history of music is owing to his having created the modern forms of instrumental music, for which he had certainly found in the sons of J. S. Bach valiant predecessors. The whole gamut of Viennese joyfulness, from naïve fervour to the wildest extravagance, vibrates in Haydn's music; but when he strikes earnest, passionate tones, he rises far above his contemporaries, and leads directly to Beethoven. It was further his merit to have individualised the instruments of the orchestra, and to have given to them independent speech. They are not only notes, chords, which we hear in his symphonies, but living natures of varied character and temperament which carry on a lively conversation. The

number of H.'s works is exceedingly great; a complete edition does not as yet exist. H. wrote no less than 125 symphonies (including overtures), the earlier ones in addition to the stringed orchestra containing only two oboes and two horns; the great English ones are written for stringed orchestra, flute, two oboes, two clarinets, two bassoons, two horns, two trumpets and drums. Some of them are distinguished by special names: "The Surprise" ("Mit dem Paukenschlag"), 1791; "Mit dem Paukenwirbel" (1795); the "Oxford Symphony" (1788); "The Farewell Symphony" ("Abschiedssymphonie" (1772); "La Chasse" (1780); the "Kindersymphonie," etc.; also the instrumental Passion, "Die sieben Worte am Kreuze" (written for Madrid), belonged originally to the symphonies (afterwards arranged for stringed quartet; also as an oratorio by Michael H.). H. himself counted among the symphonies the numerous (sixty-six) divertissements, cassations, sextets, etc. To these must be added twenty pianoforte concertos and divertissements with pianoforte, nine violin concertos, six 'cello concertos, and sixteen concertos for other instruments (double-bass, baryton, lyre, flute, horn), seventy-seven stringed quartets, thirty-five trios for piano, violin, and 'cello, three trios for piano, flute, and 'cello, thirty trios for stringed instruments and other combinations, four violin sonatas, 175 pieces for baryton (q.v.), six duets for solo violin and tenor, fifty-three pf. sonatas and divertimenti, variations (notably those in F minor, almost in Beethoven's style), fantasias for pf., seven nocturnes for lyre (q.v.), besides menuets, allemandes, marches, etc. At the head of the vocal works stand the two oratorios, *The Creation* and *The Seasons*. He wrote besides: an oratorio (*Il ritorno di Tobia*), fourteen masses, two Te Deums, thirteen offertories, a Stabat Mater, several Salve, Ave, sacred arias, motets, etc., and some cantatas *d'occasion*, among which "Deutschlands Klage auf den Tod Friedrichs d. Gr." for a solo voice with baryton. H. composed also twenty-four operas, most of which were only works for the limited resources of the Marionette Theatre of Eisenstadt and Esterház, and H. himself did not wish them to be produced elsewhere. Only one (*La vera costanza*) was written for the Vienna Court Theatre (1776), but the production was postponed through intrigues. The autograph score was supposed to be lost, but was found amongst the manuscripts which the Paris Conservatoire acquired at the dissolution of the Théâtre Italien in 1879 (the opera was given in Paris in 1791 under the title, *Laurette; cf.* Riemann's "Opernhandbuch"). In 1794 H. began in London an *Orfeo*, but it was never finished. Besides twenty-four operas, he also wrote a series of detached arias, a solo scena ("Ariadne auf Naxos"), thirty-six songs, a collection of Scotch and Welsh three-part songs with piano, violin and cello, the "Ten Commandments" (also as "Die zehn Gesetze der Kunst," vocal canons), and many vocal duets and pieces for three and four voices. He, especially in his early days, was little concerned about the publication of his works, and many appeared in print without his participation; and that is the reason why, especially in foreign countries, so many works appeared in his name which he never wrote. H.'s life and works have been described by : S. Mayr, "Brevi notizie storiche della vita e delle opere di Gius. H." (1809); A. K. Dies, "H.'s Biographische Nachrichten von J. H." 1810); G. A. Griesinger, "Biographische Notizen über Joseph H." (1810); G. Carpani, "Le Haydine" (1812 and 1823); Th. G. Karajan, "J. H. in London 1791 and 1792" (1861); K. F. Pohl, "Mozart and H. in London" (1867). The first comprehensive biography of the master was begun by K. F. Pohl ("Joseph H.," first vol.: first half, 1875; second half, 1882). After the death of Pohl in 1887, the completion of the work was undertaken by E. v. Mandyzewski. On May 31, 1887, a monument erected to H. was unveiled at Vienna.

(2) Johann Michael, brother of the former, b. Sept. 14, 1737, Rohrau, d. Aug. 10, 1806, Salzburg; from 1745-55 he was chorister, likewise solo sopranist, at St. Stephen's, Vienna, in 1757 capellmeister to the Bishop at Grosswardein, in 1762 orchestral conductor to the Archbishop of Salzburg, afterwards leader and cathedral organist there. He held this highly honourable post up to his death, and refused all other offers. He was happy in his marriage with Maria Magdalena, the daughter of the cathedral capellmeister, Lipp, an excellent soprano-singer, and he had a true, devoted friend in Pfarrer Rettensteiner; so he spent forty-four happy years in Salzburg, highly esteemed as a composer. Michael H. wrote specially church music: twenty-four Latin and four German masses, two requiems, 114 graduals, sixty-seven offertories, also many responses, vespers, litanies, etc., besides six canons à 4–5, songs, part-songs, cantatas, oratorios, and several operas. Of his instrumental works (which are, however, considerably inferior to those of his brother) have been preserved : thirty symphonies, some serenades, marches, minuets, three stringed quartets, a sextet, several partitas, and fifty preludes for organ. Some of his compositions appeared under the name of his brother Joseph. He was, indeed, altogether opposed to the publication of his works, and even refused offers made by Breitkopf & Härtel, so that most of his works remained in manuscript. In 1833 the Salzburg Benedictine monk, Martin Bischofsreiter, published, under the name "Partitur-Fundamente," a collection of thorough-bass exercises which M. H. wrote for his pupils, among whom were Karl M. von Weber and Reicha.

Hayes, (1) William, b. 1707, Hexham, d.

July 27, 1777, Oxford; he was first organist at Shrewsbury, in 1731 at the cathedral, Worcester; in 1734 organist and choir-master of Magdalen College, Oxford; he became Mus.Bac. in 1735, and in 1742 succeeded Goodson as professor of music at Oxford, and was elected Mus.Doc. in 1749. H. composed psalms, glees, catches, canons (for many of which he received prizes from the Catch-Club), was one of the editors of Boyce's "Cathedral Music," and wrote "Remarks on Mr. Avison's Essay on Musical Expression" (1762), and "Anecdotes of the Five Music Meetings" (1768).

(2) Philip, son of the former, b. April, 1738, Oxford, d. March 19, 1797, London; became Mus.Bac. in 1763, in 1767 member of the Chapel Royal; in 1777 he succeeded his father as organist and professor, and was named doctor at the same time. He died in London, whither he had gone to attend a musical festival, and was buried with great pomp at St. Paul's. He composed anthems, psalms, an oratorio (*Prophecy*), an ode to St. Cecilia, and a masque, *Telemachus*. He edited the *Harmonia Wiccamica* (sung at the Meeting of Wykehamists), published church music, and completed the Mémoires of the Duke of Gloucester, commenced by Lewis.

Haym, (1) (Hennius), Gilles, chapel singer and canon at Liége, afterwards Electoral capellmeister at Cologne, finally to the Duke of Pfalz-Neuburg. He published: "Hymnus S. Casimiri" (à 4–8, 1620); "Motetta sacra" (à 4 with continuo, 1640); four "Missæ solemnes" (à 8, 1645); and six "Missæ 4 vocum" (1651).

(2) (Aimo) Niccolò Francesco, b. about 1679, of German parents, at Rome, d. Aug. 11, 1720, London; he received a good training, especially in poetry and music; came to London in 1704, and associated with Clayton and Dieupart in introducing Italian Opera in London. In 1706 he produced his opera *Camilla*, in 1711 *Etearco*, and also arranged other Italian operas (by Scarlatti, Bononcini, etc.). On the production of Clayton's *Arsinoe* he was 'cellist in the orchestra. Both these operas were sung partly in English and partly in Italian. The arrival of Handel in London (1711) was the death-blow to this undertaking; the protest against the "new style" of *Rinaldo* availed nothing. After that H. lived for some time in Holland, and returned to London and united with Handel, for whom he wrote many opera libretti, as he also did for Ariosti and Bononcini. H. was an excellent numismatist, and published a description of rare coins (1719-20, two vols.). He also wrote: "Notizie de libri rari nella lingua italiani" (1726, 1771), and published two books of sonatas for two violins, with bass, as well as the prospectus of an "History of Music."

Head-voice. (*See* REGISTER.)

Heap, Charles Swinnerton, b. 1847, Birmingham, gained the Mendelssohn Scholarship, from 1865–67, studied at the Leipzig Conservatorium under Moscheles and Reinecke, and still in 1867 was an organ pupil of Best's at Liverpool, and since 1868 has been esteemed as a conductor and pianist in Birmingham. In 1870 he took the degree of Dr.Mus. at Cambridge. He has written chamber music, overtures, cantatas, anthems, organ pieces, songs, etc.

Hebenstreit, Pantaleon, b. 1669, Eisleben, d. Nov, 15, 1750, Dresden, violinist and teacher of dancing, known as the inventor of the instrument called after him, "Pantaleon," or "Pantalon" (q.v.). It was a large-sized and improved dulcimer (q.v.). H. made the instrument at Merseburg, whither, heavily in debt, he had fled from Leipzig. He made concert tours with the "Pantalon," and attracted considerable notice at the court of Louis XIV. (who gave the instrument its name) and other places. In 1706 he was appointed chapel-director and court capellmeister at Eisenach, in 1714 chambermusician at Dresden. The instrument naturally disappeared after the pianoforte had been evolved from it.

Hecht, Eduard, an able pianist, b. Nov. 28, 1832, Dürkheim (Rhine Palatinate), d. March 7, 1887, Didsbury, near Manchester, was trained at Frankfort, and was for a long time choral conductor at Manchester and Bradford, and from 1875 professor of harmony at Owens College; he was also a composer.

Heckel, Wolf, master of the lute at Strassburg. In 1562 he published there a "Lautenbuch," one of the most interesting memorials of old instrumental music (there is a copy of it in the Hamburg town library).

Heckmann, Georg Julius Robert, excellent violinist, b. Nov. 3, 1848, Mannheim, d. Nov. 29, 1891, Glasgow, whilst on a concert tour; from 1865–67 he was a pupil of the Leipzig Conservatorium (David), 1867–70 leader of the "Euterpe" at Leipzig. He travelled for some time, lived from 1872 in Cologne as leader (up to 1875, and again for a short time in 1881), and was the head of a famous stringed quartet party.—His wife Marie (née Hartwig), b. 1843, Greiz, d. July 23, 1890, Cologne, was an able pianist.

Hédouin, Pierre, b. July 28, 1789, Boulogne, lawyer in Paris, d. Dec. 1868. He wrote a large number of opera libretti and words to songs, etc., was contributor to the "Annales romantiques," "Annales archéologiques," and to several musical papers; also composer of many romances. He wrote: "Éloge historique de Monsigny" (1821), "Gossec, sa vie et ses ouvrages" (1852), "De l'abandon des anciens compositeurs," "Ma première visite à Grétry," "Richard Cœur de Lion de Grétry," "Lesueur," "Meyerbeer à Boulogne sur mer," "Paganini," "Joseph Dessauer," "Trois anecdotes musicales" (on Lesueur, Mlle. Dugazon,

and Gluck), the last-named also in "Mosaïque," a published collection of his miscellaneous articles (1856); also "Gluck, son arrivée en France" (1859), etc.

Heeringen, Ernst von, b. 1810, Grossmehlza, near Sondershausen, d. Dec. 24, 1855 Washington; in 1850 he attempted a reformation of musical notation (by abolishing ♭ and ♯, having the white notes for the seven fundamental sounds, black for the five intermediate sounds, simplified time-signatures and clefs etc.). Vexed at the failure of his plans, he went to America, where he died.

Heermann, Hugo, b. March 3, 1844, Heilbronn, had a very musical mother, and hence received musical training from an early age (violin); he attended the Brussels Conservatoire for five years under Meerts, De Bériot, and Fétis, and then went to Paris for three years for further training. After successful concert tours, he received in 1865 a post as leader at Frankfort, where he has been principal teacher of violin-playing at the Hoch Conservatorium since it was founded in 1878. The quartet of which he is leader (H., Naret-Koning, Welcker, Hugo Becker) is one of the best of the present day.

Hegar, (1) Friedrich, b. Oct. 11, 1841, Basle, where his father was a music-seller; from 1857–61 he studied at the Leipzig Conservatorium, was for a short time leader in Bilse's band; after a short stay in Baden-Baden and Paris, he became musical director at Gebweiler (Alsace), and since 1863 has been living at Zürich, at first as leader, from 1865 conductor of the subscription concerts, and from 1868 head of the "Tonhalle" orchestra. H. has also been director of the Zürich School of Music since it was opened in 1876, and from 1875–77, and again from 1886–87, also conductor of the Male Choral Society, "Harmonie," and has given lessons in singing at the Canton School. H. has published "Gesangsübungen und Lieder für den Unterricht." Of his compositions may be mentioned an oratorio, *Manasse,* besides a violin concerto in D, and effective male choruses ("Todtenvolk," etc.).

(2) Emil, brother of the former, b. Jan. 3, 1843, Basle, pupil of the Leipzig Conservatorium, in 1866 first 'cellist in the Gewandhaus orchestra and teacher of 'cello-playing at the Conservatorium; but, owing to a nervous affliction he was forced to give up playing on his instrument, on which he so excelled, and studied singing. He now lives as a concert singer (baritone) and teacher of singing at the School of Music at Basle.—Another brother, Julius, is first 'cellist of the "Tonhalle" orchestra at Zürich.

Hegner, Otto, b. Nov. 18, 1876, Basle, son of a musician, pupil of Franz Fricker, Hans Huber, and Glaus there; he appeared when young at Basle, Baden-Baden, etc., as a pianist, in 1888 in England and America, and, at the end of 1890, at the Gewandhaus, Leipzig. He has also made a *début* as a composer with some pf. pieces.

Heidingsfeld, Ludwig, gifted composer, b. March 24, 1854, Jauer, pupil of the Stern Conservatorium; in 1878 he became musical director at Glogau, in 1884 at Liegnitz; but he is now teacher at the Stern Conservatorium, Berlin. He has written orchestral works, pf. pieces, pleasing songs, etc.

Heinefetter, Sabine, famous opera singer, b. Aug. 19, 1809, Mayence, d. Feb. 18, 1872, at the lunatic asylum, Illenau; was "discovered" as a strolling harpist, and made her *début* in 1825 at Frankfort, whereupon she sang under Spohr at Cassel. She afterwards studied under Tadolini at Paris, and also in Italy (Italian singing), and was engaged, after some brilliant appearances at the Italian Opera, Paris, Berlin, etc., at Dresden, 1835; but already in 1836 she went on tour. She retired from the stage in 1842 and married in 1853 M. Marquet at Marseilles. Her mental disorder showed itself only shortly before her death.—Also her sister Clara (by marriage Stöckel), b. Feb. 17, 1816, an excellent singer, died in a lunatic asylum (Feb. 23, 1857, Vienna).—A third sister, Kathinka, b. 1820, d. Dec, 20, 1858, appeared with success as a singer at Paris and Brussels.

Heinemeyer, Ernst Wilhelm, b. Feb. 25, 1827, Hanover, d. Feb. 12, 1869, Vienna, son of the well-known flautist, Christian H. (b. 1796, Celle, d. Dec. 6, 1872, as royal chamber musician at Hanover); in 1845 he became flautist, together with his father, in the court band, Hanover; in 1847 chief flautist in the imperial band, Petersburg, and in 1859 retired on his pension to Hanover; but, owing to his dislike to the Prussians, he moved after 1866 to Vienna. H. wrote concertos, solo pieces, etc., for flute, which are highly esteemed by flautists.

Heinichen, Johann David, b. April 17, 1683, Krössuln, near Weissenfels, d. July 16, 1729, Dresden; he received his musical and school training at St. Thomas's, Leipzig, under Schelle and Kuhnau, but studied also jurisprudence, and exercised for some time the career of a lawyer at Weissenfels; he, however, soon gave this up and returned to Leipzig, made his *début* there as an opera composer, and published his method of thorough-bass ("Neu erfundene und gründliche Anweisung, etc.," 1711; 2nd edition as "Der Generalbass in der Komposition, oder Neu erfundene, etc.," 1728). The work attracted notice, and a councilor Buchta, of Zeitz, offered to take H., free of cost, to Italy, so that he might make further study in opera there. He was in Italy from 1713–18, stopping for the greater part of the time in Venice, where he produced several operas (he was, however, in the meantime engaged at the Cöthen court, and travelled with the Prince through Italy).

In 1718 he accepted an engagement as court capellmeister to Augustus the Strong of Saxony and Poland, and lived from that time until his death in Dresden. He only conducted the opera there for a short time, for in 1720 he quarrelled with Senesino, and the king disbanded the whole company, so that, afterwards, H. merely exercised the functions of conductor of the sacred music. The opera was only revived in 1730. (*See* HASSE, 2.) H. was a distinguished contrapuntist (the royal library at Dresden possesses the following of his compositions: seven masses, two requiems, six serenades, fifty-seven cantatas, eleven concertos, and three operas).

Heinrich, Joh. Georg, b. Dec. 15, 1807, Steinsdorf, near Hainau (Silesia), d. Jan. 20, 1882, Sorau, was organist at Schwiebus and Sorau; in 1876 royal musical director. He wrote an "Orgellehre" (1861), and "Der Orgelbau-Revisor."

Heinrichs, (1) Johann Christian, b. 1760, Hamburg, lived several years in Petersburg, where he published "Entstehung, Fortgang und jetzige Beschaffenheit der russischen Jagdmusik" (1796).

(2) Anton Philipp ("Father H."), b. March 11, 1781, Schönbüchel, in Bohemia, d. May 3, 1861, New York. He composed a number of good instrumental works, some of which appeared in London, some in Boston.

Heinroth, Joh. August Günther, b. June 19, 1780, Nordhausen, where his father was organist. In 1818 he succeeded Forkel as musical director at the University of Göttingen, where he died June 2, 1846. H. endeavoured to oust the notation by figures, which had then come into use in the primary schools, and to introduce a simplified notation; and this he succeeded in doing in Hanover. To him also belongs the credit of reforming the music of the synagogue (jointly with Jacobson). He threw life into music at Göttingen by introducing academical concerts. He was not a prolific composer (169 chorale melodies set à 4 [1829], six three-part songs, six four-part choruses for male voices). His writings are: "Gesangunterrichts-methode für höhere und niedere Schulen" (1821–23, three parts), "Volksnoten oder vereinfachte Tonschrift, etc." (1828), "Kurze Anleitung, das Klavierspiel zu lehren" (1828), "Musikalisches Hilfsbuch für Prediger, Kantoren und Organisten" (1833); and articles in G. Weber's "Cäcilia," Schilling's "Universallexikon," etc.

Heintz, Albert, b. March 21, 1822, Eberswalde, known by his articles on the themes in Wagner's operas, and by paraphrases (for two and four hands) on themes of Wagner. He is organist of the "Petrikirche," Berlin.

Heinze, (1) Gustav Adolf, b. Oct. 1, 1820, Leipzig, where his father was clarinet-player in the Gewandhaus orchestra. H., already in

1835, was engaged as clarinet-player in the same orchestra, and made extensive concert tours as a virtuoso. In 1844 he was appointed second capellmeister at the Breslau Theatre, where he produced his operas, *Lorelei* (1846), and *Die Ruinen von Tharandt* (1847), the libretti of which were written by his wife, Henriette H.-Berg; and in 1850 he accepted a call to Amsterdam as capellmeister of the German Opera, undertook there in 1853 the direction of the " Euterpe Liedertafel," in 1857 that of the " Vincentius " concerts, and in 1868 that of the " Excelsior " society for church music. The following of his compositions enjoy a good reputation : the oratorios *Auferstehung*, *Sankta Cäcilia*, *Der Feenschleier*, and *Vincentius von Paula*, three masses, three overtures, numerous cantatas, hymns, songs, and choruses for male voices.

(2) Sarah, *née* Magnus, b. 1839, Stockholm, an excellent pianist, pupil of Kullak, Al. Dreyschock, and Liszt, She lived in Dresden, afterwards in Hamburg, and since 1890 has been again in Dresden.

Heise, Peter Arnold, b. Feb. 11, 1830, Copenhagen, d. there Sept. 16, 1879. In 1852–53 pupil of the Leipzig Conservatorium, 1858–65 teacher of music at Sorö, lived then again in Copenhagen. H. was a noted composer of vocal music, especially of songs; he wrote also a ballad, " Dornröschen," and produced with great success the operas *Die Tochter des Pascha* (1869) and *König und Marschall* (1878).

Heiser, Wilhelm, popular composer of songs, b. April 15, 1816, Berlin, originally an opera singer, lived at Stralsund, Berlin, and Rostock, was (1853–66) bandmaster of the regiment of the Fusilier Guards, and afterwards devoted himself entirely to the teaching of singing. Died Sept. 9, 1897.

Helicon, (1) a mountain in Bœotia sacred to the muses (hence the " Heliconian " Muses).—(2) A four-cornered stringed instrument of the Greeks; it had nine strings, but, like the Monochord, served only for tone determination, and not for the practical exercise of music.—(3) A new brass instrument used especially in military music; it is of very large dimensions (Contrabass Tuba), of wide measure (Ganzinstrument), and of circular form; it is placed over the shoulders. There are helicons in F, E♭, C, and B♭.

Heller, Stephen, b. May 15, 1814, Pesth, d. Jan. 14, 1888, Paris. He showed early, and special signs of talent for music, and hence his father took him in 1824 to Vienna to Anton Halm, then highly esteemed as a pianoforte teacher. In 1827 he had made such progress that he played in public several times in Vienna; and in 1829 he undertook with his father a great concert tour through Germany as far as Hamburg; on the return journey, however, he fell ill at Augsburg, where he was taken notice

of by some art-loving families, and he settled there, leaving that city in 1848 as a man of ripe views and ability. From that time H. lived in Paris, where he soon came into friendly intercourse with pianistic celebrities (Chopin, Liszt, also Berlioz, etc.), and attained great fame as a concert-player and teacher; his compositions, on the other hand, only made way slowly, although Schumann, in the *Neue Zeitschrift für Musik*, had already spoken favourably about them when H. was still at Augsburg. The works of Heller (over 150 in number, exclusively for pianoforte) occupy in modern pianoforte literature an important and quite unique position. Apart from a few easy instructive pieces, or *salon* music, written during the early Paris period to satisfy publishers, these hundreds of detached pieces are so many specimens of genuine true poetry. H. lacks the passion and boldness of combination of Schumann, but rises above Mendelssohn in the choice, originality, and character of his ideas. H. differs from Chopin in that he displayed greater harmonic clearness, and more pregnant rhythms. Heller's speciality was a genuine, healthy, natural freshness; as a true poet he revels in fragrant woods and lonely fields. The Supplement to Fétis's " Biographie Universelle " gives an almost complete catalogue of his works; the greater number are short pieces, of from one to a few pages, with characteristic titles, such as: " Dans les Bois " (Op. 86, 128, and 136), " Nuits blanches " (Op. 82), " Promenades d'un solitaire " (Op. 78, 80, 89), " Voyage autour de ma Chambre " (Op. 140), "Tablettes d'un Solitaire" (Op. 153), etc.; further, several " Tarantelles " (Op. 53, 61, 85, 137), excellent " Études," (especially Op. 125, 47, 46, 45, 90, 16, in which order they are progressive), " Preludes " (Op. 81, 119, and 150), four pf. sonatas, three sonatinas, scherzi, caprices, nocturnes, ballads, Lieder ohne Worte, variations, waltzes, Ländler, mazurkas, etc. H. Barbadette wrote a biographical sketch of H. (1876; English, 1877); *cf. also* L. Hartmann's paper on H. in Westermann's " Monatsheften," 1859 (also in his " Bilder und Büsten ").

Hellmesberger, (1) Georg (father), distinguished teacher of the violin, b. April 24, 1800, Vienna, d. Aug. 16, 1873, Neuwaldegg, near Vienna. He received his first musical training as chorister in the Imperial chapel, became in 1820 pupil of the " Conservatorium der Musikfreunde," under Böhm (violin), 1821 assistant teacher (violin), in 1825 titular, and in 1833 actual, professor (among his pupils were H. Ernst, M. Hauser, J. Joachim, L. Auer, and his sons Georg and Joseph); in 1829 conductor at the Court Opera, in 1830 member of the court band, and he received a pension in 1867. He published a stringed quartet, two violin concertos, and some sets of variations; also solos for violin (and pianoforte; likewise with accompaniment of stringed quartet or orchestra).

(2) G e o r g (son), b. Jan. 27, 1830, Vienna, d.
Nov. 12, 1852, as leader at Hanover; he produced
here two operas, *Die Bürgschaft* and *Die beiden
Königinnen*, and left much music in manuscript.
(3) J o s e p h (senior), brother of the former,
b. Nov. 23, 1829, Vienna, d. there Oct. 24,
1893, became in 1851 artistic conductor of the
' Gesellschaft der Musikfreunde," *i.e.* conductor of the concerts there and director of
the Conservatorium; when, in 1859, these
became separate functions, H. retained the
directorship of the Conservatorium, whilst
Herbeck (formerly choirmaster) became concert conductor (artistic director). From 1851–
1877 H. was violin professor at the Conservatorium. Then in 1860 he received the appointment of leader of the Court Opera orchestra, became in 1863 solo violinist of the
court band (Institute for the Performance of
Sacred Music), and in 1877 court capellmeister.
He also obtained great fame, from 1849, as
leader of a quartet party. H. was at the Paris
Exhibition of 1855 as member of the jury for
musical instruments.
(4) J o s e p h, son of the former, b. April 9,
1855, Vienna; from 1870 member of his father's
quartet (second violin), became in 1878 solo
violinist of the court band and Court Opera, and
was appointed violin professor at the Conservatorium; also capellmeister at the Opéra
Comique and at the "Karl" Theatre; in 1884
conductor of the ballet music and leader at
the Court Opera, and in 1886 Court Opera
capellmeister. Six of his operettas were produced between 1880–90 at Vienna, Munich, and
Hamburg (*Kapitan Ahlström, Der Graf von
Gleichen, Der schöne Kurfürst, Rikiki, Das Orakel*,
and *Der bleiche Gast*); also a ballet, *Fata Morgana*.
(5) F e r d i n a n d, brother of the former, b.
Jan. 24, 1863, Vienna; from 1879 'cellist in the
court band, from 1883 in his father's quartet;
in 1885 teacher at the Conservatorium, 1886
solo 'cellist at the Court Opera.—A daughter of
Georg H. (2), R o s a, made her *début* as singer
at the Court Opera (1883).

Hellwig, K. Fr. L u d w i g, b. July 23, 1773,
Kunersdorf, near Wriezen, d. Nov. 24, 1838,
Berlin; pupil of Gürrlich, G. A. Schneider, and
Zelter at Berlin; in 1793 member of the " Singakademie," in 1803 vice-conductor, cathedral
organist, and teacher of singing at several
schools in Berlin. He composed the operas
Die Bergknappen and *Don Sylvio*, besides male
choruses (for the Liedertafel founded by Zelter),
sacred compositions, etc.

Helm, T h e o d o r, b. April 9, 1843, Vienna,
son of a professor of medicine, studied law,
and entered into government service, but
in 1867 devoted himself entirely to musical
criticism, and was, from that time, contributor
to various musical papers (*Tonhalle*, 1868;
Musikalisches Wochenblatt, from 1870 up to
the present), musical critic to the *Wiener

Fremdenblatt (1867), *Pester Lloyd* (since 1868),
the *Deutsche Zeitung* (since 1885), and has been
since 1874 teacher of the history of music and
esthetics at Horak's School of Music. H. is
one of the best critics in Vienna. He has
written " Beethoven's Streichquartette, Versuch
einer technischen Analyse im Zusammenhang
mit ihrem geistigen Gehalt " (1885 ; appeared
first in 1873 in the *Musikal. Wochenblatt*).

Helmholtz, H e r m a n n L u d w i g F e r d i-
n a n d, b. Aug. 31, 1821, Potsdam, studied medicine at Berlin, became, in 1842, assistant at the
" Charité;" in 1843, military physician at Potsdam; in 1848, teacher of anatomy for artists,
and assistant at the Museum of Anatomy; in
1849, professor of physiology at Königsberg, in
1855 professor of anatomy and physiology at
Bonn; in 1858, professor of physiology at Heidelberg, and in 1871, professor of natural philosophy at Berlin. This distinguished *savant*, to
whom natural science owes so many clever and
exhaustive works (" Ueber die Erhaltung der
Kraft," 1847; " Beschreibung eines Augen-
spiegels," 1851; " Handbuch der physiologi-
schen Optik," 1859–66, etc.), has opened up
quite new paths by his deep investigations in
the department of acoustics and the physiology
of hearing ; and he has, for the first time, established a complete scientific basis for musical
laws. In place of the dialectic treatment of
the theory of music, as pursued by Hauptmann (1853), one, of a purely scientific character, has recently come into vogue, the impulse to which was given by H. in his " Lehre
von den Tonempfindungen als physiologische
Grundlage der Musik " (1863 ; 4th ed. 1877).
The observation on which Rameau's system
(1722) was based, namely, that the consonance
of the major chord is explained by the tones
of musical instruments and voices which are
compounded of a series of simple sounds (*see*
CLANG), was further investigated and defined,
so that the comparability (relationship) of
various sounds rests on that combination; and
a succession of sounds which can be explained
as belonging to a compound sound is nothing
else than a partial identity of that compound
sound (or clang). H. was much occupied in investigating the various clang colours of musical
instruments, as well as the interruptions in a
compound sound (combination-tones and beats).
Of intense interest is the survey of the musical
systems of the ancients, of the Arabians, etc.,
the investigations of determinations of tone for
the various scales which have been handed
down to us, and the attempt to establish the
laws of musical part-writing on a scientific
basis. But although Helmholtz's work is one of
great merit and is epoch-making, still it is not
an infallible codex of the science of music. A.
v. Oettingen (" Harmoniesystem in dualer Entwickelung," 1866) and H. Lotze (" Geschichte
der Aesthetik in Deutschland," 1868) have
clearly discovered the weak point of Helmholtz's

system; both the minor consonance and the nature of dissonance receive in it only a negative explanation. For the minor consonance Oettingen returns to Hauptmann's polar opposition of major and minor, and provides for it a scientific basis; in the duality of clang representation he discovers the nature of dissonance. The compiler of this Dictionary has joined the ranks of these opponents of Helmholtz's system, and he has evolved a new method for the practical teaching of the science of harmony. Died Sept. 8, 1894, Charlottenburg.

Hemiolia, or **Hemiola** (*Proportio hemiolia*), was the term used in measured music for the more or less extended groups of *blackened* notes which appeared here and there amongst the white notes, which had been in use since the 15th century. (*Cf.* MEASURED NOTE and COLOR.) The black note was a third less in value than the white one of similar shape: hence the name H. (from Greek ἡμιόλιος = 2 : 3; Lat. *sesquialter*); in special cases the note lost only a fourth of its value. In Perfect Time, syncopations occurred with the H. thus in Prolatio major ☉:

$$\blacklozenge \; \blacklozenge \; \blacklozenge = \left(\tfrac{3}{2}\right)$$

and in Imperfect Time, triplets; thus in the *Prolatio minor* ℭ :

$$= \left(\mathcal{C}\!\!\!|\right)$$

The shortening by a fourth occurred in ○ :

$$= \left(\tfrac{3}{1}\right)$$

Hemitonium, Greek term for the half-tone; Lat. *Semitonium*.

Henkel, (1) M i c h a e l, b. June 18, 1780, Fulda, d. there March 4, 1851, as town cantor, episcopal court musician and teacher of music at the Gymnasium. He composed sacred works, organ and pf. pieces, and published several chorale books, school song-books, etc. His sons are:

(2) G e o r g A n d r e a s, b. Feb. 4, 1805, Fulda, d. there April 5, 1871, as teacher of music at the Training School, and Dr.Phil. He composed also much church music, overtures, marches, etc.

(3) H e i n r i c h, b. Feb. 16, 1822, Fulda, pupil of Anton André and Ferd. Kessler for theory, etc. He is an able pianist, and has been living since 1849 as teacher of music at Frankfort, was one of the founders of the music school there (with changing directorship), and has published, besides pf. pieces (of a specially educational character) and songs, a pianoforte Method for beginners, and a "Vorschule des Klavierspiels" (technical studies), also a biography of Aloys Schmitt, a new edition, in abridged form,

of A. André's "Lehrbuch der Tonsetzkunst" (1875), "Mitteilungen aus der mus. Vergangenheit Fuldas;" and, finally, instructive violin pieces for one, also for several performers. In 1883 H. received the title of Royal Musical Director.

His son, K a r l, pupil of the Berlin High School, lives in London, and is esteemed as a teacher of the violin (finger exercises).

Hennen, three brothers (1) A r n o l d, pianist, b. 1820, Heerlen (Limburg), pupil of the Liége Conservatoire; he lived for a long time in London, and is now at Antwerp.

(2) F r e d e r i k, violinist, b. Jan. 25, 1830, Heerlen, studied under Prune at Liége, was leader of various orchestras in London from 1850-71, and now lives in his native town. He has composed violin pieces.

(3) M a t h i a s, pianist, likewise trained at Liége, since 1860 teacher at the Antwerp Conservatoire (he has written trios, quartets, etc.). A son of Frederik H., C h a r l e s, b. Dec. 3, 1861, London, is also a violinist, and lives at Antwerp.

Hennes, A l o y s, b. Sept. 8, 1827, Aix-la-Chapelle, d. June 8, 1889, Berlin; he was, from 1844-1852, post-office official, attended for some time the Rhenish School of Music at Cologne under Hiller and Reinecke, and lived afterwards as pianoforte teacher at Kreuznach, Alzey, Mayence, Wiesbaden; and from 1872 at Berlin, where in 1881 he became teacher at X. Scharwenka's Conservatorium. H. became known by his "Klavierunterrichtsbriefe," in which he showed himself a clever composer of educational pieces. —His daughter, T h e r e s e H., b. Dec. 21, 1861, was for many years a youthful prodigy; from 1873 she studied with Kullak, and made a successful appearance in London as a pianist (1877 and 1878).

Hennig, (1) K a r l, b. April 23, 1819, Berlin, d. there April 18, 1873, as organist of the "Sophienkirche." He composed cantatas (*Die Sternennacht*), psalms, Lieder, several choruses for male voices ("Froschkantate"). In 1863 he was appointed "Kgl. Musikdirector."

(2) Karl R a f a e l, son of the former, b. Jan 4, 1845, studied jurisprudence, but turned to music (pupil of Richter in Leipzig and of Kiel in Berlin). In 1868 he accepted a post as teacher at the "Wandelt" Institute of Music at Berlin, was from 1869-75 organist of St. Paul's Church, Posen, where he founded in 1873 the "Hennig" Vocal Society, which attained to prosperity. In 1877 he became teacher of music at the Institute for Female Teachers, and received in 1883 the title of "Kgl. Musikdirector." H. wrote a searching analysis of Beethoven's Ninth Symphony and of his *Missa solemnis*, "Method des Schulgesangunterrichts," "Die Gesangsregister auf physiologischer Grundlage." He composed a cantata (130th Psalm), a pianoforte sonata, songs, also choruses for male and female voices.

Hennius. (*See* HAYM, I.)

Henrion, P a u l, b. July 20, 1819, Paris, popular French composer of songs ; he has published over a thousand romances and chansonettes. His operettas—*Une rencontre dans le Danube* (1854) ; *Une envie de clarinette* (1871) ; and *La chanteuse par amour* (1877)—only met with moderate success. A. Pougin calls Franz Abt the H. of the Germans.

Henschel, G e o r g, b. Feb. 18, 1850, Breslau, distinguished concert singer (baritone), and a composer of great taste. He studied under Götze (singing) and Richter (theory), at the Leipzig Conservatorium (1867–70) ; he received further training from A. Schulze (singing) and Kiel (composition) at Berlin. From 1881–84 he was conductor of the Symphony Concerts at Boston, and settled in London in 1885, where he has established the " London Symphony Concerts " ; from 1886-88 he was teacher of music at the Royal College of Music. Of his compositions may be mentioned : a Suite in canon form for stringed orchestra, a " Zigeuner " Serenade for orchestra, the 130th Psalm for chorus, soli, and orchestra, many songs (from the *Trompeter von Säckingen*, etc.), part-songs, etc.—His wife, *née* Lilian Bailey, b. Jan., 1860, state of Ohio, studied with her uncle, Charles Hayden, Madame Viardot, and, finally, with G. Henschel, whom she married in 1881, and with whom she has since given vocal recitals in London, and also made concert tours. She is an excellent Lieder singer (soprano).

Hensel, F a n n y C ä c i l i a, b. Nov. 14, 1805, Hamburg, sister of Felix Mendelssohn, d. May 14, 1847 ; she married the painter H. in 1829. She was an excellent pianist, and a composer of some talent (songs without words, songs, a trio) ; and her active intellectual intercourse with her brother was of quite an exceptional nature. Her sudden death was a heavy shock to him, and he followed her to the grave within six months.

Henselt, A d o l f (v o n), b. May 12, 1814, Schwabach (Bavaria), d. Oct. 10, 1889, Warmbrunn (Silesia), an eminent pianist, received his first musical training in Munich from Frau v. Fladt, then obtained a royal stipend (1831), and studied for some time under Hummel and at Weimar, and for two years under Sechter (theory) at Vienna, where he afterwards remained for some time. H., independently of his teachers, formed a style of playing of his own. It was not unlike that of Liszt's, but based rather on strict *legato*. He attached special value to the stretching power of the hand, and, for himself personally, invented extension studies of the most elaborate kind. He undertook his first concert tour to Berlin in 1836, married at Breslau in 1837, and definitely settled in Petersburg in 1838, after he had obtained such extraordinary success in that city by his concerts that he was appointed chamber virtuoso to the Empress and teacher of music

to the Princes. Afterwards he was named inspector of musical instruction at the Imperial Institutes for Young Ladies, and the order of the Wladimir was bestowed on him. From his numerous compositions stand out prominently : a pf. concerto (F min.), and valuable concert *Études* (Op. 2 and Op. 13 [No. 11] "La Gondola " ; " Poème d'amour," Op, 3 ; " Frühlingslied," Op. 15 ; Impromptu Op. 17 ; Ballade Op. 31), the latter similar to Mendelssohn's *Lieder ohne Worte*, only of richer figuration, and fuller tone. He wrote, besides, a number of pianoforte pieces, *paraphrases de concert* of delicate workmanship (39 works with opus number, and 15 without), a trio, a second pianoforte part to a selection of J. B. Cramer's *Études*, edited an excellent edition of Weber's pianoforte compositions (with *variante*), etc. *Cf.* La Mara's *Mus. Studienköpfe* III., and " Klassisches und Romantisches a. d. Tonwelt ;" also G. von Amyntor's " Lenz und Rauhreif."

Hentschel, (1) E r n s t J u l i u s, b. July 26, 1804, Langenwaldau, d. Aug. 4, 1875, as teacher of music at the training school at Weissenfels. He was one of the founders, and editor of the music paper *Euterpe*, and published school song-books and a chorale book.

(2) F r a n z, b. Nov. 6, 1814, Berlin, pupil of Grell and A. W. Bach, theatre capellmeister at Erfurt, Altenburg, and Berlin (" Liebhaber " theatre). He has composed an opera (*Die Hexenreise*), marches, concertos for wind instruments, etc. He lives as a teacher of music in Berlin.

(3) T h e o d o r, b. March 28, 1830, Schirgiswalde (Saxon Oberlausitz), d. Dec. 19, 1892, Hamburg, was trained in Dresden (Reissiger, Ciccarelli) and Prague (Conservatorium), became theatre capellmeister at Leipzig, from 1860 to 1890 at Bremen, and finally at Hamburg. He composed several operas : *Matrose und Sänger* (Leipzig, 1857) ; *Der Königspage* (1874) ; *Die Braut von Lusignan, Melusine* (1875) ; and *Lancelot* (1878) ; a mass for double chorus, songs, etc.

Heptachord, (1) The interval of a seventh.— (2) A diatonic series of seven notes.—(3) An instrument with seven strings.

Herbart, J o h a n n F r i e d r i c h, the famous philosopher, b. May 4, 1776, Oldenburg, d. Aug. 14, 1841, as professor at Göttingen. He devoted much time to the consideration of music, for he thought he could recognise important general philosophical laws in the relationship of sounds. Unfortunately, he did not view the matter from the physico-physiological standpoint, which, as would be universally acknowledged at the present day, is the only rational one to explain the facts underlying musical hearing ; and thus his ultimate conclusions rested on a false foundation. His " Psychologische Bemerkungen zur Tonlehre " (1811), and also all his philosophical writings, are therefore of the highest interest to the cultivated musician, but they are only of moderate importance towards increasing a knowledge of the natural laws of musical creative art. F. W. Drobisch (q.v.) followed in H.'s footsteps; but he, quite recently, has specially acknowledged the necessity of a standpoint based on physical science.

Herbeck, J o h a n n, b. Dec. 25, 1831, Vienna, d. there Oct. 28, 1877, son of a poor tailor. After attending the primary school, he went to the Gymnasium of the "Heiligenkreuz" monastery (Lower Austria), where he found employment as soprano singer. On the advice of G. Hellmesberger he received for two years, during the summer holidays, lessons in composition from L. Rotter at Vienna; for the rest, he was entirely self-taught. In 1847 he returned to Vienna, passed through the upper classes of the Gymnasium, and, in 1849, devoted himself to the study of law at the University, supporting himself by giving lessons in music. In 1852 he was appointed *Regens chori* of the "Piaristenkirche," and gave up law. He lost, however, this post already in 1854, but in 1856 was elected chorus-master of the male vocal society at Vienna, of which he was a member. As conductor of this society, the distinguished position of which is not H.'s least title to fame, he made himself known to very great advantage, and, specially, in rescuing Schubert's vocal works for male voices from oblivion. In 1858 the "Gesellschaft der Musikfreunde" entrusted him with the formation of a mixed choral society, and named him teacher of choral singing at the Conservatorium, which latter post, however, he resigned in 1859, when he was appointed artistic director of the society (conductor of the society's concerts). (*Cf.* HELLMESBERGER.) H. highly distinguished himself in this post by the production of the most important classical and modern works (also Berlioz and Liszt), and by the introduction of short choral numbers into the programmes. His merit was not ignored. In 1866 Preyer was passed over, Randhartinger was pensioned, and H. was created principal court capellmeister (conductor of the sacred music of the court chapel), after he had already acted for three years as supernumerary vice-capellmeister. He now resigned the post of chorus-master of the male vocal society, but remained honorary chorus-master (for festival occasions).· In 1869 the post of principal capellmeister at the Opera was given to him, whereupon he renounced the direction of the society's concerts. At the end of 1870 the Emperor entrusted to him the direction of the Opera, and under his management the *répertoire* was enriched with a great number of novelties (*Mignon, Die Meistersinger, Feramors, Aida, Die Königin von Saba, Der Widerspenstigen Zähmung;* Schumann's *Genoveva, Manfred,* etc.). Owing to intrigues, the difficult position finally became distasteful to him. He resigned in 1875, and two years before his death he returned to the "Gesellschaft der Musikfreunde," who again received him with open arms as their

conductor. The profits arising from a performance of Mozart's Requiem *in memoriam,* were set apart as a fund to erect a memorial to him in Vienna. A monument was erected to him by the choral society of Klagenfurt at Pörtschach, on the Wörther Lake, in 1878. As a composer, H. became principally known by his part-songs. The quartets for male voices ("Volkslieder aus Kärnten," "Im Walde" with horn quartet, "Wanderlust," and "Maienzeit") have spread far and wide: among them there are some ("Landsknecht," "Waldszene") with orchestra. He also published several sets for mixed choir ("Lieder und Reigen "). He wrote some sacred works, but only a grand mass appeared after his death, and, previously, a vocal mass for male voices. Of his symphonies only the fourth (with organ) was published in pianoforte score; besides this there appeared a quartet for strings (No. 2), "Symphonic Variations," and "Tanzmoment" for orchestra. His son, Ludwig H., published in 1885: "Joh. Herbeck, ein Lebensbild," with portrait and catalogue of his works.

Hering (1) **Karl Gottlieb, b.** Oct. 25, 1765, Schandau (Saxony), d. Jan., 1853, as principal teacher of music at the municipal school, Zittau. He wrote: "Praktisches Handbuch zur Erlernung des Klavierspielens" (1796), "Neue praktische Klavierschule für Kinder" (1805), "Neue sehr erleichterte Generalbassschule für junge Musiker" (1805), "Neue praktische Singschule für Kinder" (1807–1809, four small books), "Praktische Violinschule" (1810), "Praktische Präludienschule" (1810), "Kunst das Pedal fertig zu spielen" (1816), "Gesanglehre für Volksschulen" (1820); besides several chorale books, instructive pf. pieces (variations, exercises, etc.); in 1830 he founded a *Musikalisches Jugendblatt für Gesang, Klavier, und Flöte,* which his son afterwards continued.

(2) **Karl Eduard, b.** May 13, 1809, Oschatz, d. Nov. 25, 1879, as organist and teacher at a training school at Bautzen; he was a pupil of Weinlig's. He composed oratorios: *Der Erlöser* (performed several times), *Die heilige Nacht, David, Salomo, Christi Leid und Herrlichkeit,* a mass (produced at Prague), and other important works (two operas), all of which, however, remained in manuscript. Pf. pieces, songs, partsongs, a "Buch der Harmonie" (1861), and a school chorale collection were published.

(3) **Karl Friedrich August, b.** Sept. 2, 1819, Berlin, d. Feb. 2, 1889, Burg, near Magdeburg, pupil of H. Ries and Rungenhagen, Berlin, of Lipinski, Dresden, and of Tomaschek, Prague; he was, for a short time, violinist in the royal band at Berlin, and founded there in 1851 a musical institution (until 1867), was named royal musical director, published a few part-songs, also an elementary violin Method, a "Methodischer Leitfaden für Violinlehrer" (1857), and "Ueber R. Kreutzers Etüden " (1858).

Heritte-Viardot, Louise Pauline Marie, b. Dec. 14, 1841, Paris, daughter of Louis Viardot and Pauline Garcia. In 1852 she married the Consul-General Heritte, became teacher of singing at Petersburg Conservatoire, afterwards at Dr. Hoch's Conservatorium at Frankfort, and then lived at Berlin as a teacher of singing, and as composer (opera, *Lindora* [Weimar, 1879], cantatas, two pf. quartets, vocal exercises, etc.).

Hermann, (1)Matthias, Netherland contrapuntist, a native, probably, of Warkenz or Warkoing, in Flanders (hence *Verrecoiensis, Verrecorensis*), from 1538–55 cathedral maestro at Milan, not to be confused with Matthias Le Maistre (q.v.). He was the composer of a battle tonepicture, "Die Schlacht vor Pavia" (" Battaglia Taliana" [Italiana], printed in several collections: in Petrejus's "Guter, seltzamer und kunstreicher Gesang, etc.," 1544; in Gardane's "La Battaglia Taliana . . . con alcune villotte," etc., 1549, etc.), also of some detached motets, and of a book, "Cantuum 5 voc., quos motetta vocant" (1555). (*Cf. Monatshefte für Musikgeschichte*, 1871 and 1872.)

(2) Johann David, music-master to Queen Marie Antoinette of France about 1785, a German by birth; he published six pf. concertos, fifteen sonatas, potpourris, etc.

(3) Johann Gottfried Jakob, b. Nov. 28, 1772, Leipzig, d. there Dec. 31, 1848, as professor of elocution and poetry, and a highly esteemed philologist, specially Hellenist. His writings on metre stand in high repute: "De metris poetarum Græcorum et Romanorum" (1796), "Handbuch der Metrik" (1798), "Elementa doctrinæ metricæ " (1816), "Epitome doctrinæ metricæ" (1816 and 1844), and "De metris Pindari" (1817).

(4) Friedrich, violinist, b. Feb. 1, 1828, Frankfort, in 1843 pupil of the Leipzig Conservatorium, became in 1846 viola player in the Gewandhaus and theatre orchestras, and in May, 1848, teacher at the Conservatorium. In 1875 he resigned the former post in order to give his whole mind to composition and to the work of editing. In 1883 he was named royal Saxon professor. Hermann's activity as a teacher has been distinguished, and his editions of the classical works for stringed instruments (especially in Peters' and Augener's Editions) stand in the highest repute. As a composer, he has published some especially successful violin compositions (terzets for three violins, etc.).

Hermannus Contractus (Hermann Graf von Vehringen, called H. C. or Hermann der Lahme, because he was lame from childhood), b. July 18, 1013, at Sulgau (Swabia), was educated at St. Gallen, lived as a monk at Reichenau monastery, and died Sept. 24, 1054, on his family estate, Alleshausen, near Biberach. H. wrote a valuable chronicle (from the foundation of Rome to 1054, printed in Pertz's

"Monumenta," Vol. V.), which contains valuable notices, even for the history of music; also several small treatises on music, printed by Gerbert ("Script." II.). H. is an interesting phenomenon in the history of notation, as he worked out a notation unique of its kind; and it had a special advantage which neume notation lacked, viz., the designation of change of pitch. His signs are $e =$ unison (*æquat*), $s =$ half-tone (*semitonium*), $t =$ tone (*tonus*), $ts =$ minor third (*tonus cum semitonio;* in many manuscripts also a long $f = semiditonus$), $tt =$ major third (*ditonus*, also as δ), $d =$ fourth (*diatessaron*), $\Delta =$ fifth (*diapente*), and the other compound signs, Δs, Δt, Δd. By a point above or at the side of a sign H. indicated further that the interval was to be a falling one, and the absence of a point indicated a rising one; therefore $\dot{\Delta}$ or Δ. $=$ a fifth below. In the Munich Library there are some manuscripts of the 11th–12th centuries with some neume notation, in which H.'s notation is written above.

Hermes, Eduard, b. May, 1818, Memel, composer of songs and male part-songs, lives as a merchant at Königsberg-i.-Pr.

Hermesdorff, Michael, b. March 4, 1833, Trèves, d. there Jan. 17, 1885; in 1859 he took priest's orders, and became cathedral organist in that city. His chief merit consists in his having drawn information respecting old Gregorian Church Song from authentic sources; and, in order to have the means of making known the result of his labours, he founded the choral society. In the monthly supplements of the newspaper *Cäcilia* of H. and Böckeler (Aix) he began to edit the "Gradual ad usum Romanum cantus S. Gregorii" (Leipzig, 1876–1882, ten numbers), but did not live to complete it. Besides a graduale, anthems, and "Præfatio" prayers in use in the Trèves diocese, he published a "Kyriale" and "Harmonica cantus choralis (à 4), also a German translation of the "Micrologus" of Guido of Arezzo, and of his own compositions three masses; he also revised the 2nd edition of Lück's collection of celebrated sacred compositions (four vols.).

Hermstedt, Johann Simon, b. Dec. 29, 1778, Langensalza, d. Aug. 10, 1846, as court capellmeister at Sondershausen, celebrated performer on the clarinet, first played in a military musical corps at Langensalza, Dresden, and Sondershausen. Spohr wrote for him a clarinet concerto; he himself composed some works for the clarinet (concertos and variations) and for military bands.

Hernandez, Pablo, b. Jan. 25, 1834, Saragossa, was already at the age of fourteen organist in his native town, studied afterwards at the Madrid Conservatorio under Eslava, and in 1863 was appointed teacher in that institution. H. wrote a Method for organ, six organ fugues, a mass à 3 with orchestra, and a

Miserere and Ave à 3, a Te Deum with organ, Lamentations, motets, a symphony, overture, etc.; he also produced some Zarguelas (Spanish operettas) at the "Zarguela" Theatre.

Hernando, Rafael José Maria, b. May 31, 1822, Madrid, attended the Conservatorio there; he went to Paris in 1843 for further training, where he produced a Stabat Mater at the Société de Ste.-Cécile, while he sought in vain to get an opera brought out at the Théâtre Lyrique. On his return to Madrid he soon became known (1848–53) by some Zarguelas (operettas, *Las sacordotisas del sol, Palo de ciego, Colegiales y soldados, El duende, Bertoldo y comparsa, Escenas de Chamberi,* and *Don Simplicio Bobadilla,* the last two jointly with Barbieri, Oudrid, and Gaztambide, who soon supplanted him), and started the idea of exploiting this style of composition, for which the Théâtre des Variétes was granted; and H. was appointed director and composer. In 1852 H. became secretary of the Conservatorio, and, some years later, principal professor of harmony. He likewise founded a musical friendly society. He also wrote hymns, cantatas, and a grand votive mass (produced 1867). H. is one of the most important musical representatives of Spain of the present day.

Hérold, Louis Joseph Ferdinand, b. Jan. 28, 1791, Paris, d. Jan. 19, 1833, son of Franz Joseph H. (b. March 10, 1755, Seltz [Alsace], d. Sept. 1, 1802, Paris, pupil of Ph. E. Bach, and an esteemed pianoforte teacher; also a composer of sonatas), studied at first with his father, then at the Hix School, where Fétis, (at that time still a pupil of the Conservatoire) acted as assistant teacher, entered in 1806 into the pianoforte class of Adam at the Conservatoire, afterwards into the harmony class of Catel, and in 1811 into the composition class of Méhul. Already after one year and a half he received the *Prix de Rome.* After three years' study at Rome he went to Naples, where he was successful with his maiden opera (*La gioventù di Enrico Quinto,* 1815). Soon after his return to Paris, Boieldieu accepted him as colleague in an opera *d'occasion* (*Charles de France*); it was successful, and in the same year (1816) the Opéra Comique brought out H's first important work, *Les rosières,* which took the town by storm. In his next opera, *La Clochette,* he fully maintained the reputation he had won. Unfortunately H., after this, was in great need of a good librettist, and saw himself compelled, in order not to be idle, to write small pieces, pf. fantasies, etc., and, finally to accept libretti which were either bad, or else had already been set to music. In this manner arose *Le premier venu* (1818), *Les troqueurs* (1819), *L'amour platonique* (1819, withdrawn), *L'auteur mort et vivant* (1820), all of which failed, although pleasing musical numbers prevented a complete fiasco. Discouraged to a certain extent, H.

accepted in 1820 the post of accompanist at the Italian Opera, which took up much of his time, and enabled him to write only works of small calibre (pf. pieces, caprices, rondos, etc.). In 1821 he was sent to Italy, in order to engage fresh vocalists. Once again, after three years' silence, he tried his luck on the stage with the comic opera, *Le Muletier* (1823); in the same year followed at the Grand Opéra, *L'asthénie* and the opera *d'occasion, Vendôme en Espagne* (jointly with Auber); this, and also the one-act operas which immediately followed (1824), *Le Roi Réné* (*pièce d'occasion*), and *Le lapin blanc* (both at the Opéra Comique), obtained little more than an average success. In them H. had imitated Rossini's manner, and not to his advantage. Meanwhile (1824) he had exchanged his post of accompanist at the Opéra Italien for that of chorus-master; in 1827 he gave this up, and became *répetiteur* at the Grand Opéra. His occupations did not admit of that great productiveness which from his talent seemed possible; but in 1826 he made a hit with the comic opera, *Marie,* which is far superior to his old scores, and is, indeed, one of his best works. As *répetiteur* at the Grand Opéra he wrote some ballets: *Astolphe et Joconde, La sonnambule* (1827), *Lydie, La fille mal gardée, La belle au bois dormant* (1828), and the music to the drama *Missolonghi* for the Odéon Théâtre. After two new failures, *L'Illusion* (1829) and *Emmeline* (1830), and the *Auberge d'Aurey* (1830), written jointly with Carafa, followed the work which won for him a famous name, and even up to this day in Germany enjoys undiminished popularity; this was *Zampa* (Opéra Comique, 1831). Apart from the *Marquise de Brinvilliers* (a manufactured work, written by no less than nine collaborators: H., Auber, Batton, Berton, Blangini, Boieldieu, Carafa, Cherubini, and Paer) and a small work of one act, *La médecine sans médecin,* H. still wrote, after *Zampa,* the work which the French regard as the crown of his creations, *Le pré aux clercs,* for the Opéra Comique in 1832 (1000th performance given in 1871). His health had been declining for some years, but his ambition would not permit him to seek relief in a milder climate, and he succumbed to his chest malady at his villa, Maison Les Ternes. He left an unfinished opera, *Ludovic,* which was completed by Halévy and produced in 1834. M. B. Jouvin wrote a short biography of H. (1868).

Herrmann, Gottfried, b. May 15, 1808, Sondershausen, d. June 6, 1878, Lübeck, pupil of Spohr at Cassel, then violinist at Hanover, where, at the same time holding friendly intercourse with Aloys Schmitt, he became a sound pianist. He then went to Frankfort, where, jointly with his brother Karl ('cellist, afterwards chamber musician at Sondershausen), he established a quartet party; in 1831 he became organist of the "Marienkirche" at Lübeck, in 1844 court capellmeister at Sondershausen, in 1852 town capellmeister at Lübeck; also for a time conductor at the Lübeck Stadttheater and of the Bach Society at Hamburg. He composed several operas, which were produced at Lübeck, also orchestral and chamber music, songs, etc.— The daughter of his brother Karl, Klara H., who studied at the Leipzig Conservatorium, and afterwards with him, is an able pianist, and lives at Lübeck.

Herschel, Friedrich Wilhelm, the famous astronomer and inventor of the telescope which bears his name, b. Nov. 15, 1738, Hanover, d. Aug. 23, 1822, Slough, near Windsor. He was originally a musician, came to England (Durham) in the band of the Hanoverian regiment of Guards, became, afterwards, organist at Halifax, and in 1766 occupied a similar position at the Octagon Chapel, Bath; while in that city he began to turn his whole attention to astronomy, and soon neglected music. He wrote a symphony and two concertos for military band, which were published in 1768.

Hertel, (1) Johann Christian, b. 1699, Oettingen, d. Oct., 1754, Strelitz, as a ducal "Konzertmeister" (formerly occupied a similar post at Eisenach); a celebrated and remarkable performer on the gamba, and pupil of Hess at Darmstadt. He wrote a large number of orchestral and chamber works, which, however, with the exception of six violin sonatas with bass, remained in manuscript.

(2) Johann Wilhelm, son of the former, b. Oct. 9, 1727, Eisenach, d. June 14, 1789; in 1757 leader, afterwards court capellmeister, at Strelitz; in 1770 secretary to the Princess Ulrike and councilor at Schwerin. He composed eight oratorios on various periods of the life of Christ (Birth, Jesus bound, Jesus in the Judgment Hall, etc.), and published twelve symphonies à 8, six pf. sonatas, one pf. concerto, songs and "Sammlung musikalischer Schriften, grösstenteils aus den Werken der Italiener und Franzosen," etc. (1757-58, two parts).

(3) Peter Ludwig, b. April 21, 1817, Berlin, pupil of Greulich, F. Schneider, and Marx, court composer and ballet conductor at the Royal Opera House at Berlin. He wrote ballets, *Flick und Flock*, *Sardanapal*, *Ellinor*, *Fantaska*, *The Seasons*, etc.

Herther, F., pseudonym of Dr.Med. Hermann Günther, brother of Dr. Otto Günther, b. Feb. 18, 1834, Leipzig, d. there Feb. 13, 1871. He composed the opera, *Der Abt von St. Gallen* (1863).

Hertzberg, Rudolph von, b. Jan. 6, 1818, Berlin, pupil of L. Berger and S. Dehn, 1847 teacher of singing, and 1861-89 conductor of the cathedral choir, 1858 "Kgl. Musikdirector," and later on Professor. D. Nov. 22, 1893, Berlin.

Hervé (Florimond Ronger, called H.), b. June 30, 1825, Houdain, near Arras, the father of French operetta; he began his career as organist at various Paris churches. He appeared first in 1848 with his inseparable associate Kelm as singer, in a kind of *Intermède* of his own composition, *Don Quichotte et Sancho Pansa*, at the Théâtre National; became in 1851 conductor at the Théâtre du Palais Royal, undertook in 1854 the management of a small theatre on the Boulevard du Temple, to which he gave the name "Folies Concertantes." There he inaugurated that diminutive kind of dramatic composition of sarcastic, burlesque, or frivolous tendency, with which, since that time, the world has become sufficiently familiar. He possessed the gift of writing music exactly suitable for it (A. Pougin has given to it the name of *musiquette*, and describes H.'s muse as a *musette*). In 1856 H. resigned the direction of the small theatre (which was then called Folies Nouvelles, and later on, Folies Dramatiques), but continued, for a time, to write for the same, and to act parts. Later on he appeared at Marseilles, Montpelier, Cairo, and elsewhere, conducted concerts *à la Strauss* in Covent Garden Theatre, London (1870-71), was musical director at the Empire Theatre there, and in the course of years wrote over fifty operettas, which, however, owing to those of Offenbach being planned on a larger scale, fell more and more into the background. The best known are probably: *Fla-Fla* (1886), *La Noce à Nini*, *La Rousotte* (jointly with Lecocq), and *Les Bagatelles*. It is to be noted that H. wrote his own libretti. Besides operettas H. composed an heroic symphony or cantata, *The Ashantee War*, and the ballets *La Rose d'amour* (1888), *Diana* (1888), and *Cleopatra* (1889). Hervé's son, Gardel by name, produced an operetta *Ni, ni, c'est fini* (1871).

Herz, (1) Jacques Simon, b. Dec. 31, 1794, Frankfort, d. Jan. 27, 1880, Nice; went when young to Paris, and became a pupil of Pradher's at the Conservatoire there in 1807, was trained for a pianist, and was highly esteemed as a teacher of the pianoforte in that city. For several years he lived in England, but returned to Paris in 1857, and became assistant-teacher to his brother Henri at the Conservatoire. He composed a sonata for horn, violin sonatas, a pf. quintet, and solo pf. pieces.

(2) Henri (Heinrich), b. Jan. 6, 1806, Vienna, d. Jan. 5, 1888, Paris, brother of the former. He was first a pupil of Hünten's at Coblence, and in 1816 of the Paris Conservatoire (Pradher, Reicha). He afterwards developed still further, taking Moscheles as his model, and for more than a decade he enjoyed the highest fame as a pianist and composer for his instrument. He went into partnership with a pianoforte-maker (Klepfer), by which he lost money; and the dissolution of that partnership, and the establishment of a manufactory of his own with a concert hall (Salle H.), did not prove sufficient compensation. He therefore undertook in 1845 a grand concert tour through

North and South America, and after his return in 1851 worked up his manufactory to a state of great prosperity, so that at the Exhibition of 1855 he received the first prize, and, next to Erard and Pleyel, his became the most esteemed house. In 1842 H. was appointed professor of the pianoforte at the Conservatoire, which post he resigned in 1876. His works are: eight pf. concertos, many variations (which, in his opinion, were the most tasty food for the Paris public), sonatas, rondos, violin sonatas, nocturnes, dances, marches, fantasias, etc.; a "Méthode complète de Piano" (Op. 100), many études, finger-exercises, etc. He described his tour through America in the *Moniteur Universel* (also printed separately as "Mes Voyages en Amérique," 1866).

Herzberg, A n t o n, pianist and drawing-room composer, b. June 4, 1825, Tarnow (Galicia), pupil of Bocklet and Preyer at Vienna. After successful concert tours through Hungary, Poland, and Russia, he settled as teacher of music in Moscow (1866), where, having accumulated titles and decorations, he now resides.

Herzog, (1) J o h a n n G e o r g, b. Sept. 6, 1822, Schmölz (Bavaria), studied at the Teachers' Training School at Altdorf (Bavaria), from 1841-42 teacher at Bruck, near Hof, became in 1842 organist, and, from 1848, cantor, at the Evangelical Church at Munich, in 1850 teacher of the organ at the Conservatorium there, in 1854 University musical director at Erlangen, where in 1866 he took the degree of Dr.Phil., and after some years became unattached professor. He is a distinguished organist, and has composed for the organ: "Präludienbuch," "Kirchliches Orgelspiel" (three parts), "Choräle mit Vor-, Zwischen-, und Nachspielen," "Evangelisches Choralbuch" (three books), "Chorgesänge f. d. kirchliche Gebrauch" (five books), "Geistliches und Weltliches" (collections), "Orgelschule," fantasias, etc. H. retired in 1888, and since that time has lived in Munich.

(2) E m i l i e, b. about 1860, Diessenhofen (Thurgau), was trained at the Zürich School of Music (1876-78, K. Gloggner) and at Munich (1878-80, Ad. Schimon). She sang first at a concert in 1878, and made her *début* as the Page in *Les Huguenots*, and soon developed into a distinguished soubrette and coloratura singer. In 1889 she exchanged her post at Munich for one of like capacity, and under brilliant conditions, at the Berlin Court Opera.

Herzogenberg, H e i n r i c h v o n, b. June 10, 1843, Graz, was, from 1862-64, pupil of the Vienna Conservatorium under F. O. Dessoff, lived until 1872 at Graz, and then settled in Leipzig, where in 1874, jointly with Philipp Spitta, Franz v. Holstein, and Alfred Volkland, he established the "Bach-Verein," and, after Volkland's withdrawal in the autumn of 1875, undertook the direction himself. In October, 1885, he was honoured with a call to Berlin as

successor to Fr. Kiel. He is member of the Akademie, and president of an academical "Meisterschule" for composition, and director of the branch for composition at the High School of Music, with the title of Professor. As a composer, H. occupies a position of high rank: two pf. trios, and two trios for strings, Op. 27; three stringed quartets; quintet for wind-instruments; a symphonic poem, "Odysseus"; two symphonies (c min., 1885; B♭, 1890); "Deutsches Liederspiel" (for soli, chorus, and pf. for four hands); "Der Stern des Liedes" (chorus and orchestra); "Die Weihe der Nacht" (alto solo, chorus, and orchestra); 96th Psalm (Op. 34); 116th Psalm (for double chorus and orchestra); 94th Psalm (Op. 60, for soli, chorus, and orchestra); "Nannas Klage" (Op. 59); a cantata, *Columbus*; pf. works for two and four hands; Variations for two pianofortes (theme from Brahms); songs, duets, part-songs.—His wife, E l i z a b e t h, *née* v. Stockhausen (b. 1848), was an excellent pianist; she died Jan. 7, 1892, San Remo.

Heses, German term for B doubly flattened

Hess, J o a c h i m, from 1766 to 1810 organist and *carilloneur* of St. John's Church, Gouda (Holland). He wrote: "Korte en eenvondige handleiding tot het leeren van clavecimbal og orgelspel" (1766, etc.); "Luister van het orgel" (1772); Korte schets van de allereerste uitvinding en verdere voortgang in het vervaardigen der orgeln" (1810); "Dispositien der merkwaardigste kerk-orgeln" (1774); and "Vereischten in eenen organist" (1779).

Hesse, (1) E r n s t C h r i s t i a n, b. April 14, 1676, Grossgottern (Thuringia), d. May 16, 1762, Darmstadt; was at first official secretary for Hesse-Darmstadt at Frankfort and Giessen, was then trained at his Prince's cost at Paris under Marin, Marais, and Forqueray, and became one of the greatest performers on the gamba in Germany. His compositions (many sacred pieces, sonatas for the gamba, etc.) remained in manuscript.

(2) A d o l f F r i e d r i c h, b. Aug. 30, 1809, Breslau, d. there Aug. 5, 1863, was the son of an organ-builder, pupil of the organists F. W. Berner and E. Köhler, Breslau; in 1827 he became second organist of St. Elizabeth's Church, and in 1831 first organist of the Bernhardinerkirche. He was a distinguished, and much-admired organist, who, among others, attracted notice by his performances in the church of St. Eustache, Paris, and at the Crystal Palace, London. For many years H. directed the symphony concerts of the Breslau theatre band. Of his works the most important are his compositions for organ (preludes, fugues, fantasias, *études*, etc.). He also wrote an oratorio (*Tobias*), six symphonies, overtures, cantatas, motets, one pf. concerto, one stringed quintet, two stringed quartets, also pf. pieces.

(3) Julius, b. March 2, 1823, Hamburg, d. April 5, 1881, Berlin. He published: "System des Klavierspiels," and made a change in the measurement of pianoforte keys which was approved of.

(4) Max, active music-publisher, b. Feb. 18, 1858, Sondershausen, founded in 1880, at Leipzig, the publishing-house bearing his name, and, in 1883, jointly with A. Becker, a printing establishment for books and music (Hesse u. Becker). The house soon prospered, and, among other works, has published Urbach's "Preisklavierschule," Palme's choral works, Reinecke's opera (*Auf hohen Befehl*), Riemann's "Musiklexikon," and a goodly series of musical catechisms, etc.

Hetsch, Louis, b. April 26, 1806, Stuttgart, d. June 26, 1872, Mannheim; from 1846 academical musical director at Heidelberg, then musical director at Mannheim. He composed orchestral, choral, and chamber-music; his 130th Psalm and a duet for pf. and violin gained prizes.

Heuberger, Richard Franz Joseph, b. June 18, 1850, Graz, where he studied music diligently, from an early age, under the best teachers, but first followed the career of an engineer, passed the Government examination in 1875, and in 1876 turned his attention definitely to music, and became chorus-master at the academical Vienna Vocal Society, and then, in 1878, conductor of the Vienna "Singakademie." H. published a number of songs, part-songs, serenades for orchestra (Op. 7), orchestral variations on a theme by Schubert, a Suite (in D) for orchestra, overture to Byron's "Cain," rhapsody from Rückert's "Liebesfrühling" (for mixed chorus and orchestra), cantata, "Geht es dir wohl, so denk an mich" (for soli, male chorus, and orchestra), from "Des Knaben Wunderhorn," etc. Two operas (*Abenteuer einer Neujahrsnacht* and *Manuel Venegas*) were produced (the one in 1886, the other in 1889 at Leipzig), a symphony, etc.

Heubner, Konrad, b. 1860, Dresden, where he attended the "Kreuzschule"; from 1878–79 pupil of the Leipzig Conservatorium (also of Riemann at the University), then of Nottebohm at Vienna, and, in 1881, of Wüllner, Nicodé, and Blassmann at Dresden, became in 1882 conductor of the "Singakademie" at Liegnitz, and in 1884 second conductor of the "Singakademie" at Berlin. In 1890 he went to Coblence as successor of Raphael Maszkowski (director of the musical society and the conservatorium). H. is a talented composer—overtures, chamber-music, etc.

Heugel, Jacques Léopold, b. 1815, La Rochelle, d. Nov. 12, 1883, Paris; founder and head of the Paris music-publishing house "H. et Cie.," publisher and editor of the musical paper *Le Ménestrel* (from 1834). H. published the famous "Méthodes du Conservatoire" for all branches by Cherubini, Baillot, Mengozzi, Crescentini, Catel, Dourlen; also the more modern ones by Garcia, Duprez, Mme. Cinti-Damoreau, Niedermeyer, Stamaty, Marmontel, etc.

Hexachord, a scale of six degrees. The Greeks (*see* GREEK MUSIC) divided their system into *tetrachords* (four notes). The system of tetrachords lasted far into the middle ages, and maintained itself still longer until Guido d'Arezzo (or one of his pupils) established the hexachord system as basis for teaching Solmisation (q.v., and Mutation). Modern theory recognises only diatonic scales of seven degrees (*heptachords*, improperly named *octochords*, for the eighth degree, the octave, is identical with the first). The identity of the octave degree has indeed long been recognised; Virgil already speaks of *septum discrimina vocum*.

Hey, Julius, ranked by R. Wagner as the chief of all teachers of singing, b. April 29, 1832, Irmelshausen (Lower Franconia). The doubly-gifted youth was destined for the career of a painter, attended the Munich Akademie, and displayed a certain originality as a landscape-painter, but at length turned entirely to music, and studied harmony and counterpoint under Franz Lachner, and singing under Friedr. Schmitt, the recognised teacher for voice formation. The king, Ludwig II., introduced him to R. Wagner, for whose ideas he became warmly enthusiastic. From that time he conceived the idea of reforming the cultivation of singing in a German national sense, and to this task devoted his life. With this aim in view he worked under the direction of H. von Bülow at the Munich School of Music, established by Ludwig II., according to Wagner's plans; but after Bülow's departure in 1869 he met with hindrances to the realisation of his ideas, and, after many years' further struggle, he resigned his post when Wagner died (in 1883). In 1887 he went to Berlin, and settled there. The experiences gained at the preliminary rehearsals for the first *Nibelungen* performances at Bayreuth, for which Wagner had summoned him to render assistance in vocal technique, had, however, strongly convinced H., and the master himself, that only a "Stilbildungschule" (school for the formation of style) for the rendering of German musico-dramatic works could firmly establish and further develop what had been accomplished at Bayreuth in such a remarkably rapid manner. Wagner's plan, dating from 1877, to appeal to the singers with respect to this matter, failed, owing to unfortunate financial conditions; but H. considered it his duty to risk everything for the final accomplishment of the grand idea. So he first commenced working at a great Method of singing, "Deutscher Gesangsunterricht," of which four parts had been issued up to 1886 (Section I. relating to Speech; II. Tone-

and Voice-Formation of Women's Voices; III. ditto of Men's Voices; IV. Textual Explanations). The high importance of this work will be speedily recognised; in it are incorporated and clearly expounded Wagner's ideas respecting the training of our singers, not in gray theory, but step by step from the elements of tone-formation conformable to nature to a mature, artistic rendering, so that they may be fully conscious of the results of sound, practical instruction. Many singers trained by H. are to be found, as esteemed members, at the principal theatres of Germany. H. has published songs and duets, also sixteen easy songs for children, a favourite collection for elementary instruction in singing.

Heyden (Heiden, Haiden), (1) S e b a l d, b. 1494, Nuremberg; in 1519 cantor of the Hospital school, afterwards rector of the "Sebaldus" school there; d. July 9, 1561. He wrote "Musicæ, *i.e.* artis canendi libri duo" (1537; 3rd ed., as "De arte canendi," etc., 1540), a small, but very valuable little treatise on measured music, written with extraordinary clearness; the book is, unfortunately, extremely rare. Another little treatise of like contents bears the title "Stichiosie musicæ, seu rudimenta musicæ" (1529), or "Musicæ stichiosis, worin vom Ursprung und Nutzen der Musik," etc., or "Institutiones musicæ" (1535), and, judging from the year number, is probably identical with the former work.
(2) H a n s, of Nuremberg; he invented in 1610 the so-called "Geigenklavicimbal" ("Nürnbergisch Geigenwerk," which he described in "Musicale instrumentum reformatum," 1610). (*Cf.* BOGENKLAVIER.)

Heymann, (1) (H.=Rheineck), K a r l A u g u s t, pianist and composer, b. Nov. 24, 1852, at Burg Rheineck, on the Rhine, pupil of the Cologne Conservatorium and of the Kgl. Hochschule at Berlin; at the latter he has been teacher since 1875. H. has published pf. pieces and songs ("Einen Brief soll ich schreiben").
(2) K a r l, eminent pianist, b. Oct. 6, 1854, Filehne (Posen), where his father, Isaac H., was cantor (afterwards at Graudenz and Gnesen; at present principal cantor at Amsterdam), pupil of the Cologne Conservatorium (Hiller, Gernsheim, Breunung), then private pupil of Kiel at Berlin, excited the attention of the musical world as pianist, and had already published several pianoforte works, when nervous irritation compelled him for several years to attend to his health. In 1872 he again appeared as pianist with Wilhelmj, and accepted a post at Bingen as musical director, as he was ordered to be most cautious in resuming his activity as a virtuoso; yet he gradually appeared more and more frequently, and was named court pianist to the Landgrave of Hesse, and received many marks of distinction.

From 1877–80 he was teacher at the Hoch Conservatorium, Frankfort; but this mode of life did not suit him, and from that time he devoted himself entirely to the career of a virtuoso; but, unfortunately, owing to a return of his nervous complaint, not for long. His compositions are: "Elfenspiel," "Mummenschanz," "Phantasiestücke," a pf. concerto; they are brilliant, but also full of sterling merit.

Heyne (Hayne, Ayne, *i.e.* Heinrich), V a n G h i z e g h e m, mostly called merely H., a Netherland contrapuntist, of whom some motets are printed in Petrucci's "Odhecaton." He was chapel singer at the court of Charles the Bold of Burgundy about 1468.

Hidden Fifths and Octaves. (*See* PARALLELS.)

Hiebsch, J o s e f, b. Oct. 7, 1854, Tyssa (Bohemia), 1866 chorister of the Royal Chapel at Dresden, 1869 at the Seminary at Leitmeritz. He studied the violin under Dont at Vienna, and is at present teacher of music at the "K. K. Lehrbildungsanstalt," at Vienna. He has written "Leitfaden für den elementaren Violinunterricht" (1880; augmented 1884), a collection of duets of similar character (12 books), "Methodik des Gesangunterrichts" (1882 [1893]), "Methodik des Violinunterrichts" (1887, a "comparative" school, similar to Riemann's "Vergleichende Klavierschule"), "Allgemeine Musiklehre" (1890), and "Lehrbuch der Harmonie" (1893).

Hientzsch, J o h a n n G o t t f r i e d, b. Aug. 6, 1787, Mokrehna, near Torgau, d. July 1, 1856; studied at Leipzig, was for several years teacher in Switzerland, in order to master Pestalozzi's Method; in 1817 teacher of music at the Training School at Neuzelle, in 1822 director of the Training School at Breslau, in 1833 at Potsdam; from 1852–54 director of the Institute for the Blind at Berlin. H. published collections of church melodies for school use; edited, 1828–37, the educational musical paper *Eutonia;* commenced in 1856 to edit a new paper, *Das musikalische Deutschland,* which, owing to his death, stopped at the third number. He wrote, besides, "Einige Worte zur Veranlassung eines grossen jährlichen Musikfestes in Schlesien" (1825), "Ueber den Musikunterricht, besonders im Gesang, auf Gymnasien und Universitäten" (1827), and "Methodische Anleitung zu einem möglichst natur- und kunstgemässen Unterricht im Singen für Lehrer und Schüler" (1st part, 1836).

Hieronymus de Moravia, one of the oldest writers on measured music (about 1260 Dominican monk of the monastery of the Rue St. Jacques in Paris; his treatise, "De musica," is printed in Coussemaker's "Scriptores," I.).

Hignard, J e a n L o u i s A r i s t i d e, b. May 22, 1822, Nantes, became a pupil of Halévy at the Paris Conservatoire in 1845, and received the second composition prize in 1850. In 1851 he produced his maiden opera, *Le visionnaire,* at

Nantes, and then, with good success, at the Théâtre Lyrique, Paris, the following : *Colin-maillard* (1853), *Les compagnons de Marjolaine* (1855), *L'auberge des Ardennes* (1860) ; besides at the Bouffes Parisiens *Monsieur de Chimpanze* (1858), *Le nouveau pourceaugnac* (1860), and *Les musiciens de l'orchestre* (1861). These are all comic operas. A tragédie lyrique, *Hamlet* (the preface to the score explains the attempt herein made at a new species of composition), was published, and also carefully analysed (by E. Garnier, 1868), but was only produced in 1888 at Nantes. Of H.'s numerous other works may be mentioned the "Valses concertantes" and "Valses romantiques" for pianoforte (four hands), besides songs, male and female choruses, etc. He died early in 1898, at Vernon.

Hildach, (1) E u g e n, b. Nov. 20, 1849, Wittenberge-on-the-Elbe, was intended for some branch of the building trade, and attended the Building School at Holzminden. Not until the age of twenty-four was he trained for a singer ; he was a pupil of Frau Professor El. Drey-schock at Berlin, where he made the acquaintance of the lady who afterwards became his wife :
(2) A n n a, *née* S c h u b e r t, b. Oct. 5, 1852, Königsberg-i.-Pr., who after her marriage settled in Breslau. In 1880 Fr. Wüllner invited both to be teachers at the Dresden Conservatorium, where they remained until 1886. Since then they have devoted themselves entirely to concert singing. Eugen H. is an able baritone singer ; Anna H. possesses a sonorous mezzo-soprano voice.

Hildebrand, Z a c h a r i a s, b. 1680, d. 1743, eminent German organ-builder ; he built the organ for the Catholic Church at Dresden. His equally famous son, J o h. G o t t f r i e d H., built the organ of the great "Michaeliskirche " at Hamburg.

Hiles, (1) J o h n, b. 1810, Shrewsbury, d. Feb. 4, 1882, London, organist at Shrewsbury, Portsmouth, Brighton, and London ; he wrote, besides pf. pieces and songs, a series of musical catechisms (pianoforte-playing, organ, harmony, and general-bass, part-singing) and a Dictionary of Musical Terms (1871). His brother and pupil
(2) H e n r y, b. Dec. 3, 1826, Shrewsbury, held also various posts as organist, from 1852–59 travelled round the world for the sake of his health, received the degrees of Mus.B. Oxon, 1862, and Mus.D. 1867, and resigned his post as organist (finally, 1864–67, at St. Paul's, Manchester). In 1880 he became lecturer on harmony and composition at Owens College ; in 1882 he was engaged in the foundation of the National Society of Professional Musicians. He edited, from 1885, the *Quarterly Musical Review*, wrote a "Grammar of Music," two vols. (1879), besides " Harmony of Sounds " (1871, 3rd ed. 1879), " First Lessons

in Singing " (1881), and " Part Writing ; or, Modern Counterpoint " (1884), and composed an oratorio (*The Patriarchs*), cantatas (*Fayre Pastorel, The Crusaders*), psalms, anthems, services, and part-songs ; he has also written a small opera : *War in the Household*.

Hilf, A r n o, distinguished violinist, b. March 14, 1858, at Bad Elster (came of a musical family), pupil of his father, W. C h r. H., from 1872 a pupil of David, Röntgen, and Schradieck at the Leipzig Conservatorium ; in 1878 second leader and teacher at Moscow Conservatoire, in 1888 in similar capacities at Sondershausen Conservatorium, and, in the same year, successor to Petri as leader at the Gewandhaus, Leipzig. H. has the qualifications of a great virtuoso.

Hill, (1) W i l l i a m, English organ-builder, d. Dec. 18, 1870, introduced, in conjunction with Gauntlett, the CC compass.
(2) T h o m a s H e n r y W e i s t, violinist, b. Jan. 3, 1828, London, d. there Dec. 26, 1891. He was Director of the Guildhall School of Music.
(3) K a r l, celebrated stage and concert singer (baritone), b. 1840, Idstein, Nassau, d. Jan. 21, 1893, in a lunatic asylum at Sachsenberg (Mecklenburg), was at first a post-office official, and only appeared occasionally as a concert singer ; but in 1868 he went on the stage, and worked from that time at the court theatre, Schwerin. In 1876 H. sang the *rôle* of Alberich at the Wagner Festival, Baireuth.
(4) W i l h e l m, pianist and composer, b. March 28, 1838, Fulda, has been living since 1854 at Frankfort (pupil of H. Henkel and Hauff). His opera, *Alona*, in 1882 received the second prize (Reinthaler received the first for *Käthchen von Heilbronn*) in the competition for the opening of the new opera-house at Frankfort. Of his compositions that have appeared in print may be mentioned : violin sonatas (Op. 20 and 28) ; trios (Op. 12 and 43) ; a pf. quartet (Op. 44) ; songs, pf. pieces, etc.

Hille, E d u a r d, b. May 16, 1822, Wahlhausen (Hanover), studied from 1840–42 philosophy at Göttingen, and music under the direction of the academical musical director Heinroth ; but he afterwards devoted himself entirely to music, and lived for several years as teacher of music at Hanover, where he established the " Neue Singakademie," and conducted a male choral society. H. was intimate with Marschner, and corresponded with Moritz Hauptmann. In 1855 he was named academical musical director at Göttingen, where he founded—after long journeys, for the purpose of study, to Berlin, Leipzig, Prague, Vienna, etc.—the " Singakademie," and revived the academical concerts. As a composer H. has made himself principally known by spirited songs and part-songs.

Hiller, (1) J o h a n n A d a m (Hüller), b. Dec. 25, 1728, Wendisch-Ossig (near Görlitz), where his father was cantor; d. June 16, 1804, Leipzig. After the early loss of his father, he obtained, owing to his beautiful soprano voice, a scholarship at the Gymnasium, Görlitz, and later at the Kreuzschule, Dresden, where he studied the harpsichord and thorough-bass under Homilius. In 1751 he attended the University of Leipzig, earning his daily bread by teaching music and taking part in grand concerts under Doles, now as flautist, now as singer. In 1754 he became tutor in the house of Count Brühl at Dresden, accompanied his pupil in 1758 to Leipzig, and from that time settled there, refusing favourable offers from abroad. In 1763 he revived, at his own expense, the Subscription Concerts, interrupted by the Seven Years' War, and held them under the titles " Liebhaberkonzerte " and " Concerts spirituels " (on the model of those at Paris), until 1781; but when K. W. Müller founded the Concert Society, the Institution assumed a more general character and the concerts were transferred to the " Gewandhaus." H. was now appointed conductor, and laid the foundation of the fame of the " Gewandhaus " Concerts (q.v.). Already in 1771 he had set up a school of singing, which was of advantage in the formation of a good choir for the concerts. In 1789 he succeeded Doles as cantor at St. Thomas's School, from which post he withdrew in 1801, on account of the infirmities of old age. As a composer H. acquired special importance by his " Singspiele," which formed the point of departure of the German " Spieloper," and which were developed on independent lines side by side with the Italian *opera buffa* and the French *opéra comique*. H.'s principle in writing them was that common folk ought to sing in a plain song fashion, but personages of high birth in arias ; the songs of his operettas acquired an astonishing popularity. H.'s operettas are : *Der Teufel ist los* (1st part, *Der lustige Schuster*, 1768; 2nd part, *Die verwandelten Weiber*, 1766), *Lisuart und Dariolette* (1767), *Lottchen am Hofe* (1760), *Die Liebe auf dem Lande*, *Der Dorfbarbier*, *Die Jagd, Die Musen, Der Erntekranz, Der Krieg, Die Jubelhochzeit, Das Grab des Mufti* (= *Die beiden Geizigen*), and *Das gerettete Troja* (1777, all produced at Leipzig). Apart from the stage, he cultivated the song-form. He edited Ch. Felix Weisse's " Lieder für Kinder," also " 50 geistliche Lieder für Kinder," " Choral-melodien zu Gellerts geistlichen Oden," " Vierstimmige Chorarien," a " Choral-buch," cantatas, etc. The 100th Psalm, a Passion cantata, funeral music in honour of Hasse, etc., remained in manuscript; also symphonies and partitas. H. also enriched musical literature to a considerable extent ; he wrote ; " Wöchentliche Nachrichten und Anmerkungen, die Musik betreffend " (1766–70, actually the oldest musical paper (*cf.* NEWSPAPERS) ; " Lebensbeschreibungen berühmter Musikgelehrten und Tonkünstler " (1784; Adlung, J. S. Bach, Benda, Fasch, Graun, Händel, Heinichen, Hertel,

Hasse, Jomelli, Quanz, Tartini, etc., containing also an autobiography) ; " Nachricht von der Aufführung des Händelschen Messias in der Domkirche zu Berlin 19 Mai, 1786 "; " Ueber Metastasio und seine Werke" (1786) ; " Anweisung zum musikalisch richtigen Gesang " (1774) ; " Anweisung zum musikalisch zierlichen Gesang " (1780) ; " Anweisung zum Violinspiel " (1792). He prepared also the second edition of Adlung's " Anleitung zur musikalischen Gelahrtheit " (with comments, 1783), arranged Pergolesi's Stabat Mater for four-part chorus, and published Handel's Stabat Mater, Graun's "Tod Jesu," and Hasse's " Pilgrime auf Golgatha." As teacher he could pride himself on brilliant results; Corona Schröter was his pupil. (*Cf.* MARA.) Two Polish ladies, the sisters Podleski, induced him to go to Mitau in 1782, where he so impressed the Duke of Courland that the latter established a band, of which he made H. capellmeister with a pension. His son

(2) Friedrich Adam, b. 1768 at Leipzig, d. Nov. 23, 1812, Königsberg, was likewise a capable musician, singer, and violinist ; in 1790 theatre capellmeister at Schwerin, 1796 at Altona, and 1803 at Königsberg. He wrote four operettas, six stringed quartets, also small vocal and instrumental works.

(3) Ferdinand (von), celebrated composer and clever writer on music, b. Oct. 24, 1811, Frankfort, d. May 10/11, 1885, Cologne, son of well-to-do parents, studied first with Aloys Schmitt and Vollweiler at Frankfort, in 1825 with Hummel at Weimar, visited Vienna with Dehn (1827), where he was presented to Beethoven. After a short stay in his father's house, he resided seven years in Paris (1828–35), where he made the acquaintance of celebrated musicians, and was on friendly terms with Cherubini, Rossini, Chopin, Liszt, Meyerbeer, Berlioz. He acted for some time at Choron's Institute for Music as teacher, and made himself a name by giving concerts and playing at *soirées* with Baillot ; he was specially successful as an interpreter of Beethoven. The death of his father called him back to Frankfort, where in 1836 he conducted the Cecilia Society as deputy for Schelbe ; then he went to Milan, and, in 1839, with Rossini's help, brought out an opera at the Scala, *Romilda*, which had scanty success. The following year he lived at Leipzig, near Mendelssohn, with whom he was already well acquainted ; he there completed his oratorio, which he had commenced in Milan, *Die Zerstörung Jerusalems*, and produced it in 1840 at the Gewandhaus. In 1841 he paid another visit to Italy, this time under Baini, at Rome making an earnest study of the masters of sacred music, but returned in 1842 to Germany, and undertook during the winter of 1843–44, for Mendelssohn (who was in Berlin), the direction of the Gewandhaus Concerts at Leipzig. He produced at Dresden the two operas, *Traum*

in der Christnacht (1845) and *Konradin* (1847), was called to Düsseldorf in 1847 as capell-meister, and in 1850 to Cologne in a similar capacity, with the commission to organise the Conservatorium. From that time H. laboured as conductor of the concert society, and also of the concert choir, two bodies which united for the Gürzenich Concerts and also for the Rhenish musical festivals; and, as director of the Conservatorium, he rendered valuable ser-vice, and was considered the most famous musical notability of West Germany. On October 1, 1884, he retired into private life. From 1851 to November, 1852, he conducted at the Opéra Italien (Paris). He was not only a distinguished pianist, conductor, and teacher, a well-schooled, skilled in form, prolific, and refined composer, but, in addition, a brilliant and amiable feuilletonist. He began his career as a writer by contributing attractive feuilletons to the *Kölnische Zeitung*, some of which appeared in collected form as " Die Musik und das Pub-likum" (1864); " L. van Beethoven" (1871); "Aus dem Tonleben unsrer Zeit " (1868, two vols.; new series 1871). Other writings from H.'s finely cut pen are : " Musikalisches und Persönliches " (1876); "Briefe von M. Hauptmann an Spohr und andre Komponisten " (1876); " Felix Mendels-sohn-Bartholdy, Briefe und Erinnerungen" (1876) ; " Briefe an eine Ungenannte " (1877); " Künstlerleben " (1880) ; " Wie hören wir Musik ? " (1880), and " Goethes musikalisches Leben " (1880), " Erinnerungsblätter " (1884). The composer H. belongs thoroughly to the Schumann-Mendelssohn group. The number of his works reached almost two hundred, among which are six operas : *Der Advokat* (Cologne, 1854), *Die Katakomben* (Wiesbaden, 1862), *Der Deserteur* (Cologne, 1865), and the three already named ; also two oratorios, *Die Zerstörung Jerusalems* (1840), and *Saul* (1858) ; cantatas : *Lorelei, Nal und Damajanti, Israels Siegesgesang, Prometheus, Rebecca* (Biblical idyll), *Prinz Papagei* (dramatic legend); *Richard Löwen-herz*, ballad for soli, chorus, and orchestra (1883), psalms, motets, etc. (" Sanctus Dominus," for male chorus [Op. 192] ; " Super flumina Babylonis," " Aus der Tiefe rufe ich," for solo with pf.), " Palmsonntagmorgen " (for female chorus, solo, and pf.) ; quartets for male chorus, mixed chorus, and female chorus ; some pf. and chamber-music (works much in request, for they are elegant, and grateful to the performer), among which a concerto (F sharp minor), sonatas, suites, many books of small pieces (Op. 191, " Festtage "), études, " Operette ohne Text " (for four hands), violin sonatas, canonical suite for pf. and violin, 'cello sonatas, five trios, five quartets, five stringed quartets, several overtures, three symphonies, etc. H.'s lectures on the history of music, with illustra-tions (Vienna, Cologne, etc.), were most success-ful. The University of Bonn conferred on H. the title of Doctor (1868).

(4) **Paul**, b. Nov., 1830, Seifersdorf, near Liegnitz ; from 1870 he was sub-organist, and from 1881 organist, of St. Maria-Magdalena at Breslau. He wrote pf. pieces, songs, etc.

Hillmer, Friedrich, b. about 1762, Berlin, d. there May 15, 1847. In 1811 he was tenor player in the court band, received a pension in 1831, and made experiments in the con-struction of new and improved stringed and keyed instruments, without, however, obtaining recognition for any one of them ("Alldrey," " Tibia," and an improved " Polychord "). A son of his is highly esteemed in Berlin as a teacher of singing.

Hilpert, W. Kasim Friedrich, b. March 4, 1841, Nuremberg. a German 'cellist of great distinction, pupil of Friedrich Grützmacher at the Leipzig Conservatorium, one of the founders, and for eight years (1867–75) member of the famed " Florentiner Quartett." (*See* BECKER, 8.) He was afterwards solo 'cellist in the royal court opera at Vienna, then at Meiningen, and in 1884 teacher at the Royal School of Music, Munich. Died Feb. 6, 1896, Munich.

Hilton, John, English composer of sacred and secular music, graduated at Cambridge (1626), organist of St. Margaret's, Westminster (1628), buried March 21, so probably died March 19–20, 1657. He published : " Ayres, or Fa-las for Three Voyces " (1627 ; lately reprinted by the Musical Antiquarian Society), and " Catch that catch can" (1652 ; collection of catches, rounds, and canons). Single works of his are to be found in "Triumphs of Oriana," and Rim-bault's "Cathedral Music," and Lawes's "Choice Psalmes" ; there are some manuscripts in the British Museum.

Himmel, Friedrich Heinrich, b. Nov. 20, 1765, Treuenbrietzen (Brandenburg), d. June 8, 1814, Berlin. He at first studied theology, but then, having received a royal stipend, went to Dresden to study composition under Naumann. Friedrich Wilhelm II. also sent him for further training to Italy, and H. produced there two operas—*Il primo navigatore* (1794, Venice), and *Semiramide* (1795, Naples). In 1795 H. suc-ceeded Reichardt as court capellmeister, made (1798 to 1800) a journey to Russia (opera *Ales-sandro* at Petersburg) and Scandinavia, also in 1801 to Paris, London, and Vienna, and then resumed his duties in Berlin. After the political events of 1806 he went first to Pyrmont, and then to Cassel and Vienna, returning finally to Berlin. His operas formerly enjoyed great popularity. In Berlin he produced *Vasco de Gama* (1801, Italian), and the operetta *Frohsinn und Schwärmerei* (1801), *Fanchon* (1804, his best-known work), *Die Sylphen* (1806) ; in Vienna, *Der Kobold* (1811). His first compositions of importance were an oratorio, *Isaaco figura del redentore* (1791), and the cantata *La danza* (1792). Also many of his songs were much in vogue, as, for instance, "An Alexis ' and " Es kann ja nicht immer so bleiben." He wrote besides, psalms, a Paternoster, vespers, a mass, many pf. sonatas, a pf. concerto, a quartet for pf., flute, violin, and 'cello, a sextet for pf., two violas, two horns, and 'cello, pf. fantasias, rondos, etc.

Hinke, Gustav Adolf, distinguished oboist, b. Aug. 24, 1844, Dresden, son of Gottfr. H. (d. 1851). He introduced the bass tuba into the Dresden band. He studied at the Dresden Conservatorium (oboe, Hiebendahl), and from 1867 was principal oboist at the theatre, and in the Gewandhaus orchestra, Leipzig.

Hinrichs, Franz, b. cir. 1820, Halle-a.-Saale, d. Oct. 25, 1892, Berlin, as Oberjustizrath; friend and brother-in-law of Robert Franz, composed songs in the style of Franz and wrote:—" R. Wagner und die neue Musik" (1854, very temperate). The wife of Robert Franz—Marie H (b. 1828, d. May 5, 1891, Halle-a.-S.) was also known as a composer of songs.

Hintersatz (Ger., behind-set), was the name given in old organs (*cf.* Prätorius, "Syntagma II.," p. 102, on the restoration of the organ at Halberstadt Cathedral in 1495) to pipes of the mixture kind placed behind the Principal (Prästant), which served to strengthen the latter, and therefore formed a special stop.

Hipkins, A. J., one of the principal contributors to Grove's "Dictionary of Music," and a contributor to the "Encyclopædia Britannica. He has compiled very valuable descriptive catalogues: "Guide to the Loan Collection of Musical Instruments, etc., at the Albert Hall" (1885); "Old Keyboard Instruments;" and "Musical Instruments, Historic, Rare, and Unique" (1883).

Hirn, Gustav Adolph, an esteemed man of science, b. Aug. 21, 1815, Logelbach (near Colmar-i.-E.), d. Jan. 14, 1890, Colmar. He lived in his native place as director of a meteorological institute. Among his numerous works specially relating to physics there is one in which music is concerned—" La musique et l'acoustique" (1878), in which it is denied that the beautiful in music can be explained by physical causes.

Hirsch, Dr. Rudolf, b. Feb. 1, 1816, Napagedl (Moravia), d. March 10, 1872, Vienna; he was composer, poet, and musical critic, and wrote "Mozart's Schauspieldirector" (1859), an apology for Mozart.

Hirschbach, Hermann, b. Feb. 29, 1812, Berlin, d. May 19, 1888, Gohlis (near Leipzig). He studied with Birnbach, was (1843–45) editor of the paper *Musikalischkritisches Repertorium*, and became so hated on account of his immoderate critical sharpness that he retired entirely into private life. He was a highly prolific composer of original tendency. He wrote thirteen stringed quartets (Lebensbilder, Op. 1, etc.), two stringed quintets with two

violas, and two similar works with two 'celli, two quintets with clarinet and horn, one septet, one octet, fourteen symphonies ("Lebenskämpfe, Erinnerungen an die Alpen," "Faust's Spaziergang," etc.), overtures (*Götz von Berlichingen, Hamlet, Julius Cäsar*, etc.), and two operas (*Das Leben ein Traum* and *Othello*). He sought, above all, after music which should be characteristic in so far as it was related to the perception of an idea.

Hirschfeld, Robert, writer on music, b. 1858, Moravia, attended colleges at Breslau and Vienna, and studied at Vienna, attended likewise the Conservatorium. He took his degree of Dr.Phil. (monograph on "Johannes de Muris") 1884, and, in the same year, was appointed teacher of musical esthetics at the Vienna Conservatorium, having already given lectures there since 1882. Further may be mentioned his polemical pamphlet against Hanslick in defence of old *a-cappella* music, to foster which he founded the "Renaissance-Abende."

His, German term for B raised by a sharp

Hitzler, Daniel, b. 1576, Haidenheim (Würtemberg), prior and ecclesiastical councillor at Stuttgart, d. Sept. 4, 1635. He wrote "Newe Musica oder Sing Kunst" (1628), in which he argued in favour of Bebisation with *la, be, ce*, etc., against Calvisius, and Bocedisation. (*Cf.* BOBISATION.) He also published a collection of figured chorales (1634).

Hobrecht (Obrecht, Obreht, Obertus, Hobertus), Jakob, one of the most important Netherland contrapuntists, contemporary of Josquin, b. about 1430, Utrecht, and capellmeister of the cathedral there in 1465. In 1492 he succeeded Jacques Barbireau as capellmeister at Notre Dame, Antwerp; in 1504 a chaplaincy was granted to him, and he lived quietly until his death, about 1506. Numerous masses, motets, and chansons of this master have been preserved. Petrucci printed a volume of his masses: "Missæ Obreht" in 1503—the masses: "Je ne demande," "Grecorum," "Fortuna desparata," "Malheur me bat," "Salve diva parens"; and in the first book of the "Missæ diversorum" he produced also a mass by H. entitled "Si dedero." The "Missæ XIII." of Graphäus (1539) contain "Ave regina cœlorum" and "Petrus Apostolus" by H. Other masses of his are to be found in manuscript in the Papal Chapel archives, Rome. The Munich library contains in the manuscript No. 3,154, besides two already named ("Si dedero" and "Je ne demande"), the otherwise unknown "Scoen lief" and "Beata viscera." Motets by H. are to be found in Petrucci's "Odhecaton" (third and fourth books, 1503 and 1505); further in the first book of Petrucci's motets à 5 (1505), and in K. Peutinger's " Liber selectarum cantionum " (1520); a passion à 4 in G. Rhaw's " Selectæ harmoniæ" (1538), hymns à 4 in Rhaw's " Liber primus sacrorum hymnorum " (1542), chansons in Petrucci's " Odhecaton," " Canti B " and " Canti C," detached numbers in Glarean and S. Heyden. (*Cf.* the first Kyrie of the mass " Ave regina " by H. under MEASURED MUSIC.)

Hochberg, Hans Heinrich XIV., Bolko, Graf von H., baron of Fürstenstein (as composer: H. Franz), b. Jan. 23, 1843, at the castle of Fürstenstein, composed the operas *Claudine von Villa bella* (1864) and *Der Währwolf* [= *Die Falkensteiner*] (1876), also symphonies, etc. For many years he maintained a quartet-party (the " Hochberg ") at Dresden, and in 1876 established the Silesian musical festival (conductor: Deppe). After the death of Hülsen (1886), count Hochberg became general intendant of the royal Prussian court theatre.

Hodges, Edward, b. July 20, 1796, Bristol, d. Sept. 1, 1867, Clifton. In 1819 he was organist at Bristol. He took his Doctor's degree at Cambridge (1825), in 1838 became organist at Toronto, and in 1839 of St. John's Chapel, New York; in 1846 he presided at the new organ, Trinity Church, but, owing to ill-health, resigned in 1859, and returned to England in 1863. H. did much towards the development of musical life in New York. He wrote " An Essay on the Cultivation of Church Music " (1841), was for a long time a contributor to the *Quarterly Musical Magazine* and to the *Musical World*, and composed services, anthems, etc.— His daughter, Faustina Bach H. (d. **Feb.,** 1896), was organist of two churches in Philadelphia, and a composer.—His son, John Sebastian Bach H., rector of St. Paul's Church, Baltimore, is also an excellent organist.

Hoeck-Lechner, Frieda, b. April 5, 1860, Rastatt (Baden), pupil of Frau Schröder Hanfstängl. She first turned to the stage, and made her *début*, at the end of 1883, at Detmold, in the *rôle* of Gabriele (*Nachtlager von Granada*). Since her marriage (1884) she has bidden farewell to the stage, and is now highly esteemed as a concert-singer.

Hoffmann, (1) Eucharius, b. Heldburg (Franconia), cantor, afterwards rector, at Stralsund. He published, among other works, " Doctrina de tonis seu modis musicis," etc. (1582); " Musicæ præcepta ad usum juventutis " (1584); also " Deutsche Sprüche aus den Psalmen Davids mit vier Stimmen " (1577), and " Geistliche Epithalamia " (1577).

(2) Ernst Theodor Amadeus (really Wilhelm), b. Jan. 24, 1776, Königsberg, d. June 25, 1822, Berlin, the well-known fantastic poet, devoted with his whole soul to music, and even, for a time, a professional musician. He studied law, became assessor at Posen, but, on account of offensive caricatures, went (1802) as councilor to Plozk, was sent to Warsaw in 1803, and, in 1806, having been reduced to poverty by the war, he gave lessons in music, and in 1809 became musical director of the Bamberg theatre; but when this was closed he again had recourse to private teaching. He worked for the Leipzig *Allgemeine Musikalische Zeitung*, contributing fantastic articles under the name " Kapellmeister Johannes Kreisler " (this character—his own portrait—which is likewise chief personage in " Kater Murr," incited Schumann to his Op. 16, entitled " Kreisleriana "), and conducted the orchestra of the " Sekondasche Schauspielergesellschaft " at Leipzig and Dresden (1813–14). In 1816 he was again appointed councilor of the Supreme Court of Judicature at Berlin. H. was a man possessed of diverse rare talents, a sound jurist, a clever draughtsman, a composer rich in imagination, and a gifted poet. In Posen he produced Goethe's Singspiel, " Scherz, List und Rache " (1801); in Plozk, " Der Renegat " (1803) and " Faustine " (1804); in Warsaw, Brentano's " Lustige Musikanten " (1805), and the operas *Der Kanonikus von Mailand* (1805), and *Schärpe und Blume* (1805, libretto written by himself); in Bamberg *Der Trank der Unsterblichkeit* (1808), *Das Gespenst* (1809), and *Aurora* (1811); in Berlin, *Undine* (after Fouqué), 1816, the score and H.'s own scenery sketches of which were lost when the Opera House was burnt down; and, finally, the music to Werner's " *Kreuz an der Ostsee.* He left in manuscript the opera *Julius Sabinus* (only the first act complete), a ballet, *Harlekin*, and, besides, a mass, a Miserere, a symphony, an overture, several other vocal works, pf. sonatas, and a quintet for harp and strings. His poetical works contain many intelligent remarks about music, especially the " Phantasiestücke in Callot's Manier" (1814), and " Kater Murr " (1821–22). (*Cf.* Hitzig, " Hoffmanns Leben und Nachlass " [1823], and Funk, " Aus dem Leben zweier Dichter " [H. und Fr. G. Wetzel, 1836].)

(3) Heinrich August (H. von Fallersleben), b. April 2, 1798, Fallersleben (Hanover), d. Jan. 29, 1874, at Castle Korvei; the well-known poet and philologist, librarian in 1823; in 1830 assistant, and in 1835 professor in ordinary of the German language at Breslau. In 1842 he was dismissed from his post and exiled on account of his political opinions; he became, finally, librarian to Prince Lippe at Korvei. He published: " Geschichte des deutschen Kirchenliedes " (1832; 2nd ed. 1854); " Schlesische Volkslieder mit Melodien " (1842); " Deutsche Gesellschaftslieder des 16–17 Jahrhunderts " (1844), and " Kinderlieder " (1843).

(4) Richard, pianist, b. May 24, 1831, Manchester; he went to New York in 1847, where at his first public appearance he played Thalberg's " Sonnambula " fantasia; afterwards he performed repeatedly at the Philharmonic

Concerts. H. is highly esteemed as a pianoforte teacher, and has published many high-class *salon* pf. pieces.

Hoffmeister, F r a n z   A n t o n, b. 1754, Rotenburg-on-the-Neckar, d. Feb. 9, 1812, Vienna; church capellmeister and owner of a music business at Vienna. In 1800 he established, jointly with Kühnel, the " Bureau de musique " (now firm of C. F. Peters) at Leipzig, but in 1805 ceased to be associated with the undertaking, and returned to Vienna. H. composed nine operas, and published hundreds of works for flute (concertos, duets, trios, quartets, quintets), forty-two quartets for strings, five pf. quartets, eleven pf. trios, eighteen trios for strings, twelve pianoforte sonatas, symphonies, serenades, a Paternoster, etc. His works, written in a flowing style, but without originality and depth, were, in their day, popular. (*Cf.* Riehl, " Mus. Charakterköpfe," I., 249 ff.)

Hofhaimer (Hofheimer, Hofheymer), P a u l u s (v o n), b. 1459, Radstadt (Salzburg), 1493, court organist at Vienna, promoted to the rank of a nobleman by Maximilian I., d. 1537, Salzburg. He was looked upon in Germany as a master of the organ without a rival, and he was also highly esteemed as a composer ; H. is, in fact, one of the oldest German composers of importance. The following of his works have been preserved ; " Harmoniæ poeticæ " (odes of Horace and other Latin poets set for voices à 4 by H. [thirty-three] and L. Senfl [eleven], 1539; republished by Achtleitner, 1868) ; German Lieder à 4 (arranged, considering the period, in an exceedingly pleasing manner, and in a modern spirit as regards tonality) are to be found in the collections of Erh. Oeglin (1512), Chr. Egenolff (" Gassenhawerlin," 1535 ; " Reutterliedlein," 1535), and of G. Forster (" Auszug," etc., Part I., 1560 and 1561). Up to now only a set of his organ pieces, in the handwriting of Kleber, about 1515, has been discovered (Royal Library, Berlin); of these one has been printed in the supplement of the *Monath. f. Musikg.*, " Das deutsche Lied," Vol. II., p. 171.

Hofmann, (1) C h r i s t i a n, cantor at Krossen about 1668, published " Musica synoptica " (guide to the art of singing, 1670; frequently republished under different titles).

(2) H e i n r i c h   K a r l   J o h., b. Jan. 13, 1842, Berlin, studied at Kullak's Akademie, especially under Grell, Dehn, Wüerst, and is one of the most famous of living composers. Up to 1873 he gave private lessons, but since then works only at composition. He achieved a notable success, first of all with his " Hungarian Suite " and " Frithjof " symphony. Of his numerous works—which, if they do not show marked originality, are full of feeling for the beautiful—may be specially named the pianoforte duets " Italienische Liebesnovelle " (arranged for pf. and violin), " Liebesfrühling," " Trompeter von Säckingen," " Eckehard," " Steppenbilder," " Aus

meinem Tagebuche," etc. ; also the choral works " Nonnengesang," " Die schöne Melusine," " Aschenbrödel," " Editha " (1890), " Nornengesang " for solo, female chorus, and orchestra, " Lieder Raouls le Preux an Iolanthe von Navarre " (baritone and orchestra), a cantata for alto solo, chorus, and orchestra (Op. 64) ; part-songs for mixed and for male chorus, pf. pieces, songs, duets, a 'cello concerto, a pf. trio, pf. quartet, stringed quartet, octet (Op. 80) ; suite, " Im Schlosshof," for orchestra (Op. 78) ; " Festgesang," for chorus and orchestra (Op. 74) ; serenade for strings and flute, sextet (Op. 65), serenade for strings (Op. 72), concertstück for flute (Op. 98), orchestral scherzo, " Irrlichter und Kobolde " (Op. 94) ; violin sonata (Op. 67), 'cello serenade (Op. 63), etc. H. commenced writing for the stage with *Cartouche* (1869), after which followed *Der Matador* (1872), *Arnim* (1872), *Aennchen von Tharau* (1878), *Wilhelm von Oranien* (1882), and *Donna Diana* (1886).

(3) R i c h a r d, b. April 30, 1844, Delitzsch, where his father was town musical director. He studied under Dreyschock and Jadassohn, and now lives at Leipzig as teacher of music, and has published there a special series of Methods for ˜the various instruments of the orchestra, also a catechism of musical instruments, a Method of instrumentation, likewise many compositions, for the most part instructive, for pianoforte, strings, and windinstruments.

(4) J o s e f, pianist, b. June 20, 1877, Warsaw. He gave recitals in London, New York, etc. (1887).

Hofmeister, F r i e d r i c h, b. 1781, d. Sept. 30, 1864. In 1807 he established at Leipzig the music-publishing business which bears his name, and from 1838 published the *Musikalischlitterarische Monatsbericht* (a guide to all the musical works which appeared in Germany from month to month), which has been continued by his heirs. His son and successor, A d o l f   H. (d. May 26, 1870), brought out a new edition of Whistling's " Handbuch der musikalischen Litteratur " (1845, music, books on music, musical papers, portraits, etc.), and also a series of supplementary volumes to it (extracts from several of the yearly issues of the *Monatsberichte*), an undertaking which has also been continued by the firm, of which the present proprietor is Carl W. Günther.

Hogarth, G e o r g e, b. 1783, London, d. Feb. 12, 1870. He originally studied for the legal profession, and held an official post in Edinburgh. He was an amateur of music, afterwards musical critic and historian. From 1830 he was a contributor to the *Harmonicon*. In 1834 he became sub-editor and musical critic of the *Morning Chronicle*, and from 1846 to 1866 musical critic of the *Daily News*. In 1850 he became secretary to the Philharmonic Society. He wrote: "Musical History, Biography, and Criticism" (1835; 2nd ed., in two vols., 1838); "Memoirs of the Musical Drama" (1838; 2nd ed. as "Memoirs of the Opera"); "The Philharmonic Society of London, 1813–62" (1862). He also published a few glees and songs.

Hohlfeld, Otto, distinguished violinist, b. March 10, 1854, Zeulenroda (Voigtland), received his first instruction there from cantor Solle, and afterwards at the Training College, Greiz, from cantor Urban and the musical director Regener. He then went for three years to the Conservatorium at Dresden (Rietz, Lauterbach, Kretschmer). He joined the court orchestra at Dresden for a short time, but in 1877 went as leader to Darmstadt, whence he often made excursions for the purpose of giving concerts. H. published a quartet for strings, songs, violin pieces, and also pf. pieces (" Zigeunerklänge "). D. May 10, 1895, Darmstadt.

Hohlflöte (Flûte creuse; Hohlpfeife, an instrument of smaller dimensions), a lip-pipe stop of wide measure, for the most part with beards, of soft, dull tone (somewhat hollow, hence the name H.). It is generally of 8 feet, also 4, seldom 16 and 2 feet. As a quint stop it is called Hohlquinte.

Hol, Richard, b. July 23, 1825, Amsterdam, received instruction in music from the age of five, first from the organist Martens, and afterwards at the royal school of music in that city. After some journeys (also to Germany) for the purpose of study, he settled in Amsterdam as teacher of the pianoforte, became (1856) conductor of the Liedertafel "Amstels Mannenchor," and of the Vocal Union of the Society for the Advancement of Musical Art, and is at present town musical director as successor to J. H. Kufferath, and organist of the cathedral, also director of the municipal School of Music at Utrecht; likewise director of the Diligentia Concerts at the Hague and of the Classical Concerts at the People's Palace, Amsterdam. H., distinguished by high orders and honours of various kinds, among others his appointment (1878) as member of the French Académie, is not only one of the most esteemed conductors and teachers in Holland, but a composer whose name is known and honoured beyond the limits of his native land, and one who adheres to the modern school of thought. Up to the present he has published ninety works, among which a symphony (Op. 44), which has also been performed in Germany; several ballads for soli, mixed chorus, and orchestra, among which Op. 70, " Der fliegende Holländer," an oratorio, David (Op. 81), an opera, Floris V. (produced at Amsterdam), masses, many songs (for the most part to Dutch, some to German, words), chamber-music, etc. H. has also won laurels as a writer: criticisms in the Dutch musical paper, Cæcilia, and a

monograph on J. P. Sweelinck ("Swelingh, jaarboekje aan de toonkunst in Nederland gewijd," 1859–60), etc.

Hold, a pause. This term is obsolete.

Holding Note, a note sustained by one part whilst other parts are moving.

Hollander, (1) Jans (de Hollandere), also Jean de Holland, contrapuntist, of whom chansons à 4–6 are to be found in the first and twelfth books of the collection of chansons published by Tylman Susato (1543 and 1558).

(2) Christian Janszone, son of the former, chapel singer at St. Walburga, Audenarde, from 1549 to 1557, chapel singer to the Emperor Ferdinand I. 1559–64, after whose death all trace of him is lost. The statement of Lipowski that he became capellmeister at Munich is incorrect. His friend, J. Pühler, at Schwandorf (Bavaria), published collections of his works (and in 1570 speaks of him as dead): "Neue teutsche geistliche und weltliche Liedlein " à 4–8 (1570; 2nd ed. 1575), and "Tricinia" (1573). Forty motets are to be found scattered in collections of the 16th century; Commer reprinted a number of motets and songs.

Holländer, (1) Alexis, pianist, b. Feb. 25, 1840, Ratibor (Silesia). After attending the Gymnasium at Breslau, he became a pupil at the school of composition at the Royal Academy, Berlin, and, at the same time, private pupil of K. Böhmer. In 1861 he became teacher at Kullak's Academy, in 1864 conductor of a choral society, and in 1870 conductor of the "Cæcilia" (important choral works with orchestra). He has published a pf. quintet, pf. pieces, songs, part-songs, a cappella songs à 5, etc. Specially worthy of mention are his studies as preparation for choral singing (2nd book: methodical exercises for singing a lower part!) and an instructive edition of Schumann's pianoforte works (Schlesinger). In 1888 H. was elected Professor.

(2) Gustav, an excellent violinist, b. Feb. 15, 1855, Leobschütz (Upper Silesia), studied first with his father, a skilful physician, appeared in public as a youthful prodigy, attended the Leipzig Conservatorium (David) from 1867 to 1869, and from then up to 1874 the Kgl. Hochschule, Berlin (Joachim, and Kiel for theory). In 1874 he entered the court opera band as royal chamber musician, and at the same time became principal teacher of the violin at Kullak's Academy. In the same year he gave concerts with Carlotta Patti in Austria, and from 1871 to 1881 subscription chamber-music concerts with X. Scharwenka and H. Grünfeld at Berlin. In 1881 he became leader of the band at the Gürzenich concerts in place of O. von Königslöw, and teacher at the Conservatorium, Cologne, and became, besides, leader at the Stadttheater in 1884. On the retirement of Japha, he undertook the leadership of the " Professoren-Streichquartett," with which he had

been previously connected, taking the first violin alternately with Japha. H. has given many concerts in Belgium, Holland, and Germany, and has published a number of works for the violin (concertos, suites, etc.).

(3) **Victor**, b. April 20, 1866, Leobschütz, studied under Kullak. He has composed operettas, pf. pieces, etc.

Holly, Franz Andreas, one of the oldest and most admired composers of German operettas (Singspiele), b. 1747, Luba (Bohemia), musical director with Brunian in Prague, with Koch in Leipzig, and, finally, with Waser in Breslau, where he died May 4, 1783. He set to music a whole series (fifteen) of the Singspiel texts current at that time ("Der Bassa von Tunis," Berlin, 1774, "Die Jagd," "Das Gespenst," "Der Waarenhändler von Smyrna," "Der lustige Schuster," etc.).

Holmes, (1) Edward, b. 1797, d. Aug. 28, 1859, music-teacher in London, musical critic of the *Atlas*. He was an excellent writer, whose Mozart biography O. Jahn considered the best before his own. "The Life of Mozart" was published in 1845 (2nd ed. E. Prout, 1878). He also wrote "A Ramble among the Musicians of Germany" (1828, an account of a journey of observation through Germany); a life of Purcell for Novello's "Sacred Music"; an "Analytical and Thematic Index of Mozart's P.F. Works," as well as many articles for the *Musical Times* and other musical papers.

(2) William Henry, b. Jan. 8, 1812, Sudbury (Derbyshire), d. April 23, 1885, London. He was one of the first pupils of the Royal Academy of Music, received training as a pianist, became sub-professor in 1826, subsequently professor of the piano and senior of the teaching staff of the Academy. Bennett, the brothers Macfarren, and Davison were his pupils. He composed many instrumental and vocal works, symphonies, concertos, sonatas, also an opera, songs, etc., but published little.

(3) The brothers Alfred, b. Nov. 9, 1837, London, d. March 4, 1876, Paris; and Henry, b. Nov. 7, 1839, London, violinists, were trained entirely by their father, a self-taught musician, with the help of Spohr's "Violin School," and later, the French school of Rode, Baillot, and R. Kreutzer. They already played in public at the Haymarket Theatre in 1847, but did not appear again until 1853, after further diligent study. They both left London in 1855, and went to Brussels, where they remained for some time, performing repeatedly with great success. In 1856 they made a concert tour through Germany as far as Vienna, and settled for two years in Sweden; in 1860 they were in Copenhagen, in 1861 in Amsterdam, and in 1864 in Paris. Alfred settled there, but made frequent concert tours. Of his compositions are to be named the symphonies "Jeanne d'Arc," "The Youth of Shakspere," "Robin

Hood," "The Siege of Paris," "Charles XII.," and "Romeo and Juliet"; the overtures: *L. Cid* (1874), and *Les Muses*, and an opera—*Inez de Castro*. His brother Henry left Paris in 1865, and, after a fresh tour through Scandinavia, returned to London, where he was for a time professor of the violin at the Royal College of Music. He has written five symphonies, a concert overture, a violin concerto, two stringed quintets, violin soli, two cantatas (*Praise ye the Lord* and *Christmas*), and songs. He has also edited violin sonatas by Corelli, Tartini, Bach, and Handel. H. died Dec. 9, 1905.

(4) Augusta Mary Anne (known also as composer under the *nom de plume*, Hermann Zeuta), b. Dec. 16, 1847, Paris; she began her career as a prodigy pianist, but studied composition diligently under Lambert and Klosé, and César Franck, and soon made herself known by important works (opera, *Héro et Léandre;* psalm, "In exitu," 1873; symphonies, "Orlando Furioso," "Lutèce" [third prize in the competition instituted by the city of Paris], "Les Argonautes" [honourably mentioned at the city of Paris competition, 1880]; symphonic poems, "Irlande" and "Pologne" (1883); also a cycle of songs, "Les Sept Ivresses." All these works have assured to Mlle. H. a position among the best French composers.

Holstein, Franz von, b. Feb. 16, 1826, Brunswick, d. May 22, 1878, Leipzig. He was the son of an officer of high position, and destined for a military career. He studied at the cadet school at Brunswick, and received instruction there from K. Richter in the theory of music. Already in 1845, as a young lieutenant, he produced in private circles a small opera, *Zwei Nächte in Venedig.* He sent an opera, planned on a large scale—*Waverley* (after W. Scott)—from Seesen, where he was adjutant, to M. Hauptmann, who encouraged him to enter the musical profession. In 1853 he gave up his position as officer, went to Leipzig, and became a pupil of Hauptmann at the Conservatorium. After long journeys, and residence for the purpose of study in Rome (1856), Berlin (1858), and Paris (1859) he settled definitely in Leipzig, devoting himself entirely to composition. Bodily sufferings, however, often compelled him to husband his strength, and his life came to a close just as he had commenced his fifty-third year. A rich legacy for the benefit of music students without means will perpetuate his memory. H.'s compositions are not void of originality, yet they are scarcely strong enough to defy time. Three operas have spread his name in wide circles: *Der Haideschacht* (Dresden, 1868); *Der Erbe von Morley* (Leipzig, 1872); and *Die Hochländer* (Mannheim, 1876). H. always wrote the libretti himself; he was, in fact, not only a poet, but skilful with his pencil. In addition may be named the overtures *Lorelei* and *Frau Aventiure* (posthumous); a solo scena from Schiller's

"Braut von Messina"; "Beatrice" (soprano with orchestra); many songs ("Waldlieder," Op. 1 and 9); part-songs for mixed and for male chorus; chamber-music (trio); in all about fifty works. "Nachgelassene Gedichte" appeared in 1880.

Holten, Karl von, b. July 26, 1836, Hamburg, pianist and composer, a pupil of J. Schmitt, Avé-Lallemant, and Grädener, and from 1854–55 at the Leipzig Conservatorium under Moscheles, Plaidy, and Rietz. He lives at Altona, and is much sought after as a teacher of music, and since 1874 he has been teacher at the Hamburg Conservatorium. H. has published a violin sonata, a trio, a pf. concerto, a children's symphony, pf. pieces, songs, etc.

Holzbauer, Ignaz, b. 1711, Vienna, d. April 7, 1783, Mannheim. He was to have studied law, but worked hard, and in secret, at music. He was first of all capellmeister to Count Rottal in Moravia, and in 1745 musical director at the Vienna court theatre (where his wife was also engaged as singer). In 1747 he travelled to Italy, became court capellmeister at Stuttgart in 1750, was called to Mannheim in a similar capacity in 1753, where (with Cannabich sen. as leader) he brought the orchestra into the highest repute. From Mannheim he visited Italy several times, and produced various operas. During the last years of his life H. was completely deaf. Mozart thought highly of him as a composer. His principal works are a series of Italian operas, of which the first is *Il figlio delle selve* (for the court theatre, Schwetzingen, 1753); a German opera, *Günther von Schwarzburg* (Mannheim, 1776), 196 instrumental symphonies, eighteen quartets for strings, thirteen concertos for various instruments, five oratorios, twenty-six orchestral masses à 4 (one German), motets, etc.

Hölzel, (1) Karl, a favourite song-composer, b. April 8, 1808, Linz, d. Jan. 14, 1883, as teacher of singing at Pesth.
(2) Gustav, also a favourite singer and song composer, b. Sept. 2, 1813, Pesth, d. March 3, 1883, Vienna. He was engaged at the opera as buffo bass, and received a pension in 1869. ("Mein Liebster ist im Dorf der Schmied.")

Hölzl, Franz Severin, b. March 14, 1808, Malaczka (Hungary), d. Aug. 18, 1884, as capellmeister of Fünfkirchen Cathedral. He was a pupil of J. Chr. Kessler and Seyfried at Vienna, composed much church music, also an oratorio (*Noah*).

Homeyer, Paul Joseph Maria, a distinguished organist, b. Oct. 26, 1853, Osterode, Harz (son of Heinrich H., organist at Lamspringe, b. 1832, d. Dec. 31, 1891, grandson of Joh. Just. Adam H., editor of a Roman Catholic choral-book, "Cantus Gregorianus"), attended the Josephinum Gymnasium at Hildesheim, also the Conservatorium and University at Leipzig. He appeared in public in the latter city, and with great success, but continued his studies under his uncle, J. M. Homeyer, in Duderstadt, and was afterwards appointed organist at the Gewandhaus, and, at the same time, teacher of the organ and of theory at the Leipzig Conservatorium.

Homilius, Gottfried August, b. Feb. 2, 1714, Rosenthal (Saxony), d. June 2, 1785, Dresden. He was a pupil of J. S. Bach, and teacher of J. A. Hiller. In 1742 he was organist of the Frauenkirche, Dresden, in 1755 cantor at the Kreuzschule, and musical director of the three principal Dresden churches. He was highly esteemed in his day as a sacred composer, and his works are not yet quite forgotten. He published a "Passion" cantata (1775), a Christmas oratorio (*Die Freude der Hirten*," etc., 1777), *Sechs deutsche Arien* (1786), and the following remain in manuscript: a "Mark" Passion, church music (for a whole year), many motets, cantatas, fugued chorales, a General-bass Method, a chorale-book, etc., most of which are in the Berlin library.

Homophone (Gr.) is a term frequently applied to a mode of composition in which one part stands out as melody, whilst the others are restricted to the *rôle* of simple accompaniment; it is used in contradistinction to *polyphone*. (*Cf.* ACCOMPANYING PARTS.) With regard to its etymological meaning, the word is used inversely, for the word is identically the same as unison ("sounding the same"), and hence only applicable to ancient or early Middle-Age music—to music, in fact, in one part or two parts moving in octave. *Accompanied* would be a better term for music described as H. Helmholtz, in his "Lehre von den Tonempfindungen," distinguishes the periods of *homophonic, polyphonic,* and *harmonic* music.

Hook, James, b. 1746, Norwich, d. 1827, Boulogne; organist and composer at Marylebone Gardens from 1769 to 1773, and engaged in the same capacity at Vauxhall Gardens from 1774 to 1820. He was for many years organist of St. John's, Horsleydown. He was a prolific vocal composer, wrote music for many stage works, gained many prizes at the Catch Club. His songs, catches, etc., exceed two thousand (!) in number. He composed concertos for organ or harpsichord, sonatas, and a book of instruction for the pianoforte, "Guida di musica" (1796).

Hopffer, Ludwig Bernhard, composer, b. Aug. 7, 1840, Berlin, d. Aug. 21, 1877, at the hunting-seat, Niederwald, near Rüdesheim. He was a pupil of the Kullak Akademie up to 1860. He wrote orchestral works (symphonies, overtures); two operas—*Fritjof* (Berlin, 1871), and *Sakuntala;* and the festival play, *Barbarossa* (Berlin); the choral works, *Pharao, Darthulas Grabgesang;* the twenty-third Psalm, chamber-music, songs, etc.

Hopkins, Edward John, b. June 30, 1818,

Westminster, was chorister of the Chapel Royal under Hawes, in 1833 private pupil of Walmisley. He occupied various posts as organist in London, but was at length appointed to the Temple Church in 1843, and the service there under his direction has gained a high reputation. H. has composed anthems, psalms, and other sacred works, but is best known as an authority on the organ and author of "The Organ, its History and Construction" (with an "History of the Organ" by Dr. Rimbault as an introduction, 1855; 5th ed. 1877). He edited Bennet's and Weelkes' Madrigals for the "Musical Antiquarian Society," and also the musical portion of "The Temple Church Choral Service." John, brother of the former, b. 1822, Westminster, organist at Rochester, and a cousin, John Larkin H., organist at Cambridge, b. Nov. 25, 1819, Westminster, d. April 25, 1873, Ventnor, have also published anthems, etc.

Hoplit. (*See* POHL [RICHARD].)

Hoquetus. (*See* OCHETUS.)

Horæ canonicæ is the term applied in the Catholic Church service to the offices prescribed for the seven periods of the day (*Horæ*): 1, Matins and Lauds (*Laudes matutinæ*); 2, Prime, Tierce, Sext, None, Vespers, and Compline, when certain fixed psalms, canticles, and hymns are sung.

Horak, (1) Wenzel Emanuel, b. Jan. 1, 1800, Mscheno-Lobes (Bohemia), d. Sept. 5, 1871, Prague; studied with Türk and Albrechtsberger at Vienna, chorus-master at Prague, esteemed in his country as a composer for the church.

(2) The brothers Eduard, b. 1839, Holitz (Bohemia), and Adolf, b. Feb. 15, 1850, Jankovíc (Bohemia), founders and principal teachers of the "Horak" Pianoforte School established at Vienna, and which speedily rose to a state of great prosperity (three sections —at Wieden, Mariahilf, and in the Leopoldstadt). Adolf published "Die technische Grundlage des Klavierspiels," and with his brother a "Klavierschule" (2 vols.); Eduard, jointly with Fr. Spigl, published "Der Klavierunterricht in neue natürliche Bahnen gebracht" (1892, 2 vols.).

Horn (Ital. *Corno*, Fr. *Cor*), the brass wind-instrument distinguished from all others by its tenderness of tone. It is either a *natural* instrument (natural H., *Waldhorn, Corno di caccia, Cor de chasse, French horn*), or (without exception now) provided with valves, *i.e.* with a mechanism which lengthens the tube by the insertion of small crooks (likewise the modern system of non-combining valves [*Pistons indépendants*] invented by Ad. Sax, which, by cutting off a larger or smaller portion, shortens the tube), and hence displaces the natural scale (valve H.). The H. is a so-called "half-instrument," *i.e.* of such narrow measure that the lowest tone

only speaks with very great difficulty. Although the sound-tube is about sixteen feet long (in spiral form), the lowest note of the C Horn that can be safely taken is the 8-ft. (great) c. The usual compass of the H. extends from the lowest natural available sound (the second of the overtone series) to *c″, c♯″,* or *d″* (twice-accented), *i.e.* the limit downwards is according to the tuning (key) of the instrument (they are rarely tuned in D, C♯ and F♯):—

Horn in B♭ C D E♭ E F G A♭ A B♭ C
low   high

As for horns the natural scale is always written in c, these boundary notes downwards must all be expressed by the note

Those notes of the horn, however, which are written in the bass clef, are sometimes written an octave lower than would be the case if they were in the treble clef, so that

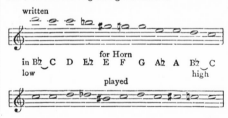

are identical. While the compass downwards is always limited by the same note (2nd tone of the natural scale, which can be lowered by means of stoppers [*see* below] 1–2 semitones, but by ventils about 6 semitones; *cf.* VENTILS), the limit upwards is determined by orchestral use; hence the highest good note is

written
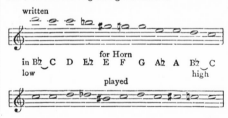
in B♭ C D E♭ E F G A♭ A B♭ C
low   high
                played
played

The scale of natural notes of the H. shows ever-increasing gaps downwards, and these are, in part, filled up by *closed* notes; for the player, by putting his hand into the bell, can lower each natural note by a half-tone, or, at need, even by a whole-tone. The closed notes of the H. have an oppressed sound, used by composers to express anguish, etc. Those lowered by a whole-tone (doubly closed) are rough and uncertain of speech—thus, *b♭, d′, f,* and especially *a♭′.* The notes *a* and *d♭′* with triple stopping are not in use. The introduction of valves removes the necessity for using closed notes, but the possibility of using them remains; the composer can demand them from players of instruments with valves, and for any note, at his pleasure. A distinction is made in the orchestra between *first* and *second* H.; and in fuller scoring there are groups each of two Hs., of which the one (first and third) is treated as high, the other (second and fourth) as low H. The first H. ranges over the highest, the second over the lowest notes : the former has a narrower mouthpiece than the latter. A medium instrument, on which the highest, likewise the lowest, notes are obtained with difficulty, but which has at command a wide middle compass, is the *Cor mixte* used by French horn players. The Hunting Horn of the 16th century (as described by S. Virdung) was a small primitive kind of instrument. About 1680 the great hunting horns (*Trompes de chasse*) came into use in France, whence Count Sporck is said to have transplanted them into Germany. In 1760 Hampel, of Dresden, discovered closed notes, and used the trumpet crooks for the H. About the same time Haltenhof provided it with the tuning-slide. Rudolph at Paris (1765) was the first H. virtuoso. Blühmel and Stölzl, natives of Silesia, were the inventors of the Valve H., 1815. (*Cf.* also EICHBORN and SAX.) The H. as a solo instrument is much in vogue, and, though H. performers who make concert tours are now scarce, on the other hand, there are H. soli of greater or less length in orchestral works, while in operas they are very frequent. Famous performers on the H. were and are : Rodolphe, Mares, Stich (Punto), Lebrun, Domnich, Duvernoy, J. K. Wagner, Amon, Belloli, Kern, Stölzel, Artôt, Meifred, Gallay, Dauprat, the family Schunke, Lindner, Gumbert, etc. (*Cf.* the respective biographies.) Of the not over rich literature for H., the three H. concertos by Mozart and Schumann's concerto for four Hs. (Op. 86) deserve special mention.

Horn, (1) K a r l F r i e d r i c h, b. 1762, Nordhausen, d. Aug. 5, 1830, Windsor. He studied with Schröter, came to London in 1782, where the Saxon Ambassador, Count Brühl, introduced him into the best circles as teacher of music, and he was appointed music master in ordinary to Queen Charlotte and the Princesses (up to 1811), and in 1823 became organist of St. George's Chapel, Windsor. H. published : pianoforte sonatas, twelve sets of variations for the pianoforte, with an accompaniment for flute or violin, " Military Divertimentos," and a treatise on thorough-bass. He also prepared (jointly with Wesley) an edition of Bach's "Well-tempered Clavier."

(2) C h a r l e s E d w a r d, son of the former, b. 1786, London, d. Oct. 21, 1849, Boston ; he lived in London for several years as operasinger and opera-composer, went in 1833 to New York, where, on the loss of his voice, he taught music, and established a music business (1842, opera, *The Maid of Saxony*). From 1843–47 he was again in London, but went to Boston and became there conductor of the

Handel and Haydn Society. Besides twentysix English operettas (1810–30), he wrote the oratorios : *The Remission of Sins* (New York), *Satan* (London, 1845), and *The Prophecy of Daniel* (1848) ; a cantata, *Christmas Bells;* canzonets, glees, songs, etc.

(3) A u g u s t, b. Sept. 1, 1825, Freiberg, Saxony, d. March 25, 1893, Leipzig, pupil of the Leipzig Conservatorium ; he made a name by his excellent arrangements of symphonies, operas, etc., for the pianoforte (for four and eight hands). He also wrote some orchestral works and an opera—*Die Nachbarn* (produced at Leipzig 1875). Besides his arrangements, only small pf. pieces, songs, and part-songs appeared in print.

Hornemann, J o h a n n Ole E m i l, b. 1809, Copenhagen, d. there May, 1870, popular Danish song composer (" Der tappere Landsoldat ").—His son, E m i l C h r i s t i a n, b. Dec. 17, 1841, Copenhagen, likewise song composer, lives at Copenhagen, where he is director of a school of music.

Hornmusik (Ger. ; Fr. *fanfare*), music for brass instruments only. (*Cf.* HARMONIEMUSIK.)

Hornpipe, an old English dance, called after an instrument known only by name. It was greatly in vogue during the last century ($\frac{3}{2}$, also $\mathbf{C}$ time ; in the former, much syncopated :

♩♩ ♩ ♩♩; in the latter with the rhythm :

♩♩ | ♩ ♩ ♩, etc.).

Hornquinten (Ger., horn-fifths), an old term for the " hidden " fifths which can be produced by the natural tones of the horn, and which are allowed even by ultra-pedantic teachers :

or reversed. (*Cf.* PARALLELS.)

Hornstein, R o b e r t v o n, b. Dec. 6, 1833, Stuttgart, d. June 19, 1890, Munich, pupil of the Leipzig Conservatorium, was teacher of the Royal School of Music at Munich. He wrote the operas *Adam u. Eva* and *Der Dorfadvokat,* also music to Shakespeare's *As You Like It* and Mosenthal's *Deborah,* besides songs, pf. pieces, etc.

Horsley, (1) W i l l i a m, b. Nov. 15, 1774, London, d. June 12, 1858. He suggested the establishment of the Concentores Sodales (1798–1847), similar to the catch and glee clubs. He graduated Mus. Bac. (Oxford, 1800) ; and was organist of various London churches. He published five collections of glees, forty canons, a collection of psalm tunes with interludes, sonatas, pf. pieces, songs, etc. He also edited a collection of the glees, etc., of Callcott (with biography and analysis), and Book I. of Byrd's " Cantiones Sacrae."

(2) Charles Edward, son of the former, **b**. Dec. 16, 1822, London, d. Feb. 28, 1876, New York. He studied with his father and Moscheles at London, afterwards with Hauptmann at Cassel, and finally with Mendelssohn at Leipzig. He lived for a long time at Melbourne, afterwards in North America. Of his compositions the following oratorios became known by being performed at musical festivals in England; *Gideon, David, Joseph;* he wrote, besides, an ode, " Euterpe " (soli, chorus, and orch.), music to Milton's *Comus*, and a " Text-Book of Harmony " published after his death.

Horwitz, Benno, b. March 17, 1855, Berlin, pupil of the Royal High School; he also studied with Kiel and Alb. Becker. He is violinist and composer (chamber-music, songs, part-songs, and vocal works of considerable extent).

Hostinsky, Ottokar, a clever writer on musical esthetics, b. Jan. 2, 1847, Martinoves (Bohemia), attended the Gymnasium at Prague; he studied in that city, first law, and afterwards philosophy (at Prague, and from 1867–68 at Munich). He took his degree of Doctor of Philosophy at Prague, and then resided in Salzburg and Munich, travelled to Italy in 1876, passed the teachers' examination at Prague University for esthetics and the history of music (1877), and in 1884 was appointed professor of esthetics. He published a small biography of Wagner in the Bohemian language (1871), also " Das Musikalisch-Schöne und das Gesamtkunstwerk vom Standpunkt der formalen Aesthetik " (1877, German); " Die Lehre von den musikalischen Klängen " (1879, German); " Ueber die Entwickelung und den jetzigen Stand der tschechischen Oper " (1880); and " Ueber die Bedeutung der praktischen Ideen Herbarts für die allgemeine Aesthetik " (1883). H. is in sympathy with the latest progress in the knowledge of the nature of harmony (Hauptmann, Helmholtz, v. Oettingen, etc.).

Hothby (Hothobus, Otteby, Fra Ottobi), Johannes, composer and theorist of the 15th century, English by birth, d. commencement of Nov., 1487, London. From 1467–86 he lived in the Carmelite monastery of St. Martin, Lucca, highly esteemed as a teacher. His treatise, " Calliopea leghale " (Italian), is printed in Coussemaker's " Histoire de l'harmonie ; " a second, " De proportionibus et cantu figurato, etc.," in his " Scriptores " III. ; two more, " Ars musica " and " Dialogus," and smaller ones, have been preserved in manuscript (Florence). There are copies of some compositions à 3 in the handwriting of Padre Martini. (*Cf.* " Kirchenmus. Jahrbuch," 1893.)

Hotteterre, Louis, surnamed " Le Romain," chamber-musician (flautist) at the court of Louis XIV. and XV. He sprang from an excellent French musical family (the father, Henri H., was chamber-musician, a highly esteemed instrument-maker, and a performer on the musette). He wrote ; " Principes de la Flûte traversière ou flûte d'Allemagne, de la flûte à bec ou flûte douce et du hautbois " (without year, probably 1699; repeatedly republished and reprinted); in Dutch, " Grondbeginselen over de behandeling van de dwars-fluiten " (1728); " Méthode pour la musette " (1738); " L'art de préluder sur la flûte traversière, sur la flûte à bec," etc. (1712; 2nd ed., under title " Méthode pour apprendre, etc.," about 1765) ; and, besides, a whole set of pieces, sonatas, duos, trios, suites, rondes (*chansons à danser*), and menuets for flute.

Hoven, J., pseudonym for Vesque von Püttlingen (q.v.).

Howling is an organ term applied to the unintentional continued sounding of a note, and this always arises either from the fact that the valve does not properly close the groove in an ordinary wind-chest, or that the separate pallets in the " cone-box " do not properly shut off air leading to the pipes. This faulty closing may actually arise from various causes, and may be sought for in every part of the mechanism from the key to the valve (warping of a key, " binding " of a tracker, crooked roller, entangled spring, sticking of a valve, dust between pallet and groove, etc.).

Hrimaly, Adalbert, Bohemian composer and conductor, b. July 30, 1842, Pilsen; he studied at the Prague Conservatorium, was trained by M. Mildner, and became an able violinist. Afterwards he was conductor of the orchestra at Gotenburg (1861), at the Bohemian national theatre, Prague (1868), at the German theatre there (1873), and from 1875 at Czernowitz (Bukowina). His opera *Der verzauberte Prinz* (1871) is in the *répertoire* of the Bohemian national theatre.

Hubay. *See* HUBER (3) and (6).

Hubek, Gustave Léon, b. April 14, 1843, Brussels, pupil of the Conservatoire there, professor of harmony at the Conservatoires of Ghent and Antwerp. He composed the oratorio *De laatste lonnertral*, an orchestral suite, a pf. concerto, etc.

Huber, (1), Felix, d. Feb. 23, 1810, Berne, a famous poet and composer of songs, popular in Switzerland (" Schweizer Lieder," " Lieder für eidgenössische Krieger," " Lieder für Schweizer jünglinge," etc.).

(2) Ferdinand, b. Oct. 31, 1791, d, Jan. 9, 1863, St. Gallen, was also a popular composer of songs in Switzerland.

(3) Karl (Hubay), b. July 1, 1828, Varjas (Hungary), d. Dec. 20, 1885, as professor of the violin at the Pesth Conservatorium, and conductor at the national theatre there. He wrote the operas *Szekler Mädchen* (1858), *Lustige Kumpane*, and *Des Königs Kuss* (1875).

(4) Joseph, an original composer, b. April 17,

1837, Sigmaringen, d. April 23, 1886, Stuttgart. He studied first under L. Ganz (violin) and Marx (theory) at the Stern Conservatorium, Berlin, and afterwards under Eduard Singer and Peter Cornelius at Weimar, where Liszt exercised a powerful influence over him. He was for a time member of the band of the Prince of Hechingen at Löwenberg, in 1864 leader of the Euterpe orchestra, Leipzig, and in 1865 member of the court band at Stuttgart. Personal intercourse with Peter Lohmann at Leipzig prompted the particular study of musical form, to which he afterwards remained faithful. He rejected ready-made, stereotyped forms (the so-called "architectonic"), and demanded of a musical work of art that it should be freely developed from the poem or idea on which it was based ("psychological" form). H. has published two operas, *Die Rose von Libanon* and *Irene* (libretti by P. Lohmann), four one-movement symphonies, songs, instrumental melodies, etc. H. despises key signatures, and appears, therefore, to be always writing in c major or A minor.

(5) Hans, b. June 28, 1852, Schönewerd, near Olten (Switzerland), attended the Leipzig Conservatorium from 1870 to 1874 (Richter, Reinecke, Wenzel), was afterwards private teacher of music for two years at Wesserling, and teacher at the school of music at Thann (Alsace); afterwards teacher, then Director of the music school, Basle, where he now lives. The university of Basle conferred on him the title of Dr. Phil. h. c. in 1892. The strings set in vibration by H's strong, sound talent give out Schumann and Brahms sounds, yet the influence of Wagner and Liszt is also clearly perceptible; while to this is added a nervous rhythm, a powerful, poetical impulse emanating entirely from himself. Besides opera, H. has attempted nearly every branch of musical art (piano pieces, sonatas and suites for two and four hands, fugues, songs, part-songs, cantatas [*Pandora*, for soli, chorus, and orchestra, Op. 66, and *Aussöhnung*, for male chorus and orchestra], violin sonatas (Op. 18, 42, and 67), suite for pf. and violin (Op. 82), trios (Op. 30, 65), "Triophantasie" (Op. 84), suite for pf. and 'cello (Op. 89), 'cello sonata (Op. 33), pf. concerto (c minor, Op. 36), violin concerto (Op. 40), overtures, "Lustspiel" overture (Op. 50), "Tell," symphony (Op. 63), "Sommernächte" serenade (Op. 87), Carneval for orchestra, a new "Wohltemperiertes Klavier" (four hands), quartets for strings, etc.

(6) Eugen (Jenö Hubay), distinguished violin virtuoso, b. Sept. 14, 1858, Budapest, son and pupil of Karl Huber (*see* above, 3), studied afterwards under Joachim at Berlin. He first gave concerts (1876) in Hungary, and, recommended by Liszt, appeared with great success at a "Pasdeloup" concert, Paris, where he was favoured with the friendship of the most distinguished Paris musicians, especially of Vieuxtemps. In 1882 he

was appointed principal professor of the violin at the Brussels Conservatorium, but in 1886 exchanged this post for a similar one at the Pesth Conservatorium, as his father's successor. H. has also made a name as composer (forty-two opus numbers, among which a violin concerto ["Concerto dramatique," Op. 21], "Sonate romantique" for pf. and violin, "Szenen aus der Czárda" [Op. 9, 13, 18, 32–34, 41] for pf. and violin, other violin pieces; also songs, a symphony, and three operas [*Aljenor*, 1891; *Der Geigenmacher von Cremona*; and *Der Dorflump*]).

Hubert, Nicolái Albertowitsch, b. March 7, 1840, d. Sept. 26, 1888. He was professor of theory at the Moscow Conservatoire, and after N. Rubinstein's death (1881), director of that institution. H. was also an active and brilliant writer of musical feuilletons in the *Moscow News* (*Wedomosti*).

Huberti, Gustave Léon, b. April 14, 1843, Brussels, pupil of the Conservatoire of that city, received in 1865 the *Prix de Rome*, and thus travelled through Germany, Italy, etc.; he became director of the Conservatoire at Mons, but resigned in 1877. He lived as conductor and private teacher at Antwerp and Brussels until, in 1886, he was appointed professor of harmony at the Brussels Conservatoire. H. has composed the oratorios, *De laatste Zonnestral*, *Verlichting* (1884), the choral work *Wilhelm von Oraniens Tod*, *Bloemardinne*, two children's oratorios, ballads, hymns, a symphony, orchestral suite, a pianoforte concerto, etc.

Hucbald (Hugbaldus, Ubaldus, Uchubaldus), a monk of St. Amand monastery, near Tournay, b. about 840, d. June 25 or Oct. 21, 930, or June 20, 932, St. Amand. He first studied with his uncle Milo, who directed the singing-school there. For a time he was at the head of a school of singing at Nevers, and afterwards succeeded his uncle. The following treatises under H.'s name are printed by Gerbert ("Script." I.): "De harmonica institutione," and "Musica enchiriadis" (or "Enchiridion musicæ," "Liber enchiriadis"), fragments entitled "Alia musica," and, finally, "Commemoratio brevis de tonis et psalmis modulandis." In the publication of "Musica enchiriadis," Coussemaker ("Scriptores" II.) has given various readings of interest from different manuscripts, and to him we are also indebted for an interesting monograph on H. (1841). According to the most recent investigations of Dr. Hans Müller ("Hucbald's echte und unechte Schriften über Musik," Leipzig, 1884), of all the works named, only the "Harmonica institutio" (entitled also "Liber de musica") is to be ascribed to H., though it is not impossible that the author of "Musica enchiriadis" may have been a learned monk of the same name, who lived about a century later. Hence, for a long period, the name of the monk of St. Amand was incorrectly associated with the beginning of music in several parts (*see* ORGANUM); also the Dacian notation, with the signs

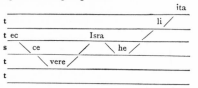

for the four finals (*d, e, f, g*) of the Church Modes, and various transformations of the same for their under- and upper-fifths, and octaves, did not emanate from him. On the other hand, the merit belongs to H. of having first employed parallel lines to show exactly the rising and falling of pitch :

The distances of whole-tones and semitones were shown at the commencement (*s* = *semi-tonium, t* = *tonus*). So long as no one else is clearly proved to be the author of " Musica enchiriadis " (in which the Organum is explained and also the Dacian notation employed), it will be well to describe the writer as pseudo-H. (or H. the younger). The long-contested meaning of the Dacian notation has probably been explained in a thoroughly clear manner by Spitta (*Vierteljahrsschrift f. M.-W.,* 1889, pp. 443–482; and 1890, pp. 283–309).

Hueffer, Fr a n c is, b. 1843, Münster, d. Jan. 19, 1889, London; he studied modern languages and music in London, Paris, Berlin, and Leipzig, settled in London, from 1869, as a writer on music, and, from 1878 until his death, was musical critic of the *Times.* In 1869 he gained the degree of Dr.Phil. at Göttingen with a critical edition of the works of the troubadour, Guillem de Cabestanh; in 1874 there followed " Richard Wagner and the Music of the Future " (eulogium of Wagner), and in 1878 " The Troubadours." He also published a collection of his *Times* articles, translated the correspondence of Wagner and Liszt into English, etc. H. was likewise the librettist of Mackenzie's *Colomba* and *The Troubadour,* also of Cowen's *Sleeping Beauty.*

Hugo von Reutlingen, surnamed " Spechz-hart," b. 1285 or 1286, d. 1359 or 1360. In 1488 appeared, in several editions at Strassburg, the well-known treatise with commentary entitled " Flores musice omnis cantus Gregoriani " (translated into German by Carl Beck in the publications of the " Litterarischer Verein, Stuttgart," in 1868. *See Monatsh. f. M.-G.,* II., 57, and a correction of errors in the new edition, II., 110).

Hullah, J o h n P y k e, b. June 27, 1812, Worcester, d. Feb. 21, 1884, London. In 1829 he became a pupil of W. Horsley, and entered the Royal Academy of Music in 1832 to study singing under Crivelli. Between 1836 and 1838 he produced the operettas *The Village Coquettes, The Barbers of Bassora,* and *The Outpost.* In 1840 he studied at Paris Wilhem's method of popular instruction in singing, and in 1841 established at Exeter Hall a school of singing on Wilhem's system (*see* WILHEM) for schoolteachers. It met with remarkable success, and grew to large dimensions. In 1847 a concert hall (St. Martin's Hall, inaugurated 1850, destroyed by fire 1860) was built for public performances by his pupils. Between 1840 and 1860 not less than 25,000 persons attended H.'s classes. In 1844 H. was appointed Professor of Vocal Music at King's College, from which post he withdrew in 1874, retaining, however, a similar appointment at Queen's College and at Bedford College. From 1870 to 1873 he was conductor of the Royal Academy concerts, and for many years of those of the Children of the Metropolitan Schools at the Crystal Palace. In 1872 he was appointed Inspector of Training Schools. In 1876 the University of Edinburgh conferred on him the degree of LL.D. ; he was also member of the Musical Academy, Florence, and of the Society of St. Cecilia, Rome. In 1858 H. succeeded Horsley as organist at the Charterhouse. As a composer he wrote songs which, for the most part, became popular. Numerous collections of vocal music were edited by him : " The Psalter " (psalm-tunes in four parts, 1843); " The Book of Praise Hymnal " (1868); " The Whole Book of Psalms with Chants "; " Part Music " (2nd ed., " Vocal Music "); " Vocal Scores "; " Sacred Music " (1867); " The Singer's Library "; " Sea-Songs," " English Songs of the 17th and 18th centuries " (Augener, 8844), etc. He edited, besides, Wilhem's " Method of Singing adapted to English Use," and wrote a series of theoretical and historical works :— " A Grammar of Vocal Music "; " A Grammar of Harmony "; " A Grammar of Counterpoint "; " The History of Modern Music " (1862); " The Third or Transition Period of Musical History " (1865) ; " The Cultivation of the Speaking Voice "; " Music in the House " (1877) ; also articles for newspapers.

Hüller. (*See* HILLER [1].)

Hüllmandel, Nicholas J o s e p h, b. 1751, Strassburg, d. Dec. 19, 1823, London, nephew of the famous performer on the horn, Rodolphe, pupil of Ph. Em. Bach at Hamburg. He was a distinguished pianist (also performer on the Harmonica [q.v.]) ; he went in 1775 to Milan, in 1776 to Paris, and lived there for ten years as a fashionable teacher of the pianoforte (he transplanted the German style of playing into France, and there formed the taste for German pianoforte music). He married a wealthy heiress, but, through the Revolution, lost his fortune; for he went to London in 1790 and his property was confiscated. Under Napoleon he recovered a portion. From 1780 H. published: twelve pf. trios (Op. 1–2; opus numbers according to the Paris editions); fourteen violin sonatas with pf. (Op. 3, 4, 5, 8, 10, 11); also six sonatas (Op. 6); a Divertissement (Op. 7); and two sets of airs and variations for pianoforte alone (Op. 9); all these works rank among the best of their time.

Hüllweck, Ferdinand, b. Oct. 8, 1824, Dessau, d. July 24, 1887, Blasewitz, near Dresden, pupil of Fr. Schneider, sub-leader of the royal band at Dresden in 1844, excellent solo and ensemble violin-player. He was teacher at the Dresden Conservatorium, but retired in 1886. He published, especially, educational works for the violin.

Hülskamp, Henry (really Gustav Heinrich), a native of Westphalia, founded in 1850 at Troy (State of New York) a pianoforte manufactory, which soon became prosperous. His "symmetrical" pianofortes gained a prize at New York in 1857, and at London in 1862; in 1866 he moved his manufactory to New York.

Humfrey (Humphry, Humphrys), Pelham, b. 1647, London, d. there July 14, 1674. In 1660 he was a chorister at the Chapel Royal under H. Cooke; in 1664, and, by means of a royal stipend, he was sent to France and Italy, and studied principally under Lully at Paris, became in 1667 gentleman of the Chapel Royal, in 1672 succeeded Cooke as master of the children and composer for the royal private orchestra (violins to his Majesty, in imitation of the twenty-four *Violons du Roy* of Louis XIV.). H. was one of the most important of the old English composers. Anthems of his are to be found in Boyce's "Cathedral Music," other sacred compositions in "Harmonia Sacra" (1714), and secular songs in "Ayres, Songs, and Dialogues" (1676–84), and in J. S. Smith's "Musica Antiqua."

Hummel, (1) Johann Nepomuk, b. Nov. 14, 1778, Pressburg, d. Oct. 17, 1837, Weimar. He was the son of the music teacher of the military school at Wartberg, Joseph H., who, when that institution was dissolved in 1786, became capellmeister of Schikaneder's theatre at Vienna. It was through this that H. made the acquaintance of Mozart, who took an interest in him and gave him lessons for two years. From 1788 to 1793, accompanied by his father, H. made concert tours as far as Denmark and England, but afterwards devoted himself to serious study under Albrechtsberger and Salieri. After he had occupied, as deputy, the post of capellmeister to Prince Esterhazy (1804–11), which had become vacant owing to Haydn's infirmities of old age, he lived for some years,

without appointment, as teacher of music and composer in Vienna, was called to Stuttgart in 1816 as court capellmeister, but in 1819 exchanged this post for a similar one at Weimar. From there, travelling in the suite of the Grand Duchess Marie Paulowna, he visited, among other places, Petersburg in 1822, where he was received with unusual honours; and, leave of absence being liberally granted, he made frequent concert tours in foreign countries, including England. This mode of life continued up to his last years, when he became an invalid and was often compelled to take the baths. His compositions are a faithful reflection of his mode of playing; garlands of passages hide a lack of passion, and atone for an absence of warmth of feeling. The influence of his teacher Mozart upon his style of writing is undeniable; nevertheless, he does not approach Mozart, by a long way, in nobleness of melody, while the mechanical element, most likely brought about by the easy action of the Vienna pianos, predominates. Of his compositions the following still live: the third (A minor), the fourth (B minor), and the sixth (A♭) of his seven concertos; the D minor septet (for pf., flute, oboe, horn, viola, 'cello, and double-bass); the sonatas in F♯ minor (Op. 81), A♭ (Op. 92; four hands), and D (Op. 106); the rondos, Op. 122 ("Villageois"), 55 ("La bella capricciosa"), 11 (E♭), 109 (B minor); and the Bagatelles, Op. 107. His works amount in number to 124, among which there are five pf. sonatas for two, and three for four hands; eight violin sonatas; six trios; many rondos, caprices, fantasias (Op. 18, 49), variations (Op. 8, 9, 10, 21, 40, 57), studies, etc.; "Symphonie concertante" for pf. and violin, pf. fantasia with orchestra ("Oberons Zauberhorn"); military septet (with trumpet, Op. 114); pf. quintet (Op. 87); serenade for pf., guitar, clarinet, and bassoon; three quartets for strings; one overture (in c); three masses for four voices, orchestra, and organ; one gradual and one offertory; four operas (*Mathilde von Guise*, 1810); five ballets and pantomimes, and some cantatas. H.'s "Anweisung zum Pianofortespiel" (1828) was one of the first books to give a rational method of fingering; but it appeared, unfortunately, at a time in which the lighter, more elegant style of playing began to make way for one of greater nobility, and hence was of little avail. (*Cf.* the obituary notice of C. Montag in the *N. Z. f. Musik*, 1837; also the articles on H. by Kahlert in the *N. Z. f. Musik*, 1883.)—H.'s wife, Elisabeth, *née* Röckl, b. 1793, d. March, 1883, Weimar, was, in her youth, an opera-singer.

(2) Joseph Friedrich, b. Aug. 14, 1841, Innsbruck, studied at the Munich Conservatorium, from 1861 to 1880 theatre capellmeister at Glarus, Aix-la-Chapelle, Innsbruck, Troppau, Linz, Brünn, and Vienna. Since 1880 he has been director of the Mozarteum at Salzburg,

teacher of music at the Training College, and conductor of the Liedertafel.

(3) Ferdinand, prolific composer, b. Sept. 6, 1855, Berlin, was the son of a musician, who trained the musical talent of the boy from an early age. When only seven years old he was a small harp virtuoso, and a royal stipend facilitated further study. Between the ages of nine and twelve H. made concert tours through Europe in company with his father, and then, at last, he began to study composition regularly, first at Kullak's Akademie (1868–71), and then, up to 1875, at the Royal High School of Music, and at the school for composition of the Akademie. For pianoforte H. became the pupil of Rudorff and Grabau, and for composition, of Kiel and Bargiel. The catalogue of H.'s published compositions (Op. 1–34) includes, amongst other works, four 'cello sonatas; Phantasiestücke for 'cello and pf. ("Märchenbilder," and "Waldleben"); a Notturno for 'cello, harp, and harmonium; a pf. quintet and pf. quartet; a violin sonata; a horn sonata; a pf. suite for four hands; an overture (Op. 17); "Columbus" and "Jung Olaf" (for soli, mixed chorus, and orchestra); some songs; a Concertstück for piano (Op. 1); two concert polonaises for piano; and many other pianoforte pieces. A speciality of H.'s are the "Märchendichtungen," for solo and three-part female chorus: "Rumpelstilzchen," "Frau Holle," "Hänsel und Gretel," "Die Meerkönigin," "Die Nayaden." A concert fantasia for harp and orchestra, and a symphony, are still in manuscript, but both have been frequently performed.

Hummel, or **Hümmelchen** (Ger.), (1) a drone, (2) an obsolete organ stop with two drone pipes—either c, F or c, G.

Humor (Ger.), Humour; *Mit Humor,* humorously.

Humoreske (Ger.), a humorous piece.

Humperdinck, Engelbert, b. Sept. 1, 1854, Sieburg, on the Rhine, pupil of the Cologne Conservatorium, won the Mozart scholarship in 1876, and went to the Royal School of Music at Munich. With the Mendelssohn scholarship in 1879, he went to Italy until 1881, when he gained the Meyerbeer scholarship. From 1885–87 he was teacher at the Barcelona Conservatoire, then returned to Cologne, and in 1890 became teacher at the "Hoch" Conservatorium, Frankfort. Among his compositions are the choral works, "Das Glück von Edenhall," "Die Wallfahrt nach Kevlaar," and the opera *Hänsel und Gretel* (1894).

Hungarian. Considering the number of modern instrumental works, great and small, bearing the title H., an approximate definition, at least, of the term is needed. It is hopeless to attempt an exact definition, for music in Hungary is by no means shut out from foreign influences. The common characteristics of H. music are great freedom and variety of rhythm, a refined ornamentation of melodies by means of appoggiaturas, short shakes (Pralltriller), slides (Schleifer), turns, etc.; and in the matter of harmony, a far more powerful amalgamation of major and minor than is to be found in modern minor as represented by the so-called harmonic minor scale. We may venture to assume that the free formations of H. music are not the results either of reflection or of caprice, but the outcome of a natural development. We may glean from them, as it were, a picture of old Grecian or Arabian music in its prime, etc. The music of the Hungarians—which, for the most part, is identical with that of the Gipsies—is based, not on polyphony but monody; at any rate, up to the present day, it is of a solo kind—*i.e.* one part is prominent, while the others, like accompanying instruments, take a subordinate part. Hence the many stand-still, melody-lacking basses, and the many tremolos under a melodic, richly-moving, principal part. The rhythmic development of Gipsy music was not, as in Western musical art, hemmed in by pedantic rules and combinations (counterpoint), neither was its melody fettered by a dogma (Church Modes). Our instrumental music, written according to art-rules, was evolved from the sacred vocal music formerly predominant, and only slowly acquired that movement and rhythmical variety which the monodic instrumental music of the early Middle Ages undoubtedly possessed; but, on the other hand, the instrumental music of the Gipsies, and of other peoples living in a state of nature, was developed without restraint, and they have only assimilated what they could of Western musical art, what was possible without injury to their own; hence the similarity of the music of all peoples not influenced by the development of Western musical art. The same rhythmical peculiarities are to be found in the music of the Highlanders, Norwegians, Russians, etc. The subject is an interesting one, and might be treated in a comprehensive monograph. A few special features peculiar to H. music—such as are commonly found in Schubert and Brahms, and other ancient and modern composers—may be mentioned. Syncopation, even in the melody, frequently occurs in H. music, change of time very frequently; likewise periods of three, six (five, seven) bars, instead of two, four, and eight. The rhythmical motive 𝄾𝄾 is extremely common, likewise the suppression or delay of the chief metrical accent at the beginning of a bar by a short pause. Especially characteristic are the ornaments of the turn kind on the closing tonic:

A minor scale with leading-note before the fifth (*b*) is often spoken of as an "H. scale," or a "scale of Gipsy music"; it would be more correct in a pure minor sense (*see* MINOR KEY) to note it down from principal minor tone to principal minor tone (*c*).

The *f♯* is introduced, instead of *f*, for the same reason that *b* is taken in place of *b♭*, viz., to obtain a semitone progression (*f♯–g*). The augmented chords of the sixth are peculiar to those scales (*d*). Naturally, such a scale is not

based on any special principle, as is the case with the minor-major of Hauptmann, or our ordinary mixed minor (major-minor); it may, however, help to make clear to us the meaning of the exceedingly numerous scales, for instance, of the Arabians.

Hunke, Joseph, b. 1801, Josefstadt (Bohemia), d. Dec. 17, 1883, Petersburg, chapel master of the court choir in that city. He composed numerous sacred works, a Method of harmony, and one of composition.

Hünten, Franz, favourite pianoforte composer, b. Dec. 26, 1793, Coblence, d. there Feb. 22, 1878. He was the son of an organist, and, after good training from his father, went to the Paris Conservatoire in 1819, and studied with Pradher, Reicha, and Cherubini. He settled definitely in Paris, was much sought after as a pianoforte teacher, and still more as a fashionable composer. His easy and pleasing pianoforte pieces were very highly paid. Besides rondos, divertissements, fantasias, etc., he also wrote a trio, two violin sonatas, and a Method for the pianoforte. From 1837 he lived in his native town.—The two brothers of H. (Wilhelm, pianoforte teacher at Coblence, and Peter Ernst, engaged in a similar manner at Duisburg) also published pianoforte music of a light style.

Hurdy-gurdy (Ger. *Drehleier;* Fr. *Vielle;* Ital. *Lira tedesca* or *Ghironda ribeca, Stampella, Viola da orbo;* it was also called *Bettlerleier,* and earlier still, *Bauernleier* [*Lyra rustica, Lyra pagana*]). It is a quaint stringed-instrument of great antiquity, which was formerly very popular, and from the 10th to the 12th century played a *rôle* similar to that of the pianoforte at the present day. The construction of the H. is almost the same

now as it was nine hundred years ago. Over a sound-box, similar to that of bowed-instruments, are stretched several strings, of which one (or two tuned in unison) can be shortened by means of a keyboard; while the other two (or four tuned in pairs in unison) are free, and always give the same notes (a fifth in the bass, as in the bagpipe). A rosined wheel, thrown into motion by a handle, sets all the strings in vibration at the same time. The oldest name for the instrument was *Organistrum* (10th to 12th century). There exists a guide to the measurement and action of the keys of the Organistrum dating from the 10th century (*cf.* Gerbert, "Script." I.), according to which the instrument had a compass of eight keys (an octave); the best instruments of the 18th century had up to two octaves with chromatic notes. From about the 12th to the 15th century the H. was called *Armonie* or *Symphonie,* corrupted into *Chifonie,* also *Zampugna, Sambuca, Sambuca rotata;* in the 15th century, when it fell into discredit, the name *Vielle* (a term formerly applied to Viols) was given to it. Virdung (1511) does not consider the H. (which he calls simply *Lyra*) worthy of a description; and Pretorius (1618) speaks of it in terms of contempt ("Bawrenoder umblaufende Weiber Leyer"). Nevertheless it became (especially in France during the 18th century), together with the Musette, an extraordinarily popular instrument. Performers on the H. appeared at concerts (Laroze, Janot, Baton, and others); Methods were written for the instrument (Bonin and Corrette); instrument-makers (Baton, sen., Pierre and Jean Louvet, Delaunay, all at Paris; Lambert at Nancy, Barge at Toulouse) improved it; while composers (Baptiste) wrote sonatas, duets, etc., for it, and writers (Terrasson) sang in praise of it. At the present day it has sunk to the level of a beggar's instrument, and seems to be disappearing.

Hurel de Lamare, Jacques Michel, a distinguished 'cellist, b. May 1, 1772, Paris, d. March 27, 1823, Caen, pupil of Duport the younger. H. was engaged at the Théâtre Feydeau in 1794, travelled 1801–9 through Germany and Russia, and in 1815 retired into private life. The compositions (four 'cello concertos) which were published under his name were written by his friend Auber.

Hurtig (Ger.), quick, brisk, nimble.

Hutschenruijter, Wouter, b. Dec. 28, 1796, Rotterdam, d. there Nov. 18, 1878. He at first devoted himself to the violin, but afterwards to the horn, seriously studying theory at the same time, and making early attempts at composition. In 1821 he founded the band of the National Guard, which remained under his direction, and in 1826 the "Eruditio musica," one of the best musical societies of the Netherlands. He became, gradually, teacher at the school of music of the Society for the Advancement of Music, conductor of the "Eruditio musica" concerts, municipal musical director at Schiedam (near Rotterdam), and director of various societies there; he also organised a church choir at Schiedam, received the honorary title of capell-meister at Delft, was member of the St. Cecilia Society at Rome, etc. H. was one of the most active and meritorious of Dutch musicians. Of his numerous compositions may be mentioned: an opera, *Le Roi de Bohême*; four symphonies, two concert overtures, one overture for wind-instruments, over 150 works, partly original, partly arranged, for wind-band; a "Concert-stück" for eight kettledrums with orchestra, several masses, cantatas, songs, etc. His son, Willem, b. March 22, 1828, was also a famous performer on the horn.

Hüttenbrenner, Anselm, b. Oct. 13, 1794, Graz, d. June 5, 1868, Ober-Andritz, near Graz. He was the son of a prosperous land-owner, studied composition under Salieri at Vienna, and was on friendly terms with Beet-hoven (by whose death-bed he stood) and Schu-bert. H. composed five symphonies, ten over-tures, three operas, nine masses, three requiems, many quartets for male voices and songs, two stringed quartets, one stringed quintet, pf. fugues, sonatas, and pf. pieces; most, however, remained in manuscript. Schubert held H. in high esteem as a composer, but his works are already forgotten. Gottfr. Ritter von Leitner wrote an obituary notice of H. (Graz, 1868).

Hydraulis (*Organum hydraulicum;* Ger. *Wasser-orgel*), an instrument of the organ kind con-structed by Ctesibios at Alexandria (180 B.C.), in which the pressure of the wind was regulated by water. It was described by Hero of Alex-andria ("Spiritalia seu Pneumatica"); and this was translated into German in Vollbeding's translation of Bedos de Celles' "History of the Organ" (1793).

Hykaert, Bernhard (Ycaert), composer and theorist, of Netherland origin, during the last quarter of the 15th century, at Naples, of whom have been preserved two Lamentations (printed by Petrucci, 1506), and a Kyrie and Gloria in manuscript; also three secular songs.

Hymeneos (Gr.), a wedding-song.

Hymn (*Hymnus;* Ital. *Inno*) was originally a term of somewhat general meaning, without any indication of the poetical or musical form, as may be seen by comparing the so-called hymns of Homer and Pindar, of which the former were written in hexameters, the latter, in rhythms of the freest kind. The word H. acquired a definite meaning in the Western Church. The singing of hymns is ascribed to Hilarius (d. 368), but, probably, was introduced into the church

at a still earlier period. It was distinguished from the Alleluia and Gradual singing, in that it had no jubilations (*colorature*, as we should say nowadays); it was simpler, and more precise, and had only one note, or, at most, a neume or two notes, to one syllable of the words. The singing of hymns in the Catholic Church very much resembles, therefore, the later Prose and Sequence singing, and really only differs from it in the matter of words (the Sequences have no really regular metre, but only syllables counted off). Certain hymns bear special names, those which, for instance, are not really hymns in the old sense: the "Hymnus angelicus"; "Gloria in excelsis Deo," etc.; the "Hymnus Trinitatis" (the *Trishagion* of Good Friday); "Sanctus Deus, sanctus fortis, sanctus im-mortalis, miserere nobis"; the "Hymnus tri-umphalis"; "Sanctus Dominus, Deus Zebaoth," etc. Also the hymns arranged in several parts, when the art of counterpoint was at its zenith, are very simple in their rhythm. On the other hand, hymns of modern date, in works of various form, are mostly written with a view to grandeur of effect, for a great choir, with accompaniment of brass instruments, etc., and are of secular, as well as sacred contents.

Hymnaire (Fr.), a hymn-book.

Hymnus Ambrosianus, same as Ambrosian Hymn of Praise (q.v.).

Hypate. (*See* GREEK MUSIC.)

Hyper (Gr.), over; *Hyperdiapente,* upper-fifth; *Hyperdiatessaron,* upper-fourth, etc. In the ter-minology of the Greek transposition scales, H. has the meaning of "situated a fourth higher," *e.g.* Phrygian *g—g'*, Hyperphrygian *c'—c"*. On the other hand, the Hypermixolydian transposi-tion scale (according to Ptolemy) lay *only one* degree above the Mixolydian. In Latin H. is expressed by *Super-* (*Superdiapente*, etc.).

Hypo (Gr.), under; *Hypodiapente,* under-fifth; *Hypodiapason,* under-octave, etc. In the Greek octave species those marked H. were always a fifth lower than the plain ones; but in the transposition scales, and likewise in the Eccle-siastical Modes of the Middle Ages, only a fourth lower. Thus Dorian (octave species) *e—e'*, Hypodorian *A—a;* Dorian (transposition scale) *f'—f"* (with five flats), Hypodorian *c'—c"* (with four flats); Dorian (first Ecclesiastical Mode) *d—d'*, Hypodorian (second Ecclesiastical Mode) *A—a*. In Latin terminology H. is re-presented by *Sub-* (*Subdiapente*, etc.).

Hypoproslambanomenos (Gr.), the note below the Proslambanomenos—namely, G.

Hzbl., abbreviation of German "Holzblas-instrumente" (wood-wind instruments).

I.

I (Ital.), the masculine article, plural of *il*. (*Cf.* Gli.)

i, letter of the alphabet by which Kirnberger indicated the natural seventh (the seventh overtone), and which, by way of experiment, he introduced into composition and notation. The idea was not a new one, for, already in 1754, Tartini (" Trattato, etc.," p. 18) had used *w* in a similar manner :

It is, of course, immaterial whether tuning as a natural seventh be indicated by an *i* or a *w*. In tempered music the distinction of the natural seventh has no meaning, since, of course, like the other notes of the chord (third, fifth), it is subject to temperament. (*Cf.* the tables under Tone, Determination of.) On the other hand, theory is justified in hesitating to class the seventh, together with the third and fifth, as a fundamental interval. (*See* Seventh, Chord of the.) For experiments with instruments tuned according to just intonation (and not equal temperament) it is absolutely necessary to indicate the seventh together with the third and fifth; and Tartini's, Kirnberger's, or any other method can be adopted (*e.g.* the figure 7 could be placed against the note).

Iambus, a metrical foot consisting of a short and a long syllable : ◡ —.

Iastian. (*See* Church Modes.)

Ibach, Johannes Adolf, b. Oct. 20, 1766, d. Sept. 14, 1848. He founded a pianoforte and organ manufactory at Barmen in 1794, and from 1834 (when his son C. Rudolf entered the firm) traded under the name, " Ad. Ibach u. Sohn," and from 1839 (when his son Richard joined) as " Ad. Ibach Söhne." In 1862 the third son (Gustav J.) founded a business of his own, and from that time the old house was known as " C. Rud. u. Rich. Ibach." C. Rudolf died in 1862, and in 1869 Richard I. took the organ-building on his own account, while Rudolf (a son of C. Rudolf) continued the pianoforte department alone under the title, " Rudolf Ibach Sohn " (with a branch at Cologne), and brought the same into high repute (purveyor to the Prussian Court, prizes, etc.). He died July 31, 1892, Herrenalb (Black Forest).

Idillio (Ital.), an idyl.

Idyl (lit. " a little image "), a short pastoral composition.

Idylle (Fr.), an idyl.

Il (Ital.), the masculine, and the neuter article before consonants, with the exception of *s* followed by a consonant. (*Cf.* Lo.)

Il doppio movimento (Ital.), a movement twice as fast as the preceding one ; the time twice as fast as before.

Il fine (Ital.), the end.

Ilinski, Johann Stanislaus Graf, b. 1795 at the Castle Romanow in Poland, studied composition under Salieri and Kauer at Vienna, and wrote many sacred works (three masses, two requiems, a Te Deum, De profundis, Stabat Mater ; also a symphony, three overtures, two pf. concertos, eight quartets for strings, etc.). In 1853 I. was named privy councilor, chamberlain, and member of the senate of the Kiev University.

Il più (Ital.), the most ; *Il più presto possibile*, as quick as possible.

Imboccatura (Ital), (1) the mouthpiece of a wind-instrument ; (2) the mode of producing the tone of a wind instrument.

Imbroglio (Ital., *i.e.* " confusion "), the name given to certain intricate rhythmical combinations which confuse the time measure.

Imitando (Ital.), imitating.

Imitation is one of the most essential formative laws of musical art. As in architecture a capital of a column, a rosette, and, in fact, the whole construction of a cathedral, is the result of the working out of a limited number of patterns, so in music, a pregnant theme, a whole movement, consists, as a rule, of the repetition of a few small motives. This repetition is certainly not a simple reproduction, as is frequently the case in architecture, where an eighth or quarter of the rosette or capital corresponds completely to the rest, or where dozens of columns, turrets, windows, have similar dimensions. On the contrary, in the repetition of motives, there is not strict likeness, yet a similarity more or less marked. As musical form is determined by a great number of esthetic laws acting simultaneously, I. occurs in a variety of ways. The rhythmic-melodic motive may be literally repeated, but, by the accompanying harmony, receive each time a different meaning. Or the motive may be exactly repeated, only with change of accent, especially when it does not follow the bar measure ; or it may be repeated on other degrees of the scale, etc. The repetition of a motive on different degrees is the most frequent form of I., from which spring the high art forms of canon and fugue (q.v.), as well as " rosalias " (q.v.), which are condemned as amateurish and mechanical. At the flourishing period of the imitative style (15th to the 16th century), the art of I. had been developed to an almost incredible extent, and frequently, indeed, at the expense of expression or beauty (*cf.* COUNTERPOINT) ; and although a well-schooled composer will not entirely forego the imitative combinations which offer themselves, yet nowadays, with the best masters, imitations are quite secondary matters, and no longer the core and particular aim. The most important kinds of I. are—(1) I. by parallel motion; (2) I. by contrary motion (Inversion) ; (3) I. by augmentation ; (4) I. by diminution. Either of the last two can be combined with either of the first two. The contrapuntists from the 15th to the 17th century used, besides, the succession of notes in reverse order (*Cancrizans*), *i.e.* the whole read backwards : a piece of art-work without value, inasmuch as the listener cannot be aware of the fact that a *cancrizans* canon is being carried out; and these contrapuntists worked out, besides, all kinds of artifices (omission of the rests, or of the notes of smaller value, etc.).

Imitation pipes are those wooden pipes covered with tinfoil in " prospect," merely for the sake of ornament, in small organs. There are also " imitation " stops which do not speak, but which are added for the sake of symmetry. They often have amusing names, as, for example : *Manum de tabula* (Fingers off !), *Exaudire, Nihil, Vacat, Ductus inutilis* (Useless stop), *Noli me tangere*, etc.

Imitative Counterpoint. (*See* COUNTERPOINT, IMITATION, and CANON.)

Imitazione (Ital.), imitation.

Immer (Ger.), always, continuously; *Immer schwächer*, becoming softer and softer.

Immutabilis (Lat.), one of the *accentus ecclesiastici*.

Immyns, J o h n (year of birth and place unknown), d. April 15, 1764, at his residence in Coldbath Fields (London), originally an attorney, but he played excellently on the flute, violin, gamba, and harpsichord. Through some indiscretion he had to give up the profession of attorney, and became copyist to the Academy, and amanuensis to Dr. Pepusch. In 1741 he founded the Madrigal Society. He was a distinguished savant and collector of the music of early masters. In 1752 he was appointed lutenist at the Chapel Royal, after learning at the age of forty to play upon the lute.

Impaziente (Ital.), impatient.

Imperfection (Lat. *imperfectus*), (1) the divisibility of the notes of Measured Music (q.v.) into two equal portions. This always took place when, by a Modal Sign, Imperfect Measure

(q.v.) was indicated ; but it could also occur under special conditions with the Modal Sign for Perfect Measure. The note intended by the Modal Sign to be divided into three portions was rendered *imperfect* by writing after it a note of half its value (*e.g.* a minim after a semibreve), this note being followed by a greater one or by a Point of Division (*Punctum divisionis*) (*see* POINT NEXT THE NOTE); or it became *imperfect* if followed by more than three notes of half its value.

(The values reduced by one-half.)

—(2) *in Ligatures* (q.v.) when the last note was a breve. This value was always determined for the two last notes by the use of the *Figura obliqua* (q.v.).

Imperioso (Ital.), imperious, haughty.

Impetuoso (Ital.), impetuous.

Imponente (Ital.), imposing.

Impresario (Ital.), a manager of a theatre or concert.

Impromptu, same as IMPROVISATION ; an instantaneous thought (Lat. *in promptu*), but in modern times the title of pianoforte pieces, in the more developed song form, with the construction A-B-A (*cf.* FORM) carried out in their three principal sections (like extended minuets and marches, yet without their characteristic rhythm), as in Schubert, Chopin, Heller, etc.

Improperia (Lat.), *i.e.* "The Reproaches," the complaint of suffering love on the cross, antiphons and responses which are sung on Good Friday in place of the ordinary mass, and, indeed, to old Gregorian melodies. Only in the Sistine Chapel at Rome have the I. been sung since 1560 to *Faux bourdons*, arranged by Palestrina in several parts, in plain style, note against note.

Improprietas (Lat.), *i.e.* "improper value"; in Ligatures (q.v.) of Measured Music, the value, not of a Breve but of a Long, attached to the opening note. This takes place when, with a rising second note, the first has a stroke hanging downwards to the right or left ; also with a falling second note without stroke. (*Cf.* PROPRIETAS.)

Improvisation (from Lat. *ex improviso*, "without preparation"), an extemporaneous performance, without notes previously written down ; the name for instantaneous production whether of poetry or music. Most of the great composers have been celebrated for their I. on the pianoforte or organ. A distinction is made between I. and free fantasia ; by the first is understood strict adherence to some one form. Thus, formerly, a capable musician was expected to be able to improvise a fugue on a given theme. Bach could accomplish wonders in this line. This kind of I. presupposes immense concentration of the mental powers, while the so-called fantasia-playing is giving free rein to the fancy, and it yields moods of various colours, producing a kaleidoscopic effect. Between the two stands the varying of a given theme—a fantasia on a melody—of which every ordinary musician ought to be capable. I. is sometimes used as identical with Impromptu.

In altissimo (Ital.); thus are called the notes from g''' to f''''.

In alto (Ital.), or **in alt.**; thus are called the notes from g'' to f'''.

Incalzando (Ital.), spurring on, hastening = *stringendo*.

Indeciso (Ital.), undecided.

Indifferente, Indifferentemente, Con indifferenza (Ital.), careless, with indifference.

In distanza (Ital.), indicates that a passage has to be performed as if the sound came from a distance.

Indy, Paul Marie Vincent d', b. March 27, 1851, Paris, pupil of Diemer, Marmontel, and Lavignac, afterwards (1873) of César Franck at the Conservatoire. In 1875 he became chorus-master under Colonne, and, in order to obtain experience in orchestral detail, became drummer for three years; he then devoted himself entirely to composition, and obtained great success thereby. In 1874, Pasdeloup produced the second part ("Piccolomini") of his "Wallenstein-Trilogie" (symphonic poem). This was followed by a symphony, "Jean Hunyade"; overture to *Antony and Cleopatra*; a symphonic ballad, "La forêt enchantée"; a symphonic pf. concerto on an Alpine theme; legend for orchestra, "Sauge fleurie"; scena for baritone and orchestra; "La Chevauchée du Cid"; a pf. quartet (in A); and a suite for trumpet, two flutes, and stringed quartet; a "Lied" for 'cello and orchestra; pf. pieces, sacred and secular songs. The one-act comic opera, *Attendez-moi sous l'orme*, met with but little success (1882); but, on the other hand, the dramatic legend, *Le chant de la cloche* (1884) gained the prize offered by the city of Paris. I. pays homage to the modern school (Schumann, Berlioz, Wagner).

Infernale (Ital.), infernal, hellish.

Inflatilia (Lat.), wind instruments.

Infrabass (Lat.-Ger.), an organ stop of 16-feet pitch, a sub-bass.

In fretta (Ital.), in haste.

Inganno (Ital.), lit. "deceit"; a deceptive cadence or close (q.v.).

Ingegneri, Marco Antonio, b. about 1545, Venice, was, already in 1576, maestro di cappella of the principal church at Cremona, afterwards in the service of the Duke of Mantua. He was the teacher of Monteverde. He published a

book of masses à 5 and 8 (1573); a book of masses à 5 (1587); four books of madrigals à 4 and 5 (1578, 1579, 1580, 1584); "Sacræ cantiones" à 5 (1576); "Sacræ cantiones" à 7 and 16 (! 1589), and "Responsoria hebdomadæ sanctæ" (1581). Separate madrigals are also to be found in Hubert Waelrant's "Symphonica angelica" (1594), likewise in Pierre Phalèse's "Madrigali pastorali a sette" (1604), and "Madrigali a otto voci" (1596). Dehn in his "Sammlung älterer Musik aus dem 16. und 17. Jahrhundert" (1837) gives one of I.'s motets.

Ingressa. (*See* INTROITUS.)

In lontananza (Ital.). The same as *in distanza*.

Inner parts. Those parts which lie between the extreme parts, *i.e.* between the highest and the lowest part.

Inner pedal, a sustained, or holding, note in an inner part.

Innig (Ger.), with deep, genuine feeling.

Inno (Ital.), a hymn.

Innocente (Ital.), innocent.

In partito (Ital.), in score.

Inquieto (Ital.), restless, uneasy.

Insanguine, Giacomo, Neapolitan opera composer, b. 1744 Monopoli (Naples), d. 1796, Naples, pupil of the Conservatorio di Sant' Onofrio, and, for a short time, teacher at that institution. He then devoted himself entirely to dramatic composition, and, from 1772 to 1782, produced nine operas, for the most part serious (*Didone, Arianna, Adriano,* etc.). He also wrote some sacred works, and pieces for organ and clavier. He lacked originality.

Insensibilmente (Ital.), imperceptibly.

Inständig (Ger.), urgent, pressing.

Instante (Ital.), urgent, pressing.

Institut de France is the great French institution to the various sections of which the name Académie is given. (*Cf.* ACADEMY.) The *Prix de l'Institut* (bestowed, among others, on Félicien David in 1867) is something quite different from the *Grand Prix de Rome*, which can be obtained every year by a pupil of the Conservatoire. The *Prix de l'Institut* was founded in 1859 by Napoleon III., and is offered every second year (20,000 francs), but in turn to the five sections of the Institut, so that it is offered by the Academy of Arts only once in ten years; the recipient of the prize can be a poet, painter, sculptor, or musician. The prize is bestowed, without competition, in order to encourage serious efforts in the department of art or science.

Instrumental Music is, in contradistinction to vocal music, music performed by instruments. As it is usual to count vocal music accompanied by instruments as vocal music, the term I. M. has come commonly to mean music performed by instruments *only*, from which, therefore, song is entirely excluded. Historically, however, the development of accompanying I. M. goes hand in hand with that of I. M. generally, but not with that of vocal music, as it is dependent upon the development of instruments. Whether pure or accompanied I. M. be the older, is a vexed question; yet it is reasonable to suppose that *wind instruments* were first used apart from singing, but *stringed instruments* first for accompanying the voice; for one person could sing and play upon a stringed instrument at the same time, but not sing and blow simultaneously. Music, however, played by several persons (so soon as it is something more than the marking of a rhythm) represents a higher stage of development. With the Greeks we find solo flute-playing (Aulesis) already developed to such a high pitch in the 6th century B.C. that Sakadas of Argos (cir. 585), at the Pythian games, claimed equality for it with the other arts. Also independent cithara-playing was, not long after (cir. 559), said to have been brought into high repute by Agelaos of Tegea. The accompanying I. M. of the ancients was nothing more than joining-in in unison or in the octave. Until late in the Middle Ages *brass instruments* were not used for really musical purposes, but only in the army, for signals, or in processions and at sacrifices, where a massive effect was the special aim (Tuba, Lituus, Buccina). It was only in the festivals of the Middle Ages at royal weddings, or at the Mysteries (sacred dramas), that there was a beginning of instrumental music in several parts, and of an artistic nature.

A new phase of development of I. M. begins with the appearance of stringed instruments. The earliest traces of instruments of the violin genus in the West occur in the 9th century A.D., if not still further back. (*Cf.* INSTRUMENTS, STRINGED.) The instrument for accompaniment, or for solo, of the Troubadours, or the favourite instrument of travelling musicians, with which, wherever they went, they accompanied the dance, was the fiddle (Fidula mentioned by Ottfried, Viola, Vielle, Giga, Gigue, Geige). This instrument quickly developed, and passed through all sorts of forms, so that at the beginning of the 16th century we find a great number of stringed instruments, which, constructed of various sizes, were used to strengthen, or replace voices in the performance of complicated vocal pieces of the great contrapuntists. The oldest pieces in several parts specially written for instruments are dances, which, however, have no decided instrumental character. The movement characteristic of instrumental compositions first appeared in the course of the 16th century in the solo-playing of keyboard instruments and lutes; when these imitated a sustained vocal composition, "colouring" had to make amends for the lack of tone. This manner was transplanted from the clavier to the organ, until at last, when the original cause

had fallen into oblivion, it was used both for stringed and wind instruments. Modern I. M. has three points of departure: compositions for (*a*) organ, (*b*) lute, and (*c*) accompanied solo vocal music. Organ music developed further in the direction indicated, imitating the forms of vocal music in a free, ornamental manner; the highest pitch was reached in the organ and clavier fugues of Bach. Writing for lute led directly to the light clavier style of the French (Couperin, Rameau) and of the Italians (through D. Scarlatti), which in Bach, and especially in his sons Friedemann, Phil. Emanuel and Joh. Christian, was amalgamated with that of the organ. The accompanied solo songs, both in the opera (q.v.) as in the church (Viadana's concertos), became the models for the accompaniment of an instrumental melody (or of several concertante melodies) by a bass instrument (likewise with indications of the harmony; *see* CONTINUO). Thus arose the violin sonatas à 2 and à 3, which play an important *rôle* in the history of I. M. As first forms of pure I. M. (absolute music) there were in organ music, and in clavier writing derived therefrom, the Intonations, Ricercari, Canzone, Sonatas, Toccatas, and Fugues; in lute and French clavier style, the dance movements, which gradually developed into characteristic pieces, terminating in the suite (chamber sonata) in the monodic instrumental style (violin music), and in arias varied, etc.; so that, finally, the church sonata, *i.e.* our sonata of to-day, was completely prefigured. The orchestral music, in which at first the four vocal parts were merely replaced by instruments (the introductions and ritornelli of the earliest operas), profited gradually by these progresses of the various styles and adopted the results obtained. Thus the symphony gradually turned into the orchestral sonata, not directly, but by way of the *Concerto grosso* (*Cf.* SONATA, SYMPHONY, SUITE, CHAMBER MUSIC, etc.)

Instrumentation, distribution of the parts of an orchestral composition among the several instruments. One must imagine the composer as first sketching his work, *i.e.* a purely musical conception without any regard to instruments, and afterwards filling in details, and allotting to the various instruments their respective parts. It is usual also to speak of the I. of a Beethoven sonata, etc., if the same be arranged for orchestra. Old orchestral works, if revived, require a change of I., because many of the instruments (Theorbo, Gamba, etc.) in use during the 17th and 18th centuries are obsolete. Since Haydn gave an independent character to the instruments of the orchestra, of which each speaks a different language, it is no longer right for a composer first to compose and then score; rather must he keep in mind the full apparatus of the orchestra selected, and thus the sketch is only an abbreviated form of notation.—A *Method of Instrumentation* teaches the pupil the tone, compass, quality, technical treatment, and suitable combinations of instruments; useful directions are to be found in Marx's " School of Composition " (Vols. III. and IV.), and Lobe's (Vol. II.), as well as in special treatises on I. by Berlioz, Gevaert (translated into German by Riemann), Riemann's " Katechismus der Musikinstrumente " (1888 ; in English, " Catechism of Musical Instruments " [Augener, 9201]), etc. *Cf.* Lavoix, " Histoire de l'instrumentation " (which obtained the Académie prize in 1878). (*Cf.* ORCHESTRA.)

Instruments. (*Cf.* Articles of words in italics.) Musical instruments can be divided into stringed I., wind I., and I. of percussion. (1) *Stringed I.* may be subdivided into *bowed* I. and *harp* I. (From lack of a proper word the latter one is coined. It is surely better than to speak of I. which are plucked, or pinched, or pulled, and which do not, besides, include I. of the clavier kind.) *Bowed I.* can be subdivided into such as have frets (*Viols, Lyres* : obsolete), and into those without frets (*Rebek, Vielle, Gigue, Violin, Viola, Violoncello, Double Bass, Trumbscheit*) ; the stringed I. with keyboard (*Hurdygurdy, Schlüsselfiedel*, and *Bogenflügel*) form a special class. (2) *Wind I.* are divided into *wood-wind* and *brass*, or, better still, from the mode of producing the sound into *lip-* (labial-) *pipes* and *reed-* (tongue-) *pipes ;* the *organ,* together with instruments related to it (*Harmonium, barrel-organ, regal, orchestrion*, etc.), consists of a combination of many wind instruments. (3) *I. of percussion* are of two kinds. Those which are properly tuned have, relatively speaking, a higher artistic value (*kettle-drums, bells* [carillon, Stahlspiel], *straw-fiddle*), and those of indefinite pitch (*drums, cymbals, triangle, tam-tam, castanets, tambourine*, etc.). The *Adiaphonon* (Gabelklavier) is an instrument which cannot well be included in any of the above-mentioned classes. The Æolian Harp can scarcely be reckoned among musical instruments, but it is otherwise with the *Anemochord*, formed after it. From among the numerous ephemeral inventions may be named the *Harmonica,* the *Clavicylinder,* the *Euphonium,* and the *Pyrophone.* I. for the purpose of investigations connected with acoustics are the *monochord,* the *tuning-fork*, and the *siren.* (*Cf.* AUTOMATIC MUSICAL MACHINES.)

Intavolare (Ital.), to write in tablature notation, *i.e.* to transcribe the usual (measured) notation into the special kind of notation specially used for the organ, likewise for the lute, etc. (*Cf.* TABLATURE.)

Integer valor (*notarum*), the average time value in measured music, the ordinary note value (mean time value) in contradistinction to that changed by diminution, augmentation, or proportion (*see* the respective articles) ; *Prolatio major* also changed the *tempo.* The determinations usual at the present day (*Allegro, Adagio*, etc.) only came into vogue about 1600 ; before

that there were no exact time determinations. The I. V. changed considerably from the period of the invention of the measured note (q.v.) up to 1600, *i.e.* the Brevis of the 13th century had a value somewhat similar to the Minima of the 16th century, and to the Semi-minima (the crotchet) of the 17th century. Michael Pretorius (1618) fixed the I.V. (mean time value) of the Brevis at about $\frac{1}{16}$ of a minute, *i.e.* the crotchet at eighty of the Mälzel Metronome, which agrees fairly well with the usage of the present day.

Interludium (Lat.), interlude, especially in connection with the transition on the organ from one verse of a chorale to another.

Intermedio, Intermezzo (Ital.). This was the name given to the musical entertainments, introduced between the acts of a play, which sprang up in Italy towards the end of the 16th century. They were used, first in tragedies, but, later on, also in serious opera. At first the *Intermezzi* between the various acts were not connected, but each treated of a different mythological subject ; gradually, however, an *Intermedio* was evolved from the *Intermezzi,* *i.e.* a second action, of a kind more or less humorous, as a contrast to the action of the principal piece, which was played in sections with the latter. Pergolesi's *La serva padrona* was an *Intermedio* of this kind. The next step was the loosening of this humorous small opera, which had gradually increased in dimension, from its unnatural entanglement with one of a serious kind, and the *Opera buffa* sprang into existence. The oldest Intermezzi were by no means written in the *stilo rappresentativo* of the Florentine music-drama, but were composed of madrigals; also, they were at times relieved by instrumental performances (likewise madrigals). Later on the *ballet divertissement* took the place of the I. At the present day we are strict with regard to the purity of style of the I., and of the principal piece ; and the only form in which they still exist (in the drama) is that of the intercalated ballet, and that of *entr'acte* music.

Intermezzo, same as Episode (*cf.* INTERMEDIO), probably used for the first time by Schumann as the name for a connected series of pianoforte pieces (Op. 4) without any reference to the word-meaning. S. perhaps regarded them as *hors d'œuvre*, intermediate numbers for a concert programme ? Heller and Brahms have also made use of the title I.

Interrogativus (Lat.), one of the *accentus ecclesiastici*.

Interrotto (Ital.), interrupted.

Interval is the ratio of two tones with regard to their pitch, vibration numbers, or length of sound-waves (length of strings). Intervals are distinguished as consonant and dissonant. (1) *Consonant Intervals* are those which together form tones of one clang (of a major or a minor chord), viz.: (a) the *Unison* (duplication of the same tone), with vibration and string-length ratio 1 : 1; the *Octave* (the repetition of the same tone in the nearest higher, and in the nearest lower position: the ratio of the fundamental- to the second over-tone (cf. OVER-TONE), with the vibration numbers 1 : 2, and the ratio of the string-lengths 2 : 1 (in vibration ratios the smaller figure always belongs to the lower tone, and in string-lengths ratios, on the other hand, to the upper; both ratios are reciprocal to one another); the *Double Octave* 1 : 4 (4 : 1), triple octave 1 : 8 (8 : 1), and thus all octave extensions of the unison. (b) The *Fifth*, with the ratio of the first tone to the fifth 2 : 3 (3 : 2); the *Twelfth* (the octave extension of the fifth ratio of the fundamental tone to the third over-tone) 1 : 3 (3 : 1); the *Fourth* (inversion of the fifth by placing the fifth degree below, or the fundamental tone in the octave above) is the ratio of the first degree of the scale to the fourth, 3 : 4 (4 : 3); the *Eleventh* (octave extension of the fourth, 3 : 8, also 8 : 3), likewise all further octave extensions of the eleventh and the twelfth. (c) The (major) *Third*, the ratio of the first tone to the third in the major scale, 4 : 5 (5 : 4); the (major) *Tenth* (octave extension of the major third), 2 : 5 (5 : 2); the (major) *Seventeenth* (second octave extension of the major third, ratio of the fundamental tone to the fifth over-tone), 1 : 5 (5 : 1); the *Minor Sixth* (inversion of the major third; cf. FOURTH), 5 : 8 (8 : 5); the *Minor Thirteenth* (octave extension of the minor sixth), 5 : 16 (16 : 5), likewise all further extensions of the major seventeenth and minor thirteenth. (d) The *Minor Third*, the ratio of the first tone to the third of the minor scale, 5 : 6 (6 : 5); the (major) *Sixth* (inversion of the minor third, ratio of the third to the fifth over-tone), 3 : 5 (5 : 3); the (major) *Thirteenth* (octave extension of the major sixth), 3 : 10 (10 : 3); the *Minor Tenth* (octave extension of the minor third), 5 : 12 (12 : 5); the *Minor Seventeenth* (second octave extension of the minor third), 5 : 24 (24 : 5), and all other octave extensions of the major sixth and minor third. Expressed in notes, the consonant intervals are as follows:—

—(2) *Dissonant Intervals* are those which are composed of tones which do not belong to the same clang; the vibration figures (likewise ratios of string-length) are easily found, if fifth and third steps are taken from one of the two tones of the interval until the other tone is reached. The superfluous octave extensions are got rid of by shortenings with the help of the number 2. For practical purposes, the best plan is to take

the figure 3 as factor for every fifth-step, and the figure 5 for every third-step; the vibration number of the second tone is then found, and that of the other is the nearest smaller, or nearest larger power of 2 (according as it lies below, or above the second tone). The I., thus determined, is always less than the octave. If it be required to extend it by an octave, one has only to multiply the greater vibration figure by 2. For instance, take $c : d$ the major second; from c, d is reached by two fifth-steps (c-g-d), and the factors are therefore 3.3 = 9; the 9 is the vibration figure for d, and if the nearest smaller power of 2 (= 8) be taken, the second $c : d = 8 : 9$; but if the nearest greater power of 2 (= 16), then the minor seventh, $d : c' = 9 : 16$. In a similar manner the augmented second $c : d\sharp$ will be found from c-g-b-d$\sharp$ (one fifth-step, two third-steps = 3.5.5), to be 64 : 75, and its inversion, the diminished seventh 75 : 128. The number of dissonant intervals is very great, as many of them can be determined in various ways, for instance: $c : d\sharp$ as c-g-b-d$\sharp$, or c-g-d-a-e-b-d$\sharp$ (one fifth and two thirds, or five fifths and one third). The most important are:—(1) the *chromatic second*, 24 : 25 or 128 : 135 (the string-length ratios are always the inversions of the vibration ratios); (2) its inversion, the *diminished octave*, 25 : 48 or 135 : 256; (3) the (diatonic) *minor second*, 15 : 16; (4) its inversion, the *major seventh*, 8 : 15; (5) the *major second*, 8 : 9 or 9 : 10; (6) its inversion, the *minor seventh*, 9 : 16 or 5 : 9; (7) the *augmented second*, 64 : 75; (8) its inversion, the *diminished seventh*, 75 : 128; (9) the *diminished fourth*, 25 : 32; (10) the *augmented fifth*, 16 : 25; (11) the *augmented third*, 512 : 675; (12) its inversion, the *diminished sixth*, 675 : 1024; (13) the *augmented fourth*, 18 : 25 or 32 : 45; (14) its inversion, the *diminished fifth*, 25 : 36 or 45 : 64. In notes, the dissonant Is. mentioned (counting from c taken as 1) are as follows:

The *augmented octave* is an octave extension of the chromatic second, the *minor ninth* an octave extension of the diatonic minor second, etc. Consonant intervals are either *perfect* (unison, octave, fifth, fourth, and their extensions), or *major* or *minor* (thirds, sixths, tenths, thirteenths, seventeenths); dissonant Is. are either *major* or *minor* (seconds, sevenths, and ninths), or *augmented* or *diminished*. The inversions of perfect Is. are perfect, those of major, minor and *vice versâ*, those of augmented, diminished, and *vice versâ*.

Intimo (Ital.), inward, heartfelt.—*Con intimo sentimento*, with deep, genuine feeling.

Intonation (Ger. *Anstimmung*) is (1), in Catholic Church music, the introductory chant of the priest in antiphons, psalms, etc. The I. fixes the mode in which the melody is set, and this differs on high and ordinary festivals, and on ordinary week-days. One speaks of a psalm being *intoned*, of a priest *intoning* the Gloria, etc.—(2) In connection with instruments the term I. is used to express the equalisation of the various tones, *i.e.* by perfecting all the parts and placing them together, or the last touches given to remove any small inequality of clang-colour; also, in the organ, small changes in the wind-way of lip-pipes, or in the tongues of reed-pipes; in the pianoforte, the exact position of the hammers, inspection of the leather coverings, etc.—(3) The term I. is also used in connection with the human voice, and refers to tone-formation, especially in reference to pitch (pure or faulty I.; for the latter the Germans have the expression " Detonieren ").

Intoniereisen (Ger.; " tuning-knife "), an instrument used by organ-builders in the first tuning of pipes; it must not be confused with the Tuning-horn (q.v.). The instrument is knife-shaped at one end, so as to widen or narrow at pleasure the wind-way; or, eventually, to be able to cut away a piece from the upper-lip or from the mouth of the pipe.

Intrade. (*See* ENTRÉE.)

Intreccio (Ital.), intrigue; a short stage-piece.

Intrepidamente (Ital.), fearlessly, boldly.

Introduction (Lat.), a term used specially for the short *Largo*, *Adagio*, *Andante*, or similar movement which precedes the *Allegro* of symphonies, sonatas, etc.

Introitus (Lat. " entry "), in the Ambrosian Ritual named *Ingressa.* It was originally a whole psalm sung by the choir, while the celebrant, holding the mass, moved from the sacristy to the altar; but it was afterwards shortened. Next was added to the psalm the " Gloria patri et filio," the " Gloria " by the celebrant, and the " Patri et filio, etc." by the choir, and then followed the antiphon. At the present day the I. is again coming somewhat more into vogue.

Inventions (Lat.), a term used in a sense similar to Impromptus. (*Cf.* Bach's two-part I.; the three-part I., on the other hand, he called " Symphonies.")

Inventionshorn. According to the statement of the Dresden " Hofmusiker," A. J. Hampel, this was the Waldhorn as improved by the instrument-maker J. Werner, at Dresden, about 1760. This was accomplished by applying crooks of various lengths to the tube of the horn, thus altering its natural scale. The system of crooks was also transferred to the trumpet (*Inventionstrompete*). Since the introduction of valves, crooks are rarely used.

Inversion (Ger. *Umkehrung*) is an exchange of the relationship of above and below, so that what was above becomes below, and what was below, above. Varied is the *rôle* which I. plays in the theory of composition. There is—

(1) an I. of *intervals*, which is simply an octave transposition of the upper note below the lower, or of the lower above the higher. The I. of an interval is always that other interval which completes the octave. There are the following Is. :—

   (1) Second—Seventh;
   (2) Third—Sixth;
   (3) Fourth—Fifth;

and further, after I., a perfect interval remains perfect, a major becomes minor, and a diminished augmented, and *vice versâ*.

(2) *I. of chords.*—By this is understood the change of bass note, *i.e.* all chords are named I. which do not have the natural bass note. Now the natural bass note, according to the usual definition, is the one which is lowest when the notes of the chord are placed one above another at the distance of a third, each from the other. There are therefore three positions of the Triad (q.v.), for instance, *c-e-g*, and its two Is. :

   (a) *Fundamental position* (bass note *c*).
   (b) 1st *Inversion* (bass note *e*) = chord of 6-3, *e, c, g.*
   (c) 2nd *Inversion* (bass note *g*) = chord of 6-4, *g, c, e.*

The *chord of the Seventh* (q.v.) has three Is.; for example: *g, b, d, f.*

   (a) *Fundamental position* (bass note *g*).
   (b) 1st *Inversion* (bass note *b*) = chord of 6-5, *b, d, f, g.*
   (c) 2nd *Inversion* (bass note *d*) = chord of 6-4-3, *d, f, g, b.*
   (d) 3rd *Inversion* (bass note *f*) = chord of 2, *f, g, b, d.*

(3) *I. of a Motive* (theme in *contrary motion*), one of the most interesting devices of imitation. It consists in this, that all the melodic progressions of the theme are made in reverse direction (rising instead of falling, falling instead of rising), in Italian *per moto contrario* or *al rovescio.* The I. of the theme occurs occasionally in

Fugue, also in the Gigue which has fugal working.

Invitatorium (Lat.; "invitation") is the name given in the Roman Catholic service to the antiphon sung at the Nocturnes, *i.e.* the one beginning the service for the following day.

Ionian (Iastian) Mode. (*See* CHURCH MODES and GREEK MUSIC.)

Ira (Ital.), anger, wrath, passion.—*Con ira,* angrily, passionately.

Irato (Ital.), angry, passionate.

Irgang, Friedrich Wilhelm, b. Feb. 23, 1836, Hirschberg (Schleswig), pupil at the school of composition of the Royal Academy, Berlin (Grell and Bach), received further training from Proksch at Prague, opened a music school at Görlitz (1863), became organist of the Dreifaltigkeitskirche there in 1878, and in 1881 organist and teacher of music at the Paedagogium at Züllichau. Besides various pianoforte pieces, I. brought out an "Allgemeine Musiklehre" (several times republished), and a "Harmonielehre."

Ironicamente (Ital.), ironically.

Isaak, Heinrich (Isaac, Izac, Ysack, Yzac; in Italy also Arrigo Tedesco [Heinrich der Deutsche], or in barbaric Latin Arrhigus), one of the most distinguished contrapuntists of the last quarter of the 15th, and first of the 16th century, probably a contemporary of Josquin, *i.e.* born about 1450. Though Glarean speaks of him as Tedesco or Germanus, I. appears to have been no German, but a Netherlander, for in his will he is named "Ugonis de Flandria." Documents testify to the fact that I. resided for a time in Ferrara, and that he was afterwards organist to Lorenzo di Medici, surnamed the "Magnificent." From there he went to Rome, and, finally, received an appointment at the court of the Emperor Maximilian I. as "Musicus" ("Symphonista regis" is the title given to him in the documents, probably the overseer of the instrumentalists), which he held until his death (about 1517); and then his pupil, L. Senfl, received the appointment, and held it until 1519, the year of the death of the Emperor Maximilian I. The following masses of I. have been preserved: *Charge de deuil, Misericordia domini, Quant jay au cor, La Spagna, Comme femme* (these five were printed by Petrucci as "Misse Henrici Izac," 1506); *Salva nos, Frölich Wesen* (in Graphäus' "Missæ XIII.," 1539); *O præclara* (in Petrejus' "Liber XV. missarum," 1539); *Missa solemnis; De Apostolis [Magne Deus, Kyrie]* (in Isaak's "Chorale Constantinum," 1550); *Carminum* and *Une musque de Biscay* (in Rhaw's "Opus decem missarum," 1541); besides masses in manuscript at the Munich, Vienna, and Brussels libraries, ten of which have not been printed. Motets are to be found in Petrucci's "Odhecaton," "Canti B," and "Canti C" (1501–5),

in his first book of the motets à 5 (1505), in Kriesstein's "Selectissimæ . . . cantiones" (1540), and in many other collections, especially German ones of the 16th century. The part-songs of I. are models of their kind, many of which, in the form in which he wrote them, produce an excellent effect even at the present day; they are to be found in Ott's "115 guter newer Liedlein" (1544) and Forster's "Auszug guter teutscher Liedlein" (1539). The Munich court and state library is especially rich in manuscripts of I.'s compositions, and these became part of the music treasures of the court chapel, probably through Senfl.

Isidorus (Hispalensis), St., Bishop of Seville, b. about 570, Cartagena, d. April 4, 636. He wrote in his "Originum sive etymologiarum libri XX." much valuable information concerning music; Gerbert collected the special passages and printed them as "Sententiæ de musica" in his "Scriptores" (I.).

Isnardi, Paolo, b. Ferrara, monk, afterwards superior, of the cloister Monte Cassino, and maestro at Ferrara. He composed numerous masses, psalms, faux-bourdons, motets, and madrigals, which appeared in a special edition between 1561–94.

Isouard, Niccolò (also simply Niccolò de Malta), b. 1775, Malta, d. March 23, 1818, Paris; he was intended for a banker, but, contrary to his father's wish, gave his attention to music, and studied at Palermo under Amendola, and at Naples under Sala and Guglielmi, while employed in a banking firm. In 1795 he entirely gave up the career of a merchant and made his *début*, under the name of "Niccolò," at Florence with his opera *L'Avviso ai Maritati*, which, however, met with scanty success. After he had written for Livorno an *Artaserse* which pleased better, he became organist of St. John's of Jerusalem at La Valette, and afterwards maître de chapelle to the Order of Malta. After the suppression of the order, he wrote a series of operas for a theatre at La Valette, and went to Paris in 1799, where he found a devoted friend in R. Kreutzer. Already in the same year he produced a comic opera, *Le Tonnelier,* which was quickly followed by some others. He first made his mark with *Michel Ange* (1802), and reached the zenith of his fame with *Cendrillon* (1810). The return of Boieldieu (q.v.) from Russia resulted in a lively competition between the two composers, who enjoyed almost equal popularity; this had a most beneficial influence on I., and was instrumental in producing his best works, *Jeannot et Colin* and *Joconde*. A disorderly course of life, and sorrow caused by the preference shown to Boieldieu, who was elected by the Institut as successor to Méhul, soon brought about his death. Altogether I. wrote fifty operas, a number of masses, motets, psalms, cantatas, canzonettes, and songs.

Israel, Karl, famous writer on music, b. Jan. 9, 1841, Heiligenrode (Electoral Hesse), d. April 2, 1881, Frankfort; he first studied theology at Marburg, became a pupil of the Leipzig Conservatorium and settled in Frankfort, where he became highly esteemed as musical critic. He published: " Musikalische Schätze in Frankfort-a.-M." (1872), and " Musikalien der ständischen Landesbibliothek zu Kassel " (1881), two comprehensive catalogues of importance to musical bibliography; besides " Frankfurter Konzertchronik von 1713–80 " (1876), and, from 1873–74, also contributions on bibliography to the *Allgemeine Musikalische Zeitung.*

Istesso (Ital.), the same; *L'istesso tempo,* the same *tempo.*

Istromento (Ital.), instrument.

Italian Sixth. The chord of the Italian sixth consists of a bass note, its major third, and augmented sixth—for instance, $a\flat$, c', $f'\sharp$.

Ite missa est (Lat.), the concluding words of the mass.

Ivry, Marquis Richard d', b. Feb. 4, 1829, Beaune (Côte d'Or), a gifted amateur, since 1854, at Paris; wrote the operas : *Fatima, Quentin Metzys, La Maison du Docteur, Omphale et Pénélope,* and *Les Amants de Vérone (Romeo and Juliet,* 1864, under pseudonym Richard Yrvid, lately thoroughly revised) ; also songs, hymns, etc.

Izac. (*See* ISAAK.)

J.

Jachet (Jaquet). (*See* BERCHEM.)

Jachmann-Wagner. (*See* WAGNER [9].)

Jack, (1) in the harpsichord the upright slip of wood on the back end of the key-lever, to which is attached a crow-quill or piece of hard leather projecting at right angles. The quill or piece of leather served as a plectrum with which the corresponding string was plucked.—(2) A part of the action of the pianoforte, the escapement lever, which is also called " hopper."

Jackson, (1) William, b. May, 1730, Exeter, d. there July 12, 1803 ; for a time pupil of John Travers at London, and, for a long time, teacher of music at Exeter ; in 1777 organist and master of the choristers at the cathedral there. He composed several operas (*Lycidas, The Lord of the Manor,* and *The Metamorphosis*), a large number of pf. sonatas and sacred works (of no importance); he also wrote " Thirty Letters on Various Subjects " (1782, some on music) ; " Observations on the Present State of Music (1791) ; and " Four Ages, together with Essays on Various Subjects " (1798).

(2) William, b. Jan. 9, 1816, Masham, son of a miller, and completely self-taught, d. April 15, 1866, organist of St. John's Church and afterwards of the Horton Lane Chapel (Bradford) ; conductor there of the Choral (male voices), and of the Festival Choral Society. He composed many sacred and secular works, and also published a " Manual of Singing " which passed through several editions.

Jacob, (1) Benjamin, b. 1778, London, became organist of Surrey Chapel 1794, d. Aug. 24, 1829, London ; one of the most famous organists of his time. He composed psalm tunes (" National Psalmody ") and glees.

(2) Fr. Aug. Leb. (*See* JAKOB.)

Jacobs, Eduard, 'cello virtuoso, b. 1851, Hal (Belgium), studied under Servais at the Brussels Conservatoire ; he was first engaged in the court band at Weimar, and, in 1885, succeeded his teacher at Brussels.

Jacobsohn, Simon E., excellent violinist, b. Dec. 24, 1839, Mittau (Courland), pupil of the Leipzig Conservatorium, 1860 leader of the band at Bremen, and 1872 of Thomas's orchestra, New York, afterwards teacher at Cincinnati Conservatorium ; he resides now in Chicago.

Jacobsthal, Gustav, b. March 14, 1845, Pyritz (Pomerania), studied from 1863–70, and qualified himself in 1872 at the Strassburg University as lecturer on music, and became, in 1875, unattached professor. His treatise, " Die Mensuralnotenschrift des 12. und 13. Jahrhunderts" (1871), is a meritorious work.

Jacotin (real name Jacob Godebrye), Dutch contrapuntist, chaplain at Nôtre Dame, Antwerp, about 1479, d. March 24, 1529. Some of his compositions are to be found in Petrucci's " Motetti della Corona " (1519) ; in Salblinger's " Concentus octo, sex," etc. (1545) ; in Ott's " Novum opus musicum " (1537) ; chansons in Rhaw's " Bicinia " (1545) ; in the collections of Attaignant (1530–35, in fifth, sixth, and ninth books) ; in Le Roy and Ballard (in sixth book of the " Chansons nouvellement composées," 1556) ; and in " Recueil des recueils," 1563–64. Masses in manuscript at Rome.

Jacquard, Léon Jean, b. Nov. 3, 1826, Paris, d. there March 27, 1886, distinguished 'cellist, pupil of Norblin at the Conservatoire, where from 1877 he was professor of his instrument.

Jadassohn, Salomon, b. Aug. 13, 1831, Breslau, studied at the college there, then became pupil of the Leipzig Conservatorium (1848), went from there to Liszt at Weimar (1849), and at last became special pupil for composition of Hauptmann's at Leipzig. At the conclusion of his studies he settled as teacher in Leipzig, became in 1866 conductor of the choral society "Psalterion," from 1867–69 was capellmeister of the "Euterpe," and, finally, in 1871 was appointed teacher of theory, composition, and specially of instrumentation, at the Conservatorium. Next to Reinecke, J. exercises at the present moment the strongest influence as teacher. In 1887 he received from the University of Leipzig the title of Dr. Phil. h. c. Especially well known are his works written in canon form—the serenade for orchestra (Op. 35), the pf. serenade (Op. 8), the four-hand ballet music (Op. 58), and the vocal duets in canonic form (Op. 9, 36, 38, 43). In all, J. has written over a hundred works, among which are :—four symphonies, two overtures, four serenades, pf. concerto in F minor (Op. 89), three pf. trios, two pf. quintets, pf. quartet (Op. 77), two quartets for strings, preludes and fugues for pf., etc. For chorus and orchestra : Psalm 100 (à 8, with alto solo, Op. 60), "Vergebung" (with soprano solo, Op. 54), "Verheissung" (Op. 55), "Trostlied" (with organ ad lib., Op. 65) ; for male chorus and orchestra : "An den Sturmwind" (Op. 61) ; further, Psalm 13 (for soprano, alto, and organ, Op. 43), motets, part-songs, pf. pieces, etc. His thoroughly conservative method of teaching as theorist is expounded in his practical instruction books : "Harmonielehre" (1883, 2nd ed. 1887), with key (1886) ; "Kontrapunkt" (1884), with key (1887) ; "Kanon und Fuge" (1884) ; "Die Formen in den Werken der Tonkunst" (1889) ; and "Lehrbuch der Instrumentation" (1889), all of which have also appeared in English. His wife Helene (d. Dec. 31, 1891) was an esteemed teacher of singing.

Jadin, (1) L o u i s E m m a n u e l, b. Sept. 21, 1768, Versailles, d. July, 1853, Paris, son of the court violinist Jean J., "page de la musique" to Louis XVI., pianoforte pupil of his brother Hyacinthe, 1789 accompanist at the Théâtre de Monsieur (until 1792), member of the band of the Garde Nationale at the time of the Revolution, for which he wrote marches, hymns, etc. In 1802 he succeeded his brother as professor at the Conservatoire, then, in 1806, became conductor at the Théâtre Molière, and "Gouverneur des pages," 1814–30. After this he retired, composed about forty operas and operettas for various Paris theatres, several patriotic choruses ("Ennemis des tyrans," "Citoyens levez-vous," etc.), symphonies, overtures, concertantes, sextets for wind instruments, quintets, quartets, trios in great number for ensembles of various kinds, pf. concertos, a concertante for two pianofortes, sonatas, pf. pieces, songs.

(2) H y a c i n t h e, b. 1769, Versailles, brother of the former, 1795 professor of the pianoforte at the Conservatoire, d. 1802. He wrote fifteen quartets and six trios for strings, four

pf. concertos, five violin and five pf. sonatas, among which one for four hands.

Jaëll, A l f r e d, b. March 5, 1832, Trieste, d. Feb. 27, 1882, Paris, son of the violinist Eduard J., esteemed in his time at Vienna, and by whom he was trained, first in violin-, and afterwards in pianoforte-playing. J. made his *début* as pianist in 1843 at Venice in the San Benedetto theatre, after which he led a very active life, making concert tours, and often changing his place of residence (Paris, Leipzig, Brussels, etc.). His playing—smooth and brilliant rather than imposing, insinuating rather than energetic—received due recognition. In 1866 he married the pianist Marie Trautmann. As a composer, J. has only written *paraphrases de concert* (transcriptions), and brilliant pieces for pf. with titles of various kinds. His wife also composes, and appears, indeed, to devote herself to works of large calibre (concerto in D, pf. quartet, waltzes for four hands, etc.).

Jagdhorn (Ger. ; Ital. *corno di caccia*), huntinghorn. (*See* HORN.)

Jahn, (1) O t t o, distinguished archæologist, philologist, and art critic, b. June 16, 1813, Kiel, d. Sept. 9, 1869, Göttingen ; he went to the convent school Pforta, studied at Kiel, Leipzig, and Berlin, travelled for the purpose of study to France and Italy (1836–39), qualified himself in Kiel as lecturer on philology, in 1842 became unattached professor of archæology at Greifswald, 1845 professor in ordinary, and in 1847 occupied a similar post at Leipzig, was dismissed, however, in 1851, on account of his political opinions ; he became professor of archæology and director of the academical art museum at Bonn in 1855, and, later on, director of the philological college ; he was called to Berlin 1867, and d. at Göttingen after a prolonged illness. Besides many works on philology and archæology of high value, we are indebted to J. for the classical biography of Mozart (1856–59, four vols.; 2nd ed., 1867, two vols. ; 3rd ed., revised by H. Deiters, one vol., 1889; translated into English by P. D. Townsend, three vols., Novello), not only an excellent and exhaustive work, but one of immense importance for musical literature in that it deals closely with musical history by philological and critical methods, and, in this sense, is epoch-making. It became a model to later biographers and historians of music (Chrysander, Spitta). J. wrote besides : "Ueber Mendelssohns Paulus" (1842), for the "Grenzbote," polemical articles on Berlioz and Wagner, reports of the Lower Rhine musical festivals of 1855 and 1856, a notice of Breitkopf u. Härtel's complete edition of Beethoven's works, etc., afterwards published in the "Gesammelte Aufsätze über Musik" (1866). He gives proof of solid musicianship in his thirty-two songs, full of feeling (in four vols.; the third and fourth contain Low German songs from Klaus Groth's "Quickborn "), and a volume of four-part songs for mixed choir. He also brought out a critical edition in vocal score of Beethoven's *Fidelio*. His biography of Mozart arose, almost against his will, as the result of ever-increasing preparatory studies and collections of material for a Beethoven biography : materials were also accumulated for a biography of Haydn. Death prevented the carrying out of these schemes ; his preparatory work was, however, made use of and developed by illustrious men :—Thayer (Beethoven) and Pohl (Haydn).

(2) Wilhelm, distinguished conductor, b. Nov. 24, 1835, Hof (Moravia), 1852 chorister at Temeswar, capellmeister at Pesth (1854), then at Agram, Amsterdam, Prague (1857–64), from 1864–81 at the royal theatre, Wiesbaden, and since then director of the Opera, Vienna, re- signed 1897 ; hitherto he has only published songs.

Jähns, Friedrich Wilhelm, b. Jan. 2, 1809, Berlin, d. there Aug. 8, 1888, highly-esteemed teacher of singing, conducted a choral society of his own at Berlin which enjoyed a good reputation (1845–70). By his special enthusiasm for K. M. v. Weber—which has led to important results for musical literature and history—J. has made for himself a lasting name. He diligently collected everything which had any relation to Weber or proceeded from him. J.'s collection, unique of its kind, of Weber's works (prints, manuscripts, sketches, letters, etc.) became, by sale in 1883, the property of the Royal Library at Berlin, where it is set in a place apart. With his treasures and experience as basis, J. wrote " K. M. von Weber in seinen Werken " (1871), the best book on Weber, and containing, besides, one of the best thematic catalogues (in chronological order, with excellent critical remarks, etc.) ; in addition, " K. M. v. Weber " (1873, sketch of his life) ; also articles for musical newspapers. In 1849 J. became " Königlicher Musikdirektor," and in 1870 " Königlicher Professor " ; from 1881 he was teacher of rhetoric at Scharwenka's Conservatorium. The following of his compositions deserve mention : a pf. trio (Op. 10), and " Schottische Lieder."

Jakob, Friedrich August Leberecht, b. June 25, 1803, Kroitzsch, near Liegnitz, d. Liegnitz, May 20, 1884, cantor at Konradsdorf, near Hainau (Silesia), 1824–78, published books of school songs, quartets for male voices, songs, a "Fassliche Anweisung zum Gesangsunterricht in Volksschulen" (1828), and his most important work—a "Reformiertes Choralbuch" (with Ernst Richter, Berlin, 1873 ; 2nd ed. 1877). He was for a long period co-editor of the *Euterpe*, and wrote various articles for educational papers. J. received a pension in 1878, and from that time lived at Hohenwiese, near Greiffenberg (Silesia).

Jaleo, a Spanish national dance in ⅜ time of moderate movement (solo dance), with castanet rhythm :

Jalousieschweller : a chest, enclosing delicate stops, with a movable lid acted on by a knee-lever ; by means of it dynamic shading is possible on the organ. A similar apparatus was long used in England for the pianoforte, and was transferred by Green (in 1750) to the organ. (*Cf.* CRESCENDO.)

Jan, Maistre. (*See* GALLUS, 2.)

Jan, Karl von, philologist, b. 1836, Schweinfurt, graduated in 1859 at Berlin with the essay " De fidibus Græcorum " (" The Stringed Instruments of the Greeks "), worked at the Graues Kloster as teacher under Fr. Bellermann, further at Landsberg-a.-W., where, in 1862, the instruction in singing was handed over to him. He left this town in 1875 on account of differences with the municipal authorities respecting an organ which he had procured for the college hall from the proceeds of concert performances arranged by him. He laboured then at Saargemünd in the same way as formerly, cultivating music at the same time, until, in 1883, he was called to the Lyceum at Strassburg. J. has published several valuable articles on the history of music, some of which appeared in the *Allgemeine Musikalische Zeitung* (1878, on Old Grecian Modes ; 1881, on the Diaulos), others in philological papers. Again, he wrote on Greek stringed instruments in the " Programm " of the Saargemünd College ; also in the Halle Encyclopædia, under signature " Citharodik," giving new explanations concerning the cithara and lyre. In 1891 J. wrote a searching analysis of Bacchius's " Eisagoge " (" Programm " of the Strassburg Lyceum), on the metrics of Bacchius in the Rhenish " Museum f. Philologie " (vol. 46), on the " Hymnen des Dionysios und Mesomedes," in 1890, in Fleckeisen's " Jahrb. d. Philologie," on the " Harmonie der Sphären " (" Philologus," vol. 52), on " Rousseau als Musiker " in the " Preuss. Jahrb." (vol. 56).—Hermann Ludwig (von Jan), the biographer of Kastner (q.v.), is related to Jan.

Janissary Music, an orchestra composed of wind and percussion instruments (big drum, cymbals, and even triangle and crescent) ; special military music.

Jankó, Paul von, b. June 2, 1856, Totis (Hungary), son of Michael von J., manager of the estates of Count Esterhazy ; he attended the Polytechnic at Vienna and the Conservatorium (pupil of Hans Schmitt, J. Krenn, and Ant. Bruckner), besides (1881–82) the University at Berlin, as mathematical student, and at the same time received instruction in the pianoforte from H. Ehrlich. In 1882 J. invented a new

keyboard, which must be regarded as a development of Vincent's idea of a chromatic keyboard, but which seems to promise better results,
inasmuch as it leaves the fundamental scale
(c major) capable of being recognised by the
eye. J.'s keyboard consists of six rows of keys,
which lie in terrace-form one above the other,
but only represent one single chromatic scale,
since the four upper rows are only repetitions of
the two under ones (each lever is represented by
a key in three of the boards). The J. clavier
has decidedly attractive qualities (only five-
sevenths of the usual stretch for the octave), and
is capable of many new effects. (*Cf.* GLISSANDO.)
Its principal defect is the weight, in playing, of
the highest rows of keys. J. described his keyboard in a pamphlet of considerable size, and,
since 1886 has produced it with success on concert tours. Hans Schmitt has written études,
etc., for the new keyboard, and a number of
pianists (Gisela Gulyas, Wendling, and others)
have adopted the new speciality.

Jannaconi (Janacconi), G i u s e p p e, b. 1741,
Rome, d. March, 1816 ; one of the last repre-
sentatives of the traditions of the Romish
School (*see* PALESTRINA-STYLE), was a friend of
Pisari, teacher of Baini and Basili (1811), Papal
maestro of St. Peter's Church as successor to
Zingarelli when the latter undertook the direction of the Conservatorio at Naples. J. ranks
high among church composers. His works
remain in manuscript, and are preserved at
Rome. They are as follows : a mass, Te Deum,
Magnificat, " Dixit Dominus " and " Tu es
Petrus " in sixteen parts, thirty more masses up
to eight parts, with or without organ and instruments ; forty-eight psalms with or without
instruments, many motets, offertories, antiphons ; canons : one in sixty-four, another in
twenty-four parts; two in sixteen, one in twelve;
and several in eight and in four parts with
several subjects.

Jannequin (Janequin, Jennekin), C l é m e n t,
important Belgian or French contrapuntist,
but of whose life nothing at all is known. He
was a pupil of Josquin de Près. The following
of his works have been preserved : masses in
manuscript (Rome) ; " Sacræ cantiones seu mo-
tectæ 4 voc." (1533) ; chansons (mostly the
same, some in greater, some in smaller number) in special editions by Attaignant (1533,
1537), Jacques Moderne (1544), Tylman Susato
(1545), Le Roy et Ballard (1559) ; " Proverbes
de Salomon mis en cantiques et ryme français "
(1555) ; " Octante psaumes de David " (1559).
Detached pieces are to be found in Gardane's
" Di Clément Jannequin et d'altri eccelentis-
simi authori vinticinque canzoni francesi " (four-
part, 1538), " Selectissimæ nec non familiarissimæ cantiones ultra centum" (four-part, 1540),
" Trium vocum cantiones centum " (1541), also
in books 11–17 of the great collection of chansons by Attaignant (1542–45), in books 7 and 8

of the " Chansons nouvellement composées "
(1557 to 1558), and in the tenth book of the
" Recueil des recueils " (1564). The most
famous chansons (Inventions) of J., which show
him to be the programme-musician of the 16th
century, bear the titles " La bataille " (the
battle near Malegnano [1515], originally in four
parts, to which a fifth has been added by
Verdelot), " La guerre," " Le caquet des
femmes," " La jalousie," " Le chant des oiseaux "
(twice), " La chasse de lièvre " " La chasse au
cerf," " L'alouette," " Le rossignol," " La prise
de Boulogne."

Janowka, T h o m a s B a l t h a s a r, b. about
1660, Kuttenberg (Bohemia), licentiate in philosophy, and organist at Prague, the compiler
of the oldest musical lexicon (with exception of Tinctor's (" Diffinitorium "), entitled
"Clavis ad thesaurum magnæ artis musicæ"
(1701).

Jansa, L e o p o l d, b. 1794, Wildenschwert
(Bohemia), d. Jan., 1875, Vienna; he studied
law at Vienna, but soon changed to music,
and trained himself for a violinist ; he became
member of the Imperial band 1824, also, in
1834, conductor of music at the University,
and arranged regular quartet evenings. He
was particularly noted as the best leader in
Haydn's Quartets ; it was also J. who, together
with Czerny, played Beethoven's Kreutzer
Sonata to the composer immediately after it
was written. In 1849 he took part in a concert
at London for the benefit of the banished Hungarian insurgents, and was, in consequence, dismissed from Vienna. He remained in London
until 1868, highly esteemed as a violin teacher,
and then, having obtained an amnesty, returned
to Vienna and received a pension. J. composed
many works for the violin (fantasias, variations,
rondos), also several concertos, sonatas, quartets
and trios for strings, violin duets, a *Rondeau
concertant* for two violins with orchestra, and a
few sacred works (offertorium for tenor solo
and solo violin, chorus and orchestra). His most
distinguished pupil was Mme. Norman Neruda.

Jansen, G u s t a v F., b. Dec. 15, 1831, Jever,
royal musical director and cathedral organist
at Verden. He wrote " Die Davidsbündler
aus R. Schumanns Sturm und Drangperiode "
(1883), a somewhat fantastic description of the
most interesting period of Schumann's artistic
life, the statements of which were contradicted,
perhaps in too sober a manner, by J. von Wasielewski (" Schumanniana "). J. also edited
" Robert Schumann's Briefe ; neue Folge "
(1886).

Janssen, (1) N. A., organist at Louvain, for
a time, Carthusian monk ; he wrote " Les vrais
principes du chant grégorien " (1845), translated into German by Smeddinck as " Wahre
Grundregeln des Gregorianischen oder Choral-
gesangs " (1847).

(2) J u l i u s, b. June 4, 1852, Venlo (Holland),

pupil of the Cologne Conservatorium; from 1872–76 music teacher and pianist in South Russia; and, from 1876, conductor of the Musical Society at Minden. Since then he has been conductor of the Musical Society and Male Choral Society at Dortmund, and in 1890 he became town musical director there (conductor of the first and second Westphalian music festivals); in some songs he has shown himself a talented composer.

Janssens, Jean François Joseph, famous composer, b. Jan. 29, 1801, Antwerp, d. there Feb. 3, 1835; he was trained by his father, who was director of the church music, and for two years by Lesueur in Paris; he then studied law, according to the wish of his family, and in 1826 became notary at Hoboken, near Antwerp, attracting attention at the same time by the performance of great works, and was appointed conductor of a musical society. In 1829 he became notary at Berchem, in 1831 at Antwerp. The siege of Antwerp (1832) frightened him away to Germany; and in Cologne, through the burning of the hotel at which he was staying, his manuscripts and other things of value were destroyed. Fear and vexation disturbed his reason, and, after a long illness, brought about his death. J. was one of the most important of Belgian composers. His principal works are: five orchestral masses à 4, a Te Deum, motets, psalms, hymns, etc., with orchestra, several cantatas (*Missolonghi, Le Roi*), a symphony which obtained a prize at a competition at Ghent; another, *Le lever du soleil,* two comic operas (*Le père rival, La jolie fiancée*), fantasias for wind band, and songs.

Japha, (1) Georg Joseph, b. Aug. 12, 1835, Königsberg, d. Feb. 25, 1892, Cologne; 1850–53 pupil of the Leipzig Conservatorium, especially of Ferd. David, and Raimund Dreyschock (violin); he studied in 1853 under Edmund Singer, who remained for a time at Königsberg, and then again under Alard in Paris; from 1855–57 he was member of the Leipzig Gewandhaus orchestra, appeared repeatedly at concerts as a violinist, made a concert tour to Russia during the winter of 1857–58, lived from 1858–63 as a private teacher at Königsberg, where he established (1863, jointly with Adolf Jensen) regular chamber-music evenings; he appeared with success in London as violinist, both as a solo and quartet player, became leader of the "Gürzenich" concerts, and was appointed teacher at the Conservatorium, Cologne.

(2) Louise (Langhans-J.), b. Feb. 2, 1826, Hamburg, where she received her first musical training from Fritz Warendorf (pianoforte), G. A. Gross and Wilh. Grund (theory and composition). She married W. Langhans (q.v.) in 1858, is an excellent pianist, has also written pf. pieces, stringed quartets, songs, etc. In 1853, under Robert and Clara Schumann at Düsseldorf, she went through a higher course of development in pianoforte-playing and composition. She was looked upon in Paris (1863–69) as one of the most remarkable of German pianists, especially in Schumann's music. She has given many concert tours in Germany, and since 1874 has been living at Wiesbaden.

Jaquet. (*See* BUUS.)

Jarnovic (Giornovichi), Giovanni Mane, violinist and composer, b. 1745, Palermo (nevertheless of Polish origin), d. Nov. 21, 1804, Petersburg. He was a pupil of Lolli's, also a member of the *Concert Spirituel* at Paris in 1770, and both as player and composer soon became the hero of the day. On account of an affair of honour he was, however, forced to quit Paris, and went in 1779 to Warsaw, Petersburg, Stockholm, meeting everywhere with success, and in 1792 to London, where he soon put Viotti to the rout. From 1796 to 1802 he lived, without appointment, in Hamburg, and then went again through Berlin to Petersburg. His light and attractively written works are: sixteen violin concertos (with strings, two oboes, and two horns), some of which, however, are said to have been composed by Saint-George; six quartets for strings, many violin duets, and a book of violin sonatas with bass.

Jean le Coq. (*See* GALLUS, 2.)

Jehan. (*See* GALLUS, 2.)

Jehin, (1) Léon, b. July 17, 1853, Spa, pupil of the Brussels Conservatoire (Léonard), was orchestral conductor at Antwerp and Brussels (Théâtre de la Monnaie and Vauxhall), also in 1879 assistant teacher of theory at the Brussels Conservatoire. Since 1889 he has been conductor at Monaco (compositions for orchestra and for violin).

(2) François J.-Prume, b. April 18, 1839, Spaa, likewise trained at Brussels, an able violinist who lived 1875–83 at Montreal, Canada, and since then at Brussels.

Jelensperger, Daniel, b. 1797, near Mülhausen (Alsace), d. there May 31, 1831. He came to Paris as a copyist for a lithographic printing firm, then studied theory under Reicha and became his "Répétiteur," and finally assistant professor. In 1820 he undertook the management of a publishing-house established by several professors of the Conservatoire for the purpose of bringing out their own works (Reicha, Dauprat, and others). About that time he wrote the Method (published after his death) entitled "L'harmonie au commencement du 19ième siècle et méthode pour l'étudier" (1830); in German by Häser (1833). He also translated into French J. Hummel's "Klavierschule" and Häser's "Chorgesangschule."

Jelinek, Franz Xaver, b. Dec. 3, 1818, Kaurins (Bohemia), d. Feb. 7, 1880, Salzburg, pupil of the Conservatorium at Prague, 1841 teacher of the oboe and archivist of the Mozarteum at Salzburg, afterwards director of the cathedral choir. He wrote church choral works, part-songs for men's voices, etc.

Jenkins, J o h n, b. 1592, Maidstone, d. Oct. 27, 1678, Kimberley(Norfolk), lute-player and violist, chamber-musician to Charles I. and Charles II.; he composed numerous *Fancies* (Fantasias) and *Rants* (Caprices) for organ, viols, etc., which, for the most part, are preserved in manuscript at Oxford, and of which some were printed in Playford's "Courtly Masquing Ayres" (1662), "Musick's Handmaid" (1678), and "Apollo's Banquet "(1690). He himself published : "Twelve Sonatas for two violins and a Base, with a Thorough-base for the Organ or Theorbo " (1660-64). He also wrote "Theophilia " (airs to several parts of a poem by Benlowe, 1652) ; an elegy on the death of W. Lawes, printed at the end of Lawes' "Choice Psalms " (1648) ; two rounds in Hilton's "Catch that catch can" (1652) ; and songs in "Select Ayres and Dialogues " (1659) ; and "The Musical Companion " (1672), etc.

Jennekin. (*See* JANNEQUIN.)

Jensen, (1) A d o l f, b. Jan. 12, 1837, Königsberg-i.-Pr., d. Jan. 23, 1879, Baden-Baden. This thoughtful song-composer, who unfortunately died at so early an age, was, for the most part, self-taught, and when he had studied only two years with Ehlert and Marpurg his talent had already begun to put forth beautiful blossoms. In 1856 he was teacher of music in Russia, became capellmeister at Posen theatre in 1857, and in 1858 went to Copenhagen to Gade, whose artistic spirit was akin to his. He returned to Königsberg in 1860, where he soon made a name both as composer and as teacher. From 1866 to 1868 he was teacher for advanced pupils at Tausig's school at Berlin, but on account of his uncertain health, withdrew, first to Dresden, and in 1870 to Graz, and spent his last years in Baden-Baden, where he suffered long from an affection of the chest. J. has a better right than Robert Franz to the title of Schumann's heir in the composition of songs, and yet the reproach cannot be brought against him of being an imitator : depth of feeling, new birth of the poem in the melody—these are things which cannot be imitated. His numerous sets of songs, from the first (Op. 1) to the last (Op. 61), are a treasure-house of poetical and musical feeling. The greater number have plain titles, as "6 Lieder " (Op. 1), "7 Lieder " (Op. 11), etc., while some form cycles with a general title, as "Dolorosa" (Chamisso's "Thränen," Op. 30), " Gaudeamus" (twelve poems by Scheffel, Op. 40), two books, each of seven songs, from the "Spanisches Liederbuch" of Geibel and Heyse (Op. 4 and 21), "Romanzen und Balladen " (Hamerling, Op. 41), etc. J. also composed some books of part-songs (Op. 28 and 29), two songs for chorus with two horns and harp (or pianoforte, Op. 10); two selections of his songs appeared as

"Jensen Albums." J. takes high rank among lyric composers for the pianoforte, the cultivators of small *genre* pieces. The following deserve mention : "Innere Stimmen " (Op. 2) ; "Wanderbilder" (Op. 17), ; "Idyllen " (Op. 43) ; "Eroticon " (Op. 44); "Hochzeitsmusik " (four hands, Op. 45) ; Sonata (Op. 25) ; a "Deutsche Suite" (Op. 36) ; "Romantische Studien " (Op. 8) ; Studies (Op. 32) ; "Phantasiestücke," dances, romances, nocturnes, etc. ; finally, "Jephthas Tochter," for soli, chorus, and orchestra, and "Der Gang der Jünger nach Emmaus," for orchestra. J. also left an opera (*Turandot*) with score complete. (*Vide* Niggli's essays on J. in the *Schweiz. M.-Zg.*, 1879.)

(2) G u s t a v, b. Dec. 25, 1843, Königsberg-i.-Pr. He studied with S. Dehn, F. Laub, and J. Joachim ; violinist and composer ; from 1872 professor of counterpoint at Cologne Conservatorium. He has written chamber-music (suite, Op. 3, for pf. and violin; trio, Op. 4; violin sonata, Op. 7; quartet for strings, Op. 11; 'cello sonata, Op. 26), orchestral works (3 Charakterstücke, Op. 33 ; symphony in b♭), pf. pieces, songs, choruses, etc.; he has likewise arranged a number of works by old masters for violin and pf. (Classische Violin Musik, Vortragsstudien, Corelli's Op. 5, etc. [Augener & Co.]). Died Nov. 26, 1895, Cologne.

Jeu (Fr.), an organ stop; *J. à bouche,* fluestop ; *J. à anches,* reed-stop ; *Grand J., Plein J.,* full organ.

Jew's Harp (Lat., *Crembalum; * Ger.*Brummeisen Maultrommel*), an old primitive instrument consisting of an elastic steel tongue, which is riveted to a small piece of iron of horseshoe shape, held by the teeth. The buzzing tones produced with almost closed mouth have a peculiar, melancholy colour. The J. H. is to be met with here and there among bear-leaders, etc.

Jimmerthal, organist, b. 1809, Lübeck, d. there Dec. 17, 1886. He wrote a monograph on Dietrich Buxtehude (1877).

Joachim, J o s e p h, the classical violinist without a rival, b. June 28, 1831, Kittsee, near Pressburg; he was a musical prodigy, and made a public appearance at the age of seven with his first teacher, Szervaczinski, leader at the Pesth theatre. In 1838 he became a pupil of Böhm's at the Vienna Conservatorium, and made such rapid progress under him that he appeared, first at a concert given by Viardot-Garcia at Leipzig (1843), and soon after, (November, 1843) at the Gewandhaus, before a very critical public, and with brilliant success. During the following six years J. remained in Leipzig, at a time when Mendelssohn and Schumann were at the zenith of their fame, and his talent was further developed, especially under the influence of the former. In 1844 he appeared at the Gewandhaus with Bazzini (who was making a prolonged stay at Leipzig), Ernst, and David, in Maurer's concerto for four violins.

It may well be imagined that Leipzig, where art was encouraged in so distinguished a manner, was of decisive influence in his development, and that he found there the richest nourishment and the safest guidance in his high aim after that which was noblest. He added to his artistic fame by occasional concert tours from Leipzig, and already, in 1844, on Mendelssohn's recommendation, he appeared in London, which he visited again in 1847 and 1849, and often afterwards, until, in fulfilment of a brilliant engagement, he became a yearly guest. In 1849 he was leader of the band at Weimar, but was too little in sympathy with the new German tendencies centred in the person of Liszt to feel that he could settle there, and therefore in 1854 he exchanged his post for that of leader and "Kammervirtuos" at the court of Hanover. In 1863 he married there Amalie Weiss (really Schneeweiss; b. May 10, 1839, Marburg, in Styria), a distinguished contralto singer who, after short engagements at Hermannstadt and at the Kärntnerthortheater, Vienna, became (1862) a member of the opera company at Hanover. Frau J. withdrew from the stage, and devoted herself entirely to concert singing. Her fame as a *Lied* singer is scarcely inferior to that of her husband as a performer on the violin. As an interpreter of Schumann's songs, especially, she is without a rival. Soon after the events of 1866, the two artists went to Berlin, as J. was appointed director of the newly established High School of Music (1868), which, developing year by year, grew to large dimensions. (There has lately been a change in the organisation of this institution, and J. is now only artistic director of the branch for stringed instruments.) A goodly number of violin-players, especially, gathered around the master. Since David's death the school for violin-playing has changed from Leipzig to Berlin. J. has a splendid technique; and if indeed virtuosi like Sarasate, by brilliancy and fascinating colouring, attract musicians for a time, J., by his transcendent greatness and classic repose, remains conqueror. J. is one of those masters to whom the intentions of the composer are the highest ideal, to whom effect is a despicable thing; one of those masters who do not excite and bewitch, but who instruct and inspire reverence. It is indeed profitable to compare J.'s interpretation of the Beethoven or the Mendelssohn concerto with that of other distinguished violinists. J. is as celebrated a quartet- as he is a solo-player. It would indeed be difficult to hear finer renderings of Beethoven's last quartets than those given in Berlin by J.'s quartet party (de Ahna[†], Wirth, Hausmann, etc.). For many years J. has been the chief attraction of the London season (New Year to Easter), playing at the Popular Concerts, Philharmonic Concerts, also at the Crystal Palace. As a composer J. has produced hitherto only a few works for violin:

three concertos (G minor, Op. 3; "Hungarian," Op. 11; and G [1890], variations for violin and orchestra); "Andantino and Allegro" (with orchestra), Op. 1; six pieces with pf. (Op. 2 and 5); notturno for violin and orchestra; variations on an original theme (viola and piano); Hebrew melodies (viola and pf.). Besides these, several overtures (*Hamlet, Demetrius*, and *Dem Andenken Kleists*, etc.); marches, and the "Szene der Marfa" (from *Demetrius*), for alto solo and orchestra. His music is akin to that of Schumann.

João (John) **IV.**, King of Portugal, b. March 19, 1604, Villa Viçosa; 1640 King; d. Nov. 6, 1656, Lisbon. He wrote "Defensa de la musica moderna contra la errada opinion del obispo Cyrillo Franco" (anon. 1649), and "Respuestas a las dudas que se puzieron a la missa, 'Panis quem ego dabo' de Palestrina" (1654); both works are translated into Italian. He composed, besides, twelve motets (1657), Magnificat à 4, "Dixit Dominus à 8," "Laudate Dominum à 8," "Crux fidelis à 4," etc.

Jobst Brant. (*See* BRANT.)

Jöcher, Christian Gottlieb, b. July 25, 1694, Leipzig, professor of philosophy and librarian there, d. May 10, 1758. He published "Allgemeines Gelehrtenlexikon" (1750, four vols., enlarged by Dunkel 1755–60, continued by Adelung 1784–87, republished and continued by Rotermund 1810–22, six vols.), which also contains biographies of musicians; his essay for the Doctor's degree appeared under the title "Effectus musicæ in hominem" (1714).

Johannes Cotto. (*See* COTTO.)

Johannes Damascenus, really Johannes Chrysorrhoos, of Damascus, b. about 700 A.D., d. about 760 as monk in the Saba monastery, near Jerusalem. He is a saint both of the Greek and the Roman Church, the oldest theologian of the Greek Church, and also the arranger of the liturgical song, and reformer of the Byzantine notation. Up to the present the system of Byzantine notation has not been thoroughly investigated; and, indeed, the whole Byzantine liturgy requires to be expounded in a thoroughly exhaustive manner. As aids to work of this kind may be named Cyriakos Philoxenos' Δεξικον της ελληνικης εκκλησιαστικης μουσικης (1868); W. Christ's "Beiträge zur kirchlichen Litteratur der Byzantiner" (1870, reprint from the session reports of the Royal Bavarian Academy of Sciences); M. C. Paranikas' "Beiträge zur byzantinischen Litteratur" (1870, ditto); Riemann's, "Die Μαρτυριαι der byzantinischen liturgischen Notation" (1882, ditto); Tzetzes' "Die altgriechische Musik in der griechischen Kirche" (1874, Dissertation), and Gardthausen's "Beiträge zur griechischen Päläographie" (1880, from the session reports of the philologico-historical class of the Royal Saxon Society of Arts); and H. Reimann, "Zur Geschichte und Theorie der

byzantinischen Musik " (1889). (Cf. BYZANTINE
MUSIC.)

Johannes de Garlandia. (See GARLANDIA.)

Johannes de Muris. (See MURIS.)

Johannes Gallus. (See GALLUS, 2.)

Jommelli (Jomelli), N i c o l a, one of the most
distinguished opera composers of the Neapolitan school, b. Sept. 10, 1714, Aversa (Naples),
d. there Aug. 25, 1774. He received his first
musical instruction from Canon Mozzilo at
Aversa; at the age of sixteen he became a pupil
of Durante's at the Conservatorio di Sant'
Onofrio, Naples, but went afterwards to the
Conservatorio della Pietà, where Leo and Feo
developed his talent for composition. With
the exception of some small vocal pieces, his
first works were ballets, with which he obtained
little success. In 1737 he made his first attempt
as an opera composer with *L'errore amoroso*, which
was given out as the work of an indifferent
musician named Valentino; it was a brilliant
success, and, already in 1738, J. produced his
first grand opera, *Odoardo*, under his own name.
His reputation spread rapidly, and in 1740 we
find him in Rome (*Ricimero, Astianasse*), and
in 1741 in Bologna (*Ezio*). He remained for
some time in the latter city, and still studied
counterpoint under Padre Martini. The success
of his opera *Mérope* (1741) at Venice gained for
him the post of director of the Conservatorio
degli Incurabili, in which capacity he wrote
several sacred works for double choir. In 1749
he was appointed coadjutor of Bencini as
maestro of St. Peter's, Rome, and remained
there until he was called to Stuttgart as "Hofcapellmeister" at the end of 1753. During his
fifteen years of activity in this post he gained
an intimate knowledge of German music, and
his part-writing and treatment of the orchestra
in his operas were greatly influenced thereby.
Much as this transformation raised him in the
eyes of the Germans, it alienated from him the
favour of his countrymen; and when the Stuttgart Opera was disbanded (March 29, 1769) and
he returned to Naples, he was looked upon as a
foreigner by the Italians, and could not regain
his old reputation. His last, and perhaps best
works, *Armida* (1770), *Demofoonte* (1770), and
Ifigenia in Aulide (1773), made no impression on
the public of the San Carlo Theatre. J. had
retired, with his family, to his native place,
Aversa, and lived alternately there or in the
neighbourhood of Naples. The failure of his
last works hastened his end; he died shortly
after he had written his famous Miserere for
two sopranos and orchestra. In all, fifty-five
operas and divertissements of J.'s are known
by name; but those which were preserved at
Stuttgart were, with few exceptions, destroyed
at the burning of the theatre in 1802. He wrote,
besides, a Passion, the oratorios *Isacco, Betulia
liberata*, and *Santa Elena al calvario, La Natività
di Maria Vergine*, several cantatas, masses,

psalms, graduals, responses, and other sacred
works, besides those for double choir: Dixit
à 8, Miserere à 8, Laudate with four solo
sopranos and double choir, "In convertendo"
(with six solo voices and double choir), Magnificat (with echo), and a Hymn to St. Peter for
double choir.

Jonas, É m i l e, b. March 5, 1827, Paris, entered
the Conservatoire there in 1841, where Lecoup-
pey and Carafa were his teachers; he received
several prizes, and, finally, in 1849, the second
state prize (medal) for composition. J. turned his
attention to the composition of operettas (*genre*
Offenbach), and made his *début* in 1855 at the
Bouffes Parisiens with *Le duel de Benjamin*,
followed by a number of other works of a
similar kind (so aptly described by the French
as "Petite musique," or "Musiquette"): *Le
duel de Benjamin, La parade, Le roi boit, Les petits
prodiges*. From 1847-66, J. was professor of an
elementary class (*Solfège*) at the Conservatoire,
and from 1859-70 professor of harmony in a
class established for pupils studying military
music. At the Exhibition of 1867 he was entrusted with the arrangement of the performance of military music. In his capacity of
musical director of the Portuguese Synagogue
(J. is of Jewish descent) he published, in 1854,
a "Recueil de chants hébraïques" for synagogue use.

Joncières, F é l i x L u d g e r (named Rossignol), Victorin de J., b. April 12, 1839, at
Paris, studied at the Conservatoire under Elwart
and Leborne, but left the institution in consequence of a dispute with Leborne about Richard
Wagner, whom J. honours (in 1868 he travelled
to Munich for the first performance of the
Meistersinger). In addition to his great activity as
composer, J. became musical critic to the *Liberté*.
The following of his compositions rank amongst
the best: music to *Hamlet*, the operas *Sardanapal* (1867), *Le dernier jour de Pompéi* (1869),
Dimitri (1876, all three performed at the Théâtre
Lyrique), *La Reine Berthe* (Grand Opéra, 1878),
Chevalier Jean (1885, Opéra Comique), also a
"Symphonie romantique," a choral symphony
("La mer"), a Hungarian serenade, an orchestral suite ("Les Nubiennes"), a "Slave"
march, a violin concerto, a concert overture,
etc. J. is extremely modern in his tendency,
but his works lack purity of style.

Jones, (1) R o b e r t, celebrated English performer on the lute at the beginning of the 17th
century. He published: "The First Booke of
Ayres" (1601); "The Second Booke of Ayres"
(1601); "Ultimum vale; or, the Third Booke
of Ayres" (1609); "A Musicall Dreame; or,
the Fourth Booke of Ayres" (1609), and "The
Muse's Garden for Delight; or, the Fifth Booke
of Ayres" (1611, "for the lute, the basse viol,
and the voyce"); besides a book of madrigals à
3-8 (for viols or voices). Some of his compositions are to be found in the "Triumphes

of Oriana" (1601); Leighton's "Teares and Lamentacions" (1614), and Smith's "Musica Antiqua" (1812).

(2) John, d. Feb, 17, 1796, as organist of Middle Temple, Charterhouse, and St. Paul's. He published: "Sixty Chants, Single and Double" (1785), one of which greatly impressed Haydn by its naïve and expressive style of melody.

(3) William (J. of Nayland), b. July 30, 1726, Lowick (Northamptonshire), d. Jan. 6, 1800, Nayland (Suffolk). He wrote a "Treatise on the Art of Music" (1784), and published in 1789 ten pieces for organ and four anthems. He also wrote a large number of famous works not relating to music.

(4) William, celebrated Orientalist, b. Sept. 28, 1746, London, d. April 27, 1794; he was judge at Calcutta for a long period, where he had leisure to study Indian manners and customs. In the sixth volume of his collected works (1799) there is a treatise: "On the Musical Modes of the Hindus," which Dalberg made the foundation of his work on the same subject.

(5) Edward, b. 1752, Henblas, near Llanderfel (Wales), d. April, 1824, London, sprung from a Welsh family of bards; he went to London in 1775, and in 1783 became bard to the Prince of Wales (afterwards George IV.). He published: "Musical and Poetical Relicks of the Welsh Bards, with a General History of the Bards and Druids and a Dissertation on the Musical Instruments of the Aboriginal Britons" (1786 [1794]; 2nd volume: "The Bardic Museum," 1802; the 3rd volume came out about the time of his death, and the rest was published soon afterwards; the work contains altogether 225 Gaelic melodies. His other publications are: "Lyric Airs" (1804, Grecian, Albanian, Wallachian, Turkish, Arabian, Persian, etc., popular melodies), "The Minstrel's Serenades," "Terpsichore's Banquet" (a pendant to the "Lyric Airs"), "The Musical Miscellany," "Musical Remains of Handel, Bach, Abel," etc., "Choice Collection of Italian Songs," "The Musical Portfolio" (English, Scotch, and Irish melodies), "Popular Cheshire Melodies," "Musical Trifles calculated for Beginners on the Harp," "The Musical Bouquet" (popular melodies).

(6) Griffith, English writer at the beginning of this century; he wrote for the "Encyclopædia Londinensis" a sketch of the history of music, printed separately as "Music," which in 1819 appeared in a new edition as "A History of the Origin and Progress of Theoretical and Practical Music" (1819, German by Mosel: "Geschichte der Tonkunst," 1821).

Jongleurs (Lat. *Joculatores;* Ger. *Gaukler;* Old Fr. *Joglars, Jongleors*), itinerant players; the word is identical with Minstrels (*Ménétriers*). (*See* TROUBABOURS and GUILDS.)

Joseffy, Rafael, b. 1852, Presburg, a pianist of excellent technique, pupil of Tausig. He has published pf. pieces, and lives at New York.

Josquin de Prés. (*See* DEPRÈS.)

Jota Aragonese, a lively Spanish national dance with castanet rhythm

with a melody played by the mandoline—

which is given alternately while the dancers rest and a stanza is sung; it is always repeated in varied form.

Jouret, (1), Théodore, b. Sept. 11, 1821, Ath, Belgium, d. July 16, 1887, at the Kissingen baths. He was professor of chemistry at the military school at Brussels, composer of songs and quartets for male voices, also of a one-act comic opera (*Le Médecin Turc* [1845], jointly with Meynne). From 1846 he was musical critic of various Belgian and foreign political and musical newspapers (*Guide musical, L'Art*).

(2) Léon, brother of the former, b. Oct. 17, 1828, Ath, studied at the Brussels Conservatoire, since 1874 professor of a vocal ensemble class at the Brussels Conservatoire, made a name, since 1850 as composer of many songs, part-songs, cantatas; also sacred works. Two of his operas were performed at the "Cercle artistique et littéraire" with great success: they are entitled *Quentin Metsys* and *Le tricorne enchanté.*

Jubilus, a term used in the Middle Ages, answering to neume; a long melodic phrase on a vowel (coloratura).

Judenkunig, Hans, a native of Schwäbisch-Gmünd, was a performer on the lute at Vienna, and published "Ain schone kunstliche underweisung . . . auf der Lautten und Geygen," etc. (1523), a small work of great interest in connection with the history of instruments (Vienna Library).

Jue, Édouard, b. 1794, Paris, trained at the Conservatoire, afterwards a pupil of Galin (q.v.), and, finally, a teacher according to the method (Meloplast) of the latter. He published "La musique apprise sans maître" (1824, etc.); "Solfège méloplaste" (1826); and "Tableau synoptique des principes de la musique" (1836).

Jula, obsolete name of a Quint stop 5⅓ ft.

Julien (Jullien), Louis Antoine, b. April 23, 1812, Sisteron (Basses-Alpes), d. March 14, 1860, Paris; he studied under Halévy at the Paris Conservatoire, but was not a steady worker, and, on account of his inclination towards dance music, was dismissed from that institution. His dances, marches, potpourris, etc., were extremely popular, and he made a name as conductor of the ball concerts of the Jardin Turc; but he fell into debt, was compelled to leave Paris, and went in 1838 to London, where he gathered together an excellent orchestra and established promenade concerts, and travelled through England, Scotland, and Ireland, and even America, with his whole orchestra. In order to derive greater benefit from his compositions, he set up a music business in London. He was completely ruined by an operatic undertaking which he set on foot for the purpose of producing his opera *Pietro il grande*. Escaping once again from his creditors, he was arrested for debt in Paris and imprisoned. Shortly after his liberation he lost his reason.

Jullien, (1) M a r c e l B e r n a r d, b. Feb. 2, 1798, d. Oct. 15, 1881, Paris. He was general secretary of the "Société des Méthodes d'Enseignement" at Paris. He wrote: "De quelques points des sciences dans l'antiquité; physique, métrique, musique" (1854); "Thèses supplémentaires de métrique et de musique anciennes," etc. (1861); and "De l'étude de la musique instrumentale dans les pensions des demoiselles" (1848).

(2) J e a n L u c i e n A d o l p h e, son of the former, b. June 1, 1845, Paris, writer on music, contributor to the *Revue et Gazette Musicale, Le Ménestrel*, the *Chronique Musicale*, and musical critic of several political papers. He wrote: "L' Opéra en 1788" (1873); "La musique et les philosophes au XVIII. siècle" (1873); "Histoire du théâtre de Mme. Pompadour, dit théâtre des petits cabinets" (1874); "La comédie à la cour de Louis XVI., le théâtre de la reine à Trianon" (1873); "Les spectateurs sur le théâtre" (1875); "Le théâtre des demoiselles Verrières" (1875); "Les grandes nuits de Sceaux, le théâtre de la Duchesse du Maine" (1876); "Un potentat musical" (1876); "L'église et l'opéra en 1735"; "Mademoiselle Lemaure et l'evêque de Saint-Papoul" (1877); "Weber à Paris" (1877); "Airs variés; histoire, critique, biographie musicales et dramatiques" (1877); "La cour et l'opéra sous Louis XVI.; Marie Antoinette et Sacchini, Salieri, Favart et Gluck" (1878); "La comédie et la galanterie au XVIII. siècle" (1879); "Histoire des costumes au théâtre" (1880); "Goethe et la musique" (1880); "L'opéra secret au XVIII. siècle" (1880); "La ville et la cour au XVIII. siècle" (1881, contains some of the aforenamed); "La comédie de la cour . . . pendant le siècle dernier" (1883); "Paris dilettante au commencement du siècle" (1884); finally "Richard Wagner, sa vie et ses œuvres" (1886); and "Hector Berlioz" (1888) —the last two are works of great merit, and splendidly got up in large 4to, with many illustrations.

Jumilhac, D o m P i e r r e B e n o î t de, b. 1611,

at the castle of St. Jean de Ligour, near Limoges, d. April 21, 1682, as adjunct to the general of the order of the Benedictines (congregation of St. Maur). He wrote "La science et la pratique du plain chant" (1673), a learned and exhaustive work with many musical examples, republished by Nisard and Leclerc (1847).

Junck, B e n e d e t t o, gifted Italian composer, b. Aug. 24, 1852, Turin (his father was a native of Alsace). Though he showed early signs of talent, he was sent to a business house at Paris. When, in 1872, his father died, he followed his inclination and became a pupil of Mazzucato and Bazzini at Milan, where he lived from that time. His works up to now are: Op. 1, "La Simona," twelve songs (libretto by Fontana), for soprano and tenor (1878); Op. 2, eight romances; Op. 3, two songs (Heine and Panzacchi wrote the words to Ops. 2 and 3); Op. 4–5, violin sonatas in G and D; Op. 6, a quartet for strings in E (1886).

Jungmann, (1) A l b e r t, b. Nov. 14, 1824, Langensalza, d. Nov. 7, 1892, at Pandorf, near Krems, business manager of the house of Spina, Vienna, composer of many drawing-room pieces, songs, etc.

(2) L o u i s, b. Jan. 1, 1832, Weimar, d. there Sept. 20, 1892, pupil of Töpfer and Liszt, teacher of music at the "Sophieninstitut." He published pf. pieces, songs, etc.

Jüngst, H u g o, b. Feb. 26, 1853, Dresden, where, from 1871–76, he was pupil of the Conservatorium, in 1876 founder and conductor of the Dresden Male Choral Society, also conductor of the Julius-Otto Association. He has composed many choruses for male voices.

Junker, K a r l L u d w i g, b. about 1740, Oehringen, d. May 30, 1797, as pastor in Rupertshofen, near Kirchberg. He composed three piano concertos, a cantata (*Die Nacht*, with violin and 'cello), a melodrama (*Genoveva im Thurm*), etc. He wrote: "Zwanzig Komponisten; eine Skizze" (1776; 2nd ed. under the title of "Portefeuille für Musikliebhaber," 1790); "Tonkunst" (1777); "Betrachtungen über Maler-, Ton- und Bildhauerkunst" (1778); "Einige der vornehmsten Pflichten eines Kapellmeisters oder Musikdirectors" (1782); "Ueber den Wert der Tonkunst" (1786); "Musikalischer Almanach" (1782, 1783, 1784); and "Die musikalische Geschichte eines Autodidakts in der Musik" (1783). He also contributed articles to Meusel's "Miszellaneen" and "Museum für Künstler."

Jupin, C h a r l e s F r a n ç o i s, b. Nov. 30, 1805, Chambéry, d. already June 12, 1839, Paris, a distinguished, early-developed violin-player, pupil of the Paris Conservatoire; for several years he was maître de chapelle at Strassburg. He composed a violin concerto, a trio for strings, a trio for pf., fantasia for pf. and violin, and several sets of variations.

Jürgenson, Peter, b. 1836, Revel; he founded in 1861 the important music-publishing business at Moscow bearing his name (specially works of Russian composers : Tschaïkowsky, etc.), and added a printing establishment to it in 1867.

Just Intonation is the intonation of intervals exactly according to the requirements of the mathematical determination of tone—for example, of the fifth as 2 : 3. The J. I. of an interval is possible with the help of combination tones, but, if logically carried out, this leads to results of an extremely complicated nature; and the question as to which of the two (J. I. or equal temperament) (*see* TEMPERAMENT) is the more advantageous must probably be decided in favour of the latter. (*Cf.* HARMONIUM.)

K.

Káan, Heinrich von (Albést-K.), b. May 29, 1852, Tarnopol (Galicia), pupil of Blodek and Skuhersky at Prague, pianist and composer (chamber-music, pf. concertos, symphonic poem "Sakuntala," ballet "Bojaja," "Frühlingscklog- ner" for orchestra); he lives at Prague, where he was appointed professor at the Conservatorium, 1890.

Kade, Otto, b. 1825, Dresden, pupil of J. Otto and J. G. Schneider; after residing for a year and a half in Italy for the purpose of study, he founded (1848) the Cecilia Society (for old church music) at Dresden, where he was musical director of the Neustadt Church, and in 1860 became Schäffer's successor with the title of "Grossherzoglicher Musikdirektor," and undertook the direction of the palace music at Schwerin, in which post, both as director and composer, he displayed extraordinary activity. In 1884 he received the title of *Dr. Phil. hon.c.* from the Leipzig University. K. wrote many compositions in old Gregorian style for the liturgy of the Evangelical Church ("Kantionale," in three parts; 3rd part 1880), a "Choralbuch" for Mecklenburg-Schwerin (1869), etc. K. has also been an active investigator in the department of musical history, and to him we are not only indebted for valuable articles in the *Monatshefte für Musikgeschichte*, in the *Allg. Mus. Zeitung*, but also for a pamphlet, "Der neu aufgefundene Luther- Kodex vom Jahr 1530" (1872); monographs on Le Maistre and Heinrich Isaak, and a translation of Scudo's "Le Chevalier Sarti." He also edited the musical supplements to the 3rd vol. of Ambros' "Geschichte der Musik" (1881, forming a 5th vol.). In 1893 K. commenced a remarkable publication, consisting of old "Passions" (thirty-four numbers, extending from Obrecht to H. Schütz), and it is to be hoped that the undertaking will be brought to a successful close.

Kaffka, Johann Christian, b. 1759, Ratisbon, pupil of Riepel, actor, singer, and composer; he appeared on the boards at Breslau, Petersburg, Dessau, in 1803, and established a publishing-house at Riga. K. wrote a series of operettas, ballets, also two oratorios, besides symphonies, masses, vespers, a requiem, etc.

Kafka, Johann Nepomuk, *salon* composer, b. May 17, 1819, Neustadt-a.-d.-Mettau (Bohemia), d. Oct. 23, 1886, Vienna; he first studied law, but turned to music, and wrote a large number of brilliant but easy pf. pieces K. was an enthusiastic collector of autographs.

Kahl, Heinrich, b. Jan. 31, 1840, Munich, d. Aug. 6, 1892, Berlin, attended school and the Conservatorium at Munich, and entered the court chapel; from 1857–66 leader of the royal band, Wiesbaden; then became theatre capell- meister at Riga, Stettin, Aachen; in 1872 chorus director at the Berlin Court Opera, and in 1880, royal capellmeister.

Kahlert, August Carl Thimotheus, worthy writer on music, b. March 5, 1807, Breslau, d. there March 29, 1864. He first studied jurisprudence, and was already refer- endary when he decided to study philosophy, and in this new vocation became professor of philosophy at Breslau. From youth upwards he was thoroughly grounded in music, and became a diligent contributor to Dehn's *Cäcilia*, and to the *Allg. Mus. Ztg.* He also published on his own account: "Blätter aus der Brief- tasche eines Musikers" (1832), and "Ton- leben" (1838); some of his songs also became popular.

Kahn, Robert, b. July 21, 1865, Mannheim, studied under Vincenz Lachner, Kiel, and Rheinberger. Since 1891 he has been con- ductor of a ladies' choral society at Leipzig, and has shown himself a talented composer of terzets and quartets for female voices, songs, pf. pieces, and some chamber music (quartet for strings, pf. quartet, trio, violin sonata).

Kahnt, Christian Friedrich, b. May 10, 1823, founder, and up to 1886 proprietor, of the Leipzig music publishing firm bearing his name. From 1857 he was publisher, and after Brendel's death (1868) nominal editor, of the *Neue Zeit- schrift für Musik;* he is also treasurer of the "Allg. deutscher Musikverein," "Grossherzog- lich sächsischer Kommissionsrat," etc. Among other important works the house has published a series of compositions by Liszt. On the 1st of July, 1886, the firm, together with the editor- ship of the *N. Zeitschr. f. M.*, was acquired by Oskar Schwalm, who carried on the business under the title of "C. F. Kahnt Nachfolger." In 1888 the property passed into the hands of Dr. Paul Simon (b. Jan. 22, 1857, Königsberg), who also undertook the editorship of the *N. Zeitschr. f. Musik.*

Kaiser, (1) Karl, b. March 12, 1837, Leipa (Bohemia), d. Dec. 1, 1890, Vienna; he studied philosophy at Prague, was then an officer in the army 1857-63, but at length turned to music, and in 1874 established a school of music at Vienna, which soon became popular; it is now under the direction of his son Rudolph.

(2) Emil, b. Feb. 7, 1850, Coburg, military bandmaster at Prague. He composed the operas: *Die Kavaliere des Königs* (Salzburg, 1879), *Der Trompeter von Säkkingen* (Olmütz, 1882), *Andreas Hofer* (Reichenberg, 1886), *Der Kornet* (Leipzig, 1886), and *Rodenstein* (Brünn, 1891).

Kalamaika, a lively Hungarian national dance in quick $\frac{2}{4}$ time.

Kalbeck, Max, b. Jan. 4, 1850, Breslau, showed at an early age a taste for poetry, music, and painting, devoted himself especially to the first, and, already in 1870-72, through the good offices of Holtei, published poems (" Aus Natur und Leben "), soon exchanged the study of jurisprudence for that of philosophy, and in Munich, whither he had betaken himself for the purpose of study, devoted himself entirely to poetry; in this matter, however, he quarrelled with his father, and now chose music as a vocation (pupil of the Munich School of Music). In 1875 he undertook the post of musical critic and feuilletonist to the *Schlesische Zeitung* at Breslau, and assistant in the management of the Silesian Museum, but soon fell out with the director of the Museum, resigned the last-named post, and exchanged the first for one of a similar character on the *Breslauer Ztg.* In 1880, on the recommendation of Hanslick, he became a writer on the *Wiener Allg. Ztg.* At present he is musical critic of the *Wiener Montags Revue* and " Burgtheater " critic for the *Neue Wiener Tageblatt.* Apart from his activity as a critic, K. first became known in musical circles by his studies on Wagner's music-dramas (*Nibelungen*, 1876; *Parsifal*, 1880). In 1881 there appeared a collection of his articles (" Wiener Opernabende "). He won great merit by new poems and translations of opera libretti (da Ponte's *Don Giovanni* [1886, for the Mozart-Don-Juan secular festival at Vienna], also Mozart's *Bastien und Bastienne* and *Gärtnerin aus Liebe, Die Maienkönigin,* with arias by Gluck; Massenet's *Cid* and *Werther,* Verdi's *Otello* and *Falstaff,* Mascagni's *Freund Fritz* and *Rantzau,* Smetana's *Verkaufte Braut* and *Dalibor,* Smareglia's *Vasall zu Szigeth,* Hubay's *Geigenmacher von Cremona,* Giordano's *Mala Vita,* and Cilea's *Tilda*). A selection of his poems appeared under the title " Aus alter und neuer Zeit."

Kalischer, Alfred, b. March 4, 1842, Thorn, studied philology and took his degree at Leipzig, then studied music at Berlin under Const.

Bürgel and C. Böhmer. He has since lived in that city as teacher and writer; he edited (1873) the *Neue Berliner Musikzeitung,* has contributed much to the *Klavierlehrer* and the *N. Z. f. Musik,* and published important works: " Beethoven's Beziehungen zu Berlin," " Luther's Bedeutung für die Tonkunst," " Lessing als Musikästhetiker," " Musik u. Moral," etc.

Kalkbrenner, (1) Christian, b. Sept. 22, 1755, Minden, d. Aug. 10, 1806, Paris; when young he went to Cassel, where his father was town musician. K. lived there for many years in a subordinate post as chorus-singer at the Opera, although he had already published numerous compositions, and had been named honorary member of the Liceo Filarmonico at Bologna. In 1788 he was at last appointed capellmeister to the queen at Berlin, and in 1790 to the prince Heinrich at Rheinsberg, but resigned this post in 1796 for unknown reasons; he lived for a time in Naples, then in Paris, where in 1799 he was appointed *répétiteur* at the Grand Opéra. K. achieved nothing remarkable either as composer or writer. His operas written, some for Rheinsberg, some for Paris, met with no success; of instrumental music he published some trios, violin sonatas, pf. variations, etc. His writings are: " Kurzer Abriss der Geschichte der Tonkunst " (1792; afterwards in revised form as " Histoire de la musique," 1802, two small vols.); " Theorie der Tonsetzkunst " (1789); " Traité d'harmonie et de composition par Fr. X. Richter " (compiled from the manuscript by K., 1804).

(2) Friedrich Wilhelm Michael, son of the former, b. 1788, on a journey between Cassel and Berlin, d. June 10, 1849, Enghien-les-Bains, near Paris. In 1799 he became a pupil of Adam's for the pianoforte at the Paris Conservatoire, afterwards studied harmony with Catel; in 1803 his father sent him to Vienna, in order to withdraw him from the dangers of Parisian life. He studied there for a time under Clementi. Owing to the death of his father, he returned to Paris, 1806, appeared with great success as a pianist, and was very much sought after as a teacher. From 1814 to 1823 he lived in London, and in 1818 joined Logier in making known the Chiroplast (q.v.), invented by the latter. In 1823 he travelled through Germany with Dizi the harp virtuoso, and in 1824 settled in Paris as a partner in the Pleyel pianoforte manufactory. Madame Pleyel was one of his pianoforte pupils. K.'s system was to render the fingers as skilful as possible without using arm power; he also originated modern octave technique (from the wrist). He devoted especial attention to the left hand, for which he wrote special pieces (sonata, Op. 42, " pour la main gauche principale "), Fugue à 4 for the left hand only, in his Méthode. To pedal technique he likewise devoted much attention. Many of his pianoforte compositions are of a light, drawing-

room *genre* (fantasias, caprices, variations, etc.), but he wrote also many larger and solidly-planned works : four concertos (one for two pianos), rondos, fantasias, and variations for orchestra, one pf. septet, one pf. sextet, two pf. quintets, one pf. quartet, pf. trios, violin sonatas, ten piano sonatas for two, and three for four hands, which still well deserve attention ; studies (Op. 20, 88, and 143 are still of value at the present day), etc.; finally a pf. Method, "Méthode pour apprendre le piano-forte à l'aide du guide-mains" (1830; *cf.* Chiro-plast), and a "Traité d'harmonie du pianiste" (1849).—His son A r t h u r, d. Jan. 24, 1869, well known in Paris through his eccentric and dissipated life, published *salon*-music.

Kalliwoda, (1) J o h a n n e s W e n z e s l a u s, an able violinist and estimable composer, b. Feb. 21, 1801, Prague, d. Dec. 3, 1866, Carlsruhe. He was a pupil of Dionys Weber and Pixis at the Prague Conservatorium, from 1823–53 capellmeister to the Prince of Fürstenberg at Donaueschingen, and then lived at Carlsruhe. He wrote seven symphonies, several overtures, violin concertos, and other solo pieces for violin, three string quartets, a concertante for two violins (Op. 20), and the much-sung Austrian "Deutsches Lied," etc.   *Cf.* the articles by Tottmann (Ersch and Gruber's Encyclopædia, II., vol. 32), Hiller ("Erinnerungsblätter," p. 110, etc.), and Gathy (*N. Z. f. Musik*, 1849).

(2) W i l h e l m, son of the former, b. July 19, 1827, Donaueschingen, d. Sept. 8, 1893, Carlsruhe ; at first a pupil of his father, studied afterwards at the Leipzig Conservatorium. He was an able pianist and composer of pf. pieces and songs, and was for a long time, as his father's successor (1853), court capellmeister at Carlsruhe ; in 1875 he retired into private life.

Kallwitz (Kalwitz). (*See* CALVISIUS.)

Kamienski, M a t t h i a s, b. Oct. 13, 1734, Oedenburg (Hungary), d. Jan. 25, 1821, Warsaw, was the first Polish opera composer ; his *Nendza Uszesliwiona* was produced in 1775 at the National Theatre at Warsaw. He also wrote five other Polish operas for Warsaw, two German operas (not produced), several sacred works, and a cantata for the unveiling of the Sobieski memorial.

Kammercantate (Ger.), chamber cantata.

Kammerconcert (Ger.), a chamber concerto, or a chamber concert.

Kammerlander, K a r l, b. April 30, 1828, Weissenhorn, d. Aug. 24, 1892, as cathedral capellmeister at Augsburg ; song writer and composer.

Kammermusik (Ger.), chamber music.

Kammersänger (Ger.), a singer in the service of a prince.

Kammerton (Ger.), "Chamber pitch," concert pitch. (*Vide* Chor-Ton.)

Kammervirtuose (Ger.), a virtuoso in the service of a prince.

Kandler, F r a n z S a l e s, b. Aug. 23, 1792, Klosterneuburg (Lower Austria), d. Sept. 26, 1831, Baden, near Vienna, as royal military draughtsman. He obtained a thorough musical training (soprano singer in the Vienna court choir, afterwards a pupil of Albrechtsberger, Salieri, and Gyrowetz), and during his eleven years' official service at Venice and Naples (1815–26) he found time to study Italian music and its history. We are indebted to him for numerous articles in the Vienna *Musikalische Zeitung* (1816–17), in the *Allgemeine Musikalische Zeitung* (1821), in the *Cäcilia* (1827), *Revue Musicale* (1829), etc., and for the pamphlets " Cenni storico-critici intorno alla vita ed alle opere del celebre compositore Giov. Adolfo Hasse, detto il Sassone" (1820) ; " Ueber das Leben und die Werke des G. Pierluigi da Palestrina, genannt der Fürst der Musik " (1834 ; extract from Baini's work, published by Kiesewetter), and " Cenni storico-critici sulle vicende e lo stato attuale della musica in Italia" (1836, from posthumous papers and articles in the *Cäcilia*).

Kanoon (Quânon), an Oriental stringed instrument not unlike our Zither. The name points to the ancient Canon, *i.e.* the Monochord, on which, already in ancient times, several strings were stretched, in order to be able to show at the same time the ratios of different sounds.

Kapelle (Ger.), a chapel. A musical establishment—consisting of a choir of singers, of a band of instrumentalists, or of both—connected with a church or a court, or in the pay of a nobleman. Now the expression is generally applied to a band of instrumentalists. (*Cf.* CAPPELLA.)

Kaps, E r n s t, b. Dec. 6, 1826, Döbeln, d. Feb. 11, 1887, Dresden, as pianoforte-maker to the Saxon court ; his speciality was the semi-grand piano.

Kapsberger, J o h a n n H i e r o n y m u s v o n, German by birth, lived first at Venice (1604), and then at Rome, where he attracted notice as an excellent performer on the theorbo, lute, chitarrone, etc., also as a composer in the modern (Florentine) style, who by fulsome flattery understood how to win favour at the Papal Court (Urban VIII.). He appears to have died about 1650. K. was a very vain man, but by no means a bad musician. His tablature for lute instruments differs from that of his contemporaries, and is very much simpler. His principal works are : " Intavolatura di chitarrone " (three books ; 1604, 1616, 1626) ; " Villanelle a 1, 2, e 3 voci " (in tablature for chitarrone and guitar ; six books : 1610, 1619 [à 2 and 3], 1623, 1630, 1632) ; " Arie passegiate " (in tablature, three books : 1612, 1623,

1630); "Intavolature di lauto" (two books: 1611, 1623); madrigals with continuo à 5 (1609); "Motetti passegiati" (1612); "Balli, gagliarde e correnti" (1615); "Sinfonie a 4 con il basso continuo" (1615); "Capricci a due stromenti, tiorba e tiorbino" (1617); two books of Latin poems of Cardinal Barberini (Pope Urban VIII.) for one voice with figured bass (1624, 1633); "Die Hirten von Bethlehem bei der Geburt des Herrn" (dialogue in recitative form, 1630); "Missæ Urbanæ" (à 4–8, 1631); "Apotheose des heil. Ignatius von Loyola" (K. was especially friendly with the Jesuits; A. Kirchner was his admirer); besides several wedding cantatas and a musical drama, *Fetonte* (1630). He left in manuscript many other works of a similar character to those already mentioned.

Karajan, Theodor Georg von, b. Jan. 22, 1810, Vienna, d. April 28, 1873, a sub-director of the Vienna Court Library and president of the Academy of Sciences; he was an authority on German literature and music, and writer on literature. He published: "J. Haydn in London 1791 and 1792" (1861), a valuable monograph, which contains the correspondence of Haydn with Marianne v. Genzinger.

Karasowski, Moritz, b. Sept. 22, 1823, Warsaw, d. April 20, 1892, Dresden; he received lessons on the pianoforte and 'cello from Valentin Kratzer; became 'cellist in the orchestra of the Grand Opera, Warsaw, in 1851, and, from 1858–60, made tours for the purpose of study to Berlin, Vienna, Dresden, Munich, Cologne, Paris; from 1864 he was royal chamber-musician ('cellist) at Dresden. Besides some pieces for 'cello with pf., he published several treatises on the history of music, namely, in Polish: "History of the Polish Opera" (1859), "Mozart's Life" (1868), "Chopin's Early Days" (1862, 2nd ed. 1869), and in German: "Friedrich Chopin, sein Leben, seine Werke und Briefe" (1877; 2nd revised ed. 1878; 3rd ed. 1881).

Karow, Karl, b. Nov. 15, 1790, Alt-Stettin, d. Dec. 20, 1863, as teacher of music at a training school at Bunzlau (Silesia), was an esteemed teacher, and wrote motets, organ and pf. pieces, a "Choralbuch" and a "Leitfaden für den Schulgesangunterricht."

Kässmeyer, Moritz, violinist and composer, b. 1831, Vienna, d. there Nov. 9, 1884, pupil of the Vienna Conservatorium (S. Sechter and Preyer), was violinist in the Opera orchestra, wrote masses and other sacred works, songs and part-songs, five stringed quartets (printed). He was an excellent musical humorist.

Kastner, (1) Johann Georg, composer, theorist, and musical investigator, b. March 9, 1810, Strassburg, d. Jan. 19, 1867, Paris. Although from an early age he showed talent for music, he was trained for the church, and attended the Protestant theological college of

his native town, but at the same time studied music seriously. In 1830 he became bandmaster of a militia regiment of his native city, definitely abandoned theology in 1832, and in 1835, owing to the successful production of one of his German operas, the town council of Strassburg gave him the means of going to Paris, where he completed his musical studies under Berton and Reicha. With his "Traité général d'instrumentation," which appeared in 1837 (the first of the works of a similar kind in France), he commenced the long series of excellent educational treatises approved of by the Académie, and adopted by the Conservatoire:—"Cours d'instrumentation considéré sous les rapports poétiques et philosophiques de l'art;" "Grammaire musicale;" "Théorie abrégée du contrepoint et de la fugue;" "Méthode élémentaire d'harmonie appliquée au piano;" "Méthodes élémentaires de chant, piano, violon, flageolet, flûte, cornet à piston, clarinette, cor, violoncelle, ophicléide, trombone, hautbois;" "Méthode complète et raisonnée de Saxophone;" "Bibliothèque chorale;" "Méthode complète et raisonnée de timbales;" "Manuel général de musique militaire." The two last-named works deal with their subject also from an historical point of view. Kastner's treatise on instrumentation was soon forgotten when Berlioz published his work on orchestration based on Kastner. A comprehensive work, "De la composition vocale et instrumentale," a "Cours d'harmonie moderne," and a "Traité de l'orthographie musicale" remained unpublished. K. was also a prolific and successful composer. Besides five German operas written at Strassburg, he composed another of the same kind, *Beatrice* (1839; libretto after Schiller by G. Schilling), also the comic opera *La Maschera* (1841), which was produced in Paris; the grand Biblical opera, *Le dernier roi de Juda* (1844, words by M. Bourges; K.'s most important work); the comic opera, *Les Nonnes de Robert le Diable* (libretto by Scribe, 1845), and a number of vocal and instrumental compositions, large and small, especially choruses for male voices. K.'s most characteristic creations are his "Livres-Partitions," great symphonic tone-poems, including also treatises on the various subjects from a musico-historical and philosophical point of view; "Les danses des morts" (Paris, 1852); "Les chants de la vie" (collection of male choruses, Paris, 1854); "Les chants de l'armée française" (Paris, 1855); "La harpe d'Éole et la musique cosmique" (Paris, 1856); "Les voix de Paris" (Paris, 1857); "Les Sirènes" (Paris, 1858); "Parémiologie musicale de la langue française" (Paris, 1866). K. was also an active contributor to French and German musical papers, to Schilling's "Lexikon der Tonkunst," etc. K.'s enterprise was fully acknowledged, and, among other distinctions, he was named *Dr. hon. causâ* of the University of Tübingen, member of the

Institut de France, and of various foreign societies, member of the " Comité des Études " of the Paris Conservatoire, " Officier de la légion d'honneur," etc. His activity was displayed in every branch of musical art, especially in France for the " Orphéons " and military music; in connection with the latter K. was the originator of the " Concours européen de musiques militaires " at the Paris Exhibition of 1867. K. was one of the founders, and afterwards vice-president, of the " Association des artistes-musiciens." A happy blending together of German and French natures, together with his own artistic individuality, explains, for the most part, that fascinating originality which distinguishes the compositions of K., and the valuable services which he rendered to the history of music. His biography, " J. G. Kastner ein elsässischer Tondichter, Theoretiker und Musikforscher," was written by Hermann Ludwig (von Jan), and published at Leipzig by Breitkopf and Härtel (two parts in three vols.). A German version of K.'s chief works has been commenced. K.'s library was sold and dispersed.

(2) G e o r g F r i e d r i c h E u g e n, son of the former, b. Aug. 10, 1852, Strassburg, d. April 6, 1882, Bonn, physicist, inventor of the " Pyrophon " (" Flammenorgel "). His investigations with regard to the laws of vibration are worthy of note ; these are explained in his " Théorie des vibrations et considérations sur l'électricité " (3rd ed., Paris, 1876; German, " Theorie der Schwingungen und Betrachtungen über die Electrizität," Strassburg, 1881), and in " Le pyrophone, flammes chantantes " (4th ed., Paris, 1876). (Cf. the Biography of Joh. Georg K., last section of the third volume.)

(3) E m m e r i c h, b. March 29, 1847, Vienna, pupil of Bibl, Pirkert, etc. He lives at Vienna as a writer on music, edited for some time the Wiener Musikalische Zeitung (afterwards Parsifal) and published a " Richard Wagner Katalog." His " Neuestes und vollständigstes Tonkünstler und Opern-Lexikon " (1889, A—Azzoni) appears not to have been continued.

Kate, A n d r é t e n, 'cellist and composer, b. 1796, Amsterdam, d. July 27, 1858, Haarlem, pupil of Bertelmann ; he wrote several operas, of which Seid e Palmira (1831) and Constantia (1835) were successfully produced at Amsterdam, also chamber-music, part-songs, etc. He did much to improve the state of music in Holland.

Kauer, F e r d i n a n d, b. Jan. 8, 1751, Klein-Thaya (Moravia), d. April 13, 1831, Vienna. He was formerly a famous composer of Viennese Singspiele, and alternately capellmeister at the Josephstadt, Graz, and Leopoldstadt Theatres ; and, in his old days, when no longer à la mode, tenor-player at the Leopoldstadt theatre. He composed about two hundred operas and operettas, of which Das Donauweibchen and Die Sternenkönigin were published,

and the first of these is to this day in the répertoire of minor theatres. He wrote besides, symphonies, chamber-music, concertos, over twenty masses, several requiems and other sacred works, oratorios, cantatas, songs, etc., which were nearly all destroyed at the overflowing of the Danube, March 1, 1830.

Kauffmann, (1) E. F., professor at the Heilbronn Gymnasium about 1850–65, noteworthy song composer in a simple, but noble and expressive style (a selection of thirty-six songs [six books, each of six], published by E. Ebner, Stuttgart). His son Emil has been for some years musical director at the Tübingen University.

(2) F r i t z, b. June 17, 1855, Berlin, where he studied with Mohr, became druggist at Hamburg, then attended the Royal High School of Music at Berlin (Kiel), won the Mendelssohn scholarship, and went to Vienna in 1881 for further training. In 1889 he succeeded Rebling as musical director at Magdeburg. K. has composed pf. sonatas, a trio, a quartet in G minor, variations for stringed quartet, a symphony in A minor, a comic opera (Die Herzkrankheit), etc.

Kaufmann, (1) G e o r g F r i e d r i c h, b. Feb. 14, 1679, Ostramondra, near Kölleda (Thuringia), d. beginning of March, 1735, as " Hofkapelldirektor " and organist at Merseburg. He wrote many works for harpsichord and organ, sacred compositions, also a treatise—" Introduzione alla musica antica e moderna," i.e. " Eine ausführliche Einleitung zur alten und neuen Wissenschaft der edeln Musik." All his works remained in manuscript except " Harmonische Seelenlust " (sets of chorale preludes à 2–4, 1735–36).

(2) J o h a n n G o t t f r i e d, b. April 14, 1751, Siegmar, near Chemnitz (Saxony), mechanician at Dresden, d. 1818, at Frankfort, while on a journey to display his inventions. He constructed musical clocks, and, among other things, a harp and a flute clock.

(3) F r i e d r i c h, son of the former, b. 1785, Dresden, d. there Dec. 1, 1866. His trumpet-automaton (1808) attracted considerable notice. His " Belloneon," constructed jointly with his father, also his " Klaviaturharmonichord " and " Chordaulodion," must be classed among fugitive experiments in the construction of instruments. On the other hand, his " Symphonion " (1839) was the predecessor of the " Orchestrion," completed in 1851 by his son, Friedrich Theodor (b. April 9, 1823, Dresden, d. there Feb., 1872), an instrument which came into great demand as substitute (?) for a small orchestra in coffee-gardens, etc.

Kayser (Kaiser), (1) P h i l i p p C h r i s t o p h, composer and pianoforte virtuoso, b. March 10, 1755, Frankfort, d. Dec. 23, 1823, Zürich, son of the organist Matthäus Kayser (d. Feb. 18, 1810, Frankfort, at the age of eighty). He was on friendly terms with Goethe. (*Cf.* " Goethe und der Komponist Ph. Chr. Kayser," Leipzig, 1879.)

(2) H e i n r i c h E r n s t, able teacher of music, b. April 16, 1815, Altona, d. Jan. 17, 1888, Hamburg, where from 1840-57 he was a member of the orchestra. His études for violin, Op. 20, "position" studies, Op. 28, daily studies, and the études, Op. 30, also his method for violin, are well known and highly esteemed.

Kazynski, V i k t o r, b. Dec. 18, 1812, Wilna, studied under Elsner at Warsaw. He produced his opera *Fenella* at Wilna in 1840, and two years later another (*Der ewige Jude*), at Warsaw and also Wilna, and in 1843 settled in Petersburg, whence he made a journey with General Lwoff through Germany for the purpose of improving his musical knowledge; the results of this tour he described in an attractive travelling-journal (1845). Soon afterwards he was appointed capellmeister at the Imperial Opera. Besides another opera (*Mann und Frau*), which met with little success (1848), he wrote many instrumental works, also cantatas and *salon* pieces for pianoforte.

Keck von Giengen, J o h a n n, about 1450 Benedictine monk at Tegernsee, author of " Introductorium musicæ," printed in Gerbert (" Script." III.).

Keinspeck (Keinsbeck, Künspeck, incorrectly, Reinspeck), M i c h a e l, Nuremberg. He was the author of the oldest printed theoretical work on music, and especially Gregorian Song: " Lilium musicæ planæ" (Basle, 1496; Ulm, 1497; Augsburg, 1498 and 1500; Strassburg, 1506). K. describes himself on the title-page of the book—" Musicus Alexandrinus " (?).

Keiser, R e i n h a r d, b. Jan. 9, 1674, Teuchern, near Weissenfels, d. Sept. 12, 1739, Hamburg, was trained at Leipzig (St. Thomas's School and the University). Already in 1692 he wrote a pastoral (" Ismene "), and in 1693 a grand opera (*Basilius*), for the court at Brunswick, and went in 1694 to Hamburg, which henceforth became his home. Both as regards quantity and (exception being made of Handel's few operas written for Hamburg) also quality, K. was the most important composer of the Hamburg theatre, as is well known the· earliest public stage for opera in Germany (from 1678). He was possessed of extraordinary gifts, especially in the matter of melody: unfortunately, he lacked patience, and the strength necessary for serious work. For Hamburg (which on several occasions he was forced to leave on account of debt) he wrote not less than 116 operas, the last of which, however, shows no improvement on the first. Their merit consists in not being merely modelled on the Italian style. The subjects of his operas are, for the most part, taken from ancient mythology and history, and such as had been repeatedly used in Italy ; the popular

subjects of the day (in part very coarse) stand alone of their kind (*Störtebecker und Goedje Michel, Die Leipziger Messe, Der Hamburger Jahrmarkt, Die Hamburger Schlachtzeit*). In 1700 he established a series of winter concerts, with an excellent orchestra and the most famous soloists ; and at these concerts provision was made, not only for the soul, but also for the body, in the shape of a choice supper. In 1703, jointly with Drüsicke, he took a lease of the Opera House, but they were not successful, and Drüsicke disappeared. K. continued on his own account still up to 1706. After several years' absence (in Weissenfels), he reappeared with his portfolio full of new operas, married a wealthy lady (his wife, and, afterwards, his daughter, were excellent singers), resumed his concerts in 1716, remained at the Stuttgart court from 1719-21 in the hope of being appointed capellmeister ; he went, after useless waiting, to Copenhagen in 1722 as Royal Danish capellmeister, and in 1728 returned to Hamburg as cantor and canon of Saint Catherine's Church. He was opera conductor at Moscow and Petersburg 1729-30, also, for some time, at Copenhagen, where his daughter had an engagement, and finally again at Hamburg. Besides his operas, K. wrote many sacred works (passions, motets, psalms), oratorios, cantatas, of which the following appeared in print: *Gemüts Ergötzungen* (1689), *Divertimenti serenissimi* (1713),·*Musikalische Landlust* (1714), *Kaiserliche Friedenspost* (1715), etc.

Kéler Béla (really A l b e r t v o n Kéler), b. Feb. 13, 1820, Bartfeld, Hungary, d. Nov. 20, 1882, Wiesbaden. He first studied law, then took to farming, and in 1845 turned his attention to music, and studied at Vienna under Schlesinger and Sechter ; after that he worked for some time as violinist at the Theater-an-der-Wien, and became known by his dances and marches. In 1854, for a short time, he was conductor of the orchestra (formerly known as the Gungl Band) at Berlin, and then returned to Vienna as the head of the orchestra of Lanner, lately deceased (1855), and was then bandmaster at Vienna (1856-63), and from 1873 at Wiesbaden. After that he lived in retirement in the latter town.

Keller, (1) G o t t f r i e d, pianoforte teacher of German origin who lived in London. He published " A Complete Method of Attaining to Playing a Thorough-bass upon either Organ, Harpsichord, or Theorbo-lute " (Method of general bass, 1707; several times republished); also six sonatas for two flutes and bass ; and six others for two violins, trumpet, or oboe, viola and bass.

(2) M a x, b. 1770, Trossberg (Bavaria), d. Dec. 16, 1855, as organist at Altötting. He published many sacred concertos (masses, litanies, Advent songs, etc.), also several books of organ pieces (preludes, cadenzas, etc).

(3) Karl, b. Oct. 16, 1784, Dessau, d. July 19, 1855, Schaffhausen; an excellent flautist, court musician at Berlin (up to 1806), Cassel (from 1814), Stuttgart (up to 1816); he then travelled as a virtuoso, and in 1817 became court musician, afterwards theatre capellmeister at Donaueschingen, where his wife (Wilhelmine Meierhofer) was engaged as opera singer. On receiving his pension (1849), he returned to Schaffhausen. His compositions were written mostly for flute (concertos, solos, duets, variations, polonaises with orchestra, divertissements, etc.). His songs became extremely popular ("Kennst du der Liebe Sehnen?" "Helft, Leutchen, mir vom Wagen doch," etc.).

(4) F.... A.... E.... one of those who have sought, by means of self-acting machinery, to solve the problem of recording free improvisations on the pianoforte (Melograph, etc.); he named his apparatus "Pupitre Improvisateur," and published "Méthode d'improvisation ... fondée sur les propriétés du pupitre improvisateur" (1839).

Kellermann, Christian, b. Jan. 27, 1815, Randers (Jutland), d. Dec. 3, 1866, Copenhagen. He was a distinguished performer on the 'cello, and studied under Merk at Vienna. After travelling and giving concerts for many years, he was appointed solo 'cellist in the royal band at Copenhagen (1847). On a concert tour in 1864 he had a stroke of apoplexy at Mayence, and from that time was disabled. K. only published a few solo pieces for his instrument.

Kelley, Edgar S., b. April 14, 1857, Sparta (Wisconsin), pupil of Clarence Eddy, afterwards of Krüger and Speidel at Stuttgart; he was successful in America with orchestral and choral compositions.

Kellner, (1) David, musical director of the German church at Stockholm, published "Treulicher Unterricht im Generalbass" (1732, and up to 1792 was republished nine times; in Swedish by Miklius, 1782).

(2) Johann Peter, b. Sept. 24, 1705, Gräfenroda (Thuringia), d. there, as organist, over eighty years of age. He published "Certamen musicum" (preludes, fugues, and dance pieces for piano, 1748–49), "Manipulus musices" (organ pieces), also sets of figured chorales. He left in manuscript a Good Friday oratorio, cantatas (a complete set for the year), organ trios, etc.

(3) Johann Christoph, son of the former, organist, b. Aug. 15, 1736, Gräfenroda; studied with his father and Georg Benda at Gotha; after a long residence in Holland, he became court organist at Cassel, where he died in 1803. He published seven pf. concertos, trios, pf. sonatas, organ pieces, fugues, etc., also a "Grundriss des Generalbasses" (1783, several times republished). An opera (*Die Schadenfreude*) was produced at Cassel.

(4) Georg Christoph, writer and teacher at Mannheim, d. Sept. 1808. Besides some historical novels, he wrote: "Ueber die Charakteristik der Tonarten" (1790); "Ideen zu einer neuen Theorie der schönen Künste überhaupt und der Tonkunst insbesondere" (in Egger's *Deutsches Magazin*, 1800); also an elementary Method for pf., organ pieces, songs, etc.

(5) Ernst August, a descendant of Johann Peter K., b. Jan. 26, 1792, Windsor, d. July 18, 1839, London. He was one of the youngest of musical prodigies. At the age of five he played at court a Handel harpsichord concerto (his father was violinist to the queen). He afterwards became an excellent singer, went to Italy in 1815, studied still under Crescentini at Naples, achieved double triumphs as pianist and singer in Vienna, London, Petersburg, and Paris, and finally settled down as organist of the Bavarian chapel in London. A biographical notice of K. appeared at London in 1839 ("Case of Precocious Musical Talent," etc.).

Kellogg, Clara Louise, b. July, 1842, Sumterville, South Carolina, celebrated stage-singer (lyric and *soubrette* parts). She made her *début* in 1861 at New York as Gilda in *Rigoletto*, and in 1867 as Margherita in Gounod's *Faust*, London, where, since that time, she has sung repeatedly. In 1874 she successfully organised an English troupe at New York, and sang in it during the winter (1874–75) 125 times.

Kelly, Michael, b. 1762, Dublin, died Oct. 9, 1826, Margate (his full name was Michael O'Kelly, and he was called by the Italians Occhelli); he was a famous singer and a prolific composer. He studied under the best Italian teachers in London, and also under Aprile at Naples. He appeared in that city in 1781 with great success, was then engaged from 1784–87 at the "Hoftheater," Vienna, and enjoyed the friendship of Mozart. In 1787 he returned to London, won triumphs on the stage and in the concert-room. He made his *début* as an operetta composer with *False Appearances* and *Fashionable Friends*. In the course of the next thirty odd years he wrote music for more than sixty stage pieces, as well as English, French, and Italian songs. In 1802 he opened a music shop, but failed in 1811; about the same time he retired from the stage. After that he was engaged in the wine trade. His wines, however, appear to have been bad, and his compositions not always original. "Grove's Dictionary" relates that the wit Sheridan described him as a "composer of wines and importer of music." In 1826 he published his Memoirs ("Reminiscences of the King's Theatre;" *see* an epitome in the *Allg. Mus Ztg.*, 1880).

Kemangeh (or Kemantsche), an old Arabian Instrument with a small sound-board (cocoa-nut shell covered with serpent's skin), long neck and foot, and only one string. (*Cf.* M. Fürstenau, " Geschichte der Bogeninstrumente," 1882, pp. 16 and 17.)

Kemp, J o s e p h, b. 1778, Exeter, d. May 22, 1824, London. He was a pupil of William Jackson ; in 1802 organist at Bristol, and in 1809 at London. In 1808 he took his Mus.Bac., and in 1809 the Mus. Doc. degree at Cambridge, and was one of the first who introduced into London the system of teaching music to numbers simultaneously. He gave lectures to prove the suitability of this method, and published a pamphlet, " New System of Musical Education." He composed anthems, psalms, songs, duets, some melodramas, also " Musical Illustrations of the Beauties of Shakespeare," " Musical Illustrations of *The Lady of the Lake*," and published the *Vocal Magazine*.

Kempis, N i c o l a u s a, organist of Ste. Gudule, Brussels, in the middle of the 17th century, probably of Italian descent, for he is quoted as Florentino. He published at Antwerp " Symphoniæ 1, 2, 3 violinorum " (1644), " Symphoniae 1–5 instrumentorum, adjunctae 4 instr. et 2 voc." (two books, 1647 and 1649), for stringed instruments and voices (1644–49), likewise a book of masses and motets à 8 with continuo (1650). His chamber-music ranks among the best of his time. (*See* the sonata in Riemann's " Early Chamber Music.")

Kempter, K a r l, b. Jan 17, 1819, Limbach, near Burgau (Bavaria), d. March 11, 1871, as capellmeister of Augsburg Cathedral. He composed many sacred works (masses, graduals, etc.; likewise several oratorios, *Johannes der Täufer*, *Maria*, *Die Hirten von Bethlehem*, *Die Offenbarung*), and published a collection (" Der Landchorregent ") for the use of small churches.

Kenn, J., famous horn-player, German by birth. He went to Paris in 1782, became second horn at the Grand Opéra in 1783, entered the band of the National Guards in 1791, and in 1795 became teacher of the horn at the newly established Conservatoire (with Domnich and Duvernoy); but in 1802, when the staff of teachers was reduced, he was dismissed. Dauprat became his successor at the Opéra in 1808. Fétis praises K. as a horn-player remarkable for his low notes. K. published duets and trios for horn, also duets for horn and clarinet.

Kent, James, b. March 13, 1700, Winchester, d. there May 6, 1776, chorister of the Chapel Royal under Croft, organist at Cambridge up to 1737, and then at Winchester. He retired from active life in 1774. It was only in the decline of life that K. published twelve anthems; a Morning and Evening Service, and eight more anthems appeared after his death. K. assisted Boyce in his edition of " Cathedral Music."

Kent Bugle, an improvement of the Key Bugle ; so named because a performance on it, shortly after its invention, took place in presence of the Duke of Kent.

Kepler, J o h a n n e s, the celebrated astronomer, b. Dec. 27, 1571, Weil (Würtemberg), d. Nov. 15, 1630, Ratisbon. In the third and fifth books of his " Harmonices mundi libri V." (1619), he treats in detail of music from a philosophical point of view.

Keras (Gk.), horn, a wind instrument of the ancient Greeks.

Keraulophon (Gk., " horn-flute "), an 8-feet English organ stop, of wide measure, and of full, sombre tone ; half stop (discant). A small hole is bored in the body of the pipe, near the mouth. (*Cf.* HORNPIPE.)

Keren (Heb.), a Hebrew trumpet.

Kerle, J a c o b v a n, Netherland contrapuntist, early contemporary of Orlandus Lassus, b. Ypern ; he was choirmaster and canon at Cambrai. He afterwards entered the service of the Cardinal Prince-Bishop of Augsburg, Otto von Truchsess, followed his master, lived with him in Rome, and returned with him to Augsburg (1562–75). It is extremely doubtful whether, as generally supposed, he was ever in the service of the Emperor Rudolph II. He must have died about 1583. His works which have been preserved are : " Sex missæ " (à 4–5, 1562) ; " Sex missæ, 4 et 5 voc. et Te Deum " (1576) ; " Quatuor missæ " (with a Te Deum, 1583) ; a book of motets à 5–6 (1571 ; also as " Selectæ quædam cantiones ") ; " Moduli sacri " (à 5–6, with a " Cantio contra Turcas," 1572) ; " Motetti a 2, 4, e 5 voci et Te Deum laudamus a 6 voci " (1573) ; " Mutetæ 5 et 6 voc." (with some hymns, 1575) ; " Sacræ cantiones " (motets à 5–6 with some hymns, 1575) ; a book of madrigals à 4 (1570) ; the first chapter of Petrarch's " Trionfo d'amore " (à 5, 1570) ; " Gebete für den guten Ausgang des Tridentiner Konzils " (1569), and finally, " Kurfürstlicher Rath " there. About 1673 he resigned his post on account of the intrigues of the chapel singers (Italians). He is then said to have been organist of St. Stephen's, Vienna (?), but he died at Munich, March, 1684. Of his organ works only the following have been preserved : "Modulatio organica super Magnificat octo tonis" (preludes, interludes, postludes, 1686), besides clavier suites and toccatas ; also a trio for violins and bass viol in manuscript. His vocal works, which have been preserved, are more numerous : "Sacræ Cantiones" (à 4 with organ bass, 1669) ; two books of masses (1669, à 2-5, and 1669, à 4-6, among which is a Requiem for the Emperor Leopold I.) ; also in manuscript, several masses and portions of masses, among which a "Missa Nigra" only in black notes (small note values from the Semiminima and Hemiolia), with which he took his revenge on the chapel singers in Munich, for they could not sing it. Finally, there exists at the Munich Library a Requiem à 5 composed in 1669, and written out by copyists in the same year ; but it is not printed.

Kes, Willem, b. Feb. 16, 1856, Dordrecht, studied there under Nothdurft, Tyssens, and Ferd. Böhm, went, 1871, to David at the Leipzig Conservatorium, and, with a stipend from the King of Holland, to Wieniawski at the Brussels Conservatorium, finally to Joachim at Berlin. He is a gifted violinist and composer, became leader of the "Park" Orchestra in 1876, and of the "Felix meritis" Society at Amsterdam. He was, for some years, conductor of the "Gesellschaftkonzerte" at Dordrecht, in 1883 became conductor of the "Parkschouwburg" concerts, Amsterdam ; after then he lived at Dordrecht, and is now conductor of the "Concertgebow" concerts at Amsterdam.

Kesselpauke (Ger.), a kettle-drum.

Kessler, (1) Ferdinand, b. Jan., 1793, Frankfort, d. there Oct. 28, 1856. He was an able violinist and teacher of music, studied with his father, who was a double-bass player, and learnt theory from Vollweiler. He was an excellent teacher of theory (Fr. Wüllner was his pupil), and published pf. sonatas, rondos, etc. ; some works, on a large scale, remained in manuscript.

(2) Friedrich, in 1819 appointed pastor at Werdohle (Sauerland), published, jointly with Natorp, Rinck's "Choralbuch" in figure notation (1829, 1836) ; he wrote, besides, "Der musikalische Gottesdienst" (1832) ; "Kurze und fassliche Andeutungen einiger Mängel des Kirchengesangs" (1832), and "Das Gesangbuch von seiner musikalischen Seite aus betrachtet" (1838).

(3) Joseph Christoph (really Kötzler), b. Aug. 26, 1800, Augsburg, d. Jan. 14, 1872, Vienna. He lived at Prague (1803-7), Feldsberg (up to 1811), Nikolsburg (up to 1816), and Vienna (up to 1820). Only from his seventh to his tenth year did he receive regular instruction in pianoforte-playing (from the organist Bilek at Feldsberg) ; for the rest, he was self-taught, and became an excellent pianist and teacher of that instrument. He taught, from 1820-26, in

he house of Count Potocki at Lemberg and La ndshut, lived after that at Vienna until 1829, then until 1830, at Warsaw, 1830-35 Breslau, 1835-55 (a part from a temporary residence at Castle Graz and a journey to Carlsruhe) again at Lemberg, and, finally, from 1855, at Vienna. K.'s Études (Op. 20 [1825], 51, 100) are of lasting value, and have, in part, been incorporated in the Methods of Kalkbrenner, Moscheles, etc. As material for study they represent a somewhat high standard of technical development (more difficult than Czerny's "School of Virtuosity," and, musically, occupying a place between Hummel and Chopin). The nocturnes, variations, preludes, bagatelles, etc., were merely fugitive pieces ; yet among them there are some which do not deserve to be consigned to oblivion (Op. 29, 30, 38, also Op. 104 ["Blüthen und Knospen"]). (*Cf.* Fr. Pyllemann's personal reminiscences of K. in the *Allg. M.-Ztg.*, 1872.)

Ketten; Henri, well-known pianist and drawing-room composer, b. March 25, 1828, Baja (Hungary), d. April 1, 1883, Paris.

Kettenus, Aloys, b. Feb. 22, 1823, Verviers, pupil of the Conservatorium at Liège, in 1845 leader at Mannheim, and lived since 1855 in England. K. composed an opera (*Stella*), pieces for violin, etc. He died Oct. 3, 1896.

Ketterer, Eugen, pianist and favourite drawing-room composer, b. 1831, Rouen, d. Dec. 17, 1870, Paris.

Kettle-drum (Ital. *Timpani;* Ger. *Pauken;* Fr. *Timbales*), musically considered, the most valuable of instruments of percussion. It consists of a hemispherical kettle with stretched polished skins, which, by means of screws at the edge, can be tightened or loosened, so that the pitch of the sound of the membrane can be exactly regulated. The name of "machine-drum" is given to a K. in which the moving of the separate screws, a process which takes up a certain time, is replaced by a so-called machine which acts equally over the whole periphery. There is a small hole (sound-hole) underneath the kettle, from which extends a wide bell in the direction of the membrane ; it is about six inches high, and from eight to ten inches wide at the mouth. In the modern K. the sound-hole and the bell are frequently omitted. As a K. without fresh tuning can only produce one sound, at least two drums, standing near to each other, are always used, so as, on the one hand, to avoid frequent retunings, and, on the other hand, not to limit the composer too much in his use of the K. Within recent times the number of K.s in the orchestra has been increased to three (Berlioz, Liszt, Wagner, etc.) —a great advantage, of course, both to the composer and to the drummer. It were greatly to be desired that there should be really three K.s in all orchestras of any importance. K. are constructed in two sizes : the so-called large drum has a compass from *F—c*, and the small one from *B♭—f*. Originally they were tuned in

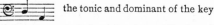

the tonic and dominant of the key of the trumpets before the time of Bach and Handel. For the principal theme of the scherzo of his Ninth Symphony, Beethoven made use of the lowest note of the large drum, and of the highest of the small one :

Formerly, when very scanty use was made of the K., and when it was regularly tuned in tonic-dominant, it was treated in notation as a transposing instrument, *i.e.* the key was indicated at the beginning of the piece : Timpani in *E♭, B♭*, or in *D A, B♭ F*, etc., but the notation was always *C G*, or rather, *c G :—*

Effect :

Notation :   This custom was done away with when composers (Beethoven) ventured to use other degrees than those of tonic and dominant; the actual notes are now written. The kettle-drum-sticks have either heads of wood, leather, or sponge; the first produce a hard, the other two an extremely soft sound. For special effects it is advisable to prescribe which kind of stick should be employed.

Keurvels, Edward H. J., b. 1853, Antwerp, studied under Benoit, was, at first, for some years, chorus-master at the Royal Theatre, Antwerp, and, since 1882, has been conductor at the " National Vlaamschen Schouwburg " (the Flemish national theatre), into which, in 1890, he introduced lyric drama (opera with dialogue: Benoit's *Pacificatie van Gent* and *Charlotte Corday*, Waelput's *Stella*, Beethoven's *Fidelio*, etc.). He himself wrote much for the stage (operas, *Parisina, Rolla, Hamlet;* several small operettas) ; also cantatas, a mass with organ, ballads, songs, etc.

Kewitsch, Theodor, b. Feb. 3, 1834, Posilge (West Prussia), was musician in the band of the 21st Regiment, then teacher and organist at Wabcz, Schwetz, and Graudenz; in 1866 teacher at the Berent seminary for music-teachers, in 1873 upper-teacher, from 1884–85 " Direktoriatsverwalter." In 1887 he was pensioned, and since then has lived at Berlin, where, from 1891–92, he edited the *Musikkorps.* At present he is editor of the *Hannoversche Musikerzeitung*, and contributor to other musical papers. For many years K. was " Diöcesanpräses " (diocesan president) of the " Caecilienverein " for Kulm. He has composed sacred vocal pieces, etc.

Key is a word of manifold signification ; the front part of the levers by which the pianoforte, organ, etc. are played, the levers of wood wind instruments, also the scale in which a piece of music is written. (*See* below.)

Key is the term for the mode (whether major or minor), and for the degree of the scale on which a composition is based. Instead of the two modes in use at the present day, the ancients (Greeks, Romans, Arabians, Indians, and the West during the middle ages) made use of a larger number. (*Cf.* GREEK MUSIC, ARABIANS, CHURCH MODES.) For the meaning of these various octave species and of scales generally, *cf.* SCALES. Each octave species can, at pleasure, be transposed—*i.e.* the same succession of intervals can be established starting from any note. The Greeks already had fifteen transposition scales ; the Church Modes were, indeed, for a long time, only transposed in the fourth, and only at a later period in the fifth and major second below. The introduction of other transpositions in the 16th and 17th centuries was already a sign of the decay of the old system. At the present day the transpositions of the two fundamental scales (c major and A minor) may, from the following table, be easily recognised and remembered (*cf.* FIFTH) :

	Major Keys.	
Flats.		Sharps.
7 6 5 4 3 2 1	0	1 2 3 4 5 6 7
C♭ G♭ D♭ A♭ E♭ B♭ F	C	G D A E B F♯ C♯ G♯ D♯ A♯
7 6 5 4 3 2 1	0	1 2 3 4 5 6 7
Flats.		Sharps.
	Minor Keys.	

The various sharps and flats are needed to rectify the succession of intervals of the fundamental scale. For instance, if the succession from the note c

is to be imitated, it will at once be seen that the fundamental scale between *e′* and *e²*, instead of having the half-tone steps between the third and fourth and seventh and eighth degrees, has them between the first and second and fifth and sixth degrees :—

The second degree must therefore be moved further away from the first, *i.e.* raised (♯ before *f*) ; but by this there results a half-tone between the second and third degrees, so that the latter must be raised so as to have the half-tone in the right place. In the same manner the second half-tone must be moved from its false to its true place (5–6) by raising the sixth and seventh degrees :—

Keys with flats are formed in a similar manner by moving the half-tone steps downwards, for example, F:

And this, as an aid to memory, may be added: the keys of the (upper and under) fifth of the fundamental scale have one chromatic sign; those of the (upper and under) whole tone, two; those of the minor third, three; of the major third, four; of the minor second, five; of the tritone, six; and of the chromatic half-tone, seven.

Key Relationship. (*Cf.* Tone Relationship.)

Keys, Auxiliary (Ger. *Nebentonarten*), the keys nearest related to the principal key of a piece of music, especially the parallel key, and the dominant keys.

Kiel, F r i e d r i c h, one of the most important of modern composers, b. Oct. 7, 1821, Puderbach, near Siegen, d. Sept. 14, 1885, Berlin; he was first trained by his father, the village schoolmaster. K. taught himself the pianoforte and composition, and several sets of dances and variations were written already 1832–34. Prince Karl of Wittgenstein-Berleberg perceived the boy's talent, and he himself taught him the violin (1835). Already at the end of a year K. played a concerto by Viotti, and became a member of the Prince's orchestra. His first works of importance were two sets of variations for violin with orchestra. After further training in theory, under Kaspar Kummer at Coburg (1838–39), he became, in 1840, leader of the court band and music-teacher to the ducal children. His next works (1837–42) were two overtures (B minor, c), solo pieces (variations, fantasias) for piano, violin, oboe, with orchestra; a cantata, four pianoforte sonatas, pf. pieces, songs, and part-songs. On the recommendation of the Prince, and as the result of the compositions which he exhibited, he received a stipend from Friedrich Wilhelm IV., and for two and a half years (1842–44) went through a severe course of counterpoint with S. W. Dehn. From that time K. resided in Berlin. In 1850 he published his first works: Op. 1, fifteen canons, and Op. 2, six fugues; the number of his published works barely exceeds eighty. He soon acquired fame, especially after (Feb. 8, 1862) the production of his first Requiem (Op. 20) by the Stern choral society; this work was composed 1859–60, revised and published 1878; a second Requiem (Op. 80 A♭) was produced a few years before his death. The Stern choral society first brought to a hearing K.'s " Missa solemnis " (March 21, 1867; composed 1865) and the oratorio *Christus* (April 4, 1874; composed 1871–72; up to 1878 performed six times at Berlin). Although these, his four chief works, are not remarkable for

thorough artistic individuality—rather, indeed, for their affinity to Bach and Beethoven, still they display such mastery, power of self-criticism, and fine esthetic instinct, that they, undoubtedly, lay claim to be ranked among the best contributions to modern musical literature. Already in 1865 K. was appointed member in ordinary of the Academy of Arts, and in the following year became teacher of composition at the Stern Conservatorium, and contributed greatly towards the reputation of that institution. After the title of professor had been bestowed on him, in 1868, he was appointed (1870) teacher of composition at the newly established " Hochschule für Musik," and elected, at the same time, member of the Senate of the Akademie. K., from the time when he had outgrown Dehn's theory, himself trained many distinguished pupils. He taught pf. playing only until his appointment at Stern's Conservatorium. To the works of K. already named may be added : The Stabat Mater (Op. 25, 1862), the 130th Psalm (Op. 29, 1863; both for female chorus, soli, and orchestra), a Te Deum (Op. 46, 1866), and two songs (Op. 83) for mixed choir with orchestra. He distinguished himself in the department of instrumental music; besides many pf. works for two hands (especially the variations Op. 17 and 62, three gigues Op. 36, and the smaller pieces, Op. 55, 59, 71, 79), and some for four hands, a pianoforte concerto (Op. 30), and four marches for orchestra (Op. 61), he wrote four violin sonatas, a 'cello sonata (Op. 52), sonata for tenor (Op. 67), seven trios (Op. 3, 22, 24, 33, 34, 65, the last containing two trios), three pf. quartets (Op. 43, 44, 50), two quintets (Op. 75, 76), two stringed quartets (Op. 53), and two series of " Walzer für Streichquartett " (Op. 73 and 78). *Cf.* the articles on K. by Bungert (*N. Z. f. Musik*, 1875), Saran (*Allg. M. Ztg.*, 1862), and Gumprecht (Westermann's *Monatshefte*, 1886).

Kiene. (*See* Bigot.)

Kienle, A m b r o s i u s, b. May 8, 1852, Siegmaringen, entered the Benedictine monastery, Beuron (Hohenzollern), 1873. He made a deep study of Gregorian melody, and wrote, besides many valuable essays in journals, a " Choralschule " (1890), a " Kleines kirchenmusikalisches Handbuch " (1892), and translated Pothier's " Les mélodies Grégoriennes " (" Der gregorianische Choral," 1881).

Kienzl, W i l h e l m, b. Jan. 17, 1857, Waitzenkirchen, in Upper Austria. He attended the Gymnasium at Graz (pianoforte pupil of Ignaz Uhl and Mortier de Fontaine), studied composition with Dr. W. Mayer (W. A. Remy), studied 1874 at Graz, 1875 at Prague, 1876 at Leipzig, 1877 at Vienna, where he took his degree of Dr.Phil. (" Die Musikalische Deklamation," published 1880). In 1879 he went to Bayreuth to Wagner, gave lectures at Munich (1880) on music, then became capellmeister of the Opera at Amsterdam and Crefeld, in 1886 conductor of the Styrian "Musikverein" at Graz, and in 1889 capellmeister of the theatre at Hamburg. As a writer, K. not only contributed articles to newspapers (collected as "Miscellen," 1886), but wrote miscellaneous essays and a compressed version of Brendel's History of Music. K. is also a composer of a light *genre* (chamber-music, pf. pieces, songs, opera *Urvasi* [Dresden, 1886], *Heilmar der Narr* [Munich, 1892], *Der Evangelimann* [1895]; he also completed Ad. Jensen's posthumous opera *Turandot*).

Kiesewetter, Raphael Georg (Edler von Wiesenbrunn), a famous writer on music, b. Aug. 29, 1773, Holleschau (Moravia), d. Jan. 1, 1850, Baden, near Vienna. He was trained for government service, and was imperial councillor of war; in the fulfilment of his duties he frequently changed his residence, and in 1845 received his pension as Imperial Councillor. From early youth K. was a zealous friend of music, made extensive collections of old musical works, which gradually led him to historical investigations; he studied, besides, theory and counterpoint (1803) under Albrechtsberger and Hartmann, and became, finally, an authority on matters connected with the history of music. Outward recognition of his services, which, indeed, could not be denied, was not lacking; he became successively member, likewise honorary member of several institutions (Berlin, Vienna) and musical societies. K. was the uncle of A. W. Ambros. His principal works are: " Die Verdienste der Niederländer um die Tonkunst" (which gained the prize offered by the Netherland Academy, 1826 ; Dutch, 1829) ; " Geschichte der europäisch-abendländischen oder unserer heutigen Musik" (1834 ; 2nd ed. 1846) ; "Ueber die Musik der neuern Griechen, nebst freien Gedanken über altägyptische und altgriechische Musik" (1838) ; "Guido von Arezzo, sein Leben und Wirken" (1840) ; " Schicksale und Beschaffenheit des weltlichen Gesangs vom frühen Mittelalter bis zur Erfindung des dramatischen Stils und den Anfängen der Oper" (1841); "Die Musik der Araber" (1842 ; *see* Riemann, "Studies on the History of Notation, pp. 77–86) ; " Der neuen Aristoxener zerstreute Aufsätze"(1846) ; "Ueber die Oktave des Pythagoras" (1848) ; " Galerie alter Kontrapunktisten" (1847; catalogue of his collection of old scores, which he bequeathed to the court library). He wrote, besides, a series of valuable articles for the Leipzig *Allgemeine Musikalische Zeitung*, 1826–45 (on the notation of Gregory the Great, on Franko of Cologne, on old tablatures, on Compère, Josquin, on Schmid's "Petrucci," etc. K. supervised the publishing of Kandler's "Palestrina"; several theoretical works remained in manuscript.

Kin, obsolete Chinese instrument of the zither kind, the strings of which (5–25) were made of silk threads.

Kindermann, (1) Johann Erasmus, b. March 29, 1616, Nuremberg, organist of St. Aegidien there ; he published up to 1652 a large number of sacred songs. (See *Monatsh. f. Mus. Gesch.* XV., 37 and 138.)

(2) August, b. Feb. 6, 1817, Potsdam, d. March 6, 1891, Munich, an excellent stage singer (baritone) ; he commenced his career at the age of sixteen as chorus-singer at the Berlin Opera, and Spontini chose him to take small solo parts. He was engaged at Leipzig 1839–46, and worked himself up from second bass to principal baritone, and was afterwards one of the greatest favourites of the public at the Munich Opera.

(3) Hedwig (Reicher-) K. (*See* REICHER-KINDERMANN.)

King, Chinese instrument of percussion consisting of stone bars tuned to different notes.

King, (1) Robert, chamber-musician to William III. of England, Bachelor of Music (Cambridge, 1696) ; he published " Songs for One, Two, and Three Voices, Composed to a Thorough-bass for the Organ or Harpsichord." Some of his compositions are to be found in collections of his time (" Choice Ayres," 1684 ; " Comes Amoris," 1687–93 ; " The Banquet of Music," 1688–92 ; *The Gentleman's Journal*, 1692–94 ; " Thesaurus musicus," 1695–96).

(2) Charles, b. 1687, chorister at St. Paul's under Blow and Clark, Mus.Bac. (Oxford, 1707), d. March 17, 1748 ; in 1707, almoner and master of the choristers at St. Paul's, organist of St. Benet Fink (1708), finally vicar choral of St. Paul's. He composed much sacred music (services, anthems, etc.), some of which were published separately, some in Arnold's " Cathedral Music " and in Page's " Harmonica Sacra," and some remained in manuscript.

(3) Matthew Peter, b. 1773, d. Jan., 1823, London. He wrote a number of English operas for the Lyceum Theatre, published pf. sonatas, songs, a cantata, produced an oratorio (*The Intercession*), and wrote a " General Treatise on Music " (1800; 2nd ed. 1809), and " Thorough Bass made Easy to Every Capacity " (1796).

Kinkel, Johanna, the wife of the well-known poet (*née* Mockel, divorced Matthieux), b. July 8, 1810, Bonn, d. Nov. 15, 1858, London. In 1832 she married the bookseller Matthieux, but left him after a few days. She was then trained at Berlin, and in 1843 became the wife of Gottfried K., whom she had followed, after his escape from the Spandau prison, to England. Her best-known works are the " Vogel-Kantate " and the operetta *Otto der Schütz;* she also wrote " Acht Briefe an eine Freundin über Klavierunterricht " (1852).

Kinnor, old Hebrew zither, or a stringed instrument of the harp kind.

Kipke, Karl, b. Nov. 20, 1850, Breslau, studied music at Leipzig, where, not counting his labours as conductor for a time at Pilsen, he has always resided. He is highly esteemed as proof-reader, also as editor of the *Sänger-halle*, etc.

Kipper, H e r m a n n, b. Aug. 27, 1826, Coblenz; pupil of Auschütz and H. Dorn. He lives as a teacher of music and musical critic at Cologne, and has made himself known by some humorous operettas: *Der Quacksalber* (*Doktor Sägebein und sein Famulus*), *Inkognito* (*Der Fürst wider Willen*), and *Kellner und Lord*.

Kirchenmusik (Ger.). (*See* CHURCH MUSIC.)

Kirchenstyl (Ger.), the ecclesiastical style, the style of church music.

Kircher, A t h a n a s i u s, b. May 2, 1602, Geisa, in the former bishopric of Fulda, d. Nov. 28, 1680, Rome; a learned Jesuit, professor of physics at Würzburg University; in 1635 he fled from the terrors of the Thirty Years' War to Avignon, and settled in Rome in 1637. Of his numerous works the following treat especially upon music, also acoustics: " Musurgia universalis sive ars magna consoni et dissoni," etc. (1650, two vols. [1654 ? 1662 ? 1690]; an epitome in German by Hirsch, 1662), and " Phonurgia nova, sive conjugium mechanico-physicum artis et naturæ," etc. (1673, German from " Neue Hall- und Tonkunst," by Agathos Cario). Both works are examples of the most extraordinary mixture of scientific proofs and of credulity beyond belief; but they also contain much of the highest interest for the history of music, and also for acoustics. Some musical peculiarities are to be found in his " Ars magnetica" (1641, and frequently), and in " Œdipus Ægyptiacus " (1652–54, three vols.).

Kirchl, A d o l f, composer of songs for male voices, b. June 16, 1858, Vienna, lives there as choir-master of the Schubertbund.

Kirchner, (1) T h e o d o r, b. Dec. 10, 1823, Neukirchen, near Chemnitz, a gifted pianoforte composer, especially of miniature pieces treated in a manner quite peculiar to himself. He went to Leipzig in 1838, and, on the advice of Mendelssohn, studied with C. F. Becker (organ and theory), J. Knorr (pianoforte) ; and in the summer of 1842 with Joh. Schneider at Dresden (organ). In 1843 he became a pupil of the Leipzig Conservatorium (but only for six months), from 1843–62 was organist at Winterthur, and for the following ten years acted as conductor and teacher of music at Zürich. After a year's residence at Meiningen as teacher of music to the Princess Maria (1872–73), he worked as director of the royal " Musikschule," Würzburg, lived for eight years at Leipzig, went in 1883 to Dresden, where he became teacher at the royal Conservatorium, and in 1890 to Hamburg. Besides pf. pieces, some songs (" Sie sagen, es wäre die Liebe ") have especially made K.'s name known in wider circles. Here is a complete list of his original compositions : Op. 1, ten songs ; Op. 2,

ten pf. pieces; Op. 3, " 6 Mädchenlieder ;" Op. 4, four songs ; Op. 5, " Gruss an meine Freunde ;" Op. 6, four songs ; Op. 7, " Albumblätter ; " Op. 8, Scherzo ; Op. 9, preludes (two books) ; Op. 10, " Zwei Könige " (ballad for baritone) ; Op. 11, " Skizzen " (three books) ; Op. 12, " Adagio quasi fantasia ;" Op. 13, " Lieder ohne Worte ;" Op. 14, " Phantasiestücke " (three books); Op. 15, " Ein Gedenkblatt " (serenade in B major for pf., violin, and 'cello) ; Op. 16, " Kleine Lust- und Trauerspiele ;" Op. 17, " Neue Davidsbündlertänze ;" Op. 18, " Legenden ;" Op. 19, ten pf. pieces (transcriptions of his own songs ; five books) ; Op. 20, stringed quartet ; Op. 21, " Aquarellen " (two books) ; Op. 22, romances (two books) ; Op. 23, waltzes (two books); Op. 24, " Still und bewegt " (two books) ; Op. 25, " Nachtbilder " (two books) ; Op. 26, Album ; Op. 27, caprices (two books) ; Op. 28, nocturnes ; Op. 29, " Aus meinem Skizzenbuch " (two books) ; Op. 30, " Studien und Stücke " (four books); Op. 31, " Im Zwielicht ;" Op. 32, " Aus trüben Tagen ;" Op. 33, " Ideale ;" Op. 34, waltzes (two books) ; Op. 35, " Spielsachen ;" Op. 36, " Phantasien am Klavier " (two books) ; Op. 37, four elegies ; Op. 38, twelve études ; Op. 39, " Dorfgeschichten ;" Op. 40, three songs (words by F. v. Holstein) ; Op. 41, " Verwehte Blätter ;" Op. 42, mazurkas (two books) ; Op. 43, four polonaises ; Op. 44, " Blumen zum Strauss ;" Op. 45, six pf. pieces ; Op. 46, " 30 Kinder- und Künstlertänze; Op. 47, " Federzeichnungen ;" Op. 48, Humoresken ; Op. 49, " Neue Albumblätter " (two books) ; Op. 50, six songs ; Op. 51, " An Stephen Heller ; " Op. 52, " Ein neues Klavierbuch " (three parts) ; Op. 53, " Florestan und Eusebius ;" Op. 54, Scherzo ; Op. 55, " Neue Kinderscenen ;" Op. 56, " In stillen Stunden ;" Op. 57, twelve pieces for four hands ; Op. 58, children's trios (for pf., violin, and 'cello) ; Op. 59, " Trio-Novelletten"; Op. 60, " Plaudereien am Klavier ; " Op. 61, six characteristic pieces (three books) ; Op. 62, Miniatures ; Op. 63, " Romanze und Schlummerlied," for pf. and violin ; Op. 64, gavottes, minuets, and lyric pieces ; Op. 65, sixty preludes (Op. 66 is wanting) ; Op. 67, " Liebeserwachen " (song); Op. 68, " Nähe des Geliebten " (song) : Op. 69, four poems by Goethe (for male chorus) ; Op. 70, five sonatinas ; Op. 71, one hundred small studies ; Op. 72, " Stille Lieder u. Tänze " (two books) ; Op. 73, " Romantische Geschichten " (four books) ; Op. 74, " Alte Errinerungen ;" Op. 75, nine pf. pieces ; Op. 76, " Reflexe " (six waltzes) ; Op. 77, polonaises, waltzes, and Ländler ; Op. 78, " Les mois de l'année " (illustrated) ; Op. 79, eight pieces for pf. and 'cello ; Op. 80, 9 Albumblätter Op. 81, six songs : Op. 82, " Gedenkblätter " (for the inauguration of the new Leipzig Conservatorium); Op. 83, " Bunte Blätter " (twelve trios) ; Op. 84, pf. quartets ; Op. 85, variations for two pianofortes. Without opus number have appeared a second "Triosonate" (cf. Op. 15) in E, Polonaise for two pfs., two études in C and D minor (the latter in the Pianoforte School of Lebert-Stark); "Lieblinge der Jugend" (thirty small études), and "Alte Bekannte im neuen Gewande" (piano duets), and some songs. K. has lately transcribed a great number of songs by Jensen, Brahms, etc., for pf. solo. Cf. A. Niggli's "Th. K." (1880).

(2) Fritz, b. Nov. 3, 1840, Potsdam, pupil at Kullak's Akademie (Kullak, Wüerst, Seyffert), where he became teacher (1864) until the staff was disbanded (autumn, 1889). He was a diligent composer, especially of constructive pieces for pf.; also vocal pieces. Died April 11, 1907.

(3) Hermann, b. Jan. 23, 1861, Wölfis (Thuringia); concert-singer (tenor) and composer, lives at Berlin.

Kirkman, (1) Jacob (really Kirchmann), founder of the London pianoforte manufactory, K. and Sons; he came before 1740 to London and worked for Tabel, where also Shudi (Tschudi), founder of the Broadwood factory, was engaged. K. married Tabel's widow, and died a wealthy man in 1778. His harpsichords enjoyed a high reputation. As he had no children, he was succeeded by his nephew Abraham K. The business was amalgamated with that of the Collards in 1896. A subtle solution of the problem how to prolong sound on the pianoforte was shown in the "Melopiano" (reiterated blows by special small hammers) which Caldera invented, and which was successfully employed by K.

(2) Johann, Dutch by birth, 1782 organist of the Lutheran Church, London; d. 1799. Trios, violin sonatas, pf. sonatas, organ pieces, etc.

Kirnberger, Johann Philipp, b. April 24, 1721, Saalfeld, Thuringia, d. July 27, 1783, Berlin, one of the most esteemed theorists of the last century. His name must be mentioned side by side with those of Rameau and Tartini, yet the services which he rendered have often been exaggerated. K. studied with Kellner (sen.) at Gräfenroda, with Gerber (sen.) at Sondershausen, and for some time with J. S. Bach at Leipzig. From 1741–50 he occupied various posts as private teacher of music and musical director in the houses of Polish noblemen, and finally at the convent, Lemberg. He returned to Germany in 1751, studied the violin at Dresden, and became a member of the royal band at Berlin, and in 1754 teacher of composition and capellmeister to Princess Amalie (q.v.), in which post he found abundant leisure for composition. The works of K. are now forgotten (lessons, pieces, suites, fugues, etc., for clavier and for organ; twelve minuets for two violins, oboes, flutes, horns, and continuo; soli for flute; trios for two violins and bass; songs, odes, motets, etc.). The best-known and most important work of K. is "Die Kunst des reinen Satzes" (1774–79, two

vols.). His first work was "Konstruction der gleichschwebenden Temperatur" (1760, cf. TEMPERAMENT). There appeared besides, under his name (cf., however, J. A. P. Schulz), "Die wahren Grundsätze zum Gebrauch der Harmonie" (1773). Fundamental chords, according to K., are: major chord, minor chord, diminished triad, major chord with major and with minor seventh, likewise the minor chord and diminished triad with minor seventh. The assertion of K. that there are only two fundamental chords (triad, and chord of the seventh) must therefore be taken cum grano salis. He wrote besides: "Grundsätze des Generalbasses als erste Linien der Komposition" (1781, often republished); "Gedanken über die verschiedenen Lehrarten der Komposition als Vorbereitung zur Fugenkenntnis" (1782); "Anleitung zur Singkomposition" (1782); "Der allzeit fertige Menuetten- und Polonaisen- Komponist" (1757), somewhat of the nature of a musical joke, a precursor of the well-known musical game of dice. K. was a contributor to Sulzer's "Theorie der schönen Künste;" he also published numerous vocal works by Hasler and Graun. (Concerning K.'s i, cf. the article "i.")

Kist, Florent Corneille, b. Jan. 28, 1796, Arnheim, d. March 23, 1863, Utrecht, worthy Dutch musician; he was originally only an amateur, studied medicine and practised as doctor at the Hague until 1825; but at an early period became an excellent performer on the flute and horn, and diligently studied singing and composition. Already in 1821 he was one of the founders of the musical union "Diligentia" at the Hague, and displayed (after he had given up medicine) an extraordinary activity as organiser. He founded at Delft a choral society, and a branch of the union for the advancement of music at the Hague, the "Cäcilia" society, and presided over, besides the above-named, the "Collegium musicum" at Delft, and the "Harmonie" at the Hague. In 1841 he went to Utrecht, edited for three years the Nederlandsch muzikaal Tijdschrift, and afterwards founded the Caecilia, which, to the present day, is the most important musical paper of Holland. For several years he was also member of the Utrecht concert society ("Collegium musicum Ultra-jectinum"), and founded amateur concerts ("Symphonie") as well as a choral society ("Duce Apolline"). Besides many articles in both his above-named musical papers, as well as in the German Signale, Teutonia, and Gassner's Zeitschrift für Dilettanten, he wrote "De toestand van het protestansche kerk gesang in Nederland" (1840); "Levensgeschidenis van Orlando de Lassus" (1841); and also translated into Dutch Brendel's "Grundzüge der Geschichte der Musik" (1851). His printed compositions are vocal pieces for one and several voices, and a volume of variations for flute; important cantatas, etc., remained in manuscript.

Kistler, Cyrill, b. March 12, 1848, Gross-Aitingen, near Augsburg, was from 1867–76 school-teacher, and then received his musical training from Rheinberger at Munich. He became, in 1873, teacher at the Conservatorium at Sondershausen, and lives, since 1885, as teacher of music at Kissingen. His romantic opera (*Kunihild*) was given at Sondershausen in 1884, and at Würzburg in 1892; two others have not been performed. He is the author of "Harmonielehre" and a "Musikalische Elementarlehre," and publishes the *Musikalische Tagesfragen* (critical notices, personal news, etc.).

Kistner, Friedrich, b. March 3, 1797, Leipzig, d. there Dec. 21, 1844; he undertook in 1831 the Probst musical business, and from 1836 traded under his own name. The publishing-house of K. developed into one of the most important in Leipzig under him and his son Julius (d. May 13, 1868), but especially under K. F. L. Gurckhaus (b. April 17, 1821, d. May 22, 1884, Leipzig), who in 1866 became the proprietor.

Kit is the name for the old pocket violin. (*Cf.* POCHETTE.)

Kitchener, William, rich London physician and famous gourmand, also a trained amateur, d. Feb. 26, 1827 (fifty years old). He wrote "Observations on Vocal Music" (1821), and edited the collections "The Loyal and National Songs of England" (1823), "The Sea Songs of England" (1823), and "A Collection of the Vocal Music in Shakespeare's Plays." He also wrote an operetta, *Love among the Roses; or, The Master Key.*

Kittel, Johann Christian, b. Feb. 18, 1732, Erfurt, d. there May 9, 1809, the last pupil of J. S. Bach; he was, at first, organist at Langensalza, from 1756 up till his death at the "Predigerkirche," Erfurt, with a very small salary (but he was protected from want by means of a small pension from Prince Primas of Dalberg, also by the proceeds of some concert tours), and went finally in 1800 to Hamburg and Altona, where he remained a year. K. enjoyed a distinguished name as organist, composer, theorist, and teacher. K. H. Rinck was his most celebrated pupil. Only a few of his works appeared in print, and of these the following deserve special mention: "Der angehende practische Organist oder Anweisung zum zweckmässigen Gebrauch der Orgel beim Gottesdienst" (1801–8, three parts; new edition 1831); "Neues Choralbuch" (for Schleswig-Holstein, 1803); "Grosse Präludien," for organ; two chorales with variations, for organ; six pf. sonatas (Op. 1); twenty-four chorales (with eight figured basses for each); "Hymne an das Jahrhundert," à 4 (1801), and a book of pf. variations.

Kittl, Johann Friedrich, b. May 8, 1809, Castle Worlik (Bohemia), d. July 20, 1868, Polnisch-Lissa, son of an officer of justice; he studied jurisprudence, but, with special prefer-ence, music (principally under Tomaschek at Prague); from 1840 he devoted himself entirely to music, and, after the death of Dionys Weber, was elected director of the Prague Conservatorium. After more than twenty years' active and salutary service, he withdrew in 1865 to Polnisch-Lissa. K. wrote several operas—*Daphnis' Grab, Die Franzosen vor Nizza* (= *Bianca und Giuseppe,* libretto by Richard Wagner!), *Waldblume, Die Bilderstürmer*—which gained for him high repute. He also wrote a trio (Op. 28), septet (pf., wind instruments, and double-bass), songs, and several symphonies, etc.

Kitzler, Otto, b. March 16, 1834, Dresden, pupil of J. Otto, Joh. Schneider, and F. A. Kummer ('cello); and after a short engagement as musical director at Eutin he studied with Servais at the Brussels Conservatoire; he was also 'cellist in the opera orchestra at Strassburg and Lyons, then opera capellmeister at Troyes, Linz, Königsberg, Temeswar, Hermannstadt, and Brünn; from 1868 director of the Brünn Musical Society and of the music school connected with it, likewise conductor of the male choral society. K. published works for pianoforte and for orchestra, also songs, which show him to be a well-schooled musician.

Kjerulf, Halfdan, Norwegian composer, b. 1818, d. Aug. 11, 1868, Christiania, where a monument was erected to him. By his songs and part-songs he became extremely popular in his native country; but he also wrote excellent pianoforte works (published by Heinrich Hofmann and Arno Kleffel), which made his name known in Germany.

Klafsky, Katharina, dramatic stage-singer (dramatic soprano), b. Sept. 19, 1855, St. Johann, in Hungary, d. Sept. 22, 1896. She was the daughter of a shoemaker, who, like her mother, was musical, and sang in church choirs. Her mother died when she was young, and, as her father married again, she left home, and went first to Ödenburg, and, later on, to Vienna. There her voice attracted notice, and Hellmesberger persuaded Mme. Marchesi to give the young lady lessons gratis. In 1875 she appeared on the stage at Salzburg in small parts; but in 1876 she married a merchant, retired from public life, and went to Leipzig. Unfortunate circumstances compelled her to return to the stage (Leipzig), and, with ever-increasing success, she soon became an artist of the first rank, and succeeded Hedwig Reicher-Kindermann in Angelo Neumann's travelling Wagner company. Neumann first took her to Bremen, but from 1885 she belonged to the Hamburg stage. In the *rôle* of Fidelio, Frau K. had, in her lifetime, few rivals.

Klangboden (Ger.), sound-board.

Klanggeschlecht (Ger.), genus of sounds; the diatonic, the chromatic, and the enharmonic genus.

Klangschlüssel ("Clang Key") is the term applied by the compiler of this Dictionary to the new method of designating chords which he has developed and exclusively employed in his theoretical works, and which he would use in place of general-bass figuring, since the latter does not indicate in a satisfactory manner the clang meaning of chords. (*Cf.* GENERAL-BASS.) In K., as in general-bass, the figures 1–10 are employed, but the intervals are determined not from the bass note, but from the principal note of the clang in the sense of which the chord must be conceived. The usual (Arabian) figures are used for major, the Roman, for minor chords; the former indicate the intervals from the principal tone upwards, the latter, downwards. The figures have the following meaning: 1 (I), principal tone; 2 (II), major second; 3 (III), major third; 4 (IV), perfect fourth; 5 (V) perfect fifth; 6 (VI) major sixth; 7 (VII) minor seventh; 8 (VIII) octave (used exceptionally, for instance, after 9 (IX), in place of 1 [I]); 9 (IX), major ninth; 10 (X), major tenth (in exceptional cases for the third). All the figures, with exception of 1, 3, 5 (8, 10), likewise I, III, V (VIII, X), indicate dissonant tones; for only principal tone, third-tone, and fifth-tone are constituent parts of the (major or minor) clang. (*See* CLANG.) When the seven or ten fundamental intervals mentioned above undergo change, < indicates raising by a semitone, and > lowering by a semitone ; *tones doubly raised or doubly lowered are inconceivable from a musical point of view.* The abbreviated sign + stands for the major chord (upper clang) in place of $\frac{5}{3}$, and the sign ° for the minor chord (under-clang) in place of $\overset{\text{I}}{\underset{\text{V}}{\text{III}}}$. The sign + is, however, only used in opposition to, or alternately with, ° ; the absence of any sign indicates the major clang of the given tone. K. differs from general-bass figuring in that it is not confined to a bass part, but can be employed at pleasure for any part. A pupil under the old method had no opportunity of learning good progressions for a bass part, but in K. such opportunity is granted to him in fullest measure. Instead of indicating clangs concretely according to their principal tone (*c*+, °*e*, etc.), the compiler of this dictionary has recently used the more general letters which, at the same time, indicate the *tonal function* :—T (tonic), D (dominant), and S (subdominant), with + and ° for major and minor. The harmonic meaning is rendered quite independent of pitch, and thus important means is offered for training scholars to think harmonically. *See* Riemann's "Vereinfachte Harmonielehre" (London, 1893). (*Cf.* TONAL FUNCTIONS OF HARMONY.)

Klangvertretung (Substitution of Clangs), a conception of modern harmony theory, relating to the special meaning which a note or interval obtains according as it is conceived in the sense of this or that clang. For example, c has quite a different meaning in the logic of composition, if it is thought of as the third of the chord of A flat, from that which it has as third of the chord of A minor (°e, *cf.* KLANGSCHLÜSSEL); in the former case it is closely related to D flat, and to the D flat chord; in the latter, to B and to E major and the E minor chord. Each note can form an essential part of six various clangs (*cf.* CLANG); for instance, the note c can be the major principal note of the c upper-clang, the major (upper) fifth of the F upper clang, the major (upper) third of the A flat upper-clang, the minor principal note of the c under-clang (F minor chord), the minor (under) fifth of the G under-clang (c minor chord), and, finally, the minor (under) third of the E under-clang (A minor chord) :—

If the note c appears as dissonant note to any other clang, or in the place of one of its chord notes as suspension, or as altered note (*see* DISSONANCE), its meaning must always be determined in the sense of one of these six clangs, and, indeed, of the nearest related.

Klappe (Ger.), a key of wind-instruments like the flute, clarinet, bassoon, Kent bugle, etc.

Klauser, (1) K a r l, b. Aug. 24, 1823, Petersburg, went in 1850 to New York, and lived, from 1855, as a highly esteemed teacher of music at Farmington (United States). K. has made a name by his numerous pf. arrangements of classical and romantic orchestral works, also by editing celebrated pianoforte works for the firm of Schuberth & Co. His son and pupil

(2) J u l i u s, b. July 5, 1854, New York, from 1871–74 at the Leipzig Conservatorium (Wenzel), lives, an esteemed teacher of music, at Milwaukee. He has published : "The Septonate and the Centralisation of the Tonal System" (1890), a harmony book of modern tendency.

Klauwell, (1) A d o l f, b. Dec. 31, 1818, Langensalza (Thuringia), for many years teacher of the third, afterwards of the fourth, "Bürgerschule" in Leipzig, where he d. Nov. 21, 1879. He was a well-known teacher, and published elementary school-books and instructive pianoforte pieces, of which "Goldnes Melodien-Album" is specially popular. His daughter M a r i e (Lang-K.), b. Jan. 27, 1853, is a much-admired concert-singer (soprano).

(2) O t t o, composer and writer on music, b. April 7, 1851, Langensalza, nephew of the former, was trained at the Schulpforta Gymnasium; from 1870–71 he took part in the war against France, and afterwards studied mathematics at the Leipzig University, but then followed his own wishes, and, in 1872, turned

entirely to music, studying under Reinecke and Richter (theory and composition) at the Leipzig Conservatorium, and in 1874 took his degree of Doctor of Philosophy at the Leipzig University. In 1875 he became teacher of the pianoforte, theory, and history at the Cologne Conservatorium, and in 1884 undertook the direction of the pianoforte training-classes established by Fr. Wüllner. K. is a talented composer; he has written overtures, chamber-music, pf. pieces, also an opera (*Das Mädchen vom See*), and songs, most of which were published. The following of his pamphlets also deserve mention: "Die historische Entwickelung des musikalischen Kanons" (1874, dissertation), an interesting collection of aphorisms; "Musikalische Gesichtspunkte" (1881); also "Der Vortrag in der Musik" (1883); and "Der Fingersatz des Klavierspiels" (1885).

Klee, Ludwig, b. April 13, 1846, Schwerin, pupil (1864–68), and afterwards (up to 1875) teacher, at Kullak's Academy, Berlin, and since then president of a school of music of his own. He published a number of educational works, of which the "Die Ornamentik der Klassischen Klaviermusik" especially deserves mention.

Kleeberg, Clotilde, b. June 27, 1866, Paris, pupil of the Conservatoire (Mme. Retz and Mme. Massart). She made her first public appearance at the Pasdeloup concerts in 1878, when she performed Beethoven's c minor concerto; since then, as a refined pianist, she has acquired European fame.

Kleeman, Karl, b. Sept. 9, 1842, Rudolstadt (Thuringia), was intended for the book trade, but, under the court capellmeister Müller at Rudolstadt, studied music and began his practical career as a conductor of a vocal society in Westphalia. In 1878 he went for several years to Italy, devoting himself diligently to composition, and on his return was appointed second opera conductor and ducal musical director at Dessau. Of his compositions the following have appeared: music to Grillparzer's *Der Traum ein Leben*, symphonic fantasia, *Des Meeres und der Liebe Wellen*, two symphonies, songs, choral works, and pf. pieces, etc.

Kleffel, Arno, b. Sept. 4, 1840, Pössneck (Thuringia), attended the Leipzig Conservatorium for a short time, but was chiefly a private pupil of Moritz Hauptmann's. From 1863–67 he was conductor of the musical society at Riga, then theatre capellmeister successively at Cologne, Amsterdam, Görlitz, Breslau, Stettin, etc.; from 1873–80 at the Friedrich Wilhelmstadt Theatre, Berlin, at Augsburg and Magdeburg; 1886–92 Cologne, then teacher of theory at Stern's Conservatorium, Berlin, Capellmeister, Hamburg, 1898. K. has composed an opera (*Des Meermanns Harfe*), which was produced at Riga in 1865, music to the Christmas legend "Die Wichtelmännchen," besides music to

Goethe's *Faust*, overtures, choral works, songs, pf. pieces, part-songs, a stringed quartet, etc.

Klein, (1) Johann Joseph, b. Aug. 24, 1740, Arnstadt, d. June 25, 1823, Kahla, near Jena, lawyer at Eisenberg (Altenburg). He wrote: "Lehrbuch der praktischen Musik" (1783); "Lehrbuch der theoretischen Musik" (1801); "Neues vollständiges Choralbuch" (1785, with an introduction on chorale music); also various articles for the *Allgemeine Musikalische Zeitung* (1799 to 1800).

(2) **Bernhard,** b. March 6, 1793, Cologne, d. Sept. 9, 1832, Berlin, an excellent composer of sacred works, received his early musical training at Cologne, where his father was double-bass player. He went to Paris in 1812, where he worked for some time under Cherubini, and studied diligently at the library of the Conservatoire. On his return he was appointed musical director at Cologne Cathedral. In 1818 he went as government inspector to the musical schools at Berlin, but settled there, where, in 1820 he was appointed teacher of composition at the newly established Royal Institution for Church Music, and, simultaneously, musical director and teacher of singing at the University. K.'s chief works are his oratorios *Jephtha*, *David*, and *Job*, a mass, a Paternoster à 8, a Magnificat à 6 (with triple fugue), responses à 6, besides eight books of psalms, hymns and motets for male voices (well known and held in high esteem), pf. sonatas, variations, etc., songs and ballads ("Erlkönig"), cantata, *Worte des Glaubens* (Schiller), two operas, *Dido* (1823), and *Ariadne* (Jan. 22, 1825), two acts of a third (*Irene*), music to Raupach's *Erdennacht*, etc.

(3) **Joseph,** younger brother of the former, b. 1802, Cologne, d. there 1862, likewise composer; he lived at Berlin and Cologne.

(4) **Bruno,** Oskar, b. June 6, 1856, Osnabrück, pupil of his father, of the musical director Karl K., and of the Royal School of Music at Munich. K. was appointed organist of St. Francis Xavier, New York, in 1879. He has made himself known as a composer by orchestral pieces, a violin sonata, a suite for pf. and violin, etc.

Kleinmichel, Richard, composer and pianist, b. Dec. 31, 1846, Posen, received his first instruction from his father, who was bandmaster there, and afterwards at Potsdam, and finally went to Hamburg, where he enjoyed further, and sound training. From 1863–66 he was a pupil of the Leipzig Conservatorium, then lived as teacher of music at Hamburg, and in 1876 settled in Leipzig, where in 1882 he became musical director of the "Stadttheater." His wife is the singer Clara Monhaupt. He has appeared frequently as a pianist, and with success, but of late is mentioned mostly as a composer. He has published, up to now, various pf. works (excellent études), songs.

chamber-music, two symphonies and two operas (*Manon=Schloss de Lorme* [Hamburg, 1883], and *Der Pfeifer von Dusenbach* [Hamburg, 1891]).

Klengel, (1) A u g u s t A l e x a n d e r, b. Jan. 27, 1783, Dresden, d. there Nov. 22, 1852, son of the landscape-painter K., pupil of Milchmayer, and of Clementi (1803), with whom he went to Petersburg, where he remained up to 1811. After a residence of two years in Paris, he returned to Dresden in 1814, which he only left for a passing visit to London in the following year. In 1816 he was appointed court organist at Dresden. K. is known under the name "Kanon K." on account of his complete mastery of this severest of imitative art-forms. He himself, towards the close of his life, published twenty-four canons under the title, "Les avant-coureurs;" his chief work ("Kanons und Fugen," 1854; an attempt to outdo the "Well-tempered Clavier," but unsuccessful, in that it is pedantic and lacking in imagination), to which the above-named forms the introductory steps, was published by Moritz Hauptmann after K.'s death. In his early years he wrote: two pf. concertos, one concert polonaise for pf., flute, clarinet, viola, 'cello, and bass; one trio, one pf. fantasia for four hands, several pf. sonatas, and many pieces; a concerto and a quintet remain in manuscript. Younger relatives of K., though not by direct descent, are :
(2) P a u l K., b. May 13, 1854, Leipzig, able violinist and pianist, composer of pleasing songs; Dr.Phil., with dissertation "Zur Aesthetik der Tonkunst" (Leipzig); from 1881–86 conductor of the "Euterpe" concerts at Leipzig, then, for some years, second Hofkapellmeister at Stuttgart, and 1893 conductor of the academical choral society "Arion" at Leipzig. His brother
(3) J u l i u s, b. Sept. 24, 1859, Leipzig, a 'cellist of the very first rank, principal 'cello in the Gewandhaus orchestra, and teacher at the Leipzig Conservatorium ('cello concerto, Op. 10, concertino, Op. 7, stringed quartet in G, suite for two violoncelli, and other compositions for violoncello).

Kliebert, K a r l, b. Dec. 13, 1849, Prague, studied jurisprudence at Vienna, took his degree of Dr.Jur. at Prague, but then devoted himself entirely to music, and was trained by Rheinberger and Wüllner at Munich. After acting for some time as theatre capellmeister at Augsburg, he was called to Würzburg (1875) to reorganise the Royal School of Music, and in 1876 succeeded Kirchner as director of this institution, which, under his guidance, has greatly prospered.

Klindworth, K a r l, b. Sept. 25, 1830, Hanover, distinguished pianist, pupil of Liszt's at Weimar, lived from 1854–68 in London, highly esteemed both as teacher and player. From 1861–62 he established orchestral and chamber-music concerts, which, however, owing to the

heavy expenses, he was obliged to give up. From 1868–84 he was professor of the pianoforte at the Moscow Conservatoire, then settled in Berlin in order to conduct the Philharmonic Concerts jointly with Joachim and Wüllner, and established in Berlin a "Klavierschule" which, with the co-operation of Bülow (one month per year), was successfully inaugurated (1893, incorporated with the Scharwenka Conservatorium). As a composer, K. is only known by a few interesting pianoforte pieces, but his remarkable editorial work is of very great importance, especially his pf. scores of Wagner's complete "Nibelungen-Trilogie," an edition of Chopin's works, new edition of Beethoven's sonatas, etc.

Kling, H e n r i, b. Feb. 17, 1842, Paris, teacher of music at the schools at Geneva, and bandmaster. He has written several operas, as well as instrumental and vocal music, all of little intrinsic value; he is also the author of a Method and studies for horn, a Method for drum, a treatise on instrumentation (German), frequently republished.

Klingenberg, F r i e d r i c h W i l h e l m, b. June 6, 1809, Sulau (Silesia); he studied theology at Breslau, but gave it up and turned to music, undertook the direction of the Breslau "Akademischer Musikverein," afterwards of the "Künstlerverein." In 1840 he was called to Görlitz as cantor of the Peterskirche, and in 1844 was named "Königlicher Musikdirector." In 1885, owing to a severe injury to one of his feet, he was compelled to resign his appointments. As conductor of the church choir, as well as of a large vocal society of his own (the "Görlitzer Musikverein"), he did much for musical life at Görlitz. As composer, he became known by a number of sacred and secular vocal works.

Klitzsch, K a r l E m a n u e l, b. Oct. 30, 1812, Schönhaide (Saxon Erzgebirge), studied philology at Leipzig, took his degree, and was appointed teacher at Zwickau College (pensioned in 1886). He studied music at the same time, and, although for the most part self-taught, he undertook later on the direction of the concerts of the musical society and of the a-cappella "Musikverein," and was also musical director of the two principal churches at Zwickau. For many years K. was a zealous contributor to the *Neue Zeitschrift für Musik*. He published songs, the ninety-sixth psalm, etc., under the name "Emanuel Kronach."

Klosé, H y a c i n t h e É l é o n o r e, famous clarinet-player, b. Oct. 11, 1808, on the island of Corfu, d. Aug. 29, 1880, Paris. When young he went to France; was, at first, bandmaster, and in 1839 succeeded his teacher, Berr, as professor of the clarinet at the Paris Conservatoire, and received his pension in 1868. He applied the Boehm system of ring keys to the clarinet (1843); he also published solo, and instructive works for clarinet (soli, duets, fantasias, studies, a "Grande méthode pour la clarinette à anneaux mobiles"), also marches, parade pieces for military band, and three Methods for the various kinds of saxophones.

Klotz (Clotz), the name of an old family of violin-makers at Mittenwald (Bavarian Alps); A e g i d i u s K. is named as the oldest representative, and his son M a t t h i a s, about 1660–96, established the reputation of the family. Sons of the latter are S e b a s t i a n and J o s e p h; later descendants (in the 18th century) G e o r g, K a r l, M i c h a e l, and A e g i d i u s K. A great many of the violins made by K. pass for those of Steiner.

Klughardt, A u g u s t F r i e d r i c h M a r t i n, b. Nov, 30, 1847, Cöthen. After attending the Dessau Gymnasium, he became a pupil of Blassmann and A. Reichel at Dresden, and commenced his public career, at the age of twenty, as theatre capellmeister at Posen, Lübeck (each a season), and Weimar (four years), where he was appointed musical director to the Grand Duke. In 1873 he became court capellmeister at Neustrelitz, and now occupies a similar post at Dessau. His stay at Weimar, especially the intercourse with Liszt, had a beneficial effect on K.'s talent for composition: he was drawn in the direction of the .new German school, proof of which, among other things, is given by his "Leonore" symphony. Besides this, the following works were published, likewise produced: the overtures "Im Frühling," "Sophonisbe," and "Siegesouvertüre;" the symphonies, "Im Walde," and Op. 37 in D; festival overture; orchestral suite, Op. 40, A minor (in six movements); pf. quintet, Op. 43; trio, Op. 47; sextet and quartet (Op. 42) for strings; operas: *Mirjam,* (Weimar, 1871), *Iwein* and *Gudrun* (Neustrelitz, 1879 and 1882); *Die Hochzeit des Mönchs* (Dessau, 1886; as *Astorre,* at Prague, in 1888); "Schilflieder" ("Phantasiestücke," after Lenau, for pf., oboe, and viola), and eight books of songs.

Knecht, J u s t i n H e i n r i c h, b. Sept. 30, 1752, Biberach (Würtemberg), d. there Dec. 1, 1817. In 1792 he became organist and concert director in his native town, in 1807 court capellmeister at Stuttgart, but, owing to intrigues, the post became distasteful to him, and, already in 1809, he returned to Biberach. As organist K. enjoyed extraordinary fame, and only Vogler was considered his superior. His compositions have ceased to live; the following may be mentioned : a symphony (" A Tone-picture of Nature," having a programme identical with that of Beethoven's Pastoral Symphony; he treated the same subject in an organ sonata, " Die unterbrochene Hirtenwonne "); concert duet, " Mirjam und Deborah " (from Klopstock's *Messias*) ; psalms, a Te Deum for double choir, masses, several operas and vaudevilles, melodrama, *Das Lied von der Glocke*

(Schiller); organ pieces, pf. variations, sonatinas, flute duets, arias, hymns, two chorale books (for Würtemberg and Protestant Bavaria), etc. As a theorist K. represents the extreme school of third-building up to the chords of the eleventh, on all degrees of the scale (!). He wrote " Erklärung einiger . . . nicht verstandener Grundsätze aus der Voglerschen Theorie" (1785); " Gemeinnützliches Elementarwerk der Harmonie und das Generalbasses " (1792–98; four parts); " Kleines alphabetisches Wörterbuch der vornehmsten und interessantesten Artikel aus der musikalischen Theorie " (1795); " Vollständige Orgelschule für Anfänger und Geübtere " (1795–98, three parts; a French plagiarised version of it was published by J. P. E. Martini at Paris); " Theoretischpraktische Generalbassschule" (without year of publication); " Kleine Klavierschule für die ersten Anfänger" (1800 and 1802; two parts; 2nd ed. as " Bewährtes Methodenbuch," etc.) ; "Allgemeiner musikalischer Katechismus" (1803, several times republished); " Luther's Verdienst um Musik und Posie " (1817). Many theoretical articles by K. are to be found in the first year of the Leipzig *Allg. Musik. Zeitung,* some also in Speier's *Musikalische Realzeitung.*

Kniegeige (Ger.), a Viola da Gamba, or Violoncello.

Kniese, J u l i u s, b. Dec. 21, 1848, Roda (Altenburg), received his school training in Altenburg, where W. Stade was his music-teacher; and he received further musical training (1868–70) from Brendel and Riedel in Leipzig. After he had become known as an able pianist and organist, he undertook (1871–76) the direction of the " Singakademie " at Glogau, became in 1876 conductor of the Rühl Choral Society and of the " Wagner-Verein " at Frankfort, and in 1884 succeeded Breunung as musical director at Aix. Since 1889 K. lives at Baireuth, where he has been, since 1882, chorus-master at the festival plays. Four of his books of songs have been printed, and a symphonic poem, " Frithjof," and the prelude of an opera, *König Wittichis,* both in manuscript, have been produced at the " Tonkünstlerversammlung," Wiesbaden (1879).

Knight, J o s e p h P h i l i p, b. July 26, 1812, Bradford-on-Avon, d. June 1, 1887, Great Yarmouth, studied under Corfe at Bristol. He was a popular English song composer, lived 1839–41 in the United States, was afterwards ordained to the charge of St. Agnes in the Scilly Isles, where he resided for two years. He published over two hundred songs, duets, terzets, etc., which enjoy great popularity (among which " She wore a wreath of roses "). He also wrote an oratorio, *Jephtha's Daughter.*

Knorr, (1) J u l i u s, distinguished pianoforte teacher, b. Sept. 22, 1807, Leipzig, d. there June 17, 1861. He at first studied philology at Leipzig, but soon turned entirely to music, **and**

made a successful appearance as pianist at a Gewandhaus concert in 1831. He lived as teacher of the pianoforte at Leipzig, was on intimate terms with Schumann, and for the first year editor of the *Neue Zeitschrift für Musik*. The educational works of K. are: " Neue Pianoforteschule in 184 Uebungen " (1835 ; 2nd ed. as " Die Pianoforteschule der neuesten Zeit ; ein Supplement zu den Werken von Cramer, Czerny, Herz, Hummel, Hünten, Kalkbrenner, Moscheles," etc., 1841) ; " Das Klavierspiel in 280 Uebungen " (" Materialien zur Entwickelung der Fingertechnik ") ; further, " Materialien für das mechanische Klavierspiel " (1844) ; " Methodischer Leitfaden für Klavierlehrer " (1849, frequently republished) ; " Wegweiser für den Klavierspieler im ersten Stadium (elementary ; c. 1853) ; " Ausführliche Klaviermethode " (first part " Methode," 1859 ; second part " Schule der Mechanik," 1860, Leipzig, Kahnt) ; " Führer auf dem Felde der Klavierunterrichts Litteratur " (without date) ; " Erklärendes Verzeichnis der hauptsächlichsten Musikkunstwörter " (1854). He also revised an edition of the Pianoforte Method of J. G. Werner (1830) and A. C. Müller (1848). K. was the first who established " technical preparatory exercises " as an essential element of study (since his time, the tripartite division : technique, studies, pieces).

(2) Iwan, b. 1853, Mewe (West Prussia), pupil of the Leipzig Conservatorium (Reinecke, Richter), in 1874 became teacher of music at an institution at Charkow (South Russia), and from 1878 director of theoretical instruction at the " Kaiserl. Musikgesellschaft " section there. At the reorganisation of Dr. Hoch's Conservatorium in Frankfort, he was appointed, on the recommendation of Brahms and Wüllner (1883), teacher of theory and composition. As a composer K. was active in the departments of orchestral and chamber-music (also " Ukrainische Liebeslieder," for mixed chorus and pf.).

Knyvett, Charles, d. 1822 as organist of the Chapel Royal, London. He was in his younger years (from 1780–90) a distinguished concert singer (tenor), and established, jointly with S. Harrison, the Vocal Concerts (1791–94). His elder son, C h a r l e s (b. 1773, d. Nov. 2, 1852, London), pupil of Webbe, re-established them, jointly with Greatorex, Bartleman, and his brother William (1801). He has also become known by publishing a Selection of Psalm Tunes (1823) ; he was for a long time organist of St. George's, Hanover Square, and was a gifted teacher of the pianoforte and of theory. More important is his brother William (b. April 21, 1779, d. Nov. 17, 1856, London) ; was already appointed from 1797 gentleman (paid) singer of the Chapel Royal, where he succeeded Arnold as composer. For a long time he was the best London concert singer (tenor), conducted from 1832–40 the Concerts of Ancient Music, from 1834–43 the Birmingham Festivals, also the York Festival of 1835. As a composer he only wrote

some glees and anthems for the coronation of George IV. and of Queen Victoria.

Kobelius, J o h a n n A u g u s t i n, b. Feb. 21, 1674, Wählitz, near Halle, d. Aug. 17, 1731, Weissenfels, studied under Schiefferdecker and J. Phil. Krieger ; " Kammermusikus " at Weissenfels, organist and capellmeister at Sangerhausen and Querfurt, finally capellmeister to the Duke of Weissenfels. Between 1716–29 he wrote for the court there twenty operas, for the most part on ancient and mythological subjects.

Kobsa, primitive instrument of the lute kind used in Russia Minor to accompany the Dumka.

Koch, (1) H e i n r i c h C h r i s t o p h, b. Oct. 10, 1749, Rudolstadt, where his father was member of the Prince's band, d. there March 12, 1816 ; under the patronage of this prince K. received musical training, first at Rudolstadt, and then from Göpfert at Weimar. In 1768 he became violinist in the band at Rudolstadt, and rose to be . " Kammermusiker " (1777). K. was not a composer of importance (cantatas for court festivals, a " Choralbuch " for wind-band, etc.), but rendered valuable service as theorist. He published a " Musikalisches Lexikon " (1802, in two parts, a meritorious work. An epitome appeared in 1807 under the title " Kurzgefasstes Handwörterbuch der Musik," another one, anonymously, in 1828, and an excellent new revised version by Arrey v. Dommer in 1865) ; also " Versuch einer Anleitung zur Komposition " (1782–93 ; in three parts, likewise a work of high excellence, which, in its day, appears to have been entirely overlooked) ; " Handbuch bei dem Studium der Harmonie " (1811) ; " Versuch aus der harten und weichen Tonart jeder Stufe der diatonischchromatischen Leiter vermittelst des enharmonischen Tonwechsels in die Dur und Molltonart der übrigen auszuweichen " (1812). In 1795 he attempted the publication of a *Journal der Tonkunst*, but soon had to give it up. Theoretical articles and reviews of his are to be found in Speier's *Musikalische Realzeitung* (1788–91), in the Leipzig *Allg. Mus. Zeitung*, and in the *Jenaer Litteraturzeitung*.

(2) E d u a r d E m i l, hymnologist, b. Jan. 20, 1809, at Castle Solitude, near Stuttgart, d. April 27, 1871, Stuttgart, 1837 pastor at Gross-Aspach, in 1847 at Heilbronn, in 1853 superintendent, which post he resigned in 1864 in order to devote himself entirely to historical studies. The work of his life is " Geschichte des Kirchenliedes und Kirchengesanges, insbesondere der deutschen evangelischen Kirche " (1847, third edition [eight volumes] 1866–76 ; the eighth volume edited by R. Lauxmann).

Köchel, L u d w i g (afterwards Ritter v o n), b. Jan. 14, 1800, Stein-a.-d.-Donau (Lower Austria), d. June 3, 1877, Vienna ; he studied law, was from 1827–42 teacher to the royal princes, was named imperial councillor in 1832, raised to the rank of a nobleman in 1842, was member of the Board of Public Instruction from 1850–52 at Salzburg, and lived from that time up to his death at Vienna. K. was an enthusiastic botanist and mineralogist, but had a solid musical training, and enriched musical literature with some valuable works : " Ueber den Umfang der musikalischen Produktion W. A. Mozarts" (1862), a forerunner of his famous catalogue, "Chronologisch-systematisches Verzeichnis sämtlicher Tonwerke W. A. Mozart's" (1862; supplements by K. himself in *Allg. M.-Ztg.*, 1864) ; also " Die Kaiserliche Hofmusikkapelle zu Wien von 1543–1867 " (1868), and " Johann Joseph Fux" (1872).

Kocher, Konrad, b. Dec. 16, 1786, Ditzingen, near Stuttgart, d. there March 12, 1872, studied the pianoforte at Petersburg under Klengel and Berger, and composition under J. H. Müller. In 1819 he travelled to Italy for the purpose of studying *a-cappella* music, and, on his return, founded a church choral society at Stuttgart ; became, in 1827, musical director of the " Stiftskirche " there, and, in 1852, *Dr. Phil. hon. c.* of Tübingen University. K. wrote : " Die Tonkunst in der Kirche" (1823), published " Zionsharfe " (treasury of chorales of all centuries), and also composed two operas, an oratorio, etc.

Kogel, Gustav Friedrich, b. Jan. 16, 1849, Leipzig, where his father was trombone player in the Gewandhaus orchestra. He studied at the Leipzig Conservatorium (1863–67), lived for some years in Alsace as teacher of music until driven home by the war. He then began to work for the Peters house, and from 1874 led a busy life as theatre capellmeister at Nuremberg, Dortmund, Ghent, Aixla-Chapelle, Cologne, Leipzig (1883–86), became in 1887 conductor of the Philharmonic orchestra at Berlin, and in 1891 conductor of the " Museum " concerts at Frankfort. As composer K. is only known by a few pianoforte pieces for two and four hands. On the other hand, he has been an industrious editor of pianoforte and full scores of operas (among which, for the first time, Spohr's *Jessonda*, Nicolai's *Merry Wives of Windsor*, and Marschner's *Hans Heiling*).

Köhler, (1) Ernst, b. May 28, 1799, Langenbielau (Silesia), d. May 26, 1847, Breslau, where from 1827 he was principal organist of the " Elisabethkirche." K. was an important organ and pianoforte player ; his published organ and pf. works are not so well known as they deserve to be. He also wrote twelve church cantatas, twelve important vocal works with orchestra, nine overtures, two symphonies, etc.
(2) Chr. Louis Heinrich, b. Sept. 5, 1820, Brunswick, d. Feb. 16, 1886, Königsberg-i.-Pr., was first a pupil of A. Sonnemann (pianoforte), Chr. Zinkeisen, sen., J. A. Leibrock (theory), and Chr. Zinkeisen, jun. (violin), at Brunswick ; then from 1839–43, at Vienna, he

received further training from Simon Sechter, J. von Seyfried (theory, composition), and also, in pianoforte-playing, from K. M. v. Bocklet, on the advice of Czerny. After being theatre capellmeister for a brief period at Marienburg, Elbing, and Königsberg, K. settled in Königsberg in 1847 as teacher, conductor of the vocal society, critic, and director of a school for pianoforte-playing and theory. In 1880 he was named professor. K. was noteworthy as a composer (music to *Helena* of Euripides, three operas, *Prinz und Maler, Maria Dolores* [Brunswick, 1844], and *Gil Blas ;* a ballet, *Der Zauberkomponist* [Brunswick, 1846]; Paternoster for four female and four male voices [Op. 100]) and was esteemed as a teacher. K. was, without doubt, one of the most zealous pianoforte teachers of our time, the heir of Czerny ; his " Systematische Lehrmethode für Klavierspiel und Musik " (1st part ; " Die Mechanik als Grundlage der Technik," 1856 ; 2nd ed. 1872 ; 3rd ed. 1888 [revised by Riemann]; pt. 2, " Tonschriftwesen, Harmonik, Metrik," 1858) enjoys a very wide circulation ; also his numerous études, of which a number exist for each stage of musical training ; but their extreme dryness prevents most teachers from using them. His " Führer durch den Klavierunterricht " (6th ed. 1879) is a valuable handbook, though at times the author is somewhat too much in the foreground. The following writings of K. have still to be mentioned : " Der Klavierfingersatz " (1862), " Der Klavierunterricht, Studien, Erfahrungen und Ratschläge " (4th ed. 1877); " Die neue Richtung in der Musik " (1864) ; " Leichtfassliche Harmonieund Generalbasslehre" (3rd ed. 1880); "Brahms und seine Stellung in der neuern Klavierlitteratur " (1880); " Der Klavierpedalzug " (1882) ; " Allgemeine Musiklehre " (1883). K. was also a zealous contributor to various musical papers (*cf.* his articles, likewise the History of Pianoforte Music in the *N. Z. f. Musik,* 1867–69, 1872, 1875, 1878 ; and in the *N. Berliner M. Ztg.,* 1871, 1875, and 1876).

Kohnt, Adolf, b. Nov. 10, 1847, Mindszent (Hungary), writer on music, lives at Berlin (" Weber-Gedenkbuch," " Fr. Wieck," " Leuchtende Fackeln," etc.).

Kolbe, Oskar, b. Aug. 10, 1836, Berlin, d. there Jan. 2, 1878 ; pupil of the Royal Institute for Church Music and of the school for composition of the " Akademie." From 1859–75 he was teacher of theory at the Stern Conservatorium, and was appointed royal " Musikdirektor " in 1872. He published several books of songs, and in 1872 produced an oratorio, *Johannes der Täufer.* He also wrote a " Kurzgefasstes Handbuch der Generalbasslehre " (1862 ; 2nd ed. 1872), and a " Handbuch der Harmonielehre " (1873).

Kollectivzug (Ger.), composition pedal. (*See* PEDALS, COMPOSITION.)

Kollmann, August Friedrich Karl, b. 1756, Engelbostel (Hanover), d. Easter Sunday, 1824, London: he studied music at Hanover, and in 1778 was private tutor to a Hanoverian family in London, where he became choir-master at the German Chapel, St. James's, also organist of the small organ presented to the chapel by George III. K. was by nature disposed to theory, as can be seen from the greater number of his compositions (programme symphony, "The Shipwreck:" twelve analysed fugues; rondo on the motive of the diminished seventh; and a hundred psalms harmonised in a hundred ways, pf. concertos, etc.). His didactic works are: "First Beginning on the Pianoforte" (1796); "Introduction to Modulation;" " Essay on Practical Harmony" (1796); "Essay on Practical Musical Composition" (1799); "Practical Guide to Thorough-Bass" (1801); vindication of a part of the latter (1802); "New Theory of Musical Harmony" (1806); "A Second Practical Guide to Thorough-Bass" (1807); Remarks on Logier in the *Quarterly Musical Magazine and Review* (1818); a German epitome in the *Allg. Mus. Zeitung* (1822); a paper of his own, the *Quarterly Musical Register* (1812), of which, however, only two numbers appeared, but it contained several valuable articles.

Kömpel, August, excellent violinist, b. Aug. 15, 1831, Brückenau, d. 1891, pupil of the School of Music at Würzburg, afterwards of Spohr, David, and Joachim. In 1844 he was member of the court band at Cassel, from 1852–61 of the court band at Hanover, and, after long concert tours, leader from 1863 at Weimar. He received a pension in 1884.

Königslöw, (1) Joh. Wilh. Cornelius von, b. March 16, 1745, Hamburg, d. May 14, 1833, Lübeck, where, from 1773, he was organist of the "Marienkirche." He was a diligent composer of "Abendmusiken." (*Vide* BUXTEHUDE.)

(2) Otto Friedrich von, b. Nov. 13, 1824, Hamburg, an excellent performer on the violin, received his first musical training from his father (who, however, was not a musician by profession), also for a brief period from Fr. Pacius and Karl Hafner. From 1844–46 he attended the Leipzig Conservatorium as a pupil of David (violin) and of Hauptmann (theory). From 1846 to 1858 he màde artistic tours, and from 1858 to 1881 was leader of the orchestra at the Gürzenich concerts, teacher of the violin and vice-director of the Cologne Conservatorium, and received the title of "Königlicher Professor." He now lives in retirement near Bonn.

Koning, David, b. March 19, 1820, Rotterdam, d. Nov. 6, 1876, Amsterdam. A composer and pianist of note, who studied under Aloys Schmitt in Frankfort (1834–38), and received a prize from the Netherland Musical Society in 1839 for an overture (Op. 7). In 1840 he settled in Amsterdam, and undertook the direction of the choral society "Musæ." He also visited London, Paris, and Vienna, but always returned to Amsterdam, where, for the space of ten years, he was secretary, and afterwards president, of the Cecilia Society, and was highly esteemed as a teacher of music. Of his compositions the following deserve mention: "Domine, salvum fac regem," with orchestra (Op. 1), several stringed quartets and pf. sonatas, études, songs, (" Zuleika "), part-songs for male voices, female voices, and for mixed chorus, concert scenas, a comic opera, *Das Fischermädchen* (which gained a prize); the "Elegie auf den Tod eines Künstlers" (Op. 22), chorales, (à 4), etc. He also translated a theoretical work, "Beknopte handleiling tot de kennis van de leerstellingen der toonkunst," from the English of C. C. Spandler.

Konradin, Karl Ferdinand, b. Sept. 1, 1833, St. Helenenthal, near Baden (Lower Austria), d. Aug. 31, 1884, Vienna; a favourite operetta composer (1860–67; eleven operettas for Vienna.

Kontski, (1) Antoine de, b. Oct. 27, 1817, Cracow, distinguished pianist, who, in numerous concert tours, won applause by the smoothness and delicacy of his playing. He lived for some years in Paris, then in Berlin, where he was appointed court pianist, and from 1854–67 in Petersburg. After that he settled in London. Of his numerous *salon* compositions, "Le reveil du lion " is universally known. His opera, *Les deux distraits*, was given in London in 1872.

(2) Apollinaire de, brother of the former, b. Oct. 23, 1825, Warsaw, d. there, June 29, 1879. In his day he was a very famous violin virtuoso, studied with his eldest brother, Charles de K., and became a player at an astonishingly early age; later on he enjoyed instruction from Paganini at Paris. From 1853–61 he was imperial chamber virtuoso at Petersburg, and then founded the Conservatorium at Warsaw, of which he was director up to his death. His violin compositions are of no importance. Also

(3) Charles de K., b. Sept. 6, 1815, Cracow, afterwards pianoforte teacher in Paris, d. Aug. 27, 1867, and

(4) Stanislaus de K., b. Oct. 8, 1820, Cracow, violin teacher in Paris; these were both brothers of the above-named, and published pieces of a light *genre* for pianoforte and violin.

Kopecký, Ottokar, able violinist, b. April 29, 1850, Chotěboř, Bohemia, attended the Gymnasium at Pilsen, from 1864–70 the Prague Conservatorium, and then played in orchestras at Brünn, Vienna, Sondershausen, etc. At present he is leader of the Philharmonic society at Hamburg, also teacher at the Conservatorium and conductor of the "Schäffer" orchestral society.

Kopfstimme (Ger.), head-voice, *falsetto*.

Koppel (Ger.), a coupler.

Korgánoff, J e n n a d i O s i p o w i t s c h, b. April 30, 1858, Kaschetin (Caucasus), d. Feb. 23, 1890, Rostroff on the Don (in a railway carriage), pianist and composer (fantasia "Bajati" on Caucasian themes). He studied under Reinecke at Leipzig, and under L. Brassin at Petersburg.

Körner, (1) C h r i s t i a n G o t t f r i e d, b. July 2, 1756, Leipzig, d. May 13, 1831, Berlin, chief privy councillor (father of the poet Theodor K.). Meetings of a choral society were held in his house at Dresden, in which city, for many years, he held office. He composed music and wrote, among other things, for the " Horen " of 1775, " Ueber den Charakter der Töne oder über Charakterdarstellung in der Musik."

(2) G o t t h i l f W i l h e l m, b. June 3, 1809, Teicha, near Halle-a.-S., d. Jan. 13, 1865, Erfurt. He attended the Training School in the latter town, laboured for several years as school teacher, and in 1838 founded there the music publishing-house which still bears his name, and which is especially rich in works for the organ (1886 incorporated with C. F. Peters). In 1844 he founded the still existing musical paper *Urania* (for lovers of the organ; editor Gottschalg).

Kornmüller, U t t o, "novice-master," prior, and regens chori of the Benedictine monastery, Metten, b. Jan. 5, 1824, Straubing, ordained priest July 16, 1847, declared his vows Nov. 30, 1858. K. wrote various masses, motets, several pamphlets on questions of liturgy and theory of music, also many articles for the " Kirchen- musikalische Jahrbücher " and the *Monatshefte für Musikgeschichte*. He is, at present, diocesan president of the Cecilia Society of the diocese of Ratisbon.

Koschat, T h o m a s, composer, b. Aug. 8, 1845, Viktring, near Klagenfurt. He attended the national Gymnasium at Klagenfurt, and commenced the study of physics at Vienna, but then joined the chorus of the court opera, and devoted himself entirely to music. In 1874 he became a member of the cathedral choir, and in 1878 of the Hofcapelle. In 1871 appeared his first Carinthian quartets for male voices. They made a furore, and there were many imi- tations of them. K. was both poet (in the Carinthian dialect) and composer of these songs, which gave a typical picture of the in- tellectual life and the character of the Carinth- ian people, but they are altogether of simple structure. He also published two small volumes of similar poems without music (" Hadrich " and " Dorfbilder aus Kärnten "), also a vaude- ville (*Am Wörther See*), which was repeatedly performed at Vienna and elsewhere.

Köselitz, H e i n r i c h, b. 1854, Annaberg (Saxony), pupil of the Leipzig Conservatorium (Richter), in 1875 under Nietzsche at Basle. Since then he has lived for the most part in Italy. He is a gifted composer of operas (up

to now has only been produced—"*Die heimliche Ehe*, Danzig, 1891, under pseudonym Peter Gast. *Cf.* Dr. Karl Fuchs, " Thematikon " of this opera.).

Kosleck, J u l i u s, b. Dec. 3, 1835, Neugrad Pomerania, performer on the trumpet and the *cornet-à-pistons ;* in 1852 he joined the band of the 2nd regiment of the Guards in Berlin, and, after some years, was appointed member of the royal band, and, in 1873, teacher of the trumpet and trombone at the royal " Hochschule." K. is known as the founder and head of the famous " Kaiser-Kornett-quartett." Besides numerous arrangements for this quartet society, K. pub- lished a Method for trumpet and *cornet-à-pistons*.

Kossak, E r n s t, b. Aug. 4, 1814, Marien- werder, d. Jan. 3, 1880, Berlin; he studied philology at Königsberg and Berlin, and took his degree of Dr.Phil., but devoted himself entirely to the career of a journalist, and excelled espe- cially as a writer of musical *feuilletons*. He was also a frequent contributor to the *Neue Berliner Musik Zeitung*, to the musical paper *Echo* (which he founded, and of which he was for a long time editor), and to the *Zeitungshalle* (afterwards called *Berliner Feuerspritze, Berliner Montagspost*), which was also started by him.

Kossmaly, K a r l, b. July 27, 1812, Breslau, d. Nov., 1893, Stettin, pupil of L. Berger, Zelter, and Klein at Berlin (1828–30), then opera capellmeister at Wiesbaden, Mayence, Amsterdam (1838), Bremen (1841), Detmold and Stettin (1846–49), where he became teacher of music and concert-conductor. He has made a name as composer of songs and some in- strumental works. As a writer he was of still greater importance: " Schlesisches Ton- künstlerlexikon " (in parts, 1846–47) ; " Mozarts Opern " (1848, after Ulibischew) ; " Ueber die Anwendung des Programms zur Erklärung musikalischer Kompositionen " (1858) ; " Ueber Richard Wagner " (1874, anti-Wagnerian). He contributed much also to the *Neue Zeitschrift für Musik, Neue Berliner Muzik Zeitung*, and the *Stettiner Zeitung*. Died Dec. 1, 1893, Stettin.

Köstlin, (1) K a r l R e i n h o l d, professor of esthetics and history of art at Tübingen, b. Sept. 28, 1819, Urach (Würtemberg), d. April 12, 1894, Tübingen, a man of high musical culture, of which his " Aesthetik " (1863–69, two vols.), also the " Aesthetik " treating specially of music, written by him for the third volume of F. Th. Vischer's comprehensive " Aesthetik," and his pamphlet on R. Wagner, give signal proof.

(2) H e i n r i c h A d o l f, writer on music, b. Oct. 4, 1846, son of the celebrated Tübingen professor Christian Reinhold K., a lawyer versed in criminal law, and also a poet, and of Josephine Lang-K. (q.v.), the excellent song- composer. He received from a tender age a sound musical education, but, after his father's premature death (1856), studied theology at

Tübingen, went in 1869 as private tutor to the Würtemberg ambassador at Paris, was chaplain in the army during the war of 1870, was tutor at the theological training-school at Tübingen (where he gave lectures on the history of music), from 1873–75 deacon at Sulz.-a.-N., organised in 1875 the union of the choirs (the three towns Sulz, Kalw, Nagold) for the practice of church music, which in 1877 was extended into the "Evangelischer Kirchengesangverein" for Würtemberg, the festival performances of which he conducted for many years. He was called to Maulbronn in 1875, and to Friedrichshafen in 1878, where he became preacher, and likewise conductor of the Oratorio Society. In 1881 he went to Stuttgart, and in 1883 was appointed professor at the Friedberg (Hesse) training-school, but in 1891 was removed to Darmstadt as member of the supreme consistorial court, and superintendent. His critical notices of musical books (in *Deutsches Litteraturblatt* and the Augsburg *Allgemeine Zeitung*) are worthy of mention; also his "Geschichte der Musik im Umriss" (1875; third, and considerably enlarged edition, 1883), and "Die Tonkunst. Einführung in der Aesthetik der Musik" (1878); and "Josephine Lang-K." (biography of his mother).

Kotek, Joseph, b. Oct. 25, 1855, Kamenez-Podolsk (Government Moscow), d. Jan. 4, 1885, Davos, pupil of the Moscow Conservatoire. After further study under Joachim, he became, in 1882, teacher of the violin at the Royal High School of Music, Berlin. He composed studies, solo pieces, and duets for violin.

Kothe, (1) B e r n h a r d, b. May 12, 1821, Gröbnig (Silesia), d. July 25, 1897; he attended the Royal Institution for Church Music, Berlin, enjoyed also, for a time, instruction from A. B. Marx, and in 1851 was appointed church musical director and teacher of singing at the school at Oppeln, from which town in 1869 he went to Breslau as teacher of music at the seminary. K. founded there the Cecilia Society for Catholic sacred music; he published collections of sacred songs for male chorus ("Musica sacra"), besides organ pieces, a "Praeludienbuch" for organ, motets, a Method of singing ("Singtafeln," for training in schools), also the pamphlets "Die Musik in der katholischen Kirche" (1862) and "Abriss der Musikgeschichte für Lehrerseminare und Dilettanten" (1874), revised the 4th edition of Seidel's "Die Orgel und ihr Bau" (1887), and collaborated with Forschhammer in a "Führer durch die Orgellitteratur" (1890).—His two brothers—(2) A l o y s (b. Oct. 3, 1828, d. 1868 as teacher of music at the seminary, Breslau); and (3) W i l h e l m (b. Jan. 8, 1831, teacher of music at Habelschwerdt seminary)—made a name by their sacred compositions and vocal works for school use.

Köttlitz, A d o l f, b. Sept. 27, 1820, Trèves, an excellent violinist; he lived for several years in Cologne, and, under Liszt's patronage, for three years in Paris. From 1848–56 he was leader at Königsberg, and, while on a concert tour through Siberia, settled at Uralsk as musical director, where an accident in the hunting-field put an end to his life on Oct. 26, 1860. Of his compositions, two quartets for strings deserve mention.—His wife (K l o t i l d e, *née* Ellendt, d. 1867) lived at Königsberg esteemed as a teacher of singing.

Kotzeluch (Koželuch), (1) J o h a n n A n t o n, b. Dec. 13, 1738, Wellwarn (Bohemia), d. Feb. 3, 1814, as capellmeister of St. Veit's Church, Prague. He was trained at the Jesuits' College at Brzeznitz, afterwards at Prague (pupil of Seegert and chorister of St. Veit's) and Vienna (pupil of Gluck and Gassmann). He was musical director of a church at Vienna, then at Prague at the Kreuzherrenkirche; finally, capellmeister of the Metropolitankirche. He wrote several operas, oratorios, masses, etc., which, during his lifetime, were held in high esteem, but were not published.

(2) L e o p o l d A n t o n, cousin of the former, prolific composer, b. Dec. 9, 1752, Wellwarn, d. May 7, 1818, Vienna; he went through his school and university studies at Prague, but, after a successful production of a ballet of his at the Prague National theatre (1771), devoted himself entirely to composition, and wrote, during the following six years, twenty-four more ballets, three pantomimes, and other incidental music for the theatre. He went in 1778 to Vienna, and was soon appointed teacher of music to the Archduchess Elizabeth. The post of leader, as Mozart's successor, of the band belonging to the Archbishop of Salzburg was offered to him (1781), but this he refused; on the other hand, after Mozart's death, he replaced him as imperial court composer (1792). K. wrote with extraordinary ease, but without much self-criticism. His works, especially those for pianoforte, were very popular in Germany, and most of them were published by a brother of his at Vienna. Besides the ballets already mentioned, he wrote several operas (*Didone abbandonata*, *Judith*, *Deborah und Sisera*), an oratorio (*Moses in Aegypten*), numerous arias, cantatas, choruses, etc., about thirty symphonies (only a few of which were published), thirteen pianoforte concertos (all of them published; one for four hands and one for two pianofortes), fifty-seven pf. trios, three *Symphonies concertantes* for strings, many pf. sonatas (for two and four hands), pf. pieces, six 'cello concertos (two published), two clarinet concertos, two concertos for basset-horn, etc.

Kotzolt, H e i n r i c h, the founder (1849) and, up to his death, conductor, of the Kotzolt *a cappella* vocal society at Berlin, b. Aug. 26, 1814, Schnellwalde, near Neustadt (Upper Silesia), d. July 3, 1881, Berlin. From 1834–36 he studied philology at Breslau, but then turned to music, and, from 1836-38, worked at theory in Berlin under Dehn and Rungenhagen. In the latter year he became principal bass at the Danzig opera, settled in that city (1839-42) as teacher of singing, and, after some long concert tours, became principal solo bass of the cathedral choir, Berlin, and in 1862 sub-conductor of the same. From 1865 he was also teacher of singing at the Königstadt high school, and from 1872 at the Joachimsthal Gymnasium; he was appointed royal musical director in 1866, and named professor in 1876. K. was an excellent teacher of singing and conductor; he published an *a cappella* method.

Kraft, (1) A n t o n, b. Dec. 30, 1752, Rokitzan, Bohemia, d. Aug. 28, 1820, Vienna. He was a distinguished 'cellist, and was a member of the bands of the Princes Esterhazy (1778-90), Grassalkowitsch (up to 1795), and Lobkowitz (up to 1820) at Vienna. He studied composition for a time with Haydn. K. wrote a 'cello concerto, six 'cello sonatas, three *duos concertants* for 'cello and violin, two duos for two 'celli, a divertissement for 'cello and bass, and several trios for two barytons (the favourite instrument of Prince Esterhazy, on which K. also was a performer) and 'cello.

(2) N i k o l a u s, son and pupil of the above, was also a distinguished performer on the 'cello, b. Dec. 14, 1778, Esterház, d. May 18, 1853, Stuttgart. He was a member of the celebrated Schuppanzigh Quartet. When young he travelled with his father, in 1796 became chamber-musician to Prince Lobkowitz, at whose expense he studied under Duport at Berlin, joined the court opera orchestra in 1809, and went, in the same capacity, to Stuttgart in 1814. In 1834 he received a pension. He added valuable works to the literature of the 'cello, among others, five concertos, one fantasia with stringed quartet (Op. 1), three divertissements for two 'celli, six duos for 'celli, characteristic pieces, one polonaise, bolero, etc. —His son, F r i e d r i c h, b. Feb. 12, 1807, was for many years 'cellist in the court band at Stuttgart.

Krakowiak (Fr. *Cracovienne*), a Polish dance in $\frac{2}{4}$ time. Like the Mazurka and other Polish, Hungarian, and Bohemian dances, its characteristic feature consists in the frequent accentuation of unaccented beats, and in the employment of syncopation—

(♪♩ ♪);

but it is lively and graceful rather than passionate.

Krantz, E u g e n, the present director of the Dresden Royal Conservatorium, b. Sept. 13, 1844, Dresden. He was the son of a painter, studied the pianoforte, first under G. Funke and R. Reichardt, received further training,

from 1858-65, at the Dresden Conservatorium (H. Döring, E. Leonhard, Ad. Reichel, I. Rietz, M. Fürstenau, etc.). He then became private teacher of the pianoforte and theory at Dresden, in 1869 chorus-master of the Hofoper (up to 1884), and at the same time at the Conservatorium, at first only for the pianoforte, in 1877 also for ensemble singing and operatic music, likewise, inspector of the seminary. In 1884 he undertook the highest choral class, and, in 1890, acquired the institution by purchase. At the same time K. was active as critic (1874-76 of the Dresden *Presse*, from 1886-87 of the *Dresdener Nachrichten*). K. is an able pianist, since 1862 highly esteemed as accompanist at concerts, also a good Bach player (at the " Tonkünstlerverein "). As a composer he has produced only a few songs, but has many works of large compass in manuscript. His " Lehrgang im Klavierunterricht " (1882) is a work of merit. In 1882 he received the title of " Kgl. Sächs. Professor."

Krause, (1) C h r i s t i a n G o t t f r i e d, b., according to Ledebur, 1719, Winzig, where his father was " Stadtmusicus," attended the University at Frankfort, went in 1747 to Berlin, where, in 1753, he became a lawyer, and died July 21, 1770. He was composer, writer, editor, and collector of the " Lieder der Deutschen," likewise contributor to the *Allgem. deutschen Bibliothek*. He wrote: " Von der musikalischen Poesie " (1753, 484 octavo pages, a sharpsighted, worthy work, which compares well with similar works in the older literature); " Vermischte Gedanken über Musik " (in Marpurg's " Kritische Beiträge, vols. 2 and 3, 523 pages).

(2) K a r l C h r i s t i a n F r i e d r i c h, philosopher, b. May 6, 1781, Eisenberg (Altenburg), d. Sept. 27, 1832, Munich, whither he had just come (for the purpose of qualifying himself as private lecturer at the University) from Göttingen, where he had long waited in vain for a professorship. He published philosophical works of the highest interest (" Urbild der Menschheit," " Logik als philosophische Wissenschaft," " Philosophie des Rechts," etc.), and historical works on freemasonry, " Darstellungen aus der Geschichte der Musik " (1827), " Anfangsgründe der allgemeinen Theorie der Musik " (1838, posthumous), and a technical educational work for the pianoforte (" Vollständige Anweisung," etc., 1808).

(3) T h e o d o r, b. May 1, 1833, Halle, pupil of Fr. Naue, E. Hentschel, M. Hauptmann, and E. Grell (theory), and Eduard Mantius and Martin Blumner (singing). He was founder of the church choir of St. Nikolai and of St. Marien at Berlin, conductor of the Seiffert vocal society (*a cappella*), musical critic of the *Deutsche Rundschau*, of the *Reichsboten*, and of the *Berliner Zeitung*, etc.; he lives at Berlin as rector. K. attempted to simplify the teaching of singing in schools by means of the so-called " Wander-

note." As a composer he has produced songs, part-songs, also sacred works. In 1887 the title of "Königl. Musikdirektor" was bestowed on him.

(4) Anton, a highly esteemed teacher of the pianoforte, conductor and composer, b. Nov. 9, 1834, Geithain (Saxony), pupil of Fr. Wieck, Spindler, and Reissiger, and, from 1850–53, at the Leipzig Conservatorium. Since 1859 he has been conductor of the "Konkordienkonzerte," of the town vocal society, and of the Liedertafel at Barmen, where he also established regular performances of chamber-music. K.'s compositions are principally confined to instructive pieces for the pianoforte (sonatinas and sonatas for two and four hands, also some for two pianofortes, études, etc.), which, owing to their simple structure, are held in high esteem. K. has also published expressive songs, a Kyrie, Sanctus, and Benedictus, for soli, chorus, and orchestra, likewise two operas.

(5) Emil, also an esteemed teacher of the pianoforte, b. 1840, Hamburg, pupil of the Leipzig Conservatorium under Hauptmann, Rietz, Moscheles, Plaidy, and Richter; he has been living as teacher of the pianoforte and theory at Hamburg since 1860, has been active as a musical critic since 1864, and, since 1885, as teacher at the Conservatorium. Of his publications, the "Beiträge zur Technik des Klavierspiels" (Op. 38 and 57, the latter as foundation to the higher development of pianoforte-playing), and his "Aufgabenbuch für die Harmonielehre," deserve special mention. He also wrote chamber-music, three cantatas, Ave Maria à 6, double chorus for female voices, songs, etc.

(6) Prof. Dr. Eduard, b. March 15, 1837, Swinemünde, d. March 28, 1892, Berlin, studied science, but at the same time pianoforte and theory under Kroll and Hauptmann at Leipzig. In 1862 he settled at Stettin, where, as pianist, composer, and teacher of music, he worked most successfully. He has become favourably known as the author of several philosophico-musical treatises.

(7) Martin, b. June 17, 1853, Lobstädt-i.-S. After attending the teachers' seminary, he joined the Leipzig Conservatorium (1874–76), was then active in Switzerland and at Bremen as pianist and teacher of his instrument. In 1882 he settled permanently at Leipzig, founded in 1885, jointly with Friedheim, Siloti, Nikisch, Dayas, F. Stade, Fritzsch, etc., the "Liszt-Verein," a society which, under his energetic presidentship, has become an essential element of Leipzig musical life. As a pianist (of Liszt tendency; for by many years intercourse he had become imbued with the master's principles), and as a critic of advanced views, he has won for himself a distinguished position. The Duke of Anhalt, in recognition of his merits in connection with music, and especially the cause of Liszt, bestowed on him the title of

professor, and the Knight's Cross, first class, of the "Albrecht" order.

Kraushaar, Otto, b. May 31, 1812, Cassel, d. there Nov. 23, 1866. He studied with Moritz Hauptmann, whose idea with regard to the oppositeness of the major and the minor consonance he adopted; and, before the appearance of Hauptmann's "Natur der Harmonik und der Metrik," he developed the same in a small pamphlet (" Der akkordliche Gegensatz und die Begründung der Skala" 1852), and in a more logical manner even than Hauptmann; for in contradistinction to the major scale he placed the minor scale as its opposite. The charge of plagiarism brought against him by Hauptmann in the preface to the above-named work is therefore altogether unjustifiable. Besides numerous articles in musical papers, K. wrote "Die Konstruktion der gleichschwebenden Temperatur ohne Scheiblersche Stimmgabeln" (1838). He also published several books of songs and " Lieder ohne Worte."

Krauss, Gabriele, opera-singer (soprano), b. March 24, 1842, Vienna, pupil of the Conservatorium there. She was engaged at the Vienna court opera from 1860–68, and since then has been one of the chief attractions of the Paris Grand Opéra. Among other distinctions, she was made honorary member of the society of the concerts of the Conservatoire, and in 1880 officer of the Académie. She plays great dramatic *rôles*, such as Aida, Norma, etc.

Krebs, (1) Johann Ludwig, b. Oct. 10, 1713, Buttelstädt, near Weimar, where his father, Joh. Tobias Krebs (b. 1690, pupil of Bach's at Weimar), was cantor and organist, d. beginning of January, 1780, Altenburg. He attended the Thomasschule at Leipzig (1726–35), became a private pupil of Bach's, and occupied various posts as organist at Zwickau, Zeitz, and Altenburg. Bach considered him his best pupil for the organ. His published compositions are: "Klavierübungen" (1743–49), sonatas for clavier and flute, flute trios, a clavier concerto and preludes for clavier. A complete edition of his compositions, remarkable for the purity of their style, was issued by Heinrichshofen at Magdeburg.

(2) Karl August, b. Jan. 16, 1804, Nuremberg, d. May 16, 1880, Dresden; an excellent conductor, composer, and pianist. His real name was Miedcke, but he afterwards took the name of his adoptive father (the opera-singer J. B. Krebs), to whom he was indebted for a good part of his artistic training. After one year of further study under Seyfried at Vienna, he commenced his career as conductor in 1826 as third capellmeister at the Vienna court opera, but went, already in 1827, as capellmeister to Hamburg, and became an important factor in the musical life of that city. He was called to Dresden in 1850 as court capellmeister, and for many years displayed great and beneficial

activity, until he retired in 1872. For a time his compositions, especially songs, were known and admired far and wide; several operas (*Silva*, 1830; *Agnes Bernauer*, 1835, revised 1858) were produced; and he also wrote a Te Deum, masses, pf. pieces, etc.

His wife (3) A l o y s i a K. M i c h a l e s i, b. Aug. 29, 1820, Prague, married 1850, was a famous opera-singer (Hamburg, Dresden).

Of two daughters, (4) M a r y (married Brenning), b. Dec. 5, 1851, Dresden, distinguished pianist (pupil of her father's), appeared already in 1865 at a Gewandhaus concert at Leipzig, and, after long journeys, settled in Dresden.

(5) K a r l, writer on music, b. Feb. 5, 1857, Hanseberg, near Königsberg-i.-W., attended the Gymnasium in the latter city. He first studied natural philosophy, then music at the Royal High School of Music, Berlin; he attended lectures on the theory and philosophy of music at the University (Spitta), and for his treatise "Girolamo Dirutas Transilvano" was created Dr.Phil. by the University of Rostock. K. gradually undertook the musical notices for the *Vossische Zeitung*, the *Moderne Kunst* and the *Deutsche Rundschau* (Rodenberg). Up to the present he has contributed a number of treatises of the highest value on the history of music to the *Vierteljahrsschrift für Musikwissenschaft*, the *Preussische Jahrbücher*, and to the science supplements of the *Vossische Zeitung*, etc.

Krebsgängig (Ger.), retrograde, backward, in reference to motion.

Krehl, S t e p h a n, b. July 5, 1864, Leipzig, studied at the Leipzig Conservatorium, and also at Dresden; since 1889 he has been teacher of the pianoforte and theory at the Carlsruhe Conservatorium. He is a highly talented composer (pf. pieces, songs, etc.).

Kreipl, J o s e p h, composer of "Mailüfterl" (words by Kleesheim), which has become a Volkslied, etc.; he was b. 1805, and d. May, 1866, Vienna.

Kreischend (Ger.), shrieking, screeching.

Kreisler, J o h a n n e s. (*See* HOFFMANN [2].)

Kreissle von Hellborn, H e i n r i c h, the worthy biographer of Schubert, b. 1812, Vienna, d. there, as Imperial Finance Secretary, April 6, 1869. He was member of the board of directors of the Gesellschaft der Musikfreunde. His two works are: "F. Schubert, eine biographische Skizze" (1861), and some years later, an exhaustive biography—"Franz Schubert" (1865; English by Arthur Duke Coleridge, 1869; an epitome by Wilberforce, 1866).

Krejči, J o s e p h, b. Feb. 6, 1822, Milostin (Bohemia), d. Oct. 19, 1881, Prague, a distinguished organist, pupil of Witassek and Proksch at Prague; in 1844 organist of the "Kreuzherrenkirche" of that city, in 1848 chorus director of the "Minoritenkirche;" in 1853 he occupied a similar post at the "Kreuzherrenkirche," in

1858 became director of the organ school, and in 1865 director of the Conservatorium. K. composed organ pieces, masses, and other instrumental and vocal works.

Krempelsetzer, G e o r g, b. April 20, 1827, Vilsbiburg (Lower Bavaria), d. there June 9, 1871; he was for many years a cloth-weaver, but resolved to devote himself entirely to music, for which he showed disposition and talent. F. Lachner, of Munich, became his teacher. He soon successfully produced some operettas (*Der Onkel aus der Lombardei; Der Vetter auf Besuch; Die Kreuzfahrer; Das Orakel in Delphi; Die Geister des Weins; Der Rotmantel*). For a time he occupied the post of capellmeister at the "Aktientheater," Munich (1865), and was afterwards similarly engaged at Görlitz (1868) and Königsberg (1870).

Kremser, E d u a r d, b. April 10, 1838, Vienna, from 1869 choir-master of the Vienna Male Choral Society. He has composed pf. pieces, songs, part-songs, and operettas: *Eine Operette* (1874), *Der Botschafter, Der Schlosserkönig, Der kritische Tag* (1891; all at Vienna).

Krenn, F r a n z, b. Feb. 26, 1816, Dross (Lower Austria), organist and composer, pupil of Seyfried, occupied several posts as organist at Vienna, and became in 1862 capellmeister of the "Michaels (Hof-) Kirche," and in 1869 professor of harmony at the Conservatorium of the "Gesellschaft der Musikfreunde." His compositions consist for the most part of sacred and secular vocal works: fifteen masses, Te Deum, Salve regina, several requiems, cantata, oratorios (*Bonifacius; Die vier letzten Dinge*), part-songs; yet he also wrote pieces for the organ and pianoforte, quartets, a symphony, an organ Method, and one of singing, etc. D. June 19, 1897.

Kretschmann (Krečman), T h e o b a l d, b. 1850, Vinos, near Prague, solo violoncellist at the Vienna court opera, and conductor of the chamber concerts.

Kretschmer, E d m u n d, b. Aug. 31, 1830, Ostritz (Saxon Oberlausitz), where his father was director of the Realschule, pupil of Jul. Otto and Joh. Schneider at Dresden, where he continued to study zealously by himself, became organist in 1854 of the Catholic "Hofkirche," Dresden, court organist in 1863, conductor, from 1850–70, of various societies there, and founded a Cecilia Society, since dissolved, of which he was conductor. K. is of importance as a composer, and his merit fully recognised. In 1865 Rietz, Abt, and J. Otto awarded him a prize for his "Geisterschlacht," and in 1868 he gained the prize at the national competition at Brussels with a Mass. He wrote, besides, three other masses, also "Pilgerfahrt" for chorus, soli, and orchestra; "Festgesang," for chorus and orchestra; "Musikalische Dorfgeschichten," for orchestra; but, above all, the grand operas *Die Folkunger* (Dresden, 1874), *Heinrich der Löwe* (Leipzig, 1877; of which he also wrote the libretto), and the operetta *Der Flüchtling* (Ulm, 1881), the first two of which were successfully produced at the most important theatres. His most recent works are : *Schön Rohtraut* (romantic opera, Dresden, 1891) and " Sieg im Gesang " (for soli, chorus, and orchestra). K. was specially stimulated and assisted by J. Rietz, who at once rightly estimated the value of *Die Folkunger*, and by Franz Lachner, with whom he opened up correspondence; the latter happened to be one of the judges, together with Fétis, at the Brussels competition.

Kretzschmar, Aug. Ferd. Hermann, b. Jan. 19, 1848, Olbernhau (in the Saxon Erzgebirge), received his first musical instruction from his father, who was cantor and organist. He attended the Kreuzschule at Dresden (received instruction in music from J. Otto), studied philology at Leipzig, obtained his degree of Dr.Phil. in 1871 with a dissertation on the notation signs anterior to Guido d'Arezzo, and became teacher in the same year at the Leipzig Conservatorium, where he had formerly been pupil (under Paul, Richter, Papperitz, and Reinecke). As at the same time he displayed great activity as a conductor (Ossian, Singakademie, Bach-Verein, Euterpe), his strength gave way, and, in 1876, he was compelled to resign all his Leipzig appointments. After resting for a short time, he undertook, still in the same year, the post of theatre capellmeister at Metz, and, in 1877, became musical director of the Rostock University, and in 1880, town musical director, and soon caused musical matters at Rostock to stand in high repute. In 1887 he succeeded Hermann Langers as musical director of the Leipzig University, and became conductor of the " Paulus." Also as member of the commission to examine students in theology, of the municipal professional Verein, and of the directorate of the Bachgesellschaft, also as conductor of the " Riedel " Society, he received in 1890 the title of Professor. In the same year he started the " Akademische Orchesterkonzerte " (with historical programmes). The few compositions for the organ which he has published, and some secular and sacred choruses, show him to be a sound musician. In addition, K. is an excellent performer on the organ, and has acquired fame as a musical critic (*Musikalisches Wochenblatt, Grenzbote,* etc.). His great literary works are reports on " Chorgesang, Sängerchöre," etc., on " Peter Cornelius " (1880, in Waldersee's Collection), the " Führer durch den Konzertsaal," which soon became popular (three vols., 1887 [2nd edition, 1890], 1888, 1890), and valuable articles in the *Grenzbote* (" Das deutsche Lied seit Schumann," 1881 ; " Die deutsche Klaviermusik seit Schumann," 1882 ; " Brahms," 1884). At present K. is at work on a vast monograph of the Opera, which was preceded in 1892 by an article in the *Vierteljahrsschrift für Musik-Wissenschaft* on " Venetian Opera," especially on Cavalli and Cesti.

Kreubé, Charles Frédéric, b. Nov. 5, 1777, Lunéville, d. 1846, at his villa, near St. Denis. He studied under Rod. Kreutzer, and was principal conductor at the Opéra Comique from 1816–28. Between the years 1813–28 he wrote sixteen comic operas for Paris.

Kreutzer, (1) Rodolphe, b. Nov. 16, 1766, Versailles, d. Jan. 6, 1831, Geneva, son of a violinist of the Chapelle du Roi. Under the guidance of his father and of Anton Stamitz, he became an excellent violinist at. an early age, and, already at thirteen, wrote his first violin concerto, before he had received any instruction in theory. His father died when he was sixteen years old, and he then took his place in the court band, and in 1790 was appointed solo violinist at the Théâtre Italien, and, holding this post, was able to bring out an opera. His *Jeanne d'Arc à Orleans,* produced in 1790, opened the goodly series of nearly forty operas, which, up to 1823, he wrote, partly for the Grand Opéra, partly for the Opéra Comique ; most of them were favourably received, but all have fallen into oblivion. On the other hand, his fame as a virtuoso and teacher of the violin still lives. In 1795 he was appointed professor of the violin at the newly established Conservatoire, and in 1796 his reputation was established abroad by a grand concert tour through Italy, Germany, and Holland. When Rode went to Russia in 1801, K. took his place as solo violinist at the Grand Opéra, became second conductor there in 1816, and principal one in 1817 ; at the same time, from 1802, he became chamber-musician to Napoleon, and, from 1815, to Louis XVIII. He retired from public life in 1826. The last years of his life were embittered by the disdainful refusal to produce his last opera, *Mathilde,* on the part of the directors of the Grand Opéra. The work which will secure the most lasting fame to K. as composer is his " 40 Études ou Caprices," for violin alone. He wrote, besides, for his instrument:—nineteen concertos, two double concertos, a similar one for violin and 'cello, fifteen stringed quartets, fifteen stringed trios, several violin sonatas with bass, violin duets, variations for solo violin with orchestra, also for two, three, and four violins. K. published, jointly with Rode and Baillot, the great Violin Method of the Paris Conservatoire. Beethoven dedicated his violin sonata (Op. 47, K.-Sonata) to Rodolphe K.

(2) Auguste, b. 1781, d. Aug. 31, 1832, brother of the former, and his pupil at the Conservatoire ; he was also a distinguished performer on and teacher of the violin. From 1798 he was a member of the orchestra of the Opéra Comique, and belonged to the Grand Opéra from 1802–23, also to the court band of Napoleon, Louis XVIII., and Charles X. up to 1830 ; he succeeded his brother as professor of the violin at the Conservatoire in 1826. He

published for the violin: two concertos, two duets, three sonatas with bass, also some solo pieces and variations.

(3) Charles Léon François, son of the latter, b. Sept. 23, 1817, Paris, d. Oct. 6, 1868, Vichy; he was an intelligent, but severe, musical critic, and wrote especially for the papers *La Quotidienne, L'Union, Revue et Gazette Musicale* (1841, a series of valuable articles, "L'Opéra en Europe"), and *Revue Contemporaine* (Studies on Meyerbeer). An edition of the article which he wrote, jointly with Fournier, for the "Encyclopédie du XIX. siècle" appeared separately in 1845 under the title "Essai sur l'art lyrique au théâtre" (up to Meyerbeer). K. was also highly gifted as a composer, and published pf. sonatas, stringed quartets, a trio, songs, a prelude to Shakespeare's *Tempest*, etc.; also a treatise on modulation. Two symphonies, two operas, etc., remained in manuscript. A. Pougin wrote a biographical notice of him (1868).

(4) Konradin (Kreuzer, according to certificate of baptism), b. Nov. 22, 1780, Mösskirch (Baden), d. Dec. 14, 1849, Riga, was the son of a miller, but, already from an early age, received regular instruction in music. After the death of his father (1800) he devoted himself entirely to music (already in 1800 his first Vaudeville, *Die lächerliche Werbung*, was produced at Freiburg-i.-Br.). He started for Vienna, but remained for some years in Constance; only in 1804 did he arrive in Vienna, where he became the pupil of Albrechtsberger. His talent for composition soon showed buds of promise, and by a performance of a piano concerto of his own K. soon became favourably known. The production of his grand operas *Konradin von Schwaben* and *Der Taucher* was prevented, but he had a pleasing success with his *Æsop in Phrygien* (1808) and *Jery und Bätely* (1810). A performance of the opera *Konradin* at Stuttgart (1812) procured for him the post of capellmeister at the Würtemberg court. He now wrote several new operas for Stuttgart, but went in 1817 to Donaueschingen as capellmeister to Prince von Fürstenberg. In 1822 he returned to Vienna, produced there his *Libussa*, and was for many years (1825, 1829-32, and 1837-40) capellmeister at the "Karntnerthor" Theatre, and from 1833-37 at the Josephstadt Theatre. From 1840-46 he was capellmeister at Cologne, from 1846-49 again at Vienna, in place of O. Nicolai. For the sake of his daughter Cecilia, whom he trained as an opera-singer, he went to Riga, where she was engaged, and he died there. In all K. wrote thirty operas, some incidental music, and an oratorio, *Die Sendung Mosis*, but only *Nachtlager von Granada* (Vienna, 1834) and *Der Verschwender* are still played. His instrumental compositions (septets, quintets, pf. quartets, three pf. concertos, trios for pf., flute and 'cello, one for pf., clarinet and bassoon, fantasias, variations, etc.), and his songs are

forgotten. Only some male quartets are popular in the best sense of the word ("Der Tag des Herrn," "Die Kapelle," etc.). (*Cf.* Riehl, "Mus. Charakterköpfe.")

Kreuzer. (*See* KREUTZER, [4].)

Krieger, (1) Adam, b. Jan. 7, 1634, Driesen (Neumark), pupil of S. Scheidt at Halle, d. June 30, 1666, as court organist at Dresden. He wrote arias à 1–5, with instrumental *ritornelli*, of which he published one in 1656; sixteen others appeared after his death in 1667.

(2) Johann Philipp, b. Feb. 26, 1649, Nuremberg, d. Feb. 6, 1725, Weissenfels, organist at Copenhagen, then, from 1672, for some years chamber composer and capellmeister at Baireuth; but, owing to the French war, for a long time he had no duties to perform, and received permission to travel in Italy. He held office in Cassel, Halle-a.-S., for periods of various lengths, and, from 1685, was court capellmeister at Weissenfels. The Emperor Leopold raised him to the rank of a nobleman on the occasion of a court concert at Vienna. K. wrote several operas for Dresden, Brunswick, and Hamburg. Of his works are preserved: twenty-four sonatas for two violins with bass (Op. 1, 1687; Op. 2, 1693); "Lustige Feldmusik" (pieces for four wind instruments); and "Musikalischer.Seelenfriede" (twenty sacred arias with violin and bass, 1697; 2nd ed. 1717).

(3) Johann, b. Jan. 1, 1652, Nuremberg, d. July 18, 1736, Zittau, pupil and brother of the former, and his successor at Baireuth; in 1678 court capellmeister at Greiz, also for a time at Eisenberg; and in 1681, musical director and organist at Zittau. His works are: "Musikalische Ergötzlichkeit" (1684, arias à 5–9); "Musikalische Partien" (1697, dance pieces for clavier); and "Anmutige Klavierübungen" (1699, preludes, fugues, ricercari, etc.). Motets and portions of masses of his are preserved in manuscript in the Berlin library. K. had the reputation of being one of the most celebrated contrapuntists of his day.

(4) Ferdinand, b. Jan. 8, 1843, Waldershof (Upper Franconia), pupil of the teachers' seminary at Eichstätt and of the Munich Conservatorium; from 1867 music-teacher at the teachers' preparatory institution at Ratisbon. He published: "Die Elemente des Musikunterrichts" (1869); "Die Lehre der Harmonie nach einer bewährten praktischen Methode" (1870); "Studien für das Violinspiel;" "Technische Studien im Umfang einer Quinte für das Pianofortespiel;" "Der rationelle Musikunterricht, Versuch einer musikalischen Pädagogik und Methodik" (1870).

Kriesstein, Melchior, music-printer at Augsburg in the 16th century; he published two collections of Siegmund Salbinger's—"Selectissimæ nec non familiarissimæ cantiones ultra centum" (1540), and "Cantiones 7, 6 et 5 vocum" (1545).

Krigar, Julius Hermann, b. April 3, 1819, Berlin, where he d. Sept. 5, 1880. He first studied for the career of a painter, but turned entirely to music in 1843, attended the Leipzig Conservatorium, and lived as a teacher of music in Berlin, where he established a vocal society. For some years he conducted the " Neue Berliner Liedertafel," and in 1857 was named royal musical director, and in 1874, professor. He only produced a few small pieces. From 1873–74 K. published a " Musikerkalender."

Krisper, Anton, Dr.Phil. at Graz. He wrote " Die Kunstmusik in ihrem Prinzipe, ihrer Entwickelung und ihrer Konsequenz " (1882), a highly interesting historico-theoretical study on a harmonic-dualistic basis.

Krizkowsky, Paul, famous Czeckish national and church composer, b. Jan. 9, 1820, d. May 8, 1885, Brünn; he was an Augustine monk, and councillor of the archbishop's consistory.

Kroll, Franz, b. June 22, 1820, Bromberg, d. May 28, 1877, Berlin, pupil of Liszt at Weimar and Paris, lived from 1849 in Berlin, where he also appeared with success as a pianist. From 1863–64 he taught at the Stern Conservatorium. A disorder of the nerves prevented him from work of any kind during the last years of his life. His name stands high through his excellent critical edition of Bach's "Well-tempered Clavier" (published by Peters, and in the fourteenth year of the Bach Society edition), the " Bibliothek älterer u. neuerer Klaviermusik " (Dresden, Fürstner, c. 1891), and, also, some pianoforte compositions of his own.

Krolop, Franz, excellent stage-singer (bass), b. Sept., 1839, Troja (Bohemia), d. May 30, 1897. He studied law at Prague, commenced his career as army auditor, but gave this up in 1861, and studied for the stage under Richard Levy at Vienna. In 1863 he made his *début* at Troppau in the *rôle* of Ernani, and from that time rose to a position of high eminence. He was engaged at Troppau, Linz, Bremen, Leipzig, and since 1872 was one of the attractions of the Berlin court opera. He had an extensive *répertoire;* he sang, for instance, the Commandant and Leporello, and also Masetto, in *Don Juan.* In 1868 K. married the singer Vilma v. Voggenhuber (q.v.).

Krommer, Franz, b. May 17, 1760, Kamenitz (Moravia), d. Jan. 8, 1831, Vienna, an excellent violinist and composer ; he was trained in organ-playing by an uncle who was *Regens chori* at Turin. After occupying a post as organist for some time, he entered the private band of Count Styrum at Simonthurm (Hungary) as violinist, became *Regens chori* at Fünfkirchen, then bandmaster of the Karoly regiment, went as capellmeister to Prince Grassalkowitsch at Vienna, and, after the death of the latter, gave lessons and composed until he received the post of Imperial "Kammerthürhüter," from which, after the death of Kotzeluch (1814), he was advanced to that of court capellmeister. His chamber compositions, especially the sixty-nine stringed quartets, are flowing and pleasing, and to some extent original ; but, at a time when Haydn, Mozart, and Beethoven were writing, their merits were not fully recognised. He wrote besides: eighteen string quintets, one stringed trio, violin duets, five violin concertos, five symphonies, music for wind band, marches, etc., flute and clarinet concertos, quartets and quintets for wind instruments, and concertante pieces of various kinds. (*Cf.* Riehl's " Mus. Charakterköpfe," I.)

Kronach, Emanuel. (*See* KLITZCH.)

Krotalon, a species of clapper, used by the ancient Greeks to mark the time in dancing.

Krückl, Franz (Krükl), Dr. Jur., an excellent stage-singer (baritone), b. Nov. 10, 1841, Edlspitz (Moravia) ; he was already officially employed by the government as a jurist when he resolved to study for the stage under Dessoff. He made his *début* in 1868 at Brünn, and after that appeared at Cassel, Augsburg (1871), Hamburg (1874), Cologne (1875), from 1876 to 1885 again at Hamburg, and then became teacher at Dr. Hoch's Conservatorium, Frankfort. Since 1892 he has been director of the Stadttheater, Strassburg. K. has written:—" Der Vertrag zwischen Direktor und Mitglied der deutschen Bühne " (1889).

Krug, (1) Friedrich, b. July 5, 1812, Cassel, d. Nov. 3, 1892, Carlsruhe, was opera-singer (baritone), afterwards court musical director at Carlsruhe (operas: *Die Marquise,* Cassel, 1843 ; *Meister Martin der Küfer und seine Gesellen,* Carlsruhe, 1845 ; also *Der Nachtwächter,* in 1846).

(2) Dietrich, b. May 25, 1821, Hamburg, teacher of music there, d. April 7, 1880. He wrote a number of easy, melodious pianoforte works, also studies and a Pianoforte Method.

(3) Arnold, son and pupil of the former, b. Oct. 16, 1849, Hamburg, received further training afterwards from Gurlitt. In 1868 he became pupil of the Leipzig Conservatorium, and in 1869 obtained the Mozart foundation scholarship, and thus became the pupil of Reinecke and Kiel (1871), and for pianoforte-playing, of E. Frank. From 1872–77 he was teacher of the pianoforte at the Stern Conservatorium, Berlin, and went (from 1877–78, as holder of the Meyerbeer scholarship) to Italy and France. Since then he has been living at Hamburg as conductor of his own Gesangverein, and, from 1885, as teacher at the Conservatorium and conductor of the Altona "Singakademie." K. possesses a sound talent for composition, and in his music there is no straining after effect. Among his published compositions are a symphony, the symphonic prologue to *Othello,* a suite, Romanesque dances for orchestra, " Liebesnovelle " and " Italien-

ische Reiseskizzen" for orchestra of strings, a violin concerto, a choral work ("Sigurd") for chorus, with soli and orchestra, "An die Hoffnung" for mixed choir and orchestra, "Italienisches Liederspiel," a pf. quartet, trio, waltzes for four hands, pf. pieces, songs, part-songs, a psalm, etc.

(4) W e n z e l J o s e f (Krug-Waldsee), b. Nov. 8, 1858, Waldsee (Upper Suabia), pupil of the Stuttgart Conservatorium, from 1882–89 conductor of the Stuttgart " Neuer Singverein," from 1889–92 chorus director at the Hamburg Stadttheater; at present he is capellmeister at the Brünn Stadttheater. Besides solo and part-songs, his choral works, " Harald," " Geiger zu Gmünd," and especially " König Rother," have been repeatedly performed. A one-act comic opera, *Der Prokurator von San Juan*, still awaits production.

Krüger, (1) E d u a r d, musical theorist, b. Dec. 9, 1807, Lüneburg, d. Nov. 9, 1885, Göttingen. He attended the Gymnasia at Lüneburg, Hamburg, and Gotha, studied philology at Berlin and Göttingen, but at the same time made a thorough study of music. He was, for a long time, teacher at the Gymnasium, and, after that, director of the seminaries at Emden and Aurich. For some time he was editor of the *Neue Hannoversche Zeitung*, and in 1861 was appointed professor of music at the University of Göttingen. K. was one of our most learned and thoughtful musicians; his critical articles in the *Göttinger Gelehrten Anzeiger* are dignified, and show great knowledge of his subject; and the same can be said of his notices of novelties in the *Neue Berliner Musikzeitung* and the *Allgemeine Musikalische Zeitung*. His works—" Grundriss der Metrik " (1838), Beiträge für Leben und Wissenschaft der Tonkunst " (1847), and especially the " System der Tonkunst " (1866)—are a rich treasure-house of thoughtful investigation. He also wrote numerous pamphlets, among which his dissertation for the degree of doctor, " De musicis Græcorum organis circa Pindari tempora " (1830). Of his compositions only a few small pieces have been printed.

(2) W i l h e l m, b. 1820, Stuttgart, d. there June 17, 1883, son of the former flute virtuoso, royal Würtemberg chamber-musician, Gottlieb, b. 1790, Berlin. He was an excellent pianist and composer of elegant (sometimes bordering on the " Charakterstück ") drawing-room music. He lived (from 1845–70) in Paris, after that again in Stuttgart as royal court pianist and teacher at the Conservatorium. — His brother, (3) G o t t l i e b, b. May 4, 1824, d. Oct. 12, 1895, Stuttgart, was a distinguished performer on the harp, and member of the court band at Stuttgart.

Kruis, M. H. v a n, b. March 8, 1861, Oudewater, received his first musical training from his father, became, in 1877, a pupil of Nikolai's at the Hague, and, in 1881, organist and musical director at Winterswyk. In 1884 he went to Rotterdam as organist and teacher at the School of Music, and, in 1866, established the monthly paper, *Het Orgel*. K. has composed pieces for pianoforte and organ, choruses, eight overtures and three symphonies for orchestra, and the Dutch opera, *De bloem van Island*. He has also made himself known as a writer :— " Beknopt Overzieht der Muziekgeschiedenis " (1892).

Krummbogen (Ger.), a crook for changing the key (pitch) of a horn or trumpet.

Krummhorn (Kromphorn, Krumhorn, from which the French *Cromorne* and Ital. *Cormone*; Ital. also *Cornamuto*, or, briefly, *Storto*)—(1) an obsolete wood-wind instrument allied to the Bomhart, which was blown by means of a double reed fixed in a kettle-shaped mouthpiece; it differs from the Bomhart through the semicircular bend of the lower portion of the sounding tube, and through the marked narrower compass (a ninth). In the 16th century the K. was constructed in from three to four different sizes (as discant-, alto- [tenor], and bass instrument), and in the straight portion of the tube it had six key-holes. The tone of the instrument was melancholy; an imitation of its clang colour is given by the (2) K. (Cormorne, Cremona, also Photinx), an organ stop frequently to be found in former days in small organs, and in the echo-work of larger ones (8 ft., 4 ft.; in the pedals also as 16 ft. as *Krummhornbass*), a half-covered reed stop, of conical shape below, and of cylindrical above.

Krumpholtz, (1) J o h a n n B a p t i s t, famous performer on the harp, b. about 1745, Zlonitz, near Prague, d. Feb. 19, 1790, Paris; he was brought up in Paris, where his father was bandmaster of a French regiment. In 1772 he gave concerts in Vienna, and settled there as teacher; was, from 1773–76, member of the band of Prince Esterhazy, and enjoyed instruction in composition from Haydn. Meanwhile his reputation had spread, and he undertook a great concert tour through Germany, and then went to France. In Metz he trained Fräulein Meyer, who became an accomplished performer on the harp. He married her and went to Paris, where he celebrated great triumphs, especially after that Nadermann, according to his suggestion, constructed harps with a loud and soft pedal. K. also suggested the idea of double pedal harps to Erard. From sorrow caused by the unfaithfulness of his wife, who ran away with a young man, he drowned himself in the Seine. His compositions for the harp (six concertos, fifty-two sonatas, variations, quartets with violin, viola, and 'cello, harp duets, symphony for harp, two violins, flutes, two horns and 'cello, etc.) are still of value.

(2) W e n z e l, b. about 1750, brother of the former, was in 1796 member of the opera orchestra in Vienna; he was on friendly terms with Beethoven, and died May 2, 1817. Beethoven

dedicated to his memory the "Gesang der Mönche." K. published "Abendunterhaltung" for violin solo, and "Eine Viertelstunde für eine Violine."

Kruse, Johann S., excellent violinist, b. March 23, 1859, Melbourne, Australia (his father had migrated from Hanover); in 1876 he studied under Joachim at Berlin, became leader of the Philharmonic orchestra, and went, in 1892, as leader, to Bremen.

Krustische instrumente (Ger.; from Gk. χρούειν, to "strike"), instruments of percussion.

Kucharcz, Joh. Baptist, b. March 5, 1751, Chotecz, Bohemia, d. after 1815, distinguished organist, studied under Seegert at Prague, became organist of the Heinrichskirche in that city, in 1790 at the Strahower Stiftskirche, in 1791 capellmeister of the Italian Opera. He was also an esteemed composer of organ concertos, operas, ballets, etc., arranger of the first pianoforte scores of Mozart's operas, and wrote recitatives to the *Magic Flute.*

Kücken, Friedrich Wilhelm, b. Nov., 1810, Bleckede, near Hanover, d. April 3, 1882, Schwerin, son of a peasant, received his first musical training from his father's brother-in-law, the court organist Lürss at Schwerin. K. played various instruments in the court orchestra at Schwerin, but even at that time attracted notice by his simple songs, which quickly became popular (the Thuringian Volkslied "Ach wie war's möglich dann"), and he was appointed teacher of music to the princes. In 1832 he went for further study to Birnbach at Berlin, and obtained a lasting success there with an opera (*Die Flucht nach der Schweiz*). He still studied afterwards with Sechter at Vienna (1841) and with Halévy at Paris (1843); but, in spite of all this zeal for knowledge, K. never got beyond the standpoint which suits the general public. In 1851 he was called as court capellmeister to Stuttgart, at first jointly with Lindpainter, after whose death he became sole conductor; but he resigned in 1861 and retired to Schwerin. The number of K.'s compositions, especially of songs and duets, is exceedingly large (among them are "Gretelein," "Ach wenn du wärst mein eigen," "Du schönes blitzendes Sternlein," etc.); in addition may be mentioned "Der Prätendent" (Stuttgart, 1847), violin sonatas, 'cello sonatas, quartets for male chorus, etc.

Kudelski, Karl Matthias, b. Nov. 17, 1805, Berlin, d. Oct. 3, 1877, Baden-Baden; 1830 at Dorpat as quartet-player, in 1839 there as capellmeister to a Russian prince, from 1841–51 conductor at the Imperial Theatre, Petersburg; and then lived for a long time at Baden-Baden. He wrote a Method of composition, a 'cello sonata, violin concerto, trios, and string quartets.

Kufferath, (1) Johann Hermann, b. May 12, 1797, Mülheim-a.-d.-Ruhr, d. July 28, 1864, Wiesbaden; an excellent violinist, pupil of Spohr and Hauptmann at Cassel, in 1823 musical director at Bielefeld, in 1830 town musical director at Utrecht, teacher of singing at the School of Music, and conductor of several musical societies; and he was held in high consideration for the musical services which he rendered to that city. In 1862 he withdrew to Wiesbaden. K. composed several festival cancatas, overtures, motets, etc., and published in 1836 a Vocal Method for schools (which gained the prize at the Netherland Musical Society).

(2) Louis, b. Nov. 10, 1811, Mülheim, d. March 2, 1882, near Brussels, brother of the former, pianist, pupil of Fr. Schneider at Dessau; from 1836–50 director of the school of music at Leeuwarden, also conductor of the societies "Euphonia-Crescendo" and "Tot nut van t'algemeen," and founder of the "Groote Zang Vereeniging." After 1850 he settled in Ghent, devoting himself entirely to composition and private lessons. He published a mass à 4, with organ and orchestra, 250 canons, one cantata (*Artevelde*), many pf. compositions, songs, part-songs, etc.

(3) Hubert Ferdinand, b. June 11, 1818, Mülheim, brother and pupil of the two former; he studied from 1833–36 under Fr. Schneider at Dessau, and under Mendelssohn and David at Leipzig; from 1841–44 he was conductor of the male choral society at Cologne, settled in 1844 at Brussels, and in 1871 became professor of composition at the Conservatorium. He published a symphony, several pf. concertos, songs, etc. Died June 23, 1896, Brussels.

(4) Maurice, son and pupil of the former, b. Jan. 8, 1852, Brussels; he studied also the 'cello under the two Servais, then attended the University and studied jurisprudence and philology. In 1873 he was named editor of the *Indépendance Belge* (for foreign politics), and, likewise, editor, later on, proprietor, of the *Guide Musical.* K. is zealously in favour of musical progress, and has published a great number of works of small compass: "R. Wagner und die 9. Symphonie," "Berlioz u. Schumann," "Le théâtre de Wagner de Tannhäuser à Parsifal," "L'art de diriger l'orchestre" (2nd edition), a biography of H. Vieuxtemps, a report on the musical instruments at the Brussels Exhibition of 1880. He has also translated the texts of works by Wagner, Brahms, and other composers (pseudonym: Maurice Reymont). His younger sister, Antonia, pupil of Stockhausen, is favourably known for her rendering of Lieder by Brahms; she married the son of the well-known song composer Ed. Speyer at Frankfort.

(5) Fredrich Wilhelm, pianist, composer, and esteemed teacher, died April, 1885, Cologne.

Küffner, Joseph, b. March 31, 1776, Würzburg, d. there Sept. 9, 1856; he composed seven symphonies, ten overtures, many works for wind- and military-band, stringed quartets, a viola concerto, quintet for flute and stringed quartet, duets and trios for flutes, duets for clarinets, etc. His works for military band met with special favour.

Kugelmann, H a n s, principal trumpeter to Duke Albrecht of Prussia, published a book of sacred songs à 3 for church use in Prussia; to this work was added, by way of supplement, a series of art-songs à 2–8. K. died at Königsberg, 1542. (Concerning his importance in connection with sacred song, *see* Winterfeld, " Evang. Kirchenges." I., 265; *cf. Monatsh. f. Mus.-Gesch.*, VIII., 65 f.)

Kuhe, W i l h e l m, b. Dec. 10, 1823, Prague, pupil of Tomaczek there, pianist and composer of pleasing pianoforte pieces; he has lived for a long time as a teacher of music in London, and since 1886 has been professor at the Royal Academy.

Kuhhorn (Ger.), a cow-horn; Alpine horn.

Kuhlau, F r i e d r i c h, b. Sept. 11, 1786, Uelzen (Hanover), d. March 18, 1832, Copenhagen; he sang for alms in the streets at Brunswick, and studied harmony there under Schwencke. He fled to Copenhagen in 1810 to escape the French conscription, and there, at the commencement of 1813, became (without salary) royal chamber-musician. He gave instruction in pianoforte-playing and theory, received, in 1818, a salary and the title of court composer, and in 1828 was named Professor. K. wrote for Copenhagen the operas *Die Räuberburg* (1814), *Elisa, Lulu, Die Zauberharfe, Hugo und Adelheid*, dramatic scena *Euridice*, and music to Heiberg's *Erlenhügel* (1828); all of these were favourably received, but are now forgotten. His instrumental compositions (three quartets for flute, *trios concertants*, duets, soli, etc., for flute, two piano concertos, eight violin sonatas, pf. sonatas and sonatinas for two and four hands—the last still popular and of great educational value for beginners [Op. 55, 20, 59], rondos, variations, divertissements, dances, etc.) have been in part preserved; but of his once popular songs and quartets for male voices nothing more is heard. (*Cf.* K. Thrane's " Fr. Kuhlau," on the occasion of the hundredth anniversary of his birthday, 1886.) A relative of K.'s, F r i e d r i c h K., an esteemed 'cellist, d. Aug., 1878, at Copenhagen.

Kühmstedt, F r i e d r i c h, b. Dec. 20, 1809, Oldisleben (Thuringia), d. Jan. 10, 1858, Eisenach. It was intended to train him for the church, but at the age of nineteen he ran away from the Gymnasium at Weimar, and studied composition for three years under K. H. Rinck at Darmstadt. His desire was to become a pianoforte virtuoso, but paralysis in the left hand frustrated this plan. After living for some time at Weimar as teacher of music, he was appointed in 1836 teacher at the Eisenach College, was then named musical director, and, finally, professor. K. composed several oratorios (*Auferstehung, Triumph des Göttlichen*),

a mass à 4 with orchestra, motets, and also secular choral pieces, songs, piano concertos, rondos, etc., which are all forgotten. On the other hand, the following are held in esteem: " Gradus ad Parnassum " (preludes and fugues as preparatory training for Bach's organ and clavier works), also his numerous organ works (preludes, postludes, fugues, concert double-fugue, " Fantasia eroica," etc.), his " Kunst des Vorspiels für Orgel " (Op. 6), and his " Theoretisch praktische Harmonie u. Ausweichungslehre " (1838, for self-instruction).

Kuhnau, J o h a n n, b. April, 1660, Neugeising (Saxony), d. June 5, 1722, Leipzig; he was a pupil at the " Kreuzschule " and chorister (" Ratsdiskantist ") at Dresden, but fled from the plague in 1680, and returned to his home. He was, for some time, cantor at Zittau, in 1684 successor of Kühnel as organist of St. Thomas's Church, Leipzig, and in 1700 musical director of the University and cantor of St. Thomas's. J. S. Bach was his successor. K. was not only an excellent musician, but had also studied languages and jurisprudence, and made translations from Greek and Hebrew, etc. His compositions which have been preserved are: " Neue Klavierübung " (1689 and 1695, two parts); " Frische Klavierfrüchte oder sieben Sonaten von guter Invention," etc. (1699), and " Musikalische Vorstellungen einiger biblischen Historien in sechs Sonaten auf dem Klavier zu spielen " (1700). In pianoforte literature K. occupies an important place as the first who transferred the form of the chamber sonata in various movements to the clavier; K., however, does not write in the " galant" style of Ph. E. Bach. The works of K. on music are: " Jura circa musicos ecclesiasticos " (1688); " Der musikalische Quacksalber " (1700, a satire on Italian music). His " Tractatus de tetrachordo " and " Introductio ad compositionem musicalem " remained in manuscript.

Kühner, K o n r a d, b. March 2, 1851, Marktstreufdorf, Meiningen, pupil of the Stuttgart Conservatorium, lives at Brunswick as teacher of the pianoforte. He has written a " Technik des Klavierspiels," romances, nocturnes, and a symphonic poem, " Maria Stuart."

Kuhreihen, or **Kuhreigen** (Ger.), the name of the simple melodies sung, or played on the horn, by the Swiss herdsmen when driving the cattle out or homeward.

Kujawiak, Polish dance of Kujawien similar to the Mazurka.

Kullak, (1) T h e o d o r, b. Sept. 12, 1818, Krotoschin (Posen), where his father was " Landsgerichtssekretär," d. March 1, 1882, Berlin; at an early age he showed talent for music, and attracted the attention of Prince A. Radziwill (q.v.), who superintended his training under Agthe at Posen, so that at the age of eleven K. made his *début* at a court concert at Berlin. The death of the Prince disturbed the musical plans made for the future. K. attended the Gymnasium at Züllichau, and went in 1837 to Berlin in order to study medicine. Here he found his old teacher Agthe proprietor of a music institution, and he was soon once more on a musical path, gave pianoforte lessons and studied harmony under Dehn. In 1842 he continued his studies under Czerny, Sechter, and Nicolai at Vienna, and in 1843, after a successful concert tour through Austria, was appointed music-teacher to Princess Anna, daughter of Prince Friedrich Karl, and was afterwards teacher to all the princes and princesses of the royal house. In 1846 he was appointed court pianist. In 1850, jointly with J. Stern and A. B. Marx, he founded the Berlin (Stern) Conservatorium, but withdrew from the direction in 1855, and founded the "Neue Akademie der Tonkunst," which celebrated the twenty-fifth anniversary of its foundation with a hundred teachers and over a thousand pupils. Theodor K. was not only an excellent pianist, but also a teacher of the first rank (pupils : Hans Bischoff, M. Moszkowski, X. and Ph. Scharwenka, and many others); his " School of Octaveplaying " (Op. 48) is a work which every pianist ought to possess. Also his " Materialien für den Elementarunterricht" (three books), and the practical part to the Method of pianoforte-playing of Moscheles and Fétis (two books) are excellent educational works. His compositions amount altogether to about 130, consisting mostly of *salon* music and brilliant paraphrases, fantasias for pianoforte. But he also wrote a pianoforte sonata (Op. 7), a " Symphonie de piano " (Op. 27), pf. concerto (Op. 55), three duos with violin (Op. 57, jointly with R. Wüerst), one Andante with violin or clarinet (Op. 70), one trio (Op. 77), and some songs (Op. 1 to 10), and the universal favourite, " Kinderleben " (two parts, Op. 62 and Op. 81).

(2) Adolf, b. Feb. 23, 1823, Meseritz, d. Dec. 25, 1862, Berlin ; brother of the former, attended the Gymnasium of the Graues Kloster, Berlin, studied philosophy there, and took his degree of Dr.Phil., but then devoted himself entirely to music (Agthe and Marx were his teachers), was contributor to the *Berliner Musikzeitung,* and gave lessons at his brother's Akademie. Besides various pf. pieces and songs, he wrote : " Das Musikalisch-Schöne " (1858), and " Aesthetik des Klavierspiels " (1861 ; 2nd ed., by H. Bischoff, 1876; an excellent book).

(3) Franz, Dr. Phil., son of Theodor K., b. April 12, 1844, trained at his father's Akademie, after whose death he became director ; the institution was, however, suddenly dissolved in 1890. He has published careful editions of classical pianoforte concertos, and by an opera, *Ines de Castro* (Berlin, 1877), has proved himself a worthy heir of his father.

Kummer, (1) Kaspar, b. Dec. 10, 1795, Erlau, near Schleusingen, performer on the

flute, was appointed member of the court band (Coburg) in 1813, d. May 21, 1870; he published numerous works for the flute (concertos, quartets, and quintets with stringed instruments, duos, fantasias, variations, etc., and a Method for flute.

(2) Friedrich August, b. Aug. 5, 1797, Meiningen, d. May 22, 1879, Dresden, son of an oboe-player in the Meiningen court band, and soon called in a similar capacity to Dresden. Young K. studied the 'cello under Dotzauer, but, as there was no post vacant for that instrument, he was first appointed oboist in 1814, and 'cellist, only in 1817. K. soon became known as one of the best performers on his instrument, whether as solo, quartet, or orchestral player; he was an especially good teacher (Cossmann, J. Goltermann, and others were his pupils). In 1864 he celebrated his fiftieth anniversary as member of the Dresden band, and retired therefrom, but still remained teacher at the Conservatorium. His published compositions are : concertos, variations, divertissements, and other pieces for 'cello, a Method for that instrument, and much incidental music to plays. Like his father and his brother, his sons and grandsons were also able musicians. His grandson, (3) Alexander K., is especially worthy of mention. He was b. July 10, 1850, and is an excellent violinist, pupil of the Leipzig Conservatorium ; he lives in England.

Kümmerle, Salomon, b. Feb. 8, 1838, Malmsheim, near Stuttgart ; from 1853 he was trained as teacher at the Tempelhof Seminary ; from 1860-66 tutor at Nice, and, at the same time, organist of the German church there ; from 1867-68 teacher of music at the seminary for female teachers at Ludwigsberg, Würtemberg ; from 1869-74 teacher at the High School for girls at Schorndorf, Würtemberg ; from 1875-90 teacher (Professor) at the lower school at Samaden, Switzerland. Up to the present the following works of his have appeared . " Musica sacra," master-works of old, especially old-Italian, church composers (for male chorus, two parts, 1869-70) ; " Grabgesänge," for male voices (1869) ; " Zionsharfe," a collection of sacred songs, motets, etc., for mixed voices (two parts, 1870-71) ; " Choralbuch für evangelischen Kirchenchöre " (three hundred compositions à 4 and 5 for mixed choir, by the masters of the 16th and 17th centuries, and by modern composers—first part, 1887 ; second part, 1889) ; " Encyklopädie der evangelischen Kirchenmusik " (first vol., 1888 ; second vol., 1890 ; third vol., in the press).

Kündinger, (1) Georg Wilhelm, b. Nov. 28, 1800, Königshofen (Bavaria), was " Stadtkantor " and musical director at Nördlingen in 1831, occupied similar posts at Nuremberg in 1838 ; but in consequence of bodily infirmities he withdrew from all his public appointments,

and lived at Fürth. K. wrote many sacred
pieces. His sons are:—

(2) A u g u s t, b. Feb. 13, 1827, Kitzingen,
violinist and composer for that instrument,
member of the Imperial court orchestra at
Petersburg.

(3) K a n u t, b. Nov. 11, 1830, 'cellist, since
1849 member of the Munich court orchestra.

(4) R u d o l f, distinguished pianist and
teacher, b. May 2, 1832, Nördlingen, pupil of
his father (see above, 1) and of Blumröder for
theory, went in 1850 to Petersburg as private
music tutor to Baron Bietinghoff, made yearly
appearances at the concerts of the Imperial
Musical Society, and in 1860 became teacher
of music to the children of the Grand Duke
Constantin Nikolajewitsch. Since that time
K. has confined himself to teaching at the Imperial court and to giving lessons to the present
Empress, and he has received high honours.
A professorship of the pianoforte at the Conservatoire was offered to him in 1879, but he resigned after the expiration of a year. Of his
compositions only a trio and some piano pieces
have been published.

Kunkel, F r a n z J o s e p h, b. Aug. 10, 1808,
Dieburg (Hesse), d. Dec. 31, 1880, Frankfort,
rector of the town-school and teacher of music
at the Bensheim College for teachers; he was
pensioned in 1854. He composed sacred vocal
works, organ pieces, a "Choralbuch," and
wrote "Kleine Musiklehre;" "Die Verurteil-
ung der Conservertorien zu Pflanzschulen des
musikalischen Proletariats" (1855); "Kritische
Beleuchtung des K. F. Weitzmannschen Harmonie Systems," and the pamphlet "Die neue
Harmonielehre im Streit mit der alten" (1863).

Kunstfuge (Ger.), a fugue in which the
composer introduces all imaginable scholastic
contrivances. *Meisterfuge* and *Ricercata* are
synonymous expressions.

Kuntze, K a r l, b. March 17, 1817, Trèves,
d. Sept. 7, 1883, Delitzsch, pupil of the Royal
Institution for Church Music at Berlin (A. W.
Bach, Marx, Rungenhagen), organist at Pritz-
walk, was appointed royal musical director in
1852, in 1858 organist at Aschersleben, in 1873
teacher of music at the Delitzsch College for
teachers. He is well known as the composer
of humorous and comic quartets for men's
voices, songs, duets, terzets, etc. He also supervised the third edition of J. J. Seidel's "Die
Orgel und ihr Bau" (1875).

Kunz, K o n r a d M a x, b. Dec. 30, 1812,
Schwandorf (Bavarian Upper Palatinate), d.
Aug. 3, 1875, Munich; he began the study of
medicine in the latter city, but maintained himself by giving music lessons, and finally devoted
himself entirely to music. He was conductor
of the Munich Liedertafel, and in 1845 chorus-
master of the court opera at Munich. K.
wrote a very large number of quartets for male
voices, which gained extraordinary popularity

("Elstein," "Odin, der Schlachtengott," etc.).
He also wrote the satirical pamphlet, "Die
Gründung der Moosgau-Brüderschaft Moos-
grillia."

Kunzen, (1) J o h a n n P a u l, b. Aug. 30, 1696,
Leisnig (Saxony), d. 1770 as organist at Lübeck.
In 1718 he was capellmeister at Zerbst, in 1719
concert director at Wittenberg, and lived later
on in Hamburg. K. is praised by Mattheson
as one of the best composers of his time (several
operas for Hamburg, a Passion, cantatas,
overtures, oratorio *Belsazar*, etc.).

(2) K a r l A d o l f, son of the former, b. Sept.
22, 1720, Wittenberg, d. July, 1781, Lübeck; he
was a youthful musical prodigy, who, at the age
of eight, attracted notice in Holland and England
as a pianist. In 1750 he was capellmeister at
Schwerin, and in 1757 succeeded his father at
Lübeck. K. published twelve pf. sonatas; his
other numerous works remained in manuscript
(symphonies, concertos for violin, flute, oboe;
oratorios, cantatas, etc.).

(3) F r i e d r i c h L u d w i g A e m i l i u s, son of
Karl Adolf K., b. Sept. 24, 1761, Lübeck, d.
Jan. 28, 1817, Copenhagen; he attended the
school at Hamburg and the University at Kiel;
went in 1787 to Copenhagen, where he made a
success with his maiden opera *Holger Danske*
(*Oberon*); and from there to Berlin, where, jointly
with Reichardt, he published the *Musikalisches
Wochenblatt* (1791), and the *Musikalische Monatsschrift* (1792). For a brief period he was theatre
capellmeister at Frankfort and Prague, until at
last he was called as court capellmeister to
Copenhagen. K. wrote, in addition to *Holger
Danske*, twelve other Danish and German operas
(*Holger Danske* and *Das Winzerfest* appeared in
pf. score), further, several oratorios, cantatas,
overtures, sonatas, etc.

Kupfer-Berger, L u d m i l l a, opera-singer
(soprano), b. 1850, Vienna, daughter of a manufacturer named Berger, pupil of the Vienna
Conservatorium. She made her *début* in 1868
at Linz as Marguerite in Gounod's *Faust*, and
in the same year took the place, at Berlin, of
Harriers-Wippern, who was retiring. At Berlin
she married a rich merchant (Kupfer by name),
and soon exchanged the Berlin court opera for
the one at Vienna, where she shares with Frau
Materna the great dramatic soprano *rôles*.

Kurpinski, K a r l K a s i m i r, Polish composer
of operas, b. March 5, 1785, Luschwitz, near
Fraustadt (Posen), d. Sept. 18, 1857, Warsaw, son
of an organist. He was, first of all, second, and,
from 1825–41, first, capellmeister, as successor
to Elsner at the National Theatre, Warsaw;
finally, from 1819, imperial Russian court conductor. Between 1811–26 he wrote not less
than twenty-six Polish operas for Warsaw.

Kurrende (Ger.; from Lat. *currere*, "to run").
This was the name given to the needy pupils
belonging to the lower-class municipal schools,
who, under the direction of one of the older

pupils (the "Präfekt") sang sacred songs for scanty alms in the streets, at funerals, etc. This custom was kept up, especially in Thuringia and Saxony, until the present century, and in Hamburg even beyond the year 1860. The boys wore small black round capes and flat cylinder hats. *Cf.* Schaarschmidt's "Geschichte der K." (1807).

Kurschmann, *v.* CURSCHMANN.

Kusser (Cousser), Johann Siegmund, b. about 1657, Pressburg, d. 1727, Dublin, an extraordinarily gifted conductor and esteemed opera composer, to whom the Hamburg opera is really indebted for its fame. According to the testimony of Walthers (in his "Musikalisches Lexicon"), he was a restless spirit who never could remain anywhere long, so that "probably a place could not easily be found where he was not known." K. lived for six years in Paris in intimate friendship with Lully. In 1693 he took a lease of the Hamburg opera-house, together with Jakob Kremberg von Schott, and so distinguished himself as director up to 1695, and as wielder of the *bâton,* that Matthesen (in his "Vollkommener Kapellmeister") named him as a model to conductors. After being capellmeister of the Stuttgart opera from 1698 to 1704, he went to England and became conductor of the band belonging to the Viceroy of Ireland. The works of K. that have been preserved are his operas : *Erindo* (1693) ; *Porus* (1694) ; *Pyramus und Thisbe* (not produced); *Scipio Africanus* (1694); and *Jason.* He published: "Apollon enjoué" (1700, six overtures and some arias); "Helikonische Musenlust" (1700, pieces from the opera *Ariadne*); a birthday serenade for King George I. (1724); a funeral ode for Miss Arabella Hunt ; a "Serenata teatrale" in honour of Queen Anne is mentioned by Chrysander (*Allgemeine Musikalische Zeitung,* 1879, 26) as a recently discovered manuscript.

Küster, Hermann, b. July 14, 1817, Templin (Ukermark), d. March 17, 1878, Herford (Westphalia); he studied under A. W. Bach, L. Berger, Rungenhagen, and Marx, at the Royal Institute for Church Music and the School for Composition of the Berlin "Akademie ;" from 1845-52 he was musical director at Saarbrücken, lived afterwards in Berlin as teacher of music, where he founded the "Berliner Tonkünstlerverein," became musical director and court and cathedral organist in 1857, and Professor in 1874. K. composed several oratorios, and other vocal and instrumental works, but his writings are of higher importance : "Populäre Vorträge über Bildung und Begründung eines musikalischen Urteils" (1870–77, four books) ; "Ueber Händels *Israel in Aegypten*" (1854) ; and many detached articles in Berlin musical papers. In 1872 he published a "Methode für den Unterricht im Gesang auf höhern Schulanstalten."

Kwast, James, distinguished pianist, b. Nov. 23, 1852, Nijkerk (Holland), pupil of his father and of Ferd. Böhme (a pupil of M. Hauptmann). He held the scholarship of the "Maatschapij tot Bevordering van Toonkunst' from 1869-74, and afterwards benefited by a royal stipend and studied under Reinecke and Richter at the Leipzig Conservatorium, under Th. Kullak and Wüerst at Berlin, and under L. Brassin and Gevaert at Brussels. In 1874 he succeeded Gernsheim as teacher at the Cologne Conservatorium, and, since Oct., 1883, he has been professor of the pianoforte at the Frankfort Conservatorium. In 1877 K. married the daughter of Ferd. Hiller. As a composer, K. has successfully produced a trio (a work belonging to his Leipzig student-days), an overture (which gained a prize at the competition instituted by the King of Holland), a pf. concerto in F (which he has repeatedly played with approval at concerts), and some other pianoforte works.

Kyrie is the name given to the first portion of the Mass (q.v.) which immediately follows the Introit. The words consist of a threefold appeal for mercy—"K. eleison ! Christe eleison ! K. eleison !" One speaks, therefore, of a first and a second K.; the first precedes, the second follows the "Christe eleison."

L.

L', the Italian article (in place of *lo, la*) before vowels.

La, (1) in Italy, France, Belgium, Spain, etc., the name which the Germans, Dutch, and English give to the note called A (q.v.). (Concerning *la, mi, re, la, fa,* etc., *cf.* SOLMISATION, also MUTATION.)—(2) In Italian the feminine article (the), before vowels, *l'.*

Labarre, Théodore, famous harp-player, b. March 5, 1805, Paris, d. March 9, 1870, pupil of Bochsa and Nadermann, also at the Conservatoire under Dourlen, Fétis, and Boieldieu, became well known by concert tours ; he lived alternately in Paris and London. He produced several operas at Paris, was, from 1847-49, *chef d'orchestre* of the Opéra-Comique, then went again to London, but in 1851 returned to Paris as *chef* of the private band of Napoleon III., and in 1867 succeeded Prumier as professor of the harp at the Conservatoire. With the exception of four operas and five ballets, L. wrote chiefly for the harp (soli, fantasias, nocturnes; duets with piano, violin, horn, oboe; trios with horn and bassoon, etc.), a "Méthode complète pour la harpe," and a number of romances which became popular.

Labatt, Leonard, celebrated stage-singer (dramatic tenor), b. 1838, Stockholm, pupil of the Academy of Music there, and of Masset at Paris. He made his *début* at Stockholm in 1866 in the *rôle* of Tamino, and from 1868 to 1882 was one of the most esteemed members of the Court Opera, Vienna.

Labialpfeife (Ger.), a flue-pipe in the organ.

Labialstimme (Ger.), a flue-stop in the organ.

Labisation, a somewhat rare term for Hitzler's Bebisation. (*See* BOBISATION.)

Labitzky, Joseph, b. July 4, 1802, Schönefeld (near Eger), d. Aug. 19, 1881, Carlsbad; a favourite dance composer of the Strauss and Lanner *genre.* He was at first member (violinist) of the "Kurorchester" at Marienbad, and afterwards at Carlsbad, where in 1834 he founded an orchestra of his own, with which he made successful concert tours as far as Petersburg and London, by which his waltzes, quadrilles, etc., became widely known. His son, August, b. Oct. 22, 1832, Petschau, pupil of the Prague Conservatorium, and of David and Hauptmann at Leipzig, undertook the direction of the orchestra in 1853.

Labium (Lat.), the lip of an organ-pipe.

Lablache, Luigi, b. Dec, 4, 1794, Naples, d. Jan. 23, 1858, was, on his father's side, of French descent; a celebrated singer (bass), pupil of the Conservatorio della Pietà, he first became basso-buffo at the theatre San Carlino at Naples and at Messina, but afterwards took serious parts, was engaged, with ever-increasing reputation, at Palermo, Milan, Venice, Vienna, and reached the zenith of his fame when he went to Paris in 1830. He sang up to 1852 in Paris, London, and Petersburg, then retired to his country-house, Maisons-Lafitte, and died at his villa near Naples, whither he had betaken himself on account of the mild climate. In his "Méthode de chant" L. wrote down his experiences as a vocalist.

Labor, Josef, b. June 29, 1842, Horowitz (Bohemia), became blind at an early age, and, as he showed musical gifts, was trained at the Vienna Conservatorium (Sechter, Pirkhert) at a heavy sacrifice on the part of his young widowed mother. In 1863 he appeared in Vienna as pianist, and his expressive playing met with such favourable recognition that he ventured to make a great concert tour through Germany. King Georg kept him for almost two years in Hanover as chamber pianist and teacher to the Princess. L. appeared at Brussels and London in 1865, at Leipzig 1866, then also at Paris, Petersburg, Moscow. Since then he has been living in Vienna. After 1870 he also studied the organ, and has also enjoyed great fame as a performer on

that instrument. He has published a pf. quintet, pf. quartet, pf. pieces and songs; a Paternoster for chorus and orchestra, and an Ave Maria in canonic form for female voices (à 2), were sung in the court chapel.

Laborde, Jean Benjamin, b. Sept. 5, 1734, pupil of Dauvergne and Rameau, chamberlain to Louis XV., afterwards farmer-general, guillotined at Paris July 22, 1794. He wrote several comic operas, also chansons; "Essai sur la musique ancienne et moderne" (1780, four vols.); "Mémoire sur les proportions musicales," etc. (1781, supplement to the former); and "Mémoires historiques sur Raoul de Coucy" (1781).

Lachner, (1) Franz, b. April 2, 1803, Rain (Upper Bavaria), d. Jan. 20, 1890, Munich, one of the most important of modern composers, and, especially, a distinguished master of counterpoint. He first studied with his father (1810-15), who was organist, and then, until 1819, at the Gymnasium, Neuburg-on-the-Danube, of which Eisenhofer was rector. The original plan of pursuing scientific studies was abandoned by L., who meanwhile had made various attempts as composer, and who played the pianoforte, organ, and 'cello. He lived at Munich from 1820-21, giving instruction in music, and still studying on his own account under capellmeister K. Ett. In 1822 he hastened to Vienna, which had long been the goal of his desires, and obtained a post as organist at the Protestant Church. He was an intimate friend of Franz Schubert, profited by instructive intercourse with S. Sechter and the Abbé Stadler, and was acknowledged even by Beethoven. In 1826 he became vice-capellmeister, and in 1828 principal capellmeister of the Kärntnerthor Theater, and remained in that post until, in 1834, a similar one was offered to him at Mannheim. On the way thither he produced at Munich his D-minor symphony; the result was an engagement as court-capellmeister, but he could not act as such until 1836, when his engagement at Mannheim expired. From that time he displayed wonderful and profitable activity as conductor of the Court Opera, of the sacred performances of the Court Band, and of the concerts of the Musical Academy at Munich; but he also found time to enrich musical literature every year with new and excellent works. He also conducted the Musical Festivals at Munich (1854 and 1863), at Aix-la-Chapelle (1861 and 1870), etc. Already in 1852 he was named general musical director, so as to connect him with Munich by lasting ties. The Wagner-worship gradually springing up in Munich, towards which L. was by no means sympathetic, caused his post to be an unpleasant one, so that in 1865 he proffered a request for his pension, which at first was given to him in the form of leave of absence, but in 1868 made absolute. In 1872 the University of Munich bestowed on him the degree of *Dr. Phil. honoris causâ.* Of the works published by L., and amounting to about 190, the principal are: his suites for full orchestra, Op. 113, 115, 122, 129, 135, 150, and 170 ("Ballsuite"), real show-pieces of contrapuntal art, and an eighth, completed in 1881; further, his eight symphonies (*Symphonia appassionata*, Op. 52, gained a prize from the "Gesellschaft der Musikfreunde" at Vienna in 1835); the operas: *Die Bürgschaft* (Pesth, 1828); *Alidia* (Munich, 1839); *Catharina Cornaro* (ditto, 1841); and *Benvenuto Cellini* (ditto, 1849); the oratorios: *Moses* and *Die vier Menschenalter;* the Requiem, Op. 146; the solemn mass, Op. 52; two Stabat Maters, Op. 154 and 168; a series of other masses, psalms, motets, etc.; five stringed quartets, several pf. quartets, quintets, sextets, a nonet for wind instruments, a serenade for four 'celli, elegy for five 'celli, trios, violin sonatas, and sonatas, fugues, and pieces for organ, a large number of songs (to the composition of which he was most strongly prompted by his intercourse with Schubert), part-songs, songs with orchestra, etc. L. is at his best in his orchestral suites, which, as a kind of modern continuation of Bach-Handel orchestral movements, occupy a distinctive place in musical literature. Sovereign command of contrapuntal devices combined with nobility of invention will secure for them in the future greater appreciation than is accorded to them at the present day.

(2) I g n a z, brother of the former, b. Sept. 11, 1807, Rain, d. Feb. 25, 1895, Hanover, attended the Gymnasium at Augsburg, was violinist in the orchestra of the Isarthor Theater at Munich, was drawn by his brother as violinist to Vienna, became, later on, conductor, and in 1825 vice-capellmeister at the Kärntnerthor Theater, and succeeded his brother as organist of the Evangelical Church, in 1831 court director at Stuttgart, in 1842 second capellmeister, under his brother, at Munich, in 1853 principal capellmeister at the Hamburg Theatre, in 1858 court capellmeister at Stockholm, and in 1861 principal capellmeister at Frankfort; on his retirement in 1875 he lived there for a time, afterwards in Hanover. Ignaz L. was an excellent musician, and published many works of all kinds. He also wrote several operas (*Der Geisterturm*, Stuttgart, 1837; *Die Regenbrüder*, Stuttgart, 1839; *Loreley*, Munich, 1846).

(3) V i n c e n z, b. July 19, 1811, Rain, d. Jan. 22, 1893, Carlsruhe, the third or fourth of the brothers (the eldest, T h e o d o r, b. 1798, d. May 22, 1877, step-brother, was organist at Munich, and, finally, conductor at the Opera). V. attended the Gymnasium at Augsburg at the same time as his brother Ignaz, was for some time tutor in a private family at Posen, went then to Vienna to his brothers, and in 1834 succeeded Ignaz as organist of the Evangelical Church, and, in 1836, Franz as court capellmeister at Mannheim, where, with the exception of two short

breaks (London, 1842, and Frankfort in 1848), he displayed wonderful and beneficial activity as conductor and teacher, until he received a pension in 1873. After that he lived at Carlsruhe, where from 1884 he taught at the Conservatorium. Various of his compositions gained prizes (overture, pf. quartet, song); his overtures to *Turandot, Demetrius*, etc., were often performed at concerts, and his quartets for male voices were popular favourites. Two sisters (T h e k l a and C h r i s t i a n e) occupied for several years posts as organists—the former at Augsburg, the latter in her native place, Rain.

Lackowitz, W i l h e l m, b. Jan. 13, 1837, Trebbin (near Berlin), attended the Berlin school-teachers' college, studied music with his father (Stadtmusikus), L. Erk, Th. Kullak (at his academy), and Dehn. He acted for some years as municipal teacher, but soon turned his attention to music; from 1877 he edited the *Deutsche Musikerzeitung*, and published "Musikalische Skizzenblätter" (2nd ed. 1876). L. is also a botanist ("Flora Berlins," fourth ed. 1880).

Lacombe, (1) L o u i s T r o u i l l o n, composer, b. Nov. 26, 1818, Bourges, d. Sept. 30, 1884, St. Vaast-la-Hougue. As early as 1829 he studied the pianoforte under Zimmermann at the Paris Conservatoire, and in 1831 received the first prize for pianoforte-playing. In 1832 he left that institution, and made an artistic tour through France, Belgium, and Germany with his sister Félicie, and accompanied by his parents. They went, finally, to Vienna, where he stayed for eight months (1834), when he studied the higher development of pianoforte-playing under Czerny, and theory with Sechter and Seyfried. In 1839, on his return to Paris, L. devoted himself more and more to composition. He published a pianoforte quintet (Op. 26, with violin, oboe, 'cello, and bassoon), a trio (D minor), and pf. pieces; then followed the dramatic symphonies (with soli and chorus), "Manfred" (1847), and "Arva, oder die Ungarn" (1850), a second trio (A minor), a grand and widely-known octave étude for pianoforte, pf. pieces, many songs, choruses *a cappella* and with organ (*Agnus* and *Kyrie* for three equal voices), a "Lyrisches Epos" of gigantic proportions, a one-act comic opera, *La Madone* (Théâtre Lyrique, 1860), a grand four-act opera, *Winkelried* (Geneva, 1892), a two-act comic opera, *Le Tonnelier* (*Meister Martin u. seine Gesellen*, not produced), incidental music to Riboyet's *L'Amour*, etc. The best-known work of L. is *Sappho*, prize cantata at the Exhibition of 1878, which was repeatedly performed at the Châtelet and at the Conservatoire. Lyrical, graceful music was the strong point of L.'s muse; at times, as in *Winkelried*, he rises to heroic greatness, or to boldness of characterisation and tone-painting (*Manfred*). — The second wife of L. (1869), A n d r é a, *née* F a v e l, is an able singer who has published a meritorious Method of singing.

(2) **Paul**, composer, b. July 11, 1837, Carcassonne, where he was trained by a former pupil of the Paris Conservatoire (Teysseyre), made a name specially as writer of chamber-music (two violin sonatas, one trio, pf. pieces, one symphonic overture, three symphonies (the first in B♭ and the third in A each gained a prize), a divertissement for pf. and orchestra (won a prize), a serenade for orchestra, "Scène au camp," "Suite pastorale" (ditto), serenade for flute, oboe, and strings; suite for pf. and orchestra, etc.; a Mass, a Requiem, also songs (in all sixty-two published works, many in manuscript). In 1889 he received the *Prix Chartier* (for the good services which he rendered to chamber-music).

Lacome (d'Estalenx), **Paul Jean Jacques**, composer, b. March 4, 1838, Houga (Gers), was trained in his native town, went to Paris when an operetta of his gained a prize offered by the Bouffes-Parisiens (but which was not produced owing to a change of management); and since then he has lived there as composer and musical critic. Besides a number of operettas and farces (*Saynètes*), he has made himself known by compositions for wind instruments, a pf. trio, waltzes, etc., for piano, songs, psalms for one and several voices, with organ or pianoforte.

Lacrimosa, the initial word of the eighth strophe of the sequence of the mass for the dead (*see* REQUIEM); hence, in a Requiem on a large scale, the name of a special (and, as a rule, soft and mournful) section of the work.

Lacrimoso (Ital.), tearful, woeful.

Ladegast, **Friedrich**, b. Aug. 30, 1818, Hochhermsdorf (near Geringswalde), important organ-builder, was the son of a cabinet-maker; he worked under his brother **Christlieb** (b. Dec. 3, 1813), who had at that time an organ manufactory at Geringswalde, afterwards in several other places, and started on his own account at Weissenfels in 1846. One of his earliest and greatest works was the renovation of the grand organ of Merseburg Cathedral (1855), which soon made his name famous. He also built the organ of the "Nikolaikirche" at Leipzig (1859–62; four manuals and eighty-five stops).

Ladurner, **Ignaz Anton Franz Xaver**, b. Aug. 1, 1766, Aldein (Tyrol), d. March 4, 1839, Massy, son of an organist; he was brought up in a Benedictine monastery, and occupied the post of organist for some time after his father's death until a younger brother took his place. He then went for further training to Munich, and made the acquaintance of a Countess Hainhausen, whom he accompanied to her estate at Bar-le-Duc. In 1788 he went to Paris, where he was highly esteemed as pianist and teacher (Auber was his pupil). In 1836 he retired to a villa near Massy. L. published: twelve pf. sonatas, one sonata for four hands, nine violin sonatas, divertissements, variations, etc.; he also produced two operas at the Opéra Comique.

Lafage, **Juste Adrien Lenoir de**, eminent writer on music, b. March 28, 1801, Paris, d. March 8, 1862, at Charenton Lunatic Asylum, near Paris. He studied under Perne and Choron, was at first teacher of singing, then, with the help of a government stipend, went to Italy (1828–29), studied under Baini's direction the fugal style of the old masters, and on his return was appointed maître de chapelle of the church St. Étienne du Mont at Paris. He went again in 1833 to Italy, and commenced as a writer on music by completing the "Manuel complet de musique vocale et instrumentale," sketched by his old teacher Choron, who died in 1834 (1836 to 1838; six vols., in three parts). For the purpose of further investigation, L. made journeys to Italy, Germany, Spain, and England, and so overworked himself that his intellect became disordered. His principal works, in addition to the "Manuel," are "Séméiologie musicale" (1837, an elementary treatise based on the principles of Choron: in the edition of 1837 it bears the title "Principes élémentaires de musique"); "De la chanson considérée sous le rapport musical" (1840); "Histoire générale de la musique et de la danse (1844, two vols.); "Miscellanées musicales" (1844; biographical notices of Haydn, Tritto, Bellini, etc.); biographical notices of Stanislao Mattei (1839), Zingarelli (without year), Choron (1844), Bocquillon-Wilhem (1844), Baini (1844), Donizetti, etc.; reports of the organs built by Cavaillé-Coll for St. Denis (1845) and St. Eustache (1845); "Quinze visites musicales à l'exposition universelle de 1855;" "Extraits du catalogue critique et raisonné d'une petite bibliothèque musicale;" "Essais de diphtérographie musicale;" "De l'unité tonique et de la fixation d'un diapason universel (1859); "Nicolai Capuani presbyteri compendium musicale." In his later years he busied himself, from inclination, with the reform of Gregorian singing: "De la réproduction des livres de plain-chant romain" (1853); "Lettre écrite à l'occasion d'un mémoire pour servir à la restauration du chant romain en France par l'abbé Céleste Alix" (1853); "Cours complet de plain chant" (1855–56, two vols.); "Nouveau traité de plain chant" (1859); "Prise à partie de M. l'abbé Tesson dans la question des nouveaux livres de plain-chant romain;" "Routine pour accompagner le plain-chant." In 1859 L. founded a newspaper, *Le Plain-Chant*. The compositions of L., in addition to some sets of variations, fantasias, duets for flute, and some songs, consist of sacred works bearing, for the most part, Latin titles, after the manner of the 16th century: "Adriani de L. motetorum liber I." (1832–35; second book, 1837); "Psalmi vespertini quaternis vocibus cum organo" (1837), etc.; also an "Ordinaire de l'office divin arrangé en harmonie sur le plain-chant" (1832–35).

Laffert, O s k a r, b. Jan. 25, 1850, Breslau, d. May 17, 1889, Dresden. He was a pianoforte-maker and music-seller at Carlsruhe, and from 1884 director of the "Apollo" pianoforte manufactory at Dresden. L. was also active as a writer on music.

Lafont, C h a r l e s P h i l i p p e, celebrated violinist, b. Dec. 1, 1781, Paris, d. Aug. 14, 1839, nephew and pupil of Berthaume, studied afterwards under Kreutzer, Rode, and Berton (harmony); already as a child he made concert tours, and continued the restless life of a wandering virtuoso until he was called to Petersburg as chamber virtuoso in place of Rode, who was returning to France. In 1815 Louis XVIII. offered him a similar position, and thus attracted him to Paris. L. nevertheless undertook many concert tours, and finally met with his death by the upsetting of the diligence between Bagnères-de-Bigorre and Tarbes. L.'s compositions are: seven violin concertos, many fantasias, rondos, variations, etc. (partly for orchestra, partly for stringed quartet, pianoforte, harp, etc.), also about two hundred songs (romances). L. produced two small operas at Petersburg and Paris.

Lagrimoso (Ital.), tearful, mournful.

La Harpe, J e a n F r a n ç o i s de, b. Nov. 20, 1739, Paris, d. there Feb. 11, 1803, poet and critic; he was one of the antagonists of Gluck, and repeatedly attacked his music in the *Journal de politique et de littérature* (1777).

Lahee, H e n r y, b. April, 1826, Chelsea, from 1847–74 organist at Brompton, esteemed English composer of vocal music (glees, madrigals, cantatas [*The Sleeping Beauty*]).

Lahire, P h i l i p p e de, professor of mathematics at the Paris University, b. 1640, Paris, d. there April 21, 1719. He wrote, among other things, "Explication des différences de sons de la corde tendue sur la trompette marine," and "Expériences sur le son" (in the report of the Paris Académie).

Lais (Fr.; English "Lays"), popular songs of the Middle Ages, after the manner of sequences. (*Cf.* Ferd. Wolff, "Ueber die L. Sequenzen u. Leiche" [Heidelberg, 1841].)

Lajarte, T h é o d o r e E d o u a r d D u f a u r e de, b. July 10, 1826, Bordeaux, d. June 20, 1890, Paris, pupil of Leborne at the Paris Conservatoire; he produced several small operas and operettas at the Théâtre Lyrique and elsewhere. He composed marches and dances for military band, also some choruses with military music, but made his mark specially as a writer on music. Apart from his contributions to various musical papers, and his musical feuilletons and criticisms in political journals, L. wrote "Bibliothèque musicale du théâtre de l'Opéra" (1876, etc., two vols.), a work of high importance (enumeration of all pieces produced at the Paris Opéra, together with special notices of all kinds based on the archives of the Opéra, of which L. was librarian from 1873); further, "Instruments Sax et fanfares civiles" (1867); and "Traité de composition musicale" (jointly with Bisson, 1880). He also published a collection, "Airs à danser de Lulli à Méhul," and, lastly, undertook the publication of vocal scores of old French operas, "Chefs d'œuvre classiques de l'opéra français" (Lully's *Thésée*, *Psyché*, and *Armide;* also works by Rameau, Campra, Piccini, etc.).

Lajeunesse, E m m a. (*See* ALBANI.)

Lalande, (1) M i c h e l R i c h a r d (de), b. Dec. 15, 1657, Paris, son of a tailor, d. June 18, 1726, as *intendant de la musique de cour* to Louis XV. He composed sixty motets, with chorus and orchestra, which appeared at the cost of the king in a magnificent edition in twenty parts, and which gained for him great reputation in his own country. He also wrote music to Molière's *Mélicerte*, and several ballets (*Les éléments*, jointly with Destouches).

(2) H e n r i e t t e C l é m e n t i n e Méric-L., b. 1798, Dunkirk, d. Sept. 7, 1867, Paris, a celebrated vocalist, made her *début* at Nantes in 1814, and at Paris in 1822. After that she still studied under Garcia, and in Milan under Bonsichi and Banderali; she married the horn virtuoso Méric, and shone especially in Italy, Vienna, and Paris, but did not achieve success in London. She brought her dramatic career to a close in Spain in the thirties.

Lalo, É d o u a r d, b. Jan. 27, 1823, Lille, d. April 22, 1892, Paris; he was a pupil of the branch of the Paris Conservatoire at Lille, an excellent violinist and composer of note. He first became known in Paris as viola-player in the Armingaud and Jacquard chamber-music *soirées*, and soon produced chamber-music works. An opera (*Fiesque*) was subject to rare ill-fortune, so that up to the present day it has not been performed, although accepted at the Opéra both at Paris and Brussels. A second opera (his best work), *Le Roi d'Ys*, the overture of which was already played in 1876, was first produced in 1888, and a third, *La Jacquerie*, remained incomplete; a ballet, *Namouna*, became popular as an orchestral suite, and a pantomimic ballet, *Néron*, was given in 1891. Of his other works the following deserve mention: two violin concertos (I., dedicated to Sarasate; II., "Symphonie espagnole"), "Rhapsodie Norvégienne" (for orchestra), a divertissement for orchestra, a quartet for strings, two pf. trios, a violin sonata, a Duo concertant for pf. and violin, a 'cello sonata, and various characteristic pieces for violin and pf., violin, 'cello and pf., and for 'cello and pf.; finally songs ("Mélodies vocales").

La Mara. (*See* LIPSIUS.)

Lambert, (1) M i c h e l, b. 1610, Vivonne (Poitou), famous teacher of singing at Paris, father-in-law of Lully; from 1650 he was chamber-music-master to Louis XIV., and d. 1696, Paris. He published a collection, "Airs et brunettes" (1666 ; second ed. 1689), and after his death there appeared another, "Airs et dialogues" (à 1–5, 1698). Some detached pieces of his, overladen throughout with ornaments, are to be found in Paris collections, many also in manuscript.

(2) J o h a n n H e i n r i c h, b. Aug. 29, 1728, Mülhausen-i.-E., d. Sept. 25, 1777, Berlin, as "Oberbaurath" and member of the Akademie, for which he wrote several valuable works on acoustics : "Sur quelques instruments acoustiques" (1763 ; German by Huth, 1796) ; "Sur la vitesse du son" (1768) ; "Remarques sur le tempérament en musique" (1774 ; German by Marpurg in the "Historisch critische Beiträge," fifth vol.) ; "Observations sur les sons des flûtes" (1775), all printed in the reports of the Akademie.

Lambillotte, L o u i s, b. March 27, 1797, Charleroi (Hainault), d. Feb. 27, 1855, Vaugirard (near Paris), sacred composer and important writer on music. He was at first organist at Charleroi, then at Dinant, about 1822 maître de chapelle at the Jesuit Institution at St. Acheul, in 1825 joined the same order, after seriously studying the dead languages, and lived in various houses of that order, finally at Vaugirard. His compositions are : four grand masses, among which one in the fifth Church Mode (Lydian), besides motets, hymns to the Virgin Mary for great and small festivals, cantica à 2 ; he also published a good collection of organ pieces, fugues, etc., "Musée des organistes" (1842–44, two vols.). His writings are : "Antiphonaire de Saint Grégoire" (1851, a facsimile of the Antiphonary of St. Gall in neume notation, with historico-critical treatises) ; "Quelques mots sur la restauration du chant liturgique" (1855, posthumous) ; "Esthétique, théorie, et pratique du chant grégorien restauré d'après la doctrine des anciens et les sources primitives" (1855, posthumous). Père Dufour, editor of the last two works, published also the "Graduale" and "Vesperale" according to L.'s reforms in chorale notes, and with transcription into modern notation (1856). (*Cf.* POTHIER.)

Lamentabile, Lamentōso (Ital.), mournful.

Lamento (Ital.), lamentation.

Lamoureux, C h a r l e s, violinist and conductor, b. Sept. 28, 1834, Bordeaux, studied under Girard at the Paris Conservatoire, played, at first, in the orchestra of the Gymnase and of the Grand Opéra, and, after further study under Tolbecque, Leborne, and Chauvet, established a society for chamber-music (jointly with Colonne, Adam, and Rignault), founded, in 1873, a *Société de Musique sacrée* (oratorio concert), and, *per saltum*, became one of the

most esteemed conductors of Paris. In 1875 he conducted the Boieldieu Jubilee Concert at Rouen, and in 1876 was associated for a time with Deldevez, but in 1878 succeeded him as chief conductor at the Grand Opéra. From 1872–78 L. was sub-conductor of the Conservatoire concerts. In 1881 he resigned his post, and established the Nouveaux Concerts (Concerts L.), which, at the present day, rank amongst the most important concert institutions of Paris. He withdrew from their conductorship in 1897.

Lampadarius, (1) J o h a n n e s, Byzantine church composer and musical theorist of the 14th century, was chapel-singer at St. Sophia, Constantinople. His work on Grecian church music is entitled, "Τεχνολογια της μουσικης τεχνης" (at the Vienna library).

(2) P e t r u s, b. about 1730, Tripolitza (Morea, hence named "the Peloponnesian" to distinguish him from the former), was likewise a composer of the Greek Church. His brother, G r e g o r i u s L., together with Chrysanthus of Madytos (q.v.), reformed the new Greek liturgical notation, and arranged at Paris an edition of "Triodia" (songs for Lent), with music by Petrus L., in the new notation (1821).

Lampadius, W i l h e l m A d o l f, Protestant clergyman, b. 1812, d. April 7, 1892, Leipzig, author of the well-known biography of Mendelssohn (q.v.).

Lamperen, M i c h e l v a n, b. Dec. 26, 1826, Brussels, from 1859 librarian of the Brussels Conservatoire ; since 1870 he has been publishing a complete catalogue of the library under his charge. He has also published a number of sacred compositions.

Lampert, E r n s t, b. July 3, 1818, Gotha, d. there June 17, 1879, as court capellmeister, pupil of Hummel at Weimar, and of Spohr and Hauptmann at Cassel. He published a great number of instrumental and vocal compositions, also produced several operas at Gotha and Coburg.

Lamperti, F r a n c e s c o, b. March 11; 1813, Savona, d. May 1, 1892, Como, famous teacher of singing, pupil of the Milan Conservatorio, established his reputation as director of the "Teatro filodrammatico" at Lodi (jointly with Masini). He became (1850) professor of singing of the Milan Conservatorio, and worked with great success up to 1875. After that he withdrew from that institution, and only gave private lessons. From among his famous pupils may be mentioned the two Cruvellis (mother and daughter), Artôt, La Grange, Albani. L. published at Ricordi's, Milan, a vocal Method, also several books of études, shake-studies, etc. M. G. B. L., who has likewise published instructive vocal works, must not be confused with Francesco L.

Lampons (Fr.), a kind of drinking-song.

Lampugnani, G i o v a n n i B a t t i s t a, Italian opera composer, b. 1706, Milan, d. about 1772.

He wrote for Milan, London (1744–55), etc., a large number of operas, mostly serious and in the style of Hasse, in which the recitative is treated in a highly expressive manner.

Landgraf, J. Fr. B e r n h a r d , celebrated clarinettist, b. June 25, 1816, Dielsdorf (Weimar), d. Jan. 25, 1885, Leipzig ; from 1840 principal clarinettist in the Gewandhaus orchestra.

Landi, S t e f f a n o , Papal chapel singer (evirato) about 1630, previously church capellmeister at Padua, a sound church composer. He published : madrigals à 4 (1619) ; madrigals à 5 (1625) ; " Poesie diverse in musica " (1628) ; " Missa in benedictione nuptiarum " (1628) ; eight books of arias à 1–2 (1627–39) ; psalms à 4 (1629) ; a music drama, *Sant' Alessio* (1634) ; one pastoral, " La morte d'Orfeo " (1639) ; and one book of masses (*a cappella*) à 4–5.

Landino, F r a n c e s c o , known under the name of Francesco Cieco (the blind), or Francesco degli Organi, a highly famous organ-player and composer, b. about 1325, Florence, where he d. 1390. Of his compositions there have only been preserved some canzone à 2 and 3, which Fétis found in the Paris Library, and one of which he published in his *Revue musicale* (1827). For an appreciation of L. *see* A. G. Ritter's " Geschichte des Orgelspiels " (1884), p. 3.

Ländler (Länderer, Dreher), old term for the so-called Landel (Austria beyond the Enns), originally a native slow waltz, danced in quiet, equal steps (3–4 time) :—

The L. has now become a characteristic dance, *i.e.* the name of one of the many types of instrumental music (*cf.* the Ländler of Beethoven, Schubert, Heller, Jensen, etc.) of characteristic rhythm, melody, and tempo. The melody of the L. generally moves along in quiet quavers. (*Cf.* the Waltz in the *Freischütz.*) The *Tyrolienne* (q.v.) is a French imitation of the L.

Landolfi (Landulphus), C a r l o F e r d i n a n d o , a renowned violin-maker at Milan, from 1750–60, whose 'celli stand even in higher repute than his violins. L. imitated Giuseppe Guarneri with great success.

Lang, (1) (L. Köstlin), J o s e p h i n e , b. March 14, 1815, Munich, d. Dec. 2, 1880, Tübingen, daughter of the court musician Theobald L., and of the famous singer Regina Hizelberger L. (for whom Peter Winter wrote the *rôle* of Myrrha in his *Unterbrochene Opferfest*) ; she was an excellent composer of songs, pupil of her mother, afterwards of Frau Berlinghof-Wagner, and, for theory, of Mendelssohn (1831), who held her in high esteem. After teaching singing and pianoforte for some time privately in Munich, she became one of the singers at the court. She married, in 1842, the Tübingen professor of law, Chr. Reinhold Köstlin (as poet, Karl Reinhold), who died already in 1856, and then she turned again to the teaching of music. A large number of songs and pf. pieces have appeared in print ; many are still in manuscript. Her son, H. A. Köstlin, wrote her life (in the *Sammlung musikalischer Vorträge*, 1881).

(2) B e n j a m i n J., b. Dec. 28, 1839, Salem (Massachusetts, North America), excellent pianist (trained in Germany), to whom Boston is musically indebted. He has been for twenty-one years organist of the Handel and Haydn Society, also conductor of the Cecilia Society (mixed choir) and of the Apollo Club (male choir).

Langbecker, E m a n u e l C h r i s t i a n Gottlieb, b. Aug. 31, 1792, Berlin, d. there Oct. 24, 1843, as secretary to Prince Waldemar of Prussia. He made a deep study of the history of the origin of the Protestant chorale, and wrote on that subject : " Das deutsch-evangelische Kirchenlied " (1830) ; " Johann Crügers . . . Choral Melodien " (1835) ; " Gesangblätter aus dem 16. Jahrhundert (1838) ; " Paul Gerhardts Leben und Lieder " (1841).

Langdon, R i c h a r d , d. Sept., 1803, Armagh, Mus.Bac. (Oxford, 1761), organist at Exeter, Bristol, and finally at Armagh. He published : a collection, " Divine Harmony " (1774, two vols., Psalms and Anthems), also twelve glees, two books of songs, and some songs of his own composition.

Lange, (1) O t t o , b. 1815, Graudenz, d. Feb. 13, 1879 ; he was a school-teacher, also musical reporter to the *Vossische Zeitung*, edited (from 1846–58) the *Neue Berliner Musikzeitung ;* he was also active as a teacher of school-singing in Berlin, and died as professor *em.* at Cassel. L. published several educational pamphlets, among which, " Die Musik als Unterrichtsgenstand in Schulen " (1841).

(2) S a m u e l de, organist and composer, b. Feb. 22, 1840, Rotterdam, where his father, of like name, was organist of St. Laurens Church and teacher at the school of music of the Society for the Advancement of Art (b. June 9, 1811, Rotterdam, d. there May 15, 1884). L. received his first education from the latter, and was further trained by A. Winterberger (Vienna), Damcke and Mikuli (Lemberg). L. is a distinguished organist, made concert tours from 1858–59 in Galicia, then settled in Lemberg for four years, and became organist and teacher at the Rotterdam Music School (*Maatschappij tot bevordering van Toonkunst*), whence he made concert tours in Switzerland, and appeared at Leipzig, Vienna, Paris, etc. From 1874–76 he was associated with the school of music at Basle, and, after a short stay in Paris, in 1877 became teacher at the Cologne Conservatorium, where he was conductor of the male choral society, and also of the " Gürzenichchor "

In 1885 he undertook the direction of the Oratorio Society at the Hague, also of some smaller societies. Of his compositions should be mentioned especially the five organ sonatas Op. 5, 8, 14, 28, 50, besides one pf. concerto, two stringed quartets, one trio, quintet, violin sonata, part-songs for male-chorus, etc. A symphony of his was produced in 1879 at Cologne, and an oratorio, *Moses*, at the Hague in 1889. In 1893 he received a call as teacher and deputy-director at the Stuttgart Conservatorium. His brother

(3) **Daniel de**, b. July 11, 1841, Rotterdam, studied under Ganz and Servais ('cello), also Verhulst and Damcke (composition), from 1860–63 teacher at the Lemberg School of Music, then studied the pianoforte at Paris under Madame Dubois, working all the time by himself until he became an able organist; he was appointed organist of the evangelical community of Montrouge, and of the "Freie Gemeinde," and conductor of the German "Liedertafel." In 1870 (during the war) he went to Amsterdam as teacher at the music school (which, afterwards, was raised to the rank of Conservatoire), then became secretary of the "Maatschappij tot bevordering van Toonkunst," was for a long time Coenen's deputy as conductor of "Amstels Mannenkoor," then conductor of several vocal societies at Leyden and Amsterdam, with which he repeatedly produced old Dutch *a-cappella* music with phenomenal success (in 1888 and 1894 at London, and in 1892 in Germany). For many years L. has been musical critic of the *Niews van den Tag*, and has composed two symphonies (in c and D), several cantatas, an opera (*De Val van Kuilenburg*), overture ("Willem van Holland"), incidental music to *Ernani*, a mass *a cappella*, a requiem, twenty-second Psalm, for soli, chorus, and pianoforte; a 'cello concerto, songs, etc. Daniel de L., next to Fuchs, is the first who ventured in orchestral-playing to make use of the principles of phrasing as established by H. Riemann (concerts at Amsterdam, 1886 and 1887).

(4) **Gustav**, b. Aug. 13, 1830, Berlin, composer of some popular drawing-room pieces.

Langer, (1) **Hermann**, b. July 6, 1819, Höckendorf (near Tharandt), d. Sept. 8, 1889, Dresden, studied philosophy and music at Leipzig, where, in 1843, he was appointed musical director of the University and organist; he was for some time conductor of the Euterpe Concerts, and conducted several vocal societies at Leipzig ("Männergesangverein," "Leipziger Gau-Sängerbund," "Zöllner-Bund"). In his official capacity at the University he conducted the "Pauliner-Gesangverein," lectured, as *Lector publicus*, on Protestant liturgy, the theory of harmony, etc., and was held in high consideration in the musical circles of Leipzig. In 1859 the University granted him the degree of

Dr. Phil. hon. causâ. In 1882, at the sixtieth jubilee of the "Pauliner-Verein," he received the title of Professor. L. published "Repertorium für den Männergesang," edited the "Musikalische Gartenlaube," and wrote "Der erste Unterricht im Gesang" (1876–77, three courses). He was called to Dresden in 1887 as "Kgl. sächs Orgelbaurevisor."

(2) **Viktor**, b. Oct. 14, 1842, Pesth, pupil of R. Volkmann, attended the Leipzig Conservatorium, and became very active in his native town as conductor, teacher of music, and composer (partly under the pseudonym of Aladar Tisza), also as editor of an Hungarian musical paper.

(3) **Ferdinand**, opera composer, b. Jan. 21, 1839, Leimen (near Heidelberg), son of a schoolmaster; without the help of any teacher of fame, he obtained the post of 'cellist in the Court Theatre at Mannheim, of which he is now second capellmeister. With his operas—*Die gefährliche Nachbarschaft* (1868), *Dornröschen* (1873), and *Aschenbrödel* (1878), *Murillo* (1887)—L. obtained pleasing, though somewhat local, success.

Langert, Joh. August Ad., b. Nov. 26, 1836, Coburg; he was active as conductor of the theatres at Coburg, Mannheim (1865), Basle (1867), Trieste (1868), and then lived in retirement at Coburg, Paris, and Berlin. In 1872 he became teacher at the Geneva Conservatoire, and then received a call in 1873, as court capellmeister, to Gotha. He wrote the operas: *Die Jungfrau von Orleans* (1861), *Des Sängers Fluch* (1863), *Die Fabier* (1866, these three for Coburg), *Dornröschen* (Leipzig, 1871), and *Jean Cavalier* (Coburg, 1880, and again as *Die Kamisarden*, 1887).

Langhans, Fr. Wilhelm, violinist and writer on music, b. Sept. 21, 1832, Hamburg, d. June 9, 1892, Berlin, where he received his school education at the Johanneum; he became a pupil of the Leipzig Conservatorium in 1849, and studied under David (violin) and Richter (composition), was also private pupil (for violin-playing) of Alard in Paris. From 1852–56 he was a member of the Gewandhaus orchestra at Leipzig, from 1857–60 leader at Düsseldorf, then teacher and concert-player at Hamburg (1860), Paris (1863), Heidelberg (1869), where he received the doctor's degree. In 1874 he become teacher of the history of music at the "Neue Akademie der Tonkunst" (Kullak), but left that institution in 1881 and joined X. Scharwenka's newly established Conservatorium. L. published a concert Allegro for violin (with orchestra), violin studies, a violin sonata, There remained in manuscript a quartet for strings (which gained a prize at Florence, 1864), a symphony, overture ("Spartacus"), songs ("Parerga"), and violin solos. L.'s activity as a writer is of greater importance: "Das musikalische Urteil" (1872: second ed. 1886), "Die königliche Hochschule für Musik in Berlin" (1873), "Musikgeschichte in zwölf Vorträgen" (1878; Dutch by Ed. de Hartog, 1885), and a cleverly compiled continuation of Ambros' "Geschichte der Musik" under the title, "Die Geschichte der Musik des 17. 18. 19. Jahrhunderts" (1882–86, two vols.), an addition to literature for which students ought to be grateful. L. was an honorary member of the "Liceo filarmonico," Florence, 1878, and of the St. Cecilia Academy at Rome, 1887. In 1858 he married Luise Japha (q.v.). Their son Julius, b. 1862, Hamburg, has been living at Sydney since 1886, where he is highly esteemed as a teacher of music.

Langlé, Honoré François Marie, b. 1741, Monaco, d. Sept. 20, 1807, Villiers le Bel (near Paris), studied under Cafaro at the Conservatorio della Pietà at Naples. He was for some time musical director at Genoa, and went in 1768 to Paris, where the production of an important vocal work gained for him a name. In 1784 he became teacher of singing to the "École royal de chant et de déclamation" (until its suppression in 1791). When the Conservatoire was established in 1794, he was appointed librarian and professor of harmony, but when, in 1802, the teaching staff was reduced, he lost the latter appointment, but retained the former. L.'s compositions are of no importance (several operas, cantatas, etc.), but his theoretical works are of value: "Traité d'harmonie et de modulation" (1797; building up of chords by thirds); "Traité de la basse sous le chant" (1798); "Nouvelle méthode pour chiffrer les accords" (1801); "Traité de la fugue" (1805).

Langsam (Ger.), slow; *langsamer,* slower.

Languendo, Languente (Ital.), in a plaintive manner.

Languette (Fr.), (1) The tongue of a harpsichord jack.—(2) The tongue of a reed-pipe in the organ.—(3) The stem of the keys of wind instruments.

Laniere, Nicholas, b. about 1590, London, d. there between 1665 and 1670. He was the son of an Italian musician who had emigrated twenty years previously. L. was a man of many talents—composer, singer, painter, engraver. To him must be ascribed the merit of having introduced the *Stilo rappresentativo* into England, of which he made use in his "Masques" (*i.e.* small stage pieces with allegorical action). L. became, in 1626, court musical director to King Charles I., which post he lost during the Revolution, but, after the death of Cromwell, regained it from Charles II. Of his compositions, pieces written for special occasions (funeral hymn for Charles I., new year songs, etc.) have been preserved, also some songs in the collections: "Airs and Dialogues" (1653, 1659); "The Musical Companion" (1667); "The Treasury of Music" (1669); "Choice Airs and Songs" (fourth book, 1685).

Lanner, Joseph Franz Karl, famous dance composer, b. April 12, 1801, Oberdöbling (near Vienna), d. there April 14, 1843; he learnt violin-playing and composition by himself, began his career as leading violinist in an amateur quartet party (with Joh. Strauss as viola-player), for which he arranged operatic pot-pourris and composed dances; and from that simple beginning was evolved a full orchestra. The L. orchestra soon gained extraordinary popularity, and his waltzes, galops, and Ländler, etc., were played everywhere. L. created the Viennese waltz (before his time [in Beethoven, Clementi, and Schubert] the waltz was a short dance piece with a few repeats and a trio), and gave to it a broader, more melodious character. Strauss followed in his footsteps, but introduced into it piquancy and instrumental refinement—new elements which J. Strauss, jun., amalgamated in the happiest manner with the former. Besides Vienna, L. gave concerts only in the provincial towns of Austria. (*Cf.* H. Sachs' "J. L." [1889], also Oettinger's "Meister Strauss u. seine Zeitgenossen" [comic novel, 1862].)—His talented son, August Joseph, b. Jan. 23, 1834, soon followed him to the grave, Sept. 27, 1855.

Lans, Michael J. A., b. July 18, 1845, Haarlem, Roman Catholic priest; in 1869 teacher at the priests' training college at Voorhout, near Leyden, since 1887 clergyman at Schiedam. In 1876 he founded the *Gregorius-blad* (newspaper for Catholic church music), and in 1878, the Gregorian Society. He has written a "Lehrbuch des (strengen) Kontrapunkts" (1889), and has himself composed cantatas, a mass, etc.

Lapicida, Erasmus, was a composer well known in his time (16th century), for it seems that he was often briefly named Rasmo, or merely designated by his initials, E. L. Of his life absolutely nothing is known; his name is evidently Latinised ("stone-cutter"). There are compositions of his to be found in Petrucci's "Motetti B." (1503), in his "Frottole" in Book VIII. (1507), in Book IV. of the motets à 4 (1507), and in Book II. of the Lamentations (1506), also in Petrejus' "Auszug guter alter und neuer deutscher Liedlein" (1539), in G. Rhaw's "Symphoniæ jucundæ" (1538), etc.

Laporte, Joseph, Jesuit father, afterwards Abbé, b. 1713, Béfort, d. Dec. 19, 1779, Paris. He wrote: "Anecdotes dramatiques" (1775, four vols.; an enumeration of all kinds of stage pieces); "Dictionnaire dramatique" (1776, three vols.); and "Almanach des spectacles de Paris, ou Calendrier historique de l'opéra, des comédies françaises et italiennes et des foires" (1750–94, 1799–1800, 1804, forty-eight vols.; continued by Duchesne and others).

Larga (Lat.) is a name used by writers on mensural music of the 14th and 15th centuries for a note-value which never attained to practical importance; it was greater than that of the *Maxima*, from which it differed in sign in that several *caudæ* (strokes) were added to the bodies of the notes: -| or ┬┬┬, etc.

Largamente (Ital.), broadly, largely.

Largando (*slargando, allargando*), Ital. "broadening"; as a rule it is united with *crescendo*.

Larghetto (Ital.), somewhat broad (a diminutive of *Largo*, q.v.); a time-indication falling between *Largo* and *Andante*, somewhat the same as *Andantino*, perhaps rather slower. The term L. is frequently to be met with as the superscription of the slow movement in a symphony, sonata, etc.; in such cases the whole movement is called the L.

Largo (Ital., "broad"), an indication of the slowest movement, except perhaps *molto* L., which, after all, conveys pretty much the same meaning. Whole movements bearing the superscription L. are rare; on the other hand, the term L. is frequently applied to the introductions of symphonies. The reason for this is that excessive heaviness is the characteristic feature of the L., and this is not removed by figuration. For a whole movement it is, for the most part, too oppressive, whereas for a limited number of bars it is of excellent effect. *Poco* L. is a somewhat indefinite term; it occurs also in an *Allegro*, and indicates a moderate modification of the principal *tempo*.

Larigot, an obsolete French name for the quint-stop ($1\frac{1}{3}$ ft.), also called *Petit nasard*. Originally, L. was the name of an instrument of the flageolet kind (small beak-flute).

Laroche, Hermann Augustowitsch, b. 1845, Petersburg; in 1862 was pupil there at the Conservatoire, in 1866 teacher of theory and musical history at Moscow. He is esteemed as a critic (articles on Glinka), and has composed vocal and instrumental works.

La Rue, Pierre de (*Larue,* ♭═╣ *rue* [the note *d = la*], Petrus Platensis [in Glarean], Pierchon, Pierson, Pierazzon), one of the most distinguished Netherland contrapuntists from the 15th to the 16th century, contemporary of Josquin, and, like the latter, a pupil of Okeghem. The dates of his birth and death are unknown, but it has been shown that from 1492 to 1510 he was chapel-singer at the Court of Burgundy, and in 1501 became prebend of Courtrai. L. was *facile princeps* in the most complicated arts of imitative counterpoint, yet his works are not lacking in feeling and grandeur. The following of his printed works have been preserved: a book of masses, published by Petrucci 1513 ("Beatæ Virginis," "Puer nobis est," "Sexti Toni," "Ut Fa," "L'homme armé," "Nunquam fuit poena major"); besides the mass "De Sancto Antonio" in Petrucci's "Missæ diversorum" (1508); the masses "Ave Maria" and

"O Salutaris hostia" in "Liber XV. missarum" of Antiquis (1516); "Cum jocunditate," "O Gloriosa," and "De Sancto Antonio" in the "Missæ XIII." (1539); "Tous les regrets" in "Liber XV. missarum" (1538); and a mass in the fourth Church Mode in Petrucci's "Missæ Antonii de Fevin" (1515). Among the manuscripts of La Rue stand prominently forth the magnificent seven masses in the Brussels Library, which the Regent of Burgundy, Margaret of Austria (d. 1530), ordered to be made (à 5, "De conceptione Virginis Mariæ," "Ista est speciosa," "De doloribus," "Paschale," "De Sancta Cruce;" à 6, "Ave Sanctissima Maria;" à 4, "De feria"). Another magnificent manuscript, also prepared by order of Margaret, is to be found at Mechlin (masses à 4, "Fors seulement," "Resurrexit," "Sine nomine," "De Sancta Cruce;" and à 5, "Super Alleluja"). Finally, there is still a manuscript of two masses at Brussels, "De septem doloribus" (the mass à 5 already mentioned, and one à 4); in the archives of the Papal Chapel at Rome, besides those à 4 already named, there are "L'amour de moy," "Pour quoy non," "De Virginibus," and "O gloriosa Margarita;" and at Munich the masses à 4 "Cum jocunditate" (three copies), "Pro defunctis" (three copies), and one à 5, "Incessament." The following works of L. have also been preserved: a Credo in manuscript (Munich), a Stabat Mater à 5 on "Comme dame de réconfort" (Brussels), five "Salve regina" à 4 (Munich MSS. 34), and several chansons (Munich MSS., 1508). A "Salve regina" is printed in the fourth book of "Motetti della Corona" (Petrucci, 1505), a motet ("Lauda") in Vol. III. of the Nuremberg collection, 1564; and some chansons are to be found in Petrucci's "Odhecaton," "Motetti A" and "Motetti B" (1501-3), and G. Rhaw's "Bicinia" (1545), also some madrigals in Gardane's "Perisone" (1544).

Laruette, Jean Louis, b. March 27, 1731, Toulouse, d. there Jan. 1792; he was one of the first French composers of vaudevilles (*La fausse aventurière*, Paris, 1756; *L'heureux déguisement; Le médecin de l'amour*, etc.).

Larynx. The human larynx belongs, as musical instrument, to the reed-pipe species. The vocal cords (of which there are two, as in the oboe) take the place of reeds, and lie opposite to, and slightly inclined to each other, between the two movable shield-like (thyroid) and the two ladle-like (arythenoid) cartilages forming the real L. The vocal cords, either throughout or partially, are tightly stretched or relaxed by means of numerous muscles; a condensation or, on the other hand, rarefaction of these cords is possible, especially at the edges, as the two sets of cartilages can easily move to and from each other, whereby the depth and breadth of the L. become changed.

It is not possible consciously to set in action these or those muscles, and the physiological experiments for investigating the conditions under which this or that modification of the sound of the human voice arises are therefore of no practical use in singing, and only of scientific interest. Unfortunately, even for the latter, unquestionable results cannot be recorded. (*Cf.* EMBOUCHURE, REGISTER, etc.) To those who may desire further knowledge in this matter, Merkel's "Anthropophonik" may be recommended (1857). Necessary details will be found in that work also about the laryngoscope, etc.

La Salette, J o u b e r t de, b. 1762, Grenoble, French officer, finally brigadier-general, d. 1832, Grenoble; he was an enthusiastic writer on the theory and history of music. His works are: "Sténographie musicale" (1805, an attempt to revive German tablature [q.v.] for France); "Considérations sur les divers systèmes de la musique ancienne et moderne" (1810); "De la notation musicale en général et en particulier de celle du système grec" (1817); "De la fixité et de l'invariabilité des sons musicaux" (1824), etc.

Lasner, Ignaz, b. Aug. 8, 1815, Drosau, Bohemia, d. Aug. 18, 1883, Vienna, studied under Goltermann at Prague, and under Merk and Servais at Vienna. He was an able performer on the 'cello, and played in orchestras at Vienna and Arad, and wrote valuable pieces for 'cello. His son and pupil, Karl, b. Sept. 11, 1865, Vienna, attended the Conservatorium of that city, and is now 'cellist in the Philharmonic orchestra at Laibach.

Lassen, E d u a r d, b. April 13, 1830, Copenhagen, whence his father removed two years later to Brussels. At the age of twelve L. became a pupil of the Brussels Conservatoire, received the first prize for pianoforte in 1844, and for harmony in 1847, and in 1851 the *Prix de Rome*, awarded every two years. He travelled for the purpose of study, first to Germany, staying at Cassel, Leipzig, Dresden, Berlin, and Weimar, and then to Italy, remaining a long while in Rome. His opera, *Landgraf Ludwigs Brautfahrt*, owing to Liszt's patronage, was performed at Weimar in 1857, and procured for him, in 1858, the post of court musical director to the Grand Duke. In 1861, on the retirement of Liszt, he was appointed court capellmeister, and there soon followed the operas *Frauenlob* (1860, French) and *Le captif* (Brussels, 1868). The following compositions of L. also deserve mention:—the music to Hebbel's "Nibelungen" (eleven characteristic pieces for orchestra), to Sophocles' *Œdipus Colonos*, Goethe's *Faust*, and *Pandora* (1886), and Devrient's version of Calderon's *Circe* (*Ueber allen Zaubern Liebe*), two symphonies, several overtures, cantatas (Op. 56, *Die Künstler*), Bible pictures (vocal, with orchestra), *Der Schäfer putzte sich zum Tanz*

(soprano, with orchestra), also a number of songs which have become popular. The University of Jena conferred on him the title of *Doc. h. c.* He died Jan. 15, 1904.

Lasso, (1) O r l a n d o di (Orlandus Lassus, b. 1532, Mons, d. June 14, 1594, Munich, next to Palestrina, the greatest composer of the 16th century. He was chorister in the church of St. Nicholas, and was several times carried off on account of his beautiful voice. With the consent of his parents, he was taken by Ferdinand Gonzaga, Viceroy of Sicily, to Sicily, and afterwards to Milan. When his voice broke, he went to the Marquis of Terza, and, in 1541, through the influence of the Cardinal Archbishop of Florence, he became director of the choir at the Lateran, Rome, as Rubino's successor. He held this post until 1548, when, after long journeys through France and England, he settled in Antwerp 1555, where he published Book I. of Madrigals à 4, and at the same time, at Gardano's, Venice, Book I. of Madrigals à 5. In 1557 Duke Albert V., of Bavaria, invited him to the court chapel at Munich, the direction of which L. undertook in 1562 and held the post until his death. The last years of his life, however, were spent in a pitiful state of melancholy caused by excessive mental exertion. L. was not only the most prolific composer of the 16th century, but probably of any period. The number of his works exceeds two thousand. His contemporaries placed him above all masters, and surnamed him "Prince of Music," the "Belgian Orpheus," etc. His works have defied time, and still excite astonishment at the present day. As complete a catalogue as possible has been given, by R. Eitner, of the printed works, as a supplement to the fifth and sixth yearly series of the *Monatshefte für Musikgeschichte;* the Munich Library has a large number of those still unprinted. (*Cf.* J. J. Maier's Catalogue, 1879.) Eitner gives the beginnings of no less than forty-six masses, and the Munich Library contains, besides, unprinted ones on "Je suis déshéritée" (à 4), "Triste départ" (à 5), "On me l'a dict" (à 4), "Jesus ist ein süsser Name" (à 6), "Domine Dominus noster" (à 6), "Si rore aënio" (à 5). From the great number of his works the following deserve special mention; the Penitential Psalms of David—a work which is as well known as Palestrina's Improperia ("Psalmi Davidis pœnitentiales," printed in 1584; in a new score edition by Dehn, 1838; in manuscript [1560-70], magnificently got up with miniatures, at Munich) The "Patrocinium musices" (1573-76, five vols., prepared at the expense of the Duke of Bavaria) is also splendidly got up; it contains:—(i.) twenty-one motets; (ii.) five Masses; (iii.) offices; (iv.) Passion, vigils, etc.; (v.) ten Magnificats. L. composed one hundred Magnificats (published and unpublished appeared together in 1619 under the title "Jubilus

Beatæ Virginis"), about twelve hundred motets ("Cantiones sacræ, etc.;" the "Magnum opus musicum" of 1604 contains 516 of them), not to mention the chansons, madrigals, and German *Lieder* which appeared in Italian, German, French, and Netherland publications, likewise pirated. The style of L., as compared with that of Josquin, Obrecht, etc., is far more developed in the matter of harmonic clearness. L. was one of the morning stars of modern times, although he held fast to the imitative style of composition, and repeatedly wrote over a *Cantus firmus*. The ease with which he moved, on the one hand, within the various forms of the Mass, motet, etc., and, on the other hand, within those of the madrigal, villanella, chanson, etc., shows that he was gifted in many ways—nay, a universal genius. New score editions of L.'s works are to be found, in varying number, in the collections of Proske, Commer, Rochlitz, Dehn, and others. Biographical notices of L. have been written by Delmotte (1836; in German by Dehn, 1837), Matthieu (1838), Kist (1841), and Baümker (1878). E. van der Straeten published letters of L. in 1891. For the tercentenary (1894) of his birth, Breitkopf and Haertel announced a complete edition of L.'s works, under the editorship of Dr. Ad. Sandberger of Munich. (*Cf.* Sandberger, "Beiträge zur Geschichte der bair. Hofkapelle unter O. d. L."—I., 1893.)

(2) Ferdinand, eldest son of the former, d. Aug. 27, 1609, as court capellmeister at Munich. He published a volume of motets ("Cantiones sacræ suavissimæ" (1587), and edited, jointly with his brother Rudolf, the "Magnum opus musicum" of his father.

(3) Rudolf, the second son of Orlando di L., organist, teacher of singing and composition to the Munich Court Chapel (from 1587), d. 1625. He published: "Cantiones sacræ" (à 4, 1606); "Circus symphoniacus" (1609); "Moduli sacri ad sacrum convivium" (à 2–6, 1614); "Virginalia eucharistica," à 4, 1616); "Alphabetum Marianum" (fifty-seven antiphons, 1621). Three Masses and three Magnificats are to be found in manuscript in the Munich Library.

(4) Ferdinand, grandson of Orlando di L., son of Ferdinand L., was sent to Rome by the Duke of Bavaria in 1609, to complete his musical education; in 1616 he was appointed court capellmeister, but was dismissed in 1629 and entrusted with a post as administrative officer. He died in 1636. Of his compositions—written for the most part for double choir (à 8–16) in the style in vogue in Italy at the commencement of the 17th century—few have been preserved. He only published "Apparatus musicus" (motets à 8 for two choirs).

Lassu. (*See* CZARDAS.)

Latilla, Gaetano, b. 1713, Bari (Naples), d. about 1789, pupil of Gizzi at Naples, had success with his operas at an early age, was appointed, already at the end of 1738, second maestro at St. Maria Maggiore, Rome, but, owing to a severe illness, was unable to attend to his duties. In 1741 he was dismissed, and lived in Naples for the sake of his health. In 1756 he was appointed teacher of choral singing at the Conservatorio della Pietà, Venice, where in 1762 he also became second maestro of St. Mark's Church. A refusal to raise his salary gave him an opportunity of returning to Naples in 1772, where, highly esteemed as a teacher, he ended his life. L. was the uncle of N. Piccini. He wrote twenty-seven operas, mostly for Naples and Venice, only known by name; *Orazio* (Rome, 1738, etc.) had the most success. L. was one of the best Neapolitan composers of opera, and also wrote some excellent sacred works and an oratorio.

Laub, Ferdinand, celebrated violinist, b. Jan. 19, 1832, Prague, d. March 17, 1875, Gries (near Bozen), pupil of Mildner at the Prague Conservatorium, succeeded Joachim as leader of the band at Weimar (1853), from 1855–57 teacher of the violin at the Stern Conservatorium, Berlin, afterwards leader of the court orchestra and "Königlicher Kammervirtuose" (until 1864). After long concert tours he was appointed professor of the violin at Moscow Conservatoire, and leader of the Russian Musical Society; he spent his last years, suffering from a painful illness, at Carlsbad (1874), and finally at Gries (near Bozen). L. only published a few solo pieces for violin.

Laudes (Lat.; Ital. *Laudi*), songs of praise (hymns, simply constructed motets).

Laureate (Lat., "crowned with laurels"), the winner of the *Grand Prix de Rome* (q.v.) at the Paris or Brussels Conservatoire.

Laurencin (d'Armond), Ferdinand Peter Graf, b. Oct, 15, 1819, Kremsier (Moravia), d. Feb. 5, 1890, Vienna, took the degree of *Dr. Phil.* at Prague, studied music under Tomaschek and Pitsch, and lived as a writer on music at Vienna. He wrote the small pamphlets, paying homage to the new German tendency:—"Zur Geschichte der Kirchenmusik" (1856); "Das Paradies und die Peri von R. Schumann" (1859); "Dr. Hanslicks Lehre vom Musikalisch-Schönen" (1859); "Die Harmonie der Neuzeit" (1861; this gained a prize, but is only strong in negation); also many articles in the *N. Z. f. M.*; *cf.* Schuchs's Nekrolog. in *N. Z. f. M.*, 1890.

Laurent de Rillé, François Anatole, b. 1828, Orléans, pupil of Elwart in Paris, where he was inspector of school-singing. He wrote numerous choruses for male voices (*Chœurs orphéoniques*) which were popular in France; and, since 1858, sixteen operettas, mostly of one act, for Paris and Brussels, but also a number of small Masses and other sacred pieces, songs, a Vocal Method, exercises for male chorus, and a musical novel—"Olivier l'orphéoniste."

Laurenti, (1) Bartolomeo Girolamo, b. 1644, Bologna, d. Jan. 18, 1726, as principal violinist at St. Petronio. He published: Op. 1, "Sonate per camera a violino e violoncello" (1691), and Op. 2, " Sei concerti a 3, cioè violino, violoncello ed organo " (1720).

His son (2) Girolamo Nicolo, d. Dec. 26, 1752, Bologna, likewise principal violinist at St. Petronio, studied under Torelli and Vitali, published concertos for three violins, viola, 'cello, and organ.

Lauska, Franz Seraphinus, excellent pianist, b. Jan. 13, 1764, Brünn, d. April 18, 1825, Berlin. He was a pupil of Albrechtsberger at Vienna, was first engaged by an Italian duke, then became chamber musician at Munich, and in 1798 settled as pianoforte-teacher in Berlin, where he was held in high consideration in private circles and at the court. His published compositions, mostly in the style of Clementi, are: sixteen pf. sonatas, one ditto for four hands, a 'cello sonata, rondos, variations, etc., a Pianoforte Method, some male quartets and songs.

Laute (Ger.), a lute.

Lauterbach, Johann Christoph, eminent performer on the violin, b. July 24, 1832, Kulmbach, attended the Gymnasium and the School of Music at Würzburg, continued his musical studies under De Bériot and Fétis at Brussels, and so distinguished himself that, at the end of two years, he was able to act as deputy for Léonard. He was appointed in 1853 leader, and teacher of the violin at the Conservatorium, Munich, but in 1861 accepted a call to Dresden as leader of the orchestra (he was pensioned in 1889); at the same time he was teacher of the violin at the Royal Conservatorium, but resigned in 1877. Of L.'s compositions the following may be named: Concert polonaise, Reverie, Tarantelle, and concert-pieces.

Lavigna, Vincenzo, b. 1777, Naples, pupil of the Conservatorio della Pietà, d. 1837, Milan, where he had been for a long while teacher of singing and accompanist at La Scala. His first opera—which, on the recommendation of Paesiello, he was commissioned to write for La Scala (1802)—*La muta per amore (Il medico per forza)*—proved his best work. He wrote, besides, eight other operas and two ballets.

Lavignac, Albert, professor of the Paris Conservatoire, published in 1882 "Cours complet théorique et pratique de dictée musicale," a work which was the means of musical dictation (q.v.) being introduced into all conservatoria of any note.

Lavigne, (1) Jacques Émile, famous French tenor, b. 1782, Pau, from 1809–25 was engaged at the Grand Opéra, Paris, afterwards lived in retirement at Pau, and d. in 1855. L. was second tenor (A. Nourrit was principal), but he won triumphs in all the *rôles* left to him by Nourrit, and abroad in all principal *rôles;* and, on account of his powerful voice, he received the surname " L'Hercule du chant ; " his post was embittered by intrigues.

(2) Antoine Joseph, famous oboe-player, b. March 23, 1816, Besançon, pupil of the Paris Conservatoire. He lived from 1841 in England, where he was, at first, in the orchestra of the Drury Lane Promenade Concerts, but afterwards joined Hallé's excellent orchestra at Manchester. L. partially applied the Boehm ring-key system to the oboe.

Lavoix, Henri Marie François, b. April 26, 1846, Paris, d. Oct., 1892, Paris, son of the " Conservateur " of the numismatic cabinet of the Paris National Library (from whom he is distinguished as " L. fils "). He attended the Paris University, graduated, and became pupil of Henri Cohen for harmony and counterpoint, and, from 1865, librarian at the National Library. L. has distinguished himself by clever monographs:—" Les traducteurs de Shakespeare en musique" (1869) ; "La musique dans la nature " (1873) ; " La musique dans l'imagerie du moyen-âge " (1875) ; " Histoire de l'instrumentation " (1878 ; honourably mentioned by the Académie, 1875) ; " Les principes et l'histoire du chant " (with Th. Lemaire) ; " La musique au siècle de Saint Louis." L. was also musical feuilletonist of the *Globe,* and one of the most active contributors to the *Revue et Gazette Musicale,*" and other musical papers. (*See* LEMAIRE, 2.)

Lawes, (1) William, pupil of Coperario, chorister at Chichester Cathedral, 1603 member of the Chapel Royal, London, and afterwards chamber-musician to King Charles I. He fell in the Civil War as a soldier in the Royal army during the siege of Chester, 1645. Anthems and other sacred and secular works of his are to be found in Boyce's " Cathedral Music " and other English collections of the period (" Catch that Catch Can," 1652 ; " Select Musical Ayres and Dialogues," 1653, 1659 ; " The Treasury of Musick," 1669, etc.).

(2) Henry, brother of the former, b. end of December, 1595, d. Oct. 21, 1662, London, was likewise pupil of Coperario, entered the Chapel Royal in 1625, and also received an appointment at court. Like his brother, he was a sound Royalist. The fall of Charles I. cost him, not his life, but his post. In 1660 he was reappointed under Charles II. Henry L. was the more important of the two brothers. He wrote music for masques, and published : "A Paraphrase upon the Psalmes of David " (1637) ; " Choice Psalmes put into Musick for Three Voices" (1648, jointly with William L.) ; "Ayres and Dialogues for One, Two, and Three Voyces " (1653, 1655, and 1658 ; three books). Other works are to be found in the above-mentioned collections.

Lawrowskaja, Elisabeth Andrejewna,

Russian singer, b. Oct. 12, 1845, Kaschin (Government Twer), pupil of Fenzi at the "Elisabeth" Institution, afterwards at the Petersburg Conservatoire under Frau Nissen-Saloman, made her *début* in 1867 as Orpheus (Gluck), and, after continuing her studies abroad (London, Paris) at the expense of the Princess Hélène, she was engaged at the Imperial Opera-house, Petersburg. Pecuniary differences with the management led her, after four years of stage work, to travel, and she appeared at the theatres and in the concert-rooms of the most important cities of Europe. She only returned to the stage in 1878, and is one of the chief ornaments of the Petersburg Opera (as Vania in Glinka's *Life for the Czar*, as Ratmir in the same composer's *Ruslan und Ludmilla*, as Princess in Dargomizsky's *Russalka*, as Grania in Serow's *Wrazyia Sila*, etc.). L. married Prince Zeretelew.

Layolle (Layole, dell' Aiolle, Ajolla), François, composer of the 16th century at Florence, probably French by birth; he composed motets, madrigals, masses, psalms, etc., which are scattered in the collections of Jacobus Modernus (1532 up to 1543), Petrejus (1538–42), Rhaw (1545), and Antonio Gardano (1538–60).

Lays (Fr. *Lais;* Ger. *Leiche*), songs of a popular character during the Middle Ages, after the manner of sequences. (*Cf.* Ferd. Wolff, "Ueber die Lais, Sequenzen u. Leiche" [Heidelberg, 1841].)

Lazarus, Henry, b. 1815, studied the clarinet under Blizard and C. Godfrey. In 1838 he was appointed second to Willman at the Sacred Harmonic Society. From 1840 he was principal clarinet at the Opera, and at all provincial Festivals and London concerts. He retired after fifty years of public life, and d. March 6, 1895.

Lazzari, Sylvio, b. 1858, Bozen, studied jurisprudence at Innsbruck and Munich, passed the government examinations, but then followed his own inclination, and in 1882 attended the Paris Conservatoire, making, at the same time, his *début* as a composer, with some songs. In Paris he studied especially under César Franck. L. is a composer of modern tendency (symphonic poems, pantomimic ballets, chamber-music, also a music-drama, etc.), and he has also contributed articles to various musical papers.

Le (Ital.), the feminine article in the plural (before vowels *l'*).

Leader (Konzertmeister ; Fr. *Violon solo*), the first violin, or solo violin, of an orchestra, who has occasionally to act as the conductor's deputy.

Leading-note is a note leading to another, causing the same to be expected, especially the semitone below the tonic (*Subsemitonium modi;* Fr. *Note sensible*), for example, *b* in c *major, f♯* in G *major,* etc. Such a L. is always the third of the dominant chord. But there is another kind of L. which is of equal importance with the *subsemitonium,* viz., the L. from above—the *Suprasemitonium.* Every sharp or flat which raises or lowers a note of the tonic triad, or of the dominant chord, introduces a note which produces the effect of a L., *i.e.*, which leads one to expect a half-tone progression upwards (♯) or downwards (♭). Thus, in c major an *f♯* has the effect of a L. to *g*, a *b♭* of L. to *a*, *d♯* of L. to *e*, *d♭* to *c*, and so on. The acoustic ratio of the L. to the following note is always 15 : 16 or 16 : 15, *i.e.* that of the fifteenth overtone (5.3, *see* CLANG, *i.e.* the third of the fifth), likewise of the fifteenth undertone (the under-third of the under-fifth) to the principal tone (likewise of its fourth octave, the sixteenth over- or under-tone), for example, *c*, (*g*), *b*, or *c, f, d♭*.

Le Bé, Guillaume, was one of the first in France to make music-types, and indeed of two kinds. In the oldest kind (1540) notes and lines were printed simultaneously—*i.e.* each type contained a note and a portion of the five-line stave. The later one (of 1555) gave the notes and the lines separately, so there had to be two printings, as in Petrucci. L. also prepared types for tablature works : all his punches passed into the hands of Ballard (q.v.).

Le Beau, Louise Adolpha, b. April 25, 1850, Rastadt, pupil of Rheinberger and Fr. Lachner, lived at Munich, Wiesbaden, Karlsruhe, as an able pianist and esteemed teacher of music. She has published various pianoforte pieces, songs, and chamber-music, which display talent.

Lebègue, Nicolas Antoine, b. 1630, Laon, d. July 6, 1702, as court organist, Paris; he published several sets of organ pieces, pianoforte pieces, and "Airs" à 2–3, with continuo.

Lebendig (Ger.), lively, active, vivacious.

Lebert, Siegmund (Levy, named L.), b. Dec. 12, 1822, Ludwigsburg (Würtemberg), d. Dec. 8, 1884, Stuttgart; he received musical training at Prague under Tomaschek, Dionys Weber, Tedesko, and Proksch, worked for several years as pianoforte-teacher at Munich, where he was highly esteemed, and founded (1856–57), jointly with Faisst, Brachmann, Laiblin, Stark, Speidel, etc., a Conservatorium at Stuttgart. L. was a renowned pianoforte-teacher, and, in addition to his activity as such, he became celebrated for the educational works for pianoforte which he published. At the head of these stands the "Grosse Klavierschule," which he published jointly with L. Stark, and which up to now has been issued in German, French, English, Italian and Russian editions : but it is far too pedantic, especially in the first and second sections, and hence is gradually losing in public estimation. Further, an instructive edition of the classics (jointly

with Faisst, Bülow, Ignaz Lachner, Liszt);
a "Jugendalbum" (jointly with Stark); Clementi's "Gradus ad Parnassum," etc. He received the honorary degree of Dr.Phil. from
the Tübingen University, and the King of Würtemberg bestowed on him the title of professor.
J a c o b L e v y, b. 1815, d. Oct. 19, 1883, Stuttgart, professor of the pianoforte at the Conservatorium, was his brother.

Lebeuf, J e a n, b. March 6, 1687, Auxerre,
d. there April 10, 1760, as Abbé, canon, and
sub-cantor of the Cathedral, from 1740 member
of the Paris Académie. He was a diligent
writer on music: "Traité historique et pratique
sur le chant ecclésiastique" (1741), and a series
of articles on Gregorian song (plain-chant) in
the *Mercure de France* (1825-37), and great historical works—"Recueil de divers écrits pour
servir d'éclaircissements à l'histoire de France"
(1738, two vols.), and "Dissertations sur l'histoire ecclésiastique et civile de Paris" (1739-45,
three vols.), which also contain matters relating to music.

Lebhaft (Ger.), lively, animated.

Leborne, A i m é A m b r o i s e S i m o n, b.
Dec. 29, 1797, Brussels, d. April 1, 1866, Paris,
pupil of Dourlen and Cherubini at the Paris
Conservatoire, winner of the *Grand Prix de
Rome* (1820), already in 1816 assistant teacher
at the Conservatoire, in 1820 teacher in ordinary of an elementary class, in 1836 successor of
Reicha as professor of composition, and in 1834
librarian of the Grand Opéra, afterwards music
librarian to Napoleon III. He was especially
famous as a teacher, but also attempted composition with success, and brought out several
comic operas ; a Method of Harmony remained
in manuscript ; he also republished Catel's celebrated "Traité de l'harmonie."

Lebrun, (1) L u d w i g A u g u s t, very famous
oboe-player, b. 1746, Mannheim, d. Dec. 16,
1790, Berlin ; he was appointed from 1767 in
the court orchestra at Munich, whence, liberal
leave of absence being granted, he gave concerts at home and abroad, and made a reputation. His published compositions are: seven
oboe concertos, trios for oboe, violin and 'cello,
and flute duets. His wife, F r a n z i s k a (*née*
Danzi, b. 1756, Mannheim, d. May 14, 1791,
Berlin), sister of Franz Danzi, was one of the
most distinguished singers of her time (high
soprano), and obtained equal triumphs at Mannheim, Munich, Milan, Venice, Naples, London,
and Berlin. She had scarcely entered upon an
engagement in the last-named city when her
husband died. Grief so overcame her that she
soon followed him to the grave. Also their
daughters, S o p h i e (afterwards Frau Dulken,
b. June 20, 1781) and R o s i n e (b. April 13,
1785), both made a name—the former as a
pianist, the latter as a vocalist.
(2) J e a n, b. April 6, 1759, Lyons, excellent
horn-player, and one who has scarcely ever

been surpassed in the production of the high
notes ; from 1786-92 he was principal horn-player
at the Grand Opéra, Paris, then for a long time
at the Berlin Court Opera. In 1806 he returned
to Paris, but could obtain no engagement, and
in 1809 committed suicide by suffocation.
(3) L o u i s S é b a s t i e n, b. Dec. 10, 1764,
Paris, d. June 27, 1829 ; from 1787 to 1803 he was
opera-singer (tenor) at the Grand Opéra, and
for some time at the Opéra Comique, then *répétiteur* at the Grand Opéra, in 1807 tenor singer
at the royal chapel, and, from 1810, director of
the singing there. He successfully produced a
large number of operas (especially *Le Rossignol*,
1815, which kept the boards during several
decades), also a Te Deum (1809), a "Messe
solennelle," etc.
(4) P a u l H e n r i J o s e p h, b. April 21, 1861,
Ghent, studied at the Conservatoire of that city,
received in 1891 the *Prix de Rome* for composition, and, for a symphony, the first prize of the
Belgian Académie.

Le Carpentier, A d o l p h e C l a i r, b. Feb. 17,
1809, Paris, d. there July 14, 1869, pianist and
composer (Methods, exercises, fantasias, etc.).

Lechner, L e o n h a r d, a gifted and diligent
composer of the 16th century, b. in the Etschthal, and probably for a time chorister in the
chapel of the Duke of Bavaria. About 1570
he occupied a position as teacher at Nuremberg, became capellmeister in 1584 to Count
Eitel Frederick of Hohenzollern at Hechingen,
but afterwards went to Stuttgart ; in 1595 he
became court capellmeister, and died Sept. 6,
1604. For a catalogue of his compositions
(motets à 4-6, German songs of the Villanella
kind, à 2-3, German songs and madrigals à 4-5,
masses à 5-6, etc.) *see* the *Monats. f. Mus. Gesch.*,
I. 179, and X. 137.

Leclair, J e a n M a r i e, eminent violinist,
b. Nov. 23, 1697, Paris, murdered there Oct. 22,
1764. He was originally a ballet-dancer, and
became ballet-master at Turin, but at the
same time cultivated violin-playing with such
energy and success that Somis took notice of
him and accepted him as a pupil. In 1729 he
went to Paris, but only succeeded in obtaining
a post as ripieno-violinist at the Grand Opéra ;
in 1731 he became a member of the royal band,
but only for a short time, as he could not obtain
the post of leader of the second violins. After
that he lived as a private teacher and composer
until, from motives unknown, he was murdered.
His works are: forty-eight sonatas for violin
with continuo (Op. 1, 2, 5, 9) ; duets for two
violins (Op. 3, 12) ; six trios for two violins
with continuo (Op. 4) ; easy trios for two violins
with continuo (Op. 6, 8) ; *Concerti grossi* for three
violins, viola, 'cello, and organ bass (Op. 7, 10) ;
an opera, *Glaucus und Scylla* (Op. 11, produced
1747) ; overtures, and sonatas as trios for two
violins and bass (Op. 13) ; and, finally, a posthumous sonata (Op. 14). Ferdinand David

revived two of his sonatas in his "Hohe Schule des Violinspiels." L.'s sonata No. 4 has been arranged for violin and pianoforte by G. Jensen. A younger brother of L., Antoine Remi, also a violin-player, published in 1739 (not 1760) twelve viola sonatas.

Leclercq, Louis. (*See* CELLER.)

Lecocq, Alexandre Charles, b. June 3, 1832, Paris, was a pupil of Bazin (harmony), Halévy (composition), and Benoist (organ) at the Conservatoire, and was active from 1854 as teacher of music. His *début* as composer was in 1857, when an opera—*Le docteur Miracle*, written jointly with G. Bizet—gained a prize in a competition instituted by Offenbach. It was only moderately successful. His operetta, *Huis clos*, in 1859, met with even a cooler reception, and also the following pieces : *Le baiser à la porte* (1864), *Liline et Valentin* (1864), *Les Ondines de Champagne* (1865), *Le Myosotis* (1866), *Le cabaret de Ramponneau* (1867), and the comic opera *L'amour et son carquois* (1868) only achieved moderate and ephemeral success. It was only with his *Fleur de thé* (April, 1868) that he completely won the ear of the public ; within a short time it was performed a hundred times, and found its way abroad. From that time L. ranked amongst the most favourite composers of the general public. He differs from Offenbach and Hervé, and to his advantage, in the greater carefulness and correctness of his writing. In addition to above-named works there are the comic opera *Les jumeaux de Bergame* (1868) ; the vaudeville *Le carnaval d'un merle blanc* (1868), the operettas *Gandolfo* (1869) ; *Deux portières pour un cordon*, *Le Rajah de Mysore*, *Le beau Dunois* (1870) ; *Le Testament de M. de Crac* (1871) ; *Le barbier de Trouville*, *Sauvons la caisse* (1872) ; *Les cents vierges*, *La fille de Madame Angot*, *Giroflé-Girofla* (1874) ; *Les prés de St. Gervais*, *Le pompon* (1875) ; *La petite mariée* (1876) ; *Kosiki*, *La Marjolaine* (1877) ; *Le petit duc* (1878) ; *Camargo*, *La petite Mademoiselle* (1879) ; *Le Grand Casimir*, *La jolie Persane* (1880) ; *Le Marquis de Windsor*, *Janot* (1881) ; *La roussotte*, *Le jour et la nuit*, *Le cœur et la main* (1882) ; *La princesse des Canaries* (1883) ; *L'oiseau bleu* (1884) ; and *Plutus* (1886) ; *Les grenadiers de Monte-Cornette* (1887) ; *Ali Baba* (1887) ; *La volière* (1888), and *L'Égyptienne* (1890). Besides his stage works, L. published also : "Les Fantoccini" (ballet pantomime for pianoforte), a gavotte and twenty-four characteristic pieces (" Les miettes ") for pf., a number of vocal pieces with pf. (Mélodies, Chansons, Aubade, etc.), sacred songs for female voices ("La chapelle au couvent," 1885), and a pf. edition of Rameau's *Castor et Pollux* (1877).

Le Couppey, Félix, b. April 14, 1811, Paris, d. there July 5, 1887, pupil of Dourlen at the Conservatoire, was, from 1828, assistant teacher in an elementary harmony class, in 1837 teacher in ordinary ; in 1843 he succeeded Dourlen as professor of harmony, in 1848 became deputy for Henri Herz, who had departed on his travels, and soon after that, professor of a new pianoforte class for young ladies. The published compositions of L. are principally educational works for the pianoforte : an " École du mécanisme du piano," " L'art du piano " (fifty Études with remarks), and a pamphlet, " De l'enseignement du piano ; conseils aux jeunes professeurs " (1865).

Ledebur, Karl Freiherr von, b. April 20, 1806, Schildesche (near Bielefeld), was a cavalry officer in Berlin, but, in consequence of a fall from his horse, resigned in 1852, and from that time devoted himself especially to musical studies. L. published a "Tonkünstlerlexikon Berlins von den ältesten Zeiten bis auf die Gegenwart" (1860–61), a work compiled with great care.

Ledent, Félix Étienne, b. Nov. 20, 1816, Liége, studied at the Conservatoire of his native city under Daussoigne, Lambert, Conrardy, and Jalheau. In 1832 he won the first prize for pianoforte-playing, and in 1843 the *Prix de Rome* for composition. Since 1838 L. has been professor of the pianoforte at the Liége Conservatoire ; he is also a composer.

Ledger lines or **Leger lines,** the short auxiliary lines above or below the stave.

Lee, the brothers Sebastian (b. Dec. 24, 1805, Hamburg, d. there Jan. 4, 1887) and Louis (b. there Oct. 19, 1819), celebrated 'cellists, pupils of J. N. Prell. Sebastian L. from 1837–68 was solo 'cellist at the Grand Opéra, Paris, lived afterwards in Hamburg, and published fantasias, variations, rondos, and duets for 'cello, also a much-used 'cello Method. Louis L., at the early age of twelve, gave concerts in Copenhagen and through Germany, then became 'cellist at the Hamburg Theatre, lived for several years in Paris, established in Hamburg chamber-music *soirées*, together with Hafner, afterwards with Böie ; and was for many years principal 'cellist of the Philharmonic Society, and, until 1884, was also teacher at the Conservatorium. His printed compositions are : a pf. quartet (Op. 10) and pf. trio (Op. 5), a 'cello sonata (Op. 9), sonatina (Op. 15), violin sonata (Op. 4), sonatina (Op. 13), pieces for pf. and 'cello, and for pf. alone ; the following are in manuscript, but have been performed : symphonies (one under Spohr at Cassel), two stringed quartets, and music to Schiller's *Jungfrau von Orleans* and *Wilhelm Tell*. Their brother, Maurice (b. Hamburg, Feb., 1821, d. June 23, 1895, London), was a composer of popular drawing-room pieces, and resided in London as pianoforte teacher.

Lefébure, Louis François Henri, b. Feb. 18, 1754, Paris, d. 1840 in the French Government service, finally sous-préfet at Verdun ; from 1814 he lived in retirement at Paris. He wrote : "Nouveau Solfège" (1780), in which he expounded a new method of Solmisation which Gossec introduced into the École Royale du Chant, and " Revues, erreurs, et méprises de differents auteurs célèbres en matière musicale" (1789); he also composed several cantatas and oratorios.

Lefébure-Wély, Louis James Alfred, b. Nov. 13, 1817, Paris, d. there Dec. 31, 1869, son of the organist of St. Roch, Antoine L., who published pf. and violin sonatas, a mass, Te Deum, etc. (d. 1831). L. studied with his father, and, at the early age of eight, was his deputy, at the age of fourteen becoming his successor. Shortly after this appointment he entered the Conservatoire, where Benoist (organ), Zimmermann (piano), and Berton and Halévy (composition) were his teachers, and he received several prizes. At the same time L. was a private pupil of Adam (composition), and of the organist of St. Sulpice, Séjan (organ). In 1847 he exchanged his post of organist of St. Roch for that of the Madeleine with its magnificent organ built by Cavaillé-Coll. He resigned in 1838 in order to devote himself entirely to composition, yet succeeded Séjan at St. Sulpice in 1863. L., who is principally known as the composer of the pianoforte piece "Les cloches du monastère," was a distinguished musician, and especially skilled in organ improvisation. He attempted almost every branch of music :—opera, *Les recruteurs* [1861]; cantata, *Après la victoire* [1863]; two masses for organ, one mass for orchestra, three symphonies, etc., numerous *salon* pianoforte pieces (three great collections of études). L. was also a distinguished performer on the harmonium, and a composer for that instrument.

Lefebvre, (1) Jacques (Le Febvre, Jacobus Faber), b. about 1435 or 1455, Étaples, near Amiens (hence called "Stapulensis"), d. 1537 or 1547, Nérac, in the service of the kings of Navarre as tutor to the royal children. He wrote "Elementa musicalia" (1496; 2nd ed. 1510, under the title "Musica libris IV. demonstrata," with a similar superscription in a great mathematical work of Lefebvre's of 1514, and in another of 1528, which also contains "Quæstiuncula prævia in musicam speculativam Bœtii;" finally in 1552 as "De musica quatuor libris demonstrata").

(2) Charles Edouard, b. June 19, 1843, Paris, son of the painter of that name. He first studied jurisprudence, then entered the Conservatoire, gaining the *Prix de Rome*, 1870. After long tours he settled in Paris, and devotes himself solely to composition (choral works [concert opera], *Judith*, 1879; fantastic legend : *Melka;* choral work, *Elva;* chamber-music, psalms, several operas : *Zaïre*, 1887; *Le Trésor* [one act], *Djelma*).

Lefèvre, Jean Xavier, celebrated clarinet-player, b. March 6, 1763, Lausanne, d. Nov. 9, 1829, Paris ; pupil of Michel Yost in Paris, for

many years member of the orchestra at the Grand Opéra, 1795–1825 professor of the clarinet at the Conservatoire, from 1807 member of the Imperial, and, since the restoration, Royal Chapelle ; he wrote the official clarinet Méthode of the Conservatoire (1802 ; also in German), also concertos, concertantes, duets, sonatas, etc., for his instrument, which he had improved by the addition of a sixth key. He refused to entertain the idea of any further addition of keys.

Legando (Ital.), slurring, binding ; playing or singing smoothly.

Legatissimo (Ital.), the superlative of *legato*, very smoothly. (*See below,* LEGATO.)

Legato (*ligato*), tied, *i.e.* without a pause between each note. L. is obtained in singing when, without break, *i.e.* without interrupting the current of air, the degree of tension of the vocal cords is changed so that the first sound really passes into the second. A similar process takes place in wind instruments, where, likewise, the current of air is not interrupted, but only the fingering or position of the lips changed. On stringed instruments sounds are tied (1) when they are played on the same string, with only change of fingering, and without the bow leaving the string ; (2) when they occur on different strings, while the bow glides quickly from the one to the other. The connecting of notes on keyed instruments is effected by only leaving the first key while the second is being pressed down. On the pianoforte then the strings of the first note are free from the damper, and therefore sound till the second note is struck. On instruments of the organ kind (Harmonium, Regal, " Positiv ") the valve admitting wind to the channel remains open until touching a new note opens a new valve. (*Cf.* SLUR.)

Legatura di voce (Ital.), smooth execution of a succession of notes in one breath.

Legend, a term much used of late for musical works of an epico-lyrical character, of which the subject (text or programme) is the legend of some saint.

Leggiero (Ital.), light, nimble. A mode of touch in pianoforte-playing between *legato* and *staccato;* it differs from the former, in that it is the result of a blow, and not of pressure. It differs from *mezzo-legato*, in that it is not the nervous touch, but merely the springing-back to which the player has to pay attention.

Legno (Ital.), wood. *Col legno*, with the stick of the bow (not with the hair).

Legouix, Isidor Edouard, b. April 1, 1834, Paris, pupil of the Conservatoire of that city, composer of a number of comic operettas, mostly of one act, but of too distinguished a character to gain the ear of the million.

Legrenzi, Giovanni, eminent composer, b. about 1625, Clusone (near Bergamo), d. May 26,

1690, Venice. He was a pupil of Pallavicino, organist of Santa Maria Maggiore at Bergamo, afterwards director of the Conservatorio dei Mendicanti at Venice, and, from 1685, also maestro of San Marco. L. considerably increased the orchestra of that church, so that there were thirty-four players (eight violins, eleven small viols [violette], two tenor viols, three gambas and contrabass viols, four theorbos, two cornets, one bassoon, three trombones). L. wrote seventeen operas (mostly for Venice), which, especially in the treatment of instrumental accompaniment, showed an advance on his predecessors. He published: "Concerto di messe e salmi a 3 e 4 voci con violini" (1654); two motets à 2–4 (1655); motets à 5 (1660); "Sacri e festivi concerti, messe e salmi a due cori" (1657); "Sentimenti devoti" (à 2–3; 1660, two books); "Compiete con litanie ed antifone della Beata Virgine Maria" à 5 (1662); "Cantate a voce sola" (1674); "Idee armoniche" à 2–3 (1678); "Echi di reverenza," fourteen cantatas for solo voice (1679); "Motetti sacri a voce sola con 3 stromenti" (1692); "Sonate a 2 e 3" (1655); "Suonate da chiesa e da camera a tre" (1656); "Una muta di suonate" (1664); "Suonate a due violini e violone" (with continuo for organ, 1667); "La cetra" (sonatas for 2–4 instruments, 1673); "Suonate a 2 violini e violoncello" (1677); "Suonate da chiesa e da camera" à 2–7 (1793). Lotti was his pupil.

Lehmann, L i l l y, distinguished dramatic vocalist (soprano), b. May 15, 1848, Würzburg, was, from 1870, for many years an ornament of the Berlin stage, but she broke her contract and went to America, where she married the tenor singer Kalisch. In 1890 she returned to Germany, appearing occasionally on the stage.

Leibrock, J o s e p h A d o l f, b. Jan. 8, 1808, Brunswick, d. Aug. 8, 1886, Berlin; he studied philosophy, and took the degree of Dr.Phil., but turned to music, and became 'cellist and harpist in the court orchestra at Brunswick. Besides compositions of the most varied kind (music to Schiller's *Räuber*, songs, part-songs, very many arrangements for pf. and 'cello, etc.), he published a "Musikalische Akkordenlehre" (1875), which is interesting in that L. seeks to establish the relation of chords in the tonal system of harmony, and, in so doing, recognises the peculiar importance of the under-dominant in a logical system of writing. L. wrote also a history of the ducal "Hofkapelle" at Brunswick (in the *Braunschweig Magazin*, 1865–66). Latterly he resided at Leipzig.

Leidenschaft (Ger.), passion, emotion. *Mit Leidenschaft*, with passion, with strong emotion.

Leierkasten (Ger.). (*See* HURDY-GURDY.)

Leighton, William Knight, English composer about 1614, in which year he published; "The Teares or Lamentacions of a Sorrowfull Soule," containing fifty-four psalms and hymns, partly à 4 with accompaniments for lute, etc., partly à 4–5 *a cappella;* the first eight pieces are by L. himself, the others by J. Bull, Byrde, Coperario, J. Dowland, A. Ferrabosco, O. Gibbons, Th. Weelkes, J. Wilbye, etc.

Leisinger, E l i s a b e t h, distinguished dramatic vocalist (soprano), b. May 17, 1864, Stuttgart, pupil of the Stuttgart Conservatorium, and of Mme. Viardot-Garcia at Paris; since 1884 she has been a highly esteemed member of the Berlin Court Opera.

Leite, A n t o n i o d a S i l v a, Portuguese composer and theorist, maestro at the Conservatorio at Oporto about 1787–1826; he wrote "Resumo de todas as regras e preceitos de cantoria assim da musica metrica como da cantochão" (1787); also a guitar Method (1796), six sonatas for guitar with violin (Rebek) and two trumpets, a "Tantum ergo" à 4 with orchestra, a hymn for the coronation of King John VI. of Portugal, etc.

Leitert, J o h a n n G e o r g, excellent pianist, b. Sept. 29, 1852, Dresden; he made his first appearance at the early age of thirteen, and afterwards studied seriously under Liszt, whom he followed to Rome. He made extensive concert tours (among others, with Wilhelmj, 1872), and became well known beyond Germany. From 1879–81 he was teacher at the Horak's Institution, Vienna. L. has published compositions for the pianoforte.

Leitmotiv (Ger.), is the name given in operas, oratorios, programme-symphonies (especially in Wagner, who first gave to the L. the important *rôle* which it now plays), to an oft-recurring motive, of rhythmic, melodic, or even harmonic, pregnance, which, by the situation in which it first occurred, or by the words with which it was first connected, receives a particular meaning, and thus, whenever used, recalls that situation. The idea of the L. was by no means unknown to the classic writers, but with them it appears mostly in the form of a general characteristic of the various personages. (*Cf.* the Leporello thirds in *Don Juan,* the "Caspar" bass figures in *Freischütz,* etc.). It first appeared with full meaning in the *Flying Dutchman* and *Lohengrin.* In his later operas Wagner has made greater, and indeed extraordinary, use of the L., and thus throughout developed real unity. Yet it is not easy to trace it everywhere, and, as a matter of fact, for less-gifted hearers, or for those not well prepared, the numerous "Führer durch Wagners Bühnenwerke" constitute help by no means to be despised.

Leitton (Ger.), leading note (q.v.).

Leittonwechselklänge, the term given by Dr. Riemann in his new theory of harmony ("Harmony Simplified," Augener & Co.) to chords of opposite genus (the one major, the other minor), the primes of which are leading notes to each other, *e.g.* e, g, b, ←——→ c, e, g. L. may be substituted for one another in a similar manner to parallel chords (Parallelklänge).

Le Jeune, Claudin, French contrapuntist; his compositions appeared from 1585 up to 1610 (chansons, madrigals, psalms, airs, etc.); he is not to be confused with Claudin de Sermisy, who flourished fifty years earlier.

Lemaire, (1) according to Rousseau, "Dictionnaire de musique," and Mersenne, "Harmonie universelle," p. 342 (1636), the one who proposed to introduce seven, instead of six, Solmisation syllables, *i.e.* to do away with Mutation (seventh syllable, according to Rousseau *Si;* according to Mersenne, *Za*). According to Fétis ("Biographie universelle"), there was a Guillaume le Maire among the twenty-four violons of Louis XIV., who might have been the innovator in question; as, however, according to Calvisius, "Exercitatio musicæ III." (1611), the name *Si* for the seventh syllable appears to have been already well known about 1611, this statement can scarcely be correct; and the priority must be refused to L., or the period at which he flourished placed earlier.

(2) Théophile, b. March 22, 1820, Essigny le Grand (Aisne), pupil of Garcia (singing) and of Michelot (opera), and Moreau-Sainti (comic opera) at the Conservatoire. In consequence of a violent attack of pleurisy, he gave up his contemplated operatic career as vocalist, and devoted himself to the teaching of singing, for which he made deep studies of all Methods, ancient and modern, which came within his reach. These studies led him to translate Tosi's " Opinioni dei cantori antichi e moderni," 1823 (" L'art du chant, opinions," etc., 1874); he also worked in collaboration with H. Lavoix (q.v.) at a "Histoire complète de l'art du chant."

Le Maistre (Le Maître), Mattheus, Netherland contrapuntist, appointed court capellmeister at Dresden in 1554, pensioned in 1568, d. in 1577. He published: " Magnificat octo tonorum " (1557); " Catechesis numeris musicis inclusa et ad puerorum captum accomodata tribus vocibus composita " (1563, for the Dresden choir-boys), " Geistliche und weltliche teutsche Gesänge " (1566, à 4–5), a book of motets à 5 (1570); " Officia de nativitate et ascensione Christi " (1574, à 5); " Schöne und auserlesene teutsche und lateinische geistliche Lieder " (1577). The Munich Library possesses in manuscript three Masses, twenty-four offices, and four versicles, which are not printed. Fétis has confused L. and Matthias Hermann. (*See* HERMANN; *cf. also Monatshefte für Musikgeschichte*, 1871 [12]; also the monograph of L. by O. Kade, 1862).

Lemière de Corvey, Jean Frédéric August, b. 1770, Rennes, d. April 19, 1832, Paris, French officer of the time of the

Revolution; also under Napoleon. He wrote a goodly series (twenty-three) of vaudevilles and comic operas, the former at Rennes when he was quite an amateur; but the latter, from 1792, as pupil of Berton, for Paris, and not without success. He also prepared in French several operas of Rossini, and published violin sonatas, pf. sonatas, potpourris, military music, a trio for harp, horn, and pianoforte, romances, etc.

Lemmens, Nicolas Jacques, celebrated performer on the organ, b. Jan. 3, 1823, Zoerle-Parwijs (Belgium), d. Jan. 30, 1881, Castle Linterport (near Malines); he was a pupil of the Brussels Conservatoire under Fétis; then (1846) sent at the government expense to Hesse at Breslau, and became professor of organ-playing at the Brussels Conservatoire, 1849. In 1857 he married the vocalist Miss Helen Sherrington (b. Oct. 4, 1834, Preston, d. at Brussels May 9, 1906), highly esteemed in London as a concert, church, and opera singer; from that time he resided much in England. In 1879 he opened a training college for organists and choirmasters at Malines under the auspices of the Belgian clergy, and it was well attended. L. wrote many excellent compositions for the organ (improvisations, sonatas, studies, etc.), also a great "École d'orgue," (adopted by the Conservatoires of Brussels, Paris, etc.), a method for the accompaniment of Gregorian chants, various sacred vocal works, symphonies, etc.

Lemoine, (1) Antoine Marcel, b. Nov. 3, 1763, Paris, d. there April, 1817; he was a performer on the guitar, played the viola in 1789 at the Théâtre de Monsieur, and was for some time conductor at small Paris theatres, but founded in 1793 a music-publishing house, which was carried on by his son. (*See* 2.) He published a Guitar Method.

(2) Henri, son of the former, b. Oct. 21, 1786, Paris, where he died, May 18, 1854, pupil of the Conservatoire there (1798–1809), and still of Reicha in 1821 for harmony, was much sought after as a pianoforte teacher, but in 1817 took over his father's publishing business, and brought it into high repute. L. himself compiled pianoforte, harmony, and solfège Methods, and, besides, "Tablettes du pianiste"; mémento du professeur de piano " (1844), also a number of good pf. pieces (sonatas, variations, etc.).

(3) Aimé, b. 1795 (date of death unknown), was a pupil of Galin (q.v.), taught according to his method, and also published two new editions of his " Méthode du méloplaste," but finally returned to the ordinary method of instruction.

Lemoyne, Jean Baptiste (Moyne, called L.), b. April 3, 1751, Eymet (Périgord), d. Dec. 30, 1796, Paris; he was at first conductor at small French provincial theatres, then studied under Graun and Kirnberger at Berlin, became second capellmeister to Frederick the Great, returned, however, to Paris and professed to be a pupil of Gluck, but was disavowed by the latter, whereupon he began to copy Piccinni's style of writing. In spite of his lack of individuality, L. was successful with some of his operas (*Nephté* was the cause of a call for the author, a thing unheard of before in Paris).

Lenaerts, Constant, b. March 9, 1852, Antwerp; he studied under Benoit, was already, at the age of eighteen, director of the (Flemish) national theatre, and is now teacher at the Antwerp Conservatoire.

Lenepveu, Charles Ferdinand, b. Oct. 4, 1840, Rouen; he was to have been a lawyer, and even studied jurisprudence at Paris, but at the same time music, under Servais, and, after he had gained a prize for a cantata, became a pupil of the Conservatoire (1865), and in 1866 obtained the *Prix de Rome*. His comic opera, *Le Florentin*, first produced in 1874, also gained a prize in a competition (1869). In 1882 followed a grand opera, *Velleda* (London). Meanwhile, L. had been appointed professor of harmony at the Conservatoire (as successor to Guiraud, who had become professor of composition).

Lentando (*Slentando*), Ital., becoming slower, slackening.

Lento (Ital.), has a meaning somewhat similar to that of *Largo; non L.*, not dragging.

Lenz, Wilhelm von, b. 1808, d. Jan. 31, 1883, at the infirmary, Petersburg, Imperial Russian Councillor. He wrote: " Beethoven et ses trois styles " (1852–55, two vols.); " Beethoven, eine Kunststudie " (1855–60, five vols., of which Vols. III.–V. appeared separately under the title " Kritischer Katalog der sämtlichen Werke nebst Analysen derselben " [1860], and the first as " Beethoven, eine Biographie " [2nd ed. 1879]); finally, " Die grossen Pianoforte Virtuosen unsrer Zeit " (1872, concerning Liszt, Chopin, Tausig, Henselt). The books of L. on Beethoven are not so much the result of serious and sober investigation as of a warm enthusiasm; they are therefore not of so much importance for the history of music, as for the understanding of the artistic character and individuality of Beethoven, and awakening enthusiasm for his genius.

Leo, Leonardo, b. 1694, San Vito degli Schiavi (Naples), d. 1746, Naples; he studied under A. Scarlatti and Fago at the Conservatorio della Pietà, Naples, and afterwards under Pitoni at Rome. On his return he was appointed teacher at the Conservatorio della Pietà, in 1716 organist of the royal chapel, and in 1717 maestro of Santa Maria della Solitaria. He afterwards exchanged the post of teacher at the above-named Conservatorio for a similar one at the Conservatorio Sant' Onofrio. He died quite unexpectedly while seated at the clavichord. L.

was one of the most distinguished representatives of the Neapolitan school, was one of its original founders and most famous teachers; Jomelli and Piccinni, among others, were his pupils. L. wrote nearly sixty dramatic works; in 1712 his oratorio, *S. Alessio*, was produced at the Conservatorio. He made his first attempt at a real opera in 1719 at the Teatro San Bartolommeo, Naples (*Sofonisbe*); his last opera was *Il nuovo Don Chisciotte* (completed in 1748 by Pietro Gomez). The titles of his other works are those common to all Italian composers of operas: *Tamerlano, La Clemenza di Tito, Siface, Demofoonte*, etc. Before *Sofonisbe* he had only produced some " serenades " for birthdays, weddings, etc. To the operas must be added the oratorios: *La Morte d'Abele, Santa Elena al calvario, Dalla morte alla vita;* further, a mass à 4 in the Palestrina style, two masses à 5 with organ, a mass à 4 and one à 5 with orchestra, several Credos, Dixits (one à 10 for two choirs and two orchestras), Misereres (one noble one à 8, *a cappella*), Magnificats, responses, motets, hymns, etc. Finally are to be named six 'cello concertos with stringed quartet, a number of clavier toccatas, two books of organ fugues, solfeggi and figured basses for the purpose of practice. The greater number of his works are in manuscript at Naples, Rome, Paris, and Berlin. In modern publications some few pieces of L. are to be found: in Braune's " Cäcilia " (" Credidi propter, Tu es sacerdos, Miserere 4 voc."); Rochlitz' " Collection," etc. (" Di quanta pena, Et incarnatus est "); the Miserere à 8, a real polyphonic pearl *a cappella*, is reprinted in Rochlitz, Commer (" Musica sacra," eighth vol.), Weber (" Kirchliche Chorgesänge," only a portion), and in a separate edition by Schlesinger (Berlin), also formerly by Choron (Paris); a " Dixit dominus " à 8 by Stanford (London), a " Dixit dominus " à 5 by Kümmel (" Collection," etc), a great number of solfeggi with bass in Lévesque and Bèche's " Solfèges d'Italie," etc., an aria from *Clemenza di Tito* and a duet from *Demofoonte* in Gavaert's " Gloires de l'Italie," etc.

Léonard, Hubert, distinguished violinist and teacher, b. April 7, 1819, Bellaire (near Liége), d. May 6, 1890, Paris, was first trained by a teacher named Rouma, in 1836 attended the Paris Conservatoire as a pupil of Habeneck, and, at the same time, soon acquired a post as violinist, first at the Théâtre des Variétés, then at the Opéra Comique, and, finally, at the Grand Opéra. In 1839 he left the Conservatoire, but remained in Paris until 1844. He then travelled much, giving concerts and making a name, and in 1848 received an appointment at Brussels as principal violin professor at the Conservatoire (successor to Bériot, who had become blind). In 1851 he married Antonia Sitcher de Mendi, an excellent vocalist, niece of Manuel Garcia. In 1867, for the sake of his health, L.

resigned his appointment at Brussels, and went to live in Paris, where he still trained many pupils. His publications are for the most part educational : " Gymnastique du violoniste," " Petite gymnastique du jeune violoniste," " 24 études classiques," " études harmoniques," " École Léonard " (Violin Method), " L'ancienne école italienne" (studies in double-stopping), six sonatas, and the " Trille du diable " of Tartini's, with accompaniment written out from the composer's figured bass; also five concertos with orchestra, six concert pieces with pianoforte, many fantasias, characteristic pieces, a serenade for three violins, a concert duo for two violins, valse-caprice, many duos with pianoforte on operatic motives, among which transcriptions on themes by Wagner, four duos with pianoforte (jointly with Litolff), and three with 'cello (jointly with Servais).

Leoncavallo, Ruggiero, b. March 8, 1858, Naples, the second of the sensational Italian composers of serious operettas (*cf.* MASCAGNI). His *Pagliacci* was produced at Milan May 31, 1892, and his *Medici* in 1893. The public will soon forget him; and the art criticism, with respect to L. and also Mascagni, pass to the order of the day. A small maiden opera, *Songe d'une nuit d'été,* was privately performed at Paris in 1889 ; also L.'s songs appeared first at Paris, where he lived for a time.

Leonhard, Julius Emil, b. June 13, 1810, Lauban, d. June 23, 1883, Dresden, became professor of the pianoforte at the Conservatorium at Munich in 1852, and received a similar appointment at Dresden in 1859. The following of his compositions may be mentioned : the oratorio *John the Baptist,* a symphony (E *minor*), overture to Oehlenschläger's *Axel und Walpurg,* a pf. sonata (which gained a prize), two violin sonatas, three trios, one pf. quartet, three cantatas for chorus, soli, and orchestra, and other vocal works.

Leoni, Leone, maestro at Vicenza during the last decades of the 16th and the beginning of the 17th century. He was one of the masters who, in 1592, paid homage to Palestrina by dedicating to him a volume of psalms à 5. L. published : five books of madrigals, à 5 (1588, 1595 [2], 1598, 1602) ; one book of motets, à 6 and one à 8 (1603, 1608) ; two books of motets, with organ bass, à 2–4 (1606, 1608 ; 2nd ed. under title " Sacri fiori," 1609–10) ; two books of motets, with organ bass, à 1–3 (1609–11) ; " Omnis psalmodia solemnitatum 8 vocum " (1613) ; and " Prima parte dell' aurea corona, ingemmata d'armonici concerti a 10 con 4 voci e 6 instromenti " (1615). Detached pieces by L. are also to be found in Gardano's "Trionfo di Dori" (1596), in Schade's " Promptuarium," in Bodenschatz' " Florilegium Portense," and other collections.

Leonowa, Daria, distinguished Russian vocalist (contralto), b. 1825, Government Twer,

entered the Imperial Opera School at Petersburg at the age of thirteen, and at the age of eighteen made her *début* as Vania in Glinka's *Life for the Czar* at the " Marientheater." Since then she has been one of the chief supports of Russian National Opera (*Russlan und Ludmilla, Rogneda, William ‚Ratcliff, Boris Godunow, Das Mädchen von Pskow,* etc.). She has travelled and made a name; in 1874 she journeyed round the world.

Le Roy. (*See* BALLARD.)

Lesage de Richée, Philipp Franz, performer on the lute, and composer, studied under Mouton, published in 1685 (Breslau ?) the " Kabinet der Lauten," ninety-eight pieces arranged in twelve suites, which rank among the best things of this branch of literature typical of the French clavier style. (*Cf. Monatshefte für M.-G.,* 1889, No. 1.)

Leschetizki, Theodor, pianist and excellent pianoforte-teacher, b. of Polish parents in 1831, Lemberg. He was for many years professor at the Petersburg Conservatoire, but resigned this post in 1878, and has lived since then as private teacher in Vienna. In 1880 he married his pupil, A. Essipoff. L. has published many clever, elegant, and effective pianoforte pieces ; an opera, *Die erste Falte,* was successfully given in 1867 at Prague, and in 1881 at Wiesbaden.

Leslie, Henry David, excellent conductor and composer of note, b. June 18, 1822, London, played at first the 'cello in the orchestra of the Sacred Harmonic Society, became secretary of the Amateur Musical Society in 1847, and in 1855 was appointed conductor of the same until its dissolution. In 1855 he founded a choral society of his own for *a-cappella* singing, which attained to high fame, and gained the first prize at the Paris international competition in 1878. In 1864 he was placed at the head of the National College of Music, but that institution broke up after a few years. The chief compositions of L. are : an opera, *Ida* (1864) ; operetta, *Romance; or, Bold Dick Turpin* (1857) ; two oratorios (*Immanuel,* 1853 ; *Judith,* 1858, for the Birmingham Musical Festival) ; several cantatas (*Holyrood,* 1860; *The Daughter of the Isles,* 1861) ; a festival anthem, " Let God Arise ;" Te Deum and Jubilate (1846); symphony (1847); overture, "The Templar" (1852). D. Feb. 4, 1896.

Lessel, Franz, composer, b. about 1780, Pulawy (Poland) ; his father was musical director to Prince Czartoryski ; d. March, 1839, Petrikow. L. went to Vienna to study medicine, but became a pupil of Haydn and devoted himself entirely to music. Haydn held him in high esteem, and L. remained with the master until his death. In 1810 he returned to Poland to the Czartoryskis, and, after they were driven away by the revolution of 1830, led a restless romantic life, and died as teacher at the college at Petrikow—it is said, of a broken heart. Some of his pianoforte sonatas and fantasias appeared in print.

Lessmann, W. J. Otto, b. Jan. 30, 1844, Rüdersdorfer Kalkberge (near Berlin). He studied under A. G. Ritter at Magdeburg, afterwards at Berlin under H. v. Bülow (piano), Fr. Kiel (composition), and Teschner (singing). After having been private tutor, for two years, at Pförten in the house of Count Brühl (in which capacity he frequently came into contact with A. W. Ambros at Prague), he became teacher at the Stern Conservatorium, Berlin, then at Tausig's school for the higher development of pianoforte-playing until 1871 (when Tausig died). For a short period he was proprietor of a music school of his own at Berlin, and since 1872 he has been director of musical instruction at the "Kaiserin Augusta-Stiftung" at Charlottenburg; also for some time he conducted the singing at X. Scharwenka's Conservatorium. L. is principally known as musical critic, but has also been active as a composer, and has produced some successful songs, etc. Since 1882 L. has been proprietor of the *Allg. Musik-Zeitung*, and edits the same with remarkable tact.

Lesto (Ital.), nimble, quick.

Lesueur (Le Sueur), Jean François, b. Jan. 15, 1760, Drucat-Plessiel (near Abbeville), d. Oct. 6, 1837, Paris: the "predecessor of Berlioz" as programme musician. He was chorister at Abbeville, and afterwards at Amiens, where he attended the College. In 1779 he broke off his school studies, and took the post of *maître de musique* at Séez cathedral, which, six months after, he exchanged for that of *sous-maître* at the Church of the Innocents, Paris, where Abbé Roze became his instructor in harmony. The restless, ambitious spirit of L. was not satisfied with a subordinate position, and thus, within a small space of time, we find him *maître de musique* at the cathedrals of Dijon, Le Mans, and Tours, in 1784 *maître de chapelle* of the Innocents at Paris, and further, in 1786, of Notre Dame. Gossec, Grétry, and Philidor were favourably disposed towards the young man. L. was allowed to have a full orchestra at Notre Dame, and he now wrote for the services, Masses, motets, etc., with orchestra; among other things, a grand instrumental overture, which created quite a sensation, and raised a storm of *pros* and *cons*. L. himself defended his principles in the pamphlet, " Essai de musique sacrée, ou musique motivée et méthodique " (1787), and, on receiving an anonymous reply, published a second, " Exposé d'une musique imitative et particulière à chaque solennité " (1787). Unfortunately the orchestra was reduced in the same year, and L. resigned. As, at the same period, his opera *Télémaque* was refused by the Grand Opéra, he withdrew dissatisfied to the country

at Champigny, where, from 1788–92, he devoted himself to composition, whilst the horrors of the Revolution were being enacted in Paris. In 1793 he reappeared in Paris, and produced the operas *La Caverne, Paul et Virginie* (1794), and *Télémaque*, all at the Théâtre Feydeau. When the Conservatoire was founded he was named one of the inspectors, and was elected member of the *comité des études;* he also drew up, jointly with Méhul, Langlé, Gossec, and Catel, " Principes élémentaires de Musique " and " Solfège du Conservatoire. A new conflict ended in a manner still more unpleasant for L. than the first. Two operas (*Ossian* [*Les Bardes*] and *La mort d'Adam*) sent in by L. to the Grand Opéra were discarded in favour of Catel's *Sémiramis*. L. opened up a stormy discussion with the " Lettre à Guillard sur l'opéra de *La mort d'Adam* " (1801), which finally degenerated into an attack on the Conservatoire (" Projet d'un plan général de l'instruction musicale en France," 1801), which brought about L.'s dismissal (1802). Thereupon he experienced bitter anxiety as to his means of living, until, in 1804, Napoleon named him his *maître de chapelle*, as successor to Paisiello, and thus at one stroke he received the highest musical post in Paris. His *Bardes* was now produced and met with Napoleon's special approval. After the Restoration (1814), L. became royal principal *maître de chapelle* and court composer, and, on the reopening of the Conservatoire, professor of composition; finally he was loaded with honours of all kinds, and, already in 1813, elected member of the Institut, etc. To the dramatic works of L. must be added the divertissements " L'inauguration du temple de la Victoire " and " Le triomphe de Trajan " (both jointly with Persuis, 1807), also the operas *Tyrtée, Artaxerce,* and *Alexandre à Babylone*, which were not produced. Of his numerous masses (thirty-three), oratorios, motets, etc., only a Christmas oratorio, three *Messes solennelles*, the oratorios *Deborah, Rachel, Ruth et Naémi, Ruth et Boaz*, three Te Deums, some motets, two Passion oratorios, a Stabat Mater, and a few *pièces d'occasion* (Coronation March for Napoleon) appeared in print. L. was also the author of " Notice sur la mélopée, la rythmopée et les grands caractères de la musique ancienne " (Paris, 1793). He wrote, likewise, a biographical notice of Paisiello (1816). The following wrote about L.: Raoul-Rochette (1837), Stéphen de la Madeleine (1841), and Fouqué (" L. comme prédécesseur de Berlioz ").

Letter Notation, *i.e.* the indication of sounds by means of letters. It appears to be the oldest form of notation; anyhow, it was already in use among the Greeks. (*Cf.* GREEK MUSIC.) Their notation—at least in the treatises of the theorists—was preserved in Western Europe up to the 10th century A.D.; though from about the 6th century, and possibly earlier, notation by means of neumes (q.v.) was in practical use. In the

10th century, however, we meet with a new kind of notation, the one with Roman letters; the first seven letters, in fact, of the alphabet. *A B C D E F G* were used for the seven sounds of the diatonic scale, but their former differed from their present meaning: they corresponded rather to our *c d e f g a b*. Above *G* came *A*, and below *A*, *G*, as at the present day. According to the testimony of writers of the early Middle Ages, this notation was first used for stringed instruments (Psalterium, Rotta), and was generally adopted for the organ, then coming into vogue. But the Western monks soon changed the meaning of the letters by adapting them to the old Grecian system (a minor scale through two octaves). *A*, consequently, acquired its present meaning, *i.e.* in the old letter notation *C D* and *G A* were half-tone steps, but in the reformed one (called the "Odoistic," after the name of Odo of Clugny, who died in 942, and who probably made the change), *B C* and *E F*. Already in the 10th century differently formed letters began to be used for each octave. A note was added to the system of the Greeks, viz. our capital G; this was indicated by the Greek Gamma (Γ). Then followed the octave of the capital letters *A B C D E F G*, and after that the small ones, *a b c d e f g;* if higher notes were required, these were doubled, *aa bb cc dd ee*, or thus: $\frac{a\ b\ c\ d\ e}{a\ b\ c\ d\ e}$. Instead of the small letters for the second octave, the alphabet characters were sometimes continued thus; *H I K L M N O P*. This notation *A—P* (falsely called the "Notation Boétienne") occurs in the old system (*H* = our *c*), and in the "Odoistic," in which *H* stood for *a;* both were in use up to the 12th century. Once the knowledge of the origin of the double meaning of the letters had become lost, it was natural that they should be used with various meanings, and this actually was the case; the meaning of the letters changed according to the tuning of the instrument for which they were employed. In the theoretical treatises of the 12th and 13th centuries the employment of letters as pitch-signs was, therefore, quite arbitrary; for example, *A* is to be found in the sense of our *F*, and so on. For a long time letter notation for practical use passed out of sight. Through Guido d'Arezzo's invention or arrangement of our modern notation on lines (cir. 1025), which, however, as shown by the clefs placed at the beginning, was only a shortened and more distinct letter notation—letters, at least for the notation of vocal music, fell gradually into disuse, while, on the other hand, they were employed more than ever by instrumentalists. Unfortunately, we have no notation of instrumental compositions older than the end of the 15th century. About this time letter notation was revived, under the well-known name, in fact, of *Organ Tablature* (q.v. *Tablature*). The meaning of letter notation, viz., the "Odoistic," now becomes

fixed, for it passed into the Guido note system with lines, and became the basis of *Musica Mensurata notation.* On the other hand, the *order* of letters, with regard to octave division, varies. Together with the old Γ, *A—G*, *a—g*, etc., we find *f̱—e, f—e, f̄—ē*, and occasionally *G—F, g—f*, etc.; also already at the beginning of the 16th century we catch glimpses of our present octave division, which always begins with *c* (as the oldest always began with *A*, answering to our *c*). We find the present system fully developed at the commencement of the 17th century in Michael Prætorius (1619); but the old octave division *A—G, ā—g, a—g*, and extended downwards *A—G*, was maintained so long as the Tablature was in use (up to the last century). The following octave division with *B* and *H* (*B rotundum* and *quadratum*) is also to be found in the 16th century (*see* FUNDAMENTAL SCALE and CHROMATIC SIGNS), *A B H C D E F G A B h c d e f g a b h̄ c̄ d̄ e*, etc. With regard to rhythmical value and pause signs of the Tablatures, *see* TABLATURE 2. Although letter notation is no longer in practical use, it is used by theorists, both in the past and present, to express acoustical relationships, etc., but always with the division starting from *c*. A different use of capital and small letters has, however, recently come into vogue. *Letters with chord meaning* were first employed at the beginning of this century (Gottfried Weber); a capital letter indicated the major chord of the sound expressed by the letter (irrespective of the position in this or that octave), and in like manner a small letter, the minor chord; for example, *A* = *A* major, *a* = *A* minor. A small nought marked the diminished triad, *e.g. a⁰* = *a : c : e♭*. (For another meaning attached to *nought, see* KLANGSCHLÜSSEL.) By *A* is also understood the key of *A major*, and by *a* that of *A minor*. Moritz Hauptmann and his pupils, again, use capital and small letters in another sense, viz. to distinguish *fifth-sounds* and *third-sounds*. If, for instance, four steps of a fifth are taken upwards from *C*, the sound *E* is reached (to be considered apart from the octave position); this sound does not exactly coincide with the third of *C*, but is somewhat higher. The vibration number for the 4th fifth is 81 (= 3⁴); the nearest *c* below is the nearest smaller power of 2, *i.e.* 64. (*Cf.* INTERVAL 2.) This so-called Pythagorean third has, then, the ratio 64 : 81; but the ratio of the major-third is that of the fourth to the fifth partial tone (*see* SOUND) = 4 : 5, or, which is the same, 64 : 80, *i.e.* the third is lower than the true fifth by 80 : 81. This difference is called the *comma syntonum*. Hauptmann indicates all tones obtained by fifth steps by capital letters, and third-tones by small ones; for example, *C e G, a C e*, etc. This method would not be sufficiently accurate for scientific purposes: the second upper-third of *C*, as third of *e*, would be written again with a capital letter,

G♯, i.e. no distinction would be made between it and the 8th fifth, higher by two commas. Helmholtz, therefore, in the first edition of his " Lehre von den Tonempfindungen," contrived to indicate the lower pitch by means of a horizontal stroke under the capital letters for the second upper third, *c e, e G♯,* and a similar mark, above the letter, to indicate higher pitch for the second under-third, *a♭ c, F♭ a♭.* This method was simplified by A. v. Oettingen, for, while adopting the horizontal strokes, he did away with capital letters. A horizontal stroke above a letter signified an upper-third, and one below, the under-third ; the second third was indicated by two strokes, the third by three, etc., so that the letter notation showed exactly the vibration number of the interval, thus ;

$$c : \bar{e}, \ \bar{e} : \overline{\overline{g}} ♯, \ \overline{\overline{g}} ♯ : \overline{\overline{\overline{b}}} ♯, \ a\underline{♭} : c, \ f\underline{♭} : a\underline{♭}, \text{ etc.}$$

Every stroke indicates the lowering, likewise the raising, of the tone obtained by plain fifth-steps by 80 : 81. For theoretical purposes this is a great gain, as the harmonic meaning of the interval is directly perceived by the letter notation ; for example, if *c̄♯* be the third of the fourth fifth from *c* (*c—g—d—a—c♯*), *c̄♯,* on the other hand, is the second third of the under fifth of *c* (*c—f—ā—c̄♯*), etc. Helmholtz, unfortunately, in accepting this improvement in the second edition of the above-named work, has given reverse meaning to the horizontal strokes above and below the letters. One must, therefore, carefully note in reading as to whether the Oettingen plan, or the more widely known one of Helmholtz (which alone is used in this Dictionary) is employed.

Leuckart, F. Ernst Christoph, established a music business at Breslau in 1782, which was taken over by Constantin Sander in 1856. The latter moved the business to Leipzig in 1870, and enlarged it by purchasing the publishing houses of Weinhold and Förster of Breslau, Damköhler of Berlin, and Witzendorf of Vienna. Of works brought out by this very enterprising firm may be mentioned compositions by Robert Franz, Ambros' Musical History, etc.

Levasseur, (1) Pierre François, performer on the 'cello, b. March 11, 1753, Abbeville, pupil of Duport junior, member of the orchestra of the Grand Opéra, Paris, 1785 to 1815, after which he soon died. He published twelve 'cello duets.

(2) Jean Henri, likewise performer on the 'cello, b. 1765, Paris, pupil of Cupis and Duport junior, member of the orchestra of the Grand Opéra from 1789 to 1823, and professor of 'cello-playing at the Conservatoire, from 1795 to 1823 member of the Imperial, named after 1814 the Royal, chapel. He published 'cello duets, sonatas, and études, and was one of the chief contributors to the 'cello Method of the Conservatoire.

(3) Rosalie, was a famous singer at the Paris Grand Opéra 1766–85, and especially remarkable in the chief *rôles* of Gluck's operas until the appearance of Madame Saint Huberty.

(4) Nicolas Prosper, celebrated bass singer, b. March 9, 1791, Bresles (Oise), d. Dec. 7, 1871, Paris, pupil of the Conservatoire, played serious *rôles* at the Grand Opéra 1813–45, teacher of singing at the Conservatoire 1841–70.

Levé (Fr.), the upward movement of the foot or hand in beating time ; it corresponds with the unaccented part of the bar.

Levens, church maître de chapelle at Bordeaux. He published ; " Abrégé des règles de l'harmonie " (1743), in which he places the under-tone series (*progression arithmétique*) over against the upper-tone series (*progression harmonique*) ; *i.e.* he accepts two principles for the consonance ; he is, therefore, an harmonic dualist like Zarlino (1558), Tartini (1754), Hauptmann, and others.

Levey, William Charles, b. April 25, 1837, Dublin, d. Aug. 18, 1894, trained at Paris, opera conductor and composer of operettas, incidental music to plays, and cantatas ; he lived in London.

Levi, (1) Hermann, excellent conductor, b. Nov. 7, 1839, Giessen, studied under Vincenz Lachner at Mannheim (1852–55), attended the Leipzig Conservatorium (1855–58), was musical director at Saarbrücken (1859–61), capellmeister of the German Opera, Rotterdam (1861–64) ; from 1864–72 he was court capellmeister at Carlsruhe, and in 1872 was called to his present post as court capellmeister, Munich.

(2) Jakob (Levy, Lewy). (*See* LEBERT.)

Lewandowski, Louis, b. April 3, 1823, Wreschen, Posen, d. Feb. 4, 1894, Berlin, pupil of the School of Composition of the Berlin " Akademie " ; from 1840, musical director of the Synagogue at Berlin. He composed many orchestral, vocal, and chamber works. L. was one of the first founders of the Institution for Aged and Indigent Musicians, which, owing to his direction, already disposes of a colossal fortune.

Lewy, (1) Eduard Constantin, performer on the French horn, b. March 3, 1796, St. Avold (Moselle), d. June 3, 1846, Vienna. He was a French military musician, and from 1822, after long concert tours, principal horn-player at the Vienna Court Opera, and teacher at the Conservatoire. Also his brother and pupil, Jos. Rudolph (L.-Hoffmann), b. 1804, Nancy, d. Feb. 9, 1881, Oberlössnitz, near Dresden, was a distinguished performer on the French horn.

(2) Charles, son of E. C. L. (1), pianist and drawing-room composer, b. 1823, Lausanne, d. April 30, 1883, Vienna.

(3) Richard (Levy), brother of the former, b. 1827, Vienna, d. there Dec. 31, 1883, was originally a performer on the French horn, and

already at the age of thirteen, member of the court orchestra. Later on, he was appointed chief inspector and *régisseur* of the Court Opera. As a teacher of singing he trained Mallinger, Lucca, and Sembrich. (*See* LEBERT.)

Leybach, I g n a c e, b. July 17, 1817, Gambsheim (Alsace), d. May 23, 1891, Toulouse, received his musical training, first at Strassburg, afterwards at Paris under Pixis, Kalkbrenner, and Chopin, and in 1844 became organist of the cathedral of Toulouse. L. was an excellent pianist, and published a great number of drawing-room pieces which became popular, also a harmony Method, concert pieces for the harmonium, a great organ Method (" L'organiste pratique," three vols., containing 130, 120, and 100 pieces), and some books of songs and motets with organ.

Liaison (Fr.), (1) a bind, a syncopation.— (2) The playing or singing of a series of notes with one stroke of the bow, in one breath.— (3) A ligature.

Libitum (Lat. *ad libitum*, abbr. *ad lib.*), at pleasure.

Libretto (Ital., " little book "), the name given to the text (the text-book) of important vocal writes, especially operas ; *Librettist*, poet who writes the words for an opera.

Licenza (Ital.), freedom, deviation from strict rules (for example, *Canone con alcune licenze*, canon with certain licence).

Lichanos. (*See* GREEK MUSIC.)

Lichner, Heinrich, b. March 6, 1829, Harpersdorf (Silesia), pupil of C. Karow (Bunzlau), Dehn (Berlin), Mosewius, Baumgart, and Ad. Hesse (Breslau), cantor and organist of the Church of the Eleven Thousand Virgins, Breslau, and conductor there of the " Sängerbund." He is a diligent composer (psalms, choral pieces, songs, many pf. pieces). His much-played sonatinas are shallow and unoriginal.

Lichtenstein, Karl August Freiherr von, b. Sept. 8, 1767, Lahm, Franconia, d. Sept. 10, 1845, Berlin, successively intendant of the court theatres of Dessau, Vienna, and Berlin (1805), wrote words and music of operettas and operas : *Knall und Fall* (1795) ; *Bathmendi* (1798) ; *Die steinerne Braut* (1799) ; *Ende gut; alles gut* (1800) ; vaudeville, *Mitgefühl* (1800) ; all given at Dessau. *Kaiser und Zimmermann* (Strassburg, 1814) ; *Die Waldburg* (Dresden, 1822) ; *Der Edelknabe* (Berlin, 1823) ; *Singethee und Liedertafel* (Berlin, 1825) ; and *Die deutschen Herren vor Nürnberg* (Berlin, 1833).

Lichtenthal, Peter, important writer on music, b. 1780, Pressburg, d. Aug. 18, 1853, Milan, studied medicine, but devoted himself entirely to music, and in 1810 settled in Milan. His published compositions are : a stringed quartet, a pf. trio with violin and 'cello, ditto with violin and viola, and some works for pf. alone. For the Teatro della Scala

he wrote three operas and four ballets. His writings are : " Harmonik für Damen " (1806) ; " Der musikalische Arzt " (1807, on the healing power of music; also in Italian, 1811) ; " Orpheik, oder Anweisung, die Regeln der Komposition auf eine leichte und fassliche Art zu erlernen " (1807) ; " Cenni biografici intorno al celebre maestro W. A. Mozart " (1814) ; " Mozart e le sue creazioni " (1842, on the occasion of the unveiling of the Mozart memorial at Salzburg) ; " Estetica ossia dottrina del bello e delle belle arti " (1831) ; but his chief work is : " Dizionario e bibliografia della musica " (1826, four vols., the third and fourth vols. containing bibliography).

Lie, Erica (married Nissen), excellent pianist, b. Jan. 17, 1845, Kongsvinger (near Christiania), was trained by her father and Kjerulf, afterwards by Kullak at Berlin ; she has made herself known by numerous concert-tours on the continent and in England.

Lié (Fr.), slurred, tied.

Liebe, Eduard Ludwig, b. Nov. 19, 1819, Magdeburg, where he received musical training, was afterwards a pupil of Spohr and Baldewein at Cassel, then musical director at Coblenz, Mayence, Worms, for several years teacher of music in Strassburg, and finally in London. L. has composed numerous vocal and instrumental works, of which only songs have appeared in print and enjoyed popularity, and pf. pieces. An opera (*Die Braut von Azola*) was given in 1868 at Carlsruhe.

Liebich, Ernst, b. April 13, 1830, Breslau, d. there Sept. 23, 1884, was a distinguished maker of violins at Breslau, where his father and grandfather had already been similarly engaged. L. worked under Vuillaume (Paris), Hart (London), and Bausch (Leipzig), and received many first prizes for his instruments.

Liebig, Karl, the founder of the Berlin " Symphoniekapelle," b. July 25, 1808, Schwedt, d. Oct. 6, 1872, Berlin ; he was at first clarinet-player in the Alexander regiment, and from 1843 established symphony concerts in various halls with a band playing on a co-operative system. These met with such great success that the band was engaged for concerts by the Berlin Vocal Societies (" Singakademie," the Stern " Gesangverein "). In 1860 he received the title of royal musical director. In 1867 the band became unfaithful to him, and placed itself under the direction of Stern, whilst L. founded a new orchestra, but with only moderate success. His son Julius, b. 1838, Berlin, d. there Dec. 26, 1885, was for many years capellmeister at Ems.

Lieblich (Ger.), sweet, lovely, delicious. This word occurs often as an epithet in the names of organ stops, as *L.-Gedackt*, *L.-Bourdon*, etc.

Lied, the union of lyric poetry with music, in which the words are sung in place of being spoken, so that the musical elements of rhythm and cadence belonging to speech are intensified so as to become real music, rhythmically planned melody. (*Cf.* SINGING.) The characteristic feature of the L. is plain periodic division. The so-called L.-form (also for instrumental compositions) has two themes in the following order : theme I. II. I. ; and in further development also with like division of the three parts: I. *a b a ;* II. *c d c ;* III. *a b a* (extended L.-form, *cf.* FORMS). *L. ohne Worte* (song without words), since Mendelssohn, has become a common expression for somewhat short melodious instrumental pieces of all kinds (formerly " Aria "). The L. proper (the poem composed for song) is either a strophe L. or through-composed (*durchkomponiert*) ; *i.e.* when the poet adheres to a definite strophe, the composer can follow him and write a melody which is repeated for each strophe, or he has a number of strophes sung to the same melody, but perhaps for the last, or for a middle one, introduces either a new melody, or the first one with certain modifications. The through-composed L., on the other hand, follows the poet's meaning more closely than the strophe L. ; it not only gives the general mood, but enters into detail, characterises, paints. Thus each strophe is set to a new melody, and if, for the sake of roundness of form, one is repeated, it appears modified. (*Cf.* VOLKSLIED.)

Liederspiel (Ger.), a vaudeville ; a dramatic piece interspersed with light, easily comprehensible music—songs, duets, choruses, etc.

Liedertafel, male choral union with social tendencies. The first real L., founded in 1809 by Zelter at Berlin, was composed of members of the Singakademie, and it was followed in 1815 by those at Leipzig and Frankfort-a.-O., in 1819 by the "Jüngere L." at Berlin, etc. In England there existed already in the former century clubs (*cf.* CATCH, GLEE and MADRIGAL) of a similar character ; but the German L. have a special meaning, inasmuch as they fostered German patriotism at the time of the ignominious oppression of German nationality. The members of a L. are called "Liederbrüder," the president is " Liedervater," the conductor "Liedermeister," and the vocal festivals of the " Sängerbunde," composed of a large number of Liedertafel, are named " Liederfeste." The united choral societies of the " Deutscher Sängerbund," numbering about fifty thousand singers, are usually named after some county or province (Suabian, of the Palatinate, Lower Saxon, Silesian, Franconian, Bavarian, Thuringian, Baden, North German, etc., Sängerbund), occasionally after the names of towns (the Berlin, Dresden, Bromberg Sängerbund), or of persons (the Zöllner-Bund, Julius Otto-Bund, Molck's Sängerbund, etc.). The " Deutscher Sängerbund " held imposing festivals at Dresden in 1865, at Munich in 1874, at Hamburg

in 1882. (*Cf.* H. Pfeil's " Liedertafel-Kalender." In France, male choral unions have of late grown in importance. (*See* ORPHÉON.)

Lienau, Robert, music publisher, b. Dec. 28, 1838, Neustadt (Holstein), bought in 1864 the publishing business of Schlesinger at Berlin, and in 1875 that of Haslinger at Vienna ; so that he is now the proprietor of one of the largest music-publishing firms.

Ligato. (*See* LEGATO.)

Ligature (Lat., *Ligatura*), tie, (1) a term in modern counterpoint equivalent to syncopation. It occurs in writing when, of two notes against one, the first is tied to a note of the preceding beat of the bar ; for example :

(2) In mensural music, groups of notes connected together in which the rhythmical value of the notes does not depend upon their form, but on their position. When mensural music was developed in the 12th century, it took from the Choralnote (q.v.) not only the simple notesigns but also the complicated neume-forms (*see* NEUMES) which now, as L.s, constitute one of the most difficult chapters in the theory of mensural music. The following scheme enables one to see at a glance the value of the initial and concluding notes of L.s :

Initial note :		Concluding note :	
Brevis			Longa
Longa			Longa
Brevis			Brevis
Longa			Brevis

{ Here, on the other hand, the first two notes are Semibreves.

Every note of a L. which is not first and last is a Breve, with exception of the second in the last cases given, where it is a Semibreve. (*Cf.* the articles PROPRIETAS, IMPROPRIETAS, PERFECTION, and IMPERFECTION.)

Liliencron, Rochus Freiherr von, b. Dec. 8, 1820, Plön, Holstein, youngest son of the Danish Land-, and afterwards Army-commissary-general, v. L. He attended the colleges at Plön and Lübeck, studied first theology, then jurisprudence, at Kiel and Berlin, finally Teutonic philology, and graduated in 1846 with the treatise " Ueber Neidhardts höfische Dorf Poesie " (1848), pursued old-Northern studies in Copenhagen up to 1847, and then went to Bonn and qualified himself as Privatdozent ; but, as about this time (1848) the first Schleswig-Holstein war broke out, L. placed himself at the disposal of the provisionary government, and became secretary in the bureau of foreign affairs. At the end of the year, however, he was sent to Berlin as official deputy, with full authority, from the " Gemeinsame Regierung," which meanwhile had come into power. In the latter city he represented the government in office when the war broke out afresh. After the conclusion of peace between Prussia and Denmark, L. betook himself, in the autumn of 1850, to Kiel, where he entered on the professorship of Northern languages which had been offered to him. As, however, he was not recognised by the Danish Government, he accepted the invitation of Michaelis in 1852 to Jena as professor of the German language and literature. L. published, jointly with the then musical director of the University, Wilh. Stade, a collection of " Lieder und Sprüche aus der letzten Zeit des Minnesangs " (Weimar, 1854); L. wrote the Introduction and the translation of the text, Stade the (modern) harmonisation in four parts. In 1855, L. accepted a call to Saxe-Meiningen as chamberlain and cabinet councillor (afterwards privy cabinet councillor) to Duke Bernhard; he also undertook for a time the intendantship of the ducal chapel, but soon exchanged it for the post of director of the ducal library, and then undertook for the historical commission founded in Munich in 1858 the task of collecting and annotating the historical German folk-poems of the Middle Ages. These " Historische Volkslieder der Deutschen vom 13.–16. Jahrh." were published by Vogel at Leipzig (1865–69) in four volumes and a supplement, which contains chiefly melodies and a treatise on the melodies of the 16th century. When he had completed this work, he was further commissioned by the same body to undertake the editing of the " Allgemeine deutsche Biographie," of which a plan had been already sketched. In order to prepare himself for this important—and, at the present day, far-advanced—publication, L., who had been appointed foreign member in ordinary of the Bavarian Academy of Sciences, 1869, made a short stay in Brunswick, and in the same year settled in Munich, where, after the death of Wilh. Wackernagel, he was elected member in ordinary of the historical commission. As soon as the work was sent to press, Professor von Wegele, of Würzburg, became chief editor of the politico-historical section of the biographies. Besides many historical studies, L. wrote:—" C. E. F. Weyse und die dänische Musik seit dem vorigen Jahrh." (eighth yearly series, 1878); " Ueber den Chorgesang in der evang. Kirche " (questions and discussions of the day, No. 144, 1881). Further must be mentioned his biography of J. B. Cramer in the " Allg. d. Biographie." He also assisted in the " Deutsche National Litteratur," edited by Kürschner, and published by Spemann : it

consisted of two volumes, one under the title " Deutsches Leben im Volkslied um 1530," containing the finest German popular songs of the 16th century, together with their melodies. At the same time he published the treatises " Ueber Kirchenmusik und Kirchenkonzert " (Second Yearly Report of the Society for Evangelical Church Music); " Ueber Entstehung der Chormusik innerhalb der Liturgie" (*Magdeburg. Evang. K.-Ztg.*); " Introitus," Graduale, Offertorium, Communio (Siona X. 9 to XI. 4).

Limma. (*See* APOTOME.)

Limnander de Nieuwenhove, Armand Marie Ghislain, b. May 22, 1814, Ghent, d. Aug. 15, 1892, at his castle, Moignanville (Seine-et-Oise); he studied under Lambillotte at the Jesuit college, Freiburg, afterwards under Fétis in Brussels, lived first at Malines, where he married and founded a vocal society ("Réunion Lyrique"); he then lived in Paris, where he brought out several stage works. His best productions are comic operas: *Les Monténégrins* (1849, at the Opéra Comique); *Le Château de Barbe-Bleue* (1851, Opéra Comique); and *Yvonne* (1859, Opéra Comique); the grand opera *Le maître chanteur* (1853, at the Grand Opéra); *Scènes Druidiques;* a Te Deum, Requiem, Stabat Mater, a 'cello sonata, a stringed quartet, many songs, etc.

Lincke, Joseph, b. June 8, 1783, Trachenberg (Silesia), d. March 26, 1837, Vienna, was an excellent 'cellist, member of the famous Rasumowsky quartet party; he played at Schuppanzigh's quartet *soirées*, occupied afterwards some posts in the provinces, then became chamber virtuoso to Countess Erdödy, afterwards principal 'cellist at the Theater an der Wien, and finally at the Vienna Court Opera. L. published some variations for 'cello.

Lind, Jenny, b. Oct. 6, 1820, Stockholm, d. Nov. 2, 1887, at her villa, Wynds Point, Malvern Wells, probably the most wonderful singer of our age, surnamed " The Swedish Nightingale." Bewitching were the sympathetic, elegiac tone of her noble soprano voice; astonishing were her coloratura, her perfect shakes, and her *staccato;* and her incredible leaps were as worthy of admiration as were her expressive and artistic performances. She received her first training at the opera school connected with the Stockholm Court Theatre (Lindblad), made her *début* at Stockholm, in 1838, in the *rôle* of Agathe, and for three years was the most brilliant star on the court stage. In 1841 she went to Paris and put herself under Garcia. She sang to Meyerbeer quite privately, and with pianoforte accompaniment, in the operahouse; but, from the recently published " Memoirs of Madame Jenny Lind-Goldschmidt, 1820–51," by H. S. Holland, M.A., and W. S. Rockstro (two vols., 1891), there seems to be no ground whatever for the general impression that in consequence of no engagement having been offered to her she had taken a profound artistic dislike to Paris. In 1844 she studied German at Berlin, and appeared with brilliant success in Meyerbeer's *Camp of Silesia* (*Feldlager in Schlesien*), the principal *rôle* (Vielka) of which had been written for her by Meyerbeer. After repeated triumphs at Berlin, Stockholm, also at Hamburg, Coblenz, Leipzig, Vienna, she made a victorious *début* in London in 1847, where, by every possible means, her appearance was delayed in order to raise to the highest pitch the curiosity of the public. After that she sang principally in London and Stockholm ; but already in 1849 she retired altogether from the stage, and devoted herself entirely to concert-singing. From 1850–52 she travelled through North America with J. Benedict and the impresario Barnum ; she married Otto Goldschmidt (q.v.) at Boston in 1852 and returned to Europe with a balance of £30,000, two-thirds of which, however, she devoted to benevolent institutions in Sweden. After a long stay in Germany (Dresden), she returned with her husband to London. From 1883–86 she taught singing at the Royal College of Music. Goldschmidt was for a time conductor of the " Bach Choir," and Madame Lind-Goldschmidt took part in the rehearsals and performances. Her last public appearance was at the Rhenish Musical Festival, Düsseldorf, in her husband's oratorio, *Ruth* (1870). The fame of the vocalist has been celebrated in various biographical sketches : " Jenny Lind die schwedische Nachtigall " (1845 ; in Swedish 1845) ; " Jenny L.," by A. Becher (1846) ; " G. Meyerbeer and J. L.," by J. B. Lyser (1847) ; " Memoirs of Jenny Lind " (1847) ; and the above-named " Memoirs " by Holland and Rockstro (1891).

Lindblad, A d o l f F r e d r i c k, b. Feb. 1, 1801, on the family estate at Löfvingsborg (near Stockholm), d. there Aug. 23, 1878 ; pupil of Zelter in Berlin ; from 1835 he lived at Stockholm. He composed a great number of Swedish songs of thoroughly national colouring, and original both as regards melody and harmony ; their merit was generally recognised, and they were frequently sung by, among others, L.'s pupil, Jenny Lind. His instrumental works, a symphony (produced at the Gewandhaus, Leipzig, 1839), a violin sonata, etc., were highly praised by the critics, but are little known.

Linden, K.a r l v a n d e r, composer, b. Aug. 24, 1839, Dordrecht, pupil of J. Kwast, senior (pianoforte), and of F. Böhme (theory) ; otherwise self-taught. After a long residence, for the purpose of study, in Paris, Belgium, and Germany, he became, in 1860, conductor of the " Harmonie at Dordrecht, also, successively, conductor of the " Liedertafel " (1865), " Ido's Mannenkoor," bandmaster of the National Guard at Dordrecht (1872), and, in 1875, conductor of the grand concerts of the Netherland " Tonkünstlerverein." L. is one of the most esteemed musicians in Holland ; he conducted the Musical Festival at Rotterdam (1875), also at Dordrecht (1877 and 1880), and was member of the jury at the great musical competitions of Ghent (1873), Paris (1877), and Brussels (1880). Among his compositions that have appeared are the cantatas *De starrenhemel* and *Kunstzin* (both for soli, chorus, and orchestra), and numerous songs. He also wrote seven overtures for grand orchestra, two operas, part-songs, for male, female, and mixed voices, with and without accompaniment, sonatas and pf. pieces, and many works for wind band.

Linder, G o t t f r i e d, b. July 22, 1842, Ehingen, pupil of the Stuttgart Conservatorium, from 1868 teacher at that institution, and in 1879 named Professor. He wrote the operas : *Dornröschen* (1872) and *Konradin von Schwaben* (1879), a " Waldlegende " for orchestra, an overture (" Aus nordischer Heldenzeit "), trios, songs, etc. L. belongs to the new German school.

Lindley, R o b e r t, excellent 'cellist, b. March 4, 1776, Rotherham (Yorkshire), d. June 13, 1855, London. He was a pupil of Cervetto, and first received an engagement in the theatre orchestra at Brighton, and in 1794 succeeded Sperati at the Royal Opera, London. His 'cello compositions (four concertos, duets for violin and 'cello, also for two 'celli, solos, variations, a trio for strings) are not of importance.

Lindner, (1) F r i e d r i c h, b. about 1540, Liegnitz, d. as cantor of the " Aegidien " Church, Nuremberg : he published two books of " Cantiones sacræ " (1585–88), a volume of Masses à 5 (1591), and the two collections, " Gemma musicalis " (4–6, and various madrigals, for the most part by Italian masters and by himself ; 1588, 1589, 1590, three parts) and " Corollarium cantionum sacrarum " (motets of Italian masters à 5-8 and of L., 1590, in two parts).

(2) A d o l f, distinguished French horn virtuoso, b. 1808, Lobenstein, d. April 20, 1867, Leipzig. He was at first court musician, then " Stadtmusikus " at Gera, from 1844–46 member of Gungl's travelling band, then of the orchestra of the Potsdam Theatre, and from 1854 was at the Gewandhaus, Leipzig.

(3) E r n s t O t t o T i m o t h e u s, for many years editor of the *Vossische Zeitung*, b. 1820, Breslau, d. Aug. 7, 1867, Berlin ; he was an excellent musical connoisseur, and on friendly terms with Dehn, Stern, and Rust. He conducted for a time the Berlin " Bach Verein," wrote many musical articles in his newspaper, also in the *Echo*, gave lectures on music at various places, and published " Meyerbeer's 'Prophet' als Kunstwerk beurteilt " (1850), " Die erste stehende deutsche Oper " (1855, two vols.), " Zur Tonkunst. Abhandlungen " (1864), and " Geschichte des deutsches Liedes im 18. Jahrhundert " (1871, posthumous ; edited by L. Erk).

(4) August, excellent 'cellist, b. Oct. 29, 1820, Dessau, d. June 15, 1878, Hanover, studied under K. Drechsler, since 1837 member of the court band at Hanover; he composed various works for his instrument.

Another of the same name, likewise 'cellist, formerly member of the theatre orchestra, Stuttgart, d. Aug. 9, 1887, Heidelberg.

Lindpaintner, Peter Joseph von, conductor and composer, b. Dec. 9, 1791, Coblenz, d. Aug. 21, 1856, Nonnenhorn (Lake Constance), while on a holiday trip; from 1812–19 he was musical director at the Isarthor Theater, Munich, then court capellmeister at Stuttgart. L. was a distinguished conductor, and brought the Stuttgart band into high repute. He was more prolific than original as a composer; he wrote twenty-one operas, several ballets and melodramas, six Masses, a Stabat Mater, two oratorios, cantatas, symphonies, overtures ("Faust"), concertos, chamber music, and many songs, of which "Fahnenwacht" achieved great popularity.

Linley, (1) Thomas (senior), composer, b. 1732, Wells (Somerset), d. Nov. 19, 1795, London, musical director and part proprietor of Drury Lane Theatre, for which he wrote several pieces (*The Duenna, Selima and Azor, The Camp, The Carnival of Venice, The Gentle Shepherd, Robinson Crusoe, Triumph of Mirth, The Spanish Rivals, The Strangers at Home, Richard Cœur de Lion, Love in the East*); he also published six elegies for three voices (probably his best work) and twelve ballads. After his death there appeared, together with some works of his son, of the same name, two volumes of songs, cantatas, and madrigals. His three daughters, Eliza Ann, Mary, and Maria, distinguished themselves as concert singers.

His eldest son, (2) Thomas, b. 1756, Bath, d. Aug 7, 1778, Grimsthorpe (Lincolnshire), drowned through the upsetting of a boat; he was an excellent violinist, studied under Boyce, then went to Florence to Nardini, and on his return became solo violinist at Bath, and afterwards at Drury Lane Theatre, London. He wrote music to Shakespeare's *Tempest*, an anthem with orchestra, "Let God arise;" an "Ode on the Witches and Fairies of Shakespeare"; an oratorio, *The Song of Moses*, etc.

(3) George, b. 1798, wrote many songs, ballads, etc. He also composed music for *The Toy Maker*, produced at Covent Garden in 1861. L. died Sept. 10, 1865.

Linnarz, Robert, b. Sept. 29, 1851, Potsdam, studied under Haupt at Berlin, teacher, in 1877, at the Bederkesa Seminary, occupied in 1888 a similar position at Alfeld-a.-L. He wrote *Alldeutschland* (Festival cantata), songs, choruses for male voices, Methods for violin, for organ, and one on the art of teaching singing.

Lipinski, Karl Joseph, famous performer on the violin, b. Oct. 30 (or Nov. 4), 1790, Radzyn (Poland), d. Dec. 16, 1861, at his country house, Urlow (near Lemberg). He received his first instruction from his father, a gifted amateur, but otherwise was self-taught. Already in 1810 he became leader, afterwards, from 1812–14 capellmeister, of the theatre at Lemberg. In 1817 he went to Italy in order to hear Paganini, and became intimate with him; but the two met again in 1829 at Warsaw as rivals, and their friendship was disturbed. In 1839, after long triumphant concert-tours throughout Europe, L. became leader at Dresden until he received his pension in 1861. L. was a player of broad tone and was skilled in double-stopping. His compositions are; four violin concertos (second in D, Op. 21 [military concerto], still often played), a number of caprices for violin alone, rondos, polonaises, variations, fantasias, a stringed trio, etc.: he published a collection of Galician melodies, with pianoforte accompaniment (1834, two vols.).

Lip-pipes, those pipes in which sound is produced by a thin stream of air forced against an edge; this stream excites alternately condensation and rarefaction in the body of the pipe, and is thus drawn inwards and outwards. (*Cf.* WIND INSTRUMENTS.) Of orchestral instruments only flutes belong to the lip-pipe species; the oboe, clarinet, bassoon, and brass wind instruments, on the other hand, to that of reed pipes. According to the scale, or measure (q.v.), also according to the height and breadth of the mouth, a distinction is made between the various lip-pipe stops in the organ: *Diapason, Gamba, Flute,* and *Hohl-flute* stops, etc.; the *Gemshorn, Pyramidon,* also *Bifara* and *Double Flute* differ in the shape of their pipe bodies. (*Cf.* separate articles.) Stopped and half-stopped L. (Rohrflöte) form a special section. The following differ, not in the mode of construction, but in that of their use: *Quint* and *Third stops, Mixtures, Cornet, Progressio harmonica, Sesquialtera, Tertian.* (*Cf.* MUTATION STOPS.)

Lips (from Latin, *Labium*), the name given to the edges above and below the mouth of lip-pipes (q.v.). The under-lip forms with the core of the pipe the windway through which a narrow stream of air is directed against the sharp-edged upper-lip situated exactly above.

Lipsius, Marie, a lady writer, known under the pseudonym of "La Mara," b. Dec. 30, 1837, Leipzig. She belongs to a family of savants, and is the authoress of "Musikalische Studienköpfe" (1873–80, five vols.; several times republished), "Gedanken berühmter Musiker über ihre Kunst" (1877), "Das Bühnenfestspiel in Baireuth" (1877), a translation of Liszt's "Chopin" (1880), "Musikerbriefe aus 5 Jahrhunderten" (1886, two vols.), "Klassisches u. Romantisches aus der Tonwelt" (1892), and other works, which, in regard to modern composers, prove trustworthy sources. L. writes in an intelligent and attractive style.